Judith Gould Omnibus

Sins
The Love Makers

Also by Judith Gould

DAZZLE
NEVER TOO RICH
THE TEXAS YEARS
FOREVER
TOO DAMN RICH
SECOND LOVE
TILL THE END OF TIME
RHAPSODY
TIME TO SAY GOODBYE
A MOMENT IN TIME
THE BEST IS YET TO COME
THE GREEK VILLA

Judith Gould Omnibus

Sins
The Love Makers

JUDITH GOULD

timewarner
paperbacks

A *Time Warner* Paperback

This omnibus edition first published in Great Britain by Time Warner Paperbacks in 2004
Judith Gould Omnibus Copyright © Judith Gould 2004

Previously published separately:
Sins first published in Great Britain by
Futura Publications in 1993
Reprinted 1984, 1985 (twice), 1986 (twice), 1987 (twice), 1991
Published by Warner Books in 1992
Reprinted 1993 (three times), 1994, 1995, 1997
Copyright © Judith Gould 1982

The Love Makers first published in Great Britain by
Futura Publications in 1985
Reprinted 1985, 1986, 1988 (twice), 1990
Published by Warner Books in 1992
Reprinted 1993, 1996, 1998, 1999
Copyright © Judith Gould 1985

A CIP catalogue record for this book is available from the British Library

ISBN 0 7515 3644 X

Printed and bound in Great Britain by
Mackays of Chatham Ltd, Chatham

Time Warner Paperbacks
An imprint of
Time Warner Books UK
Brettenham House
Lancaster Place
London WC2E 7EN

www.TimeWarnerBooks.co.uk

Sins

ACKNOWLEDGMENTS

No book is the result of the author's efforts alone, and grateful acknowledgment to the many people who have unstintingly given of their time, expertise, experiences, and suggestions is due:

For starting the whole creative process—Gladys Allison.

The team at NAL—Alison Husting, Angela Rinaldi, Elaine Koster, and Mary Anne Wilson.

For his fine-tooth-comb copy-editing—Raymond Phillips.

For his initial commitment—Evan Marshall.

For her enthusiasm and continued support—Maria Carvainis.

For research, anecdotes, and generous support—Lucy Gaston, Lynn Contrucci, Janice Resnick, Lola Peters, Maria and Albert Gardini, Annette Bodzin, Virginia Martin, Florence Pybus, John M. Severt, Jr., Harold B. Eisner, Helmut Schmidt, Rhea and Kathryn Gallaher, Gunther and Erna Bienes, and Alberto Silveira, who said: "You do a little bit at a time, and before you know it . . ."

And, of course, Gala, who lay patiently at my feet for thousands of hours. Here's a steak, little darlin', before Momma sits back down for another few years.

**To
Thomas E. Hill
who helped make it possible**

Of what is't fools make such vain keeping?
Sin their conception, their birth, weeping:
Their life, a general mist of error,
Their death, a hideous storm of terror.

John Webster, *Duchess of Malfi*, Act IV

TODAY

Tuesday, January 9

1

Through the porthole of the jet she could see the double strands of lights shimmering through the swirling mist as the plane touched down on the solitary runway. She was seated alone in the small passenger section, anxious for her signal to disembark.

The man was waiting for her at the end of the runway. For as long as he could remember, there was only one thing he had ever wanted that had eluded him, and that was the woman who was stepping off the jet. She could be as soft as creamery butter, as fragrant as wildflowers, yet as hard as nails. For years he had waited patiently for her. She had called him less than an hour earlier.

And now she was at the bottom of the stairs, her lithe body bathed in the lights. She broke into a run and headed toward him, her high heels clicking on the concrete. He ran forward to meet her, and halfway, they suddenly collided into each other's arms. Closing his eyes as she fiercely gripped him, he felt her shift slightly as she pulled away from him.

"Darling," he said softly. "I jumped in the car as soon as you called. How long do we have?"

"I've already lost an hour with this detour. Another hour and I've got to be off again."

"It's that bad?"

She nodded slowly.

Together they walked toward the car. When they reached it, he held the passenger door open for her and she slid inside, carefully smoothing her skirt over her knees. He walked to the driver's side and slipped in beside her, while he wordlessly reached into his breast pocket and took out a folded slip of paper. It was a cashier's check for eleven million dollars.

A veil seemed to drop over her eyes. "No," she said under her breath. "This isn't why I interrupted the flight."

"Please let someone help you for once. Take it," he gently urged.

Apologetically she smiled. "I'm sorry, I can't." She turned away and stared out the windshield, her eyes focused in the distance on something only she could see.

"If you change your mind . . ." He pursed his lips, sighed, and put the check on the dashboard within her reach. Fifteen yards away, the wing- and taillights of the jet blinked on and off, and the round portholes were ghostly circles of yellow light.

An hour later, he sat in the car alone, hearing the high-pitched whine of jet engines as the plane swept up off the ground and was once again lost to the black night.

Long after the runway lights clicked off, he still sat there staring up into the dark. Even in the hour of her greatest need, all she had wanted was to be near him.

The check was still on the dashboard.

2

In his luxurious apartment at the Hotel Pierre, Karl von Eiderfeld glanced at his seven-thousand-dollar Piaget wristwatch. One minute past eight, the thin gold-and-lapis dial read. A little less than five hours to go, he thought grimly. He sat in a French chair, tapping his fingers up and down its graceful arms. It was very unlike him to be nervous. Everyone who knew him said that Karl von Eiderfeld was always in control of his own destiny, as well as the destinies of others.

Emaciated and tall, von Eiderfeld carried his air of haughty aristocracy to perfection: people almost tended to forget that he was an albino. His flesh was cadaverous, and his head, crowned with thinning white hair, was narrow and skull-like in shape. His eerie pink eyes and strange coloring could not detract from his imperious posture, his aquiline nose with its long, thin nostrils, or his arched white eyebrows. But then, neither could his steel mills, his fleet of oil tankers, his refineries, and his many millions.

Karl von Eiderfeld had founded and forged his industrial empire out of the ashes of postwar Germany. The Reich that was to rule for a thousand years had collapsed. The spirit of his country had been spent. Tank treads crisscrossed the land once walked by a proud Barbarossa. The cities were smoldering. Germany was one vast ruin.

But von Eiderfeld had not been unhappy. He didn't believe in the bitter taste of defeat. Besides, vast sums of money were pouring in from America under the Marshall Plan. . . . Yes, he recognized it as a golden opportunity for those who would have a hand in rebuilding the vanquished Fatherland. And it was an even greater opportunity for those with foresight, imagination, and daring—for those who *knew* things. Little things. Little things such as where certain desperately needed items could be obtained. Items people were willing to pay for. Dearly.

Yes, he had known where forgotten stockpiles of much-needed propane gas were stored. By cover of night he quietly dug up the cylinders from their secret depots and transported them in horse-drawn wagons to a deserted winery on the Moselle River. It took him two months, but that winter it paid off. Nature was on his side and brought the coldest winter in ten years. Fuel was in short supply. He sold the propane, found his fortune, and financed his first steel mill.

In 1946 Karl von Eiderfeld emerged as one of the architects of the postwar industrial boom. In no time at all, his steel mills were helping rebuild the burned cities and bombed railroad tracks by pouring girders and rails. His refineries processed the oil that was needed to keep the railroad and construction machinery running. And his ships brought that oil to Hamburg, Bremen, and Bremerhaven. Soon nothing was beyond his reach. And he was making a most pleasant discovery. The more he accumulated, the quicker everything seemed to multiply. It was magic. Money indeed made money.

By 1949 he was a millionaire. By 1960 his companies had reached out and expanded into an enviable worldwide network with seventeen foreign branches. And now? Now his position as one of the three wealthiest and most powerful men in the entire Ruhr Gebiet was secure.

His piercing gaze swept around the dim, luxuriously furnished living room. It was on the fifteenth floor of the Hotel Pierre and had six windows facing Fifth Avenue. The view of Central Park was spectacular, but he never saw it. The heavy damask draperies were always kept drawn. Without the natural protection of pigmentation, his delicate eyes were painfully sensitive to light.

There was nothing remotely Germanic about von Eiderfeld's New York apartment. In style it looked as if it had been transplanted from Versailles. The walls of the living room were covered with authentic Régence paneling that had been carefully dismantled from a château in France and shipped to New York. It had been installed under the fastidious eyes of both a decorator and an art historian. From the ceiling hung a splendid pair of Venetian-glass chandeliers; over the marble mantel, a Venetian mirror flashed silvery. Scattered all about were Louis XVI settees and chairs, all genuine and upholstered in ancient blue damask. Like the chairs, the fabric was genuine eighteenth-century: worn thin, faded, and tattered. On the walls hung three gilt-framed Monets, two Goyas, and a small Fragonard.

His inspection over, von Eiderfeld rose from the chair with a thoughtful expression on his face and slowly paced the length of the room. Today was the day for which he had waited all these years.

By all rights I should be feeling triumphant, he was thinking, just like all those other times when I exacted my revenge. But this time was different. Vengeance somehow has a way of tasting bitter when you have to wait too long.

He sighed and shook his head. He had always destroyed his enemies as neatly and swiftly as an avenging angel. With the power of the mighty Von Eiderfeld Industrien G.m.b.H. behind him, that never posed any sort of problem. But to every rule there is an exception. His exception was Hélène Junot. Opposing her, he was as powerless as Goliath against David. Her weapon was, however, one he could well appreciate: she knew things. Just as he had once known things. But her knowledge had not become obsolete over the years. Instead, it seemed to increase in importance as time went by. It had brought her control—over people. And she had used him. He had been coerced into becoming one of the shareholders in her publishing firm. He had wanted no part of it. But he had given in. It was either that or . . . No, he still didn't want to consider the alternative. She had made that

6

only too clear. It still loomed over his head like Damocles' sword. And he knew she wasn't bluffing. He knew it only too well.

Yes, he thought, Hélène Junot, founder of Hélène Junot International, Inc., and publisher of *Les Modes,* the world's most successful fashion magazine, was more than just a woman. Far from it. She was a beautiful, iron-willed, erotic, blackmailing *monster.* In short, dangerous. She had the power to destroy him. She had almost used it once, and he could remember it only too well. It had been a far-too-close shave.

He had no illusions. It could happen again.

The familiar hatred prickled hotly behind his ears. Gott im Himmel! How he despised her!

But today he and the others were finally prepared to wage war. Her time had finally come.

It was forty minutes past eight EST and Marcello d'Itri picked at his first-class, yet still bland Alitalia breakfast. Leaning back in his seat, he held out his empty champagne glass to the stewardess for a refill.

"Right away, sir," she said with a smile.

He smiled back at her as she filled his glass with more Piper Heidsieck. An extraordinarily lovely girl, he thought. He took an appreciative sip of his champagne. Ah, yes, *everything* was lovely today. The muted, steady roar of the Boeing engines coming from the rear pleased him. He couldn't remember when the thick sea of clouds far below had seemed more beautiful, and for once he didn't mind the blinding sunlight that poured in through the little square window. He wasn't going to pull the shade down. Not today, he wouldn't. Even the tasteless eggs he decried on every flight were a special joy.

Because in two hours he would land at Kennedy Airport and then, finally, all the little wheels he had so meticulously arranged would be set into motion.

A warm glow of satisfaction spread through his body.

Marcello d'Itri was forty-two years old, olive-complexioned, and of medium height. His hair was graying black, thick, and looked perpetually—almost calculatedly—unkempt. His cheeks had a constant blue-green tint from his thick beard that no amount of shaving could erase. He was dressed in a stylish gray velvet jacket, pleated gray trousers, a red-plaid shirt, and a thin gray tie. Other than his disheveled hair, he was superbly groomed; his fingernails were manicured, his hand-sewn loafers gleamed, and the thin belt around his small waist was fashioned from cobra skin and fastened with an eighteen-carat gold buckle. The gray leather briefcase beneath his seat sported a pattern of continuous diagonal initials—*Md'I . . . Md'I . . . Md'I*. He was quite content carrying the same "signature" luggage as thousands of other travelers. Especially since the initials were his.

Although he was now accepted as *the* leading Italian fashion designer of the past decade, d'Itri's chances of even moderate success had in the beginning been very slim. His fantastic, sometimes outlandish designs, as well as his humble peasant origins, had horrified both the industry and customers alike. In an age of aristocratic couturiers—when the titles Prince, Princess, Count, and Countess were expected on every fashion label—his simple "Marcello d'Itri" was enough to send customers scurrying.

But a fairy godmother had come to his aid. Hélène Junot had seen his designs and liked his potential. Enough overexposure in her fashion magazines had single-handedly put him firmly on the fashion map, even ahead of that other darling of society women, Valentino. But the setup, d'Itri discovered much later, was costly. Hélène had infiltrated his business like an elegant octopus whose tentacles were everywhere. She ended up controlling not only Marcello d'Itri fashions but also Marcello d'Itri himself.

He sighed, thinking back. Ah, well, it could have been worse. At least the success she had created for him had one wonderful compensation. Money. And so, little by little and very quietly, under the cover of various dummy corporations, Marcello had used his growing fortune to buy into Hélène Junot International, Inc. Before Hélène knew what was happening he was sitting on the board.

Now, after all these years of suffering at Hélène's beautiful hands, it would come to an end.

Her creation was going to help destroy her.

In the exclusive enclave of Manhattan's Sutton Place, Z.Z. Bavier gloated as she looked thoughtfully out at the East River through the giant beveled-glass French doors of her seventeenth-floor penthouse apartment. Outside, the icicle-draped yew bushes sat in their frozen, sun-drenched tubs on the terrace. Below, traffic on both levels of the Fifty-ninth

Street Bridge looked miniaturized, and sunlight flashed off chrome.

Z.Z. stood there, her Dunhill cigarette curling acrid smoke upward past the violet moiré draperies. She had just replaced the receiver of her ivory telephone after a short but highly satisfactory conversation. Hélène Junot was already back in town, ahead of schedule, the caller had informed her. Hélène Junot, that beautiful, ill-bred, high-fashion whore was smelling trouble through those pretty nostrils of hers, no doubt. Probably running scared, Z.Z. thought with sadistic pleasure. Oh, that was so delicious. And what a reception she'd get! After nearly ten years, the showdown was at hand at last.

Simply delicious!

Z.Z. Bavier was thirty-eight years old, spiteful, bone-thin, and deceptively short. She wore a puce-and-violet Pucci caftan, a gold necklace fashioned from ancient Byzantine coins, and gold sandals. Her hair was honey-colored and starched stiff from too much spray, her predatory nose had a sharp upward tilt, and her lynx eyes were small, green, and alert. She breathed the very elegance she had dedicated years to achieve. Of all her far-flung social contacts, none knew what her first name actually was, nor even what the letters Z.Z. stood for. Z.Z. delighted in the speculation.

She turned around from the window and stalked the length of the generously scaled living room, the Byzantine coins around her neck clunking softly against one another.

She snorted as she thought back to how it had all begun almost ten years ago. Ten long years ago when she had been Mrs. Siegfried Bavier, the lovely wife of the legendary financier who had had a celebrated nose for sniffing out sound investments and whose effortless wealth seemed to grow in leaps and bounds.

Then, in 1965, everything fell apart. Her darling Sigi had forced her into divorce. He didn't seem to care that she was pregnant at the time. His only concern was for Hélène Junot. Well, Z.Z. had let him have her, believing that it wouldn't be long before he'd come crawling back on his knees, begging for forgiveness. She was as certain of that as she was of receiving an invitation to Earl Blackwell's next party, being listed in the *Celebrity Register,* or having her latest wardrobe described by Suzie. And when Sigi came crawling back, what then? Well, she would punish him for a suitable time and then finally relent. It had happened before, but not to the point of divorce. She would simply wait patiently until this fling was over. And of course she had received a handsome settlement by any standards. Seven million dollars, the co-op apartment on Sutton Place and the house in Easthampton, two Picassos and one Braque, a collection of Georgia O'Keeffes, and a trust fund for the unborn baby.

But the unthinkable had happened. Her Sigi never came back. The day after their divorce was final, Sigi and that Hélène woman exchanged vows in a civil ceremony downtown. Two months later, he dropped dead on the floor of the stock exchange, leaving Hélène with fifteen million dollars, leaving Z.Z. to give premature birth to his son.

How desperately she had wanted to have their baby! She had banked on its bringing Siegfried back. They would be closer than ever; surely fatherhood would force him to stop his philandering and settle down. She had even decided on a name. Carla if it was a girl. Wilfred if it was a boy.

But when the Jamaican nurse had brought her face to face with the baby boy, her hands had flown up to her face to cover her eyes. In one glance she had seen enough of that horrible, distorted little creature. She had caught sight of the little pink face with the wide-set eyes, an inheritance from her, the little red mouth lolling open, the expression of utter helplessness. She had caught sight of that face scrunching up into hideous distortions. Her baby had survived his early birth, but he had suffered irreversible brain damage.

"Mine?" Her hoarse whisper seemed to echo from the green-and-white walls.

The nurse nodded solemnly.

Z.Z.'s eyes widened in horror. "It can't be," she wailed in a shocked voice, shaking her head. "It's *not* mine! It can't be! It *can't* be!" She had shrunk against the metal headboard, sobbing violently.

She couldn't believe it. She had given birth to a monster! The realization brought on a nervous breakdown.

When she recovered, Z.Z. told all her inquiring friends that the baby had been stillborn. And she had accepted their apologies and condolences and clucking ministrations for that which she wished so badly could only have been.

She was never able to erase Wilfred from her mind. Her rejection of him haunted her day and night. Did he ever wonder about his mother? she asked herself over and over. And what was he like now?

She shut her eyes and shivered. Always that same thought came back to her: *What was he like now?* But she had always been afraid to find out.

Hélène would pay for this, Z.Z. had sworn. Oh, yes, she would pay. It was all that whore's fault. If it hadn't been for Hélène, she would have inherited twenty-two million dollars instead of the paltry seven she'd had to settle for. And above all, she wouldn't have had to be alone while giving birth to Sigi's . . . She swallowed. Sigi's . . . *child.* She wouldn't have had to carry all by herself the horrible burden, the hidden stigma, of bringing a malformed child into the world. Sigi would have been there to share the anguish, and it would have seemed less.

And so, as it had become available, Z.Z. found herself buying three million dollars' worth of stock in Hélène Junot International, Inc.

She felt it was worth every penny. It was very satisfying to sit on the board, countering every move made by that woman she hated with all her being.

But *that* had only been petty warfare. The real offensive was just beginning.

The big Mercedes limousine fought its way through the dense morning traffic. Seated on the plush gray velour was a single passenger, the Comte de Léger. He was on his way from his fashionable brownstone on East Sixty-eighth Street to the Junot Building, the Fifth Avenue headquarters of Hélène Junot International, Inc.

A banker, a wine grower, and second cousin to the prime minister of France, the Comte was a member of the board of Hélène Junot, as well as an alcoholic. A sour, red-faced Frenchman with the handsomely cruel features that women tended to find irresistible, he had a flat stomach and stood six feet, two inches tall. His eyes were coal black and hard, and his abundant graying hair was swept back as if to offer less wind resistance. He was elegantly dressed in a blue suit that had been custom-tailored on Savile Row, highlighted by a black raw-silk tie. His cufflinks were engraved with the de Léger crest, a lion and a salamander supporting a shield between them. They were a family heirloom, passed down from one comte to the next. They had been fashioned from ancient gold earrings that had been a gift to the first Comtesse de Léger by King François I in 1546. The lion and the salamander symbolized the alliance of the de Légers to the French throne.

At the moment, the Comte was oblivious of the start-and-stop traffic, and he felt sick. He was oblivious of the traffic because he had more important things on his mind. He felt sick because he had spent a sleepless night drinking heavily. In the middle of the night he had received a telephone call from Paris. Hélène Junot had chartered a Lear jet and left Orly Airport in a tearing hurry, the faint crackling voice had informed him.

The significance of the Lear jet was not lost on the Comte. Obviously she hadn't taken the company's lavishly decorated Grumman Gulfstream II because she didn't want to alert anyone to her unexpected return.

She didn't want anyone to have time to prepare. He smiled. As if there was anything she could do now. Didn't she realize it was too late?

How naive she was to think that she could outsmart them! Especially when they had all waited so patiently and for so long.

Well, he was nobody's fool. He had expected a sudden move on her part, and he'd been prepared. She had been shadowed to Orly, and before the Lear jet had received flight clearance he had already known about it. And when the jet landed at Kennedy Airport a mere fifteen minutes ago, he had known that, too. The only thing that surprised him was that it had taken this long for her to make a move.

Ah, it felt so good to be on top of it all. Poor Hélène. She thought she was a queen when she was, in reality, only a pawn. His pawn.

She had been a fool. Somewhere along the way she had been lulled into a false sense of security. It was so easy to feel omnipotent just because of a few items in a lawyer's vault. He smiled secretly. Even the most secure vaults have a way of opening.

He felt the limousine lurch to another stop. The queasiness in his stomach returned. Better have another drink to dull that feeling, he told himself.

He opened the door of the built-in bar cabinet and splashed a generous portion of Armagnac into one of the Baccarat snifters. He drained it in one greedy gulp.

Ah, that felt good, he thought as the warm glow of the

brandy spread through him like a much-needed caress. Then he poured himself another.

Suddenly his lips compressed angrily as he slammed a fist into the velour seat. "Je suis bête!" he exclaimed. How stupid to have overlooked the obvious. He should have noticed it before.

Two hours were unaccounted for. He hadn't realized it at first, but Hélène's flight had taken 140 minutes more than the usual flight time. He had been notified upon both takeoff and landing. But what had she done during those two unaccountable hours? Surely she hadn't flown circles over the middle of the Atlantic. A Lear jet didn't carry enough fuel for that.

Yes, she must have interrupted the flight. She had landed somewhere. But where? And whatever for?

He picked up the limousine's mobile telephone. Someone would have to talk to the pilot and find out.

The Comte's black limousine was nearing the Junot Building just as James Cortland Gore III placed another syrup-drenched pancake into his mouth. Gore sat in the breakfast room of his baronial mansion in Greenwich, Connecticut, a mere forty-five-minute drive from mid-Manhattan. The small bright room was covered with a green fern-patterned wallpaper, and the floor was laid with dark gray flagstones. Sitting across the wrought-iron-and-glass table, his wife was silently looking out the big bay window. It was a moment of fantasy. The morning sunshine was throwing elongated shadows of trees across the blinding snow, making the lawn look like a zebra-skin rug.

Then she glanced back at her husband.

Gore was a short, porcine man of sixty-one with sagging jowls, pursed red lips, and innumerable chins. He had a bald head, and the beady gray eyes peering out of the sagging pouches beneath his stiff salt-and-pepper eyebrows were focused on the front page of *The Wall Street Journal* spread out beside him. His pinstriped suit reflected his position. As a successful banker he had a $150,000-a-year salary, generous expense accounts, and memberships in the exclusive clubs that cater to working gentlemen. He was at the pinnacle of his career.

Gore lifted his eyes from the newspaper and peered across the table.

One look at Geraldine left no doubt but that she was a

pampered woman. She was fifty-seven years old but looked no more than thirty-nine. Painfully thin, she had striking Indian-like cheekbones and her skin was dark with the unmistakable Palm Beach tan from weekends spent in Florida. Her lemon gown trimmed with matching ostrich feathers had come from Martha's in Bal Harbour. Her ash-blond hair was bleached almost white by the sun and hung thinly to her shoulders. It was styled each Thursday afternoon at Susumu's salon on Fifth Avenue before her Friday flights to Palm Beach. Her nose was thin and delicate. More than fifteen years earlier it had been "redone" in an exclusive clinic outside Lausanne. A sparkling canary-diamond bracelet hung from her bony wrist. She'd picked it out at Bulgari a week ago, and since then it hadn't left her wrist for a moment.

Gore cleared his throat. "By the way, dear, there's some bad news." His chins quivered as he spoke.

"Bad news?"

"I'll have to work late tonight."

"Oh, no, darling," she said with a moan. "Don't tell me! You . . . you can't! Not tonight. You *promised* nothing would interfere with tonight. We're invited to the Asburys' for dinner, remember?"

Gore was annoyed. Remember? How could he forget? "Sorry, dear," he said calmly. "You'd better call them up and cancel."

"Oh, d-a-m-n!" Another fine evening spoiled by his work. And she'd been so looking forward to this one. The Asburys had houseguests from France, and Geraldine was dying to show off her half-forgotten Sorbonne French and the taffeta Grès gown she'd bought in Paris last year. It was gorgeous, in geranium, port, and bottle green. There was no doubt about it—the Grès was a masterpiece. It hugged her body where it was supposed to, but not too tightly; rather it . . . yes, it *caressed* her.

Now the evening was ruined. She couldn't go to the Asburys' unescorted. It just wasn't *done*. S-h-i-t, she spelled out in her mind. Careful, she told herself. Simmer down. Be dignified. She glanced at her husband.

Across the table, Gore, not content with one helping of pancakes, was engrossed in sating his unusually limitless appetite. He was, however, genuinely sorry for ruining Geraldine's plans. Nobody knew better than he how much she'd been looking forward to dinner with the Asburys and their French guests. He didn't enjoy disappointing her. But tonight he had other plans. Tonight he was going to make one of the most important decisions of his life.

Just three days were left, he thought. *Just three more days and the Junot bank loan would be due. If it could not be repaid on time, then it would be up to the bank—up to him—to decide the fate of the collateral: 20 percent of the entire stock of Hélène Junot International, Inc. A juicy 20 percent of Hélène Junot's personal 51 percent of the corporation, for it had been a personal loan. And members of the board of Hélène Junot International, Inc., had approached him—discreetly at his clubs, openly through associates and attorneys, and even secretly with mysterious telephone calls. There were whispered offers of what he would receive. One million dollars, tax-free, as long as Hélène did not get an extension and the bank decided to distribute the shares to the other stockholders for their market value.*

Like greedy vultures, they were all waiting to pounce on her. For one reason or another, each of them seemed determined to have her out of the way.

Oh, what a million dollars couldn't solve. There had never been a time he needed it more. He enjoyed living comfortably, and Geraldine demanded a life-style that . . . well, that had practically gone out of style. There was the mansion in Greenwich and the house in Palm Beach, both so very necessary socially, and both so prohibitive financially. Both were mortgaged to the hilt. On the landing strip outside town sat the Beechcraft Bonanza that they used each weekend to commute to Palm Beach. The honey-gold-and-champagne Bentley sat in the heated garage between the brand-new Cadillac Seville and the late-model Lincoln Continental. Then there were the shopping sprees in Paris, where Madame Gore was becoming an increasingly well-known fixture. The red carpet was already being rolled out for her at the couturiers' and she was even getting front-row seating during the shows. And finally there was the sixty-foot Chris Craft yacht Geraldine was determined he buy for her. After all, she reasoned with typical rationale, the house in Palm Beach looked stark naked with an empty dock. His suggestion that they tear out the dock had not been met with disapproval. It had been met with horror.

And then, two months ago, the most expensive habit of all had surfaced. "Picking up trinkets" at Harry Winston or Bulgari. He glanced at the diamonds sparkling on her wrist and winced.

All that was so difficult to manage on $150,000 a year. Geraldine didn't know it, and God knows he couldn't bear to break her pretty heart by telling her, but his finances were looking very bleak.

Already he had "borrowed" from the bank, discreetly giving himself loans from time to time. He always planned on repaying them when he had a windfall, or sometime when Geraldine wasn't costing him so much.

Damn her! he thought angrily. It was so hard to say no.

The million dollars offered for throwing Hélène Junot's shares in the other stockholders' directions was irresistible. An answered prayer.

And best of all, no one need ever know.

He tossed the newspaper aside. It was far more pleasurable to think about a million dollars than to scour the news.

That was how he missed a three-column headline on page two. It read: "SHAKE-UP AT JUNOT PUBLICATIONS?"

The icy wind stung bitterly at his face as the Chameleon snapped the phone-booth door shut behind him. Frowning, he inserted a dime in the phone and punched out the number of another pay phone somewhere across town. He listened to the soft rings. Once. Twice. Three times. He replaced the receiver on the cradle and his dime jingled back into the return slot. He fished it out and waited twenty seconds. All around him he heard the noisy turmoil of Times Square.

Paper and garbage flew in the wind while neon flashed gaudy advertisements. The record and shoe shops weren't open yet. The porno theaters were quiet. No one dashed in and out of massage parlors. It was too early. Altogether, Times Square looked seedy, an ancient dowager turned bag lady. Still, it wasn't too bad, the Chameleon thought to himself. Times Square never looked too bad at nine-thirty A.M. But at nine-thirty at night it was a whole different story.

Last night it had looked like a Babylonian carnival. Rows of movie marquees were festooned with cutouts of voluptuous nudes. Peep-show parlors promised a glimpse of Sodom for a quarter. Hookers in rabbit coats paraded around with bare, frozen thighs. Drag queens strutted on shaky heels, their coats open wide to show off rock-hard, expensive breasts. Hungry-eyed boys in tight Levi's were posed to accentuate their firm round bottoms. All available, for a price.

At Forty-fourth Street a Puerto Rican girl had stepped out of the shadows. She wore white plastic boots and a short skirt. Her long bare legs were red from the cold.

"You give me light?" she asked softly. Shiny black eyes looked at him over her cigarette.

He fished in his pocket for his lighter. As the flame flared up, he caught a glimpse of tawny skin and wet red lips. Her cheeks were powdered but gray, the shivering fingers holding the cigarette too thick, too masculine.

He shook his head and continued walking. Another drag queen. He liked real pussy, not a queer prick tucked out of sight. He sighed. Weren't there any women working these streets anymore?

At a red light he set his suitcase down on the sidewalk and lit a cigarette. Then he looked for a hotel.

On Forty-eighth Street, just off Broadway, he found one. He stared up at it. A real fleabag. Eight stories high, bricks painted an ugly gray. There was an alley beside it that led to a parking lot in the rear. Around the corner he could see an elaborate fire escape that led down to it. "HOTEL ZANZIBAR," the flashing red neon on the front announced. "Rooms $5.00 and up. Permanents and Transients Welcome," a rusty sign read.

It was the type of place that offered total anonymity, where no one asked any questions. Pay for your flop in advance, and then come and go as you like.

Perfect.

He tossed his cigarette into the gutter and watched it land with a shower of sparks. Then, whistling softly, he went up the concrete steps, opened the door, and walked into the lobby.

The lobby was something else. It was tiled and looked like a cross between a Turkish bath and a 1920's theater lobby. The sconces along the walls were of surprisingly good quality, but dented and rusty and missing their shades. The tear-shaped bulbs glared harshly. From one of the rooms down the hall a radio was on full blast. It was loud, tinny salsa, distorted and painful to the ears. Steam radiators hissed and clanged like snorting locomotives.

To the right, just inside the door, was a glass-and-wood

17

booth. It almost hid the short, tired-looking blond who sat behind it reading a confession magazine.

He cleared his throat.

Reluctantly she put the magazine down on the counter and her pale face looked up at him. "Yeah?" she rasped unenthusiastically.

He set his suitcase down. "I want a room," he said softly.

"Well, there's not much choice," she answered in a hoarse voice. "All I got's one." She snapped her bubble gum. "Rest's full up."

"Does it face the street?"

She shook her head. "Nope, out back. Looks down on the parking lot. Third floor. Real quiet."

"How much?"

"Twenty bucks a night."

"Twenty bucks a. . . ? But the sign outside says five!"

"Yeah," she said wearily, "I know. It's an old sign. Take it or leave it." Her voice sounded annoyed. She wanted to get back to the confession magazine.

He sighed. "All right, I'll take it."

"How long you want it for?"

He considered. "Oh . . . make it a week."

She shoved the registration book toward him and watched him bend over and sign in. "A. Samuels," the legible script read, from Washington, D.C. A change, she thought, from all the illegible John Smiths that filled the ledger. She turned around and took a key from one of the cubbyholes behind the desk. He reached out for it.

"Uh-uh," she said with a shake of her head. "That'll be a hundred and forty bucks. In advance."

He reached for his wallet and counted out three fifty dollar bills.

"Room's number three-oh-four," she said, slapping a ten and the key down on the linoleum counter. "That's on the third floor. Elevator's over there, on your right." She nodded vaguely in the direction. "And leave the key here at the desk whenever you go out. The management don't like their guests takin' off with their keys."

"Sure," he said, picking up his suitcase. Then he walked to the elevator.

Room 304 was everything he had expected. It was small and shabby, the paper-stiff sheets on the bed hiding a stained, lumpy mattress. In the bathroom, a leaky faucet endlessly dripped into the green-stained sink. Rough voices and rock music filtered through the thin wall from the room next door.

He pushed aside the faded curtains and peered out into the darkness. He couldn't have chosen a better place. All around were the backs of old office buildings. At this hour of the night they were empty. Below, the parking lot was dark and deserted, strewn with garbage. And right outside his window, the fire escape led down to that parking lot. A grimy private staircase. He would be able to come and go up and down that fire escape anytime after nightfall. If he was cautious, maybe even during the day. And best of all, the Hotel Zanzibar was far removed from that glittering world of high society he'd have to come into contact with. He might end up getting bitten by bed bugs, but at least he wouldn't be connected with the job. When it was done, the police would scour among the Beautiful People, not the city's cheap hotels for an anonymous stranger. Anyway, by that time he planned to be long gone.

He drew the curtains, turned away from the window, and went over to the bed. He placed the suitcase on it and unlocked it. So far, everything was going according to plan. In the bus terminal he'd found the key and the suitcase in two separate lockers.

The suitcase was neatly packed with stiffly folded clothes. Unceremoniously he dumped them on the floor. Taking out a pocketknife, he slashed apart the lining inside the lid. Then he slid his hand between the lining and the vinyl shell.

The Chameleon smiled. His fingers felt paper. "Oh, baby," he whispered to the suitcase. "Sweet, sweet baby. I could come all over you."

He pulled twenty-six envelopes out from behind the lining. First he tore open the twenty-five thick ones. Each was filled with crisp new hundred-dollar bills. He stacked them neatly in a pile. Then, wetting his finger, he quickly counted. The amount checked out: $50,000.

The down payment on a murder.

Finally he tore open the twenty-sixth envelope. It felt empty. But inside was a single newspaper clipping, neatly folded. Slowly he unfolded it.

He let out a low whistle and blinked. Then he sat down on the edge of the bed and stared at the photo of the first female target he'd ever had. Such a pity, he thought. God, she was a beautiful dame. She didn't stand a chance. Not against him.

The Chameleon was the best contract killer in the business. He lit a cigarette and glanced again at the photo with its simple caption: *Hélène Junot.*

3

The Junot Building was located on the northeast corner of Fifth Avenue and Twelfth Street. In the midst of that sedate old neighborhood it stuck out like a dazzling, blinding diamond. Hélène had hired Kevin Roche, John Dinkeloo, and Associates to design the nineteen-story structure.

"I want something spectacular," she had told the architects. "Something dazzling and chic, yet something with panache and *guts.*"

And that, exactly, was what she got. It literally stopped traffic. A small-scale forerunner of their spectacular U.N. Plaza Hotel, Roche, Dinkeloo, and Associates had designed an award-winning structure of angular walls of mirrored glass. In the morning light the Junot Building looked frosty and ice-cube-cold. During the day it caught movement and activity and seemed alive. At night it was almost as if a million candles shimmered inside the facade. But at sundown it was at its most spectacular. It faced west, and the dying sun turned its faceted mirror walls to fire.

The building's facade loomed cold and silvery at nine-thirty when Hélène emerged from her white Rolls-Royce Silver Cloud, New York license plate HJII. The mirrors threw reflections of the car all over the building as the gray-liveried chauffeur held the door open for her. On the sidewalk, several passersby looked at her. Hélène was the type of woman who naturally made heads turn. Wherever she went, she was noticed. This was due in part to her celebrity status, in part to her extraordinary beauty.

Anyone who did not know her would have laid odds that she was under thirty and a fashion model. Actually she was thirty-eight and owned the controlling shares of Hélène Junot

International, Inc., the publishing empire that bore her name. She had founded and forged the corporation that printed the world's most influential and widely read fashion magazines. She was slender, stood five feet, ten inches tall in her stocking feet, and held herself with regal poise and grace. Her exquisitely pale oval face was as delicate as a Dresden figurine's, and she had the most strikingly violet eyes. Set in her face like radiantly rare jewels, their exact coloring was dependent on the lighting around her. Fluctuating somewhere between smoky amethyst and translucent violet, they were speckled with the tiniest flecks of sapphire. Her luxuriant hair was raven black. Drawn back into a chignon, its severity only emphasized the delicate cheekbones that were as pronounced as a Bolshoi ballerina's. Her lips were full and sensual and her teeth had the gleam of new porcelain. The collar of her lush Blackglama mink coat was turned up and hid her long, graceful neck.

She glanced down Fifth Avenue toward Washington Square. This was basically a residential area: the sidewalks were nearly deserted. At the foot of the avenue the arch gleamed white in the sunlight. In front of it the giant Christmas tree was still up. Her lips tightened when she saw it.

Merry Christmas, she thought, shaking her head unhappily. Such a sad holiday, so sad because it is always what others seem to celebrate. Others, all those secure, nameless families snowbound in quaint little houses with creaking rocking chairs and colorful quilts and wonderful relatives with whom they can share the holidays.

I had a wonderful family once.

She felt a shiver, but it was not from the cold. Instinctively she drew the mink lapels closer to her throat and held them there.

"Madame?" a voice said gently from behind her.

She came out of her reverie and turned around. The chauffeur was still holding the car door open, unable to close it. She was in the way.

"Oh! I'm sorry, Jimmy," she said in her throaty, French-accented voice. Her breath made little white clouds of vapor in front of her face. Quickly she moved aside.

He shut the door. "Shall you be needing the car for lunch, madame?"

She considered. "No . . . five-thirty will do."

"Very well, madame. Will you be needing anything else?"

She shook her head. "No. Thank you, Jimmy. Just drop the luggage off at the apartment." She could not help smiling faintly as he clicked his heels together, Prussian fashion, giving a slight bow while touching his visored cap with his fingertips. A moment later the Rolls-Royce engine purred and the big car slid silently down Fifth Avenue.

Nothing had changed in the week she had been gone. Except for the Junot Building, nothing on the block had changed for decades. Across Fifth Avenue, the massive gray hulk of the Forbes headquarters squatted with the invincibility expected of a financial soothsayer. It amused her that the solid, classical temple had to face her building. The Junot Building did not fit in with Malcolm Forbes's pillared tabernacle to the almighty dollar. Nor did it fit in with the haughty elegance of the prewar apartment buildings that lined the avenue down to the arch.

But the location fit. After all, her empire was to the fashion world what Forbes's was to economics. Her name had become just as synonymous with haute couture as the Fairchild empire housed in the squat, ugly factorylike building next door. Fairchild, the downtown publisher of *Women's Wear Daily* and *W*, was not a Junot competitor like snooty uptown Condé Nast was with *Vogue*, or Hearst was with *Harper's Bazaar*. Regardless, jokes abounded about two fashion publishers rubbing elbows on the same block.

Smiling faintly, she pivoted on her heel and walked to the entrance of her building. The blatant snobbery of New York's "glamour" industries never failed to amuse her; they always insisted on being associated with the posh Upper East Side. After all, where was Condé Nast? Where were all the modeling agencies? But she showed them. She alone had been responsible for shifting glamour's axis back downtown. When she'd decided on the tranquil Twelfth Street location for the building, the whole boardroom had been in shock.

Would the ridiculous snobs never learn? If uptown was always pictured as being so very fashionable, what, then, was *more* fashionable than fashionable lower Fifth Avenue? What could compare with the peaceful elegance reminiscent of Paris, and the stateliness associated with London?

The glass doors of the Junot Building slid open electronically, and she entered the warm, cavernous lobby. Nodding to the receptionist seated behind the marble desk, she crossed the lobby to her private elevator. Though she had entered its doors countless times, she still looked around with pride. This was her world, the world she had created, the world over which she alone reigned. Employees on errands rushed around purposefully, their brisk footsteps echoing on the black marble floor. Voices became part of the low murmur that drifted to the ceiling, and occasional coughs rang out like the dull tolls of a cracked bell. Faintly she could hear the relentless ringings of telephones in the distance. This was the way she liked it. Her world was alive and well.

She glanced up at the enormous silver block letters on the lobby wall above her. "HJII." they read. And underneath, smaller letters translated: "Hélène Junot International, Incorporated." It was a ritual with her to always check those letters. Just to be sure she wasn't dreaming.

"Good mornin', Miz Junot," a cheerful voice said from behind her. She turned. Henry, the uniformed daytime guard, was following her. His wizened black face wore a wide, toothy grin. "Happy New Year," he said.

Hélène smiled. "And a very Happy New Year to you, too, Henry," she answered.

"Thank *you*, ma'am."

They had reached her private elevator. He punched the button outside it, and the door slid silently open. Courteously he held it aside for her.

"Have a real nice day, Miz Junot," he said, meaning it.

"Thank you, Henry, I will," she replied in spite of what she knew. She stepped into the small walnut-paneled elevator and pressed the button marked nineteen.

The nineteenth floor was the executive floor. The windowless reception area was dim, spacious, and lavishly appointed. Here the dollar-and-cents value of the empire was translated into tangibles for all to see. No expense had been spared. Even the blond receptionist behind the enormous ellipsoid marble desk was gorgeous, chicly dressed in a peach-colored designer shift. The floors were carpeted in thick mahogany pile which ran all the way up the walls to the acoustic-tile ceiling. Suede-upholstered conversation pits—by Brueton, $24,000 per sofa—were scattered all around, with brass tables holding neat stacks of the latest Junot magazines. The magazines were not listed on a roster by name. Instead, all around on the walls they were represented by the covers of their most recent issues. Lit by all but invisible lights, the shadowboxed blowups hung at evenly spaced eye-level intervals like twelve small movie screens. Without fail, they were changed each month at the exact moment the issues hit the newsstands.

Hélène's imperious gaze swept over them. She had seen each cover hundreds of times, and had the final say on each one, had helped choose the layout and the color, style and size of the typeset, and still she felt a thrill of maternal pride coursing through her. Her babies, and she was their proud mother. Each one of them called by the name she had baptized it:

Les Modes	**Les Modes**
(American edition)	(English edition)
Les Modes	**La Moda**
(French edition)	(Italian edition)
Mode	**Les Modes Homme**
(German edition)	(French edition)
La Moda Uomo	**Glamorous Miss**
(Italian edition)	**Ladies' Bazaar**
Bride's World	**Yachting and Boating**
Beauté	

All beautiful slicks with a combined monthly circulation of almost twenty-eight million copies. Worldwide. All part of a publishing empire that spawned new vogues and changed life-styles around the globe.

The cover girl behind the reception desk glanced up with visible surprise. "Miss Junot!" she said quickly. "We . . . we hadn't expected you back so soon. Not until this afternoon . . ."

Hélène began to unbutton her mink. "I decided to come back early, Maggie."

Maggie glanced around suspiciously, and her voice dropped to a conspiratorial whisper. "The Comte de Léger is already here. He came in twenty minutes ago. Almost as if he knew you were arriving this morning instead of this afternoon."

Hélène stopped unbuttoning her coat. Hubert de Léger? As usual he was too well-informed. She had left no word that she was coming back early. There was only one way he could have known: he probably had someone in Paris watching her Île St.-Louis apartment. Spying on her. So it had come to

24

this. She had suspected that sooner or later it would. "And he's the only one?" she asked.

Maggie nodded. "So far. But the grapevine's on Red Alert. Rumor has it the whole board will be here by this afternoon."

This came as no surprise. She herself had scheduled the board meeting more than a month ago. For those not in the know, it was a routine formality. For those in the know . . . She felt a strange tightening of her throat. In a faraway voice she murmured, "Yes, they'll all soon be here."

Maggie gave her a strange look. "Are you all right, Miss Junot?"

Hélène managed a smile and nodded. "Yes. Thank you, Maggie."

The reception phone rang and Maggie picked up the receiver. Hélène turned and walked down the long, plushy carpeted corridor to her office. Vaguely she could hear snatches of Maggie's conversation drifting after her. "Yes . . . she's already here . . . just came in . . ." But Hélène wasn't paying attention. Over and over she kept thinking: It's another winter, another one of those cold, dreadful winters.

"Miss Junot!"

She stopped and turned around. Albert Lourie, her executive secretary, was running to catch up with her. He was a thin, pasty-complexioned man in his thirties with mousy brown hair. In one hand he clutched a folded newspaper.

"Why, Albert!" Hélène said. "You *are* in a hurry!"

"Thank *God* I caught you," he said breathlessly. His face was flushed. "Maggie just told me you came in. There's something I think you ought to see right away."

From his discomfiture, Hélène could tell it was something serious. Albert was not one to sound false alarms. "Well?" she asked.

"Not out here." He gestured to a small conference room off the corridor.

Hélène nodded. They went into the walnut-paneled room, closed the door, and sat opposite each other on rich brown leather Tucroma chairs. "Now," she said, "what is this matter of life and death?"

"This." Morosely Albert tapped the newspaper in his hand. "Today's *Wall Street Journal*. Have you seen it yet?"

"I haven't had a chance. And. . . ?"

Without answering, he handed her the paper and jabbed an accusing finger at an article on page two. Hélène stared at it.

The three column headline seemed to scream at her: "SHAKE-UP AT JUNOT PUBLICATIONS?"

Her lips went dry as she read the second bank of headlines: *"Publishing Giant in Serious Trouble?"* Stunned, she read on:

A formal, but unannounced meeting of the board of directors of Hélène Junot International, Inc., is expected to commence today. A reliable source who wished to remain anonymous disclosed that the meeting will focus on what seems to be a secret power struggle for control of HJII. It is no secret, however, that Miss Junot is overextended with loans, and that *You!*, Junot's new magazine oriented toward the working woman, has been a commercial failure, with a loss of millions. Observers in the publishing industry and on Wall Street speculate that a power struggle at this time could conceivably harm HJII's financial footing and already tenuous stock value.

The power behind the publishing giant has always been Hélène Junot, the legendary French publisher who began the magazine *Les Modes* in 1957 in Paris and who built it into a worldwide publishing conglomerate noted for its ability to set fashion trends and arbitrate taste.

Two years ago, Miss Junot used a large portion of her personal shares in HJII as collateral for a massive loan to finance Junot Publications, a separate corporate entity held exclusively by Miss Junot. That note reportedly is shortly due. If Miss Junot is unable to meet her commitments on time, the huge bloc of HJII voting shares may become property of the ManhattanBank N.A., which can then, in turn, sell them as it sees fit. This would leave the founder and president of HJII, Miss Junot, with only a minor portion of voting stock, barely enough to exercise a veto concerning a public offering of HJII stock. . . .

There was the crunching of newspaper as Hélène flung the paper aside. Her face was grim. She knew what this article meant. Someone on the board of HJII had deliberately leaked the story to the press, determined to undermine her position as president of the corporation and to weaken her standing with the banks. It was a sneaky tactic designed to throw doubt on her ability to lead. Also, it was a way to publicize her steadfast refusals to allow the company to go public, and thereby pressure her to reconsider. While the other members of the board would realize an enormous profit if she agreed to it, none would gain as much as she. But the thought of unknown investors invading the company she had fought in countless ways and against innumerable odds to create, only to speculate for higher and higher profits, terrified her. In the search for the corporate dollar, quality would undoubtedly slip. To Hélène that was unthinkable. After all, what was HJII but a trend-setter of quality? HJII had a handful of stockholders, and that was the way she wanted it to remain.

Albert squirmed nervously in his chair. "I . . . I'm awfully sorry, Miss Junot," he stammered. "I just thought you should see it before . . ." Helplessly he spread his hands apart.

She looked at him. "Yes. Thank you, Albert," she said in her throaty voice. "I appreciate it. Really."

Then she got up, clapped a weary hand on his shoulder, left the conference room, and walked slowly down the corridor to her office. I've been betrayed, she thought miserably. And not for the first time, either. The only thing that doesn't change is the dirty taste it leaves in your mouth.

Of course HJII had problems, she admitted to herself. What company didn't? But to leak such problems under the guise of "news" to *The Wall Street Journal* was despicable and inexcusable. Who was the culprit? De Léger? She wouldn't put it past him. Still, she couldn't be sure; the others were not much better.

She could be absolutely certain of only one thing. The leakage to *The Wall Street Journal* was not a warning shot across the bow. It was an open declaration of war. And long or short, she knew it would be a bitter conflict. One or all of the board wanted control of Hélène Junot International, Inc. They had for years. And she knew why. Not because they cared for a single share of their Junot stock. Not even because they cared an iota for money or fashion or publishing. But because they hated her enough to try to take from her the only thing she'd ever loved and cared for—her corporation.

She made a left turn at the end of the corridor and stopped in front of a polished teak door. At eye level, the small gold letters spelled a single word: "President." It looked so alien. So weighty. She wished her title would read "Founder and Artistic Director" instead. That was what she was proudest of.

She put her hand on the knob and opened the door. The steady droning of a typewriter greeted her as she stepped into the outer office. Julie, her secretary, was busy attacking a pile of letters that had accumulated over the holidays. Throughout the building and behind her back Julie was known as "The Sphinx." Her reputation for guarding the entrance to Hélène's inner office was legend.

At the sound of the door opening, Julie glanced up suspiciously, her fingers never leaving the keyboard. Her dark brown eyes fluttered with surprise. "Why, Miss Junot!" she exclaimed. Abruptly she stopped typing, her fingers poised in midair.

Hélène smiled. "Good morning, Julie."

"You're back early! There wasn't even notification that the plane . . ."

"Yes, I know," Hélène answered. "I thought I'd rush back very quietly, so I chartered a Lear jet." She paused and said slowly, "Not quietly enough, it seems. I hear the Comte is waiting."

Julie made a face. "Inside," she said. Then she frowned, leaned forward, and placed an ear beside the intercom on her desk.

Hélène looked at her strangely. "What in—?"

Julie put a finger to her lips to silence her. Then she straightened with satisfaction and pointed at the intercom. Hélène understood. She nodded, leaned close, and listened carefully. She could hear a faint humming sound. Hubert de Léger had switched it on from the inside office. He was eavesdropping.

Hélène shook her head. This didn't surprise her in the least. She knew the Comte better than anyone else did. He was sly and brash and managed to force his way in wherever it pleased him to do so. Even the Sphinx's determination was no match for his will. Nothing short of armed guards could have kept him out. Hélène shrugged. "Any messages?"

"These." Julie handed her a sheaf of small pink message memos. "Also, your brother called. He wants to see you privately before the board meeting this afternoon. He says it's very important."

Hélène nodded. She would see Edmond as soon as she got rid of the Comte. "Thank you, Julie," she said. "And please make certain we're not disturbed. Hold all calls."

Julie nodded and went back to her typing. Hélène walked

over to the inner office door and began to turn the knob, but stopped and waited. She closed her eyes for a few seconds as she steeled herself for the confrontation with de Léger. Then she entered her office.

It was a corner office that actually consisted of four rooms—office, kitchenette, bedroom, and bath. All the rest of the offices and corridors in the Junot Building had been decorated by an expensive design firm, but Hélène had warned them about touching her office. "Hands off this one!" she had told the aging decorator whose firm she had chosen. He had been horrified. "You try to touch this suite and I'll have your head on a platter!" she warned.

In the large room which served as her office, the two outside walls were floor-to-ceiling windows. One faced the solemn Forbes Building; the other looked down Fifth Avenue to the stately arch guarding the entrance to Washington Square Park. She had chosen this corner for her office expressly for that view. The arch reminded her of the Arc de Triomphe in her beloved Paris.

The inside walls were an innocuous white and the floor covering was nubby beige wall-to-wall wool carpet. In these respects it looked like any other corner office in New York. However, Hélène had used her personal stamp of good taste, style, and memories to create her own luxurious yet eminently comfortable environment.

The walls were hung with framed fashion sketches, her favorites from past issues of *Les Modes*. The furniture was her own, lovingly hunted-down pieces of ancient French furniture whose meticulous restoration she had personally directed. Whether she was in town or not, a vase of fresh flowers always sat on her desk.

One glance told Hélène that the Comte had made himself at home in her sanctuary. He sat in the delicately carved French chair behind her Louis Quinze desk. The vase of fresh flowers had been moved aside, and both of his damp patent-leather loafers rested informally on the highly polished marquetry top. In one red hand he held a glass of Napoleon brandy that he had served himself from the bar behind her desk, in the other a cigarette with an enormous ash cocked on its end.

Hubert de Léger blew a stream of smoke skyward and looked at Hélène. Amusement glinted in his jet-black eyes. "Entrez!" he slurred. The ash fell away from the cigarette and landed on the spotless beige carpet. "My beautiful Hélène," he said in French. "I have been expecting you. Please. Come in. I do not bite. And even if I did, I am not suffering from rabies at the moment." He broke into a series of thin, hollow laughs.

Hélène closed the door quietly behind her. For a moment she looked at him; then she turned her face away. There was repulsion in her eyes. She knew he drank heavily. But my God, she thought, not to this extent at nine-thirty in the morning.

"Can I offer my beautiful Hélène a drink?" he asked mockingly as he hoisted his glass. "The bar in this office is most superbly stocked."

"Thank you, no," she replied coldly.

"Hmm. C'est dommage." He made a childish face.

For an instant she remembered how he had once looked with his youthful, dashing good looks, his raven-black hair, his stiff posture, his lean, athletic physique, his sober black eyes and determined cleft chin. Now his jaw had slackened, his hair was gray, and his once-sober eyes were glassy from drink. Could this be the same man she had known since childhood? Was this the Hubert de Léger who had at one time wooed her so ardently?

Tightening her lips, she crossed the room and wordlessly looked down at his feet. Anger surged through her. He was playing games, seeing just how much he could get away with. Suddenly she grabbed his feet and pushed them off.

He heaved a sigh and let them drop heavily to the carpet. "My dear, that was not very nice of you," he said reprimandingly.

"Hubert," she said in a peculiar warning tone, "you take far too many liberties."

He raised his eyebrows, but she didn't notice. She was moving the vase back to the spot where it always stood, and then slipped out of her mink. Haphazardly she flung it over the back of one of the two little Louis Quinze chairs facing her desk. Both were upholstered in ancient cracked green leather. Then she walked over beside his chair and stood there for a moment looking down at him. He stared back up at her with a pretended lack of understanding.

"Hubert? Must you be reminded?" she finally asked. "This is *my* office."

He looked at her with a blank expression. Then he slapped

the palm of his hand against his forehead in mock forgetfulness. "How thoughtless of me!" he said. "Of course, it still is, isn't it? How silly of me." He frowned ostentatiously, peered deep into his brandy, and said slowly, "Well, we might as well be truthful. It *still* is your office. And it will be, at least until this week is up."

"At least," she said, her voice curt and razor-sharp. "My chair, Hubert . . ."

"Your . . ."

"Chair. If you insist on plaguing me with your company, I'm afraid you shall have to do it from there." She pointed to the empty chair in front of her desk.

He raised his glass in a silent, airy toast and took his time getting to his feet. His lips were twisted into an ugly smile. After making a courteous, if ungenuine display of helping her into her seat, he sat where she'd specified.

"Charming office . . . such a marvelous view," he said approvingly. "But the place needs some changes. Too feminine for my tastes . . . too many curlicued French touches."

Hélène stiffly folded her hands and stared down at them. If she said nothing, perhaps he would burn himself out.

"You know," he said, "by next Monday I may have to call up a design firm and have them redecorate this place. 'Tear it all out!' I'll demand. 'Make it sleek and masculine.' "

She was only half-listening; her mind was racing over the possibilities of how to get him out of the office. Some way that was quick, yet wouldn't give him a chance to create a scene.

He stubbed out his cigarette in a crystal ashtray. Then, pretending to notice her mink for the first time, he reached over to the chair beside him and hoisted up one of the sleeves. "The famous Blackglama?" he asked.

"Yes," Hélène said quietly.

He laughed. "How marvelous! Every woman in this city would commit arson to get one. But you? All *you* have to do is model one coat for Richard Avedon and . . . presto! You're a living Blackglama 'legend.' Ergo, Hélène Junot, who by the way has whole closets full of furs, gets another one for free. And not only that, but the title 'legend' as well!" He leered at her. "You've always wanted a title, eh, Hélène?"

Hélène looked at him steadily. "I don't think you came here to discuss the coat, Hubert," she said dryly.

He let the sleeve drop. "As a matter of fact, I didn't."

31

"Then why *did* you come?"

"Our mutual business interests," he replied. "Hélène Junot, of course. The corporation *and* the woman."

She stiffened, her violet eyes flashing warily. "In that case, I'm afraid we have nothing to discuss."

"Nothing?"

"Nothing whatsoever. As you're only too well aware, the board meeting is this afternoon. I suggest you discuss any pertinent complaints you have regarding my publishing policies—or me—openly at that time."

"Bring the dirty laundry out into the open and it disappears, eh?" He clucked his tongue. "My, but such a display of courage. But then, you were never a quitter, were you, Hélène? You've always gotten everything you set that iron heart of yours on, haven't you?"

"Hubert," she said wearily, "please get to the point."

He lit another cigarette. "Ah, but you see, I'm getting there. I've come to warn you. I want you to be prepared before you set foot in that boardroom."

"Prepared? Whatever for?"

"Corporate slaughter, my dear."

YESTERDAY

I
MURDER

1

Paris, 1944

It was after three o'clock, and Hélène was playing in the park. The January afternoon was cold and windy and the narrow streets were nearly deserted. It was very quiet. Overhead, the sky was clear blue and the sun was shining. Completely surrounded by buildings, the little park was in deep shadow.

Across the street was her house. It was almost identical to the other grim, crooked houses that sagged against one another like rows of tired dominoes, each dependent on the next for support. But her house stood out proudly from the others. The windows on the ground floor were covered over with thick iron bars twisted into fanciful curlicues, and the front door was painted bright yellow. *Canary* yellow, Maman called it. And above the snow-covered rooftop she could glimpse the white dome and cupolas of Sacré Coeur gleaming in the sunshine.

She thought she heard something. She stopped playing with Antoinette, her porcelain doll, and listened carefully. It was a rumbling noise, still far away. But it was coming closer. A truck is headed this way, she thought with surprise.

She waited in anticipation. Motorized traffic in this working-class section of Paris was rare. There were no taxis or private automobiles. Parisians rode bicycles everywhere. Only the Boches and their collaborators experienced the luxury of traveling in cars and trucks. The streets of Montmartre were old and crooked, many of them too narrow to accommodate even the smallest automobiles.

The noise of the truck engine grew louder, and she put her lips close to Antoinette's ear. "Watch, Antoinette," she instructed the doll in a soft whisper. "Watch and you'll soon see your first truck!" She straightened the yellowed lace of

35

Antoinette's gown. After all, Antoinette was a lady, and ladies must look their best when they are seen in public.

Two minutes later a gray truck came roaring around the corner from the rue Durantin.

As she watched, it switched into low gear and rattled uphill, coming closer. The snow chains clattered and the gray tarpaulin stretched over the back flapped in the wind. Plainly she could see the swastika stenciled on the sides of the cab. Even as a child she already knew what it meant.

In a moment, the truck had passed by. She wrinkled her nose at the offensive stench of gasoline fumes. Curiously she stared after it. She wondered what it was doing in Montmartre. Then there was the sound of grinding gears as it turned a corner and disappeared. The noise of the motor slowly died away. A minute later there was silence. But a cloud of gray exhaust still hung heavy in the air.

She looked around to see if she was being watched. She wasn't. Then she did what she had seen other people do many times. She spat in the street. She was only seven years old, but she had already picked up the habits of older Parisians. One could not spit directly at the Boches. That was too dangerous. But one could spit after him when his back was turned.

It was almost half an hour after the truck had gone by that she had the feeling something was wrong. She had been building miniature snowmen on the slats of the park bench for Antoinette. Suddenly, somehow, she just *knew*.

She felt a sudden prickling of her spine.

Something was wrong.

She glanced across the street at her house. Everything appeared normal and peaceful. Nothing seemed amiss. Nothing . . . except the front door was open a crack and a woman was standing outside it. Hélène couldn't see her face underneath the black wool scarf, but she thought she recognized Madame Courbet, the wife of a switchboard operator at the Prefecture of Police. Still, she couldn't be certain. Whoever it was gestured frantically to someone inside, all the while throwing furtive glances over her shoulder. Then the woman hurried off. Hélène still wasn't able to see her face. The scarf was pulled too far forward, and the woman's face was in shadow.

Hélène would never know what gave her that feeling, but the moment she felt the prickling along her spine, she knew

Maman needed her. She didn't waste any time. She picked up Antoinette and ran across the street and up the three steps to the canary-yellow door.

It opened before she even reached it.

"Quickly!" Michelle, Maman's huge, plump servant, hissed at her. Michelle didn't even wait for Hélène to stomp the snow off her shoes. Roughly the thick fingers of her hands grabbed hold of the girl and pulled her inside. She slammed the door shut behind her and bolted it. The foyer was dark. The curtains were drawn, and between them, a chink of light showed.

Hélène looked up into Michelle's tense red moon face. "What's the matter?" she asked.

Michelle shrugged and brusquely turned away. Perhaps she was moody because it was so cold in the house, the week's coal rations already depleted. Despite her size, Michelle didn't take well to the cold.

Michelle had big peasant bones and enormous breasts. She was the maid, housekeeper, and nanny all rolled into one. Like a member of the family, she was devoted beyond endearment. Hélène knew that Maman couldn't afford to pay Michelle wages anymore, not with Papa gone all the time. Yet Michelle stayed on.

Hélène glanced around the little foyer. Maman was standing at one of the foyer windows, with her back turned. She was anxiously peering out through a crack in the drawn curtains, nervously wringing her slim hands. Hélène noticed that her belly looked larger than ever, and she knew why. Recently Maman had explained to her that a little brother or sister was on the way.

Maman was tall and bone-thin. Hélène remembered when her face had been unlined, her blond hair untouched by gray, and her eyes clear and lively. Suddenly, almost overnight, they looked tired. Still, she was a thoroughly elegant woman. Even the lean Occupation years could not put a dent in her poise.

And a working mother. She had held her job as a seamstress for Madeleine de Rauch ever since 1939. That was when Chanel, for whom she used to work, closed her doors.

Oh, and could Maman sew! Like an angel, she spun out one creation after another at her archaic pedal-operated machine, or even by hand. And after her long hours at

Madeleine de Rauch's salon, sewing for the fat German women she despised, Maman would bring work home. Sometimes she even did small jobs for neighbors as well—neighbors who could pay with precious rations instead of money.

Now Maman stopped peering out the window. If she noticed Hélène, she didn't let on. Instead she nervously paced back and forth in the foyer. "Mon dieu!" she said breathlessly. "Catherine is still not coming. Those acting lessons should be over by now."

"Then we must leave without her," Michelle said flatly. "If she wants to become the new Sarah Bernhardt so badly that she spends all her time at that theater—"

"Leave without Catherine?" Maman looked at Michelle in horror. "We *must* wait for her."

Michelle made clucking noises and threw her fat red hands up in despair. "There is no time! You heard what Madame Courbet said. She risked her life coming here to warn us. We haven't a moment to lose. We *cannot* wait!"

"We *must* wait," Maman said through clenched teeth. "You'll see. She'll be here any minute."

"Minute!" Michelle shouted. Her voice was shrill. "We don't have minutes. Seconds count!"

Maman wrung her hands. "Michelle. We have to wait. Can't you understand that? Catherine is my daughter!"

"And she is like mine also!" Michelle retorted.

"See, then you understand," Maman said without logic.

Michelle let out a frustrated growl. "There is no getting through to you," she snapped. "I might as well get whatever is in the pantry. If anything. We'll need food. It's a long journey."

Maman nodded absently and moved toward Hélène.

"Edmond!" Michelle called out. She hurried to the kitchen faster than Hélène had ever seen her move before.

Maman looked down at Hélène through tired eyes. Then she stooped over and wrapped her thin arms around the child. She held her very tight, too tight, and it hurt. Hélène felt frightened. More than ever, she knew something was terribly wrong.

"*Edmond!*" Michelle's voice came from the kitchen at a dangerously high pitch. "Give me a hand, you lazy good-for-nothing!"

"I'm coming, I'm coming!" Hélène's eleven-year-old

brother came down the stairs wearing his warmest winter clothes.

"Maman?" Hélène said, looking up at her.

"Yes, ma petite?"

"Is Papa coming home soon?"

Maman didn't answer. Her eyes looked moist and she wiped them with the back of her hand. From the nursery upstairs, little Marie began crying. She was hungry or lonely or wet.

Gently Maman pushed Hélène away. "Go upstairs," she said, her voice soft. "Go and put some warm clothes on Marie. The blue wool suit and the warm coat. Then bring her right down. And hurry!"

"Are we going somewhere, Maman?"

She nodded. "We're going on a journey."

Hélène's eyes sparkled. A journey? That sounded like fun. She loved journeys. "Can we take the train, Maman?" she pleaded. "Oh, please, let's do take the train. I love the train."

"Yes, ma petite," Maman whispered. "We'll take the train. But you must hurry. Otherwise we might miss it."

Hélène wrapped her arms around Maman and hugged her tightly. "I'll hurry!" she promised.

Maman smiled a strained little smile and tousled Hélène's hair affectionately. Hélène ran upstairs. From the top of the landing she looked down. Maman was at the window again, anxiously peering out through the crack in the curtains. Her lips weren't smiling anymore. Maman looked very frightened.

Hélène ran down the hall and entered the nursery. Marie stopped crying as soon as she saw her, and her tiny pink face broke into laughter. Her eyes were wide, luminous, and blue, like Maman's.

Hélène sat Antoinette down on top of the dresser and took Marie's blue wool suit and tiny winter coat out of a drawer. Then, carefully but quickly, she dressed her. Marie giggled and squirmed playfully as she put her into the clothes and buttoned them. Usually Marie's laughter would bring Hélène laughter. Not today. Today something was terribly wrong. Hélène didn't know what, but that only made her all the more uneasy.

Carefully Hélène took Marie into her arms and carried her downstairs. Maman was still pacing the foyer. She had put on her thick brown winter coat. Michelle and Edmond stood silently to one side. Each carried a string bag filled with rutabagas. Inwardly Hélène groaned. She hated rutabagas. It seemed that fried rutabagas were all there ever was to eat anymore, and there were never enough of those.

Once again Maman parted the curtains a crack and peered out. This time she let out a sharp little cry. "She's coming!" she exclaimed. "Catherine is coming!"

"Well, then, tell her to hurry!" Michelle snapped.

Maman ignored her, unbolted the door and let Catherine in, then threw the bolt back into place.

Hélène's sister Catherine was thirteen years old but looked older. Already she'd lost most of her baby fat. She had large brown eyes, shoulder-length brown hair which she wore pinned up, and she was growing into a stunning-looking young woman. Hélène knew this was true because of the special looks men gave Catherine on the street. Hélène had no doubt but that Catherine would become an actress when she grew up.

At the moment, Catherine stared at everyone in silence. A puzzled look come over her face. "Are you going someplace?" she asked.

"*We* are! We all are!" Michelle cried hysterically. Her big bosom rose and fell excitedly. "Now, run and put your warmest clothes on. We haven't a moment to lose!"

"What's the matter?" Catherine asked. "What has happened?"

Michelle's eyes flashed dangerously. "Never mind what's happened!" she snapped. "Just do as I say. Get dressed warmly! Now!" There was no mistaking the authority in her voice.

Catherine shot a questioning look at Maman, who nodded gravely. Without another sound, Catherine turned and went upstairs to change. Gently Maman took Marie out of Hélène's arms and held her close. Her hands were shaking.

Two minutes later, they were all set to leave.

"Hurry!" Michelle, who was clearly in charge, urged. "We're going out the back way—through the garden!"

At the kitchen door, Hélène suddenly remembered that she had forgotten something. She stopped and turned to Edmond. "Antoinette," she said. "I forgot Antoinette."

"Forget it," Edmond said roughly. "She's only a doll."

"She is not!" Hélène retorted angrily. "She's my friend."

Maman touched Hélène gently on the shoulder. "There is

no time, ma petite," she said. "We'll have to come back and get her later."

Hélène stood where she was, resolutely refusing to budge. "I want to get Antoinette. I want her now! I won't leave until I have her!"

Michelle rolled her eyes and let out a murderous sound. If looks could have killed, hers would have mowed Hélène down right on the spot. Then Michelle glanced at Maman.

Maman's mouth tightened. She sighed. "Oh, very well," she said. "But hurry!"

Hélène smiled as she ran upstairs to the nursery. No, she wouldn't leave Antoinette behind. Not for anything in the world. Maman had given her the doll for her birthday. She was the first doll that was really hers. All the others had once belonged to Catherine.

Antoinette was sitting on top of the dresser where Hélène had left her. She picked her up and hugged her tightly. As she was going out the door, she heard an ear-shattering roar outside on the street. She rushed to the window, pushed the lace curtains aside, and looked down.

Led by a motorcycle escort, a long, shiny black Daimler and several gray trucks pulled to a halt outside the door. Pennants were affixed to both front fenders of the car. Hélène recognized those flags. Who wouldn't have? They flew all over Paris, a constant, hated reminder of subjugation and defeat.

Her heart skipped a beat and she shivered. The Boches.

A sudden dread came over her. They want me! she thought. Because I spit in the street after their truck had gone by.

As she watched, the tailboards of the trucks dropped with a crash and soldiers spilled out and scrambled to line up alongside the curb. Their heavy, cleated boots clattered loudly on the cobblestones. Within seconds they snapped to attention in a precise straight line. Their chests were thrust out like pigeons' and their rifles were affixed with bayonets. Some of them were dressed in gray, others in black. It was the ones in gray who wore the coal-scuttle helmets and who were lined up. They had hopped down from the backs of the trucks. Hélène started to count them but stopped. There were at least twenty. The ones in black silver-trimmed uniforms, riding breeches, peaked caps, and highly polished boots stood casually to one side of the stiff formation. There were three of them. By a sudden barked order, the ones in gray broke out of line and half of them rushed the door. With a noisy clatter, the other half double-timed it down the street and turned the corner, disappearing out of sight.

"Hélène!" Maman was calling. "Quickly! Quickly!" Her voice quivered with fear.

Hélène left the window and started for the stairs. She looked down at Maman. Her face had gone white and she was pacing the foyer, Marie in her arms.

Michelle stood at the foot of the stairs. "Get down here!" she screamed hysterically. "*Now*, you little ingrate!" There was panic in her voice. Apparently Hélène still wasn't moving fast enough for her, because she took a deep breath and began to charge up the stairs. Her face glared at Hélène and her huge breasts rose and fell with the effort of the climb. As soon as she reached the girl, Michelle grabbed her arm roughly with one hand and pulled her along, all the while muttering prayers under her breath.

A moment later there were thuds at the front door. Maman let out a gasp and froze. The door shook but held fast. They hadn't bothered to knock. Instead, they were hurling all their weight against the door.

"Come *on*," Michelle wailed at Maman. "Quickly! We haven't a second to lose! Or did you forget about the little ones?"

Maman came out of her terror and found her feet. Hélène shot a last frightened look back as they rushed into the kitchen. Behind them, the front door was quivering. Wood creaked each time there was a thud. Suddenly Hélène wished she hadn't gone back for Antoinette.

Maman solemnly handed Marie over to Catherine. Then she slowly opened the kitchen door a crack and peered out. It led out to a courtyard where the neighboring buildings shared vegetable gardens.

Maman let out a gasp, slammed the door shut, and shot the bolt in place. There were soldiers out back too.

A hunted look crossed Maman's face. She closed her eyes and shrank back against the kitchen wall. "The Boches!" she whispered.

Michelle looked at her in horror and let go of the string bag. It hit the floor with a dull thump and precious rutabagas spilled out, rolling in all directions across the linoleum. Nobody took any notice of them.

"The children!" Maman whispered. "Where are we going to hide the children?"

"I don't know," Michelle replied. "Where in all France can one hide anything from the Boches?"

Suddenly there was a terrible crash at the kitchen door, accompanied by a heavy cracking noise that sounded like thunder. Michelle let out a shriek and crossed herself. Marie began to wail. They all backed away from the door.

"Sssssh, little one," Catherine said softly as she rocked Marie back and forth in her arms. "Sssssh."

Maman looked around in desperation. "There must be *some*place . . ." Her voice trailed off.

They backed into the dining room. Hélène lost her grip on Antoinette and dropped her. She knew better than to try to retrieve her. Not now.

"Why, of course!" Michelle suddenly cried out. "The dumbwaiter!" Her plump red hands lost no time in shoving the children toward it. Then she pulled at the old oak doors that were set in the wall and slid them apart. They rattled like a warped window that had not been opened for ages.

So we're going to play games, Hélène thought. She, Edmond, and Catherine had used the dumbwaiter many times playing hide-and-seek.

She remembered when Michelle had once caught them at it. She had boxed their ears mercilessly.

"You imbeciles!" she had ranted. "Are you trying to kill yourselves? That thing is as old as the revolution! The wood's rotted, most likely. Or God forbid the cable should break! You want you should fall and die at the bottom of the shaft?"

And now she was trying to shove them into the very dumbwaiter she had fought so hard to keep them out of in the past. Hélène's mind was in a whirl. Had Michelle gone completely crazy? Had the world?

"Get in there!" Michelle ordered. "All of you!"

From her voice they knew they'd better do exactly as she said. She held the double doors open. Catherine handed Marie to Maman and then climbed in. Edmond and Hélène followed. The floor of the dumbwaiter shook as Maman handed Marie back to Catherine,

"And not a sound!" Michelle warned. Her dark eyes looked oddly hostile as she waved her fist threateningly. "If I hear as much as a single peep, I'll come and wallop all four of you, but good!"

Hélène shrank back, frightened.

Maman leaned forward into the dumbwaiter and her hand shook slightly as she touched each of them gently on the forehead, her thumb sketching the sign of the cross upon them. Maman was not a religious woman, but somehow a great strength had come to her at this moment. Her face was no longer haunted by terror. Instead, her pale blue eyes were composed and brave and her lips were set in a sad but gentle smile.

"Edmond," Maman said softly, "you are forced to become a man much sooner than nature intended. My son, be strong like your father, whose place you must now take. And you, Catherine. You are the oldest. You will take my place. Together the two of you must take care of Hélène and little Marie. Do so with your lives! Then, if you have the chance, forget everything, and when it's safe . . . run. Your Tante Janine is a good Christian woman. She lives in Saint-Nazaire—that's at the mouth of the Loire, on the Bay of Biscay. I don't know how you'll do it, but get to Tante Janine's. God will forgive you for what you may have to do in order to get there! It won't be easy, but take heart. Soon the British and the Americans will land there. Then you will be safe forever. They are not pigs like the Boches. You'll see, another year and they'll drive the pig Boche out of France and back to his pigsty across the Rhine!"

Ca-rack! The doorjamb at the front door gave way and crashed into the foyer with a piercing sound. Hélène jumped with fright. Maman shot a glance behind her.

"It is now time to say good-bye, my children. Never forget, my darlings, that your Maman loves you more dearly than you'll ever be able to know."

"Yes, Maman," Catherine whispered gravely in a very grown-up voice. She reached for Maman's hand and kissed it. "We love you, too."

Maman suddenly snatched her hand back and fumbled with her fingers. The children watched her silently. She was pulling off her gold wedding ring. Awkwardly she pressed it into Edmond's hands. "Take this, my son," she whispered. "It is all I can give you. Use it to bargain with."

His hands closed over it.

"Go with God, my children," Maman whispered. "May he

44

love and protect you." She wasn't crying, but her pale eyes were moist and sorrowful.

Edmond had to turn his face away. He was ashamed of the tears in his eyes.

"Remember what I told you!" Michelle warned in a thick wavering voice. "Not a sound!" She sniffed and wiped her red nose with the back of her hand. Her eyes were glassy, too, just like Maman's. Gently she pulled Maman away and slammed the dumbwaiter doors shut. They banged together like the jaws of a toothless whale and the children were enveloped in darkness. The thuds and crashes were now muted.

From their games in the dumbwaiter, Hélène had learned where to peek out without being detected. There was a hole in the wood on her side. It had once been a knothole that had since been punched out. Soon her eyes adjusted to the darkness, and the hole in the wood stood out clearly. It let a thin stream of light through, in which danced a million tiny dust motes.

The cracking and banging noises at the door continued, this time followed by a horrible splintering noise. Something else had given. Hélène reached for Catherine's hand and held it tight as the thuds grew louder and louder. Catherine's hands was clammy and trembling.

Suddenly there was an ear-splitting crash. It sounded like the whole roof had caved in. The dumbwaiter shook and Hélène let out a cry. Marie began wailing, and Catherine rocked her back and forth, sticking a thumb in her mouth. Hungrily Marie began sucking on it.

"The roof," Hélène whispered to Catherine. "The roof has fallen in."

"No," she whispered back. "It's the door."

"But Maman—"

"Keep quiet!" Edmond hissed.

Boots thudded inside the house now, and sharp orders were barked in German. Hélène placed her ear against the knothole to listen, but she couldn't understand a word. She knew only a few random words of German. Then she peered out.

Her view was restricted to a small portion of the room and all she could see were headless figures. The knothole was located too far down to see anything taller than a child. She did see starched uniforms and shiny black boots. Then she recognized Maman's gray-woolen-stockinged legs and old worn shoes. They were a sad contrast to her dress and coat. "Thank goodness I can sew," she used to joke. "Unfortunately, even I can't sew shoes or weave silk stockings."

Hélène didn't need to see her head to recognize Michelle. Her unmistakable tublike shape was backed against the wall beside the kitchen door. Hélène was puzzled by something, and then it came to her. Uncharacteristically, Michelle's hands were folded behind her back. Michelle always had her hands at her hips, never behind her back.

Hélène shifted her gaze to the right. She caught sight of Antoinette lying on the floor. As she watched, a shiny boot stepped on her. She winced as the porcelain face so dear to her shattered with a crunch. Then the boot kicked at the pieces, scattering them.

Suddenly Hélène heard a stilted Boche voice speaking awkward French, so she moved again to peer out in Maman's direction. She was speaking to one of the Germans dressed in black, but her voice was too low to carry. Suddenly there was a resounding slap. Maman's torso jerked as she screamed out in pain.

Edmond recognized Maman's scream. With a strangled cry of rage he started to reach for the dumbwaiter doors to jump out and protect her.

Catherine sucked in her breath and dug her fingernails deep into his arm. "Didn't you hear what Maman and Michelle said?" she hissed at him. "We're to take care of the little ones! Or do you want to have all of us killed?"

He settled back stiffly and let out an angry sigh. Catherine was right. Maman and Michelle had given explicit orders.

The Nazi asked something else, again in French. His accent was so bad Hélène had to strain her ears to understand.

"Jacqueline Junot," she heard Maman reply.

"What?" the sharp voice snapped. "I can't hear you. Louder!"

"Jacqueline Junot!" Maman yelled back at him. "Jacqueline Junot!"

"Don't you *dare* raise your voice at an officer of the Reich!" the Boche barked. There was a crack as another slap rang out. Maman's cry for help was lost in her scream.

"What did you say?" the Boche asked.

"N-nothing," Maman said in a trembling voice.

"So . . ." The Nazi voice took on a tone of satisfaction. "Now are you ready to talk?"

"Yes," Maman said in a hoarse whisper. "Yes."

"Then where is the transmitter?"

"Transmitter?" Maman asked. "I don't know what you mean. What on earth—"

Smack! Yet another resounding slap rang out, this time much harder and louder. Maman moaned and tumbled to the floor, not more than four feet in front of the dumbwaiter. Hélène could see all of her now. She was doubled over on her knees, her head touching the floor. Hélène knew she was in great pain. Her face was flushed. She coughed and vomited, her nose and mouth pouring blood. In shame she turned her face away from the dumbwaiter. Hélène's stomach wrenched in sorrow for her. Above all, Maman would never have wanted her children to witness her humiliation.

The Boche moved toward Maman where she cowered. From Hélène's vantage point all she could see were boots and black breeches standing over her. He made a production of clearing his throat. "About this transmitter . . ."

"I don't know what you're talking about!" Maman cried, her voice gurgling from the blood in her mouth. "I swear I don't *know*!"

"Liar!" One of the boots flashed as it kicked out at her, catching her in the belly. An agonized, bile-filled scream reverberated around the room and into the confines of the dumbwaiter. Edmond covered his ears with his hands. He was sobbing quietly.

Hélène closed her eyes. She couldn't bear looking at Maman any more. Maman had drawn herself up as tightly as she could, her arms wrapped protectively around her swollen belly, around the baby boy or baby girl who was shortly to arrive.

"Maman," Hélène whispered painfully without making a sound. "What are they going to do to you, Maman?"

A Boche issued a command. Curious, Hélène opened her eyes. Instantly the soldiers in gray split into four groups. The thuds of their boots echoed clearly as they stomped up the stairs and down into the cellar. Hélène heard doors banging, and then there was a crash as glass shattered. Their voices were muffled as they smashed furniture and tore the house apart. A tremendous crash from above shook the whole house.

"We're going to die," Hélène whimpered.

"Keep quiet!" Catherine whispered.

It seemed to go on forever. Then someone yelled from the top of the stairs. The Nazi who stood over Maman squatted, grabbed her by the hair, and pulled her head up a foot.

"You fool!" he laughed at her. "They've already found it. Was it worth it to hold out on the Gestapo? Was it?"

Maman drew back and winced. Then he spat in her face. Hélène saw her grimace and blink as the spittle hit her and ran down her cheek. He let go of her hair and·her head dropped back onto the carpet. But not before Hélène caught a glimpse of his face under the visor of his peaked cap.

She stared at him incredulously. His face was as lean and narrow as a skull, with lips that were thin and cruel and bloodless. A tiny crescent-shaped scar stood out on his cleft chin. But it was his coloring that left her in shock. His skin was as pale as a corpse's, while his eyes were hideously pink. If he'd had horns, he would have looked like the devil himself.

He got to his feet, straightened his tunic, and went upstairs. Hélène felt a wave of relief when he had gone. Somehow she was more terrified of his ugliness than of his cruelty. Two soldiers in gray came and stood guard over Maman. Each time she moved as much as a finger they swiftly delivered her a vicious kick.

Hélène shifted position and peered toward Michelle. She hadn't moved from the kitchen door. There was a grim expression on her moon face, and her arms were still behind her back.

She heard the thuds of many boots coming down the stairs. They were all returning to the dining room. Apparently they had found what they'd been looking for. One of the soldiers carried it downstairs. It was a bulky, complicated-looking metal box covered with little dials and switches. Hélène had never seen it before.

The sinister, white-faced Boche gestured to the men standing guard over Maman. "Show her how we punish liars and traitors," he said in an authoritative voice. "And when you're through, take her to headquarters!" Then he left the room, the back of one gloved hand tucked into the small of his erect back.

The guards clicked their heels. "Zu befehl!" they chorused. Then they glanced down at Maman. She was silent, but her eyes were wary. Two of the soldiers bent over and pulled her to her feet. She stood swaying unsteadily. As Hélène watched, one of the Boches in black approached her and made a fist. Suddenly he slammed it into her belly.

"Traitor!" he shouted.

Maman let out a wrenching scream and collapsed. "My baby!" she screamed. "I'm losing my baby!" Tears were pouring down her cheeks.

Again the fist punched into her belly. Again she screamed. Hélène was filled with a murderous hatred.

Suddenly she noticed movement by the kitchen door. With the stealth of a huge cat, Michelle crept forward toward the soldiers. One of her fat red hands moved slowly from behind her back, and Hélène's eyes caught something flashing—a kitchen knife. It was the longest and sharpest one in the house.

With a cry Michelle dived forward upon the nearest Boche and plunged the knife into his back. He let out a howl and sank to his knees. Blood spewed from his gaping mouth and his eyes widened as if in surprise. Then they froze in a glassy, unseeing expression. He pitched forward, and Hélène saw that the knife was buried in his spine. The dark brown haft still quivered.

The others faced Michelle with a mixture of shock and surprise. One of them pointed his rifle at her. Instinctively she raised her hands out in front of her. There was an orange flash and the room seemed to explode. Michelle was jerked backward against the kitchen wall. Then, like a limp puppet, she slid downward into a ludicrous sitting position. In her lap, a large red spot was forming. Her glazed eyes seemed to stare straight through the knothole at Hélène.

Angry Nazi hands clawed at Maman and dragged her outside to the trucks. She was hunched over, her face smeared with blood. Suddenly Hélène noticed that her gray-stockinged legs were stained with blood too. Twice she tripped and fell to her knees, and each time she was pulled along and kicked.

"Vive la France!" Maman shouted with a last surge of strength. "Vive la République!" The brave words echoed gloriously into the street like a forbidden song. Even in the confines of the dumbwaiter, the cowering children heard it clearly. Then there was a moment's heavy silence before the motors of the car and trucks roared to life and drove off.

Two soldiers, however, still remained in the room to guard the house and wait for a detail to clear away the bodies.

They had taken off their helmets and leaned their rifles against the kitchen doorframe beside Michelle.

One of them struck a match and lit a cigarette. The other was talking in moody tones. Cursing, he kicked at a chair and it overturned.

It was then that Marie started crying.

The soldier who had kicked the chair turned and listened. Then he walked over to the dumbwaiter. Hélène's view from the knothole went dark. Suddenly the doors flew open with a clatter and blinding light streamed in.

2

They blinked in the sudden light.

"Ach, seh' mal was ich hier gefunden habe!" the soldier called out. His face was a shadow against the bright room behind him. He turned toward his partner and gestured him over.

Edmond and Hélène huddled closer to Catherine. They clung together like frightened puppies who had been abandoned. Hélène could feel Catherine's shivers. Eyes downcast, she was holding Marie tightly against her breast. Marie's cries were louder now, and Hélène could see her squirm fitfully.

The second soldier came over and peered in for a moment. Then he grunted, and there was the scraping of a match. In the flickering light Hélène saw both of the Boches' faces clearly, their lips spread in hungry grins. Their eyes ignored her, Edmond, and Marie, staring greedily at Catherine with the same look Hélène had seen on children eyeing the cakes in the windows of the neighborhood pâtisserie. Catherine, though the oldest of them, suddenly looked the most helpless and frightened. Her lips were tense, her brown eyes wide and wary.

"You," the second soldier said to her in bad French. "You come out from in there."

Catherine looked up at him but did not move. She stayed

cowering as the children clutched each other tighter than ever.

"You!" the soldier said in a cold voice. "Do I have to pull you out?"

Trembling, Catherine solemnly handed Marie over to Hélène. Then without a word she pushed Edmond aside and slid slowly out of the dumbwaiter. Clumsily she stumbled onto her knees.

"Ah-hah!" the Boche exclaimed, leering at her with appreciation while, like a shark, he slowly circled his prey.

The other soldier threw the remains of his cigarette on the carpet, carelessly ground it out with the hee. of his boot, and looked at his comrade with a hard expression. "Ich gehe zuerst," he announced with finality. For emphasis he poked a thumb toward his chest.

The other one vehemently shook his head. "Nein! Ich habe Sie von dort 'raus gebracht!" He gestured toward the dumbwaiter.

Still on her knees, Catherine stole a glance over her shoulder. Her eyes met Hélène's. Her lips were pressed tightly together and her body had gone limp. Hélène had seen that look far too often on the streets—the look of defeat.

Ashamed, Catherine turned away from her and looked toward the stiff, awkwardly seated Michelle. Hélène looked too. The blood that stained the front of Michelle's dress with a huge maroon splotch had already coagulated. A horrible nausea swept over Hélène and she looked quickly away.

The Boches' arguing had now turned to grumbling. One fished in his pocket and took out a leather change purse. He unzipped it, poked through it, and extracted a coin. Going through a weird ritual, he rubbed it, kissed it, and tossed it high into the air. It spun and flashed and then fell. Expertly he caught it with a swift downward motion of his hand and slapped it onto his wrist.

They both peered closely at it. The Boche who had won Catherine grinned widely. The other one mumbled sourly.

The victor carefully replaced the coin in his change purse and put it back in his pocket. Then he bent down and grabbed Catherine by the shoulders of her coat. With one swift movement he jerked her to her feet.

"A pretty young thing," he said in his bad French. "Well, we will soon see just how pretty you really are. Probably too skinny." He made a face. "All French are too skinny." He patted one of her cheeks with his big hand.

Instinctively Catherine flinched and pulled away.

Amusement glinted in his eyes. "She's a virgin," he said to the other Boche. "I can always tell. A nice sweet virgin. Really nothing like it."

The other shrugged. "I've had virgins," he replied in equally weak French. "No big deal."

Hélène exchanged glances with Edmond. "What are they going to do?"

Edmond's eyes were cold as he looked at her. "Do not be afraid," he whispered in a voice far more mature than his years.

She nodded solemnly. "I'll try not to be."

There was a shout from across the room. "Silence!"

Hélène jumped. Edmond gave her hand a reassuring squeeze and smiled. But she noticed that his eyes were not smiling.

At the other side of the room, the Boche had stuck his face close to Catherine's. "It is not every day a man finds for himself a virgin, is it?" he taunted in a loud voice.

Suddenly he let out a shriek, spun Catherine around, and threw her away from him. With a thud she landed against the edge of the dining-room table. Her hair was hanging over her face and she was gasping for air.

The Boche cursed and gingerly touched his lower lip. It was bleeding. He glanced at his finger, grunted, and wiped the blood on his thigh.

The other Boche giggled hysterically. "Mensch," he called out. "Kannst Du nicht einmal ein Mädchen handeln?"

The bitten one glared at him. "Halt's maul!" he snarled. Then he lunged savagely at Catherine. His hands tore at her coat and pulled it off.

"No!" Catherine screamed. "Oh, please God, no!"

The Boche grinned and licked his lips. Catherine backed against the table, her steepled fingers held pleadingly out in front of her as if in prayer. Hélène could hear fabric ripping as he tore the dress Maman had sewn for her. Buttons popped and bounced on the tabletop. The dress fell around Catherine's ankles.

"Please," Catherine whimpered. "Please . . ."

Something else ripped; her brassiere. Desperately she held

on to it, but it was torn out of her grasp. Protectively her hands flew up to cover her small breasts.

"Please . . . please don't," she begged in a low voice.

"Quiet!" There was a sharp report as he slapped her across the face. She recoiled as if stung. Then she curled her fingers into claws, and with a cry of rage she fiercely swiped his cheeks with her nails. Almost instantly four red streaks seeped to the surface.

"Verdammt!" Hélène heard him curse under his breath. Then more slaps rang out as he flung her onto the tabletop. Catherine kicked and squirmed as he pulled her wool stockings and panties down to her ankles. She was naked now, her tears streaming. He grabbed her and yanked her off the table. She struggled to get her footing, tripped on the garments collected around her ankles, and fell headfirst to the carpet. Not wasting a second, the Boche loosened his pants and pounced on her.

3

A searing rage tore at Hélène's stomach. She had never known hatred, but she had her first taste of it that afternoon as her sister was spread-eagled to the floor, a Nazi pinning her down. Nausea rose from her churning stomach to her throat like gaseous fire, and it took everything in her to swallow and hold it down.

"No," Catherine gasped. "No!" Her firm, boyish breasts rose and fell with each terrified breath.

"Let her go!" Hélène suddenly screamed.

Amused, the soldiers glanced toward the dumbwaiter and grinned. Then the one holding Catherine down by the wrists glanced at her groin. She tried to raise her hands, but her strength was no match for his. Her wrists were held down firmly, and her arms only reddened and trembled uselessly under the pressure. She bit her lips in pain.

"Mensch, mach's schnell!" the watching soldier snapped impatiently.

The Boche atop Catherine ignored him.

Edmond almost imperceptibly nudged Hélène and slowly glanced toward the kitchen door. She followed his gaze. Surely Edmond didn't expect her to stare at Michelle. No, there must be something else. Something very important . . . Then she understood. Beside Michelle, the soldiers' rifles were propped against the doorframe. She glanced back toward her brother. Their eyes met grimly, and she nodded ever so slightly. Even without speaking she knew what they had to do. Carefully she set Marie down on the dumbwaiter floor. Then they awaited their opportunity.

The Boche pinioning Catherine to the floor placed his groin close to her and with one vicious thrust of his body entered her. Catherine's drawn-out scream seemed to hang in the air forever. For one long, agonized moment her back arched and Hélène was certain her sister was going to throw him off, but after a moment Catherine slumped back wearily, horrible sobbing sounds escaping through her teeth.

Hélène shared in Catherine's humiliation and pain. So did Edmond. He sucked in his breath sharply. "Soon," his lips mouthed soundlessly. "Soon."

Hélène answered with a blink.

Flesh slapped obscenely against flesh while Catherine tossed her head from side to side in agony, horrible grimaces deeply etched on her face. The eyes of the other soldier were fixed on the rape taking place at his feet. He undid his belt and let his pants drop around his boots in anticipation of his own turn.

Edmond nudged Hélène. It was time. She watched as he hopped soundlessly out of the dumbwaiter. He waited a second and glanced cautiously at the men. They were too intent on Catherine to notice. Like a crab, Edmond scuttled behind the dining-room table and motioned Hélène to follow.

Trying to imitate his ease and nonchalance, she followed, joining him behind the table. She had reached it unseen. He gave her hand a reassuring squeeze.

"For God's sake, *stop* it!" Catherine's voice rang out.

Hélène glanced around the edge of the tablecloth, but Edmond grabbed her arm and pointed toward the kitchen door. He wanted her to follow on his heels. She nodded. From across the room, the noises rose and fell.

"Oh God!" Catherine was crying. "Oh God, *where are you?*"

Edmond nodded. Together he and Hélène began to crawl slowly and cautiously toward the stiff body of their beloved Michelle. Toward the rifles.

"*Aghhhhh . . .*" the soldier hammering at Catherine bellowed.

Edmond and Hélène were halfway between the table and Michelle. Fascinated, they stole another glance backward. The soldier was thrashing against her much faster now. Sweat poured from his flushed forehead, and the purple veins on his temples protruded so far Hélène thought they would burst.

"*Aghhhhh! Aghhhhh! Aghhhhh . . .*" Spasms racked his body.

Edmond prodded Hélène to move on. She hastily crawled after him, and they didn't look back until they had reached Michelle. By that time the soldier, eyes squeezed shut, was beginning to catch his breath. Catherine was sobbing softly. Hélène felt another wave of nausea rising in her throat, but she didn't need to do much to stifle it. The German did it for her. He was staring straight toward her and Edmond. "Verdammte Scheiss Kinder!" he roared abruptly. He pointed an angrily shaking finger.

Marie began to wail again, her cries sounding hollow coming from inside the dumbwaiter.

"Quickly!" Edmond shouted. "Quickly—get behind me!"

Hélène was frozen to the spot. "I . . . I can't move!" she whispered.

Edmond grabbed her arm and yanked her toward the kitchen door. Wasting no time, he took advantage of the soldiers' surprise. He picked up the rifle nearest him and swung it straight out in front of him, narrowly missing Michelle's head. The barrel glistened blue-black and oily. It was heavy. A man can hold such a rifle steady. In the hands of a child it wavers. But hatred makes adrenaline flow freely, so it was hatred that held up that rifle, not Edmond Junot.

Edmond squinted as he peered along the barrel the way he had seen actors do in cowboy films. But cinemas do not teach a boy how to shoot. Tanks and rifles had been common in Paris for years now, and Edmond and his friends had studied them from close and afar, exchanged notes on the mechanics of them. Thus it was that Edmond, a mere eleven-year-old child, knew where the safety catch was. And now he released it.

The Germans didn't miss this action. Both stiffened perceptibly. There was hatred in their eyes. That and something else that hadn't been there a few moments earlier. Fear.

"Runter, du verdammtes Schwein!" the Boche on top of Catherine yelled, too unnerved to search his mind for the elusive French words. With his hands he motioned Edmond to lower the rifle and put it down. The other soldier bent over and pulled his pants up, but his angry eyes never left them, not even while fastening his belt. He took a step in Edmond's direction.

Hélène was terribly afraid. "Now!" she cried. "*Now*, Edmond. Shoot!"

Frowning, her brother hesitated. The heavy rifle swung back and forth in an arc in his trembling hands.

The soldier slowly stepped closer. His angry face was flushed, and his dark eyes flashed. "Come on. Hand it over," he coaxed in bad French.

Edmond stared at him dully.

"Come on, put it down." His voice was gentler now. "Nothing's going to happen, boy."

Hélène knew it was a trick to get the rifle out of Edmond's hands. And if that happened, then what? Would they all be killed? All she knew was that Edmond mustn't hand the rifle over.

"Come on," the soldier said in a calculating soft voice. "Be a good boy and lay it down."

Oh, how Hélène despised that deceptive voice. And now the German was attempting a benign smile. Her heart was pounding wildly. Oh, Edmond please do something. Don't be fooled! Do something quickly . . . while there's still time.

The Boche was closer now. His left hand reached out for the rifle. He approached slowly, like a man nearing a cobra, with infinite caution. "Lay it down," he said in a soft whisper. "Nothing's going to happen." His voice was seductive. You have a chance, it seemed to say. A chance not to do anything monstrous you'll be sorry for later.

Instinctively Edmond took a step backward toward Hélène.

"Edmond," she warned between clenched teeth. "Edmond . . ."

The Nazi's eyes flashed angrily upon her. He was afraid

her pleas might influence her brother. The other soldier was staring with a grim expression on his face. Marie was quiet.

The Boche's hand had almost reached the barrel. It was trembling. "Come on. Steady," the voice said softly. "That's right. Steady, boy . . ."

"Edmond!" Catherine screamed as she tried to sit up and push the other soldier away. Hélène looked over at her. Catherine's eyes were frightened ovals. "Edmond!" she screamed. "For God's sake—"

"Halt's maul!" the soldier screamed suddenly, and backhanded her viciously. She fell back with a screech of pain as her head hit the carpet with a dull thud.

A strangled cry of rage issued forth from the depths of Edmond's throat, and he pulled the trigger. There was a flash. Simultaneously, a blast shook the room. Maman's good china in the armoire rattled. From the dumbwaiter Marie let out a high-pitched wail. And then, as suddenly as the room had seemed to explode, it was so quiet that Hélène dared not breathe. She was afraid it would intrude on the silence. Even Marie suddenly quieted down. The acrid odor of cordite passed over them like a curse. For the first time that afternoon Hélène noticed the steady, persistent ticking of the grandfather clock by the front door. Then she glanced at Edmond and sucked in her breath.

He still held the rifle out in front of him, but his face was dull, dazed. He didn't seem to realize that he was hurt. A stream of blood ran down his neck from his mouth, and he was missing two front teeth. When he had squeezed the trigger, the butt of the rifle had hit him squarely in the jaw as the recoil threw him back against Hélène. But he had managed to retain his footing, and he still squinted along the barrel.

The soldier in front of Edmond was no more. At point-blank range, he'd had no chance. The bullet had smashed into his chest, and his ribs and lungs had shattered into a million flying fragments that slammed haphazardly against the wall as he'd been flung backward. Bits of bone and bloodied flesh were embedded in the wallpaper.

There was one less Nazi on French soil. He was a Boche no more. Just like Michelle was no more.

I never even screamed, Hélène thought.

The other Boche stared at Edmond with stone-cold eyes.

Edmond gestured at him with the rifle. "Pull up your pants," he said in a hollow voice.

There was a moment of quiet tension. Then the Boche started to bend forward.

"Very slowly," Edmond warned. "Otherwise . . ." Unspoken, the threat hung heavy in the air.

Slowly the Boche pulled up his pants and tucked in his shirt. His face was expressionless, but Hélène saw that his eyes were wary. They never left Edmond, not for a fleeting instant. When he finished buckling his belt he let his hands drop alongside his thighs. His fingers were splayed and rigid. Instinctively Hélène knew why. He was waiting for an opportunity to pounce.

Edmond lowered the rifle slightly and looked toward Catherine. "Get up," he told her gently.

She turned her tear-streaked face toward him. With the palms of her hands she wiped her eyes.

"Go and fetch some clothes," Edmond said. His voice was thick with emotion. "Go. Get dressed."

Catherine nodded. Eyes downcast, she managed to stagger to her feet. Feebly her hands covered her pubis. She looks so haggard, Hélène thought. So . . . so *ashamed*. A hot, prickling humiliation began to spread through Hélène. Then with a shock she noticed that Catherine's thighs were smeared with blood. Quickly she averted her eyes.

Suddenly the Boche made his move. Hélène's eyes caught the blur of movement, and her heart jumped. In vain she tried to cry out a warning. Her throat was frozen with terror.

She heard Edmond's gasp. He saw too, but it was too late. For one split second he had taken his eye off the Boche, and that instant was all it took.

With split-second timing the Boche dived at Catherine and tackled her legs. She toppled back to the floor and grunted as the wind was knocked out of her. Then, pulling her up in front of him, using her limp body as a shield, the Boche got 'o his feet. He had one arm wrapped around her neck and something flashed in his hand. A pocketknife, the point of it pressed against her throat. Not hard enough to puncture, but enough to depress the soft skin where the point of the blade rested. Her eyes were wide with terror; her mouth was open and gasping for air.

"Drop the rifle or I'll slit her throat," the Boche said quietly. His eyes were narrowed and he looked at Edmond with contempt.

Hélène stared at the Boche. There was no mistaking that

he meant every word. Edmond didn't move. His somber face was wet. He had broken out in a cold sweat. There was nothing he could do now, but still he held the rifle in front of him.

The knife point pressed harder against Catherine's throat. Then a bead of blood appeared and slid slowly down her neck.

"Drop that rifle," the Boche repeated.

Helpless, Edmond let go of the rifle. With a clatter it fell at his feet.

The Boche's lips spread into a thin cruel smile. He eased the pressure of the knife but still held it close to Catherine's throat. Clumsily he stepped forward.

He was face to face with Edmond now. With one swift movement he kicked the rifle behind him, toward the foyer. "You fools," he hissed. Hélène could smell the garlic on his breath.

She felt the shiver of gooseflesh and slowly let her eyes roam toward the door. Something told her that they were not the only ones in the house anymore. She had heard nothing, but she sensed someone else's presence. She was right. She saw a man slip stealthily from the shadows of the foyer into the dining room. This was no Boche. She stared at him in recognition. Could it be? Her heartbeat quickened. Yes, it was Monsieur Laval, Papa's friend. Hélène's eyes met his. He paused and held a finger to his lips, not five feet from the Boche, when a floorboard creaked. Startled, the Boche let go of Catherine and spun around. He cursed and his arm shot out in a wide arc. Hélène heard the knife whistle through the air. Monsieur Laval ducked low, but the blade grazed his winter coat, slicing open the thick wool down to the lining. Hélène shuddered. Beside him, swaying dizzily, stood Catherine.

"Catherine!" Hélène screamed. "Catherine!"

Catherine stared at her with blank eyes. She was lost in some fog only she was aware of.

"Catherine!" Hélène screamed again. "Move away from them!"

Now her words penetrated the fog. Catherine snapped out of it and scrambled out of the way. Hélène took her ice-cold hand.

Once again the knife sliced through the air. Hélène could hear it before she saw it. Monsieur Laval flung himself to one side, brought up his knee, and slammed it into the Boche's groin. The Boche let out a scream of pain and doubled over. The knife fell from his grasp and his face turned a sickly gray. Then he slumped to the floor. He lay on one side in a fetal position, hands pressed against his groin.

Monsieur Laval took a handkerchief out of his coat pocket and wiped his forehead. He was still breathing rapidly from the exertion of the fight. He was no longer a young man.

"Monsieur Laval!" Hélène said suddenly. Fiercely she tugged at his coat. "They've taken Maman away! The Nazis have taken Maman!"

As he looked down at her she saw the compassion in his tired brown eyes. He put his hands on her shoulders and pressed her close to him, the way Maman always did. But his belly wasn't warm like hers, or soft like Michelle's. His coat was cold and rough. Hélène didn't like the scratchy feel of it. It didn't comfort her at all. For the first time that afternoon she began sobbing.

Gently Monsieur Laval pushed her away and squatted down until both their faces were level. He looked deep into her eyes. "Yes, Hélène," he said quietly. "They took your Maman. But we mustn't let them take you, must we?"

She shook her head silently.

"Good. Then you be a brave girl and wipe your eyes."

She sniffed and nodded and did as she was told.

"There. That's better." He forced a smile with his lips. "Now, I want you to listen carefully. Will you do that?"

"Yes." Hélène's wavering voice was thick.

"You have to leave this house right now," he said, "It isn't safe for you here. Do you understand?"

Again she nodded her head.

"Good. I will take you someplace where you will be safe." Monsieur Laval got to his feet and glanced toward Catherine. For the first time he noticed her bloodied thighs. He stared at her in shock. "You poor girl," he murmured, shaking his head. "They are worse than animals!"

Catherine turned her face away in shame.

"Don't!" Monsieur Laval said sharply. "Don't be ashamed! Ever! You have done nothing wrong. You must remember that!"

"Yes." Catherine's voice was a whisper. "Yes. I'll remember."

"Now, run upstairs and put some clothes on," he told her. "But don't wash up. There isn't time."

Catherine nodded and dashed from the room.

Monsieur Laval looked at the Boche, then at Edmond. "I'll need a towel and a sturdy rope."

"Will a laundry line do?" Edmond looked at him questioningly.

Monsieur Laval nodded. "A laundry line will do just fine."

Without another word, Edmond left. Hélène heard him rummaging in the kitchen. A minute later he came back out, holding the towel and a length of white rope. Monsieur Laval kicked the Boche over on his belly, then bent down and with the rope began to truss him expertly. That done, he gagged him with the towel. The Boche whimpered with fright. So he wasn't that brave after all, Hélène thought with satisfaction.

Catherine came back downstairs already dressed. Without looking at anyone, she headed straight for the dumbwaiter, picked up Marie, and held her close.

Monsieur Laval looked around. "Everyone ready?" he asked.

In silence the children nodded. They didn't waste another moment going through the kitchen and out the back door. Behind them, a single gong from the grandfather clock announced that it was three-thirty. Less than a half-hour had passed since Hélène was playing in the park with Antoinette. Less than a half-hour, and her life had changed. Forever.

With Monsieur Laval in the lead, they ran across the brittle, crusty snow lying frozen on the ground of the courtyard. It crunched beneath their feet. They passed the rusty old barrel that was used to collect rainwater for the garden. It was covered with ice. Something deep inside Hélène told her she would never see it again. High above their heads, the familiar laundry lines crisscrossed the courtyard. Laundry hung stiffly in the biting wind. Then they ran through the dark, tunnellike passageway of the building across from theirs.

They were on the run. For their lives.

4

The house was located at the end of a short, dark alley that branched off the one they traveled. Monsieur Laval halted in front of the door of 17 rue Jules Talet and hit the buzzer three times in quick succession.

The building was ancient and dingy and gray. Like all the other houses in the district, it looked like the tenants had always lived in a near-poverty level. There was a mailbox next to the door, but it didn't have any name tags on it. Hélène looked up. All the windows were dark,

Just when she thought no one was home, the door opened abruptly and a flood of yellow light poured out into the alley. A bald, heavyset Negro giant was silhouetted dimly against the light. His massive black arms were folded in front of his chest.

Monsieur Laval took off his beret and murmured something under his breath.

The giant turned toward the children, his eyes hard and appraising. Then he stepped aside and motioned them to enter. Silently they slipped past him into the hallway. The heavy door shut behind them.

Hélène glanced at Edmond. His eyes had widened as much as hers. Outside, the house had looked old and dilapidated. Inside, it was luxurious to a fault. The first thing Hélène noticed was how warm it was. Their own home had always been cold and drafty; this one was practically a blast furnace. The furnishings were antiques. There were crystal chandeliers, fine blue-and-white Oriental vases, and thick rugs. The walls were covered with rich red fabric, and to either side of a pair of handsome double doors stood massive bronze torchères. These torchères were in the shape of muscular Moors. Each held a many-branched candelabrum aloft.

The giant motioned them to wait. He walked toward the big doors, knocked once, and entered. For a moment Hélène could hear the hum of conversation and the clear tinkling of a woman's laughter suspended in the air. Then the doors closed behind him and there was silence.

Hélène glanced around the hallway. Catherine was leaning wearily against the wall. After a half-hour of carrying Marie, her arms seemed to sag under the weight. Edmond was gingerly touching one of the torchères. He behaved as if it might suddenly come to life and bite him. Monsieur Laval was standing back to back with him, his lower lip jutting out slightly and his squinting eyes thoughtful. His beret was clutched limply in his hands.

A moment later the doors opened and the giant came back out. He was followed by a tiny lady who walked with slow, delicate steps. She was Oriental. Hélène stared in rapt fascination. Never before had she seen anyone so exotic. There were the murmur and scent of faraway places, of orchids and water lilies and unspoken taboos. Her skin was pale and her hair was jet black. Worn loose, it hung all the way to her waist. Her eyes shone brightly in the lights of the torchères. They were slanted, black and shrewd. Her red gown was of shiny silk and fit snugly, cut low to emphasize her figure. Though she was very slim, her breasts were large. From around her neck a platinum chain dangled a huge marquise-cut diamond into the cleft of her bosom. In the winter of 1944 that sparkle was obscene.

The giant hovered at a discreet distance, but the woman made no move to dismiss him. Nor did she give any indication that she noticed Catherine, Edmond, or Hélène. She came straight toward Monsieur Laval and held out a hand as delicate and white as new porcelain.

Hélène watched as Monsieur Laval shook her hand. He held it gently, with a grace Hélène was unprepared for.

The woman was very short and had to look up to him. "Monsieur," she said. Her singsong voice was high-pitched but clear. It was then that Hélène realized that the crystalline laughter she had heard was hers.

Politely Monsieur Laval inclined his head. "Madame Chang," he said in a respectful voice, "it is good of you to see me."

She bowed her head. Without prologue she said, "Monsieur, I know you are here because you are in trouble. Do not misunderstand me; I will help you if I can. However, I want to know absolutely nothing about this trouble." Her voice

63

was still soft and delicate, but her tone was now brusque and businesslike. It was almost as if a chill wind had touched upon the most delicate of blossoms. "Do we understand each other?"

"Perfectly, madame. Your discretion is both wise and highly appreciated."

She looked up into his eyes. "Now. What is it that you wish me to do?"

Monsieur Laval gestured toward the children. "They need a safe place in which to stay."

Madame Chang's face was impassive. "That is not such an unusual request. But you realize, Monsieur, that I cannot be expected to close my establishment for the night. Not because of four children."

"I realize that," he said.

"Good. Then we understand each other." Her almond eyes bore into his. "How long do they need to remain here?"

"Until tomorrow sometime. I shall return and take them elsewhere."

She nodded. "It is settled, then. But remember. I shall expect you to pick them up no later than three o'clock in the afternoon."

Monsieur Laval practically prostrated himself with a profusion of thanks. "Madame is too kind," he began. "An—"

Madame Chang held up a hand to silence him. Hélène noticed that her fingernails were long and lacquered red. "I must have one guarantee," she said.

They all stared wordlessly at the woman.

"They must keep very quiet," she said. "The older ones are capable of keeping the baby silenced?" She looked questioningly at Catherine.

Catherine nodded gravely.

"Very well, then." Madame Chang turned to the giant. "Take them upstairs to Gisèle's room."

Wordlessly the giant bowed. With his hands he motioned the children to follow.

Hélène hesitated and glanced beseechingly at Monsieur Laval. He was the only familiar face in these strange surroundings, and the thought of being separated from him terrified her.

He noticed her reluctance. "What are you waiting for?" he asked. "Go . . . go along with him. I will pick you up tomorrow afternoon."

She looked at him skeptically. "Is that a promise?"

He nodded. "I promise. Now, do not worry. Everything will be all right."

On an impulse, Hélène flung her arms around Monsieur Laval and gave him a massive hug. Then, just as suddenly, she disengaged herself from him and followed the giant. Edmond and Catherine walked behind her.

Catherine was feeding Marie from a makeshift bottle when Edmond spoke to Hélène. "You better be careful. You could fall out the window."

She ignored him. Gisèle's room was in the attic and had a dormer window. By standing tiptoe on her bed Hélène could look out over the jagged rooftops. Night had fallen and it was almost pitch black out.

"Have it your way, then," Edmond said. "See if I'll help if you start to fall."

"Children," Gisèle warned. "Keep quiet! Madame Chang doesn't want you to make a sound!" She glanced at Edmond and patted the mattress.

He made a face but sat down obediently beside her on the edge of the bed. Hélène could feel the mattress shift under his weight. It had good springs.

After a few minutes she left the window and joined them. It was too dark out to see anything anyway. From below she could hear a piano playing, and several times there were shrieks of high-pitched laughter. It sounded like a party going on.

Gisèle said she was one of twenty girls in the house. Right now she would normally have been sitting downstairs with the others, waiting for clients to arrive. But she was having her "delicate condition," and Madame Chang wouldn't hear of her girls working during those times.

Gisèle was tall and full-breasted. She just missed being pretty. Her misfortune, she lamented, was her torso. It was too short-waisted for her to ever hope for a lean, elegant figure. She would forever seem to be slightly dumpy. Her large breasts made her look more like a woman in her early twenties than the seventeen-year-old girl she actually was. A year ago she had come to Paris from the suburb of Auteuil. Ever since then she had worked for Madame Chang.

There were certain advantages for the girls who worked at Madame Chang's. The pay was good and, unlike the rest of

Paris, which was starving, there was always enough food in the larder here. But best of all, a girl who worked here could afford a pretty wardrobe. That was an almost unheard-of luxury.

Some of the other, more beautiful girls had luxurious high-ceilinged rooms and clothes designed by the most expensive couturiers. Jocelyne, Gisèle said, almost reverently, was the most ravishing and highest-priced of them all. Men who could afford her claimed she was the most sensational creature in all of Paris. But to afford her, a man had to be able to part with six thousand francs for one hour. A fortune.

"I'm getting bored," Edmond grumbled. Gisèle's story did not interest him.

Hélène nodded. "Me too. I hate just sitting around here doing nothing."

Gisèle thought for a moment. Then her face brightened. "I know what!" she said. "I'll sketch all of you! Would you like that?"

Edmond made a sour face.

"I'm quite good, actually," Gisèle said quickly. "That is, as long as you promise to sit still. Let me get my sketchpad." She hurried over to the dresser, where she kept her pad and a supply of blue-leaded pencils. Then she made a production out of moving one of the chairs to just the precise spot she wanted. Finally satisfied, she sat down in it and faced them. With a frown she studied the children one by one. Then she motioned Hélène to sit still. With deft strokes of the pencil, Gisèle began to draw.

Hélène sat in self-conscious silence and watched Gisèle's hands. They were small, the fingers too stubby. They were capable-looking hands, but a far cry from Madame Chang's exquisitely lacquered claws. Hélène wondered if all short-waisted people had little hands.

Edmond cleared his throat, and Hélène glanced at him. The moment their eyes met, he began to make funny faces. Hélène started to giggle.

Gisèle shot her a warning look. "Sit still!" she said angrily.

It took Gisèle a half-hour to draw all four. Then, with a sudden fanfare, she held up the sketches. "What do you think?" she asked eagerly.

Hélène studied them closely. They were quite good, and she recognized Catherine instantly; it was her spitting image. She was disappointed by the way she herself had turned out,

66

though. She thought Gisèle had drawn her too young and sweet, and it wasn't at all what she saw when she looked at herself in the mirror. Edmond's was a pretty good likeness, but then again, it didn't *really* look like him. The nose was all wrong and the eyes were set too close together.

Gisèle looked at Hélène. "Well?" she asked.

Before Hélène had a chance to voice her opinion they heard footsteps in the corridor and then a knock on the door. Catherine jumped and turned toward it, a frightened-animal look in her eyes.

Gisèle smiled gently and patted Catherine's hand. "Don't worry. It's only Roland." She got up, put the sketchpad back in the dresser, and unlocked the door.

The black giant came inside carrying a tray. On it were several domed lids with steam escaping from under them. He set the tray down on the dresser and left.

"He's not very friendly, is he?" Hélène asked when he was gone.

"Why do you say that?" Gisèle asked.

"Well, for one thing, he never says a word."

"That's because he's a mute," Gisèle said. "He cannot talk."

"Oh." Hélène was curious. "How come?"

Gisèle shrugged. "I do not know."

"But he can hear us and understand us?"

She nodded, walked over to the dresser, and lifted the domed lids off the tray. Billowing clouds of steam rose from the big platters as the delicious aroma reached Hélène's nostrils. Her mouth fell open. It had been a long time since she smelled anything so mouth-watering. Suddenly she forgot all about Roland the giant and his lack of speech. She was ravenous.

Gisèle spooned the food onto gilt-trimmed china plates. Hélène stared at her helping with wide-eyed wonder. On her plate she had thick slabs of beef with a mushroom sauce, steamed green vegetables, and potatoes. She looked over at Catherine's and Edmond's helpings. Figuring that they were older and had bigger appetites, Gisèle had piled their plates even higher. And as if all this were not enough, a plate of petit fours had been included for dessert. For a moment Hélène closed her eyes and savored the aromas of the food. Then she wasted no time in attacking it.

* * *

Hélène was wide-awake. Groggily she looked around, trying to figure out what had awakened her. She listened carefully. Then she heard it again. Someone was gently tapping on Gisèle's door.

Slowly her night vision adjusted to the darkness. She glanced over to the bed and could make out Gisèle as a sound-asleep shadow. On the comforter spread out on the floor, Catherine, Edmond, and Marie were still curled up, fast asleep.

Again Hélène heard the tapping, a little louder this time. She wondered whether she should answer the door, but Gisèle had reprimanded her when she tried to go out and use the toilet and had made her use the chamber pot behind a screen. The door had to stay locked at all times. The order had been emphatic.

Hélène turned to Edmond. For a moment she hesitated, then shook him awake.

He sat bolt upright. "What the—"

Hélène clapped a hand over his mouth. "Sssssh!" she whispered. "There's someone at the door."

He cocked his head to listen.

Again the tapping. This time it must have reached through Gisèle's shroud of sleep. She moaned and lifted her head off the pillow. "Go away," she called out in a sleepy voice.

"Gisèle!" a woman's hoarse voice called softly. "It's me! Jocelyne. Open up! I need to talk to you!"

Gisèle moaned again and sat up. "Oh, all right," she said grumpily. She stretched wearily and rubbed her eyes. Then Hélène heard the bedsprings creak as Gisèle swung her legs over the side.

Edmond and Hélène lay back down as Gisèle stumbled over to the door. By the time the key turned in the lock, the children's eyes were closed in pretended sleep.

The door creaked open and weak, flickering yellow light shone into the room. Whoever was standing out in the hallway was holding a candle.

"Jocelyne," Gisèle said in a whisper. "What are you doing out there? What time is it anyway?"

"Almost four o'clock," the throaty voice replied.

Gisèle shook her head. "What do you want at this unearthly hour?"

"Sssssh." There was a pause. "Are they asleep?"

"How do you know about them?" Gisèle's voice was guarded.

"Simple. I saw two of them going up the stairs yesterday afternoon. I know that there must be more. There were far too many little footsteps. Besides, I saw the dinner tray being brought up." Hélène saw her trying to peer into the room over Gisèle's shoulder. In the shimmering candlelight she caught sight of the most extraordinarily beautiful woman she had ever seen. She was tall and blond, and under the voluminous pale blue chiffon of her peignoir, her figure was voluptuous but slender. "Come on, Gisèle," Jocelyne coaxed. "Let me in for a moment. I have to see them."

Gisèle shook her head in exasperation. "Why? There must be a reason."

"All right, all right. I'll tell you." Jocelyne looked around conspiratorially and her voice dropped an octave. "There may be money in it for both of us."

"Money?" Gisèle's voice sounded explosive in the night.

"Sssssh!" Jocelyne hissed. "Don't wake them up! Just let me in to see them. I'll tell you about it later."

Gisèle placed her hands on her hips. "Suppose you tell me now."

"Oh, all right. One of my visitors tonight was that Standartenführer who's so crazy about me."

"Yes, yes. The bald regular. I know the one."

"Well, he told me they're scouring Paris for four kids."

"*Four* kids?"

Four kids. Hélène felt a shiver slither down her back. Beside her, Edmond stiffened.

"Yes, four. An older boy and a girl, and a little one of seven or eight. Plus a baby."

"But why should the SS be out looking for children?" Gisèle asked.

"They're killers."

Gisèle laughed. "Killers? Those sweet little darlings?"

"Don't be fooled." Jocelyne's voice was serious. "They're killers, all right. They shot a Boche yesterday. There were two of them, but only one came out of it alive. He told the story, and now there's a reward out for information leading to their capture."

"A reward?"

Jocelyne nodded her head vigorously.

"How much?" Gisèle's eyes flashed greedily as she glanced toward the children.

Jocelyne was silent for a moment. "Half a million francs."

"Half a mil . . ." Gisèle sucked in her breath. "Good God! That's a *fortune*!"

"And half of it would be yours," Jocelyne said quickly. "Just think! A quarter of a million francs apiece. We could go out and get three, maybe four dresses at the couturiers'. . . . Now, are you going to let me in or not?"

Gisèle still hesitated. "But Madame Chang—"

"Madame Chang need never know. Trust me. I can arrange that."

"But—"

"But nothing." Jocelyne smiled faintly. Gently she reached up and touched Gisèle's face with slender, tapered fingers. "And another thing, darling. I've seen the special way in which you constantly watch me. I can tell, you know. You don't want the men. You prefer the women." The smile was wider now. "But that's no crime. I myself am sometimes attracted to other women. Maybe I will even let you come down to my room." The air was heavy with promises.

Gisèle's voice was a choked whisper. "Come to your room. . . ?"

Jocelyne nodded. Slowly she parted the front of her peignoir. Her breasts were as firm and perfectly shaped as a Greek statue's. Hélène heard Gisèle gasp.

"And not only that," Jocelyne continued in a lilting voice. "I will let you do whatever you want." She paused. "I will even part my legs for you so that you may eat my écu."

With trembling hands Gisèle pulled the door wide open and stepped aside. "Come in," she whispered.

Jocelyne swept into the room. Edmond poked Hélène. They both closed their eyes simultaneously and he began breathing regularly, as if in a deep sleep. Hélène copied him and snored gently. A moment later she could feel the women's presence as they came close and shone the candlelight over them. She could smell Jocelyne. Lavender.

"Is that them, do you think?" she heard Gisèle whisper.

"They seem to match the descriptions, all right," Jocelyne whispered back. "I'm certain it's them."

Then Hélène heard them move away, and she ventured to open her eyes. The women were back at the door.

"Jocelyne . . ." Gisèle's voice was a tremor.

"Yes?"

"I want to come with you down to your room. Now."

Jocelyne looked at her in surprise. Then she smiled and took Gisèle in her arms. Noisily she kissed her on the lips. "Come along, then. But you'd better come back up here in an hour to check up on them. Besides, I have to get *some* sleep. I have to go and see the Standartenführer first thing in the morning." She shuddered. "He'll probably *insist* that I lunch with him at that horrible café on the Champs-Élysées."

Then the door snapped closed behind them. Once again the room was in total darkness. Hélène waited for the key to turn in the lock, but in her haste Gisèle must have forgotten about it.

Edmond didn't speak until their footsteps receded in the hallway. Then he sat up straight as a board. "Wake up Catherine," he ordered grimly. "Then get dressed."

Hélène sat up. "A half million francs!" she said. "Imagine! There cannot be so much money in the world."

"Hurry!" Edmond hissed at her. There was no mistaking his tone; obedience was called for.

He was on his feet already, tiptoeing over to Gisèle's nightstand. After fumbling around in the darkness, he found what he was looking for. Hélène heard the scratch of a match and then saw the flame leap up. By the time he had the nightstand candle lit, she had already shaken Catherine awake.

5

Their progress was tedious. The alley was unlit, and several times they slipped on the treacherous ice. There were no streetlights; electricity was too precious a luxury. Paris got only one-half hour of it each evening.

Hélène shivered from the cold and pulled the collar of her winter coat up around her chin. The temperature had plummeted during the night and her coat was not thick enough. Her ears stung from the cold and she needed a cap.

On her left, Catherine trudged along in stony silence. In her arms, Marie was a small, quiet bundle. The sudden exposure to the cold couldn't be doing her any good, Hélène thought. It was dangerous to expose a baby to sudden cold.

It was even more dangerous to be caught out on the streets after the midnight curfew. They had heard enough stories from Michelle to know what happened to curfew violators. Any Frenchman caught by the night patrols was taken to the Feldgendarmarie headquarters. There, either of two things happened. If they were lucky and it was a peaceful night, the curfew violators would spend the night polishing the Boche's boots. If they were not so lucky and the Resistance killed a German during the night, the curfew violators were the reprisal victims. They would be shot by a firing squad.

Yesterday afternoon, Edmond had killed a Boche. Now with a heavy heart Hélène wondered what innocent Frenchmen—unknown and faceless—would end up paying for that deed. For someone would surely have to pay. The Boche always saw to that.

Bitterly she wondered which was the harsher fine—the loss of their own lives if they were caught, or the subsequent attack on their consciences if they were to live. Instinctively she knew that somehow they would all eventually have to pay. If they were to be delivered from danger now, they would probably be guilt-ridden for the rest of their lives. How else could they ever begin to do penance for those who substituted for them—those who would suffer such a brutal, final solution in their place?

Still, it is survival—not sacrifice—that is the foremost of human instincts. The fight for survival was now on—consciously and subconsciously. Their first move was only too clear. As quickly as they could, they had to get out of Paris. That was their only hope for survival. They had to follow Maman's instructions and try to reach the safety that beckoned to them from Tante Janine's house in faraway Saint-Nazaire.

Saint-Nazaire. Oh, but how distant it sounded! And Hélène had never been farther from Paris than Rambouillet. Then she frowned, and the magic in the name crumbled like ashes in the wind. Travel took money.

"We don't have any money," she found herself worrying aloud. "Why, we can't even get on the métro. How will we ever get out of Paris?"

"We have money," Edmond said softly.

"We do?" Catherine asked. There was surprise in her voice.

"Yes," Edmond said. "We have Maman's wedding ring, along with a pile of francs. Over two thousand."

"Two thousand francs!" Catherine whispered. Then her voice turned suspicious. "Where did you get it?"

"From Gisèle's nightstand, of course. Where else?"

"But . . . but that's *stealing*," Catherine said.

Edmond didn't bother answering. Hélène could imagine him shrugging his shoulders. Then she spoke up in his defense. "I'm glad he did it," she whispered to Catherine. "Gisèle was a monster! She deserved it! She wanted to sell us to the Boche!"

"But still, stealing—"

Edmond cut Catherine off. "What do you want?" he hissed savagely. "To stay in Paris and get caught? Have them repeat what they did to you? Is that what you want?"

His words had the effect of a slap across her face. She recoiled and fell silent. All Hélène could hear were Catherine's quick footsteps in the darkness. Then she heard another sound, and it hurt her to hear it. Catherine was crying softly.

Edmond heard, too. He was helpless against tears. "I'm sorry," he told her gently. "I . . . I didn't mean to hurt you. God knows, you've suffered more than enough. But please try to understand. If we're to reach Saint-Nazaire at all, we'll need that money. That and more. *Believe* me."

Catherine sniffed, and they walked on in silence.

6

Her feet were sore, her legs were sore, even her back and neck were sore. She couldn't tell whether it was because of the cold or all the walking they'd done. It was days now since they had left Paris. Edmond had bribed a vélo-taxi driver to take them out of the city, but the danger hadn't ended there.

Now they had to battle the Boche-infested countryside. Instead of the roads, they had stayed on the dirt paths that crisscrossed the fields. By doing this, they not only managed to avoid any traffic—namely the Boches—but also skirted most of the villages along the way. The earth must have been soggy just before winter set in; the paths all had deep wheel ruts frozen into the dirt. As a result, walking was treacherous.

It was Edmond's turn to carry Marie. He held her in such a way that she could look backward over his shoulder. He was singing softly to her.

Suddenly Hélène stopped walking. "I have to take a short rest," she announced wearily.

Edmond turned to her. "We'll rest for five minutes," he said. "But then we'll have to move on again."

"Thank heaven," Catherine murmured gratefully. "For the last half-hour I thought my legs were going to give out on me."

Keeping her hands in her pockets, Hélène looked out across the endless barren fields and past the villages that dotted the landscape up ahead. Way in the distance, where the earth met the sky, thin twin spires poked up out of the horizon.

"Hey . . . what's that over there?" she asked.

Edmond looked around. "What's what?" he asked.

"In the distance," Hélène said, pointing toward the spires. "See? Those two little things."

Edmond squinted. Then he shrugged. "Looks like a church or something," he answered.

Catherine shook her head excitedly. "It's got to be Chartres! Michelle once told me that after Ablis, you can already see the cathedral. Well, we've just passed through Ablis."

Ablis was one town they hadn't managed to bypass, but they had stayed near the outskirts to avoid being seen by too many people.

Edmond nodded thoughtfully. "If Michelle was right, that has to be Chartres," he said slowly. "There's no other cathedral around here that I've ever heard of."

Once again Hélène glanced at the distant spires. "Do you think it's far to Chartres?" she asked.

He smiled. "On foot, everything is far."

She poked him angrily. "I meant in kilometers."

He frowned. "I don't know. But it could be ten, maybe fifteen kilometers."

To Hélène, fifteen kilometers sounded a world away. "I hope it isn't as far again to Saint-Nazaire as it is from here to Chartres," she murmured. "I don't think my feet could stand it."

Weakly Edmond smiled down at her.

Suddenly Hélène had an inspiration. She gripped his arm. "Couldn't we take the train the rest of the way?" she asked eagerly.

He shook his head. "I'm afraid not. We'd need travel permits and money to do that. We don't have either."

"Oh." Her face fell. "But I thought we had money."

"It's all gone. I paid the vélo-taxi driver with it."

"But we still have Maman's ring," Hélène pointed out. "Can't we use that instead of money?"

Edmond tapped the pocket where he kept it, just to make sure he hadn't lost it. "We're not going to touch the ring if we can help it," he said flatly. "It's the only thing Maman could give us. It's . . . well, it's like an . . . an heirloom."

"Couldn't you steal some more money, then?" she asked.

Catherine shot Edmond a triumphant look. "Fine things she picks up from you. Before we know it, she'll become a pickpocket."

An expression of hurt crossed his face. Hélène glanced sharply at Catherine. "What's a pickpocket?" she demanded.

"Someone who reaches into other people's pockets and steals their money," she said harshly.

Hélène shook her head. "No, I don't think I'd like that," she said thoughtfully. "It doesn't sound very nice." Then she looked at Edmond curiously. "You weren't a pickpocket when you took Gisèle's money, were you? I mean, it wasn't actually in her *pocket*."

Edmond put a hand on her shoulder. "Just remember one thing, Hélène," he said quietly. "Whether you lift something from a person's pocket or from a nightstand or a chicken coop, it amounts to the same thing. Stealing is stealing, no matter how—or why—you do it. It's wrong, and nothing can ever make it right." He glanced sharply at Catherine. Her face reddened and she turned away in shame.

Hélène took Edmond's hand and squeezed it. "But if it's wrong, then why did you. . . ?" Her words trailed off uncomfortably.

He smiled sadly. "Because I had no choice. Remember what Maman said. She told us that God would forgive us for what we might have to do. But that still doesn't make it right."

Hélène digested this in silence.

Suddenly Edmond clapped his hands. "All right," he said gruffly. "Five minutes is up! It's time to get moving again."

"Already?" Catherine moaned.

"Already," he said with finality. "We still have far to go." He looked up at the sky. Hélène's eyes followed his. The sun was starting to go down and the sky was graying again. She knew that as soon as the sun dropped down, so did the temperature. Another couple of hours and it would get dark. And much colder.

They hadn't continued walking for five minutes when Catherine cried out sharply. Startled, Edmond and Hélène stopped and looked over at her. She was bending down, rubbing her left ankle with her hand.

Swiftly Edmond lowered Marie into Hélène's arms; then he touched Catherine gently on the back. "What's the matter?" His voice was concerned.

She looked at him sideways, her hair falling down over her face. Between strands of hair, Hélène could see her eyes. They were glazed over in pain. "It's my ankle," she moaned. "I . . . I twisted it in that rut."

Edmond knelt on the ground, his fingers gently probing around her ankle. Hélène could hear her sucking in her breath in pain.

He stood back up, placed a hand under Catherine's armpit, and pulled her to an upright position. "Do you think you can walk?" he asked.

She took a few tentative steps and nodded her head. "I'll be all right," she said.

Edmond looked thoughtfully across the fields, his eyes roving to the distant road. "We'll get off the path and stick to the road," he said with finality. "That way, walking will be a lot easier for you."

"The road?" Catherine said in a worried voice. "Do you think it's safe?"

"Right now it's a lot safer for you than the path. You could have a sprain, and these ruts won't help it any. Besides, I doubt that anyone's out here searching for us. The Boches may be looking for us in Paris, but they can't scour all of France. Not for us, anyway. We're not that important."

Catherine nodded. What he said made sense.

"Come on," he said. "Hélène can carry Marie for a while. You just hold on to me, and I'll help support you. That way we'll take some of the weight off your leg."

Even though they switched over to the smooth asphalt road, their progress had now slowed considerably. But Hélène had to credit Catherine with having guts. She tried to make light of her pain, although she limped noticeably, and much as they wanted to, she wouldn't hear of stopping so she could rest. And she was right. They had to keep on going. Already it was about time to look for a place to spend the night. So far, they hadn't come across a single shelter that looked suitable.

It was almost half an hour before they encountered any traffic. Then they heard the lonely drone of a car somewhere in the distance.

Hélène glanced at Edmond and pointed questioningly at the ditch. "Do you think we should. . . ?"

He shook his head. "I don't think that's necessary. But in case anyone asks, your names are Sara and Denise. Mine is Jacques. We live in Ablis and we're on our way to visit our sick grandmère in Chartres. Got that?"

Catherine and Hélène nodded in unison. Quickly they decided that Catherine was Sara and Hélène would be Denise.

It was just as well that they had the story prepared. Less than a minute later, a black car coming from the direction of Ablis pulled to a halt alongside them. A plump, red-faced Boche in a field uniform rolled down the window and leaned out, gesturing for them to come over.

Hélène glanced at Edmond hesitantly. He nodded, and they drew toward the car. Then, while he and Catherine talked with the driver, Hélène stood on tiptoe and peered curiously in through the back window. She was surprised to see that there were no passengers. Only a big bundle, wrapped up with brown wrapping paper and tied with a string, was on the backseat.

"Where are you headed?" she heard the driver ask in surprisingly fluent French.

Catherine tossed her head brusquely. "Our grandmère is sick," she said in a cold voice. "We are on our way to visit her."

The driver's mouth curved into a faint smile as he stared at Catherine longer than was necessary. "Where does she live?"

Catherine pointed in the direction of the distant spires. "Chartres."

"I noticed you were limping."

"I twisted my ankle," Catherine said with a shrug. "It's nothing."

"Even without a twisted ankle it's a long walk to Chartres," the Boche said. Suddenly his smile widened. "I tell you what. I shall drive you there." He leaned sideways and opened the front passenger door from inside. "Get in."

It sounded more like an order than an offer. Catherine didn't move. "What about my brother and sisters?" she asked stiffly.

"They can get in the back."

Once again Hélène looked at Edmond. Grudgingly he nodded his head, and she stood aside as he opened the back door. He shoved the package against the far side and let her climb in first.

Hélène glanced around excitedly. This was all new to her. She had never been in a car before. The seats were soft and bouncy and smelled faintly of leather; the dashboard was paneled with polished wood. She felt very important to be riding in such style.

After they piled in, the Boche expertly put the car in gear and drove off smoothly. While driving, he kept glancing sideways at Catherine. She didn't mask her distrust for Germans. She leaned against the door, as far from his reach as she could get. In frosty silence she stared out the windshield at the lifeless flat scenery up ahead.

"What is your name?" the Boche asked finally.

"Sara," Catherine answered softly. She didn't bother to look at him.

"My name is Kurt," he said. "I am from the Rhineland. From Koblenz. Where do you live?"

"In Ablis."

With curiosity Hélène inspected the wrapped bundle on the seat beside her. The brown paper crunched when she touched it. "What's in here?" she asked loudly.

The driver's eyes glanced back at her through the rearview mirror. "Newspapers. Every day I have to drive to Paris and pick up the *Pariser Zeitung*, *Paris-Soir*, and *Le Petit Parisien* for the general staff in Chartres."

"Oh!" The package might as well have been a snake; instinctively Hélène withdrew her hand. Even she knew what those newspapers were. Every kiosk in Paris sold them. The *Pariser Zeitung* was Paris' daily German newspaper. The others were French collaborator papers.

Good Parisians didn't read them.

"You can look at them if you like," the driver said. "You have plenty of time. Chartres is still a long way off. Over twenty kilometers."

"No, thank you," Hélène declined politely.

He chose not to hear her. He took one hand off the wheel, reached for a folded newspaper on the seat beside him, and handed it back over his shoulder. "If you don't want to tear the package open, here's a loose copy."

She had no choice but to take it. She murmured her thanks, and since she didn't want it, she handed it to Edmond. He started unfolding it.

Suddenly he let the paper drop facedown on his lap. He stared out the window thoughtfully.

Puzzled by this reaction, Hélène decided to find out what had triggered it. She lifted the newspaper and saw that it was a copy of *Paris-Soir*. The headlines screamed at her: "A MOTHER'S ANGUISH." Smaller headlines underneath it read: "Countrywide Search on for Kidnapped Children—One-Million-Franc Reward Offered." There was a blurred photo of a fat woman whom Hélène had never seen before. And below that, three pencil sketches.

Nausea rose up in her throat. The drawings had been reduced in size, but how well she recognized them! *They were Gisèle's sketches!* And Catherine's likeness was incredibly accurate, unmistakably recognizable. . . .

A series of chills swept through Hélène. The tactics were clear. The Boches were after them—but good. And in their search, they were even trying to enlist the aid of the unsuspecting French populace. Had it been spelled out that they were wanted for murdering a Boche, they'd be overnight heroes. Any good Frenchman would have welcomed—and helped—them with open arms. But instead, they had been "kidnapped," and their tearful "mother" was anxiously awaiting their return. The romantically inclined French loved children. They would go out of their way to reunite them with their "mother." Hélène had no doubt that whoever recognized them now would quite innocently head for the nearest police station and report seeing them.

And their "mother" in the photo? She would probably turn out to be a Gestapo agent.

Suddenly the Boches were no longer all they had to fear. Now every Frenchman was their potential enemy too.

Now they couldn't trust anyone. Under any circumstances.

Edmond turned away from the window. His face wore a grim expression. Carefully he laid the paper on his lap and turned it to face the front seat. He tried to make his voice light. "Look, Sara," he said. "Isn't this interesting?"

It took Catherine a moment to respond: she wasn't quite used to her new name yet. Then she twisted around in her seat.

Edmond pointed at the pictures.

Catherine's expression didn't change, but her face went white. Slowly she turned back around and stared blankly out the windshield.

There was a little more traffic on the road now. They passed a platoon of soldiers marching in the direction of Chartres. The sight of them only increased Hélène's dread. She couldn't help wondering what would happen if the driver recognized them. But she already knew the answer to that. He would turn them in—without giving it a second thought. In fact, at this very moment he might already be driving, not to Chartres, but to the nearest police station. Or worse, Gestapo headquarters.

The driver glanced over at Catherine again and frowned. "You know," he said slowly, "you look familiar. Somehow I can't get over the feeling that I've seen you somewhere before."

"I don't think that's possible," Catherine replied quickly.

"No, I'm sure of it. Maybe it was in Ablis. I often drive through there."

"Of course!" Catherine lied. "I remember now! I've seen you before too!"

Suddenly he hit the brakes. With a tremendous jolt, the car screeched to a halt. "Ach du lieber Himmel!" the driver exclaimed. He twisted around in his seat and snatched the newspaper off Edmond's lap. Then he peered closely at the drawings on the front page and rattled the paper. "You . . . you're the kidnapped children! The ones the whole country is being searched for!" He stared at Catherine.

Suddenly she began to laugh. It was a laugh Hélène had heard her practice over and over in her room at home. Perhaps her acting lessons would now pay off, after all.

"What is so funny?" the driver asked.

Catherine pretended to be out of breath. "Don't you see?" she gasped. "We weren't kidnapped. We ran away from home!"

He hesitated. "But . . . why?"

Catherine's face took on a spiteful look. "Because Maman is a monster!" she spit out vehemently. "We had to get away from her. She beats us till we're black and blue."

"But why are you going to Chartres?"

She took a deep breath. "A friend of mine named Yves happens to live there. It's the only place we have to go."

"But . . . the newspapers," the driver said with disbelief. "They wrote that you were kidnapped. Newspapers don't tell lies."

Catherine laughed bitterly. "Don't they?" She looked into his eyes.

"But why?"

"Simple. Maman's a very clever woman. She must have felt that people would look harder for us if they thought we were kidnapped."

He nodded slowly. "How could she arrange all this publicity?"

Catherine smiled. "For a year now she has been seeing a high-ranking German. He's head over heels in love with her, and she can make him do anything." She tapped the newspaper in his hand. "Even arrange for things like that."

He shook his head slowly. "It sounds so farfetched. Yet I believe you. But much as I hate to do it, I'll have to report you to the authorities. That's my sworn duty."

"I know," Catherine said. Suddenly she lowered her eyes. "I'm too old to let Maman run my life," she said in a whisper. "I've grown up so quickly that she never even noticed my needs. She only seeks gratification for her own."

The driver's interest quickened. "Needs?" he asked. "What needs?" Hélène caught a glimpse of his eyes. They shone brightly.

"Oh, you know." Catherine shrugged. "Being a woman and not being able to do anything about it."

He sat up straight. "Don't you have any other friends? I mean, men friends who will . . ."

"Other than Yves?" Catherine shook her head and sighed painfully. "Not really. You see, most men I've met aren't really men. They're all simply terrified of Maman. Only Yves has ever had the courage to face up to her." She paused suddenly and stared at him intently. "Would you stand up to her?"

"I . . . I think so," he stammered.

She smiled and reached out slowly, her fingers gently exploring his crotch.

"No," he said. "You must not do that. I have to drop you off at a police station. We shouldn't lose any time."

She smiled at him again and unbuttoned her coat. Then she took his hand and placed it on her breast. "I am not a child," she said. "I am a woman."

Nervously he pulled his hand back and drove on again. He wasn't paying much attention to the road now.

"Do I excite you?" Catherine asked.

His voice was a whisper. "Yes."

Once again, Catherine's hand began to explore. "You're getting hard," she said in an admiring tone. "My, but it's big."

"Bigger than your boyfriend's?"

"Much bigger."

The driver preened visibly. "Then why don't you undo my fly and get down on it?"

She smiled promisingly. "No, it's much too big to do just that. I want it . . . *inside* me."

The car swerved.

She glanced quickly out the windshield. On the right, a small forest of evergreens was coming up.

"I tell you what," she said. "See those trees up ahead? We can pull in there for a few minutes. Nobody will see the car if you drive in far enough."

He hesitated. "They could send me to the Russian front if they found out."

"Don't worry, they won't. Who is there to tell them? Certainly not those little monsters in the backseat."

Hélène was getting a bit annoyed. Catherine was pushing it a little too far. Monsters, indeed!

"Come on, it won't take long," Catherine said. "Afterward you can drop us off at the police station. But first I want you to treat me like the woman that I am."

The Boche's face broke into a smile. Suddenly he hit the

brakes and made a sharp turn onto a dirt road that branched off into the forest. Dipping evergreen branches brushed the sides of the car. It was darker here among the trees. They blotted out a lot of light.

After about ten meters, they pulled into a clearing. It was a log-splitting area; chopped yellow firewood was stacked up in neat piles. Between the graceful boughs of the pines they could catch glimpses of the road, but for anyone to see them, they would have to draw quite a bit of attention to themselves.

The Boche switched off the engine. "Do you want to send the kids out for a walk?" he asked.

Catherine shook her head. "It's too cold. Besides, this is nothing new for them. They've seen it before."

"Whatever you say." He lifted his hips off the seat and undid his fly.

Hélène felt a hand on her arm. She glanced over at Edmond. His eyes were expressionless. He was motioning for her to slip the string off the bundle on the seat beside her.

"It's even bigger when it's out!" Catherine's voice sounded impressed. "So big and red and swollen."

Hélène had the string off now. Impatiently Edmond snatched it away from her. Grimly he wrapped some of it around his hands, then stretched the remainder of it taut. At first Hélène thought he was going to play cat's cradle. Then suddenly she realized what he was going to do, why Catherine had lured the Boche into this secluded clearing. She held her breath and waited.

"First take it in your mouth," the driver was saying. "It will get even harder that way."

With a cry, Edmond pounced forward. He brought the string down in front of the driver's neck and pulled back hard, choking him.

The Boche's face began to get beet red. He made horrible gasping noises and his hands flew up to his throat, fingers clawing at the string. Catherine let out a shriek. She shrank into the corner of her seat. Then she leaned down and groped under the seat for something to club him with. She came up with a heavy flashlight. Savagely she began pounding him over the head with it. But the Boche could take a lot of punishment. With a sudden surge of strength he managed to tear the string loose. He shook his head, trying to clear it. In a rage, he lunged at Catherine.

Edmond immediately jumped out of the car. Hélène followed right behind him. There were pieces of firewood lying around on the ground. Without hesitation, he picked up the nearest piece and yanked the driver's door open.

The Boche had his big hands clamped around Catherine's throat. Her mouth hung open, desperately gasping for air, her body slumped in the seat. She was suffocating.

With the log, Edmond began to pound the Boche on the back of the neck. The Boche turned around with a snarl, but his hands wouldn't leave Catherine's throat.

Hélène looked around in desperation. Then she saw a metal tool lying next to a stack of chopped wood. It was a spike, the kind used for splitting logs. The point looked very sharp. She tried to pick it up, but it was too heavy. She tugged at Edmond's arm. "Use this!" she screamed. "Use this!"

Edmond threw down his piece of wood. He grabbed hold of the spike with both hands. Once again he flung himself on the Boche. This time, he was armed with a weapon that could destroy. Swiftly he plunged the spike into the Boche's belly.

The Boche screamed. His hands left Catherine's throat and his eyes moved down to his belly. In shock he stared at the protruding spike. Then came the blood.

But he wasn't dead yet.

At that moment Hélène heard the steady footfalls of marching feet coming from the road. Her heart began thumping even faster. That sound could mean only one thing. The platoon they had passed earlier would soon be upon them.

The Boche must have heard it too, for suddenly he rallied his strength and tried to cry out. Quickly Catherine pressed her hands over his mouth to muffle the cries. She winced as he sank his teeth into her fingers, but she held on. Then, struggling fiercely like some wounded animal, he tried to crawl out of the car. "His legs!" Edmond hissed at Catherine. "Grab his legs!"

She let go of his mouth and grabbed his pants, trying to pull him back into the car.

Hélène glanced toward the road. Between the pine boughs she could see the platoon. It was just passing by. And when she looked back at the car, she could see something else. The Boche was trying to reach for the center of the steering wheel. *For the horn!*

Catherine let go of his legs and tugged at his arm. Each time she pulled it away from the horn, he managed to reach for it again. And again. And again.

Grimly Edmond grabbed the driver by the hair. He pulled his head halfway out of the car and began slamming the door shut on it. The Boche grimaced and groaned, but he didn't cry out. Hélène could hear one sickening thud after another as Edmond pounded the door against his skull. The fifth time, there was a horrible crunching sound and the blood began pouring from the head. And slowly the Boche gave up the fight. His body went limp.

Finally he was dead.

The platoon was gone now, the sounds of marching receding into the distance. The road was clear.

Fatigued, Edmond threw himself to the ground. He sat there, a weary expression on his face. Right beside him, the Boche's head hung out of the car. From the backseat, Hélène could hear Marie's whimpers starting up. Incredibly, she had slept through the entire incident.

Catherine stumbled out of the car. She had to hold onto the car to steady herself as she came around it. She took one look at the driver, then bent over and vomited.

"The newspapers," Edmond said in a whisper. He was still breathing heavily. "We'll have to . . . carry them . . . a distance away. Burn them. Or bury them. They mustn't get to Chartres."

Catherine nodded wearily and dropped to the ground beside him.

They rested for fifteen minutes. By then Edmond and Catherine had some of their strength back. Hélène helped them lug the newspapers to a spot about fifty meters from the car and burn them. To hide the evidence of a fire, they covered up the charred remains with pieces of wood and pine boughs.

85

It was pitch dark by the time they found shelter for the night. They had discovered it by accident. They had walked more than three kilometers along the road to Chartres when they saw a car's yellow headlights bobbing in the distance.

"Quick!" Edmond said. "Into the ditch!"

They scrambled off the road, and there it was, right in front of them. A large round culvert that connected the ditches that ran along both sides of the road. Here, directly under the road, they would be well hidden. The bottom was filled with water, but it had long since turned to ice. Although cold, they would at least be safe.

After the car passed by overhead, they set out to make the shelter as comfortable as possible. Edmond had them pull out shrubs from the roadside. He figured that they could stuff them at each end of the pipe, thereby blocking out some of the wind. But the shrubs were stubborn: their roots were frozen into the ground. All they managed to collect were some bare branches. These they spread out over the ice. Then they lay down on top of them.

They slept curled up together, cold and hungry, using their body heat to try to warm each other, to try to draw some comfort from their closeness. But Hélène didn't sleep well; Marie cried a lot that night. And when dawn finally came, Hélène awoke shivering, her teeth chattering noisily. Even before she opened her eyes, she sensed that Edmond was gone.

An hour later, he returned. He had been to loot a house in a nearby village, and he brought back some milk, small slabs of cheese, two thin sausages, and a little sugar. The sugar was still in its blue-and-white ceramic bowl. He had also come across a bottle of brandy. He pulled out the cork, and taking turns, they each took a swig. It tasted bitter and burned all the way down their throats, but then they would feel a comforting warm glow spreading through them. They even wet Marie's lips with a little taste of it. To their surprise, it quieted her down.

"The brandy seems to silence her," Edmond said. "We'll give her some whenever we need to keep her quiet."

After they finished eating, they moved on. They headed southwest across yet more barren fields and then through forests which lacked underbrush. Over the centuries, the bushes and brambles had been cleared away, and Hélène imagined that in summer the earth would be carpeted with moss. Right now it was covered with yellowed pine needles and fallen cones. Overhead, the sky was thick and gray, looking like snow.

In the afternoon, it began to sleet.

It caught them unawares, while they were still in the middle of the forest. Numb with cold and soaked to the skin, they finally found a shelter. It was a deserted woodcutter's cabin, and it even had a fireplace. Stacks of chopped wood were piled up along the outside walls, and they carried some into the cabin. Edmond built a fire. Wet wood doesn't burn well, and the cabin got very smoky. It made their eyes water, but they were grateful for the warmth.

Realizing that they might be snowed in for days, they ate sparingly in order to stretch their rations. And when there was no more milk, they fed Marie a mixture of sugar and warm water.

It looked like the storm would continue for some time, so they took the opportunity to wash Marie's diaper. It must have suited her well, for that night she slept soundly.

But getting soaked hadn't done them any good. Catherine and Hélène came down with colds. They both sneezed and coughed a lot, and Catherine got laryngitis on top of it. That night, the sleet turned to snow.

Two days later, the weather cleared. They stepped outside the cabin and gazed around in wonder. The temperature had plunged even lower, but the air was crystalline and pure. The sky overhead was of the palest blue, and everything was covered with a blanket of thick, glistening snow. Even the branches of the trees looked as if someone had piled cotton on top of them. To a young girl it was a fairyland.

"Isn't it beautiful?" Hélène said to Edmond.

He nodded. "Yes, it is very beautiful," he agreed. But beauty, apparently, didn't weigh heavily on his mind right now. There were more important things to think of. He turned to Catherine. "Is there any sugar left?"

"A little." Her voice was a hoarse croak.

"Mix whatever there is in some warm water and give it to Marie," he said. "Then, when she's done eating, prepare her for the cold. We shall be moving on shortly."

Catherine nodded obediently and went inside the cabin to wake Marie. A moment later, she rushed back outside.

Edmond stared at her. "Is something wrong?"

"It's Marie," Catherine said huskily. "She's burning up. I think she has a fever!"

Edmond pushed her aside and entered the cabin. Swiftly he crossed over to where Marie was lying and touched her little forehead with his hand. "I'm afraid you're right," he told Catherine grimly. "She really is sick."

Hélène did as he had done and laid her hand on Marie's forehead. It was wet with perspiration, but ice cold. "What are we going to do?" she asked.

Edmond stared down at Marie. "What we must do," he murmured. "Find a doctor for her."

Catherine looked at him. "No doctor will come here."

"Then we must go to him," he replied simply.

Catherine took him firmly by the arms and shook him. "But it's too cold!" she said sharply. "It's dangerous to take her outside in her condition!"

Edmond began to strip off his coat. Hélène watched as he gently wrapped Marie in it. "This will keep her warm," he said.

"But what about you?" Catherine asked. "What are you going to wear?"

He shrugged. "I'll be all right. I don't have the fever."

Catherine stared at him. "Have some sense! You'll freeze to death!"

"Maybe," he said. "But that can't be helped." Then he raised his voice. "Enough of this. Hurry up and get ready. We'll leave right away."

Catherine threw up her hands in exasperation. Then she stomped around the cabin gathering up their few belongings.

As Hélène buttoned her coat she looked at Edmond. "Don't doctors cost money?" she asked.

He nodded.

"Does that mean you'll steal some?" she whispered hopefully.

"No, I will not," he said sharply.

"Oh." She frowned. "Then how are we going to pay the doctor?"

He patted his breast pocket. "We'll have to use Maman's ring. Although I hate to part with it, I think Maman would understand."

Hélène nodded. He was right. Under these circumstances, Maman would.

Each time they neared a village, Edmond had them wait out of sight while he took Marie and went off to find a doctor. Doctors, it turned out, were a scarcity in the country. It was only after a few hours that he finally found one. He left Marie there and hurried back to where Catherine and Hélène waited. Once again, he was wearing his coat. "Come along," he said. "The doctor's house is nice and warm. A little heat won't hurt us."

Catherine looked at him with apprehension. "Do you think the doctor can be trusted?" she asked.

"I hope so," he answered. "Anyway, we have little choice. I left Marie with him."

"Is the doctor in the village?" Hélène asked, pointing at the sleepy clusters of houses in the distance. "Or is he in one of the farmhouses?"

"In the village. Come along." Their footsteps crunched on the snow as he led the way up the peaceful main street. At the last house, he opened a gate into a small front yard, and then they waited on the steps while he knocked on the door. It was opened by a heavyset middle-aged woman. She recognized Edmond. "Come in, come in," she said, herding them inside with her hands. "The doctor is upstairs with the little one."

They stepped into a dark, narrow hallway. After the woman closed the door behind them, she gestured at their feet. "Take off your shoes, they're probably soaked through. Leave them by the door. Then come along with me."

They followed her down the hallway. She opened a door with opaque glass panels set into the frame. This was the kitchen. There was a huge enamel-and-tile stove in the corner, and a lot of heat radiated from it. Quickly the children drew around it, holding out their hands over the glowing top, trying to warm them.

"Sit down," the woman said, gesturing at the table. "You look like you could do with some food. I was just preparing a hot lunch."

"But Marie—" Edmond began.

"The little one is fine," a man's voice said from the doorway.

The children turned and looked across the room at him. He was elderly and white-haired, with deep wrinkles etched into his face. He wore silver-rimmed glasses and a thick wool sweater. "She's upstairs, asleep."

"Is it anything serious?" Edmond asked anxiously.

The doctor looked at Edmond. "She is but a baby," he replied. "At her age anything is potentially serious. The little ones have very little resistance." Then he smiled reassuringly. "But I think she will be all right. What she needs right now is to stay out of the cold. Let's hope the fever breaks soon. If it does, I don't think it should take more than a few days until she can travel again."

"A few days!" Edmond exclaimed. "We don't have that long, doctor. We . . . we've got to be on our way soon."

The doctor frowned. "You're not from anywhere around here, otherwise I'd have recognized you. That means you must still have far to go. Am I right?"

Silently Edmond nodded.

The doctor sat at the kitchen table and gestured for them to sit down. "You can trust me," he said with compassion. "Would you like to tell me about it?"

Edmond looked at him in silence. After a moment's hesitation he nodded. Seated around the table, and over steaming cups of cocoa, he told the doctor everything that had happened, beginning with Maman and Michelle and the Boche banging the canary-yellow door down. . . .

Four days later, Marie was fit to travel. The children were well rested; the stay had done them good. Hélène's cold was gone, and so was Catherine's laryngitis.

When it was time to say good-bye, tears filled Hélène's eyes. The doctor and his housekeeper had both gone out of their way to be kind, and she hated to leave. They had made them feel welcome and at home, when they had no right to expect it, and now it suddenly felt as if they were saying good-bye to close friends.

Hélène buried her face in the woman's big soft bosom and gave her an enormous hug. "I'll miss you," she whispered.

"And I will miss you, too," the woman said quietly, looking down at her. "Take care of yourself, and may God bless you."

Edmond took the doctor aside. He reached into his pocket for Maman's ring. "We owe you so much," he said. "This is all we can pay you with."

The doctor shook his head. "I can accept nothing."

"But you saved Marie's life," Edmond insisted.

"It was my duty—as a Frenchman and as a doctor."

Edmond nodded. "Thank you," he said softly. "And for the new clothes, too."

The doctor shook his head. "No, it is we who must thank you. Although they are a small minority, there are those who collaborate with the invaders of our country and blacken our pride. Yet you—mere children—have the courage to fight the Boche. You are an inspiration. We are grateful to you."

Carefully the housekeeper lifted Marie, bundled up in a thick new blanket, into Catherine's arms. "Take care of the little angel," she told Catherine.

Catherine smiled. "I will."

The woman wiped her moist eyes and sniffed. "Sometime, when all this is over, let us know how your journey went. Even if it is years from now." She hugged Edmond tightly and then fumbled with the silver chain that hung around her neck. Attached to it was a little religious medallion. Solemnly she fastened it around his neck. "You have our blessings. We shall pray for you." Then she reached up to the table and handed Edmond a heavy basket which she had filled with the choicest foods from the larder. "For your journey," she said simply.

Edmond stood on tiptoe and kissed her cheek. "Thank you," he whispered.

Suddenly they heard the ringing of bells coming from outside. "What's that?" Hélène asked, rushing to the window. Her eyes widened. A big sleigh pulled by two chestnut drays had slid to a halt on the snowy street in front of the house.

"That will be Claude Sorel," the doctor said. "He's a poor farmer who owes me a favor. Last year I saved his wife's life. He couldn't afford to pay me, so now I am letting him work off his debt. I arranged it so that you will spend the night on his farm. Tomorrow he will drive you in his sleigh to

Châteaudun. Once there, head south for sixty kilometers. Then you will be at the Loire. Follow the river westward until you reach the sea. There you will find Saint-Nazaire."

8

When they reached his farm, Claude Sorel pulled up in front of the house and turned around in the driver's seat. "We're here," he said, his deep-set, penetrating eyes looking down at the children.

Without another word, he hopped to the ground and waited as they climbed out of the sleigh. They stretched their legs. They had been riding for well over an hour, and they were numb with cold despite the thick old lap blanket that they had pulled up around them. Sorel didn't bother unhitching the horses. He tethered them to a post, where they stood twitching their tails and snorting noisily. Their chestnut bodies heaved from exertion and gleamed with sweat. He had been driving them mercilessly, flaying them when they weren't flying fast enough across the softly powdered fields.

"Come along," he said tersely.

They started toward the front door, and Hélène looked up at the house. It was large and cheerless, a drab rambling blight on the fairytale landscape. Like most of the buildings in the province, it was ancient. Roughly built and picturesque in its very neglect, at each end rickety wooden lean-tos—obvious afterthoughts—sagged against the stone walls for support. The small square windows punctuating the thick walls were few and far between, lending the building the look of a forbidding fortress. Each of the windows had weathered wooden shutters; some of them were pulled closed, a few were loose and banged in the wind. The solitary chimney gave the only evidence of habitation. Out of it trailed a meager wisp of smoke.

On the doorstep they stopped to stomp the snow off their

shoes. Then Sorel grunted, pushed open the door, and they entered.

Inside the dim hall, the ceilings were so low that Sorel had to duck through the doorways. The walls were whitewashed with chalky paint that rubbed off on your fingers if you touched them.

They went through another door and found themselves in the kitchen. Like the hall, it was dimly lit. The floor of roughly hewn boards was bleached almost white from decades of scrubbing. Some antlers and stuffed deer heads hung on the walls. The deer were half in shadow, but their eyes caught the light coming in from the window and glinted malevolently. Hélène couldn't understand why people wanted to decorate their walls with such frightful objects.

"Hey, woman!" Sorel called out in a loud, abrasive voice.

They heard a door opening and closing. Then a woman shuffled listlessly in from a room in the back. "Yes?" she mumbled. Her speech sounded slurred; then Hélène saw why. Her lip was swollen.

Hélène stared at her. She was much shorter than her husband, her face red and tired-looking. Her thick, frizzy hair was plaited. Somberly dressed, she wore a heavy black skirt, a thick black sweater with sleeves that were too long, and a faded blue apron. There was something about the way her shoulders sagged that reminded Hélène of an animal whose spirit had been broken.

"Can't you see that we've got visitors, you lazy woman?" Sorel shouted. "Don't just stand there stupidly! Hurry up and put some food on. Then fix them a place to sleep!"

"Yes, Claude," she said dutifully. Hélène noticed that the woman's face had reddened. Hers would have too, if she were treated like that in front of strangers.

The woman glanced at them and gestured that they sit around the rough-hewn table. It was only then that Hélène realized how young the woman really was. Young and worn out.

"Make sure you put 'em to bed early," Sorel grumbled. "Tomorrow I'm supposed to drive them to Châteaudun. We got to get an early start."

She looked at him over her shoulder. "Yes, Claude."

He grunted again, lifted an earthenware jug down off a shelf, uncorked it, and took a swig. Hélène could smell the cider as it spilled down his chin. He wiped it off with his sleeve, brought the jug over to the table, and set it down with a bang. He scraped a chair back and sat down, putting his boots up on the spotless table.

Hélène could see the disapproval flickering in the woman's eyes, but she kept prudently silent.

Sorel took another swig of cider and pushed his chair back heavily. He got to his feet. "I'll be back later," he growled. "Make sure they're bedded down early."

"Where are you going?" the woman asked. Hélène could recognize the fear in her voice.

"To the village."

She turned to him, nervously twisting a corner of the apron between her fingers. "Claude, please, no," she begged. "You just went there last night and came back . . ." He scowled at her and she fell silent.

"Shut up, woman!" He waved his warm threateningly. "You want a shiner to match your lip?"

"No, Claude," she said wearily. With a sigh of resignation she turned back to the stove as he stomped out.

"I don't like these people," Catherine said.

Edmond nodded in reply. He was sitting on one of the hard lumpy mattresses. Occasionally he would bounce Marie up and down on the creaky springs. Each time he did, she squealed with delight while thick clouds of dust rose up in the air around them. They all wore their coats. The upstairs of the house was unheated. Once in bed, under the ancient feather quilts and moth-eaten blankets, they'd be nice and warm, but not until then. The room was in shadows, gloomily lit by a solitary oil lamp.

Hélène got to her feet and went over to the tiny window. It was barely big enough for a pigeon to squeeze through, but it was at one of the gable ends of the house, and when she stood on tiptoe she could look down to the farmyard, two stories below. The moon was out. White and almost full, it bathed the landscape and cast long night shadows across the snow.

Edmond settled back against the splintery headboard. "It's the farmer," he said. "His wife isn't too bad, but she's terrified of him. Did you see her lip? He must have punched her real good."

"I can't understand why the doctor has anything to do with

them," Catherine said with a toss of her head. "Doesn't he know that the farmer is . . . well, not quite right?"

"Maybe he feels sorry for the wife. Or maybe the husband doesn't show his real feelings in front of him," Edmond said thoughtfully. "Don't you remember how he smiled when we got into the sleigh, and how friendly he was to the doctor?"

Catherine nodded slowly. "Yes, it must have been an act."

Hélène balanced herself on her toes and looked out the window again. All she could see were dim yellow fields of snow, and then the darkness that stretched beyond. Somewhere out in that darkness was the village where the kind doctor lived . . . and his housekeeper with the warm bosom. And even farther out, somewhere way to the south, was the Loire. The river of kings, they called it, lined with massive castles and majestic white châteaus. All they'd have to do was to follow the meandering riverbed, and eventually they'd end up in Saint-Nazaire, where they would find Tante Janine, an aunt they'd never even met, and wait with her for the Boche to be driven out of France, for Maman and Papa to come and get them and take them back to Paris.

Suddenly she heard the faint jingling of bells. She peered out in all directions. Far in the distance she could see the sleigh. She watched as it came closer and pulled up out front. This time, instead of jumping, the farmer climbed unsteadily down from the seat. He didn't bother tying the horses to the post. He stumbled, straightened, and then reeled into the house. From the floor below came a sudden deafening crash.

Catherine jumped. "What was *that*?"

"It's the farmer," Hélène said, turning away from the window. "He just came back. He must have fallen over something." She giggled. "I think he's drunk."

"I sure hope he's sober enough by morning to drive us to Châteaudun," Edmond mumbled. He cocked his head to one side and listened. The farmer was coming heavily up the rickety stairs. When he reached the landing, he lumbered toward the door. There was a moment's silence before he stumbled on down the narrow corridor, his footsteps fading. Finally a door slammed.

Then they heard his voice through the walls. "Woman, are you in bed already!"

A conversation followed, but it sounded one-sided; only his words were spoken loud enough for the children to catch.

There were banging noises, and the sounds of drawers being opened and slammed shut.

Finally they heard the wife's voice adding to the commotion. "Claude, don't!" she shrieked in rising hysteria. The door down the hall was flung open, and once again his footsteps echoed out in the hall. Hélène could hear the woman as she ran after him. "No, Claude, don't! Please, I beg of you!"

"Get your hands off me!" he snarled. There were the sounds of a scuffle. Hélène winced as a sharp slap rang out. The woman moaned. She must have tumbled to the floor, because it suddenly shook. "You fool woman!" he spit out. "What do you want? For us to be poor the rest of our lives?"

"No, Claude," she sobbed. "That's *not* what I want. But I don't want blood money, either!"

"Shut your mouth, bitch!"

There was a short silence, after which he approached the children's door. Hélène held her breath. For a moment she was afraid that he was going to come in and beat on her, too. But instead he inserted a key in the lock.

She stared at the door in horror. Somehow, this was even more terrifying than if he'd tried to attack. She flinched when she heard the key turn. Then she saw the door handle lowering as it was tested from the outside.

A sudden dread knowledge came over her. The worst possible thing had happened.

They had become prisoners.

"There—they're locked in," the farmer said with gruff satisfaction. "They can't go anywhere now."

Hélène stared first at Catherine, then at Edmond. "What are we going to do?" she whispered.

"Sssssh!" hissed Edmond. "Be quiet!"

The farmer grunted. "Get up, woman! Go and get dressed. I want you to be presentable when the Germans arrive. They'll soon be here." He paused. When he spoke again, it was with awe in his voice. "Just imagine—a million and a half francs! Me, Claude Sorel, a millionaire!"

Hélène shook her head in despair. So the reward for our capture had gone up once again, she thought. At Madame Chang's, it had been half a million francs; in the newspapers six days ago, a million. Now it had been increased by yet another half-million. If, somehow, they did manage to get out of here—and that seemed a remote possibility at best—the reward would soon be so astronomical that anyone, perhaps even Tante Janine, could be induced to turn them over to the Boche.

"But you don't even know it's them," the woman wailed.

Claude Sorel laughed. "There was a newspaper in the tavern. Sure as hay, the pictures were theirs. Especially the older girl's. The paper claimed that they'd been kidnapped. Isn't that funny?" He laughed again. "If it hadn't been for the doctor telling us otherwise, I'd have believed that story myself. Anyway, it's a good thing I went out drinking. If I'd listened to you and stayed home, I would never have found out about the reward. That's how fortunes are made, by being in the right place at the right time. Good thing the gendarme was there, too. He let me use his telephone."

The woman's voice was barely a whisper. "Who did you call?"

"Since I knew who was really searching for them, the Gestapo, of course. Going through the Feldgendarme might take days. I wanted to make sure there'd be no delay with the reward. You know how long paperwork takes to process."

The woman was sobbing uncontrollably now. Hélène could imagine her red face getting even redder. "How could you?" she screamed. "We're *Frenchmen*! And the doctor is a friend! He *trusted* us! And we're in his debt!"

"You mean *you're* in his debt. Anyway, *he's* not about to give us one and a half million francs, is he?" Sorel rationalized. "Well, it's none of his business, then. So stop worrying and wipe your eyes. I can't stand it when they're all bloodshot and puffy. You're ugly enough as it is!"

It was with an empty feeling that Hélène heard their footsteps receding. She had hoped the woman would stay behind. Perhaps she could have been cajoled into stealing the key from her husband and unlocking the door.

Edmond put Marie down and rose from the bed. "We have to get out of here," he said softly.

Catherine nodded. "But how? We're locked in." She looked over at Hélène. "Can that window be opened?"

Hélène nodded. "Yes, but it's too small. Even Marie couldn't squeeze through it."

Edmond picked up the oil lamp and walked around the room, shining the light into the dark corners, feeling along the walls with his fingers, staring in thoughtful silence around the ceiling, down at the floor. But there were no other exits except for the door—no trapdoors to the roof, no forgotten blocked-up doorways behind the moldy wallpaper. Even a mouse would have had a difficult time of it escaping.

"Well?" Catherine asked. Her large brown eyes were watching Edmond intently.

He shook his head glumly. "I'm afraid we'll have to choose between the frying pan and the fire. There's only one way we can get out of here."

Catherine raised her eyebrows questioningly.

He glanced at her and sighed. "We'll have to set the place on fire."

She stared at him. Then she slowly nodded. "And hope they'll come and unlock the door in time?"

He didn't answer. "We'd better get started," he said. He snapped his fingers. "Help me drag the mattresses over toward the window."

He set the lamp down on a crate and they began to tug at the mattresses. Stuffed with horsehair, they were stiff and heavy. When they were all piled against the wall, Edmond made sure they wouldn't fall as soon as they started to burn. Then he wiped his dusty hands on his trouser legs. Catherine picked up Marie.

"Cover her face with her blanket," he said. "That way, she won't inhale too much smoke."

Catherine nodded. She kissed Marie's forehead and gently tucked the soft cover up around her tiny pink head. "There, baby," she whispered soothingly. "Don't be frightened."

"Now, back up against the door and stay put," Edmond ordered.

He grabbed a blanket and draped it over Hélène's and Catherine's shoulders.

"Pull this over your heads and hold it there. It should shield us from some of the heat." He glanced questioningly first at Catherine, then at Hélène. Nothing needed to be said. They understood.

Edmond held the lamp high. Hélène watched as he gracefully tossed it toward the window. The glass globe shattered against the wall and fell to the pile of mattresses, soaking them with oil. Instantly a pillar of furiously crackling flames shot up to the ceiling.

From that moment on, instinct took over. They began stomping on the floor and banging on the door with their fists.

"Fire!" Hélène screamed abruptly. "Fire!" There was genuine terror in her voice.

Catherine's eyes were wild with fear. "Help!" she shouted. "Fire!" From the pitch of her voice, Hélène knew that Catherine's terror was no less real than her own.

She glanced backward. The mattresses were all ablaze now. As she watched, the quilts caught, too. Within seconds the whole far side of the room was a roaring sheet of flame. The stench of burning hair and feathers was nauseating. Then suddenly she couldn't breathe. It was as if the fire were sucking all the air out of the room. Her eyes burned and teared. She began to hammer even more furiously on the door, and screamed again.

"Fire!"

"Help! Help!"

Now the smoke was like a thick black screen. It burned raw in their lungs and they couldn't see a thing. Then they heard quick footsteps outside in the hallway. The farmer was cursing.

The woman let out a shriek. "Smoke!" she screamed. "Pouring out from under the door! Claude, *do* something! The house will burn down!"

Once again they could hear the key turning in the lock. Then the cylinder clicked. There was a rush of sudden fresh air as the door opened.

Choking and coughing, the children stumbled blindly out into the hall. Claude Sorel pushed past them and ran into the inferno. He tore off his jacket and began beating the flames with it. It was futile. On all sides, the wallpaper was a solid wall of flame, and already tongues of fire licked up from the dry wooden floor. The noise was awesome: the fire roared.

The woman was in hysterics. She held her arm up in front of her face to shield it from the heat. "Claude!" she kept screaming. "Put it out!"

And then the children rushed down the rickety stairs, almost falling over themselves in the process. There was a dull crash from upstairs as something gave way and fell. The woman shrieked and drew back. Hélène looked up and saw that a massive blazing beam had burned itself loose from the ceiling. One end of it was poking crazily out into the hall; the other still slanted up to the ceiling inside the room. Now it was only a matter of moments before the hall would be engulfed in fire too. And the stairs.

Less than a minute later, they were outside in the clear, icy night. Never had fresh air felt so good. Hélène took deep lungfuls of it and wiped the perspiration off her forehead; her whole body was soaked with sweat.

For a moment they stood there in the snow, staring up at the house. The tiny window at the end of the gable flashed brightly, and the snow on the roof had begun to melt from the heat. Water was pouring down off the eaves. Then suddenly a huge tongue of fire leaped up through the snowy roof into the black sky, licking at the white moon and sending showers of sparks high into the night. Everything around was now yellow, flickering as though it were alive. The house. The barn. The snow. Hélène felt a tug at her sleeve.

"Come on!" Edmond hissed. He was starting off across the snow.

"Wait," Hélène cried, pointing. "The sleigh! Can't we take that?"

He nodded. "You two hop in," he said. "I'll drive."

They hurried toward it, but just then part of the roof caved in with a crash. Terrified, the horses reared and neighed. They broke into a gallop and shot off into the night, pulling the empty sleigh. Edmond ran after them, but in vain. They were halfway across the fields already. He made a gesture of defeat and sprinted back, panting and out of breath.

Once again the children headed across the fields on foot. Only this time they left clear tracks in the snow. Like Hansel and Gretel and their trail of bread crumbs, Hélène thought. Only with us, the birds won't come to peck at them and erase our path.

Edmond seemed to read her thoughts. "I wish it would start snowing again," he murmured. "At least then our footprints would be covered." He glanced hopefully up at the sky, but it was obvious that there would be no snow coming.

After they had gone about a hundred meters, Hélène turned around and glanced back at the house. The fire completely engulfed the downstairs now, and two little figures—one shorter than the other—were silhouetted against the blaze, rushing around frantically. For a moment Hélène thought about the woman's immaculately scrubbed floors, brushed almost white by her and generations of women before her. Now blazing like kindling. But this was no time for pity. Already she could see the bobbing headlights of vehicles in the distance. We have less time than we thought, Hélène said to herself.

The Boches were fast approaching.

This time, they had dogs.

They could hear them baying in the distance. Hélène's lungs were burning and raw from all the running, but she didn't dare to stop and rest for an instant. Whenever she looked back, she could see tiny flashlight beams cutting through the night.

In their hurry, they had no time to waste choosing the best, safest, or easiest routes. They crashed through scratchy winter foliage, stumbled over frozen fields, and plunged past barren orchards. The dark and the snow were enemies, too, hiding obstacles in their path—rocks, stumps, tree trunks, and fallen branches. Often they fell, but the snow, the culprit that hid the dangerous traps, ironically lent them a helping hand in the process, providing a soft cushion each time they fell.

Every minute, it seemed, the baying of the dogs drew closer. Whenever they glanced back, the waving flashlights had definitely gained on them.

When they reached a narrow, frozen creek with two long boards stretching across it as a kind of bridge, Edmond had them stop for a brief moment so that they could catch their breath. Gratefully they took deep lungfuls of air. Marie was crying, but there no longer was any brandy to silence her with. It was in the burning house, along with the basket of food the doctor's housekeeper had given them. From where they stood, they could still see the fire. The whole sky to the north was tinted with a rosy glow. All of a sudden the glow flared.

"It must be the barn," Edmond said. "It must have gone up too. The sparks probably carried over from the house."

Catherine spit in the snow. "Serves them right," she said.

Edmond stared at the plank bridge in the moonlight. "Listen," he said excitedly. "I've got an idea."

Hélène turned to him. "What is it?"

"We'll split up."

Catherine stared at him. "Split up? But—"

"No buts," he said roughly. "We must, especially since they have dogs. Besides, two of us won't be as easily recognized as four. Four children are what they're looking for."

101

Hélène was trembling. "I don't think I like this," she whined. "We should all stick together."

"We can't," Edmond said with finality. He took a deep breath. "Catherine, you take Marie. You cross the creek. Once you're over, Hélène and I will remove the planks. That way, the dogs won't follow you. We'll head south along the creek, throwing them off your track."

Hélène had a sudden sinking feeling. "No!" she cried. "I want us to stay together."

"Shut up!" Edmond hissed. He looked at Catherine.

Her face was pale in the moonlight. She nodded solemnly. "I'll take good care of Marie," she promised quietly.

"Take care of yourself, too," Edmond said. "We'll meet at Tante Janine's."

A veil dropped over Catherine's eyes; even in the moonlight Hélène could see it. "Yes, we'll meet at Tante Janine's," Catherine said softly.

Quickly they kissed each other good-bye. For a moment Catherine clung to Edmond, her eyes staring into his. "I'm sorry," she said.

"What for?" he asked.

"For being such a fool. About the stealing. I had no right."

He dug his foot in a pile of snow and looked down. "Forget it," he said. "Once we meet in Saint-Nazaire, we'll be able to exchange notes on who stole what."

She smiled. "Yes. We'll do that. Good-bye, Edmond. Good-bye, Hélène."

Suddenly Edmond reached into his pocket and pressed something into Catherine's hand. "Maman's ring," he whispered. "You may need it more than us."

She nodded. Then, tears in her eyes, and gently holding Marie against her breast, she carefully crossed over the plank bridge. Once she got to the other side, she stood on a mound of snow watching as Edmond and Hélène knocked the planks loose. Edmond lifted them up and tossed them to the other side. With a fallen branch he brushed snow over where the bridge had been.

It was no longer possible to tell that it had ever been there. Edmond's tracks, and Hélène's, would head along the creek, throwing off the pursuers. For the time being, Catherine and Marie would be safe. It was a small comfort, but at least they had a good head start.

Edmond straightened up and tossed away the branch. For

a moment he and Hélène stared over at Catherine. She looked like a forlorn Madonna holding her child. Hélène lifted her arm in a wave. Gravely, Catherine waved back. Then Hélène and Edmond headed south, quickly running along the creek.

Hélène sniffed and wiped her nose with her hand. Her vision was blurred by tears. She wondered if she would ever see Catherine and Marie again.

9

It was half an hour later when they realized they'd lost their pursuers. Hélène could no longer hear the baying of the dogs. When she looked back, the night was black and peculiarly silent. The flashlight beams had vanished. It was clear the Boche weren't following. She tapped Edmond's arm excitedly. "They're gone!" she exclaimed. "Look behind us!"

He stopped and turned around. "So they are," he said in surprise.

She took what she thought was a well-deserved rest and flung herself down on a felled log. She looked up at Edmond. "Perhaps they gave up?" she said hopefully.

He turned to her and shook his head. "Fat chance," he said soberly. "They don't give up *that* easily. Especially not after all the trouble they went through to try to capture us in the first place."

A terrible thought suddenly took shape in Hélène's mind. Unconsciously she got to her feet. She stared at him. "You don't think they . . ." Her words trailed off. She couldn't get herself to finish the sentence; it was too horrible to put into words.

Edmond's face clouded over. "You're wondering whether they've managed to follow Catherine instead of us," he said heavily.

She nodded.

"I can't answer that. All I know is that she should be safe. I thought we covered her tracks rather well."

"Maybe they got suspicious," Hélène said. "They followed three sets of tracks from the farmhouse, and one set petered out at the stream. Don't you think they might have decided to have a look around?"

"I suppose it's possible," Edmond said softly. He kicked the log with the tip of his shoe. "Maybe they went back to get horses. If they decided to do that, they may have knocked off for the night. After all, they can continue the search in the morning and still catch up with us. Our tracks won't disappear overnight." He smiled grimly. "They'll be here for days to come."

She nodded. "So what do we do?"

"We trick them. We won't leave any tracks for them, nor any scent for their dogs."

She looked at him suspiciously. "How?"

"We keep following this creek and hope that it joins up with an even bigger stream. One that's faster moving, and not covered with ice. Then we'll wade through the water. They should be completely thrown off."

"Brrr . . ." The mere thought of it made her shiver. "But won't the water be too cold?"

"It will be freezing," he replied. "But it's our best bet." He punched her playfully. "We better get moving."

They trudged on. They came across several creeks, but it was only after about three hours that they found an angrily moving stream that was free of ice except at the very edges. Fearfully Hélène stared at this dark caldron boiling angrily over a bed of rocks and boulders.

Ever resourceful, Edmond grabbed a stick and tested the depth of the water. It proved to be pretty shallow. Then he threw the stick in. Quickly it was swept downstream.

He nodded to himself and took Hélène by the hand. "The current's strong," he cautioned. "I want you to hold on to me. If you don't, it might sweep you downstream."

She nodded. "I'll be careful," she said.

Slowly he stepped into the water, and she followed gingerly. She winced, and it took everything for her not to cry out. The water came up to her knees. It was so cold that she thought a knife had suddenly cut off her legs. A second later, she could no longer feel them. She supposed that in a way it was a kind of blessing.

Edmond sensed her distress. "Bear with it," he said. "We're not going to stay in here any longer than we have to."

But it seemed to her that they waded through that tricky current forever. Several times she lost her footing or a loose rock in the riverbed gave way under her feet. Then only her hold on Edmond saved her from being swept away.

When they reached a low wooden bridge, Edmond drew to a halt underneath it. "Hold on to something," he warned. "I'm going to let go of you. I want to have a look."

Hélène wrapped her arms securely around an ice-encrusted piling. She watched as he knocked some icicles loose from the edge of the bridge, grabbed hold of it, and pulled himself up. After he had a quick look, he lowered himself back down into the water. She looked at him questioningly.

He smiled. "It's a little road," he said. "It's been traveled on quite a bit lately. Which is good, because our tracks won't be the only ones. Come on."

They got out of the water, and Edmond climbed up the steep, snow-covered embankment. She followed him, her numb fingers clutching at dead clumps of weeds. When she nearly reached the top, he grabbed hold of her arm and pulled her up the rest of the way.

She was glad to be out of the stream, but strangely enough, she felt even colder now. She guessed it was because some of the feeling was returning to her legs. She looked down. Her stockings and shoes were dripping water. She could hear her teeth chattering.

Edmond's eyes roved over the dark countryside. Thank God for the moonlight, Hélène thought. Once again it had turned into an ally. Without it, they wouldn't be able to see a thing.

"We mustn't lose any time," Edmond said. "We've got to find a place where we can get warm. Someplace where our clothes can dry. Otherwise we're sure to come down with pneumonia."

10

It happened seven days after they had fled the blazing farm-house. The sky was pale with the first light of dawn. The crystalline air was freezing. It was the kind of cold that turned the mucus inside Hélène's nose to frost and made her ears feel like chunks of ice ready to break off. They never even heard the Boches. Suddenly they were just there. The fir branches rustled as the rifle-wielding figures swept soundlessly out from behind the trees and formed a circle around them. Mechanically, one of them stepped forward and checked them for weapons. Then he grunted and drew back.

Hélène was confused and frightened. She glanced at Edmond. He nodded his head, warning her to keep quiet and do as she was told.

Swiftly they were marched uphill to the nearest road. Here four tarpaulin-covered trucks were parked on the shoulder. The Boches pushed them toward the back of the third one. They climbed inside. A couple of armed guards followed behind them.

The truck had two rows of wooden benches facing each other. They sat down on one side, the guards on the opposite. It was much colder now that they weren't moving. Hélène wrapped her arms around herself, briskly rubbing herself with her hands, trying to keep warm.

The truck engine wheezed, coughed, and backfired. There was a sudden lurch as the truck began moving. The road was full of potholes, and they bounced around on the bench.

Hélène looked at Edmond. "Do you think—" she began.

He cut her off by nudging her roughly. "They may under-stand French!" he hissed. "Watch what you say!"

"*Silence!*" one of the guards said harshly.

Edmond smiled bleakly. But Hélène could tell he was sat-isfied that he'd at least managed to say this much. He looked sort of funny with his short, ragged hair. She supposed she looked pretty strange, too. They'd had to cut each other's hair because of lice.

After they'd ridden for a few kilometers, Edmond leaned over and put his head between his knees. Hélène could hear him singing softly to himself. The roar of the engine and the rattling of the truck was so noisy she could barely hear him. At first she didn't pay any attention. Then suddenly she concentrated carefully. Because he wasn't singing to himself. He was singing to her!

It was a tune she knew well, but he was substituting words of his own:

> We're just simple peasant children from the town of Saumur.
> We have never been to Paris, and no farther than Tours.
> Just stick to that story, and even if they know better,
> You must stick to what I'm telling you, right to the letter.
> Our Papa grew champignons in a cave before he died,
> And our dear, sweet Maman she is dead, buried at his side.
> Not a brother or sister have we, we are all alone.
> Your name will be Eloise and mine is Henri Goyon.
> In case they force the issue, maybe get nasty, or what,
> Act crazy, have tantrums, do anything to throw them off.
> Should they show us the pictures of our sister, remember:
> Do not flick an eyebrow, get nervous, or recognize her.
> So whatever will happen, little sister, Eloise,
> If you understand what I'm saying, won't you poke me, please?

She gave Edmond a poke with her elbow. He stopped singing and sat back up. They exchanged glances and she gave him a little smile.

Yes, she understood. She was Eloise Goyon, and he was her brother, Henri. Catherine and Marie were alien to them. Both Papa and Maman were dead. Papa grew champignons (in a cave like the one they'd spent last night in, no doubt). And if the Boches got violent (like they had with poor Maman), Hélène was to act crazy or childish. That should not be too difficult, she thought. Michelle had often been exasperated by her fits and tantrums.

They stared out the open back of the truck, but their view was restricted to the truck that followed behind theirs and the skeletal trees that lined the road. Once in a while, when they turned corners, she caught glimpses of a frozen-over river. By its size she could tell that it was not the Loire. It was one of the smaller tributaries. Then suddenly they arrived at the Boche headquarters. She was surprised at the beauty of the building. But of course, she thought; the Boches always appropriated the best of everything. So too with their headquarters. It was located in a breathtaking old château that had been built right over the willow-lined river.

Built of pale white stone, it rose in splendor above the iced-over water, which, she assumed, served as a sort of reflecting pool in warmer weather. There were four corner turrets, massive cornices and machicolations and large double-mullioned windows. The green mansard roofs sported decorative dormers and fairly bristled with chimneys.

It would have been a beautiful château at any given time, and still was, but the imprint of the Boches was unmistakable. Part of the Italian gardens had been bulldozed flat in order to make a dirt parking lot. The entrance steps were flanked by stiff, gray-uniformed guards. Two huge flags hung from poles extending out from the machicolations. One was the ubiquitous swastika banner. The other sported twin Z-shaped S's.

Hélène had yet to discover what the S's stood for.

The tailgate of the truck dropped with a clatter and one of the guards prodded them with his rifle. Edmond and Hélène hopped down onto the parking lot. Then they were hurried up the wide, imposing steps and through the heroically carved double doors. Hélène was wide-eyed. Never before had she seen such luxury. But it was cold luxury. There was no central heating, only the enormous, inefficient fireplaces.

They stopped in the long, high-ceilinged hallway. She looked around in fascination. Here were painted wooden beams, massive tapestries, elegant silk-upholstered bergères, and gleaming parquet. All this beauty was marred by the ugly, functional pieces necessary to the bureaucracy. Metal filing cabinets and masses of telephone cables incongruously vied for attention with a magnificent ormolu desk.

The soldier escorts drew themselves up and stiffly saluted a bald, monocled officer who sat behind it. There was an exchange of words, but it was all in German so Hélène couldn't understand any of it. Finally the monocled officer nodded. He picked up his telephone receiver and spoke softly into it. A moment later a young, fair-haired Boche arrived.

Papers were signed and exchanged, and the Boches who had brought them here drew themselves up again and thrust out their right arms.

"Heil Hitler!" they chorused.

Wearily the officer returned a haphazard salute. "Heil Hitler," he murmured dryly. Snappily the two Boches turned on their heels and strode off.

Now the fair-haired young guard was in charge. He led Edmond and Hélène through the château. They passed an elegant, balustraded staircase, turned right into a gloomy corridor, and then descended a steep flight of much less elegant steps to what was obviously the cellar of the château.

The basement room was round, probably located in one of the turrets on the shore side. It was damp, cold, and windowless. It smelled of mildew. Indeed, in the garish glare of the solitary bulb that was screwed into the ceiling, they could see that the stone walls were white with mold.

The worst thing of all was the waiting. She and Edmond must have been kept in that room for half a day. They were seated on a hard wooden bench that faced a long trestle table and a comfortable-looking tapestry-covered chair. Hélène had to pee badly. Each time she told the Boche, he gave her a blank stare. She thought he didn't understand French.

Whenever she heard footsteps out in the corridor, she would look up with a mixture of hope and dread. Hope that perhaps someone would come to release them. Dread that it could just as easily be their executioner. But always the footsteps passed by, and then she would hear a door opening and closing.

For what must have been the hundredth time, she looked up. Once again she could hear voices and footsteps outside in the corridor. Then suddenly the door flew open with a clap and the guard snapped to attention. Two more gray-uniformed Boches marched into the room. Behind them was a fat, red-faced sergeant. And behind *him* . . .

Hélène's eyes widened in shock and she began to tremble. She could feel Edmond jabbing her with his elbow, warning her to keep her composure. She tried to keep from shaking, to make her face look natural. But how could she? She was sick.

Sick, because the German in the elegant black breeches and gleaming knee boots was all too familiar. His face was cruel, narrow, and skull-shaped, his chin was cleft, his lips bloodless. His skin was white and colorless, and the polished visor of his peaked cap was pulled down low over his eyes. Still, she could glimpse those eyes. Those pinkish, satanic eyes that seemed to glow evilly from within when the light lit them.

He was the one who had spit into Maman's face.

He was the one who had barked: "Show her how we punish liars and traitors."

He was the Evil One himself.

When he entered the room, he had one gloved hand tucked in the small of his back. Suddenly he looked away, as if to shield his eyes. He made a rapid gesture at the bulb on the ceiling.

The fat sergeant puffed his belly out importantly. "Zu befehl, Herr Obersturmbannführer!" he shouted. Without needing to be told, his plump red fingers hit the light switch and the room was plunged into darkness.

Now the only light came from out in the corridor. Against it, the Boches were demon silhouettes throwing grotesque shadows across the floor. It was easy to imagine that the eerie yellow light was the glow of hell's fires.

The sergeant hurried off down the hall and disappeared, his heels clicking swiftly on the stone floor. A few minutes later he returned carrying a lamp. It must have been the only lamp he could get his hands on quickly. The base was ormolu and sprouted into a large onyx ostrich egg. The shade was silk. Promptly this lamp was set down on the trestle table and plugged into an outlet. The silk shade glowed delicately. In that dismal room it was an anachronism of luxury.

While the others stood stiffly against the wall, the white-faced Boche sat down in the tapestry-covered chair and crossed his legs. Once again he made a rapid gesture with his hand. Instantly the sergeant stepped forward and produced a sheet of paper.

The Boche held up the paper and studied it intently. It was illuminated from behind by the lamp, and Hélène could see through it. She held her breath. Printed on the other side were three sketches. *Gisèle's sketches.*

Edmond noticed them too. He pressed his leg against hers, trying to ease her fears.

The pink eyes flickered between the pictures on the paper

110

and the children. The white face showed dissatisfaction, un-
sureness.

The Boche twisted around and looked up at the sergeant.
"Es könnte diese Kinder sein," he said. "Ich weiss nicht.
Jeder der Ihnen gesehen hat, hatte bei diese Gleichnisse
geschworen. Aber"—he rattled the paper ominously—"Ich
bin nicht zufrieden." He glanced sharply at the sergeant.
"Schmidt! Bringen Sie mir das Mädchen!"

"Jawohl, Herr Obersturmbannführer!" The sergeant clicked
his heels together and once again hurried off.

Schmidt, Hélène thought. That must be the sergeant's
name.

The white-faced Boche stared coldly at her. Then he
pointed a gloved finger at Edmond. "What is your name?" he
demanded in the same badly accented French Hélène
remembered hearing when they hid in the dumbwaiter.

"Henri Goyon," Edmond replied. His voice sounded calm
enough, but Hélène could feel his leg twitching spastically
against hers.

Swiftly the Boche's finger switched directions. The pink
eyes were on Hélène now. "What is *your* name?"

"Eloise Goyon," she said with dignity.

The Boche leaned back in his chair and steepled his gloved
fingers. He regarded Hélène thoughtfully. "And where do
you live, Eloise Goyon?" he asked coldly.

"In Saumur."

"Where is your mother?"

She sniffed and wiped her nose. "Maman is dead."

"And your father?"

"Dead, too."

"What did he do for a living?"

"He worked under the ground."

The Boche looked at her sharply. "He was in the underground?"

"No, monsieur," Edmond cut in quickly. "He worked in a
cave."

The pink eyes narrowed suspiciously, and Hélène could almost feel their malevolent heat. "A cave?"

"Yes, monsieur," she said. "Papa grew champignons. See?"
On an impulse, she reached into her pocket for one of the
mushrooms they'd picked two days ago and held it out
toward him.

He wrinkled his nose in distaste and motioned for her to

111

put it away. Then he turned and glared up at the Germans who had led him to this room. Both of them seemed to shrink against the wall. They knew he was displeased. Hélène hoped it was because he thought he was wasting his time. That she and Edmond had convinced him they were not the children he was looking for. After all, Gisèle's sketches of Edmond and her didn't really look like them. Especially not after they had to cut each other's hair.

Now she could hear two sets of footsteps coming down the hall. The sergeant must be returning with someone, she thought. She wondered who it could be.

The footfalls got louder as they approached. "Mach's schnell!" the sergeant snapped impatiently.

"All right, all right, I'm hurrying," a low voice replied.

Hélène's heart began to thump wildly. How well she recognized that voice.

It was Catherine's.

So she, too, had been captured by the Boches. Then Hélène froze, realizing the enormity of Catherine's presence. The Boches were going to use her to help identify Edmond and herself. And unsuspectingly, Catherine would come into the room and throw her arms around them. It would be the kiss of Judas in all sincerity. In all innocence.

Faintly, so very faintly that even she could barely hear it, Edmond began to hum a tune. It was the same tune he had sung in the truck.

He was trying to tell Hélène something. But what? Her mind raced. Then the words of his song came back to her:

Should they show us the picture of our sister, remember:
Do not flick an eyebrow, get nervous, or recognize her.

Suddenly she understood. He was telling her that they must turn their backs on Catherine. That she mustn't give any indication of knowing her. Hélène looked hesitantly at the door, and her soul was in torment. She must treat her sister like a stranger.

It was an agonizing position to be put in. Hélène wanted to rush out into the hall and throw her arms around Catherine. Yet the situation demanded her to denounce her, to deny the fact that she was her flesh and blood. But even if she did that, what was the use? Whether they pretended to know her or not, Catherine would still recognize them.

112

Hélène couldn't ponder the situation any further, because the footsteps had reached the door. The sergeant gave Catherine a push and she stumbled into the room ahead of him.

11

Hélène mustered a blank expression and looked up at her sister. It was Catherine, all right, but she had changed. The gaunt, stringy-haired girl who stood there clutching a baby against her breast looked haggard and broken. Spiritless. Her eyes were without life, and her body seemed to sag. Hélène noticed that Maman's ring gleamed on her finger.

"Look!" the white-faced Boche said tauntingly. "We have found your brother and sister!"

Catherine turned her head and looked at Hélène. Hélène thought her eyes flickered for a moment, but it was so brief that she couldn't be sure. "Who are they?" Catherine murmured listlessly.

"You don't recognize them?" he asked.

Catherine shook her head slowly. "No," she whispered hoarsely. "Should I?"

"You mean you've never seen them before?"

She shook her head again.

The pink eyes narrowed. "If we find out that you're lying, you are going to die. Do you know that?"

"Yes," she said quietly.

"And it's not them?"

Catherine's face was expressionless. "No. I already told you that."

"I don't believe you!" he accused.

She shrugged sadly. "Believe what you want," she said wearily. "It doesn't make any difference."

The Boche sighed. Slowly he pushed himself to his feet and came around the table toward Hélène. His hand shot out and caught her by the collar and pulled her to her feet. He shook her roughly. "Is she your sister?"

Hélène looked over at Catherine and shook her head. Then all at once he lashed Hélène across the face. She grunted as the pain shot through her, and she tottered toward the table. Her hand flew up to her nose. Her fingers touched something wet. Blood.

He looked at Catherine. "You still don't recognize them?" he shouted.

"No," Catherine persisted.

He hit Hélène again. This time she tumbled to the floor. For a moment she lay there crying softly. When he turned away from her, Edmond squatted down, helping her back up.

The Boche reached into one of his pockets and selected a cigarette from a gold case. Deliberately he tapped the end of it on the case. The sergeant leaped forward to light it.

The Boche inhaled deeply, staring thoughtfully at Catherine. "Put the baby down," he ordered.

Catherine looked around for a place to put Marie.

"On the table."

She hesitated. Then gently she carried Marie over to it and laid her down. She whispered softly, soothingly stroking her little head.

"Now step back."

Reluctantly Catherine obeyed. There was a knowing look of fear in her eyes.

The Boche handed the cigarette to the sergeant and pointed to Marie. Noisily Catherine drew in her breath. "No!" she cried. "Don't! *Please!*" She reached for the Boche's sleeve and tugged it desperately. "I beg of you!"

He threw her loose and slapped her. Instantly her cheek turned white, his handprint standing out clearly. Grimly he turned and then faced Edmond and Hélène in turn, his bleak eyes gleaming evilly. There was a crooked smile on his face. Then he spun back around and faced the sergeant. "Jetzt!" he commanded.

In horror Hélène watched the sergeant unbuttoning Marie's little suit. Slowly he brought the glowing end of the cigarette down on her belly and held it there. Marie let out a terrible shriek and began to kick her little legs frantically. Her screaming seemed to go on and on. The two Boches standing against the wall looked away. Catherine's face was pale, and tears rolled down her cheeks.

And it was then that Hélène swore it. Someday, she thought. Someday, if they managed to get out of here, she would make those horrible creatures pay for what they were doing. She would make them pay and pay and pay. She didn't know how. She didn't know when. She didn't know much, but at least she knew the sergeant's name. That was a start.

"Please!" Catherine begged. "Leave the baby alone!"

The cruel smile was frozen on the bloodless lips. "Well? Are you ready to admit that these children are your brother and sister?"

Hélène held her breath and watched Catherine. She seemed to slump in agony, but her voice was calm. "How many times do I have to tell you? It's not them."

Angrily he brought his fist down on the table. Marie shrieked again as the lamp toppled over. The shade cushioned the bulb from the fall, but now it glared in the Boche's eyes.

He turned away from the table and motioned for the sergeant to draw back. Then he faced the other two. "Release them," he spat out in French, pointing at Edmond and Hélène.

Hélène glanced at her sister. For a moment a triumphant look glinted deep within Catherine's eyes. Then it was gone.

The Boche's voice rose. "As for the idiots who brought them here, I want to see them immediately. They are going to be sent to the Russian front!"

Schmidt cleared his throat and pointed questioningly at Catherine.

"The girl and the baby get the usual treatment." The Boche made an irritable gesture. "Arrange for their transportation to Poland."

Catherine's expression didn't change, but her body no longer seemed to sag. She held herself with a kind of quiet dignity. It was the same kind of pride Hélène had often seen in Maman's bearing. Maman would have been proud of Catherine.

Then angrily, as if he didn't want to waste another precious second, the white-faced Boche strode out of the room.

Schmidt stayed behind. He grabbed Catherine by the arm. She nodded wordlessly.

Hélène was the only one who noticed that Catherine had worked Maman's ring loose from her finger. When she bent down to pick Marie back up, she quickly slipped the ring under the lampshade.

For a moment the two sisters' eyes met. "Take the ring," Catherine's expression seemed to say. Hélène nodded imperceptibly.

Then Catherine was gone.

Once again Edmond and Hélène were on their way. The wind had picked up, and they pulled their coats tightly around them. They didn't know where they were. The surrounding countryside was hilly, densely forested, silent, and dark. Though they knew they must still be somewhere near the Loire, they couldn't see the river anywhere. It was late afternoon, and soon night would fall. Already the patches of light between the trees were no longer blue. They'd have to find shelter fast.

Only one thing gave Hélène strength. Hate. Already, so young, she was becoming consumed with destroying those who had separated her from her family. Those who had tortured first Maman, and now Marie. Yes, she was going to exact a heavy vengeance. Even if it took years. After all, she was young. She could afford to wait.

Schmidt, she thought once again. She mustn't forget that name, ever. A fat, red-faced sergeant named Schmidt. That was where she would begin, and by the time she was through, she would cut down the sinister white-faced Boche. But she would do it slowly. That way he would suffer.

These thoughts of revenge were sweet. At the moment, they were the only way she could fight the Boche, the only way she could vent her fury and hatred.

When the doors of the château banged shut behind her and Edmond, she had waited until they were out of earshot before she gave Edmond Maman's ring. She explained to him how Catherine had slipped it under the lampshade, and how she had managed to snatch it up without being seen. He clenched his hand fiercely around the little band of gold, and then he slowly opened his fingers one by one, looking down at the ring as if it might disappear at any moment. On a sudden impulse he brought it to his lips and kissed it reverently.

Then his face darkened. His arm was trembling as he raised it and flung it high into the air. The ring flashed once before it disappeared in a distant clump of bushes.

Slowly Edmond dropped to his knees. He pressed his cheek

116

against the frozen ground, and his body heaved with pain as he wept aloud. Hélène stood there helplessly, unable to comfort him. She could feel the tears running down her cheeks. She wondered what she had done wrong.

Just as the last light of day faded, they came upon a clearing. It was like a narrow, dark valley cut out between the pine trees, and a pair of gleaming railroad tracks ran along it. They followed the tracks for a while and spent the night alongside them in an unheated tool shed. Edmond managed to jimmy the door open and they sat down on pieces of equipment, leaning back against the walls of the shed as they ate the rest of their champignons. They were ice cold and the chill hurt Hélène's teeth, but once she chewed them well, they seemed somehow warmer. At least they soothed the gnawing emptiness in her belly. Then they cleared a bit of floor space, made a makeshift bed out of pieces of tarpaulin, and curled up together to go to sleep.

But it was an uneasy sleep. As soon as she shut her eyes, the bad dreams began. She dreamed of Paris, but it was not the Paris she knew. This was a grotesque, nightmarish world of distortion in which Sacré Coeur was stretched out of shape into an evil black minaret, the Seine was like an ocean, and all the bridges were gone. The wide-open Place Vendôme was threateningly cramped and dark, like some medieval alley, and the Bois was filled with treacherous cliffs and monstrous trees that had massive gnarled roots. Then Saint-Nazaire entered the dream, and that was strange, because it looked exactly like the beautiful Paris she remembered. And then there was a terrible noise. The earth shook, the buildings trembled, and Saint-Nazaire tumbled to the ground. She awoke suddenly, sweating profusely.

It was the middle of the night and a train was roaring past outside. So that was why I dreamed of an earthquake, she thought with relief. The entire shed was shaking. She got to her feet, stumbled over to the door, opened it a crack, and peered out. A blast of icy air rushed past her. The night was pitch black, and the locomotive spewed showers of reddish sparks high into the sky. This hellish spectacle frightened her so much that she quickly shut the door, huddled close against Edmond's warmth, and closed her eyes. Before she knew it, she was asleep again. And the dreams continued.

This time she was in a pitch-black wide-open space. All around her she could see sparks glowing in the distance. Then she realized that they were slowly moving . . . steadily approaching her. As they got closer, she saw that she had been mistaken. The sparks were actually white-faced Boches brandishing cigarettes. In horror she watched as they closed in on her. The nearer they got, the hotter the heat of the cigarettes felt. She tried to draw back, but she was surrounded. They pressed closer. Closer.

And suddenly they lunged forward, their cigarettes searing her skin and burning deep into her flesh.

She began to scream and scream and scream, and Edmond was saying: "Hélène! Wake up! Wake up!" Then she felt his hands shaking her awake. "Wake up!" he said. "Wake *up!* You're having a bad dream."

She opened her eyes and clung to him tightly, still trembling with fear. He stroked her head reassuringly. It was morning already. Outside, the light was soft and gray.

After she calmed down, they ate some more champignons. Then they continued walking westward along the railroad tracks. They still had no idea where they were. Only that they had to head west. Always west. Every so often they would hear a train approaching, and whenever they did, they quickly fled out of sight and stayed behind the trees, waiting until it chugged past. Hélène noticed that most of them were freight trains, long serpentines of boxcars and flatcars loaded down with heavy machinery.

In the afternoon, the tracks brought them to a railway freight yard on the outskirts of a large town. There were quite a few signs around with the name of the town printed on them. At least now they knew where they were. Angers.

The signal tower was built in the middle of the yard. It was thin and ugly and had huge windows at the top that went all the way around, giving a 360-degree view. Occasionally Hélène would catch glimpses of figures sitting behind the glass. Those were the controllers, directing the traffic.

When they reached the far perimeter of the yard, where the maze of rails once again funneled into two solitary tracks, Edmond put a restraining hand on her arm.

She stopped and looked at him.

"What do you say we take a train?" he asked slowly.

"You mean . . . actually ride on one?"

"Yes. All we have to do is catch one heading west and hop aboard. A lot of them seem to stop up ahead, waiting for the signal to change. See?" He pointed to where a long freight train was halted, the locomotive looking like it was floating on a cloud of steam. As they watched, the signal changed and the locomotive chugged, wearily starting to pull its burden.

Hélène looked back at Edmond. "Would a train take us all the way to Saint-Nazaire?" she asked hopefully.

He shrugged. "I don't know. But they're sure to go part of the way, at least."

"And if they turn off somewhere and start going in the wrong direction? What then?"

"Then we'll have to jump off."

Less than half an hour later they sat in a big boxcar half-filled with bulky crates, with the sliding door cracked partly open and the countryside flashing by outside. In the late afternoon they were shunted onto a siding somewhere and the train stopped. Hélène could see cranes swinging enormous tapered cylinders onto the flatcars at the rear of the train. These cylinders were of dark gray metal and sprouted sleek sharklike fins at the bottom. Edmond told her they were rocket bombs. The place was swarming with uniformed Boches. Some of them were slowly making their way from the rear of the train to the front, sliding open the doors of the boxcars and inspecting them.

"They're headed this way," Edmond whispered. "Quick, we have to get off before they find us."

He pushed open the sliding door on the other side of the car and looked out. The coast was clear. On this side of the train there was no activity: a steep shrub-covered hill sloped up from the edge of the tracks. Silently he and Hélène hopped down off the train and scuttled uphill. For a while they walked along a plateau. Then abruptly they drew to a halt. They could go no farther. A sheer abyss plunged a hundred meters down to a dry, boulder-strewn riverbed. There was no way that they could climb down it, cross the riverbed, and then get back up the sheer cliff on the other side. They would have to find another way to cross it. A quarter of a kilometer to their left, a strange structure bridged the abyss. The top was level with the plateau, and trees and bushes grew up out of it, giving it a bizarre, almost theatrical look.

Hélène pointed at it. "What's that thing?" she asked.

"An aqueduct," Edmond replied. "The Romans built them in order to channel water across valleys."

"It leads westward," she noted.

They headed toward it. When they got there, she froze. From far away it had looked delicate but sturdy. Close up, it looked ready to collapse. Stones were missing, the edges were crumbling, and there was no railing of any kind, just a low curb that barely came up to her ankles. The channel where water had once flowed was now filled in with dirt, and here the trees and bushes had taken root.

Fearlessly Edmond stepped onto the narrow aqueduct and started across. Hélène hung back, staring at it in apprehension. The aqueduct seemed to hang in space before her, devoid of any visible support. She turned sideways and looked down at the dry riverbed. That was a mistake. Quickly she averted her eyes.

It was a long drop.

Edmond turned around. "Well?" he demanded. "What are you waiting for?"

"It . . . it looks awfully dangerous," Hélène stammered in embarrassment.

He stared at her for a moment. Finally he spoke. "It's safe," he said gently. "It's probably stood here for over a thousand years. It's not likely to come tumbling down now." He gestured for her to follow him. "Come on."

Reluctantly she took a few steps. She realized immediately that it was even worse than she'd imagined. They had to pick their way carefully around the tree trunks and bushes, sometimes forced to stand at the very edge of the parapet.

Suddenly she stopped in her tracks. Her head was spinning crazily. It was impossible for her to go on. She would never get across this way. Not with her sanity intact.

Edmond turned around again. "For God's sake, Hélène!" he called over his shoulder. "Come on. Don't you want to get to Saint-Nazaire?"

That did it. She forced herself to look her fears in the face. Slowly she began to follow him again. Her hands were clammy and she found herself breaking out in a sweat. "Just don't look down," she kept repeating over and over to herself. "It'll be all right as long as you don't look down!"

So she kept her eyes on Edmond's back. She emulated his every move. When he skirted deep holes where the aqueduct had begun to cave in, she skirted them in exactly the same manner. When he climbed over piles of rubble, so did she.

The wind was strong now. It buffeted them as it howled

by, sometimes almost throwing them off balance. It got so strong that after a while they prudently dropped to their knees and crawled on all fours. Once her fingers dislodged a stone and it fell over the edge. For what seemed an eternity, she heard nothing. Then finally a faraway clatter. Slowly she crawled on.

When they were halfway across, she could hear a train in the distance. She had to squint against the wind as she glanced over at the railroad bridge. From here it looked tiny, like a pattern of rusty toothpicks. As she watched, the front of the locomotive came into view. Slowly it chugged westward across the bridge. It must have been the very train they had abandoned earlier. It had boxcars followed by flatcars loaded with evil-looking cylinders. When the locomotive reached the middle of the bridge, some of the cars were still out of sight. It was a long train indeed.

She stared at it wistfully, wishing she was still aboard. She'd have much preferred crossing the abyss in the shelter of a boxcar to having to crawl over the aqueduct.

A moment later she took back her wish.

It began with a droning in the skies above. She looked up. An airplane had broken out of the cloud cover and came swooping down toward the bridge. Suddenly tiny figures appeared to be swarming all over the train; it must have taken on a battalion of Boches. She heard the sharp cracking of gunfire and the chattering of machine guns. Then there was a shrill, ominous whistle.

"Duck!" Edmond screamed. "Lie flat and keep your head down!"

Hélène did as she was told, but she kept her face turned sideways, toward the bridge. She saw that something had fallen out of the belly of the plane. Whatever it was seemed to float lazily through the air. It wasn't until a moment later that she realized it was a bomb.

It missed the bridge and landed on the floor of the abyss. Suddenly the earth shook and there was a massive explosion. Debris and fire and smoke and destruction blew high into the air. Hélène let out a shriek. In the reverberation of the blast she could feel the aqueduct shaking. The stones under her actually lifted up and shifted. Then they finally settled back into place with an audible sigh. Before her eyes, a row of curbstones crumbled away and fell down out of sight.

When the smoke cleared, she saw that the distant bridge

was still standing, and the train continued to chug steadily across it. When they had seen the bomb coming, some of the Boches had hit the roof of the cars; now they were getting back on their feet. She could see one Boche hanging on to a girder of the bridge, his tiny legs futilely kicking air. As she watched, he lost his grip and fell down into the abyss, his body doing a wild spiral.

Another airplane droned and broke through the clouds. She started to pray hysterically, but it didn't help. This plane, too, dived at the bridge, spit fire, and then dropped its bomb. There was another terrible whistling noise, and then the earth shook again. And again. And again. Debris was raining down all around her, and with each explosion the stones of the aqueduct did their terrible dance, rippling like a swift tide from one end to the other before settling back down.

And then one of the bombs hit its mark. In a single frozen, blinding split second, the bridge broke in half. The train buckled gently like a snake in midair, and then it plunged headlong down into the abyss. Now came the worst explosions imaginable. One after the other, the rocket bombs went off.

The aqueduct shook spastically. The stones rattled like millions of chattering teeth. Rocks and earth and pieces of the train rained down all around them. A section of twisted track shrieked through the air, landed not five meters away from Hélène on top of the aqueduct, and impaled itself on the stones like an angry, quivering piece of sculpture.

Suddenly Hélène caught the smell of burned hair. It was a moment before she realized what she was smelling. Her own hair, singed by the distant holocaust.

Then there was silence, an intense, shell-shocked silence the likes of which she had never heard before. Slowly she turned her head and looked around. The spot the bridge had spanned was now three times the width it had been. Neither bridge nor train was anywhere in sight. What hadn't been blasted to pieces or scattered was buried under tons of rock and rubble.

This way one shipment of rocket bombs that would never reach the coast, would never fall on the place called London.

And then she began to whimper. Softly at first, increasingly louder, until finally her body shook uncontrollably and she started to weep. She wept for herself, for Catherine and

Marie, for Maman. She wept for the bridge. For Paris. For all of France.

Edmond crawled toward her. "Are you all right?" he asked softly.

She raised her head and looked at him through tear-streaked eyes. "Yes," she managed to croak. "And you?"

He nodded and shrugged. "I've a few scratches, nothing serious."

It was a miracle. They had come through unscathed. Not very pretty, with most of their hair singed off and their faces beet red, but their hair would grow back and they weren't badly burned. Just superficially. Yes, it was a miracle.

She stopped weeping long enough to dry her eyes and said a silent prayer of thanks. Then they lost no time crawling across the rest of the way. Now she didn't give the aqueduct a second thought. Her fear of heights was a small thing compared to what they'd just lived through.

Five minutes later they stood on the far side of the abyss. For a long moment they looked around in silence. Then they continued walking.

They had gone only a few meters when they were surrounded by a motley group of men pointing rifles at them. Hélène counted a dozen of them.

Not again, she thought with a sinking feeling. Not the Boches again. Not after what they'd been through already.

She didn't see the men lowering their rifles. She didn't notice the ragged clothing they wore or the strange assortment of weapons they wielded. All she knew was her hatred and her fear. It had been walled up deep inside her for too long. Now it burst like a boil. She flung herself upon the nearest man. She clenched her fists and furiously hammered him in the stomach. She kicked and clawed and bit. He stood there stonily, staring down at her in silence.

"My God!" one of the others exclaimed in the soft speech of Touraine. "She's a savage! An animal!"

Savage? Animal? She whirled around. What did that idiot know? And why was he speaking such good French? And then it hit her. He must be a collaborator. She spat. Collaborators were even worse pigs than the Boches. Then she attacked him in a fury, beating him until she was ready to drop from exhaustion. When she looked up, she saw that he was looking down at her, not with pain, but in surprise.

I'll make you hurt, you pig, she thought. I'll make you hurt good! She bent down, grabbed a big rock, staggered up, and began to raise it over her head. She was going to smash him with it. Smash him like a bug!

Effortlessly the man reached out, took the stone out of her hands, and tossed it away.

Suddenly she began to tremble. What was the use of fighting any longer? she asked herself. They were captured once again. And now she had no more energy, no more fight left in her. She was surrendering, and it hurt her more than she could bear. Especially with Catherine's and Marie's sacrifices having been in vain.

Numbly she slid down into a sitting position. Tears streamed down her cheeks. She found herself howling like a mortally wounded animal.

"We're your friends," the stony-faced man said gently. He squatted down in front of her and looked her in the eyes. "Where are you from?"

She looked away in silence. They wouldn't get a word out of her. Not a single word. Even if they tortured her. Even if they burned her like they had burned Marie.

"What about you?" she heard the man ask.

"Paris," Edmond answered. His voice sounded foggy and far away, as if in a dream. Things were becoming unfocused, focused, unfocused again.

"Paris!" the man exclaimed. "And you came all this way? Alone? What's your name?"

"Edmond Junot."

"And hers?" He pointed at Hélène, but she couldn't see it. She was slipping into the unfocused zone again.

"She's my sister Hélène. My other two sisters and our mother were carted off by the Boches. The Boches are looking for us everywhere. They claimed that we were kidnapped. We weren't! We killed some Boche, and now they want to kill us! Maman had a transmitter hidden in our house. That's how it all started. It was the right thing to do, having a transmitter, wasn't it?"

"Indeed it was," the stony-faced man said. "Your mother fought for France. You have much to be proud of."

Maman! Suddenly Hélène could see her blurry shape standing in front of her. She tried to reach out and touch her, but her arms felt like lead. Then everything came into focus again. It wasn't Maman . . . it was the stony-faced man.

124

And Edmond was speaking with him. She was becoming very confused.

"So you're the so-called kidnapped children," the man said thoughtfully. "And you managed to hide all this time?"

Hélène saw Edmond nodding. "We're going to our aunt's."

"Where is that?"

"Saint-Nazaire."

The blurry men exchanged glances. "That's still a long way off," one of them said finally.

Then Hélène blacked out. The last thing she remembered was being lifted up by the stony-faced man. He smelled strongly of sweat, and somehow that was comforting. "Come with us, Little French Girl," he whispered softly. "We will see to it that you get safely to Saint-Nazaire."

TODAY

Wednesday,
January 10

1

It was ten-fifteen in the morning when Hélène walked into the conference room and shut the door softly behind her. She wore a champagne Chanel suit and her hair was pulled back in the ubiquitous no-nonsense chignon. Her only piece of jewelry was a large gold brooch pinned to her lapel.

The board members were already seated around the table, waiting. Before she came in she had heard the buzz of their conversations, but now the room had suddenly fallen silent. Smiling tightly, she came around to her place at the head of the table. She remained standing, her fingertips poised on the oiled teak, her violet eyes alert and appraising.

They were all in their usual places. Wearing dark sunglasses, von Eiderfeld nevertheless sat with his chair pushed away from the table, which was flooded with light from the overhead tracks. Next to him was the Comte, who looked up at Hélène, red-faced and mocking. She noticed that his hands were trembling. Beside him, like an elegant black widow, sat Z.Z. She was dressed in a black silk shantung suit, long leather gloves, and a little hat with a veil half-covering her face. She smiled and chain-smoked malevolently, the smoke picked out by the lights like swirling veils. Opposite her, d'Itri was doodling on a piece of paper, a bored expression on his face.

The Sphinx was present to transcribe the meeting. She was in the far corner of the room, legs crossed, steno pad on her lap, pen poised.

The door opened abruptly and Edmond walked in briskly. Wordlessly he crossed the room, pulled up a chair beside Julie, and sat down.

Hélène looked at him. Almost imperceptibly he shook his head from side to side. She looked thoughtful, masking her emotions. He had just returned from a meeting at ManhattanBank. The day after tomorrow, the ten-million-dollar loan was due. He had gone to fight for a desperate last-ditch extension.

The shake of his head told her all she needed to know. There would be no extension. Unless some sort of miracle happened, the bank would seize her collateral—20 percent of HJII stock—and throw it to the vultures. Or perhaps even to some higher bidder she did not know of. Either way, the outcome would be the same. She would lose control over HJII. The others would end up owning 69 percent of the total voting stock and her remaining 31 percent wouldn't amount to a hill of beans. Out of hatred and revenge, they would continue to band against her, this time armed with enough power to topple her. Almost certainly they would elect a new president. It was a grim prospect, but one she had to face. After all, Hubert had gone so far as to spell that out.

The idea of him—or one of the others—sitting in her office, running HJII, was revolting. She felt like a mother must feel when her baby is about to be snatched away from her. After all, HJII *was* her baby.

But this was no time to show her feelings. She had to be impassive. Composed.

Like an actress about to make an entrance, she took a deep breath. "Good morning," she began. Her crystalline voice rang out clearly, impersonally. Without a hint of her inner turmoil. "The board of directors' meeting is called to order.

"I know that time is a precious commodity for each one of us. Therefore, I strongly suggest we stick to the subjects listed on today's agenda. Let's try not to stray from them as we did the last time. However"—she looked down at Hubert, who was grinning up at her with amusement—"I do want you to know that I have noted the criticisms you voiced over how I run this corporation. I'm afraid I can do little about those complaints that dealt with my personality. But when I have the time, I will review those that directly affect HJII's publishing policies.

"Now, to the first item on the agenda. In front of each of you is a bound copy of this year's projected plans. If you would be so kind as to open them, we can then discuss the items, one by one." Hélène sat down, reached for her copy, and opened it to the first page.

They all stared down at their reports, but not one of them made a move to pick them up.

Z.Z. smiled slowly. Then she reached out and pushed hers

aside. "I realize that these plans are most important," she said craftily. "However, I feel that I *must* move that we drop the subjects on today's agenda so that we may discuss something far more important to HJII's future."

Hélène folded her hands and looked wearily at Z.Z. This move came as no surprise; she had expected something of this sort to happen. "Such as?" she asked calmly.

Z.Z.'s smile broadened. She lifted her little black veil and slowly pushed it over the top of her hat. "Something that concerns each and every one of us." She paused. "Leadership."

"All right," Hélène said with resignation. "Say what you have to say."

Z.Z. rose to her feet. Hélène could detect the excitement flashing in her narrowed green eyes. She knew that look only too well. It would be another day of cat-and-mouse games.

"Last night," Z.Z. purred, "the gentlemen sitting around this table and I had a private . . . chitchat, you might call it. We all agreed that for the past few years HJII has been faring quite well. However, separate though it may be from HJII, the disaster produced by that new magazine you insisted on publishing puts everything in a different . . . *perspective*. We're quite concerned about the fact that you are having personal financial difficulties. Of course, under ordinary circumstances that would be none of our business. However, the fact that you used twenty percent of HJII stock as collateral for a loan you will not possibly be able to repay affects us immensely."

Hélène stared at Z.Z. numbly. *Not be able to repay*! Those vultures were disgustingly well-informed. They knew things they had no business knowing. Yesterday's *Wall Street Journal* article speculated on her inability to pay back the loan; today it was known for certain that she could not. She wondered if someone at the bank had been shooting his mouth off. Gore, perhaps?

"After all," Z.Z. continued self-righteously, "what would happen if ManhattanBank sells those shares to someone none of us knows? If some outside stranger would buy them and just walk right in? It could be disastrous, that's what! After all, they'd be owning one-fifth of this corporation.

"So we discussed it, the gentlemen and I. And we've come to an agreement." Z.Z. stopped and smiled sweetly at Hélène. "We hereby offer to help you weather the storm. We are willing to buy twenty percent of your HJII shares for eleven million dollars. That's ten million plus the million interest. In that way, you could pay off ManhattanBank, your collateral would be returned, and we wouldn't have to worry about having an outsider sitting on the board. This way we'd *all* benefit."

Sure, *you'd* benefit, Hélène thought. You'd get your claws into the business without my putting up a fight.

"If you were to sell us twenty percent of HJII," Z.Z. continued, "we would certainly have to look upon that action as a gesture of goodwill. It would ease our fears of outside . . . invasion. It would also boost our confidence in your leadership ability." She turned to the others and smiled shrewdly. "Am I correct, gentlemen?"

"That you are," Hubert said heartily.

Z.Z. spread her hands apart. "So you see?" she said sweetly. "It's as simple as that." She sank down into her seat.

Hélène cleared her throat and chose her words carefully. "It seems that 'outside invasion' of HJII weighs heavily on your minds. Let me try to put your fears to rest.

"In my opinion, you would all be best off to wait and see *if*—and I stress the word 'if'—the bank does indeed seize my collateral shares. Should that occur, I believe you have nothing to worry about. As I understand it, you would be in a position to bid for them." She glanced across the room at Edmond. "Am I correct in assuming that?"

"Yes," Edmond agreed in an expressionless voice.

"There is your answer," Hélène said with finality. "No matter what happens, you'd have your chance to block 'outside invasion' of HJII. And if you did that, you would also be in a position to elect a new president. Then my leadership abilities wouldn't need to concern you." She looked around. "I believe that for the time being, at least, this closes the discussion brought up by Mrs. Bavier. Now, as far as this year's projected plans are concerned—"

"Not so fast, my dear," Hubert chimed in quickly. "I move that we suspend *all* the items on today's agenda and adjourn this meeting until Monday morning." He smiled. "That way, we'll all be wiser as to the future of HJII. After all, anything we might discuss today could be a waste of time. As you pointed out, we may be in a position to elect a new president on Monday. If we do that, all of HJII's policies would have to change."

Hélène forced her face to remain expressionless. His tactic was clear. The loan was due on Friday; the following banking day was Monday. If they had already convinced the bank to sell them the shares—and she wouldn't put that past them—it would not take more than a few minutes for the transaction to take place. Then the buyer could rush back uptown for the meeting and use the shares for a showdown vote. Cutting her out. *Throwing* her out of HJII. She would be nothing more than a minority shareholder with her hands tied.

As for the board of directors, she wondered which of them actually planned to buy the shares. Von Eiderfeld and Hubert were both filthy rich. Either one could afford it.

Z.Z. and d'Itri were worth quite a lot of money, but they didn't have eleven million dollars to squander. Perhaps they would all chip in; that way, they would get what they wanted and not even notice the dent in their pocketbooks.

Hélène rose to her feet suddenly. "All right," she said. "The meeting is adjourned until Monday morning at ten." Swiftly she strode out of the conference room. Her eyes had hardened. She knew what she had to do. She would set up her own meeting with Hubert and von Eiderfeld. She couldn't do anything about Z.Z., and d'Itri was a small fry; without Hubert and von Eiderfeld, they'd disband like third-rate criminals. But Hubert and von Eiderfeld . . . Yes, she just might be able to do something about them.

Much as she hated to, she'd use her hold over them for one last time. It shouldn't be too difficult.

After all, it had worked in the past.

An hour later, Hélène had Jimmy bring the Rolls around and she and Edmond rode uptown and had lunch at 21. The restaurant was already crowded when the captain led them to her usual table. On the way, they nodded and greeted many acquaintances.

To anyone who saw her, she never looked more beautiful and relaxed. But Edmond knew better. She was composed, yes. But she was very tense. He thought of the enormous pressures she was under and wished he could do something about them. For the past year she'd been working herself half to death. It seemed that each time she managed to win a round, something else popped up from behind her and knocked her back down. "How about a drink?" he asked.

She shook her head. "I could use one, but I think I'll stick to club soda. Today I decided that the best remedy for a lousy day would be to act like a woman." She smiled. "So I'll have my hair done. I called up Susumu's, and they'll squeeze me in after lunch."

He nodded and ordered soda for her and a martini for himself. When the captain left, Edmond lit a cigarette and leaned over the table. He kept his voice low. "I know you won't want to hear what I've got to say, but as your lawyer and brother, I think I owe it to you."

She nodded. "You're going to try to convince me to go public," she predicted calmly.

His voice dropped an octave. "Yes. I know you hate having to do it, but it's the only way you can keep control of HJII. This morning, after the bank turned down the request for an extension, I took the liberty of asking if they'd consider it were you to go public. They will, but only on that condition, because then they'll be virtually guaranteed that you will make a fortune. I must say that the well-fed Mr. Gore was quite beside himself when I brought the subject up. For some reason, he doesn't seem anxious for that to happen." Edmond frowned. "I really don't like that man. Never have. There's something odd about him. Something sneaky."

"I don't trust him, either." She looked thoughtful. "Perhaps Hubert or one of the others got to him."

Edmond shrugged. "I wouldn't put it past them."

She started to say something but fell silent as their drinks arrived. She sipped her soda slowly. "I talked to von Eiderfeld and Hubert," she said. "I'm going to go and see them this evening. I may be able to get them off my back."

"Yes, but it still won't raise the money," Edmond pointed out. "If you can't do that, they'll be able to walk right in and take HJII over. And you can't let that happen. Take my word for it, Hélène. Go public. Otherwise everything you've worked for will go down the drain."

She nodded soberly. "How long do I have before I need to come to a decision?"

"Tomorrow afternoon at the latest."

She looked down at her glass. That wasn't much time. Still . . . Suddenly she looked back up. "All right," she said, "I'll give you my answer at noon tomorrow. I'll seriously consider it."

"Please do." He reached across the table abruptly and covered her hand with his, his eyes pleading. "The way I see it, you stand to make an enormous profit by selling public stock. Forty million dollars. Perhaps more. And, Hélène, you really wouldn't be losing anything. You'd be chairman of the board. You'll still own fifty-one percent of the corporation."

She sighed wearily. "Yes, Edmond. We've been through that before. Remember?"

He nodded. "I remember," he said.

He did, too. Ever since he had first brought it up, she had been dead set against it. In a way, he could understand her reasoning. But one thing didn't make sense. If she felt so strongly about keeping HJII "private," why had she ever let the vultures in?

"Don't forget," he said. "Things are different now than they were a year ago. Going public's your only chance."

She shook her head slowly. "No, it isn't. I have another choice that nobody knows of. Even you."

He gave her a strange look. "What on earth are you talking about?"

Her voice was soft. "Nigel offered to lend me the money."

Suddenly he sat up straight. This news changed everything. Nigel Somerset, the Duke of Farquharshire, was the third-richest man in England.

"Why didn't you tell me this before?" Edmond asked.

She toyed with her glass. "Because I don't know if I should accept his help."

"Why? Because he loves you?"

"No," she said gently. "Because I'm in love with him." She paused and looked Edmond in the eye. "He's asked me to marry him again."

"And?"

"I still haven't given him an answer. I told him I'd have to think about it."

"But *why*? You said it yourself—you love the man!"

"Because I don't want to get married before the problems at HJII are sorted out. Somehow it wouldn't be . . . right."

Edmond rolled his eyes. "Oh, my God! Don't tell me! You don't want him to think you're marrying him because of the money. Is that it?"

She shook her head. "No . . . because *I* want to make certain I'm not."

2

Susumu's Fifth Avenue salon is reputed to be one of the finest beauty parlors in the world. It was here that Hélène had her hair done in a private room on the eighth floor. She watched in the mirror as the slim, Japanese hairstylist expertly wrapped her head up in a soft, thick turban. On a stool beside her sat the manicurist, busily working on her nails.

"Could you please excuse me for a moment?" Hélène asked apologetically. "I would like to go to the powder room."

"Of course, madame," Susumu said. "I believe you know where it is."

Hélène nodded. The hairstylist helped her solicitously out of her chair and smiled. The manicurist smiled too. They were expensive smiles. Having your hair done at Susumu's cost a fortune, especially if Susumu did it personally.

She crossed the room to the door. The stylist got there first and held it open for her. Just as she was about to step out into the corridor, a woman was being led to one of the other rooms. Hélène waited in the doorway for her to pass.

The woman looked up at Hélène and stopped. "Why, Miss Junot," she bubbled. "It has been *ages!*"

Hélène looked confused. "Yes?" she said, wondering who in the world this emaciated, blond, deeply tanned caricature of a woman could be.

"We met last year, remember? I'm Geraldine Gore. My husband handles your accounts at ManhattanBank."

Hélène smiled. "Of course. How do you do?"

Geraldine Gore extended her bony hand, and Hélène couldn't help noticing the two bracelets encircling her wrist. Both were identical, except that one was made of canary diamonds while the other was of bloodred rubies. Both were unmistakably from Bulgari. Both were unmistakably expensive.

"Oh, what lovely bracelets," Hélène admired.

Geraldine held up her wrist and smiled contentedly. "They are, aren't they? I just picked the ruby bracelet out a few minutes ago. I've been feeling *so* depressed lately. I told myself that just having my hair done simply won't be enough to make me feel better. It's amazing, isn't it, how shopping for little trinkets always helps one get over a depression."

"Yes, it really is."

Geraldine suddenly made a face. "But I hate to have to face my husband. I think he'll commit suicide when he sees it." She glanced at her attendant, who waited a discreet distance away. "Well, I'd better be going or else they'll never get finished with me on time. Usually I come in on Thursdays, but I'm flying to Palm Beach a day early this week. Virginia Simonsen is going to hold the most marvelous masked ball!" She sighed heavily. "I do so love masked balls, don't you?"

"Yes, I do," Hélène, who had never been to one, answered politely.

"Well, I *must* be going. It was so *nice* to run into you. Ta!" Then Geraldine started down the corridor after her attendant.

Hélène stared after her. What an abominable, name-dropping woman, she thought. But she did credit Geraldine with having one thing. Exquisite—if expensive—taste.

Vaguely Hélène wondered how the Gores could afford such high living.

Politely Karl von Eiderfeld took the Comte's hat and coat, hung them in the hallway closet, and led him into the living room. Even though it was already dark outside, the heavy damask curtains were still drawn tightly. Only two very dim lamps were lit.

Von Eiderfeld waved his guest into a faded French chair. "Sit, my dear Comte. It should not be long before our *friend* arrives. Meanwhile, would you care for a drink?"

"Armagnac, if you have it," the Comte said.

"I do." Von Eiderfeld crossed the room to the massive armoire. When he opened the double doors, Hubert saw that the inside had been converted into a bar, complete with refrigerator and sink. Von Eiderfeld brought the drink over. "You have the envelopes?" he asked.

Hubert nodded and snapped open his briefcase. He took

out a large manila envelope and placed it on the Directoire table beside him. "They arrived by courier from Paris less than an hour ago."

"You think they are what she is coming to see us about?" von Eiderfeld asked.

Hubert looked thoughtful. "It's possible," he said. "But I rather think she doesn't even know they're missing yet. I hired the best safecracker available. He stole only what I paid him to steal. Then he locked the vault shut again. There was no evidence of a break-in."

Von Eiderfeld smiled with satisfaction. "I commend you on your good work. She will have no hold over us now. Did you manage to discover where she stopped off yesterday when she interrupted her flight?"

"I did." The Comte took a big swallow of Armagnac. "She landed at a private airstrip in England. Our sweet Hélène travels in some very high circles. The airstrip in question belongs to Nigel Somerset."

Von Eiderfeld started. "She's still seeing him?"

"I believe so."

Von Eiderfeld digested this piece of information thoughtfully. "That is not very welcome news, I'm afraid. Somerset is one of the richest men in England. What if he comes up with the eleven million dollars for her? Then we'll have lost the battle."

"I don't think that will happen," Hubert said confidently. "Otherwise, it would already have been arranged. You don't know Hélène as I do. She wouldn't wait until the last possible moment—she would have arranged everything long ago. Besides, her ethics would never permit her to accept charity, even in the form of a loan. No, my friend. She's squirming right now. She'll never be able to raise the money."

Von Eiderfeld looked gloomy. "I hope to God you're right."

At that moment, the telephone began to ring. Von Eiderfeld crossed over to the Directoire table and picked up the receiver. "Yes?" He looked at Hubert and nodded. "Have her come right up." He replaced the receiver and smiled grimly. "That was the desk. She's on her way up."

A few minutes later, Hélène arrived. She hadn't had time to change. She wore her Blackglama coat open, and the champagne Chanel suit still showed underneath it. Her hair

138

was no longer in a chignon. It hung thickly to her shoulders, casually cut, yet eminently elegant, framing her face in lustrous waves. "Hello," she said stiffly.

Awkwardly von Eiderfeld motioned for her to come in. "Please. The Comte is already here. Can I take your coat?"

She shook her head. "I don't think I'll be staying that long."

Von Eiderfeld shrugged and led her into the living room, where Hubert was comfortably sprawled in his chair. He made no move to get up. "Ah," he said with a wicked grin. "So the president has stooped to socializing with mere stockholders. Do have a seat." He leaned sideways and patted the chair next to his.

"No, thank you," she said coldly. "I prefer to stand."

"As you wish. Now, what did you want to see us about?"

Hélène chose her words carefully. "I have come by in order to remind you that you would both find it more . . . agreeable, let's say . . . to stop fighting me. To stop playing cat and mouse. As you may recall, we've had this kind of discussion once before."

Hubert smiled and rose to his feet. He walked over to the fireplace, where a log and kindling sat on the grate. He squatted down and carefully lit it. Slowly the kindling started to burn, and after a few minutes the log caught fire. The blaze threw flickering yellow light around the dim room. Hubert made a noise of satisfaction and got to his feet. "I suppose you're referring to the 'hold' you have over us?" he asked.

"Yes," Hélène said.

Hubert smiled. "Take my advice, my dear. Go home and forget all about it. You see, we're no longer quaking with fear."

"I think you should take this matter more seriously," Hélène warned. "I could ruin you both." She turned and fixed a glacial stare on von Eiderfeld. "I could have you charged for war crimes. You would be hung." Then she turned back to Hubert. "And you. You, too, would be hung. For murder."

Hubert began to laugh. "That's preposterous! Who would believe you? You'd need proof to make these slanderous accusations stick!"

Her eyes narrowed. "Stop playing games, Hubert! You

139

know very well that I have the proof. The evidence is locked in a lawyer's vault."

He laughed again and went over to the Directoire table. He picked up the manila envelope and tore it open. Reaching inside it, he extracted a smaller white envelope.

"Do you recognize this?" he asked, holding it up. Scrawled across the sealed flap was her signature.

They could hear her sharp intake of breath. "Yes," she whispered. "Where did you get it?"

"Let's just say it's found its way here from a lawyer's vault in Paris. Don't blame your solicitor. It wasn't his fault. In fact, he doesn't even know that anything is missing yet." Hubert tore the white envelope open and pulled out some old, yellowed documents. He unfolded them and held them dramatically up in the air. "Evidence of war crimes," he announced in a loud voice. He handed the papers to von Eiderfeld. "Will you do the honors, my friend?" he asked softly.

Hélène watched in horror as von Eiderfeld accepted them gravely, walked toward the mantel, and tossed them into the fire. Greedily the flames sprang up and licked at them; then they blackened and curled.

"And now, this!" With a flourish Hubert produced a second white envelope, this one bulkier than the first. It, too, was sealed, the unbroken flap signed with Hélène's signature. "And do you recognize *this*?" he asked, taunting.

For a moment she shut her eyes. This can't be happening, she thought. *It can't be.* She opened her eyes. But it was.

Hubert tore open the second envelope.

Inside it was a reel of recording tape. He held it high. "Evidence for murder?" he called out laughingly. Then he clucked his tongue in mock sympathy. "Really, my dear. You should have known better than to resort to *blackmail*."

He walked slowly toward the fireplace and with a motion of disgust threw the reel into the flames. A portion of the tape unwound and snaked out onto the carpet. With his foot, he kicked it into the hearth. Then he turned to Hélène.

Her face was white. She was staring into the fire, mesmerized. As she watched, the recording tape began to melt, exuding a stench of burning plastic.

"See, my dear?" Hubert said pleasantly. "You no longer

have a hold over us. The past is gone and forgotten." He snapped his fingers. "Just like *that*."

She stared numbly into the flames. No, it wasn't. For her, the past would never be gone. Could never be forgotten.

YESTERDAY

II
RAPE

1

Saint-Nazaire, 1950

Tante Janine lived on the outskirts of Saint-Nazaire and made a modest livelihood off her plant nursery. Her house was on a raised piece of property a quarter of a kilometer from the sea. It was built of weathered gray stone, was two stories high, and had a steeply sloping roof. On a clear day you could even see down to where the Loire emptied into the sea. That was two kilometers to the south.

The nursery surrounded the house on all sides. Every square centimeter of space was put to good use. There were four big hothouses and dozens of long, glass-covered pits in which Tante Janine grew the seedlings which the townspeople would buy in the spring to plant in their own gardens. All around these odd structures, the earth was tilled and used for planting seasonal vegetables and flowers. There wasn't a patch of useless grass to be seen. Wooden planks served as paths between the flowerbeds and the vegetable patches.

Two additional structures were situated quite some distance from the house—a smelly three-sided bunker used for storing manure and compost, and a shed where the gardening tools were kept and in which they made wreaths or floral arrangements for funerals or an occasional wedding. For a long time, funerals had outnumbered weddings by ten to one.

A stone wall surrounded the property. Attached to it was a big wooden sign that faced the road. It read: "JANINE JUNOT." The black-and-white paint was peeling and blistered.

During Edmond's and Hélène's first winter there, things had not gone well at the nursery. At that time, Saint-Nazaire was considered to be of extreme strategic importance by both the Allies and the Nazis.

First, there were the German installations—namely the U-boat base. Many of the U-boat wolf packs that infested the

Atlantic originated from here. They depended on the Saint-Nazaire base for supplies, servicing, and repairs. It was the ideal spot, since much of the equipment they needed was already there from before the war. Saint-Nazaire had been known for its shipyards since the nineteenth century.

Second, and more important, the town was part of what the Allies called the Saint-Nazaire Pocket. This was considered to be the chief infiltration point into France from the Atlantic coast. As a result, Saint-Nazaire was nearly devastated.

Each time the British and the Americans pounded the installations, Tante Janine would burst into tears. Not that she was sorry about the U-boat base being demolished. But the nearby explosions reverberated all the way to her nursery and shattered the glass that covered her hothouses and pits. When that happened, the vegetables she had been nurturing so diligently would be in danger of exposure to the cold. For a while she managed to patch up everything as best as she could. Then came a particularly heavy bombing and the glass was shattered beyond repair. In a single night, every last seedling had frozen and died. When spring came, there was nothing to sell. It was a very lean year.

But 1944 did bring a moment of jubilation. On August 26, General de Gaulle marched triumphantly down the Champs-Élysées. At last, Paris was liberated. Frenchmen were in tears. The war was as good as over. Just like Maman had predicted, the Boches were being driven out of France and pushed back across the Rhine.

Like everyone else, Edmond and Hélène had greeted this news with joy. Now it would not be long before the family was reunited. But as month after month crept by with still no word from Maman, Papa, Catherine, or Marie, they slowly began to lose all hope of ever seeing them again. From the grown-ups, terrible fragments of stories about the Germans filtered down to them. Stories that were beyond their comprehension. Stories that just couldn't be true. Stories about what happened to those who were carted off by the Nazis. Stories about the camps.

In the beginning, Tante Janine had been relatively friendly. Then in May 1945 she "turned." Perhaps the realization that Edmond and Hélène were now solely her responsibility finally dawned on her. One thing was only too clear. She was stuck with two hungry mouths to feed. Two growing bodies

146

to clothe. And times were bad. As a result, she began to strike out at the "cause" of her frustrations. The children.

Hélène would never forget the first time she and Edmond were subjected to Tante Janine's fury. It was on the fifteenth of May, a day that had started out smoothly enough. The afternoon sun was still shining strongly, and there was a sharp nip in the air. In the distance, Hélène could see the fishing boats bobbing out in the bay. Their bows bit into the waves and their gray patched sails billowed in the wind. Trouble seemed far away.

Instead of playing by herself, Hélène decided to help Edmond repair a section of the shattered hothouses, so they went out scavenging for pieces of broken glass. These would be cut into smaller squares, which would then be inserted into the hothouse frames. Luck was with them that afternoon. They found a large piece—big enough to cut into at least six squares. Carefully they carried it back to the nursery, and everything went fine until Edmond tried to cut it. For one reason or another, the piece splintered into shards.

Tante Janine threw a fit. Viciously her hand slashed across Edmond's face. Then she yanked his hair so hard that she tore out a fistful.

That was the beginning. For over a year, this kind of abuse continued. There was no telling what might trigger it. Edmond and Hélène were helpless. Their only relief came when Tante Janine made one of her sudden, unexplained trips to Paris. There was nothing they could do but suffer these rages in silence, and usually it was Edmond who had to take the brunt of them. Perhaps because he was the elder. Perhaps because he had the bigger appetite. Every night Hélène prayed fervently, begging God to have Maman and Papa come to rescue them from Tante Janine. But God turned a deaf ear.

Then, a year later, everything came to a head. Weeding among tiny lettuce seedlings, Hélène accidentally mistook some of them for weeds.

"Which of you idiots pulled these?" Tante Janine demanded.

"I did," Edmond lied. He knew that a beating was imminent and that his body could absorb the blows much more easily than Hélène's.

"You idiot!" Tante Janine raged. "You good-for-nothing!" She reached down, snatched up a slat of wood that was lying there, and angrily began to beat him across the back with it. Hélène screamed for her to stop it, while Edmond took the blows in silence. When it was over, he got to his feet, swayed unsteadily, and stumbled into the house.

Hélène ran after him. There were only two bedrooms. Tante Janine slept in one; they shared the other. When Hélène got upstairs, Edmond was already throwing his few belongings together.

"What are you doing?" Hélène asked in sudden panic.

He laughed mirthlessly. "What does it look like? I'm packing."

"But, Edmond!" Her voice was desperate. "Why?"

"I'm leaving, that's why! I can't stand living here any longer."

"I'm sorry, Edmond!" she pleaded. "I'll make it up to you. It was all my fault!"

He shook his head. "No, it wasn't your fault. It's that woman. She's a bitch!"

"Please don't talk like that."

Savagely he turned to her. "Well, she is! And I'm not going to stay here waiting to be beaten half to death. Anyway, I'm tired of slaving away for her."

"But where are you going to go?"

"I'm joining up with the fishing fleet. Let the old bitch look after her own stinking weeds!"

Hélène's eyes glistened with tears. "And me?" she asked softly. "What about me, Edmond?"

He came close and took her in his arms. He was wet from perspiration and smelled strongly of sweat. "Little French Girl," he said gently, "until I can arrange otherwise, you're going to have to stay here."

"But I can't!" she sobbed. "Not without you!"

"You can and must. To get away from here will take money. I swear I'll save every penny I earn. Then we can go away together." Gently he extricated himself from her and stuffed his belongings into a pillowcase. "Now, wipe your tears."

She nodded solemnly. Sniffing, she wiped her eyes. "Edmond . . ."

He looked up. "Yes?"

For a moment she didn't speak. Then she clutched him in sudden desperation. "You won't leave me here for good with her, will you?"

He looked at her. The fear and loneliness in her violet eyes tugged at his heart. "No, Little French Girl. All we have is each other. Nobody can ever separate us. Not after what we've gone through together. Neither the Boches nor that bitch can keep us apart."

Fearfully she looked up into his eyes. "And the sea?" she asked softly. "What if the sea separates us?"

Suddenly he grinned. He looked very sure of himself. "Even the sea won't be able to do that."

2

Hélène sat in the back of the classroom. Mademoiselle Gribius always put her best-behaved pupils there. This way the troublemakers would be in the front where she could keep her eye on them. The bell sounded. The girls automatically glanced toward the door. From out in the hall came the noises of slamming doors and the stampeding of feet. Restlessly they looked back at Mademoiselle. They were anxious to be dismissed. Home economics was the last class of the day.

Mademoiselle slowly got out of her chair and walked around to the front of her desk. Her hawklike eyes searched the room through the thick lenses of her eyeglasses. There was a look of approval on her thin lips. Not one girl had moved a muscle. Their eyes, yes. But that was all. They knew better. If one of them made an attempt to gather up her things before class was dismissed, they would all be kept behind for an extra five minutes.

"Ecoutez!" Mademoiselle's sharp, clipped voice carried to the back of the room.

The girls sat in tense misery, trying their best to look attentive.

Mademoiselle was not to be hurried. "By now most of you should have *some* inkling of how to sew. As you all know, there are only ten more periods of this class until the summer recess. Every year at this time it is traditional that my classes show me what they have learned."

There was a collective groan from the girls. Their faces fell. They knew what was coming. Mademoiselle's pet project.

Most of the girls hated to sew. The needles pricked their fingers, the threads got tangled, and Mademoiselle was ever unsatisfied. She complained endlessly about their buckling hems, their sloppy stitches. More often than once, each of them had experienced the humiliation of Mademoiselle's wrath: with her tiny scissors she tore out whole rows of stitches, and the tearful girl would have to start over from scratch.

Mademoiselle continued. "You are each assigned to sew a dress. The dress shall be something utilitarian. Something simple. You will design and cut out your own patterns. You will supply your own fabric. You will sew it without help. All work shall be done in this classroom. What you sew, and how well you do it, will determine your final grade." She paused. "Do I make myself clear?"

"Oui, mademoiselle," the girls chorused.

Mademoiselle raised her chin. "Girls!"

They all sat stiffly at attention.

"Class is dismissed!"

There was much scraping of chairs, a stampede out the door. On the other side of the building the boys would be waiting.

Usually Hélène was the last one out. She had nowhere to rush except home to Tante Janine. But today she sailed happily out the door with the rest of them. Her heart pounded. Of all the girls in the class, she was the only one who greeted the news of the sewing project with delight.

"What's with *her*?" Jeanne-Marie Berty asked loudly, staring after Hélène. "I've never seen her in a hurry before."

Jeanne-Marie's friend Edith Loiseau said something in a whisper, and the girls glanced at Hélène, giggling noisily.

Hélène could feel her face flushing, but she ignored them. Jeanne-Marie and Edith thought they were better than everyone else. Monsieur Berty owned a shipyard and Monsieur Loiseau was the head of the local fish cannery. They were the wealthiest families in town and the two girls were vain, stuck-up, and vicious. They got their jollies making fun of other people. Hélène always went out of her way to avoid them. But often their loud wisecracks followed her and caught her off guard.

Today she didn't care. Let them snicker, she thought. She'd show them! Her heart did another joyous leap. She had not only a talent for sewing but also a secret passion for it. Perhaps it was a legacy from Maman.

She smiled to herself. She would have ten classes—ten Saturdays—on which to work on her project. And eleven Saturdays from now was the annual Feux de St.-Jean festival. For that the townswomen would don their traditional costumes with the fantastic starched lace caps and celebrate proudly. But she? She would celebrate *beautifully*.

Hélène stopped hurrying for a moment in order to catch her breath. She leaned against a stone wall and shut her eyes. Yes, she could see it already. At the festival she would wear a beautiful dress. Something besides the humiliating hand-me-downs that Tante Janine collected from neighbors on whose children Hélène had seen the same shapeless outfits a year or two before. Yes, for once she would dazzle. She would be Cinderella, the festival her ball.

It wouldn't be difficult. She had the talent and she had a little money. For the past few years she had squirreled away a few francs that people had given her when she ran errands for them. A few francs Tante Janine didn't know about.

Hélène smiled again. On the way home she would stop at Madame Dupré's shop. Madame Dupré was the local seamstress. But she didn't only sew. She sold fabrics by the bolt or by the meter. Most of them were simple, inexpensive fabrics. But a few—ah, a few were fabulous!

And best of all, Madame Dupré had back issues of fashion magazines—copies of *Paris Vogue* and *Elle* and *L'Officiel*. Hélène would flip through them, carefully selecting a style for the dress she was going to sew.

She skipped along the steep cobblestoned streets, past the stone houses that had turned pale gray under the onslaught of the salt winds. Within a few minutes she would pass Madame Dupré's and peek in the window. And on Monday, right after school, she would march in armed with her precious francs.

3

On the following Monday, Hélène stood paralyzed in front
of the door to Madame Dupré's. In the window was a breathtaking dress on a headless wooden dummy, and underneath it
a photo clipped from one of the Parisian fashion magazines.
Hélène saw that the dress was a copy of the one in the picture. Only the fabric was different.

She was enthralled.

Slowly she opened her hand and looked down in her palm
to make certain that the money was still there. It was. Then
she fortified herself with a deep breath, opened the door of
the shop, and went in.

The shop was dim. Through an open door she could see
the brightly lit workroom in the back. There were two girls
sitting there. One was sewing meticulously by hand; the other
sat facing a machine, pedaling with her feet and spinning a
large wheel with one hand.

But what caught Hélène's eye was the long counter in
front of her. Displayed on it were bolts of beautiful cloth.
She stared at them but didn't dare touch them. One fabric in
particular fascinated her. It was gray and had tiny nubs, like
imperfections, scattered all over it. Instinctively she realized
that they were not imperfections; they were indigenous to the
fabric.

"May I help you?" a cultured voice said from behind her.

Startled, she turned around and looked up in awe.
Madame Dupré herself was standing there. She was a tall,
imposing woman. Hélène thought she was the most elegant
woman in the world. She wore a striped silk blouse with a
delicate lace bow at the collar. Her eyes were brown and
gentle, her hair elegantly gray, and she smelled faintly of perfume. Next to her, Hélène felt extremely shabby and
awkward. For a moment, a feeling of panic seized her. She
wanted to turn and run right back out. But something gave

152

her courage. Perhaps it was the way Madame Dupré looked at her.

"Bonjour, madame," Hélène said meekly.

"Bonjour, mademoiselle," Madame Dupré returned with extreme politeness. "May I be of assistance?"

Hélène took a deep breath and clutched her handful of francs tighter. "I would like to buy some beautiful fabric."

Madame Dupré smiled wisely. "All fabrics are beautiful," she said. "It depends on how they are sewn. What is it that you would like? I have cottons, woolens, linens, silks and satins, velvets . . ."

"Oh!" Hélène looked a bit deflated. Then she composed herself. "Something like that"—she pointed a trembling finger at the nubby gray material—"how much would that cost?"

"You have good taste, mademoiselle," Madame Dupré said with approval. "That is raw silk, from the Orient. It is the only bolt I have. It is very expensive. But oh, so fine." She looked at Hélène warmly. There was something about the way the girl took to the fabric that reminded her of herself when she was young. Having an eye for fabrics was a rare gift. And the girl had it. She smiled. "Would you like to feel it?"

Hélène's eyes lit up. "May I?"

"But of course, mademoiselle."

Madame Dupré watched Hélène as she reached out and reverently stroked the fabric. Then she held a corner of it between her fingers and caressed it. The woman nodded to herself. The girl was getting the feel.

To Hélène the cloth seemed to have a lifeblood of its own. She could feel it coursing between her fingertips. The texture was luxurious to the touch. The sheen was soft, like subtle moonlight on a tranquil sea.

"It would make a beautiful gown, n'est-ce pas?" Madame Dupré said.

Hélène was breathless. "Oh, yes! How much is it?"

"Ah." Madame Dupré looked at her shrewdly and wagged her finger. "You must not think that raw silk is all there is. The woolens are sturdy, coarse and warm, or they can be soft and subtle. The linens are crisp. The velvets are like the deep colors of the night. And the cottons are cool. Each fabric has its own personality and characteristic. You yourself must judge what fabric will suit your needs best. Royal fabrics like silk and velvet must never be used to make aprons or housedresses. But a ball gown—yes! Linens and cottons are for the summer. Woolens for the winter. There are fabrics for every season of the year. For every function in the world!"

Hélène's eyes shone with rapture. The door to a whole new world was opening before her. And she was dazzled.

There was the sound of someone coming into the shop. Madame Dupré turned around automatically. Discreetly Hélène examined a bolt of navy-blue linen, comparing its texture to the raw silk.

"Bonjour," Madame Dupré said.

"We need fabric," an all-too-familiar voice said loudly.

"Yes, something simply extravagant!" a second voice chimed in.

"For mademoiselle's annual sewing project, no doubt," Madame Dupré said dryly.

"Oui." Suddenly there was a shriek. "Jeanne-Marie! Look who got here ahead of us!"

Hélène glanced sideways at Edith and Jeanne-Marie. The two girls put their heads together and started whispering and giggling. Hélène clenched her fists. It was as if a dark cloud blotted out the sunshine. Those two malicious creatures didn't deserve to be here, she thought. Not among all these bolts of beautiful cloth.

Edith looked at Hélène. "Which fabric are you going to buy?" she called over.

"I . . . I don't know yet," Hélène murmured.

The girls whispered and giggled again. Madame Dupré glanced at them sternly. She felt sorry for Hélène, but she didn't dare chase the two other girls out. Their mothers were her best customers; most of their dresses were sewn at the shop. That was how Madame Dupré really made her money. Selling fabric was only a sideline. No, to chase them out was impossible, but she would try to get rid of them quickly.

"Could you excuse me for a moment?" she asked Hélène.

Hélène nodded and withdrew to a corner. Silently she stood there and waited. She watched in horror as Edith immediately homed in on a bolt of bottle-green velvet, pawing it like a bundle of rags. Jeanne-Marie was in no hurry. Slowly she examined each bolt, all the while watching Hélène out of the corner of her eye. When she reached the gray raw silk, she saw Hélène stiffen.

Jeanne-Marie smiled triumphantly and looked up at

Madame Dupré. "I'll take six meters of this," she said sweetly.

Hélène's heart sank. In panic she looked pleadingly at Madame Dupré.

The woman looked at her stoically. Then she turned to Jeanne-Marie. "That's a very expensive fabric," she told her. "Perhaps—"

"The cost doesn't matter," Jeanne-Marie said firmly. "Maman said I was to choose whatever I want. You're to put it on her bill."

"Very well," Madame Dupré said with a sigh. The sight of Hélène tugged at her heart. The girl stood trembling in the corner, clutching her coins pathetically.

A few minutes later the two girls left, their noses in the air. Their fabrics were wrapped up in brown paper parcels and tucked under their arms. They were chattering happily, grandiosely planning their dresses. Edith had the bottle-green velvet; Jeanne-Marie walked away with the raw silk.

"I thought those two would never leave," Madame Dupré murmured wearily after the door closed behind them. "Ill-mannered girls! What they both need is a good spanking!" Then she turned to Hélène. "Now, mademoiselle," she said gently, "let me teach you something."

Hélène didn't speak. She remained in the corner, staring up at her. There was deep hurt in her eyes.

"Come, come," the woman said knowingly. "This is not as tragic as you think. The raw silk and the velvet are all wrong. They are not for dresses. They are for gowns or beautiful suits. And gray does not become Mademoiselle Berty at all. Not with her terrible pallor. It will make her look all washed out. Neither does green suit the other one. Her skin is much too dark."

Hélène nodded slowly. She thought she understood what Madame Dupré was trying to say. "But . . . it's just . . ."

"Never mind, my dear." Madame Dupré made a gesture that looked as if she were waving away an irritating fly. "Let them make fools of themselves. They have no taste. You are smarter, non?"

Hélène gave a tentative nod. She felt a little better. Not much, but enough. Still, the excitement was gone from her eyes. Her pleasure had turned sour.

Madame Dupré touched Hélène on the shoulder. "Fortunately I have no fittings scheduled this afternoon. Come upstairs to my apartment with me. We will have some tea and I will teach you a lesson that you should never forget. Danielle!"

The sewing machine in the back of the shop stopped chattering. The skinny girl who operated it came out front. "Madame?"

"I am going upstairs, Danielle. You're in charge of the shop while I am gone."

Hélène looked up at the elegant wall clock. It was three o'clock. They had been talking for almost two hours.

Madame Dupré rose from her chintz-upholstered chair. "That's enough of a lesson for one day," she said, smoothing her skirt. "Now, go home and digest what you have learned. Don't forget what I told you—that there are two approaches to design. The first?" She looked questioningly at Hélène.

Hélène took a deep breath. "Designing the pattern and then finding a fabric to suit it."

"Bon. And the second?"

"Designing the dress around the fabric."

"Correct. And which will you do?"

Hélène did not hesitate. "I shall design a dress that will look good on me. Then I'll use whatever fabric best suits it *and* me."

Madame Dupré looked at her with respect. The girl learned fast. With the right tutoring, she might even get someplace.

4

It was ten Saturdays later that Mademoiselle Gribius came around from behind her desk. She clapped her hands sharply, bringing the class to order.

The girls sat erect, nervously looking up at her. On the table in front of each of them was a neatly folded garment.

Mademoiselle cleared her throat. Her face was impenetrable and her voice was emotionless and dry. "As you all know, this is the last class until September. I have tried to teach you well. Now we shall see what you have absorbed during the past year."

She was silent for a moment. Her sharp eyes swept through the room. "You will all change into the outfits you have sewn. You will remain dressed in them for the remainder of the day. However, you will not wear them home. Upon dismissal you will change back into your school uniforms."

She frowned. "I think this is prudent, since it will spare you much embarrassment. I have been watching you while you were sewing, and it saddens me to realize how little some of you have learned. I do not think your parents would appreciate the humiliation of your looking like clowns on the way home."

She paused. "All right, girls! Change into your dresses!"

Hélène's heart began to hammer. She took a deep breath. Slowly she reached for her dress and began unfolding it. For a moment, the rest of the class slipped out of her consciousness. All she had eyes for was her new dress.

During the past ten weeks, Mademoiselle had indeed kept her eye on the girls' progress. However, she offered no advice or comments. No approval or disapproval. Not one girl knew what she thought. Mademoiselle never smiled. Her stern face gave nothing away.

Edith had the most trouble. Her constant "ouches" and muttered curses were greeted with muffled giggles from the rest of the class. She found it very difficult to sew and drape the green velvet. The fabric was thick and difficult to handle. Somehow or other, it got so much wear and tear that the nap was already beginning to wear off in a lot of places. Each Saturday, Edith was ready to burst into tears.

Jeanne-Marie had no fewer problems, but she attacked them with gusto, if only to spare herself ridicule. Each time she stuck herself with her needle she refrained from cursing or crying out. But her sharp intakes of breath were enough. The hisses carried to the back of the classroom. She was discovering—too late—that the raw silk she had bought out from under Hélène was no easier to sew than the velvet, for silk has its own characteristics. It "crawls" right out from under the needle. A beautifully fluid fabric, it also tends to

157

show off flaws in workmanship more easily than "everyday" cloths such as cotton or linen.

Adding to their misery were their designs. Mademoiselle's instructions for a "simple" dress were interpreted differently by each girl. But no interpretations were as ambitious—or bizarre—as Edith's and Jeanne-Marie's. Clearly both of them got carried away. They tried to create updates of lavish eighteenth-century court dresses. This process required repeated visits to Madame Dupré's. Almost daily they bought multicolored ribbons and frothy white or gold lace. Each time they saw a new item, they would pounce on it. Madame Dupré was no help. Knowing that they would return, she shrewdly put all her ribbons, laces, and bows out on display. It was too much for Edith and Jeanne-Marie. They knew no restraint. They had to have everything. And everything was destined to go on their dresses.

Hélène was grateful for Madame Dupré's tutelage. She took what she'd learned to heart and designed the simplest dress imaginable. She had gotten the idea for it from a picture she saw in *L'Officiel*. It had an unadorned bodice and a modest skirt and was supposed to be the latest rage in Paris. The sleeves were short, and the neckline, although low, was not low enough to be scandalous. For fabric, she'd chosen a lightweight cotton that was itself simple and easy to work with. The rich shade of burgundy would go dramatically with her raven hair. For adornment she sewed a belt out of the same fabric and used the beautiful buckle Madame Dupré had given her as a gift.

The pure simplicity of the dress gave it its elegance.

Slowly the girls began to change into their dresses. Most of them did it with trepidation.

"Hurry up!" Mademoiselle snapped. "We haven't got all day."

Unhappily, they hurried. Then Mademoiselle instructed them to walk around the room one by one. When they reached the front of her desk, they had to do a pirouette before returning to their seats. The girls sitting up front went first.

When Edith got up, a burst of laughter reverberated through the room. She stood there blushing helplessly. Her dress was a disaster. One sleeve was longer and fuller than the other, the hemline was crooked, and she'd pleated so much velvet at the waist that it made her look pregnant. All the trimmings she had applied were a horror. It looked as though a dozen bakers—none of them talented—had frosted the same cake over and over. Even Jeanne-Marie couldn't help giggling. But the laughter soon died in her throat. She was next.

Slowly Jeanne-Marie got to her feet. For once her poise and assurance deserted her. She walked meekly around the room. From a distance the raw silk did not look too bad. Close up, it was a nightmare of loose threads, bunched-up fabric, and sloppy seams. There was something so pathetic about her serious demeanor that no one laughed. But when she did her pirouette, everyone noticed something odd about her back. The dress buckled terribly, making her look hunch-backed. The class erupted in gales of laughter. Even Mademoiselle's lips held the hint of a smile.

Hélène was last. When Mademoiselle called out her name, a feeling of dread passed through her. She froze. Heads turned, looking back at her. Mademoiselle called her again. She forced herself to get up.

She walked slowly, self-consciously. Every step was an effort, and she felt as if her feet didn't belong to her. She held herself stiffly and her hands were clenched awkwardly. She could feel the perspiration breaking out on her forehead and under her arms. She kept thinking: This dress is new and now I'm going to soil the armpits.

When she finally reached the front of the room, she stood there while insecurity bombarded her. Her temples were throbbing.

Finally she did her pirouette. The girls gaped at her. Their mouths hung open. A sudden, spontaneous "ah" filled the classroom. It was a moment before she realized what it meant. Slowly her eyes began to glow with pride. Her dress was a success.

For the first time she was drunk with excitement.

She had found her métier. Fashion.

5

When school was dismissed, the girls all clustered around Hélène. They wanted to know about the dress, begged to have a close look at it, asked a million questions. Where did she get the idea for it? How could such a common fabric look so beautiful? How could such a simple cut be so dazzling?

Hélène had never been happier. Suddenly she found herself in the midst of an admiring crowd. The dress had shot her to popularity. Even Edith and Jeanne-Marie grudgingly came over.

Jeanne-Marie looked hesitantly at Hélène. "Could you design and sew a dress for me?" she asked. "For money, of course."

Hélène had never felt the warmth of adulation before. Tante Janine kept her from making friends by clamping down on her socializing. There was Mass to attend, the nursery to be worked in. There was time for nothing else. But now she basked in the sweetness of acceptance.

When Hélène came out of the big school door, she squinted in the sunlight. She was clutching the string bag in which she carried the dress. She was still surrounded by the chattering girls.

Suddenly a deep voice whispered into her ear from behind. "Hello, Little French Girl."

Hélène spun around. Edmond was standing there, his grin white against his deeply tanned face. His smile was marred only by the two missing top teeth which had been knocked out so long ago by the recoil of a rifle in Paris. For a moment she just looked at him. Then she flung her arms around him, and effortlessly he lifted her high into the air. "Edmond!" she shrieked. "Oh, Edmond!"

The fishing fleet had just come in. He hadn't bothered to take the time to wash up. His cheeks felt scratchy from his beard. He stank of fish. But she didn't care. At the moment it was the best smell in the world.

When he finally put her down, she looked proudly up at him. It had been almost two months since she'd seen him last. His chin looked stronger, and he seemed to have grown taller. He looked more ruggedly handsome than ever. His shoulders were broader. There was a weather-beaten, outdoor quality about him. The manual labor was packing hard muscle onto his body. She could feel it through his shirt.

Suddenly she put her face against his chest and started to cry.

He looked down at her in surprise. "What's the matter?" he asked softly.

She smiled through her tears. "I know it sounds silly. But . . . oh, Edmond, Edmond! I'm so happy to see you." She sniffed and wiped her eyes.

He grinned widely. "Tell you what. I just got paid. Come on, I'll buy you a meal in the best restaurant in town. I'll eat anything as long as it's not fish. And we can have a long talk."

"Don't you want to come . . . home with me? We can talk there."

His expression darkened and he shook his head. "No!" he said vehemently. "I don't want to see that bitch."

She nodded soberly. His attitude hadn't softened. He still didn't want to see Tante Janine, didn't care if he never saw her again. When he was in port he rented a room in a boardinghouse near the waterfront.

They walked in silence for a while. Then he took her hand suddenly. "I've got ten days' leave till we go back out to sea."

She smiled contentedly. "Then you're going to take me to the Feux de St.-Jean festival?"

"You bet. You'll be the second-prettiest girl there."

She stopped walking. She stared at him dumbly. "Second!" she said bewilderingly. "Who's the first?"

"Someone you'll meet at the restaurant."

Suddenly a strange fear passed through her. "Is . . . is it a . . . a girlfriend?" she asked weakly.

He nodded slowly. "I met her last time we were in port." He saw the look of pain in her eyes. "Oh, come on. Jeanne is special. But she can never take your place." He smiled. "You're my Little French Girl."

She smiled back, but her smile was tight. Some of her happiness had died. She wasn't the only girl in his life any longer. He had a girlfriend. She had wondered how long it would take. He was too handsome not to have one. No, she hadn't wondered. She had worried.

Suddenly she knew what she felt. Jealousy.

The restaurant was called Au Petit Caporal. Hélène had passed it often but she'd never been inside. They had to go down two steps from the sidewalk and pass through an old but clean kitchen to the dining room in the back. It was almost empty. It had a low vaulted ceiling, white stone walls, and a flagstone floor.

They sat down on cane chairs at a round table covered with a checkered tablecloth. Beside them was a small window. Geraniums grew in the flower boxes, and beyond that were rows of moored fishing boats. The sunlight reflected the squirming water on their hulls.

Hélène recognized Edmond's girlfriend instantly: she could tell by the way the young waitress looked at him. Hélène stared at her disapprovingly, comparing the girl's looks with her own. She was Edmond's age, almost eighteen. Her hair was brown, almost mousy, but her face was kind and her brown eyes were soulfully gentle. She looked very pretty when she smiled.

Edmond got to his feet and kissed her cheek. Once again Hélène could feel a stab of jealousy. She looked away.

"Hello, Jeanne," she heard him say. There was a peculiar warmth in his voice that she had never heard before. "This is my sister, Hélène. Hélène, my . . . Jeanne."

Hélène looked up. "Hello," she said awkwardly.

Jeanne smiled. "How do you do," she said warmly. She sensed that Hélène felt threatened by her presence. She pulled up a chair and sat down. Then she reached out, took Hélène's hand, and looked earnestly into her eyes. "I like Edmond very much," she said honestly. "And I know how much you love him. He's told me. If you'll let me, I . . . I want us to be close friends."

Somehow Hélène felt immediately better. She looked at Jeanne with respect. "I would like that," she said. "I've never had a good friend before."

The day of the Feux de St.-Jean festival dawned warm and clear. The sun shone brilliantly and there wasn't a cloud in the sky. Tante Janine even closed down the nursery for the festivities.

Early in the morning, Hélène filled the big kitchen pots with water and put them on the stove. When it boiled, she washed herself carefully, scrubbing the gardening earth out from beneath her fingernails, shampooing her hair and combing it out. She took infinite care with her appearance. Today she would wear her new dress. She hadn't shown it to anyone yet. Not Tante Janine, Madame Dupré, or Edmond. She would surprise them all! Especially Edmond. He and Jeanne would be waiting for her outside the nursery gate at exactly twelve o'clock.

"It's time you got dressed," Tante Janine snapped at eleven-thirty. She was already wearing her long traditional black dress with the white lace collar. Her gray braid was wrapped around her head and the high, stiffly starched lace cap was pinned to it. It made her look somehow invincible, bigger than life.

Hélène nodded obediently and went upstairs to her bedroom. She wasn't about to tell Tante Janine that she was planning to leave without her. Nor did she dare mention Edmond's name. Tante Janine would fly into one of her rages.

No, Hélène had a better plan. When her back was turned, she'd simply slip out of the house.

She dressed carefully. The burgundy cotton felt good and new against her clean skin. She had gotten up in the middle of the night, heated a brick in the oven, and put it inside the iron. Then she had surreptitiously pressed the dress. It didn't have a single crease or wrinkle.

Happily she did a pirouette, watching the fabric swirl around her hips. She wished she had a mirror so she could see what she looked like. But Tante Janine didn't believe in mirrors. They were a sign of weakness. Of vanity.

She parted the flimsy curtains and looked down. She could already see Edmond and Jeanne waiting for her at the gate. Edmond was leaning against one of the posts, smoking a cigarette. She waved to him. He saw her and waved back.

Quickly she smoothed the dress, ran a hand through her hair, and opened the door a crack. Tante Janine was nowhere in sight. She took a deep breath. Quietly, gritting her teeth against each creaky step, she descended to the kitchen.

Hélène had never looked lovelier. The dress seemed to

have a life of its own. It even made her skin tone look warmer. In the excitement of the occasion, her violet eyes glittered like jewels. She felt truly beautiful.

She tiptoed across the room to the door. When her hand touched the handle, a staccato voice froze her in her tracks. "Where do you think you're going!"

Hélène turned around slowly. Tante Janine was standing near the wardrobe. Her eyes were wide and her hands rested on her gaunt hips.

Hélène gestured to the door. "Edmond is waiting for me at the gate."

Tante Janine approached her with the crafty stealth of a spider. "Running out to see your brother, are you?" she spat contemptuously.

"Yes," Hélène said coldly.

Tante Janine laughed shrilly. "All dolled up, too." Then her lip curled. "Where did you get that dress?"

"I made it."

"Don't lie to me!"

"I did make it! It was Mademoiselle's year-end project."

"And the fabric? Where did you get that sinful color? Red is the color of the devil!"

"It's not sinful!" Hélène said. "Even the Abbé wears red robes sometimes!"

Suddenly Tante Janine flew at her. "You wicked, cursed beast! How dare you equate that lascivious garment with the Holy Church!" Her hand slashed out to slap Hélène, but Hélène effectively blocked it with her forearm. Tante Janine sucked in her breath in pain. Then suddenly she grabbed hold of the bodice of Hélène's dress. She jerked downward with all the strength her bony fingers could summon.

There was a terrible ripping sound as the bodice tore. Hélène let out a cry and looked down in despair. Her dress—her dazzling Cinderella dress—was ruined! The bodice hung in shreds around her waist. Her white slip was all that covered her small breasts.

"I hate you!" Hélène cried out. "I despise you!"

"Get dressed into something decent," Tante Janine snapped. "You're going to confession."

"I am not," Hélène said quietly. Then she drew herself up. Her eyes flashed. "I'll tell the Abbé what a wicked woman you are! How you . . . you . . ." Hélène lifted up the sagging bodice and smiled suddenly. "How you attacked me so that you could see me naked!"

"You wouldn't dare tell a lie like that!" Tante Janine whispered. "God would punish you like he punishes all sinners! You'll see!" Then she turned, her black dress rustling as she stormed out the door.

6

Summer passed, autumn came, and winter followed. Then once again the seasons slipped into their perpetual cycles. Spring, summer, autumn, winter. On the sixth of January 1952, Hélène turned fifteen. She was invited to spend the Sunday afternoon with Edmond and Jeanne.

When she arrived at Jeanne's gray apartment house, Jeanne answered the door. "Hello." She smiled. "Edmond's here already. Come in."

Hélène was led to the familiar kitchen. It was off the narrow hallway, separated by a door that had wavy, opaque panels of glass set into it. Edmond was sitting at the table. When Hélène came in he got up and kissed her.

"Now my two favorite girls are here," he said, smiling.

Hélène slid down beside him on the wooden banquette while Jeanne crossed the room and disappeared into the pantry. She came out holding a bottle of white wine. She took three glasses from the credence. Carefully she filled them and set one down in front of each of them. Then she slipped into the banquette on Edmond's other side. She raised her glass. "To Hélène," she announced. "Who in another year will be graduated from school."

Edmond raised his glass. "À votre santé," he said.

Hélène smiled. "À votre santé."

By the time she sipped her second glass of wine, Hélène felt a warm glow settle over her. The wine made her relaxed and content. Her favorite hours were those idly spent in this little apartment that Jeanne's mother had "inherited" after

165

her grandmother died. It was cozy, warm, and cheerful. Edmond still rented his room at the boardinghouse whenever he was in port. But he spent most of his days here, going back to his room only at night.

For a while they exchanged small talk and gossip. Then Jeanne took Edmond's hand. Her face was serious as she looked at Hélène. "We have something to tell you," she said hesitantly. She glanced at Edmond and squeezed his hand, signaling for him to do the talking.

He nodded and she looked away. "Jeanne and I . . ." He paused and took a deep breath, his brown eyes flickering nervously. "We're going to get married."

For a brief moment Hélène stared at them openmouthed while she let the news sink in. When it did, she jumped to her feet. Her heart thumped and she was beaming. She bent down, grabbed hold of Edmond, and hugged him tightly. He looked up at her with surprise. Then she rushed around the table and hugged Jeanne. "Congratulations!" she cried with excitement. "When's the big day? Did you set a date? Just think!" She shook her head unbelievingly. "I'll have a sister-in-law! My present to you will be the wedding gown," she announced. "I will sew it myself!"

"Would you?" Jeanne looked pleased.

Hélène lifted her glass. "I propose a toast," she said.

Edmond and Jeanne reached for their glasses, and a blush came to Hélène's face. It was the first time she had ever proposed a toast.

"To my brother and sister-in-law," she said quietly. "Both of whom I love dearly."

She walked back to Tante Janine's alone. The town was quiet and there was no traffic on the dirt road that led to the nursery. The sky had grown dark and the fog rolled heavily along the ground. The wind had picked up. Icy gusts tugged at her clothes, but she didn't seem to notice. Her mind was in another world. The world of fashion. Of Paris. Of magazines.

Yes, when she graduated from school she would immediately get a job and scrimp and save; when she'd saved up enough, she would buy a one-way ticket to Paris. That was where fashion reigned supreme. Once there, she would be able to start along the road that would lead to the fulfillment of her dream. Her glossy dream. Her magazine. A magazine more beautiful than all the others she had looked through at

Madame Dupré's. More beautiful even than *Elle*. More glamorous than *L'Officiel*. More powerful than *Vogue*. The thought of it made her drunk with excitement. She loved designing and sewing dresses. But she didn't want to do that. She had talent, true, but she also instinctively knew that she didn't have *enough*. Not to compete with such geniuses as Madame Grès and Christian Dior and Hubert de Givenchy. Her talent lay elsewhere. In recognizing fine things. Fine fabrics. Fine jewelry. Fine design. She had what Madame Dupré called an "eye."

When she got to the house the lights were glowing weakly in the ground-floor windows. Now that she'd have to face Tante Janine her dreams evaporated. With this return to reality came the sudden knowledge that it was very cold, and she shivered.

She found Tante Janine sitting in the kitchen with a visitor. She recognized the man instantly. He was an unemployed riveter who had worked in the shipyard and now spent most of his time frequenting the waterfront taverns. Hélène didn't like him one bit. He was tall, dark-haired, dark-eyed, and had a crafty look. Several times when she'd passed him on the street he had directed lewd remarks at her. His name was Pierre Péguy.

"Come here, Hélène," Tante Janine said sternly.

Dutifully Hélène crossed the room toward the table.

"Sit down." With her bony hand Tante Janine indicated an empty chair.

Hélène was suspicious of this sudden hospitality. It was the first time Tante Janine had ever asked her to sit and join her. Slowly she pulled out the rickety wooden chair and sat down stiffly.

Tante Janine looked at her expressionlessly. "I think it is only fair that you should know something," she said in a flat voice. Her dark eyes glanced at the man beside her. "Monsieur Péguy has asked me to marry him."

Hélène was staggered. Her mouth hung open as she stared at Tante Janine, then at Pierre, then back at Tante Janine. Her mind was reeling. Tante Janine marrying? And a penniless, drunken dockworker for a bridegroom? Surely this was a bad joke! She looked deep into Tante Janine's eyes. No, this was no joke.

"I have given Monsieur Péguy my answer," Tante Janine said. "I have accepted his proposal."

Hélène looked at her in horror. Abruptly she got to her feet.

"Where are you going?" Tante Janine demanded. "I haven't dismissed you yet."

"I . . . I don't feel well, Tante Janine," she stammered.

She started to leave the room. In her hurry she overturned her chair. It fell on its side with a clatter. Quickly she bent over and righted it. When she rose, her eyes met Pierre's. He had been staring at her derrière. She shivered. She didn't like the look in his eyes.

It was the same look the Boche had given Catherine.

Hélène awoke sometime during the night of Tante Janine's marriage. The room was dark. Pierre and Tante Janine were still up. She could hear mumbled snatches of their conversation coming from the next room. She frowned sleepily. Somehow it did not sound like the type of things that were said on a wedding night.

"Of course there's a house," Tante Janine was saying.

"You're sure . . . this?" Pierre asked.

"Absolutely. In Mont . . ."

The conversation was lost on Hélène. They were talking about a house in Mont Something-or-other. Montluçon? Montlivault? She yawned and dismissed it from her mind. A moment later she turned over. She was fast asleep again.

When she awakened in the morning the sun shone brightly through the window. She sat up, yawned noisily, and stretched. Then quickly she got dressed and went downstairs. She paused at the foot of the stairs and looked around the kitchen. Pierre was sitting hunched over the table, sipping steaming coffee out of a big enamel mug. Monsieur Champagne, the cat, sat alertly on a cold portion of the big stove, intently watching Tante Janine scrambling eggs, his pink nose sniffing the air. The kitchen smelled deliciously of frying ham.

Hélène's mouth watered. Perhaps marriage had softened Tante Janine, she thought hopefully. She had certainly never cooked such lavish breakfasts before. Usually there was only bread, accompanied by the weak coffee into which they dipped pieces of it. Or, in especially cold weather, hot oatmeal. But today even the coffee smelled strong and delicious.

"Bonjour," Hélène said. She covered her mouth to stifle a yawn. "It smells good."

Tante Janine grunted but didn't turn around.

Hélène went over to the table and pulled out a chair. As she sat down, she stubbed her toe on something. She looked under the table. It was a suitcase. "Is someone traveling?" she asked in a surprised voice.

Pierre looked up at her for a long moment. "I am," he said hoarsely. Then his eyes fell back to his coffee.

"Where are you going?"

"Paris."

"Paris!" Hélène's eyes lit up.

"That's enough!" Tante Janine snapped. She turned around from the stove and flashed Pierre an angry look. "It's none of the girl's business!"

He shrugged and sipped noisily at his coffee. A moment later, Tante Janine put an enamel plate down in front of him. On it were eggs and ham and bread. Greedily he picked up his fork and began to eat.

"You get yours later," Tante Janine told Hélène. "He's got a train to catch."

Pierre returned from Paris on the afternoon train eight days later. Hélène and Tante Janine were hoeing the ground near the gate when a car pulled up. They stopped working and watched as Pierre stumbled out, paid the driver, and unsteadily lugged his suitcase toward the house.

Tante Janine sensed that something was wrong. Stiffly she put down her hoe and wiped a strand of hair away from her eyes. Then she walked up to him and gripped his arm. "Why didn't you walk from the station?" she hissed.

He looked at her with puffy red eyes. "I didn't feel like it," he growled. He laughed when he saw her expression. "Don't worry! We can afford it. We're rich now!"

"You've been drinking!" she accused contemptuously. "I should never have allowed you to go by yourself!"

He jerked his arm free from her grip. "Leave me alone, woman!" he growled.

Tante Janine glowered at him. "How dare you speak to me like that!" For the first time she noticed his clothes. "That suit!" she shrieked. "Where did you get it?"

"I bought it."

"In Paris, no doubt." She drew herself up. "That sinful city! Thank God, now that the house is gone there's no more need to go there!"

Hélène frowned. House gone? In Paris? What house?

Suddenly it dawned on her. There was only one house she knew of in Paris. A shudder passed through her. Not Maman's house, she thought. Oh, God, no! Not the house in . . . Montmartre! Suddenly she remembered the conversation she'd overheard the night of Tante Janine's wedding. The "Mont" meant Montmartre, of course! Why hadn't she thought of it? She closed her eyes. That was the house, all right. She could still see it in her mind. The canary-yellow door and the curlicued window bars and the white domes of Sacré Coeur rising in the distance. The little park across the street. Oh, God, no. She had never given any thought as to whether Maman had rented or owned it.

Another wave of dread passed through her. If it had been owned, it would have been hers! And Edmond's! A place where she could have lived in Paris! Why hadn't she thought of it before? Perhaps she'd blocked the house from her memory because of the bad things that had happened there.

Slowly she approached Tante Janine and Pierre. "What are you talking about?" she asked in a whisper.

Tante Janine glowered at her. "It is none of your business! Get back to work!"

Hélène stood her ground. "It was Maman's house, wasn't it?" she said with sudden knowledge.

Tante Janine looked away. "What if it was?"

"You had no right to sell it!" Hélène cried. "It belonged to Edmond and me!"

Tante Janine whirled around and stabbed a finger at her. "You ungrateful child! Who took care of you for all these years! Who fed you and clothed you? Who took you in?"

Yes, Hélène thought dully. Who indeed? Who went around collecting castoff clothes for her? Who fed her the cheapest, starchiest foods money could buy? Who made her slave away in the nursery? Who indeed?

"Edmond's not going to like this," Hélène said between clenched teeth.

"Is that supposed to frighten me?" Tante Janine asked shrilly.

"Who's Edmond?" Pierre asked drunkenly.

Tante Janine glared at him. "Her brother."

"Yes," Hélène said. "My brother. Tante Janine knows what he's capable of. Don't you, Tante Janine?" Hélène looked at her tauntingly. "When he was eleven he murdered

170

the Boche who raped Catherine! I wonder what he'll do to the thieves who stole Maman's house."

Pierre's eyes flashed and dimmed.

"I don't want to hear any more!" Tante Janine snapped in a wavering voice. "Get back to work!"

7

Hélène felt Jeanne's hand on her arm. She turned and looked at her future sister-in-law. Jeanne's eyes were reassuring and her gentle touch gave Hélène courage. Together they went into Monsieur Lefèvre's dim, musty-smelling office.

Hélène was nervous. She had been to the lawyer's only once before. That must have been more than six years ago. She could still remember the day. Tante Janine had made sure that she and Edmond were scrubbed pink and clean, and then she dressed them in their Sunday clothes. Even then, this office had smelled musty and oppressive. But what she remembered most was that an interminably long and boring discussion that she couldn't understand had taken place. It seemed that she and Edmond had to sit stiffly for hours, well-behaved and confused, while vague things about their future were being discussed. Hélène remembered that her legs hadn't quite touched the floor when she sat in the chair.

Now she was back in this office because she had told Jeanne about Maman's house having been sold out from under them.

Monsieur Lefèvre heard the complaints, pursed his pink lips, and went over to an old wooden filing cabinet. Slowly he dug through a stuffed drawer. Finally he pulled out a worn folder. "Here it is," he said. "Junot, Edmond and Hélène." He went around behind his desk, sat down, and slowly flipped through the pages, humming softly to himself as he read.

Hélène glanced at Jeanne. Jeanne nodded and smiled encouragingly.

Monsieur Lefèvre finally closed the file, folded his fat hands on the desktop, and looked at Hélène. "The paperwork was filed between 1945 and 1946. In April 1946 your aunt, Janine Junot, filed for formal adoption of you and your brother. For some reason or other, she never followed through with it. She was, however, appointed your legal guardian."

"Which means?"

"Which means, quite simply, that she was considered legally fit and competent for raising you and your brother and looking out for your best interests."

Hélène leaned forward suddenly. "Tell me, Monsieur Lefèvre," she said in an oddly quiet voice. "Was the adoption procedure abandoned before she was appointed our guardian or after?"

He looked at her with respect. She certainly caught on fast. "After," he replied.

Hélène nodded slowly. So Tante Janine had been ready to adopt her and Edmond until she found out that it wasn't really necessary. She'd have complete control over them anyway.

"What about the property my father and mother owned?" Hélène asked. "Is Tante Janine free to dispose of it?"

"Property such as what?"

"There was a house in Paris. Tante Janine and my . . ."—Hélène swallowed—"my new uncle just sold it. Don't my brother and I have any claim to it?"

The lawyer sighed heavily. "I'm afraid not. You see, your aunt was placed in a position of trust. As long as it is related to your welfare, any decisions regarding you and your property can be made as she sees fit until you are twenty-one."

As the weeks wore on, Hélène found excuses to spend less and less time at home. Pierre's drunkenness—worse since the sale of Maman's house—had made life there increasingly unpleasant for her. For days at a time Pierre would go off on drunken binges or sit sullenly in the kitchen with his bottles of wine. Tante Janine would stare venomously at her husband, but instead of doing something about it, she let her anger fester. When it exploded, it was vented on Hélène.

Hélène retaliated by purposely flunking a series of mathematics and history exams. As usual, this ensured her staying late after school. Then, defying Tante Janine's orders to head straight home, she would go to Jeanne's apartment and wait there until Jeanne got home from work.

A close friendship had developed between the two young women. Jeanne was the first real friend Hélène had ever known. She helped Hélène to open up, to gain self-confidence, and it was from Jeanne that Hélène learned about the intricacies of womanhood. Like an older sister, Jeanne was always there when she was needed. And she was needed more and more as Hélène's home situation deteriorated.

"Where is Tante Janine?" Hélène asked. Pierre was sitting alone in the kitchen with a half-empty bottle of wine in front of him.

He took a swig out of the bottle and laughed. "Out," he said drunkenly. He staggered to his feet and came toward her. She drew back. His hot breath smelled sour from the wine, he hadn't shaved, and his face was purplish-red. "You're sort of pretty, you know," he said, lurching forward.

Adroitly Hélène sidestepped him and he stumbled against the table.

"I can make you feel real good," he whispered. "You got meat on you. Not like that bag of bones I married."

"Stop it!" Hélène whispered. She was becoming frightened. "Stop it!"

He leered at her. "Don't you want to feel good? Pierre knows how to make a woman feel like a woman!"

Hélène turned to go upstairs, but he caught her arm and pulled her toward him. Suddenly he pressed his scratchy face against hers, sloppily trying to kiss her. His mouth missed her lips and he ended up kissing her nose. She grimaced and pushed him away. With her sleeve she wiped his saliva off her face. "You pig!" she hissed. "If you ever touch me again, you're finished! I'll tell Tante Janine and she'll throw you out of the house!"

He laughed. "No she won't!" he cackled. He looked at her craftily. "She'll blame you! I'll tell her that you led me on."

Suddenly she was furious. Without warning she slapped him across the face. "You wouldn't dare!" Then she turned and ran upstairs. But even when she closed the door of her room she could still hear his drunken laugh.

That night she wedged her chair against the door handle before going to sleep. It wouldn't keep him out, but if he tried to come in, it would fall over. The noise would wake her. At least she would be warned.

Despite her preparation, she lay awake for hours, expecting to see the door handle moving in the pale moonlight that filtered in through the thin curtains. Finally she decided that he must have passed out in the kitchen, and she allowed herself to fall asleep. It was an uneasy sleep. She kept waking up, expecting to find him standing at the foot of the bed. But he didn't try to come into her room that night. When she was awakened in the morning, it was by a different sound. The cacophony of trucks.

Curious, she got out of bed, found her slippers, and went over to the window. She pushed the curtains aside, swung the window wide, and leaned out. The morning air felt brisk and cool. She watched as a small convoy of construction vehicles ground to a halt outside the nursery gate. She counted a bulldozer, a big cement-mixing machine on a flatbed truck, and two dump trucks. The big engines idled noisily and the air was filled with the odor of gasoline.

She leaned farther out to get a better view. Men were jumping down off the vehicles. Then she saw Tante Janine striding purposefully toward the gate. She was pointing to the left and the right, shouting instructions Hélène couldn't hear over the din of the idling motors.

Quickly she closed the window, got dressed, moved the chair away from the door, and ran down the stairs two at a time. A few seconds later she was outside. She found Tante Janine standing in the midst of a group of workmen. Hélène went over to her and touched her arm. "What's going on?" she asked.

Tante Janine looked at her with irritation. "They're going to do some work around here," she said tersely. Then she went on talking to the men.

Hélène then wandered around trying to piece together bits of information she overheard. She had no idea what—or how much—work was going to be done. Not until she stopped to listen to two of the men.

One of them was lighting a cigarette. "She bought two hectares of adjoining land," he said as he extinguished the match by waving it in the air. "All with cash. I know because my sister sold it to her."

The other one was impressed. He let out a whistle. "What did she do? Win the lottery?"

"Either that or she robbed a bank." He laughed at his own joke. "She's got fifteen giant hothouses going up."

Hélène stood there with a stunned expression on her face. She couldn't believe what she had just overheard. Suddenly she turned and ran into the house.

Tante Janine was expanding the nursery. Hélène didn't need to ask where the money had come from. She already knew.

From the sale of Maman's house.

She knew if she stayed with Tante Janine much longer she would go crazy. She had to get out. The time had come to break free. She would go see Madame Dupré the next day.

8

"Bonjour, madame," Hélène said politely.

Madame Dupré came around from behind the counter and smiled warmly. "It's a pleasure to see you again. It has been too long."

Hélène nodded. "I was afraid of bothering you, madame."

"Nonsense!" Madame Dupré said reprovingly. "You are never a bother. You should know better!"

For the first time, Madame Dupré looked closely at Hélène. The girl had changed, she suddenly realized. She had grown taller. But that wasn't all. She looked older. And she was certainly turning into a remarkable-looking young woman. Especially with those eyes. Strange, she'd never really noticed how vividly violet they were. All Hélène needed to do was lose some of her baby fat.

"I beg your pardon?" Madame Dupré said. "My mind was wandering." She smiled apologetically at Hélène. "I must be getting senile."

Hélène swallowed nervously, her throat tight and dry. "I was asking . . ." Suddenly she seemed to have lost her voice. Somehow she felt undignified, like a beggar. "A job, Madame Dupré!" she finally blurted out desperately.

175

Madame Dupré looked at her in surprise. "But aren't you still going to school?"

"Oui, madame. But I'm going to quit."

Madame Dupré frowned. She went over to the window and looked out thoughtfully. There was something pathetic about Hélène's lack of composure. The girl wasn't asking for a job because of her love for fabrics and her talent for sewing. There was another, more desperate reason. She could see it written all over her face. Yet underneath, she somehow knew there still lurked a cold ambition.

Madame Dupré hesitated, but only for a moment. She knew that Hélène's talent was exceptional. Something—instinct, perhaps—told her that she should hire Hélène. Anyway, she rationalized, Danielle, the girl who operated the sewing machine, wouldn't be working for much longer. She would soon be getting married. Hélène would learn very quickly at the machine.

Madame Dupré turned and looked at Hélène. The girl was tense, clearly preparing herself for a refusal. Madame Dupré smiled. "You have yourself a job," she said.

The desperation suddenly vanished from Hélène's face. She looked young again and her eyes shone joyfully. She wanted to fling her arms around Madame Dupré and show her how happy she was, but she stopped herself just in time. It wouldn't do to embrace one's employer.

"Don't be too excited," Madame Dupré warned. "The hours are long and the wages are low."

"I don't care," Hélène whispered. She took a deep breath. "When can I start?"

"Whenever you wish."

"Tomorrow?" Hélène asked eagerly.

Madame Dupré nodded. "Tomorrow morning, then."

For a moment Hélène shut her eyes. This was too good to be true! Not only was she getting away from Pierre and Tante Janine, but also she was taking the first step—the first *concrete* step—toward going back to Paris. Only there could she pursue her dream.

"You *what*?" Tante Janine said. Her voice was quivering with rage.

"I found a job," Hélène said quietly.

"I gave you no permission to go and look for one," Tante Janine snapped. "Besides, you're still going to school."

"I'm going to work," Hélène said firmly. "And nobody's going to stop me."

"What about the nursery?" Tante Janine asked. "I thought you were going to work here once school was out."

Hélène was silent.

"Well? Where are you going to live now that you're such a big shot?"

"I thought I would live here until I can afford to move."

Tante Janine's lips were compressed in a tight, ugly smile. "Why don't you move out of here right this minute, then?" Her voice had an ugly, cutting edge to it.

Hélène recognized the taunt that lay behind her words. Tante Janine was trying to pressure her to stay and work in the nursery, or leave and be done with. Either way, she would make it look like it had been Hélène's choice.

Hélène clenched her fists. She wasn't about to fall into the trap that easily. Much as she wanted to, she couldn't just pack up her things and go. She had no money. She still needed a place to live. Jeanne's? she thought suddenly. She squashed that thought immediately. No, it wasn't fair to Jeanne. What she had to do was to make Tante Janine see reason. And assert her own position, making it clear that she was no pushover.

"And if I decide to go to work and still live here?" Hélène asked. "What then?"

"I'll throw you out."

"You can't do that."

Tante Janine smiled tightly. "Try me. It's your choice. The nursery or your job," she said.

"I'm going to stay here until I can afford to move. And I'm going to work," Hélène said.

She looked at Tante Janine for a long moment. What she said next was going to be a gamble. She wasn't sure just how far she could go, but she'd push it.

"According to Monsieur Lefèvre," Hélène said in a quiet voice, "you are my guardian—and Edmond's, too—until we are both twenty-one. Only under the power of guardianship, *which you would relinquish by throwing me out*, are you allowed to dispose of our property." Hélène forced herself to smile triumphantly. "If you throw me out, you'd no longer be my guardian, would you, Tante Janine? I could even take you to court and win Maman's house back. Of course, it isn't there anymore. There's just the new nursery. Since my

177

money—and Edmond's—was used to build it, we might end up owning it. Then you'd have competition right next door." She paused. "Would you like that, Tante Janine?" she asked softly.

Hélène had to say one thing for her aunt. Tante Janine knew when she was beaten. Pale-faced and angry, she marched stiffly out of the room.

9

Slowly life for Hélène became sweeter. Her world revolved around the shop. She went to work early every morning and left late at night. The wages were low but Madame Dupré had told her confidentially, "Danielle will be leaving in three months. You will get a small raise then."

In the meantime, Danielle was in charge of her. She taught Hélène how to use the pedal-operated sewing machine and the exact way to stitch and hem to Madame's satisfaction (Madame was far more demanding and exacting than Mademoiselle Gribius had ever been). Hélène caught on to the thousands of little jobs that Madame found it necessary to farm out to the girls. And she learned quickly. By the time a week had passed, she was more adept at the sewing machine than Danielle had ever been. Her eager mind soaked up the craft like a sponge.

But her favorite hours were after closing time. When everyone left the shop, she would stay behind, turn out all but one of the lights, and sit on the floor beside the counter. With her knees drawn up to her chin and a studious expression on her face, she would leaf through the precious back issues of Madame Dupré's fashion magazines. That was when Hélène would enter what she considered the "real" world, the world of style and fashion and international vitality that transcended national borders and natural boundaries. In silence she would study each page of each magazine. Each layout, each advertisement, each model, each dress, each pose, each photograph. Nothing escaped her sharp eye. She learned to detect the subtle differences among the designers. There were the greats—Odile Joly, Schiaparelli, Dior, Madame Grès, and Chanel—and a crop of talented young hopefuls. (She decided that when she had *her* magazine, she would devote one feature in each issue to new talent.) She became aware of each designer's "mark," each one's *style*. It was by this unique style that she was able to recognize their garments as easily as she could recognize persons by their faces, their walks, their mannerisms. She even became adept at predicting what Madame Grès might do next, and what Dior would definitely *not* do. (Although she couldn't in her wildest imagination have foreseen that Chanel would come out with *costume* jewelry.) She was, however, able to understand the subtle differences between Chanel's classical simplicity and Schiaparelli's boldness; Dior's elegance and Madame Grès's daring. And above all, there was the great Odile Joly, the grande dame of fashion, who reigned supreme among even the high chieftains of fashion. Somehow, she always managed to melt all the differences of the competition into a single fluid style. Her style was so distinctive, so different, and yet so elegantly subtle that it transcended pure magic and astounded all the other magicians of design.

Hélène absorbed and absorbed until she could absorb no more. And still she studied the magazines again and again until she found a tiny something she had overlooked—and then she absorbed that, too. Her favorite days were those when the postman delivered new issues of *Elle* or *L'Officiel* or *Paris Vogue*. Madame Dupré understood Hélène's excitement and let her have the first look at them.

With trembling fingers Hélène would rapidly tear off the brown wrapping paper and stare at the colorful, glossy covers with awe. Always she felt the thick paper with the palm of her hand before turning the pages. She loved feeling the luxurious, slick texture against her fingers.

Finally the day came when Hélène looked at a photograph and frowned. She said to herself: "I could do that better. I would have placed the model differently. I would have had her wear the Grès gown in the other photo instead of the Schiaparelli. I would have had the camera focus upward, from below, instead of just head-on." That was the moment she knew she was learning.

Madame Dupré watched Hélène's progress with interest.

There was no doubt in her mind: Hélène was a natural. A natural seamstress, a natural learner, a natural barometer of taste. Instinctively she could differentiate between the good and the bad. And under Madame Dupré's subtle tutelage— making Hélène think she was actually discovering everything by herself instead of being taught—Hélène learned to tell the difference between the good and the exceptional. Between the exceptional and the sublime.

One day Madame Dupré stopped at the sewing machine and silently watched Hélène at work. The girl had a deftness, a professional assurance in handling fabric, that usually came only from years of experience.

Hélène stopped sewing and looked up at her.

"Come upstairs to my apartment, Hélène. I would like to have a private talk with you."

Hélène nodded. "Oui, madame." Quickly she took the dress she was sewing out from under the needle, carefully folded it, and followed Madame Dupré upstairs. Nervously she wondered what she had done wrong.

When they got to the little apartment above the shop, Madame Dupré switched on the parlor lights and directed Hélène to one of the floral-chintz-covered chairs.

Hélène uncomfortably folded her hands in her lap and watched as her employer sat in the chair opposite and elegantly crossed her legs.

Madame Dupré hesitated a moment. "How long have you been working here now?" she asked.

Hélène looked at her dumbly. "I . . . I'm not sure, madame. A month?"

Madame Dupré smiled and shook her head. "*Three* months to the day," she corrected her.

Hélène's mouth hung open. "It . . . it doesn't seem possible!"

Madame Dupré smiled. "It does. When you become my age, the weeks can drag by like years."

Hélène nodded. How strange, she thought. Every minute she spent at Tante Janine's was an eternity, and yet months here seemed mere minutes.

"In two weeks, Danielle will be leaving. On that day you will take over her job completely."

Hélène's lips broke into a smile. "Oui, madame," she said.

Madame Dupré raised an eyebrow. The girl showed no

nervousness about the added responsibility. She was confident that she could do the job well.

"It appears that you like your job," Madame Dupré said slowly.

"Oui, madame. I have never been happier."

Madame Dupré looked at her shrewdly. "And yet you are not satisfied." It was a statement, not a question.

Hélène hesitated a moment. Then she nodded. "I am satisfied for right now, madame," she said carefully. "And I'm very grateful for the opportunity you've given me."

"Ah. But it's not what you really want to do, is it?"

Hélène shook her head. "Not really."

Madame Dupré leaned forward. Her eyes met Hélène's evenly. "Tell me about it. What is it that you want to do?"

Hélène started to say something, then stopped. She got up and walked over to the window, parted the lace curtains and looked down at the cobblestoned street and the row of stone houses. She turned to face Madame Dupré. "I can sew and stitch well, madame. I can even design clothes adequately. But I'll never be very good at it. I borrow too much from other people's work. But . . ." She paused and then continued in a low, earnest voice. "But I can *see* what's good. Instinctively I know how to put things together."

Madame Dupré nodded. The girl was wise beyond her years. "Go on," she said gently.

Hélène took a deep breath. "I want to return to Paris," she said fervently. "I want to start my own . . . fashion magazine."

Madame Dupré did not look surprised. She had felt the currents of Hélène's ambition and yearning stirring restlessly beneath the surface. Lately she had felt the current gathering strength. She sighed. Yes, she too once had a similar ambition. But now it was too late. Somehow she had become too entrenched in her comfortable life-style. Perhaps her ambition hadn't burned strongly enough. But Hélène's did.

"I wanted to move to Paris once," Madame Dupré said. There was a faraway look in her eyes.

Hélène looked surprised. "Why didn't you?"

Madame Dupré shrugged her shoulders elegantly. "One falls into a trap. One is too comfortable. One is afraid of adventure. Of starting anew." She paused. Suddenly her voice was very quiet. "Or one doesn't have enough talent."

Hélène stared at her. She had always thought Madame

Dupré was strong-willed and extremely talented. She didn't think there was anything she couldn't do, once set on it. Suddenly she remembered the first time she had gone into the shop, and the beautiful dress that was displayed in the window. The *copy* in the window, she corrected herself. Now she knew what it had been. A Grès.

Madame Dupré rose to her feet suddenly. "Come with me," she said.

Hélène got up and followed her into an elegant little bedroom. The walls were papered with a forget-me-not pattern; there were a pale blue dresser with a mirror and two big wardrobes.

Madame Dupré motioned for Hélène to sit down. "I want to show you something," she said softly. "I visited Paris once and brought something back." She opened one of the wardrobe doors and took out a wooden clothes hanger draped with a long sheet. She flung the sheet away.

Hélène let out a gasp. The gown had to be a Dior. It was the most beautiful garment she had ever seen. Even on the hanger it had a life of its own. The pale satin shimmered with a luminosity that came from within.

"It is beautiful, non?"

Hélène was speechless. She was barely capable of nodding. Then slowly, delicately, she reached out to touch the gown. She laid it carefully out on the bed and examined the design, the workmanship, the fabric. It was a culmination of everything that was genius. Slowly, reverently, she lifted a corner of it to her lips and kissed it.

Madame Dupré watched her. "Now do you understand that I am a . . . a failure?" she asked.

Hélène looked at her compassionately.

"Never would I be capable of creating something like that," Madame Dupré said in a whisper. "But oh, how I *longed* to. Now I've learned to accept my shortcomings. My lack of genius. But I learned it too late. After too much hungering. Strange, how every so often something reminds me of my failed ambition." She smiled painfully. "This time it was you."

Hélène nodded solemnly.

Suddenly Madame Dupré grasped Hélène's hands in her own. "Leave Saint-Nazaire!" she whispered. "As soon as you can! You are lucky. You know your ambitions. Your limitations. Leave and become successful with your magazine!"

Hélène swallowed. "Yes, madame. As soon as I can, I will."

Carefully Madame Dupré covered the gown with the sheet and hung it back inside the wardrobe. She snapped the door shut and they went out to the parlor. For a moment, neither of them spoke.

"I have promised you a raise," Madame Dupré said finally. She crossed the little room to a delicate desk and opened the top. She took a thin booklet out of a pigeonhole and handed it to Hélène.

"What's this?" She looked at it curiously. "It's . . . a bankbook!"

"In your name. I have taken the liberty of depositing the first month's difference between your salary and your raise. Bank it every month from now on." She looked into Hélène's eyes. "For Paris," she said softly.

"Yes . . ." Hélène whispered. "For Paris!"

The night was dark and cool as she walked home. The road to the nursery was treacherous because it was hard to see the ruts and bumps without any moonlight. But Hélène liked the quiet solitude of the night and the distant, reassuring rumbling of the surf. It gave her time to think. To plan. Madame Dupré was right—she would have to leave Saint-Nazaire soon. There was no future here. Sadly she recalled Madame Dupré's own shattered dreams and lost hopes, a lesson to remember. She mustn't fall into the same trap. She must keep her ambition burning.

She rounded a familiar bend more by instinct than by sight. In the distance she could see the lights glowing in the Brocqs' house. She put her hands in the pockets of her coat. Yes, she thought, she'd learned a lot today. She smiled to herself. She was judging each day by what she had learned.

"There's my pretty!" a voice hissed out of the darkness.

Hélène suddenly froze and her heart pounded against her ribs. Pierre! In terror, her eyes searched the darkness around her, but she couldn't see anything. What was he doing out here? It was still a good kilometer till she'd be home. Suddenly she knew what he was doing here. Lying in wait. Setting his trap. For her.

The whisper came again. *"My pretty. Pierre is waiting!"*

Hélène whirled around. "Where are you?" she cried out.

The foliage on the trees to her left suddenly rustled. She turned to face them. But it was only the wind.

"I'm over here, my pretty!" Now the voice seemed to come from her right. She whirled in that direction.

"No, no, no. Pretty mustn't run! Pierre is in front of you!"

She drew back instinctively—right into his arms. He clamped them around her.

He hadn't been in front of her! He'd tricked her! He'd been behind her all along!

She started to scream, but a cold hand covered her mouth.

"Pretty better not scream," he whispered, his breath hot against her neck.

She let out a muffled wail. Her mind raced. She had to do something. Anything. For a moment she sagged in his arms. He loosened his grip in surprise, and suddenly she dived out of his grasp. He tried to grab her again, but she twisted around and brought her knee up in his groin. She could hear him grunt. Then, as fast as her legs could carry her, she started off across the dark fields. She plunged past trees whose branches tore at her dress and scratched her face. Every branch held a special terror. To Hélène they seemed like fingers, as she ran out of their reach. She tripped over a rock and fell, and for a fleeting instant she thought Pierre had tripped her. With a grunt she struggled back to her feet and continued running, never stopping to listen to see if he was following. She had lost all sense of direction.

After a while she felt as if her lungs were going to burst. For a moment she stopped running, her breasts heaving as she swallowed mouthfuls of air. Her heart hammered like it had gone out of control.

"Pierre's waiting!"

"No!" she screamed, and covered her ears. "No no no no no *no!*"

And suddenly she felt herself slipping into nothingness. For a moment she swayed unsteadily, and then she could feel herself falling. She was aware that he was very near, but she wasn't quite sure where. She thought she could feel his thighs clamping around her face. It was all so . . . so dreamlike. So unreal. In the distance she heard breathing. It sounded shallow and faraway.

After a while things slowly focused again. She felt drops of warm liquid falling on her face. Had it begun to rain? she wondered in surprise. Then the pressure left the sides of her face and she heard a noise moving away in the underbrush.

She moaned and lay there without moving. He was gone. She shook her head to clear it and realized that there was liquid on her lips, too. For a moment she caught the taste of it. It was strangely salty.

Suddenly she knew what it was. Semen. In disgust, she started to wipe it away with her wrist. But she never finished. The nausea rose instantly. Before she could bend over, she threw up.

When the lights in the shop went on, Hélène looked up and blinked. Madame Dupré was standing in the doorway, a coat over her nightgown, her hair in metal curlers. Her eyes were red and swollen; she looked like she'd just awakened. "What are you doing here?" she asked. "It's after midnight!" Then she sucked in her breath. "What's happened to you? Your face—it's got scratches all over it!"

Hélène trembled. She looked away. "I couldn't stay at home, madame. So I came here. I tried to let myself in quietly. I'm sorry. I didn't mean to wake you."

"That's all right. I heard noises and came down to investigate." Madame Dupré came close and examined Hélène's face. Her elegant features suddenly contorted with rage. Her voice was sharp. "Who did this to you? You look as if you were beaten!"

"Please . . ." Hélène begged. "Don't make any trouble."

"Trouble!" Madame Dupré snorted. "Somebody certainly made trouble, but it wasn't I!" She looked at Hélène. "Well?" she demanded. "Was it one of the boys?"

Hélène shook her head slowly.

Suddenly Madame Dupré's eyes widened. "Don't tell me it happened at home!"

Hélène nodded.

Madame Dupré frowned crossly. "Was it your aunt?"

"Please . . ." Hélène's voice was a small, timid whisper.

"All right, we won't talk about it, then." Madame Dupré shook her head. "But tell me—is this why you wanted the job so badly? To get away?"

Hélène nodded again. "I had to get away from home, madame. I was trying to save up to get my own apartment."

Madame Dupré wrapped her arms around Hélène. "You poor girl! Don't worry, you won't have to go back. And you won't have to spend your money on an apartment, either. You must use it to get to Paris!"

Hélène nodded. "But where will I live?"

"I know just the place."

Hélène looked at her questioningly.

Madame Dupré smiled and pointed at the ceiling. "Upstairs, in the garret. There's an old iron bed up there and a few sticks of old furniture. It will be your own room."

Hélène brightened. "Really, madame?"

Madame Dupré nodded. "Come with me. I'll get you some sheets and pillowcases. Tomorrow you can go back to your aunt's and get your things." She wagged a warning finger. "But don't you go alone!" she said sternly.

"Non, madame. I'll have my brother's fiancée come with me."

"Bon. It is settled, then. Come along. Let us see how you like your new room."

They went up two flights of stairs. The garret was on the third floor, right under the beams of the eaves. The roof was steep, and they could stand up only in the center of the room. It smelled musty and the air was full of dust. Clotheslines crisscrossed it from one end to the other.

"You'll have to clean it up a bit," Madame Dupré said as she threw open one of the little dormer windows. "But it should be comfortable enough."

Hélène nodded. "I don't know how to thank you."

Madame Dupré shrugged. "It's nothing. Just try to get a good night's sleep. And take tomorrow off." She clapped the dust off her hands and walked over to the door. "Good night, Hélène."

"Good night, madame."

Hélène waited until Madame Dupré's footsteps disappeared down the stairs. Then she walked over to the open window and looked out. Over the rooftops she could see down to the dimly lit quay where the fishing boats tied up. Right now, it was strangely deserted, with barely a boat in sight. Beyond it, the bay was dark, melting into an equally dark sky. She smiled to herself. From up here she would be able to see Edmond's ship when the fleet came in.

Jeanne flapped the dust rag out the window and made a face. She coughed and turned to Hélène. "Sprinkle the floor with some more water before you go on sweeping. Otherwise we'll be choking to death!"

They were dressed almost identically, in Jeanne's old housedresses, with scarves tied around their heads.

Jeanne shook her head and giggled. "If we don't look like two housewives."

Hélène smiled and bent down as she carefully swept out a corner with the horsehair broom. "Once it's cleaned up, it should look rather nice."

Jeanne looked around the garret. "It's certainly big enough for one person," she said in an impressed voice. "And just think! It's a place of your own." Her voice suddenly became angry. "At least you'll never have to go back to those horrible people anymore!"

Hélène sighed and sank down into a broken chair. "I can't tell Edmond the truth though, Jeanne. That hurts me, because we've never kept any secrets from each other. But I'm scared . . ."

Jeanne looked over at her. "I know. You don't have to worry about me—I won't breathe a word. But what *are* you going to tell him?"

"Part of the truth, at least. That I couldn't bear living with Tante Janine any longer. That this place is very convenient, since I only have to go downstairs to go to work. That I'm just biding my time till I go to Paris."

"Good. Then our stories will match."

Suddenly Hélène came over to Jeanne and embraced her. "When we first met, you told me that you wanted us to be friends," she said softly. "Well, I want you to know how happy I am that we are."

"I know," Jeanne replied. She gave Hélène a squeeze. "But we'd better get working. Edmond will be back on shore this weekend. We want him to be impressed when he sees this place, don't we?"

Hélène nodded. She was studying Jeanne.

"What are you staring at?" Jeanne asked.

Hélène smiled and turned away. "Nothing," she said vaguely.

But that wasn't quite true. She had been studying Jeanne's height and build and figure. Her seamstress mind instinctively appraised it and sized it. Tonight, after Jeanne left, she would begin designing her wedding dress. After all, the wedding was only four months off.

There was a knock at the door.

Hélène turned toward it. "Come in," she called.

Madame Dupré came in carrying a wooden tray covered with a napkin. "I thought you both might use some lunch," she said with an apologetic smile. "I took the liberty of making you a little something." She set the tray down on the bed. Then she looked around. "Good gracious! I never thought this place would clean up so well!"

"We've barely started," Hélène said.

"Perhaps you should take up interior decoration instead of fashion."

Hélène smiled. "That's stretching it a bit, I'm afraid. But I have a feeling about this place." She gave the room a proprietorial look. "I guess everybody does about the first place of their own."

"Yes," Madame Dupré said. "I'll never forget mine. A small room with peeling wallpaper. Chinese flowers . . ." She made a limp gesture with her hand. "Anyway, I'm sure you have better things to do than listen to an old woman rambling on. I'll leave you two in peace." When she reached the door she turned around. "Oh, Hélène . . ."

"Oui, madame?"

"I got a letter from the Comtesse de Léger this morning, confirming her fittings. I don't believe I told you."

"No, madame."

Madame Dupré sighed. "Every year the Comtesse goes to Paris and orders an entire wardrobe from the couturiers. Unknown to everyone but me, she never wears her good clothes except for special occasions. She has me make a copy of each of the garments she buys. This way she has an identical—cheaper—wardrobe to 'wear around the house.' This project usually takes me four weeks. I close the shop for the duration, since the work is done at the de Léger château." She paused. "I always take my best seamstress with me. I am planning to take you."

Hélène's eyes shone. "I'd love to go, madame. When is it?"

"The entire month of September."

Hélène's face fell.

"What's the matter? I thought you'd be pleased."

"I am. It's just that Jeanne and Edmond . . ." Hélène turned around and looked desperately at Jeanne. "They're getting married then, and—"

Jeanne interrupted. "Hélène, I want you to go," she said

firmly. "Edmond and I will postpone our plans. We'll marry in December instead."

"But—"

"Quiet! This is the opportunity of a lifetime. You've never been in a château, have you?"

Hélène didn't answer. She didn't want to remember back that far, not to a Nazi-occupied château on the Loire, and Catherine and Marie . . .

"Besides, who knows?" Jeanne said lightly. "You might meet a handsome Comte." She glanced at Madame Dupré. "There is one, isn't there?"

"Oh . . . yes. But he's married to the Comtesse. However, he does have a rather handsome young son, the future Comte. His name is Hubert, I believe. Yes, Hubert de Léger." She looked thoughtfully at Hélène. "Actually, he's only a year to two older than you are."

10

The sky was cloudy and looked like rain when Hélène and Madame Dupré got off the train in Bordeaux. They were met on the platform by an elderly white-haired man in a dark blue uniform with brass buttons, gleaming high boots, and a visored cap. He recognized Madame Dupré instantly and clicked his heels smartly, giving a low bow. He gestured to her luggage.

Madame Dupré smiled. "Bonjour, André. Yes, those are ours."

Quickly the suitcases were loaded onto a trolley and André led the way out to the parking lot, where an old black Citroën limousine was waiting. André held the rear doors open for them, stowed the luggage in the trunk, and then got in behind the wheel. As they drove off, Hélène pressed the velour seat with her hand. It was firm but soft. She smiled to herself. This was luxury indeed.

They rode slowly through the narrow streets of the town.

Hélène pressed her nose against the window. Bordeaux was much larger than Saint-Nazaire. In a way, it seemed part of a different country. The stone houses were large and ornate. Some of them even had balconies. There were many shops and cars. They passed a bustling open-air marketplace where bright umbrellas and awnings had been set up over tables piled high with cheeses, breads, fruits, and vegetables. She could see intricately braided heads of garlic hanging from the vegetable stalls.

They drove through the dark tunnellike arch of the Great Clock Tower. This was a bizarre building. On its facade, high above the arch, was a big square clock. And even higher up, in another arch flanked by stone turrets, hung the big bell, proudly silent after its morning's cry that harvesttime had come once again to the vineyards of Bordeaux. When they drove back out into the daylight, Hélène twisted around in her seat and looked out the rear window. After a moment, she could see the clock on this side. Its giant gold-colored hands read five-thirty.

Soon they left the town behind and headed north. Green pastures, vast pine forests, and timeless villages flew past in a blur. They had to slow down whenever the road cut through the villages, and then Hélène would catch sight of ancient stone houses and window boxes overflowing with pale pink impatiens and deep red geraniums. Often the countryside opened up into gently sloping hills that looked as if someone had run a comb through them. These were the vineyards that were the heart and soul of Gascony. After they had traveled a while longer, Hélène turned to Madame Dupré. "How much farther is it?"

Madame Dupré patted her hand. "Another hour and a half. So you just relax. The de Léger châteaux are in the Médoc."

Hélène perked up. Her voice was incredulous. "*Are*? You mean there is more than one?"

"There are two." Madame Dupré settled back comfortably. "There are the Château Hautecloque-de Léger and the Château Loustalot-de Léger."

"And both of them are real castles?"

Madame Dupré nodded. "Both of them, and each with its own vineyard. But the Comte and the Comtesse live in the Château Hautecloque. It's the larger and by far more luxurious one." She smiled slightly. "Also, it's the more prestigious."

An hour later, they arrived at the edge of the de Léger estates and Madame Dupré pointed out the sights. These vineyards were by far the biggest they'd yet come across. The gently sloping hills seemed to stretch from horizon to horizon.

"It's the single biggest vineyard in all of France," Madame Dupré said.

Hélène nodded. She was speechless. Never had she seen so many furrowed slopes in her life.

"Look quickly! There on your left!" Madame Dupré pointed to the window on Hélène's side of the car.

Hélène turned her head and gazed out. All around, workers were swarming through the chest-high rows of vines, bending over and picking grapes, looking up at the ever-darkening sky with worried eyes. She noticed that a complex maze of paved roads crisscrossed the vineyard. And in the distance, bathed by the tranquil waters of a large moat, was a sprawling château. Medieval stone turrets and crumbling retaining walls merged nicely with the elegant additions of the Renaissance.

"That is the Château Loustalot-de Léger," Madame Dupré said. "What you see all around it are more than two thousand acres of grapes."

"It's so . . . so enormous!" Hélène said.

Madame Dupré nodded. "Two years ago the château produced almost two million bottles of wine. Can you imagine!"

Hélène shook her head in awe. "The de Légers must be very rich," she said.

Madame Dupré smiled but said nothing. Yes, she thought. They were very rich indeed. But the Comtesse had inherited the typical shrewd frugality of the French. Instead of spending an additional ten thousand francs at the couturiers' for a second wardrobe, she was having copies made for three thousand. It was unbelievable. A woman worth multimillions went out of her way to save seven thousand francs!

"And the Château Hautecloque-de Léger?" Hélène asked. "What about it?"

"It is a little farther to the north. It covers only two hundred and thirty acres. We'll be there soon."

Just as they got there, heavy splatters of raindrops were starting to fall. André grunted and mumbled something about the grapes. He slowed the big car down and they drove through the gates of the château.

Hélène leaned down and peered up through the arcs of glass that the thumping windshield wipers were clearing. She caught a blurry glimpse of a large stone plaque on top of the gate. Carved in relief were a lion and a salamander supporting a crest between them. The crest of the de Légers.

They rode down a long poplar-lined drive. To either side of it was the vast park attributed to Le Nôtre, the landscape architect who had designed the gardens of Versailles. Even through the heavy sheets of rain Hélène could see the Château Hautecloque-de Léger. She took a deep breath. It was unlike any château she had ever imagined. There were no towers, no turrets. This was an elegantly noble building, and yet there was a haughty coldness about its perfect symmetry. It consisted of a narrow pavilion flanked by two wings that had larger pavilions at each end. It was three stories high, its steep dark roofs rounded off to support lanterns. In the center was a sweeping marble staircase.

They drove around the building and pulled up to a small door in the back. André produced a huge black umbrella, hurried out, held their doors open, and kept them covered as they ran to the building.

A fat red-faced woman dressed in white flung the door open and they rushed inside. André hurried back to the car.

Hélène looked around. They were in a massive kitchen. Copper and steel pots and pans hung from the walls and ceiling. At a wooden table, a young girl with her sleeves rolled up was expertly kneading dough. Hélène couldn't help but feel a certain disappointment that they hadn't pulled up to the majestic staircase in the front.

The fat woman was obviously a cook. After she closed the door, her face broke into a cheerful smile and she wiped her large hands on her apron. "Bonjour, madame," she said in a friendly voice. "Did you have a pleasant journey?"

Madame Dupré returned her smile and brushed some raindrops off her sleeves. "Bonjour, Thérèse. Yes, the journey was fine until the rain began."

Thérèse lifted her red hands in despair. "This weather! We have had such a dry summer, and now all this rain! It is not good for the poor grapes." She shrugged her shoulders philosophically and sighed. "I suppose you cannot hope for every year to be good."

192

"I suppose not," Madame Dupré said.

"The Comtesse has instructed me to put you in your usual room," Thérèse said. "Is that all right with you?"

Madame Dupré smiled. "That will be fine, merci."

"Then I will take you upstairs at once. I'm sure you're anxious to wash up and change."

Madame Dupré looked at Hélène. "Come along. Our luggage will be brought to us."

Hélène followed them up a steep staircase to the servants' quarters. They were located on the top floor of the château, under the gently rounded roof. Their rooms were identical, connected through an adjoining door.

Hélène sat down heavily on her bed and looked around miserably; the plaster walls were cracked and the furniture was comfortable but plain. There was one circular window so low to the floor that she would have to bend down in order to look out.

Once again Hélène couldn't help but feel a bit resentful. She had expected a stately suite with a canopied bed and rich furnishings. She bit down on her lip. She must be careful to say nothing. The chauffeured limousine aside, it was obvious that they were considered slightly superior to the rest of the servants but far below the lordly station of the de Légers.

Late the next afternoon the Comtesse summoned them to the Embroidered Room. A liveried manservant led them through the house and down a stone staircase. This staircase, unlike the servants', was delicately carved with fruits and flowers. Hélène saw that the interior of the château was lordly indeed. The rich architecture was well-preserved, looked almost fresh and new. Everywhere there were seventeenth- and eighteenth-century paintings, Flemish tapestries, Chinese lacquered commodes, and Aubusson carpets. The exquisite furnishings were of the Louis XV style. "All genuine!" Madame Dupré whispered.

Hélène let out a cry as the manservant opened the giant double doors of the Embroidered Room. The walls were covered in red-and-gold-painted moldings set with the fanciful needlework panels that gave the room its name. Again, the furnishings were Louis XV bergères and fauteuils. But there were no paintings in the Embroidered Room. Instead, Chinese and Japanese porcelains were everywhere. There were blanc-de-chine figurines, covered vases, and mandarin dolls. A delicate table held a lavish arrangement of flowers. Seated on an embroidered settee behind it was the Comtesse de La Brissac et de Léger.

The Comtesse could trace her genealogy all the way back through the Brissac-Orléans; one of her far-distant ancestors was Anne de Bretagne, the wife of King Louis XII. The Comtesse was thin and elegant, as haughty-looking, Hélène thought, as the facade of the château. Her hair was uniformly gray and immaculately set. Her pale skin was almost porcelain-toned, but her hands, in which she held a small Maltese spaniel, attested to her years. They were spotted with a faint sprinkling of age spots. She had a very distinguished Roman nose, a perpetual frown, and a network of tiny wrinkles in the corners of her cool, stony dark eyes. She sat stiffly erect and wore a simple white silk blouse and a beautiful pale yellow suit. A Chanel, Hélène thought.

Madame Dupré curtsied politely. "Bonjour, Comtesse," she said formally.

"Bonjour, madame." The Comtesse's clipped voice was loud and clear. She pronounced each syllable precisely.

"May I introduce my new seamstress, Hélène Junot." Madame Dupré gestured gracefully to Hélène.

Hélène curtsied as Madame Dupré had instructed her to, but her movements were somewhat awkward. She could feel a blush coming over her face. "Bonjour, Comtesse," she whispered nervously.

The cool dark eyes swept imperiously over Hélène. "But she is very young!" the Comtesse said with surprise.

"Oui, Comtesse," Madame Dupré said quickly. "She is the most talented seamstress I have ever had. She will go far."

"Is that so?" Once again the Comtesse's dark eyes looked at Hélène, this time with keen interest. "She is rather an attractive young lady."

Hélène could feel another flush of embarrassment coloring her face. She rarely received compliments, and when she did, she didn't know how to accept them graciously, so she remained silent. From the Comtesse's pleased expression, Hélène knew that her silence had been misinterpreted as modesty.

The Comtesse pulled a bell rope that hung beside the settee. A moment later a young maid in black uniform appeared soundlessly.

"Lise, I want you to give Madame Dupré and her associate all the assistance they may require."

"Oui, Comtesse."

"Bon. You may take them upstairs to the sewing room. Then I want you to bring them the clothes that have arrived from the couturiers. Everything except for the gowns."

"Oui, Comtesse."

"That is all." The Comtesse made an imperious gesture of dismissal.

Madame Dupré glanced at Hélène. Once again they curtsied, then followed Lise out of the room.

The sewing room was on the second floor of the northeastern wing. At one time it must have been a sumptuous bedroom. There were high carved ceilings, boiserie-paneled walls, and big mullioned windows that allowed maximum light. Sheet-draped objects stood around the room like ghostly white sculptures. The room was cold and dusty and needed airing. Hélène went over to the windows and threw them open. A blast of fresh air and a sprinkling of raindrops came blowing in. For a moment she stood there looking out at the sweeping view of Le Nôtre's park.

With a snapping motion of her wrist Madame Dupré went around the room pulling off the white sheets. Hélène saw that they had draped the sewing machine, a big paper-covered table, the dressmaker's dummy, a coatrack in the corner, a three-paneled screen (behind which the Comtesse could dress or undress with delicacy), and a tall three-paneled gilt-framed mirror. Then Madame Dupré crossed the room to the carved wardrobes and threw open the doors. Inside were bolts of fabric, threads, needles, pincushions, shears, trimmings, and all other tools of the dressmaker's trade.

"The Comtesse insists on many fittings," Madame Dupré told Hélène in a low voice. "That is why the sewing room is not in the servants' quarters!"

Hélène pushed her plate away. "I'm full," she announced.

Madame Dupré looked at her sharply and wagged her finger. "A lady never says 'I'm full,' " she said sternly. "In society a lady says 'I've had plenty, thank you.' You must not underestimate the importance of these social graces. Once you get to Paris, they can make the difference between success and failure."

Hélène nodded and filed this bit of information. They were

having dinner on the little table in Madame Dupré's room. This arrangement was the result of a bizarre etiquette that placed them in a no-man's-land: their social status was far below the de Légers' but somewhat above the servants', so they could dine with neither. Madame Dupré explained to Hélène that if there had been a governess in the house, she would have been an acceptable dinner companion for them, but since there were no small children there was no governess, and thus they had to eat alone in Madame Dupré's room. Hélène was somewhat annoyed at such intricacies of the social ladder and wondered how many rungs there could possibly be.

Carefully Madame Dupré placed her fork and knife in an X on her plate, signifying that she, too, was finished. Delicately she dabbed her lips with her napkin.

"Thérèse will bring us coffee and dessert later," she said. "She knows I like it a few hours after dinner."

Hélène nodded, sipping delicately at her wine. "I can't wait until tomorrow," she said. "The dresses are so beautiful! And the Chanel suits—I can't believe their quality. I'd have never thought of sewing tiny chains into the hems to make them fall better."

Madame Dupré nodded. "Chanel is a genius," she said simply. She rose and walked over to the little round window. She bent down, parted the filmy curtains, and looked out. She let the curtains drop back in place and turned to Hélène. "It has stopped raining. Shall we take a walk?"

Hélène pushed back her chair and got to her feet. "I'd love some fresh air. Let me get my coat."

They went downstairs and walked out through the kitchen door. It was still daylight, but dusk would soon begin to fall. The rain had made the dull autumn lawn appear green and springlike. A fine mist had settled over the countryside. The clouds overhead were thinning and looked like a gray watercolor wash. All at once they parted and a glimmer of weak sunshine broke through.

Madame Dupré glanced at the sky and smiled. "Perhaps there is hope for the tender grapes after all," she said. "Let's take a look around."

When they had walked for some minutes, the sprawling stables suddenly came into view. Hélène marveled at their size. "The de Légers must have a lot of horses to need so many stables."

Madame Dupré smiled. "They do. The de Légers pride themselves on horsemanship. They hold fox hunts and even race horses." She stopped talking as they both heard the approach of pounding hoofbeats. They turned around.

Hélène let out a shriek and threw herself at Madame Dupré. A magnificent black Arabian stallion was charging across the grass toward them. It looked as if the equestrian had lost control, but at the last moment he expertly drew in the reins and the big horse whinnied and skidded to a halt barely a meter away from them. Bits of earth flew up all around. Hélène could feel the animal's heat. It must have been galloping for some time.

The shadow of the rider fell across Hélène and she looked up. He was undeniably handsome, with dark hair, a determined cleft chin, and deep, flashing eyes. They were the same eyes as the Comtesse's, but whereas hers were cold, his were mischievous. Under the serge riding habit she could sense a wiry, athletic physique, and his bearing bespoke an aristocratic heritage. This had to be the Comtesse's son.

Hubert de Léger grinned suddenly and touched the little visor of his cap with his riding crop. "Ah, Madame Dupré," he said.

Madame Dupré gave a curt little nod. "You scared us half to death," she said with quiet fury.

He ignored her and nodded his chin at Hélène. "Who are you?"

Hélène could feel his dark eyes boring through her. There was something virile and powerful about him that made her suddenly afraid. She felt paralyzed. "Hélène Junot," she murmured softly, and looked away.

"You're a lot better-looking than that woman Madame Dupré brought with her last year." He looked at Madame Dupré and smiled disarmingly. "Isn't she?"

"I think it's all a matter of personal taste," Madame Dupré replied stiffly. "I wouldn't know."

Hubert de Léger threw back his head and laughed heartily, showing strong white teeth. Then his expression became serious as he looked at Hélène. "Do you ride?"

Hélène looked confused. "You mean . . . horses?"

He grinned easily. "What else is there?"

"I . . . I've never tried."

"It's easy to learn." He kept his hands on the reins; the stallion was restless.

"I'm not sure I like horses," she said quickly.

"You will," he said confidently. "You'd cut a fine figure on a horse. We have many in the stables. Some of them are quite gentle. Perhaps I should teach you to ride." He paused. "You should be flattered."

Hélène looked flustered. She fidgeted with her hands and turned her face away. "Maybe some other day," she murmured.

"Tomorrow?" he said quickly.

"No, I'm afraid I've work to do tomorrow," she said firmly, then looked at Madame Dupré, clearly wanting the woman's backup.

Madame Dupré took her cue. "I'm afraid your mother would be very displeased if her garments weren't finished on time."

He grinned slyly and bowed to Madame Dupré. "But I know better. You never work after six o'clock, madame." Then he looked at Hélène. "We'll have the lesson here tomorrow at half-past."

Before Hélène could refuse again, he neatly smacked the stallion with his crop and dug in his spurs. Instantly horse and rider went flying across the lawn, hooves pounding and kicking up pieces of earth. Soon he disappeared.

Hélène turned to Madame Dupré. "What do I do now?" she moaned.

Madame Dupré shrugged. "Hubert does not easily take no for an answer. He has inherited the determination of the Brissac-Orléans."

Hélène looked uncomfortable. "Perhaps I should go and speak with him later."

Madame Dupré shook her head. "That would be a waste of time. He is charming but evasive. You can search everywhere, but you'll never find him until six-thirty tomorrow afternoon. I'm afraid you'll just have to go."

11

A little after six o'clock the next afternoon, Madame Dupré chaperoned Hélène as far as the stables and helped her into one of the riding habits that were kept on hand for guests. When Hélène was fully dressed, Madame Dupré stood back to study the effect. She frowned thoughtfully. "It's a little big in the bust, but otherwise it suits you quite handsomely." She stepped closer to rearrange the wisps of veil that hung off the top hat. "Yes, *quite* handsomely," she repeated with satisfaction.

Hélène walked over to the tilted dressing-room mirror and stood in front of it awkwardly. She stared at her reflection. The outfit *was* beautiful. The long black skirt was just short enough to show off the gleaming boots that had been murder to pull on and that didn't quite fit. They were too narrow in the ankles—"A lady really needs custom-made boots," Madame Dupré had growled as she helped Hélène struggle into them. The black coat and white blouse were slightly too big, but elegantly cut, and the black bow tie was a dressy touch. Still, Hélène felt ill-at-ease, as if wearing a costume she didn't belong in.

They went out into the pine-paneled saddle room, fragrant with the smells of leather and wood. A glass-fronted vitrine was filled with racing trophies and dressage ribbons, and the walls were hung with tack, saddles, brass hunting horns, and framed engravings of horses that the de Légers had raced at Chantilly and Longchamps.

Hélène took one look at the paraphernalia and turned to go back into the dressing room. "Maybe I'd just better—"

Madame Dupré caught her arm. "Oh, no, you don't! You are going to have to go through with it."

"But—"

"Silence!" Madame Dupré gestured in agitation. "Just be yourself! Right now you're too stiff and self-conscious. Relax!

Don't give anything a second thought." Then her voice softened. "Remember, you look lovely."

"I'm hungry."

Madame Dupré rolled her eyes. "A little dieting won't hurt," she said between clenched teeth. "You can stand to lose a few pounds."

Just then they heard approaching hoofbeats outside.

"Out you go," Madame Dupré said firmly. She pushed Hélène toward the door. "There's nothing to be afraid of. Have fun and . . . be careful." She gave Hélène an obscure look.

Hélène blushed. Silently she cursed herself. She was blushing all the time lately. She'd have to find some way to bring it under control. It wouldn't do to walk around with a red face half the time. But what had Madame Dupré meant about being careful? Careful of what? The horse or . . . Hubert?

When he saw her, Hubert de Léger expertly swung down off his saddle and strode toward her, leading his Arabian by the reins. "You look marvelous in that getup, but of course, I *knew* you would."

"Thank you," she said coldly. Her lips trembled angrily at his arrogant self-confidence.

"Come," he said. "I will tie up Sheik here and have a boy bring your horse around. We'll stay in the corral for a while."

She nodded nervously and he called out to one of the stableboys. A few minutes later, her horse was led out. It was a huge chestnut mare with a sidesaddle. Hélène looked up at it and cringed. "It . . . it looks so high."

"You'll manage."

"If you say so," she said doubtfully.

For the next half-hour he taught her only to mount and dismount. She had the sneaking suspicion that this exercise was being practiced so diligently because it gave him the opportunity to put his arms around her, hold her by the hips, and "accidentally" brush against her as he lifted her up. With surprise, she found that she rather liked the feel of his body against hers. She sensed a certain rough power in him, a cruel streak perhaps, but to her he was gentle and polite. Several times his face was close to hers, and for a few seconds they would stare at each other. Then she would look quickly away and he would continue with the lessons as if nothing had happened.

He was playing a game, she thought, smiling to herself. Two could play such a game. She would simply alter the rules and play a game of her own—learning quickly how to mount and dismount. She was strangely pleased when she saw his disappointment over her quick progress. Hélène one, the hungry lion zero, she thought.

"Now we ride," Hubert said at last. "Just a slow trot around the corral for practice, and then once around the park." He reached into his pocket for a lump of sugar and held it out to the mare. She nuzzled his hand as she took the sugar gently from him.

Hélène practiced riding around the corral. Then slowly she was graduated to the park. She had to admit that she enjoyed it immensely. It took concentration and skill, and she was catching on quickly. For a moment she even brought the mare to a canter, and the wind felt exhilarating against her face.

When they returned to the stables, Hubert told Hélène to stay put. Then he leaned low over the Arabian's neck, dug in his spurs, and headed toward a fence. Hélène drew in her breath. He was going to try to jump the fence! She saw that there was a series of hurdles in varying heights inside the enclosure.

Neatly the Arabian leaped over the fence and Hubert took it through its paces over the hurdles. The horse cleared each one. Hélène shook her head unbelievingly. Hubert was showing off for her, she knew, and dangerously so. Yet it was a beautiful, graceful demonstration of the unity of man and beast.

The hurdles completed, he headed the stallion back over the fence and galloped toward Hélène. When he drew up alongside her, he looked at her questioningly. She said nothing, but she thawed with a smile. Apparently satisfied with that reaction, he hopped to the ground and motioned for her to dismount. They handed their reins to two stableboys.

Hubert looked at Hélène. "Are you tired?"

She nodded. "Yes, but it's a rather thrilling tiredness."

He nodded. "I know what you mean. Feel sore from the saddle?"

She looked at him challengingly. "Not a bit."

He grinned. "You will tomorrow."

Together they walked across the park back to the château. Dusk was at hand and the sky was turning deep purple. For a few minutes they were silent. He still carried his riding crop and kept slapping it against his boot.

"I made you miss dinner," he said finally. "You may have it with me."

She looked at him. "I'm not hungry."

He smiled. "I won't take no for an answer."

"But . . . I'd have to get changed." She gestured at her riding skirt.

"Then get changed."

She paused. "No," she said firmly. "I'm afraid I can't." She shook her head. "It wouldn't be right."

He looked at her queerly and stopped tapping his boot with the crop. "What wouldn't?"

"My having dinner with you."

"Why?" He looked at her with amusement. "Because I'm a de Léger?"

She flushed. "Yes," she said softly.

But he was very persuasive. She could have countered him if he had ordered her to dine with him. But he hadn't. Instead, he threw himself at her mercy and begged. Finally she laughed. It was impossible to refuse. She suspected that he knew this was the only way she'd agree to it. But she no longer really cared. Too much virility and a potential cruel streak aside, he was very charming.

When they reached the house, they parted company for an hour. She ran upstairs, waited for one of the maids to come out of the bathroom they shared (what took her so long!) and quickly drew a bath. For several minutes she luxuriated in the tub, then hurried to her room and dressed with care. When she was finished, she looked in the mirror approvingly. The dress was black and plain, almost severe, but it was acceptable for anything from taking a walk to attending a funeral. At any rate, it was the only decent thing she owned. In her excitement she'd forgotten to close the connecting door between her room and Madame Dupré's. With a start she realized that Madame Dupré was watching her with amusement from the doorway.

"Do I . . . look all right?" Hélène asked hesitantly.

"That depends on where you are going."

"Downstairs. Hubert has asked me to dine with him."

"In that case, you look beautiful," Madame Dupré said. She frowned slightly. "But a bit severe."

Hélène looked at her in panic. "What do you mean?"

"We'll have to break up the gloominess of all that black. Black is elegant, but not by itself." Madame Dupré reached behind her neck and unfastened one of the thin gold chains she wore. "Here, I'll lend you this."

Hélène shook her head. "I couldn't."

Madame Dupré smiled. "Don't worry. You won't break it."

Hélène nodded. "I'll be very careful with it."

Madame Dupré smiled and fastened the chain around Hélène's neck. Hélène had never looked better. There was a color in her face that did not come just from riding. It was a flush of happiness and excitement. Love? she thought suddenly. She hoped not. Hubert de Léger was too wild. Too youthful and playful for a sensitive girl like Hélène.

The same manservant who had taken them to see the Comtesse arrived to escort Hélène downstairs. Suddenly Madame Dupré reached out, grabbed Hélène's hand, and squeezed it. "Enjoy yourself," she said. Then her voice dropped to a whisper. "Remember your manners."

Eagerly Hélène nodded. "I will," she replied quietly. Then she was gone.

Hubert was waiting for her in the Salon de la Rotonde on the first floor. He crossed the Savonnerie carpet and looked at her appreciatively. "We'll have to wait a few minutes. My mother and father will be right down."

Hélène's pulse seemed to stop. "You mean . . . they haven't eaten yet, either?"

He shook his head. "No. We usually dine late." He smiled. "Don't worry. They do not bite."

Nervously Hélène fingered Madame Dupré's necklace. She had counted on dining alone with Hubert, not with the Comte and the Comtesse. She hadn't even met the Comte yet, but the Comtesse had unnerved her enough. She was too imperious, too studiously elegant and refined. Her cold dark eyes frightened Hélène. For an instant she was tempted to murmur her excuses and flee. Instead, in a voice that sounded as if it belonged to someone else she said, "What a lovely painting," and gestured to one of the gilt-framed canvases on the pale blue moiré-covered walls.

"Let's go closer and take a look," Hubert said. He touched her arm to lead her around the room.

A faint flush came over her face as he touched her, and it gave her skin a beautifully rosy glow. She looked at him and smiled nervously. He let his hand drop and stood back watching her as she went from painting to painting. For a long time she lingered in front of a small canvas over one of the couches. It was very old, and she could see that the paint had developed a network of fine cracks. It depicted a young boy with a beatific smile and half-closed eyes. "This is the most beautiful one of all," she said softly.

"You have good taste, mademoiselle. That is a Raphael," a woman's voice said.

Hélène stiffened and turned around slowly. She knew that clipped voice, with its precise pronunciations, only too well. Swiftly she curtsied. She was surprised that it came off so gracefully. "Good evening, Comtesse," she said politely.

"Good evening, mademoiselle." The Comtesse smiled coolly and came toward her. "The Comte will be down shortly." Her dark eyes looked at Hélène curiously. "I had no idea you appreciated fine art. Sometime, perhaps, I must show you around. The château has many fine examples of Italian and French paintings. It is said that we have the largest collection of Claude Lorraines in Europe. One of my ancestors was a devoted romantic."

Hélène nodded politely. "I would like very much to see them, Comtesse."

The Comtesse turned to Hubert. "Did you ride today?" she asked.

He grinned. "Yes, as a matter of fact I rode with Mademoiselle Junot."

The Comtesse's eyebrows lifted a fraction. "She rides, also?"

"I . . . I'm just learning," Hélène said quickly.

"Every young lady should learn to ride," the Comtesse said flatly. "When I was young, I won many ribbons and trophies in dressage."

"Really?" Hélène asked. She had no idea what dressage was, but she looked at the Comtesse with surprise. The elegant woman hadn't struck her as an equestrienne.

A moment later, Hélène saw the Comte enter the room. She curtsied, once again surprising herself with her own grace. It was from him, she realized at once, that Hubert had inherited his stature and physique. But Hubert's face, with its dark eyes and cleft chin, clearly came from the Comtesse, for the Comte's eyes were bright blue. His graying hair still showed streaks of its natural blondness, and he was, Hélène decided, very distinguished-looking.

"Shall we?" he asked, hooking his arm into the Comtesse's. The Comtesse nodded. Hubert touched Hélène's elbow, and she started. It was as if a spark of electricity crackled in his touch. She could feel it coursing down to her groin and erupting into an exquisite pain. Why does he do this to me? she wondered.

Then they went into the dining salon.

The dining salon was rich in elegant woods. It had gleaming dark parquet-de-Versailles flooring, lustrous Régence boiserie walls, a marble mantel, an antique Waterford chandelier over the table, and shiny caned French chairs. The sterling candelabra with their slim beeswax tapers, the heavy silverware, the fine Limoges plates, and the Baccarat crystal were set directly on the polished wood table. There was no tablecloth.

Hélène saw four table settings with baffling rows of forks, spoons, and knives laid out with military precision. A liveried footman stood behind each of their chairs. Hélène had never imagined splendor such as this.

Solicitously the footmen held their chairs away from the table. Hélène waited until the Comte and the Comtesse were seated before she sat down. She followed Madame Dupré's instructions: "If you're in doubt about anything—any fork or glass or finger bowl—watch to see what the others do. Just follow their example and you can't go wrong." Hélène glanced at the Comtesse. She was delicately unfolding her linen napkin and placing it on her lap. Hélène did likewise.

The dinner was long; most of the conversation was dull. But to Hélène it was the most exciting evening of her life. She felt pleased that she had been invited. She knew that she had not succeeded in breaking down any impermeable social barriers, but she had been invited, and that was a minor victory in itself. It proved that entrance to the upper stratum could be gained. It was a matter of meeting the "right" people. Staying in the class was a different story. By being beautiful and charming, by having exquisite manners and developing her wit, it could probably be accomplished.

Mentally Hélène thanked Madame Dupré when a footman held the soup tureen filled with crayfish consommé out to her for a second helping. "I've had plenty, thank you," she murmured politely despite the fact that she was ravenous. She knew she had been right in declining when she saw that no one else took a second helping.

Hélène was dazzled by the food. It looked even more delicious than it tasted. After the consommé came a course of sherbet. At first she thought this was dessert. It wasn't. It was served merely to clear the palate. Then a sterling platter was carried from person to person. On it was a whole pike stuffed with scallop mousse. The fish's back was artfully draped with lettuce leaves lined with little florets. All around the big fish, the platter was decorated with mushroom caps. This course was served with a white butter sauce and was accompanied by a bottle of Pouilly-Fuissé. It had been sitting uncorked on a sideboard to give it time to "breathe." Hélène raised her glass and savored the bouquet of the wine. The Comtesse once against raised her fine eyebrows. Delicately Hélène sipped at the wine. She couldn't believe how delicious it tasted. Her only wish was that she could have shared this moment with Madame Dupré.

Most of the conversation eluded Hélène. It centered around vintages, antique cars, politics, and a piece of gossip about a certain Baronne de Savonnières and her beautiful daughter, Mirielle. Hélène listened in silence, content just to be there hearing these things discussed in her presence. She was surprised to find that the gossip wasn't whispered. It was told amusingly and straightforwardly but with the deadly wit of a rapier.

Then the subject changed to one she could appreciate. Apparently a fancy-dress ball would be held at the château the night before she and Madame Dupré were to return to Saint-Nazaire.

The Comte flashed a quick look at his wife. "Did you invite the Baronne de Savonnières?" he asked.

"But of course," the Comtesse replied as if it was the most natural thing in the world.

He raised an eyebrow and his voice took on a worried tone. "But don't you think that with this recent scandal it would have been wise not to?"

The Comtesse's lips curved into a faintly malicious smile. "Au contraire, Philippe. Everyone will love me for it! You know how I adore throwing people together—especially enemies!" She wrinkled her Roman nose in delight. "It makes for such delicious stories afterward."

For a while, no one spoke. The silence was broken only by the sounds of silverware scraping on china. Hélène's eyes glowed with excitement. The round window in her room looked down over the front drive. From it she would be able to see the guests arrive. She wondered how she might recognize the notorious Baronne de Savonnières and her beautiful daughter.

Dessert was served: enormous velvety peaches on Limoges plates. Hélène was about to pick the fruit up with her fingers, but caution intervened. Discreetly she glanced at the others for guidance. They were picking up their dessert cutlery. Carefully she followed suit. She had never imagined that there were people who ate fruit with knife and fork. It proved that she had a lot to learn.

Hubert smiled across the table at her. "You're invited to come, of course," he said. "As my guest."

Hélène stared at him blankly. She had been too engrossed with watching the Comtesse slice her peach to pay attention. Now she was puzzled. Invited? To what? "I beg your pardon?" she asked politely.

"The ball, of course," he said matter-of-factly. "You shall come as my guest."

Suddenly a thrill of excitement coursed through her. The ball! She hadn't dared hope for an invitation, but now Hubert had asked her. And right in front of the Comte and the Comtesse! Quickly she looked at them, expecting some sort of negative reaction, an imperceptible shake of the head perhaps, or a widening of the eyes, or a faint arching of the brows. But she saw none of these.

Modestly Hélène lowered her eyes. "I . . . I don't know," she said softly.

"Why not?" he demanded. But as soon as the words tumbled out of his mouth, he cursed himself. He knew why. For the same reason she had tried to turn down the dinner invitation. Because he was a de Léger and she would feel out of place. "You'll be quite at ease," he assured her quickly. "Believe me, you will be a success."

"Thank you," Hélène said, fighting to keep her voice level. "I will think it over and let you know."

Satisfied that her reply was as good as an acceptance, he continued eating his dessert.

Hélène suddenly felt sick. She cut off a tiny piece of her peach and chewed it dumbly. Would Hubert never understand her dilemma? She *wanted* to go to the ball. Oh, but *how* she was dying to go. She wasn't frightened any longer. She wasn't even worried about being out of place. But she had nothing to wear to a fancy-dress ball. The severe black dress she had on certainly wouldn't do. And that was the best one she had. The feeling of disappointment was like a dull ache that spread outward from her heart and extended to her limbs until even her fingertips were numb. She sighed to herself. There was nothing she could do. She would just have to make the best of it.

After dinner they went back to the Salon de la Rotonde for coffee and brandies. Hélène sipped her coffee but declined brandy. She was not used to liquor, and the wine had already made her feel peculiarly light-headed.

Carefully the Comte lit a cigar. He and Hubert sat facing each other in chairs at the far side of the salon, discussing business and politics. The Comtesse was sitting beside Hélène on a couch, pointing out some of the paintings in the room and reciting the history behind each one. She seemed to enjoy having a captive audience. As she talked, her cold dark pupils flashed with excitement, as if each historical detail was unfolding right before her eyes. Hélène fell under the spell. It seemed that centuries of de Légers had had their fingers in many pies—in government, in wine, in art. She was fascinated with the Comtesse's copious knowledge, and flattered that the woman was so open with her. Greedily she filed away everything she learned.

Finally the Comte rose to his feet. Then he and the Comtesse excused themselves and retired. A footman closed the door softly behind them. Hubert smiled at Hélène. "Did we bore you?" he asked in an amused voice.

"On the contrary!" she countered. "I found it fascinating."

He changed the subject. "How about going for a ride?"

She shook her head. "I'd have to change again. Besides, you warned me about getting saddle sore."

He laughed. "Not a horseback ride. I meant in a car. To the village. I know—we could go to Chez Gaston for a nightcap! There's music there."

"I'm not sure I should," she said quickly.

He looked at her challengingly. "Do I detect fear in your voice?"

She looked at him sharply. "Of course not."

"Then get your coat. I'll see about a car. I'll pick you up in front, at the entrance."

For a moment she couldn't believe her ears. She stared at him. "Up front?" she asked slowly. "You mean . . . at the big marble staircase?"

"Of course. That's the entrance, isn't it?"

Is it? she thought uncharitably. Maybe for you it is, Hubert de Léger. But for Madame Dupré, Thérèse, the rest of the servants, and me, the entrance is the kitchen door. But she said none of these things. Instead, she found herself saying: "I'll be there in five minutes."

He smiled. "Make that ten. I'll have to gas up the car first."

She hurried up the servants' staircase and rapidly entered her room. The connecting door to Madame Dupré's room was still open. When the woman heard her come in, she put down the book she was reading and came to the door. "You look excited," she observed shrewdly.

Hélène nodded breathlessly. "Hubert de Léger is taking me to the village."

Madame Dupré stared at her. "He's certainly rolling out the red carpet," she remarked dryly. "He seems quite taken with you."

Hélène caught the undercurrent in Madame Dupré's voice. She looked at her hesitantly. "You think I shouldn't go?" she asked.

Madame Dupré smiled weakly. "You go," she said, wagging an admonishing finger at Hélène. "Just be careful. Hubert de Léger is a headstrong womanizer. He usually ends up with what he sets out to get."

"I'll be careful," Hélène promised. On an impulse, she hurried across the room and kissed Madame Dupré lightly on the cheek. Then she grabbed her coat and rushed back out, leaving the door slightly ajar.

Chez Gaston wasn't in the next village. It was located in Saint-Médard, ten kilometers north of Bordeaux, in the cellar of an old building. The stone walls had been whitewashed; the place was dark and noisy and the air was blue with smoke. The music was American, played on a scratchy, blaring phonograph.

Hélène surprised herself. She was a very good dancer. Perhaps it was because she gave herself over to Hubert and let him lead her. His arms were around her and she responded naturally, holding on to him, her head resting on his chest. She thought she could smell the animallike manliness of him. For a while she closed her eyes and let herself go, feeling the delicious strength of him as he moved her gracefully around the floor.

When the slow dance stopped, she opened her eyes and smiled tiredly up at Hubert. He took her hand and led the way back to their little table. Her steps were slow and she walked very carefully, as if she was not sure in which direction her feet were taking her. He helped her into the rush-seated chair and then sat down across from her. He lifted the champagne bottle out of the ice bucket to refill their glasses.

She covered her glass with her hand and shook her head. "I think I've had enough," she said thickly. She frowned. It seemed to take a lot of effort to form the words.

"Come on," he coaxed. "A little more won't hurt you. Besides, it will loosen you up."

She met his eyes. "Do you think I need loosening up?" she asked softly.

He grinned and made a gesture with his thumb and fore-finger. "Just a little."

She looked at his other hand. He was still holding the bottle over her glass. Or was it the second bottle? She pursed her lips thoughtfully. Then she shrugged and threw caution to the wind. She removed her hand and he filled both their glasses to the brim. "À votre santé," he said.

"À votre santé," she repeated. She drained half the glass in one long swallow. She hadn't realized she was so thirsty. It must be the dancing and all the smoke.

He fixed his eyes on her and reached across the table. Again a thrill coursed through her body. "You're very beauti-ful," he said. "Do you know that?"

A red flush rose up her face. She was suddenly grateful for the dim lighting. At least it hid her constant blushes.

"Do I make you nervous?" he asked softly.

She nodded slowly. "Yes."

He smiled. Then his eyes fell to her breasts and lingered there. She forced herself not to look down at herself. What's the matter? she thought. Is the dress torn? Did I spill cham-pagne on myself? What *is* it? But suddenly, instinctively, she knew what it was. Abruptly she pushed her chair back and got unsteadily to her feet. "I . . . I think we'd better dance," she said in a serious voice.

He sensed her discomfiture and nodded. He followed her to the dance floor. For a moment she stopped and looked down at her feet. They felt strangely light, as if she were walking on cushions of air.

When they got to the floor, the music changed to a slow dance. She wrapped her arms around his neck and he embraced her. Slowly she moved her body in rhythm with his. She closed her eyes, once again smiling contentedly. Now she felt safe. Here on the floor, he didn't look at her with longing or say things that made her feel uncomfortable. Here it was just him and the music, the firmness of his body, the grace with which he led her. Again she caught that peculiar male smell. Or was it just sweat? Or her imagination?

His hand moved down to the small of her back and he pressed her tightly toward him. Suddenly she was aware of his groin pushing against her hips. She took a deep breath. The familiar, exquisite pain was growing inside her again. Fiercely she tried to push it out of her mind, but the harder she tried, the more painful and insistent it became. Suddenly she could feel a strange moistness between her legs.

He lowered his head so that his lips were at her ear. "I want to make love to you," he whispered.

Slowly she opened her eyes and looked up at him. "I think I'm drunk," she said slowly.

"That doesn't matter," he said quickly. "It won't change the way I feel about you."

Her eyes held a questioning look. "How do you feel about me?" she asked softly.

"I want you."

She turned away, suddenly disappointed. Her voice was tight. "Is that all?"

He shook his head. Then he pressed her face against his chest. He stared over her head at the dance floor and grimaced. His voice was bored, but she didn't seem to notice. All she heard was the whispery echo of his words, and they were the words she wanted to hear.

"I love you," he said.

12

They left the noise of Chez Gaston and went out into the quiet of the moonlit night. The air was cold and smelled clean and fresh after the stuffy, smoke-filled cellar. Hélène breathed deeply and clung tightly to Hubert's arm. Their heels made sharp slapping sounds on the cobbled street.

He helped her into the car, banged her door shut, and got in on the driver's side. He smiled over at her. Her face looked pale in the moonlight, and she was huddled against the door. Suddenly he leaned toward her and took her in his arms. He kissed her deeply with moist, hungry lips. Her hands clung to him fiercely.

Slowly he pulled himself away from her and started the car.

"Where are we going?" she asked in a weak voice.

"I thought we'd go to a hotel."

She reached out and touched his arm. "Not a hotel, Hubert," she said in a small voice. "Someplace romantic."

He tapped his hands on the steering wheel, thinking quickly. Then he made a grunting sound, switched on the headlights, and put the car into gear. "I know just the place."

"Where?" she asked.

He grinned. "You'll see soon enough."

The roads were deserted and he drove swiftly. The reflecting markers on the roadside picked up the glare of the headlights and flashed past in a blur.

Less than half an hour later they approached the Château Loustalot-de Léger. From a distance it looked like a brooding black shadow against the dark sky. As if on cue, the moon came out from behind some clouds and washed the battlements, the fat, medieval turrets, and the newer, more elegant Renaissance additions in a magical pale white light. The moat looked like liquid silver. Hélène gasped at the drama of the scene.

"Is this romantic enough?" he asked.

She nodded. "Yes," she said softly. "It's beautiful."

Hubert threaded the car through the dark web of roads that crisscrossed the vineyards of Loustalot. Several times the hills sloped up in front of them or the road made a turn and they lost sight of the château. Then it would appear again, looming in front of them, always larger than before.

Finally they drew to a halt alongside the moat. From here the Renaissance additions could not be seen, only the towering rock walls of the Middle Ages. In the moonlight these battlements and turrets looked mighty and impregnable.

Hubert placed his arm around her waist and led her to the entrance, a permanent stone bridge that had long since replaced the drawbridge.

"What if someone sees us?" Hélène whispered. She glanced up at him out of the corners of her eyes.

He laughed, and his teeth gleamed in the moonlight. "Don't worry," he told her. "I am a de Léger, not a thief. Anyway, we keep only a handful of servants here. We'll never even see them. I've been known to come and go at odd hours."

Suddenly she froze in her tracks. "With . . . women?" she asked. What a stupid question! she thought angrily. Whom was she trying to fool? Of course Hubert came here with other women! What was it Madame Dupré had called him? A womanizer. A veil dropped down over Hélène's eyes. Before Hubert could reply, she drew herself up with dignity.

"Take me back, Hubert," she said firmly. "To Haute-cloque."

They drove back in silence. Hubert was angry, and he kept the accelerator pressed down to the floorboard. Hélène was afraid to speak. Afraid to beg him to slow down. She sat white-faced in her seat as the dark vineyards flew past. We're going to have an accident, she thought as fear constricted her throat, clamped her chest like a vise. We'll both be killed.

When he stopped to let her out at the marble steps, she looked at him and hesitated. She wanted to say something— beg him not to be angry with her, explain how she felt. But the situation was too awkward. She fumbled with the door handle (this time he didn't treat her like a lady and hold it open for her), got out of the car, and closed the door. It didn't shut the first time and she had to close it a second time more firmly. Then he gunned the engine, turned the car around, and sped back down the poplar-lined drive toward the road. Back to Saint-Médard? she wondered. Back to Chez Gaston? Back to some woman he'd once had who would welcome him with open arms and hungry lips?

She stared up at the white marble steps. Suddenly they looked too imposing, too cold and regal. She shuddered. Quickly she began to walk around the château, finally letting herself in through the kitchen door.

She was angry with Hubert. And the more she thought about it, the angrier she became. He had plied her with champagne, probably suspecting her low resistance to alcohol. And after doing that, he had tried to trick her into going to bed with him.

But she was even angrier with herself. She should have known better than to go out with him in the first place.

She didn't see Hubert anymore, nor did he try to contact her. Clearly their friendship was over. He was either as elusive as Madame Dupré had said he could be whenever he didn't want to be found, or else it was she who was elusive. At any rate, they had few opportunities to run into each other. He was in the lavish parts of the château; she was in the servants' quarters. Most of her day was spent in her room or in the sewing room. She did her best to stay indoors. The rare times she went outside were when she took walks with Madame Dupré. Hélène had never told her what had happened, and Madame Dupré was sensitive enough not to bring up the subject.

The day of the ball drew near. Hélène no longer had any desire to attend. In fact, she wished she didn't have to be in the same house where it was being held. Everything had been soured by the . . . the misunderstanding with Hubert, as she thought of it. And the ball would only be a painful reminder.

The day before the ball, Madame Dupré sent word to the Comtesse that her wardrobe was completed. Despite the flurry the household was in, the Comtesse's manservant came to announce the Comtesse's arrival in half an hour.

"She will try on all the outfits," Madame Dupré said. "Let's hope she will be pleased."

Hélène looked at her. "I don't feel well," she stammered. "Could I be excused?"

Madame Dupré frowned. "Sit down," she said, gesturing to one of the chairs.

Hélène sat down nervously and looked up at her.

Madame Dupré's eyes narrowed. "I don't know what did or did not occur between you and Hubert de Léger," she said. "However, that is between you and him. I do assume that the Comtesse is in no way involved?" She arched her eyebrows questioningly.

Hélène was silent for a moment. Then she shook her head. "No," she said finally.

"In that case, I think it is your duty to be here. After all, you worked very hard on her wardrobe, and you are partially responsible for its success or failure. If the Comtesse has any praise or criticism, you should also hear it."

Hélène looked away. "But I . . . I don't feel well," she said weakly.

Madame Dupré shook her head. "I believe you feel fine," she said firmly. "I insist that you stay."

Hélène nodded morosely.

The Comtesse was punctual. Exactly half an hour later, there was a knock on the tall door. A footman threw it open and stepped aside as the Comtesse swept in. She was dressed in a flowing, belted robe of an Oriental fabric. Her silvery hair was carefully coiffed and gleamed like the silver thread embroidered into her robe.

Madame Dupré flashed Hélène a quick look. Both of them curtsied gracefully. Immediately the footman withdrew and closed the door. The Comtesse crossed the room and went behind the three-paneled screen while Madame Dupré brought her one outfit at a time. They were on satin-covered hangers. The sleeves of each garment were carefully stuffed with lengths of tissue paper, the tops of the hangers padded with a "neck" of more tissue paper so that the collars of each garment would fall naturally.

First Madame Dupré brought out the copy of the Comtesse's pale yellow Chanel suit. This was followed by two more Chanels—one in pale blue, the other in a tweed. Then came a startling red Schiaparelli dress and two Balenciagas—one white, one black. Finally there were three Givenchys—two suits and one dress—in varying earth tones.

Each one fit the Comtesse to perfection. Madame Dupré eyed them with satisfaction. Even a professionally trained eye would find it difficult to distinguish the copy from the original, she thought.

The Comtesse stood in front of the three-paneled gilt-framed mirror in each garment. She carefully scrutinized herself from all angles, moving her arms, twisting her thin body. Finally, after trying on the last Givenchy, she nodded approval. "You have done well, madame," she told Madame Dupré.

Madame Dupré looked pleased. "It was a pleasure, Comtesse," she replied modestly.

The Comtesse nodded and went back behind the screen. When she reappeared in her Oriental robe, she said, "I will have Lise collect the clothes in a few minutes."

Madame Dupré nodded.

The Comtesse turned her dark eyes on Hélène. "I had hoped we would see more of you, mademoiselle," she said reproachfully.

Hélène felt herself flushing. "Oui, Comtesse," she murmured. "I had hoped so also."

"I recall that my son invited you to the ball tomorrow. You *are* coming?"

Madame Dupré started. This was news indeed! Quickly she looked at Hélène. The girl's eyes seemed to dull; the violet pupils turned to smoky amethyst.

"I'm afraid I won't be able to accept your kind invitation, Comtesse," Hélène said. "I hope you will excuse me."

Madame Dupré gasped and the Comtesse looked at Hélène in surprise. "But that is not possible! My son will be very upset if you do not appear. He has asked me to tell you personally that he will expect you in the Salon de la Rotonde at eight o'clock tomorrow evening."

Hélène's heart gave a joyous leap. Did Hubert really say that? Was it possible that he still wanted to see her? Was he no longer angry with her? The sudden news made her curiously light-headed. But she couldn't go to the ball. She had nothing to wear. She would have to make up some excuse.

"I'm sorry," Hélène said. "I thought he . . . I . . ." She looked helplessly at Madame Dupré, her eyes begging for help. Almost imperceptibly Madame Dupré shook her head sideways.

The Comtesse reached out, touched Hélène's chin with her elegant fingers, and gently turned her face toward her. "I do not know whether you are very dumb or very clever, mademoiselle," she said softly. "My son was extremely agitated by your behavior."

"I . . . I'm sorry."

"Do not be. Apparently you are the first woman who has ever dared to refuse him." For a moment the dark eyes flashed with amusement. "He was very hurt, but strangely enough, he respects you for it. As do I." She smiled. "You will be in the Salon de la Rotonde at eight?"

"I'm sorry, Comtesse." Hélène made a helpless gesture with her hands. "It is such short notice. I thought I wouldn't be welcome, so I didn't prepare anything to . . ." Her eyes fell. ". . . to wear."

The Comtesse frowned thoughtfully. Then she glanced at Madame Dupré. "Could you quickly sew something for her, madame?"

Madame Dupré bowed her head. "Of course, Comtesse. But there is the matter of fabrics."

"There are still some in the wardrobes, non?" The Comtesse gestured toward them.

"Oui, Comtesse. But they are mostly fine white silks."

The Comtesse smiled. "Use as much as you want, but make it beautiful. You shall be paid extra for it."

"Oui, Comtesse." Suddenly Madame Dupré looked at the Comtesse with inspiration. "I know it is asking too much, Comtesse, but the greenhouses . . ."

"Yes?" The Comtesse looked at Madame Dupré quizzically.

"Some flowers. For decorating the dress. Might I have the gardener bring me some?"

"Fresh flowers for a dress?" The Comtesse frowned. "That sounds rather bizarre. But as long as it is beautiful, take all the flowers you want."

"Thank you, Comtesse," Madame Dupré said.

The Comtesse started toward the door. Quickly Hélène and Madame Dupré curtsied. Suddenly the Comtesse turned around in the doorway. She gazed at Hélène. "Eight o'clock tomorrow, then. In the Salon de la Rotonde."

And the tall door closed.

Hélène let out a painful sound and sank into a chair. She pushed her fingers through her hair. "What do I do?" she wailed.

Madame Dupré looked at her with delight. "I know what *I* shall do. For once, I am going to design and sew a dress that truly inspires me!" Her eyes flashed with excitement. She made an agitated gesture with her hands. "Quickly—get undressed! I shall measure you immediately! We have no time to lose!"

Madame Dupré ate no lunch or dinner. "There is no time!" she cried. "I have a gown to sew—overnight!"

Hélène began to feel an excitement growing within her as she watched the woman deftly attacking the bolt of silk with her shears. The fabric parted smoothly in two as the sharp blades slid through it. Hélène reached out and touched the silk. It was soft and white and fluid. It seemed to shimmer with the radiance of sunshine on new snow.

Madame Dupré's pace never flagged. She seemed to know exactly what effect she was striving for. What style the gown would be. How much fabric to use. She worked without a pattern and with a speed and surety Hélène had never seen before. Madame Dupré seemed to have burst out of the shackles that had bound her creativity. She was creating a garment that was totally original, that would be spectacular. There would be no "borrowing" from Givenchy, Balenciaga, Odile Joly, or Dior.

As the hours passed, the gown slowly began to take on a shape. Hélène could see that it would have a square, low-cut neckline and an enormous full skirt. There would be no sleeves, only loose over-the-shoulder straps.

From time to time Madame Dupré would pin the pieces of silk around Hélène. Then she would step back, her mouth full of pins, and study the effect with a critical frown. She would make a quick tuck here, a swift chalk line there. Then everything would be spread back out on the paper-covered table.

Madame Dupré did everything by hand. Hélène was astonished. It seemed that the woman was quicker with the needle than the machine. Her fingers flew.

When it was nearly midnight, Hélène could no longer hold her eyes open. She fell asleep in her chair. Madame Dupré glanced at her and smiled. Hélène's legs were stretched out, her feet crossed, and her hands were folded in her lap. Her head was tilted sideways against one shoulder, her black hair tumbling down over her face. Ah, the sleep of the young, Madame Dupré thought. How peaceful and rejuvenating it was. Well, Hélène would need every wink she could get. Attending a ball was going to be exhausting.

When morning came, Madame Dupré was still at work. Strangely enough, she didn't feel a bit tired. It was as if the thrill of her creativity superseded her need for sleep.

Hélène suddenly stirred. She opened her eyes and blinked. She yawned noisily, and with her fingers she rubbed the sleep from her eyes. Sunlight was already streaming in through the big windows. She looked over at Madame Dupré with surprise. "Why . . . it's morning!"

Madame Dupré smiled. "It is, and a beautiful morning at that!"

Hélène let out a gasp. She had seen the gown lying on the table. Slowly she got to her feet and came toward it. Already it looked finished. As the sunlight hit its whiteness, the silk seemed to dazzle and threw blinding light back at her. She had to squint.

"It's beautiful!" she breathed.

Madame Dupré smiled and glanced at Hélène out of the corner of her eye. "It shall be, but that will be many hours from now. Did you sleep well?"

Hélène nodded, rubbing her shoulder briskly; it felt sore from sleeping in the chair. "Yes, well enough. But you didn't get a wink!"

"I will once this gown is finished. Now I need you to try it on quickly before I continue. Then I want you to eat a very light breakfast and a tiny lunch. The emptier your stomach, the better you will look. We must make you appear to be very slim."

Hélène nodded. "And I'll need to take a bath and wash my hair and do something with it—"

"Don't do anything with your hair except wash it!" Madame Dupré said sharply.

"Why not?"

Madame Dupré smiled secretly and got to her feet. "You'll see. Now, stand over here and we'll have a fitting."

Quickly Hélène slipped out of her clothes and Madame Dupré helped her into the gown. The low-cut bodice fit snugly, and Hélène noticed that it pushed her small, firm breasts upward, making them appear larger and more shapely than they actually were. The skirt was huge and magnificent—kilometers of soft, voluminous silk billowing like a cloud. On an impulse, she walked over to the three-paneled mirror and whirled around. She caught sight of her reflection. The skirt shimmered as it sailed around her legs, and she could hear the soft rustling of the silk.

"It . . . it's lovely!" Hélène said. She whirled around again, and a look of despair suddenly marred the excited look on her face. Her body seemed to slump. She had seen her shoes. They were the only pair she owned and certainly couldn't be worn with the gown. Her heart sank. It was an impossible situation.

"What's the matter?" Madame Dupré asked, instantly catching her dismay.

Wordlessly Hélène lifted the skirt to display her shoes.

Madame Dupré smiled. "I know that," she said soothingly. "So don't worry, I have already thought of it."

Hélène looked relieved. She posed in front of the mirror, watching the folds of silk shift and fall. The gown seemed to have a lifeblood of its own. Then she turned questioningly to Madame Dupré. "What have you thought of for shoes?"

"I shall sew silk slippers with soft leather bottoms. They will tie around your ankles with white silk ribbons, rather like ballet slippers."

Hélène beamed. On an impulse she hugged Madame Dupré. "You're a genius!" she said happily.

Madame Dupre looked pleased, but her voice was gruff. "Careful!" she said. "You're crushing the dress! Now, off with it! I want to finish it on time. We have less than ten hours until the ball." She helped Hélène to undress. "You go and eat. Before you take your bath, look in my nightstand. I have some scented bath seeds. Pour a handful into the tub."

By four o'clock Hélène had completed her grooming. She had bathed twice and carefully washed her hair. When it was dry, she did what Madame Dupré had told her to do—winding it as tightly as possible around her head and pinning it in place. Then she went back down to the sewing room.

The gown was nearly finished. Hélène just stood there staring at it, transfixed. She shook her head in disbelief. She had never seen anything quite so lovely. It lay on the table, and Madame Dupré was deftly sewing a surfilage along the hem. The surfilage wasn't necessary, but it was an added luxurious touch. Hélène knew that only the finest garments had this finishing touch that would keep the hem from fraying. Not that the gown would be worn enough to fray. But she knew that Madame Dupré wanted it to stand up to the most lavish designer gowns at the ball.

"There. Fini." Madame Dupré sighed with approval and let the hem fall back down on the table. "Try it on once more," she said. "I've got to see if it needs any last-minute adjustments."

Eagerly Hélène slipped into it. Her eyes glowed and her breath came in short, excited gasps. The gown was spectacular indeed. Its very simplicity gave it a style of its own. Madame Dupré stepped back to study the effect. She nodded with satisfaction.

"It's more beautiful than anything I've ever seen in *Vogue*," Hélène said in a hushed voice.

Madame Dupré nodded. "It fits perfectly. Thank God, no adjustments are needed. Now, slip out of it and hang it up on one of the hangers. I'm going to work on the slippers now. In the meantime, I want you to go and see the gardener. Tell him the Comtesse said it was all right to deliver enormous bunches of baby's breath to me immediately."

Hélène frowned. She had forgotten all about the flowers. She wondered what on earth they were for.

At seven-thirty she got dressed. Madame Dupré was like a fussing, clucking mother hen. First the slippers. Hélène slipped into them and tied the silk ribbons around her ankles. She tried walking around the room in them. It was like walking on air. They let her move with a grace she'd never known she had. Then the gown. After Madame Dupré approved the way it fell, she reached for a matching silk turban she had sewn and slipped in over Hélène's head. It covered her skull tightly, hiding her ears and framing her face. It made her forehead look elegantly peaked.

Then came the crowning touch. The flowers. Madame Dupré picked up a cluster of baby's breath she had tied together with almost invisible wires and pinned it to the back of the turban. The flowers looked like a lacy halo growing up out of the silk. Then she reached for an enormous thick boa of more baby's breath. This, too, she had wired carefully together. She draped it around Hélène's shoulders and bodice. Then she got out her needle and deftly stitched it on.

Hélène let out a gasp when she looked at herself in the mirror. It was a fairy-tale gown. The lacelike flowers were far more elegant and beautiful than jewels could ever be.

Madame Dupré glanced at her watch. It was five minutes until eight. She stood back and smiled with satisfaction. She knew that for the first time in her life she had sewn a masterpiece. A masterpiece that was not a copy, that had not been inspired by anyone except herself. Suddenly she felt very tired. Soon she would be able to rest.

"You look beautiful!" she told Hélène proudly.

Hélène's eyes were moist with tears. "I don't know how I can ever thank you."

Madame Dupré's eyes narrowed. She said hoarsely, "Wipe away those tears! You don't want to have puffy red eyes, do you?"

Vehemently Hélène shook her head and wiped her eyes.

Madame Dupré took her hand and squeezed it affectionately. "Enjoy yourself."

And then there was a knock at the door. A footman in red satin livery had come to escort Hélène downstairs.

The guests were already arriving as Hélène swept down the carved stone staircase behind the footman, and she could hear the faint sounds of an orchestra somewhere within the château. She tried not to show her nervousness. Delicately she lifted the skirt of her gown so that she wouldn't trip on the hem. She caught sight of herself in an ornate pier glass and gasped. She still couldn't quite believe that the reflection she saw there was hers.

Several guests were milling about at the foot of the stairs, the men in hand-sewn tuxedos, the women in lavish gowns and elaborate jewels. Hélène's eyes caught the flashing of diamond chandelier earrings, the sparkle of weblike necklaces of diamonds and emeralds, the deep fiery flashes of rubies, the cool moonglow of sapphires. She could see the expressions on the guests' faces as they looked curiously up at her. They were all stunned.

They stepped aside for her as the footman led her through the open double doors of the Salon de la Rotonde. The room was crowded with guests. The Comte and the Comtesse were standing inside the door, greeting the guests as they arrived. Hélène could see Hubert at the far end of the room. He was impatiently pacing up and down, looking at his gold pocket watch. With a quick motion he snapped it shut. He looked very handsome in black tuxedo and white silk shirt and bow tie.

Suddenly all conversation in the room stopped. For a moment Hélène wondered why. Then she knew. She could feel all their eyes upon her.

For a moment she hesitated. Then gracefully she dropped a curtsy in front of the Comte and Comtesse. When she got back up, Hubert was suddenly beside her, touching her arm.

The Comtesse smiled at Hélène. "Extraordinary," she murmured. "You are quite lovely. And Madame Dupré is a genius. You must tell her for me."

"Thank you, Comtesse. I shall do that."

The Comte smiled at Hélène, his blue eyes looking at her with quickening interest. Then Hubert led her aside. A manservant presented a silver tray with glasses of champagne. Hélène took a glass and sipped delicately, looking at Hubert over the rim. But she drank very slowly. She had decided to have no more than two glasses all night long. She would be above reproach.

"Who *is* she?" she heard a young woman in an apricot Dior gown ask an older one.

"I do not know, chérie. But I'm going to have to find out where that gown came from."

Hubert smiled at Hélène. "You are quite a sensation. I had no idea you were so beautiful."

She smiled, genuinely pleased.

"Would you like to go to the ballroom?" he asked.

She nodded, and he took her arm and led her down a long hall. She gasped in amazement. The hall was lined with linen-draped tables. Spread out on them were lavish hors d'oeuvres: bright red "trees" of crayfish; silver tubs filled with escargots; platters of scallops, mussels, oysters, and clams; tiny quail eggs on beds of Iranian caviar. There was an abundance of everything, all artfully arranged around a dazzling ice sculpture. Predictably, it depicted the familiar lion and salamander holding the crest of the de Légers.

Hélène was even more dazzled when they entered the ballroom. For a moment she could only stand there staring. She had never seen anything so festive. The room was enormous, with a high, fanciful trompe l'oeil ceiling and columned walls. All around the room were palms from the hothouses. Concealed among the graceful branches were flowerpots whose orchids gave the appearance of growing among the palm fronds. Overhead, the crystal chandeliers sprouted forests of slender white candles, and the walls danced with flickering light. At the far end, on a small stage, an orchestra was playing waltzes.

"Would you care to dance?" Hubert asked, executing a solemn little bow.

Hélène looked out across the shiny floor. It was still early. No one was dancing yet. She nodded, handed her champagne glass to a passing footman, and let Hubert pull her into his arms. Soundlessly he swept her across the room. Her gown rustled and billowed like a graceful white cloud, and the baby's breath looked like hundreds of snowflakes frozen around her.

When the waltz ended, another one started up. A few more couples were whirling around them now, moving across the floor with the grace of lithe swans. One waltz melted into another. And another. And another. Hélène had no idea how many they danced. "I think I need a rest," she said finally.

Hubert hooked his arm into hers and led her away from the swirling guests. She saw that the Comte and Comtesse were now standing at the edge of the dance floor. The guests must have all arrived, she thought.

The Comte made a little bow to Hubert and smiled at Hélène. She could feel his penetrating blue eyes upon her. She felt herself flushing.

"May I have the pleasure of this dance?" he asked.

Then she felt his hand on her arm. She started. Whatever she had felt at Chez Gaston with Hubert was nothing compared to the powerful surge that now coursed through her body. Was she to feel this with every man who touched her? she wondered.

"You look lovely," the Comte told her softly as they swirled around the floor. "May I compliment you on your gown?"

"Thank you," Hélène murmured politely. "You are too kind."

"White suits you so much better than black," he declared. "You should wear white always."

Her heart pounded and she looked up at him. He remembered what she'd worn at the dinner three weeks ago! Was it possible? They hadn't exchanged two sentences. He had hardly looked at her.

When the music stopped, he led her back to Hubert. The Comtesse smiled. For the first time, Hélène noticed the Comtesse's jewelry. She wore nothing but gold earrings. They were large and looked very old. Raised in relief on them were the salamander, the lion, and the crest of the de Légers. Hélène realized that the Comtesse must own much fine jewelry, but since she chose to wear these, they must be quite precious.

"My dear Comtesse," a fawning, woman's voice said from behind.

They all turned. "Why, Baronne, how delightful that you could come," the Comtesse said smoothly. "For a while I didn't think you were going to make it."

The Baronne laughed a high, brittle laugh. "I'm afraid I'm always late."

Hélène stared at the Baronne. She was in her mid-thirties, red-haired, sharp-eyed, and bony. She wore a Balmain gown of scarlet satin and her neck was draped with blood-colored rubies. A palsied, very old gray-haired man stood on one side of her, a beautiful young woman in green on the other. The young woman wore an emerald necklace and matching earrings and held herself with cool self-confidence.

Curiously Hélène wondered if the red-haired woman could be the Baronne de Savonnières. She glanced at the poised beauty. Was that Mirielle? Were they the ones the Comtesse had gossiped about during the dinner, so delighted that she'd invited them?

The Comtesse smiled and introduced Hélène. So it *was* the Baronne de Savonnières and Mirielle. And the old man was the Baron.

Mirielle gave Hubert a reproachful look and touched him on the arm. Her face was close to his. "I haven't seen you for ages," she said in a husky voice.

He smiled uncomfortably at her. "I'm afraid I have been kept very busy. I must apologize for the neglect."

The Baronne's eyes flashed and she smiled like a shark. Her teeth were long and pointed. "Aren't you going to ask her to dance?" she said slowly.

Hubert knew when he was cornered. He bowed to Hélène. "Please pardon me for a few minutes," he said. She watched as he dutifully hooked his arm into Mirielle's and led her across the floor.

"They make a charming couple, don't you think?" the Baronne said approvingly.

The Comtesse nodded wordlessly. Smoothly she changed

the subject and brought Hélène into the conversation. After one dance, Hubert returned with Mirielle.

"What is the matter?" the Baronne asked with undisguised acidity. "Only one dance? Don't tell me you have become stingy!" She flashed Hubert a disapproving look.

Hubert smiled politely and gestured to Hélène. "I have invited Mademoiselle Junot to the ball. I'm afraid it is my duty as her escort to show her some attention." Before the Baronne could reply, he bowed to Hélène. "May I have the pleasure?"

Hélène couldn't help smiling at Mirielle's vitriolic look as they waltzed away.

"Who is *she*?" the Baronne asked angrily, watching Hélène.

"A friend of the family's," the Comtesse replied vaguely. "A very charming young lady."

"Yes . . ." The Baronne's voice trailed off as she gazed sharply around the room. "Come, Mirielle. I see some Rothschilds over there . . ." She pointed a splintery finger to a cluster of people standing at the far side. Immediately they hurried toward them, the old man limping along behind. The Rothschilds saw them coming and fled onto the dance floor, waltzing in the opposite direction.

"What a dreadful woman," the Comte said when the Baronne had left. "I can't understand why you always invite her."

The Comtesse smiled wisely. "To add spice to the party, of course. People love tension, and the Baronne supplies it naturally." She looked over the dance floor with satisfaction. So far, the ball was a huge success. Her eyes caught sight of Hélène. "Hubert and the girl look well together, don't you think?"

The Comte nodded. "They certainly do," he said slowly. "She is very beautiful. And she dances well."

"Yes," the Comtesse said with a sigh. "It is a pity that she has no title." She glanced up at her husband. "Well, Philippe. Aren't you going to ask me to dance?"

He turned away from the dancing couple. "Of course," he said. He bowed gallantly and waltzed the Comtesse across the floor. She moved very elegantly but with an economy of movement that precluded natural grace. Every now and then he would catch a glimpse of Hubert and Hélène. Yes, the girl was quite stunning, he thought with sudden longing. And she moved well. Like an angel. Somehow, she made you know that she was a woman and you were a man.

Hélène left the ball at one o'clock. Hubert caught her arm. "Where are you going?"

She smiled. "Upstairs. I have a long journey ahead of me tomorrow. I'll need my rest."

"You're leaving, then." His voice was flat.

She nodded. "Yes. Our work here is over."

"But don't you want to stay?"

She looked into his eyes. There was a painful shadow within the black pupils. "I'd like to stay, but I can't, Hubert. There are things that I must do."

"What kind of things?"

She was silent for a moment. How could he ever understand what she had to do? How could she explain to him that her dreams were glossy pieces of paper glued together to become a magazine? She was certain that he would never understand her need to create something. For him, life was glittering parties, beautiful women, fragile grapes. "I have to go, Hubert," she said firmly. "I'm sorry."

He looked at her sullenly. "I thought you loved me," he said.

Silently she looked out across the crowded dance floor. She saw the beautifully dressed couples moving elegantly in time to the music. She saw the jewels of the women glittering around their patrician throats like the chandeliers high above their heads. She saw the self-assurance of these women, the bearing and style and confidence that could come only from a high-placed birth. That was the type of woman Hubert needed. Someone elegant and cultured and composed. Someone who knew how to make small talk, which wines to serve with dinner, what types of people to invite in order to make a party a success.

"I thought I loved you, too, Hubert," she said softly. "But I'm not ready for love. And I'm not right for you."

He reached out and grasped her hand. "We could get married!" he said quickly. "I am the future Comte. You would be the future Comtesse. We could live in the Château Loustalot while my parents are alive. Then we'd move in here." He squeezed her hand in desperation. "In time, you would learn to love me."

She stared at him. For a moment she didn't know what to say.

Then she smiled sadly. She shook her head. "It wouldn't work, Hubert," said gently. "I'm sorry."

When she got to the servants' quarters she could no longer hear the sounds of the ball. Although the connecting door to Madame Dupré's room was shut, Hélène was very quiet. She knew that the woman must be exhausted, and she was afraid of waking her up.

Slowly Hélène took off her turban, slipped out of her gown, and hung it carefully on a clothes hanger. In the morning she would remove all the baby's breath and then carefully pack the gown. Cinderella's ball had not lasted long. Five beautiful, exciting hours. Now she was a seamstress again. Suddenly she realized that she was tired and that her feet were aching from all the dancing.

She sat down on the edge of the bed and unlaced her slippers. At last she had time to think. Thoughtfully she massaged her feet, kneading her ankles with her hands. Had Hubert been serious about his proposal? she wondered. Probably. But there were two things she believed a successful marriage needed. Love, and acceptance from the family. She knew that she did not love Hubert enough to become his wife. She was not sure that he loved her. Perhaps he had mistaken infatuation for love. And acceptance from the family? She had no family to speak of, but he did. Would the Comte and Comtesse have allowed a marriage between their heir and a seamstress? She couldn't be certain, but she believed they wouldn't.

Abruptly she got to her feet and walked over to the round window. She bent down, parted the curtains a crack, and looked out. The night was dark and misty. In the light of the gaslights, one after the other, she saw chauffeured limousines pulling up to the marble steps. The guests were departing. The ball was over. For everyone. But not as much as for her.

13

"I want to hear everything!" Jeanne said excitedly when Hélène returned to Saint-Nazaire. "Did you see the Comte? Was his son handsome?"

Hélène looked across the kitchen table at Jeanne and smiled weakly. She cupped her hands around the warm coffee mug and looked quietly down into it. "Yes," she said slowly. "He was very handsome."

"Did you fall madly in love with him?"

It was supposed to be a joke, but Hélène couldn't laugh. She shook her head. "At first, I thought I did. I'm afraid he was more taken with me than I was with him."

Jeanne stared at her. "You mean he . . . ?"

Hélène nodded. "He asked me to marry him."

"You're not serious!" Jeanne gave Hélène an appraising look. Then her voice took on a quiet respect. "You *are* serious."

Hélène nodded.

Jeanne looked sharply at Hélène. "Don't tell me you turned him down!"

Hélène smiled. "I did."

"Well, that does it! Now I have to hear every last detail!"

They talked far into the night. Hélène didn't omit a thing. When she got to the part about the ball, Jeanne shook her head. She couldn't believe it. It all sounded too lavish for this world.

"You'll have to see my gown," Hélène said wistfully. "It was the most beautiful one there."

Jeanne's eyes brightened. "I can't wait to see it."

Suddenly Hélène smiled. She reached across the table and put her hand on top of Jeanne's. "Tell you what. I'll give it to you. It'll need a little taking in since you're so skinny, but it will make the perfect wedding gown."

Jeanne shook her head. "I could never accept it," she said in a tight voice. "It . . . it means too much to you."

Hélène smiled. "You must accept it. I wanted to make a dress for you, but this one is just perfect. I want you to look beautiful. After all, you get married only once, right?" She waited for Jeanne's nod. "And you want to look beautiful for Edmond, don't you?"

"Yes, but . . . you might need to wear it someplace . . ."

Hélène shook her head. "I'll never have the opportunity to wear it again."

Jeanne looked doubtful. "But what about when you get to Paris?"

Hélène sighed. "That's still a long way off, I'm afraid. Madame Dupré gave me a generous bonus, and I've saved quite a bit of money already, but it's not enough. Not for Paris." Suddenly her face broke into a smile. "How is Edmond?"

"He was here for only two days," Jeanne said. "He decided we could use the extra money, so instead of taking his month's vacation, he went back out to sea. It seems that your ambition is rubbing off on him."

"What do you mean?"

Jeanne suddenly clapped a hand over her mouth. "Oh-oh. Now I've let the cat out of the bag."

Hélène's eyes narrowed. She leaned across the table. "Out with it," she demanded.

"I'm not supposed to tell you," Jeanne said hesitantly. "Edmond wanted to tell you himself."

Hélène chuckled. "You told me this much; now I might as well hear the rest."

Jeanne sighed and shook her head. Then her voice dropped an octave. "We're saving up so that Edmond can go to school."

Hélène's eyes widened in surprise. This was news, indeed. "School," she repeated aloud, rolling the word on her tongue. A sudden keen intuition came over her. Edmond was right. An education would serve him well.

Jeanne's eyes burned with earnestness, but when she spoke, it was in a curiously soft voice. "Edmond wants more out of life than just being a fisherman, Hélène. He wants a future. He wants to be somebody. And when we have children, he wants them to be somebody, too. So he's thinking of going into law." She paused. "Just like you, he decided that in order to do it, he needs to return to Paris."

"Paris!" Hélène's eyes lit up and she could feel her heart beginning to pound. "That's *wonderful!*" she said.

Breathlessly Jeanne plunged on. "We've got it all worked out. For the next two years we'll scrimp and save. Then, as soon as we can afford it, we'll follow you to the city. They say there are many jobs there, so I shouldn't have any trouble finding work as a waitress. That way, I can help pay his way while he's going to the university!" She looked at Hélène proudly.

It's too bad that we no longer have Maman's house in Montmartre, Hélène thought bitterly. Then none of us would have to wait to get to Paris. But instead of voicing these thoughts, she asked brightly, "When's the fleet due in?"

"Next Friday. And the wedding is on the following day. Just think, Edmond's getting a whole week off!"

Hélène grinned. "Good. There'll be enough time for two celebrations, then."

Jeanne frowned. "Two?"

"Of course. One for your marriage, the other for your future." Suddenly Hélène sprang to her feet and began to pace thoughtfully up and down the kitchen. She tapped an index finger against her lips. "Let me see, now . . . there's the wedding. Are all the preparations made?"

Jeanne nodded.

"Good. And we'll have to plan a big dinner and . . . Good Lord! There's still so much to be done. We have no time to lose! You'd better come by my place this Sunday. I'll have to do the alterations on the gown immediately! And if I can find the right fabric by then, I'll sew your veil, also."

Jeanne stared at her. Suddenly she started to laugh.

Hélène stopped pacing and looked at her. "What's so funny?"

"You look so nervous, everyone would think you're the bride!"

14

The wedding was beautiful and Jeanne was the picture of the bride that all women dream they will be one day. Hélène sighed. This was a fairy-tale dream that happened once in your life. And Edmond was waiting for his lady, understandably nervous, yet visibly anxious for her arrival, for their hands to be joined forever.

Now it was over and Hélène realized that her time had come—not to meet her love, but finally to return to her beloved Paris to pursue her own dream.

She was ready.

Carefully she stepped over two sets of railroad tracks to the third platform. Edmond set her cardboard suitcase down at her feet. She turned around and looked at the small party of well-wishers who followed her. The only friends she had were here. Jeanne, Edmond, and Madame Dupré. And now she would be separated from them. Tears stung at her eyes. How long would it be until she saw them all again? she wondered.

She could hear the faint chugging of a locomotive. She glanced down the tracks. In the distance, a plume of white smoke marked the approaching train.

"It's coming," Jeanne murmured.

Hélène held her breath. She nodded with apprehension.

Madame Dupré gave Hélène a small package. "I've made you some sandwiches," she said.

Hélène nodded gratefully.

"Wait a second, there's one more thing." Madame Dupré reached into her pocketbook, took out an envelope, and pressed it into Hélène's hand.

Hélène looked at it curiously. "What is this?"

"A little something that might come in handy," Madame Dupré said vaguely.

232

Slowly Hélène lifted the flap of the envelope. She could see money inside. "No," she said firmly.

"You'll need it," Madame Dupré said, pushing Hélène's hand aside. "There isn't much. I didn't have a chance to go to the bank. It was all there was in the cash drawer."

Hélène embraced Madame Dupré. For a moment she couldn't speak. "Thank you," she said finally, her voice husky. "For everything. I'll never forget all you've done for me."

Madame Dupré's eyes were moist. "You just become successful!" she whispered. "You just take Paris by storm!"

"I will," Hélène promised. She turned to Jeanne. "Goodbye, friend."

Jeanne's lips quivered. Then she drew Hélène wordlessly toward her.

"You'll take care of Edmond?" Hélène asked softly.

Jeanne nodded. She looked ready to burst into tears.

Hélène turned to Edmond.

"Well, it looks like you're finally on your way, Little French Girl," he said softly.

Hélène found herself sniffling. She threw herself into his arms. He wrapped them around her, and she could feel his gentle strength. "I'm frightened, Edmond," she whispered.

He looked at her in surprise. "What of?"

"Paris."

"Don't be," he said solemnly.

"I don't like to be all alone."

"Don't worry. We'll join you there as soon as it's possible. And Jeanne will write to you every week."

Hélène nodded and looked up at him. She smiled through her tears. "If I'm rich before you, I'll send for you and put you through school."

"And if I get through school before you're rich, Little French Girl, I'll start a magazine for you."

The train rolled in with a metallic screech and then crawled to a stop with a mighty hiss and a jolt. Hélène looked up at the rows of grimy green cars. Then she glanced at her friends. There was nothing more to be said.

"Off you go," Edmond said cheerfully, extricating himself from her arms. "To Paris."

A lump rose up in her throat. "To Paris," she repeated softly.

TODAY

Thursday, January 11

1

It was after ten o'clock in the morning when James Cortland Gore III spun his swivel chair around to face his office window. It overlooked New York harbor to the right and the East River to the left. Idly he switched his gaze directly downward. Twenty-one stories below, he could see the tourists already swarming around on the decks of the antique tall ships that were docked at the South Street Seaport.

He spun back around to face his desk and pulled open the top drawer, where he kept his cigars. Opening the wooden box, he selected one, sniffed it, held it to his ear, and carefully rattled it. Satisfied, he trimmed the end off, leaned back, and lit it slowly. He folded his hands over his ample stomach as the expensive aroma of the Havana filled the office. Contentedly he puffed at it.

Things were certainly looking up, he thought with satisfaction. In fact, in a few days he might even surprise Geraldine by ordering the half-million-dollar Chris Craft Roamer she had been hungering after. He thought about it for a moment. Yes, a yacht might be very nice indeed. After all, there would be nothing to do on board but eat and drink, and he loved to do both. Best of all, it would even be affordable. Because only last night he had received another telephone call. . . .

He had been at home going over some documents in the big paneled study, a redolent pine fire sparkling in the fireplace when the call came.

"Do you know who this is?" the familiar voice asked softly.

His heart had begun to pound wildly and he looked around to make sure he was alone in the room. Geraldine had an unnerving habit of entering a room quiet as a mouse, and you'd never even know she was there. "Yes," he whispered into the receiver as if the walls might overhear.

"Well? Have you come to a decision?"

He took the silk handkerchief out of the breast pocket of his red silk smoking jacket and mopped his forehead. He had broken out in a sweat.

"Yes," he finally answered. "I have decided."

"And your answer?" the voice demanded.

He hesitated, but only fractionally. "I'll do it," he whispered. "She will not get an extension. I will arrange it so that you will get her shares."

"Good." The voice sounded satisfied. "The moment we sign the papers, you will receive a briefcase containing one million dollars."

"Consider it done."

The phone clicked and went dead, and it took him a moment to realize that the caller had hung up. His chins were quivering as he replaced the receiver. He felt relief. Yes, and at the same time, he was very nervous. As nervous as he was each time he "wrote" himself a loan. . . .

The intercom on his desk buzzed. He leaned forward and pressed the button. "Yes, Alice?"

"Mr. Gore, there are two men from accounting here to see you."

He stared at the intercom, his face going pale. Men? From accounting? Once again he began to break out in a sweat. Good God, not the auditors, he prayed. Not at a time like this. Not when he'd be able to replace all his "borrowings" in less than a week's time. Dear, sweet, merciful God, no. Then he put the brakes on this ridiculous train of thought. He was just feeling guilty and panicky. There really was nothing to fear. After all, it was part of his job to deal with the accounting department. It would not do to panic each time he had to talk things over with them. That thought made him feel better, but one thing was certain. As soon as he got his hands on the million, he'd lose no time in replacing the missing funds.

After a long moment he cleared his throat. "Send them in," he said.

Seconds later, Alice opened the door and ushered them into his office. His heart began to thump and he thought he was going to be sick. Instantly he realized that he had reason to panic. These were not just two men from accounting. He recognized them. The short, stocky one was Paluzzi, the tall blond one O'Rourke. They were part of the bank's internal auditing team.

Gore's mind began to race. If he didn't think fast, he'd find his whole world, his dreams, indeed his whole life come crashing down all around him. Somehow he'd have to stall them; somehow he'd have to find a way to gain a week in order to dig himself out of this mess. Above all, he must conceal his fears. His guilt.

"Gentlemen," he said with a forced smile. "Won't you have a seat?"

They nodded expressionlessly and sat down in the two overstuffed chairs that faced his desk.

Gore quietly folded his hands on the polished mahogany surface. It did not surprise him to find that his hands were shaking. Trying to keep his voice natural, he favored the men with the friendliest look he could muster. "What can I do for you?"

Paluzzi looked curiously at him. A sturdy Italian with thick black hair and extremely broad shoulders, he looked more like a weight lifter than an accountant. But looks can deceive. Gore knew that Paluzzi's reputation at ManhattanBank was secure. He was the best auditor they had.

"Mr. Gore," Paluzzi said softly, "we've been going over your accounts dating back over the last five years. The first forty-three months are in order. But beginning seventeen months ago, we've found some discrepancies."

"Discrepancies?" Gore could feel his blood pressure rise. "What kind of discrepancies?"

Paluzzi's dark eyes were steady. "I think you already know, Mr. Gore."

This can't be happening, he told himself over and over. It's only a nightmare. A *nightmare*. It'll be over when I wake up.

Now O'Rourke spoke up. "Don't you want to know the amount of the discrepancy, Mr. Gore?"

No! He didn't want to hear another word. He couldn't bear it any longer. But in a faraway voice he found himself murmuring, "How much?"

"Exactly five hundred thousand, ninety-five dollars," Paluzzi said. "All of it missing from your accounts."

Gore forced a thin laugh. The moment it came out, he realized how unconvincing it sounded. "You must be mistaken," he said. "You have the ledgers?"

"In our office. They are correct."

Gore pushed back his chair and rose to his feet. "I would like to go over them with you, if it won't be inconvenient. Could you wait outside for me? I would like to make a telephone call first." He caught them exchanging glances. He puffed his chest out with dignity. "No, gentlemen," he assured them, "I'm not going to call a lawyer. I have no need for one."

O'Rourke looked questioningly at Paluzzi. The shorter man shrugged. Then both got up and went back into the outer office, closing the door softly behind them.

Gore covered his face with his hands. It was over. He didn't stand a chance now. He would be branded a thief, put in jail, ostracized from his clubs, never find another job. At least not in another bank. No bank in the world would ever touch him again. He was a thief.

One more week, and everything would have turned out differently. But now? Now it was too late. Suddenly he wondered what Geraldine would think. He smiled bitterly. She'd probably be mad as all hell that after all her years of working so hard at being a social item, it would be gone down the drain in one fell swoop. She would despise him.

Geraldine didn't like losers.

Slowly he walked toward the door, then stopped and turned around to stare out the window. From here, all he could see was the sky. Like a siren, it seemed to beckon sweetly.

Suddenly he knew what he had to do. It was the only way out.

He took a deep breath. Then, before he could change his mind, he charged forward, holding his hands out in front of him. They smashed through the plate glass, his knees caught on the thigh-high air-conditioning and heating ducts, and as he plunged through the window, his body did a grotesque, graceless somersault.

The sudden rush of cold air felt strangely exhilarating. He let out one short scream, and then it was all over.

Geraldine had been right. Her husband did kill himself. If not because of the Bulgari bracelet, then because of some others.

2

Hélène was standing behind her desk, her back to the windows. She looked down at the artboards that completely hid the beautifully inlaid marquetry. There was a thoughtful expression on her face. The artboards were all mock-ups of Junot magazine covers. The tissue paper protecting each picture had been carefully folded back behind each board, and a sea of glossy faces stared coldly up at her. She studied each one closely.

There was *La Moda*, with a fiercely scowling super-model; French *Les Modes* showing a tart with glossy, pouting lips; the German *Mode* cover girl, almost in too aggressive a pose; and a sweet-faced, airbrushed blond for American *Les Modes*.

It was funny, Hélène thought, that the average American woman preferred the sweet-looking girl-next-door-type model to the angular Amazonian Venus the Europeans adored. Her eyes roved on.

The English edition of *Les Modes* showed a full figure in a billowing summer dress by Halston, and *Yachting and Boating* had a photo of two "New Wave" girls in blue suede bikinis at the helm of an outrageously expensive Riva speedboat.

All the covers were fantastic, and she knew it. Yet there was something about each one that didn't quite suit her. At first she couldn't put her finger on what it was, but then it dawned on her: they were the covers for the June issues, and outside it was still midwinter. Even after years of preparing the magazines four to six months ahead of their issue dates, she still hadn't learned to get used to seeing bathing suits and chiffons in winter, wools and furs in summer. There was something oddly obscene about it. It made her feel like a clairvoyant when the issues—and clothes—finally came out, and it was a rather creepy feeling. Each season confronted her with this peculiar sense of *déjà vu*.

241

She heard the door opening and looked up. It was Edmond. He hadn't bothered to knock. He was the only person permitted to walk in unannounced, but usually he did not exercise this prerogative. As a matter of courtesy to Julie and herself, he always let himself be announced. The fact that he hadn't bothered with formalities aroused Hélène's misgivings. Something very important must have happened. She could remember only two times before that he had rushed in like that. Both times had been emergencies.

He walked briskly toward her and didn't wait for her to ask what had happened. "You've just gained a week's extension!" he said excitedly. "ManhattanBank has decided it won't call in the loan tomorrow."

She frowned in silence, digesting this unexpected turn of events. Stretching the deadline by a week wouldn't help her in the long run. Still, it was a nonrenewable note. As such, the extension *was* significant. "I don't understand," she said.

"Why don't you have a seat and I'll explain it to you."

She nodded and they sat down in the fragile French chairs that faced her desk. She crossed her legs and waited while he lit a cigarette.

"I just found out that Gore is no longer handling your accounts," he said. "Whoever is appointed to replace him will have to acquaint himself with them, review your financial predicament, and come to a decision. He'll need a week—maybe more—to catch up on it."

Hélène gave him an odd look. "But why? Has Gore quit his job?" she asked curiously. She couldn't imagine the well-fed banker doing anything of the sort.

Edmond shook his head and watched her closely. His voice was soft. "He committed suicide. Jumped out of his office window."

Hélène went pale. An uncontrollable chill rushed through her. "I think someone just walked over my grave," she said quietly.

"What do you mean?"

Hélène looked down at her hands. "Only yesterday, I ran into his wife at Susumu's. She showed me a bracelet she'd just bought at Bulgari, and do you know what she said?" Edmond shook his head in silence. "She said: 'My husband will probably kill himself when he sees it.' Those were her exact words!"

Edmond stared at her. "That's too bad," he said sympathetically. "I only hope the poor woman won't blame herself for it." He paused. "But mercenary as it may sound, Gore's done you an enormous favor. It's gotten you an extension. Even if it is only for a week or so."

She nodded slowly. At least now she'd have more time to think everything over carefully, to weigh the alternatives and arrive at the right decision. But there was still one thing she couldn't understand. "Edmond, *why* did he do it?"

He shrugged and took a deep drag on his cigarette. "I'm not certain, but the rumors are flying. ManhattanBank tried to put a lid on them, but word's leaked out anyway. They say he's embezzled a lot of money. Apparently he must have thought death was the only way out."

Hubert de Léger waited in his upstairs library until the house phone rang. "Monsieur le Comte," the soft-spoken butler said in French, "they are all here."

"Very well, Eduard," the Comte said. "I'll be down shortly. See that they're made comfortable. Serve them drinks."

"I already have, sir."

"Good." The Comte replaced the receiver and finished the letter he was reading. He was in no hurry. Let them wait, he thought with a smirk. It would only add to their suspense. He had hastily summoned them little more than half an hour ago, and each one had pointedly inquired about the reason for the urgent meeting. He had been purposely mysterious, and none of them had lost any time in getting here. Now he would let them speculate.

He made some notes on a pad, wrote out a telex, finished his inevitable Armagnac, and finally got to his feet. By now they would be bursting with impatience.

He took the small suede-lined elevator down to the foyer. At the living-room doors he hesitated. Then he flung them aside and strode in.

Slowly he looked around the big, Empire-furnished room. Seated on chairs with sphinx heads for arms and on couches with gilt claws for legs were Z.Z. Bavier, Karl von Eiderfeld, and Marcello d'Itri. A look of satisfaction showed in the Comte's eyes. No, not one of Hélène's enemies had wasted a second getting here. All of them had drinks in their hands.

The Comte could feel the hostility in his guests' eyes, and his lips spread into a sudden smile. "My friends," he announced with a quick nod of his head, "I am pleased to see that you could all come so quickly. Especially on such short notice."

Z.Z.'s lynx eyes narrowed. "Is that why you kept us waiting for so long?" she hissed in annoyance.

The Comte smiled easily. "Of course not, my dear Z.Z. I was delayed by a most urgent call." He came toward her, bent down, kissed her cheek. "My heartfelt apologies."

She looked at him doubtfully. Suspicious bitch, he thought to himself. He crossed the room to the bar, poured himself a glass of Armagnac, and leaned against the marble fireplace. Since they were all seated, he preferred to remain standing. It gave him a certain feeling of dominance.

"Well?" Z.Z. demanded. "Would you mind explaining what is so urgent that we had to drop everything and rush over here?"

The Comte sipped his Armagnac. "An unexpected development has come up. It requires that we revise our plans."

Z.Z. looked at him sharply. "An unexpected development? What the hell has happened?"

"Gore," he answered softly. "The banker."

D'Itri exchanged glances with Z.Z. "What about the banker?" the Italian designer asked. "Has he had a change of mind? Won't he sell us her collateral?"

The Comte looked at d'Itri. "It's not that he won't sell it. It's that he *can't*."

D'Itri looked puzzled. "I don't see any difference between 'won't' and 'can't.' "

"Ah, but there *is* a subtle distinction," the Comte said.

"You mean she's actually managed to pay it all *back*?" Z.Z.'s voice was incredulous.

All at once d'Itri and von Eiderfeld began to talk excitedly.

The Comte raised a hand to silence them. "No, she hasn't paid it back. But she's gotten a week's extension."

"An extension!" Z.Z. wailed. "*How*! It's a nonrenewable loan!"

The Comte smiled grimly. "At ten-forty-five this morning, Mr. Gore made a rather untimely departure from this life. He committed suicide."

"Verdammt!" Von Eiderfeld slammed his palm down on one of the sphinx heads of his chair. "I knew we should not have trusted that man!"

D'Itri stared sullenly at the Comte. "So what do we do now?"

"What *can* we do!" Z.Z. shrieked. She stared accusingly at the Comte. "You assured us that it was all arranged! That nothing could go wrong!" With trembling fingers she lit a Dunhill.

The Comte was calm. He wasn't about to be goaded into an argument. "This was beyond even my control," he said patiently. "I like it as little as you do. It seems that Gore had been embezzling money. It just so happens that he got caught at the worst possible moment."

"Oh, Christ!" Z.Z. swore. She drained her drink in one long swallow.

"Now that Gore is gone," von Eiderfeld murmured thoughtfully, "where does that leave us?"

The Comte shrugged. "Someone else will have to take Gore's place. We'll just wait patiently and see who it is. Then we'll approach him."

"And if he can't be bribed?" d'Itri snapped. "What then?"

"My dear Marcello." The Comte's tone was cold. "Everyone has his price. You should know that better than anyone."

D'Itri flushed. "Just what do you mean by that?" he demanded angrily.

The Comte smiled. "All I mean to say is that of all of us, you are the one with the scantiest excuse for hating Hélène. Without her, you'd be nothing. Oh, maybe you'd have a third-rate dress shop somewhere. But face it—she made you. She set you up, and now you don't like the price." He paused. "Marcello, you're biting the hand that feeds you."

D'Itri's hands shot up to cover his ears. "Shut up!" he screamed. "Shut up!" Angrily he jumped to his feet. "What about you?" He pointed an accusing finger at each one of them in turn. "And you? And *you*?"

The Comte smiled benignly. "We have other reasons, Marcello. Better reasons. With us it's not a simple matter of turning our backs on a debt."

"Well, fuck you!" With his hands, d'Itri made an obscene gesture and left, slamming the door behind him.

For a moment the others sat in stunned silence. Then Z.Z. began to laugh. "My, my! Such a vulgar outburst!"

The Comte crossed the room and poured himself another glass of Armagnac. "Marcello is a peasant," he said derisively. "He may have money, but in the end, class always tells. There is nothing worse than the nouveau riche." He looked at von Eiderfeld and smiled apologetically. "Excepting yourself, of course. I do not consider you to be in that category."

"I should hope not," the industrialist said with dignity. He rose to his feet. "As soon as you contact the new banker, you will let us know?"

The Comte nodded. "Of course."

"Good. And now I must regretfully be going. I have an important appointment, and I am already late." Von Eiderfeld stiffly shook hands with the Comte, and the butler showed him out.

When they were alone, Z.Z. shook her head. "Von Eiderfeld never fails to give me the creeps," she said. There was a note of disgust in her voice. "All that dreadfully white skin and those bloodless eyes. He reminds me of something out of a monster movie." She shuddered.

The Comte was silent, and she took it as a cue.

"Well, I suppose it's time for me to go also," she said with a sigh. "After all this bad news, I might as well stop at Bendel's and buy a little something to cheer me up."

The butler came with her silver-fox coat and she took her time slipping into it. Then the Comte personally escorted her to the door, drink in hand.

In the foyer, she halted, turning to face him. Her lips formed a mocking smile, and there was a glint of wicked amusement in her eyes. "You never mentioned why *you* hate Hélène Junot so much, my dear Comte. Could it be too unladylike for my delicate ears to hear?"

He stared down at his glass. His face looked suddenly haggard with pain, and she couldn't help wincing. For an instant she felt genuinely sorry that she had brought up the subject.

When he spoke, his words came out so softly that she almost didn't catch them. "I . . . was in love with her once."

Z.Z. glanced at him sharply. Curiosity had replaced her momentary pity. "So? What happened?"

Suddenly he began to tremble, then gripped his glass so hard that the delicate crystal shattered in his hand. She stared at his fingers; they were starting to bleed, and pieces of jagged crystal were embedded in the flesh. She heard what sounded like a strangled sob in his throat.

"What *happened?*" he screamed. Then his hysterical laughter reverberated around the foyer.

YESTERDAY

III
ADULTERY

1

Paris, 1953

A lump came up in Hélène's throat as the train sped into Paris. She got to her feet, pushed down the window, and leaned her head out. She had to squint as the cold wind hit her face and rushed through her hair. She swallowed her first deep gulps of Parisian air and the tears sprang to her eyes. In the distance, through the tears, she could see the Eiffel Tower. For a while she stared out at it in rapt fascination. It seemed to spring triumphantly up from among the endless sea of gray and black rooftops like a welcoming beacon. Then it disappeared as the train began the drawn-out, grating screech that signaled its approach to the station.

When the train jolted to a halt, Hélène carefully stepped down onto the platform. Up front, clouds of steam billowed up from under the hissing locomotive. It sounded like a weary giant letting out a deep sigh. Overhead, the metal gird-ers of the Gare Montparnasse soared up to the glass roof in apparent defiance of the laws of gravity. She put down her suitcase and looked around. The first thing that caught her eye was that the travelers looked fatter and healthier than the Parisians of her memory, and they were far better dressed. All around her was the vibrant air of life that the French called joie de vivre. Gone were the dark things that had left a smudge on her memory: the haunting silence, the frightened looks on people's faces and the constant furtive glances over their shoulders, the fumblings with those all-important documents—official, stamped papers. Missing, too, were the swastikas and the sharp-eyed, ever-present Boches. Paris was different. She could feel it, and it felt good.

An old porter came up to her. "Mademoiselle?" he asked. He looked at her questioningly.

Quickly she shook her head. "Non, merci," she said softly.

Porters cost money, and she didn't have as much as a sou to throw away on such an extravagance. She grabbed her old suitcase and lugged it out to the street. The sunlight was bright and hurt her eyes. She blinked, but not because of the sun. In front of the station was the most incredible sight she had ever seen. Rows of gleaming black taxis. She shook her head in wonder. Would miracles never cease? And the streets—it was the first time she had ever seen the streets of Paris so crowded. Gone were the horse-drawn wagons, the vélo-taxis, and the hordes of bicycles. Instead, there were cars of every shade of the rainbow. How different everything looked from the Occupation! If only Maman were here to see it, she thought with regret.

"Taxi, mademoiselle?" A driver with a mustache held the door of his Renault open.

Hélène hesitated and peered inside. The seats were thickly upholstered and looked inviting. For an instant she almost splurged and got in. It would be nice to celebrate her return and ride down the Champs-Élysées and through the narrow streets of the Right Bank in style. But like the porter, it was a waste of money. Quickly she tightened her grip on the suitcase and walked away. She would need every last precious sou she had. Her first priority would be to find an inexpensive place to live. And then to buy food.

Wearily Hélène climbed the four narrow flights to her apartment. Another useless day, she thought listlessly as she unlocked the door. She threw the key down on the rickety kitchen table, kicked the door shut behind her, and slipped out of her clothes. Then she flopped down on the bed. The mattress sagged under her weight. In silence she stared up at the cracked ceiling. She was bone-tired. When she first arrived, her hopes had known no ceiling. Anything was possible. Now reality was crushing her hopes slowly but inextricably.

Still no job, she thought miserably. For three weeks she'd been looking now, and still nothing. Meanwhile, all Paris was bustling while she was pounding the pavement. And today had been the worst day yet. She closed her eyes.

Today she had answered an advertisement for a brassiere manufacturer looking for models. It was not the kind of job she wanted, but in desperation she'd gone anyway. It had been a gross mistake. The "manufacturer" had turned out to be nothing more than a front for a low-class whorehouse. And the disgusting fat pig who ran the place took one look at her and chased her around the filthy "office." She shuddered in disgust. Luckily she had managed to outwit him, get to the door, and flee. Now what would she do?

She had less than fifty francs left to her name. There was nothing in the tiny cupboard but two eggs, plus the bottle of milk she kept out on the windowsill to stay cool. The rent was due in two days.

She sighed and opened her eyes. Then she sat up and looked around the apartment. It was unbelievable. One room in a crummy Montmartre garret. She shook her head. In the expansive letters she had sent Edmond and Madame Dupré, she had written that it was small but charming, and had a splendid view. So they wouldn't worry about her, she had even lied and written that she had several job possibilities lined up. And that she'd have to think each over carefully to choose the one she thought would best suit her future.

Future? What future? Job opportunities? Being chased around by a pervert who smelled of cheap wine? Was that a job possibility?

Suddenly she began to laugh.

Charming apartment? She began to laugh even harder. Sure it was charming, she thought. The walls were covered with dirty white paint, the linoleum floor was cracked, and three of the nine panes of glass in the one small window were broken and boarded over. And the view she had written home so warmly about? She was in gales of laughter now. The view was the window of an apartment across the court-yard. In it lived a shaggy young artist who masturbated with more frequency than he painted. When Hélène had discovered that, she lost no time in yanking the tattered tablecloth off the kitchen table and draping it across the window. She was only too happy to spare herself that view.

And the size of her apartment? Also laughable. It was a single room, twelve feet long and not quite nine feet wide. There wasn't even a closet. All her clothes were hanging from hooks on the wall that some previous tenant had put up. The toilet out in the hall was unheated. She shared it with three other tenants on the floor. There was no bath.

She despised the place.

Her eyes came to rest on a heap of fabric on the floor. It was the dress she had been wearing. Tonight she'd once again have to wash it out in the sink, hang it up to dry, and then borrow the concierge's iron. Tomorrow she'd have to wear it to go back out and pound the pavement again.

Suddenly her laughter turned to tears and she buried her face in the pillow. Violent sobs began to rack her body. Oh, what was the use? she asked herself. Surely this was the end of the road.

Just then there were heavy footsteps outside on the stairs, followed by a loud knock on the door. A frown crossed her face. She wasn't expecting anyone; so far, she knew no one in Paris. As she lifted her head from the pillow, a feeling of dread went through her. Perhaps it was the concierge. Could she already be coming around to collect the rent?

The thought sent a chill of terror through her. She didn't have enough money left to pay the rent. She hesitated and stared at the door. Perhaps if she kept really quiet the old hag would go back downstairs where she belonged.

The knocks came again, louder this time.

Hélène sighed. "Just a minute," she finally called out in a weary voice. She struggled up and swung her legs over the edge of the bed. She took her robe down off the hook, slipped into it, and quickly wiped her eyes dry with the palms of her hands. Clutching the front of her robe together, she went over to the door and opened it a crack.

She stood there and stared up at him in surprise, He was a tall man. Very tall. He must have stood at least six-feet-four, had unruly red hair, a red beard, an engaging smile, and she had never seen him before. His eyes were gentle and sky blue. In the crook of his arm he carried a half-full bottle of wine and a rolled-up newspaper with the tip of a loaf of bread sticking out.

She blinked. "Who are you?" she asked.

He grinned. "I'm Guy Barbeau," he said easily. "Artist and ne'er-do-well, by my own admission. I live across the hall." He held out his free hand.

"Oh. I'm Hélène Junot," she said awkwardly. They shook hands. When he let go of her hand she pointed vaguely behind her. "I . . . uh . . . I live here."

He laughed and peeked past her into the room. "I can't believe it!" His voice was incredulous.

She was confused. "Believe what?"

"You've got even more space than I've got!"

Despite herself, she laughed. "I can't believe anything could be more cramped than this pigeonhole."

"You'll be surprised. You should see my dump. May I come in?"

The request took her by surprise. She hesitated. Should she entertain a man in her room? Although she wasn't frightened, she wondered if it were proper. Then she pushed the thought out of her mind. She nodded and stepped aside. Guy Barbeau came in and set the wine and bread down on the kitchen table.

"Have you had your supper yet?" he asked.

"Have I . . . ?"

"I see you haven't." He acted very sure of himself. "We'll sup together, then. Have you got two glasses and a knife?"

She blushed. "I haven't got any glasses," she said shyly. "Will two small milk bottles and a knife do?"

"Splendidly. The height of luxury. Thank God your kitchen is better equipped than mine." He scraped the table closer to the bed and unwrapped the newspaper. Besides the bread there was a chunk of Roquefort, a tin of sardines, and a length of hard salami. Expertly he opened the can of sardines, smoothed out the newspaper, and artfully arranged the food on it. When she finished rinsing out the bottles in the sink, he was already sitting down on the edge of the bed.

"It looks delicious," she said politely as she sat down beside him.

He laughed. "It's merely poverty food. Fuel for our bodies. Alas, not enough to nourish our souls." He poured a few fingers of wine into each milk bottle. "Santé."

"Santé."

She let the glass door of the boutique slam shut behind her. It was still raining out, and she pulled the collar of her coat up high around her neck. Another dead end, she thought morosely. She sighed deeply. Today the rent was due.

She turned right and headed toward the Boulevard St. Germain. She had applied for a job as a salesgirl in a smart new boutique opposite Sainte Clotilde. The owner, Madame d'Arbeuf, had interviewed her in a little office in the back of the store.

Madame d'Arbeuf held a lot of faith in first impressions. Through her elegant blue-framed glasses, her stern eyes had studied Hélène. What she saw did nothing to inspire her.

Even Hélène's best dress was a sad contrast—an embarrassment, actually—to the posh refinement of her shop. Worse, it had begun to rain and Hélène had gotten caught in it. She was soaked.

"What experience do you have in retail sales, mademoiselle?" Madame d'Arbeuf purred smoothly.

"I . . . I've worked in a dress shop," Hélène replied.

"Oh. Where was that?"

"In Saint-Nazaire."

Madame d'Arbeuf frowned. "Saint-Nazaire? Let me see, now, Saint-Nazaire . . ." She shook her head. "I can't seem to recall where that is. Is it near Cannes?"

Hélène couldn't help but smile. Saint-Nazaire might as well have been a million light-years from Cannes. "No, madame. It's on the Bay of Biscay."

"Oh." Madame d'Arbeuf rose to her feet. "Actually, we're looking for someone with more . . ." She smiled thinly. "More sophistication. More polish. You see, the Boutique Chat Blanc has an international clientele, mademoiselle. I'm afraid . . ."

Hélène's desperation was written all over her face. "But, madame! I'm very clever! I learn quickly! You'll see . . ."

Madame d'Arbeuf looked at her with distaste. "It's no use," she said sternly. "I'm sorry to have wasted your time."

2

Hélène's concierge was right at the foot of the stairs when she came in. There was no avoiding her. She was on her knees scrubbing the linoleum with a stiff brush. When she saw Hélène she struggled to her feet and wiped her red hands on her apron. "Mademoiselle! The rent is due today."

Hélène looked at her. "I'm sorry, Madame Guérin. I don't have it yet. Perhaps tomorrow."

"Tomorrow!" Madame Guérin stormed. "I have my orders to collect it the day it is due. That is today. That, too, was our agreement when you moved in."

"I know. Just give me a few days," Hélène begged. "Please. My brother will send it."

"I'm sorry, mademoiselle. In this building we collect the rent in advance. It's either pay now or move out now!"

Behind them the front door creaked open. The person entering evidently had second thoughts about coming in and started to leave again. Hélène turned and caught a glimpse of Guy Barbeau slinking away like the cat that caught the canary.

"Monsieur Barbeau!"

Madame Guérin's shrill voice froze Guy in his tracks.

"You also! Like I was telling Mademoiselle Junot, the rent is due!"

Sheepishly he came toward them, rain pouring off his overcoat. His soaked red hair was plastered against his head. Wearily he smiled at Hélène. "Hello again."

"Hello," she replied.

"Had any luck?" he asked.

She shook her head. "No," she said softly.

Madame Guérin placed her hands on her hips and looked up at him. "Do you have the money?" she demanded.

He sighed heavily and looked down at his feet. "Just a few days. Please."

"We've been through that often enough now. Go upstairs and start packing before I call the police."

"But my paintings! The canvases! It'll take days to move them." In desperation he looked at Hélène. "You wouldn't by any chance . . ."

She shook her head. "I'm being tossed out too, remember?"

All of a sudden he grabbed her by the arm and pulled her aside. "Listen," he whispered excitedly. "How much money have you got?"

She was puzzled. "About forty francs. Why?"

He did some quick calculations. "And I've got fifty!"

"So we're both broke. What good will that do us?"

"Don't you see? Your rent's seventy francs, right?"

She nodded.

"So we'll let my apartment go and move into yours! We'll be roommates."

She hesitated. "I don't know," she said slowly. "It'll be awfully cramped."

"It's either that or the streets for both of us."

It made sense. Slowly she nodded. "As long as it's strictly platonic," she stipulated.

He held up his right hand. "As God is my judge."

She smiled. "Monsieur Barbeau, we've just bought ourselves a month's reprieve."

Five minutes later, it was all arranged and they went upstairs to move his things into her apartment. At his door, Hélène's eyes opened wide. Leaning against one wall was an enormous canvas. It was almost the length of the room. She backed against the far wall and squinted at it. "It's extraordinary!" she exclaimed.

"It's my best work to date," Guy said. He moved a stack of small canvases aside and stood beside her. "I'm calling it *The Hyperbolic Ascension*. I've been working on it for nine months now. Another couple of days and it should be finished."

Hélène couldn't take her eyes off it. It depicted a surrealistic Madonna exploding in space, her body all in shards against a background of light. It looked as if someone had placed a charge of dynamite inside her and then frozen the picture in the midst of the explosion.

"As soon as it's finished, it'll go to the Lichtenstein Gallery," he explained. "André Lichtenstein himself came by to see it a couple of weeks ago. He's willing to handle it. He's big-time. They say he's the most important art dealer in Paris."

"That's wonderful!" Hélène said warmly.

He nodded. "Hopefully a buyer will think so, too."

She smiled. "I don't think you need to worry about that. I'm certain it'll be snatched up right away. And whoever gets it will be very lucky."

He looked at her curiously. "You really believe that, don't you?"

Without taking her eyes off the painting, she nodded her head. "It's more beautiful than most paintings I've seen in the Louvre. It reminds me of Raphael, only there's so much more depth." She shook her head. "It's really incredible."

On Saturday they ate a light breakfast of bread and fruit. The bread was hard and stale. The loaf had been two days old, but as a result they had gotten it for next to nothing.

Hélène had cut up the fruit into little cubes and made a

salad out of it. It looked delicious. Actually, she had prepared it that way so it wouldn't look too depressing. The night before, Guy had scavenged among the crates of throwaways at Les Halles. Since each piece was partially spoiled, it called for surgery. She decided it was much more appetizing to eat a salad than fruit with big chunks pared out of it.

When they had finished eating, Guy picked up the table and set it down in the far corner out of the way. "Food for the muses," he murmured. "You didn't warn me that you could cook. Besides a roommate, I seem to have gained a first-class chef as well." He stifled a burp. "Well done. It was rather a nice change from biting into amputated apples."

She smiled. She was glad he appreciated her effort. "You're going to start painting now?" she asked.

He nodded.

"Good. Then I'm going to take a long walk. I've spent two weekends catching up on culture in the Louvre, and every weekday for three weeks chasing down dead-end jobs. Today I intend to walk around for the sheer joy of it." She reached behind *The Hyperbolic Ascension* and felt around for her brown wool skirt and heavy knitted sweater. She would wear the sweater outside, over the skirt, and then fasten her brown leather belt around it. Already she was picking up fashion pointers from chic Parisian women she saw in the streets. Perhaps she would even pin up her hair. The idea made her smile. She wondered how it would look.

"Want me to go outside while you change?" Guy asked.

She shook her head. "No, I'll use the toilet. At least there's a mirror in there."

He nodded, took the tablecloth down off the window, and opened it. The sun was shining and light flooded the room. A chill wind blasted in along with it.

"You better wear a coat or you'll catch cold," she suggested.

He nodded absently. Already he was in another world, his eyes searching the big canvas. He didn't even hear the door snap shut behind her.

She walked for hours. At first it was aimless wandering. She left the old streets of Montmartre behind and took one of the arched bridges over to the Left Bank. The sidewalks were crowded with Saturday shoppers and families out taking a stroll. Even some of the sidewalk cafés already had a few hardy customers braving the chill. Spring was not long off. In Paris, you could smell it coming.

Passing a lingerie shop, between the ghostly shapes of brassieres, she caught sight of herself in the glass. Could that be me? she asked herself. She stepped closer. It *was* her. She couldn't believe it. Pinning up her hair made all the difference in the world. She looked taller, more mature, but still youthful. And to her surprise, the past few weeks of fasting hadn't taken their toll. Instead, they had done the exact opposite. Gone forever was her baby fat. She was no longer slender; she was very thin. But not in the way malnourished people are emaciated. Rather, in the way that fashion models are slim, statuesque.

She looked closer. Her cheekbones, too, had gained new prominence, and her eyes seemed larger and oddly luminous. The belt around her sweater accentuated her tiny waist. She pivoted, checking the profile of her body. Satisfied, she made a mental note to remember to take in all her clothes at the waist.

As she continued walking, she found herself humming softly to herself. She felt suddenly more beautiful, more confident, more stylish. More like a real Parisienne. Now she had only to gain a little polish. She would study the elegant ladies. She would pick up their walks. Their mannerisms.

Each time she passed a shop window, she found herself sneaking quick glances at her shadowy reflection. Yes, it was really true. She had changed.

When she reached the Boulevard St. Germain, the jugglers were already out in full force. They were entertaining a pack of little children who shrieked and clapped their hands in delight. Smiling, Hélène stopped and watched them in idle amusement. But as she looked at the jugglers, she saw other jugglers from the past. The amusement in her eyes dimmed. Other jugglers, from years ago. Years ago, with Michelle.

Years ago . . .

Suddenly she found herself slipping back in time. Perhaps it was triggered by the mesmerizing effect of the little red balls that were being tossed and caught with such hypnotic repetition. Maybe it was the shrieks of the children. Or even the smell of spring in the air. Whatever it was, something had unlocked the long-shut door to the memories of her childhood and laid them bare for her to see. For a moment she felt a wave of nausea. It was like she was on a merry-go-round and the world was reeling all around her.

As if in a trance, she turned and began to walk on. This time it was not with the aimless pace of a Saturday-afternoon stroller but with purpose. It was almost as if some unexplainable power—some magnet—was drawing her toward a certain destination.

All the background noises of the city were now muffled. Behind her, the shrieks of the children were distorted whispers in the afternoon. Loud in her ears was the sound of her heels clacking faster and faster on the sidewalk. Each footstep seemed to reverberate louder than the last, like a distant roll of thunder that was fast approaching. Even the sidewalk seemed to warp, a ribbon of undulating waves.

Then the peal of thunder was upon her. She felt a sudden blast of heat and then began to fall. An iron lamppost was within reach, and she wrapped her arms around it to steady herself. For a moment she just hung on.

An old man stopped and looked at her. "Mademoiselle?" he asked in a concerned voice. "Are you all right?"

She took a deep breath and slowly nodded. The man moved on. Was she all right? No, she wasn't all right. But there was nothing anyone could do to help.

For the next half-hour she walked briskly, without stopping. The vertigo was gone, and in its place was new understanding. She knew her destination.

She had no trouble finding the flights of twisting stone steps that led up to the top of the Butte. It had been almost ten years, but it all came back to her as easily as if it had been yesterday.

Halfway up, she reached the little park. It was still there, and so was the bench where she used to play with Antoinette. So, too, were the acacia trees. They were bare, like the last time she had seen them. Only they were much bigger now. Acacia trees grow quickly.

And there, across the alley, stood the house. She looked at it curiously. It looked much smaller now that she was grown. But she could still recognize it, even if it did look seedier and more modest than the house of her memory. The front door was different; it was of varnished dark oak. Gone forever was the canary-yellow door. But the ground-floor windows were still covered with the curlicued bars, and above the rooftop, the domes of Sacré Coeur gleamed whitely. Odors of greasy food hung heavy in the air. Someone was cooking pork.

This was where she would be living now if Tante Janine hadn't sold the house out from under her, she thought bitterly. Rightfully the house had belonged to her and Edmond.

But it was no use harping on that now, she told herself savagely. Be practical. Be realistic. She and Edmond no longer had any claim to it. It had been stolen from them. Her lips tightened. *Stolen.*

She stared at the house. If . . . *If* it were still theirs, it would have solved so many of her problems. She would have lived on the ground floor and converted the dining room into a bedroom. Perhaps put up a cheerfully patterned wallpaper. There would have been a separate living room and kitchen as well as access to the garden out back. There would have been no need to share a claustrophobic closet with Guy Barbeau. She would even have been assured a steady income by renting out the upstairs. There would have been no financial woes, no pleading with dour concierges, no scavenging for rotten fruit . . .

Suddenly the vertigo started up again. Her head began to spin and she sank down onto the cold hard slats of the bench.

Like a series of slow-motion negatives, a chain of distorted pictures flashed through her mind. She saw Maman being punched mercilessly in the belly by the Boche. Even now she could still hear her screeches of pain echoing through the neighborhood. Once again she heard the ear-shattering blast of the gunshot that threw Michelle against the kitchen doorway and made her collapse like a limp sack of potatoes.

Abruptly Hélène got up and quickly began to walk away. Tears blurred her vision. Fiercely she wiped them away with her hands. She could deal with many things. This house was not one of them. She never wanted to see it again. Ever.

"It's just as well that that thief Pierre sold it," she said to herself as she stumbled along the cobblestones. "I could never live there. *Never.* It's no use trying to live in a house full of ugly ghosts."

She headed straight home, strangely glad that Guy would be there. His company would be a comfort.

The window was still open when she got back. The room was icy. Guy didn't speak. He was sitting on the floor with

260

his back against the wall. He looked exhausted. His eyes were on *The Hyperbolic Ascension.*

Hélène stepped over his palette and sat down on the floor beside him. She stared up at the canvas, which seemed to explode off the wall with a force of its own. She didn't need to be told. It was finished.

In silence she got to her feet and went back out. Ten minutes later she returned with a bottle of champagne. She had splurged recklessly. It had cost every last sou they had left. When she opened it, the cork flew across the room and out the open window. She heard it land in the courtyard below. Carefully she filled their drinking bottles and handed one over to him. They clunked the bottles together.

She looked into his eyes. "To your masterpiece," she toasted in a solemn whisper. "To your future."

He nodded. Even he couldn't help but admit that *The Hyperbolic Ascension* had turned out to be a masterpiece. And with André Lichtenstein at his side, even the impossible was possible. The art dealer was an acknowledged genius when it came to discovering new talent.

Guy smiled. Suddenly the road to his fame and fortune looked paved with promise. He would be not only a respected artiste but perhaps also even a member of the small, close-knit community of financially successful artists as well. Who could tell? He might even become another Picasso, another Dali. Anything seemed possible.

But it never happened.

3

Breathlessly Hélène dashed past a startled Madame Guérin and ran up the steep flights two steps at a time. When she flung open the door and burst into the room, sweat was pouring down her forehead and her breast was heaving from exertion. She had run all the way.

Guy was standing at the sink. He twisted around and looked at her red face in surprise. "Where's the fire?"

She took deep gulps of air and plopped herself down on the bed. "The news . . . I couldn't wait . . . to tell you . . . I ran . . ."

"First catch your breath," he said calmly. "Then tell me everything. Can I get you a glass of water?"

She nodded and waited impatiently while he went over to the sink and filled the bottle under the tap. Water dripped down on the floor as he carried it to her.

"Thanks." She held the bottle between her trembling hands and drank thirstily.

He sat down beside her. "Caught your breath?"

Excitedly she nodded her head. With the back of her hand she wiped the water from around her mouth. "We're rich!" she blurted out. "I got a job!"

His eyes widened. "What?" He hugged her tightly and then held her at arm's length by the shoulders. "Where? How?"

Her eyes shone. "I answered an ad. I didn't tell you about it because I didn't want to give you false hopes. I didn't really think for a moment that I would get it! But finally we'll have some money! Now we'll be able to buy food and even be able to cover the rent!"

Jumping to her feet, she raised her hands above her head and broke into a flamenco. Fiercely she snapped her fingers and stomped her heels. Her dress swirled around her. "We're rich!" she sang. "We're rich!"

From the floor below, someone began banging on the ceiling. Undaunted, Hélène danced on. Finally she collapsed on the bed. She was out of breath again.

"Well?" Guy demanded. "Are you going to dance all night? Or are you going to tell me about it? What kind of job is it? Where is it?"

"It's nothing, really. Just a hat-check job. But it's not far from here, and I'll be able to walk to work. Even in the rain. I think the very first thing I'll buy myself will be an umbrella." Her eyes were shining. "Then I'll go out every time it rains just to luxuriate under it. I'll never have to get wet again!"

"You'll be a hat-check girl?" he asked softly.

"That's what I said." She waved her hand deprecatingly. "Oh, I know. It's no big deal. But they told me the tips are good."

He looked at her questioningly. "Where is it?" he asked hesitantly.

"On the rue de la Tour-d'Auvergne."

He nodded slowly. "It wouldn't by any chance happen to be the Folies de Babylon?"

She looked at him in surprise. "You've been there!"

He shook his head, and their eyes met. "No, I haven't been there. But I've heard enough. It's not a good place, Hélène. It has a . . . reputation, let's say."

She turned at him angrily. "Not good? Reputation? What are you trying to say? That I shouldn't work there because it's a nightclub?"

"Not because it's a nightclub. Because it's where men go to pick up girls. Girls who aren't nice. You know what I mean."

"Prostitutes. Yes, I know," she said wearily. "I've been in Paris long enough to know that there is such a thing as prostitution. So what? I'm not a prostitute and I certainly don't intend to become one. I'm merely the hat-check girl."

He shrugged. "Have it your way, then. You won't last there anyway. They've got a fast employee turnover."

"Then I'll work twice as hard. Three times as hard. I'll make sure I keep my job."

He fell silent and got to his feet. He shoved his hands deep into his pants pockets and started to pace the room in annoyance.

She looked up at him for a while. Finally she spoke. "You don't want me to work there, do you?"

He stopped pacing. "I can't tell you what to do."

She reached out, grabbed his sleeve, and shook it. "We need the money, Guy. Can't you understand that? This is a chance! Another two weeks and the rent will be due again." She motioned around the room. "This is no way for human beings to live! We need money to live well. To eat well." She looked at him pleadingly. "Please understand me. I want to eat some good food for a change. I'm tired of going through garbage cans and chasing away the flies just to get at other people's leftovers!"

"Don't you understand?" he asked softly. "It's worse at the Folies de Babylon. There *you'll* become garbage."

"Then I'll become as rotten as the garbage I eat!" she declared angrily. "I know the taste well enough by now. Do you really think working in a trash bin is any different than eating out of one?"

He reached up and grabbed his coat off a hook on the wall. "I'm taking a walk." He looked at her in disgust. "I need the clean air."

She looked stunned as he stalked out. She was about to open the door and call after him when she had second thoughts. She sighed and turned away. No, it wouldn't be of any use. He was too stubborn to listen.

Suddenly she noticed that something about the room was different. Then she realized what it was. *The Hyperbolic Ascension* was no longer there. André Lichtenstein must have had it picked up while she was out. Now she understood. With the excitement of her pitiful job offer, she had stolen Guy's thunder. No wonder he felt so hurt.

She rushed over to the door and flung it open. "Guy!" she screamed. "Guy! Please wait!"

But it was too late. Her calls were answered by the angry slamming of the front door. Even four flights up, she could hear the panes of glass rattling in the frames.

"You fool!" Madame Guérin's shouts echoed shrilly in the stairwell. "Are you trying to tear the whole house apart?"

Slowly Hélène shut the door and slumped heavily against it. She let out a deep breath. She wished she had the time to sit down and relax, to get all the ill feeling out of her system. But she'd have to start getting ready soon. In less than two hours she would have to report to work.

Her lips twisted bitterly. This was a hell of a way to start off her first working day.

She got to the nightclub on the rue de la Tour-d'Auvergne half an hour before opening time. The night was dark but the tall red neons over the entrance hadn't been turned on yet.

For a moment she hesitated in front of the big glass double doors. They had been painted over with lilac paint so that people couldn't peek in without paying admission, but to her it only made it appear that much more ominous and foreboding. Already she was so nervous that her teeth were chattering like castanets. She had never before worked in the city, let alone in a nightclub, and she was filled with fears. Perhaps people would look down on her like Madame d'Arbeuf had, and think she was provincial. Or worse yet . . . Her heart began beating heavily. Perhaps the Folies de Babylon was an even worse fleshpot than Guy had let on. For an instant the impulse to flee seized her. Then she forced herself to stifle it. Think of the money, she told herself grimly. Or do you want to starve? She stared at the lilac doors. Then, fortifying herself with a deep breath, she pulled open the heavy doors and walked in. She tried her best to act casual, but her legs felt weak. They were trembling as if she had the ague.

The bright overhead lights inside the club were still on, and in the glare everything looked tawdry and cheap. She couldn't help wrinkling her nose at the odor of stale tobacco and spilled drinks that hung in the air. Passing the hat-check room, she paused to give it a brief inspection. Then she wove her way past the sea of tiny tables toward the stage that took up the entire front of the massive room. As she walked, she looked around the club.

Right away her worst fears began to vanish. She had half-expected to be met by a fire-breathing dragon, but instead it all looked rather amusingly threatrical. Whoever had decorated the place must have had two things in abundance, she thought. No end of bad taste and a fixation on lilac and pink. The walls were lilac and embedded with pink sequins, and so was the heavy curtain drawn across the stage. On each side of the stage, an enormous cutout of a turbaned Negro woman was attached to the wall. Except for the faces, these, too, were heavily decorated in lilac with pink sequins.

Squeezed into the room must have been a hundred tables. Each one was draped with a pink cloth and held a little pink-shaded lamp, a large pink card with a big black number printed on it, and a pink French-style telephone. Instinctively she knew what the phones were for. You could use them to call from one table to another just by dialing the number of the table you wanted. It was supposed to be a discreet way for people to contact each other. She was highly amused.

Behind the pink bar, two middle-aged, bored-looking Algerians were polishing glasses. In front of the bar a big Algerian bouncer was seated on a stool. He scowled across the room at her. He had been cleaning his fingernails with a pocketknife. Carefully he folded it up and snapped his thick fingers at her. She came over and looked at him questioningly. His dark eyes shone at her from under thick black eyebrows.

"Front door for customers only," he growled in bad French. "Employee door in side alley." He nodded to his left.

Hélène looked confused. "I'm sorry," she said. "They didn't tell me."

"Well, don't forget for future. This club belong to Monsieur Blond. Monsieur Blond don't like mistakes. Especially not from pretty ladies." He eyed her up and down. "Around here, you gotta do what Monsieur Blond says."

She nodded and smiled tightly. "I'll try to keep that in mind."

"You be smart girl and do that." He reached in his pocket for a cigarette and looked at her as he lit it. He took a deep drag and nodded to himself. She was fresh-looking and healthy, not like all those worn-out, pasty-faced showgirls and painted hookers. Yes, she really was quite beautiful. In fact, if Monsieur Blond didn't take a fancy to her, then perhaps . . . His face broke into a smile. "Now, be a good girl," he said in a friendlier voice. "Run along and go behind stage. Ask for Mother. She get you in costume and tell you what to do."

Costume? Hélène thought. What costume? Nobody had said anything about a costume. Then she shrugged. She turned around, skirted the bar, and climbed up the steps to the stage. She groped around the curtain for a while. Then she found an opening and slipped backstage.

From the look of things, there was a lot going on. The overhead lights were much brighter back here than out in the club, and they burned with a stifling heat. Hélène saw tall, long-legged showgirls in sequined bikinis and mountains of feathers, muscular showboys in sequined stretch tuxedos or obscene-looking loincloths. They all stood around looking bored, smoking cigarettes in groups. Close up, their makeup looked garish. Their skin underneath the greasy, powdered surface was pimply and uneven. With surprise, she noticed that even their bodies had makeup. The girls' breasts were rouged and the boys' washboard stomachs were outlined in brown greasepaint.

She noticed immediately that it was not the performers but the stagehands who were panic-stricken. They were rushing around seeing to this and that, screaming at the repairmen who were hammering away on a damaged set. In a corner, an ambivalent orchestra was tuning up. A clarinet squeaked.

Hélène was dazzled by the shabby glamour of it all. The set facing the curtains was big and garish and glittery. She looked up at it in awe. Prancing atop a wide, gold-painted pyramid were three stuffed stallions with colorful plumes on their heads. Hélène gazed farther up, at the ceiling. There were more flat sets up there, suspended above the height of the stage, ready to be lowered at a moment's notice.

Suddenly the floor under her began to move. She looked down in horror. Then she realized that she was standing on a revolving stage. When it stopped moving she quickly hopped off the big platform. She found herself in the midst of a group of gossiping girls. Most of them wore pink bikinis and massive headdresses sprouting pink ostrich plumes. They held their heads curiously straight, afraid that their elaborate headgear would slip off.

"I can't stand wearing all this crap," one of the girls complained crossly. She was wearing a thick, arched ponytail on her rear and another atop her head. "Monsieur Blond's a sadist for making us get ready so early. My feet hurt and I want to sit down!" She snorted and stamped her feet. The tail bounced up and down, and it rather looked like the movements of a horse. Hélène couldn't help giggling.

The girl turned around, her heavily made-up eyes flickering up and down Hélène. She placed her hands on her bare hips. "Would you like to share the joke?" she demanded.

Hélène clapped a hand over her mouth and drew back. "N-no, mademoiselle," she stammered in embarrassment. "Excusez-moi, I wasn't laughing at you. It's just . . . I'm looking for Mother."

"Humph!" The girl's eyes narrowed. "You're new around here, huh?"

Hélène nodded. "I'm the new hat-check girl."

"Listen, honey, we've all been hat-check girls. Right, ladies?" She looked at the others and winked.

They all burst out laughing. Hélène felt a deep blush coming on.

One of the girls stepped forward. "Don't mind Angélique," she said gently. "She's just pissed off because she's pregnant and she'll have to foot the bill for the abortion herself. Come on, I'll take you to Mother." She took Hélène by the hand and scowled at Angélique. Then she looked back at Hélène and smiled. "My name is Denise."

Hélène smiled shyly. "Mine's Hélène."

They walked on farther back, through a dim, narrow corridor. "Don't mind the girls," Denise said. "They're not that bad, really. They just like to sound tough. And all these feathers get hot and heavy, believe me. It's amazing that tempers don't fly more often. Ah, here's Mother."

They had stopped at one of the dressing-room doors. It was open, and Hélène could see inside. An old, limp-wristed little man with short brown bangs and a ruffled white shirt was touching up one of the showgirls' makeup.

"I can't see through these eyelashes, Mother!" the girl wailed. "They feel like stiff brushes!"

The man gave a high-pitched cackle and tossed his wrist. "Don't worry, chérie. The worst they'll do is poke your eyes out." He made a minor adjustment on her eyes. "*There.*" He stepped back to study the result and rubbed his hands together. "You look very chic."

Hélène glanced at Denise curiously. "*Th-that's* Mother?" she whispered incredulously, pointing at the man.

Denise nodded. "Except for his tongue, he's really quite harmless. If you're a girl, that is. The showboys don't like him, since he's constantly trying to grab them. The reason we call him Mother is because he's a pouf. Actually, he rather likes being called that, since it makes him feel he's one of us."

"One of us?"

"Sure. Us girls." Denise smiled. "Anyway, he mothers all of us. He's like an old hen, but we love him dearly."

Hélène shook her head. It was all so bizarre. Women with horses' tails. Stiff false eyelashes. A man called "Mother" who liked to grab the boys.

She watched as the showgirl bent close in to a mirror and blinked her eyes. "I'll probably be blind in five minutes," she wailed.

Mother put his hands between her bony shoulder blades and propelled her to the door. "Off you go, chérie." Suddenly he stopped in his tracks and stared at Hélène. He knocked his hand against his forehead. "I think I'm going to faint!" he shrieked. "Where did this wholesome creature come from? Mon Dieu! I'm supposed to make *her* look like a painted hooker? Yes, I think I *am* going to faint!"

"She's the new hat-check girl," Denise said.

Mother minced over to Hélène, looking her over. "How *do* you do? Hmmm. You do have lovely skin. Perhaps I'll give you the milkmaid outfit," he mused, a thoughtful pinkie resting on his lips.

Hélène looked perplexed. "The . . . milkmaid outfit?" she asked cautiously, glancing at Denise.

Denise narrowed her eyes. "He wouldn't dare! It's one of his peasant costumes. It's simply the ugliest thing we've ever laid eyes on. So far, all the girls have refused to wear it. It's got a low-cut bosom so that your tetons practically hang out, with a little lace edging and one of those god-awful Marie Antoinette peasant caps. Ugh!" She shuddered involuntarily.

Mother put an angry hand on his hip and snapped, "What do you mean 'ugh'? I designed it myself! Peasant top, net stockings, and all. It's very flattering."

"It's very disgusting," Denise snapped. "Have you got cataracts? Where's your taste? Can't you see that this girl's got class? Now, give her something decent so she won't look like a hooker. Otherwise, we'll all gang up on you and cut off your pecker!"

He let out a shrill scream. "You naughty girls! You wouldn't dare!"

It was six o'clock in the morning when the girls finally poured out through the employee door into the side alley. Already the blue light of dawn was in the sky. Hélène blinked. After the carnival atmosphere of the club, the big dark room with the pink-shaded lamps, the false energy onstage, the men's evening suits and the women's gowns, it was startling to be out in the fresh air and find that it was daylight.

Guy was waiting for her in the alley. As soon as she saw him, her heart lifted.

He grinned at her. "How'd it go?"

She smiled happily. "Come to think of it, not bad at all."

It was true. In a strange sort of way, she had actually enjoyed it. Perhaps it was because she was finally working. Or maybe it was the girls. Denise had been right. They really weren't a bad bunch.

"Good," he said. "I want to hear all about it."

Hélène felt a hand tugging on her arm. She turned around. It was Denise, her face pale and ordinary without all the makeup, her red hair hidden underneath a scarf. "See you tonight," she said. She glanced at Guy out of the corner of her eye and leaned forward, putting her lips to Hélène's ear. "That's some handsome man you got," she whispered. "And a gentleman, too. Imagine, waiting up this long just to escort you home! You'd better keep your claws in him and get a ring on your finger real fast!" Then her voice rose to normal. She raised her hand in a wave. "Bon nuit!" she sang.

269

Hélène laughed and returned the wave. "Bon nuit, Denise."

Guy hooked his arm through Hélène's. "You look tired," he said, leading her home.

"I'm beat! I've never worked so hard in my life. I've been on my feet since nine o'clock. You know the first thing I'm going to do when I get home? I'm going to boil a big pot of water and soak my feet in it."

He grinned. "You're going to do nothing of the sort. You're going to sit down and I'll boil it for you."

They walked in silence for a few minutes. Then she stopped and looked up at him. "Listen, Guy," she said softly, "I'm sorry."

"What about?"

"This afternoon. In all my excitement I didn't even realize that the painting was gone."

He shrugged tolerantly. "Well, look at it this way. We've both managed to get something positive accomplished on the same day." He paused and looked ruefully into her face. "I'm sorry, too, about the way I talked to you. I had no right to say what I did. You'll never be trash, Hélène." He smiled gently. "You'll still come to the gallery for the show?"

"You can count on it. I wouldn't miss it for the world."

He looked pleased. "Of course, I'm not the only one who's going to be exhibited. You've got to have twenty or thirty paintings to have a show of your own. Still, it's a start. And Monsieur Lichtenstein thinks that the chances of fetching a decent price for my painting are good. As I told you, he only picks winners. Now, about you. How did it go?"

She fumbled in her pocket and held out a wad of money. "Look!"

"Good Lord! How much is there?"

She shoved the money back in her pocket and laughed. "I haven't even counted it yet. I get one-third of the tips. The house keeps a third and Yvette, the other hat-check girl, gets a third. Listen, what do you say we find a café that's open at this ungodly hour and celebrate with some breakfast?"

He frowned. "Do you think we should?"

"Certainly. It's only money."

"Spoken like a true millionairess."

Half an hour later they finished their coffee and croissants in a little hole-in-the-wall frequented by early risers of the working class. Hélène set her cup down on the tiny marble table. She looked at Guy as his laughter reverberated around the tiny room.

"Really, Guy!" she said. "I'm serious. I had no idea! I was assured that I wouldn't have to . . . put out, you know? With men. But anyway, this old white-haired man took a fancy to me. He wanted me to sit with him and have some champagne. I didn't want to, but Yvette told me I couldn't possibly refuse. So I left the hat-check room and went over to his table. He was very courteous and invited me to sit down. Then one of the waiters—they're *all* Algerians, you know—came over and said, 'Would you like a drink, mademoiselle?' And I said, 'Yes, please. I'll have a glass of mineral water.' Anyway, not three minutes had passed when the waiter returned with orders for me to see Monsieur Blond immediately. He's the boss, you know. Well, I thought he was going to insist I go to a hotel or someplace like that with the old man. On the way to the office, I started making up all sorts of excuses. But when I got there, I received the worst tongue-lashing of my life! 'Mademoiselle,' Monsieur Blond said in a cold, quiet voice"—she mimicked him, her own voice taking on a chilly, whispery tone—" 'I do not know what remote region of this country you hail from, but let me make something clear to you. Do you have any idea how we make our money?' I looked at him stupidly. 'From the cover charge?' I asked in confusion. 'No, mademoiselle. Off the house champagne. Anytime a customer wants to buy you a drink, you order champagne. Is that clear?' "

Guy was laughing so hard that the tears were rolling down his cheeks. It was contagious. She found herself laughing hysterically too.

"You know," he said, "if anybody can single-handedly destroy that place's reputation, it will be you!"

4

A week later, just past midnight, Jocelyne came into the Folies de Babylon. Casually she dropped her fur coat over the hat-check counter, took the plastic tag stamped 47, and floated after the maître d' to table 21. She was seemingly unaware that every male eye was hungrily following her. In her path she left behind the thick sweet scent of lavender.

Lavender. The bitch still wore lavender, Hélène thought as she clutched the counter and found herself slipping back in time, back to 1944 in Nazi-occupied Paris, to a luxurious bordello run by an elegant, diminutive Madame Chang. Back to the night they had spent hidden in Gisèle's room and she had been awakened by furtive taps on the door. Jocelyne had worn a peignoir of pale blue chiffon then, and her conversation with Gisèle had been a throaty whisper.

"But why should the SS be out looking for children?" Gisèle had whispered.

"They're killers," Jocelyne hissed.

Gisèle had laughed. "Killers? Those sweet little darlings?"

"They're killers, all right . . . they shot a Boche soldier yesterday . . . now there's a reward out for information leading to their capture . . . half a million francs . . . we could go and get three, maybe four dresses at the couturiers'!"

That was what the price had been. Four children delivered into Nazi hands in exchange for three, maybe four dresses. For Jocelyne and Gisèle, dresses were expensive, but life was cheap.

Hélène stared after Jocelyne. The initial shock was wearing off, and she could feel the chill of deadly hatred beginning to swell up inside her.

Yvette looked at Hélène. "Is something the matter?" she asked in a worried voice.

Grimly Hélène continued to stare out over the counter.

There was a faraway look in her eyes. "Nothing's the matter!" she said huskily.

"Well, hurry up and hang up the coat, then."

Hélène drew back from the fur as if it were covered with snakes.

"Pardon *me!*" Yvette glared at Hélène, grabbed Jocelyne's coat, and went to hang it up.

Hélène kept her eyes on Jocelyne all night long. Jocelyne had presence; she had to credit her with that. The moment she was in a room, everybody became aware of her. She was graceful and poised. Not once did she glance up at the tawdry show on the stage. It was as if she was the star of the Folies de Babylon. In a way, she was.

She was even dressed like a star. She wore a strapless red evening gown and white shoulder-length gloves. She still had that captivating beauty. That slender body that burst into voluptuousness at her breasts. That spun-gold hair, those thin gold eyebrows. Only the blue eyes had changed. They looked curiously vacant now.

So Jocelyne wasn't working in a high-class bordello anymore, Hélène thought to herself with satisfaction. She had become a common bar hustler. But she deserved far worse! That whore had blown the whistle on Edmond, Catherine, Marie, and her. She was a traitor. A collaborator.

Hélène's eyes narrowed. Jocelyne had been responsible for having Gisèle's sketches plastered all over the Boche newspapers. She was as responsible for Catherine's and Marie's fate as the Boches themselves. It was because of her that Marie had been burned with the cigarette. That Catherine and Marie had disappeared, never to return.

Yes, fate had been kind to Jocelyne. Much too kind.

For an hour Jocelyne sat at her table sipping champagne, chain-smoking cigarettes, and answering her pink telephone. But as time dragged on, she began losing her composure. She looked worried about something. Hélène wondered what. Certainly not about finding a man. Her phone was ringing off the hook.

Finally a tall dark man with a beard approached Jocelyne's table. Hélène perked up. He didn't sit down. He exchanged a few words with Jocelyne, discreetly put one of his hands into a pocket, and slipped her something. Jocelyne palmed it, and the man went away. Then she glanced around warily and rose to her feet. Hélène thought she was leaving. Instead, she headed for the powder room.

Hélène hesitated a moment, then turned to Yvette. "I have to go to the bathroom. Can you cover me?"

"Sure. Are you all right?"

Hélène nodded. "It's something I ate," she said quickly. Before Yvette could ask any more questions, she let herself out and followed the path Jocelyne had taken.

The powder room was located off a little corridor. When Hélène closed the door, she stood in the starkly illuminated room for a moment. It was relatively quiet in here. The sounds of the show were weak and distant. She glanced at the three doors leading to the toilet stalls. She knew that they had locks. She knew, too, that the locks were broken. The girls said it was because Monsieur Blond didn't like hanky-panky going on in the toilets. One of the hookers had once brought a john in there.

She crossed over to the first door and pulled it open. The stall was empty. The second was empty, too. Then she pulled open the third. She stifled a gasp.

Jocelyne was sitting on the toilet. Her eyes were closed, the long white glove on her left arm was rolled down, and a hypodermic needle was stuck in the crook of her arm.

Quickly Hélène closed the door. In her oblivious euphoria, Jocelyne hadn't even noticed her. Quickly she left the powder room and went back outside. For a moment she just stood there. Then she noticed the pay phone on the wall beside the powder-room door. She pursed her lips thoughtfully. Suddenly she knew what she had to do. But she needed small change. She rushed back to the hat-check room.

Yvette looked at her suspiciously. "What do you need change for?" she asked.

"Don't be so nosy. I've got a telephone call to make."

Reluctantly Yvette reached into the tip box and handed her a coin. "Make it fast. Monsieur Blond doesn't like to see his employees goofing off."

Hélène looked over her shoulder, but Jocelyne still hadn't come out of the powder room. "Thanks for the advice," she said dryly. Then she hurried off to call the police. One of the bouncers passed her while she was on the telephone. She stopped talking until he was out of earshot.

When she returned to the checkroom, Hélène kept her eyes peeled for the gendarmes. She had given them Jocelyne's description, the location of the powder room, her table number. Anxiously she turned to Yvette. "What time is it now?"

Yvette sighed and looked at her wrist. "Two minutes later than the last time you asked," she said wearily. She looked suspiciously at Hélène. "What's the matter? You waiting for somebody?"

Hélène shook her head. "No . . ." Suddenly she stiffened. Jocelyne was returning to her table. Hélène watched her sit down. The whore was no longer nervous. The heroin was doing its stuff. One of the waiters came over, took her champagne bottle out of the ice bucket, and refilled her glass. She smiled up at him. Then she answered her telephone, looked across the room, and smiled professionally. Her head bowed in a kind of little nod. A moment later Hélène saw a short fat man in an evening suit getting up from table 16. He waddled excitedly across the room toward Jocelyne, pulled up a chair, and leaned across the table, lighting her cigarette.

A few minutes later there was a commotion at the door. Hélène leaned out over the counter. Two uniformed gendarmes were pushing the bouncers aside. They looked around and walked straight over to Jocelyne's table. Jocelyne looked up in surprise. The short fat man shot to his feet, gesturing nervously. One of the gendarmes grabbed Jocelyne's purse, dumped its contents out on the table, and then pulled her to her feet. She let out a shriek. Roughly he yanked her gloves down. She stood there motionless, her shoulders sagging, her hair falling down over her face as she stared at the floor. Conversation in the club had come to a halt. Monsieur Blond and one of his bodyguards hastily approached the table. The club owner's dark suit and sunglasses contrasted with his yellow-dyed hair. He took one of the gendarmes aside. His face was devoid of expression as he tried to throw oil on the troubled waters. Onstage, the orchestra didn't skip a beat and the showgirls were doing their best to continue the performance. But no one was watching. Customers were signaling for their checks. The hookers were gathering up their purses.

"What's going on?" Yvette asked curiously. She pushed Hélène aside in order to get a better view.

"They're arresting somebody," Hélène said softly.

Yvette looked at her accusingly. "It was you, wasn't it? You called the police. That's why you needed the change for the telephone. That's why you were so nervous!"

Hélène looked down silently.

"You bitch!" Yvette hissed. "Don't you know that this place is already operating at the very fringes of the law! Do you want it to be closed down? Do you want all of us to lose our jobs?"

Hélène shook her head. "I'm sorry," she murmured. "I didn't think of that."

"You didn't think! For God's sake, where are your brains? If the others hear about this, they'll scratch your eyes out!"

"You won't tell them, will you?"

Yvette's face suddenly broke into a smile. "Not this time. Jocelyne's the nastiest cunt I've ever met."

After Jocelyne was taken away, the atmosphere in the club slowly returned to normal. Monsieur Blond quickly spoke to each departing customer; most of them were persuaded to stay. Then Hélène saw one of the bouncers whispering to Monsieur Blond and pointing toward her. It was the same bouncer who'd seen her use the telephone. Then Monsieur Blond nodded and went back to his office. The bouncer walked over to the hat-check room. He gestured at Hélène. "Monsieur Blond wants to see you," he said gruffly. "Now in his office."

Yvette shot Hélène a worried look. Hélène smiled tightly and followed the bouncer.

Monsieur Blond's office was located at the end of the same corridor where the powder room was located. When she was shown inside, Monsieur Blond was sitting behind his desk. He was still wearing his sunglasses. She had never seen him without them.

He looked up at her expressionlessly and pointed to the bouncer. His voice was thin and cold. "Houari tells me he saw you using the pay telephone in the hallway."

Hélène took a deep breath. It was useless to deny it. Any number of people might have seen her leave the hat-check room. "Yes," she said softly.

"And you called the police?"

Hélène nodded.

Monsieur Blond steepled his fingers. "Would you mind telling me why?"

Hélène looked down at the expensive carpet. It was an antique gold-colored Tabriz. Her eyes followed the intricate pattern. Finally she shook her head. "It's personal," she said softly.

276

"You are full of surprises, mademoiselle. It seems that you are intent on ruining us."

"I didn't mean to cause any trouble," she said hastily. Then she bit down on her lip. She felt like a fool. What could she say? That calling the police had been a personal vendetta? That she hadn't given the repercussions any thought?

"I'm afraid you leave me no choice, mademoiselle," Monsieur Blond said flatly. "As of this moment, you no longer work here."

Hélène looked up at the imposing stone building on the Faubourg St.-Honoré. It was Parisian architecture at its best. Solid, eighteenth-century neoclassical. It had a facade covered with columns and was crowned with a steep mansard roof. It looked more like a palace than a commercial building. The André Lichtenstein Gallery took up most of the ground floor.

"It looks rather awesome," Hélène said nervously.

Guy laughed. "Don't let all that grandeur intimidate you."

"I just feel somewhat out of place. I don't think I'm ready for high society."

"Who says they're ready for you? Come on, let's go in." He took her arm and led her to the big glass door. The doorman held it open for them.

The gallery was full of people. Most of them were in fancy dress. Hélène could tell the artists from the buyers. They were more poorly dressed and their hair was unruly. She noticed at once that *The Hyperbolic Ascension* had the place of honor. It was hanging high on the back wall of the main room, opposite a mezzanine, so that it could be appreciated from two levels.

A waiter circulated with a tray of glasses. Guy reached for two of them and handed one to Hélène. She smiled and clinked her glass against his. "To *The Hyperbolic Ascension*," she said.

"Amen."

André Lichtenstein made his way through the crowd toward them. He was a tall, distinguished-looking man in a perfectly tailored evening suit. He looked more like a stockbroker than an art dealer. But then, art was fetching a lot of money nowadays, Hélène thought. His hair was dark, his temples streaked with gray, and he wore small gold-rimmed glasses. "How's the genius?" he asked in a smooth voice.

Guy smiled nervously. "All right, I guess."

Lichtenstein turned to Hélène. "And who is your beautiful companion?"

"Mademoiselle Junot," Guy said. "Hélène, meet Monsieur Lichtenstein."

Hélène smiled, shifted the glass to her left hand, and extended her right. Lichtenstein surprised her by taking her hand, bowing over it, and kissing it. She could barely feel the breath of his lips. He straightened and smiled. "You are very beautiful, mademoiselle." Then he turned to Guy. "I want you to come and meet a couple who have expressed an interest in buying your painting."

Guy's mouth dropped open. "Already? Are they serious?"

Lichtenstein nodded. "They're serious," he said soberly.

Hélène looked at Guy. Her eyes were shining with eagerness. "Did you hear that?" her expression seemed to say.

Lichtenstein turned and looked around for a moment, his eyes searching the room. "They're probably still upstairs," he said. He put his hand on Hélène's elbow and led the way to the center of the room, where a circular Plexiglas staircase rose up to the mezzanine.

From the mezzanine, most of the main room could be seen and *The Hyperbolic Ascension* appeared to be exploding in midair, the multicolored shards of the virgin hanging in frozen suspension.

André Lichtenstein fell all over a middle-aged couple. He clicked his heels together and bowed. "Madame Vanel, I would like the pleasure of introducing to you the artist who painted *The Hyperbolic Ascension*, Guy Barbeau."

Monsieur and Madame Vanel belonged to that new, moneyed breed indigenous to the twentieth century, the nouveau riche. Monsieur Vanel had made his fortune quite by accident in the bakery business. He was short and plump, with a ruddy complexion and steel-gray hair. He was still perplexed by his sudden wealth, and although he was a millionaire, he looked like he still spent all day standing in front of an oven. Madame Vanel was another story entirely. She enjoyed the money with a vengeance. She was bone-thin and her hair was brown and stiff and carefully coiffed. She wore too much jewelry and too much makeup. Both her clothes and her voice were loud.

Guy smiled at Madame Vanel, his nervousness showing. "How do you do?" he said formally.

Madame Vanel held out her hand. He bent over it and kissed it awkwardly. She preened visibly.

Lichtenstein smiled at Monsieur Vanel. "Monsieur Barbeau is delighted to answer any questions you may have regarding the painting. Please feel free to discuss it with him. As soon as you have reached any decision, just have me paged."

Monsieur Vanel nodded absently. He reached for a glass of champagne from a passing waiter. Madame Vanel took Guy aside. Art was her territory. She didn't know what surrealism was, but she did know that the best homes had art that nobody understood hanging on the walls. It was a sign of culture, and she was determined to show that she had it. She was about to purchase one of those hideous, puzzling paintings. And she was socializing with a real artist. One whom André Lichtenstein had assured her was indeed a rising star. "Get him now while he's cheap," Lichtenstein had whispered to her in confidence. "In a few years his prices will skyrocket."

Lichtenstein smiled at Hélène and led her away. "Let's leave them to talk," he said. "The painting is as good as sold."

They halted abruptly as Lichtenstein made some small talk with a buyer. Not wishing to eavesdrop, Hélène looked around. Suddenly her heart began to pound. She recognized the old woman who was holding court in the midst of a small group. She had seen her photograph in all the fashion magazines. She was one of her idols. She was the living legend, Odile Joly, the most exalted couturière of the twentieth century. Hélène couldn't keep from staring at her.

Odile Joly was so tiny that she looked like a young girl. Actually she was seventy years old and bony as a starved bird. Her neck was thin and stringy, the cords standing out like taut wires. Her thick glasses were encased in tortoiseshell, and her bobbed black hair under the bowllike hat was a daring anachronism for her age. She was dressed in a suit of her own design. It was a pale pearl color, the fabric suggesting just the vaguest hint of gold. Stories circulated that it was the only suit she owned. When she smiled she looked like she was grinning from ear to ear, and her gestures were extremely emphasized. Her hands fluttered like an agitated bird learning to fly; for some reason or other—nervousness perhaps—she kept tugging at the hem of her jacket. She smoked incessantly, holding her cigarette with her elbow bent, her hand constantly at chin level. Her huge brown eyes darted about continuously. Although few people understood exactly what she was saying in her raspy voice, everyone listened raptly to her every word, absorbing them as if they were divine decree.

Suddenly Odile Joly looked up and caught sight of Hélène. The giant eyes flashed—studying, visualizing, deciding, all in one sweeping glance. Then she slowly stepped forward. The group surrounding her parted and let her through.

Hélène's heart began to pump even faster. Was it possible? Was Odile Joly approaching *her*?

"Always wear white, chérie," Odile Joly commanded imperiously, her cigarette hand sweeping dramatically through the air. "Never, never wear dark blue like you're wearing now." She frowned disapprovingly. "No, not even white. White is too startling. Too flashy. It *glares*. Wear champagne. Yes, that's it! *Champagne*." She rolled the word on her tongue, tasting the color with her lips.

Hélène was afraid to breathe. She cast a quick glance at the others. They were staring at her, digesting the great Odile's edict and nodding in agreement.

Finally she found her tongue. "I . . . I will wear champagne from now on," she stammered.

Odile Joly gave a birdlike nod. "Good. Champagne first and foremost, but anything very, very pale will do. But never, never wear pastels or sherbets. They are *non*colors. They are for cowards. For people who wish to look 'safe' and end up looking like ice-cream cones." Her eyes roved up and down Hélène. "You have a wonderful figure for clothes. A model's figure. Your proportions are fantastic. Tell me, chérie. Are you a fashion model?"

"N-no," Hélène managed to say. She could feel herself perspiring.

"Well, what is it you do, then?"

"Nothing at the moment, I'm afraid."

The huge, famous eyes glinted shrewdly. "You should be a model. If you're interested, come and see me at my atelier. The Maison d'Odile Joly. It's just up the street."

Hélène found herself nodding. This was the last thing in the world she would have dreamed could happen. She had heard about being in the right place at the right time, but who would have thought it was here? And to think that she hadn't even wanted to come to the gallery in the first place.

Not after losing her job and being without work for over a week. She had only come for Guy's sake. And what had happened? She had met the great Odile and been offered a job as a fashion model! Without a job interview, without any experience. It was too good to be true.

"Thank you," Hélène told Odile in a quivering voice, "I . . . I shall be at the atelier on Monday."

Still shaking, Hélène stammered her excuses and retreated unobtrusively into a quiet corner. Although the crowds milling around her sounded like a thousand chattering magpies, she cut them from her mind completely. She needed time to mull over the extraordinary luck which had fallen her way. She had met the distinguished Odile Joly. Not only that, but the greatest couturière in the world—and the most formidable—had sought her out and offered her a job. Was it possible? Truly? She felt like pinching herself. It was more than she had ever dared hope for. When she had first arrived in Paris, she had been filled with naive dreams. Slowly they had evaporated. The truly successful, like the very rich, were part of a social orbit which was totally, hopelessly out of reach. Now, suddenly, not only was she mingling with an assortment of people she never thought she could meet but also she had met the one person she had idolized for years.

She had been alone in her corner no more than five minutes when a tall, attractive man came over to her. He smiled and handed her a glass of champagne. "I'm not intruding?" he asked politely in French. His French, she noticed, was heavily accented with the mellifluous tones of upper-class English.

"No, of course you're not intruding," she assured him quickly.

He smiled. "What do you say we mingle and look at the art? No one else seems to."

If we can see anything past the crowds, she thought. But aloud she said, "I'd love to."

He took her gently by the arm and guided her expertly around the pockets of people, pointing out various paintings here and sculptures there. She felt shy and as though she were dream-walking.

As they were standing in front of a faceless white Brancusi sculpture with only clean lines hinting at the features, she let her eyes dart sideways to have a good look at him. He was watching her with an expression of amusement.

Quickly she averted her eyes. I'm behaving like a schoolgirl, she chided herself.

"I don't even know your name," he said.

She looked at him again and swallowed. "Mademoiselle Junot."

He gave a little bow. "My name is Nigel."

"How do you do, Monsieur Nigel?" she said gravely.

He flung back his head and laughed.

She looked suddenly stricken. "Have I . . . have I said something wrong?"

"No, no. Not at all. You see, Nigel is my first name. Somerset is my last. You may call me Nigel."

Her heart began to beat faster. She felt suddenly drawn to him. What was happening? First Odile Joly, and now this intriguing stranger.

"Nigel . . ." she said slowly, as if to herself. "It's a very pretty name. Mine . . . mine is Hélène."

"Also very pretty. Stately, too."

She looked to see if he was joking; she was grateful to see that he wasn't.

"I hope I'm not too forward," he said, "but I was wondering if you would like—"

A scream suddenly reverberated around the high walls of the gallery. At once everyone stopped talking.

"Oh, my God, no," Hélène heard André Lichtenstein murmuring under his breath. Then she saw him quickly pushing his way through a crowd of well-dressed people.

"For Christ's sake!" a voice boomed out from the edge of the mezzanine. "Green! What are you, some kind of moron? Whoever heard of matching a painting to your living-room sofa!"

Hélène went pale. The voice was Guy's. What was he doing? Who was he screaming at? "I . . . I'm sorry," Hélène said quickly to Nigel. She handed him her champagne glass and started after Lichtenstein. They found Guy at the edge of the mezzanine, his face red, the veins on his temples popping out and throbbing. Madame Vanel was cowering against her husband, her eyes wide in fear.

"He's crazy!" Madame Vanel whispered in a frightened voice. "Crazy!"

Guy turned around to face the others. "This . . . this

woman"—he pointed a shaking finger at Madame Vanel—"wants me to change the colors in my painting. In *that* painting!" He whirled around, pointing at *The Hyperbolic Ascension*. "She wants me to prostitute my talent like a common whore!"

Lichtenstein reached Guy and took him by the arm. Angrily Guy threw him off.

Hélène came up beside Guy. "Come on, Guy," she said quietly. "I think it's time we went home."

He laughed derisively. "Home? What home? Some shitty rat hole? What's there? No one cares about art or how artists live. None of these people give a fuck about anything except their matched sofas and their bank accounts!"

She shook his arm. "Guy, come *on*," she whispered desperately.

He laughed again and pushed her away. There was a crazed look in his eyes. "Not without the painting, I won't! It's too good for these . . . these . . ." At a loss for words, he threw his fists high into the air. His body was trembling. Suddenly he rushed at the silent crowd. Frightened, they drew back. He ran down the Plexiglas stairs two at a time. Now everyone on the mezzanine crowded forward to see what was going on. Hélène grabbed hold of the steel railing and looked down. Guy was pushing through the crowd on the ground floor. Then he stood under the painting, staring up at it. He let out a cry of agony. "You're too good for this world!" he screamed at the painting. "You're too good! Do you hear that?"

The painting hung there in silence.

André Lichtenstein's face was stony. "He's finished!" he hissed under his breath. "I'll see to it that every gallery in this city will be closed to that maniac!"

Hélène closed her eyes. Why was Guy doing this? Everything had been going so well. The painting had been as good as sold! Why hadn't he just told Madame Vanel quietly that her request was impossible? Why create such a scandal? Why? *Why?*

Suddenly a gasp swept through the crowd. Hélène's eyes flew open. Guy was jumping up at the painting. He missed it the first time. On the second try, he managed to grab hold of the bottom edge of the frame. The painting was hanging away from the wall, and he hung suspended in midair, his feet off the ground. For a moment *The Hyperbolic Ascension*

283

just swung sideways. Then one of the wires connecting it to the ceiling snapped abruptly. Guy lost his grip and fell, rolling across the carpet. The left corner of the frame missed him as it crashed to the floor, the big canvas wobbling under the impact. For a moment Guy looked stunned. Then he staggered to his feet. He picked up a chrome-and-leather bench and began attacking the painting, smashing the legs of the bench through the canvas. Once the holes were punched, he threw the bench aside. He grabbed hold of the canvas with both hands and began tugging at it.

The same fingers that had painted *The Hyperbolic Ascension* tore it to shreds.

5

With her forearm, Hélène wiped the perspiration off her brow. Then she put the paint roller back in the pan. She wiped her hands on a rag, placed them on her hips, and looked around the room. She was pleased. It was amazing what a can of paint could do. The old dirty-white room was transformed by a coat of bloodred paint that covered up the unevenness of the walls and all the little cracks in the plaster. Already the second coat was nearly dry.

The three-panel screen she'd bought at the flea market, which she'd also painted red, hid the sink and the little stove. With the fabric she had bought in a shop on the Right Bank, the transformation would be complete. The inexpensive bolt of red paisley had a pattern of deep blue and ivory. From part of it she had made a tablecloth that she would drape over the kitchen table. The square of glass she had bought would cover the top. Now that she had a little money to play with, she decided to buy a few things. A shaded lamp and the cracked old landscape in the gold frame she had seen at the flea market—no Rembrandt, mind you, but nice enough. She would be lavish with the paisley curtains, though. Skimpy curtains looked so cheap. For the bed she had sewn a cover of plain deep blue cotton, as well as some slipcovers for the cushions. They were of the same blue, and a few others were paisley. Now the bed would look nice and could double as a sort of couch. And very cleverly she'd suspended a rod over the far end of the room. It would hold a massive curtain of more paisley. She'd nailed all the hooks against this one wall, and now it would function as a makeshift closet. At least her clothes would be out of sight.

She looked down at the floor with distaste. Between the newspapers she had spread out, she could see hideous patches of yellow linoleum peering up at her. The next priority would be to put something over it. Perhaps she could find an inexpensive roll of glossy deep red linoleum somewhere. If she kept it waxed, it could look quite stunning.

She sat down on the edge of the bed. Now that she had finished painting, the room seemed awfully quiet. With Guy gone, she missed the incessant talk, the laughter, the humming while he painted. When he had stomped out of the gallery, he had gone off alone and gotten drunk. Then on Saturday morning he had returned sheepishly to the apartment and packed his things.

"Where are you going?" she had asked him.

He smiled grimly. "Back home."

"Not to Strasbourg!"

His gentle blue eyes were sad. "Yes, back to Strasbourg."

"But, Guy!" she protested. "You have so much talent!" Her voice took on a tone of sadness. "It would be such a pity to waste it."

He shook his head. "I can't paint anymore," he said quietly. "Not while the buyers are people like the Vanels."

Hélène sighed and got to her feet. She brought the roller, the paint pan, and the brush over to the sink and carefully rinsed them off. When they were spotless, she picked the newspapers up off the floor, got the apartment in order, and made herself a salad. She had to watch her weight and figure now that she was a model. After she cleared away the dishes, she sat down at the table to write some letters. Thoughtfully she chewed the eraser on the end of the pencil. She began to write:

Paris, July 30, 1953

Dearest Jeanne and Edmond,

I know I have been very lax in writing to you, and I feel

terribly guilty about it. Will you believe my excuse that I've been so busy I couldn't find the time?

I am a fashion model now. Not in the magazines but in a real couturière's atelier, the Maison d'Odile Joly. Sounds impressive. But until now I've only been a kind of dressmaker's dummy for Odile Joly. She designs all her clothes in the most peculiar manner. She uses live models instead of dummies, and some of the other girls and I have to stand there for hours, draped under tons of fabric, while the great Odile cuts the patterns with scissors and then pins them together.

Next week is the Big Event, the winter showing, and I've graduated from dummy to part-time runway model. It's going to be quite exciting. All the important buyers will be there, as well as the press and photographers from all over the world. Imagine me in the newspapers and magazines! If I can get hold of any of the pictures, I'll be sure to clip them and send them on to you.

I hope everything is going well for you both. I can't wait until you can come to Paris. It is so exciting here, and I'm sure you'll love it.

All *my* love always,
Your Little French Girl
in Paris

Hélène read it over, folded it carefully, slipped it into an envelope, and kissed the seal before she licked it. Then she wrote another letter:

Paris, July 30, 1953

Dear Madame Dupré,

I know this is only my second letter, but I have been very busy working at odd jobs. Finally I have landed one I'm crazy about—I'm a fashion model in the Maison d'Odile Joly. Really! So I must tell you exactly what goes on there.

First of all, everybody always calls Odile Joly by both names—never just "Odile" and never "Madame Joly." On the other hand, according to those in the know, Jacques Fath is always called just "Jacques," Coco Chanel is plain "Chanel," Dior is "Christian," and Madame Grès is "Madame Grès." I'm becoming a storehouse of trivia.

Odile (to save words I'll call her just plain "Odile," woe

286

to my fate if she ever finds out) is very short and tiny. As you know, she is known mostly for her suits, although she designs dresses, gowns, and coats, too. You probably also know that she always wears funny little (or big) hats, and that she lives in an apartment in the Plaza Athénée. But did you know that she chain-smokes? Anyway, the atelier is on the Faubourg St.-Honoré, in one of those grand buildings Paris is so famous for. She owns the whole building, and the smaller one next door as well. One of the other models told me that over a thousand women work for Odile. Last year she sold more than thirty thousand garments—and you know how expensive they are! A poor family in Saint-Nazaire could live on one of those suits for a year. But this is not Saint-Nazaire. This is Paris!

So far, I have spent most of my time in the atelier. The atelier is everything but the showroom itself. There are many rooms where Odile creates her garments, and she'll work on a dozen different ones at the same time. Usually, though, she works in a big gray-linoleum-floored room. Here's her method. She'll drape yards and yards of shantung or wool or whatever around me and stand back, poke here and there with shears—snip, snip-snip, stand back, snip some more—put a pin here or there, have her whole mouth full of pins (and literally using her own sweater and skirt as pincushions, so that she'll constantly stick herself), and go scampering around the floor *on her knees, for heaven's sake,* trying to get a view from every angle. This is the way the originals are handled. Odile also has a ready-to-wear line which she exports (mainly to America). Can you imagine—over 500 midinettes copy and sew her garments day and night, day in, day out?

Last week was the first time I set foot in the showroom. That's because I was promoted. I'm still going to continue to be Odile's favorite dressmaker's dummy, I'm afraid—it kills your feet—but I'll be in the winter show as a runway model. Isn't that exciting? I've promised Jeanne and Edmond newspaper and magazine clippings if I'm in them, and I'll send you some, too.

If you want to know what's new on the fashion scene, I'm going to tell you. The favorite item I'm going to model in the show is one of Odile's suits. It's furry alpaca wool, champagne-colored. You wouldn't believe the finishing touches!

As soon as you come to Paris, I'll try to arrange for you to attend one of the shows. The showroom is actually five rooms, all connected by the runway. They are lavishly decorated, and remind me of Château Hautecloque. They are all carpeted, and the main room has a big staircase going up to one of Odile's workrooms. The staircase is supposed to be where the superimportant buyers and columnists sit during the shows. The walls of the rooms are white boiserie, and they have theater-type spotlights, crystal chandeliers, and wall sconces with silk shades.

At any rate, that's all the news I have right now. As soon as there's more, I promise to write.

Affectionately,
Hélène

She reread the letter carefully, wondering whether there was anything she should add in a postscript. Briefly she thought of mentioning the intriguing British gentleman she had met at the art gallery, but then thought better of it. She had thought of Nigel quite a bit since then, wishing that she had not had to run off after Guy, but it was too late now. It would be best if she just forgot him, chances being that she would never again run into him. She sighed, wrote out the envelope, and licked the flap shut. It felt good to be able to write the truth for once.

The unventilated dressing room behind the heavy velvet curtain was like an oven. The hot spell had hung over Paris for nearly two weeks now. All Parisians hoped for a cooling rain, but none as much as the models at Odile Joly's. The winter clothes were hot and heavy.

Nervously Hélène looked at her reflection in the three-paneled mirror. She watched as one of the dressers deftly buttoned up the back of her blouse. Then the fat, middle-aged woman stood back, frowned thoughtfully, stepped closer, and began to fuss with the collar. The heavy tweed jacket would be put on only at the last moment. All around the room, the other dressers were helping the models into their clothes. Lining the walls were metal garment racks on casters. On them hung Odile Joly's winter collection for 1953–1954.

For once, Odile Joly was not in the atelier. This was her moment of glory. She stood at the top of the famous circular staircase in the main showroom. From here she could watch everything. She could keep one eye on the models and the other on the most important buyers and the most powerful journalists. But she would watch no one as closely as the crème de la crème. They would be sitting at the places of honor—below her on the sweeping steps of the carpeted staircase.

Odile Joly's face had settled into an inscrutable expression. Despite the heat and the momentous occasion, she was relaxed and calm. Her work was finished, the Collection complete. She knew that it was good. For a moment she closed her eyes. She could feel the crackling excitement that hung in the air like invisible bolts of electricity in the summer skies. It was the same kind of excitement that can be felt in a theater before the curtain goes up. But she could not share in it. Her excitement derived from the pleasure of creating. From cutting. From pinning. From discovering a new style, creating a new pocket, designing a new button.

She looked down at the carpeted models' catwalk. It was laid out like a figure X. The center of the X was in the main room, and each end of the X extended into one of the four other rooms. But only the people in the main room counted. Those in the other rooms were yokels. Tourists whose hotel concierges had arranged for them to attend the show. Very minor journalists who insisted on covering the collection. People who were known never to buy anything.

Her large dark eyes darted around, absorbing what was going on. All the big French windows were open, trying in vain to catch a breeze that did not exist. Already the showrooms were filling up. The vendeuses were showing people to their seats. Right below her, the honored few started to take their coveted places on the staircase. There were two princes. The older one, Alfonse, was practically destitute. Odile Joly knew how he had fought against the Germans during the war, helping to preserve some of France's great national treasures from destruction, and she loved him for it. Ever since, she made certain the Prince and Princess were seated in the places of honor. Also, she insisted that the Princess was dressed at no charge.

There were two other princesses. One of them, ancient and stiffly coiffed, had been a Cleveland divorcée who had married a Danish prince. She was famous for never paying for anything in her life—not for a single lunch in the expensive restaurants she frequented, not for her lavish hotel suites, nor even for her clothes. Those bills of hers which *were* paid were footed by her "walker," the young American automobile heir who admired her and escorted her everywhere. The dotty old Prince did not mind. The young man in question was a known homosexual; thus the princess was in "safe" company. Odile Joly was one of the few on his list of creditors to be paid, as she refused to dress the Princess otherwise.

Odile smiled down at the wife of an exiled Far Eastern monarch. In the past three years, Sammyo Kittilongkhon had bought more than three hundred and fifty different outfits at the Maison d'Odile Joly. She was by far the best customer in the house.

Then there was a duchess, a German actress, and that American politician's wife, Barbara Sennett. The fabulously wealthy Mrs. Sennett, who had the irritating habit of squinting while perpetually grinning, had created a minor scandal the year before by altering her twenty-five-thousand-dollar sales slip from the Maison d'Odile Joly to read twenty-five hundred dollars. Her crude alteration had been caught by U.S. customs officials at Idlewild Airport. Then there were the truly powerful journalists.

Odile Joly's eyes roved over the gilt chairs that lined the models' catwalk ten chairs deep. Scattered among the rich social set were more journalists, their status decreed by the row in which they sat. First row was highly acceptable, last row was "Siberia." This hierarchy was strictly observed, closely watched, much gossiped about when someone gained or lost a row.

In the front row, Odile Joly saw Pauline Monnier, the society reporter from the *Couture Magazine*. Pauline deserved the back row, but she had come in with her inseparable companion, Daphne Epaminondas. Madame Epaminondas was the first wife of one of the world's wealthiest men, the Greek shipping tycoon Zeno Callicrates Skouri. She was worth thirty outfits a year. Also in the first row but on the opposite side of the catwalk was Cynthia Skouri, the tycoon's current American wife. And only two chairs away was Ariadne Cosindas, a renowned ballerina with a passion for haute couture. This seating arrangement would be talked about for a long time to come, because it was common knowledge that Ariadne Cosindas had been Zeno Callicrates Skouri's mistress through both his marriages. Now the three women who on different occasions had shared the bed of the same man were studiously avoiding each other's eyes.

Still in the main room but banished to the most inferior back-row seats were the representatives from *Women's Wear Daily*'s Paris bureau—one reporter, one sketch artist, one photographer. *Women's Wear Daily* would ordinarily have been steered into one of the four other rooms, but Odile Joly had foresight. She predicted that within ten years *WWD* would be the most powerful fashion instrument in the world. But for now, even giving them the worst seats in the main room was being more than generous. As *WWD* progressed in stature, Odile Joly would begin moving them forward row by row.

Beside the *WWD* group sat the Comte and Comtesse de la Brissac et de Léger. Odile Joly's old face cracked into a malicious smile. The Comte and Comtesse had been relegated to these seats because of a photograph that she had seen of the Comtesse. There had been a local polo-pony tryout in Bordeaux. Although it would have gotten no press coverage under ordinary circumstances, the unexpected appearance of the Comte's first cousin—a former army colonel and now a rising politician—had made the event newsworthy. The Comtesse had been caught with her pants down, so to speak. Her full-page four-color photograph had appeared in *Paris Match*, and Odile Joly had seen it. Her eagle eyes had immediately recognized the Comtesse's "Odile Joly" suit as a copy. Since the Comtesse was a relatively steady buyer, and a social item at that, Odile Joly couldn't very well ostracize her from the main room. But she could—and did—kick the Comte and Comtesse from their usual second-row seats to the least important row in the back. This snub would be duly noted and reported and gossiped about. In the future, the Comtesse would be more careful. And more important, Odile Joly was certain that the Comtesse would now buy three times her usual amount of clothes to try to make up for her treachery and secure the usual second-row seats for the future. This gave Odile Joly a sense of satisfaction, a feeling of power.

Odile Joly's eyes swept down the catwalk into one of the adjoining rooms. She could see just a portion of it. Suddenly she stiffened. Someone looked all too familiar. She frowned, trying to place the face that went with the blond wig and the big glasses. Then the woman lit a cigarette. When she inhaled, she held it between her thumb and forefinger.

Quickly Odile Joly signaled for a vendeuse. The dark-haired woman in the black dress hurried over to the side of the staircase. Odile Joly leaned over the railing. "Room three, chair thirty-seven!" she whispered angrily. "How did she get in?"

The vendeuse turned around discreetly and glanced through the open doorway. The woman in chair thirty-seven wore large glasses, a wide-brimmed ocelot hat, and a silk blouse with a huge lace bow at the collar. The vendeuse turned and looked back up at Odile Joly. "The concierge at the Hotel Cusset called in her seat reservation. I don't see anything—"

"You fool!" Odile hissed. "That's Simone Doucet! Can't you tell?"

The vendeuse looked again. Her face suddenly paled. "By God, it is!" she said in a grief-stricken whisper. "I . . . I can't tell you how terribly sorry I am! I didn't recognize her in that getup."

Odile Joly snorted. "Getup indeed! You mean disguise. That lesbienne spy came sneaking in here dressed as a lady! Throw her out immediately!"

Quickly the vendeuse hurried off. Simone Doucet was on the design team of one of the lesser houses that thrived on stealing designs from the great couturiers. There was a strictly enforced rule in each maison de couture that the doors were shut to workers from all other houses. With satisfaction, Odile Joly watched the vendeuse dealing with the matter. Simone Doucet was being escorted to the door.

Odile Joly gave a little signal with her hand. Immediately the chandelier lights dimmed and the klieg lights clicked on. The show was ready to begin.

The dressing room was getting hotter by the minute. The models were sweating. They were lined up in order of appearance. The harried dressers, nervous despite years of experience, made last-minute adjustments to the models' hair or smoothed their hands over the skirts and jackets, dabbing the perspiration from their carefully made-up faces with tissues. Everything had been timed to the second. Within ninety seconds of leaving the dressing room, the first model would be back. Four others would be on the floor during that time. Each model had three minutes in which to get changed into the next outfit and be ready to go back out again. Each model had to make seven such changes of clothing.

Hélène was last in line. She watched nervously as the first model slipped out through the curtain. She could hear a smooth voice from outside explaining the garment. Four more models slipped out. Then the first model returned, quickly shed the outfit she was wearing, and was hurriedly dressed in the next.

Then there was only one other girl in front of her. The girl turned around. "Good luck," she whispered.

Hélène smiled faintly. "Thanks, Liane. Good luck to you, too."

And it was Hélène's turn. Her hands were shaking. Quickly she took a deep breath and slipped out through the curtain. She pretended that this was just a practice run. For the past week, all they had done each day was practice walking. Choreographing each step. From the audience's point of view it would all look effortless and natural. Only the models and Odile Joly knew how difficult it actually was. It had been planned so that four models would be on the catwalk at the same time, each on a different end of the X, but in precisely the same spot as the others. Then they would meet at the center of the X and switch lanes.

Graceful as a swan, she glided toward the main room, looking vacantly ahead, seemingly unaware of the hundreds of eyes that were upon her. There was scattered, polite applause. The popping flashbulbs from the cameras momentarily blinded her vision, but she did not falter. All the people were a blur. She felt Odile's eyes on her from atop the staircase and ignored them.

She pirouetted at the end of each catwalk, returned to the main room, took the branch-off into rooms one, two, three, and four, and finally returned to the dressing room.

The Comtesse de Léger recognized Hélène immediately. The cold patrician eyes narrowed, and the paper with which she was fanning herself stopped in midair. Quickly she recovered. It was a shock to see the girl here—the girl who knew about her copied garments. She wondered whether Hélène had tattled on her about Madame Dupré and the copied clothes. She glanced down at her lap. Or had it been that unexpected picture in *Paris Match*? She knew that the only person who could recognize one of Madame Dupré's expert copies of an Odile Joly suit—even from a distance or from a photograph—was Odile herself. Damn that photograph! Was that why Odile had put her and the Comte in these miserable seats this year? It was scandalous. Everyone would talk! The only thing she could do was to pretend it had never happened and to placate Odile Joly by placing an order for an enormous wardrobe.

Once again Hélène came back out from behind the curtain onto the runway. At the intersection of the X she passed Liane, who was floating gracefully back to the dressing room. Hélène was now wearing the alpaca suit. There was a spontaneous murmur of appreciation.

The Comte de Léger nudged his wife. "Isn't that the girl who was at the château?" he whispered.

The Comtesse nodded absently.

"What was her name?"

"Junot something or other. No, Hélène Junot." Irritably the Comtesse made a note on the paper with her pencil. She wanted the alpaca suit. In fact, if it would help regain her second-row seat, she was prepared to buy everything in sight. The miserable back-row seats rankled her.

When Hélène got back to the dressing room, there was a sudden commotion.

"Liane's fainted!" one of the models whispered.

A dresser came rushing over to the prostrate Liane.

"It's those lights!" another model hissed. "In this hot spell . . . they're too much!"

"Never mind!" the dresser snapped angrily. "One of you others is going to have to double for her." Quickly she glanced around. Her expert eyes rested on Hélène. "You're closest to Liane's size. It'll have to be you. Now you only have a minute and a half to change between each garment. You'll be out there twelve more times. The announcer will have to shuffle your sequence. Let's hope she can ad-lib. Now, quick! Up with your hands! There isn't a moment to lose!"

Hélène was dressed in Liane's outfit in record time. Two dressers helped her, Liane's and her own. One of them deftly pinned the sides of the dress to make it tighter. She felt herself perspiring enormously. Then she found herself pushed out through the curtain. Automatically, she smiled vacantly.

All at once, she was no longer nervous. Modeling was second nature already.

* * *

In the morning a delivery boy arrived at the atelier with a long slim box from a florist's on the Champs-Élysées. Puzzled, Hélène scratched a pen across the yellow delivery slip and took the box. When the boy left, she lifted the lid. A dozen long-stemmed red roses lay inside. She frowned.

"Any idea who they're from?" Liane asked from the doorway.

Hélène looked up and shook her head wordlessly. Then she reached down and picked up the small white envelope. She pulled out the card. It was engraved with an unmistakable coat of arms. The lion, the salamander, and the crest of the de Légers. She turned the card over. On the back, the blue ink read: "Tomorrow night at nine. Will expect you at Maxim's. Just ask for my table." It was signed simply "Philippe de Léger."

Hélène sank down into a rickety chair.

"Are you all right?" Liane asked.

Hélène nodded. "Yes," she said in a quivering voice. "You won't mind if . . . if I have a little while to myself?"

Liane shook her head. "No, of course not. I'm sorry to intrude. I'll talk to you later." She waved with her fingertips and closed the door softly behind her.

Thoughtfully Hélène turned the card over in her hand, alternately glancing at the crest on the front and the message on the back. She had been in Paris for more than six months now; she was no longer a naive child from the country. In Paris, you learned fast. In six months you knew all there was to know. And she knew that a man like Philippe de Léger didn't invite a girl to Maxim's just because she'd once been in his wife's employ or because he'd once danced with her. Then there was the matter of Maxim's itself.

Maxim's was a restaurant, not only a restaurant but one of the finest in the world. It was on the rue Royale. In the early years of the century the cocottes went there with their gentlemen; now it had turned into a highly respectable place. Everyone went there to see and be seen. The best of society. The tourists. You only had to be rich and not bat your eyelashes at the prices.

She puckered her lips thoughtfully, tapping the card in the palm of her hand. Perhaps a cocotte was what Philippe de Léger fancied, but on the other hand, she didn't necessarily need to become one. More important, the card had no address on it. He had given her no chance for declining.

Hélène smiled to herself. It was probably only a dinner, and here she was making a big fuss about nothing. Going to Maxim's was probably no more exciting for the Comte than going to the corner food market was for her. Keep things in perspective, she warned herself.

Tonight she would stop by the restaurant and wait outside to see what the women were wearing. She had a little money saved up. Not enough for a Dior or an Odile Joly, but enough to buy a simple black dress at Bon Marché or Au Printemps. The red linoleum she'd seen in a little shop on the rue Victor-Masse would have to wait.

Hélène purposely stayed late at the atelier. Before she left at seven-thirty, she put the roses back in the box, tucked it under her arm, and walked down the Faubourg St.-Honoré. When she came to the rue Royale she made a right turn, crossed the street, and stayed on the opposite side of the street so that when she got to Maxim's she could look over to the other side. She didn't want to stand right outside the door, looking obvious. Fifteen minutes later, she knew all there was to know. A plain black dress would be perfectly acceptable.

The next morning she got to the atelier at her regular time. By midmorning a series of delivery boys had arrived with boxes. All for Hélène Junot. "What is going on?" Liane asked.

Hélène looked confused. "I . . . I don't know."

Liane lit a cigarette and inhaled deeply. She gestured at the boxes. "Aren't you going to open them?"

Hélène glanced over at them. "I guess I'd better."

Liane smiled. "Don't tell me! You have a secret admirer! Yesterday roses, today . . ." She stopped in mid-sentence, her mouth suddenly hanging open.

Hélène looked distressed. "What's the matter?"

"You'd better not let Odile Joly see them."

"But why?"

"The top and bottom boxes. Don't you recognize them?"

"No. Should I?"

Liane smiled grimly. "Odile Joly would. They're from the competition. Those boxes are from the House of Dior."

Hélène nodded, and they went over to the boxes. They began with the one on top. Inside was a pair of elbow-length red silk gloves.

"They're beautiful!" Liane breathed. She held one up. Then she smiled sideways. "He isn't kinky by any chance, is he?"

"I don't think so," Hélène said good-humoredly.

Next was a box from Germaine Guérin. Hélène took out a red Moutin silk evening bag. The box underneath that one came from Charles Jourdan. In it was a pair of elegant red high heels. The next box held identical red shoes, a size larger. Altogether there were four different pairs, all in different sizes. Hélène began to laugh.

Slowly she lifted the lid off the big Dior box. She parted the soft tissue paper and let out a gasp.

"My God!" Liane said quietly. "It's the dinner suit!"

Carefully Hélène lifted the ruby-red silk dinner jacket out of the box. It was bloused and had flaring hips, huge elbow-length sleeves, narrow lapels, and a thin red belt. The matching skirt was narrow and calf-length.

Liane let out a whistle. "He must be enamored of you," she stated.

Hélène turned away and stared across the room. She was silent for a moment. "I don't know. It seems too much to accept."

"But you can't return it!" Liane said quickly. "It would break the poor man's heart." She looked at Hélène. "He must be very rich."

Hélène nodded. "He is."

Suddenly there was a knock at the door.

"Just a minute!" Hélène called out. Quickly she folded the dinner suit, placed it in the box, and put the lid back on. She looked around, spied a piece of cloth, and quickly draped it over the boxes. Then she wiped her brow and went over to the door.

"Another messenger," one of the old ladies who worked in the atelier said dryly, gesturing to the young man beside her.

Quickly Hélène signed another delivery slip, took a small package, and closed the door.

Liane looked up. "Where was he from?"

"I don't know," Hélène murmured. "I didn't think of looking at the slip."

Liane placed her hands on her hips. "Well, unwrap it!" she ordered.

Silently Hélène undid the ribbon and tore off the paper. She let out a gasp. The leather-covered little box was imprinted with gold letters: "Chaumet." With trembling fingers she lifted the lid.

Two diamond-and-ruby earrings in the shape of parrots shimmered against the velvet-lined box.

"Well . . ." Liane said in an impressed voice. "Now comes the jewelry."

6

Gracefully Hélène followed the maître d' through Maxim's. She walked slowly, her full champagne-colored Balmain gown sweeping the floor, her full-length Révillon mink touched with glistening drops of melting snowflakes. By order from Liane, her hair was in a chignon, offsetting her cheekbones. She wore the canary-diamond clips on her ears.

As she walked, she smiled at the people she knew. Twice she stopped at tables, exchanging cheerful greetings and gossip as the maître d' waited patiently.

"She's like one of the old time cocottes," one ancient woman said in a dry whisper, her voice like a wind sweeping across desert sands. She sighed wistfully as Hélène swept by. "This place used to be full of them. You could hear the satin rustling, I tell you! They wore the most exquisite gowns. That was the way you could tell a cocotte, you know—sweeping gowns, enormous hats. They were worn with pride. It was like the Chinese empress who never cut her fingernails. It showed that she was not a common laborer."

"I heard she works," the younger woman beside the ancient one said. "Although, granted, she doesn't need to."

"Yes, she's a fashion model. But still she's the closest thing to those darling cocottes. I'll never forget one night in here . . ." The ancient woman's face took on a faraway look. "It was 1913, I think. Or was it 1914? Anyway, one of the cocottes broke a bottle of wine and slashed her lover across the face with it. All because he was with another woman! Those were the exciting days!"

298

The Comte smiled as Hélène sank down into the red banquette and shrugged off her mink, letting it fall back off her shoulders. The strapless Balmain gown showed her figure off to perfection. He took her hand and brought it up to his lips. "You look more beautiful all the time," he said. She looked into his eyes. The bright blue pools held that intent look that she knew only too well. He lowered her hand and brought it down between his legs. His shaft was swollen hard.

She smiled and removed her hand as a bottle of champagne and a massive silver ice bucket were automatically brought to the table. They spent so much time at Maxim's that no one needed to ask what they would drink. Everyone who worked there knew that they always had champagne first, followed by a bottle of Château Hautecloque-de Léger with dinner (if they ate fish, they ordered Château Haut-Brion blanc instead), and after a café moka they had Cognac Prince Eugène. Hélène never had more than half a glass of wine and champagne, and only a few sips of the cognac.

"I'm sorry I couldn't meet you at the house," the Comte said smoothly. He gave an elegant shrug.

Hélène nodded. She knew what that shrug meant. The Comtesse had been in town. She took a sip of her champagne. The only times he mentioned the Comtesse were when he'd been detained by her visits. The Comte reached into his pocket, took out a long skinny box from Van Cleef, and handed it to Hélène. "Just so that you don't feel too left out, I brought you a little gift."

She smiled and opened the box. The cool sapphires surrounded by loops of diamonds flashed fire up at her. She took a deep breath. It was the most extravagant gift he'd given her to date.

"Like it?" he asked lightly.

She looked up. "I love it," she said softly. Immediately she removed her canary-diamond earrings and let him hang the sapphires around her throat. She reached up and felt their coldness with her fingers. She was glad to have them. Now the canary diamonds could be put to good use. To the same use as she had put the ruby-and-diamond parrot earrings. Then, the next time he gave her a jewel, she would "retire" the sapphire necklace. It would go where all the other jewels had gone.

Was it possible that seven pieces of jewelry had already gone that route? she asked herself. Could it be possible that she had been seeing the Comte for six months already? That she'd been going regularly to Maxim's ever since then? She would never forget the night she had first come here.

She had followed the maître d' to the Comte's table, walking her graceful model's walk and staring vacantly ahead. Silently she thanked Odile Joly for making her practice it over and over. Now it served her well. It covered up her nervousness, her trembling legs. It made her look self-confident. Aloof. Blasé.

She had been intimidated by Maxim's. The big rooms were all Art Nouveau. They had patinated murals of wine-sipping nymphs. Behind the banquettes were yellow fleur-de-lis lamps overlapping on the huge, swirling wood-and-beveled-glass mirrors. The dim overhead lights looked like inverted umbrellas. She walked past a spiral staircase, wood-edged pillars, black iron columns, and old brass that shone with newness. The tablecloths and napery were crisp and white, the silver flashed, the crystal gleamed. The women were elaborately gowned and decked out in expensive jewels. The men were in elegant dinner jackets and evening suits.

The murmur of conversation suddenly stopped as if someone had switched it off. Hélène could feel everyone's eyes watching her with curiosity. The people were leaning toward one another, whispering. It was almost too much to bear. She knew that the whispers were about her.

"Dior," she heard one woman whisper.

"She's beautiful!" another added. "Look at those cheekbones!"

It was a moment before Hélène understood. She laughed scornfully at herself. What a fool she had been to worry. It was *they* who were in awe of her!

Now she dared look around. She was glad that she had decided to wear the red dinner suit after all. Just one glance told her that she was the most beautifully dressed woman there. Suddenly she felt invincible. Good clothes gave her a confidence she hadn't known could exist.

The Comte rose to his feet, the maître d' held the table away, and Hélène sat down. The Comte ordered champagne. For a moment he and Hélène just looked at each other in silence.

"It was quite a shock to receive all the packages," she said haltingly. "I didn't want to embarrass you by coming here in rags, so I took the liberty of accepting the clothes."

"I'm glad you did. I knew that they would look stunning on you."

Hélène opened the evening bag. With trembling fingers she took out the little box from Chaumet. She put it on the table.

He was watching her with amusement.

"But I can't possibly accept these," she said quietly. "They're far too valuable."

He laughed suddenly. "You're being distressingly correct, mademoiselle."

She could feel one of her blushes working up. She looked down at the table. As suddenly as the blush had begun, it receded before it could rise to her face. She looked back up, steadily meeting his eyes. "I'm being dishonest," she said with sudden wisdom. "There is no difference between accepting clothes from Dior and jewels from Chaumet."

He looked at her in surprise. Then he nodded, reached for the case, and lifted the lid. The parrots caught the light from the fleur-de-lis lamps and beveled mirrors behind them and flashed red and white sparks. Slowly he picked up the earrings and put them gently on her ears. "They look as if they were made for you," he said, slowly withdrawing his fingers.

"And the payment for all this?" she asked in a quiet voice. "What is it that you want from me?"

For a moment he didn't speak. He leaned back against the velvet banquette and lit a cigarette. He waved out the match and tossed it into the ashtray. He watched her closely. "I'm not asking for repayment," he said finally. "However, I have a proposition to make. You may accept it or turn it down. I will give you all the time you need to make up your own mind."

She looked at him questioningly. Her lips were suddenly numb. She could feel that intense electricity she had felt when he had first touched her at Hautecloque, asking her to dance. Only this time he didn't need to touch her. She felt it all the same.

"And what is this proposition?" she whispered, knowing very well what it would be.

He didn't mince words. "I want you as my mistress," he said honestly.

She looked at him levelly. So she had been right. He wanted a cocotte. It didn't shock her. It didn't even surprise her. She was only glad that he hadn't been evasive, that he hadn't tried to glamorize the possible relationship, that he didn't try to frost it up with sweet words of love. Besides, he *was* very attractive. She'd never be able to forget the thrill she had felt when he had taken her into his arms at the ball at Hautecloque. And now that same feeling had been reawakened in her. Who knows? she thought—what the Comte was suggesting could even turn out to be . . . quite interesting.

For a moment her lips tightened. Then she smiled coolly. "And what would we both gain by such a . . . relationship?"

He brought the cigarette to his lips and inhaled calmly. "I would gain a mistress," he said flatly. "I'm usually in Paris for two days each week. I would expect to spend those evenings with you. As for you, I am prepared to give you the use of a town house I own on the Boulevard Maillot. You would have a certain monthly income and charge accounts at the better shops. You would receive gifts every now and then."

"But I have a job," she said evenly. "I don't want to give that up. It gives me a sense of security."

He nodded. "You don't need to give up your job," he said.

For a long time she sat in silence, her eyes focused on nothing in particular. But her mind was racing. The Comte was offering her a town house in one of the best sections of Paris and charge accounts at God-only-knew what expensive shops. But most important, she could not only keep her job at Odile Joly's but also receive an extra income. Plus "gifts every now and then." Jewels, probably. It was the type of offer that any "nice" girl turned down immediately. Without second thoughts. Hélène knew that being kept by a man would categorize her as a "mistress" at best—and as a "whore" at worst. Yet there was another side to it, one she didn't dare overlook.

Long ago she had sworn to herself that she would seek out and find two Nazis—a sergeant named Schmidt and an albino with a thin, cruel face—perpetrators of senseless violence. She had sworn to bring to justice the animals who had made Maman, Catherine, and Marie suffer and disappear. Finding those monsters would be no easy task. It would take money. Much money.

She had sworn, too, that if she became successful before him, she would help Edmond. He and Jeanne were stuck in Saint-Nazaire with nothing but a bleak future looming in front of them. There would be no way for Edmond to escape

Saint-Nazaire. Not on his own. He would need help. Again, only one thing stood between her helping him and not. Money.

And last, but certainly not least, there was her own dream. Her magazine. Starting it would require more money than she could ever lay her hands on in the normal course of events.

She gave a painful inner sigh. Everything she wanted to accomplish took money. True, she had a decent job at Odile Joly's. But she wasn't earning nearly enough as a model to make a single one of her ambitions come true. Probably never would. And worst of all, models had a short, expendable lifespan. Once she began to show signs of aging—then what? Then her future would be as bleak as Edmond's and Jeanne's was right now. It was time to insure her future— time to think of her dream. Time to work fast. Time to make all her ambitions a viable reality.

The Comte's offer would be the first step toward it.

The champagne arrived. Hélène watched the waiter uncork the bottle and pour. When they were alone again, she sipped delicately. Her violet eyes looked at the Comte over the rim of her glass. She had come to a decision.

She would make a deal with the devil.

"Monsieur le Comte"—she smiled softly—"you have yourself a deal."

He had given her two more gifts that night. A ruby-and-diamond necklace to match the earrings and a solid gold key—the symbolic key to her new home. For practical use, he had also given her a regular key. After dinner they rode to the house in the black-and-burgundy Rolls. When they got there, the chauffeur held the rear door open. Hélène looked out at the house in awe. The old white building behind the small garden looked like a little palace. It was four stories high. Above the big double doors were balustraded balconies on the second and third floors. The top floor, with its mansard roof, had five small oval dormers. All the rest of the windows were big and mullioned.

"Do you find it agreeable?" the Comte asked.

Hélène turned to look at him. She was speechless. She didn't know what to say. Finally she managed to nod her head.

"Shall we go inside?" Without waiting for her reply, the Comte placed the palm of his hand on her elbow and led her through the garden and up the marble steps. She took out her key and unlocked the front doors of her new home for the first time. Unbelievingly she looked around the foyer. The marble floor gleamed and the walls were lined with pilasters. She was dying to explore the rest of the house, to go from room to room and acquaint herself with all that a new home has to offer. But that would have to wait until morning. Tonight she sensed that the Comte had something far more urgent on his mind.

Immediately they went upstairs to the huge, dimly lit bedroom overlooking the Bois de Boulogne. She watched as he went over to the window and pulled the heavy draperies together. She knew what was expected of her. Wordlessly she got undressed.

When he was naked, she stood there staring at him. His penis was erect and pulsing. Suddenly she was afraid. She went over to the giant bed, pulled down the cover, and lay stiffly on the Porthault sheets, watching him with frightened eyes.

Slowly he came over to her. He sat on the edge of the bed and reached down, tracing his fingertips across her nipples. At first she was tense. She refused to submit to her longings. Then suddenly she stopped resisting. She closed her eyes and gave herself up to the tingling sensation that swept through her body in little waves. Her breasts rose and fell with each breath, her nipples rising under his touch. After a while he rolled on top of her and their arms and legs intertwined. His face found hers and his tongue darted deep into her throat, probing, exploring, licking. She could feel his stiff penis rubbing against her legs. She moaned softly, her head making a slow pendulum motion on the pillow. A current of excitement surged through her body. She struggled to free her lips from his. "Love me," she whispered, giving herself over to him completely.

She felt him moving away from her, freeing her from his grasp. Then there was a delicious sensation between her legs. She looked down. His head was buried in her pubis, his tongue licking her clitoris. She shuddered, feeling the beginnings of her first orgasm. He waited for her excitement to ebb. Then in one savage thrust he entered her. She gripped him fiercely, relishing the sensation of his body against hers. Abruptly he pulled out of her.

"Don't stop!" she cried.

He grabbed her by the ankles and held her legs high in the air, over her head. Her buttocks were now off the bed. Without warning, he forced his penis up into her anus. Instinctively she clamped her sphincter tight. With one massive thrust he pushed deeper. Her hips jerked, her body shuddered. She writhed in agony. The pain was excruciating. A scream burst forth from her lips.

"Whore!" he hissed. His hand shot out and slapped her across the face. The sting of his slap erupted on her cheek. The scream died in her throat.

"Whore!" His voice was louder now, and he raised his hand to strike her again. She flinched and whipped her head sideways. Suddenly he let out a cry. A spasm shook his body and he emptied his juices into her. He let go of her legs and let them drop back down on the bed. He bent forward and buried his face in her breasts. "Mother!" he sobbed. "Mother!"

Hélène looked down at him and stroked his head gently. She could feel his tears rolling down the cleft of her breasts.

The uniformed maid knocked gently on the door. Then she entered the bedroom and crossed soundlessly over to the window. The curtains blocked out all the light. In two swift draws she yanked them aside and the faded winter sun came weakly into the room. Hélène stirred on the big bed and rolled over, burying her face in the pillow. The maid went over to the marble mantel and got to her knees, placed kindling in the grate, stacked some logs on top of it, and lit a fire. She fanned the flames until they burned evenly, then got back to her feet. She looked at Hélène. "It's time for your breakfast, mademoiselle."

Wearily Hélène sat up and blinked. She yawned and wiped her eyes. "What time is it, Marthe?"

"Eight-thirty, mademoiselle. You requested that I wake you, remember?"

Hélène nodded. Now she remembered. It was Saturday. Odile Joly had given her the day off, but she had an important errand to run. Quickly she looked over at the pillow beside hers. The Comte had left already; all that remained of his spending the night was the depressed shape of his head in the pillow.

Hélène sighed. "All right, Marthe. I'll have breakfast now."

Efficiently Marthe marched out. She returned a moment later with a wooden tray. She set it down on the nightstand, waited for Hélène to lean forward, and plumped the pillows up behind her. Carefully she placed the tray on Hélène's lap and poured a cup of coffee from the china pot into one of the delicate gold-bordered cups. Hélène took a sip and shuddered. She put the cup back down. She hated black coffee. She liked it sweet, with cream and sugar, but she had to watch her weight. She looked down at the plate. On it was a single flaky croissant, hot and steaming. On the tiny side plate was a minuscule dab of country butter and a teaspoon of red raspberry jam. It had been a long, exhausting night. The Comte had been insatiable. After sex, she always had an appetite. Now she was hungry as a horse. Perhaps if she ate very slowly the croissant would be enough to fill her. She sighed, broke the croissant in half, and began to butter it carefully.

"Is there anything else you need, mademoiselle?"

Hélène looked around the room. She saw the Balmain gown draped across the back of a French chair. "Send the gown to the cleaner's. Oh . . . and don't forget to change the bedsheets."

Marthe gave a little curtsy. "Oui, mademoiselle." She would have changed the sheets automatically anyway. After the Comte stayed overnight, Mademoiselle always insisted on fresh sheets.

"That's all, Marthe, thank you."

The maid picked up the Balmain, left the room, and gently shut the big carved door behind her.

Hélène took a bite out of the croissant and chewed it slowly. Then she looked at the rest of it and dropped it on the plate. Suddenly she didn't feel hungry anymore. There was too much to do today.

She lifted the tray, set it back on the nightstand, and threw off the covers. She walked across the soft carpet and went into the big marble bathroom. She leaned over the tub, spun the gold-plated faucets, and watched the steaming water crash down onto the smooth, contoured enamel bottom. She leaned over the tub for a moment, letting the clouds of steam rise up into her face. This was luxury, she thought. Hot running water. Not like the single ice-cold low-pressure tap at Tante Janine's or Jeanne's.

Humming softly, she poured a generous portion of scented bath oil into the water. She sat down on the edge of the tub, rolled up one sleeve of her peignoir, and reached down into the water, stirring the oil around with her hand. Then she rose and dried her hand. She slipped out of the peignoir and tossed it over the back of the vanity chair. Carefully she stepped into the tub. The water was hot and delicious. She spun the taps, and immediately the water stopped. She sank down into the tub and soaked for a few minutes. Then she began to lather herself with the almond cold-cream soap. She lathered her pubis well, rinsing it off with the shower attachment when she was done. Her private parts had gotten her to the Boulevard Maillot. They, too, might help make her dream come true. She smiled to herself. Her dream. Her magazine. It seemed more important than ever to start it soon.

When she finished dressing, she looked at herself in the mirror. She used very little makeup; with her complexion she didn't need to. Only her right cheek was thickly made-up. Every time the Comte approached orgasm, he called her a whore and slapped her across the face. Then he would become the repentant little boy, crying "Mother! Mother!" and fall asleep on her breasts, his face streaked with tears. Hélène shook her head. It was bizarre, and she didn't understand it. She only wished he didn't hit her so hard. Her cheek bruised easily, and only her artful mixing of four different shades of makeup covered up his handprint. What will be will be, she told herself. She bent close to the mirror. Even under the harshest lighting, neither the bruise nor the makeup would show.

She tore herself away from the mirror and crossed the room to where a gilt-framed painting hung on the wall. She felt along the frame, released a catch, and the painting swung forward on its hinges like a window. Behind it was a small wall safe. Deftly she spun the intricate combination. She heard the familiar click and pulled down on the iron handle and swung the heavy door open. She reached inside and felt for the Cartier box with the canary-diamond earrings.

"Good-bye, Cartier," she whispered.

* * *

Baghat Cheops picked up the loupe and held it close to his right eye. He closed his left eye and studied one of the canary-diamond earrings through the magnifying lens. Then he pushed the earring aside and reached for the second one. He studied it as closely as the first. Finally he replaced the loupe carefully in its velvet-lined case. His face was expressionless as he looked at Hélène. "They are not bad," he said.

Hélène's face was a mask. She knew what the dark little Egyptian was trying to do. Bring down the price. Start by offering her a fraction of what the stones were worth. He knew, and she knew, that they were flawless. Each earring had three diamonds, one three-carat, one two-carat, one half-carat. Cartier's asking price must have been enough to buy six Citroën limousines. Baghat Cheops would begin by offering her a sixteenth of their value. They would end up by agreeing on about a twelfth of their value. Then he would turn around and sell them for double or triple what he'd paid. Hélène's only consolation was Cheops' assurance that he would sell them only to transient foreigners. She knew that the jewelry was all recognizable, one-of-a-kind pieces. She couldn't afford to take them back to Cartier's. Even discreetly. They'd be right back on the market. That was too dangerous. The Comte might find out that she'd been selling the jewelry he was giving her, and he'd be furious.

Carefully Cheops laid the canary-diamond earrings side by side on a velvet cloth. He lined them up by tapping them with his nicotine-stained fingernail. They winked with yellow light. "Twelve thousand," he said, smiling. His gold tooth gleamed.

Hélène's face was impassive. It was the most ridiculous starting offer he'd ever made. Obviously the little Egyptian thought he'd found an easy touch. Someone who gambled. Or who had an expensive drug habit. Deliberately she reached out, took the earrings, and put them back in the box. Lazily she dropped it into her purse. "Good-bye, Monsieur Cheops," she said. "It is a pity we could not do business again." She started out of the room.

The Egyptian watched her shrewdly, calculating the chances of her seriously walking out of the shop. He smiled. Once at the door, she would have second thoughts. She would turn around. He had seen it happen often enough.

Hélène closed the door behind her, looked up and down the street, and began walking briskly down the sidewalk. At

308

the next corner, a breathless Cheops grabbed her by the arm. He had been running all the way. It was her turn to smile.

"Twenty thousand," he said between gulps of air.

Marthe was on the telephone when Hélène let herself into the town house. "Un moment, Monsieur le Comte," the maid said quickly. "Mademoiselle has just come in." She held her hand over the mouthpiece. "It's the Comte!" she said in a flustered voice.

Hélène nodded, hurried over to Marthe, and took the receiver. "Philippe?" she said softly. "Where are you?"

As usual, the Comte was in a hurry. He spoke quickly. "I'm at Orly. My flight departs in a few minutes."

"Orly! Where are you going?"

"Scandinavia."

She stared at the receiver. This was news. He'd made no mention of it last night.

"Something's come up," he explained quickly. "I'll be there on business for a week."

Her heart leaped hopefully. This might give her the time she needed to put her plan into action. She made her voice sound disappointed. "Does that mean you won't be here on Tuesday?" she asked carefully.

"Yes," he said irritably. "I'll see you on Friday and Saturday instead. Keep both days open."

Hélène smiled to herself. Good. She would have Marthe call up the Maison d'Odile Joly on Monday and say she was sick. And as soon as the Comte hung up she would make a reservation for the train. Suddenly she spied the neat stack of mail lying next to the telephone. She picked it up and leafed idly through the envelopes. Bills from the electric company. From Hermès. From the telephone company. A letter. She tossed all the envelopes but this one back down. She recognized the handwriting instantly. Jeanne's.

"Are you there?" the Comte asked coldly.

"Yes, of course," Hélène said automatically. He was certainly being irritable today! she thought. In the background she could hear a tinny voice.

"They're announcing my flight," the Comte said, "I've got to go."

"Have a good trip," she said.

But he didn't hear it. Already he'd hung up. Hélène made a face at the receiver and put it back down in the cradle.

309

Quickly she tore open Jeanne's letter, reading it as she walked into the salon.

Saint-Nazaire
January 30, 1954

Dear Sister,

Here everything is so quiet, as Edmond is still at sea. He won't be back for a week. Things are always so hectic when he's around, so I thought I'd better quickly write to you now, before he returns. I pity him out there, especially in this cold. Every time he's gone I say prayers for him.

I have seen Madame Dupré quite a few times. She always asks about you. You can't imagine how proud she is of you! She has your clippings hanging up in the shop. For a while, she even had them in the shop window! Ours are on the doors of the kitchen credence. You are the most famous person in Saint-Nazaire, did you know that?

I saw your aunt in town once. She wouldn't speak to me. I never saw anyone giving me a more hateful look in my life.

I haven't had the chance to tell Edmond yet, since he is at sea, so you're the first person to hear the news. Hélène, I'm *pregnant*! I'm going to give Edmond a child! I know he'll be as delighted as I am. And I'll make certain that if it's a girl, she'll be named after you! I'm only worried that Edmond will treat me like an invalid when he finds out I'm carrying his baby. How I wish you could be here for the christening. Of course, here I am, already planning something that's still so far off!

Don't ever forget, we both love you dearly.

Your sister,
Jeanne

Hélène put down the letter and smiled. Was it possible? Jeanne a mother? Already? Suddenly she felt the tears pressing out of the corners of her eyes. Jeanne and Edmond were so lucky, she thought with a flash of jealousy. They had each other. They were sustained by love.

For the first time, she found herself feeling sorry for herself. What did she have to sustain her? Angrily she wiped her tears away. Plenty, she told herself. You have your dream, your ambition. Your magazine. You have your work and your vows. You want money and power. You have a lot to look forward to. But love? And children? She looked blankly down at the letter on her lap.

She had never even given them any thought.

7

The black Gothic stone spires of the cathedral were menacingly poised against the angry gray wash of sky as Hélène came out of the train station. She put her suitcase down and pulled the collar of her mink coat tighter around her neck. She looked up at the cathedral. The wind was like ice. It swept in from the Rhine and battered the imperturbable flying buttresses that leaned heavily against the massive nave. "Köln," the signs on the train platform had read. Cologne. The cathedral in front of her had stood for centuries. It had accumulated the grime that blackened it through storms and pestilence and bombings.

The narrow streets were busy. It was rush hour. Soon it would be dark. She watched the old women who hobbled out of the cathedral, their heavy dark scarves tied firmly under their chins. She saw the young couples gathered around the lit store windows. She looked to see what was so fascinating. On display were shiny Grundig radios, Telefunken record players, Siemens appliances. She noticed that the best-dressed women wore Persian-lamb coats. Children walked quietly beside their parents, well-disciplined and neat. Everything was orderly, everyone was polite.

Once in the hotel she found the air less oppressive. Tourists and businessmen stood around the spotless lobby. There were the sounds of many languages, not just the guttural staccato German Hélène remembered that the occupiers of her country spoke. Somehow she hadn't expected Cologne to be so cosmopolitan. Then she understood. Bonn was the new capital. It was a small town, just downriver. Cologne was bound to catch some of the international overflow.

The pride of the German woman in postwar years was the

311

Persian-lamb coat. To everyone, it showed that the woman had wealth and status. But nothing impressed anyone as much as mink. The chief desk clerk took one look at Hélène's coat and fell over himself. "Darf ich—"

"Hélène Junot," she said coldly, and added in French: "I have a reservation."

"Oui, madame," he replied, smoothly slipping into French. "One moment, please." He consulted the ledger, his lacquered fingernail sweeping down the page. A veil fell over Hélène's eyes as she watched him. She couldn't help but wonder whether he had been in France during the war. He had been of age. He spoke French well enough. Had he learned it in Paris? Had he been in the Gestapo? Or had he been an ordinary Wehrmacht soldier? Stop it! she told herself harshly. You've been asking yourself that same question every time you've seen an adult German.

The clerk looked up and smiled professionally. "Here it is, Madame Junot. Five days, room seven forty-three." He reached for one of the keys hanging from the cubbyholes on the back wall. Wordlessly she opened her purse and handed him her passport. She scribbled her signature in the register. Then she pushed it back toward him.

"Your passport will be returned to you shortly, madame," he said.

She nodded. "Also, I would like to have something locked in the vault." She gave him a thick envelope. In it was money. A lot of money. Everything she had gotten from Baghat Cheops. Tomorrow, it would be deposited in a German bank.

Hélène paused in front of the frosted-glass door. The gold block letters outlined in black read: "K. Häberle." And underneath it: "Privat Detektiv."

It was the eleventh such office that she had been to in the last three days. For one reason or another, the other ten hadn't suited her. Before she could change her mind about this one, she pushed down on the brass handle and went inside.

She found herself in a secretary's office. A young blond was sitting behind the desk, a beige cardigan draped across her shoulders. She looked up at Hélène and smiled pleasantly. "Guten Morgen," she said.

Hélène forced a smile. "Parlez-vous français?" she asked.

312

The woman smiled and made a motion with her thumb and forefinger. "Un peu," she replied. "Won't you have a seat?" She gestured to the dark varnished wooden chair in front of the desk.

Hélène shook her head. She had learned that service tended to be swifter if you looked uncomfortable. "No, thank you," she said. "I prefer to stand. Is Herr Häberle in?"

The blond's smile broadened. "Yes, of course. One moment, please." She pushed her chair back, got up, and walked over to another frosted-glass door. She opened it and spoke to someone inside. Hélène could overhear the conversation but she couldn't understand any of it. She had never bothered to learn German.

The secretary gestured for her to come over. Quickly Hélène crossed the room and entered the inner office. The secretary closed the door behind her and stayed outside.

Behind a beat-up secondhand desk sat a slim young man with thick, prematurely gray hair. His blue eyes were gentle, but sharp and appraising. His suit was dark and loose; his white shirt, washed-out gray. The collar was unbuttoned, the tie was loosened. He got to his feet and held out his hand. "I am Karl Häberle," he said formally in French. "You must excuse my vocabulary and pronunciation. I'm afraid it has been a few years since I studied French."

Solicitously Häberle pulled up an upholstered chair and Hélène sat down. "Would you like a cup of coffee?" he asked.

She shook her head. "Thank you, no."

"You don't mind if I smoke?"

"Of course not."

Häberle went around his desk and sat down behind it. He reached for a pack of HB's, fished a cigarette out, and stuck it in his mouth. He struck a match and held it to the cigarette. Then he leaned comfortably back in his chair. He eyed her curiously. "Tell me, mademoiselle—it is mademoiselle?" Hélène nodded. "Why do you require the services of a private detective?"

She looked down at her lap as if the answer somehow lay there. For a moment she was silent. Then she looked back up and met his eyes squarely. "I wish to locate someone," she said quietly.

Karl Häberle nodded slowly through the blue cloud of smoke. "Who?"

313

"A man. A man who served in France during the war."

He gave her an obscure look. "A German."

"Yes," she replied softly. "A German."

He nodded to himself, his keen blue eyes boring through hers. "And why do you wish to find this man?"

She looked away. "Because he was kind to me. He . . . he saved my life."

Häberle shook his head. "You are lying, mademoiselle. You hate the man."

Hélène stared at him. Then suddenly she leaned forward. Her eyes blazed. "Yes!" Her voice was a whisper that echoed around the thick old walls. "I hate him!"

"And why is it that you want him found? To bring him to justice or in order to . . . exact vengeance?"

Hélène's voice was shaky. "He must pay for what he has done."

"I shall have to know what that is."

Painfully Hélène closed her eyes. Her voice grew dull and heavy, almost weary. "In 1944 I was seven years old," she said. "The Ger—I'm sorry, the Nazis—came to our house and broke down our doors. My mother was in the underground. She was pregnant at the time. Very pregnant. They found a radio transmitter hidden somewhere in the house. They beat my mother in the belly until . . . until . . ."

"One moment, mademoiselle."

Hélène started and her eyes blinked open. They were confused and startled, like a dreamer's who is suddenly awakened from a nightmare. Häberle was reaching into his desk. He brought out a bottle of schnapps and splashed some into a glass. He leaned across the desk and handed it to her. She nodded gratefully and drank it down. Her fingers were trembling.

"Please continue," he said gently.

Hélène nodded and swallowed. She put the glass down on the desktop. "My mother miscarried, Herr Häberle. I'll never forget seeing the blood running down her gray stockings. Then they took her away and she was never heard of again. Our maid, Michelle, was shot trying to protect her. My brother, my older sister, Catherine, my baby sister, Marie, and I managed to escape. We got separated. A few weeks later, the Nazis caught up with my brother and me. They took us to their headquarters. They had Catherine and Marie. Catherine pretended not to know us and my brother and I managed to get freed. They tortured Marie, though. Right in front of our eyes. What kind of men are those who torture a baby?"

Häberle was silent. There was nothing that he could say.

For a moment she could find no more words. "I never saw my sisters again," she said finally. "I think they were sent to Poland."

Häberle looked at her with compassion. "And you know who was responsible for these atrocities?"

Hélène nodded. "I will never forget him."

Häberle's voice was gentle. "It's possible that he may already have been convicted for war crimes. Or that he has been tried and acquitted. Have you given that any thought?"

"Yes. But deep inside I know that he *hasn't* been caught. That he's walking around free somewhere. In Berlin, or Munich, or Buenos Aires. Perhaps even here in Cologne. I can feel it!"

"You should also realize that many Germans served in France during the war, mademoiselle. Many of them were transferred elsewhere. Some to the Russian front, some back here to Germany, others to Italy, to Holland . . ." He shrugged. "And many died. There were also a lot of cases of the men's service records having been destroyed. It is difficult to trace the events and people in a time of chaos."

"I realize that," she said.

He looked at her closely. "You could go to the Americans or to the Jewish organizations," he said. "It would be much less expensive."

"No!" She shook her head vehemently and tried to keep her voice under control. "No," she repeated softly. "I don't want that. I don't want them to get hold of him. I want him for myself."

He ground out his cigarette in the kidney-shaped ashtray. "Do you have his name?"

"No."

"Do you know where he was from?"

"No."

Häberle heaved a sigh. "Then it will be very difficult."

Suddenly Hélène leaned forward. She reached for his arm and gripped it tightly. Her face was determined. "He must be found," she said grimly.

"As you wish. But I cannot promise you any results. And it will be very expensive. Personally, I recommend that you

315

do not go through with this. It may be a waste of money."
He looked at her sympathetically. "And emotions," he added
gently.

Hélène instinctively liked this young man. He was refreshingly honest. Not like the others, who she felt would have gouged her for everything they could get.

"I am prepared to pay whatever it costs," she said with finality. "I want you to give this case your undivided attention."

"It could take months," he warned. "Years, even."

Her voice took on the hard edge of a knife. "I have time," she said. She reached into her purse and took out a thick envelope. She tossed it on the desk. "Here is your retainer."

Idly he undid the flap and thrummed the stacks of money like a deck of cards.

"Twenty thousand deutsche marks," she said. "Cash. And if you find him, I am willing to pay you a bonus on top of your fee. Two hundred thousand marks have been deposited in a branch of the Dresdener Bank in anticipation of your finding him."

Häberle let out a whistle. "You must want this man very badly," he said.

"I do, Herr Häberle. And you? Do you want to take this case?" There was a challenging look in her eyes.

He grinned. "With wages such as you're offering, I would be a fool not to. Now, tell me everything you know about the man you want found."

Hélène nodded. "First, I know that he was acquainted with a sergeant named Schmidt. A fat man."

"There are hundreds of thousands of Schmidts all over this country. It is one of the most common German surnames. Can you describe him better?"

Hélène nodded. "I would say he was rather short. Dark hair. Red-faced. He looked large to me as a child, but then, all grown-ups do when you're so small." She smiled mirthlessly. "Also, he had a mole on his chin. About here." She put a finger on her own chin.

"Anything else?"

"I'm sorry. No."

"And the man you want?"

She gave an ugly laugh. "I know his rank, I know that he

was in the SS, and I can describe him very well. He is tall. His face is shaped like a skull." She paused. "He is very ugly, Herr Häberle. You see, he is an albino."

8

Politely the Comte helped Hélène slip out of her mink. He tossed it carelessly over the back of one of the velvet seats. She sat down carefully so as not to wrinkle her gown and leaned over the balcony of the Comte's private box.

She loved going to the opera. She enjoyed dressing up for it and seeing the other people in their finery. She felt a thrill whenever she climbed the magnificent great staircase. But above all, she loved losing herself in the musical world of make-believe drama that unfolded onstage. Somehow it was so unreal, and yet at the same time so very real. She had never sat through a single performance without constantly breaking out in gooseflesh.

Her eyes roved around the enormous theater. There was marble of all colors everywhere: the pale, stony shades of white and rose, the deeper, richer hues of green and red and blue. The gleaming chandelier hanging from the domed ceiling was enormous. It was said that it weighed six tons.

She looked down at her program as the Comte took his seat beside her. "*Alceste*," the title read. "Christoph Willibald Gluck." She opened the program and began reading it with quickening interest. She had never heard of this particular opera, and that made it twice as exciting.

The Comte leaned toward her. "Front row, orchestra center. Do you see the old man with the white hair?"

Hélène frowned and stretched her neck like a swan. She looked down at the front row and then back at the Comte. "Yes," she said. "Who is he?"

"Stanislaw Kowalsky, the pianist."

Hélène nodded without speaking. She didn't need to be told who Kowalsky was. Neither did half the schoolchildren in France. He was one of the world's finest concert pianists. For once, even the hard-boiled critics and enthusiastic audiences agreed: he was more accomplished than even Rubinstein and Horowitz.

The door in the back of the box suddenly opened. "Sorry," a deep voice said. "I didn't realize anyone was here."

Hélène and the Comte turned around in their seats. Behind the elegant velvet swags stood Hubert de Léger. Beside him was a young aristocratic lady in a pink gown. She appraised Hélène coldly.

For an instant Hélène locked eyes with Hubert. Then he turned to the girl beside him. "Lille, could you be an angel and wait outside for a moment?"

The girl looked confused. Then reluctantly she nodded and left, closing the door behind her.

Hubert stepped forward. "I thought Lille and I would go to the opera, since the family box is never used," he said quietly. "But I see that I was mistaken."

"Invite her back in," the Comte said easily. "There are enough seats."

Hubert gave a low laugh and looked at Hélène with a sudden knowledge in his eyes. "Don't tell me where you're living. On the Boulevard Maillot?"

She was silent.

"Father always lends that house to his current favorite. Did you know that?"

"I'll forget that remark, Hubert," the Comte said softly. "Now, I think you'd better apologize to Hélène and leave us be. Go back to the university. Your grades could stand your studying some more."

Hubert's face flushed. "Why are you trying to get rid of me? So you can be alone with your whore?"

Hélène rose to her feet. Her face was devoid of expression as she looked at the Comte. "I don't feel like the opera suddenly," she said quietly.

The Comte nodded and got up. He picked up her fur and draped it over her shoulders.

"Leaving won't help," Hubert said tightly. "It won't change a thing. A whore's a whore."

Hélène started for the door. She had almost reached it when Hubert caught her arm and spun her around. "Hélène," he said in a yearning voice. "Leave him. Come with me."

She turned away. "Let me go," she said dully.

"In a minute." He pulled her closer. "You sleep with him, don't you?" he demanded in a hissing whisper, glancing at the Comte, then back at her. "But you wouldn't sleep with me. What's the matter? Is it money you're after? I have a trust fund. Or do you naturally like old men?"

Angrily she tried to pull her arm free. His fingers dug deeper into her wrist. "You're hurting me," she said from between clenched teeth.

"Why did you turn me down?" he asked. "Just so you could turn around and rush off with him? Does his title turn you on?"

"Let her go," the Comte said in a whisper, the muscles twitching in his cheeks.

Hubert looked at him. "You like to steal my girls, don't you, father? That's what it takes to make you feel like a man, isn't it?"

Hélène's free hand suddenly lashed Hubert across the face. He let go of her arm and looked at her in surprise, his fingers gingerly touching his reddening cheek.

"I may be a whore," she whispered, "but you? You don't deserve your father. You don't even deserve me!" Then she pushed past him and started out of the box.

The thickly leafed chestnut trees in the Bois de Boulogne were turning yellow as the taxi pulled to a stop alongside the curb. "Here we are," Hélène said.

Madame Dupré started to reach into her purse. Hélène shook her head. She put a restraining hand on her friend's arm. "You are my guest," she said firmly.

Madame Dupré hesitated. Then she smiled. "All right. Thank you."

They got out of the taxi and watched the driver lifting Madame Dupré's valise out of the trunk. He set it down on the sidewalk. Quickly Hélène paid him and grabbed the valise by the handle.

"What a lovely house!" Madame Dupré said. She gazed up at it, shaking her head in amazement. "And in such a chic neighborhood, with the Bois right there."

"Yes, it is nice," Hélène said.

"I shall take many walks through the Bois." Madamé Dupre smiled. "I love autumn in Paris. I'd almost forgotten how beautiful it can be. There is nothing like Paris in the spring and the fall." She followed Hélène up the marble steps and waited for her to unlock the front door. Hélène held it open for her.

"After you," she said, gesturing inside with a flourish.

Madame Dupré stepped into the foyer. She looked around in surprise. "Why . . . I thought this was an apartment house!" she said. She turned to Hélène.

Hélène turned around and smiled wryly. "I never said it was." She started to close the door but stopped. A young man in uniform was coming up the steps. She waited until he was at the door.

"I have a telegram for Mademoiselle Junot," he said.

"I am she."

He handed her an envelope and she signed for it. He started to leave.

"Just a moment," she said. She fished in her purse for some coins and gave them to him.

"What was that?" Madame Dupré asked.

"A telegram," Hélène said thoughtfully. She frowned as she tore the envelope open. Then she pulled out a paper, unfolded it, and quickly read it:

LITTLE FRENCH GIRL STOP WE HAVE A DAUGHTER YOU HAVE A NIECE STOP JEANNE INSISTS CHRISTENING HER HELENE STOP SO WE DON'T CONFUSE YOU TWO SHE WILL BE PETITE HELENE STOP LOVE YOU STOP PROUD MOTHER AND FATHER JEANNE AND EDMOND

"Jeanne's just had her baby!" she cried excitedly. She thrust the telegram into Madame Dupré's hand.

Madame Dupré read it and shook her head. "She must have been born while I was on the train!"

Hélène grinned. "Imagine me—an aunt!" Then softly she said, "Petite Hélène. It's got a nice ring to it, doesn't it?"

Madame Dupré nodded. "It certainly does. And I know she must be a beautiful baby," she said warmly. "Jeanne must be very happy."

Hélène nodded solemnly. "She'll make a wonderful mother." Then she smiled. "Well, I'd better show you to your room. I know the trip must have been exhausting. You'll want to wash up and maybe take a nap. You'll need all the rest you can get. I've got the next few days all planned out, and it'll be a grueling schedule. Tomorrow I've got to work, but I've reserved a seat for you at Odile Joly's for the show. It's only the daily showing, and not at all as exciting as the big summer and winter shows, I'm afraid. But you'll get to see all the clothes." Hélène hugged Madame Dupré fiercely. "I'm so happy you could come and visit!" she said. "Even if it is only for five days."

Madame Dupré smiled. "And I am happy, too."

"Come, let's go upstairs."

Madame Dupré started to reach for her valise.

"Just leave that there for now," Hélène said. "Marthe will bring it up later."

"Marthe?"

"She's the maid," Hélène said with embarrassment.

Madame Dupré nodded wordlessly. Then she followed Hélène upstairs. When they got to the guest room, Hélène flung the door open and stepped aside. "Voilà!"

Madame Dupré stepped into the room. The draperies had been pushed aside, and the room was filled with the autumn air. She looked out at the Bois and around the cream-colored room. Against one wall was a big four-poster bed draped with kilometers of cream-colored satin. "It's beautiful!" she said.

Hélène smiled and led the way. She flung open some doors. "This is the closet, this is the bathroom. Soap, towels, it's all here. You can get washed up even before Marthe brings up the valise."

Madame Dupré nodded. "Such luxury," she said with a smile. Then her smile faded as she spied the thick white bath towels. Woven into them was a familiar crest. The crest of the de Légers.

Hélène saw the look on Madame Dupré's face. "Back to square one, right?" she joked quietly. "Only this time it isn't the servants' quarters."

Madame Dupré came closer and held Hélène's hand. Within her brown eyes was a sad and worried look. "Be careful," she said softly. "When a woman is in a position . . . What I mean is . . ." She hesitated, clearly embarrassed.

"I know," Hélène said, forcing her voice to sound light. "I'm a kept woman who could be thrown out at any moment."

Madame Dupré turned away. "It's not that that worries me. We French are very forgiving. We know all about affairs of the heart. Just remember . . ." She shook her head. "I'm sorry. It's none of my business. I will say no more."

Hélène's face was expressionless. "No. Go ahead."

Madame Dupré made an agitated gesture and turned to face her. "Hubert is . . . well, like I warned you at Haute-cloque, he's a womanizer. He doesn't believe in being faithful to one woman. He doesn't even believe in having just a wife and one mistress like his father. He's a playboy. He loves *all* women. Now that he's got you, I'm afraid that his interest will wane. I'm afraid for you, Hélène. I don't want to see you hurt."

Hélène suddenly began to laugh. She sat down on the edge of the bed and looked down at her feet.

"What's so funny?" Madame Dupré asked.

The laughter subsided and Hélène's face grew serious. She looked up into Madame Dupré's eyes. "I am not seeing Hubert," she said softly. "I'm the Comte's mistress."

Punctually at seven o'clock they had dinner in the big dining room. Hélène had had a hand in everything, and it showed.

"It looks lovely," Madame Dupré said.

Hélène smiled. She had made a special effort tonight and was glad it was appreciated. She had even gone so far as to get a bottle of Château Hautecloque-de Léger from the wine cellar. She had opened it and then left it on the sideboard, letting it breathe. Now she picked up the dusty, mold-covered bottle and carefully strained the wine of sediment as she poured it into a silver-filigreed crystal decanter. She brought it over to the table and poured a little into Madame Dupré's glass. Then she stood back.

Madame Dupré brought the glass up to her nose and inhaled the fragrance of the grapes. She looked at Hélène with a smile of excitement. Then she took a sip. She put the glass back down and closed her eyes, savoring the taste. "Superb," she proclaimed finally.

Hélène looked pleased. She poured some more wine into the glass and sat down opposite Madame Dupré. After Marthe served the first course, Hélène dismissed her. She wanted to be alone with Madame Dupré. "Is the beef rib all right?" she asked.

Madame Dupré made a gesture with her fork. "Delicious. I've never tasted anything so fine."

"Marthe is quite accomplished," Hélène said.

They ate on in silence for a while. Then Madame Dupré laid down her cutlery. "Have you given your magazine any further thought?" she asked.

Hélène nodded and toyed with her meat. "Yes, but it's still too early to think about. To start a magazine takes a lot of money."

"How about the Comte? I mean . . . not as a gift," Madame Dupré added quickly, dropping her eyes. "As a loan or an investment." She looked across the table at Hélène. "Have you brought the subject up?"

Hélène smiled sadly. "Yes, but unfortunately he's very old-fashioned. He still believes that a woman's place is in the home. I'm afraid he has enough trouble trying to accept the fact that I'm working at Odile Joly's."

"Have you tried explaining to him that there's not much difference between working for someone else and working for yourself?"

"Yes." Hélène sighed. "He thinks women are not cut out for business."

"Indeed!" Madame Dupré's eyes flashed. "Have you pointed out to him that there are many women who are successful? Look at all the designers! Chanel, Schiaparelli, Madame Grès, Madame Vionnet."

"And Odile Joly," Hélène added with a smile.

"Above all, Odile Joly," Madame Dupré said. "They've all been enormously successful!"

"I'm afraid the Comte just doesn't see it that way. Actually, I think he's afraid that if I start a magazine, I wouldn't have enough time left over for him."

"Then what are you going to do?"

"I don't know. I do know that I'll never be able to start a magazine on my salary from modeling. It's simply not enough. Nor can I hope to start it with the Comte's help and blessing." She sighed helplessly. "Sometimes it just eats at me. It's as if my hands were tied."

Madame Dupré nodded. "It's very difficult to build up something from scratch. Twice as difficult if you're a woman."

"So what do I do?"

"You wait," Madame Dupré advised gently. "You wait patiently and bide your time until the opportunity comes. If nothing else, I've learned one thing from life: everyone has a

323

time when his moment comes. The secret is for you to recognize it for what it is, and have the courage and stamina to let yourself be carried away with it. And follow through with it. When that times comes, you must not be afraid. I've had my opportunity, and I didn't take advantage of it. It's ironic, but I didn't even realize it was there until it was too late."

"So I wait," Hélène said slowly. "But how long?"

"You are young," Madame Dupré said. "So very young. Give yourself time." She smiled. "You perhaps don't realize it," she went on, "but in a way, you have already begun."

Hélène felt a ripple of excitement strumming through her body. "I don't think I understand," she said slowly.

Madame Dupré's dark eyes were gentle and wise. "Don't you see it? The magazine is your destiny. It's in your blood. And everything that has happened to you so far is another step toward it. The first time you set foot in my shop was the first step. The month at the château was the second. Now you are in the third stage. You are seeing the inside of the fashion industry. You are headed toward it steadily but surely. Mark my words, Hélène. You will make it. It is like the grapes that make the wine. They must be picked at the moment they are the ripest. Not before, not after. You are not yet ripe. But soon you will be."

Baghat Cheops smiled with self-importance as the slim young man led him into the private office. "Monsieur Bonnard will be with you shortly," the young man said smoothly.

Cheops nodded and smiled. "I am at his service," he said as he took a seat opposite the desk, which was cleared of everything but some high-intensity lamps. When the young man withdrew, he drummed his fingers on the briefcase on his lap and looked around the room.

The sparsely furnished office was on the second floor of number nine, Place Vendôme. In many ways it was like the other luxury shops on the square. The first floor was devoted to selling, the second to management and buying. On the ground floor, the gold script on the arched windows was duplicated on the scalloped white awnings. It read: "Claude Jassel."

Cheops lit one of his brown Egyptian cigarettes and inhaled the pungent smoke nervously. He put his briefcase down, rose to his feet, and started to pace the room. He never liked to be kept waiting. Even less by a snob like Bonnard. He was impatient to exchange the piece of jewelry he had brought along for a nice six-figure check. He glanced at his cigarette. The ash was long and cocked. He looked around the office, but as usual there was no ashtray in sight, and so he was forced to tap the ash into his trouser cuff. He made a mental note to brush it out once he got home. He always forgot, and his cuffs were filled with ash and cigarette butts.

A few minutes later a tall, distinguished-looking man dressed in an exquisite suit came into the office. "Bonjour, Monsieur Cheops," he said briskly.

Cheops stopped pacing and looked at him. "Bonjour, Monsieur Bonnard," he replied, his voice suddenly smooth as oil. He sat back down in the chair, carefully pinched the end of the cigarette between his fingers, and placed the butt in his trouser cuff.

Bonnard walked over behind the desk and sat down, folding his hands. "What may I do for you today, Monsieur Cheops?" he asked brusquely.

Cheops smiled nervously, his gold tooth catching the light flooding in through the window. He could feel the sweat breaking out on his face and he reached for his rumpled handkerchief. "I have another piece of jewelry which I would like to dispose of," he murmured, mopping his forehead. "Discreetly, of course."

"Of course." Bonnard permitted himself a slight smile. Cheops was anything but discreet. He had conveniently picked up the word that every society matron down on her luck used. The matrons, however, insisted that the stones of their jewelry be reset before being resold, so that their friends would not recognize the jewels and find out about their reduced circumstances. Cheops, however, used the word loosely; he never insisted on having anything reset. To him, "discreetly" merely meant not disclosing to whom the jewelry had belonged.

"It is the most magnificent item yet," Cheops said in a gushy voice. "The stones are of the highest quality. It is a necklace fit for an empress."

"May I see it, please?" Bonnard held out his hand.

"Of course," Cheops said, Hastily he released the catch on his briefcase and lifted the lid. He took out a long slim box and put it on the desktop, pushing it toward Bonnard. It slid halfway across the polished desk. The box was imprinted: "Van Cleef & Arpels."

Nonchalantly the jeweler lifted the lid. He took a velvet cloth out of a drawer and deftly spread the necklace out on it. The sapphires were smoldering blue, surrounded by icy white diamonds. Cheops sucked in his breath, but Bonnard barely glanced at them. He switched on the high-intensity lamps. His face was inscrutable as he took out his loupe. Then he studied the stones closely but impersonally. To him, the most beautiful gem was no different from the plainest wedding band. It was merely a piece of merchandise. Only when he showed it to prospective customers would his attitude change. Then he would become fawning, praising the necklace with sumptuous words.

Cheops watched him eagerly. "The best piece yet, eh?" he said with a grin.

Bonnard was silent. He studied each stone carefully.

Snob, Cheops thought to himself. He always thinks he's better than everyone else. But he consoled himself for the snub by doing some quick mental calculations. He'd probably be able to get about half of what the necklace was worth. He knew it had a retail value of at least 250,000 francs. He congratulated himself on what he'd paid for it; a mere 15,000 francs. He'd probably end up getting 125,000 from Bonnard. A 110,000-franc profit was not bad for making a single trip to the jeweler's. No, it was not bad at all. He only hoped that the woman who sold it to him would continue bringing him more pieces. She probably would, as long as she didn't stop by at the better jewelers. Because he wasn't selling them to tourists and foreigners as he had promised. Most of the jewels had been bought in shops around the Faubourg St.-Honoré. And most of them ended up no more than three blocks from where they'd been bought.

He mopped his forehead again. He hoped she wouldn't find out too soon. She was the goose who was laying his golden eggs. Twenty-four karat eggs, at that.

9

It was after two o'clock. The room was dark and the snow was coming down heavily as Hélène sat in the window seat. Her knees were drawn up to her chin and her head leaned back against the window frame. She had been sitting in that position ever since the snow started to fall. That was hours ago.

Her eyes stared out into the night. Through the thick lead glass, the world outside looked distorted. As if everything were either stretched out of shape or compressed, depending on the angle she looked at it. Sort of like funhouse mirrors, she thought. She pursed her lips. Only nothing was funny. It was all frightening. Too frightening.

Up until now everything had been going quite well. Even she had to admit it. She was a top model at Odile Joly and she enjoyed the advantages of the Comte's affections. From him she had gotten the closets full of fashionable clothes, the jewels she had been pawning to pay Häberle, the three fur coats. From him, too, she had gotten the use of the big town house on the Boulevard Maillot. She had managed to put a hundred thousand miles between herself and the grimy labyrinths of Montmartre and the horrors of Saint-Nazaire. There was no doubt about it. She was on her way up.

But now? She turned her head away from the window and stared wearily down at her hands. Now suddenly the tables had turned. She had missed her period. She was never late, but at first she had told herself that that was all it was. So she waited. Then she missed the second month. Then the third. Finally she had panicked and gone to see the doctor. He had confirmed her worst suspicions. She was three months pregnant. Biting down hard on her lip, she wondered what would happen to her now.

She was a fashion model. She didn't have to be told what happened to pregnant fashion models. There weren't any. She knew she was lucky to even have a job modeling. She knew, too, that there were hundreds, even thousands, of beautiful girls already lined up, ready to jump into her place. Ruthlessly awaiting their opportunity. And she had heard somewhere that giving birth left stretch marks. So what if they eventually went away? She couldn't just take a leave of absence and go off to have a baby. When she got back, her job would be gone. And without a job, how could she ever expect to support and feed the baby? She shook her head. It was a malicious cycle that fed on itself.

Then, there was the matter of the Comte. She no longer had any illusions left as far as he was concerned. To him she was nothing more than an exceptionally constructed toy in a lavish dollhouse. He would never tolerate a pregnant mistress. As soon as he found out about it, she would be kicked out, back into the cold. The most she would be able to expect from him would be a financial settlement of some sort. Along with a notice to vacate the town house and find her own place to live.

Finally, and most important of all, there was her dream. Her secret ambition. Her magazine. She had already picked out a name for it. *Les Modes*. And she knew that *Les Modes* was the only child she would ever really want to have. She shook her head in despair. The baby. The baby. It wasn't even born yet, but suddenly everything revolved around the baby.

On an impulse she stretched out her legs. Then with her fingers she felt her belly. It was still flat and hard. It didn't feel a bit different. Not yet. It wouldn't be noticeable for a couple of months, but it was there, all right, deep down inside her. She could almost feel it growing, that infinitesimal spark of life.

She closed her eyes and took a deep breath. Over the past few hours a vague plan had been hovering nearby. At first it had been an ugly, shapeless cloud and she kept pushing it away. But now she let it metamorphose into the ugly dark shape that it was. It was a way out.

TODAY

Friday, January 12

1

Hélène and Edmond got off the elevator on the twenty-first floor of the ManhattanBank Building. Hélène looked extremely elegant. She was wearing a sable coat, a sable hat, an ivory-colored Givenchy suit with a sable-colored blouse and a single strand of pearls. Her handbag and shoes matched: they were made of choice lizard skin. The attaché case she carried came from Botega Veneta on Madison Avenue and had cost two thousand dollars.

This morning, Hélène had dressed with special care. She had gone through her wardrobe and chosen each item piece by piece. The result was an outfit that made her look rich, and yet it had the elegant understatement and conservative style that was associated with "old money." It was a bit of camouflage, since her money certainly wasn't "old," but today some camouflage wouldn't hurt. The pearls, she decided, were a good touch. They were not too much; not too little. You could never go wrong with pearls, she thought. She decided that she must look cautiously conservative and extremely restrained. Even aloof. Appearances were all-important.

She looked at the familiar block letters on the wall above the reception desk: "International Commercial Banking Division." This part of ManhattanBank, as well as the personal banking division on the floor below, was a side of the banking world that most people never saw. Here the important clients were handled *by appointment only* in plush private offices. When millions of dollars were involved, there was no waiting in line for surly bank tellers or nasty "officers." Up here, everything was strictly first-class. Very professional. Very efficient. Very slick.

The receptionist looked up at Hélène and Edmond and smiled professionally. "May I help you?" she asked in a polite voice.

"We have an appointment with Mr. Rowen," Edmond said.

The receptionist reached for the call directory and lifted the receiver. "Who should I say would like to see him?"

"Miss Junot," he replied.

"One moment, please." The receptionist smiled apologetically, punched a four-digit number, and murmured softly into the receiver. A moment later she hung up and smiled again. "Room two-one-oh-seven," she said. She pointed down the hall. "It will be on your right. Mr. Rowen's expecting you."

"Thank you," Edmond said. He touched Hélène's sable sleeve and guided her down the blue-carpeted corridor. Framed color renderings of worldwide ManhattanBank branches hung on the white walls.

At room 2107 they found a young man sliding a brass nameplate into the metal slot on the door. Hélène looked at it curiously: "R. ROWEN, Vice-President." When the man finished, he noticed them and stepped aside. "I'm sorry," he apologized quickly. "I didn't realize . . ."

Hélène smiled automatically. "That's all right," she said. But her smile faded when she saw the old brass sign in his hand. It was engraved: "J. C. GORE III, Vice-President."

She shivered. How quickly the new replaces the old, she thought. Only a single day had passed since Gore's death, and already all evidence of his tenure was being obliterated. Suddenly the hallway was oppressive, stifling. She was glad when Edmond opened the door and they entered the office. A dead man's office.

Alice, Gore's middle-aged secretary, looked up from her desk. Her eyes were red and she looked like she'd been crying.

"Hello, Alice," Hélène said softly.

"Good morning, Miss Junot." Alice sniffed and wiped her nose with a Kleenex. "Mr. R-Rowen is expecting you."

"I'm sorry about Mr. Gore," Hélène said.

"Thank you, Miss Junot." Alice composed herself, rose to her feet, and walked with dignity toward the veneered door of the inner office. She knocked twice and opened it. "Miss Junot and Mr. Junot are here to see you, Mr. Rowen."

Alice stepped aside, waited for Hélène and Edmond to enter the office, and quietly closed the door behind them. Hélène started. The office seemed strangely dim: a huge plywood board covered one of the big expanses of window, blocking out some of the light and most of the view. She shuddered.

Mr. Rowen got to his feet and came around from behind the desk. He shook hands firmly with Hélène and Edmond. "I'm Robert Rowen," he said in a friendly, reassuring voice. He gestured for them to take a seat.

Hélène unbuttoned the sable and let it slip back on the chair as she sat down. Edmond took a seat beside her, and Rowen went back behind the desk. Hélène couldn't help noticing that with the plywood over the window, she could see Rowen's face clearly. It used to be difficult for her to read Gore's expressions with all the light coming in from behind him. She also found it a bit disconcerting that Gore's successor was so unlike his predecessor. She hadn't realized that she'd gotten quite used to Gore's obesity and wheezy self-importance. This man was in his mid-thirties, slim, and dark-haired. He was part of the new breed, one of the Bright Young Men who'd made it. For his age, he was somberly dressed. He wore the traditional pinstriped suit and Turnbull-and-Asser shirt indigenous to the banking profession.

Rowen pushed a stack of computer printout aside and cleared his throat. He chose his words carefully. "For the time being, I have been designated to act as Mr. Gore's replacement. I have no idea whether this is a permanent position. However, I will try to handle everything to your satisfaction." He looked at Hélène. "Hélène Junot International, Incorporated, seems to do the bulk of its American banking with ManhattanBank. I cannot pretend that you are anything but a highly valued client." He smiled, showing straight white teeth. "As well as my wife's favorite publisher, I might add."

Graciously Hélène smiled back. It was expected of her.

"At any rate," Rowen continued, "our only immediate concerns are to ensure a continued smooth relationship between yourself and ManhattanBank, and to come to a mutually satisfactory decision regarding your ten-million-dollar loan." He looked at Hélène. She nodded slowly. "In order to acquaint myself more fully with the circumstances involved, I do not want to make any decision concerning the loan until Monday."

Hélène nodded again, but she remained silent. Edmond had told her to let him do the talking. Now he spoke up.

"Mr. Rowen, I fully understand ManhattanBank's position. But as the head of HJII's international legal department, as well as Miss Junot's personal adviser and brother, I have requested this meeting in order to familiarize you with the urgent need for an extension.

"As you may know, HJII is the world's largest and most powerful fashion instrument. We have subscribers on six continents. One word in our magazines can make or break a major designer or manufacturer. We have helped push many of today's most successful couturiers into the forefront—Halston, d'Itri, Armani, Geoffrey Beene, to mention a few. Our faithful readers—we have a monthly circulation of over twenty-eight million copies—trust us implicitly and spend almost six hundred million dollars a year buying our magazines. Our advertising revenues—"

"You don't need to acquaint me with Hélène Junot International's success, Mr. Junot," Rowen said quietly. "The fact of the matter is, the ten-million-dollar loan was not made to the corporation but to *Miss* Junot."

Edmond shook his head. "Miss Junot *is* HJII," he said smoothly. "And since she used a portion of her HJII shares as collateral, you must admit that the loan does indeed affect the corporation. Especially since her control over the corporation hinges on your decision."

Rowen steepled his fingers. "I can appreciate that," he said carefully. "But I do not quite understand what it is you're trying to get at."

Edmond reached for his cigarettes. "May I?" he asked, holding up the flat eighteen-karat-gold Tiffany case.

"Certainly."

Edmond selected a cigarette, tapped it on the case, and slowly lit it. It was a device he had invented long ago in order to stall for time to think. Rowen was sharp, he realized. He would not be as easy to handle as Gore had been.

Edmond blew the smoke out through his nostrils. "All I'm trying to get at, Mr. Rowen, is that without Miss Junot's leadership, taste, and expertise, the corporation would be in extreme danger of losing its appeal. Without her, HJII would probably close its doors and go bankrupt within five years. Maybe less. It is therefore vital that the collateral shares held by ManhattanBank are *not* sold.

"Like any big institution or wealthy person, Miss Junot occasionally has cash-flow problems. I am sure that you can appreciate that. Much of her money is tied up in investments.

You can be assured that her cash-flow problems are very temporary.

"Also, I would like to reiterate what you yourself have stated—that the bulk of HJII's banking is done with ManhattanBank. That is due entirely to Miss Junot's discretion. Should her collateral shares be sold, she would lose control over HJII and you would have no guarantee that ManhattanBank would continue getting HJII's business. I don't think I need to tell you that more than one hundred and sixty million dollars a year flow through our ManhattanBank accounts. I'm sure you already know that."

Rowen nodded. "I do. And as I said to you over the telephone yesterday, I shall consider all these factors before coming to a decision."

Nonchalantly Edmond leaned forward and stabbed out his cigarette in the big ashtray. His eyes met Rowen's. "Mr. Gore . . . he was mainly in charge of our accounts, wasn't he?" he asked lightly.

"Yours and several others," Rowen replied carefully.

Edmond sat back. "I take it, though, that HJII was his single largest account?"

"I'm not certain. I would have to check that out. I can only presume so."

Edmond smiled agreeably. "Which means, of course, that if Mr. Gore did indeed 'borrow' money from various accounts, more money would be missing from HJII's accounts than any of the others?"

"Mr. Junot, let me assure you that this institution is fully insured and *if*—and I stress the word 'if'—this turns out to be the case, we would immediately be able to cover your losses."

"I understand that," Edmond said easily. "And I'll try to make Miss Junot understand that, too. But you must agree that it would be rather . . . unfair if we were the victims of having our accounts fraudulently mishandled, and at the same time be doing business with an unresponsive bank?"

"What exactly do you mean?"

"I'm certain most corporations would not look lightly upon their bankers 'borrowing' money from their accounts. But Miss Junot fully understands the problems of having many employees. She has hundreds of them herself, all around the world. Any corporation—even a bank—can have one rotten apple in a barrel of good ones."

Rowen leaned across the desk. "Mr. Junot," he said quietly, "you wouldn't by any chance be trying to blackmail ManhattanBank into giving Miss Junot an extension, would you?"

Edmond grinned suddenly. "Not at all, sir. I'm only saying that as far as HJII and ManhattanBank are concerned, we hope that our mutually successful business relationships in the past can be smoothly continued in the future. Miss Junot would hate having to take one hundred and sixty million dollars' worth of annual business elsewhere." Edmond rose to his feet and looked down at Hélène. She got up, and he helped her into the sable. Then he turned back to Rowen. "It was very kind of you to see us, Mr. Rowen. We know that you must be extremely busy, and we don't want to take up any more of your time."

Then they left the office. Only after they had gone did Rowen realize that Hélène had not spoken one word.

2

The snow was coming down in flurries when Robert Rowen climbed into the back of the Checker cab. He let out a sigh of relief. At last he was on his way home. He rubbed his eyes. They hurt fiercely. He had been straining them all day and far into the night going over the Junot accounts. Finally he had called it quits and telephoned for a cab. Then he waited in the lobby of the ManhattanBank Building for it to arrive. After business hours, Wall Street became a morgue and you couldn't find a cab if your life depended on it. Every time it snowed, it was the same old story.

Finally, after he'd waited more than forty-five minutes, the cab had pulled up in front of the building. He hurried out through the swirling flakes. "Park Avenue and Seventy-second," he told the driver.

During the ride uptown, he kept thinking about the Junot accounts. He hadn't realized just how mind-boggling they were until he'd really started going over them. There was no end to the number of accounts. There were some into which bank drafts and letters of credit were paid, there were separate accounts for each of the advertising agencies (twenty-seven in all), several for payroll, a few for taxes, one for the shareholders' dividends, one for billing, one for receiving, one for receiving funds from each overseas branch, one for each New York department, another for travel expenses, a miscellaneous account, a slush fund, a petty-cash fund, and no less than seven personal accounts for Hélène Junot. The list was endless.

His mind was still on the accounts when the cab pulled up in front of the prewar Park Avenue building. "Good evening, Mr. Rowen," the doorman said as he held the door of the cab open.

Rowen paid the driver through the little slot in the scratched-up Plexiglas divider and climbed out of the cab. "Good evening, Pedro," he said in an annoyed voice. He fished in his pocket for a quarter and silently cursed the doorman for running out and making a tip necessary.

Pedro held the lobby door open and Rowen hurried out of the cold and into the warmth. He crossed the lobby to the old elevator, punched the button, and waited an eternity for it to arrive. When it did, he stepped inside the varnished wooden cage and pressed the button marked 12.

When the elevator door slid open, he turned right, walked down the tiled hall, fished for his keys, and began to unlock the door of apartment 12C. It opened just as he was turning the key.

"Hi, honey," Jennifer said softly. She wrapped her arms around him, stood on tiptoe, and gave him a long, hard kiss. Then she drew back, smiling up at him. Her brown hair, with its preppy cut, shone softly in the light. "Have a tough day?"

He shrugged and nuzzled her ear. "How's my baby?"

She giggled. Then her face turned serious. "Honey, I missed you."

"I missed you, too."

"Martini?"

"You said it." He followed her into the living room. It was furnished with the heavy mahogany pieces she'd inherited from her mother. He watched as she took two glasses from the sideboard, then disappeared into the kitchen. She opened

337

the freezer and reached for the martinis they kept on ice in a glass shaker.

"Honey? Are you hungry?" she called out.

"I can wait," he called back.

She tossed an olive into her glass, *gently* lowered a grape into his, and poured the martinis. Carefully she carried them out to the living room.

He was loosening his tie. Wearily he sank onto the camel-back sofa. She handed him his drink and sat down beside him, curling her legs under her torso in that peculiar manner of hers. She watched him take a swallow of his martini.

"So tell me," she said finally. "How did your day go?"

"Well, come to think of it, I met a rather interesting person. A woman."

Her eyes narrowed teasingly. "Was she beautiful?"

He looked suddenly thoughtful. "Yes."

"More beautiful than me?"

He looked at Jennifer. This was an old game between them. Whenever he met a woman, she would always ask that. He would invariably hesitate, she would pretend to be cross, and finally he would say, "No, honey, you're the most beautiful woman in the world." Then she would be content and they would kiss happily.

"Well?" Jennifer demanded with mock petulance.

"She was . . . very beautiful," he said slowly.

She sat bolt upright. She looked suddenly cross. "You're serious, aren't you?"

He nodded.

"So she's that special," she said bitterly. She shook her head angrily, but her eyes were frozen.

Now he knew she was really upset. He sighed helplessly. He should have known better and stuck to the rules of the game.

"Well?" she demanded. "Who was this . . . this Helen of Troy?"

He couldn't help but smile at her unintentionally appropriate metaphor. "Hélène Junot," he said. "The publisher."

She tried to laugh lightly, but it came out sounding very ugly. He looked at her with surprise.

"So she got to you, too," she said accusingly.

He looked at her blankly. "What do you mean?"

"What do I mean! Really, Robert! Don't you know anything about her? According to the columnists, she leaves a path of destruction wherever she goes."

He looked at her angrily. "Come off it, Jennie. It's nothing personal. Hey . . ." He reached out to stroke her cheek, but she drew back coldly. "I didn't even speak to her. Her brother did all the talking." Once again he looked thoughtful. "You know what?" he said, thinking aloud. "They're a very slick pair of operators."

Despite her anger, she looked at him with deepening interest. "What do you mean?"

"Well . . ." He took another swallow of his drink. "It was strange. I got the idea she was there just as window dressing. You know what I mean?" She nodded. "He did all the talking. Come to think of it, she never even said 'hello' or 'good-bye.'" He shook his head. "Her brother's real sharp. Almost *too* sharp. And yet . . . she's the power behind it all. You can almost feel it. It's sort of . . ." He paused, searching for the right word.

"Scary?" she offered.

"Hmmm . . . I guess you could call it that."

Suddenly the telephone rang. They glanced across the room at it.

"I'll get it," Jennifer said quickly. She uncurled her legs, got up, and crossed over to the round mahogany fern table that they used as a telephone stand. "Hello?" A moment later she put her hand over the mouthpiece and turned to Rowen. There was a peculiar look on her face. "Honey . . ."

"Who is it?"

"I don't know. A man, I think. He says he wants to talk to you."

"Well, find out who he is."

"Honey, he sounds kind of creepy. He's *whispering*."

Rowen saw the expression on her face. He sighed, got up, and crossed the room. She handed him the receiver and then put her ear close to his, trying to eavesdrop.

"Robert Rowen here," he said.

For a moment there was silence. Then a whispering voice echoed in the telephone. "*Mr. Rowen*," it said, "*how would you like to make a million dollars?*"

YESTERDAY

IV

ABORTION

1

Paris, 1955

The snow had stopped falling but the air was like a breath of ice as Hélène hesitated on the doorstep of the old building. For a moment, she couldn't move. It was as if the snow had frozen her feet to the sidewalk. She glanced up. The building looked like any of the countless ugly gray buildings which the tourists found so picturesque. Only there was nothing picturesque about what went on in this one.

Determinedly she bit down on her lip. It was a moment before she realized the force of the bite. Then she could taste the thick warm sweetness of her blood. Slowly she opened the door and began to climb the dark, steep flights of stairs which were illuminated by a single naked bulb. There was trash piled high on the landings, and the stench of urine and cat feces hung foul in the air. Halfway up, she stopped suddenly and gripped the banister. She could feel the fear in her heart hammering against her ribs. She closed her eyes. She was frightened and depressed and alone. She had been feeling like that ever since she had come to a decision and gone to see Angélique.

She hadn't known whether Angélique still danced in the revue at the Folies de Babylon, but she had hoped so. She had never forgotten her first day there. Angélique had been testy because she was pregnant and had to pay for her abortion herself. She smiled grimly. Angélique was the only person she had ever known who had gotten an abortion.

At six in the morning Hélène had waited outside the employee door of the Folies de Babylon. She had stayed awake all night long, and her exhaustion showed. Her eyelids were red and puffy from lack of sleep, and she had to wait in the snowy darkness for almost an hour; inside the nightclub, closing and cleanup were running late. Finally the door had opened and the girls poured out into the narrow street. She drew deeper into the shadows so that she would not need to speak to anyone she knew.

She recognized Angélique immediately, and a lump rose up in her throat. She waited while the tall showgirl stopped to light a cigarette. Then she watched her pull her coat tightly around her and hurry down the alley, the footsteps of her flat heels noiseless in the snow. Quickly Hélène slipped out of the shadows and fell in step behind her.

"Angélique?" she said in a small, timid voice, a band of fear suddenly constricting her chest.

The showgirl stopped and looked at Hélène in the dim light of a streetlamp. "Yes?"

Hélène pushed her hat back from her face. "Remember me? I used to work with Yvette in the hat-check."

Angélique looked at her blankly. "There's no job opening right now," she said in a bored voice and continued walking. "Look someplace else," she said over her shoulder.

Hélène ran after her and caught her arm. "I'm not looking for a job," she said quickly. "I need your advice."

Angélique laughed. "Listen, chérie. It's been a grueling night. My legs ache, I'm tired, and I want to go home."

"Please," Hélène begged. "I've just got one question."

Angélique stopped and faced Hélène wearily. "All right, what is it?"

"I remember you had to get an abortion—"

"Listen, young lady!" Angélique snapped. "What I do or don't do is none of your business!" She squinted and frowned. Then her eyes flickered with recognition. "Now I remember you," she said, giving a short laugh. "You're the wholesome one."

Hélène felt her cheeks stinging as if she'd been slapped. She looked down at her feet. "I need to know where I can get an abortion," she said quietly.

Angélique laughed. "Don't tell me! So you're not that wholesome after all!"

"No," Hélène said tightly. She looked back at Angélique. "Please," she whispered. "I need to know where I can go."

Angélique looked at her. Suddenly the girl's misery sank through. She thawed immediately. "All right," she said in a gentler voice. She put her arm around Hélène's shoulders. "Hey, you're crying!"

Hélène nodded and wiped her eyes.

"You really want to keep the baby, don't you?"

Hélène's voice trembled. "Yes. But I . . . I can't."

"Come on," Angélique said, smiling. "I'm suddenly not that tired after all. How about some breakfast?"

"I'm not hungry," Hélène said. "But I'll have a cup of coffee."

Angélique smiled. "Then I know just the place. Henri has the worst coffee in Paris, and nobody drinks it. But he keeps the best brandy under the counter."

The brandy was served in coffee cups. Hélène looked down at hers and smiled faintly.

"Henri can't get a liquor license," Angélique explained. "So in his typically sneaky fashion he circumvented the liquor laws by serving drinks in cups. Not that it's legal. It just looks aboveboard to the casual observer. Even the gendarmes on the beat drop in for a cup of his 'coffee' every now and then." Suddenly she reached across the table and took Hélène's hand. "Listen," she said softly, "how far gone are you?"

Hélène's lips twitched. "Three months," she whispered heavily.

Angélique was silent for a moment. "It'll be difficult," she said quietly. "Once you've carried a child for that long, it gets very tricky."

Hélène stared at her.

"You're sure you want to . . . get rid of it?"

Hélène winced at the expression. Slowly she nodded.

Angélique toyed with the cup. "I know this intern . . ." She smiled humorlessly and shrugged. "At least he says he's an intern. If you decide to go ahead with it, I'll have to call him and recommend you. Then he'll get in touch with you. Just think it over carefully first. If you do it, there's no going back, you know. Once it's done, it's done."

Hélène nodded. "I've thought it over already," she said. "I have to do it."

Now she felt a tightening in her throat as she knocked three times on the door on the top floor. A muffled voice came from inside. "Who is it?"

"Angélique's friend, Hélène. I . . . I have an appointment?"

There was the sound of a key turning in the lock and then the door jerked open. A sloppy, fat young man stood in front

345

of her, scratching his beard. Behind him, the room was dark and musty. He stared at her. "Well, don't just stand there! Quick! Come in."

Hélène quickly stepped past him. He glanced suspiciously out into the stairwell and lost no time in shutting the door and locking it behind her. She looked around, a nervous smile masking her disgust. There were newspapers spread out over the floor, and cats were everywhere. Licking their paws, sizing her up, slinking around.

The fat man shuffled over to her, the soles of his mules slapping against the newspapers. "Three thousand francs," he said, holding out his hand.

Hélène nodded. Nervously she reached into her coat pocket. "Don't take a purse," Angélique had advised her. "Don't take anything you'll have to carry. You'll feel very weak afterward." She peeled off some bills and handed them to him. Wordlessly he wet his finger and counted them. Then he grunted and stuffed them into his trouser pocket.

"Follow me," he said, gesturing with his hand.

Hélène hesitantly followed him into the kitchen. Here, too, the floor was covered up with newspaper. There was a pot of water boiling on the stove and dirty dishes in the enamel sink. In the center of the room was a large wooden table. The top was covered with a thick layer of newspapers.

"Take off your clothes and lie down on there," he said.

She stared at the table. "On . . . here?" she asked hesitantly, pointing at it.

"You don't see no other place, do you?"

She shook her head. "No," she said softly. Self-consciously she began to unbutton her blouse. Then she stepped out of her skirt. She glanced at him. He had his back to her, washing his hands in the kitchen sink. Quickly she stepped out of her slip and shrugged off her brassiere. She draped her clothes neatly over a chair. The room felt suddenly cold. She shivered and rubbed her arms with her hands.

He turned around and looked at her indifferently. Instinctively she tried to cover herself. "I told you to get on the table," he said.

Her face turned scarlet. She looked at him without replying. She took a deep breath and then climbed onto the table.

"Lie down on your back," he said. With his foot he pushed a metal trashcan over beside the table.

"What's that for?" she asked with a sudden fear.

"Let me worry about that."

She nodded hesitantly. Stiffly she lay back, her head hanging over the edge of the table.

"Slide farther down," he said. "And put your legs up. You know, like someone's going to shove something up your pussy."

She bit down on her lip and did as she was told. Then she watched him reach for a long, thin piece of wire with an ugly hook at the end. He tossed it into the pot of boiling water. A minute later he fished it back out, holding the end of it with a rag. Some water dripped down onto the burner and hissed.

Hélène closed her eyes. She hadn't had any idea that it would be like this. She had thought it would be nicer, somehow. Cleaner. More professional. Dignified.

"Spread your legs apart," he said. "And keep still."

She took a deep breath. Her legs were trembling as she splayed them. Then she felt his fingers brushing her pubic hair aside. She tensed, her hands gripping the sides of the table, her breasts rising and falling with her quiet breathing. A moment later he began to push the warm metal hook inside her. It felt foreign, like an object that didn't belong. Something deep within her made her want to cry out, but she fought against it, biting down on her lip. She felt the wire going in deeper. Deeper. Probing, moving around. Then the hook hit against something.

"No," she cried, hammering her head against the tabletop. "No!" she screamed as she felt the hook digging in. The pain shot through her belly as the something inside her was being poked and jabbed and jostled loose.

She knew what it was. Her baby. The spark of life which she and the Comte had produced and which her body had been nurturing for more than three months. The tears pushed out of her eyes, running down her cheeks.

Now the pain was gaining in strength. She forced herself to open her eyes and look down at the man. He was holding the end of the wire, moving it around within her, poking still farther in and then giving it short, swift tugs. Suddenly the pain burst through her like a flash of red-hot lightning. Her body convulsed and she screamed in agony as her baby was wrenched from her womb.

"Don't look," he advised grimly.

She opened her eyes and pushed herself forward into a sit-

347

ting position. "I want to see," she whispered in an anguished voice. "I *have* to see."

Then she saw and she let out a cry of terror. The newspaper under her was soaked with thick, sticky blood. On it lay the motionless little fetus. It had an oversized pink head, short little limbs, and a network of fine blue veins crisscrossing the misshapen body. Its umbilical cord still snaked up inside her.

Now she knew what the trashcan was for. Her baby.

The door behind her crashed shut and then there was silence. It was the kind of unearthly silence you would experience if you were the only person alive on earth.. She looked slowly up and down the alley. It was still daylight. What time was it? she wondered. Slowly she pulled back her sleeve and looked at the watch on her wrist. Could it be possible? she asked herself. She had been upstairs for less than half an hour. Yet she seemed to have aged a few years.

She stumbled along the sidewalk, veering like a drunkard. Her face was pale. She leaned against a wall and shut her eyes. There was a terrible pain within her; suddenly she felt hot. She wiped her sleeve across her forehead. It was wet and her hair was plastered against her head. But there was snow on the ground. Why should she feel so hot?

Then she slumped to the ground.

2

Hélène twisted her head to one side and a moan came through her lips. Slowly she opened her eyes and stared straight ahead, a puzzled look on her face. All she could see was one dark, unfocused blur and a vague vertical line of light that kept changing shape as it danced in front of her.

She frowned and blinked her eyes. Slowly her vision focused. The room was dark, but it was daylight outside; straight ahead there were chinks of light between the drapes.

The window was open, and the light kept shifting as the draperies moved. So that was the dancing, changing shape. She had imagined it to be many things. A whirling ballerina, a nightmare creature, a white horse prancing in front of her. But never draperies.

She tried to sit up in bed, but her body felt like lead and refused to obey. Frustrated, she sighed deeply and let her head sink back down on the pillow. What had happened? What was wrong with her?

Then she remembered. She wrinkled her nose in disgust. Still she could almost smell the offensive odor of urine and cat feces. She could almost see the dingy apartment covered with newspapers and the fat bearded man holding the long piece of wire that had the hook on the end. And now she also remembered the cats stalking around everywhere, and the . . . the fetus . . .

Nausea rose up within her. Quickly, as if it would chase away the demons in her memory, she turned her head sideways on the pillow. She frowned again as the curtains billowed and the room was flooded with sudden light. The pillow was white. So were the bedsheets. And they were starched, not soft like the Porthault sheets embroidered with violets that she had at home.

Wearily she moved her head from side to side, her violet eyes straining to get a better view of the room. It was a large room, but one in which she had never been before. That much she knew. But it was a clean room. There were no newspapers, no cats. She felt an immeasurable relief at that.

She tried to look up as she heard a door opening. A man came quietly into the room. He approached the bed and looked down into her face. "How are you feeling?" he asked gently.

She looked up at him with curiosity. "Who are you?"

He smiled and switched on a lamp. She could feel the mattress shifting as he sat down on the edge of the bed. "I was going to ask you the same question," he said, tucking the sheet around her chin. "But that can wait." He smiled reassuringly and reached into his pocket. Then he took a pair of thick wire-rimmed glasses out of an eyeglass case. Carefully he put them on. Then he picked up a thermometer off the nightstand and shook it with short, expert jerks of his wrist. He peered closely at it, gave a nod of approval, and stuck it in her mouth. Dutifully she closed her lips over it and looked up at him.

He was short and small-framed, with narrow shoulders that seemed to sag under an enormous invisible burden. His hair and beard were of various shades of black and gray, his nose was magnificent, almost noble in its size and shape, and seemed sadly out of place in a face so deeply engraved with sadness. Under the hooded lids his eyes were dark and heavy. They were eyes that had seen too much pain in the past and could foresee a future that was filled with no less suffering.

He waited patiently. After a while he reached for the thermometer, slipped it gently out of her mouth, and held it close to his eyes. He looked pleased. "Your temperature is stable, as I suspected it would be." He put the thermometer down on the nightstand. "You are out of danger. Your fever broke yesterday."

"Yesterday!" Hélène said in a small voice. A sudden intuition came into her eyes. "How long have I been here?"

"Four days."

"Four days!" She shook her head unbelievingly. "But I just woke up . . ."

The man nodded, "You were very weak," he explained to her. "And you lost a lot of blood. But that wasn't half as debilitating as the infection."

"Infection!" Hélène struggled to sit up, but he shook his head.

"Don't try to move," he warned. "You are still too weak. It will be a few days before your body recovers its strength."

Hélène nodded obediently and lay quietly back. "Where am I?" she asked.

"Don't worry, you are under good care. I am a doctor. My name is Simon Rosen."

She relaxed a little. "How did I get here?"

"I found you and carried you here. You had passed out."

She felt a sudden stab of guilt. "I put you through a lot of trouble," she apologized meekly.

"Don't worry yourself about that. I should have taken you to a hospital, but I thought it was better to bring you here. The hospital would have been forced to call the police. They would have asked many ugly questions."

Now she understood what it was like to owe a big debt. He had not only saved her life. He had kept her name clean as well.

"I don't know how I can ever thank you," she said solemnly.

He smiled. "Just concentrate on getting your strength back." He got to his feet. "I will bring you some food in a moment."

She nodded gratefully. Suddenly she felt very tired. He noticed it. He would wait with dinner and let her sleep. It would do her more good right now than eating. But first she needed to drink some water. He reached for the glass, placed one hand under the back of her head, and held her up as he put the glass to her lips. She drank slowly. When she had had enough, she nodded. Gently he let her head back down.

"I shall be right back," he promised.

She smiled weakly and closed her eyes. Already she could feel the mantle of sleep closing in around her.

"By the way," he said. "You never told me your name."

"Hélène Junot," she whispered so softly that he could barely hear it.

Her eyes were shut so she did not see the tears behind his glasses. He shook his head. God worked in strange ways. He had seen to it that his path crossed with another Junot's. Hélène Junot. He frowned and searched his memory. There were four children. She would be the second youngest.

He took off his glasses, wiped them carefully with his handkerchief, and placed them back in the case. He rubbed the tears from his eyes with his fingers. Then he just stood there looking over at her. Her face was lost in innocence, and the sounds of her breathing were slow and regular. She was fast asleep.

He shook his head sadly. "Sleep peacefully, little one," he murmured. "Gather up your strength, for you shall need it. You should never have had to hear the story I must tell you. But God would not have crossed our paths if he did not will you to hear it."

She slept through two days and two nights. When she awoke, her strength had returned enough so that she could eat, sit up, talk, and worry. Her biggest worry was over her job. "Please," she begged Dr. Rosen. "Could you call the Maison d'Odile Joly for me and tell them that I am sick? That I can't come in to work yet?"

"Odile Joly?" Dr. Rosen asked. "You mean the couturière?"

She nodded.

He looked at her strangely; then his face broke into a smile. "I shall call immediately."

He left to place the call. When he returned, she looked at him questioningly.

He smiled. "I spoke to Odile Joly herself. She was very worried about you. She hopes that you will get well soon."

Hélène looked suddenly troubled. "You didn't tell her . . . ?"

He looked genuinely upset. "Of course not!" he said, drawing himself up indignantly. "I am a doctor. A doctor keeps his patient's illness in confidence."

"I'm sorry," she said contritely. "I should have known better." But there was a look of relief in her eyes.

That afternoon, an enormous bouquet of roses arrived from the atelier. Dr. Rosen went to find a vase and made room on the nightstand for it. Hélène pulled the stiff card out of the small white envelope. The spidery handwriting was so elegant she could barely read it. Finally she made it out: "Feel better soon. Your job is waiting. So don't worry about that. Odile Joly and all the girls."

Hélène smiled suddenly and stared at the roses. They were long-stemmed and luxuriantly pink, just barely open. The delicate petals tightly cocooned the thick fat buds, promising huge blossoms to burst forth. She could smell their sweet fragrance in the air. Odile Joly could be hard as nails, but as far as her "girls" were concerned, she had a soft spot in her heart.

The next day, Dr. Rosen sat on the edge of the bed. He was reading to Hélène from a new book that was causing a sensation. It was called *Bonjour Tristesse* and was written by an unknown young writer named Françoise Sagan. Abruptly she reached out for his hand. She gripped it fiercely. He stopped reading, carefully placed a ribbon between the pages, and closed the book.

"Dr. Rosen?" she said in a small, frightened voice.

He shook his head and smiled. "You must call me Simon. We are friends, non?"

She smiled. "Yes, we are good friends, Simon."

He smiled slowly and looked pleased. Tenderly he brushed aside the hair that fell down over her forehead. Suddenly her violet eyes clouded over. He was startled to see them change color so rapidly. One instant they had been violet; now they were a dull amethyst. It was as if a cloud had pushed its way in front of the sun.

"I have to ask you something, Simon," she said in a quiet, heavy voice. "I need to know the truth."

He nodded in silence. He knew what she was going to ask. He had wondered how long it would be until she did. But he hadn't thought it would be so soon.

She stared at him, and her voice dropped to a whisper. "Simon? Will I . . . will I be able to bear any more children?"

He closed his eyes. He who had managed to comfort so many people all his life found that words failed him at this moment.

"Thank you, Simon," she said softly. "Thank you for not trying to deny it. For not giving me false hopes." She turned her head sideways on the pillow and stared at the wall. She felt an agony like she had never thought could exist. She didn't make a sound, but the tears streamed down her cheeks. Only now did she realize the true gravity of what she had done. Her lips trembled. As far as she was concerned, she was now only half a woman. She could never have another baby. Then her lips stopped trembling. Yes, she would! She would have a baby of the spirit. She would have *Les Modes!*

Now her recovery speeded up. There was no time to lose, she told herself. Time was a luxury she couldn't indulge in. Every day she spent in bed would be a day's delay for *Les Modes*. And the very next day, she was able to walk around the room. At first she felt wobbly on her feet, but she forced herself to exercise them. Dr. Rosen was surprised by this sudden willpower, but he said nothing. He was relieved. Now he knew that she was emotionally stronger. That night he carried a little table into the bedroom and spread a cloth over it. "We shall dine together," he said.

She smiled. "That will be very nice."

A little later, he helped her into a chair and she looked down at the table. It was simply set with inexpensive white china. She thought that these simple plates were far more beautiful than any of the gold-rimmed flower-patterned Limoges or Meissen plates she had been using in the town house. Somehow the plain white looked refreshingly honest and unpretentious.

When they finished dinner, she carefully laid her knife and fork in an X across the plate. "While you were out earlier, I went into the other room and used the telephone," she said slowly. She stared down at her plate. "I'm afraid I won't be able to stay here much longer. I am expected home tomorrow."

He nodded, thinking how peculiar it was that she had wanted him to contact only Odile Joly, and no one else. Was it because she had no friends? But surely a beautiful young woman had many friends. And what about the man who had made her pregnant? "I think you will be strong enough to go home tomorrow," he said. "You have a strong will and incredible recuperative powers. But you must take it very easy for the next few weeks. You must promise me that."

She nodded. "I promise."

"And no . . ." He made an agitated little gesture.

She smiled. "I know. No sex for a few weeks."

He nodded, his face reddening suddenly. Then he cleared his throat. "Also, I insist on escorting you home. You will find that even getting in and out of a taxi takes a lot of energy."

She looked at him gratefully. "Thank you. You've been so kind. I . . . I don't know how I can ever repay you."

He waved her to silence. "Someday you shall run across someone who is sick and in need of help," he said. "You can repay me by helping them."

"I will do that," she promised solemnly.

He leaned back in his chair and looked at her. His voice was filled with sadness. "I cannot help but feel sorrow that we must part."

"I, too," she said. "I will miss you. I hope we can visit each other."

He smiled. "I would like that very much." Then he looked at her intently. "Tell me," he said carefully. "Now that you are on your way to physical recovery, how do you feel . . . emotionally?"

Her eyes dropped. "How can I feel?" she asked softly. "Except ashamed and dirty?" She gave an ugly little laugh. "It's funny, isn't it? I thought I was doing the right thing. The *only* thing. But I realize now that I was wrong. I murdered my baby." She was silent for a moment. "I saw it, you know. It even *looked* like a baby." She shook her head. "I don't know if I'll ever really get over that."

He took out a pipe and looked at it thoughtfully, turning it over and over in his hands. "I think you have a right to know what I am about to tell you," he said, looking back up at her.

354

"I do not know whether you are emotionally ready to hear it now or not. But perhaps . . . yes, perhaps it will help you feel better about yourself. You see, we all suffer, Hélène. We suffer many times in our lives. Some of us suffer more, some of us suffer less. I don't want you to misconstrue what I am going to tell you. I am not trying to show you how little you have suffered. But that we all have suffered. And that, sometimes, exposure to immense suffering helps ease our own. Do you understand what I am trying to say?"

"I . . . I think so," she said haltingly.

He filled the pipe with tobacco and lit it carefully with a match. Then he smoked in silence for a long time. Finally he spoke. "Hélène, I am a Jew. We Jews have suffered for thousands of years." He smiled bitterly. "Sometimes I tend to think we have cornered the market on suffering." Then his face grew extremely sad. "But it is no joke. Every so often someone comes along who tries to wipe us off the face of the earth. So far, we have always managed to survive somehow. We have bled and been decimated, but all the pogroms could not get rid of us as a race. I don't think I need to point out to you the last time such a tragedy occurred."

She nodded quietly. Ever since she had been a little girl in Saint-Nazaire she had heard about the camps. About the unspeakable horrors that went on in those wholesale slaughterhouses of hell. About the millions who had been shot and starved and burned and gassed to death.

"It was my lot in life to endure the last such attack on my people," Dr. Rosen said. Slowly he unbuttoned his cuff and rolled the sleeve of his white shirt up to his elbow. Hélène stared at his arm. The dark blue numbers stood out clearly beneath the light matting of his hair. Her eyes were moist and fathomless. Slowly she reached out and traced her fingers across the numbers.

"It was hell on earth," Dr. Rosen said tightly. "And the devils were in uniform." He put down his pipe as if it left a bad taste in his mouth. "You cannot imagine the horrors unless you were there."

Hélène nodded. "The concentration camps were the shame of all mankind," she said gently.

"They were," Dr. Rosen said. He took a deep breath. "But you must remember that there were two types of camps. Concentration camps and extermination camps. They were all horrible, and people suffered and died in all of them. The concentration camps were in France, Holland, Germany, and Austria. But the extermination camps? They were in Poland. Their only function was to kill millions of people. Just the names of those places still fill me with dread. Names like Belzec and Treblinka and Stutthof and Auschwitz." His voice was trembling uncontrollably, and the muscles in his cheeks twitched. "I was in Auschwitz."

"Please stop," she said softly. "Haven't you suffered enough? Telling this will only make the pain so much worse."

He shook his head. "I have to tell you. You see, not only we Jews were sent to Auschwitz. There were Gypsies and homosexuals and 'enemies of the state.'" He stared at her sadly. "There were even members of the French Resistance."

Hélène suddenly went cold. She couldn't speak. Somehow she knew what he was going to say next.

His voice suddenly rose with a cry of anguish. "I met a woman there," he said, tears flooding from his eyes. "Her name was Jacqueline Junot."

Hélène closed her eyes. For a moment she sat in shocked silence. Then she leaned across the table, her face an expressionless mask. "Tell me!" she whispered. "Tell me everything! Please. I have to know!"

And so he told her.

Maman had been gassed in Auschwitz.

3

It was ten o'clock in the morning when the two taxis swung into the Avenue Fréderic Le Play and pulled to a halt alongside the curb. The girl dresser and the tall male hairstylist climbed out of the first car and watched as the driver lifted three suitcases out of the trunk. Hélène and Jacques emerged from the second cab. While he paid the drivers, she looked down the Champs de Mars toward the Eiffel Tower. It rose up from the intricately laid lawns and swirling paths of the formal gardens high into the clean winter sky. She cringed.

She was frightened. Something told her that she should never have agreed to this. But when Odile Joly had taken her aside, it had sounded like a good idea.

"There is a very fine photographer doing a spread for *Paris Vogue*," Odile Joly had said. "He will use seven pieces from my summer collection. He saw you on the catwalk and insists that you be the model."

Hélène had been flattered and excited. The magic word, of course, was *Vogue*. How often had she leafed through the slick pages of that magazine, hungrily staring at the models? But more important, she had kept in mind what Madame Dupré had said. That perhaps she had more steps to take in order to realize her ambition. Maybe this was yet another such step. Plus there was the matter of the photographer.

Jacques Renault had already made quite a name for himself as a free-lance photographer. His trademark was "daring." He posed his models on the unthinkable—on cliffs, cranes, precipices. One winter morning, he shot various models dangerously posed on the parapets and gargoyles of Notre Dame Cathedral. The pictures had turned out to be fantastic. They were everything Jacques Renault had hoped for. The models' faces were white with fear, as if they were trying to get away from Quasimodo himself. Their fear looked very genuine for one reason. They really were terrified.

There had been only one problem. Jacques had simply taken his models, gone inside the cathedral, and climbed the steps in the north tower up to the roof. There the models threw off their coats. Underneath, they were scantily clad in slips and brassieres. The ad was for Bonaparte Lingerie.

There had been a public outcry. The film had been confiscated, and Jacques retaliated by going to court. The case was lengthy, and Jacques became a kind of *cause célèbre*. After six months, the court ruled in his favor. Overnight he became a major celebrity, a martyr for art. He had made such a sensation that Condé Nast immediately offered him a lucrative contract. Jacques signed it and had worked for *Vogue* ever since.

When Hélène discovered that the photographer who wanted to use her for the spread was Jacques, she did not hesitate. Of course, she had known that his trademark was danger. But she had thought it had been overplayed by the press.

Now, looking toward the black pig-iron girders rising up

from the edge of the Seine, she felt sick. Ever since she was a tiny girl, she had been afraid of heights. And on top of it all, it was cold out. And up there, on the second platform of the Eiffel Tower, the wind would be much stronger yet. She looked at Jacques; he was watching her.

You mustn't think of the height, she told herself as she gritted her teeth. You mustn't think of the danger. You must think only of other things. Comforting things. She smiled wryly. She knew of nothing that could comfort her. The Comte? That was a laugh. Right after Dr. Rosen had taken her home, the Comte had arrived. He had been furious that she had been gone for over a week. She knew that he didn't believe that she had been ill, so she decided not to tell him about the abortion. She had a feeling that he wouldn't have understood.

Instead, she defied Dr. Rosen's orders and dutifully went to bed with the Comte. She had to get good and drunk in order to deaden the pain that tore through her abdomen. It was a terrible pain. The wounds inside her had not yet healed completely.

She thought back to how she had quietly climbed out of the bed and gone to the bathroom when the Comte had fallen asleep. Carefully she had washed the blood from her pubis. The Comte hadn't even noticed how he hurt her. Only in the morning, when he awoke to the bloodstained sheets, did he realize that something was wrong. He had slapped her awake. "Why didn't you tell me that you were having your period?" he demanded. "You know I can't stand making love to a bleeding woman!" He threw her arm loose. "Don't ever let that happen again!"

"All right, first we'll take some shots using the tower for the background," Jacques said swiftly. He shoved his hands deep into his trouser pockets and looked around, shoulders hunched, his young face twisted in concentration. "Merde! That grass looks all dried up. That's always the trouble with shooting summer clothes in winter." Irritably he signaled to the dresser and the hairdresser. "Lug that stuff down to the water fountain."

They picked up the suitcases and started walking. The oval fountain, halfway between the Eiffel Tower and the Coeur d'Honneur, was dry. When they got there, Jacques looked pleased. He turned to Hélène.

"Good. We'll take the first pictures down in there, with the tower rising above you from behind. After that, we'll take the rest of the shots up on the second platform."

Hélène glanced over at the tower. She closed her eyes. The second platform was a dizzying hundred and fifteen meters off the ground.

Half an hour later they were standing on the roof of the second platform. Hélène had changed into a simple pale evening dress that hugged her bosom and then flared to a full skirt below the waist. With a few expert flicks of his wrist, the hairstylist dusted her face with a powder puff; then, noticing the wetness around her eyes, he dabbed them carefully with a piece of tissue. The wind was powerful. It whipped at the carefully pinned-up hair, flogged the skin of her bare back like an icy whip, and forced the tears right up out of her eyes. The makeup had been carefully applied; tears would ruin it. Hélène narrowed her eyes, fighting to keep the tears back.

A few feet away, Jacques looked through the viewfinder of his Hasselblad. He grunted and fiddled with the lens. Without needing to be told, the dresser and the hairstylist quickly got out of the way. With one hand he signaled for Hélène to move sideways.

"Hold it!" he yelled above the noise of the wind. She froze and he grinned suddenly. "That's great! The sun's right behind you, and I can see straight through your dress. Your figure's good. Very good."

"Come on, Jacques!" she shouted, briskly rubbing her arms and doing a series of quick little hops. "My teeth are chattering and I'm freezing to death!"

Suddenly he started snapping away, his mouth twisted in a frown of concentration. She began to move fluidly, like a dancer swaying to some music only she could hear. Jacques picked up the rhythm of her dance and edged closer, backed up again, stalked around her, all the time clicking his shutter. He stopped a few times to reload the camera. Each time, the hairdresser hurried over to her and dabbed her eyes.

After a while Jacques stopped. Hélène looked across at him. His face was serious now. "Move to the edge of the platform, chérie. And careful. We don't want to have to scrape you off the Champs de Mars."

She tightened her lips across her teeth. Now came the famous Jacques Renault touch. The acrobatics. She knew just what the girls straddling the Notre Dame gargoyles must have felt like. She could feel it in her gut.

For a moment she couldn't move. Then she managed to turn around, lifted one foot slowly, and began taking half-steps toward the edge of the platform. Careful, she told herself, there's no railing. Easy does it. . . .

When she reached the corner girder, she grabbed hold of one of the pig-iron struts and clung to it for dear life. She closed her eyes. She couldn't bear looking down and seeing the distance between her and the ground. It was a long drop. Forty stories.

Jacques's voice was harsh. "Come on, we're not in a church. Turn around and open your eyes, for God's sake!"

Slowly she opened them. Then she twisted around awkwardly and faced Jacques. He was crouching low, once again studying her through the camera. Suddenly he grinned. "That wasn't so bad, was it?" he shouted.

"Not bad for you, you bastard!" she called out in a frightened, wavering voice. "You're nice and safe!"

"Come on, give me a smile."

She bared her teeth.

"That's the girl. Now, step right to the edge."

She took a deep breath, loosened one hand from the strut, and cautiously backed up a few centimeters until her heels hung out over space and only the toes of her shoes were balanced on the riveted platform. With her free hand she reached down and grabbed hold of the hem of the dress. She lifted it and held it up at arm's length like one shimmering unfolded butterfly wing. The light fabric caught the wind like a sail and began to billow. She held tighter to the strut. It seemed as if the wind delighted at her vulnerability and suddenly flung even angrier gusts at her. Her teeth were chattering. All too easily an unexpectedly powerful gust could propel her backward and cause her to lose her balance.

Jacques pointed. "Look down at Paris!" he shouted. "And hang out over the edge a little!"

Her face went even whiter. Almost paralyzed, she tightened her grip, let her body angle out sideways into space until her arm was stretched stiff, and slowly lowered her head. The city sprawled beneath her like an endless sea of stone divided by the gray, snakelike S-curve of the Seine. She forced her face to assume an unafraid, blasé expression. As if hanging off the girder was the most natural thing in the world.

Finally Jacques grinned widely. "All right," he shouted. "Wrap it up!" He came close and held out his hand. She tottered forward. A few steps later, she felt him grab hold of her, and she collapsed into his arms. He caught her and held her close. She was sobbing uncontrollably. "Hey, it's all right," he said soothingly into her ear. "It's finished."

She nodded weakly, letting him push her away so that the dresser could throw a chinchilla wrap over her. Suddenly she shivered. Until now, she had only been afraid. She had forgotten how cold it was.

"Why didn't you tell me you're frightened of heights?" he asked her.

She looked at him, and a shroud seemed to fall down over her eyes. How could she explain to a virtual stranger about her ambition? That this was just a necessary step toward it?

"I'd like to use you again," he said as they took the elevator back down to the ground.

She smiled bleakly. "What's next? Hanging off the wing of an airplane in flight?"

He laughed. "Don't plant any seeds in my mind that you will be sorry for later."

"I won't be sorry," she said, "because I have no intention of becoming a stunt woman." The elevator came to a halt and she started out the door.

He described his ideas for the next layout in detail while they waited for a taxi on the Avenue Gustave Eiffel. He seemed pleased at the opportunity of having an attentive audience, and as he talked, his eyes shone and he made animated gestures. "What I have in mind is the reconstruction of a murder. A crime of passion. It will be a photo essay of five or six pictures. In the first one I'll have a woman and her lover in bed. In the second picture, the husband arrives and they quarrel. Then she shoots him. The next-to-last picture will have him lying in a pool of blood and she'll be standing over him, smoke trailing from the barrel of her revolver. And in the last picture I'll have her back in the arms of her lover."

Hélène found herself laughing. The idea sounded contrived and absurd. It was a farce. "Those are supposed to be fashion pictures?" she asked incredulously.

He looked at her with such a hurt expression that the

laughter died in her throat. "Of course," he said seriously. "They'll be a sensation. Will you model for them?"

She thought for a moment. "On one condition."

"And that is?"

"That this 'crime' takes place on terra firma."

He grinned. "You have my word." He paused for a moment. "But I need to have your word, also."

She looked surprised. "What for?"

"You know that I'm on the staff of *Vogue*?"

She nodded.

"Well, the crime pictures will be for *L'Officiel*. Sometimes I moonlight as a free-lance photographer. *Vogue* winks at it as long as my credit doesn't appear with the pictures. Of course, everyone who knows my style can immediately pick up on who did them. Just don't advertise that I did the pictures."

"You can trust me," she said, fighting to keep her face serious. "I won't tell a soul."

By the time she came home from the atelier a week after the shooting, it was, as usual, a quarter to six. She closed the front door wearily, crossed to the telephone table, put her purse down, and began to pull off her gloves. She sniffled. She hoped she wasn't coming down with a cold. She started as the telephone began to ring. Quickly she reached down and picked up the receiver.

"Hélène? It's Jacques."

"Jacques," she said, "this is a surprise."

"Listen, I called to tell you that the proof sheets are printed. The photos turned out even better than I'd expected! You're naturally photogenic. Anyway, what do you say I pop over and show them to you?"

"Now?"

"Why not?"

"I appreciate your calling, Jacques, but I'm afraid I'm tied up tonight." That was the truth. The Comte was in town and he'd be spending the night. Just thinking about it made her grimace. She'd be up half the night. What she really wanted to do was crawl under the covers and sleep for thirteen or fourteen hours. Maybe then this cold would work out of her system.

"Christ," he mumbled with bitchy disappointment. "Well, I suppose there's plenty of time for you to see them." Then his voice took on a brighter tone. "Before I forget, what do you say we take the *L'Officiel* shots on Saturday?"

"So soon?"

"Sure. Don't forget, it takes months before the issues hit the stands. The sooner they're taken, the sooner you'll be a star."

She smiled. "Saturday it is. I'll call you on Friday to confirm?"

"Fine. Talk to you then," he said. " 'Bye."

She said good-bye, and when she heard the click at his end, she dropped the receiver back down on the cradle. At the same moment she noticed a letter propped up against the vase. She recognized the envelope immediately. It was from the Karl Häberle Agency. Her heart pounded as she snatched it up. The first thought that entered her mind was that Häberle had found Schmidt and the white-faced one.

She tore open the envelope, took out the letter, and unfolded it. The type was thick, black, and smudgy, as if the typewriter it had been pounded out on was a piece of antiquity. As she read, her excitement faded. It was nothing more than a progress report—a report of no progress at all.

Hélène balled up the paper angrily and tossed it into the wastebasket. What was it with Häberle? Did she have to pound him over the head for him to realize that she was dead serious? She would have time to draft a quick letter to him. The Comte wouldn't be here for another hour.

She went into the salon, sat down behind the leather-covered desk, and took a sheet of vellum from the box in the top drawer. She dipped the pen into the inkwell, hesitated for a moment, and then swiftly scrawled the reply:

Dear Herr Häberle,
I have received your letter. I think I have made it quite clear that no matter how long or expensive the task, I am totally dedicated to finding the men who have perpetrated such evil. I shall not rest until then. Please continue and let me know if there is any progress.

Sincerely,
Hélène Junot

She read it through, wrote out an envelope and affixed a stamp on it. Then she rang for the maid. When she came,

Hélène handed her the letter. "Marthe, post this immediately, please."

"Oui, mademoiselle." The maid gave a little curtsy and hurried back out.

Hélène rose to her feet and went upstairs. After taking a quick bath, she slipped into a rose-colored peignoir and went back downstairs to the salon. Efficiently she set about arranging things just the way the Comte liked them. It was Marthe's job, but she insisted on doing it herself. That was the way she knew things would be perfect. Not that Marthe couldn't be trusted. It was just that the Comte was fussy. He insisted that everything had to be just the way he wanted it. Eggs, three minutes to the dot. Bathwater, forty-one degrees. Drinking glasses, polished.

Finally everything was ready. The big ashtray and the humidor on the cocktail table, the soft lighting, the low mood music, the iced champagne.

She turned around as the door chimes tinkled. The Comte never rang. He had his own key. She shrugged her shoulders. Perhaps he had misplaced it. She could hear Marthe's footsteps in the hall.

"That's all right, Marthe," she called out. "I'll get it."

"Oui, mademoiselle." Marthe's footsteps immediately receded.

Hélène went out into the foyer. By reflex, she ran her hands over her hair and rearranged the front of her peignoir so that her breasts appeared to push up out of her décolletage. Then she pulled the door open.

Hubert de Léger was standing there, dressed in evening clothes. He didn't say a word. He simply pushed the door wide, staggered inside, and slammed it shut behind him.

She stared directly into his eyes, her pupils completely encircled with white edges. She sensed his drunkenness even before she smelled it.

Quickly she tried to block his way. "Hubert, please. This is not the time to visit," she said.

He began to laugh and pushed her aside. "I wanted to pay my respects," he said gruffly. "Besides, this house does belong to my family, in case you've forgotten."

"It belongs to your father," she corrected him in an icy tone.

He started toward the salon. "Speaking of my father, where is he? Upstairs asleep already?"

364

"Hubert!" she said sharply. "I won't have you talking about your father like that!"

He gave a low laugh. "You're one to talk! I suspect I'll get a lecture on virtue next. Ah. The salon is nice and cozy. We can have a little chat." He rubbed his hands together and crossed the Savonnerie to the sideboard, where he poured himself a slug of Armagnac. Then he walked toward the couch, picked an ice cube out of the champagne bucket, and tossed it into the glass. He looked down at the drink as he sloshed it around in the glass. "The Americans drink everything with ice," he mumbled. "I learned it from some of the students at the university. There are a lot of Americans there, you know?" He looked at her.

"I didn't know," she said quietly.

He tossed his head back and downed the drink in one big swallow. Then he grimaced and his eyes flicked around again. "*Very* cozy, yes." He nodded slowly. "A fire roaring in the grate. Mood music. Champagne . . ." He reached for the bottle and pulled it out of its nest of ice. "Dom Perignon. Good, good." He leered at her.

She felt the heat in his eyes and pulled the peignoir tighter around her. "Hurry up and finish your drink," she said. "Your father will be here at any moment."

He grinned. "You mean you're not going to sit with me?"

She sniffed. "No, I will not." She crossed over to the window, parted the curtains nervously, and looked out. Somehow she would have to get rid of Hubert before the Comte arrived. The question was how to do it without him making a scene.

He came up behind her and caught her arm and without any preamble said, "I want you." He spun her around, his hand pulling her toward him.

She struggled to push him away. "Leave me alone!" she hissed, breathing deeply. Her eyes flashed fire.

Suddenly he let go of her arm and stepped back. "My, aren't you the coy one," he said nastily. "I'll comfort myself with the idea that I don't take hand-me-downs." He went to pour himself another drink, and she watched him toss it down. Her contempt for him was growing stronger by the minute.

He slammed the glass down on the sideboard and looked at her for a long moment. "I'll let you off the hook. I'm leaving," he said sullenly.

She didn't answer, but a breath of relief escaped her lips. She followed him out into the foyer. When he reached the front door he turned around and looked back at her. "Just remember, I turned you down," he said pointedly in an ugly voice. "You've got the distinction of being the only whore in the city who's been rejected."

She could feel a searing blush rising up her face and looked away.

He flung open the door and then drew back. The Comte was standing outside, key in hand. Hubert stared at him for a moment, then regained his unseemly composure and grinned nastily. "Don't worry, *Father*. I didn't touch her." He gave a jerky shrug of his shoulders and glared at Hélène. "Funny how the French will cheat on their wives but insist that their whores remain faithful." Then he pushed past the Comte and stumbled down the steps.

The Comte stared impassively after his son. Then he came inside and closed the door quietly. He looked across at Hélène. "You shouldn't have let him in," he said softly.

"I didn't," she said, twisting her fingers in agitation. "The chimes rang and I thought it was you. When I opened the door, he pushed his way in."

"All right," the Comte said wearily. He followed her into the salon, shrugged off his coat, and threw it over the back of a chair. He looked thoughtfully down at his feet. "Sit down. I think it's time we had a little talk."

She stared at him. "I'm sorry that you don't believe me, Philippe. He really did push his way in."

"That's not what I wanted to talk to you about."

Hélène looked surprised. "Then what is it?"

"Sit down."

She was startled by his sharp command. Slowly she took a seat, folded her hands in her lap, and looked at him curiously. She had no idea what this was about. She knew that he had many business interests in Paris. But business problems or no, he shouldn't be taking them out on her.

Idly he paced the carpet. "I've always trusted you, haven't I?"

"Yes," she said cautiously.

Unexpectedly he took one hand out of his pocket and came up with a tangle of jewels. She recognized them instantly. They were the ones she had sold to Cheops. Almost

366

casually he dropped them down on the sideboard. "Then how do you explain this?"

Her face had suddenly gone pale. Her eyes were riveted on the incriminating jewels. That slimy Cheops had lied, she thought angrily. She had been a fool ever to trust him. All along, he must have been selling the jewels to the major dealers and not to transient tourists as he'd assured her. And these dealers kept careful records of every item they sold, and to whom. They must have contacted the Comte.

"I bought them back, but what I want to know is . . . *why?*"

She tore her eyes away from the jewels and looked at him. "I needed the money," she replied.

"What for?"

Suddenly she looked weary. "It's a long story, Philippe."

"Tell me. I have all night."

For a moment she sat in thoughtful silence; then she looked into his face and shook her head. Her vow to destroy those who had destroyed her family was something she had to do alone. It couldn't be shared with anyone, least of all him. She was only beginning to realize that her past was her weakness but that it was also her greatest strength. From it stemmed her ambition, her indomitable will to survive. It did not seem right to have to bare her vulnerability for him to see. "No," she said slowly. "It's something I don't want to discuss."

"All right, you leave me no choice," the Comte replied. "It is over. As soon as possible, I want you to find another place to live."

"So it's over," Hélène said softly. "Just like that."

He smiled grimly. "I demand total honesty from everyone I deal with. I feel I can no longer trust you."

Hélène made a thoughtful face and nodded slowly. "All right," she said slowly, rising to her feet. "I shall go upstairs and pack my things immediately. It will take me half an hour. Then I shall call a taxi and go to a hotel."

"Don't forget these. They're yours." He picked up the jewels and threw them at her. Some of them hit her, others scattered on the carpet around her feet. She stared stoically first at him, then down at them. On principle, she started to turn around and walk away. But she was a practical woman. You've earned those jewels, a little voice inside her asserted. You've been at his beck and call for over a year now. You let him own you. You've even carried his baby and let it be torn out of your womb. Because of it, you'll never be able to bear children again. If you've ever worked for anything, you've worked for these. As if in slow motion, she fell to her knees and began picking them up. When she reached for the last earring, she lifted her eyes. The Comte was watching her. She got to her feet, drew herself up with dignity, and went upstairs to pack.

The next day she took all the jewels to Van Cleef and Arpels, where she sold them for an excellent price. She deposited the check in her savings account and then found a small apartment on the highly respectable rue Paul Valery, just off the Avenue Foch.

4

A week later, Jacques was set to shoot the photos for *L'Officiel*. He had borrowed an apartment on the Avenue Foch to use as a location. Besides Hélène, there were two men dressed in custom-tailored tuxedos that were clearly British. Even the French, world-renowned geniuses when it came to designing women's clothing, had to acknowledge that when it came to men's garments, the English were without peer. One of the men would pose as Hélène's lover, the other as her husband.

Hélène came out of the study which they used as a dressing room and stopped in the doorway of the salon. Jacques was sitting in an armchair; her "lover" and her "husband" were forced to stand so that they wouldn't wrinkle their tuxedos. They stared at her. She wore the latest gown from Odile Joly. It had a strapless top that encased her breasts, a narrow, form-fitting skirt that went to the calf, and was entirely encrusted with sequins and colored rhinestones shimmering in the intricate swirls of an arabesque.

Jacques got to his feet slowly and motioned for Hélène to come closer. When she was in the center of the room, he gestured for her to stop. She stood there silently, watching him. His face was expressionless. Then he walked around her in circles. Finally he stopped, frowned, and put his hand on his chin. "It's a beautiful gown," he admitted slowly.

She tilted her head forward and looked down at herself. It was one of the most exquisite creations anyone could ever have imagined. Costly, too. A house in the suburbs carried the same price tag as these few meters of fabric.

"Odile Joly calls this a gown fit for a Persian princess," she said, frowning, and slowly walking over to the pier glass between the two tall windows. She watched herself critically. Each time she moved, her body flashed with brilliance. It was as if a million gems were glued right onto her body. She turned around. "You don't like it." It was a statement.

"Go and take it off," Jacques told her. "You look like a samuri warrior. Then we'll put on our thinking caps and see how we can remedy this situation."

Hélène was disappointed, but it was obvious that Jacques had made up his mind. She shrugged her shoulders and obediently returned to the study. She let the dresser undo the back of the gown and wearily stepped out of it. She pulled on a white silk robe, tied the sash around the wrist, and went back out to the salon.

Jacques looked at her and nodded. "That's much more becoming."

"You're not going to take her picture in *that!*" one of the male models squeaked incredulously.

Suddenly Jacques snapped his fingers excitedly. "That's it! Why didn't I think of it before!" His face broke into a smile. Casually he sat back, then stretched out his legs and clasped his hands behind his head.

Hélène placed her hands on her hips. "Well?" she demanded imperiously.

"We'll do the unheard-of," Jacques said. "Instead of dressing *you*, we'll dress them. It'll be a new angle. You know, the way women would like their men to dress. We'll get them a few more tuxedos. A different one for each picture, but similar enough so they won't detract from the overall theme."

Hélène stared at him for a moment, then paced the room. "What do I tell Odile Joly?" she wailed. "She did me a personal favor by getting that gown out in time for the photos!"

369

Jacques grinned. "Tell her anything, but make sure it's diplomatic. Now, what are you doing tonight?"

Hélène sniffed. "What I do tonight is my business."

"Well said, but my intentions are honorable. I have a party to attend, and I want you to come with me."

The house was seventeenth-century, Hélène thought, and most of the guests could probably trace their lineage much farther back than that. There were ambassadors, film stars, politicians, industrialists, artists, and financiers. The guests spilled from the foyer and the salon into the music and sun rooms.

"Jacques," an elegant middle-aged woman with angular cheekbones said as they politely pushed their way through the throng clustered in the foyer.

Jacques stopped and smiled at her. She lifted her bony, jewel-studded hand grandly and he bent over and kissed it gallantly.

"You've been hiding, you naughty boy," she said with a reproachful pout.

He smiled. "May I introduce my newest model, Hélène Junot? Hélène, our gracious hostess, the Vicomtesse de Sévigné."

"How do you do?" Hélène said politely. She stared at the woman in fascination. She had read of the de Sévignés in all the society columns. They were among the richest people in France. The reclusive old Vicomte was a financier; the Vicomtesse was a partygoer, a party-giver, and the owner of a chic costume-jewelry boutique. She was also an interior designer, for friends; a hairdresser, her own; and a couturière of sorts, by insisting that the designers of the hallowed houses alter their great creations to her own specifications. They obliged, but only because they recognized the Vicomtesse's innate good taste.

"Jacques is a terribly talented young man," the Vicomtesse said to Hélène. "His photographs are works of art. And he is so handsome. He could sweep half the women in Paris off their feet." She sipped her champagne delicately.

"Unfortunately, he prefers to go to the pissoirs to pick up his bed partners," a slurry male voice said from behind.

The Vicomtesse paled beneath her carefully applied make-up. Abruptly the conversation around them ground to a stop. People began to stare; a few started to move away in embarrassment. A deep flush rose up Jacques's face and the Vicomtesse and Hélène turned around slowly. Hubert de Léger was smiling innocently at them.

Hélène felt sick with disgust. She couldn't believe that Hubert was here. Even worse, that he had just said what he had, and so loudly.

"Did I say something wrong?" Hubert asked in a charming voice.

"You bastard," Jacques said quietly. "One of these days I'll knock your filthy teeth out." He clenched his fists threateningly.

Quickly Hélène grabbed his wrists and restrained him.

"Fancy a cream puff being so brave," Hubert said with a faint smile. He turned to the Vicomtesse and gave a little shrug. "I suppose if one invites so many people, one pervert will be bound to slip in. You are forgiven, madame."

Without answering, the Vicomtesse swiftly hooked one arm through Hélène's, the other through Jacques's. "I think we should pay our respects to the guest of honor," she said quickly. "Come."

As she marched them across the salon, she apologized for Hubert's behavior. "He is worse than a peasant," she said derisively. The words were bitter, but Hélène noticed that a careful smile masked her face. Anyone looking at her would have thought that she was chatting amiably.

Halfway across the room, the Vicomtesse drew to a halt. "Ah, here is our guest of honor." She extricated herself elegantly from their arms and gently pulled an old white-haired man out of a crowd of people. "Stanislaw, chéri," she said, kissing him on the cheek.

Hélène stared at the old man. She had seen the world-famous pianist once before. It had been at the opera. While she and the Comte had been in the box, Stanislaw Kowalsky had been sitting in the front row.

The Vicomtesse made a sweeping gesture. "Stanislaw, I would like you to meet two of my friends. Hélène Junot and Jacques Renault."

The old man smiled pleasantly and bowed to both of them. "I am enchanted to meet you, mademoiselle," he said to Hélène. He took her hand and kissed it, his breath barely brushing her flesh.

Hélène was speechless. He looks so small and shrunken, she thought. Strange, that such a little man could take the world by storm. She couldn't help noticing that his arms were long, his fingers slender, flat, and elongated, the small pink fingernails clipped down to the quick. But in his own way he was impressive-looking; even the unruly tufts of white hair on his head were worn like a regal crown. His eyebrows were gray and bushy; his dark eyes beneath them twinkled with merriment.

The Vicomtesse smiled. "Mademoiselle Junot is a model. She has just done a spread for *Vogue*. Monsieur Renault took the pictures."

The old man smiled. "I am certain they will turn out to be fine pictures. With a model so lovely, who could fail to take a beautiful picture? Unless, of course, Monsieur Renault forgot to put film in the camera."

"I hope not." Hélène laughed. "He had me hanging off the second platform of the Eiffel Tower."

"Jacques!" The Vicomtesse looked horrified. "Haven't you learned enough from that Notre Dame incident!" Mystified, the Vicomtesse looked at Hélène and shook her head. "I don't know how you did it. You must be very brave. Myself, I find it difficult even to climb a flight of stairs. I'm afraid I'm a terrible coward."

"Hardly, my dear," Kowalsky said to the Vicomtesse. "You are the bravest woman I have ever met."

"Please," she protested.

He held up a liver-spotted hand to silence her. "During the war, she hid thirteen downed American fliers and two Jewish families in her château. And imagine—at the same time, the Nazis occupied another wing of the same building! She hid us right under their noses for three whole years!"

"She hid *you?*" Hélène asked in surprise.

"My family and another. She is very brave, non?"

Hélène looked at the Vicomtesse with new respect. She seemed so frail and delicate, hardly the stuff of which heroes were made. But the eyes told otherwise. If you looked deep into them you could tell that they were eyes that had lived. They were unwavering, strong, and filled with character. Still, it took courage for a woman of such social standing and wealth to put her life on the line for others. She had so much to lose.

"But what about the piano?" Hélène asked Kowalsky. "I've heard that pianists have to practice for hours every day. You must have had to start over from scratch after the war."

The old man smiled. "No, I played throughout the three years. But I played for ghosts. You see, the Vicomtesse was good enough to dismantle the keyboard of the Bechstein in her salon. She brought it to me during the middle of the night, and I was able to practice and play without anyone being able to hear it."

"It was such a pity," the Vicomtesse said. "Just think! I had the world's finest concert pianist under my roof and I wasn't able to hear a single note that he was playing! Sometimes I think it was crueler to me than anyone else, I love his music so."

Hélène nodded. She smiled gently at Kowalsky. "It must have been sad for you, too, not to be able to hear what you were playing."

He smiled. "Ah, but you see, I *did* hear it. I could imagine the sound of every note. Don't forget, Beethoven composed music when he was deaf. I think I could play even if I were. To lose one's hearing is bad, but to lose one's faculties is disastrous. Thank God, I still have them."

"Come, come. Let us not be so maudlin. This is a party," the Vicomtesse chided them. "What would people think if all we did was to discuss such weighty subjects?"

Kowalsky nodded. "Of course." Then his eyes glittered. "Is your piano tuned?"

The Vicomtesse drew a deep breath. She looked at him with surprise to see if he was serious. "Really, Stanislaw, there's no need . . ."

He patted her hand. "I would love to play a few pieces."

She was delighted. Hubert's outburst had nearly ruined the party. Having Stanislaw Kowalsky play would not only overshadow that but also make her the hostess of the season. "You really don't have to, you know," she said without meaning it.

"And that is why I shall," Kowalsky said. "For you, I would do anything."

The Vicomtesse clapped her hands. Immediately the room fell silent. All eyes were on her.

"As you know, Monsieur Kowalsky is our guest of honor," she announced in a clear, melodious voice. "I don't need to tell you that his charity concert at the opéra tomorrow has been sold out since two months ago. But tonight he has decided to honor *us*." She paused dramatically. "If you will follow us to the music room . . ."

373

An excited murmur rose from the guests. Kowalsky bowed to the Vicomtesse and Hélène. "Could I have the pleasure of being escorted to the music room by both of you?"

"We'd be delighted," the Vicomtesse said without hesitation.

Hélène turned to flash Jacques an apologetic look as Kowalsky hooked one arm through hers, the other through the Vicomtesse's. Then they led the crowd into the big, high-ceilinged music room overlooking La Cité and the floodlit rump of the cathedral. Quietly the guests pressed around the big grand piano as Kowalsky took his seat on the bench. He smiled at Hélène, stretched out his arms as if to push back his cuffs, carefully poised his hands above the keyboard, and then brought them crashing down in Chopin's "Ballade in G Minor." The resonant beginning notes gave way to a light airiness, the tune wafting effortlessly from the piano, always the clear, sweetly melodious notes mingling with the richness of the lower ones.

Hélène watched in fascination as his fingers flew effortlessly up and down the keyboard, sometimes slowing deliberately, then skipping quickly across the keys again. Behind the piano he seemed so big, so lively, so much in command. He was like a lion tamer and the piano was his lion. For him, it performed to perfection. The music swirled and flew and quickened until it reached the last deep chords. He didn't stop there. Immediately he moved into a piece by Schubert.

The guests listened intently, but none with as much rapture as Hélène. The beautiful notes climbed and fell and swirled and danced around her, finally working up to a crescendo.

For a moment the guests stood in stunned silence. Then they forgot where they were and burst into wild applause.

Kowalsky smiled and gave a little bow of his head. Then he began playing Debussy's "Serenade for the Doll." As he played, he smiled up at Hélène. She stood there mesmerized, her breath caught in her throat, her arms breaking out in gooseflesh. She had never known music to do this to her, not at the opéra or at the ballet. It was as if he were playing to her alone. When he finished the piece, he rose to his feet. The applause was like thunder. He made a courtly bow and took the Vicomtesse's hand.

"How can I ever thank you for this precious gift, Stanislaw?" she asked softly.

"Please," he said politely. "The pleasure was entirely

mine." He gave a little smile. "I think I am a bit tired. I have the concert tomorrow and I'm afraid I shall need my rest. You will excuse me?"

The Vicomtesse smiled graciously. "Of course, Stanislaw. And thank you again for the recital. My guests will be talking about it for years to come."

"I am always only too happy to accommodate you," he said gallantly. Then he turned to Hélène. "It has been a pleasure meeting you, mademoiselle."

Hélène smiled. "Not as much as mine."

"Would it be forward of me to ask you to attend my performance tomorrow? As my guest, of course."

"But . . . I thought it was sold out."

"A seat shall be found for you."

Hélène smiled at him. "I would be honored."

Once again he bowed formally. "Good night."

The Vicomtesse watched him leave. "He is such a kind man," she said softly. "I wish he did not feel so indebted to me."

"He plays beautifully!" Hélène said. "It was magic."

The Vicomtesse allowed herself a smile. "He always plays beautifully. But the 'Serenade for the Doll'? It was plain as day. He was playing that to you."

Hélène found herself blushing and turned away.

The Vicomtesse touched her arm gently. "Stanislaw is an old man," she said wisely. "He is old because of his years. But inside, he is a youth trapped in a frail body. He is seventy-two, would you believe?"

Hélène shook her head. "He certainly doesn't act it."

The Vicomtesse smiled. "He has a son and a daughter, both much older than you. They have lived in America since after the war."

"Did you hide them, also?" Hélène asked.

The Vicomtesse had a faraway look in her eyes. "Yes, but unfortunately the war drew them apart. Being cramped together in a tiny attic room for so long was not good for them. They grew to hate each other."

Hélène nodded. "You have been a good friend to him," she said softly. "I can see how much he appreciates it."

"He 'appreciates' you, also," the Vicomtesse said suddenly.

"Me? What do you mean?"

"Can't you tell? He's in love with you."

"No." Hélène looked at the Vicomtesse to see if she was

serious. The dark eyes and elegant lips held an expression of truth. "But . . . he doesn't even know me!" Hélène stuttered.

"He knows you better than you think," the Vicomtesse said. "Stanislaw has good instincts when it comes to people. Besides, the last time he played the 'Serenade to the Doll' was when he met his late wife."

Hélène shook her head and looked away. She did not know what to say. The Vicomtesse's revelation dumbfounded her. But it went deeper than that. Even if Stanislaw Kowalsky had fallen for her, he wouldn't want her. Not only was she too young for him but also there was her past to consider. Her miserable tenure with the Comte.

But she was wrong. After the concert, Stanislaw listened to her story quietly over a simple peasant dinner in a Hungarian restaurant and then smiled. He reached across the checkered tablecloth and covered her hand. "We have all done things we are not proud of," he said simply. "Sometimes we did not have much choice."

"But don't you see? I did!" Hélène told him vehemently. "I knew exactly what I was doing!"

But it did not matter to him. Three weeks later, he asked her to marry him.

For the first time in months, Hubert felt really good. He hadn't realized what a bad turn his life had taken until he'd smashed up Le Bon Coin, a little bistro near the university. Almost before the gendarmes threw him in jail, the family's slippery lawyer, Maurice Hugo, had everything under control. Before the night was out, the proprietor of the bistro had received three envelopes containing money. One for damages incurred during the brawl, one for the loss of customers during the necessary renovation, and one because he was a forgiving man of the world and could surely see that there had been a mistake, that there hadn't been a melee, merely a boisterous celebration. A fourth envelope had ended up in the hands of the gendarmes. Like magic, Hubert de Léger's name disappeared from the police files.

Any harm this incident might have produced had been quickly averted, but the Comte's face had been white with anger. Hubert's behavior had cost a great deal of money, but more important, a family branching out into politics and diplomacy did not need the black mark of a barroom brawl against it. It was not enough to just sweep such an incident under the rug. There would perhaps be another one, and then another. Somewhere along the line, one of them could spark off a major scandal and cause irreparable damage to the de Léger name. The Comte realized that his son was, in effect, a walking time bomb. The cure was not to whitewash the harm caused by his disastrous behavior, but to wipe out the cause of it. Hubert needed to be dried out and get professional counseling. Without hesitation, the Comte had him signed into an exclusive clinique near Deauville that specialized in treating alcoholism and its related emotional problems.

At first, it had been hell for Hubert. He was moody and struck out at anyone and anything. He battled constantly with the doctors and nurses, and started fights with fellow patients. Once he managed to run away and was picked up at a local bar, hardly able to stand, and taken back to the clinique. It was there, while he was drying out for the second time, that he saw the picture in *Ici Paris*. Hélène's familiar face was smiling reluctantly into the camera, and beside her was a withered old man. Hubert had to reread the headline five times before he could begin to believe it: "WORLD-FAMOUS PIANIST TO WED FASHION MODEL."

At that moment, Hubert knew what he had to do. He wouldn't say a word to anyone. He would fool the doctors with his best behavior. Then maybe they would release him from this prison in record time. He hoped that it wouldn't be too late to stop this revolting marriage from taking place. If it was, he'd just have to find a way to break it up.

His lips curled into a tight smile. At least he now knew where to find her.

Hélène looked up at the train as it labored slowly into the Gare Montparnasse. Most of the windows were down and the passengers were leaning out with expressions of expectancy. She recognized Jeanne and Edmond immediately. They were in the fourth coach from the front. Her face broke into a smile and she began waving her hand. Suddenly Jeanne caught sight of her and nudged Edmond. They waved back excitedly. Hélène hurried along the platform beside the second-class coach until the train hissed and jolted to a stop.

As soon as they stepped off the train, she flew toward them and threw herself into their arms. "I'm so happy to see you!" she cried, her voice husky with emotion.

Their embrace was long and emotional. For a moment,

none of them said anything more. They were content just to hold each other. Edmond gently stroked her hair.

Hélène looked at Jeanne. She hadn't changed much. Still the mousy hair and pale skin, the soulful but strong dark eyes, the sturdy provincial clothes. But Edmond had changed; she could see that right away. Somehow he looked thinner, and there were tight lines of tension around his mouth. He must be working himself hard, she thought. He had three mouths to feed. Suddenly she felt a tinge of guilt. Things were not going nearly as well for them as Jeanne had written. They were probably struggling to make ends meet in Saint-Nazaire while she was living it up in Paris.

"Hey, how's my Little French Girl?" he asked softly.

She burrowed her head in his chest. "How's my big brother?" Her voice sounded muffled.

He shrugged. "Getting old, I guess." He pulled her away and studied her. "You're looking good."

She smiled, stood on tiptoe, and kissed his cheek. "Maybe it's because life is finally agreeing with me."

"I'm glad to hear that."

Hélène turned to Jeanne and held both her hands. "Good, sweet Jeanne. You haven't changed a bit."

Jeanne laughed. "You should have seen me when I was pregnant. You would have thought I was carrying a whale!"

"How *is* Petite Hélène?"

"It's too bad we couldn't bring her along, but she's being well taken care of," Jeanne said as Edmond picked up the battered suitcase and began to lug it toward the exit.

"I can't wait to meet her," Hélène said with a smile. "When you write, I read the letters over and over. I've kept each one. They cheer me up to no end." Then her voice was serious. "How is Madame Dupré? I sent her an invitation but she wrote that she is ill and couldn't come."

Jeanne nodded. "She's been feeling bad for quite some time now. I'm not sure what's wrong with her, because she won't talk about it. But she doesn't look well."

"I hope it's nothing serious," Hélène said in a worried voice.

When they were out on the Boulevard de Vaugirard, Hélène signaled for a taxi.

"Why don't we take a bus or the métro?" Edmond suggested. "Taxis are so expensive."

Hélène allowed herself a laugh and shook his arm. "Don't

worry about money," she said lightly. "I'm about to become a very rich woman." She gestured at the taxi. "Hop in."

Jeanne exchanged glances with Edmond. He nodded imperceptibly and she climbed stiffly into the cab. Hélène climbed in after her and Edmond sat up front next to the driver. The driver looked at him questioningly. "Where to?" he grunted.

"The Georges V," Hélène said.

"Oui, mademoiselle." The driver sounded impressed. He put the car in gear and they swung out into the traffic. Edmond kept staring out through the windshield, his eyes thoughtful.

"It looks so different," he said, twisting around to look at Hélène. "There are so many people, so much traffic. All I've remembered were empty streets, vélo-taxis, and wood-burning trucks."

Hélène smiled at him. "Funny that you should say that. I'll never forget the day I first arrived. I thought exactly the same thing."

He turned back around to gaze out the windshield some more.

Jeanne took Hélène's hand and shook it excitedly. "Tell me about your fiancé." She gave a lively little shrug. "Is he handsome?"

Hélène smiled slowly. "No, but he is beautiful. I wrote to you that he is a pianist."

Jeanne nodded. "And that can make a man rich?" she asked.

Hélène nodded. "He performs all around the world. He has played for General de Gaulle and Queen Elizabeth."

Jeanne shook her head in wonder. "He sounds very important."

"He *is* important." Hélène turned to look out the window for a moment. Much as she hated to, she would have to warn them that Stanislaw was not a young man. Otherwise, when they met him, their shock might be too evident. But she wouldn't tell them here in the taxi. It could wait until they got to the hotel.

Jeanne looked wide-eyed around the suite. "This hotel must be very expensive," she said. "Did you see the lobby? And the way the clerk looked at us? It's our clothes, Hélène. Don't you think it would be better if we went to another hotel? One more suitable to . . . to our station? We're not elegant like you."

"Nonsense," Hélène said firmly. "A little luxury never hurt anybody. Believe me, you'll get used to it very quickly. You are going to stay here, and tomorrow I will take you shopping."

Edmond paced the big room, his hands in his pockets. He looked thoughtfully down at the thick carpet. Then he squashed his cigarette out in an ashtray. He came over to Hélène, put his hands on her shoulders, and held her at arm's length. His voice was flat. "You don't have to go through all this trouble and expense for us, Little French Girl. We're not used to living like this."

She met his eyes evenly. "Please, Edmond. Let me do things my way. I'm going to become the wife of a very prominent man. This is the way we will have to live."

"Madame Dupré said you lived in a house. Can't we stay there?"

"No," Hélène said quickly. "I don't live there anymore."

"Where do you live?" Jeanne asked curiously.

Hélène smiled. "I had an apartment, but I've just given it up. For the past few days I've lived here, in the hotel. After the wedding, I'll move in with Stanislaw. He has a house."

Edmond smiled good-naturedly. "All right," he said. "We'll be good relatives. We'll do as we're told and try not to embarrass you."

Hélène looked at him gratefully. "I . . . I have to tell you something," she said.

"I'm listening."

Nervously she clasped her hands in front of her and began to pace the room. "I want you to know that I love Stanislaw. Maybe you won't be able to understand that. It's not like the love you both share. That's something I can only hope for, but I don't think it will ever happen to me."

Jeanne looked confused. "What do you mean? Maybe if you . . ."

Hélène shook her head. "Please," she said. She looked out the window at the traffic down on the Avenue Georges V. "Let me finish. You see, Stanislaw and I respect each other. We'll be good for each other. Don't ask me to explain. I just know it."

"Why don't you just let us meet him?" Edmond said straightforwardly. "We can form our own opinion."

Swiftly she turned around to face him. Her voice was guarded. "I just want you to know something before you meet him. You see, you'll think that we can't possibly have anything in common. I just wanted to tell you that we *do*."

Jeanne and Edmond exchanged glances. Finally Jeanne came toward her and put an arm around her shoulder. "What is it?" she asked softly. "What's worrying you?"

Hélène's face was impassive. "Your reactions. You see, Stanislaw is not a young man."

Jeanne smiled and tried to put Hélène at ease. "It's not like you're marrying your grandfather!" she joked.

Hélène paled and threw Jeanne's arm off her shoulder. Her face was agonized. "Yes, it is. You see, Stanislaw is seventy-two years old."

Hélène read through the telegram and sank slowly down onto the edge of the bed. For a moment she just sat there shocked. It can't be true, she thought dully. There must be a mistake. Slowly she read the concise message again. There was no mistake.

REGRET TO INFORM YOU MADELEINE DUPRE DIED OF CANCER AT NANTES HOSPITAL THIS MORNING.

There was a quick knock on the door. Hélène didn't look up. "Yes?" she said weakly.

The door opened and Jeanne sailed into the room. "You're not even dressed yet!" she scolded. "We're due at the chapel in half an hour!" She smiled. "Hey, you're not nervous, are you? Edmond and I both think that Stanislaw is a fine man."

Hélène wiped her eyes and looked up at Jeanne. "No, I'm not nervous," she said in a small voice.

"Then what is it?"

Wordlessly Hélène handed her the telegram. Jeanne read it through and paled. "How terrible! Who would have thought that Madame Dupré had cancer?"

Hélène sniffed. "She died on the day I'm getting married." She thought for a moment and looked at Jeanne. "She was . . . my savior. I think I should postpone the wedding."

Jeanne sat down beside Hélène. "No," she said firmly. "She wouldn't want that. Otherwise she would have let us know what was wrong. She was brave, can't you see that? She didn't want you to worry."

Hélène sighed and reached for a handkerchief. "I suppose you're right, but all the same . . ."

Jeanne patted her on the back. "Come on, dry your eyes and get dressed. I'm responsible for getting you to the chapel on time."

5

The white clifftop villa Stanislaw had taken on Cap Ferrat for their honeymoon was magnificent. Palladian in style, it consisted of a two-story fifteen-room main house and a connecting six-car garage. The roofs were terra-cotta tiles and all the windows were elegant glass arches. Tucked away among a Mediterranean forest of dark cypresses, umbrella pines, and overgrown hedges, it looked like a castle in the midst of a jungle. But that was only from the road. Within, it was a whole different story. Planted like a garden, the entire estate consisted of formal rose beds, expertly pruned topiary, and oleander-filled urns. It even boasted a climatically controlled greenhouse for orchids.

In addition, there was an enormous pool pavilion set a hundred meters back from the house. Like the villa, the pavilion was Palladian. Outside it, terra-cotta greyhounds sat gracefully in niches built into the walls. Inside, it had a generously scaled living room decorated with detailed moldings and sleek dark wicker furniture.

The pool, poised near the edge of the cliff, was enormous, with rounded edges and a water fountain at each end. Its clever design presented the viewer with an optical illusion: surrounded by a raised marble coping on all sides except for the seaside, it appeared far calmer than the sea below but seemed to be a part of it.

Between the pool and the pavilion stood a relic of antiquity, a giant marble head of Apollo. From his pedestal he gazed out to the distant cliffs at the other side of the bay.

The house came with a staff of five. There were the

Gaudets—a housekeeper/gardener couple—two maids, and a cook.

Madame Gaudet welcomed Hélène and Stanislaw when they arrived. She was a stern elderly Breton dressed in somber gray and white. Hélène immediately got the impression that she ruled the house with an iron hand. The first thing Madame Gaudet did was to show them around. Throughout the tour Hélène was busy making mental notes.

She grasped the layout of the house immediately. There were two identical hallways on both floors. These were located off one central circular staircase that divided the house into symmetrical halves. The staircase was located under a large frescoed rotunda.

The public rooms were on the ground floor. One look told Hélène that the living room was perfectly suited for Stanislaw. It had two huge black Bechstein grand pianos and plenty of shelf space for his music library and recording equipment. The tall, arched French doors opened out to both the front and back gardens. No matter how hot it got, the room would always remain cool and comfortable. It had good cross ventilation and would catch the breezes coming in off the sea. Like sentinels, rows of potted palms were lined up between the doors.

The room next to it was the formal dining room—huge, marble-floored, and liberally hung with crystal chandeliers. The table would seat thirty. Fine for a banquet, Hélène decided, but hopeless for an intimate dinner for two. Depending on the weather, they would take their meals either in the greenhouselike breakfast room or out on the terrace.

All the bedrooms were on the top floor. Hélène noticed at once that their luggage had already been brought upstairs and deposited in their rooms, the suitcases serving as discreet announcements of who would sleep where. She wondered whether it was Stanislaw or Madame Gaudet who had been responsible for that. Or was it that rich people slept in separate bedrooms?

The bedroom staked out with Stanislaw's suitcase, to the left of the rotunda, was cool beige decorated with overstuffed suede furniture. French doors led to a large balustraded balcony overlooking the pool pavilion and the sea and cliffs beyond.

Hélène's suitcases were in an even more luxurious bedroom directly across the hall. It was the biggest bedroom she had ever been in, and it was entirely pink. The walls were covered in pink silk and the carpeting underfoot was thick and soft and pink. The enormous bed was canopied with miles of pink silk, and so was the silk-skirted vanity. A crystal chandelier gleamed overhead, and there were two down-filled pink couches with matching armchairs.

Hélène walked over to the windows. The curtains were pink, and even the view of the front garden was—what else could she have expected? she asked herself—pink: a massive round bed of roses in bloom. Vases of these same roses stood on the nightstands that flanked the bed.

Madame Gaudet threw open four white doors set in the pink walls. Hélène inspected them. Three opened into walk-in closets, the fourth into a pink marble bathroom. It was the most lavish bathroom Hélène had ever seen.

Overcome, she sank down into one of the pink sofas.

"Like it?" Stanislaw asked eagerly.

Hélène sighed and nodded. He wanted so desperately to please her.

She got to her feet and signaled for Madame Gaudet to leave. The housekeeper nodded and silently left the room. When the door closed behind her, Hélène stepped toward Stanislaw. "Separate bedrooms?" she asked gently.

He looked away. "I thought you'd want that."

She reached up, touched his chin, and turned his face toward hers. "I want us to share the same bedroom," she said softly. "I want to sleep with you."

"I am an old man," he whispered uncomfortably. "I . . . I no longer need to . . ." He made a quick gesture with his hands. "To do that."

Hélène looked deep into his eyes. "Why do you think I married you?" she asked. "I want to be your wife in every way."

"But I am old."

"That doesn't matter. You are my husband."

Tears welled up in his eyes. "My dear Hélène," he whispered, "you are a good woman. I do not deserve you." Gently he squeezed her hand. Her skin felt soft and young between his old, wrinkled fingers. It made him feel the difference in their ages and it saddened him.

Hélène disengaged herself from him, reached down, picked up her suitcases, and marched across the hall with them. He followed her. One of the uniformed maids was already in his bedroom unpacking his luggage. She gave a curtsy.

Hélène shook her head. "No, thank you," she told the maid. "I prefer to do it myself."

"Very well, madame."

When the maid had gone and Hélène was in the middle of unpacking, she said suddenly, "Stanislaw, what do you say we give the servants an extended paid vacation? I want you all to myself. Let's just be us two here. Alone. On a *real* honeymoon."

He thought about it for a moment. Unpacking suitcases was one thing; running a fifteen-room villa without help was another. "It's a big house," he said at last. "And the grounds are tremendous. Are you certain you can handle it?"

She smiled with eagerness. "The weeds may grow and dust may collect on the chandeliers, but I want to give it a try. Please."

He shook his head. He wondered if he would ever get to understand her; every other woman he had ever known could not be pampered enough.

He took her in his arms and looked into her eyes. They caught the light coming in through the French doors and shone like polished amethysts. She wanted so much to please, he thought. And those eyes—how could he refuse those eyes anything? Well, if taking care of him was what she wanted, then that's what she would get. He smiled. "Tell them to take a vacation."

She stood on tiptoe and gave him a quick kiss on the cheek. Then, like a delighted child who had been given a toy, she was off to dismiss the staff.

An hour later they watched from the living room as the staff piled into two black taxis. The maids were chattering happily, but Madame Gaudet gave one last disapproving look toward the house. This was her domain, her stern eyes seemed to say. God only knew what condition the place would be in when she returned.

As the cars disappeared around the circular drive, Hélène looked at Stanislaw and let out a breath of relief. "Now I finally feel like I'm at home."

He laughed. "Me, too. I'm glad they're gone. To tell you the truth, there was too much help buzzing around all over the place. I would never have been able to concentrate on my music."

Her eyes flashed mischievously. "Today *I* won't let you concentrate on it," she said. "In another few hours it will be dark. In the meantime, I'll go prepare us a light supper. Then we'll drink champagne. And afterward . . ."

Hélène tugged gently at Stanislaw's hand as she led him through the garden to the pool pavilion. Both of them had changed to belted bathrobes. The temperature had dropped and the wind had picked up. The air was scented with roses, oleanders, and pine. In the pavilion niches, the greyhounds were in deep shadow.

Holding hands, they stood wordlessly by the edge of the pool, watching as the sun set. The water fountains were turned off and silent, and the sky overhead was red and orange as the sun dropped down the burnished horizon like a blazing fireball. Far below, a lone sailboat raced across the bay.

Hélène slowly released Stanislaw's hand. She untied her robe, letting it fall around her ankles. She was completely nude, her firm breasts silhouettes against the sky. Proudly she threw back her shoulders and felt the wind rushing against her nakedness. A strange new strength coursed through her.

Stanislaw stared at her. She could hear him breathing heavily as she undid his robe. The champagne had done its bit. It had softened the edge of his inhibitions.

She took a deep breath. In the sunset his naked body did not look old at all. In fact, it glowed with vitality, and even his snow-white hair seemed golden blond.

She reached out to touch him. There was a look of anguish in his eyes. "I . . . I don't know if I still can," he said quietly.

Intuitively she understood. He was afraid. Afraid of being rejected; afraid of being humiliated. And above all, afraid of not being able to function as a man any longer.

She looked deep into his eyes. "Sssssh," she whispered solemnly. She reached up and strummed a gentle finger across his lips. "Don't say a word, my husband. Don't say anything."

Tenderly she began to run her fingertips across his back. He began to tremble. Without looking, she could sense the beginnings of passion rise up within him. Now was the moment, she knew.

6

The weeks on Cap Ferrat flew. Hélène learned a great deal about Stanislaw, and he about her. At first they were slightly nervous, but realized that this was only natural and accepted it. For a while their politeness to each other verged on awkwardness, but slowly they dropped their guard and began to enjoy each other's company.

Hélène found herself slipping quickly and easily into Stanislaw's life-style and routine. Since he rose late in the mornings, so did she. But she would wake up first and hurry downstairs to prepare him a light breakfast. Then she would run outside, cut the most perfect rose she could find, stick it into a bud vase, arrange everything on a linen-draped wooden tray, and serve him breakfast in bed. It was several weeks before she realized the truth: all along, he had been awake long before her. But he enjoyed both his breakfasts in bed and the pleasure she got from preparing them so much that he pretended sleep. When she discovered this, she served him breakfast in bed every morning whether he was asleep or not.

After getting out of bed, Stanislaw would quickly shower, dress, and go downstairs. Immediately he would sit at one of the Bechsteins and begin practicing scales and études. This would continue into the afternoon. She spent this time shopping in the Vieux Village or in Beaulieu, going to the Ile de France Museum, walking along the promenade Maurice-Rouvier and enjoying the beautiful view of the coast, or just simply working in the garden.

Every afternoon she made a lunch of fruit and salads. They ate outside on the terrace while watching the sailboats tacking into the wind in the bay below. Then he would take a nap in the pool pavilion and she would sunbathe on a chaise or swim in the pool. Sometimes she tired of the tranquil water and had a reckless craving for the sea. Then she would go to the edge of the cliff and descend the seventy-six steps carved out of the rock to the shingle beach twenty meters below. She loved swimming in the cold and powerful sea.

After an hour and a half, Stanislaw would wake up and go back inside the house to play his piano. At this time Hélène would stay close to the house so that she could enjoy the music that wafted out through the open French doors. Her favorite piece was no longer the "Serenade for the Doll," but Chopin's Mazurka in C-sharp Minor ("Opus thirty, number four," Stanislaw told her later). And when he found out that it was her favorite, he made a point of playing it over and over again. Sometimes she would tiptoe into the living room and just stand there watching him play. He always sat stiffly erect, his small body dwarfed by the big black piano while his nimble fingers flew over the "teeth," as he jokingly called the keyboard. A few hours later, they would eat a light snack (he disliked big dinners), and then he would begin working on his pet project: transcribing *Clytemnestra*. It was a "lost" opera that had recently been found, and the ancient score had to be translated note by note for modern instruments. Hélène was especially fascinated with this process, since he used his antique instruments to play through a portion of the notes before translating them. After a few hours, they would either go upstairs or outside and make love before going to bed. Always she was gentle, not only guiding him along but also encouraging experimentation. But she always managed to make him think it was his own idea. Actually, he understood what she was doing, but he never let on: he didn't want to spoil her pleasure in pleasing him.

One day, although Hélène didn't tell Stanislaw the reason why, she put an abrupt halt to their outdoor lovemaking. She missed it immediately, because it had been her favorite place for sex. She loved the feel of the elements all around her—the caressing freshness of the wind, the smell of the earth, and the cushiony softness of the grass against her skin. She loved the romance of the gorgeous sunsets and the stars overhead and the sound of the water. She stopped it because she had the feeling that they were being watched.

She had felt it for the first time when she was swimming in the pool. She told herself that she was being ridiculous. But later, when she was sunbathing, she had the feeling again. She looked up suddenly and frowned. She could swear she saw some of the thick bushes at the end of the property moving. Quietly she slipped into her heavy terry-cloth robe and went over to investigate. At first, there was no sign of anyone. But upon closer inspection she found footprints in the dirt around the bushes, and the grass was crushed.

When she looked around and discovered an overgrown path nearby, she decided to follow it. It led along the very edge of the cliff and connected their villa with the one next door, an Italianate U-shaped structure with a loggia overlooking a terra-cotta terrace. The blue shutters were closed.

She walked around the property and called out a few times, but no one answered. Finally she shrugged her shoulders and returned the way she had come.

She had just been imagining things, she tried to tell herself. But deep inside she knew better. She had seen the footprints.

The next week, Hélène discovered who was spying on her. While Stanislaw was practicing his études, she walked to the Vieux Village to get some shopping done. The day was perfect Côte d'Azur weather: sunny, cloudless, hot, but breezy. She wore one of the bright print dresses from Odile Joly.

First she ran some errands and then she stopped at the salon de coiffure. She would surprise Stanislaw with a new hairstyle she had been thinking about getting. Carefully she instructed the hairdresser to cut it into short, boyish bangs instead of giving her the wavy permanent that was so fashionable at the moment. When she finally left the salon, she stopped at a greengrocery. Once again, that peculiar feeling of being watched came over her.

Quickly she turned around and saw a fleeting shadow darting into a doorway. She lost no time going to investigate, but whoever it was had disappeared. With a weary sigh she returned to the greengrocer and finished her shopping. On the way back to the villa she walked past the secluded houses lining the boulevard. Suddenly she heard rapid footsteps behind her.

She whirled around. "What are you doing here!" she said angrily.

"I decided to be near my love," Hubert de Léger said fervently. His eyes looked glassy and they shone like a puppy's, eager to please.

She recoiled. She could smell his breath; he had been drinking. "Leave me alone!" she said coldly.

"After all the trouble I went through to be near you?"

She looked at him with distaste. "Hubert," she said softly, "I love Stanislaw and I am his wife. I have no intention of seeing any other man. Especially you!"

She started to leave, but he caught her arm. "Not so quickly, my sweet," he whispered. "It wasn't easy to get the house next door at such short notice. I expect some reward for my effort."

She stared at him. "So it is *you* who have been spying on me!" She shook her head. "I should have known!"

Suddenly she felt sick. Was there no getting away from him? Would he follow her everywhere she went? Why couldn't he just leave her alone?

"Hubert," she said quietly, "I think that from now on you'd better stay away from me. My husband won't like it when he hears about this."

He laughed silently. "Your husband! That old crow? He's old enough to be your grandfather!"

Her hand flashed out and slapped him.

He grinned. "Did I hit a nerve, love?"

She turned her back on him and started walking quickly. After a moment he caught up with her and took her by the arm.

She shook off his hand and angrily whirled around. Her voice was quietly menacing. "Leave me alone, Hubert. If you don't, I'll call the police!"

Suddenly he was angry. "Then call the police, you bitch!" he yelled. Then he laughed softly. "See if it keeps me away!"

She shuddered. Hurriedly she started walking again. Only after she'd gone a quarter of a kilometer did she dare look back over her shoulder. She let out a sigh of relief. He wasn't following.

When she got back to the villa, Stanislaw was still at the piano, and she could hear the sounds of a polonaise. He must have heard her come in, for he instantly switched to the Chopin mazurka. In spite of the harrowing incident with Hubert, she couldn't help but smile.

She left her shopping bags by the staircase under the rotunda and went into the living room. She approached Stanislaw soundlessly and kissed the back of his neck. With a flourish, his fingers swept the length of the Bechstein's "teeth." He pounded a few deep chords and then raised his hands dramatically in midair and held them there. He slid around on the bench to face her.

He raised his eyebrows. "What a lovely hairstyle," he said with an approving smile. "It becomes you."

She looked pleased. "It's not exactly what everyone's wearing. Even the hairdresser tried to get me to change my mind, but I was adamant."

"Good girl. You have more taste than all of them combined. What else did you do?"

She shrugged. "A little shopping. Errands. The usual."

She was ashamed of herself for not telling him about Hubert. But she didn't want to worry him, especially with the upcoming world tour his agent had just booked. It was her job to keep everything running smoothly.

He looked at her closely. "Is something the matter?"

She detected the note of worry in his voice. She wanted to kick herself. There, I've really done it now, she thought.

Quickly she shook her head. She forced her facial muscles to relax and tried to laugh. "No, nothing's the matter. I was just thinking about what I would wear on the tour. I *am* going with you, you know."

He took her hand and pulled her down onto his lap. "It will be the happiest tour of my life," he predicted. "Every night, I shall forget the audience is even there. I will play my heart out to you alone, as if you are the only person in the concert hall."

Suddenly she hugged him tightly. "And I shall sit in the crowds," she whispered. "And I, too, will forget that any of them are there. For me, you will be the only one in the concert hall."

7

Stanislaw waved. "Hélène!" he called out. "We have a visitor!"

"Just a moment!" She pulled off the thick gardening gloves, took off the big straw hat, and struggled to her feet. She ran a hand through her hair and saw Stanislaw and someone else walking toward her. Suddenly she stared at the visitor. She knew only one person who wore sport coats and ascots.

"Jacques!" she exclaimed with delight. Then she ran toward him and flung herself into his arms. He lifted her off the ground and whirled her around in the air a few times. Then he spun dizzily to a halt, and they laughed and embraced. He drew back and held her at arm's length.

"Let me look at you," he said with a smile. "Good God!" He glanced over his shoulder at Stanislaw. "Married life certainly seems to agree with her. I've never seen her this radiant before. You must be doing something right."

Stanislaw looked pleased.

"Well?" Hélène demanded. "What are you doing here? Don't tell me you've decided to chaperon us."

"Not at all," Jacques replied lightly. "I just had a mad impulse to see you, that's all." He grinned. "So I grabbed a cab, told the cabbie to drive me to the Gare Lyon, hopped on board the Train Bleu, and bribed the conductor into giving me a berth. And here I am on the beautiful, sunny Côte d'Azur!" His face fell. "But just until tomorrow."

"I'll get one of the guest rooms ready," Hélène said firmly. "There are plenty of empty bedrooms." She waved at the house. "Just look at this place. It's big enough to sleep an army!"

He shook his head. "No, thanks. I've already got a room at the Voile d'Or."

She was visibly disappointed. "If you insist . . ." Then she brightened. "Anyway, what brings you here?"

"Actually, I only came to drop off something. I wanted to deliver it in person."

"But . . . you've already given us a wedding present."

He smiled secretively and wagged a finger at her. "Ah, but this is not a wedding present. Come to the terrace."

Hélène looked at Jacques, then at Stanislaw. Suddenly her eyes shone with excitement. "It . . . it isn't . . ."

"It is!" Jacques said. "Advance copies of Vogue and L'Officiel. I didn't think you could wait to see them. They're up there on a chaise."

"Well, come on, then!" Hélène cried impatiently. She took each of them by the hand and pulled them toward the house. When they reached the terrace, she let their hands drop and raced up the steps. On the chaise lay the two magazines. She sucked in her breath. Her face was staring up at her from the cover of *Paris Vogue*. Slowly, as if it might be a mirage that would disappear when she touched it, she reached down and picked it up. Then she studied it intently. "Why, it's fantastic!" she said at last. She glanced at Jacques, who nodded in agreement. Then she flipped through the magazine. On page fifty-four, there she was again, dizzily hanging off the girder of the Eiffel Tower, with Paris far below her feet and the pale evening dress billowing in the wind like an enormous spinnaker. Quickly she put *Vogue* back down and snatched up *L'Officiel*.

And there she was again, this time in a five-page four-color spread. She stared at the pages silently for a moment. These were the smoking-gun photos. At first she couldn't believe that the beautiful model in the slip was her. But it was. She—Hélène Junot—was standing arrogantly over the body of a man, her legs in a defiant stance, one high heel poking the tuxedoed body, her face glaring into the camera. The barrel of the revolver was smoking. They were more than just photographs. They were works of art. She remembered laughing at Jacques, thinking the idea ridiculous. Soberly she realized that he had been right.

She shook her head, wondering if all this was indeed real. It was. And she felt strangely light-headed at seeing herself for the first time in a magazine.

Finally she turned to the men. "I . . . I simply can't believe it! They're beautiful! Stanislaw, did you see them?"

Her husband smiled warmly. "Jacques showed them to me the moment he arrived."

"These call for champagne!" she announced. She started to go inside the house.

"Oh . . . there is one more thing," Jacques said.

She looked back at him questioningly. "What?"

He reached into his sport coat and produced a long slim envelope. Puzzled, she retraced her steps and took it. Slowly she tore it open. One glance was enough. She knew what it was. A modeling contract from the most prestigious agency in Paris. Slowly she sank down onto the chaise.

Jacques grinned. "Well?" he asked. "What do you say to that?"

Wordlessly she put the contract down in her lap.

Jacques was looking at her strangely. "Is something wrong?"

She shook her head. "No, Jacques. I appreciate it. I really do . . ."

"Then what is it?"

She looked up at him and met his gaze. "I don't think I want to model anymore," she said quietly.

"Are you crazy!" He looked like someone who had just discovered a charge of dynamite in his pocket. Openmouthed, he turned to Stanislaw. "But . . . I don't get it!" he sputtered.

Hélène smiled gently. "Jacques, you wouldn't understand. And please, don't be angry or hurt." She reached out and touched his arm. "All I want right now is to be a good wife for Stanislaw. And then, if there's time . . ." She made a vague gesture. "Never mind. It's still too early to plan that."

"But the money! And the terms!" Jacques snatched the contract off her lap and waved it in front of her face. "Look what they're offering you!" He jabbed the paper with a finger. "It's astronomical! You'll be the highest-paid model in France! And next year, they're even planning to send you to New York!"

She smiled gently. "Jacques, please don't think I'm ungrateful. I appreciate everything you've done. It's just that I've already made up my mind. I know what I want to do."

He stared at her in exasperation. "Oh, Jesus! Women!"

An hour later, Jacques returned to his hotel. Hélène walked him to the taxi. When she came back inside, Stanislaw looked at her. "Is he coming back for dinner?" he asked.

Hélène shook her head. "No. He's returning to Paris tonight."

"He feels hurt," Stanislaw said with wisdom. "He was certain you'd be delighted."

"But I *was!*" Hélène protested.

"Sit down, my darling," Stanislaw said. "I think it's time we had a little talk."

Hélène raised her eyebrows questioningly, but she crossed the room and obediently sat down on the couch. The down-filled cushions were soft, and she sank deeply into them. He sat down beside her and reached for her hand and covered it with his. His eyes were sad. "You don't have to sacrifice anything for me," he told her gently. "That includes modeling."

"But I'm not!" she protested earnestly.

"Hush! Keep quiet and listen to the ramblings of an old

man for a minute!" He cleared his throat and chose his words carefully. "You are young, Hélène. Too young to sit around being bored. You must have something to keep yourself occupied. Especially since you're saddled with an old husband like me who locks himself away for hours on end transcribing old manuscripts and practicing the 'teeth.'" Again she started to protest, but he motioned her to silence. "You must have a life of your own, too. A hobby. A career. Something worthwhile."

Hélène smiled. "I'm not trying to play the martyr. Please believe me. It's just that modeling isn't for me. Of course, I would have jumped at the chance when I first came to Paris. No," she corrected herself, "I would have *killed* for the chance! But now, I'm glad I tried it. I found out that I'm not really crazy about modeling. I can't seem to get any satisfaction out of just looking pretty. Once in a while, yes. But not for a career." Suddenly she clutched him. "I want to *do* things, Stanislaw. I want to create something." She looked at him earnestly. The short haircut made her violet eyes look huge. "I want to start my own fashion magazine. I know I would be good at that. And I would *enjoy* it."

"Then that is what you must do," he said simply.

"It takes a lot of money to start a magazine," she said.

He shrugged. "I have a lot of money. Besides, what good does it do, just sitting in the bank? It's your money, too."

Her eyes were suddenly moist. He understood what she wanted to do . . . what she *needed* to do. Not like the Comte, who was afraid it would take up all her time and leave none for him. Stanislaw was secure. He just wanted her to be happy.

"Perhaps I will do it once the concert tour is over," she said thoughtfully. "I only hope that Jacques will understand the way I feel. I would hate to lose his friendship. But to create a new magazine—a new voice for couture—yes!" Her eyes shone with excitement. "I would like that!"

He smiled. "Good. Then as soon as the honeymoon is over, you shall get to work and start planning it."

She smiled back at him. "But let's not cut our honeymoon short. After all, this is the first vacation I've ever had." On an impulse, she leaned over and kissed him, then toyed with his white hair. "You know," she whispered, "I really love you. You're the first person who has ever understood me. You can't know how happy that makes me."

* * *

The following morning, Hélène helped Stanislaw set up his bulky reel-to-reel tape recorder in the living room.

"I'm going to record some of my playing," he announced. "Come up to the bedroom. I'll need your help carrying the tapes down."

She nodded and followed him upstairs. The trunks that he'd shipped there the day before the wedding were in one of the big walk-in closets. Fortunately the one with the tapes was right inside the door. They pulled it out and slid it across the carpet. Inside, it was filled to the rim with boxes of recording tape.

"Good Lord!" she exclaimed. "I've never seen so many tapes in my life! We're not going to carry this whole thing downstairs by ourselves, are we?"

He shook his head. "No, it's too heavy. We'll just take some of the boxes." He bent over, lifted out a stack, and piled them high in Hélène's arms. "You can take these downstairs," he said. "They're blanks."

At the door, she stopped and poked her head around them. "What are you going to carry?"

"Some of the recorded ones. I'll just be a minute selecting them."

A little while later, she helped him get everything ready. She tore the wrappers off the new tapes and laid the reels out on a table. Carefully he threaded one of them through the machine and tested it. She noticed that the reels he had brought down were carefully labeled and dated. They were all Chopin or Scriabin. She picked up one and peered closely at the handwritten date. He had recorded this particular one nearly fifteen years earlier. She put it back down. "What are you going to record?" she asked.

He pointed at the blank reels. "Everything I've transcribed so far on *Clytemnestra*. Then I'm going to listen to some of the old recordings I made years ago, just to compare my style with today's."

She shook her head. "That sounds like an awful lot of work." She brightened suddenly. "Maybe I can help you change the reels?"

"No, my dear. You go and do whatever you want."

"But I want—"

He gestured her to silence. "I'll need total peace and quiet for this." He kissed her gently. "I know you'd be as quiet as a mouse, but I need to *concentrate*." He smiled. "You're so pretty, I'd get distracted. Out you go." He put his hands in the small of her back and propelled her toward the door.

"Do you want me to call you for lunch or dinner?" she asked.

"No, *I'll* call *you*."

She sighed helplessly. "All right, if you say so."

"I do," he said with finality.

She spent the day in the garden. First she took a swim in the pool. Then she placed her hands on her hips and surveyed the lawn. She frowned. It was beginning to look disgraceful, but it would have to wait. Instead, she weeded some of the flowerbeds, trimmed around them with clippers, and snipped away dead blossoms. As she worked, she could hear the piano. She recognized the overture from *Clytemnestra*.

In the afternoon, Stanislaw came out onto the terrace. "I'm taking a break," he called out.

Quickly she prepared lunch. Then he took his nap and she sunbathed and swam. When he went back inside the house, she kept her bathing suit on. She'd gotten used to the sun; a little more tan wouldn't hurt.

For hours, until the sun set, she could hear him playing, often the same passages over and over. At first some of them sounded awkward and laborious, but finally they were pure magic.

Clytemnestra.

Hélène shut her eyes for a moment. The music was hauntingly beautiful and she could imagine the drama unfolding onstage. She could almost see the beautiful Clytemnestra join her lover Aegisthus in murdering her husband upon his return from the Trojan War, and then being herself killed by their son, Orestes.

"Pretty music."

Hélène jumped. Her eyes flew open and she stared at Hubert standing there in front of her. "Go away," she whispered coldly.

He reached for her hand and held it. "I've loved you," he said, "ever since that first day I saw you. I'd do anything for you. I'd even help you get rid of that old man!"

She felt a sudden chill and her eyes flashed in the sunset. She tried to pull her hand away, but he was clutching it tightly. Suddenly she was frightened. "Let me go!" she said quietly.

"Uh-uh. Not until you tell me the truth," he persisted. "That you love me and that you only married him for his money!"

She glared at him. Her voice was flat. "Hubert, there is nothing to tell. I love Stanislaw. Now, I think—"

"Aren't you at least going to admit that you love me?"

"No, Hubert," she said wearily. "I'll never admit that. You see, I *don't* love you."

Suddenly his face clouded over. Savagely he pulled her up from the chair and pressed his face against hers. His cheeks scratched her as she fought to turn away. His mouth found hers, and suddenly he pushed his tongue between her lips. She tried to shove him away. Clumsily he thrust a hand inside her bathing-suit halter and squeezed one of her nipples. She let out a cry of pain.

The music had come to a crescendo and then stopped abruptly.

"Stanislaw!" Hélène screamed. "Stanislaw!"

A moment later, Stanislaw came running out to the terrace. Hélène turned her head and looked up at him. His face went purple. She pushed away from Hubert and ran toward her husband.

"Go inside," he said in a quiet voice.

She nodded wordlessly and ran into the house. She watched from the French doors as Stanislaw approached Hubert. They were both silhouetted against the spectacular bloodred sunset. She could hear their voices raised in anger. As she watched, Stanislaw grabbed Hubert by the collar and shoved him backward. Then he raised a trembling finger and pointed to the edge of the property.

Hubert did not move. Hélène could hear his ugly, taunting laugh. Suddenly Stanislaw struck him across the face. Hubert recoiled.

Hélène shut her eyes. When she opened them, Hubert was flinging himself at Stanislaw. They began fighting with their fists.

"*Stop it!*" Hélène screamed. "*Stop it!*" She pounded her hands on the frame of the French door. The panes of glass rattled in their mullions.

The men continued grappling. They fell to the ground and started rolling around. Hélène's face had turned white.

398

Hubert was young and strong and Stanislaw was old and weak. And there were his hands to consider. His *piano* fingers. If only one got broken, it would be enough to put an end to his concert career. Suddenly she sucked in her breath. The cliff, she thought. Oh, God! She hadn't given it a thought, and now they were nearly at the edge!

Abruptly she ran out of the house, across the terrace, past the pool pavilion toward the cliff. When she was almost there, one of the silhouettes lost his balance and vanished, abruptly dropping out of sight.

The last thing Hélène saw were two clawing hands desperately clutching at air. Then a drawn-out, fading scream pierced the dusk, blending with her own.

And suddenly there was silence.

8

The Place Vendôme was very quiet at night. Even during the day, it had a kind of peaceful, secluded elegance. But it was by lamplight that one got the real ambience of the place, the illusion of what it must have been like when it was first built in the 1700's. It wasn't just the expensive shops, or the fact that it was closed off from the world by the majestic pilastered buildings on all sides, or that there were only two openings into this most exclusive enclave—one the rue de la Paix, the other the rue de Castiglione. The quiet came from the staid smell of money. It seemed to seep out through the doors and windows of the mighty Banque Rothschild; it somehow managed to escape the well-sealed vaults filled with millions of dollars' worth of gold and gems in the jewelry emporiums. It hung over the Ritz at number 15 like a sterling-silver cloud. And why not? Its wealthy international clientele were those who crossed borders with true carte blanche. These borders were not defined on maps; they were carefully surveyed and charted in the minute-by-minute fluctuations of multimillions, the dizzying plunges and peaks of power.

Hélène smiled as they got out of the taxi. For a moment she paused in front of one of the pedimented gray buildings that melted into other identical buildings that made up this side of the square. Her delicate nostrils flared as she tried to pinpoint the exact source of the elusive, quiet scent. It seemed to come from all around. There were few other places where it hit you with this impact. Palm Beach, parts of New York, Beverly Hills, Zurich, and the French Riviera.

"I used to dream of this place when I was a kid," she said, looking around with a proprietary expression. "Only then I knew I didn't belong here. I belonged in the slums of Montmartre."

"You've come a long way," Jacques said.

She sighed and looked down at her hand-sewn shoes. Then she looked back up. "Sometimes I wonder. You know, the older I get, the more I realize that distance isn't measured in kilometers. It's measured in francs and dollars and deutsche marks. Montmartre's not so far away from here. Just a little bit beyond the Opera. So how far have I really come in all these years? Three kilometers, maybe. That's not far, is it?" Suddenly she touched his arm. "I'm getting maudlin. Come, I want to show you something."

With a sigh of anticipation she led him to a recessed doorway in the arcade. On one side of the door, the lamp caught the sheen of a new brass plaque. Jacques looked closely at it. It was engraved with simple block letters:

LES ÉDITIONS HÉLÈNE JUNOT S.A.
Les Modes

He looked at her strangely and swept his finger along the lettering. "What's this?"

She reached out and touched the plaque. The brass was cold and lifeless. "I suppose it could be called the culmination of a dream," she said softly. "Ever since I was a young schoolgirl I've waited for this moment." She got the keys out of her purse and unlocked the door. "In a minute I'll tell you all about it."

He glanced at the sign once more and followed her inside. She turned on the lights and closed the door. The big rooms were empty and silent. For a moment they stood there without speaking.

She spoke finally. "I just signed the lease yesterday. The plaque went up this afternoon. You're the first person to see it."

"I'm honored," Jacques said in a puzzled voice.

She led him from one tremendous room to the next, then up a broad staircase. On the second floor she switched on another light. "This will be my office. Look," she said. She crossed the room, each hollow footstep echoing around the bare white walls. She threw open one of the six tall windows. He came up beside her.

Across the huge square, most of the buildings were dark. Except number 15. Lights were blazing at the Ritz.

She went over to a corner, bent down, and picked up a bottle of Château Mouton-Rothschild and two glasses that were sitting on the floor.

"Wine?" he asked in surprise.

She glanced at him as she poured it into the glasses. "This is a celebration. I would have had champagne, but the icebox hasn't been installed yet."

He took his glass. "You still haven't told me what exactly you're celebrating."

"My new business. Hélène Junot is now a publisher." She gave a little laugh. "Or rather, will be soon. After Stanislaw died, I found I was a rather rich young woman with a lot of free time on my hands. I had to do something."

"You could have retired in youthful splendor."

"Not me. I have to keep busy."

He raised his glass. "Congratulations." He drank the wine. "Now, tell me about this publishing company."

She stood with her back to the window, her hands resting on the sill. She chose to keep her words and voice light. "You've heard of *Elle*, you've heard of *Vogue* and *L'Officiel*." She paused. "I intend to take them down a peg or two."

He looked to see if she was joking; her violet eyes were dead serious. "That's a big ambition," he said carefully.

"Not really. I have the money to pump into it. What I need now is a staff."

"I think I'd better have some more wine," he said. Quickly he refilled his glass and drank it down. The Mouton was warm and smooth as liquid velvet. "Shoot."

"I'm offering you a job, Jacques."

"I already have a job."

"I know that. You're a photographer, and a damn fine one."

"I'm at *Vogue*. That's top of the line."

"*Les Modes* will surpass *Vogue*," she said with a certainty he had never heard in her voice. "Give me a year and you'll see."

"You haven't even set up yet. It'll be six to eight months before the first issue is ready to go out."

"It'll be out in four months. What I need now is a staff. The best people I can find. I'll need your help hiring them."

"Where are you going to get them?"

She grinned. "I'm going to pull off the biggest heist French publishing has ever seen. I intend to steal the best talent that *Vogue, Elle, L'Officiel, Marie Claire,* and *Harper's* has to offer."

He shook his head. "Why do you think *you'll* be able to do it?"

"I'm going to offer them big francs. Everyone likes to get a raise. Plus there's the matter of ego. The chance to have a hand in shaping something new."

"You seem to have it all worked out."

She shrugged. "It's one way to get things done quickly. The sooner the ball gets rolling, the sooner *Les Modes* is out. What do you say? Will you consider coming in with me?"

He looked at her cautiously. "How big are those francs you were talking about?"

"What are you making now?"

"This," he said. He took a check from Condé Nast out of his pocket. "I don't usually carry these around with me. I just got paid today and haven't been able to get to the bank."

She took the check and looked at it. It was for twenty-eight hundred francs. She handed it back. "You don't do badly taking pictures."

"As you said, I'm a damn fine photographer."

"All right, I'm prepared to offer you thirty-five hundred a month."

"That's not bad," he said slowly. He thought for a minute. Then he nodded. "I'll give notice at *Vogue*. Two weeks from tomorrow, I'm yours."

She narrowed her eyes shrewdly. "I'll make it four thousand a month and you start tomorrow. Plus, there's no moonlighting around here. God help you if you smuggle pictures to *Vogue* or *L'Officiel*, byline or none."

Suddenly he grinned. "Boss," he said, "you've got yourself a deal." He extended his hand and they shook on it. "Where do I report in the morning? Here?"

"Right here." She smiled and looked around the empty room again. Their voices sounded as if they were bouncing off the walls of a cavern. But soon that would change. She could already envision what it would look like. A thick carpet on the floor would deaden the hollow sounds. So would the furniture. Her desk would be placed diagonally in front of the window. That way, she would be able to swivel her comfortable chair around and look down at the Place Vendôme whenever she felt like it. The chairs for her visitors were another matter. They would be stiffly uncomfortable; anyone coming to see her would immediately be put on the defensive. There must never be any doubt of who was in command. There would be filing cabinets and bookcases around the office, and the only decoration on the walls would be covers from *Les Modes*. A sudden idea hit her. She would change the covers each month so that only the most recent one would hang there. She made a mental note and filed it away among the hundreds of other details that had occurred to her.

"Where *are* you?" Jacques asked. He was watching her with an amused expression on his face.

She gave an apologetic little smile. "In the future."

"That's as good a place as any, I suppose."

"Yes, it is." She nodded slowly. The future would be a good place, she thought. At any rate, it couldn't be any worse than the past.

It seemed unbelievable that her dream was beginning to take shape at long last. She frowned suddenly. Something was missing. Then she knew what it was. She should be feeling elation. Triumph. There should be excitement and electricity crackling through the air. But there wasn't. The only thing she felt was a levelheaded determination to work hard and succeed. It was as if her childish sense of wonder and joy had deserted her when she had stood over Stanislaw's crumpled body on the rocks below the cliff on Cap Ferrat. That had been the final step she had had to take toward her ambition. Strangely enough, it had endowed her with that which she needed to become successful. A new sense of awareness and maturity. The willingness to take the worst kind of situation and turn it around to her advantage.

She was breathing heavily from the exertion of the climb, but she barely noticed. The windows of the villa were red with fire. For a moment she stared at the house dumbly, her hands at her side. Then she realized that it was not on fire. The windows were merely reflecting the sunset. Slowly she held out her blood-covered hands and looked at them with a blurred expression. "He's dead," she whispered. "He's dead!"

Quickly Hubert came over to her and put his hands on her arms. His eyes were wild. He seemed to have aged thirty years. "I didn't mean for this to happen!" he said softly. "It was an accident! You have to believe that."

In a daze she pushed him away and started walking toward the house. She couldn't even feel the ground beneath her feet. It was as if she were walking on air. She could not even feel any pain. Only a dull numbness. The pain would come later.

Solicitously Hubert helped her toward the house. "Maybe you're wrong," he said quickly. "Maybe it we call a doctor he'll be able to do something. Patch him up . . ."

Hélène stopped in her tracks and pushed him away. She shook her head vehemently. "He's dead! He landed on the rocks." She turned away from him in time to see the red sun dropping into the sea. She shuddered. "It . . . it's terrible. He's all crushed, and there's blood everywhere."

"Hélène, why don't you lie down and rest? I'll take care of everything."

"No!" Her voice took on the high pitch of hysteria. "Haven't you done enough! You've killed my husband!"

"Please, Hélène . . ." He stepped toward her.

Her eyes were wide with fear. "Stay away from me, Hubert!" she warned. "Don't come near me!" Suddenly she turned and ran to the terrace.

He watched her disappear into the house. He sighed heavily. Then he ran after her. At the French doors he stopped and paled. She was on the telephone.

He rushed into the living room and snatched the receiver out of her hand. Quickly he slammed it down on the cradle. "What are you doing?" he hissed.

"I'm calling the police."

"What are you going to tell them?"

She flashed him a nasty look and reached out for the telephone. Swiftly he blocked her way. He was almost childlike. "Don't tell them," he pleaded. "Please. I'll do anything for you. Give you anything . . ."

Her voice sounded weary as she held out her hand demandingly. "Hubert, just give me the receiver."

"Will you listen to me for a moment!" His usually deep voice, now high-pitched and whining, sounded grotesque. "Do you think I wanted this to happen? It was an accident!"

She flashed him a contemptuous look. "How old are you, Hubert?"

He looked at her quizzically. "Twenty-five."

She gave a mirthless laugh and slapped her thigh. "Twenty-five! To think that you fought with a man of seventy-two! A pianist whose fingers were his life, who couldn't defend himself. And you hurled him off the cliff!"

He turned away from her. "I told you it was an accident! He lost his balance!"

"I don't believe you," she said dully.

"All right, then don't!" He whirled around savagely, his narrowed eyes blazing. "I wanted to kill him!" he spit out wildly. "You're right. Ever since the day you two first met. He was too old for you! Too damned old and too damned ugly! I'm glad I killed him!"

"Do you know what you're saying?" Her words were scarcely audible.

"Of course I know what I'm saying!" he snapped angrily. "And if you tell the police that I had any part in it, I'll deny it. I'll call you a liar! He was a frail old man." He made a disgusted gesture. "Even a woman could have tossed him down that cliff!"

She started to laugh and flung her arms out unbelievingly. "I can't believe this! You would tell the police a lie like *that?*"

"If you tell them I did it, yes! I will even say I witnessed *you* doing it. That he was just standing there admiring the sunset and that you gave him a push. You had the perfect motive. After all, you married him for his money!"

"How dare you!"

"Go on—call the police." He laughed tauntingly and started for the French doors. Halfway there, he turned around. "Come on, let's see if you have any guts."

She looked into his dark eyes to see if he was serious. For

a moment she could see straight through them into his soul. It was a dark soul, mangled and decayed, festering with venom. She closed her eyes to wipe out the terrible sight.

He's crazy, she thought. Not just drunk; this time it went much deeper than that. Somewhere along the line, the blue blood had curdled. As much as the young Hubert de Léger had once charmed her, he now repulsed her.

"Get out of here," she said quietly.

He left without a word.

Slowly she lifted up the telephone. Her fingers trembled as she dialed the police. They answered immediately.

She took a deep breath and fought to keep her voice under control. "There's been an accident!" she whispered hoarsely. "My husband is dead. Please . . . come quickly!"

While she was waiting for the police, she looked around the big airy room. There was the big black Bechstein Stanislaw had been playing, the one nearest the terrace doors. The sheet music was still leaning against it. She walked over and stared at the carefully penned score. Slowly she picked it up and leafed through it. Then she closed it. On the first page was scrawled in his precise handwriting:

CLYTEMNESTRA
An Opera by Jean Baptiste Lully
Translated and Arranged by Stanislaw Jastrow Kowalsky

And under that, newly scribbled words caught her eye:

This translation is dedicated to my darling wife, who makes me feel like a young man again.

She stared at the words, and then she pressed the paper against her breast. The heat of her tears burned her eyes. It was at this moment that the true tragedy sank in. The numbness wore off; the pain began. Quickly she replaced the score on the piano, but that didn't alleviate the anguish she felt.

Snap! A noise startled her in the silence. She jumped and spun around, her eyes darting from door to door. Then she glanced over at the table on the other side of the piano. The tape recorder had just turned itself off; a piece of the flesh-colored tape was still fluttering against the big machine as the reels did a few last spins. She let out a breath of relief. It was only the tape recorder. Funny how a little noise like that could set you off when you were all wound up. She hadn't even realized that it had been running all this time.

She caught her breath. No, not only running. *Recording.* Stanislaw had been making a tape of *Clytemnestra* when her screams had interrupted him.

Suddenly the enormity of this discovery flashed through her mind. Momentarily it even isolated the pain in a small, unimportant corner of her body. On that tape was not only *Clytemnestra* but also Hubert's incriminating confession. She had enough evidence to incriminate Hubert de Léger for the murder of her husband, regardless of what tales he'd tell the police. Stanislaw had inadvertently trapped his own killer by leaving the machine running.

Hélène's mind began to race. With this confession, she could put Hubert behind bars. There was only one problem. The de Légers were powerful. They had connections. Exactly how far-flung these connections were she could not know. But as a de Léger, Hubert would probably get off with a light sentence. Perhaps even a mere slap on the wrist. After all, his family was one of the ten most powerful in France. One didn't just throw a de Léger into a jail packed with hoodlums, common thieves, and butchers.

She took the reel off the machine and tapped it in the palm of her hand. It did not weigh much, but somehow it felt very heavy. And no wonder. As long as it was in her possession, *she* would be in a position to punish Hubert. For as long as he lived, she could make his life miserable. For a moment she hesitated. Wasn't this called blackmail? Who was she to dispense justice? She pursed her lips thoughtfully and came to a swift decision. Better she than no one.

She thrust the spool into the box labeled "Clytemnestra" and put it in a drawer of the bureau.

Then the police arrived.

Inspector Rème found her sitting on one of the soft beige couches in the living room, her lips compressed into a thin twisted line, her face chalk white. One of the lights under the palm pots threw the shadow of a knifelike frond across her face. She was a beautiful woman, he thought to himself, but like most beautiful women, grief did not agree with her. In his thirty-one years on the force, Inspector Rème had learned to tell when grief was genuine. But grief itself proved nothing. He knew of several cold-blooded women who had thought nothing of killing their husbands; afterward they had been genuinely grief-stricken for having done it.

"Inspector . . ." Her voice was barely a whisper as she began to tell him about the accident.

9

Hubert stood at the bedroom window looking out at the sea. The wind was brisk and the waves were capped with foam. He tapped his foot impatiently. What was the matter? He'd finally been able to trace her to the Grand Hotel. Why wasn't she answering?

Finally he heard a click and her voice came on the line. It sounded small and weary. "Hello?"

"Hélène? It's Hubert."

"Yes, Hubert. What do *you* want?"

"How are you?"

For a moment she was silent. When she spoke, it was as if every word were frozen. "My husband is dead and I've been questioned by the police. I don't think they believed my story. How do you think I am?"

"What did you tell them?" he asked curiously.

"I don't think this is the time to discuss that," she snapped, and then he heard a click.

He stared dumbly at the receiver. She had hung up on him. Angrily he banged it down and cursed. The worst thing was, she wouldn't even tell him what she'd told the police. If they came to question him, how was he to be sure that their stories matched?

But they hadn't come to see him, he thought suddenly. That at least indicated that she'd been wise enough not to mention him.

The press had a field day. As soon as the news of Stanislaw Kowalsky's death leaked out, reporters descended on

Cap Ferrat in swarms. Most of them were from sensational journals like *Ici Paris;* a few even came from as far away as Germany, Italy, and England. Stanislaw Kowalsky was news. In death as much as in life.

Jacques didn't bother with trains. He hopped on the first Air-Inter flight to Nice. There he hired a car to take him to the isolated, exclusive Grand Hotel du Cap-Ferrat. Hélène was in a suite consisting of two connecting bedrooms, each with its own door out into the corridor. That way, if any reporters managed to slip past the alert staff downstairs, Jacques would at least be able to come and go from his room without being harassed.

The bellboy put down his suitcase and thanked him profusely for the tip. Jacques grinned good-naturedly and looked around the room. When he heard the door close, his face grew serious. "Hélène?" he called out softly.

She opened the connecting door a crack, peered out suspiciously, and then flung it open. She rushed into his arms. For a moment he held her tightly. Her small voice was muffled in his chest. "Thanks for coming, Jacques. You don't know how much I appreciate it." She looked up at him and tried to smile.

He leaned down and kissed her cheek. Then he looked at her silently for a moment, shocked by her appearance. Her face was white and drawn, her eyes lackluster. He felt helpless. All he could do was try to comfort her. And that he did, as they talked long into the night. Finally he convinced her to try to rest. The hotel doctor had given her some pills, but she hadn't take any, not wanting to miss Jacques's arrival. Now, as Jacques handed them to her, she accepted them gratefully. After a few minutes she did what she had believed to be the impossible. She slept.

Whether it was the pills, the tiredness, or the emotional strain, something knocked her out completely. She even slept through the jangling of the phone. Finally Jacques shook her awake. She looked at him groggily.

He held his hand over the receiver. "It's Inspector What's-his-name," he said. "He wants to talk to you right away."

She moaned and struggled up. What was it with the police? Didn't they sleep like normal human beings? Or did somebody wind them up with a key like one of those mechanical toys?

She glanced at the alarm clock on the nightstand. It was still light out, but the clock said eleven-thirty. She sat up straight. Was it possible that she'd slept fifteen hours straight through? She shook her head to clear it of the fog and took the receiver.

"Madame Kowalsky? This is Inspector Rème. I hope I'm not disturbing you."

"No, not at all," she lied. "If I sound a little groggy, it's because of the pills the doctor prescribed. What can I do for you?"

Jacques stood there looking at her questioningly. She caught his look. "Coffee," she mouthed soundlessly. He nodded and quickly slipped out of the room.

"I'm all right, Inspector," she said into the phone. "Please, go ahead."

"Perhaps you will feel better once I tell you what we've discovered," Inspector Rème said. "A witness who saw the accident take place has just come forward."

She felt a sudden chill and drew the sheet higher around her neck. So someone had seen Stanislaw and Hubert fighting, she thought with dismay. How could that have been? Had someone across the bay accidentally focused binoculars their way? Had a sailboat been going by, and a member of the crew looked up as the body fell? It could have been any of a dozen things. A hundred things.

"Yes . . . ?" she said cautiously.

"It seems that the villa next to yours was rented to a certain Hubert de Léger."

Whatever sleep was still in her body shot out of her like a bullet. "I see," she said. She had to fight to keep her voice calm.

"Monsieur de Léger was in his garden, also admiring the sunset, when your husband lost his balance. He said that he saw you rushing toward him, trying to save his life."

"I didn't succeed, Inspector."

"But you tried." He paused for a moment. "I've called to let you know that you're free to leave Cap Ferrat whenever you like. The case is closed."

She forced herself not to show her relief in her voice. "Thank you, Inspector. Do you have any idea why this person did not come forward sooner?"

"It seems that he is from a prominent family and didn't want its name involved. He said he came forward after much deliberation because it was his duty as a citizen."

"I see," she said dryly.

"If you need any help leaving," Inspector Rème said, "I am glad to be of service. I can have my men try to get you past the reporters. Also, your husband's body is still in the morgue in Nice. Do you wish to have it shipped to Paris?"

"Please."

"I will be happy to arrange it."

"Thank you, Inspector. Au revoir."

Slowly she replaced the receiver. For the first time she noticed the persistent ticking of the alarm clock. Almost angrily she snatched it off the nightstand and buried it under the pillows. It didn't do any good. She could still hear the *tick-tick-tock, tick-tick-tock*. But at least it wasn't so loud that she couldn't think. Her eyes were thoughtful. Trust Hubert to be a slippery fish. He had managed to squirm out of this mess nicely, even clearing her in the process. He would probably expect her to be eternally grateful.

She smiled grimly. But he *had* done her one favor without even knowing it. He'd left himself wide open to be punished for his crime. By her.

She reached for the telephone and waited for the hotel operator to come on. "Bonjour, madame."

"Bonjour," she replied. "Connect me with the desk, please."

"Right away." There was a clicking sound; then the unctuous voice of the head desk clerk came on.

"Please prepare my bill," she said. "I'm checking out. Also, reserve two seats on the next flight to Paris." She tossed down the receiver and swung her legs over the side of the bed. She pulled on her robe. Then she got her suitcase and threw it on the bed and began to pack.

"What's the hurry?" Jacques looked at her questioningly as he came in with a steaming cup of black coffee."

"Pack your things," she said without looking up. "We're leaving."

He stared at her incredulously and slowly put the cup down. "What! Leaving! Where to?"

"Back to Paris, of course."

At the airport in Nice, they passed a newsstand in the

lobby. Hélène stopped in her tracks. A grayish color came over her skin as she stared speechlessly at a tabloid on display.

Jacques looked over at it too. He winced. It was one of the weekly scandal rags. It was enough to knot your stomach. The bold red banner read: "LUCKLESS MARRIAGE ENDS ON THE ROCKS." There was a big black-and-white paparazzo shot of Stanislaw and a half-page blowup of Hélène. It was the "smoking-gun" photo. The one from *L'Officiel*.

"Jacques, it's your photo!" she said in a tight voice. She furrowed her brow. "You didn't . . . give them permission to use it?"

He caught the look in her eyes. "No, of course I didn't. They must have pirated it from *L'Officiel. Le Monde Internationale* is always pulling stunts like that," he said angrily.

"But it's so . . . so out of context," she whispered.

"Forget it. There's nothing you or I can do about it. More important personalities than you have tried to stop them. *LMI* always wins. Your best bet is to forget about it. Let it die a quiet death. Don't even demand a retraction."

She felt a terrible surge of anger because she knew that he was right. But it wasn't fair. A person shouldn't have to take such slander. It wasn't right to have to feel so impotent. Then she had a sudden brainstorm. "Can't *L'Officiel* sue them for ripping off the photo?"

He nodded. "But it would cost them a fortune and could take forever. Years, maybe. Even then, there's no way to be sure of the outcome. *Le Monde Internationale* could get just a slap on the wrist. Listen, take my advice and forget you ever saw it."

She stared at him. "But how can I? 'Marriage Ends on the Rocks.' That's despicable!"

"Keep busy for a while," he advised her gently. "Stay out of the public eye. Do nothing, say nothing. In a few weeks, you'll be yesterday's news. In a month, no one will even remember who you are or what you look like."

But Jacques was wrong. For the rest of her life, the reporters would always be there to haunt her. She would not only be in the news. She would create constant news.

Stanislaw Kowalsky was buried on the silent slopes of the Père-Lachaise Cemetery in Paris. The grave was off the Avenue Transversale Number Three, a few graves away from

Modigliani's. It was a short, private ceremony. Besides Hélène and Jacques, the only other friend of Stanislaw there was the Vicomtesse de Sévigné. She sniffed ceremoniously into a lace-edged handkerchief, her huge black picture hat with the big black satin bow flapping perilously in the wind. The Vicomtesse was a very elegant mourner, Hélène thought, but a genuine one. The eyes that had seen so much were red-rimmed and puffy from crying.

Also at the grave were Ada and Herbert, Stanislaw's estranged children. Neither had come from New York for the wedding, but both had turned up for the funeral. Before the service, Hélène had tried to speak to them, but they had turned away. They made it clear that they did not regard her as a member of the family, and that even the Vicomtesse was a barely tolerated friend of their father's. During the service, Hélène looked over at them. They stood together at the far side of the grave, Ada with her face hidden behind the thick veil of what looked like a black beekeeper's bonnet. Her long black skirt reached almost to her swollen ankles, which were encased in black nylon stockings. Herbert, pear-shaped and wearing heavy glasses, studiously kept his eyes on the grave like an engineer studying a blueprint.

At the end of the service, Hélène picked up the tiny shovel and scooped a little symbolic earth out of the big mound beside the grave. She took a deep breath and looked stoically down at the gleaming coffin. Then she flicked her wrist awkwardly and the pebbles rained noisily down on the curved mahogany lid and slid off it into the sides of the grave. Quickly she turned away and began to walk to the exit. Jacques fell into step beside her and put his hand under her elbow. Behind her she could hear the Vicomtesse weeping as she threw her shovel of earth. "Au revoir, mon ami," she heard her cry thickly.

At the cemetery gate, the Vicomtesse caught up with Hélène. She put a hand on her arm and drew her aside. "I want to tell you that Stanislaw was very fortunate," she said, carefully dabbing her eyes with a corner of her handkerchief. "His last few weeks were the happiest of his life."

Hélène looked away, her eyes distant. "No," she said firmly. "If he hadn't married me, he'd still be alive."

The Vicomtesse put a gloved hand on Hélène's chin and twisted her face around. "Even in grief you have no right to say such a thing," she said coldly. "Stanislaw wrote me a letter the day before he died. I received it only yesterday. I've memorized every word. He wrote: 'I only regret that I did not meet her years before. She is strong and sweet, my Hélène, sensual and caring, passionate and maternal. If she had been the mother of my children, I am sure I would have had a close-knit, loving family instead of one that fell apart at the seams.' "

Suddenly Hélène's eyes filled with tears. She didn't answer. She gave her a little hug, pulled herself away, and hurried to her waiting Citroën limousine.

That afternoon, in Monsieur Duchamps's stuffy, paneled law office on the Avenue de L'Opéra, she found out just how much Stanislaw cared for her. He had made her the sole beneficiary of a single rare Stradivarius violin, a house in the sixteenth arrondissement, all his recording royalties, bank accounts, and stocks and bonds worth in excess of two and a half million dollars. He had left Ada and Herbert with a paltry twenty-five-thousand-dollar a year trust fund each.

10

Hélène sat beside Karl Häberle, the private detective, in the front seat of his battered Opel Rekord. Her posture was tensely erect, her violet eyes keen and hard, her nostrils flaring with anticipation. She ducked down again and looked out the dirty windshield at the plain four-story apartment house. The first part of her long-vowed search had ended here on the Berliner Strasse in a small town in Germany. Not even in her wildest dreams had she considered that it would end anywhere but in some dark, seedy, furtive place. The Hamburg waterfront, perhaps. Even a secluded village on the pampas of Argentina. But Seulberg sprang up from the slopes of the Taunus Mountains just north of Frankfurt. It was a new community being built from scratch. Quiet suburbs like this one were popping up all over. The postwar boom was in its heyday.

Hélène studied the building closely. It looked like a big rectangular box. There was something almost antiseptic about the sharp Bauhaus angles, the immaculate white stucco, the big plate-glass windows with gauze curtains behind them. There was no personality, no grace. No style. Only function, and in postwar Germany, form followed function as B followed A. Only one thing seemed to be more important, and that was C. Cleanliness. Neatness. Order. It was as if after the rubble of the war had been cleared away, neatness was the most strictly enforced requirement of them all. She looked over at Häberle. He was watching her curiously. "Well?" he asked. "Are you ready?"

She didn't speak. After having waited so many years for this moment, her body felt somehow leaden. She thought she had been emotionally prepared. Now she knew she was not. Slowly she reached for the door handle, pushed down on it, and swung the door open. When she stood on the sidewalk, she looked up and down the new street. The asphalt gleamed blue-black in the bright sun. On top of the hill, the bulldozers were grading more land. She nodded to herself. The air out here was country air. It smelled fresh and clean. Even the birds swooped happily in the skies above the nearby fields. The recent war was way in the past.

Häberle took her arm and led her along the concrete path to the entrance. When they reached it, she looked at the row of doorbells. Each tiny black button had a small metal slot beside it. In each was a slip of cardboard with a carefully printed name. The third one from the button jumped at her. Schmidt. A shiver of revulsion ran through her.

Häberle turned to her and raised his eyebrows questioningly.

She forced herself to smile. As soon as he wasn't looking, she bit down on her lip. She watched him push on the doorbell with his finger.

A few seconds later, a crackling voice came on over the squawk box. "Wer ist da?"

He didn't answer, just pushed the button again and again. Finally the door buzzer that released the catch sounded noisily and he pushed on the door. He held it open for her and they found themselves in an anonymous corridor with a staircase in the back. They headed toward it.

"Third floor," he said.

She nodded as they climbed the stairs. They were clean

and spotless. The smell of antiseptic was everywhere in the air.

"It smells like a hospital," she whispered.

He didn't reply. On the third floor, a door opened and a woman looked out at them just as they reached the landing. "Wer sind Sie?" she demanded in a shrill Bavarian dialect that echoed hollowly in the stairwell.

Hélène looked at her. She was tired-looking and thickset, her size accentuated by her shapeless gray housecoat. Her mangled grayish-blond hair was in the remains of a long-past permanent and a tired wave hung down over her forehead. She brushed it aside irritably with her hand.

Häberle gave a little bow and stepped forward. "Verzeihung. Mein Name ist Karl Häberle. Das ist meine Frau. Sind Sie Frau Schmidt?"

The woman looked at him suspiciously, drew back inside, and closed the door a little farther. "Ja?"

Häberle came right to the point. "Ich war in der Wehrmacht mit Hans. Ist Er zuhause?"

Hélène knew what he was saying. He had explained his tactics to her in the car. If Schmidt himself didn't answer the door, they would gain access by Häberle posing as an old army buddy.

"*Ach so.*" Some of the woman's suspicions faded and she smiled tentatively. She opened the door wide and invited them inside. "Guten Tag," she told Hélène.

Hélène smiled automatically but kept quiet. Häberle had told her not to open her mouth, her speaking French might create suspicion.

"Mein Mann ist in der Küche. Kommen Sie." The woman led the way down a narrow hallway and through a stiffly furnished parlor that looked like it was never used. Hélène looked around with curiosity. The chairs, tables, and wall unit all had long, tapered, blond wood legs. There were no pictures, no flowers, no personal knickknacks of any kind. They went into the kitchen.

Hélène let out a gasp and drew back. Her mouth was suddenly dry. There was no mistaking the man seated at the table. It *was* Schmidt. The same Schmidt who had been with the white-faced one. The Schmidt who had unbuttoned Marie's little suit and burned her on the belly with a cigarette. Now he was sitting with his back to the wall, contentedly munching on Belegte Brote. A half-full stein of beer was on the table in front of him.

Silently Hélène's eyes traveled up the wall beside the table. She stared at it in morbid fascination. It was covered with memorabilia from the war. There were medals, pictures, photographs; an Iron Cross, ribbons with swastikas. It was a long time since she had seen items such as these. She couldn't believe that anyone had the gall to display them. Then out of the corner of her eye she noticed that the man no longer had legs. She could see the scarred, rounded ends of his fleshy stumps protruding from his shorts. She looked at Häberle with a curious expression. With his eyes he motioned for her to remain silent. She tightened her lips across her teeth and nodded imperceptibly.

The woman leaned down over her husband. "Hans, Du hast besuch!" she shouted as one does to a person who is hard of hearing.

"Was? Besuch? Wer den?" Schmidt looked up, squinted, and reached for the thick wire-rimmed glasses on the table. Carefully he looped them over his ears. He frowned as he looked from Häberle to Hélène and then back at his wife. "Wer sind diese Leute? Ich kenne Niemand."

The woman frowned and looked at Häberle sharply. "Soll das ein Witz sein?" she demanded angrily. "Lassen Die doch mein Mann in Ruhe!" Protectively she put her thick arms around her husband's shoulders and pulled his head into her bosom.

Häberle turned to Hélène. "Wait in the parlor," he told her firmly in French.

She nodded gratefully and fled the stifling kitchen, the mutilated sadistic man, the evil memorabilia staring down from the wall. She sat on one of the hard upholstered chairs. From the kitchen she could hear voices raised in anger. After a while she got up, went over to the window, and parted the filmy curtains. She looked out thoughtfully. The view was uphill, and she could see bulldozers pushing at mounds of earth. She wondered what the arguing in the kitchen was all about. She thought it peculiar that the Schmidts were so violently defensive. She hadn't expected that. She had expected sincere apologies, begging for forgiveness. Anything but such a noisy battle. Weren't they sorry about what had happened? The answer now came to her. Obviously not. Otherwise, what would all those horrible medals and photographs be doing on the wall?

Ten minutes later, Häberle came out of the kitchen, Frau Schmidt at his heels. Hélène let the curtains fall back in place and slowly turned around. Frau Schmidt's eyes flashed with hatred. When she spoke, it was in badly accented, venomous French. She had obviously learned the language long ago. It was very rusty and grating, the naturally melodious pronunciations curdled by her thick, guttural Bavarian dialect.

"Do you sink ve vant the vor?" she shouted suddenly, flinging her arms around. "Ve are peaceful citizens! Vhy you come here and accuse my Hans of dese terrible sings?"

Hélène could only stare at her.

The woman made an indignant gesture toward the kitchen. "Don't my Hans suffer enough? He give his legs, almost his life! Not that he vant to! He vas . . ." She looked questioningly at Häberle.

"Conscripted," he said quietly.

"Conscripted!" she repeated almost triumphantly, rolling the word on her tongue. "Do you understand? He has no choice!"

Hélène looked at her steadily. She could no longer remain silent. She was tired of being intimidated, of being made to feel that she was the one who had done something wrong. "No, I don't understand," she said quietly.

Frau Schmidt had a challenging look on her face, "Even I—a vuman—have to vork for Hitler. Not that ve liked him. Ve had no choice! I vas in the Arbeitsdienst. Vorking on a farm to grow foods so that people don't starve. Am I a bad person vor doing this? For growing foods?"

Hélène looked at Häberle. "Did you find out about the other one?"

He nodded.

"Let's talk in the car." She shot a contemptuous glance at Frau Schmidt. "I can't stand the air in here."

"You . . . you sink you know everysing!" Frau Schmidt screamed. "How vould you like a man with no legs? I even have to stretch our government stipend by being a Hausmeisterin!"

Hélène looked puzzled.

"Sort of a concierge," Häberle explained.

Hélène whirled around and glared at the woman. She had taken just about as much of this as she could. "I had a mother, Frau Schmidt," she said disgustedly between her teeth. "She was pregnant. The Nazis punched her in the belly until her baby ran down her legs. My mother ended up in Auschwitz and was burned. My older sister? God only knows what happened to her. Probably gassed and burned. And my baby sister?" She pointed a trembling finger toward the kitchen. "That husband—that *Hans* of yours—burned her! A baby! That's right, a *baby*. Right in the belly. Here." Hélène yanked her blouse out of her skirt and jabbed at her navel. "And how do I know this?" She glared at Frau Schmidt. "*Because I saw that monster doing it with my own eyes!*" Hélène turned on her heels, marched through the hallway, flung open the front door, and stomped down the stairs. She could hear the venomous tirade coming from the landing above. "You young vons! You sink you know everysing. You alvays have a quick answer. Sure, you know everysing. How do you know vat it is like? Ve don't *like* Hitler! Every time the radio says there is a victory, we have to hang flags out the vindows. Do you sink ve like that?"

Häberle rolled down the window of the Opel and lit a cigarette. He inhaled noisily, drawing the smoke deep into his lungs. His face was pale and drawn. Hélène was shaking. Her eyes were expressionless as she stared blankly out the windshield. For a long time they sat in intense silence. Then without turning to him she asked, "What did they tell you?"

He looked at her. "Do you want to stop at a Gasthaus? You look like you could use a drink."

She twisted around in the seat and faced him. "No!" she said sharply. "Tell me here."

He tapped his fingers on the steering wheel. "All right," he said quietly, "I'll tell you. But I think the man in the kitchen speaks for himself. He is desperate and beaten."

"And all that . . . that junk on the wall? What about that?"

Häberle smiled grimly. "Don't you see? He has nothing left but the past. That is where he now lives. That was where he was a man."

She laughed. "A man? What kind of a man tortures a baby?"

"I'm not talking about that," he said irritably. "I'm talking about his physical condition."

"I know that he hasn't got any legs. I could see that for myself. I don't think that should alter anything."

Häberle laughed softly. "In the kitchen, the woman had him pull his shorts down. He doesn't have any genitals, either. He stepped on a mine in Russia."

Hélène closed her eyes. Somehow nothing was turning out the way she'd expected it to. She had imagined herself an avenging angel wielding a swift, clean sword. What kind of a sword could she lift against a legless man who was no longer a man? She shook her head. Nothing was going right. *Nothing.*

"Tell me about the other one!" she shouted, suddenly slamming her fist down on the dashboard. "The goddamn albino!"

Häberle took a drag on his cigarette. "I've got to warn you. You're opening a can of worms with that one. He's in the big leagues."

Her voice was soft. "I'm listening."

"His name is Karl von Eiderfeld and he's a pillar of respectability. About ten years ago he began to deal in oil and shipping. Since then, his company has become a behemoth; it's worth millions. It's called Von Eiderfeld Industrien, G.m.b.H. and it's based in Düsseldorf. I know nothing about von Eiderfeld himself, though. I'm pretty certain I've never come across a photograph or an article about him. Not in *Stern* or in *Der Spiegel*." He frowned thoughtfully. "Almost all of the industrialists have been written about in terms of the great postwar miracle, but never him. And he's certainly contributed to it. Yes, it is rather peculiar . . ."

Hélène ventured a guess. "His company was begun just after the war?"

"I'd have to research that, but I believe I can safely say yes."

"Then he must have had connections from the war. A huge industrial complex like that doesn't just start overnight. He's had help. Or knows things. Perhaps those who have helped him aren't even aware of it. There's got to be a shady beginning somewhere."

"It's supposed to be a very conservative company."

"I don't care." She clapped her hands together as if in prayer and inclined her head. "I want you to begin a discreet inquiry," she said slowly. "Look for anything connected with von Eiderfeld—especially from before the war. Get a dossier together. Include documents, passport photos, anything. Lie

420

in wait for him and snap his picture. I want to see it. But above all, dig for the dirt. I want his whole army career from A to Z. I want enough to charge him with to last five lifetimes. But it's got to stick. Every allegation must be documented. There has to be *proof*!" She turned to him, her eyes flashing with violent anticipation. She allowed herself a little breath of excitement. Somehow she felt—knew, she corrected herself—that she was now on the right track. Woman's intuition or no, it was a strange feeling. He was out there somewhere. Healthy and living it up.

"That's a tall order."

She allowed herself a smile. "I'm certain you're capable of it. Even if things haven't turned out well so far, you can't be faulted."

His expression became serious. "I have to warn you," he said gently. "Von Eiderfeld has more than just money. He has power."

Suddenly she smiled confidently. "So? Even Achilles had his weak spot. Von Eiderfeld will have one, too. Start digging!"

Daylight was beginning to fade as the big car finally turned into the poplar-lined drive that led up to Hautecloque. As it rolled through the gate, she caught a glimpse of the familiar crest of the de Légers chiseled into the stone. In the evening shadows, the lion and the salamander looked curiously weary and bored. She sat up straight. There in the distance Château Hautecloque-de Léger stood, its haughtiness worn like an implacably elegant mask. Against the velvet purple of the twilight, the lights shone yellow in the elongated windows and the air was very quiet. Somehow Hautecloque looked much smaller and less formidable than that first time she had seen it. For now she recognized the haughty coldness for what it really was. Simply a facade that both inflated the achievements of the early ancestors and hid the decadence of the present generation.

"Wait here," she instructed the chauffeur as she got out of the car, attaché case in hand.

He nodded courteously and closed the door behind her. When she was on top of the marble steps, she banged twice on the brass knocker. For a moment she turned and her eyes lingered on the car. The chauffeur was leaning against it, cupping his hands and lighting a cigarette against the wind.

Behind him, the green-and-black coachwork flashed snobbishly in the flickering glow of the gaslights. She smiled grimly to herself. She was facing the de Légers on their own terms. First-class.

A liveried footman opened the huge carved doors and a big square of corrugated light spilled out onto the steps. He made a production of clearing his throat. "Madame?" he said with the reserved air of self-importance that Hautecloque, by its very magnificence, seemed to demand even of its servants.

"I am Madame Kowalsky," she said formally. "I believe the Comte is expecting me."

He looked at her expressionlessly as she stepped into the big foyer. Then he slowly pushed the heavy doors shut. "Please wait here, madame. I shall inform monsieur le Comte that you have arrived."

She nodded her acquiescence. Then soundlessly he withdrew down a long corridor and disappeared. She smiled to herself. She didn't know whether it was a new rule in the house or not, but there was only one way a servant could walk so quietly. By wearing crepe-soled shoes.

As she waited, she looked around. She couldn't help remembering what a big deal it had seemed the time she had used the front door instead of the servants' entrance. In five years, some things had changed. At least for her.

A few minutes later, the footman came back into the foyer. "The Comte will see you now, madame," he announced. "He is in the Salon de la Rotonde. Please follow me."

Hélène nodded and followed him down the hall and through a succession of rooms. When they reached the salon, he opened the double doors, stepped aside so she could enter, and slowly drew the doors closed behind her. She looked around the room. It was exactly the way it had been the night she had dined with the de Légers, the night Hubert had taken her to dance in Saint-Médard and she had refused to go to bed with him. Only the pale blue moiré-covered walls seemed a shade paler. That was par for the course; fabric faded in five years. The fine old paintings all around were cast in soft pools of light coming from the brass arc lamps bowed down over the carved gilt frames. She noticed the Raphael she had admired so much. Then she saw the Comte.

He was standing motionless at one of the windows, one hand tucked in the small of his back as he gazed thoughtfully down at Le Nôtre's dark park. For a moment she thought he did not know that she was here. Then he turned around and looked at her with an expression of disapproval.

"Hello, Philippe," she said softly.

He crossed the big Savonnerie toward her. "I thought I made it quite clear that I did not wish to see you again," he said coldly.

She gave a little laugh. "It seems I have the habit of popping up like a bad penny."

"Indeed. What is it you want?"

She stared at him. "Why this brusqueness, Philippe? Are we such strangers?"

He did not reply. With his hand he made a familiar elegant gesture. She looked at the nearest settee and sank down into it. It was the same one on which she had sat with the Comtesse while the Comte and Hubert had been at the far side of the room discussing politics and business. Was it really possible that all that had been five years ago? Slowly she set the attaché case down on the floor beside her.

For a moment she was silent. She had been so awed by the de Légers, had been so easily blinded. But now she knew better. They were involved only in themselves, their own business, their own pleasure. They took and they took and they never gave. They thought everyone had a price. Dangle a bauble in front of a girl and watch her melt. The Comtesse was just as bad. Why else would she have used Madame Dupré to copy the great couturiers' creations? They played sick little games, the de Légers. To them, everyone was a pawn who could be kicked off the board without a moment's notice. Maybe they had done that with enough people to believe they really were invincible. But she could be as hard and unforgiving as they were. She smiled coolly at the Comte. If that was the way he wanted to play it, then she was willing to go along with it. She held all the aces and he didn't even know it. Her voice was suddenly brisk and businesslike. "The reason my solicitor contacted you was that I have a business proposition."

His blue eyes clouded over and he took a seat opposite her. So that was it, he thought. She was like all the others who had been jilted. He had wondered how long it would take for her greed to rise to the surface. Sooner or later it always did. They were stupid, these girls, to think that all they had to do was to keep coming around and demanding more money. He knew their ploys well enough by now. They came to see him under all sorts of pretexts. They would begin with charming small talk, casually bait the hook, and then try to pull him in. He was used to it. Not once had he given in to their offensive tactics.

"I'm in a bit of a hurry," he said wearily. "If it isn't too inconvenient, I'd appreciate it if this didn't take too long."

"Very well," Hélène said. "I don't know whether or not you are aware that I am now a widow?"

He offered no condolences. "I think I heard mention of it somewhere," he replied dryly. "It seems you've become a rather wealthy young woman."

"Wealthy, perhaps. Terribly rich, no. But I'm finding myself with a lot of time on my hands. I think that during times of mourning it is best to keep busy, non?"

He started to rise to his feet. "I don't know what it is you're getting at," he said irritably, "but I'm a very busy man. Now, if you'll please excuse me . . ."

Her voice was suddenly icy. "*Sit down!*"

He started, and met her eyes. There was something challenging in them that he'd never seen before. It was as if the soft amethyst had been suddenly cut into brilliant facets. Slowly he took his seat again.

She folded her small-boned hands in her lap. The hardness in her eyes faded as quickly as it had come, and once again her voice was low and controlled. "As you might recall, Philippe, I once made some mention of having ambitions of becoming a magazine publisher."

"Yes," he said noncommittally. "So?"

"Well, the corporation is now set up," she answered. "My solicitor has requested this meeting so that I might make you more aware of the company. You see, I'm selling stock in it."

"I'm afraid you've come to the wrong person."

She gave a low laugh. "No, Philippe. I've come to the *right* person. You are going to buy ten percent of Les Éditions Hélène Junot, S.A."

He sat back and began to relax. He looked at her with good humor. "You have a lot of nerve, I'll credit you with that."

"Don't give me credit for that which you know nothing of," she said pointedly. "Do you have a tape recorder?"

He looked at her curiously. "A tape recorder? What on earth for?"

She reached down for the attaché case, swung it onto her knee, and flipped it open. She took out a reel of recording tape and held it up. "I think you should hear this," she said in a level voice.

At first his mouth fell open. Then he began to laugh. "Why, of all the cheap tricks!" His voice took on a taunting edge. "I'm afraid that's not very original. It's been tried before by one of your predecessors."

She looked at him innocently. "What has?"

"Taping our lovemaking and then making an ultimatum."

"An ultimatum such as what?"

"Don't play the innocent," he snapped angrily. "Demanding a financial settlement . . . or the tape will be sent to my wife. I know that routine and you should be smart enough to realize that it won't work. As I told you once, I demand total honesty from everyone. Not only that. I reciprocate. You see, blackmail is not possible because the Comtesse knows all about the house on the Boulevard Maillot and what goes on there."

Hélène's eyes fell and her voice was quiet. "Don't make it sound so cheap, Philippe."

"You're the one who's being cheap," he said. "Now, I'm afraid you've taken up all the time I can spare."

"You'd better listen to this tape," she said quietly. "It's the only chance you'll get. If you haven't got a recorder, I brought one with me. It's outside in the car."

He made an impatient gesture. "I have a recorder in the library. I'll listen to the tape there."

She got to her feet and followed him into the richly furnished two-story library. He gestured at a round baize-covered table at one end. She went over to it. On it stood a radio, a record player, and a tape recorder. Her face was expressionless as she placed the reel on the recorder, carefully threaded the tape through the machine, and then turned to him. "Bear in mind, Philippe, that this is only a copy. The original is in a lawyer's vault. Need I say that it's not the same lawyer who arranged this meeting?"

"You make it sound very ominous. Go on, turn the damn thing on. Let's get it over with."

She inclined her head, smiled pleasantly, and brought a finger down on the green plastic button.

At first there was only a hissing noise. Then came the sound of footsteps and a chair scraping against a floor. Finally the first elegantly baroque notes of the overture from *Clytemnestra* filled the library.

She took a chair near the Comte's and scraped it closer. "As you know, my late husband was a concert pianist. One of the greatest in the world."

"If you say so," the Comte said dryly. "Myself, I've always preferred Horowitz."

She shrugged. "To each his own. Let's listen, shall we?"

She settled back silently as the familiar piano notes rose and fell, swirled and banged, went through all the moods and emotions that could possibly be lured out of an instrument, and then some. Suddenly the music stopped, there was an abrupt scraping sound, quick footsteps, and then silence.

"Really, Hélène—"

She held up a hand. "There's more. Be patient, Philippe."

The sudden sound of footsteps—this is where it started, when she had run through the French doors into the living room.

She watched the Comte closely. His face was an impenetrable mask.

Then there was the unmistakable sound of a telephone being dialed. Suddenly a second set of footsteps echoed loudly, and the receiver was slammed down.

"What are you doing?" a voice hissed.

Despite himself, the Comte leaned forward as he recognized his son's voice. She nodded to herself. He was starting to show signs of curiosity. Then she forgot all about him. She could feel herself starting to tremble as she slipped back in time.

"I'm calling the police."

"What are you going to tell them?" The sound of a scuffle, then Hubert's voice, humble and desperate: *"Don't tell them. Please. I'll do anything for you. Give you anything."*

"Hubert, just give me the receiver."

His voice started to whine. *"Will you listen to me for a moment! Do you think I wanted this to happen? It was an accident!"*

"How old are you, Hubert?"

"Twenty-five."

Her little laugh was strained and humorless. Then there was the sound of a slap. *"Twenty-five! To think that you fought with a man of seventy-two! A pianist whose fingers*

426

were his life, who couldn't defend himself. And you hurled him off the cliff!"

She caught the Comte's eyes flashing for a moment. Then he got to his feet and faced a wall of books so that she couldn't see his face. But she could see the sag of his shoulders as his hands fell to his sides.

"I told you it was an accident!" Hubert shouted. *"He lost his balance!"*

"I don't believe you." Her voice sounded dull and lifeless.

"All right, then don't!" Hubert screamed. *"I wanted to kill him! You're right. Ever since the day you two first met. He was too old for you! Too damned old and too damned ugly! I'm glad I killed him!"*

There was a pause. Then: *"Do you know what you're saying?"*

"Of course I know what I'm saying! And if you tell the police that I had any part in it, I'll deny it. I'll call you a liar! He was a frail old man. Even a woman could have tossed him down that cliff!"

The Comte suddenly lunged at the recorder and snatched the reel off the machine. Angrily, he threw the reel against the wall. Then he slumped over the table and grabbed hold of it. His hands were shaking. Suddenly he looked very old and defeated.

Her voice was soft. "Philippe, at the time all this happened, I didn't even know that the machine was running. Stanislaw had been recording the piece you heard and left the machine on when Hubert attacked me in the garden."

Slowly the Comte straightened and turned to face her. His eyes were pained but unwavering. "Hubert's behavior cannot be excused."

"Don't you think 'inexcusable behavior' is rather too casual a term for murder?"

He ignored her. "I don't care what you want to call it, but I will not let myself be blackmailed," he said with dignity. "Not by anyone or for any reason."

She looked at him levelly and rose to her feet. "I'm leaving now. You may keep that tape. As I told you, I have another. More copies can easily be made. I can send them to the police, to the newspapers, even to *Ici Paris* or *Le Monde Internationale*."

His mouth hung open. "You wouldn't do that!"

"No?" Her lips were grim. "Try me, Philippe."

He looked at her in silence.

"I have brought along all the documents you need for buying into Les Éditions Hélène Junot, S.A.," she continued. "I should mention that they are made out in Hubert's name and require *his* signature, not yours. The contract specifically states that he cannot under any circumstances sell his shares and that he must attend any and all board meetings as scheduled by me. He must stay in constant touch with me and let me know all his movements. That is to make certain that in case of emergencies he will always be available. Need I state that if he fails to do all this, the tape will fall into rather . . . well, into rather unsavory hands?"

He still did not speak.

"Furthermore, ten percent of Les Éditions Hélène Junot, S.A., will cost one million francs. That is the fair market price. I own ninety percent of the corporation and have put up nine million francs as required. So you see, it's not blackmail at all. You're simply being coerced into making a small investment. I should mention that dividends shall be paid quarterly."

His voice was bitter. "You've got it all figured out, haven't you?"

"I like to think so. As I said, I shall leave the documents here. You can have your lawyers go through them. I believe they will find everything in order. I will give you seven days to consider this option. If at the end of that time I do not receive the signed documents and one million francs deposited in the company account at the Banque Rothschild—" She shrugged helplessly.

The Comte slammed his fist down on the table. "I won't have it!" he roared. "I won't let myself be blackmailed!"

When she left the room, he dropped down into a chair. Suddenly he was very tired. He closed his eyes and sat there in silence.

Three days later, when Hélène returned to Paris, the documents were waiting for her. She went over them carefully. Each copy had been signed by Hubert de Léger and witnessed by one of the de Léger lawyers. She called the Banque Rothschild. One million francs had been deposited in her account. She tapped the documents in her hand. *Les*

Modes was finally on its way. But it was a way she had never expected. She was using it as an instrument of justice.

At least that was what she liked to think. But sometimes, when she lay awake at night, she wondered about it. Was it really justice? Or was it vengeance? Sometimes there seemed so little difference between the two, and then, after a while, she could no longer even tell what that difference was.

11

After she left Hautecloque, Hélène had headed for Saint-Nazaire. She had the chauffeur put in at the Hotel Soubise in Rochefort for the night. By noon the next day they reached Nantes. Then once again she was riding along the Loire. The day was overcast and gray, the clouds low and threatening, and the meandering river in its huge, sandy bed picked up the charcoal tones of the sky. At a little past one o'clock they arrived on the outskirts of Saint-Nazaire.

As soon as she saw the road sign with the name of the town on it, she felt a peculiar sensation. At first it began with a buzzing in her temples and she felt the heat of a blush coming on. The strange thing was, the blush wouldn't leave. It took her a while to realize what caused this. Self-consciousness and fright. There was something about this place that could do that to her. It wasn't just the fear of running into Tante Janine. That was part of it, but it went deeper than that. It was the fear of being recognized by *anyone*. Schoolmates, shopkeepers, customers who had come to the nursery. In Paris, she was becoming a somebody. Here she was plain Hélène Junot, the gawky kid who lived with the crazy old woman who ran the nursery. Here she would always be remembered for that. It made her feel a deep sense of shame and resentment. It was difficult to put her finger on what it stemmed from. It was simply there. When you left a place, you could never go back. Not as yourself.

She sighed. All the pain of her childhood seemed to be

capsulized in this one small, unimportant town. She felt pain in Paris sometimes, but nothing like here. She had lived here for years and still felt like an outcast. It was when she returned to Paris that she felt she was coming home.

She looked out the window. In many ways, the town had changed. A lot of construction was going on, especially on the outskirts. It reminded her somehow of Seulberg. The new houses here had the same boxy shape, the same kind of cold neatness and sharp angles and stuccoed walls. Was that what the war had done? she wondered. Was all the individual character of a place wiped out and replaced with the unimaginativeness of the new? Why was style just swept aside like antiquated dirt and forgotten? Didn't beauty count for anything anymore?

She pushed the button that lowered the glass partition between her and the chauffeur. "Drive to the church," she instructed.

She pushed the button again and the glass slid silently back up out of the seat. She stared out the window again. She should never have come here. She knew that now. She should have had Edmond, Jeanne, and Petite Hélène come straight to Paris. Saint-Nazaire was a torture.

The chauffeur had no trouble finding the church. He drove around the walled-in churchyard until they reached the main gate. Then he pulled the car expertly up alongside the curb, jumped out, and held the rear door open. Hélène climbed out slowly and looked around. On the other side of the street was the stonemason who specialized in tombstones and statues. A winged angel sculptured out of marble stood outside in the yard, keeping guard over gravestones and what looked like short marble and granite railroad ties. There were other angels, too. Some were weeping, some had their hands over their faces. Next door was a florist. That would be Herriot's. She was surprised. The familiar old stone building had been torn down and a new one had gone up in its place. Progress and prosperity had finally come to Saint-Nazaire.

She started across the street toward "Herriot's." Then she stopped. The sign over the door didn't read "Herriot." It read "*Janine Péguy.*" So the old lady was doing all right for herself, she thought grudgingly. She had expanded all the way into town.

She retraced her steps to the Rolls. The chauffeur was

stretching his legs and smoking a cigarette. As soon as he saw her, he made as if to toss it into the gutter.

"Don't bother," she said quickly. "I was wondering if you could do me a favor."

"Oui, madame?" He inclined his head, took a few quick puffs, tossed the cigarette down, and ground it out under his boot.

She snapped open her purse and took out some crisp bills and handed them to him. "Go across the street and buy some flowers." She frowned suddenly. "On second thought, make that a potted plant."

"Any preferences?"

She shook her head. "Anything, as long as it's something nice."

He gave a little bow, waited for a Simca to pass by, and hurried across the street. A few minutes later he returned carrying a big potted plant wrapped up in dark green tissue. She took the plant into her arms. "Merci. I'll be back soon," she said.

He nodded and watched her go through the gate and disappear into the cemetery that surrounded the church. He reached for his pack of cigarettes, fished one out, and lit it. Vaguely he wondered about a person who left Paris to visit a château in Bordeaux for an hour and a cemetery in the boondocks the next day. Then he gave a typically Gallic shrug. Chacun à son goût. To each his own.

Hélène looked around at the neat rows of crosses and stone memorials. The cemetery was laid out like a precisely surveyed town, the paths straight and defined, the rectangular plots marked off by thick borders of marble or granite. The earth inside each perimeter was covered with chalky white gravel. Centered in it were either minuscule flowerbeds or big stone planters. She shifted the plant around in her arms and gave a sigh of bewilderment. She had forgotten that there would be so many graves.

She turned as she heard a scraping noise. Not far off, a wizened old gravedigger was standing knee-deep in a rectangular hole. She watched as he grunted while stomping on his shovel, trying to dig it into the hard-packed soil. She walked over to him and cleared her throat. "Excuse me, monsieur," she said politely.

He stopped digging, leaned on his shovel, and looked up at her. Then he turned his face away, hawked noisily, and spit the soil up out of his lungs. He wiped the sweat off his forehead with his dirty sleeve and gave a toothless smile.

"Tell me, would you happen to know where the grave of Madeleine Dupré is?"

He screwed up his face thoughtfully for a moment, rubbing his unshaved chin as if that would help him remember. Then his eyes brightened and he pointed across the cemetery. "Over there, on the other side of the church. Third row from the wall, about in the center. It's got a small gray marker with a black plaque. I remember it because the stone was put in before the earth had a chance to settle."

She smiled her thanks and followed his directions. After a while she found the grave. She stood very still and looked down at it. The gravedigger had been right. Both the tombstone and the stone edging had been installed far too soon; they were sagging and the granite had cracked in three places as the earth underneath it had shifted. The little flowerbed in the center of the dirty gravel was sadly neglected. The weeds were even pushing up through the gravel. She looked at the graves on either side of it. They were both neatly tended, but the one on the right was big and lavishly planted. She set the pot down on the granite edging of Madame Dupré's grave and looked over at the neighboring one. The right side of the expensive, shiny headstone was blank, meaning that one of the spouses was still living. The left was inscribed in chiseled, gilt-filled letters:

PIERRE PÉGUY
1918–1955

Hélène's face clouded over and her eyes glittered. So he was dead. Of course the grave was well-tended, she thought resentfully. And she knew by whom. Tante Janine. Who else's devotion could be so blind? To her, Pierre had been some kind of saint. She shook her head slowly and looked back at Madame Dupré's sagging, overgrown grave. Then she hiked up the skirt of her Odile Joly suit, got to her knees, and began to tug at the weeds that grew from her friend's grave. Later, after she had finished and the earthenware pot of pink hydrangea was sunk halfway into the ground, she clapped the dirt off her hands and got to her feet. She surveyed her work. It helped somewhat, but it wasn't enough. Immediately she came to a decision. Before leaving, she would see the stonemason across the street about putting in a new border and a new headstone. Something nice and solid. And marble. Madame Dupré had appreciated quality.

Deftly Jeanne made shallow cuts on both sides of the small turbot. She sprinkled it with salt and pepper, dipped her fingers into the cup of congealed grease, and rubbed some sparingly on the fish. Then she carefully picked up the turbot by the head and the tail and laid it flat in the heavy iron baking pan, white side down. She opened the oven door and shoved the pan inside. There. At least there would be food to eat.

Things hadn't been going well since Petite Hélène had been born. She had fought Edmond and kept working at Au Petit Caporal right up until she was ready to give birth. Then a new girl had temporarily taken her place. Monsieur Boivin, the fat proprietor, had promised that her job would be waiting for her. When Petite Hélène was six months old, she had gone back to the restaurant to reclaim her job. Monsieur Boivin had hemmed and hawed and squirmed uncomfortably. Finally he had stammered that he couldn't fire the new girl. Her husband had just died and she was now the breadwinner of her family. Jeanne had nodded quietly and made the rounds looking for another job. There were none to be had.

Now she shrugged philosophically and turned around as she heard movement behind her. Petite Hélène was sitting in a corner, her little hands cautiously pawing through the pile of laundry. Her pink face was screwed up in deep wonder and curiosity as she inspected the colors and textures of the fabrics.

Jeanne cocked her head and studied her for a moment. There was something about watching your child that made you realize you were watching a little part of yourself. Strange, how quickly the little ones grew. It seemed only yesterday that she had pushed the child out of her womb and the midwife had held it up in the air by the legs and given it a resounding smack. She would never forget the joy she had felt when she had heard Petite Hélène's first angry cry. And now, more than ever, Petite Hélène was her pride and her joy. She was just at that age where they are getting into everything. Exploring, discovering, trying to grasp the feel of life, her tiny lips glum when the mysteries were too big to comprehend, the smiles wide with delight every time one. was solved. She was such a beautiful child, Jeanne thought. An angel, really. Her hair was neither brown nor golden, but aggressively red; yet each curly strand was as delicate as spun copper. Her eyes were big and blue and naturally wide with curiosity. Jeanne envied her. It would be years before she would find out what her lot would be—that she was poor, that the smell of fish in the walls of her home was not in homes everywhere.

More than three months ago, Edmond had left the fishing fleet and had gone to work at one of the new shipyards. The pay was much better, and they had both been happy about the job. Then, a month ago, the company went bankrupt. Ever since, something had gone out of Edmond. He seemed to be spending all his time at the taverns. There was no money for anything, but he always seemed to come up with enough for a drink. It wasn't until last week that she found out how. The wife of one of his friends had come to her, demanding that his loan be repaid.

There was a sudden hissing sound behind her. Quickly she spun around, the reality of the chore at hand forcing the thoughts out of her mind. The pot on top of the stove was boiling over. Instinctively she grabbed a rag and used it to lift the lid off. She picked up a fork and gently prodded a potato. It was soft and perfect. "Now, if only Edmond comes home on time," she said aloud, wiping her hands on her apron.

From out in the hallway she could hear someone knocking on the door. She felt a sudden chill. She listened carefully. The knocking came again. Quickly her mind raced over the possibilities of who it might be. Not Edmond; he always let himself in. No, it must be someone to whom they owed money. Not the landlady; Jeanne had already run into her earlier that morning, promising that it wouldn't be long. She wrung her hands in despair. There were so many people to whom they owed money. She sighed, went over to Petite Hélène, and picked her up. She tiptoed out into the hallway, put one hand over the child's mouth, and silently approached the door. Soundlessly she moved aside the hinged piece of metal that hung over the peephole. She blinked to make sure she wasn't dreaming. Then she let out a cry, threw aside the bolt, and flung the door open.

"Hélène!" she gasped.

"Jeanne!" Hélène stepped forward, wrapped her arms warmly around her sister-in-law, and kissed her. Then she stepped back to study Petite Hélène.

Jeanne smiled proudly and handed Petite Hélène over. "Look who's here, ma petite," she whispered. "Your aunt. See . . ."

Hélène took the child in her arms and held her tightly, swaying her back and forth. The tiny pink face broke out into an enormous smile.

"Come in, come in," Jeanne said quickly.

Hélène stepped inside and Jeanne closed the door, carefully locking it behind her. She led the way to the kitchen. "Make yourself comfortable," she said timidly. "I'm afraid everything's in a mess."

Hélène laughed. "Don't worry about it. It's my fault. I should have given you some notice instead of arriving on the spur of the moment."

"Nonsense!" Jeanne took Petite Hélène and sat her down on the dinette.

The tiny girl picked up a spoon and started tapping the table with it. "Tante Hélène! Tante Hélène! Tante Hélène!"

Jeanne and Hélène both began to laugh. "She knows my name," Hélène said.

"She'd better. I've been teaching it to her since the day she was born." Jeanne quickly slipped out of her apron and patted her hair. "She already knows more than thirty different words. She's a prodigy!" Then she took Hélène's hands in hers and her voice became suddenly sober. "I'm sorry about Stanislaw. I got your letter and heard the news. Even people here were talking about it."

"I can imagine," Hélène said dryly.

"I'm sorry we didn't send flowers." Jeanne looked away, her face suddenly red with shame. "But I wrote you a letter."

Hélène frowned. "That's strange. I never got it."

"I couldn't send it," Jeanne confessed in a quiet voice.

Hélène pulled Jeanne toward her in an embrace of understanding. "Are things that bad?" she asked softly.

Jeanne nodded miserably. "Things haven't been going well. In fact . . ." Suddenly she burst into tears.

Gently Hélène patted the back of Jeanne's head. "Do you want to talk about it?"

Jeanne nodded and wiped her eyes. "Au Petit Caporal . . . well, they wouldn't give me my job back after Petite Hélène was born. And Edmond quit the fishing fleet to work for a new shipbuilder. They went broke right away and ended up owing him three weeks pay."

Hélène listened in silence. "But why didn't you let me know?" she asked finally. "I would have sent you money."

"Edmond's stubborn, Hélène. He's so proud."

"That's ridiculous!" Hélène said angrily. "We're *family*. He should know that better than anyone! But don't you worry. You can stop crying now."

"Please . . . don't tell Edmond I told you," Jeanne begged.

"I promise I won't." Hélène smiled. "Come, now, your troubles are over."

"No." Jeanne sniffled and wiped her nose with her finger. "We're so far in the hole that we'll never be able to dig ourselves back out."

"Don't worry about that. I want you to make a list of all your creditors and give it to me. I'll take care of it. You won't even have to see them. And by the way . . ." She propelled Jeanne toward a chair, reached into her purse, and took out two thick envelopes. She handed one to Jeanne.

Jeanne looked up at her. "What's this?"

"You'll need to buy tickets, new clothes, new furniture. New *everything*."

Jeanne looked confused. "But . . . what are you talking about?"

Hélène gave her the second envelope. "And here's Edmond's tuition for the University of Paris."

"The . . . University of Paris?" Jeanne stared dumbly at the envelope.

"Did I forget to tell you?" Hélène said lightly. "There's an apartment waiting for you. It's just across the street from the Bois de Boulogne."

"But . . ." Jeanne could say no more, only stare at Hélène.

"Of course, there's a catch," Hélène said. "I've just started my own business."

"The magazine?" Jeanne asked in an awed voice.

"The magazine. When Edmond's finished with his schooling—it'll be a few years, of course—he has to help me.

I'll need a bright international lawyer I can trust." She looked around. "By the way, where *is* Edmond?"

Jeanne looked down at her hands. "Probably at the tavern," she said quietly.

"Good," Hélène said with finality. "Go and get dressed. We'll join him and a buy a round for everybody in the place."

TODAY

Saturday, January 13

1

Spruce Point was located on the Hudson a few miles upriver from West Point. It was set in a magnificent old park that sloped gently down to the railroad tracks along the river's edge. From uphill you could see the river. When you stood near the tracks, you couldn't. That was because a high stone wall separated them from the manicured lawns of Spruce Point.

From the road, Spruce Point Manor, set behind the stately blue spruces from which it took its name, looked just like it had for the past hundred-and-some years since a tin-can tycoon had erected the neoclassical folly. After his death and a much-contested will the white elephant had been sold and turned into an institution for special people. It was still a beautiful place, but there was something stifling about it. There were uniformed guards in the gatehouse, an electronic surveillance system, and the walls surrounding the property—once necessary to keep people out, now to keep them in—were high and in good repair. In a posher era, the residents of Spruce Point had dressed in furs and fabulous jewels, and the staff wore black-and-white uniforms. Now the residents looked neat but far from elegant, and the staff wore the smocks and uniforms of doctors and nurses.

At the entrance, one of the brown-uniformed guards hurried out of the gatehouse. He bent down to look through the passenger window of the long chauffeur-driven black limousine that had just pulled up. The tinted window lowered silently.

Z.Z. looked up at the guard through her dark sunglasses. "Mrs. Bavier," she said coldly. Nervously she flicked the ash from her cigarette into the ashtray. It missed and she brushed it off the seat with her fingers.

The guard consulted his clipboard. "Mrs. Bavier . . . yes, ma'am, you're expected." He signaled the second guard to open the gate. Quietly the iron doors swung open electronically. Then the Cadillac started to roll and drove past the gate and along the gravel drive between the blue spruces. The trees made the drive look dark and depressing. On an impulse, Z.Z. twisted around in her seat and looked out the rear window. Behind them, the gates were swinging shut again. She shuddered involuntarily. This place was a prison. The prison into which she had locked her . . . her *baby*.

Nervously she lit another cigarette with the butt of the old one. Her hands were shaking. What would Wilfred look like? she wondered. She had never seen him since that day in the hospital, ten years ago. The day he had been born.

Suddenly she felt a chill. Maybe he would recognize her. Maybe there would be a scene. Maybe he would go out of his mind and try to attack her. Maybe . . .

The limousine pulled to a halt in front of the colonnaded building and the chauffeur held the back door open. Flustered, Z.Z. reached for her black leather purse, pulled her mink collar closer around her neck and held it there as she got out.

A middle-aged woman with short brown bangs and large baby-blue eyes came down the portico steps. She wore a stiffly starched white smock and black leather pumps. "Mrs. Bavier?" she asked in a reassuring, friendly voice.

Z.Z. looked at her. "Yes," she replied hoarsely.

"The gate called and said that you were on your way. I'm Dr. Rogers. You had requested to see your son's doctor." She smiled and extended her hand. "I am she."

Limply Z.Z. shook the hand. For once, her self-assurance deserted her. "My . . ." She swallowed. "My . . . son's. . . . Yes."

"Won't you come in, Mrs. Bavier? We can talk in my office."

Z.Z. followed her up the stone steps and into the building. From outside, the mansion had looked neoclassical. Inside, the main hall was strictly Gothic. There were thick stone pillars, heavy dark paneling, and an oppressive vaulted ceiling. Suddenly she froze. A young nurse was leading a little boy down a corridor that branched off the main hall. Even through her sunglasses, Z.Z. could see him all too clearly. He was a boy, but close up he didn't really *look* like a boy. She winced and felt a tightness within her. He was short and

442

overweight. His eyes were close-set and slanted, his forehead flattened. His tongue was hanging out.

Dr. Rogers turned to Z.Z. "Could you please excuse me for a moment?"

Z.Z. couldn't speak. She nodded dumbly and watched her child approach the child.

"Hello, Stephen," Dr. Rogers said in a friendly voice. She squatted down so that her face was level with his. "Where are you going?"

He stared at her. When he spoke, his words sounded thick and labored, and his mouth twisted into a kind of smile. "I'm going to the craft shop."

Z.Z. forced herself to shut her eyes. What kind of monsters did they keep in this place? Oh, God, why had she come? Why hadn't she just let sleeping dogs lie? Why?

But she knew why. It was because the battle for HJII—for the destruction of Hélène Junot—reopened all the old wounds. It was because she had to *see* what Hélène had put her through. What she had made her suffer alone, without Sigi.

". . . and you be a good boy." Dr. Rogers tousled the child's straight black hair. Then she came back to Z.Z. "I'm sorry to have kept you waiting." She smiled. "But Stephen needs a little love every now and then."

Z.Z. nodded wordlessly.

Dr. Roger's office was off the main hall. It was a small low-ceilinged room with an enormous stone fireplace and more dark paneling. The metal filing cabinets and the teak-and-chrome desk looked out-of-place.

Dr. Rogers gestured for Z.Z. to take a seat in an armchair. Then she went behind her desk and sat in the swivel chair. "I must admit that your appointment to see Wilfred came as a surprise, Mrs. Bavier. Wilfred has been here for ten years, and this is your first visit." Dr. Rogers paused.

Wordlessly Z.Z. snapped open her purse and lit a cigarette. Her hands were shaking.

Dr. Rogers continued. "Your request for a visit specifically stated that you do not wish your son to know your identity. We will respect that wish." She looked at Z.Z. rather queerly. "You know, in a way, he rather looks like you."

Z.Z. stiffened. Rigidly she put her splayed fingers on the arms of her chair and started to rise.

"Please, Mrs. Bavier," Dr. Rogers said. "Do stay. I assure

you that Wilfred is quite normal physically. Except for the unfortunate fact that his brain is damaged, he is quite like any other boy his age. It would be unfortunate if you did not at least see him."

Slowly Z.Z. nodded. "Where is he right now?"

"In the craft shop."

"You mean with that . . . that . . ." Z.Z.'s voice cracked.

Dr. Rogers folded her hands on the desktop. "You mean, with Stephen?" she asked in a soothing voice.

Z.Z. nodded.

"Yes, with Stephen and quite a few of our other residents. Crafts are very popular here at Spruce Point. Stephen and Wilfred are good friends, actually. There is nothing wrong with Stephen except that he had the misfortune to be born a mongoloid."

Z.Z. smoked in silence.

"Do not worry about the residents intermingling. They do so constantly. Indeed, we encourage it. However, there is always a member of our trained staff on hand. You see, the residents are all quite harmless. To them, Spruce Point is not only their home, it is their *world*. Very few of them have ever been to the 'outside' as we call it. Their world consists entirely of the fifteen acres that comprise Spruce Point. Most of our residents have no desire to leave here. They feel safe inside these walls. In fact, the majority of them would be terrified at the prospect of going 'outside.' "

"And Wilfred?" Z.Z.'s voice was a whisper.

"Wilfred is slow but quite normal," Dr. Rogers said carefully. "He has expressed a desire for adventure."

Z.Z. leaned forward and stubbed out her cigarette. "I think I'd just better—"

"Please, Mrs. Bavier. I am not trying to put you on the spot. Just because you have expressed a desire to see your son doesn't obligate you to take him home with you."

"Does he . . . know who he is?"

"He knows nothing about his family," Dr. Rogers said gently.

"Has he . . . ?"

"Asked? Yes. Many of our residents are naturally curious. But your instructions were to keep his identity a secret." Dr. Rogers smiled warmly. "Shall we go and see him?"

Z.Z. nodded and slowly rose. She was glad that she was wearing sunglasses. They hid the moistness in her eyes.

Dr. Rogers led the way to the craft shop. When they got there, she opened the door and motioned for one of the supervisors to come out into the hall. A pretty young woman with fair hair appeared. She was wearing a smock. Z.Z. took off her sunglasses and tried to see past her into the room, but the door closed quickly.

Dr. Rogers introduced the pretty young woman as Janet Kovacs, the arts-and-crafts teacher. As soon as she saw Z.Z., a flicker of recognition showed in her eyes. Z.Z. noticed it. "Is something the matter?" she asked.

Quickly Janet Kovacs recovered. She shook her head. "No, it's nothing," she said softly. "I'm sorry."

On an impulse, Z.Z. put her sunglasses back on. For some reason, Dr. Rogers seemed to view this gesture with approval. Then she cleared her throat and turned to the teacher. "Would it be possible for us to observe the class without attracting undue attention?"

Janet Kovacs glanced at Z.Z. and thought for a moment. "I don't see why not," she said finally. "The residents are quite wrapped up in their projects. I doubt they'll pay much attention to you other than showing natural signs of curiosity. I do suggest that you stay near the door. That way, they'll be less likely to be distracted."

Dr. Rogers nodded. "Very well." Then she turned to Z.Z. and gave her a reassuring smile. "Let's go in."

Janet Kovacs opened the door and they followed her inside. Z.Z. looked around the noisy room in horror. She was suddenly dizzy. To her, this room looked like the devil's workshop. Painting, needlecraft, macrame, pottery; arts and crafts of every sort were being worked on. But it was not the projects that made her feel faint. It was the people doing them.

They were of all sizes and ages. Some were mentally retarded, some were mongoloids, some had birth defects, others had been struck down by accidents or disease. One small girl in a corner had no arms or legs, only a head and torso. Studiously she was drawing with a felt-tipped pen clenched between her teeth. Next to her, Stephen was sitting at the potter's wheel laboriously working on a piece of clay, and his already contorted face was screwed up even more in concentration. By the window overlooking the Hudson sat an old man in a wheelchair. He had multiple sclerosis. His body was as twisted out of shape as the wreckage of an automobile. For a moment Z.Z. could only stare at him.

These were some of the nameless residents of Spruce Point. They all went by their first names; their surnames were kept secret even from themselves. Only the older ones who had been struck down by disease knew who they were. The rest did not. Neither did Z.Z. She only knew that they all came from the "best" families. Their last names were those of people who moved in lofty circles, people listed in the *Social Register* or the *Celebrity Register*. People who owned Fortune 500 corporations or who made it big in politics or in the performing arts. It was ironic that the residents of Spruce Point were the would-be heirs to some of the largest fortunes in America. But they would never claim these fortunes. Spruce Point was their prison.

Suddenly Z.Z. noticed that the man in the wheelchair was modeling for a painting. She glanced over at the canvas and winced. For a long time she couldn't take her eyes off it. It was a horrible painting and yet it was beautiful. Its depiction of the twisted, crumpled body looked abstract in its very realism. Somehow it managed to convey raw power in the useless, tortured limbs. But more than just power; there was a fierce anger, and compassion, too. Tears sprang to her eyes. Then she caught her breath. She saw the artist.

He had his back to her. In his right hand he held a paintbrush. His hair was honey-colored—just like hers! My God! she thought. Wilfred! For a moment she felt a surge of maternal love. She wanted to rush toward him and throw her arms around him. Beg for his forgiveness. Promise to take him home. But she was frozen.

Suddenly he turned around. For an instant she felt the floor beginning to spin. She caught herself on the door frame.

Wilfred's retardation wasn't the worst part. The worst was his perfect face. Now she understood why Janet Kovacs had been so startled, why Dr. Rogers thought her wearing sunglasses was a good idea.

Dr. Rogers had been right. Wilfred looked absolutely normal. But the cruelest irony of all was that he looked like Z.Z. She had been prepared to come face-to-face with a horribly misshapen mutant like Stephen, or someone contorted like the man in the wheelchair. But instead, it seemed that nature had compensated for Wilfred's brain damage by giving him an extraordinarily beautiful face. He was by far the most handsome boy she had ever seen.

For a moment he stared at her. The sudden pain in his intelligent eyes seemed to burn straight through her.

Z.Z. clutched Dr. Rogers. "Get me out of here!" she whispered hoarsely. "For God's sake, get me *out*!"

2

The Chameleon had no trouble finding the place he was looking for. It was located in Westchester County, just a short drive north from Mount Kisco. When he reached it, he pulled his rented black Ford over on the shoulder, rolled down the window, and looked out. Here a narrow private drive branched off from the road. It led up to a white house set a quarter of a mile back behind some bare old oaks. At the entrance to the drive stood a big painted sign: "PAUL ROEBUCK, Master Trainer/Kennels."

A twisted smile crossed the Chameleon's lips. Yes, this was the place. Expertly he put the car in reverse, then made a left turn, forward into the drive, and drove up to the house. It was one of those colonial-style wooden buildings with a porch running all the way around it. Parked up front were a station wagon and a white van with the legend "PAUL ROEBUCK KENNELS" painted on the side. He pulled in behind the van, got out, and approached the house. When he stepped up on the porch, he found a huge German shepherd guarding the front door. Its watchful dark eyes were oddly hostile. It didn't move, but it let out a low, menacing growl. It smelled danger.

The Chameleon smiled with contempt. He never could understand what people saw in dogs. They were noisy and dumb and dirty. Still, they had their uses, he supposed. Just like he had a use for one now.

Giving the dog no more than a cursory glance, the Chameleon lit a cigarette and pressed the bell. Melodious chimes tinkled somewhere inside the house.

A tall, heavy set blond man opened the door. "Mr. Samuels?" he said easily.

The Chameleon smiled and nodded as they shook hands.

As he had expected, the man's grip was strong and firm. "I'm Erik Roebuck," he said.

The Chameleon still smiled, but he was silent for a moment. Erik Roebuck? This was something his research had overlooked. He felt like kicking himself for being so sloppy. Not that it made any difference. But in the future he'd have to be more careful. One silly mistake like that, and in the wrong situation, could mean curtains. He laughed softly. "I'm sorry," he said apologetically. "You just threw me. I was under the impression you were Paul Roebuck."

"So are many people. Paul Roebuck is my father. He founded this place twenty-five years ago. Last spring he decided to retire, and I took over for him. I hope you're not disappointed."

The Chameleon puckered his lips thoughtfully. "I was counting on getting one of his dogs."

Roebuck smiled warmly, showing straight white teeth. "Have no fears, Mr. Samuels," he said reassuringly. "My father did not restrict his training to canines. He personally trained every man who works here. That includes me."

The Chameleon smiled. "Good. Your word is enough. Now, let me explain a few things to you, if I may."

"Certainly," Roebuck said as he went behind the desk. "Won't you have a seat?"

The Chameleon sat down in the vinyl chair and made himself comfortable. He took out another cigarette and lit it. Then he looked Roebuck straight in the eye and began to recite the cover story he had come up with. "Let me be frank with you, Mr. Roebuck. My wife and I recently moved here from California, and we live near Port Washington. In a rather secluded neighborhood, I might add. I'm a businessman, and unfortunately, my work requires that I travel a great deal of the time. Sometimes for weeks on end. And my wife is frightened when she's left alone." He smiled sadly and spread his hands apart. "So I'm here."

"And you want a watchdog?"

"Precisely. Something that has both a bark and a bite."

Roebuck folded his hands and looked down at his cuticles.

"Tell me something, Mr. Samuels," he said. "Do you like dogs?"

Better to play this one straight, the Chameleon decided. The animal would instinctively sense his dislike and give him away. He shook his head. "I'm afraid I really don't care much for them."

Roebuck nodded. "You'd be surprised to find out how many people lie when I ask that question." He smiled. "Exactly what kind of dog is it that you're looking for?"

The Chameleon shrugged and pretended to think. He wanted a black Great Dane, or maybe a Doberman, but he wasn't about to say so. Let Roebuck suggest the breed, and he would think it was his own idea. "Oh . . . just something mean-looking and big. Size is no problem, since the dog will have a lot of running-around space. We have a large property, fenced in I might add. Probably short-haired . . . yes, Amanda would like that." Good touch, that "Amanda." Now his wife had a name.

Roebuck frowned. "We have quite a few short-haired breeds to choose from." He waved at the pictures on the wall. "Why don't you take a look and tell me what appeals to you?"

The Chameleon got to his feet and made a pretense of studying the photos. Finally he smiled helplessly. "It's really not my line. What do you suggest?"

"Either a Doberman or a Great Dane. Both are short-haired and fast." Roebuck smiled and got to his feet. "Would you like to go down to the kennels and see one in action? Then I'll let you decide."

A moment later they left the house and went outside. In silence Roebuck led the way and they started down a frozen dirt path to the base of the hill where the kennels were located. As they approached, the wind brought their scent toward the dogs, and suddenly they all jumped up and began to claw excitedly at the fences. The cacophony of howling and barking filled the air.

"They can smell us coming," Roebuck explained.

When they reached the nearest building, a man was there waiting for them, smiling brightly. "This is Edward," Roebuck told the Chameleon. "He's the best trainer here." Then he looked at Edward. "Bring Rufus out into the pen."

Edward's smile faded. "Rufus?"

Roebuck nodded curtly. There was no mistaking the authority in that gesture.

Edward shook his head and shrugged. Without another word he went inside the building.

Roebuck put his hands in his pockets and smiled at the Chameleon. "The pen is on the other side of the building." He led the way around the corner to the far side of the kennels. Here was the huge three-sided pen. One side of it was actually the wall of the building; the other three sides were ten-foot-high, heavy-duty mesh wire attached to sturdy steel posts. Roebuck opened a gate and they went in.

"It won't take Edward but a minute," Roebuck promised.

The Chameleon nodded patiently. He looked at Roebuck with interest. "This Rufus," he said slowly. "What's so special about him?"

Roebuck's voice was soft. "Rufus is no ordinary dog, Mr. Samuels. He's quite intelligent. He's also big and well-trained. Depending on what you instruct, he can either be gentle or mean." He paused. "He's also capable of killing a man."

The Chameleon stared at him. He was digesting this welcome piece of news in silence when Edward came out of the building leading a black Great Dane. The Chameleon studied the animal closely. Little as he knew about dogs, he could tell that this one was exceptional. Rufus looked as big as a horse but moved with the lithe grace of a swan. His bulging, taut muscles stood out clearly under gleaming short hair.

Roebuck reached into his pocket and took out a small object.

The Chameleon glanced at it. "What's that?"

Roebuck held it out. "This is a sonic dog whistle," he explained. "You and I can't hear it because our ears can't catch certain high-pitched decibels. But Rufus can. When I give two short blows, Rufus attacks. When I give a long, drawn-out one, he retreats. Watch closely." He raised the whistle to his lips, inflated his cheeks, and blew.

Rufus suddenly perked up. For a split second his ears quivered; then he trotted complacently over to them, his tail wagging.

"Sit!" Roebuck commanded in a stern voice.

The dog immediately sat, looking up at Roebuck with a questioning look in his shiny black eyes. He was an alert dog, all right, the Chameleon noticed. Then he looked over at Edward. The trainer was going back inside the building. A few minutes later, he came out again, thick, bulky padding strapped around his arms, chest, and legs. Suddenly Rufus was emitting a low, steady growl, his alert eyes concentrated on Edward, but he remained obediently seated.

"Ready?" Roebuck called out.

"Ready!" Edward shouted back.

With quickening interest the Chameleon watched the dog as Roebuck blew twice into the silent whistle. Then it happened. Rufus sprang forward and went flying down the length of the pen toward Edward. Instinctively the trainer held up his padded arms to cover his face. Seconds later, the beast collided with him, attacking in a frenzy and knocking him to the ground. The fierce snarls were carried away by the wind and sounded strangely distant, almost too quiet. For a moment the Chameleon winced. The Great Dane was sinking its teeth into the trainer's padding. Edward went rolling around, trying to protect himself, but it was impossible. Rufus was a powerful brute. He was trying to rip the padding to shreds.

The Chameleon shook his head. God help that dog's victims, he thought with new respect. Even a pro wrestler would be no match for him. And a woman? A woman would be finished off in a minute. Maybe less.

Once again Roebuck raised the whistle to his lips and blew deeply. Rufus immediately froze in his tracks. Then he looked in their direction and came trotting obediently back to them, his tail wagging. His mouth was lolling open and he was panting from the exertion, his breath making clouds of vapor as saliva dripped to the ground. For an instant the Chameleon caught sight of long white fangs.

"Sit!" Roebuck commanded. The dog sat, and he scratched it behind the ears. "Good boy, Rufus," he said gently. "Good boy."

The Chameleon's eyes wandered down toward the end of the pen. Edward was getting nimbly to his feet, unbuckling the padding.

Roebuck turned to the Chameleon. "Satisfied, Mr. Samuels?"

The Chameleon suppressed a smile. Was he satisfied! That

451

dog was perfect! It was a walking time bomb. It would tear Hélène Junot to shreds.

His voice soft, the Chameleon looked Roebuck deep in the eyes and said, "Sure thing, Mr. Roebuck. I'll take Rufus—he's exactly what I want."

YESTERDAY

V

BLACKMAIL

1

Paris, 1958

Lubov Tcherina, editor-in-chief of *Les Modes*, knocked on the door with her characteristic impatience, flung it open, stalked briskly into Hélène's office, and shut the door behind her with a decidedly firm *snap*. Hélène smiled up at her and put aside the marketing report she had been studying. She folded her hands on the desktop. "You wanted to see me, Luba?"

Luba's cracked-plaster face, with its apple-red rouged cheeks and most determined of determined chins thrust indignantly forward, was set into the haughtily ominous expression that Hélène knew could only mean she was on the warpath. With a quick motion of her hand, Luba snatched her shocking pink framed glasses off her regal nose. She threw the layouts she was carrying under her arm down on Hélène's desk.

"Yes!" Luba's voice was shrilly dramatic. She waved a quivering red-lacquered finger at the layouts. "These . . . these *things*!" she said, her red cheeks getting even redder under the flush of her outrage. "You're not really serious about printing them!"

Hélène smiled at her and picked up the artboards. Quickly she glanced through them. They were for the June-July issue and showed the summer collections. The photos were crisp and clear, the vacant-eyed models in starkly dramatic poses. Jacques had them wading around in the Neptune basin at Versailles, hiking their chic dresses and skirts up above their knees.

"Yes," Hélène said. "I think they're very good."

Luba vented a volcanic sigh. "Don't you *see*?"

Hélène looked at her with a puzzled expression. "See what?"

"They're so . . . so *ordinary*." Luba rolled the distasteful word on her tongue as if it were poison.

Hélène couldn't help smiling at Luba's overdramatizations. Everything about the woman was bigger than life. Her voice, her gestures, her looks. A White Russian refugee, whose voice was a strangely exotic mixture of mispronunciations and foreign dialects, Luba possessed a face and figure that were one of a kind. Ordinarily she would have been a tall, bone-thin woman with a long neck like all other tall, bone-thin women with long necks. But Luba was not content with that. She *worked* at her looks. She dyed her hair so pitch black that it gleamed like shoe polish, she painted her eyes with an astonishing amount of mascara, shadow, and eyeliner, and she used rouge like it was going out of style. Most important, she knew how to look vibrant, and that was what made the ugly duckling into a swan. She could never be a beautiful swan, but she settled for second best by becoming an exceptional swan. She shone like ten layers of lacquer, dressed herself in the most unusual finery—Japanese kimonos, Persian robes, Prussian boots trimmed with gold lace, scarlet dresses with purple furs—and could command the attention of an auditorium full of people. If Luba ever went to an auditorium, that is. She went to theaters, fancy-dress balls, important openings. People might have laughed at her, but her style was so deadly serious, so highly original, so indisputably tasteful despite the costumy effects, that she created new trends and styles wherever she went. One word from Luba could make or break a designer's collection.

Being editor-in-chief of a fashion magazine was a natural for Luba. The only pity was that the world lost a potentially great couturière or costume designer in the process. Still, she was already a legend in her own time. In the trade, she was reverently nicknamed "The Czarina." She had been editor-in-chief at *Marie Claire Elle*, and *L'Officiel* for years at a time. She had charted bold new courses in fashion reporting with the same inimitable flair she used in transforming herself.

A little over a year ago, Lubov Tcherina had been fired from her last job—legend had it she had been vacationing at a posh villa in Costa Smeralda when one of the houseboys brought a telephone to the poolside. She swam over and picked up the receiver. It was her magazine. It had just undergone a change in management. "You're fired," she was told, and Luba promptly sank to the bottom of the pool and nearly drowned. Hélène considered herself lucky on two counts. The houseboy was alarmed by the bubbles rising from the bottom of the pool and dived in. The Czarina was saved by mouth-to-mouth resuscitation and joined the staff at *Les Modes*.

Now Hélène carefully studied the artboards Luba had brought in. "I don't see anything wrong with them," she said carefully.

Luba threw her hands up in the air in frustration. "Summer dresses in the Neptune basin? No no, *no*! They should be on a *glacier*. On a mountain peak. An *ice* floe. In a refrigerator. This is too ordinary. Too *trite*."

Hélène slowly nodded and pursed her lips thoughtfully. She could see what Luba was getting at. More drama was called for. These photos were good, but they were staid. Almost benign. *Elle* and *L'Officiel* might have done them. And if that was the case, then *Les Modes* was certainly not going to become the leader of the world's fashion magazines.

Still, these boards had already been laid out, the copy written. Everything was ready to go to the printer in two days' time. Already the August *Les Modes* was being worked on. Each issue was completed six months before the public ever saw it. Hélène gestured for Luba to stay put. She thought for a moment, frowned and quickly pressed down on her intercom buzzer.

Her secretary's efficient voice came over the wire like a distorted squawk. "Oui, mademoiselle?"

Hélène was now going by her maiden name and insisted on being called mademoiselle instead of madame. She leaned forward and spoke directly into the box. "Eleonora, call up the travel agency. Make arrangements for . . . ten?" She glanced at Luba, who nodded pontifically. "For ten to . . ." She thought quickly.

"Chamonix," Luba said in a stage whisper. "I've already checked. They have plenty of glaciers and *cable* cars." Her dark eyes glittered wickedly.

"To Chamonix, Eleonora. Leaving tonight, returning the day after tomorrow. Make overnight arrangements at a decent hotel."

"Oui, mademoiselle."

"And, Eleonora?"

"Oui?"

"Order me a new intercom," Hélène said irritably. "One of

the new American ones. I like to be able to hear what you're saying."

"Oui, mademoiselle." Eleonora buzzed off.

Hélène looked up at Luba sternly. "Now, about those cable cars and Jacques. I want *no* accidents. *No* scandals. *No* broken bones. And *no* hysterical models marching in here in tears. I know the way Jacques works only too well."

Luba smiled malevolently and picked up the artboards.

"You may throw those away," Hélène said.

Luba sniffed the air disdainfully. "*Gladly,*" she announced, as if it were her moral duty to march straight to the nearest trashcan.

Hélène watched her leave. She knew that Luba's taste was unerring, as inbred as a champion's pedigree. Still, she couldn't get over the feeling that the older woman was constantly testing her. Almost challenging her power to see how far she could go. Hélène sighed. As far as her work was concerned, she trusted Luba explicitly. The only thing Luba would have to learn was how to descend from her lofty heights every once in a while and show a little more respect for those she worked for.

Hélène pushed her chair back and got to her feet. She came around from behind her desk and walked over to the wall where a blowup of this month's *Les Modes* cover was carefully spotlighted. She stared up at it. She had now seen it hundreds of times. During production, on the printer's proofs, on every kiosk she passed in the streets. It was the twelfth issue. Could that be possible? she wondered. Had *Les Modes* already been going strong for over a year? They put out ten issues annually; June-July and December-January were counted as one each. That meant they had been covering the French fashion scene for fourteen months already.

She studied the oversized cover as critically as she had studied all the others. She liked seeing them this big. It was easier to recognize the flaws and make certain they did not recur in the future. This particular enlargement was from the December-January issue. The glossy logo had been specially done to look like clear ice. It read:

LES MODES®
Paris

Decembre-Janvier

Centered at the bottom were more ice-cube block letters:

Spécial
Pour une nuit d'hiver

For a winter's night. She liked the theme. She herself had come up with the idea. The glossy close-up photo showed a model from the neck up. The huge stand-up collar of a Max Reby Chat lynx framed her leonine face. Her dark hair was like a mane speckled with glistening snowflakes, and her makeup was frosty, the lipstick almost pinkish-white, the Lancôme eye shadow glistening frost against the rich bronzé makeup cream. The combination was tawny; the model looked like an aggressive tigress ready to stalk the night.

Hélène congratulated herself. It was the best cover to date. Much better than the current *Vogue*. Quickly she crossed over to her desk and pushed down on the intercom again. "Eleonora?"

"Oui, mademoiselle?"

"Call the art department. Tell them to put a hold on the June-July cover."

"Consider it done."

Hélène smiled to herself. She could count on Jacques and Luba coming back from Chamonix with a spectacular new cover shot. On an impulse, she lifted a current copy of *Les Modes* off the stack beside her desk. She opened it, and as her eyes skimmed the masthead, she felt a rush of proprietorial authority and pride.

Decembre 1957/Janvier 1958   *No. 12*

LES MODES

est publié par Les Éditions Hélène Junot S.A.
Président-Directeur Général: HÉLÈNE JUNOT
Directeur des Éditions: NICOLAS DUCOUT
Rédactrice en Chef: LUBOV TCHERINA

She smiled. No matter what anyone tried to tell you, there was nothing like seeing your name in print. Slowly she flipped through the 168 pages. Even now, she could still feel a surge of electricity every time she turned a page.

To date, each issue of *Les Modes* had sold out before the first half of the month was over. Not a single copy had ever been returned from the newsstands. In fact, there was such a demand for *Les Modes* that the distributor was pressing Hélène for an increased run each printing. But Hélène was playing it cautiously. When they'd begun, it had been with a small first run of thirty thousand copies. Even then, she'd kept her fingers crossed. Now they were printing and selling out almost seven times that number. She knew that it was better to have people clamoring for more copies than being stuck with a warehouse full of unsalables. She was cautious, but she shrewdly coupled caution with daring. It was paying off. The first ten issues had been in the red, issue eleven had broken even, and now *Les Modes* was truly in the black for the very first time. Hélène knew that that wasn't bad for a magazine starting off from scratch. In fact, it wasn't bad for any new business. Sometimes it took three to five years before they showed a significant profit. She was very pleased. *Les Modes* was turning out to be a good investment.

Hélène nodded to herself. All in all, it was a magazine to be proud of. And slowly the monopoly of fashion publishers—*Vogue, L'Officiel, Elle,* and *Marie Claire*—who in the beginning had sneered contemptuously at her, were now starting to sit up and take notice. And well they should. A good number of their previously ardent readers were deserting them for *Les Modes.* Already they were feeling the bite.

The intercom sounded noisily. "Yes, Eleonora?"

"Monsieur Ducout is here. And there's a message from a Karl Häberle. He said to tell you that he's here in Paris and staying at the Sèze."

Karl Häberle was in Paris? That took Hélène completely by surprise. Suddenly she stiffened. He had found something. Why else would he have come? She knew of the Sèze. It was one of the moderately priced tourist hotels. She thought quickly.

The man awaiting her was Nicolas Ducout, her managing editor. Excepting herself, he was the most important person on the staff. Even more important than the Czarina. Because when it came down to brass tacks, it was circulation, money, and power that really counted. The first-rate quality, art, and layout were important, but the salesmanship had to come first. She had set up this meeting with him in order to discuss foreign distribution of *Les Modes* and the possibility of planning an Italian-language edition within a year.

She came to a swift decision. "Eleonora, tell Nicolas to have a seat and wait. I won't be long. Then call the Sèze and get hold of Karl Häberle. I need to talk to him right away!"

2

"I don't know what to do," Hélène said quietly. She got to her feet and paced the room restlessly. "At first, I thought it would be clear-cut and simple. But now?" She clenched one of her fists and smacked it into the palm of her other hand. "Now, I just don't *know*."

Dr. Rosen took a deep breath as he looked down at the papers scattered across the scarred desktop. He was sitting stock-still on one of the cane-backed chairs in his book-lined study. From the distance came the muffled sounds of traffic. Behind him, the curtains drawn across the window shifted slowly as they caught an elusive draft. Outside, it was dark already. Night came early in winter.

Hélène stopped pacing and watched him in silence. Behind his wire-rimmed glasses, his heavily hooded eyes were wide in horror. For the first time, she was aware of how old he really was, how truly overburdened his narrow, stooped shoulders must be. Perhaps she had been wrong in coming to him, she thought suddenly. He had already suffered so much. She should never have added to it with this. Right in front of her eyes, he seemed to have aged ten years. Even his black-and-gray hair and beard now looked much more gray than before, and the deeply furrowed skin of his face seemed to be stretched tightly across his bones. The muscles in his temples did a series of twitches.

For a moment Dr. Rosen could not speak. It was as if keeping himself under control was all he could hope to do. When he looked back up at her, she could see the tears glistening in the corners of his eyes. Once again he looked down at the papers. Everything blurred. He couldn't even see the papers on the desk clearly. Slowly he reached up and lifted his glasses off the bridge of his nose, wiped the tears from his eyes with his fingertips, and let the glasses sit back down on their prominent Roman perch. Then with a trembling hand he somehow summoned the courage to reach out and shuffle through the papers.

Hélène had never expected Häberle to come up with what he had. She had seen to it that the two hundred thousand deutsche marks she had deposited in the Dresdener Bank in Cologne had been released to him. He well deserved the reward. She wondered how he had ever managed to dig up this much dirt.

There were several photos. One had been taken recently with a telephoto lens. It showed a man in a business suit stepping into a late-model Mercedes-Benz limousine. Despite the graininess of the blowup, she had no doubt who it was. The colorless skin, the skull-shaped head, the bloodless cruel lips spoke for themselves. He was the white-faced one. Karl von Eiderfeld. The one who had ordered Schmidt to burn Marie. The one she herself had seen through the knothole of the dumbwaiter as he had ordered Maman to be "punished."

There were three other photos. Older photos, with dog-eared corners and ragged edges. All of them showed von Eiderfeld in the sleek black uniform with the silver piping. In one, he was standing among a group of men posing for the camera. Written on the back in neat Gothic script was the legend: *(Links zu Rechts): Goebbels, von Eiderfeld, Göring, Hitler, Himmler.* The photo was dated 1935 and von Eiderfeld looked almost youthful. In another, he was standing in an open SS staff car parked by a roadside, watching as an SS unit went by in single file. The men had rifles slung over their shoulders and were pushing bicycles. The third photo showed him with two other officers inspecting a platoon of rigid infantrymen. That one was taken in 1944, and he looked considerably older.

Just seeing those photographs was enough to make Hélène feel a terrible rage. It was poetic justice, she thought, that another German with the same first name as his should have come up with all this evidence.

But there was much more than just the photos. Häberle's search had turned up nineteen different documents, which he had painstakingly translated into French. Most of them were Nazi reports and requisition forms, but one was a copy of Karl von Eiderfeld's military record. Hélène had studied it closely. Karl Jürgen von Eiderfeld had been born in Rüdesheim on the Rhine in 1915. His father had been a general in the Kaiser's army and his mother had been the daughter of a Viennese merchant. In 1932 Karl von Eiderfeld had joined the SS. Almost immediately, the organization had been officially disbanded by the Weimar government. Three months later, when the SS was reinstated, Karl von Eiderfeld had joined once again. He started off on the right foot. Hitler had tried to gain an aura of respectability for the SS by recruiting members of the aristocracy, church dignitaries, and former generals to hold honorary rank. Von Eiderfeld's long-retired father had taken one such rank and had thereby managed to pull enough strings that his son rose quickly within the rigid hierarchy of this army which had been built upon a bastardization of the principles of the Order of the Jesuits. Karl von Eiderfeld had everything going for him. He was considered an outstanding officer and had been decorated numerous times. Then, in 1944, his promotions stopped abruptly and he had been transferred to the Belzec Concentration Camp in Poland. The new job was punishment for having failed what had been considered a simple mission: despite all the resources available to him, he had been unable to find two of four French children who had fled a house in Paris after wounding one German soldier and killing another.

Hélène had closed her eyes. She didn't have to see the names listed. She knew very well who those two French children had been. But there they were on the document, jumping out at her from the German type.

Edmond Junot . . . Hélène Junot. There was something obscene about their being listed in this hellish document.

Von Eiderfeld's short career at Belzec was well-documented by the other papers. He had been the deputy military liaison between the death camp and private industry. There were requisition forms and correspondence signed by him. A receipt for a trainload of Zyclon B crystals from I. G. Farben. Approval for new, fast-burning incinerator devices from Topf and Sohn in Wiesbaden. The crystals had been used for gassing victims in the chambers, the oven to burn their bodies. The last order for a new consignment of Zyclon B had been signed a scant three weeks before Belzec was liberated. That was the most terrible thing of all. Even when it was clear that everything was lost, the Germans had done nothing to stop the senseless horrors. Almost everywhere, the wheels of destruction kept on turning until the very end.

Dr. Rosen sighed painfully and pushed the papers away. The tears came into his eyes again. "This is a powder keg," he said at last. He took off his glasses and slowly put them back in their case.

Hélène nodded slowly. "I know," she whispered. "Even I had no idea there'd be all this."

He looked up at her. "What are you going to do?"

She came closer, sat down again, and looked across the desk at him. "I don't know," she said honestly. "I'll have to think about it." She glanced down at the papers and twisted her lips. "I've thought of going to the Israeli authorities."

He lifted his eyebrows. "And?"

"I'm afraid they wouldn't punish him enough. I mean, there's bound to be a big trial and a lot of publicity. But the worst he'd get is to be hung or electrocuted or shot." She gave a bitter shrug. "I don't know if that's enough."

Dr. Rosen's voice was gentle. "What would be enough as far as you're concerned?"

She reached suddenly across the table and dug her hand into his wrist. Her eyes were hard and relentless. "I want him to suffer," she whispered vehemently. "I want him to live in constant fear. He keeps himself well-hidden. When he leaves his house, he's driven directly to the garage of his office building in Düsseldorf. From there, a private elevator whisks him upstairs to his penthouse office. Few people have ever even seen him. He allows no pictures to be taken. Karl Häberle told me he posed as a reporter wanting to do an article on him for *Der Spiegel*. Not only could he not get near him, but he was warned off. Von Eiderfeld's scared, Simon. But I want him to run even *more* scared." She grabbed some of the papers, held them up, and shook them angrily. "I want to let him know I have *these*. I want to make certain he won't be able to sleep nights. I want him to worry himself sick for as long as he lives!"

Dr. Rosen heaved a big sigh. His face wore a fixed expression of sadness. "The dispensation of justice is a heavy burden," he said simply, "and vengeance an even heavier one. It exacts more from the judge than the judged."

She looked at him and nodded. He was right. The hold she had over Hubert proved that. Was it punishment enough just to dangle a constant threat over someone? The last time she'd forced Hubert to attend a meeting at Les Editions Hélène Junot, S.A., it seemed she had been more miserable than he. In fact, he had constantly challenged and taunted her to see just how far he could go.

Dr. Rosen patted her hand. "Think it over well," he advised in a gentle voice. "Don't rush into anything."

"I won't," she promised. "I'll wait until I've managed to get over some of my immediate anger. But somewhere, somehow, he's got to be made to pay!"

3

She looked out the window of the taxi as it swung onto the quiet elegance of the Boulevard Maillot. In front of the Comte's town house, she saw the familiar Rolls-Royce parked under the streetlamp.

She twisted around in her seat and looked back at the house. The lights shone in all the windows. That meant the Comte was in town.

For a moment she wished she had found Edmond a different apartment than the one on the Boulevard Maurice Barrès. The trouble was, she always had to pass the Boulevard Maillot in order to get there, because the two short streets were actually part of the same long one that ran across the top of the Bois de Boulogne. There was only one way to get around it. In the future, she'd instruct her taxi driver to make a wide detour and come down along the Ancien Cimetière de Neuilly.

It was she who had decided that Edmond should live on the Boulevard Maurice Barrès. The location had seemed only natural. Petite Hélène would be practically across the street from the Jardin d'Acclimatation with its small zoo, amusement park, ponds, Enchanted River, and the Bois de Boulogne. It was the perfect place for a child to grow up. Where else was there the same enchanting mixture of city, nature, and fantasy? She had figured—rightly—that the chances of her ever running into the Comte were almost non-existent. He was not the type of man who wasted time walking around the Bois. If he wasn't working, he was either at Hautecloque with the Comtesse or in the town house or a restaurant with his mistress. The only thing she hadn't figured on was the way she'd feel each time she passed by the town house.

When the cab pulled up in front of the big mansion which had been converted into apartments, she got out and paid the driver. As he meshed the gears and drove off, she tucked the gift-wrapped box under her right arm and went up the balustraded steps. In the lobby, she greeted the concierge and then took the little elevator to the third floor.

When it bobbed to a halt, she pushed the metal gate to one side and stepped out into the hall. Her heels clicked on the polished stone floor as she walked to the far end and rapped on the varnished-wood door.

A moment later she heard a click and the heavy door swung slowly open. Hélène looked down. Petite Hélène was standing there, bathed by the bright light from inside. Hélène caught her breath. The girl was gazing up at her almost shyly. Her eyes seemed bigger and bluer than the last time she'd seen her, her cheeks were the color of pale, ripening strawberries, and her delicate copper hair was like a fuzzy halo fashioned out of the softest down. In the back, it was gathered and tied with a dark blue silk ribbon. Her matching dress, styled along the lines of a painter's smock, was the one Hélène had given her on her last birthday, the dark blue wool trimmed with a Peter Pan collar of beautifully crocheted lace.

Petite Hélène showed off her manners to perfection and dropped a curtsy like a little princess. "Bonsoir, Tante Hélène," she sang formally.

Hélène smiled. "Bonsoir, Petite Hélène."

Suddenly the girl's cherubic face broke out in the most dazzling of smiles and her stiff manners dropped away like a veil off a painting. She flung her arms around Hélène's thighs and squeezed them. "Tante Hélène! I'm so glad you've come," she cried happily, her voice muffled as she buried her face in Hélène's skirt. "I've waited for *hours*."

Hélène reached down with her free hand and held her niece close. Then gently she began to stroke the copper hair. It felt even softer than it looked. Suddenly her eyes dimmed over. Was this what her baby would have been like? So delicate, so fragile.

Then Jeanne bustled into the foyer and by reflex wiped her hands on her apron. "You're late!" she reprimanded.

Hélène looked up and smiled apologetically. She handed Jeanne the bottle of red wine she had tucked under her arm along with the big package. "Peace?" she asked in a small voice.

Jeanne looked at the wine and made a pretense of frowning. Finally she had to laugh. "Peace," she returned, leaning forward and kissing Hélène affectionately on the cheek.

Hélène returned the kiss. Every time she was around Jeanne, she could feel the flow of warmth and love in the air. It was in every corner of this house.

Jeanne took her by the arm and pulled her into the foyer. Hélène squatted down so that her face was level with Petite Hélène's. "And this is for you, young lady," she said in a solemn voice. She handed over the gift-wrapped package.

Petite Hélène's eyes got big as she took the box. She could barely contain her excitement. "Merci beaucoup, Tante Hélène," she managed to spurt out politely. Quickly she pecked Hélène on the lips and then staggered into the living room with the box.

"You're spoiling her," Jeanne said disapprovingly as Hélène got back to her feet.

Hélène gave a little shrug. "At her age you deserve to be spoiled a little. I want her to have everything I could never have."

Jeanne smiled. "We'll see if you change that tune once you have children of your own."

Hélène felt her stomach beginning to cramp. She looked quickly away.

As they walked into the living room, Edmond looked up. He was sitting behind the big desk, his nose poked in a thick law book. He flashed a dazzlingly white grin across the room.

The dentist had done a good job, Hélène thought. Edmond hadn't wanted to go, but she had worked on him until he had finally gotten fed up with her nagging. It had been well worth it. A thousand francs was little enough to pay for replacing what the recoil of a Boche rifle had ruined when he was eleven. Somehow, she had never been able to get used to the gap when he smiled. Now she was satisfied. Edmond looked more handsome than ever. And no longer did he have that hungry look he'd had in Saint-Nazaire. He held himself with a confidence she had not seen before. The incidents with the Nazis and Tante Janine might never have happened. But she knew better.

Carefully Edmond marked his place and closed the book. Then he rose to his feet and quickly strode across the room. They embraced warmly. "How are you, Little French Girl?" he asked softly, his breath warm in her ear.

"Fine, I suppose. Busy, at any rate," she said, relishing the warm strength of his arms. For a moment she felt a foolish pang of jealousy toward Jeanne for holding title to his strength. She could remember what it had been like when they were children. How strong and protective he had been. You felt safe when you were in his arms, like nothing in the world could harm you. She wondered if she would ever find a man of her own who would be able to make her feel this way. As suddenly as they had come, the feelings of jealousy and yearning dropped away. Self-consciously she slipped out of his arms and stepped back. "And . . . and you?" she asked awkwardly. "How's school?"

"Some days are better than others."

Jeanne came over to him and punched him good-naturedly. "Nonsense," she said proudly. "Don't believe a word of it! My Edmond's at the head of his class."

Hélène looked pleased; Edmond, perpetually ill-at-ease when hearing words of praise, flushed and studied his feet.

"Come and sit down," Jeanne said. "I'll uncork the wine. It's only a few minutes until we eat. Is there anything I can get you in the meantime?"

Hélène shook her head and obediently took a seat as Jeanne headed toward the kitchen. She tried her best to avoid looking around. That way her face wouldn't register the disappointment she felt whenever she saw the apartment. Quickly she amended her thoughts. It wasn't really disappointment. Disillusionment, perhaps. It was the sort of feeling a magician must have if his rabbit crawled out of his sleeve at the wrong moment. She had tried her hand at magic and failed. She had tried to get Jeanne to spend the money necessary to buy the appropriate furnishings for this elegant apartment, but it was no use. Jeanne would purchase only fourth-rate items, insisting they would one day repay Hélène. Only Petite Hélène's little room at the far end of the hallway was lavishly decorated. This was because Hélène was determined that her niece was going to turn out to be a lady of taste and means. For her, only the best would do. She had seen to it that the bed which replaced the crib she had outgrown was fit for a princess. It was huge and soft, replete with a silken canopy, mountains of satin and lace pillows, and a shimmering white silk spread. This oasis of luxury vied for attention with the miniature French chairs she'd found in an antiques shop on the Left Bank, the small Venetian chandelier which looked like cake frosting. In one corner stood Petite Hélène's favorite item, a miniature vanity complete with neatly lined-up atomizers filled with yellow play perfume. Without Hélène's realizing it, Petite Hélène had become her surrogate child.

Now she smiled to herself as Petite Hélène knelt on the living room floor, her hands tugging impatiently at the bow of the satin ribbon tied around the package. Finally she got it off and handed it over to Jeanne, who had just come back out from the kitchen. Expertly Jeanne coiled the ribbon around her index finger, then went over to the desk and placed it in a cubbyhole. Petite Hélène started attacking the wrapping paper.

"Careful," Jeanne warned her.

"Oui, Maman," she said in a frustrated voice. What she really wanted was to rip the box apart. But obediently she unwrapped the tissue paper, smoothed it out on the floor, and folded it so that, like the ribbon, it too could be used over again.

Finally, with mounting suspense, she lifted the lid off the glossy white cardboard box. Then she held her breath as she reached in and dramatically parted the cover of white tissue paper. A cry of delight escaped unbidden from her lips.

For a long moment she could only stare at the doll that lay in a lavish nest of yet more tissue paper. Then slowly she lifted her out. It was one of the new dolls, the kind with jointed arms and legs that could be moved, soft and realistic plastic skin, and thickly lashed eyes that opened and shut. Her straight hair was so pale blond that it was almost white, and long enough to be combed and styled. Petite Hélène stroked it gently with her fingers. Each strand felt smooth and satiny, like real hair. This was more than just a doll, she was thinking. This was a beautiful little girl of her own. She was far more beautiful than any of the other dolls she had.

This one would have the place of honor. She would always keep her right on top of the bed.

But what fascinated her most was the way the doll was dressed. For it was not a frothy concoction of lace over crinoline, but a perfectly tailored replica of the suit Hélène was wearing—a pale pink Odile Joly out of raw silk with a rich smattering of tiny nubs. Pinned to the lapel was a tiny brooch. It, too, was the same as the one Hélène wore, a gold circle encrusted with diamonds, but in miniature.

Petite Hélène struggled to her feet and hugged the doll. "Ooooh! Je l'aime bien! Maman! Look, Maman!" Proudly she held the doll out.

Jeanne looked at it and shook her head. "My word . . ." she began. Then she inspected the brooch closely, and suddenly a dark expression crossed her face. She shot Hélène a knowing look. The diamonds were real. They were not carats in weight but mere points; yet each one was fully faceted and cut.

Hélène shrugged. To stave off any further lectures on spoiling the child, she jumped to her feet and sniffed the air. "Something smells like it's burning! It must be the food! And just when I'm starving!"

Jeanne had no choice now but to hurry back to the kitchen.

Hélène caught Petite Hélène's eye. They winked at each other. Then the girl studied the doll's eyes as they opened when she stood the doll up, and slowly floated shut as she was laid back down. Up again, and the eyes opened, unblinking and deep blue. Down again, and the lashes rested on the rosy cheeks.

Petite Hélène looked up. "I already know what I'm going to name her," she declared.

Hélène smiled. "Are you going to tell me?"

The little girl nodded and went over to her. "Can you keep a secret?" she asked in a semiwhisper.

Hélène nodded solemnly.

Petite Hélène's eyes were fixed on Hélène's. "There's only one name that's elegant enough for her."

"Oh? And what's that?"

"She's going to be named after a queen," Petite Hélène gestured for her aunt to bend down. Then she stood on tiptoe, placed her lips next to Hélène's ear, and whispered softly. The little girl's breath was like an icy chill. *"Antoinette!"*

Hélène froze. Her eyes were focused on another dimension. There was no way Petite Hélène could have known of her own doll, Antoinette.

"Don't you think that's a pretty name?"

"Yes, it's . . . it's a very pretty name," Hélène managed to say.

4

After Petite Hélène had gone to bed, the adults sat around the living room as they had once sat around the kitchen in Saint-Nazaire. Jeanne took out her sewing and Edmond stoked the fire in the fireplace. He smoked and drank peacefully, his feet up on a hassock. Hélène was content just to sit there, sipping her wine and soaking up the warm family atmosphere. They spoke of bygone days and caught up on the latest news. Inevitably their talk got around to *Les Modes.*

"I'll never forget the night of the publication party," Hélène said, "when the first issue came off the press. Strangely enough, no one was in a good mood that night. I guess they were all overworked. And to think that I rented the ballroom in the Georges V for the occasion! Finally I couldn't take any more of it and I just left. Well, Jacques knew where to find me. He came to the office at three in the morning, and there I was, wandering around like a lost soul, wondering where all the thrills and excitement had gone." She smiled at the memory. "I'll never forget it. He had a big paper bag, and in it was a chilled bottle of Dom Perignon and two Baccarat glasses. We sat and drank champagne till everyone came to work in the morning. Then we went home." She shook her head and smiled again. "The glasses are now on the shelf in my office."

Jeanne glanced up from the sock she was darning. "You

471

mean the ones engraved *'Les Modes,* Volume 1, Number 1'?"
she asked.

Hélène looked somewhat embarrassed. "I'd forgotten that I
must have told you that story already. Anyway enough of all
this," she said firmly, changing the subject. "Tell me what's
happening with you."

Jeanne glanced questioningly at Edmond. He nodded.

Hélène looked from one of them to the other. "Well?" she
demanded finally. "What's the matter now?"

"I'm pregnant again!"

"Pregnant!" For a moment Hélène stared at her with big
eyes. Then her face broke into a huge smile. "Oh, Jeanne!"
she cried. "That's *wonderful!"* She jumped to her feet and
crossed over to her. Then she bent down and her arms went
around her sister-in-law's neck as she hugged her happily.

Edmond lifted his feet off the hassock. "What about me?"
he asked with mock hurt in his voice. "Doesn't the father get
any credit?"

5

Luba Tcherina flung open the door to Hélène's office and
marched in, her pomegranate-lacquered fingernails sweeping
through the air. Jacques was at her heels. He closed the door
softly behind him.

Hélène was perched on her desk, one delicate shoe resting
on a chair, the telephone receiver tucked between her ear and
her shoulder as she consulted a sheaf of papers on her lap.
She glanced up, motioned for them to wait. The Czarina
sighed impatiently, her elongated fingers tapping her folded
arms. Jacques just nodded. Quickly Hélène finished her conversation and replaced the receiver. Today the Czarina was
dressed in elegant head-to-toe black. "Tartar black," she
would have called it. Black breeches, black high-heeled silver-trimmed boots, and a beautiful black wool tunic embroidered with silver thread that had an enormous monk's

cowl framing her face. On this occasion, to match her outfit, Luba wore black-framed glasses; legend had it she collected drawers full of different colored glasses to match her wardrobe. Her cheeks, like her nails, were pomegranate: two big circles liberally smeared into the wrinkled skin. Hélène couldn't help wondering if the Czarina had her own cosmetics lab at home. How else could she manage to get hold of all the long-out-of-date colors? Not only that, but make them appear the height of fashion.

The Czarina's dark eyes flashed. "I think," she exclaimed, "I've gone *blind*! I never want to see snow again for as long as I live! And I never, *ever* want to set foot in a darkroom again! You know, don't you, that the red light in there *only* makes it look like a *cheap* whore's bedroom?" She shivered with revulsion and slumped into one of the chairs, the back of one elegant hand dramatically resting across her brow.

Hélène hopped off the desk. Jacques stepped forward, gave a sweeping bow, and handed her the manila envelope he was carrying.

She looked at it curiously. "What's this?"

"Proof sheets, princess."

"Proof sheets!" Hélène parroted. Her voice was incredulous. "Already! But you must have gotten back from Chamonix in the wee hours!"

"That we did." The Czarina heaved a weary sigh, her gaunt bosom rising and falling beneath the voluminous folds of her tunic. "As soon as we got back, Jacques simply insisted that we lock ourselves in the darkroom and work all night through!"

Jacques grinned at Hélène. "I figured you'd want to see the results right away."

Luba's black eyes flashed with mischief. "The results are that when this issue comes out, the editors-in-chief at *Vogue*, *Harper's*, and *L'Officiel* are going to tear their hair out!"

Quickly Hélène began to unravel the figure-8 string that held the envelope shut. She slid out the proof sheets and lined them up neatly, sat down and took her tortoiseshell magnifying glass out of the top drawer. Silently she gave each print a cursory first glance. She nodded to herself. She had been right in allowing Luba and Jacques to go to Chamonix. Even on these miniature prints, Jacques' genius came through, as did the Czarina's dramatic posing of the models. They were a good team, Jacques and Luba.

When she finished scanning the shots, she went over them again, this time scrutinizing each one closely. She was pleased. There was something about the juxtaposing of summer couture and winter backgrounds that gave the photos the elusive "something special" she'd been after all this time. Up to now, everything *Les Modes* had done had been superb. But these? These were sublime.

She picked up a black grease pencil and began circling the ones that most appealed to her. Like the one with the giant yellow snow remover. The plow was raised high in the air and the models were posed in the giant scoop as if they'd just been bulldozed off the snow and trapped there. Or the ones where the models, in their delicate print dresses, were standing knee-deep in snow, their beautiful long legs red with cold. And . . . She felt a sudden chill and closed her eyes for a moment. There it was. The unmistakable Jacques Renault daredevil trademark. The cable car.

It was not far off the ground as far as cable cars went; it had obviously been stopped just after leaving the ground station. But still it must have been at least fifteen meters up. And any way you looked at it, a four-story drop was a long way. But it was a spectacular shot. All that could be seen was the shiny red car and the athletic models clinging to its sides for dear life. The backdrop was a pristine blue sky cut in half by thick cables.

Hélène chose the shot she'd use for the cover without hesitation. Even in its tiny state, she could see that it was perfection itself. And blown up and cropped, it would be a sensation. It showed the typical *Les Modes* cover girl, tawny and leonine, stretched out on a carpet of crystalized snow. In front of her, delicate snowdrops, like miniature lilies, had pushed their way up through the snow, each hardy bloom bowed over its pale waxy leaves like miniature bells. The model had her nose poked right in them, her chin aggressively thrust in the snow and her Cleopatra-like eyes glaring up into the camera. Her glossy red lips were barely visible behind the flowers.

"They're fantastic!" Hélène said finally. She looked up at Jacques and Luba. "Just make certain the competition doesn't hear about them until we're on the stands."

"Have no fear," Jacques said. "We went so far as to have

the models sign agreements that if they shoot their mouths off, they'll be docked and held legally liable."

"Good." Hélène looked at Luba. "Why don't you go home now and get some shut eye? You look like you could use it."

"I do, do I? Well, just this *once*, I'll let that slide." The Czarina of haut goût rose haughtily to her feet.

"Oh, and one more thing," Hélène said quickly. "Have you gone through the American *Harper's* recently?"

The Czarina nodded. Part of any editor-in-chief's job was to keep a keen eye on the competition.

Hélène picked up a sheaf of papers. "I've just gotten a translation of some of the columns. I like Diana Vreeland's column, 'Why Don't You . . .' Have you read it?"

The Czarina's eyes narrowed. She didn't favor any comparisons, no matter how exalted. "No. Is there any reason why I should?"

"I think so," Hélène said. "It's very funny and positively chic. You know, like: 'Why don't you turn your old ermine coat into a bathrobe?' That kind of thing. There are no end of possibilities with something like that."

"Indeed not." The Czarina's nostrils flared distastefully as she ticked off some quick titles on her fingers. "Why don't you . . . let's see . . . turn your old Porthault sheets into new terrace awnings? Why don't you . . . use your old diamonds to stud your bolero jacket? Why don't you turn your old gold bracelets into napkin rings? Why don't—"

"All right," Hélène said testily, "I get the idea. You don't like it."

"On the contrary," the Czarina said. "I like it. Only it's been done. We'll have to be more original than that."

"I agree. But let's try to think up a column along those lines. It's got to be something terribly useless, though, otherwise it won't be chic. When you come up with some ideas, we'll have a powwow. Now, off you go."

The Czarina rose, offered her cheek for Jacques to kiss, and then swept out of the office. When she was gone, Jacques started to gather up the proof sheets. "I'll blow up the ones you've marked after I've gotten my forty winks."

"Fine," Hélène said. "But I'd like you to do something for me first."

"Sure. What is it?"

Hélène went over to the big floor safe, knelt down and spun the combination. After a moment of fiddling, she swung the heavy door open and took out a manila envelope. She snapped the safe shut again and spun the dial around for good measure. "Let's go to the lab," she said. "I need you to take some pictures right away."

It took two hours for Jacques to finish. He snapped all the von Eiderfeld documents, developed the film, blew it up to eight-by-tens, and printed one copy of each. While it was being done, Hélène stayed in the darkroom. She wasn't about to let those precious documents out of her sight. Not after all the trouble she'd gone through to get them.

When everything was finished, they went back to her office. She studied the prints. Jacques had done a fine job. He had photographed each document carefully and they were eminently readable. Even the photos of von Eiderfeld looked better than the originals had, since he had played around some with the lighting.

She put the copies in one envelope, the originals in another, and both of them in her attaché case. She placed the negatives separately in her purse. Later, she would destroy them. There was no point in having too many copies of something this volatile floating around.

"Thanks, Jacques," she said. "I really do appreciate it. I know you're overworked and tired."

He grinned. "Anytime, princess." He paused. His voice was suddenly very serious. "That's heavy stuff." He gestured at her attaché case.

"I know that." She forced her voice to remain light. "Now, you'd better go home and get your forty winks."

"I'll do that." He started for the door. When he reached it, he turned around. "See you tomorrow. I'll be in the darkroom all morning. By afternoon, you'll have the Chamonix blowups."

She smiled. "Tomorrow, then."

As soon as he was gone, she drummed her fingers thoughtfully on the attaché case. She hadn't wanted to get Jacques involved in this. There was no need for him to know anything about it. But she needed a set of copies, and he was the only person she could trust to make them. She shrugged. Some things just couldn't be helped.

Quickly she made three telephone calls. The first was to her personal lawyer, Émile Mauriac. It was he who had the original of the *Clytemnestra* tape locked away in his vault.

She would put the von Eiderfeld originals in there along with it. And the same instructions would apply: if she didn't contact him regularly, he was to go promptly to the police. She smiled grimly to herself. She wondered what Hubert and von Eiderfeld would think if they knew what dangerous ground they were treading upon. If one of them succeeded in harming her, the other would suffer the consequences as well. She thought it rather poetic.

She had made an appointment to drop by Monsieur Mauriac's office at eleven o'clock. She glanced at her wristwatch. It was after ten already. She'd have to hurry.

Next she called Paul Clermont. He was the lawyer whose offices handled all the legal ends for Les Éditions Hélène Junot. She would meet with him after lunch. He would help her gain entrance to see the reclusive Karl von Eiderfeld. She had mapped out her strategy very carefully. She would have him send the von Eiderfeld lawyers in Düsseldorf a tiny portion of one of the documents. A cryptic portion only von Eiderfeld himself would be able to recognize. That should flush the fox out of hiding, she thought. And to keep him dangling, she would use the name Madame Kowalsky. That wouldn't set off any warning bells. And using the Clermont offices to make contact was a good idea. She'd done the same thing when she'd gone to see the Comte. This way, neither of them had any idea where the documents were.

Finally she called Edmond.

"Hey, Little French Girl," he said in surprise. "What's up?"

"Not much. Are you doing anything exciting?"

His laugh was warm. "I'm afraid not. Just cramming for exams, as usual."

"Oh, I should have known better." She hesitated, then decided that she was being a fool. Family was family. When something important came up, you just had to drop what you were doing. "Listen, would it be a great inconvenience if you took a break and met me for lunch?"

"That's no inconvenience." Then a note of worry crept into his voice. "Is anything the matter?"

"No," she assured him hastily. "It's just that I need your opinion on something. It's . . . well, it's rather important."

Hélène hung up thoughtfully after they arranged to meet. She had never meant to discuss von Eiderfeld's "punishment" with Edmond. But he had a right to know. He had been victimized by that horrid albino as much as she had. And sooner or later, when he finished school and joined *Les Modes*, he was bound to find out. Better that he knew now.

After leaving Monsieur Mauriac's office, Hélène walked to Fouquet's. It was only a few blocks down the Champs-Élysées. The attaché case in her left hand felt much lighter now; the originals of the von Eiderfeld documents were safely locked away. No matter what von Eiderfeld threatened, he wouldn't dare lift a finger against her. Not now. She had all the bases covered.

She would talk it over with Edmond and ask his advice. The only trouble was, she thought she knew what he would say. That since it was she who had set the wheels in motion, it was up to her, and her alone, to decide von Eiderfeld's fate.

She crossed the rue de Bassano and passed the TWA office without giving it as much as a glance, At the Avenue Georges V she stopped for the red light. She waved to Edmond. He was standing on the far corner, waiting for her outside the café's glass-enclosed terrace. He smiled and waved back.

The light changed and the automobiles stopped behind the zebra-striped crosswalk. As she stepped off the curb, she heard the high-pitched, clucking whine of a moped. Instinctively she stopped in her tracks and whirled around. The moped was shooting recklessly forward from the narrow space between two cars, the driver and passenger both wearing bowllike white helmets with big gray goggles. Her heart gave a leap. For a moment she was certain they were going to run her down. Then she let out a slow sigh of relief. The driver had swerved to a sudden halt. She shook her head angrily. Just as she started walking again, the passenger's leather-jacketed arm shot out, a gloved hand grabbed her purse, and the moped went roaring off in a blue cloud of exhaust.

It took a second for what had happened to register. Then Hélène let out a scream and frantically began chasing after the bike. "Thief! Stop him, somebody!" she cried. "My purse! My purse!"

But she wasn't fast enough. They burned the red light, made a sharp right turn onto the Champs-Élysées, and swiftly merged into the heavy traffic. For a moment she could see the passenger twisting around to look back at her. But all she could see was a pair of goggles.

Hélène stopped running and slowed to a halt. It was useless. She would never catch up with them. Not on foot, nor in a car. Besides, one of the heels of her shoes was coming loose.

The last thing she saw was the moped weaving in and out of the traffic. A few seconds later, it disappeared out of sight. She made an angry, futile gesture with her arm. Then Edmond was beside her and held her tightly. He, too, was out of breath. Like her, he had started to give chase on foot. Silently she let him lead her up onto the sidewalk and into Fouquet's. They were quickly shown to a sidewalk table and she sank down into a chair. She sat there motionless for a moment. Blankly she stared out the glassed-in terrace. Then she covered her face with her hands as the enormity of the situation hit her. She had not yet had a chance to destroy the negatives. They were still in her purse. Her stolen purse.

Edmond twisted around and motioned for a waiter. "Quick —a glass of brandy!"

"Oui, monsieur." The waiter hurried off.

Edmond leaned solicitously across the table. "Do you think you can remember anything about either one of those punks?"

She shook her head dumbly.

"Did you catch the license plate?"

"No," she whispered. She still stared out the window. "It . . . it all happened so fast."

He sighed and slumped back wearily. "I didn't either." Then he started to get up. "I'll be back in a moment."

She looked up suddenly. "Where are you going?"

"To call the gendarmes. It won't hurt to report this."

"No!" She gripped his arm so fiercely that he looked at her in surprise. For a brief moment he half-sat, half-stood.

"But . . . your money . . . your ID papers?"

"I don't want to go to the police," she said flatly.

He stared at her. "But . . . you can't allow them to get away with it!"

"They already have," she pointed out. Her usual practicality was quickly returning. "Besides, it's not the money that worries me." She leaned across the table and clenched her fists. "It's the film."

"The film?" He looked at her blankly and settled back in his seat. "What are you talking about?"

Her brandy arrived and she took a quick swallow. Her hands were still shaking, but not as badly as they had been. She was starting to regain her calm. She set the glass down and looked around quickly to make certain she couldn't be overheard. "Just hear me out, Edmond," she said in a low voice. "Then you'll understand."

She cleared her throat and started telling him about her search for von Eiderfeld. While she talked, she couldn't help wondering about the coincidence of her purse being snatched while the negatives were in it. She'd never had anything stolen before. She'd read of women's purses being snatched by thieves on mopeds. The papers were full of such stories. But that it should happen now? And to her? Long ago, she had stopped believing in coincidences. They were too pat an answer. And. . . . She paled suddenly. If it was really more than just a coincidence, then who could it have been? The hairs at the back of her neck prickled. Only one person knew that she'd put the negatives in her purse.

She tried to push the creeping thoughts out of her mind. No, she thought quickly. She was overdramatizing things. He would never do anything to hurt her. Jacques was a friend.

6

Hélène looked out the round porthole of the Lufthansa DC-7 as it neared its destination. Outside, on the starboard wing, she could see the twin propellers spinning in a silver blur. She could hear a muffled roar as the motors changed pitch.

The hostess came down the aisle. "Please fasten your seat belt, Fräulein," she said, leaning forward. "We're approaching Köln-Bonn airport."

Hélène turned away from the window, fastened her seat belt, and stared straight ahead. Once again, she was returning to Cologne. But this time it was different. The other trips were merely to make the arrangements that would culminate in this one visit for which she had waited so long. The moment she would face Karl von Eiderfeld. The destroyer. The butcher. The white-faced one who had filled her with such terror that sometimes she still had nightmares about him. It had been more than fourteen years since she had first laid eyes on his hideous face. Fourteen years was a long time to wait for anything, but now she was ready.

She rolled her head to one side of the headrest. She had chosen a most exquisite and fitting form of punishment. He, too, would have to buy into Les Éditions Hélène Junot; just as Hubert had had to. But this time the terms would be different. When Paul Clermont drew up the papers, he had thought the terms bizarre. But he hadn't known what she was up to.

Hélène smiled slowly. Von Eiderfeld's punishment was going to suit his crimes. She was going to prey on his greatest fear. The fear of discovery. The fear of having an accusing finger pointed at him. Well, she wouldn't be the one who'd point that finger. She would allow him to remain burrowed in his paranoid seclusion. Except, that is, for four times each year. Once every three months he would have to attend a board meeting. Otherwise, he could come and go as he wanted. But for her board meetings, the rules were stringent. She stipulated in writing (and he would have no choice but to agree to her terms, unless he wanted her to go to the Israeli authorities) that he must use second-class public transportation to get there. He could use his choice of scheduled airlines, scheduled railroads, scheduled buses. But he could not go by private or rented car, could not, in fact, charter anything—plane or bus—not even hide in a wagon-lit on a train, nor even use a taxi. Ship's travel, too, was strictly forbidden, for ships were like floating hotels. It was too easy to lock yourself up in your cabin. No, for her meetings Karl von Eiderfeld would have to travel openly with that which he feared most: crowds. She had even mapped out his airplane routes carefully. Frankfurt–Tel Aviv–Paris. Paris–Tel Aviv–Frankfurt. It was a big detour, but it wouldn't hurt him to have to set foot on Israeli soil and deal with Jewish officials every now and then, she thought. In fact, that would probably frighten him the most. Customs officials were enough to unnerve anybody. Especially somebody with something to hide.

Yes, the danger of discovery would be an all-consuming threat. Albinos were a rarity. They attracted attention and weren't easily forgotten. And somewhere, sometime, a survivor of his brutalities would put the finger on him. If not in Paris, then perhaps in Tel Aviv. Sooner or later it was bound to happen.

She nodded to herself. The more she thought about it, the more sense it made. She didn't feel proud of what she was doing, but she didn't feel ashamed of herself, either. She believed that this time, what she was doing was truly the right thing. And this time, the severity of the punishment she meted out verged on genius. Von Eiderfeld wouldn't be able to slide through with a splashy, quick trial and then feel the hangman's noose around his neck. For then, all his suffering would cease. Dead men didn't feel anything.

No, she would make certain that before that happened, he would suffer first. Slowly. Painfully. For as long as it took his past to catch up with him. Especially with such stipulations as the one which specifically stated that he could not undergo cosmetic surgery of any kind. Or the one that forbade travel under any name but his own. There was even a clause that he could not wear hats of any kind during his trips, and only those eyeglasses which were absolutely necessary and whose lenses were each no larger than six and a half square centimeters. This way, disguises of any kind were out of the question.

A grim smile tightened across her teeth. Four times a year, the fear-ridden fox would be flushed from his hole. Four times a year was enough. Between each meeting, he would have ninety days to worry about the next one.

She started as the wheels of the plane touched down on the tarmac and the fuselage gave a shudder. She straightened in her seat and looked out again. The flaps on the wings were in a vertical position. And in the distance was the terminal, surrounded by planes like a mother nursing her litter. They were already taxiing toward it. She could see the black-yellow-and-red-striped German flag that had replaced the ominous swastika banner of the war years. It was surrounded by smaller flags of many nations fluttering festively in the breeze. Now it wouldn't be long. The showdown was at hand. Only a short drive away waited Düsseldorf and Karl von Eiderfeld.

Karl Häberle was waiting for her inside the terminal.

"Welcome back to Germany," he said in French, raising his voice above the noise of the crowds and the echoes of the loudspeaker system.

She smiled. "I hope I'm not imposing," she said carefully in German. "It's just that I don't know anyone else here."

"You're not imposing at all," he assured her politely, also in German. "I hope you'll forgive me, but I didn't arrange for a car and driver as you requested. If you don't mind, I'd like the pleasure of being at your service."

She smiled gratefully and slipped her arm through his. "Thank you, I like that. Now we'd better switch back to French." She laughed as she changed languages. "I'm afraid I still have much to learn."

"On the contrary. You speak it very well. And your pronunciation is excellent."

She was pleased. She didn't bother to tell him that she was simultaneously learning English and Italian as well. She had figured that it was high time. Now that *Les Modes* had foreign distribution channels—if not foreign editions themselves, yet—it wouldn't hurt to be multilingual. Surprisingly, learning all the languages at the same time posed no problem for her. Instinctively she grasped the meanings of words and mastered the syntax and grammar of each language. She never once mixed Italian words into an English conversation, or French ones into German.

"I've got a new car," Häberle said offhandedly as they walked to the parking lot. "Thanks to your generosity, my tired little Opel could finally be retired."

She looked at him. "And you bought a Mercedes," she said slyly.

He laughed. "And I bought a Mercedes."

Hélène held her breath and hesitated. Slowly she swung her legs out of the silver-gray car and stepped out, staring thoughtfully up at the tall building that threw its shadow full force across the parking lot. Absently she pushed the car door shut. The parking lot was in the midst of an expanse of hardened, frost-touched earth that had been graded but not yet landscaped. Only the building, the road, and the parking lots had been completed. The rest looked like a lunar landscape, ugly, barren, and brown. There was an enormous industrial complex a kilometer away; like an expanding, misshapen hydra that had spawned a mind-boggling array of offspring, it sprawled hideous, twisted, and complicated beyond belief. Behind it were the huge chemical tanks, like bloated silver bellies, and from the midst of it all rose the tall chimneys that spewed forth eternal flames. As if the fires of hell had burst through the earth, she thought. A grotesque place, perfectly suited to the man she had come to see.

Karl von Eiderfeld turned away from the expanse of tinted windows and went back behind his desk. Wearily he lowered himself into the teak-and-leather chair. Several minutes ago the guards at the main gate had called to notify him that Madame Kowalsky had arrived. He had made it a point to watch her car pull up in the parking lot below. From fifteen stories up, all he could see was a man and what appeared to be a slim, attractive woman. Nothing more. Not that he had hoped to recognize her from this distance. He knew better than that. But he prided himself on his photographic memory. He could remember faces from years ago, even connect them with names.

A knifelike pain shot through his chest. His lips tightened as he touched his ribs with his hand. He knew what that pain was. His heart.

He reached into his desk drawer and took out a gold-and-enamel pillbox that had once belonged to the Czar of Russia. He didn't give the exquisite Fabergé workmanship a single glance. Quickly his fingers sought the catch and snapped it open. Inside were several minuscule pills. He popped one into his mouth and dry-swallowed it. Then he put the box away.

His heart had been acting up regularly ever since the afternoon his lawyers had forwarded the cryptic portion of an old document. Even before he opened it, he had had a terrible premonition of what was inside. The power to destroy him and all that which was his. Just when he had almost begun to believe that he had finally left his past entirely behind him. That there was nothing now that would surface. And why should it? During the war, he had been careful. Unlike most Germans, he had been a realist. He had accepted the fact that either side could win the war. And before 1943 was over, it was obvious to him that the Germans were losing. That was when he had begun rerouting shipments of propane to his secret depots and destroying the shipping forms. That was when he had seen to it that anyone who had witnessed him giving orders that he might later regret had been promptly shipped to the camps. Could anyone have survived that fate? In the beginning he had doubted it. But when the war was over, it became clear that unthinkable blunders had been made. Survivors had begun to straggle to the surface, picking out one war "criminal" after another, many of them men he had once known and marched beside. Most of them were brought to trial; a few had managed to commit suicide first. The newspapers had been full of their stories in the beginning; then they steadily dwindled, until after a while it was only a few highly publicized cases a year. Finally the public grew weary of them.

As the years passed, he had begun to sleep better. Whatever ax had descended upon the others had missed him, and for a good reason. Unlike them, he had covered his tracks well. At least that was what he liked to believe. Nor had he ever flaunted himself. Not during the war and not after. Even now, hardly anyone had ever seen or heard of him, and no one questioned his seclusion or connected it to "atrocities." All people ever heard of was Von Eiderfeld Industrien, G.m.b.H; never anything about Karl von Eiderfeld himself. Millionaire recluses never raised suspicions.

After receiving the cryptic portion of the document, he had spent whole days and nights racking his brain. He had tried to remember who might have escaped the execution he had planned, who might have gotten hold of the incriminating document. Who was this mysterious Madame Kowalsky, and why had she sent that message? To gain access to see him, of course. But that was strange, too. For she herself was coming, not the police or the Israelis. Was it blackmail she was after?

He buried his bloodless face in his white hands. For so long now, everything had been going well. He had prospered more than he had ever hoped. He had climbed to unimaginable heights of wealth and power. Yearly, six million barrels of crude oil passed through his refineries. Millions of tons of steel were being poured in his mills. His coal and iron mines were thriving. And his shipyard in Kiel was already producing seven new tankers every fifteen months. Now, all this was threatened. Everything he had built could fall like a house of cards if Madame Kowalsky took a deep breath and blew on it.

He pushed down on a white button recessed in his lacquered desk. Ahead of him, a portion of the highly polished teak wall slid soundlessly aside, exposing a large television screen.

He pushed down on the blue button and a bluish light came on within the gray screen. A moment later he had a flickering view of the inside of the elevator. There were a man and a woman. The man was German; that much he could tell. His lips, his hairstyle, his facial structure, and the cut of his clothes gave him away. But the woman was young and beautiful, expensively dressed. Her clothes were obviously Paris couture. He had never seen her before. And if he had, she must have been a child at the time. She could only be in her early twenties.

A child. He froze, cursing his stupidity. The blue face on the screen seemed to be mocking him. Angrily he pushed down on the third button. The red one. The picture faded slowly and the wall slid shut again.

His eyes narrowed in memory. He had slipped up only once—when he had let those two French children go. He should have had them killed.

Now he knew who she was.

Hélène had noticed the camera lens in the elevator the moment they stepped inside. But it was only after the car began to move that she had the feeling they were being watched. She glanced up into the thick glass lens that was focused on them. She could *feel* him now. Von Eiderfeld was watching. Waiting.

When she was shown into the hushed silence of his office, von Eiderfeld looked up slowly. His hands were folded on the desktop and his hooded pink eyes were guarded. She turned her face and smiled automatically at the secretary. The instant the door closed, her smile dropped away. She turned back around and for a long moment locked eyes with von Eiderfeld.

She shuddered and tightened her grip on the attaché case. He looked older than she'd imagined.

He waved his thin hand elegantly, his voice soft and emotionless. "Be seated, Fräulein Junot."

How could he possibly have known who Madame Kowalsky was? she wondered. Then she threw the thought away. It really didn't matter. "I prefer to stand," she replied coldly.

"As you wish."

Her eyes moved slowly around the elegant but sterile office. She forced her face to remain impassive as she took in the nightmarish Max Ernst canvases. They were very appropriate. Only a truly twisted mind could appreciate them.

"You have built quite an impressive empire," she said quietly.

He gave a modest shrug of his narrow shoulders. "It is not that difficult when one works hard."

"Or when one has no distractions and can do nothing *but* lock oneself away and work."

He looked at her calmly. The fire within his eyes seemed to dim. "What is it you want of me?"

She put her attaché case down on one of the modular units and snapped it open. "I, too, have begun an empire of sorts," she said, taking out several issues of *Les Modes*. She handed them to him.

He glanced quickly at them, and then, looking slightly puzzled, put them down on his desk. "I am afraid that fashion holds little appeal for me," he said. He folded his hands again, waiting for her to continue.

"It should," she said after a moment. "You see, I am selling stock in my corporation, Herr von Eiderfeld. Ten percent of that stock will cost you one million francs."

Von Eiderfeld looked relieved. Blackmail, by whatever name, was something he could understand. "Your company is in financial difficulties, then?"

She permitted herself a low laugh. "Quite the opposite."

"Then why is it you are selling stock?"

Hélène was silent. She reached for a thick envelope, undid the flap, and dumped the contents out on the desktop. His face was still expressionless as he looked down at the glossy black-and-white photographs, but his mind was racing. He had thought that she had somehow managed to get hold of one document. But these! There were so many. Gott im Himmel! Was so much incriminating evidence still floating around? Silently he cursed the Reich. No wonder they had lost the war! The bungling idiots in Berlin hadn't even had the sense to burn the archives.

But he betrayed none of these thoughts. His face was a studious mask. "One million francs is a small price for these," he said softly.

She shrugged. "It's not a small price," she said, "it's the fair market price."

His pink eyes narrowed suspiciously; this was no ordinary

blackmailer he was dealing with. She wanted something else besides money.

She reached into the attaché case again and took out a thick document bound in a light blue folder. "Here it is. Your copy of the stock offering. I suggest you read it through very carefully before you sign."

Something in her voice set off warning bells. He gave her a sharp look but said nothing as he took it from her.

She continued. "Need I mention that the lawyer who contacted you for this meeting is not the same one who has the originals of your documents? Or what will happen if any harm comes to me?"

He tapped the folder in his hand. "Let me ask you a hypothetical question."

She said nothing.

"If I were to purchase these . . . these shares. Then would I get the originals of the documents?"

Hélène shook her head. "I'm afraid not, Herr von Eiderfeld. You see, they are my insurance for a long and healthy lifespan. Do go ahead and read the contract."

"It's a long document," he said. "It will take time to read."

"I have time." She indulged herself in a smile and took a seat in front of his desk.

He sighed, opened the folder to the first page, and began to read. It was not long before he sat up straight. His white face seemed even whiter than before. "Th-this is preposterous!" he sputtered suddenly. "You don't really expect me to agree to such ludicrous terms!" Disgustedly he flung the document across the room.

Hélène looked over at it, then back at him. Patiently she got up, retrieved it, and placed it on his desk. She sat down again. "Yes, Herr von Eiderfeld," she said softly between clenched teeth. "I expect you to agree to all these terms. And no, this is not preposterous. What happened to my family was preposterous. Four children fleeing Paris with the Nazis on their tail was preposterous. A baby burned in the belly—that was preposterous. My mother gassed at Auschwitz—that, too, Herr von Eiderfeld, was preposterous."

He made an irritable gesture. "How would you know where she was sent?" he mumbled halfheartedly. "You were not even there."

"My mother told another survivor, who in turn told me. The camps were one giant grapevine—you should know that.

Many people told others their stories in the hopes that when it was all over, the world would hear the truth."

"The truth!" he spat out venomously. "Speculation and hearsay, that's all it is!"

Hélène shook her head. "No, it's not. You see, Herr von Eiderfeld, my mother lived almost to the very end. I have an eyewitness who was with her, a Jewish doctor. He is willing to come forward and testify. Now about those papers . . ."

His eyes met hers. "And if I decide not to sign. What happens then?"

"Then I shall not go to the German authorities." She paused. "I shall go to the Israelis."

For a moment he closed his eyes.

Her voice lowered to a whisper as she began hammering his alternatives home. "Not only will you be tried and convicted. Something even worse will happen. Let's not fool ourselves, Herr von Eiderfeld. I am a businesswoman and you are a businessman. We both know what it is that is most important to us. Our empires. Von Eiderfeld Industrien is what you live for. That, above all else. You have no shareholders. You own one hundred percent of the corporation, which would make it one of the biggest fortunes ever to be seized by the German government. You know what they would use it for, don't you?" She smiled as he winced. "To pay Israel reparations. To pay Jews who have claims against Germany for restitution." She leaned toward him. "Every asset your companies have would end up in Israel!"

He made no comment.

"Think of all the orange groves it would plant! Think of all the desert irrigation it could provide! Think of how the harbor at Haifa could be dredged and expanded!"

He looked totally defeated now, but he made one last, desperate attempt. "You forgot one thing, Fräulein," he said with weak dignity. "I am a powerful man."

"Are you?" She shook her head. "You *used* to be powerful. But that is all over. In ninety days I shall expect you in Paris for the first board meeting. You remember, don't you, what a beautiful city Paris is in the spring?"

"Why are you doing this?" he said. "*Why?*"

She shook her head unbelievingly. Had he no inkling of the difference between right and wrong? Had he no conscience beneath that hideous white skin? She wanted to grab him and shake some humanity into him, but that would have been useless. His soul was dead.

"The young man who is waiting outside for me will be the one who escorts you to and from the board meetings," she said impassively. "I suggest you start getting your passport and visas in order. As specified, you will take a bus or train from your home to the airport. Then you will fly to Tel Aviv, second class. You will remain there overnight. The next day, you will proceed on to Paris and take public transportation from the airport into the city. Just one slipup, Herr von Eiderfeld, and Israeli agents will have in their possession every original of the documents you have before you. And I know you won't try to flee to South America or some other sympathetic haven. Not after all you've built. But I'm cautious and distrusting, so I shall see to it that this company is under constant scrutiny. I advise you not to try to sell it. Before you even approached a buyer, it would be all over for you."

He looked at her with a grudging respect. "You drive a hard bargain," he said quietly.

She got up, went back to her attaché case, and snapped it shut. She looked over at him with disdain. "I don't make bargains, Herr von Eiderfeld."

She turned and started to leave. When she reached the door, she spun around. "By the way, Herr von Eiderfeld. You wouldn't know what happened to my two sisters, would you?"

"They were sent to the camps."

"And . . . ?"

He looked down at his desk. "Children were the first to be . . ." His words trailed off.

Hélène tightened her lips. "You have forty-eight hours to get those papers back to me." She glanced at her watch. "Forty-eight hours from *now*."

His eyes instinctively dropped to his wristwatch.

Thirty-six hours after her meeting with von Eiderfeld, her lawyers in Paris received the signed stock documents, and one million francs was deposited in the Les Éditions Hélène Junot account in the Banque Rothschild.

Von Eiderfeld had met her ultimatum with twelve hours to spare.

490

7

Hélène felt like a member of the Chinese acrobatic circus as she tried to contort her body every which way in front of the tall beveled mirror. She thought that this way she just might possibly be able to reach back far enough with her hands to hook together the back of the pale satin evening gown. After a minute of fumbling she let her hands drop in exhaustion.

"Merde!" she cursed uncharacteristically under her breath as the top hook, located in that elusive area between the shoulder blades and the nape of the neck, somehow still evaded her dexterous fingers. It was infuriating! She made a gesture of frustration and stared at herself in the mirror. Already she felt sweaty from all the effort, and in a minute her carefully coiffed hair would go limp. She reached for a tissue and gently dabbed the beads of perspiration from her forehead. Now her makeup, too, was in danger.

She scowled restlessly into the mirror at the gown. Then, holding it up by placing a hand flat against her bosom, she half-tripped over the hem as she stumbled to the telephone. Impatiently she lifted the receiver. As soon as the switchboard picked up, she said, "Jacques Renault, please."

"Un moment, mademoiselle," the operator sang. And a moment later, Jacques came on the line.

"Yes, boss?" he said good-humoredly.

"Jacques, get the hell up here. Right away."

"Sure, princess," he said with guarded caution. "You know I'm only downstairs. What's the problem?"

"The problem is . . ." She took a deep breath to try to calm herself. "The problem is this goddamn gown!" she said between her teeth. "I can't get it hooked up!"

He chuckled. "I'll be right up. Just let me get my pants on!"

Hélène slammed the receiver down, whirled around, and stalked across the room to the open window. The perfume of flowers was strong in the air, the lingering sweetness mixed with the tangy salt breeze from the sea. For a moment she looked out without appreciating the view.

How had she gotten into this anyway? She should never have let Jacques and Luba talk her into coming along. She'd much rather have stayed in Paris. That was where the power of Les Éditions Hélène Junot pulsed like a loud-and-clear heartbeat. On location with the models, she felt helpless. This was Jacques and Luba's territory. All she could do was stand around and get in the way.

But she thought that only now. Forever afterward, it would seem it was fate which had drawn her to the Côte d'Azur. For after the pain of Cap Ferrat, she had sworn to herself that she would never set foot in the South of France again. Added proof of fate's drawing power was the fact that this was the only time she had ever accompanied Jacques, Luba, and the models anywhere.

They had wrapped up the two-day shoot early that afternoon. The models had departed to their rooms at the less expensive Helvetia Hotel while she, Luba, and Jacques went back to the lavish Hôtel de Paris. Even after less than forty-eight hours here, the distinction was clear. There was Monaco and then there was Monte Carlo. The Hôtel de Paris was in Monte Carlo.

It was more than just a hotel. It was a spun-sugar dream imagined somewhere out of this world and set down amid a garden of paradise. Almost every hotel in the world made you feel you didn't belong, but at the Hôtel de Paris they made you feel like royalty. Upon arriving, the first thnig the worldly Luba had done was to seek out the chief concierge. He had given her a polite bow and smiled. "Madame Tcherina," he said. "I trust that everything is to your liking."

Luba had drawn herself up, her imperiousness worn like a titular crown as she demanded that the furniture in their rooms be changed to suit their tastes. And a half-hour later, after they sipped a cooling wine on the flowering terrace, their rooms had indeed been refurnished. They now looked like sumptuous palace salons filled with the best of antiques. At first, Hélène had been embarrassed by the Czarina's demands; already she was taking them for granted. The management hadn't raised an eyebrow. It was a customary request at the Hôtel de Paris, and they were only too happy to oblige. Life here was different, she thought. It was richer, more comfortable; one's every whim was magically catered to. It was easy to get spoiled.

The famous Hôtel de Paris was located diagonally across from the equally or even more famous casino with its green weathered-copper domes, twin towers, and elegant arches. The hotel's pool and sauna, like the windows of Hélène's suite, looked down to the port below. It was early evening, and despite her irritation with the gown, her anger slowly seeped out of her. There was no way you could look out and not let the view affect you. The warm Mediterranean air was slowly cooling off, the faint, fragrant breezes like gentle caresses. The expensive yachts were lined up with military precision inside the calm, sparkling breakwater. Behind the town that sloped up the hillsides rose the rocky Maritime Alps, towering and magnificent above the deep blue of the sea. It was August, and August was to see the principality in its fullest glory.

Like a dowager empress, Monaco had bedecked herself in floral jewels. Everywhere, the majestic palaces, villas, and high-rise condominiums were surrounded by fine flowering terraces, rare exotic plants, cacti, and palms whose fronds rustled in the breezes. Hélène had learned to differentiate between the stately date palms with their tall, smooth trunks and the shorter, more squat Canary palms, which had rough and scaly trunks. Lining the avenues and clustered in the parks, magnificent eucalyptus trees grew to a great height and perfumed the air with their distinctive, almost medicinal aroma.

She couldn't help feeling glad now that she had come. This was by far the most beautiful place she had ever seen. More beautiful even that Cap Ferrat, because everything wasn't walled up behind gates or hedges. And there was even a little bit of Paris here, as if to squelch any homesickness a visitor might have. The same man who had designed the Paris Opéra had had a hand in designing the casino.

A smile pushed through her frown as she thought of how Luba and Jacques had persuaded her to accompany them to the casino tonight.

"Really, I'm not one for gambling," Hélène had tried to beg off as the models had gotten dressed on the imported white stones that comprised the manmade beach.

The Czarina's coal-black eyebrows seemed to lift right off her patrician brow. "Indeed!" she snorted disdainfully. "You know, don't you, that the casino is *only* the most glamorous spot in Monte Carlo? Propriety, if nothing else, requires you to go."

"Propriety?" Hélène sputtered. "I don't see how—"

Swiftly Jacques had cut her off. "Where's your sense of adventure, princess?"

"My sense of—"

"Adventure. We shall knock on your door at seven-thirty sharp, have dinner down in the Grill, and go on to the Casino from there."

"But what a—"

Jacques placed a restraining finger on her lips. "Live, for once, princess," he coaxed with a glint of amusement in his eyes. "And don't look so indignant, for God's sake! Casinos aren't exactly low-life fleshpots. They're respectable haunts of high society."

"Take one of the models. Really, Jacques. I don't *want* to go!"

Suddenly he reached out, caught her in a tight bear hug that made it impossible for her to argue any further, and lifted her off her feet. "Say you'll go and I'll release you," he whispered.

She stared down at him. Her face was getting red, but she shook her head emphatically.

He appeared not to notice. "Oh, and don't forget to dress. You don't want to look like a yokel or an American, do you?"

"Put me down! You're hurting me!" Her voice was sharp with anger.

He grinned. "I'll let you go as soon as you agree to come. Just nod your pretty head."

She glanced up at him out of the corner of one eye. Finally she lifted her head and nodded. Then he set her down, unwrapping his arms slowly and gently.

She took a swallow of air. "You . . . you brute!" she spit out, trying to catch her breath and smooth her clothes at the same time. "That was blackmail!" She looked at him, her eyes flashing. "You forced me into agreeing! It doesn't count!" She turned her back on him.

He took her arm gently and twisted her around. "Come on, princess," he said. "A deal's a deal."

"Some fine deal," she snapped. "It was coercion, nothing more and nothing else!"

494

* * *

The casino. Now she thought about it again. Just having to go there filled her with a certain trepidation. She had never been inside a gambling palace before. As far as Monte Carlo went, she knew only what Luba and Jacques had told her, and what every schoolchild in France knew. That it was the queen of all casinos.

About gambling itself, she knew nothing. It had never interested her in the least. The lure of breaking the bank was for others, for those who still dreamed of the impossible. She didn't believe in luck, and any investment she undertook was gamble enough. But a casino, where one just threw money away? It was an obscenity that she couldn't comprehend. She'd worked too hard to get where she was; she'd done without too much in the past even to consider that such waste could be fun. And when the Czarina had reeled off the staggering array of games that could be played at the casino—baccarat, roulette, chemin-de-fer, boule, craps, blackjack, and trente-et-quarante—none of which she knew anything about, her terror only grew. But as with everything else she had tackled, she kept that terror well under control. Her quick mind had immediately seen through Monte Carlo. Like Hautecloque, it was nothing more than an elegant facade. And elegance was the one thing she knew plenty about.

That afternoon, while Jacques and Luba had taken their naps, she left her room. She took the elevator downstairs and walked through the lobby to the conciergerie.

Enlisting the aid of the chief concierge, who was familiar with the problems that could face the hotel's guests, an appointment was made at the best coiffeur in Monte Carlo—the best in the South of France. Étienne's was located just a few meters from the quay. When she got there, an indignant middle-aged woman was just leaving. She pushed stiffly past Hélène and slammed the door behind her in no uncertain terms. Hélène turned and stared after her. Then she looked around the salon. It was empty but for Étienne himself, a male assistant, and two young girls in crisp white smocks.

Étienne stepped forward. He was a tall, bearded, virile-looking man. His white silk shirt was unbuttoned halfway to the waist. His chest was hairy, and he wore a heavy gold chain around his neck, "Mademoiselle Junot?"

Hélène nodded and gestured at the door. "That woman—why was she so upset?"

He laughed as the pixie-faced girl hurried to pick up a magazine off the floor. "Madame Laprade is always upset," he said with a shrug. "I simply told her that it was impossible for me to do her today."

"But why?" Hélène asked. "Didn't she have an appointment?"

He remained discreetly silent, and Hélène felt a stab of guilt. Now it was clear. The woman's appointment had been cancelled at the last minute because of her. The chief concierge must have impressed upon Étienne how important she was when he had made the appointment. Perhaps he had even hinted that it was to his advantage to drop everything to take care of her. That he might even get exposure in *Les Modes*. It wasn't fair to Étienne, Madame Laprade, or herself, and she knew it. But it was too late to worry about that now. "Really, I . . . I should have been told," she said miserably. "I didn't mean to push my way in—"

He interrupted her. "Please, Mademoiselle Junot," he said smoothly, putting her fears to rest, "don't worry yourself about it. Madame Laprade is not going anywhere tonight. She has her hair done for the same reason that she goes shopping. To relieve her boredom. Please . . ." He gestured to the serious-faced girl. "Just follow Roxanne into the changing booth. Besides, it is not always that we have such an important client as you. See?" He nodded at the girl who was replacing the magazine that had been lying on the floor. She saw now that it was the August *Les Modes*, and it was going on top of the stack of past issues. He looked at her. "Your magazine is my clients' favorite," he announced.

"It seems that it's also their favorite weapon to fling at you," she observed archly, following Roxanne to the changing booth. Roxanne stayed outside and pulled the curtain shut with a well-practiced flick of her wrist.

He laughed and kept on talking while she changed. "In this business, one learns to take the lumps." He lowered his voice. "You've heard of Pauline Monnier?"

Hélène stuck her head out from behind the curtain and nodded. Pauline was the society reporter for *Couture Magazine*. Occasionally she'd run into her in Paris. She could still remember the first time she had ever seen her. It was from the catwalk when she'd first begun modeling at Odile Joly's. She knew, too, that the witty, unscrupulous Pauline was so often seen with Daphne Epaminondas that nasty tongues wagered they were carrying on a lesbian affair.

"The Epaminondas yacht was in the harbor all last week," Étienne was saying as Hélène pulled aside the curtain and stepped out wearing a starched white smock. She turned around and let the pixie-faced girl tie a plastic bib around her neck. Then she took a seat while Roxanne spun the taps on the sink and tested the water with her hand.

Étienne wasn't finished with his story. "Poor Pauline came in only the day before yesterday and demanded that I cut her hair in a style which I warned her was totally unsuitable," he said sadly. "Afterward, she decided I'd ruined her looks. She actually picked up a pair of shears and tried to attack me! Can you imagine that?"

Hélène suppressed a smile. She could well imagine the minuscule Pauline in a rage. She could also imagine how quickly and easily she must have been subdued. Nevertheless, she clucked her tongue sympathetically, cautioning herself to refrain from telling Étienne a thing. He might look like a masculine sailor, she thought, but he seemed a terrible gossip.

"Well, the Epaminondas yacht was here up until yesterday morning. Then, as soon as the Skouri yacht came in through the breakwater, they hauled in anchor and sailed straight out. You know that Madame Epaminondas was once Madame Skouri, don't you?"

Hélène started to nod, but he didn't wait for a reply.

"Ex-husbands and ex-wives can either be great friends or terrible enemies," he philosophized in an aggrieved voice. Then he sighed and was silent for a moment. He shook his head. "Unfortunately, they're archenemies. I've even heard it said that the casino won't allow her in while he's there. Not just because they have such public rows, but because Monsieur Skouri is powerful enough to keep her out. He's one of the directors of the SBM."

Hélène nodded. She knew what the SBM was. The Société des Bains de Mer et Cercle des Etrangers. It was the organization which controlled or owned a good portion of Monte Carlo, including the Hôtel de Paris, the casino, and the magnificently planted gardens.

"Anyway, the way I see it, Madame Epaminondas doesn't have anything to gripe about. She's come a long way, you know. Greek peasant girl makes good, that sort of thing. She got a settlement of fifteen million dollars from Monsieur Skouri, and as soon as the divorce was final what did she do? Turned around and skipped off with Monsieur Epaminondas, that's what! They say he's good for at least a hundred million. Of course, Monsieur Skouri's worth three times that, but she doesn't have anything to worry about really, now, does she?" He stopped short suddenly, "How much time have you got?"

Hélène was thrown by the sudden change of subject. "I . . . I should be back at the hotel by six-thirty."

He frowned and glanced at his wristwatch. "That gives us a little more than three hours. Nina!"

The pixie-faced girl looked up and caught his nod. Obediently she went over to the door, quickly turned the key in the lock, and flipped the "Fermé" sign around to face the sidewalk outside.

Étienne was now all business. "It will take us all of three hours," he said, clapping his hands. "Now, then, have you given any thought to the kind of hairstyle you want?"

Hélène shook her head. "Not really. But I want something very elegant." She gave a faint smile. "Even showy."

"Ah." He stepped back, strummed his lips, and frowned thoughtfully for a moment. "I take it you're going to the casino?"

She nodded.

"What are you going to wear?"

"A Marcel Manet," she answered, adding: "He's a new designer. The gown's of pale blue satin, almost white, actually, and looks sort of like a Grecian toga."

"Sounds lovely." He looked thoughtful. "Jewelry?"

"I'm not certain. Aquamarines or coral."

He came close and placed his fingers lightly on her head. While he felt her hair, her eyes went to the big round mirror. She watched him closely.

"I think we should stick with an overall Greek look, then," he suggested. "What do you say we part your hair right here in the middle and have it sprout tiny, delicate curls all the way back to here? Then, here on the back, we'll pin on a fabulous fall."

She thought for a moment; there was an unsure look in her eyes. What he was suggesting was elaborate and extremely formal. She wondered whether it was too formal for the casino.

He sensed her indecision. "It'll look spectacular," he assured her. "But I'll show you what I mean, and you can make up your own mind." He turned around. "Ambrose!"

His male assistant perked up.

"The Grecian curls. Bring out all the dark shades."

Ambrose nodded and hurried to the back of the salon. A moment later he came back out with a stack of boxes. Étienne frowned as he went through all of them. Finally he selected a thick black fall and pinned it expertly to the back of Hélène's head. "It's a fantastic look," he said. "Sort of à la Elizabeth Taylor. You could even wear a jewel on the hairpiece."

Roxanne and Nina held up hand mirrors so that Hélène could see herself from all angles. Slowly she nodded. Étienne was right. The elaborate hairdo would set off the classic simplicity of the gown sensationally. He had good taste, she thought, even if he did borrow liberally from Alexandre. But what the hell, she thought. If you had to borrow, just make sure you borrowed from the best. And she liked his idea about wearing a jewel in her hair. She knew exactly which one. The large pearshaped pearl mounted in white gold and surrounded by a spray of aquamarines. Any other jewels were out of the question. They would only detract. Her arms, neck, and ears would have to be bare. For a wrap, there was the thin satin stole that was an integral part of the gown. For footwear there were the delicate silver evening sandals. The matching white-gold-mesh clutch purse with her aquamarine initial on the clasp would be the crowning touch. There was no doubt in her mind but that she would make heads turn. And long ago, that first night when she had set foot in Maxim's, she had learned that elegant dress made a world of difference. It closed the social gulf a bit and made you feel you were at the top of the world. Yes, she would be stunning. The only thing that still bothered her were the games. Suddenly she had an idea. She knew that Étienne liked to gossip, but she decided to take that risk. Better that a few stories circulated about her than that she made a fool of herself tonight. Just as Roxanne was about to rinse her hair, she turned to Étienne. "You wouldn't happen to know how to gamble, would you?" she asked huskily.

He looked at her sympathetically. "Like everyone else, I know enough to get by."

"What's the easiest game to learn?"

He didn't hesitate. "Roulette."

Her face took on an enthusiastic expression. "I need a crash course," she said. "To tell you the truth, I've never been to a casino in my life."

"That's no problem. By the time your hair is done, you'll know everything there is to know about roulette, and then some."

Hélène looked around the roulette table as the bets were placed. The multicolor chips rose like neat clusters of miniature skyscrapers from the green baize. Each chip represented anywhere from five francs on up. She estimated that a fortune lay on that table.

Almost furtively she leaned forward to place her lone chip on the black, and then quickly withdrew her hand and stood back. She had been watching the game carefully. Étienne had taught her just enough so that she wouldn't get confused. "Bet on the red or the black," he'd said. "Forget about the numbers." So far, the wheel had run to the red. She reasoned it was time for the black to come up.

The croupier spun the wheel, and the dressed-up crowd quickly placed their last bets.

"Rien ne va plus," the croupier announced.

No more bets could now be placed, and the gamblers watched intently as the ball that was to decide the fate of their money was tossed into the wheel. It did a few hops and then began to do a wide roll.

The tension around the table was tangible. The society matrons' hooded eyes were like those of eagles, their pupils darting and flashing like the diamonds around their necks. One young blond, on the arm of a fat old German who kept mopping his brow with a handkerchief, was almost jumping with excitement. A tall, elderly gentleman watched the ball with a studiously expressionless face, but his fingers ticked nervously against his trouser seams. A younger, shorter man beside Hélène glanced at her and smiled nervously.

She smiled back at him and then watched the ball as the wheel began to slow down. The gamblers held their breath; the ladies pressed their red lips more firmly together and clutched their mink stoles tighter. Then the wheel came to a stop. The ball did a final, almost lazy roll. Hélène watched it without breathing. She was going to win! It would land in the black!

But it only looked that way. The elusive ball hesitated and then dropped neatly into the red compartment labeled thirty-four. The croupier expertly raked in the chips.

Hélène sighed and turned away. Her lone chip was being scraped away along with the others. Not that she'd really thought she'd had a chance at winning. It was just that controlled though she was, she *had* been excited during that last half-second interval when the ball had nearly dropped into the black.

She felt Jacques pull her aside as the next batch of chips was placed. "Are you winning?" he asked.

She shook her head morosely, her Grecian curls doing a little dance. "I've played five games and lost all five," she said wearily, opening her palm to show some chips. "These are all I have left."

He made a face and clucked his tongue in mock sympathy. "Poor princess. Lose much?"

"Twenty-five francs."

He laughed. "I should have known you'd be placing the unité de mise. Shame on you!" He wagged a finger at her. "A rich girl like you should be reckless. You shouldn't be in the public rooms. You should be in the Salles Privées, where the stakes are respectable."

"Is that where the Czarina is?"

He shook his head and grinned. "She's in the Salle des Amériques playing blackjack, cursing in Russian, and losing her shirt!"

Hélène smiled. "She must be a sight."

He nodded. "I'm going to try my hand at craps. Want to join me?"

She shook her head. "I think I'll stay right here."

He lifted his hand and crossed his fingers. "Good luck."

Now she looked around the roulette table again. While she and Jacques had been talking, she'd missed placing her new bet. The sharp eyes of the gamblers were already on the spinning wheel.

She shrugged, turned away from the table, cashed in the remainder of her chips, and started out of the room. When she reached the magnificent staircase, she descended to the Ganne Room. She hesitated in front of the nightclub, then decided against it and went into the tearoom instead. She was shown to the best table immediately.

"I'll have a mint tea," she told the waiter. When he brought it, he carefully poured a cupful from the pot. The spicy aroma of the mint was sweet to her nostrils, and the steam curled lazily out of the thin white china cup. She had no inkling of it yet, but luck was indeed at the casino this night. It had brought her down here to the tearoom, and it was smiling benevolently upon her.

8

"You've been sitting here for over an hour now," the man said politely.

Hélène set her third cup of tea down in the saucer and looked over at him. Vaguely she had wondered whether he was a gigolo. She had heard that that type of man hung out in the casinos and preyed on lonely women. Then, realizing how foolish this thought was, she saw that he was too re-fined-looking, too understated. She wondered where she had seen him before. He looked vaguely familiar, but she couldn't place him. He was British, probably. Only the English could cut a tuxedo so superbly. And now that he spoke, she realized her guess had been right. His French was excellent, but the accent was unmistakably upper-crust British.

She inclined her head and smiled. "I'm not terribly keen on gambling, I'm afraid."

He smiled back at her. "Neither am I," he admitted. "I came in with a group of people and managed to sneak away. What about you?"

She laughed. "I came here with friends also. They're gambling away upstairs."

"You are very wise," he observed.

"So are you," she replied.

"Would it be terribly forward of me if I joined you?"

Hélène brightened at the prospect of having company.

Luba and Jacques were both preoccupied with the games, and they were the only people she knew. Sitting alone for so long was a bore. "Not at all. I'd be delighted. Please . . ." She gestured to the empty chair opposite her.

Delicately balancing the cup, he lifted his saucer and slipped over into the chair. It was only now that she realized how tall he was, and she could smell the faint scent of his eau de cologne. His hair was brown and thick, carefully combed back, and his features were very fine. But it was his eyes which she found so fascinating. They were brown and warm, speckled with little flecks of gold.

It was then that she realized where she had met him. Years ago, at the Lichtenstein Gallery, after Odile Joly had "discovered" her. His name was Nigel Somerset and it seemed he was far more handsome than she had remembered him to be.

For the next half-hour they talked and got reacquainted with one another. She knew little about English society, but his manners, like his dress, hinted at a cultured, perhaps titled background. Still, he might be merely upper-middle-class with a good education. The rigid system of structured society was slowly changing, even in England. She learned that he lived in London and in the English countryside and sometimes spent holidays and vacations on the continent. He talked so casually, and without pretense, that she could easily envision his country home. She had seen enough pictures of quaint English cottages with thatched roofs and ancient beams and stucco to be able to do that.

She found out, too, that he worked for a living in the family business, a subject about which he was rather vague. That killed off any notion she had that he was one of the idle rich, but this revelation didn't disappoint her at all. A working person of quality was someone she could understand and identify with. Even appreciate. After all, she was a working woman. It hadn't hurt her any. If anything, she honestly believed it had only made her more interesting.

She couldn't help wondering about his personal life. He made no mention of having a wife or children, so she took it for granted that he was unmarried. When she glanced—discreetly—at his ring finger, she saw that it was bare. The only family he mentioned were his parents. They were both alive, and he would say no more except that he was here in Monte Carlo with friends; he had been invited to cruise on board their yacht.

503

She found out this much in the first twenty minutes; what he didn't put into words she saw in her mind's eye. Then, adroitly, so that she hardly knew what was happening, he turned the subject around and began asking questions about her. She was frank and talkative. It had been a long time since she had talked seriously with anyone. It felt good to do it now. Nigel Somerset, she had to admit, was a good listener, and good listeners were a rarity. She opened up easily. There was something about him that made her feel comfortable. He ordered another pot of tea, this time a strange blend she had never heard of; but then, he was English, she reminded herself, and the English were great tea drinkers. When he gently probed and asked if she had a husband, she told him that she was Stanislaw Kowalsky's widow. He didn't raise an eyebrow. If he thought it strange that the old pianist had had such a young wife he concealed it behind that implacably expressionless quality that was so much a part of the British. He simply nodded and said that he had met Stanislaw twice when he had performed at Royal Albert Hall. He thought very highly of him, both as a man and as an artist. Then he prodded some more, and she found herself telling him about *Les Modes*. Although at first she was certain she must be boring him, she realized after a while that he was genuinely interested. Then she became suspicious.

"You're sure you don't work for the competition?" she asked good-naturedly.

He grinned. "I'm afraid not."

She took a sip of tea. "You still haven't told me what you do."

He started to tell her, but at that moment Jacques appeared in the doorway, and motioned to her. She set down her cup and pushed her chair back. "Could you excuse me for a moment? It seems that one of my friends is looking for me."

"Of course." Nigel got up, gallantly held out her chair, and watched her make her way through the tables toward the door.

Jacques held the door open for her, and she went outside with him. "What is it?" she asked.

"I think I'm going to leave." He glanced impatiently down the hall, and her eyes followed his. Étienne, her hairdresser, was standing a discreet distance away. His eyes met hers and he gave a little bow in her direction.

She took Jacques by the arm and pulled him into a corner. "So you dragged me here and now you want to run off and play!"

"Have a heart, princess."

"All right, go on," she said, affecting a weary tone. She was anxious to get back to Nigel. "But when I got my hair done at Étienne's, I tipped lavishly. Now, don't you go promising him exposure in *Les Modes* in return for any . . . any favors," she warned dryly.

He shook his head. "Really, princess, when you think things like that, you disappoint me."

"Just make certain you keep business and pleasure separate."

"I always do." He sniffed. "Now, I'd better run off before he gets impatient. You just go back to Nigel Somerset and enjoy yourself." He started to turn and leave.

"Whoa." She grabbed his arm. "Not so fast. How do you know Nigel's name?"

"Everybody knows who Nigel Somerset is." He looked at her in surprise. "Don't you?"

"No, but he's a very nice man."

"He's a very nice *rich* man," Jacques corrected her. "He's the future sixteenth Duke of Farquharshire and heir to the Somerset fortune. I suppose you'll tell me next that you didn't know that his father, the fifteenth duke, just happens to be the third-richest man in England?"

The Monte Carlo Beach is in French territory. It was there that Jacques had shot the models on the imported white stones. Now Hélène glanced around the darkness as she and Nigel cautiously picked their way down the beach. It was after midnight, and the big pool was deserted, the parasols around it closed. The casino crowd, which sunned here during the day, was still at the gaming tables, and here on the beach in the middle of the night, everything was quiet, even the tiny bungalows where the rich and famous held their private beach parties. Except for one, and it was there that they were headed. About a hundred meters down the beach, the glow of fires and the sounds of a band marked where the Skouri crowd was having a Mediterranean-style luau. Nigel had insisted she accompany him to the party. When they neared it, Hélène saw that it was complete with calypso band, fiery torches stuck in the ground, and a buffet table laden with bowls of caviar stuck in ice and with all the delicacies the Mediterranean could provide. The music was nearly ear-splitting, and the flickering torches cast shadows that gave everyone an eerie reddish-bronzed hue. There must have been at least thirty or forty people there, none of whom she knew. But Nigel had been right about one thing. They were all in evening clothes. Some of the men had begun to strip to the waist as they danced to the frenetic beat of the calypso; the women had prudently taken off their delicate evening slippers.

Hélène stopped, quickly slipped out of her sandals, and carried them in her hand.

"Niggle!" a deep voice boomed out above the party sounds.

Startled, Hélène looked around. A short heavyset man with white hair and thick black-rimmed glasses was hurrying toward them. He was wearing baggy trousers and a white shirt open to the waist. He flung his arms around Nigel. Then he glanced at Hélène.

"I knew it, Niggle!" he cried excitedly. "Sooner or later, the charms of a beautiful young woman were bound to affect you!"

Hélène glanced at Nigel. He was smiling. "You think she's beautiful, Zeno?" he asked.

Zeno studied Hélène closely. Then he laughed. "I would say she's very beautiful!" Suddenly he stepped forward, embraced Hélène tightly, kissed her once on each cheek, and stepped back. "I'm Zeno Skouri," he said, not waiting for an introduction.

"I'm Hélène Junot."

"Enchanté," he said, making a production of kissing her hand as well. Then he hooked one arm through hers, the other through Nigel's. They started to walk. "Come, let us drink some champagne. We have fifty magnums on hand. It would be a pity to let it go to waste." He looked at Hélène. "You like Dom Perignon?"

She smiled. "Yes, but only a little. I'm afraid I have to be fit for travel tomorrow. I'm, returning to Paris in the morning."

Skouri frowned. "A beautiful woman like you must return to the city? I thought all beautiful people left Paris for the summer."

She laughed. "I'm afraid I'm a working girl."

He looked at her shrewdly. "A model or an actress?"

"Neither. She owns a fashion magazine," Nigel explained. "Perhaps you've heard of it. It's called *Les Modes.*"

Skouri beamed. "I've seen it," he said enthusiastically. "Ariadne swears it's the only decent one on the market."

Hélène looked pleased. Ariadne Cosindas was the world's most magnificent ballerina. She had also been Skouri's long-time mistress. Still, it was strange to hear the revered La Cosindas referred to as simply "Ariadne."

"Since you're self-employed and presumably have a capable staff, I insist that you join us for the next two weeks," Skouri stated flatly.

Hélène stared at him. "I . . . I don't think I understand," she stammered.

"The cruise. We started in Barcelona and are going to work our way around the boot of Italy and up to Venice." Skouri stopped walking and looked at Hélène. "What do you say? You'll honor us with your company?"

For a moment, Hélène looked confused. She had never before received such a spur-of-the-moment invitation. Nor had she ever had a real vacation. The chances of being invited on the legendary Skouri yacht some other time were slim. It would be nice to go, she thought. Besides, any excuse to wheedle out of it would sound skimpy. Zeno Skouri was right. Why else did she have a staff if they couldn't get work done in her absence? She could always put the Czarina in charge. Quickly she made up her mind. She leaned forward and glanced sideways at Nigel. He was smiling enthusiastically.

"Do *you* want me to go?" she asked softly.

He nodded wordlessly.

Skouri caught the nod. "See?" he boomed exuberantly. "Niggle says you must go, so you must go. It is set, then. The day after tomorrow, we sail on. I'll send a car to pick you up. Where are you staying?"

"The Hôtel de Paris."

"It's my favorite place in the world," Skouri said proudly. "That's the only reason I bought into the SBM. Because I liked the Salle Empire so much." He shot her a challenging look. "You like it?"

Hélène nodded. "It's a masterpiece of Belle Epoque," she said seriously, thinking of the big room and the opulent mural of the busty women. "I have a weakness for the period."

"Then we'll hit it off well. The salon of the *Evangelia* is all original Belle Epoque." They had reached the bar. "Now, for the champagne. And don't worry, if you get a hangover, you have all day tomorrow to recover."

Nigel patted Skouri's broad back and cleared his throat. Skouri turned around, then heaved his shoulders and sighed. "Just my luck," he said with mock resignation. "The most beautiful woman here, and spoken for." He assumed a morose expression and made his way toward a tall, smoothly exotic woman in a silver sarong.

Nigel and Hélène watched Skouri's instant jovial smile as he put a hand in the small of the woman's back, propelling her toward the beach.

Nigel grinned, hooked his arm through Hélène's. "Dance?" he asked.

She smiled at him, her face radiant and flickering in the torchlight. "Dance," she said huskily.

Till dawn lit the beach, Hélène danced and drank with Nigel, both of them losing their reserve, until dance after dance and drink after drink melted into countless others. She didn't mind at all that he wanted to keep her all to himself rather than share her with the rest of the party. And when he took her back to the hotel, the sun was already streaking the pale sky in a fan shape, and she realized only then that she had been introduced to no one but Zeno Skouri.

Nigel, she thought with a peculiar stirring, was enough. More than enough.

The next day Hélène awoke to find the bedroom dim, but afternoon sunlight shone in the bright chinks between the curtains. She looked up at Jacques, who was sitting on the edge of her bed. "I had a great time!" he said happily. "That Étienne's really something, you know that? He's not like all those fairies in Paris. He's a real man. And what he can do with his tongue!"

Hélène tried to lift her head up off the pillow. "Please," she said weakly. "Spare me the gruesome details." Gingerly she touched her forehead with the back of her hand and let her head drop back down on the pillow. She tried to swallow. Her mouth tasted stale and sour.

Jacques watched her with an expression of amusement. "What's the matter, princess? Got a hangover?"

"Please," she begged, "lower your voice. It's pounding in my temples."

He shook his head. "Poor princess." He got up, and she could feel the mattress shifting under her. He crossed over to the telephone table and picked up the receiver. He had his back to her and she could hear snatches of his conversation. "Room service . . . a tomato juice with ice, Tabasco sauce, and salt . . . and a jigger of vodka." He turned around and glanced over at Hélène.

She made a face. "Now I know I'm going to be sick."

He hung up the phone and grinned. "All I sent for was the American cure for a hangover." He clapped his hands and she winced. "Come on, princess, there's a lot we have to do today! We're leaving in three hours, remember?"

"Leaving?" Her voice was tiny. She shook her head slowly. "I can't go anywhere."

"Sure you can. It won't be long till you'll feel fit as a fiddle." He crossed the room and went from window to window, swiftly yanking aside the curtains. Sunlight poured in.

Hélène let out a gasp and covered her face with a pillow. Her voice was muffled. "Close those damn things!"

"We've got to get up, princess," he said in a hearty voice. "The trains won't wait for us. The Czarina's already packed and brunching downstairs."

She peered out from under the pillow. "What time is it, anyway?"

He pulled back his cuff to glance at his Baume and Mercier. "Five past three," he said mildly.

"Three o'clock!" she moaned. Small wonder that she was feeling so lousy. She'd come in at five-thirty, high as a kite and giggling hysterically. The last thing she remembered was Nigel bringing her up here, putting her to bed, and kissing her gently on the forehead. Could there have been more? Perhaps he . . . No, she'd have remembered if they had done anything. And how could she think such horrible thoughts, anyway? Nigel was a gentleman. Through and through. He wouldn't take advantage of a lady in distress.

Suddenly she sat bolt upright. Then she cursed herself for the sudden move as flashes of pain shot through her skull. She placed her thumb and index finger firmly on her forehead. The cruise! Good God, she'd have to let the chief concierge know that she'd be staying an extra day. And she'd have to get Luba in here and give her instructions on running the office in her absence. Or . . . An ugly thought managed to worm its way into her mind. Had the invitation for the cruise been a hallucination? No, she hadn't even started drinking when Zeno Skouri had invited her. She let her head drop to the pillow again.

"Jacques . . ."

"Yes, princess?" He came toward the bed and looked down at her.

"Call the chief concierge. Tell him I'm staying another day. Then get Luba up here."

"You're staying?"

"Just do as I say," she said wearily, closing her eyes.

"Sure, princess." He gave her a curious look and went back to the telephone table. A moment later he had the chief concierge on the wire. When he finished the call, he looked across at her, an incredulous expression on his face. "The chief concierge already knew," he said in a disbelieving voice. "You move in mighty exalted circles, princess. It seems that Zeno Skouri himself called up to extend your reservation."

Hélène opened her eyes and stared at him.

"Not only that, but I'm supposed to tell you that you're to consider yourself a *guest* of the Hôtel de Paris."

Hélène let out a sigh of relief. So the invitation hadn't been a dream. She could feel some of her energy returning. "Good," she said. "Now get the Czarina up here."

"Will do. But you still haven't told me why you're staying."

She kept her face carefully expressionless. "I've decided to take a two-week vacation, that's all. Boss's prerogative."

"Good for you! Where are you going?"

"On the Skouri yacht."

"The Skouri yacht!" He let out a low whistle. "Good Lord, a few days here, and you set Monte Carlo on fire!" He looked thoughtful. "Princess?" he said hesitantly.

"Hmmmm?"

"You wouldn't mind terribly if I stayed on here for one more day also, would you?"

"What about the pictures?" she pointed out. "They've got to be developed."

"That can wait a day. I'll get to them the instant I get back, cross my heart. Besides, we're a month ahead of schedule."

Before she could answer, there was a discreet knock on the door.

"Come in!" Jacques called out, hurrying across the room.

It was room service with the tomato-juice concoction and a perfect red rose in a bud vase. Jacques took the tray and brought it over to the bedside and held it out to her.

She grimaced.

"It works, princess. Just be a good girl and drink up."

"À votre santé," she mumbled, slowly bringing the glass up to her lips. She looked at him over the rim as she took a tentative sip.

When Luba came into the room, Hélène looked over at her from the settee. She put down the buttered croissant she had been nibbling. Luba was carrying the new *Paris Vogue* under her arm. The life-sized cover girl was glaring out at her with a spiteful expression.

"I hope I haven't inconvenienced you," Hélène said apologetically.

"Not at all," Luba said quietly. "In fact, I was going to come and see you."

Hélène nodded. "I just wanted to let you know that I'm not returning to Paris with you. I've decided to take a two-week vacation. You'll be in charge in my absence."

Luba nodded. "Before you turn the responsibilities over to me, there's something you might first like to take care of yourself," she said with gravity.

"Oh?" Hélène raised her eyebrows. "And what's that?"

"Before lunch, I noticed that the new *Vogue* was already out," Luba explained. Despite the fact that they were alone, she lowered her voice confidentially. "So I bought a copy." She glanced down at it. "Only to keep tabs on what the competition's doing, you understand," she added unnecessarily.

Hélène smiled, but her eyes looked at Luba with concern. The Czarina wasn't her usual dramatic self. Something serious was up. She nodded to a chair. "Won't you have a seat, Luba?" she said gently.

Stiffly Luba pulled the chair closer and sat down. She handed over the *Vogue*. "Pages eighty-four through eighty-nine."

Hélène glanced at her, but Luba's dark eyes were carefully veiled. Then wordlessly she opened the magazine and flipped to page eighty-four. Suddenly a horrified look crossed her

511

face. Quickly she thumbed through the following pages. Still clutching the *Vogue*, she sprang to her feet, regretting it the instant her headache started again. She began pacing the room, her lips set in a grim line. Against her specific orders, Jacques had been moonlighting. Taking pictures for the competition while he was *Les Modes*'s staff photographer. That in itself might have deserved a severe dressing-down. But he had gone further than that. A blatant credit was printed alongside each picture. It was a direct stab in the back.

After a while she stopped pacing and turned to Luba. "Thank you for showing this to me," she said.

The Czarina got to her feet. "I wasn't trying to get anyone into trouble," she said uncomfortably.

Hélène forced a smile "Of course not. I realize that, in many ways, *Les Modes* is even more important to you than to me. Don't worry, I won't tell Jacques that you brought this to my attention."

Luba smiled gratefully and started to leave the room.

"You don't mind if I keep this for a little while?" Hélène asked, holding up the *Vogue*.

Luba shook her head and went quietly out.

Quickly Hélène changed from her peignoir into a dress, ran a comb through her hair, and went in search of Jacques. He wasn't in his room. Finally she found him out on the terrace, eating under a tilted parasol. He looked up as her shadow fell across him.

He grinned. "So you're already up, princess. I told you that vodka and tomato juice work wonders. Here . . ." He leaned sideways and pulled out a chair for her. "Have a seat and we'll order you an early dinner."

She remained standing, a dark expression on her face. "No, thank you," she said quietly. She plopped the *Vogue* down on the table. "Your contract specifically reads that you may not publish pictures in any magazine but *Les Modes*."

He shrugged and looked away. "So the shit has hit the fan," he mumbled. "Surely you're not serious about binding me to that contract?"

"I not only stipulated it orally, but in writing as well. Is that binding enough for you?"

"Come on, princess—"

"Don't you 'princess' me!" she said sharply. "As of this moment, you're fired! I expect your resignation in writing immediately."

He looked dumbfounded. Then he burst out laughing. "Fired? This is Jacques, your loyal employee, remember? I helped you put that magazine together from scratch."

"I repeat, you're fired. I'm being kind enough to let you resign," she said quietly. "I suggest you give Luba all the film you've shot here."

He looked at her tauntingly. "And if I don't?"

"I'll sue, and then you're finished. Word spreads. You'll be tagged as 'unreliable.' Not one fashion publisher in the Western world will as much as look at one of your snapshots."

He picked up his napkin from his lap and tossed it on his plate. He pushed his chair back and got to his feet. "Fine. Then I won't show my face in the office until you're back. But I want us to have a talk."

She tensed. "What's there to talk about?" she asked curtly.

"My severance pay." He patted her cheek. "But that can wait. I wouldn't want to spoil your vacation, princess."

She started to reply, but he was already on his way back into the hotel, leaving her seething on the terrace. Angrily she turned away from the table. She had both liked and trusted him but he had broken the bond between them. For a moment she considered calling Skouri and canceling the cruise. Then she decided against it. The copy and pictures for *Les Modes* were ahead of schedule. Luba would find someone to develop the shots. In the meantime, they would use a freelance photographer. Maybe Cecil Beaton, William Klein, or Hiro was available. Why should she suffer because of Jacques?

9

It was midmorning and the sun was already high and white and baking, but the breezes swept in from the sea as they always did to rustle the palm fronds and cool the air. Inside the breakwater, the white yachts did a little bob in the wake of a speedboat heading out between the twin stone towers that guarded the entrance to the port.

Jacques was standing in the shade on the rue des Remparts. A pair of Zeiss binoculars hung from around his neck and there was a magnificent view of the harbor from up here on the bluff. But he hadn't come to enjoy the view. He was waiting for someone.

Meanwhile, he thought back to last night. He had seen Étienne twice now. All night, they had drunk a lot and smoked some opium which Étienne had gotten hold of. As a result, Jacques hadn't gotten nearly enough sleep. There was plenty of time for that later, he told himself. Besides, now that he had been fired, and Hélène wouldn't be back in Paris for two weeks, he really had nothing to do. He might even stay longer here. At least until the good things wore off.

Someone was approaching. Jacques turned around, his eyes fixed steadily on Hubert de Léger. Suddenly he had to smile. Hubert was headed toward him on foot, his face florid and his chest heaving from the exertion of the climb. In Monaco, no matter where you walked, it was either up- or downhill. Twice Hubert had to stop to wipe the perspiration off his face with a rumpled handkerchief. Jacques waited until he was near. "You're late," he said.

"What's so important?" Hubert asked in a surly voice. "What did you have me fly down here for at such short notice?"

"It would be well for you to learn some patience." Jacques dug his hands into his trouser pockets and nodded down to the harbor. "Nice view, don't you agree?"

Hubert was silent.

"Recognize any of the yachts?"

Hubert looked at him. His voice was belligerent. "Should I?"

"Take a look at the prime berth." Jacques took his hands out of his pockets, unlooped the binoculars from around his neck, and held them out to Hubert.

For a moment Hubert hesitated. Then he took them and squinted through the lenses. The prime berth was just inside the breakwater on this side of the port. A four-decked yacht was moored there, Mediterranean fashion, stern to the quay. He studied it for a moment. There was no doubt but that it was the biggest yacht in the harbor, long and sleek, the blinding white throwing off a dazzling glare. It was the size of a small ocean liner, three hundred and thirty feet long. The bow was rakish and sloped gracefully downward to the stern, which was gentle and rounded. The funnel was painted navy blue, and so were the two amphibious Piaggio airplanes behind the on-deck crane. Also navy blue were the canvas covers on the speedboats and the big awning stretched over the aft deck.

"Whose yacht is that?" Hubert asked.

"The *Evangelia*," Jacques replied. "The Skouri yacht. It's big, isn't it?"

Hubert lifted the binoculars again. As he watched, five Rolls-Royces pulled to a halt behind the Skouri yacht and the chauffeurs got out to hold the rear doors open. He counted twelve people getting out. He focused in on each one of them. Suddenly his face went pale and ashen. He had recognized one of the passengers. A woman wearing cork-soled sandals, a checkered dress, large round sunglasses, and a big straw hat. His eyes narrowed as he lowered the binoculars. He did not notice the way Jacques was looking at him. All he could think of was the woman he'd just seen. It was Hélène.

His hands started to shake. The desperate longing he'd once felt for her had long since curdled into something quite different and more powerful.

Hate.

After the *Evangelia* was a white speck halfway to Menton, Jacques and Hubert headed to the Ariston Bar. It was cool inside and the place was filled with tourists nursing their drinks.

They got a table in a quiet corner. They didn't speak until after the drinks arrived.

Hubert's face held a hostile expression. "I know there's no love lost between us," he said suspiciously. "Why the sudden interest?"

"Because it's to our mutual benefit to call a truce and join forces," Jacques replied smoothly. He took a swallow of his Campari. It tasted deliciously bitter and refreshing. "I know you don't like me, Hubert," he said. "You've bad-mouthed me in public once too often. But *I've* been discreet. *I* haven't told anyone a thing about you."

Hubert's florid face reddened even more. It looked like his blood vessels were about to burst. "What's there to tell?" he asked angrily.

Jacques laughed thinly. "Come off it, Hubert. You know very well."

Hubert looked down into his drink. "I was very drunk at the time," he said quickly. "It was a set-up."

Jacques stared at him steadily. "Was it?" His voice was flat. "Sure, you were only a kid of fifteen spending the week-end in Paris with his parents. But you did sneak out of the hotel and come into the *pouf* bar, didn't you? You did go home with Maurice and me. And you did suck on our pricks. Remember?"

Hubert grabbed Jacques by the collar and pulled him close. Instantly, Jacques's face reddened and he began gasping for breath. His hands flew up to his throat, tugging at Hubert's fingers. "Let me go," he rasped. "You'll be sorry."

Hubert twisted the collar in his hand, tightening the stranglehold. "Listen, you slimy queer," he snarled into Jacques's face. "I'll kill you if you say that again!"

Suddenly the conversations around them had stopped and Hubert could feel eyes upon them. He looked around. Contemptuously he released his grip and threw Jacques backward into his chair. Jacques swallowed and loosened his collar. For a moment he stared at Hubert.

"Everyone tries something like that once in his life!" Hubert hissed in a half-whisper. "I'm not a queer. It was part of growing up. All adolescents do that sort of thing."

Jacques recovered quickly. "What about the pictures, Hubert?" he asked tauntingly. "I've still got copies of them, you know. Sure, they're not exactly sex pictures. But you're naked in them. Masturbating, remember? At the time you thought posing was a great turn-on."

"It was a mistake! Can't you get that through your perverted skull? I was a kid." He brought the brandy up to his lips and took a swallow.

Jacques gave a low laugh. "Who'd believe it? The pictures speak for themselves. Me, I'll never forget that day. I had to take a cab home, remember? Because you rode home on the back of Maurice's moped. Playing with him the whole way, I might add."

"What is it you want? Money? Here." He reached for his wallet and started counting out thousand-franc bills.

Jacques shook his head and pushed the money away. "I don't want your money. I want to make a deal."

516

Hubert stared at him. "I don't think I like your deals," he said quietly.

Jacques now leaned across the table, his confidence fully restored. "But you liked *her*, didn't you? And she left you cold. I know how much you must hate her. Don't you want to get even?"

Hubert drew himself up and finished his drink. He put the glass down. "Just say what you have to and let's get this over with," he said irritably.

"All right." Jacques frowned into his Campari and toyed deliberately with the stem of the glass. "If I'm not mistaken, there are three shareholders in Les Editions Hélène Junot." he said calculatingly. "Hélène, you, and a certain German. Joining forces, you and the German hold twenty percent of the shares."

"Why would you care about that?" Hubert mumbled. "You're the one who's chummy with her."

Jacques looked at him. "And what would you say if I were to tell you that I was going to become a shareholder? That would give us thirty, maybe forty percent if we stuck together. Enough to throw some wrenches into the publishing machinery."

Hubert sat up straight now. "*You* hold shares!" he said incredulously. "How? What has she got on you?"

Jacques looked puzzled, wondering what this was supposed to mean. "Got on me? My dear boy, what on earth are you talking about?" His eyes widened suddenly as everything fell into place. "So *that's* it!" he exclaimed in triumph, answering his own question. "Now I get it!" He burst out laughing. The world had gone crazy. Jacques was crazy. Even Hélène was crazy.

Hubert looked at him sharply. "*What* do you get?"

"Why you are a shareholder. I always thought it strange. She's hated you for as long as I've known her. And she was rich enough not to need your money." Delicately Jacques sipped his Campari. When he spoke again, his voice was a whisper. "What did you do, Hubert, that she could force you into investing?"

"Nothing," Hubert answered quickly.

"Come on, I'm not a fool." Jacques looked at him shrewdly across the table. "You said you would kill me—I wonder if that would be new to you?" he said softly. "That's the key to everything, isn't it?"

Hubert said nothing. He just looked at Jacques. What he saw was a hungry, ambitious look in his eyes which he had never seen there before.

"Who would you have killed, Hubert? Let me see, now . . ." Jacques pretended to be deep in thought as he made a production of drumming the table with spiderlike fingertips.

Hubert watched the fingers in morbid fascination. They looked like they were moving slowly up and down the keyboard of a piano.

Jacques smiled widely and looked at him. "Kowalsky," he stated softly.

The decks vibrated pleasantly as the big diesels pushed the *Evangelia* through the water. Monaco was slowly slipping away behind them like just another cluster of white houses on the Côte d'Azur. When you looked away from the coast, all you could see was water, deep blue and undulating gently. The horizon was blurry. It was difficult to tell just where the sea ended and the sky began.

Hélène turned around as Zeno Skouri came up beside her. "Are you ready for the grand tour?" he asked. "Everyone's had it but you."

She laughed. "That's because I didn't know you when the cruise began in Barcelona."

"Come, I give you your tour now." He looked around. "Where's Niggle?"

"He went inside," Hélène replied. "He told me he'd be right back."

"Then we shall wait." The old Greek smiled as he planted himself against the railing. "I don't want him to think I'd kidnap you." He looked at her shrewdly. "He thinks very highly of you, our friend does."

Hélène felt a blush coming on.

"Ah, here comes Niggle now."

She turned around. The salon doors were sliding apart and Nigel came out on deck. He had changed into white shorts, a polo shirt, white knee socks, and deck shoes. She was conscious of his slim but muscular physique, his lithe, easy movements, the curls of hair on his tanned legs and arms. He grinned and walked straight toward her and Zeno. He seemed to catch her stare, and she blinked suddenly and looked away. As if she had been caught looking at something she shouldn't have.

"She is getting the grand tour," Skouri announced proudly. "You're welcome to come along, if you think you can bear to indulge an old man's whim."

"I'd be honored," Nigel said gallantly, taking Hélène by the hand.

A pleasant thrill ran through her as he wrapped his fingers around hers. His grip felt good. It was firm, yet also gentle. She raised her head. For a moment she found herself looking into his eyes. They were warm and smiling and unblinking. There was a sensual quality in his touch, and she felt herself trembling.

The grand tour lasted over an hour. The *Evangelia* was Skouri's pride and joy. Once started, it was difficult for him to stop talking. He delighted in having an attentive audience. Born into poverty on Thera, he had made a career out of wooing the rich, the famous, the accomplished. It was quite natural that his yacht should serve as public evidence of his social status in international society. The guests who had already cruised aboard were like a list lifted from *Who's Who*, the *Social Register*, and the *Celebrity Register* combined.

The *Evangelia* had been a 2,500-ton American frigate which had seen undistinguished service during World War II. Skouri had bought her in 1953, dilapidated and in mothballs, for forty thousand dollars. He then spent millions converting her into a yacht. This had been done at the von Eiderfeld shipyard in Kiel, Germany. This news distressed Hélène, but she tried her best to leave her personal feelings out of it. Probably even Skouri had not met the reclusive Karl von Eiderfeld; his shipyard had simply gained a reputation for its fine German craftsmanship.

The yacht was more than just a floating palace. From the beginning, Skouri had intended it to be his home, and he personally followed every phase of the conversion. Anxious as he had been to move aboard immediately, he had had to wait for a year and a half until the conversion was complete. In the end, it had been worth it.

Like an expectant father, Skouri descended on the shipyard without warning to inspect the work as it progressed. When he didn't like the location of the air-conditioning ducts, whole bulkheads had to be torn out and the air-conditioning shafts rerouted. His endless demands nearly drove the designers and workmen out of their minds. And then there were the special touches. Like the sunken bathtubs, which meant that the deck floors had to be raised. Or how to have a dance floor as well as a swimming pool on the aft deck. The engineer cleverly solved that particular problem by creating a hydraulic pool floor. The pool could then be drained and the floor raised and danced upon. There was even a special device that kept the seawater that was pumped into the pool several degrees below air temperature so that swimming in it would be refreshing.

Hélène marveled at all these luxurious touches. When she was finished with the tour, she was quite taken aback. And to think that she had been impressed when she was first shown to her stateroom! The door had an engraved, gold-plated plaque on it that read: "Pissarro Suite." At first she had been puzzled; then, being led down the corridor, she had noticed other doors marked "Rembrandt Suite," "Van Gogh Suite," "Picasso Suite," "Goya Suite," "El Greco Suite," "Dürer Suite," "Raphael Suite," "Dali Suite," "Matisse Suite," and "Renoir Suite." Only after she was inside her suite did she realize the significance of the name. Above a sofa in the little sitting room hung a framed, hermetically sealed Pissarro. There was another in the bedroom. She half-expected to see one in the bath as well, but there she was disappointed. It was plain marble, albeit with gleaming gold fixtures, embroidered Porthault towels, and a staggering array of soaps, perfumes, and toilet waters. By the sunken tub there was a reading lamp and a pillow so that you could soak in comfort. Never in her life had she seen such shameless luxury.

And the guests! So many socialites and celebrities. There were Magda Mond, a reclusive Hungarian film star; Sir George Broyhill, an ancient British statesman who had helped the Allies win World War II; Blanche Benois, the French sex-kitten film star who had once been the subject of a *Les Modes* article; Elena and Evangelia, Skouri's attractive twin daughters; Nikos, his son; Ariadne Cosindas, the world-famous ballerina who was also Skouri's long-time mistress and had survived his two marriages; Giorgio Marioni, an Italian menswear designer; and Paolo Ralli, a Grand Prix circuit driver for Ferrari. Conspicuous by her absence was Skouri's beautiful American wife, Cynthia.

The cruise was all mapped out. The *Evangelia* was steered on a steady course along the French and Italian Rivieras. Just past Portofino, she turned and cut straight down to Corsica.

Stops after that were to be Sardinia; Capri and Naples; Corfu; Elena, Skouri's lavish private island in the Ionian Sea; and finally Venice, where the cruise would end and all the guests would attend the event of the season, the Black-and-White Ball in an ancient palazzo on the Grand Canal.

Hélène enjoyed herself from the moment she came aboard. She managed to push Jacques's backstabbing into the farthest corner of her mind. The days were too beautiful and sun-drenched to harp on something like that; the nights were too cool and romantic. The *Evangelia* was the perfect ship to cruise aboard. It was large enough so that no one got in any-one else's hair, and yet it had the feel of an intimate vessel. Activities could either be joined or ignored. Onboard there were the usual deck games, nightly Magda Mond movies, and daily swims, either in the pool or in the sea. When they were in port, Skouri had arranged for cars ahead of time, and there were plenty of sights to see and restaurants to visit. On Corsica, Hélène and Nigel went off on their own to the chalky cliffs at Bonifacio, where in the fifteenth century the inhabitants had resisted a lengthy Spanish siege. Hélène mar-veled at the strong scent of the maquis, the dense under-growth growing all over the island, a combination of the rich perfumes of myrtle, lavender, eucalyptus, wild mint, and cyclamen.

"Napoleon once said, 'I would recognize Corsica, eyes closed, only because of its perfume,' " Nigel quoted.

On Capri, they went off by themselves again. They climbed to the top of the island, drank wine on a fragrant terrace, and later hired a boat and rowed through the Blue Grotto. It was the stuff of which romances were made.

One evening, some of the *Evangelia*'s crew played bouzouki music and everyone danced on deck and broke piles of plates. Hélène continued to be astounded by the una-bashed luxury that surrounded her. Daily, fresh bread was flown in by seaplane from Skouri's favorite bakery in Paris, and when Ariadne demanded fresh Greek lamb, it, too, ar-rived by special plane from Crete. The *Evangelia* had two chefs, one Greek and one French. To top it all off, there was even a completely stocked wine "cellar" and a sommelier. In-variably, Hélène chose to eat Greek food, and Skouri was delighted by her choice. Like him, she drank ouzo during the cocktail hour, champagne with her meal, and a sip of Cour-voisier after dinner.

"You are a Greek in soul!" Skouri cried one afternoon. "If you like, I let you send a writer and photographer onboard and they can do a big article on the *Evangelia*!"

Hélène was flattered. "I'll make sure you stick by that, Zeno," she warned.

He laughed heartily. They were sitting on the bar stools which were covered with the skin of whale testicles, and he wrote on a napkin: "I the undersigned do hereby permit Hélène Junot to send any and all photographers and writers of *Les Modes* to do a feature article on the *Evangelia*. The entire yacht is at their disposal. (signed) Zeno Callicrates Skouri." It was a memento she was to treasure forever.

The cruise was the first real vacation Hélène had ever had, and it worked wonders. She had never felt so relaxed in her life. She had vowed that she wouldn't spend a minute thinking of business, and she nearly kept that vow. Only twice was *Les Modes* mentioned, and both times the subject was brought up by someone else. The first time had been Skouri, and she had arranged with him for Luba to work on the *Evangelia* article. She knew that the Czarina would be forever grateful for the opportunity. The second mention was by Giorgio Marioni. He wanted to know why Hélène didn't create an edition of *Les Modes* for menswear. She promised to think about it.

From every place they dropped anchor, she wrote postcards to Edmond, Jeanne, and Petite Hélène.

Skouri, forever the perfect host, seemed to find time for everyone. He had that rare gift of making sure that neither Ariadne, his mistress, nor Magda Mond, his most cherished friend, was lacking in attention. But most important he gave Hélène the opportunity to get to know Nigel.

She stood on deck with him one fine evening. The lights from shore were like the stars above, twinkling and bright and moving slowly in the night. The moon was full, flooding the deck with half-light. She never remembered what they had been discussing, but suddenly he took her in his arms and pressed her against him. His lips sought hers, and she gave herself up to his kisses. They were deep and demanding. Then he held her face to his chest. "Hélène . . ." His voice was a whisper, half-carried away by the breeze.

She looked up and could see his eyes shining down at her in the moonlight. "Nigel . . ." she said huskily. "Oh, Nigel . . ."

"I love you," he said.

She closed her eyes and smiled up at him. "I love you, too," she whispered.

"Darling!" He held her tighter. She made no move to get out of his arms. She was willing to stay in them forever, enveloped and protected, loved and cherished. She could smell the powerful masculinity of him, feel the strength of his body. He needed her; she could feel that, too. And she needed him. She needed his strength.

His murmur was a caress in the moonlight, his lips a thrill of warmth as he nuzzled the nape of her neck, his breath a stir in her ear. "Is my suite all right?"

She could not trust herself to speak, but her eyes flashed her answer in the light spilling out from the open door, her pupils dark wide jewels of desire.

The off-white carpet was deep and velvety and her bare feet made no sound as she crossed over to the bed. He was stretched out naked, slim and tanned, watching her approach in the dim light.

He felt a sudden dryness come up in his throat. She had pulled the pins out of her hair, which flowed long, black, and silken down her naked back. Her skin was tanned and taut, smooth as polished alabaster, and her belly was so flat that her navel seemed to protrude. Her breasts, small but firm and perfectly shaped, rode high and proud above her taut rib cage. Her nipples were already erect, dark and hard with longing.

He moved lithely off the bed, his motions fluid as he got to his feet and reached for her hands.

Quickly her eyes moved over his body, downward past his chest and slim hips to his groin.

For a moment she stood transfixed as he held her hands and looked deep into her eyes. She could feel her heart fluttering as he brought her slim, tapered fingers up to his lips and kissed them seductively, looking directly over at her through those sparkling, gold-flecked eyes. Then he let go of her hands and moved one of his to the small of her back, tracing small circles on her flesh with his forefinger. The rousing scent of her musk was in his nostrils. "You're beautiful," he said softly. "Beautiful." His lips sought hers now. As his fingers glided smoothly up and down the ridge of her back, he felt her responding to his touch. He pressed her toward him so that she sucked in her breath as she felt the wetness seeping from within her.

Before Helene could ask him to wait, Nigel had lifted her effortlessly off her feet, and without interrupting their kiss, carried her the rest of the way to the bed.

His searching tongue parted the soft dark curls of her pubic hair. She widened her legs and thrust her hips forward and could feel his face snuggling close, his moist tongue parting her and probing inside. It was a soft and rousing sensation, and it brought a tingling warmth spreading throughout her.

Gently he rolled her over on her stomach. Obediently she complied. He continued to tease her with his tongue. Her anticipation was unbearable. She had waited too long to sleep with him. She begged him to come inside her, but he continued to touch another part of her. The inside of her thigh, the back of her knee.

Suddenly she let out a cry. "Nigel!"

He knew she was ready for him, and with a thrust of his hips he quickly slid himself up inside her. He could feel her strong muscles contracting around him, trapping him inside.

Slowly he began to thrust in and out until her breath came in gasps and she surrendered herself completely to him. Neither one had to say a thing. Never had Hélène been loved like this. Her life would never be complete without him.

Blanche Benois felt trapped. She could feel the familiar ache swelling up inside her. For the past week, it had been unbearable, but nothing compared to this. It felt as if her pubis were about to explode.

Frantically she began pacing up and down the stateroom, but it didn't do any good. Her pink lips were set in an angry pout and her huge gray eyes with the long lashes were wide with boredom. Her tight white jeans and the straining bikini top which barely covered her full breasts looked strangely out of place in the quiet luxury of the stateroom.

For a moment she stopped pacing. On an impulse she pushed aside the curtains and unlatched the porthole. She stuck her head out into the night. The air was cool and clear. She could hear the muffled throb of the diesels and the sounds of another Magda Mond movie coming from the deck above. She cursed, drew her head back in, and slammed the porthole shut again. Everyone seemed to be having a good time but her.

At first she'd thought the cruise might be fun. And it would have been, too, if that sexy American athlete hadn't had to cancel at the last minute. Only after she had boarded in Barcelona did she learn that the handsome black boxer had sustained injuries in the ring and had been hospitalized. She had wanted to get off right then and there, but she didn't. You couldn't just board Skouri's yacht, find out that a guest was unable to make it, and then pack your bags and get right off again. Skouri's empire was too far-flung. He owned a film-production company, International Artists. It was I.A. that held the option for her next three films. No, she couldn't walk out on Skouri. Not without feeling the full force of his wrath.

Who else was there to have fun with? No one. Sir George was too ancient, Elena and Evangelia had Giorgio and Paolo tied around their little fingers, Hélène had Nigel falling all over her, Ariadne had Skouri, and Nikos Skouri liked nothing better than to consort with the engineers and tinker with the engines of the Piaggio seaplanes or one of the many speedboats.

With a frustrated sigh she plopped herself down on the king-size bed and stared up at the padded-leather ceiling. What a bore this was turning out to be! And there were six more days of it. The way things were going, she'd probably be a raving lunatic by the time the cruise was over.

Blanche Benois could be characterized as a vampire. She lived on men and took from them. On screen, her sex-hungry quality reflected her sexuality, which was all-consuming. When she worked on a film, she retired to her trailer and had sex with whoever was available before she would stand in front of the cameras. That way, the film was certain to capture her torrid appeal. She knew that only a woman who had just had satisfying sex radiated a certain animal quality.

But much as she threw herself into sex, she only took from men. She sucked all the sweet juices out of their loins and never gave of herself in return. She usually only had to lie there and moan while they did all the work. And they never noticed that she did nothing, the fools! They were always too concerned with their precious penises to realize that as long as they were humping her, there was a triumphant gleam in her eyes. They thought they were showing off their prowess, when actually it was she who controlled them.

She let out another sigh and arched her body off the bed so that only her head, shoulders, and feet were firmly planted on the mattress. She undid the buttons of her white jeans and peeled them down around her ankles. When she was out of them, she shrugged off the bikini top and lay naked on her back. Deliberately she let her fingers brush across her nipples until she felt the fine, tingling sensation starting up within them. She moaned and looked down at them. They were large and plum-colored against the deep bronzed tan of her breasts. Million-dollar tetons, they were. That was what they were insured for by Lloyd's of London. They had always been perfectly shaped and big, but now they were even better since she'd had the silicone implants.

She felt her fever rising. Hundreds of thousands of men who went to see her movies hungered after those tetons, could imagine the sweetness of them between their lips. Hundreds of thousands—perhaps even millions—of men would have given anything to jump into bed with her and show her how they could make those tetons feel. And yet . . . and yet she was alone, dammit! Nobody wanted her, and her body demanded that she have a man!

She took a deep breath as she felt the moistness starting up between her legs. It was like Sister Magdalene at the Catholic boarding school had told her: she would suffer. But Sister had been wrong. Blanche's suffering was not the kind she had been warned about. She smiled now, thinking back to that time in the dormitory.

She had just turned fourteen. Sister had come into her tiny room unexpectedly, finding her naked on the iron-framed bed with both hands half-buried inside her. Blanche hadn't even realized she was there until she'd heard the gasp. Then suddenly she sat bolt upright in embarrassment. The pink face framed by the white wimple and black veil looked at her with shock.

"Blanche!" Sister Magdalene hissed harshly, trying to control her voice. "What are you doing!"

Blanche laughed now. What the hell had that old virgin thought she'd been doing? Praying?

Sister's voice had risen righteously. "Get decent immediately and then come down to the office!" Swiftly she turned on her heel, her black robes rustling and the rosary beads around her waist clicking faintly against one another as she marched back out.

Ten minutes later, Blanche was bent over the big scarred desk as Sister Magdalene brought the wooden cane down upon her bare buttocks again and again. Blanche strained her ass muscles, tightening them to lessen the sting. At first the pain had been exquisite; then it began to burn fiercely, like fire. Blanche hadn't been able to contain herself. The pain, plus the picture of a crucified Jesus being flogged by the Romans staring down at her from the wall, brought on the strongest orgasm she was ever to know.

Strange that she should think about Sister Magdalene now. She hadn't thought about her for years.

She rolled over on the bed. But that was long in the past. She needed a man now, today, and there was none.

Suddenly a calculating glint came into her eyes. She couldn't steal Giorgio or Paolo from Elena and Evangelia. Skouri wouldn't have it. But there was always Nigel.

She smiled now. All she had to do was wait a little while till they all went to bed. Till Hélène slipped out of his suite in the wee hours of the morning. She had never known a man who could say no after she'd sneaked into his room and wakened him up by flicking her tongue over his balls.

An hour and a half later, the movie ended; everyone congratulated Magda Mond on her performance and then headed to the bar or to bed. Hélène and Nigel went up on the sundeck and stood beneath the stars. They were the only ones there, and the sounds of soft music drifted up from the bar below. Hélène stood there listening to it. She was watching Nigel closely. His face was illuminated by the pale wash of moonglow. She wanted him to take her in his arms.

Instead, he said, "It was a wonderful movie. They don't make them like that anymore."

She was surprised by his small talk. It took a moment for her to find her voice. "No, they don't."

He shook his head. "It must be terrible to be a star. One's aging never shows so much as on film. It's a sad reminder of how quickly one grows old."

She nodded slowly.

Suddenly he reached out and took her hands in his. "Oh, Hélène, I know this is sudden and rash. But I want to . . . Could you . . . I mean, will you marry me?"

527

She drew in her breath and stared at him. The proposal had been sprung on her so suddenly that she was momentarily speechless. Then her heart gave a joyous leap and her eyes shone. "Are you sure?" she stammered. "You know so little about—"

He didn't wait for her to finish. "Just say yes," he said earnestly, squeezing her hands. "Darling, please say yes!"

Her eyes stared down to the deck below. She looked back up at him. "I will give you your answer tomorrow," she said in a trembling voice.

Much later, after they made love and he lay asleep, she brushed her lips against his, slipped out of his bed and back to her own suite. He said he loved her. And she was certain she loved him. Or was it only physical attraction which drew them together? No, it was more, she decided. Much more.

It took a long time for her to get to sleep. Back in her own bed, she stared up at the dark ceiling for what seemed like hours. The night was quiet save for the sounds of water slapping against the hull. She missed the warmth of his body, the steady sounds of his breathing. She could only lie there thinking of Nigel and his proposal. When she finally fell asleep, it was into a pleasant, dreamless black depth, totally at peace.

She was brought out of it by the ringing of the telephone. She opened her eyes and looked groggily at her Hermès travel alarm clock. The luminous green dial read two o'clock.

Bewildered, she reached for the receiver. "You have a call from Paris," the yacht's operator said. "Please hold." Then she could hear the ship-to-shore operator making the connection through the *Evangelia*'s radiotelephone system. A moment later a voice came on over the air, crackly and far away.

"Edmond!" she said.

"I wouldn't call you if it weren't an emergency," he said quickly in a distraught voice.

"What's the matter?" Hélène demanded, suddenly frightened. She sat up straight in bed, sleep falling away in brittle shards.

The words spilled out of him. "It's Jeanne. She's in the hospital."

"The hospital!" Hélène's voice was disbelieving. A sudden chill seized her heart. "Edmond, what *is* it?"

"The baby. There are complications."

She didn't hesitate. "I'll be there on the next plane!" she promised.

"Please hurry." He tried to say more, but his voice cracked suddenly. It took a moment for him to recover. "I . . . I don't know how much time she's got left . . ."

"I'm leaving, Edmond. Straightaway. Please tell her I'll be there!"

"I will, if she . . . if she's conscious long enough. Thanks, Little French Girl."

She hung up and sat there in the dark, stunned. The stateroom was quiet except for the low hum of the air conditioning. She covered her face with her hands. She couldn't believe it. Something wrong with Jeanne? The best friend she had? It couldn't be true. Then tears were pouring down her face. She wiped them away with her fingertips and switched on the lamp. The yellow glow spilled out over the nightstand.

She stared at the telephone. Then, without losing another second, she dialed the bridge. A moment later she got hold of the captain. Almost immediately the *Evangelia*'s diesels changed pitch and the yacht slowed to a halt. The crane on deck swung one of the Piaggio seaplanes overboard. Quickly Hélène threw on some clothes, took a sheet of the engraved *Evangelia* stationery out of the desk and hastily scribbled a note to Nigel. When she was through, she quickly read it over. It would have to do.

My darling,

A family emergency requires me to leave at once. I'll get in touch with you as soon as possible. In the meantime, my answer to your proposal is: Yes! Yes!! Yes!!!

All my love,
Hélène

By the time she folded it, the telephone rang again. It was the Captain. The Piaggio was ready for takeoff, the pilot standing by. She hurried into the corridor and stuck the note in the door of the Rembrandt Suite. Then she went up on deck. A Riva speedboat had already been lowered from the davits. A sailor was waiting for her and helped her down the portable stairs to the floating platform. Another sailor helped her into the Riva. The line was untied and he let out the clutch. The boat began to nose slowly toward the seaplane.

She could just make out its dark shape bobbing on the water a short distance away.

She didn't see Blanche Benois tiptoe to the Rembrandt Suite, take her note, read it, and tear it into tiny shreds. As Nigel awakened from his sleep to a moist tongue licking at his scrotum, the faint drone of a plane overhead hummed away into the distance.

10

The receptionist looked up at her with annoyance. "Visiting hours are from one to four," she said sternly.

Hélène stared at her. She was worried and bushed. She had tried to doze on the planes, but it had been impossible. For the four hours it had taken her to get to Paris, she'd been able to do nothing but worry. Now she had to fight to keep her temper under control as well. In a split second she sized up the receptionist. Long ago she had learned that those on the low end of a bureaucratic totem pole tended to try to exercise their power the most. There was only one way to deal with them.

She drew herself up imperiously. "Do I get to see my sister-in-law, or must I have words with whoever is in charge of this place?" Hélène turned her back on the receptionist and looked around, trying to spot a supervisor.

"I'm sorry," the receptionist said apologetically. "I didn't realize you were a relative. What did you say the patient's name is again?"

Hélène turned back around. "Jeanne Junot."

The receptionist consulted a ledger on the desk and ran her finger down a long list. Finally she looked up. "Room three-oh-nine." She leaned forward and pointed. "Make a right turn at the end of the waiting room and follow the corridor to the St.-Gatien wing. Take the second bank of elevators."

Hélène nodded her thanks, turned again, and went briskly in search of the elevators.

On the third floor, she found Edmond pacing outside

Jeanne's room, his expression blank. Hélène could feel her heart dropping. His face was pale and white. It was a face that had lost all hope.

Taking a deep breath, she hurried toward him. Her deck shoes made no sound, but he sensed her approaching. He looked up. "Little French Girl," he said in a tight voice.

She put out her hands and embraced him. Then she held him at arm's length. "How is she?" she demanded, looking up at him.

He avoided her eyes. "I don't know." There was hopelessness in his voice, too. "The doctors keep using medical terms I can't understand."

She bit down on her lip. "Can I see her?"

He shook his head. "The doctors are in there now. We have to wait."

She let go of his arms, turned away, and began to pace the corridor. Suddenly she had an idea. She stopped and whirled around. "Wait a moment! I'm going to make a telephone call."

He looked at her curiously. "To whom?"

"A friend who's a doctor. He's helped me before. He'll at least be able to unravel the mysteries of the jargon and let us know what's going on. I'll be right back." Quickly she started down the hall to find a telephone.

Dr. Rosen arrived long before the doctors were finished with Jeanne. From the corner of her eye, Hélène caught sight of him approaching. He was wearing a worn gray cardigan and his eyes were red-rimmed from interrupted sleep. Hélène felt bad at having awakened him, but she looked at him gratefully. She kissed his cheek. "Thank you for coming." She took his gnarled old hands into hers and held them silently for a moment. There was something about his quiet strength that made her feel better almost instantly.

She introduced him to Edmond and the two men shook hands. "What have the doctors told you?" he asked immediately.

Edmond made a futile gesture and looked down at his feet. "Not much. Something about fluid retention and renal failure."

Dr. Rosen was silent for a moment. "Hélène told me your wife is pregnant. What month is she in?"

"The eighth."

"The eighth." Dr. Rosen shook his head. It was the old story, he thought miserably. The wife probably knew all along that something was wrong but was afraid to tell the husband. Even without seeing her, he could guess what was the matter. Fluid retention was bad enough in itself, but renal failure probably meant toxemia. Poisoning of her body by her own fluids. "And how long has she been having the problems?" he asked.

Edmond shrugged painfully and looked away. His face was an expression of self-contempt. "I'm not certain. She didn't want to worry me, so she kept quiet. Finally I knew that something was wrong and insisted . . ." With shaking fingers he reached for a rumpled pack of cigarettes.

The door to Jeanne's room opened suddenly. A nun in flowing black robes and a starched winged hat came out. She was carrying a tray expertly balanced against her hip while she silently pulled the heavy door closed behind her.

Hélène hurried over to her. "How is she, Sister?"

The nun frowned disapprovingly and shook her head. "I cannot say. The doctors will be out shortly, I believe. They will be able to tell you more accurately than I." The nun looked past Hélène and eyed Edmond severely. "I'm sorry, monsieur, but smoking is strictly forbidden!" she announced in sepulchral tones.

Edmond took a quick last puff and looked around helplessly. Finally he dropped the cigarette on the stone floor and ground it out under his heel, shredding the tobacco. The nun said nothing, but gave him a stern look before she swept away down the corridor.

A team of doctors came out of Jeanne's room shortly after nine o'clock. By then Hélène had been waiting nearly three hours. She, Edmond, and Dr. Rosen quickly surrounded the doctors.

Edmond recognized one of them. "Dr. Dufaut, can we go in now?"

The doctor cleared his throat and held up his hands. "Yes, but only for a moment. Your wife is quite weak. She needs rest."

"How is she, doctor?" Hélène asked. "I mean, will she—"

"It's still too early to tell," the doctor cut in smoothly, sidestepping the question before it was fully formed. This was familiar territory for him. No matter how badly a patient was doing, you never admitted it. You had to leave the relatives with hope. He smiled tightly now. "Let me assure you, we're doing everything for her that we possibly can."

Dr. Rosen stepped forward. By habit, he took off his glasses and began polishing them with a handkerchief. "What, exactly, is wrong with Madame Junot?" he asked.

Dr. Dufaut frowned and looked at him closely. "Who are you?"

Dr. Rosen smiled agreeably. "I'm Simon Rosen. I'm a doctor and a close friend of the family's. I am here at their request."

The doctor took a deep breath and turned around. "You may go in now," he told Hélène and Edmond, "but the nurse won't let you stay long." Then he took Dr. Rosen aside.

The sickroom was dim and Hélène was not prepared for the sight of Jeanne lying on her pillow, breathing heavily. She didn't move. Perhaps she hadn't heard them come in.

Hélène took a deep breath and stifled her tears. This was not the Jeanne she knew and loved. The Jeanne who had waited on tables in Saint-Nazaire, who had given her the guidance and love of an older sister, who had married Edmond, who had given birth to Petite Hélène. This woman was a stranger. Her face was beet red and swollen. She was staring vacantly up at the ceiling. For a moment Hélène found herself looking up too. But there was nothing to be seen there.

"Jeanne . . ." Edmond said tentatively.

Slowly Jeanne turned her head on the pillow to face him. Her eyes were glazed. Trying hard to focus. "Edmond?" she mumbled thickly through swollen lips. "Edmond, I'm . . . I'm sorry." Her eyes brimmed over with tears. Her voice was tiny. "Edmond . . ."

He was beside her now, searching for one of her hands and holding it tightly. "You'll be all right in no time," he said, sitting down on the edge of the bed. With his free hand he stroked her forehead. "The doctors said you're making fine progress. Just keep it up, and in no time we'll have you back home."

"If things are going so well, then why are you looking away?" Jeanne asked calmly. She stared at him, and there was a sure look in her eyes as she shook her head. "No," she whispered. "I'm not going to go home. Never again."

Hélène stepped forward. "Jeanne!" she said in a choked voice. "I won't have you talking like that! You mustn't give up! You have everything to live for. You have me, Edmond, Petite Hélène, the new baby . . ."

"Hélène, dear sweet Hélène," Jeanne said gently, looking up at her gratefully. "You came. Edmond said you would, but I thought he was only saying that to placate me." Jeanne shook her head from side to side. "I know I won't get better. Just . . . just promise me one thing."

Hélène and Edmond nodded.

"Don't let Petite Hélène see me like this. Don't make her . . ." Jeanne twisted her face away from them and looked out over the side of the bed.

"Don't make her do what?" Edmond asked gently.

Jeanne closed her eyes wearily. "Don't make her . . . kiss me when I'm dead. I want the coffin closed. She's too young to have to see such . . . ugliness." With an immense effort, Jeanne fought to open her eyes. They were clear of tears. Her other hand found Hélène's, and the icy fingers closed over it like a vise. Her voice was growing fainter. "Hélène . . ." Jeanne swallowed and lifted her head. Her eyes were unwavering. "You'll . . . take care of Petite Hélène? Like your own daughter?" she asked in a small voice. "Can you promise me that?"

Hélène nodded solemnly and squeezed Jeanne's hand. "I promise," she said huskily.

Jeanne smiled and slowly let her head sink back down on the pillow. She let go of Helene's hand, the fingers unwrapping slowly.

A nurse came into the room. "Please, you'll have to wait outside for a while," she said sternly. "The patient is tired."

"Don't make them go!" Jeanne's face was suddenly contorted with fear. "Please," she begged. "Let them stay! I don't want to die alone!"

11

Jeanne did not die alone. The terrible thing was, she needn't have died at all.

When Hélène and Edmond went back out into the corridor after visiting with her, Dr. Rosen quickly slipped inside to examine Jeanne for himself. It was not long before he returned, but the wait seemed interminable. Hélène looked at him hopefully, but his face was grim. He drew her and Edmond aside and glanced around to make sure they couldn't be overheard. When he spoke, his voice was low. "We've got to move Madame Junot to another hospital."

Hélène stared at him. "But why?" she asked in surprise. "I don't—"

Dr. Rosen didn't let her finish. "Because this is a Catholic hospital," he explained, "run by nuns and priests, following the doctrine of the Church. Listen carefully, for we don't have the time to run through this twice. There isn't a moment to lose."

He turned to Edmond and looked up at him from above the glasses which were slowly slipping down his nose. He jabbed them back in place with his thumb.

"Your wife is diagnosed as having acute toxemia. That diagnosis is, unfortunately, correct. The illness was brought about by difficulties arising from her pregnancy. It is a dangerous condition, often fatal. In her case, assuredly so. The toxemia can cause"—he ticked the complications off on his fingers—"renal failure, that is, failure of the kidneys to function, which has already occurred; pneumonia, which is also beginning to set in; and pulmonary edema and cardiac failure could follow. In other words, the chances of heart failure are now great. While you were visiting her, I had a discussion with Dr. Dufaut. It is my opinion"—Dr. Rosen glanced from Hélène to Edmond—"that what Madame Junot needs is an immediate abortion!"

The word cut through Hélène's heart like a searing knife. Instantly a terrible nausea rose as a flood of memories engulfed her. Visions of her own baby that she had had cut out of her flashed before her eyes. She tried to swallow.

Edmond was visibly shaken. Somehow he found his voice. "An abortion!" He turned away suddenly. "My God, *no!*"

Dr. Rosen placed a hand on his arm. "Have courage, young man." He turned to include Hélène. "An abortion is the only thing that will spare Madame Junot her life. To do that, we've got to get her out of here. Catholic hospitals forbid abortion under any circumstances, and this one is especially strict. We must get her to a private clinic immediately."

Hélène wiped her eyes. "Where do we . . . find one?" she whispered.

"There's a good private hospital in Passy. Please, don't misunderstand me. I'm not in favor of taking a life. In this case, it is the only way in which we can save Madame Junot's life. Otherwise, both she and the child are doomed to die. Even Dr. Dufaut admitted that to me."

Sudden anger pushed through Hélène's shock. "And yet he won't perform it?" she asked incredulously.

Dr. Rosen shrugged helplessly. "He is a devout Catholic."

Edmond was silent. Hélène looked at him levelly, waiting for a moment. "Edmond," she prodded quietly, "there isn't much time."

His face was white with anguish. Then his eyes fell. "Please, Hélène," he begged huskily. "I . . . I can't make that kind of decision."

For a moment she could only stare at him. A fleeting realization came to her. Her stalwart Edmond, who as a child had bravely killed the Boche and led her on that impossibly treacherous journey halfway across France, was now hunched over in pain, indecisive and afraid.

But Hélène's mind was working swiftly. Tenderly she wrapped her arms around her brother. His body was locked in stiff tension, the muscles frozen. "I trust Dr. Rosen," she said softly. "Now's not the time to go into it, but he saved my life once. If he says an abortion is necessary, then it is."

Edmond could only nod. "It isn't me, it's Jeanne. She's so devout. She'd never allow it."

"I'll talk to her," Hélène declared briskly. "She'll listen to me."

After giving Edmond quick orders to prepare for Jeanne's transfer, she went back into the sickroom, got rid of the nurse, and went over to Jeanne and sat down on the edge of the bed. She reached for the wet sponge, wrung it out, and gently began dabbing Jeanne's forehead. Jeanne lay still. For a moment Hélène was afraid she was dead. Then slowly Jeanne's eyes fluttered open. She smiled thinly. "You came back!" she whispered. "I knew you wouldn't let me die alone."

"I won't let you die, period," Hélène said grimly. She looked down at Jeanne. "Edmond and I are transferring you to a different hospital."

536

"A different . . ." Jeanne looked suddenly confused. "But . . . they're so good to me here."

"I know that," Hélène said gently, "but another hospital can make you well again. Think of Petite Hélène and Edmond. Don't you want to live for them?"

A glimmer of hope pushed its way through Jeanne's dull eyes as she struggled to sit up. "What must I do?"

"We shall take you to a private clinic. You'll probably have to stay there for a few weeks. Then you will be as good as new."

Suddenly a look of understanding crossed Jeanne's face. She snatched her hand away and her eyes moved down the length of her body to where her swollen belly distended the blanket. After a prolonged moment her gaze moved back up to Hélène. Her eyes were penetrating. "And my baby?" she asked softly.

Hélène looked away. It was useless to lie. Her expression would give her away. "The baby must die," she whispered.

"No!" Jeanne croaked sharply. She shook her head stubbornly. "I know what it is you want them to do to me! I won't let that happen!"

"But you must!" Hélène pleaded. "Your life . . . and what about Edmond and Petite Hélène! What about them? They love you, Jeanne. Edmond needs a wife. And Petite Hélène needs a mother."

"Not one who is disgraced in the eyes of God. Please, Hélène . . ." Jeanne sought Hélène's hand again and squeezed it with the little strength she had left. "Forgive me, but I cannot."

Jeanne's last request was to die in the chapel, and she was wheeled there on a rolling stretcher to spend her last minutes lying in front of the altar rail, the stained-glass windows throwing their kaleidoscopic splotches of color everywhere. The last earthly sight she saw was the gleaming crucifix the priest held over her as he said Last Rites.

12

This house is dead, Hélène thought as she watched Petite Hélène getting dressed in a somber black dress. It was like the villa on Cap Ferrat after Stanislaw died. Something that had lived and breathed had gone out of it. Overnight, the house that had been such a happy home had become nothing more than an empty shell.

Petite Hélène finished dressing. She came toward Hélène and turned around solemnly. "How do I look, Tante Hélène?" she asked quietly.

It has already affected her, too, Hélène thought. She was more mature, more serious and grown-up. She had taken the news of her mother's death very soberly, almost without emotion. Even that morning at the funeral, she had been dry-eyed. Of course, Hélène hadn't really expected her to understand what death was. Not yet. Often it took a while for the tragedy to sink in. Especially with children.

"You look lovely," Hélène said automatically, retying the black satin ribbon in the girl's fiercely orange hair.

"Where are we going?" Petite Hélène asked.

"I thought it would be nice to walk in the Bois for a while," she answered. She forced a smile. "Afterward, we can stop somewhere and have an ice cream."

"I don't think I want an ice cream."

Hélène shrugged. "In that case, we shall just walk. Hurry, or we'll miss the sunshine."

When they got outside, the day was still bright and fresh. Aimlessly they wandered along the less-used paths in the Bois. Hélène couldn't help looking around constantly. It was as if Jeanne's soul could be found here floating somewhere among the thickly leafed chestnut trees, dancing among the fragile flowers that bent in the breezes, even soaring elusively overhead alongside the birds that swooped in the puffball skies. After an hour, they sat on a bench in the Jardin d'Acclimatation and watched the children at play. Petite Hélène was five years old, but she was in no mood for the animals and the rides. It was as if she had suddenly shed the Renoir-girl quality and outgrown the laughter and games. Instead of mingling with the children as she usually did, she sat quietly beside Hélène, her short legs not quite reaching the ground. After a long silence, she turned to Hélène with that curious, adult wisdom that some children tend to have. "Tante Hélène . . . ?"

Hélène looked at her silently.

"Maman's gone, Tante Hélène. We'll just have to keep on living, won't we?" She turned her head slightly and looked vacantly at the noisy playground. A crowd of screaming children was hanging on to the whirling merry-go-round. "Just sitting here waiting won't bring her back."

Suddenly Hélène found herself crying. She drew the girl against her, wrapping her in her arms and holding her close. The tears were streaming unchecked down her cheeks. Petite Hélène was right, she thought. Jeanne was gone. Her soul wasn't here in the Bois. It was in this girl she was holding in her arms. A soul was passed from mother to daughter, from father to son. Only, her own soul could never be passed on, for she could never have children.

Silently she let Petite Hélène go and wiped away the tears that shone on her cheeks. Petite Hélène was watching curiously. "Can I get you something, Tante Hélène?" she asked in a small voice, embarrassed at having caused the outburst.

"No," Hélène said huskily. There was a distant look in her eyes. "I . . . I'm fine." Suddenly she changed her mind and unsnapped her purse. She took out a few twenty-franc bills. "Here, go to the kiosk and buy some newspapers and magazines."

"Any particular ones?"

Hélène shook her head and nodded with her chin. "You pick them out."

Petite Hélène looked at her, quietly palmed the money and left. Thoughtfully Hélène watched her going down the path. Even the girl's walk had changed. It no longer had that awkward childish bounce. She was still many years from puberty; she was also many years from being a mere baby. The painful years were yet to come. Or were they already upon her?

When Petite Hélène returned, she carried a big stack of

newspapers and magazines. Wearily she dropped them on the bench and then plopped down beside them.

Hélène looked blankly at the publications. *Ici Paris* was on the top. She made it a point never to buy it, but she didn't want to disappoint Petite Hélène. Slowly she picked it up. For a moment she could only stare at the cover. It took a moment for it to sink in. The big color photo showed a pouting Blanche Benois on the arm of Nigel Somerset, scion of a dukedom, at the Black-and-White Ball in Venice. It was the very ball to which Zeno Skouri had invited her. Only now did she realize that things had been so topsy-turvy that she hadn't given much thought to Nigel.

Wearily she closed her eyes and let the paper drop unread onto her lap. She felt very, very alone.

Hélène drew a deep breath as she climbed out of the taxi in front of Fouquet's. For a moment, she couldn't help but stop and glance around at the pulse of the city. For the first time since Jeanne had died, she felt a little something stir inside her. The late-summer weather was on its best Parisian behavior. The café owners were jubilant; everywhere, the outdoor tables were doing a brisk business. The chestnut trees lining the avenues were deep dark green, not the lush, fresh green of spring, but that perfectly mature green when they are at their ripest.

Hélène clutched her purse more tightly now. The brilliant day had soured suddenly as harsh reality grabbed hold of her. Quickly, without another glance around, she entered the terrace of Fouquet's. At the far end, she saw Jacques already sitting at one of the sidewalk tables. He waved at her as the maître d' led her to the table and helped her into her seat.

She put her purse on the table and started to pull off her gloves. "Hello, princess," Jacques said quietly.

Hélène nodded curtly. The packed tables and the traffic beyond the sidewalk seemed suddenly to fade into the distance. Her voice was low but clear. "Well?" she asked, getting right down to business. "Why not the office? Why Fouquet's?"

"Because it's appropriate," he replied. "But all in good time. Besides, I vaguely recall your warning me never to set foot in the office again." He sat back and studied her. He made a production of frowning. "You're not looking very well," he said in a reprimanding voice. "You're all pale and washed out. Black does not suit you. You of all people should know better."

She shrugged. She no longer cared what he thought about the way she looked or anything else. Nor was she about to tell him that it was a miracle she didn't look worse after all she'd been through the past week.

"The cruise didn't seem to do you a bit of good," he continued in a bitchy tone. His eyes narrowed shrewdly. "By the way, did you happen to see the latest issue of *Ici Paris*?"

She noticed now that he had a copy beside him. He unfolded it and held it up. Nigel's face stared mockingly at her.

"His Lordship, it seems, is quite smitten with Blanche Benois." Jacques smiled smugly.

"Get to the point," she said wearily.

She knew perfectly well why he had arranged this meeting—and why Fouquet's. In Monte Carlo, he had mentioned something about severance pay. That could only mean that he had the von Eiderfeld pictures and was going to blackmail her with them. Her purse with the negatives in it had been snatched right outside here, on the crosswalk not four meters away. At the time, she had suspected he was involved. But as time had passed, and he'd made no move, her suspicions had died down.

A waiter approached. "A white wine, s'il vous plaît," she said. When he was gone, she turned back to Jacques. The best defense was an offense. "You have the photos?" she asked brusquely.

He looked at her in surprise, momentarily thrown. There was a drawn-out, uneasy pause. "So you've known all along."

She kept her voice flat. "I've had my suspicions."

"You're clever," he said with grudging respect. "I didn't think you were onto me."

She remained silent as the waiter brought her wine. She pushed it aside and looked at Jacques. "How much do you want?"

"Always to the point, aren't you?" he asked dryly.

"I find that it saves time."

He shook his head and smiled. "Still watching those precious minutes."

She didn't reply.

"I'm afraid you won't like my terms," he said.

"Go ahead, state them."

"You've got two shareholders in Les Éditions Hélène

Junot," he said slowly. "The first, of course, is Hubert de Léger. For a while I was mystified as to why he should be one. But that's cleared up now. He told me what it is you've got on him."

"And what's that?"

Jacques smiled knowingly. "He killed Stanislaw."

Hélène's face was impassive. "Go on."

"He says you had him do it. So you could inherit."

She couldn't help laughing. "To think I've always given you more credit than you deserved!"

"You told Inspector What's-his-name that it was an accident."

She shrugged. "It was simpler in the long run."

"All right, I'll take your word for it. But it doesn't add up."

"There's proof."

He smiled thinly. "I'm sure there is. Now, to the second shareholder. A certain German industrialist. Karl von Eiderfeld."

"What about him?" she asked cautiously.

"Come, come. We both know what you've got on him."

"You've got the negatives," she said frankly, "and my name's on one of the documents. It's all there for you to see."

He gave a tight little smile. "Those negatives are worth a lot, princess," he said slowly. "They're damaging enough to put a noose around his neck. Yet he's walking around scot-free. Anyone who has information like that would take it to the authorities. Obviously you haven't. Then I asked myself why. And do you know what I concluded?"

She said nothing.

"You're blackmailing him." He smiled triumphantly. "Only I still can't figure out one thing. Why? You've got plenty of money. You don't need his."

She stared at him. It was her business, not his. He had no right to know why. She would never tell him.

He sighed. "Well, then, don't tell me. But we both know that *Les Modes* is the darling of the French fashion scene," he continued. "And you know what the French think of the Germans. It's as if no time at all has passed since the war ended. As a nation, we still hate them with a passion. Sure, we let German tourists invade our cities and crowd our beaches. We want their money. Why should Spain get it all? But there isn't a Frenchman alive who wants anything to do

with a *known war criminal*. The wounds are still too fresh."
He paused again, choosing his words carefully. "What if I
were to leak the von Eiderfeld documents to . . . oh, let's say
Le Monde Internationale? Along with a copy of von Eiderfeld's last year's dividend statement which I lifted from your
files and copied some time ago. Do you have any idea of
what would happen then?"

She sat stiffly, not moving. .

"After the war, the French shaved the heads of women
collaborators," he said softly. "They don't do that now. But
Les Modes would be finished, and so would you. You
wouldn't be able to walk down the Champs-Élysées without
being spit upon."

Her eyes narrowed. "How much do you want? Ten thousand francs?"

"Ten thousand francs!" His laughter echoed crazily.
"That's chicken feed. Each share of Les Éditions Hélène
Junot is worth two hundred thousand." He lowered his voice
to a whisper. "I want a percentage of the company, princess."
He looked at her confidently. "I want, say, twenty percent?"

13

In the months that followed Jeanne's death, Hélène threw
herself into her work with an almost superhuman vengeance
that surprised even herself. She pushed herself beyond the
boundaries of her almost limitless energy until she was exhausted. She realized, of course, why she was forcing this
grueling regimen upon herself. It was to cover up the deep
pain she felt. Yet despite all her efforts, the thoughts somehow kept on coming. Busy as she kept herself, they always
managed to worm their way into her mind: Jeanne had been
the best friend and only confidante she had ever enjoyed. She
missed her terribly.

There was another hurt Hélène couldn't get over. Nigel.
Before they'd met for the second time, she had never even

heard about him. Of course, because Zeno Skouri surrounded himself with successful, brilliant people, she had known that Nigel was prominent. But she had never suspected the magnitude of his importance. Now, suddenly, it seemed that he was everywhere. Whatever he did was news. The sensational press linked him to a dozen speculative romances ranging from film stars to a certain young English noblewoman, Lady Amelia Ayers. But it was primarily his career that catapulted him into the limelight.

One morning in November, when the chestnut trees in the Bois were barren of leaves, Eleonora brought the latest bundle of magazines into Hélène's office and left them in their usual spot on the sideboard. Hélène glanced over at them but waited until the late afternoon before getting to them.

First she glanced at the covers. Suddenly she sat bolt upright. The third one from the top was the latest issue of *Time*. The yellow corner banner read: "Britain's New Breed of Leader." From within the red border Nigel stared out at her.

She looked at the picture for a long time. The lean, square jaw, the aristocratic forehead, the intense eyes—they were all the way she remembered him. Especially the eyes, flecked with tiny specks of gold, that had looked at her in the moonlight as he had proposed to her. She sat back and sighed painfully. Proposed . . . and not been heard from since.

She stared at the cover for a long time. She wasn't able to take her eyes off him. She ran her hand over the glossy paper to feel his face. But it was flat. Lifeless. No amount of imagining would bring it to life.

How long had it been now since Jeanne had died, since Hélène had left the *Evangelia* in the early hours of the morning and left the note at his door? Almost three months now.

She felt an ache stir within her. She knew that the best thing she could do for herself was to throw away the magazine unread. Nigel was part of her past, a part that had disappeared forever. But she couldn't. The way she felt about him was still there. Would probably always be there. She still loved him.

She found herself opening the magazine to a picture of Nigel sitting behind his desk.

For a moment she put down the magazine, then took a black case out of her top drawer and flipped it open. She picked her tortoiseshell magnifying glass out of its nest of baize and studied the photo closely. Nigel's desk was an ancient one, all mahogany and centuries of polish. Behind it, on the gleaming paneled wall, hung an oil portrait of a frowning, distinguished old gentleman with white hair. Was that Nigel's father, the Duke? Or was it his grandfather?

The next photo showed Nigel stepping out of a Bentley in a shipyard in Ireland. Yet another, with his back turned to the camera and his hands clasped behind his back, showed him gazing out a big window. Below him was the Thames, wide and sluggish, and in the distance, the object of his view. The Houses of Parliament.

After studying the pictures, Hélène began to read the article. Clearly Nigel was a part of the political winds of the English future. A powerful part. More than ever now, she was fascinated with this man about whom she knew so little.

She tossed the magazine down on her desk and sat back. Thoughtfully she brought her right hand to her lips and sucked on the knuckle of her forefinger. She began to see Nigel in a new light. He was more than just the charming man who drank tea at the casino and scrambled among the rocks of Corsica with her.

Suddenly she was angry with herself. On impulse she reached for the intercom. She had made up her mind. Perhaps it was up to her to make the next move. After all, it was she who had left the *Evangelia* as if she were fleeing from a fire. For her, an emergency had arisen. Perhaps the same thing had happened to him. Perhaps he didn't get her note. Perhaps . . .

Her secretary's voice came over the wire.

"Eleonora, place a call to England immediately. To Somerset Holdings, Limited. I believe they're located in London. I want to speak with Nigel Somerset."

"Right away, mademoiselle."

The call seemed to take forever.

Irritably Hélène sprang to her feet and started walking around the office. For a moment she stopped at the windows and stared down at her beloved Place Vendôme. For once, she couldn't appreciate the elegance of the square. All that appeared before her eyes was Nigel.

"Why didn't you try to contact me?" she whispered to herself, her face drawn in pain. "You know who I am. Where to find me. I've waited and waited for you."

The one person she *had* heard from was Zeno Skouri. She had sent him a thank-you note and an apology for having left so suddenly. He, at least, had taken it for granted that an emergency had arisen and forgiven her sudden departure. True to his word, he had left the yacht at *Les Modes*'s disposal for an entire week so that the article he had promised her could be done. Hélène had been tempted to go along with Luba and the photographer. But she hadn't gone. She had known only too well that the *Evangelia* would only have served as a painful reminder of Nigel.

Now, suddenly, she turned away from the window and went back to her desk. She pressed down on the intercom button again. "Eleonora?"

"Oui, mademoiselle?"

"Cancel the call to Somerset Holdings."

Wearily Hélène lowered herself into her chair. He'd had time enough to get in touch with her. He just hadn't wanted to.

She had never felt this way about any man, ever.

TODAY

Sunday, January 14

1

The Chameleon drove slowly past the rural Connecticut house in his black Hertz car. On the backseat, the huge Great Dane named Rufus sat quietly alert, his ears cocked, his shiny black eyes staring benignly out the window.

The Chameleon studied the house. It was set far back from the road in a yard of bare old maples. It had been built in the first half of the nineteenth century, was sided with gray clapboard, and stood two stories high. From the front it looked L-shaped, with a gable facing the road. The open shutters were painted black, and smoke was rising from one of the chimneys. The silvery mailbox by the driveway was neatly stenciled "E. Junot."

Satisfied, the Chameleon turned the car around and drove back in the direction from which he had come. After he'd driven a quarter of a mile, he backed into a dirt road and parked behind a screen of evergreen bushes. He looked at the quartz chronometer on his wrist. It was three-forty-five. There was time for a quick reconnaissance of the Junot property before dark. The voice on the telephone had informed him that Hélène Junot would probably be spending the weekend at her brother's. He wondered if the information was correct. Well, now he would find out.

The Chameleon left Rufus in the car and pulled the collar of his unobtrusive brown, wool jacket high around his neck. Then he got out of the car and made his way back to the house on foot. He had no desire to be seen, so he stayed well in the woods, walking soundlessly on crepe-soled shoes. It was quiet out here in the country. A little noise could travel a long way. Not like in the city, where sounds were blanketed by an ever-present cacophony.

When he reached the house, smoke was still trailing from the chimney and already the lights were turned on. For a while he stood still and listened intently. He could hear no sound of anyone outside. They must be in the house, he thought. So far, so good. He just wished it weren't winter. Winter in the country was a special bitch. It was too easy to be seen when most of the trees were bare. At least it would be a lot safer once night fell. He was an expert at working in the dark.

But night had not yet fallen, so he would have to take special care while finding out everything he needed to know.

Behind the house was the big clapboard garage. It had two windows along each side. Cautiously he .approached one of them and peered in. He could see an orange BMW coupé and a black Lincoln Continental. No white Rolls-Royce, though. Still, that didn't prove anything. She could have been driven out here in the Rolls and then had the chauffeur take it back to the city. Or maybe her brother had driven her out here in one of his cars. Or she might even have come by Conrail or bus. Even wealthy people commuted between New York and Connecticut on public transportation.

He shrugged. There was no end of possibilities. He continued his stealthy reconnaissance.

To the left of the garage was the rectangular swimming pool, covered over with heavy-duty canvas. A flagstone path ran along the side of the pool, connecting the house with a big barn set thirty yards farther back. The barn was covered with weathered cedar siding. It had big picture windows, and the lights were on inside.

He approached it stealthily and looked in through one of the Thermopane windows. He suppressed a whistle. This was no ordinary barn. It had been converted into a swanky guesthouse. He could see teak-paneled walls, a beamed ceiling, plush carpeting, and expensive furniture. The hand of an interior designer was evident, as was the fact that this was a woman's domain. He saw a handbag on the coffee table. He guessed that the voice over the telephone had been right after all. Hélène Junot must indeed be here. She was probably using the guesthouse instead of staying in the big house. Unless, of course, the handbag belonged to another woman altogether. Well, he'd just have to be careful and wait and see.

He made his way back to the car by the same route he'd come. Then he let Rufus out to sniff around and do his business. He lit a cigarette and watched the big, obedient dog lift his leg against a rhododendron. Rufus didn't stray; he stayed close by, always watching for instructions.

The Chameleon smiled. Soon now, it would be dark. In a half-hour he would return to the house.

This time with Rufus.

Hélène smiled at Edmond. He was standing over the big Jenn-Air range, apron tied around his waist. She watched as he expertly forked the two steaks onto the grill. Immediately they started to sizzle. Then he put the fork down, picked up the tongs, and opened the oven door. He took out two giant baked potatoes.

"It smells good," Hélène said in French, bending down to shut the oven door.

He turned around and grinned. "Wait until dessert. I spent all morning on it."

"What is it? *Boule de neige*? *Profiteroles*?"

"You'll have to wait to find out," he said mysteriously. "Where do you want to eat? Dining room, den, or here in the kitchen?"

"How about right here? I still can't seem to get kitchens out of my blood. Remember when we were kids? We always seemed to live in kitchens. Looking back, I've grown rather fond of them. They always smelled so good."

He grinned at her. "You've still got the peasant in you, you know that, Little French Girl?"

She laughed. "Please, keep it a secret. You wouldn't want the world to know that the queen of high fashion is nothing but a homespun kitchen slut, would you?"

He chuckled. "Cross my heart, I won't ever tell." He picked up the fork again and expertly flipped the steaks over. "What do you want to drink? Champagne or red wine?"

The Chameleon glanced at his watch. The half-hour had passed. He got out of the car and held the rear door open. "Come on, Rufus," he said quietly. The dog's ears instantly cocked. Then he got to his feet and leaped neatly to the ground. He stopped and gazed questioningly up at the Chameleon, the slack pink skin of his jaw making him look deceptively benign.

The Chameleon smiled crookedly. "Come on, dog. It's time you earned your supper."

* * *

551

"That was good," Hélène said.

She took a last sip of wine, delicately patted her lips with the pink linen napkin, and got to her feet. She started clearing away the dishes, slipping them into the slots in the dishwasher.

Edmond pushed his chair back. "I suppose I'm becoming very Americanized. Steak and potatoes are my favorite foods now."

She looked over her shoulder. "Mine, too."

"But you didn't finish your potato."

She laughed and touched her flat stomach. "I don't want to get fat," she replied. "If I do, you'll have to call me *Big* French Girl."

He chuckled and shook his head. "And you didn't even touch your apple pie," he said admonishingly.

She made a face. "Really, Edmond. Building up a dessert that took you all morning to fix! So you went into Roxbury and bought a Sara Lee to heat up in the oven." She placed her hands on her hips in mock anger. "I suppose the trip into town took you all morning?"

"Almost," he admitted. He got to his feet and stretched. "Ready to go through the financial reports?"

She nodded. "Fine, but I've got to go back to the barn first. I left my figures there."

"All right, I'll be waiting upstairs in the library."

She nodded and closed the dishwasher door, then turned the machine on. "I won't be long," she promised.

Edmond went upstairs and she took her quilted, down-filled coat from the hall closet, slipped it on, and went back into the kitchen. She snapped a switch, and the path between the house and the barn was suddenly flooded with light from fixtures hidden in the trees.

She opened the door and stepped outside. The Connecticut night felt crisp and cold against her face. She put her hands in her coat pockets and stood on the porch for a moment, taking a deep breath. The air smelled good; clean and fresh. Somehow innocent. She looked up. The skies were clear and the stars were winking brightly on a peaceful sea of black velvet. And above all, it was quiet. Very quiet. That was what she liked best about the weekends out here. The solitude. It gave her time to think. Somehow you couldn't do that in Manhattan.

She started across the flagstones toward the barn.

* * *

The moment the outside lights clicked on, the Chameleon drew deeper into the shadows. The beginnings of a tense excitement stirred within him. It was an almost sexual excitement. He always felt it when he was about to face his prey. It was the excitement of the hunt. But no matter how strongly he felt it, he always kept it under control. He never let it overstep its bounds. His first priority was—and always would be—extreme caution. In this line of business, only the fools took chances. And fools died.

An instant after the lights went on, he saw the door opening and a woman coming out of the house. For a moment she just stood there looking around. He nodded to himself. He guessed that she was on her way to the barn. But he would wait patiently until she came closer. He had to make certain that it was Hélène Junot.

With growing anticipation he watched as she came down from the porch and started walking toward the barn. Her heels echoed on the flagstones. Beside him, Rufus stiffened and emitted a low growl.

The Chameleon looked down at the dog. The canine's eyes were caught in the floodlights and gleamed yellow. "Quiet!" he whispered.

Instantly the growl died in the dog's throat. But the Chameleon could still sense the animal's tension. That was good, he thought. The dog was as excited as he was.

He smiled to himself. Anticipation wouldn't hurt. It would propel the dog to special fury.

Slowly he reached into his pocket and took out the sonic whistle. He remembered the trainer's instructions. Two short blows for attack. One long one for retreat.

The Chameleon kept his eyes glued on Hélène. He watched her with appreciation. She moved elegantly and sensually, but without any overt suggestiveness. This was one classy dame, he thought to himself. That is, if it was her. . . .

When she was halfway between the house and the barn, he caught his breath. One of the lights in the trees bathed her face and he could see her clearly. The photo hadn't done her justice. He no longer had any doubts. It *was* her.

Hélène suddenly stopped in her tracks. She stiffened as she felt a sudden prickling of her spine.

Something was wrong.

Danger lurked nearby. She didn't know what it was, but she'd experienced this feeling before. Long ago, in Paris. Before the Boche came, when she had been playing with Antoinette in the little park. Only this time, the warning was even stronger. It swept over her like a persistently pounding surf. As if this time the danger was closer.

Her eyes darted as she looked around, but she couldn't see beyond the shadows; the lights in the trees bathed only the path.

For a moment she stopped breathing and listened carefully. She couldn't hear anything, but still the feeling persisted.

She shivered, briskly rubbing her chill arms with her hands, but it was not a shiver from the cold. Then she tried to swallow her fears. "You're just being silly," she told herself. "There is nothing here to hurt you."

Nevertheless she gauged the distance between where she stood and the house and the barn. The barn was closer.

She started to run toward it.

The Chameleon frowned. What was that crazy bitch doing? Why was she running? Had she seen them? But that was impossible. They were too well hidden. And they had been quiet, so she couldn't have heard them, either.

He didn't hesitate. Swiftly he raised the sonic whistle to his lips and blew into it twice. The night remained quiet; not a sound was made that could be heard by human ears.

But Rufus' ears weren't human. They picked up the high-decibel whistle. The dog tensed, and then, with the speed of lightning, emitted a low growl and shot to his feet.

He flew silently out of the shadows toward Hélène.

The richly paneled upstairs library was warm. Far too warm and stuffy with the fire crackling in the grate, Edmond decided. He and Hélène were likely to fall asleep before they got past the first page of the financial report.

He crossed between the twin chamois-upholstered Chesterfield sofas which faced each other across the shimmering silk Tabriz rug. Four windows, burgundy velvet draperies drawn tightly across them, punctuated the wall of books. He parted one set of draperies and leaned down, slid the mullioned window open. Then he released the catch of the storm window and slid it up, too. He stuck his head out.

554

The blast of night air felt good. He looked down. The tree lights were on and Hélène was standing between the house and the barn, spotlit as if onstage. He frowned. She was oddly posed, all her weight on the ball of one foot, the toes of the other hesitantly poised as she looked around slowly. Suddenly she started to run for the barn.

Even before Edmond saw the black blur lunging out of the darkness, long-buried instinct took over. His heart crashed against his rib cage, and for a moment he couldn't breathe.

Danger, he thought automatically. *She's in danger.*

He jumped back from the window, cold fear sweeping over him as he lunged across the nearest Chesterfield. He reached across it to the desk and seized a letter opener. It was like a miniature scimitar, with a sharp, sturdy, paper-thin blade. It would be a lethal weapon as long as the porcelain handle did not break.

He weighed it in his hand for a split second. It would have to do.

He thrust it between his lips and clamped his teeth down on the handle, at the same time rushing back to the window.

He did not have to think. He was governed by reflex alone.

Got to protect her. No time to take the stairs, run through hallways and rooms. The window is the most direct way down.

He clutched the top of the window molding between both hands and like an acrobat lifted himself off the floor. He swung his buttocks backward, bringing his knees up under his chin, and then swiftly flung his legs forward and out, loosening his grip as his body caught the momentum. He ducked his head as he shot feetfirst through the open window. Mentally he blessed his workouts at the Athletic Club. He was no longer young and spry, but still sinewy, still in good shape.

He slid down the steep roof of the back porch, bumpy and abrasive and cold under him. The edge was coming up. Careful, he cautioned himself. Timing was everything. Careful . . .

He shot past the drainpipe, off the roof, and out into the open air. He brought his knees neatly under his chin and crouched forward, ready for the impact.

It came, and with a jar, the pain shooting like fire through his ankles and up his legs. He somersaulted over, sprang to his feet, and began to run across the frozen ground toward Hélène. Her screams pierced the night, and on top of them he could hear the vicious snarls of a dog gone mad. Yards ahead, he could see her struggling with it, both of them rolling around, the dog huge, its short black hair glistening in the lights. He glanced up at the tree lights as he ran. They would be on for only two minutes. Then the timer would automatically shut them off again. He wondered how many seconds of light were left.

He grabbed the letter opener from between his teeth and let out a yell.

Hélène had heard the dog before she saw it. At first there had been a heavy crashing in the underbrush. Then a menacing snarl. She could sense the muscular body racing toward her. She glanced backward and saw the flashing yellow eyes and the black sinewy blur in the glare of the floodlights. She let out a scream and began to run faster, knowing in the back of her mind that running would not be enough. The dog was faster. Much faster.

Suddenly the beast lunged at her. She dived sideways, instinctively tightening the muscles in her arms as she threw them up behind her. She could feel the rush of cold air as he missed her by inches. She rolled over on the hard ground and quickly scrambled back to her feet, continuing to run toward the barn. To safety.

In front of her, the dog, confused by the miss, skidded to a halt. Only as he turned around to attack again did Hélène realize the magnitude of her mistake. The dog was to one side of her, to be sure, but he was between her and the barn, cutting off her escape.

Fractionally she hesitated, wanting to turn and run toward the house instead. But then the dog would be behind her, and she would be blind to his tactics.

For a moment she stopped running, her pulse racing, the cold air raw in her throat. Perhaps she should have stayed near the path, keeping a tree between the beast and herself. A tree. She glanced desperately behind her. The nearest one was seven yards away. She glanced back at the dog. It was growling menacingly, already on its haunches, ready to put all its weight into another spring.

Her mind raced. It was a Great Dane; she could see that clearly now. And it was enormous; it probably weighed as much as she. Probably outweighed her, in fact. Its jaws were enormous. And she had no weapon with which to defend herself. No protection of any sort.

No, she was wrong, she realized suddenly. She did have protection of sorts. Her coat. Her down-filled coat. It was thickly padded. If she rolled herself into a ball, tucked her head down against her chest, hid her hands, and curled her legs up under her, she would be afforded some protection. Not much. But maybe enough. . . .

The dog hesitated, his eyes glittering like iridescent head-lamps. For a drawn-out second he seemed to crouch there, indecisive. Then the second was over and he lunged.

For one long frozen moment the dog seemed to be suspended in midair. Its razor teeth flashed whitely in the light from the trees, its enormous lean body, tapered as a greyhound's, showing the defined masses of hard muscle under the short gleaming hair.

Hélène ducked and dropped to the ground, readying herself for the swift maneuver of rolling herself into a ball. But the dog was too fast. He loomed larger and larger in front of her, and when she was least ready, the impact came.

Stabbing daggers of pain shot through her as the dog collided into her. She had had no idea the beast was this heavy or powerful. He had caught her on the chest, just as she had let her legs crumple and had felt herself starting to fall. She felt sleek black hair against her face, smelled the hot stench of his breath. The wind was knocked out of her lungs with a noisy *whoosh!* and her breasts were suddenly heavy and bruised as she fell backward, choking for air as any remaining wind was knocked out of her a second time as her back hit the frozen ground. But she could not wait to regain it. The air in her lungs would return. More important that she curl herself up, that she give the animal no outstretched limbs for his crazed jaws, that at all costs she keep her neck down. Dobermans went for the neck. Did Great Danes? She was taking no chances.

For the moment, the dog was not upon her. She had sensed him somersaulting over her, and the collision had stunned him momentarily. Wasting no precious seconds, she curled her knees up against her chest, wrapped her arms protectively around her, careful to keep her hands tucked far up her sleeves. She hunched her shoulders, trying to tuck her neck as far into her collar as possible, like a tortoise retracting into its shell at the first scent of danger. As the dog snarled and struggled to his feet, she quickly rolled over on her belly and pressed her face into the ground. It was hard and icy and scratchy, but she knew that her face was the most vulnerable, the most easily injured part of her body. She must keep it turned away from the dog at all costs.

The Chameleon watched in excitement. Tension welled up within him until it became almost unbearable. His penis hardened and strained against the fabric of his trousers. Rufus looked as big and powerful as a horse, yet was so light on his feet that his movements had the grace of a panther's. The woman had the same fluid grace. There was something peculiarly sensual about her.

The Chameleon's eyes glittered as he fingered his penis. He was witnessing a battle to the death—a battle between a superior brain and a superior body. A pity that they were so unevenly matched. The woman had no chance. The dog would win.

He congratulated himself for using the dog instead of his hands or a gun. There was something primordial about a duel between a human and a beast. But best of all, once the woman's body was found, her death would be blamed on a crazed animal. It would be a neat killing. A superior killing. One for which no man, however unknown, would ever be blamed. There was no chance that anyone would connect him or Rufus to the "accident." Both of them would be long gone. He on his way back to Chicago, the final installment for the murder in his pocket. The dog buried in a pit somewhere. Dead, like the woman.

All traces would be neatly obliterated. Once again, he had created a masterpiece. The perfect murder.

He raised the sonic whistle to his lips and blew into it again to egg the dog on. Not that Rufus needed any egging. He was onto the scent of blood. Any second now, and he would taste it.

The thought was almost enough to release the Chameleon's passion. Already he could sense his seminal emission surfacing. Instantly, he stopped stroking himself and willed his orgasm to die. He did not want to be racked by the splendid passion until the final moment was at hand.

Suddenly a yell rent the air. Rufus stopped in mid-attack, and turned toward the house. The Chameleon's eyes shifted. For the first time, he became aware of Edmond, head bent forward, blade in hand, racing across the yard.

Again Edmond's yell rang out clearly. This time the Chameleon could hear the word distinctly.

"*Sit!*"

The Chameleon's erection died, and he felt a cold paralysis coming on. His eyes were wide and unbelieving. The stupid dog—his goddamn killing machine—was actually backing off! Obediently starting to sit down!

The Chameleon quickly lifted the whistle again, giving two more short blows.

"Sit!"

Confused, the dog sprang to his feet, then sat hesitantly back down again. His head twisted first in the direction of the silent whistle, then to the man verbally commanding him to sit.

"Motherfuck!" the Chameleon cursed under his breath. He blew into the whistle again. The short hair stood up on Rufus' back; then the dog sprang gracefully to his feet, fangs bared.

"*Sit!*"

The dog sat obediently.

Edmond stopped running. As he slowly approached Hélène, Rufus let out a low, menacing growl.

"Sit!" Edmond commanded.

The growl died in the dog's throat, and he remained seated.

"Get up slowly, Little French Girl," Edmond cautioned softly. "Don't make any sudden moves."

Hélène raised her head slowly. The dog began to move again.

"Sit!"

The Chameleon cursed under his breath. Of all the stupid things to have happen! Why did those trainers teach a dog to obey common commands like "Sit"? They should have used code words. And he should have been more alert and noticed that yesterday.

It was too late now. He didn't even have a gun to finish the woman off himself. Nor could he rush out of the bushes and use his lethal hands or his knife. The element of surprise was gone. And now there was the man to contend with, too. He had a blade on him. No, better to retreat and try again some other time.

He whistled one last time—a single, long, drawn-out blow

to recall the dog. Rufus got to his feet, backed off slowly, and then retreated into the darkness.

Hélène took a wobbly step toward Edmond. She felt suddenly drained and collapsed limply in his arms, closing her eyes.

"It's over," he said softly, pocketing the letter opener. He held her tightly. "The dog is gone." He rocked her gently in his arms. "Are you hurt?"

She shook her head. "No," she said huskily. "But that dog—"

"Forget it," he whispered. "It's over now." He pressed her face against his chest and stared out over her head. At that moment, the tree lights clicked off. Two minutes were over. Had it lasted only that long? he asked himself. It had seemed a lifetime.

"It's over," Hélène repeated to herself, trembling. But her tremors were dying down. Edmond's presence was warm and comforting. "Thank God, it's over."

But was it? Edmond frowned into the darkness, his body still tensed. He did not have the heart to worry her by telling her otherwise.

He had heard not just the dog crashing through the bushes. He had heard something else. Something that moved with greater stealth.

A man.

2

Karl von Eiderfeld sat in thoughtful silence behind his big desk. The silk-shaded ormolu lamp cast a warm pool of light on the highly polished wood. He looked at the silver-framed photographs of his family. First there was Helga, his beautiful blond wife.

The oval photograph had been taken right after they were married. She was forty-four now and her hair had grayed, but she was still an extremely attractive woman. He hoped that this Hélène Junot business would soon be cleared up. He had just spoken to Helga long distance. She had told him that Düsseldorf was grim this winter and she wanted to fly to Marrakesh for a few weeks' vacation. He had promised that as soon as his business in New York was finished, they would fly to Morocco together.

Personally, he despised the north of Africa—all of Africa, for that matter. It was too filthy. There were too many verdammte flies. Worse, the whole continent was filled with an inferior race. As if that wasn't bad enough in itself, half the natives seemed to be missing something. Eyes. Ears. Noses. Limbs. He shook his head. Nor could his sensitive eyes take the harsh desert sun, the blinding glare of the whitewashed houses. He always stayed indoors in Marrakesh, never venturing farther during daylight hours than the cool, shady loggia.

But Helga liked the hot North African winters. She loved the Olympic-size swimming pool she had persuaded him to build at the villa.

He shook his head fondly and his white face broke into an unaccustomed smile. When he had met Helga Recknagel, she was a minor legend in Germany. She had brought a feeling of national pride to the degrading postwar years. At the 1956 Olympics in Melbourne, she had won a silver medal for the 400-meter freestyle swim event. She had clocked in at 4:55.9. Her face had been plastered in all the German newspapers and on the magazine covers. On her return from Australia, she had been met at the Bonn-Köln airport by a weeping mob. *Die Heilige Helga*, they called her. The Saintly Helga.

Unknown to everyone but him, Helga Recknagel had been born in 1936 in the first of the Lebensborn maternity homes. These were Heinrich Himmler's pet project, institutions he had set up in order to increase Germany's birth rate. Helga's mother was one of many women encouraged by the state to have an illegitimate child by an SS officer. Dutifully she had spread her legs for the Reich, let pure Aryan seed enter into her, and nine months later pushed an Aryan child out of her womb. At the Lebensborn home, with its large picture of the Führer in the lobby, both mother and daughter led a comfortable life.

Three weeks after they met, Karl von Eiderfeld married Helga Recknagel. In her he found everything he was looking for in a woman. She was a pure-blooded Aryan. Her father had been an SS officer. She was sturdy, strong, and had brought honor to her country. They honeymooned briefly on the Chiemsee in Bavaria and then he had begun building their family.

He glanced at the two smaller silver frames flanking Helga's oval portrait. Rolf and Otto. His sons.

Helga had wanted to have children, but he had refused. It had been the only major fight they had ever had. He had been afraid that the children would be born albino. He still believed in the pure Aryan ideal, and he despised himself for his own lack of physical perfection. So they had compromised. He and Helga had scoured the adoption agencies for a nice blond boy.

What they found were two boys, orphaned brothers. Actually, they had wanted a much younger child, but the boys had looked like Aryan ideals. Rolf was now twenty-three, Otto twenty-eight. They had been good-looking boys when they had been adopted, and they still were.

Otto had always been tough and unsmiling. He was very fair, with pale eyes, sensual lips, and a stern, almost judicious expression. Already Otto was embarked on a promising political career. The Christian Democrats were beginning to take notice of him as one of their future strengths, the Social Democrats as a formidable future opponent. A high position in the Bundestag was not out of the question. Who knew? In time, perhaps, Otto von Eiderfeld might even become chancellor.

Rolf had always been the prankster, the one with the sense of humor. But suddenly, almost overnight, the boy inside him had disappeared and a hardness had taken its place. Von Eiderfeld had been surprised but pleased by this change in his son. He could pinpoint the exact moment when it had occurred. The day of Rolf's first job in the family business . . . with the knowledge that he was being groomed as the heir to Von Eiderfeld Industrien G.m.b.H. Already he was surprising von Eiderfeld with his keen business acumen. His toughness when it came to dealing with hardened competitors. His German efficiency. Von Eiderfeld Industrien was assured of its future with Rolf at the helm.

The only thing that rankled von Eiderfeld about the boys was that they were not of his flesh. Not of his *blood*. But he never mentioned this. He consoled himself that with the boys, everything he had built would continue to prosper. At least the von Eiderfeld name would continue on for generations. Rolf's young wife, Monika, was already pregnant.

He sighed sadly, folded his old white hands, and looked down at them. There was no doubt but that the boys were going to surpass the parent. Of course, they had a head start. Von Eiderfeld Industrien had already been a very powerful corporation by the time they arrived on the scene. But the boys were brilliant. They would go far. In fact, either one of them was probably far better equipped for dealing with Hélène Junot than he was. But he couldn't divulge his past to them. Even Helga didn't know about it. She suspected, yes, but she never said a word. She loved him. She was devoted to him. She was German. *She understood.*

He sighed again. The incriminating evidence Hélène Junot had collected was burned. But was there more? If one person could get hold of such documents, couldn't someone else dig some up also? After all, the Reich had been one massive bureaucracy. Many documents had been destroyed, but far too many had survived. And what about human survivors? Millions had died in the camps—he alone had sent hundreds of thousands there—but some of them had returned alive. All it took was one person who might recognize him, blow the whistle on him. He took precautions, yes. He shunned publicity. He led a quiet life. He always traveled by private car, private plane, private boat. Photographers were never allowed near him. But always he walked around with a death sentence hanging over his head. *Someone might recognize him.*

The worst had happened the day Hélène Junot arrived at his office, slapping copies of the incriminating documents down on his desk. He shuddered, remembering that day. Still, was it enough that the documents were destroyed?

He pushed a weary hand through his thinning white hair. She was a witness. She had seen the documents. She could still make him stand trial for war crimes.

She was alive.

3

Jennifer Rowen rolled over in the bed and gently shook her husband awake. Her voice finally pushed through the thick blanket of his sleep. "Honey . . . wake up, honey."

He moaned and opened his eyes, looking up at her. Then he blinked and shaded his eyes with his hand against the glare of the nightstand light. He struggled to sit up. "What is it?" he asked irritably.

She held up one hand to show him. She was holding the ivory receiver of the bedroom extension phone, the cupped palm of her hand wrapped around the mouthpiece. "Honey, it's that person again," she whispered in a frightened voice. "You know who I mean."

"The whisperer?" he asked sleepily.

She nodded and handed the receiver over to him, ducking the cord. He took it and cleared his throat. "Robert Rowen speaking."

"*Mr. Rowen?*" The whisper over the wire was thin and reedy. For some reason, it sent a chill up his spine. Perhaps it was because the voice sounded so disembodied and he couldn't connect it with a face.

"*Are you there, Mr. Rowen?*"

"Yes, yes, of course."

"*Have you given any more thought to our proposition?*"

For a moment, Rowen hesitated. He glanced over at Jennifer. She was watching him with open curiosity. He wished she would take some kind of cue and leave the room, but he couldn't ask her to do that. She would get too suspicious. He kept his voice noncommittal. "Yes," he said carefully, "I've given it thorough thought."

"*And what conclusion have you arrived at?*"

Rowen didn't hesitate now. "You have yourself a deal," he said. "That is, unless she comes up with the money by five o'clock tomorrow afternoon." He glanced at the alarm clock

564

on the nightstand. "I mean, *this* afternoon," he corrected himself. "If she doesn't, the bank will confiscate the collateral and I'll make certain that we sell it as you see fit."

"A very wise decision, if I say so myself, Mr. Rowen." The voice gave a low, whispery laugh. *"She can never come up with eleven million dollars, believe me!"*

There was a pause. Rowen waited for the caller to continue.

"Say we meet in the morning? An attaché case filled with five hundred thousand dollars will be exchanged for your word. You'll receive the other half-million once the transaction is completed and the shares are in our hands. We warn you, though . . ." The whisper took on the sharp, harsh tones of a hiss. *"Do not try to double-cross us!"*

Rowen smiled into the receiver. "I wouldn't dream of doing that."

"Another wise decision, to be sure, Mr. Rowen. To show our goodwill, we shall deliver the money to you at eight a.m."

"Where shall we meet?"

"Is the Staten Island ferry terminal convenient?"

"That would be very convenient," Rowen agreed. "How will I recognize you?"

"It is I who shall recognize you, Mr. Rowen. You do have a trench coat?"

"Yes," Rowen said curiously, thinking of the London Fog raincoat Jennifer had given him last Christmas.

"Then wear it. And please, do be trite and put a red carnation in your left lapel buttonhole. I will recognize you by that. We shall meet in the men's room. Good night, Mr. Rowen."

"Good night—"

But the phone had already clicked; the caller had hung up. Rowen stared at the receiver for a moment, shrugged, and then slowly handed it back to Jennifer.

She took it and dropped it on the nightstand extension. She turned to him. "Honey . . ." She looked at him anxiously. "What's wrong?"

He forced a smile. "Nothing's wrong. It was just business." He leaned over and planted a kiss on her lips.

She stiffened and refused to respond. "At two in the morning?" she asked suspiciously. She shook her head. "By the look on your face, I know that something's up. Why can't you tell me?"

"All right, Jennie," he said wearily, "after tomorrow morning, we're going to be rich."

"Rich! Now I know you're pulling my leg!" She turned away.

"I'm serious," he said quietly.

Something in his voice caught her. "But how?" Her eyes narrowed suspiciously. "You're . . . you're not thinking of *stealing*!"

"Bite your tongue." He smiled tightly. "No, I'm not going to steal. Who do you think you married, a fool? Just trust me, Jennie." He took her hand in his and squeezed it. "You wait and see. We'll have money to burn!"

YESTERDAY

VI
DIVORCE

1

Paris 1960

Edmond stepped aside to let Hélène into the apartment. Her eyes swept down the hall to the living room. It was stuffy and hot in here. Despite the fragrant spring weather, all the windows were shut and most of the curtains were drawn against the sunlight. She shuddered. There was something dismal about it. As if he was trying to shut the world out. "I'm glad I caught you at home," she said. "I'm not disturbing you, am I?"

He smiled weakly as he closed the door and led the way into the living room. "I'm just studying." He waved helplessly toward the desk. Open volumes were illuminated by a single arc desk lamp with a weak bulb. "Can I get you something?"

"No, thanks," she said, putting her purse down on the couch and smoothing her skirt behind her before she carefully took a seat, avoiding one of the lethal exposed sofa springs. She had to fight to keep from wrinkling her nostrils. The apartment wasn't only dim, it was dirty and dusty as well. Already she could feel it irritating her nostrils. Long gone were the sounds of laughter, the smiles of contentment, the delicious smells of cooking hovering in the air.

"I just came by to have a little talk," she explained in what she hoped was an offhand voice. It took an effort for her to smile at him. She quickly forgot her own emotional disappointments when she saw him. He looked haggard and so terribly beaten. His threadbare red cardigan had holes in the elbows. If Jeanne were alive, she would have seen to it that they were mended.

"What do you want to talk about?" he asked.

"In a minute," she said, suddenly uncomfortable. "I think I'll have something to drink after all. Do you have any chilled white wine?"

569

He nodded. "I think so. I'll be right back."

She watched him walk toward the kitchen. Slowly, she shook her head. Why doesn't he snap out of it? she asked herself. Why doesn't he come back to life instead of burying his nose in his books? You can mourn for only so long. Then you have to go on living. She knew, too, that the person who suffered most was Petite Hélène. Young and resilient though she was, she had lost her mother, and now, Hélène realized she had lost her father also, albeit to the university. Only Hélène herself had profited psychologically from having to shoulder some of the responsibility for her niece. It had given her yet another task to undertake, one which filled up the last remaining gaps left by Jeanne's death and Nigel's desertion. Even more important, it had opened up a whole new vista of the future. A future so dazzling she dared not breathe a word of it to anyone.

She had given careful thought as to how Petite Hélène was to be raised. She had made her promise to Jeanne, and she was determined to stick to it. Not only for Jeanne's sake but also because it suited her own ambitious ends. Already she had carefully begun to plot Petite Hélène's future, inextricably tying it to Les Éditions Hélène Junot. Since her abortion had made it impossible for her to have children, it was only natural that Petite Hélène would be her link to the future, her insurance that *Les Modes* would be kept in the family.

It was a long way off, but that was the strength of the plan. Grooming an heir was a painstaking process that takes time, and there was sufficient time to do it correctly. Time to supervise the complicated process and make sure that it was done step by step. Petite Hélène would have everything she herself had ever lacked. The way was already paved; the wherewithal was there. Now it was only a matter of careful guidance. Petite Hélène would go to the best schools, meet the right people, attend the best Swiss finishing school, become a social item, an expert businesswoman. Hélène had it all worked out. Never once did she give a passing thought to the fact that the girl might not be cut out for a business career or that her plan might somehow fail. She thought about only one thing. It had to be done.

Since it was so far in the future, she kept her strategy to herself. She did not even tell Edmond about it. Meanwhile, she would start the process, but she wouldn't go overboard, either. Petite Hélène had to be raised like other children. She must not be deprived of a normal childhood as she herself had been. Yet the fires of long-term ambition had to be constantly fed and kept alive. After all, Petite Hélène was already six. It wasn't premature to breed a little bit of the lady into her. As far as that was concerned, one could never start too soon. Hélène knew from her own life how impressionable she had been at Petite Hélène's age. All her adult strengths had their roots there.

The only thing that took time was planning how to go about her plan. It had to be done in the best possible way for all the parties concerned. First, she had to have more control over Petite Hélène, but she couldn't just take the child and raise her by herself. Petite Hélène was Edmond's daughter. Despite the fact that he didn't see enough of her, Hélène knew that he loved her above everything else in the world. She was all that was left of his union with Jeanne. It would be cruel and terribly unfair of her to tear his daughter away from him.

For a while, Hélène entertained the idea of getting a huge apartment and living together with them. That way, she would be close to Petite Hélène. It would give her a thousand opportunities to give her niece constant guidance. But eventually she discarded this idea, also. It wouldn't do for a brother and sister, no matter how close the relationship or how big the apartment, to be living together. Not that it would raise any eyebrows. Besides, she had long ago stopped caring about what people thought. It just wouldn't have been fair. Not to Petite Hélène or to Jeanne's memory. Jeanne had been her mother; Petite Hélène must never be confused about that.

But finally Hélène had come to a decision.

Edmond came from the kitchen, careful not to spill any wine from the glass. He handed it to her.

"Aren't you having any?" she asked.

He shook his head and sat down beside her.

She took a sip and set the glass down on the table beside her. She folded her hands in her lap and watched him light a cigarette. Then he looked at her through the cloud of smoke. "I take it this is not a social call?"

She smiled uncomfortably. "I'm afraid not. And I hope you won't think I'm trying to barge in on something that's none of my business."

He smiled grimly and smoked in silence.

"Edmond, we've always been close. You know that."

He nodded his head slowly.

"Far closer than most brothers and sisters. But ever since Jeanne . . ." Hélène sighed and quickly looked down at her hands. "Ever since Jeanne died, things haven't been the same between us, and that's been a long time now."

He turned away and faced the far wall as he felt the tears springing to his eyes.

Hélène glanced sadly at him. It was said that time heals all wounds. Yet it seemed as if his were as open and bleeding as the day they were inflicted.

"If you'd rather not talk about it, I'll understand," she said quietly. "I didn't drop by to cause you any more pain."

She saw the back of his head nodding. "I know that," he said huskily.

She bit down on her lower lip and wondered how to continue. Perhaps she should just wait and broach the subject some other time? Then she took a quick swallow of wine. No, this couldn't wait. It was too important.

She shifted around on the couch and touched his arm, gently pulling him back around to face her. There was sorrow in her eyes. "Edmond, it's Petite Hélène I'm worried about. Can't you see what this is doing to her? You're never around, and if you are, your nose is buried in your books."

He nodded dumbly and stared straight through her. "What do you want me to do?"

She pressed his hand between both of hers. "To give her more attention. Get someone to cook for her. To keep her company."

"Madame Courbet is taking good care of her."

Hélène sighed and jumped to her feet. Angrily she started to pace the room. "Madame Courbet is the concierge, and she's busy. Perhaps she's adequate, but she can't focus all her attention on Petite Hélène. She's a growing child, Edmond!" She stopped pacing suddenly. "She needs company. Guidance. A family."

He jerked his hand suddenly. His cigarette had burned itself down to the filter and scorched his fingers. Quickly he half got up and tossed the butt into the fireplace. Then he sat back down.

"Edmond, Petite Hélène needs a nanny."

His lips tightened. "Nannies are for babies."

But she kept pressing him until he would finally admit that

none of the arrangements he had come up with thus far had worked out. At first, there had been an irresponsible au-pair girl; then a woman who came in every day while he was gone, took Petite Hélène to school and picked her up again in the afternoon. Hélène discovered after a while that the woman drank heavily. Several times she had even had blackouts and couldn't remember a thing that had happened. And Madame Courbet just wasn't suited for the job.

"I'd be no good at picking out a nanny," Edmond said lamely. "I don't know the first thing about it!" He looked at her beseechingly. "I know you're awfully busy, Little French Girl, but . . ."

Hélène nodded. "I'll see to it," she said with satisfaction.

Now that it was settled, she didn't waste another moment. She took a week off from work during Petite Hélène's Easter vacation and flew to England with her. After all, nannies were one thing the British were famous for, so what made more sense than trying to find one in London? After the histories of the au-pair girl and the drunk, Hélène wasn't about to compromise. Of course, the thought that she might run into Nigel while in London did enter her mind.

They stayed at Claridge's, where Hélène had booked a suite. It had a quietly luxurious living room, two bedrooms, and two baths. For once, Hélène was content to do nothing but play tourist and enjoy Petite Hélène's company. The girl's energy was boundless, her excitement infectious, her quick intelligence stimulating. Sometimes Hélène just stood back and watched her niece as she approached something new with a cautious, almost adult curiosity. Together they explored London from top to bottom, holding hands and skipping along the Thames esplanade through the fine-mist fogs and marveling at the patience of the polite English as they queued up for the double-decker buses or the Underground. They attended a performance of *Der Rosenkavalier* in the sweetly gaudy Covent Garden opera house, visited Tower Bridge, the Houses of Parliament, and saw the crown jewels guarded by the Yeomen of the Guard in their colorful uniforms in the Tower of London. They marveled at the Egyptian antiquities in the British Museum, shopped Regent Street and Harrods, visited the Old Curiosity Shop immortalized by Charles Dickens, and shuddered when they saw the wax figures at Madame Tussaud's. One afternoon, Hélène hired a chauffeured car and they drove out to the country to see Windsor Castle. On the way back, they stopped in a delightful old country inn and ate sliced roast beef and Yorkshire pudding and drank Earl Grey tea.

They were in England to look for a nanny, and every day before they went out exploring, Hélène patiently interviewed the various potential nannies the services sent over.

It seemed to Hélène that she would never find one both she and Petite Hélène could get along with. Some were dour, some patronizing, some overly sweet.

But if she had hoped to run into Nigel, it was in vain, even though the week stretched into two. She never saw Nigel, but she did finally find a nanny who was satisfactory.

Her name was Elizabeth Stewart and she was a stout Scottish woman in her late forties. She had a natural way with children—that much was obvious from the start. She and Petite Hélène immediately took to each other—something that stirred up irrational jealousies in Hélène. It was she who had insisted on getting a nanny, but at the same time, she wanted all of Petite Hélène's affections for herself.

With the nanny engaged, there were no more excuses to keep them in England, so they flew back to Paris. However, Hélène was not content with just having found a nanny. Every family needed a home, a constant refuge to go back to in times of joy and crisis, a place where they could spend the holidays together. The old house with the canary-yellow door in Montmartre would have been her home had Maman been alive. She missed not having had it. She knew, instinctively, that Petite Hélène needed such a place, too. But not in the city. It would have to be out in the country; as far as Hélène was concerned, they all spent too much time in the city. And it would have to be a secluded place. A private place.

When she found what she wanted, she signed the papers, bought it for just over a million francs cash, and took Edmond and Petite Hélène to see it one Saturday afternoon. She had kept the purchase a secret. She didn't even tell them where they were headed.

Two hours after they left Paris, Hélène rapped on the glass partition of the Citroën limousine. The chauffeur glanced back through the rearview mirror. Hélène pointed to the left, and he nodded. As soon as the next intersection came up, he slowed down and made a left turn into a bumpy, rutfilled road that branched off into a forest.

574

"Where are you taking us?" Petite Hélène asked with growing excitement.

Hélène smiled secretively. "I've just bought a little cottage in the country. I thought we should have a refuge to escape the bustle of Paris." She leaned forward, looked around Petite Hélène, and smiled at Edmond. "You don't mind my not telling you? I wanted to keep it a surprise."

Edmond smiled. "I don't mind it at all as long as you'll agree to take some time off every now and then, too."

"And likewise," she said. "Look who's telling me."

But she was pleased. Ever since Nanny had joined the household, even Edmond was starting to come back to normal. The curtains were drawn aside each morning, the rooms aired out, the cooking done. Nanny's influence even showed in their family relationship. Once again they had become close-knit.

Edmond sat up straight as the car came into a clearing. "A cottage, did you say?"

"Well . . ." Hélène shrugged and made a helpless little gesture with her hands. Petite Hélène was suddenly trying to crawl across her lap, "ooohing" and "aaahing" excitedly as she pressed her nose against the window.

Hélène couldn't help but smile as she looked out. The sun was high in the sky and bathed the clearing. The grass and moss were moist and lushly green, and the sunlight between the cathedrallike trees was like flashes of silver. The château was a brownstone island with corner turrets, a central cobblestoned courtyard, and a moat that emptied into a big green pond which had ducks and swans gliding gracefully across their own reflections.

As soon as the car came to a halt, Petite Hélène jumped out and ran over to the pond.

It was a beautifully proportioned house, Hélène thought as she looked up at it, her hands in her pockets. It wasn't nearly as lavish as Hautecloque, but it had an unpretentious charm of its own. It was neither haughty nor majestic. It was simply a manageable country château 160 kilometers south of Paris. And it was steeped in history, parts of it dating from the sixteenth century. Originally the château had been owned by Diane de Poitiers; then it had undergone various changes in family ownership. It had a caretaker's cottage, a guest house, stables, and a livable three-story stone tower on the far side of the pond.

Hélène had decided to keep on the old caretaker couple, Monsieur and Madame Greuze, to run the place. And she had bought Petite Hélène a pony of her own.

Jeanne was gone, never to be part of them except in their memories, but Hélène couldn't help thinking that Jeanne would have been pleased. Petite Hélène now had a house she could come home to, that would eventually be her own.

2

The Banco di Milano was located on the ground floor of a thirty-story office tower that rose out of the ancient pedimented buildings of old-town Milan. An inverted black cone, it dominated the skyline like a huge, uncircumcised phallus. When Hélène came out of the building, she squinted in the bright sunlight, put on her sunglasses, and took the flight of low, curving steps down to the sidewalk. There she skirted the crashing water fountains that split up the concrete piazza like an enormous ultramodern cupcake pan. The warm May breeze carried the shroudlike mist from the fountains over to her. It felt cool and refreshing.

A slight smile of satisfaction played across Hélène's lips. Things were going well. It was the second month since she had officially become a millionairess in her own right—not counting her inheritance from Stanislaw, and not in worthless lire or in so many, many francs, but from Les Modes, and in the currency that counted. Dollars. Not bad, everything considered. The first issue of La Moda, Les Modes's Italian counterpart, had already hit the newsstands.

She smiled, thinking of how Signor Piarotto, the bank president, was becoming increasingly ingratiating every time she entered the bank. He was beginning to realize her worth and saw to it that he always took care of her personally, a fawning smile on his face. How different things were now from a few years earlier, she thought, when she hadn't had as much as a sou in her pocket. When she'd arrived "fifth-class" on the Right Bank of Paris and couldn't afford to eat anything but old bread and scavanged fruit—and only when she was lucky.

She glanced at her gold watch. It was nearly ten o'clock; she'd have to hurry. She had meetings scheduled with paper suppliers and advertisers, and at noon there was a working lunch with the Czarina.

She turned right on the via Montenapoleone and headed for the offices of Edizioni Hélène Junot S.p.a. They were located several blocks away in an enormous old Medici palazzo that had been carved up into high-class commercial space. The building was shared by several fashion designers, three giftware wholesalers, a parfumerie, and *La Moda*.

On the way, she passed the newsstand where she always bought her morning paper. It was run by a wrinkled old widow. Hélène paused; something had caught her eye. There it was. A stack of *La Moda*. She watched as two blond women hesitated between it and *Vogue*. Finally curiosity won out over habit. They picked up *La Moda* and flipped rapidly through it. The expressions on their faces immediately changed: they were transported from their drab, humdrum lives into the exciting world of couture and makeup and fine jewelry, a Cinderella world where anything was possible, where a slickly photographed pair of seventy-thousand-lire Ferragamo shoes replaced the traditional glass slipper.

Hélène felt a wave of pride coursing through her. She was sharing her taste and knowledge—indeed the entire fashion world—with these women, perhaps making their lives more beautiful, more worthwhile. At any rate, bringing their dreams into perspective and putting them down on paper where they couldn't evaporate. Perhaps even giving them ideas to apply to themselves, to make them feel more beautiful and secure, desired. How well she could still remember how the magazines at Madame Dupré's had changed her life.

Without another glance at *Vogue*, both women reached into their purses and snatched up *La Moda*. Happily they began to chatter and walked off.

Hélène smiled. It was only the first issue, but already she had witnessed two tiny victories—two minor miracles—two women reaching for *La Moda* instead of *Vogue*. On an impulse she walked over to the newsstand. The old woman knew her already, but she didn't know who she was. So much the better.

"Good morning, signorina," the old woman said.

"Good morning." Hélène looked down at the stack of *La Moda*. "A new magazine?"

"Yes, signorina, but finally one that is bellissimo!" For emphasis the old woman made a circle with her thumb and forefinger and kissed it noisily.

Hélène reached into her purse, took out a thousand-lire note, and picked up a copy. It was thick and heavy.

Thanking the old woman, she left the newsstand and strode down the street, the magazine tucked proudly under her arm. When she came across a sidewalk café she took a seat under the striped canvas awning and ordered a cup of espresso; the meetings would have to wait. Then she laid the magazine faceup on the table, took off her sunglasses, leaned her elbows on the table, and proudly stared at the cover.

The block letters "LA MODA" were huge and white and dazzling.

As Hélène flipped through the magazine, she found it hard to believe how much had happened in the last two years. *Les Modes* was here to stay, a growing giant that was a power to be reckoned with. The Italian edition, *La Moda Uomo*, was out only a month behind schedule. And, most important, men's editions of both magazines—*Les Modes Homme* and *La Moda Uomo*—were in the planning stages. But that was only a fraction of what she had up her sleeve—the visible fraction. Like a deceptive iceberg, she chose to keep her ambitions and future plans well hidden. She knew—instinctively, and from experience with Stanislaw's inheritance—that it took money to make money. And she knew perfectly well that having money, like owning art, was an awesome responsibility. Once you had it, you had to make sure that it was constantly working for you, increasing steadily. What good did it do you otherwise? By simply banking it, you lost it steadily but surely. Nothing shrank as fast as idle money.

She put this knowledge to good use by expanding her empire and thinking of starting another, entirely different but related business. But as always, she combined caution with just the right amount of shrewd daring. Instinctively she sensed when to wait and when to go all-out. Her instincts had served her well in the past, and she relied upon them completely. For her, Paris and *Les Modes* had only been the jumping-off point. Italy was where her fortune would skyrocket. She knew that as surely as she knew that Thursday followed Wednesday, and she was already planning for it. She saw things happening in Italy that were not happening elsewhere. Design was new and bursting and alive; the young designers were branching out, freed from the shackles of conservatism to forge ahead and create exciting new styles previously unheard-of.

Yes, a lot was happening. And she planned to be where it was happening.

Hélène entered the building, crossed the hollow-sounding lobby, and hurried past the glass cases filled with expensive giftware. She didn't bother to glance at them. She had seen that same display a hundred times already. The air in here smelled expensive. It was the fragrance of perfume.

The glass cases belonged to the giftware wholesaler who occupied the ground floor; the scent drifted down from the parfumerie on the third. Quickly she ascended the wide balustraded staircase to the second floor and crossed the marble landing to the carved double doors. She glanced at the engraved brass plaque:

"EDIZIONI HÉLÈNE JUNOT S.p.a."

She pulled open the door on the right and went inside.

For a moment, she paused. As usual, the offices were humming with the activity of the business day. She could feel the cogs turning, could almost reach out and touch the creativity that crackled visibly in the frenetic atmosphere. The persistently ringing telephones, the clattering of typewriters and telex machines, and the fragments of raised voices coming from the conference room, where she knew a "creative meeting" was in progress, were music to her ears. The big office space reminded her of the Place Vendôme headquarters. The language here was Italian, but the flavor—for a moment she closed her eyes—the *flavor* of the Milan offices was exactly like that of the Paris headquarters. The business of reporting on and predicting style and elegance, of "making" promising new designers or sending established, staid ones to their death—not through spectacular battle, but by simply ignoring them—here the *power* of fashion pulsed strong and loud.

Hélène hurried down the plush-carpeted corridor to her private office. She was sorry to have missed the meetings scheduled for that morning and the working lunch with Luba, but she had been too involved with her plans to notice how much time had passed. It was already two o'clock.

She crossed over to her chrome-and-glass desk and put down her purse and her copy of her magazine. A pink note under the small Jean Arp bronze she used as a paperweight caught her eye. Carefully she slid the note out from under it. The writing, she could tell from a glance, was Luba's. It was as elegant and spidery as the woman herself. True to the Czarina's fashion, it was both cryptic and dramatic: *"I've found him! L."*

Hélène crumpled it up into a ball and tossed it into the wastebasket. Then she picked up her telephone and summoned the Czarina to her office. While she waited, she sat down in her upholstered swivel chair, swung around to the molded filing cabinet to her left, pulled open a drawer and took out a report. The light blue cover was stamped in red ink: CONFIDENTIAL.

She sat back, opened the report to the first page and started to read. Within a moment she was as immersed in it as a housewife reading the latest blockbuster novel.

La Moda
Projections

Issue:	November
Start Production:	June 1
Advertising Deadline:	July 1
Projected Advertising Pages:	230
Advertising Pages Sold to Date:	223
Projected Article Pages:	70

Monthly Features

Editorial:	*La Moda*'s Point of View: ?
Guest Speaker:	?
Society:	Bonacossi-Peretti wedding in June
	Charity ball in Florence (send Luba and photographer)
Cuisine:	Heartwarming Soups
	Eating with Flair: Tureens
Travel:	Sun in the Alps—Switzerland, France, and Austria
	Sun on the Beach—the Great Barrier Reef, Tunisia, and Malibu
Interiors:	John Fowler
Health:	Avoiding Skin Cancer on the Slopes and Beaches

Beauty:	New Skin Tones for Winter
	Interviews with Six Plastic Surgeons
	New Colors for Eyes and Lips

She pursed her lips thoughtfully and drummed her nails on the glass desktop. So far, everything was too predictable. Too much like the first issue. Like the others that were in production right now. What was needed was a new approach.

She had a sudden inspiration, picked up her pen, and wrote a note in the margin: *"For lipstick features, focus close up on lips and mouths. Tongues with caviar on them, lips with straws sipping Coca-Cola, etc."*

Satisfied, she laid down her pen and continued reading:

Arts:	Film—Fellini
Architecture:	Palladio
Art:	Sculptures by Marino Marini and Eduardo Paolozzi
Theater:	London This Season
Fashion:	Focus on—Valentino
La Moda's Boutique:	Our Choices for Winter
Around the World:	Finnish Leather to Alaskan Parkas
Haute Couture:	Paris, Milan, and New York
Ready-to-Wear:	This Season's Top Designers—Milan
Accessories:	Skis and Skates—New Designs for the Sixties
Jewelry:	Colombian Emeralds, Peruvian Gold, Celtic Jewelry from Ireland, Navajo Turquoise, New Pop-Art Plastics
Special Features:	Visit with Picasso at La Californie
	What's New for Winter—Paris, New York, Milan
	Furs for All Seasons (*Note: Max Reby bought 6 pages of ads!*)
	Dressing Up by Dressing Down
	Revlon's Cosmetics—a Retrospective (1932 through present)

Hélène was startled when Luba knocked on her door. She looked up. "Come in!"

Luba approached the desk with her usual purposeful pace. Hélène noticed she held a typed sheet of paper in her hand.

Hélène closed the report, put it aside, and folded her hands. "Luba," she said with a smile.

The Czarina stood confidently gaunt in a black knit shift belted at the waist with the thickest black leather strap and the biggest silver buckle Hélène had ever laid eyes on. Her black pumps had identical but slightly smaller buckles. As usual her pitch-black hair was gathered on the right side of her head and plaited into a single long, thick braid that hung aggressively down to nearly her waist.

Luba's tangerine nails slashed through the air. "I've found the patsy!" she announced in a dramatic stage whisper.

Hélène looked at her in embarrassment. "Please, Luba. You know I don't like to use that word."

Luba's black eyes flashed from within her thick sable eyelashes. "A patsy is what best describes what you're looking for."

Hélène sighed. "Patsy it is, then." She waved to a chair.

Luba made a production of consulting the paper in her hand. "His name is Marcello d'Itri. Born in Sicily, current resident of Milan. Studied fashion here while apprenticed to Missoni as a weaver. Left for New York and spent two years studying at the Fashion Institute of Technology. Came back, spent a year as a laborer in a ready-to-wear garment factory. Was one of the assistants to a fabric designer at T. and J. Vestor. That lasted six months. Tried to open his own boutique two years ago, failed miserably, and has been knocking on the doors of every designer in this city since then. He's a bachelor and a heterosexual, and that's it in a nutshell." Luba dropped the paper on Hélène's desk.

Hélène looked thoughtful. "And you think he's the one we're looking for?"

"I've kept my eyes wide open," the Czarina said. "He's the perfect patsy."

Hélène winced. She wished Luba would stop using that word. But the Czarina was right; what she wanted *was* a patsy. A handsome ladies' man, preferably Italian, who had a fashion background but was a miserable failure. She wanted someone with enough intelligence to face that fact, yet someone who wasn't so independent that he wouldn't do as he was told. He had to be someone who could never become successful on his own. Someone who was . . . weak.

Hélène glanced down at the paper that summed up one man's life in such terse, unfeeling terms. Could that really be all there was to a life? she asked herself. Was the rest just padding? Could her own life be outlined just as concisely, with only one difference—success substituting for failure?

In a way, she felt sorry for Marcello d'Itri without even having met him. Getting a start in the fashion business was like swimming in an ocean full of sharks. It didn't matter whether you were good or bad. You were a potential competitor, and as such, the others ganged up on you and cut you swiftly down to size before you even had a chance to start swimming. It was Darwinism, pure and simple. The survival of the fittest. You had to be a shark to survive.

Yet as much as she felt sorry for him, the fact that he had had such miserable luck was a plus. For her. She had been searching for someone like him for months, but until now none of the candidates met all the qualifications. And for what she wanted (as usual, she knew *exactly* what she wanted), each qualification was important. For she, Hélène Junot, was going into the fashion business. Not just reporting on fashion as she had been doing all along, but having an atelier of her own. She knew that she and Luba had an abundance of taste and foresight—and that *Les Modes* and *La Moda* were powerful enough—to assure the atelier's success. Only for once, her magazines stood in her way: she couldn't open an atelier in her own name. That would be a blatant conflict of interests. What she had to do was to own an atelier but remain a silent partner. She had to set up someone else as a figurehead. Someone who would listen to her and Luba and pretend that he was in charge. Someone who would take orders from them. Someone who had little or no talent.

Of course, an atelier needed talent, but that would remain as silently in the background as she herself would. She would simply get a design team together. Just as she had begun *Les Modes* by robbing *Vogue, Harper's Bazaar,* and *L'Officiel* of their talent, so she would snare the best design talent for her atelier. Of talent there was always a plentiful crop. It was the figurehead who was more difficult to find. And Hélène knew one thing better than even the established couturiers who gambled on the Look of the season. *She knew the exact direction in which the winds of fashion were blowing, be-*

cause she helped them blow that way. Her atelier wouldn't be a gamble. Nor would it cajole customers into buying beautiful, expensive things by relying on their own good taste. No, she would cleverly cater to them from the beginning, playing on their ingrained tastes and snobbishness. Her atelier would sell exactly what people wanted. Nothing else.

Hélène did not realize it, but she had stumbled across what was to become a trend that would continue for years. Creating a figurehead and making his name a household word, or using a figurehead to carry on a name, would become an intrinsic part of the fashion world on both sides of the Atlantic. It was coincidental whether the figurehead could design or not, although some of them could. What was important was that people would pay for the name.

Marcello d'Itri.

Hélène rolled the name on her tongue. It sounded good. Now, if only he was what she was looking for. She winced as Luba's words came back to her.

The perfect patsy.

Hélène forced herself to push the word out of her mind. She rose to her feet and smiled. "Thank you, Luba," she said.

The Czarina rose also. "Do you want me to schedule a meeting with d'Itri?"

"Please. I've got to return to Paris on Friday, so make it as soon as possible."

"Is tomorrow soon enough?"

Hélène nodded. "Tomorrow will be fine."

"Good. I'll send for him."

"No," Hélène said slowly. "I tell you what. I'll go to him instead. I want you to accompany me, of course."

The Czarina looked baffled, but she knew better than to ask why the mountains were going to visit Muhammad. She nodded.

After she was gone, Hélène thought about her decision to go and visit d'Itri. She knew instinctively that it was a good idea. You could always tell more about a person from his surroundings than if you summoned him to your office. Of course, in the office he was more vulnerable, more ill-at-ease and nervous. But she didn't want d'Itri to be any of these things. She wanted to find out the little things about him that only a shelf of books or the throw on a chair could reveal.

That was far better than seeing him disguised in his best suit.

The next day Hélène and Luba sat in the back of the company's tiny chauffeur-driven Fiat, negotiating the narrow, ancient streets of Milan.

Marcello d'Itri was sweating. He was not usually prone to sweat, but he couldn't help it now. Not with the two elegant women he faced. The tall, gaunt, aggressive one and the expensively dressed younger one. They looked so different—like an elegant old lizard and a poised gazelle. Yet undeniably they both had chic—an instinctive, intimidating chic such as he had never been exposed to before. And they wore it so naturally, so comfortably! Most people he knew felt that way only in worn sweaters and old bathrobes. Yet here they were, dressed to kill, and totally at ease. The old lizard in a turtle-neck sweater and a skirt—both of black silk interwoven with cashmere—a long gold-mesh chain knotted around her neck, and an Hermès belt around her waist; the young gazelle in a pale apricot Chanel suit with dark piping, an off-white silk blouse, and a straw hat. Her ear clips were unmistakably Bulgari—an emerald-cut diamond surrounded by baguettes and set in white gold.

But chic was not all they were. He felt something menacing under their beautiful veneers. They were powerful. He could see that in their eyes, in their self-assured poise. He knew they weren't the type to be taken in by overt displays of masculinity or suave, effusive compliments. There was something hard and businesslike about both of them. Especially the younger one.

Marcello d'Itri was slender and good-looking. His skin was olive and his eyes and hair were dark and glossy. He looked a little unkempt, Hélène thought, but it was clear that that was a matter of finances. He'd obviously done all he could to make himself presentable, even getting a haircut. Not a very good one, but probably all he could afford. His suit, though of a good fabric and cut, was worn and more than a little frayed. It had had a last-minute pressing. It was either the best suit he owned, or the only one. It was made of wool and he was wearing it in May. His white shirt was of good-quality cotton, but there, too, wear and tear showed. But she knew better than to judge him by his immediate appearance. What

585

mattered was how he *could* look. And she instinctively realized that with a little flair and some money, he could look highly presentable. His skin tone was just slightly exotic, his full lips could be construed as sensual. He was good-looking enough for any woman, and yet not perfect enough to instill an instant dislike in men. His tiny dark apartment was shabby. In one corner stood a large loom with an unfinished design woven on the hundreds of vertical strings. Hélène glanced at it disapprovingly and then caught Luba's eye. They both recognized the design instantly. Missoni.

Marcello d'Itri clearly copied from whoever was in vogue.

D'Itri fidgeted nervously with his hands, waiting for one of the women to speak. He wondered what they could possibly want from him.

"I've taken the liberty of ordering a rundown on your personal history," Hélène was saying. She smiled apologetically, looking directly into his eyes. "I hope you don't mind. However, I like to make certain I know whom I'm dealing with whenever I anticipate throwing money in any direction."

D'Itri nodded in bewilderment. He squirmed nervously in his chair. He looked as if he were facing a firing squad.

"You have an interesting background." Hélène smiled, trying to put him at ease. "Not a spectacular background, but one I'll accept. Signor d'Itri, time is my most precious asset and I don't like to waste it, so I'll come right to the point. How would you like to become a fashion designer?"

"I've already tried that route." He smiled sadly, relaxing a little.

"Unsuccessfully."

"Yes." His voice was small.

"How would you like to become famous, Signor d'Itri?" Hélène asked softly.

He gave a short, nervous laugh. Now he knew she was crazy. There was a time when he had thought he was talented. It had taken him years to find out he wasn't. Surely a woman as important and powerful as she was, a woman who was constantly tuned in to fashion, knew it even better than he.

Hélène continued. "Within a short period of time I could make you as well known as Valentino, as successful as Dior. Would you like that?"

"I'd be a liar if I said I wouldn't."

"Fine. At least you're honest. I appreciate honesty. I also appreciate the fact that on your own, you'll never make it in this business."

D'Itri sat frozen now, flushing under the sudden onslaught. It had come so suddenly that he broke out in a fresh sweat. Quickly he began dabbing his forehead with the balled-up handkerchief clutched in his fist. "Then why are you here?" he found himself saying. He seemed startled to hear his own voice.

Hélène stared levelly into his liquid eyes. They were dark and confused, as if he'd awakened to find himself in a place he'd never seen before. Quickly she told him about her plans to open an atelier. He heard her out in silence.

"You don't want a designer, then. You want a . . ." He struggled to find the right word.

"A figurehead, Signor d'Itri," Hélène said smoothly, avoiding Luba's narrowed eyes. She knew what the Czarina was thinking. *Patsy.* Quickly she continued. "The design team will do everything. But that's not to say you won't have work to do also. You'll have to work very hard. Acquiring polish, meeting people, wooing clients. Believe me, that is a job in itself."

D'Itri couldn't believe his ears. Out of the blue, just as he was at the lowest ebb of his life, came *this*! He couldn't understand it, but he was smart enough not to try to. Obviously the two women were either crazy or they knew exactly what they wanted. If they were telling the truth, all he had to do was go along with them and he'd be living like a king.

He listened as Hélène went on, his mind rapidly seizing upon the possibilities. With the power of *Les Modes* and *La Moda* behind him, he could live in a villa, travel around the world, get his picture in the papers. Sure, he'd know he wasn't doing anything. But no one else would.

"It would be like selling my soul to the devil," he told Hélène bleakly. But his mind raced. Airplanes, expensive cars, yachts . . . Suddenly all the things he had dreamed of, and some he hadn't, were possible. And a social position! The poor boy from Sicily could make good. Very good.

He forced himself to remain subdued. "What would I get out of this arrangement?" he asked, trying to appear businesslike.

"As I said, you'd become one of the foremost designers in the world. You'd get fame. Respect." Hélène paused, and when she spoke again, it was a whisper. "Fortune."

His dark eyes flashed greedily. "How much fortune?"

Hélène shrugged. "That depends on how the business fares. You'd own a small percentage of the company."

"How small?"

"Fifteen percent."

He looked disappointed. "That means I wouldn't have any say in it."

"That's right. The company would be run by projections of the market. We'd sell only what's guaranteed to sell. My policy is not to go out on a creative limb. However, you can rest assured of three things." Slowly Hélène ticked them off on her tapered fingers. "First, your name would be the name of the atelier. Second, it would be based here in Milan and have a branch in Rome before we'd branch out further. And third, *it would be the most expensive store in the world.*"

He stared at her in silence for a moment. "And fifteen percent . . . that would make me rich?"

"Very rich, Signor d'Itri. For the time being, until we begin production, I also plan to pay you a salary, which will eventually be deducted from your earnings. A salary of . . ." She paused, pretending to think it over. "Say, one and a half million lire a month?" She raised her eyebrows.

He held his breath, suddenly feeling giddy. One and a half million lire! Mamma mia! Three thousand dollars. And every month! Was it possible? Oh, sweet Blessed Mother, let it be true, he prayed.

He grinned now, suddenly feeling more sure of himself. "It sounds interesting," he said reflectively. He looked down at his lap, his mind spinning. When he looked back up at her, he said shrewdly, "I'd want twenty-five percent, though."

Hélène had expected this; she had purposely offered him fifteen percent, planning all along to let him have as much as thirty. Twenty-five suited her even better. But she didn't want to seem too eager.

"Twenty," she said firmly.

He hesitated, once again finding himself wading around in foreign territory. He felt he should demand more, but how much more? If he got too greedy, there was the danger that he would frighten her off. Then he'd lose out completely. He looked at her. She was sitting there quietly. "Twenty-two?" he asked.

"Twenty."

He looked offended. "Twenty," he agreed meekly.

Hélène smiled. "It's a deal," she said, not believing her good luck. She would own eighty percent of the atelier outright.

She and Luba rose to their feet.

"Come to the offices next Tuesday," Hélène told d'Itri. "My lawyers will have all the papers prepared."

"I'll be there," he promised. Already he was planning to stop by the Alfa Romeo showroom on the way.

When Hélène reached the door, she turned around and shook his hand. "Good-bye, Signor d'Itri."

He unexpectedly bent down over her hand and kissed it. "Good-bye, signorina." He looked up at her over her hand, his dark eyes shining. "Together, we shall be rich."

3

On an overcast day in June, Hélène attended a party held by Odile Joly. The invitation had come as a total surprise, since she knew that Odile Joly wasn't one to throw parties. The old designer had spent a good part of her life guarding her privacy as jealously as the secret to her success. But then Hélène understood. It was her eightieth birthday—which happened to coincide with the sixty-third anniversary of the Maison d'Odile Joly, which she had begun in September 1898 as a millinery shop. It was for that occasion that she threw the doors to her apartment in the Plaza Athénée open to everyone she had ever known. Or, as sharp Parisian tongues had it, to everyone she was still on speaking terms with. It was a party which lasted for half a day and far into the night. The wealthy and the famous came to crowd the apartment and pay homage to the greatest couturière of all time.

Photographers were everywhere, including a team from *Les Modes*.

Like a queen, Odile Joly received each guest individually. When the guests entered the apartment, a servant took their coats and had them line up; another servant took them, one by one, to see Odile Joly. Never one to do things by halves, she sat in lonely splendor on a mountain of cushions and Oriental rugs inside a silken tent specially erected for this occasion. The tent was lit by lanterns and lined with pots of bushy areca palms. Sandalwood incense burned in a brass brazier, and an Indian singer sat cross-legged in a corner strumming a harplike instrument and singing in a high-pitched voice. For this occasion, Odile Joly had gone all-out. She wore a sheer veil, an elegant silk sari she had bought on a recent trip to India, and gleaming gold jewelry. She allowed each guest to do two things: congratulate her on her success and longevity and pick her mind for a single pearl of wisdom by asking one, and only one, truly important question.

Odile Joly enjoyed herself immensely. She knew how everyone seized upon her every word as if it were gospel, and she made a game of it. When a model asked her for the secret to beauty, she replied elusively, "Beauty is that elusive gift that no one can find."

When a man asked her for the secret to success, Odile Joly looked thoughtful for a moment and mused, "Hmmm . . . success." She placed a finger across her lips, apparently deep in thought. Then she looked up, her dark eyes sparkling with sudden knowledge. "Success is either there or it isn't."

When asked what was the most important thing in the world, she succinctly explained, "Economy of motion."

"When should I get my first face lift?" someone else asked.

"Face lift! Non, non, non, non! Never get a face lift. Add wrinkles!" Odile Joly cried. Then with a look of self-satisfaction she settled back on her mountains of cushions. "Wrinkles," she sighed happily, "add character."

Hélène was nearly overcome by the sumptuousness of Odile Joly's apartment. She had never before been there. Though it was an apartment in a hotel that was known for its luxury, she had expected something Spartan like the workrooms in the maison where the cutting and designing went on, or at the most, a comfortable but uninspired suite of hotel rooms. She was mistaken on both counts.

The enormous suite had been decorated by Odile Joly herself, "with a little help" from the great English decorator John Fowler. Along one wall of the formal living room were built-in black-lacquered bookcases, and in front of them was a long couch filled with goosedown and upholstered in rich bone-colored suede. The two end walls were completely mirrored except for the delicately carved marble fireplaces. The coffee tables and the chairs were genuine Empire, the carpeting was a thick wool pile that looked like velvet, and life-size bronze deer stood around looking as if they were grazing upon it. There were coromandel screens, ormolu clocks, furniture inlaid with mother-of-pearl, paintings by Turner and Renoir, a pair of tiny Titians, and a collection of Kang H'si porcelains. As if all this were not enough, even the ceiling was mirrored.

As Hélène awaited her turn to see Odile Joly, she kept thinking back to how much her former employer had been responsible for her own success. For it had been Odile Joly who had sought her out so many years ago at the André Lichenstein Gallery and offered her a job as a model. It was she who had recommended her to Jacques to pose for the sensational Eiffel Tower pictures. Then, when she had begun *Les Modes,* Odile Joly had once again given her all the support humanly possible, even breaking with the High Fashion Association in order that *Les Modes* might have the jump on covering her collections. Perhaps without Odile Joly, *Les Modes* would never have become a success. Perhaps would never have come into being at all. Or would it have anyway? Were some things in life just destined to happen? Would Hélène have found another way to do it? They were questions to which she would never find the answers. All she knew was what Madame Dupré had once told her: things happened when you were ripe for them to happen.

But of one thing she was absolutely certain. Three people had helped her get to where she was today. Madame Dupré, Odile Joly, and Stanislaw. They had been her guardian angels.

At seven-thirty-three a footman came over to Hélène and bowed. "If you'd please come with me, mademoiselle? Odile Joly will see you now."

They walked down a long corridor and stopped at a door at the end. The footman opened it, stood aside, and then followed her inside.

Hélène stared curiously at the huge tent. Then the footman held the flap open and she ducked inside. She caught her breath. The tent was so beautifully exotic that for a moment she forgot she was in Paris. The singsong wail of the Indian singer, the incense, and the jungle of green palms mixed with the arabesque of the rugs and cushions were part of another world.

Instinctively she took a step backward. In one corner she had noticed movement and then heard a menacing growl. It was an ocelot, sleek and alert and sitting on its haunches. Its yellow eyes seemed to glitter hungrily.

"Don't worry, Sheba doesn't bite," a chuckling, throaty voice said.

Hélène turned her face to the left. Like a venerable guru, Odile Joly was sitting on a pile of pillows, her back as ramrod straight as a young girl's. The light from the lanterns threw a soft glow on her wrinkled face. Her deep-set eyes lit up and her face crinkled into a sudden smile. "Hélène!" She held out a gnarled hand. "Come over here and let me have a good look at you. It has been a long time."

Hélène glanced hesitantly at the big cat and noticed it was chained to a post. She smiled nervously and gave it a wide berth as she slowly walked over to Odile Joly. She looked down at her. "Yes, it has been a long time. Happy birthday, and many happy returns."

Odile Joly made a weary gesture. "I've had so many birthdays I stopped counting them half a century ago. Here, sit down beside me." Odile Joly patted the cushions.

Hélène knew what an honor this was. Everyone else had been whisked in and out within a minute. She looked around hesitantly. Then she smiled. "Are there any snakes in here?"

Odile Joly narrowed her eyes. "In here, none. But I'm sure the rest of the apartment is *filled* with vipers." She waited until Hélène had taken a seat. "You've done very well for yourself, chérie. You're one of the few people I've learned to respect—did you know that?"

Hélène blushed at the compliment. It was the last thing she had expected. "*Les Modes* would never have gotten to where it is without your help," she said.

"You've worked like a maniac. It is only too bad that your personal life did not work out as beautifully. I adored Stanislaw."

Hélène felt a sudden lump in her throat. "Yes, so did I," she said softly. "He was an exceptional man."

Odile Joly nodded. Then she looked at Hélène shrewdly. "A few minutes ago, a man asked me for the secret to success. Do you know what I should have told him?"

Hélène shook her head.

"I should have said, 'Ask Hélène Junot. She has found it.'"

"I think that's overstating it a bit."

For a while, neither of them spoke. "Well, aren't you going to ask for the answer to one important question?" Odile Joly asked finally.

Hélène laughed helplessly. "I'm afraid I wouldn't know where to begin."

"Good girl." Odile Joly paused. "You know that I don't give parties very often?"

Hélène nodded, wondering what she was leading up to.

"People are racking their brains trying to figure out why I broke down and gave this one, although they don't dare come right out and ask me. They think it's my farewell to life."

"That's ridiculous," Hélène said. To her, Odile Joly always was and always would be.

Odile Joly smiled ruefully, held her hands out, and looked at them. She shook her head. The fingernails were perfectly lacquered, but the skin was ancient and age-spotted. "I'm eighty years old now. Perhaps I'll live for another ten years, perhaps not." She shrugged philosophically. "Why do you think all these people came? To wish me many happy returns?" She laughed dryly. "No, they wanted to see how much life an eighty-year-old woman has left. They wanted to see how much I've slowed down." She leaned forward and reached down to a round brass box at her feet. She lifted the cover and took out a chunk of raw, bloody meat. She tossed it over at the ocelot, which sprang to its feet. A second later, its teeth were embedded in the meat as it started to chew.

"They came to see how life has eaten me up after all these years." Odile Joly nodded in the cat's direction. "Just like Sheba devouring the meat." She sighed and met Hélène's gaze. "I'm a dinosaur, a leftover from the last century. There are a hundred new designers out there waiting to take my place. And it's funny. I really am getting tired, you know. I can feel that deep inside my bones."

Hélène felt sorry for the old woman. She knew how hard it must be for her to have to slow down. Mentally she was so active; she'd always had the energy of the hyperactive. It

593

seemed strange that her body could be slowly wearing down. And yet, Hélène had always thought Odile Joly to be as indestructible as a French monument. It seemed peculiar to see her in another light. As just another mortal.

Suddenly Odile Joly seized Hélène's hand and held it tightly. "Make sure your photographers cover this party thoroughly!"

Hélène did not speak. A worried expression crossed her face.

"Don't look at me that way!" Odile Joly said. "There's nothing wrong with me. Tell me, what issues of *La Moda* and *Les Modes* are you preparing right now?"

"November."

"Oh." Odile Joly sounded disappointed.

"What's the matter?" Hélène asked.

Odile Joly smiled. "I was wondering if it was possible for you to stick a few extra pages into an earlier issue . . ." Her voice trailed off.

Hélène thought quickly. She knew Odile Joly well enough to realize she was sounding her out about giving her another scoop. "I could kill an article in the September issue," she said without hesitation. "That's still in page proofs. I'm afraid the others are already at the printer's or in the warehouses."

"September is fine." Odile Joly nodded and smiled in relief. "Use the party photos from tonight. And when you leave, send your photographers in here to do some nice big portraits of me. You see, chérie"—she lowered her voice confidentially—"I'm finally ready to retire."

Hélène couldn't believe her ears. "R-retire!"

"Yes, once you're eighty, I think it's high time. After all, it's important that one knows when to retire." Odile Joly smiled. "I wouldn't want people to say, 'At last.' However, I'll wait to make the public announcement. I'll wait until . . ." Her dark eyes flashed mischievously. "Until the day the September *Les Modes* and *La Moda* come out."

Hélène took both the woman's hands and squeezed them affectionately. "Thank you," she said, her voice suddenly husky. She knew at that moment how much the old woman loved her. Even as she was retiring, she was seeing to it that *Les Modes* would benefit by it.

"Now, go out and party," Odile Joly said gruffly. "The people waiting to get in here are probably lined up for kilometers!"

She smiled as Hélène left. Her former mannequin had done well. She hadn't let that turn her into a fool, either. Odile Joly had watched her closely, following *Les Modes*'s steady climb to the dizzying heights of power. Just as there would never be another Odile Joly, she thought, there would never be another Hélène Junot.

After leaving the tent, Hélène had a few words with her photographers and then she left the party. It was early evening, but her business hours didn't stop at five. There were still many things she had to do. Like approving the architect's renderings for the two d'Itri boutiques. The mock-Egyptian interiors needed a few changes. But they would have to wait. First she would call Luba and together they would start mapping out the layouts for Odile Joly's farewell from the fashion world.

As Hélène came out of the Plaza Athénée, she saw a limousine plowing through the sudden deluge and watched it roll to a halt in front of the hotel. Probably another guest coming to honor Odile Joly, she thought. She watched the doorman hurry down the steps, holding up an oversized black umbrella. Only when the passenger ducked out of the limousine did Hélène freeze.

It was Nigel Somerset.

Her knees went suddenly weak and she felt her body starting to sag. She caught hold of the balustrade and clung to it. For a moment she just stared down at him. Then, as he hurried up the steps, she averted her face so that he wouldn't see her. She tried to stem the waves of longing washing over her.

"*Hélène!*" The word was almost a whisper, low and filled with a thousand memories and promises.

He *had* seen her. He had spoken to her.

Her heart sang loudly, joyously, triumphantly. Slowly she turned around.

"Nigel!" The voice was choked and husky, a voice belonging to someone else.

Then she quickly turned away again as a woman came out of the revolving brass doors to meet him.

The voice *had* belonged to someone else. To Hélène Giraudoux.

4

Forty thousand spectators crammed the tribunes at Auteuil to watch the horse race. Two hundred thousand others surrounded the racecourse; many people had camped out there for two days. It was the first of November, the traditional date of the autumn Grand Prix. This last race of the season always drew a good crowd, but never before had a race been known to virtually stop the wheels of industry. All over the country, factories and businesses reported that fifty percent of their work forces had called in sick. The bookmakers in Montmartre were doing business as never before. Not only had the racing buffs tuned in to the race, but all of Paris was out in its finery, buzzing with low-keyed excitement. It was the same all over France. Those who couldn't be there were glued to their radios.

This season, for the first time, five horses were running neck and neck. The horses were so evenly matched that no one could even guess the odds. The way it turned out, the race had become a showdown between five of the leading families of France. Running were the de Rothschilds' Baron, the de Sévignés' Très Jolie, the de Gides' Mylène, the d'Ermos' Piper, and the de Légers' L'Afrique.

The excitement had begun on Palm Sunday and built up steadily all summer long. On Palm Sunday, the de Rothschilds' Baron won the President of the Republic Stakes.

On Whit Monday on the St. Cloud racecourse, the de Gides' Mylène placed first.

On the last Sunday in June, the same horses had run again, this time at Longchamps for the Paris Grand Prix. The de Légers' L'Afrique had come out the winner.

In Vincennes in September, the d'Ermos' Piper had won the summer Grand Prix.

At Longchamps on the first Sunday in October, the de

Sévignés' Très Jolie came in ahead of the others in the Arc de Triomphe Grand Prix.

Steadily, with each race, excitement had risen until it verged on feverish hysteria. All five winners of the season's previous races were present again for this last big race. It was clear that one of these five would be running away with the prize.

Hélène took Petite Hélène to watch. "After all," she'd explained to the nanny, "she must be exposed to all facets of society. I know she's young. But she should have some idea of what is going on in the world."

A hush had now fallen over the crowd at Auteuil as the horses shot down the racetrack. Their hooves threw up clumps of earth as the cadence of their run beat out a staccato drumbeat. Right from the start, five horses pushed ahead of all the others. Baron was in the lead. No more than half a neck behind him, L'Afrique, Très Jolie, Mylène, and Piper were already inching ahead.

Petite Hélène craned her neck and lifted the binoculars to her eyes, but the horses were past the grandstand now and it was difficult to tell just which one was in the lead. They seemed so close together.

The crowds began yelling and screaming.

When the horses turned the corner of the oval and were opposite the grandstand, L'Afrique was clearly in the lead, but not by much. The others were not far behind. It would be a very close race.

Edgardo Jiménez, the jockey hunched over L'Afrique, turned his head and glanced backward at the others. He could see Très Jolie gaining on his right, Piper on his left. He could not see the bent-over jockeys, just the horses' heads. The air roared with the sound of hooves. His face tightened with determination.

Hubert de Léger had warned him what he would do if L'Afrique placed anything other than first. He would be fired; ruined. Hubert de Léger had told him he would see to it that he never rode again. That he would be deported back to Argentina.

Jiménez dug in his knees, screamed at his horse, and beat its rump furiously with his riding crop, forcing it to fly even faster.

The others must not catch up.

Ermanno Foggi, the Italian jockey astride Mylène, smiled grimly to himself. He was at the rear, a neck behind Baron, two lengths from L'Afrique. He had let himself slow down purposely, waiting for the moment that would now soon come. It was his style always to stay near the front, but never to push his horse to its absolute limit until the last quarter stretch. Then he would summon all its remaining strength and shoot ahead, squeezing between the others and with a final burst of speed dash across the finish line first.

Ermanno Foggi needed to win. His young daughter needed expensive surgery and the de Gides family had promised him a hundred thousand francs extra if he won.

As if one, the screaming people in the grandstands rose to their feet as the horses reached the last quarter of the oval track. Piper and Très Jolie had gained on L'Afrique; now the three horses were running neck and neck.

Ermanno Foggi shot ahead now. He and Mylène were one and the same. He didn't even look sideways as he passed Baron. His eyes were focused straight ahead as he skillfully cut in front of Baron, blocking him. Now in front of him were L'Afrique, Piper, and Très Jolie. They were tightly knit. He cursed. He needed an opening.

Edgardo Jiménez was panicking. On his right, he could see the blurry chestnut form of Très Jolie. *Gaining.* Already, Très Jolie was inching ahead. He must not let that happen. Très Jolie must be stopped at all costs.

Jiménez knew that the time to make his move was now or never. He had pushed L'Afrique to his limits since the start, and the horse was tiring. If he didn't act swiftly, he would be deported.

Without thinking of the consequences, Jiménez raised his riding crop in the air and slashed out at Très Jolie's face. It came down so fast that none of the spectators in the tribunes could tell what had happened. All they saw was Très Jolie rearing suddenly and her jockey fighting to keep her under control. Then he was thrown from the horse. He landed on the track, and the thundering hooves of Baron and Mylène instantly crushed him.

A sudden hush filled the tribunes.

Ermanno Foggi felt rather than saw what had happened. For an instant Mylène's hooves had not touched earth. What they had touched was soft and pliable. Yet this was a race. He couldn't stop to give assistance. He had to keep on going.

Expertly he skirted Mylène around the rearing Très Jolie and came up alongside L'Afrique and started to pass him. For a moment he looked to his left and caught a glimpse of Jiménez's dark eyes flashing behind his goggles. Then he saw a riding crop raised high in the air. Instinctively he ducked his head. It was too late. He felt a burning slash across the back of his neck and a white fireball burst in front of his eyes. Then the world blacked out. Jiménez had whipped him unconscious. Mylène collided into L'Afrique and the two horses went tumbling.

The crowd screamed in a frenzy as Piper burst across the finish line.

After the race, Hubert de Léger and Edgardo Jiménez were standing outside the stables. Hubert's face was red with rage. Jiménez had his head wrapped in a bandage and there was a terrified look in his eyes. Behind them they could hear the sudden crack of a gunshot. Both men had been prepared for it; still, they both jumped.

A moment later the stable door creaked open and the Comte de Léger came out with stiff dignity, his face white. He stopped in front of Jiménez, towering over the tiny jockey. "Why?" he asked in a whisper, fighting to control his anger. "*Why?*"

Suddenly Jiménez went to pieces. The terror of Hubert's temper and the threat of deportation loomed like a specter in front of him. "Is not my fault!" he screamed in fright. "I had to do! *He* made me!" The jockey wiped away his tears and pointed a trembling finger at Hubert.

The Comte jerked as if he'd been struck. He turned slowly and stared at his son without speaking. Hubert lowered his head and studied his feet.

The Comte took a deep breath. What he had feared the most had finally happened. Hubert had done something which all the power and money of the de Légers could not undo. A hopeless sadness welled up inside him. Didn't the fool know that never again would any member of the family be able to hold up his head in public? Didn't he realize the disgrace he had brought down on the house of the de Légers?

Wordlessly the Comte drew himself up and walked stiffly back into the stables. Hubert glared menacingly at Jiménez. His eyes bore right through the jockey's. The little man shrank back in fear.

At that moment a second gunshot cracked the air at Auteuil.

Hubert had become the new Comte de Léger.

Nigel Somerset had sat with the d'Ermos in their private box. He did not normally go to horse races if he could help it, and for one simple reason. Just as he did not get caught up in the gambling fever in the casinos, neither could he get caught up in the spirited excitement of watching some horses flying around a track. The only reason he was here was that he had come to Paris for business dealings with the Marquis. It was he who had invited him.

"You must come," the Marquis had said. "Our Piper is racing at Auteuil. It will be the race of the year."

Nigel was no stranger when it came to horses. He had ridden all his life. The proper social upbringing of any upper-class Englishman from a wealthy family included learning to ride, attending private boarding schools, and playing polo. Nigel had been a polo player, mostly because it had been expected of him. He had had a string of polo ponies, and though he found the game diverting, he found that his mind was far better equipped for business and politics than sports. As far as races went, his social station required that he appear regularly at Ascot. Especially when the royal family—*his* family—was out in full force. He found Ascot bearable because of its pomp. Everyone dressed in stylish finery and the Royal Box was festooned with purplish-blue hydrangeas and white lilies. The Queen, a distant cousin, always sat in her place of honor under a scalloped canopy. Although Auteuil was crowded with the rich and the titled, it just wasn't the same. No one knew how to stage an extravaganza like the English. But the chief reason he did not like to attend races was that he preferred to ride horses himself rather than watch others doing it.

Until this particular race he had almost forgotten how uncivilized other countries were. The behavior of the de Légers' jockey had been deplorable. No Englishman from the lowliest cockney to the stiffest upper crust would tolerate such scandalous foul play. But sportsmanship was one thing, murder another entirely. The jockey who had been trampled was dead. Any accident casts a pall on a sporting event. This one, done so deliberately, left a foul smell in the air.

600

He had congratulated the Marquise on her heavy gold trophy and then turned around, making room for the other well-wishers who had swarmed to the box.

Suddenly he froze as he found himself face to face with a beautiful woman and a child with a freckled nose and bright orange hair. His heart began hammering. For a moment, neither he nor the woman could speak. Then he found his voice and said softly, "Hélène . . . ?"

For an instant Hélène's violet eyes widened in confusion. Then she forced herself to smile politely, but it was a sad smile. "Nigel," she said stiffly, "it has been a long time."

The moment the words were out, she realized how reproachful they sounded. She had wanted to be cold and aloof. Like a stranger, not a wronged wife. What was wrong with her?

"Yes, it has been a long time," he said quietly. "Much *too* long."

5

Hélène had loved her château from the moment she'd first laid eyes on it. Now, with Nigel, it took on a special characteristic it had never had before. She banished Monsieur and Madame Greuze, the caretakers, to their cottage and wouldn't allow them to enter the château once all week long.

Madame Greuze placed her hands on her big hips and sniffed disapprovingly. "Just make sure you're in the kitchen at six each morning," she admonished. "The barrel next to the door is filled with stale bread and rolls."

Hélène nodded. She didn't know what Madame Greuze was talking about, but as she propelled her out into the hall, she assured her that everything would be well taken care of.

Madame Greuze looked at her with indignation and heaved a sigh, her big bosom rising and falling. But obediently she untied her starched white apron, hung it neatly in the cupboard under the stairs, and left without arguing any further.

Hélène shared her bedroom with Nigel. It was her favorite room, on the second floor of one of the corner turrets overlooking the pond. It had been newly wallpapered a lovely deep blue with a continuous pattern of miniature white ovals in which blue urns sprouted thistle-like flowers. The bed was wide enough for two, in a sleeping alcove, half-hidden behind draperies. They matched the wallpaper and were lined with heavy white cotton in order to cut any drafts. The ceiling, too, was blue, and so was the wainscoting. A faded Oriental rug covered the rough-hewn reddish stone floor; the table, which doubled as a desk, was draped with another, smaller Oriental carpet. The ancient French chairs grouped around it had white-painted frames and gold velvet upholstery, and the pictures on the walls were inexpensive but charming small landscapes in simple gold frames.

They stayed up late into the night. Nigel built a birch log fire in the huge fireplace in the salon and turned off the lights. They spread cushions out on the rug and lay on them, enjoying their closeness as they talked in the snug air and drank brandy from balloon snifters.

"We have a lot to catch up on," Nigel said softly.

Yes, we have, she silently agreed. The cushions were soft and warm, and his closeness, or the brandy, or both, made her feel heady. Deliriously happy. She snuggled against his warmth, and he held her close, comforting and smelling of freshness. Now that he had come back into her life, she needed him more than she needed anyone or anything else, and she knew that he needed her in the same way. He tightened his arms around her and kissed her, his lips warm and moist and demanding, hers not at all submissive, but just as demanding as his.

Suddenly she pulled away from him. There was something she had to ask him before they made love.

"Nigel?"

He saw the anxious expression on her face, the fear and the hesitation. "Yes, darling? Is something wrong?"

"No," she said slowly, her eyes locked into his. "I just have to know . . ." Her words trailed off, and she shook her head miserably, afraid of the question she had to ask; even more afraid of his answer.

He reached for her hands and held them gently. "Tell me," he said.

She nodded and swallowed. "Why . . ." she whispered miserably, "why didn't you contact me after you got my note?"

He looked perplexed. "Note? What are you talking about, darling? What note?"

She heard the honest bewilderment in his voice, and her heart ached for both of them and that which they had almost lost. She told him about Jeanne's sudden illness and the note she'd slipped in his door aboard the *Evangelia*. They both came to the same conclusion: Blanche Benois had destroyed it.

"She told me she ran into you as you were leaving," Nigel said. "She explained that you two had a woman-to-woman talk. That you were running away because you didn't want to get any more deeply involved with me than you were." The anguish showed in his face. "I was tempted to call you a thousand times, but each time I started to call, I hung up." He smiled sadly. "What a fool I was! I thought you didn't want me."

Oh, if she'd only called him!

He wrapped her in his arms and she gave herself up to his gentle kiss. "But now we're together again, darling," he said softly, nipping her lips. He smiled down into her eyes. "And this time I won't let you slip through my fingers. I've missed you terribly."

And then she felt him urgently but gently unbuttoning her blouse. She turned as she felt the pull of silk, as it slid smoothly off her. His warm lips played on the nape of her neck, rippling the tendrils of hair, stirring her. A tingling warmth moved down her back and through her breasts, then gathered force deep within her. Yes, hers was a need that had been dormant and unsatisfied for too long. His fingers unzipped her skirt, removed her slip, pulled off her stockings. She lay on her back, the cushions warm and soft beneath her, and looked up at him, her eyes blazing with intense hunger, her lips unsmiling as he hurriedly started to unbutton his shirt.

"No!" she whispered. "Let me . . ." And she reached up. Her fingers nimbly undid his shirt front and sleeves. Finally he let it fall away from his body and carefully lay down beside her. She sat up and untied his shoes. Putting her hands on his hips, she gently pulled off his pants.

Hélène took a deep breath, running an index finger down the stiff bulge in his shorts, carefully moving to the softness of his scrotum, fondling, exploring, teasing. Mesmerized, she watched the penis tense at her touch. Then, slowly, reverently, she pulled the trunks down and his cock sprang free.

She could feel the warmth within her melting to wetness as he rolled on top of her. His hands and lips were everywhere at once, stroking, kissing, licking, caressing. His entire body felt hard against her own tight softness. Helene shuddered in expectation.

"Please. Now." Her voice was eager and tight in her chest, the words coming in whispered gasps.

"No," he whispered, his breath and tongue in her ear. "Not yet."

And then he was on his hands and knees, his lips moving down over her satiny skin, gently nipping, inexorably moving downward from her shoulders to her soft breasts, twirling his tongue around her stiff, erect nipples, moving downward still . . .

"Don't stop!" she moaned.

He paused for one endlessly suspended moment, his gold-flecked eyes looking up at her; then slowly he moved back up, finally flicking his tongue over each nipple in turn. She arched her back with a lissome feline grace as he mastered her, making her wait. Nigel teased her, drawing her on and out of herself. Suddenly he drove into her, finding her smooth, warm, and welcoming. His hips thrust against hers, as their wet bodies danced a high-precision ballet. Breaking the frantic rhythms, he abruptly threw his head back while pinning the twisting, driven woman underneath him, his orgasm melting into the ecstatic pulses of her own.

When at last they fell against each other in an exhausted sleep, oblivious of the bed awaiting them upstairs, the embers in the fireplace had long since lost their glow. They slept naked on their sides, his arms wrapped protectively around her, his body curled into hers, the back of her head contured in his neck. It was a gloriously sated, peaceful, and dreamless sleep for both of them.

In the morning, just as daylight broke, Hélène awakened to the sound of banging on the kitchen door. She rubbed her eyes, flipped a coil of loose hair from her forehead, and turned to look at her alarm clock. It was not beside her. Nor was she in bed. She was still on the cushions in the salon, beside Nigel, who was snoring softly, a smile of content on his face. She fell back on the cushions and snuggled deliciously against him, feeling the warm comfort and glow of his flesh. His arm wound sleepily around her, and she shut her eyes.

But the rude, insistent banging continued. Finally she extricated herself from his embrace, got up, slipped into her skirt, and held her blouse against her breasts as she tiptoed into the kitchen to investigate. A moment later she felt Nigel's presence behind her.

"What's going on?" he asked, mystified.

She turned and covered her mouth as she yawned. "I don't know," she said sleepily. "But I aim to find out."

She opened the back door and they burst out laughing. The swans, ducks, and geese had marched over from the pond and were clustered at the door, pecking it impatiently with their bills as they demanded their breakfast.

Hélène remembered Madame Greuze's instructions, and they took the old bread and rolls from the barrel and tossed some of them outside. With a squabble, the birds instantly attacked the food.

Every morning after breakfast, Hélène and Nigel took long walks through the autumn woods, breathing the fresh moistness of the air and feeling the cushion of fallen leaves beneath their feet. Once they wandered off the property and walked through the orchards to the fields surrounding the nearby village. The farmers were burning the cut weeds and grass, readying the land to plow in the spring. The smell of fire and roasting potatoes was in the air, and the farmers greeted Hélène and Nigel with solemn respect and offered them potatoes they had roasted under the fires. She and Nigel thanked them politely and peeled the charred skins back with their fingers. They ate the potatoes as they walked on. Neither had ever eaten anything so delicious. You could almost taste the sweetness and the strength of the land, she thought.

Determined to show off her cooking skills, one afternoon Hélène scoured the second-floor library that the previous owner had left behind. After searching for a while, she found a cookbook and proceeded to prepare an elaborate meal. She followed the laborious instructions to the letter, slaving for hours in the high-ceilinged turquoise kitchen with its solid wooden worktables, black fireplaces and stoves, tile ovens, and white enamel sinks. For a moment she couldn't help comparing herself to Marie Antoinette. Only, instead of playing shepherdess, she was playing housewife. Then her lips tightened and she shoved that thought out of her mind. She wasn't playing housewife. She was simply spending a week alone with Nigel.

The meal turned out to be delicious, and she was content. While she was preparing it, Nigel kept her company. He sat at one of the worktables reading a book he had found in the library. She felt a heady glow of euphoria just because he was so near. She thought: This is what a honeymoon must be like.

"You're going to an awful lot of trouble," he said.

She thought: I'd go through anything as long as you're beside me.

On Saturday night Nigel asked if he could use the telephone to call England.

"Of course," she said with forced lightness. "Just don't call Singapore." But the call was a painful reminder that they had less than a day left. Tomorrow evening they would drive back to Paris. And Monday morning . . . She didn't want to think of Monday morning. Monday morning would come soon enough.

She watched him heading for the telephone in the salon. Could a whole week have flown by already? she wondered. Was it possible? It seemed as if they had spent only minutes together. How much longer would she have to wait before she could once again taste his kisses and feel his strong arms around her?

When Nigel came back from making the call, he smiled apologetically. "I forgot something in England. They're sending it over by messenger tomorrow."

"But we're going back to Paris tomorrow night."

"It will get here on time," he said.

The last day began, as had the others, with the feeding of the birds. But the magic was missing. After breakfast they went to the stables and saddled the horses. Wordlessly they rode through the woods, where they had to duck the low, scratchy branches, up the crest of a hill which looked out over the fields and the village. When they got back to the château they had a subdued lunch, interrupted by the arrival of Nigel's messenger, who seemed to signal loud and clear that only a scant few hours were left. Four more. And then they would have to drive back to Paris. The minutes were racing faster and faster, and Hélène could find no way to stop the clock.

"Let's take a walk," Nigel said when they had finished their lunch.

She nodded, forced herself to smile, and changed into slacks and an old corduroy coat. They walked for an hour, followed by the Greuzes' dog. They threw sticks for him to retrieve. Hélène picked up a fallen branch and lackadaisically strummed it along the trunks of trees. She couldn't remember a time when she'd felt so miserable.

On their way back to the château, Nigel stopped in a clearing and pulled her towards him. "Hélène . . ."

She looked up at him, her eyes wide and frightened. "Nigel . . ."

As he looked down at her, he noticed the sadness in her eyes. For a long moment he held her close without speaking. He knew how she felt. He could never forget the numbness that had come over him after Blanche Benois told him that Hélène had fled the yacht. It was the kind of pain that was difficult to work out of your system.

"I can't tell you how much I've enjoyed this past week," he said softly.

Enjoyed it? *She* had *loved* it. Every last minute of it, but most of all the hours they had spent in bed. "I . . . enjoyed it also," she said under her breath.

He smiled sheepishly. "I'm afraid I don't want to leave without you."

"We'll see each other again," she said.

"I'm counting on that." He reached into his jacket pocket and took out a cubelike velvet case. For a moment he hesitated and looked down at it. "The messenger brought this," he said, holding it out to her.

She looked at him, took the case, and lifted the lid carefully.

She caught her breath. Glittering on a tiny cushion of velvet was a round diamond. It was the most enormous, most uniformly yellow stone she had ever seen.

"It's canary yellow!" she whispered, holding it up in the sunlight. She stared at it incredulously. It must weigh thirty carats.

He seemed to read her mind. "Twenty-eight."

She shook her head adamantly. "Really, Nigel. I . . . I can't possibly accept this," she protested. "It's . . . it's far too valuable." Quickly she shoved it back in the case, snapped it shut, and pushed it into his hands.

He opened the case ceremoniously, fished the ring back out, and carefully slipped it on her finger. "Yes, it's very valuable," he said slowly. "It's been in my family for centuries. It's called the Somerset Sun."

"Yes, but—"

He placed a finger on her lips. "Let me try to explain. There are certain traditions in my family. The Somerset Sun happens to be one of them." He paused and then continued. "For three centuries now, it has graced the finger of every woman in line to be the Duchess of Farquharshire."

As if paralyzed, she stared at him.

Suddenly he threw his arms around her and gave a joyous laugh. The gold flecks in his brown eyes shone brightly. "Don't you see? Darling, I'm *proposing* to you! When I'm duke, you'll be my duchess!"

She dared not believe her ears. She had hungered to hear these very words for so long. They soared and sang and she could find no words to reply.

"I love you," Nigel said. "I've loved you ever since that night in Monte Carlo. I've loved you . . . Say yes, my darling!" His voice was anguished. "Please say yes. God knows, I don't deserve you. Not after letting you down the way I have. I know I've hurt you, but I promise I'll spend a lifetime making it up to you."

This time it was she who placed a finger on his lips. "Yes!" she whispered. "Oh, Nigel, *yes!*"

They embraced again. Her heart beat wildly against her chest. They would be together. Eternally together.

It seemed too good to be true.

6

The de Havilland Comet belonging to Somerset Holdings, Ltd., flew them from Paris to England. The interior of the jet was like a house. There were a living room, two bedrooms, a kitchen, and a bath.

"I've never seen anything like it," Hélène marveled as she boarded at Orly. The living room was subdued in its luxury, with thick carpeting, polished tables, and crimson-upholstered easy chairs, even a desk.

They drank champagne, and the chef served a superb lunch which they ate over the English Channel.

"It was delicious," Hélène told the chef when she had finished.

Then they moved to one of the curtained windows as the engines changed pitch and the jet started its descent. Nigel pointed out the sights. "As far as your eye can see, up to the horizon, is Farquharshire."

She stared out at the endless fields and forests and toylike villages. She glanced at him. "You mean your family owns it all?"

He grinned. "I'm afraid not. We do own a lot of property, though. Coal and zinc mines, textile mills, farms, dairies, real estate, electrical-machinery plants, six newspapers—"

"Six!"

He nodded. "Three in England, two in Australia, and one in New York."

"So *you're* in publishing too."

Then her smile faded. She gazed back out at the checkerboard fields, the precisely surveyed property boundaries marked with hairline walls, and the thin gray ribbons of roads that seemed to float past below them. So she knew even less about him than she had thought. She wondered at the trifling things she did know, the things she'd read about him and the things she'd learned while they'd been on the Skouri yacht and during the past week they'd spent together. The thought suddenly crossed her mind that perhaps she should have waited awhile instead of accepting his proposal so quickly. After all, it was only by spending a lot of time together that people really got to know each other. And what did she know about him, anyway? That he was rich, that she loved him, that he was titled? A man like Nigel was very complex. Now she knew that it would take a lifetime to get to know him completely.

Yet he wasn't like any man she had ever met. He made her and everything around him seem to come alive. And he seemed to know so much about everything. Business, international politics, many languages, the arts. There wasn't a thing that seemed to baffle him. In a way, he overpowered her. But that was one of the things she loved about him. And yet she couldn't help feeling that perhaps she wasn't quite right for him. After all, she was a power within her own field. Perhaps a man like Nigel needed someone who had no responsibilities to anything except him. Who could be at his beck and call at any hour of the day or night. Someone dedicated to his political ambitions. A wife who had the time to entertain constantly and graciously, who could put people at ease, who could campaign for him, who knew just how to run the staggering array of residences he'd reeled off to her: Fallsworth in the autumn; the house in Mayfair when they were in London; Winthrow Abbey, the castle in Ireland, during spring; Craigmore, the lodge in Scotland; and on Mustique, the pink gingerbread house . . . Was she the kind of woman who could handle all that? Would she be a credit to him or an embarrassment?

These misgivings weighed heavily on her mind. After all, they had never even discussed how they would run both the Somerset businesses and Les Éditions Hélène Junot. Well, they had plenty of time to discuss that, she told herself. They weren't even married yet. No, not yet. But soon would be. And they would have to come to some decision regarding the businesses before then.

She glanced down at the Somerset Sun. It felt heavy and demanding, a prophecy of a thousand responsibilities that were to come. For the first time in many years she felt a real terror. Did all women who were about to be introduced to their future parents-in-law and yearned for their blessings— did they all feel this panic-stricken? Or was the fact that

Nigel's parents were the Duke and Duchess of Farquharshire, and she a commoner, only reinforcing her dread? Would the fact that she was a foreigner be a black mark against her?

Worst of all, she knew so little about the English aristocracy. She wondered if she was dressed right for the noble society she was about to mingle with. The classically demure Odile Joly suit, the high-necked silk blouse buttoned to the collar with a big bow under her chin, the wide-brimmed felt hat, and the low-heeled slippers—were they the right, understated look? She had called Luba in a panic, not trusting her own instincts for this important meeting.

"Look fashionably staid," the Czarina had specified. "And very, very modest. You know, don't you, that those kinds of people lead the most boring type of life?"

Hélène had followed Luba's instructions to the letter. Her only jewelry was gold earrings, a thin gold watch, and the Somerset Sun.

Nigel interrupted her gloomy thoughts. "We're almost there."

She turned to him and forced a smile.

"Are you nervous?"

She nodded.

"Don't be. They won't eat you alive, you know."

She wasn't so sure. The misgivings were brewing like somber dark storm clouds. She didn't know what would happen if for some reason the Somersets should reject her. She had already been through so much anguish during Nigel's long absence. How much pain would she feel if something went wrong now?

She scolded herself angrily: Get a hold on yourself!

But it was difficult. The last time she had felt this way was long ago at Hautecloque, when Hubert had proposed to her. She had felt a boundless social gulf then. Now she felt it again.

The jet made a smooth three-point landing on a long private airstrip. Hélène was surprised. She had expected that they would put down at some commercial airport.

As soon as the plane rolled to a halt, an old-fashioned boxy-looking Rolls-Royce pulled up alongside. "Good day, Master Nigel," the ancient chauffeur said, respectfully touching the visor of his cap.

"Good day, Stirling."

"Did you have a nice trip, sir?"

"Yes, thank you, Stirling."

Stirling looked at Hélène impassively. "Let me help you with that, mum."

She surrendered her cosmetics case.

As soon as their luggage was transferred, they were driven north on a winding country road to Fallsworth, the Somersets' ancestral home. It was a pleasant-enough drive, but the closer they got to Fallsworth, the more agitated Hélène became. Everything went past in a blur. The charming villages, the neat fields, the sudden forests. Everything looked civilized and well-tended.

"It's beautiful," she said.

"Not as beautiful as you, darling." Nigel took her hand. "Now, relax."

She was trying to.

Half an hour later they approached the gates of Fallsworth. The car came to a stop and they had to wait for the old gatekeeper to come out from the gatehouse. He bowed effusively and pushed the big iron gates open.

"That's Mackie," Nigel said. "He's a little slow, and although we'd gladly pension him, he loves his job. He's been in the family's service for over sixty years now, and he won't hear of retirement. That's why we don't mind waiting for him."

Hélène nodded. Hearing that, she felt a little better. At least the Duke and Duchess sounded human.

The Rolls began to move again. Hélène stared out at the tree-lined drive as they picked up speed. The road was asphalt and narrow, just wide enough for one car. The trees were big and ancient, with massive trunks and thick, powerful branches. It must look beautiful in the spring, she thought, when the leaves would be thick. Now they were all dried up, a layer of brown mulch raked high around the trunks.

"Here we are," Nigel said.

The road made a curve, they crested a hill, and the Silver Lady hood ornament dipped. Below them was Fallsworth. Any courage Hélène had left evaporated completely. Fallsworth was a sprawling stately home. By comparison, her own pitifully small château seemed to be nothing more than an inconsequential farmhouse. Fallsworth was big and elegant, but not haughty like Hautecloque. It seemed to belong on the estate, imposing and solid, its buttery sandstone walls fortified by powerful pilasters, its copper roofs green and aged, its elegant windows tall and slim. Like a colossus the house rose up from the formal gardens of clipped golden yews, the temple-style pediment ornamented with the Somerset coat of arms.

"Do you like it?"

Hélène looked at Nigel. "It's . . . impressive," she said in a shaky voice.

He shrugged. "A house is a house." Then, as if he could read her mind, he quickly added, "I much prefer your château."

She turned and stared doubtfully out at Fallsworth.

7

"Another cup of tea, my dear?"

Hélène looked at the thin, regal woman. The Duchess of Farquharshire was the kind of dignified, flawless-skinned woman the British aristocracy had been churning out for centuries. Other people in other countries changed with time, but the upper-crust British had withstood the test of wars, disease, and democracy. Hélène thought the Duchess would have looked perfectly at home on the walls lined with ancestral portraits. Someday hers would indeed hang there for posterity, looking unsmilingly down at anyone who chanced to look up into her hooded liquid brown eyes.

Fallsworth was the perfect setting for the Duchess. The gilded, high-ceilinged rooms contrasted with the comfortable no-nonsense floral slipcovers, the red-draped tables, and the ancient carpets and turned what could have been a sterile, palatial interior into understated luxury at its best.

"Please," Hélène said politely. "It's delicious tea." She handed the Duchess her cup.

The Duchess nodded and with her small, smooth hands picked up the sterling Georgian teapot. She smiled as she handed the replenished cup back to Hélène. "I subscribe to *Les Modes*," she said, smiling. "I prefer it even to *Vogue*."

"You're very kind," Hélène said. She looked over at Nigel, who smiled encouragingly. Hélène had to stifle a laugh. Beside Nigel, the frail old Duke, seated in a big armchair, looked as if the cabbage-rose upholstery had swallowed him up. He was snoring gently.

"I think you should start an English version of *Les Modes* next," Nigel said. "After all, *Vogue* is here. And there's a ready market waiting."

The Duchess nodded. "That *is* a good idea," she said.

Hélène felt her hopes rising. Unconsciously her eyes strayed down to the Somerset Sun on her finger.

A quarter of an hour later, Nigel rose to his feet. He looked at his mother. "I'd like to show Hélène around before it gets dark."

The Duchess nodded. "Don't forget the aviary." She smiled at Hélène.

Hélène rose also. "I'll make sure that Nigel shows it to me. Thank you for the tea. It was lovely."

Nigel led her from the Green Salon through the quiet, lofty marble corridors to the front entrance. They passed the great Francesco Guardi paintings, which rivaled those in the world's greatest museums and made anyone who gazed upon them feel like an inconsequential midget. Hélène realized that Fallsworth housed collections worth fortunes. Not just the fortunes of one lifetime, but the accumulation of centuries.

Nigel looked at Hélène and smiled. "Well, they *didn't* eat you alive, did they?"

She shook her head. "They're very kind."

"But formal." He grinned goodnaturedly. "That's civilized British blood. In time you'll get used to it. Come."

He took her hand and gave her the grand tour of the gardens. In the back of the house, a wide gravel path split up the park. This path came to an end at a large oval fountain where glistening bronze figures frolicked under thin arcs of water. He showed her the topiary garden, where the trees and shrubbery had been clipped to look like figures, and then to the aviary. It was a long glass-roofed building, a series of wrought-iron pavilions linked by elaborate corridors alive with the shifting colors of rainbow plumage and the cries of exotic birds.

614

Hélène was very impressed. "Fallsworth is like a country in itself," she said when they finished the tour.

He laughed. "Not a country. City, maybe. You haven't seen a fraction of it yet. We have an indoor staff of thirty-nine servants and an outdoor staff of fifteen gardeners and twenty handymen. Let's see if I can remember everything correctly." He pretended to have to frown thoughtfully. "The house has almost eight thousand panes of glass, twenty-two bathrooms, three acres of copper on the roofs, seventy-nine clocks, all of which have to be wound—"

"You're joking!"

He shook his head. "I'm dead serious." And he told her the long, complex history of Fallsworth. The story was one of restlessness and constant achievements. It began in the early sixteenth century when Sir Arthur Somerset took over the estate which was to become the ancestral home of the Somersets. He began building a small Elizabethan manor, which was now consolidated into the far wing. His firstborn son was made Earl of Farquharshire in 1573. In 1693 the fifth Earl began rebuilding the house and sheathed it with a new exterior. His son became the first Duke. Slowly Fallsworth as it looked now began to take shape, each subsequent duke and duchess building onto the original house. Gardens were uprooted and planted anew, and whole forests were imported. Even the nearby riverbed was changed and a new channel built so that it passed by in front of the house. By the time the ninth Duke came along, all the various wings were consolidated into one solid classical building. Then came even more alterations, more great wings. Famous gardeners were called in, and the greatest architects of each century found work at Fallsworth.

But each duke and duchess did more than just add onto Fallsworth. If much care was taken with the exterior, then even more love went into the interior. The notable art collections were continuously added to and upgraded: Gainsboroughs, Bouchers, Fragonards, and Reynoldses; royal Savonnerie and Aubusson rugs; Meissen and Sèvres porcelains; Limoges enamels; Beauvais tapestries, fine French cabinets. All these treasures were cared for in the most befitting manner. Blinds shielded the rooms from the harsh sunlight. The canvases were regularly cleaned and restored. Daily, the precious porcelains received light dustings only. To date, not one single item had ever been broken.

Charlotte Somerset, the fourteenth Duchess, suffered ill health and had to spend winters in the South of France. During this time, each treasure was wrapped in made-to-measure chamois pouches and packed in specially constructed boxes and crates and stored. Each spring, when the Duchess returned from France, every item was unpacked again and put in its proper place. During World War II, Fallsworth had housed three hundred children so that they might avoid the bombs falling on London. The present Duke and Duchess saw to it that Charlotte Somerset's chamois pouches, boxes, and crates were again put to use. For the first time in nearly sixty years, the treasures were once again packed and stored in the vast cellars of Fallsworth. Not one item was damaged.

Hélène listened to the history with great interest, but she felt new misgivings. Clearly Fallsworth was not a home. It was a national treasure that required the full attention, love, and dedication of each duke and duchess.

"I've never seen Nigel look so happy," the Duke said. "She's a fine young lady." He lowered the newspaper he was reading. It was the royal edition of the *Times*, which, like the edition delivered to Buckingham Palace, was specially printed on rag paper.

The Duchess got to her feet and walked over to one of the windows. She held aside the heavy curtains. For a long time she stared out at the two people walking hand in hand toward the house. Then she turned around. Her eyes were veiled. "Yes," she said slowly. "She's a rather . . . remarkable young woman."

Dinner was held in the Private Dining Room. By now Hélène had been exposed to enough of Fallsworth not to be overly impressed by this room. The walls were paneled in white and the moldings were gilded. The heavy red curtains were velvet, the marble fireplace seven feet tall. There were antique Chinese screens and large paintings by Rubens. The stemware was Waterford, the cutlery heavy Georgian silver, the candelabra gold, the prominent centerpieces on the polished Georgian table two antique Ascot gold cups won by Somerset horses in the nineteenth century.

Hélène was glad when dinner was finally over. They retired to a salon for coffee, and after a suitable amount of time she and Nigel went for another walk. It was dark out, and she breathed deeply. The air was clean, rich country air, alive with the noise of the crickets and the humming insects of the night. When they came to a wrought-iron pavilion, they sat down on the stone garden bench inside it. For a while, they were both silent.

"You're not comfortable here," Nigel said finally.

Hélène pursed her lips thoughtfully as she looked across the lawn to the multitude of yellow windows. "It's not you, Nigel. It's Fallsworth. It's like . . ." She sighed. ". . . a museum."

"I agree with you."

"You do?" She looked at him in surprise. His face was dark, but she could feel the warmth of his eyes.

He nodded. "I wasn't planning for us to live here." He sought her hand and squeezed it. "I was thinking we'd get a house of our own in London. A place we both feel at home in. I've lived my entire life in museums. What I want now," he said emphatically, "is a home."

She smiled in relief. "You don't know how happy that makes me."

He hugged her and smiled. His teeth gleamed faintly from the lights in the distant house. "Darling, I want to marry *you*, not a curator."

She laughed. "I don't want a big house," she warned him. "I want something small and manageable—"

"Without servants crawling all over it—"

"And airy and modern. I mean, we're in the 1960's. I don't want to have to live like we're part of the last few centuries—"

"Indeed not. But it must be cozy—"

"Yes! With a nice garden—"

"Where we can raise our children."

She froze. Slowly she turned and stared numbly at the huge house—the house that demanded a continuous dynasty. A dynasty which her body could not provide.

She slipped her hand from his. "No, Nigel," she said flatly.

"What is it?" he asked. "I mean . . . did I say something wrong?"

Hélène closed her eyes. A fierce pain burned inside her. Her voice was a whisper. "Nigel, I don't know why I never told you. It's just that it didn't seem important." She gave a low laugh. "I was a fool. I thought it was us that mattered."

His voice was worried. "Of course it's us that matters. Darling, what on earth are you talking about?"

"Children."

"What about children?"

"I can never have any."

"I'm sorry, darling. I didn't know." He drew her toward him and held her in silence. Finally he spoke. "It doesn't matter," he said gently. "If we want children, we can adopt some. A whole brood, if you like."

"It's not right," she said heatedly, extricating herself from his arms. "Your family's endured for centuries. If you don't have children, you'll be the end of the line."

"And you think that's so important? Doesn't our love count for anything?"

"It counts," she said frowning. "I just don't think it would be fair! Not to your parents, not to your ancestors—"

"Why are you worried about my ancestors and my family?"

"Perhaps because the war claimed most of mine," she said quietly. "Maybe that's how I know having a family is so important. Why else would you work so hard to build and achieve, if it's not going to endure beyond your own lifetime?"

"And you?" he asked gently. "Why do you push yourself so hard if you can't leave your empire to anyone?"

A note of pride crept into her voice. "There *is* someone I can leave it to, Nigel. My niece. She's like my own daughter."

"And what's wrong if she's left Fallsworth also?"

Her voice was shaky. "Do you mean that, Nigel?"

"Of course I mean that, darling. If I can't have you . . ." His voice was filled with pain. "Then what's the point of going on living?"

She knew when he kissed her that he meant every word. And she had never known such happiness to exist.

It was late at night and Hélène stood at the window of her bedroom. She had switched the lights off, and the night outside was black as only a night in the country could be. She was filled with a sense of well-being. Ever since coming to Fallsworth, she had dreaded that something unexpected would tear to shreds what she and Nigel shared. Now she felt certain that that would not happen.

618

There was a discreet knock on the door. Nigel was coming to share her bed! She tried to keep the excitement out of her voice as she said, "Just a moment!"

Quickly she switched on one of the silk-shaded lamps, hurried over to the bed, and picked up her peignoir. She slipped into it and ran a hand through her hair. Joyfully she hurried to the door and swiftly pulled it open.

Standing in front of her was the Duchess of Farquharshire. Hélène's smile froze.

"I'm sorry to bother you, my dear," the Duchess said. She made an embarrassed gesture with her slender fingers. "May I come in? I was wondering if we might have a little talk."

Hélène stepped aside. "Please . . . come in."

The Duchess stepped inside and Hélène closed the door.

8

When Nigel awoke he flung aside the covers, jumped out of bed, and went over to the windows. He opened the holland blinds. The sunlight was already bright on the outside of the window frames.

Impulsively he flung the windows wide, letting the sunshine and chilly morning air wash over his bedroom in the East Wing. For once he was oblivious of the rule of shutting out the daylight from the valuables of Fallsworth. He wanted to revel in the sunshine. To let its life-giving brightness soak into his skin. Ever since the day before yesterday, when Hélène's eyes had shone as she had cried, "Yes! Oh, Nigel, *yes*!" he had been filled with the warm, satisfied glow of love. What he and Hélène shared was a treasure that surpassed anything at Fallsworth.

As Nigel was opening the windows in his bedroom, Hélène was staring out of another window. Twenty thousand feet above England, the BOAC Comet dipped its silver port wing and she could see the English coast far below. The distant breakers looked like a smooth line of motionless white along the beaches. Then the coastline slipped out of sight and all she could see was an uneven, monotonous gray. Once again she was flying over the English Channel.

She turned her face away as the morning sun glared into her eyes. There was a numbness in her body that made it feel heavy and lifeless.

"Would you like a drink, miss?" a voice asked.

Hélène looked up at the stewardess bending solicitously toward her. She shook her head and wearily turned away again. "No, thank you," she murmured. She tilted her head sideways to avoid the sun. She looked as if she was staring out at the bank of clouds they had headed into, but what she was seeing was her bedroom at Fallsworth and the Duchess of Farquharshire standing in front of her. She could see herself, too. Staring at the imperious woman with a sudden fear. "Please," she had said, "come in."

The Duchess inclined her head and entered. Her aristocratic eyes were veiled and heavily lidded.

Hélène closed the door. "Won't you sit down?"

The Duchess sat regally on one of the petit-point-upholstered chairs. With a feeling of dread, Hélène slowly took the seat opposite her. "What can I do for you?" she asked hesitantly. But she needn't have asked. Her intuition told her why the Duchess had come.

The Duchess looked at her for a lingering moment. Then she sighed and folded her smooth hands in her lap. For a moment she looked down at them and then back up at Hélène. "My son," she said carefully in her cultured voice, "has expressed the desire to marry you."

"Yes," Hélène said in a tight voice, "we love one another."

The Duchess smiled thinly. "That is an admirable sentiment. I'm sure you love him very much." She made an agitated gesture with her hands. "We Somersets are an old family. I'm sure you realize that."

Hélène didn't answer. She nodded cautiously and waited for the Duchess to continue.

Victoria Hollingsworth Somerset, the fifteenth Duchess of Farquharshire, had been named after a queen and born of an earl. From childhood she had been groomed to make a good marriage. She had not married the Duke as much for love as for the fact that his title was better than her own. That was reason enough for matrimony. One didn't go in search of love. That was for the lower classes. Although love had not been an integral part of her own marriage in the beginning, she was an excellent chatelaine for Fallsworth. Indeed, she now shared a sincere affection with the old Duke. She also genuinely liked Hélène Junot. She respected anyone who worked hard and achieved so much, and she did not like what she had to do now. But she was the guardian of Fallsworth and she knew her responsibilities. The Somerset name had to be guarded as jealously as any of the treasures in the great house. It had to be kept within the narrow confines of the aristocracy as it had been for centuries. Not once had the Somerset strain of the blood royal ever been diluted by a commoner. It was up to the Duchess to see that it did not happen now.

The Duchess inclined her head thoughtfully. "Tell me, my dear. Has my son discussed his future with you at all?"

Hélène kept her face impassive. *His* future. Not *their* future. The implication was clear. "I'm not quite sure what you're trying to get at."

The Duchess sighed. This was difficult enough without having to do battle. "Well, let me put it this way. My son has political ambitions."

"Yes," Hélène said carefully, fearing a trap somewhere.

"And I'm sure you realize that for a future duke, the correct wife is one of the most important assets in his life."

Hélène smelled the trap and adroitly sidestepped it. "Every man needs a woman he loves," she said. "A stable marriage is important under any circumstance."

"And would your marrying him be a sign of stability?"

Hélène frowned. "I'm not sure I understand."

"Then let me try to explain. Nigel's social position is secure." The Duchess paused. "At least for the time being. But, my dear . . . a wife like you?"

"You don't like the fact that I'm a businesswoman?" Hélène asked.

"It isn't that *I* don't like it," the Duchess said smoothly. "It's the public. The average Englishman, I'm afraid, is rather ordinary and set in his ways. A man running for election who has a wife who runs her own business . . . well, the people can't be expected to accept that. It's so . . . common." She rolled the word on her tongue as if it were something dirty. "Not that I personally have anything against it, you understand. But the public looks up to us. They expect us to be . . . noble."

Hélène's intuition had borne her out. "You don't want me to marry Nigel," she said flatly.

The Duchess smiled sadly. "I want what's best for him," she said gently.

"And you think you know what that is?"

For a moment the Duchess did not speak. "I know what's best for the family."

Hélène sat there white-faced and quiet. So her worst fears had turned into stark reality. She wouldn't be welcome in the Somerset fold. She was a commoner, a foreigner. Her eyes fell to her hand. The Somerset Sun seemed to wink mockingly at her.

After a while the Duchess spoke again. "Don't you want what's best for my son? If you love him—"

"I *do* love him!" Hélène said stubbornly.

There was another silence and the two women's eyes met. Each one sized up the other. Finally the Duchess spoke again. "Don't you want Nigel to have the future that is his birthright?" she asked softly.

Hélène didn't reply.

The Duchess looked down at her lap. "Everything will have been for nothing," she said. "Everything will be over before it even begins."

Hélène leaned forward. "Nigel will have a future!" she said vehemently.

The Duchess shook her head. "Not with you, I'm afraid."

"I'll be a credit to him!"

The Duchess got to her feet. She looked down at Hélène. "If you love him as much as you say you do, for God's sake, *let him go!*"

Hélène stared at her. "I can't!"

The aristocratic eyes were hooded. "Then I'm afraid you leave me no alternative. I cannot let this marriage take place."

Hélène felt as if she was being smothered by an invisible pillow. Suddenly the luxurious bedroom took on a new personality. The poppies on the turned-down sheets looked like bloodstains and the sphinx heads on the Empire dressing table seemed to smile carnivorously. "What . . . are you going to do?" she whispered haltingly.

"I shall have to consult our solicitors about that. But I can assure you of one thing. Nigel will not inherit a penny. Fallsworth will be forever closed to him."

"I have enough money," Hélène said defiantly. "We can live on that."

The Duchess smiled faintly. "Yes, but can Nigel live with the fact that he has been ostracized from his own family? That the doors to every noble house in Great Britain will be closed to him?"

"You wouldn't do that!" Hélène said sharply.

"I would. And eventually this love which you now share would be soured. The marriage would not have a chance of lasting." The Duchess laughed a thin, brittle laugh. "Do you think my son could conceive of living off his wife?"

Hélène looked defeated. Her face was pale and her lips were trembling. "What is it you want?"

"Leave him!" the Duchess implored. "He belongs in the aristocracy. Leave him among his own kind!"

Hélène rose with dignity. For a moment she looked down at her hand. Then she worked the Somerset Sun off her finger. She handed it to the Duchess. "I would not want to become a member of such an unloving family," she said in a quivering voice. "You are not worthy of your son. Please believe me when I say I much prefer being Hélène Junot to Hélène Somerset." She took a deep breath and fought to retain her composure. "If you'll be so kind as to send your chauffeur around, I'll have my bags packed within a few minutes."

"I'll telephone the airfield to have the airplane in readiness," the Duchess said.

This time it was Hélène who smiled thinly. "I think I'd prefer a commercial airliner," she said.

"As you wish." The Duchess looked down at her feet. "What should I tell Nigel?" she asked quietly.

Hélène looked at her, but she wouldn't meet her eyes. "The truth, perhaps?"

The Duchess was silent.

Hélène's laugh sounded like a hysterical cry. "I expect you would like me to write him a note and have *me* break off the engagement?"

"If it's not asking too much."

"It is," Hélène said, "but I love Nigel too much to make him hate you for the rest of his life." Her voice dropped to a whisper. "I'd much prefer for him to hate me."

623

As it had been so often in the past, Les Éditions Hélène Junot continued to be a barometer of Hélène's personal life. When she looked back at the progress of the company, its growth and achievements seemed to leap sporadically each time she suffered a personal crisis. Ironically, what was an enemy to Hélène turned out to be a friend to the company. Although she was never consciously aware of that fact until the crisis was behind her, she worked herself mercilessly during those times, building and expanding and pushing all those around her to a level of achievement that was almost superhuman. Now that she knew she could never share Nigel's name and love, she banished him completely from her life. She refused his calls and returned his letters unopened. Once he even arrived unexpectedly at the Place Vendôme office, refusing to leave until he could at least see her. Warned by her secretary, Hélène slipped quietly out the back way, fleeing down the stairs to the delivery entrance. She could fight many things, she thought bitterly as she flagged a taxi, but not the loss of Nigel's birthright. If she became responsible for that, she knew that she would never be able to live with herself.

This crisis continued for six months. As time passed, Nigel's letters and calls got fewer and fewer, until they stopped coming completely. And then, just as she was starting to recover, the crisis peaked. She was leafing through a copy of *Paris Match* one evening when she suddenly froze. The title of the article was "A Society Wedding." And the color photo showed a young bride named Lady Pamela Grey leaning against the groom's shoulder. The groom was Nigel, and in the background loomed the unmistakable glorious elegance that was Fallsworth.

Hélène knew from the terrible pain she felt that she still loved Nigel. That for her the feelings they had shared were not over. Would never be. It was impossible simply to shut

Nigel from her life and then expect the feelings to vanish, too.

She stared at the picture for a long time. She tried to console herself with the fact that at least now Nigel would no longer be trying to get to her. But this was a defensive reaction, and she knew it. He hadn't even tried to get in touch with her for over two months now. She had wanted Nigel to find out by himself why she had cut him off so suddenly. She had hoped he would somehow manage to straighten things out. But these wedding pictures were irrefutable proof that it was too late. That everything they had shared, everything she had hoped so desperately for, was over. She was no longer even left with hope. It was clear that she was no longer a part of Nigel's life. Lady Pamela was.

Hélène narrowed her eyes as she inspected Lady Pamela's picture closely. Lady Pamela was not a beauty by any standards, although she was pretty enough in a quiet, wholesome way. The first thing Hélène noticed about her was her skin. It was flawless pink English skin. She had blond hair, conservatively coiffed under the Belgian-lace bridal veil, large dark eyes, and a ready smile. Her wedding dress matched the veil and came to a puritanically high collar. She wore no jewelry except for the ring on her finger. Her hand was casually but intentionally poised against her collarbone so that the Somerset Sun was shown to its fullest advantage.

Hélène felt physically ill. The Somerset Sun, which had graced her very own finger, and which was to announce to the world that she would become the sixteenth Duchess of Farquharshire. And beside the bride, cutting a handsome figure in his black tuxedo, Nigel seemed tall and stoic, looking expressionlessly into the camera.

He's staring at *me*, Hélène thought, catching her breath. She could almost feel the heat of his eyes, the warmth of his breath. She was pleased about one thing only. Nigel, who was supposed to be the happy groom, was not smiling on this, his wedding day. She couldn't help wondering if he were unhappy. If the Duchess hadn't arranged everything.

What a silly thought! she told herself. Of course she had. She had chased Hélène from Fallsworth and Nigel. That was arrangement enough.

In an uncharacteristic rage, Hélène suddenly ripped the page out of the magazine. Her fingers were shaking as she tore it into tiny shreds, letting the pieces flutter down to the floor. She looked down at them, her breasts heaving, and she could see one of Nigel's familiar eyes gazing up at her. She kicked at the scrap of paper until it turned over.

This time, the pain was so intense that she plunged into her work with a vengeance so fierce that all her other work binges paled by comparison. And while she herself looked unchanged, Les Édition Hélène Junot was reflecting the effects.

There was no stopping her now.

Les Éditions Hélène Junot began growing like a mushroom after a rainfall. Between Paris and Milan, the staff numbered close to two hundred. The Place Vendôme headquarters was expanded. The building next door had become vacant, and Hélène readily signed a twelve-year lease. Soon even that additional space was not enough and she had to rent yet another building on the nearby rue des Capucines. The building in which she had started her empire now housed only the administrative offices—the accounting department, the advertising offices, the circulation managers, and the legal section. The connecting building housed the creative staff—the various editors and writers and the art director and his artists. The photography studio, with its sets and darkrooms, was moved to the rue des Capucines. It was like a small film-production studio and boasted the latest in photographic equipment. It was no longer necessary to send photographers and models to a tropical beach or to the mountains. Everything but the most important layouts could be shot right in the studio. The sets were constructed in the workshop in the back of the building.

The Paris office and showroom of Marcello d'Itri were on the rue Cambon. Hélène was pleased that everything was within a few minutes' walking distance, but she was waiting for another space on the Place Vendôme to become available. She wanted to have the d'Itri office and showroom conveniently next door to Les Éditions Hélène Junot. Especially now that she lived in a suite in the Hotel Ritz, just across the square. Living at the Ritz provided her not only with unsurpassed luxury but also with the added convenience of hotel services. This way she could dedicate every waking hour to her work.

Hélène Junot was big business.

More magazines had been added to *Les Modes* and *La*

Moda. The roster now included *Les Modes Homme,* the definitive men's fashion magazine, and *Beauté,* a smaller version of *Les Modes* that was geared to younger women. *Beauté* was filled with makeup and fashion tips and with more ready-to-wear than haute couture. It was for women on a budget and it outsold even *Les Modes. Les Modes,* however, remained the top of the line. It gave the empire its prestige.

The progress was not confined to Paris. In Milan, *La Moda* gave birth to *La Moda Uomo,* the Italian equivalent of *Les Modes Homme.*

In June 1963 Edmond joined the Paris staff as a full-fledged corporate lawyer. For nine months Hélène had him do nothing but learn the ropes. When she thought he was ready, she promptly moved him up in the legal staff. In a few years he would be in charge of the empire's entire legal department. He was learning fast and becoming an expert at delegating authority. What he lacked in experience he more than made up for in intelligence and dedication.

Luba, too, was promoted. Officially, she became vice-president of Les Éditions Hélène Junot, S.A. Unofficially she also became vice-president of Marcello d'Itri, but this particular position was kept very quiet so that there would be no visible connection between the ateliers and the magazines. Hélène was afraid that if the readers put two and two together, it might stir up a conflict of interest in their minds. Although *Les Modes*'s and *La Moda*'s backing of the ateliers had been responsible for their success, for practical purposes it was important to make it appear that the magazines were unbiased and owed no allegiances.

Hélène was gratified that the ateliers in Milan, Rome, and Paris were thriving so soundly.

She had conquered France and Italy. But still she was not satisfied. If anything, she was more restless than ever. Deep inside, her craving for Nigel was raging out of control. She barely managed to keep her emotions in check by ever increasing her workload. Determinedly she saw to it that Petite Hélène's grooming followed her careful planning to the letter. Even more doggedly she plotted the course her magazines and ateliers would take. There was still one place she had to conquer in order to prove her magazines' prowess. Once you had made it there, you'd made it everywhere.

Paris and Milan were not enough. She liked the battle for

success far more than the success itself. She knew where her fashion tentacles had to reach next.

New York.

10

New York in the 1960's was a tough place to crack. The city beat with the very pulse of fashion. Odile Joly's prediction of many years earlier had become reality. *Women's Wear Daily* was now the Bible not only of Seventh Avenue but also of much of the international fashion world. Bitchy, gossipy, and all-powerful, *WWD* was read as much for its snide comments as for its fashion news. The paper had come a long way since 1954 when John Fairchild, in charge of the Paris bureau, found himself in a humiliating rear seat during the couturiers' showings.

No less powerful was *Vogue*. After twenty-seven years at *Harper's Bazaar,* Diana Vreeland moved over to the competition and reigned from *Vogue*'s lofty throne like a Wise Lady scattering crumbs of chic to a drab populace. It was Diana Vreeland who sent her photographers into the desert to shoot models wrapped in nothing but clear plastic. Everything that had never been done before was being done by Diana Vreeland. She became a thorn in both Hélène's and Luba's sides. It seemed that "the Empress," as the indefatigable Mrs. Vreeland was deferentially nicknamed, had a limitless imagination. For once, even the Czarina had met her match. For the eight years that Diana Vreeland would be at *Vogue*, American *Les Modes* and *Vogue* would run neck and neck in a constant race. This friendly running battle between the Czarina and the Empress brought about some of the most dramatic and creative concepts in fashion photography and reporting the world was ever to see.

Hélène was fascinated by New York. She knew better than anyone how a camera could be used to overdramatize anything, so she was ready to meet the challenge of the spectacular skyline that rose into the sky as the SS *United States* steamed into New York harbor. But she had not been prepared for what had happened on board the ship. She took it as an omen that New York would become *her* city. For during the transatlantic crossing, she fell in love. For the first time, she had met a man who was not overshadowed by the image of Nigel Somerset.

His name was Siegfried Bavier and he didn't look like a night in shining armor. In fact, he was everything that Nigel was not, and perhaps that was what attracted her to him in the first place. From the start, she knew that he was married because he came right out and told her. He didn't try to hide things. He was as shrewd and toughly honest with himself as she was.

They met in the cocktail lounge during one of the fiercest storms at sea the liner had ever encountered. Ninety-five-foot waves were crashing over the bow, and had she or Siegfried been afflicted with weak stomachs, chances were they never would have met. As it was, they had been the only people in the first-class lounge. At first, she had been the only one. She was seated at one of the little tables, holding on to her glass so that it wouldn't slide off and crash to the floor. Oddly, she had been aware that he was behind her even before he spoke.

She turned around slowly and looked up at him. Their eyes met. His shoulders were wide and he was powerfully built. He held a drink in his hand. His dark hair was cropped short and he looked more like a stevedore or a prizefighter than a first-class passenger. She sensed that he was ill-at-ease in his dinner suit. But there was a look in his piercing blue eyes that she recognized instantly, that drew her to him like a magnet. It was the confident look of success, and he wore it better than he wore his clothes.

"Can I buy you a drink?" he asked in English. He had a surprisingly deep, resonant voice.

"No, thank you," she said. She smiled and showed him her glass. "I have one."

"Mind if I join you? Company is kind of scarce tonight. Everyone seems to have disappeared."

"Not at all," she answered quickly. "Please . . ." She gestured to the banquette at the other side of the table. As he slipped into it, the liner suddenly listed to starboard and the deck sloped precariously. The man was caught off guard. For a moment he teetered almost drunkenly and then was unceremoniously thrown onto the banquette. Under the impact, the bourbon shot out from his glass.

Hélène burst out laughing. Then she saw his scowl and covered her lips with her fingers. She forced herself to look serious. "I'm sorry," she said contritely, removing her hand from her lips. She looked suddenly concerned. "You didn't hurt yourself, did you?"

He shook his head. "Only my pride's wounded." He looked darkly into his glass. "Hell of a waste of good bourbon, though." Then he noticed the bodice of her dress. A dark stain was spreading slowly across it. "I'm terribly sorry," he apologized embarrassedly. "It seems I've ruined your dress."

She glanced down at herself and then looked back across the table at him. "The cleaner's will get it out," she said confidently.

"You're sure?"

She nodded. "I'm sure."

She studied him more closely. He looked no more than forty years old, she thought, and there was something about him that was incredibly vibrant. He seemed more alive than many men half his age. She felt a strange and powerful feeling well up inside her. It was a feeling that had been dormant for far too long.

She watched as he settled comfortably on the banquette and took a cigar from the inside pocket of his jacket. He struck a match, carefully held it to the end of the cigar, and inhaled deeply several times. Finally he waved the match out. He leaned sideways so he could see past Hélène and signaled to get the bartender's attention. "Another bourbon!" he called out. He leaned toward Hélène. "You're positive I can't buy you a drink?"

She shook her head. "I'm positive, thank you. I've had two of these already."

He frowned at her glass. "Vodka?"

She laughed and shook her head. "Club soda."

He grimaced. "Don't see how you can drink that stuff. It gives me gas." He grinned, showing strong, even white teeth. "By the way, my name's Siegfried Bavier," he said easily. "My friends call me Sigi."

She flushed. Over the years she had met quite a few Americans, but she had yet to become accustomed to their easy familiarity. As soon as they met you, they insisted on being on a first-name basis. Europeans weren't like that at all.

"How do you do?" she said. "I'm Hélène Junot." She paused and added with an embarrassed smile: "My friends call me Hélène."

The bartender came over with the bourbon. Bavier signaled him to wait. He downed the drink in one swallow and handed the empty glass back. He laughed when he saw the intrigued look on Hélène's face. "Best cure in the world for seasickness," he explained.

"Is it?"

"Sure. When you drink too much, everything reels around you, right?"

She nodded doubtfully.

"Well, the way I figure it is this. Once you're good and drunk, everything's topsy-turvy anyway, so how are you going to notice the motions of the ship on top of it?"

She laughed. "You have made your point . . . Sigi." She looked at him closely. "But don't you like to feel the sea?" she asked. "The power of the wind and water?"

"Sure, I like it. I'm a born sailor. I sailed around the world alone on a forty-foot sailboat a few years back. Even hit a bad typhoon in Micronesia. Nothing like this . . ." He made a condescending gesture. "This is nothing compared to that. The waves must have been a hundred and twenty feet high and the sky was a solid black wall of water."

Hélène shivered. "Weren't you frightened?"

He made a face and was tempted to brag, but when he saw her serious expression, he decided against it. "To tell you the truth, Hélène"— he grinned sheepishly—"it scared the living shit out of me."

And that broke any ice that was left between them. Suddenly she felt completely relaxed in his presence, even on a first-name basis. His language was salty, to be sure, but to her knowledge, most Americans were crude. They lacked the cultured refinement and breeding of the Europeans. Yet there was something about Bavier which attracted her to him in spite of that. Perhaps it was that he had an almost French joie de vivre, which, coupled with his confident bearing, clinched her feelings toward him. He was honest and good-natured, yet there was something untamed about him. She felt secure in his company.

It was then that she saw the flash of gold on his finger.

"Your wife isn't weathering this storm well?" she asked.

His face went suddenly sad as he glanced down at his wedding band. He had been in Europe for more than a month and he realized now that he hadn't once thought of her.

Hélène dropped her eyes. Her own question had caught her by surprise. She had never asked a strange man about his wife before. "I'm sorry," she said softly. "I had no right to ask."

"Of course you did." His face creased into a warm smile. "When a strange man comes up to you and invites himself to join you, you have every right."

She smiled gratefully.

"My wife is in New York," he said quietly. He looked down at the ring and twisted it around on his finger. "I'm afraid we don't get along well."

"Oh. I'm sorry."

He smiled weakly. "Sometimes it just takes a while to find out that you're not suited to each other. It took us a few years. At first, I used to think it was all my fault. That I wasn't giving her enough of myself. Then I used to blame her." He shook his head slowly. "I've gotten wiser now. When a marriage doesn't work, you can't lay the blame on either of you. It's both your faults or neither of you is to blame. It took me a long time to realize that." He looked at her and smiled sadly. "What about you?"

Hélène shrugged her shoulders expressively. "I'm widowed. Then I was engaged again, but it turned out his family didn't like me."

The truth was, the Duchess had been downright hostile. But it was close enough. What had transpired at Fallsworth was her own business, and no one else's.

"His family are fools, then," Bavier said. "Didn't he at least put up a fight?"

It was her turn to sigh.

He shook his head. "He must be a fool too. I can't see any man not fighting for you."

She was suddenly angry at him. He hadn't said anything nasty, but she resented his attitude all the same. For some strange reason, she felt compelled to come to Nigel's defense. Her voice went cold as she said, "It wasn't his fault. I didn't give him half a chance. You see, it was I who broke it off."

He looked at her curiously. "But you still love him."

"It's over," she said sharply. Then her voice fell. "Besides, he married someone else." She gave a sad little smile. "So you see, it really is over."

He nodded. "I didn't mean to pry."

"That's all right."

"Good. Let's change the subject. What's bringing you to New York?"

"Business."

"Which do you do? Act? Model?"

"Neither." She laughed and toyed with her glass. "Whatever gave you those ideas?"

"You're beautiful. I thought most beautiful women were either actresses or models."

She glanced up at him, her eyes serious. "I'm a magazine publisher."

He looked at her with deepening respect. "Have I seen your magazines around?"

She smiled. "I don't know. They're mostly women's magazines. *Les Modes* and *La Moda*."

"Hey!" He grinned. "They're fashion magazines."

She nodded. "How did you know?"

"My wife always buys *Les Modes*," he explained. "In fact, she swears by it. But she always curses because she can only get it at Hotaling's on Times Square."

"That's going to change soon," Hélène said. "I'm setting up an American edition, and seeing to it that the European editions get better distribution outlets in the major cities across the United States."

He nodded approvingly. "You'll do well in New York."

"I hope so. It will be a challenge."

He shook his head knowingly. "Not for you. I have good instincts about people. You'll turn the city inside out in no time." He glanced at his cigar appreciatively. "You're a fighter."

She could feel her face flushing. "And you?"

"I'm a fighter too," he said. "It takes one to know one."

She looked at him and laughed. She saw the solemnity in his blue eyes.

"I'd like to see more of you when you're settled in New York," he said quietly.

"I would like that too," she said quietly.

She looked at him and then rose unsteadily to her feet. He

633

got up also. The deck lurched and she suddenly found herself in his arms.

"I've got you," he said, holding her gently.

A warmth seemed to seep from her insides as she looked into his eyes. They were bright and intense, filled with an ocean of promises.

"I think I know a good way to weather this storm," he said softly.

Hélène sank into the pale blue quilted satin spread. She rolled on her side and then settled on her back, feeling the sleek, sensual fabric beneath her. The cabin was lit by the glow coming from the sitting room and a single dim bedside lamp. The big square windows looked out onto the promenade deck. Chances were that nobody ventured out on deck in this weather, but the curtains were nevertheless drawn, ensuring full privacy and somewhat muting the lashings of the rain and the sea.

She could hear Siegfried's movements in the sitting room. There was a click as the light went out, and finally the whisper of his feet moving across the carpet. Slowly he entered, pulling the bedroom door shut behind him.

Hélène was stretched full length on the bed, the light casting shadows across the firm contours of her body. She had let her hair fall free from the chignon. It hung down her back, and would have seemed to be a single sheet of black silk in the dim light if it hadn't been for the one renegade tendril that caught on her breast.

He hesitated momentarily at the sight, and then moved toward her, unable to see her eyes until he stood a foot away. She raised her head and stared up at him, meeting his gaze. Her violet eyes moved down his tanned, muscular body. His chest was covered with small spirals of dark hair, his hips flat and narrow. From the thicket of hair at his groin, his penis pushed out, the veins sculptured in bold relief.

She reached out and took his hand, guiding it toward one of her breasts. Closing her eyes, she felt his gentle fingers kneading one nipple and his moist tongue flicking against the other. His free hand began slowly to stroke her perfumed flesh, gradually increasing momentum as it moved down to her navel and then found its way to her clitoris, one finger probing its wet, radiating warmth.

Hélène began to shudder as the pleasure began culminat-

634

ing toward pain. Just as she thought his stroking would overwhelm her, he stopped and moved over her. Straddling her gently, he pressed his lean hips down against hers. Her arms reached up, encircling his neck, and drew him fiercely downward. Siegfried's face was an inch from hers when suddenly he halted, and in that one silent moment Hélène's world stopped. Urgently her eyes flicked up to meet his, and there she saw a stare so determined, yet at the same time so unreadable. There was something fearful in the intense power she saw in those features, something that seemed to have gathered force like a dam ready to burst.

His face never moved, but she could feel his hips slowly, steadily lifting from hers. Up they rose until they stopped, seeming to hover, ready, yet hesitant. And then he drove down hard, plunging through her slick, wet walls. Hélène's body arched with the impact, as he reached her deepest recesses in that one, long-awaited drive. He then pulled away from her and began to quickly enter and withdraw, enter and withdraw in shallow, rapid thrusts.

She writhed beneath him, her legs firmly clasped around his waist, while her head moved back and forth. Hélène felt his pace slow, as if he feared he would hurt her.

"Don't slow down! Please . . ." she whispered, anxiety betraying her.

"Ssssssh."

He pulled out gradually, and in a panic she felt he was abandoning her. But then he slowly entered her again, and the joys of relief and pure physical sensation brought breathless sounds from her. Over and over he repeated the maneuver, sometimes quickening his thrusts, then easing them. Hélène's body shuddered as she climaxed again and again, each orgasm rushing over her until he, too, finally cried out, slapping into her with all his force, bringing her to still another orgasm. Siegfried came, his muscles quivering with the release of vibrant liquid energy.

She lay back as his body collapsed against her, the still-muted sea now a comforting wash of sound in the air.

Siegfried Bavier and Hélène had many things in common, but of all their shared qualities there was one which stood out above the others. Their beginnings. Both of them had begun life penniless and worked their way up from the depths of poverty and despair. As a result, each recognized and respected the restless hunger which drove the other. In Bavier, Hélène saw a mind that was a mirror image of her own. He was cunning and ambitious and enjoyed his wealth and status. Yet it hadn't gone to his head. On the contrary, during his climb to success and power he had never lost touch with his simple beginnings. He liked the whole process of making money—the work and the struggle and the skill he had to employ in order to get it. There was no reason for him to continue working. Years ago, he could easily have retired in splendor for the rest of his life. But he kept adding to his riches. Mainly because he enjoyed exercising the skill and the gambling it involved. Had he possessed a different, less creative mind, Bavier might have spent his life playing cards or gambling on horses or numbers. But he recognized these as children's games. To him, the gambles that went on daily in big business were the Big Leagues. And the winning wasn't nearly as important as the Game. He was a gambler like no others. Forty-one years old, he had been a millionaire three times, and twice in between he had gone bankrupt.

"A man who can make a fortune once, lose it all, and make it all over again from scratch has nothing to worry about," he was once quoted as saying. "If success isn't a fluke, it can be repeated a hundred times over."

And he proved it. Each time he lost a fortune, he not only regained it but also ended up with more than he had before. When Hélène met him, he was worth in the vicinity of twenty-two million dollars, was playing the stock market and investing heavily in futures and commodities. Wisely enough, he kept five million tied up in tax-free municipal bonds. The rest he used to play with.

His financial ups and downs had their roots during the war, when he had been an eighteen-year-old infantryman marching from France deep into Germany. By the time he was shipped stateside he was in one of the last waves of returning GI's. The first waves had gotten the heroes' welcomes and the ticker-tape parades. Victory had then been fresh in people's minds. But by the time he got back, there were no more parades. There were no more heroes' welcomes. There was a housing shortage and all the jobs were taken. Giancarlo Iacono, his old employer in Brooklyn, had slapped him on the back before he had been shipped off to Europe. "Just remember, Sigi-boy, you a got friends here," Iacono had promised expansively. "Your job will be a waiting for you when you a get back."

But when Bavier got back, his job was held by one of Iacono's many nephews, and his girl had married someone else. His future had never looked bleaker. When he had boarded the Liberty Ship in France, he had been ready to grab the future by the balls. He had had twenty thousand dollars tucked inside his boots. By the time he got off the ship at the Brooklyn Naval Yard, he was dead broke.

For as long as he lived, Bavier would never forget the hellish march through Germany. Day after day, he and the other GI's in his platoon were met by the same ugly sights, smells, and sounds. Nothing but death, destruction, misery, hunger, and despair. As the march progressed, Bavier had watched as half his platoon was steadily decimated, either shot to pieces or blown up by land mines or falling bombs. Somehow, almost through sheer willpower, he managed to survive. He did his duty to the best of his ability, and tried to blot out all the ugliness. But that was difficult. For the GI's, there was no such thing as even a semblance of normalcy, even for a few hours. And no recreation of any sort. There was only the promise of more fighting, the constant specter of death, tasteless cold rations, and perhaps a little much-needed sleep. But never enough. It was hard to sleep when bombs were falling all around you.

Bavier recognized the need for recreation better than anyone else, perhaps because he himself needed it so badly. More important, he recognized this as an *opportunity*.

It did not take long for him to begin the recreational program. When a pimply young boy from Idaho was shot down beside him, he lifted the deck of cards the boy carried and pocketed it. He traded his cigarettes and rations for more decks of cards. Soon he was the only person within miles who had them. Then he made a small portable roulette wheel out of junk he stumbled across. At first everyone laughed at him, but he knew that they would come around. And he was right. In the wet foxholes and the icy, windblown tents, the card games and gambling parties he organized became so popular that he had them solidly booked for a week in advance. The "recreation" was, in fact, a traveling casino, and one of the best-kept secrets in the division.

Bavier was well aware that in gambling you had to make sure people paid their debts. He couldn't let anyone slide by owing him. Especially not if the debtor could be blown to bits that very night. So before he even started the enterprise, he got together with Hector Carras, a husky fellow soldier who also hailed from Brooklyn and who, before he was inducted, used to be a minor collector for the notorious Zanmatti family. Together, splitting the proceeds fifty-fifty, Bavier and Carras had the games in the division organized to an astonishingly sophisticated degree. By the time his tour of duty was over, Bavier's share of the loot amounted to over twenty thousand dollars, which he kept carefully stashed in a plastic bag tucked safely inside his boots.

When the war was over, Bavier and Carras found themselves steaming back to New York on the same troop ship. The passengers were a restless, impatient mass of GI's. The ship was cramped and everyone was anxious to get home; the trip would take nearly a week and a half. Everyone was boasting about the women who were waiting. And as the men lay in their swinging hammocks in the dark, the sounds of their restless hands and the moans of their self-induced orgasms filled the nights.

Once again Bavier recognized the opportunity for organizing some lucrative recreation. After all, the men had nothing but daydreams to occupy themselves. Together he and Carras came up with the idea for making one last killing.

There was a big GI aboard named Luis Gonzales who kept bragging how he had been a professional prizefighter before he was inducted. Carras, too, had fought quite a few rounds professionally before he joined up with the Zanmattis. He and Bavier approached Gonzales. The ex-prizefighter agreed to a match. Then they talked to the platoon sergeant, who in turn went to see the company commander, who welcomed the fight as a way to entertain the bored men. There was only one hitch. The company commander was adamant about allowing no betting.

That didn't deter Carras or Bavier. They simply did it quietly and in a roundabout way. They bought the services of four privates, and it was they who went around making book. Betting was rampant and everyone went at it feverishly. Bavier decided to bet his entire twenty thousand dollars on Carras. It was a gamble, but if Carras won . . .

The fight was held on deck and lasted more than an hour. In the last round, Carras knocked Gonzales unconscious. Carras came out of the fight with a broken nose, some minor contusions, and forty thousand dollars on top of his twenty. Bavier also came out with sixty thousand. As was his habit, he kept his money hidden in his boots, each bill carefully marked in the right-hand corner with a tiny inverted B. He slept with his boots and socks on and took every precaution safeguarding his loot. When he had to shower, he had Carras watch over it. If Carras was on duty elsewhere on the ship, Bavier hid the money in the air duct. That was where he had hidden it when, two nights from New York, he returned from showering only to find his money missing. And Gonzales, who hadn't had a penny to his name after losing the fight, was sitting in the smoke-filled hold playing cards and betting heavily with hundreds of dollars. Bavier recognized the money instantly. It was his. His unmistakable trademark was scrawled on the corner of each bill.

The men sitting around watching the game fell suddenly silent. It was as if a gust of danger had blown through the hold, and everyone was aware of it.

Bavier grabbed Gonzales roughly by the collar and yanked him to his feet. "You stole my dough," he accused belligerently, spinning the bigger man around. "I want it back."

Gonzales looked down at him, his black eyes flashing. "I didn't steal nothing. I won it." He pushed Bavier away, turned around, and casually sat back down.

Stubbornly Bavier stayed put. He was filled with a murderous rage. Gonzales was the thief. The marked bills proved that. And he wasn't about to let him get away with it. It had taken him two years to get the sixty thousand together, and he wasn't going to let anyone walk away with it now.

He clenched his fists, and when he spoke again, his voice trembled with rage. "Come on, you thieving spic," he challenged, raising his voice a little louder. "I aim to get my dough back."

The others stared at Bavier. Slowly they shuffled to their feet and drew silently back in a circle.

Only Gonzales didn't move. He didn't even bother turning around. "I would watch who I called a spic if I was you," he warned softly.

Bavier's eyes bore into the prizefighter's back. Then he suddenly threw himself at him. Both men went crashing to the floor, rolling over and over.

The other men drew back even farther, giving the two room to fight. Normally Gonzales would have had the advantage. He was by far the bigger man, and much more experienced as a fighter. But he was caught off guard and he was still weakened from the punches he'd taken in the fight with Carras two days ago. Bavier caught him around the throat, dug his hands into the flesh, and watched his swarthy face go purple.

"Where is it?" he screamed. He clamped his fingers even tighter and shook Gonzales by the neck so that the back of his head kept banging on the steel decking. "God damn you! Where's my dough?"

At first Gonzales tried to push Bavier's face away with his hands. Then he attempted to rake his fingers across Bavier's eyes. Bavier saw what was happening and instinctively averted his face. Finally the big man felt himself weakening. In a desperate, last-ditch attempt to free himself, he tried to tear Bavier's hand loose, but to no avail. Bavier's hands were as steely as vise grips. All of his overwhelming rage was behind the choking hold.

Gonzales' frightened eyes flashed as he gasped uselessly for air, his throat making harsh noises.

Suddenly Bavier felt a pair of powerful arms around him, pulling him off Gonzales. He spun around angrily. It was Hector Carras.

Bavier's lungs were burning from the exertion of the fight and he swallowed huge mouthfuls of air. "What in hell did you go and do that for?" he demanded in a surly voice. He pointed a trembling finger at Gonzales. "That son-of-a-bitch spic stole my dough."

Carras looked at Bavier calmly and slapped him affectionately on the arm. "Cool it," he said quietly. "The CO's on his way down here. Let's split."

The other men heard it and studiously began busying themselves as if nothing had happened. Bavier glared at Gonzales, who was still sprawled on the floor. He was trying to sit up, his hands tenderly touching his swollen neck. He looked up at Bavier.

"I'm gonna kill you, you yellow-bellied thief," Bavier spat from between his teeth.

"Shut up," Carras said sharply. He pushed Bavier ahead of him through the watertight bulkhead door. "Let's get outta here before we find ourselves in hot water."

Reluctantly Bavier allowed himself to be led away. "I'll kill that son of a bitch if it's the last thing I do," he threatened.

" 'Tenshun!" Carras barked.

Both he and Bavier snapped smartly to attention and saluted as the company commander walked past. The CO returned the salute negligibly and continued walking.

Carras relaxed when they were out of earshot. He pulled Bavier into a corner. "Listen, you dumb-fuck," he hissed angrily. "Don't ever go around spouting your mouth off like that. It ain't healthy, you know? If you want to do something, just go ahead and do it. But quietly. The way things stand now, if something happened to the guy tonight, you'd be the leading suspect."

Bavier stared at Carras. His friend was right. And smart, too. It was "CYA" all over again. That was how the army was run. By making sure you Covered Your Ass. Well, in the future he'd be wiser.

But it turned out that his resolution didn't help much for the time being. The guard-duty roster put Gonzales up on deck for the night shift. When his relief came, he wasn't at his station. Nor did he show up for roll call in the morning. The entire ship was turned inside out, but there was neither hide nor hair to be found of him. The lifeboats and life preservers were counted, but none of them was missing. The dreaded alarm was sounded throughout the ship: Man Overboard! The captain promptly turned the ship around and steamed back in the direction from which they had come. He put the vessel into a pattern of ever-narrowing concentric circles. The sea was searched for four days, and a searchlight played upon the black waters for four nights, but not a trace was found of Luis Gonzales.

Bavier looked upon these four extra days as a blessing. It gave him the opportunity to search everywhere he could think of for his money. A ship of this size had a million crannies where you could hide things. If you didn't know where to start looking, chances were you'd never find it. Sixty thousand dollars can be rolled into a small bundle. And to make matters even worse, the company commander got wind of the fight between him and Gonzales and his threat to kill him. The CO decided to investigate the incident. Luckily for Bavier, it fizzled out almost before it began. He had never been out of sight that fateful night, and he was cleared of any suspicion of wrongdoing. He breathed a sigh of relief. Military justice wasn't at all like civilian justice. You weren't automatically considered innocent until proved guilty. He should have been pleased by the outcome, but he wasn't. By the time the ship docked at the Brooklyn Naval Yard, he still hadn't found his money.

Service friendships aren't long-lasting. When a tour of duty is over, everyone goes his own way. Bavier and Carras said their good-byes and made the usual well-meant promises to look each other up. Both men knew they wouldn't. And unknown to Bavier, Carras got off the ship with a hundred and twenty thousand dollars in his pocket and blood on his hands. No one had even suspected him, least of all Siegfried Bavier. While Carras got himself a suite in the Waldorf-Astoria and renewed his contacts with the Zanmattis, Bavier was wearing out his boot soles searching Brooklyn for a job. Any job.

Finally he managed to find one unloading fish from the trawlers at Sheepshead Bay. He didn't like the job one bit. It was beneath him, and would take him nowhere, but he had no choice. He had to eat.

There were times when he thought he'd never be able to get the stench of fish out of his nostrils. It seemed to follow him wherever he went. And it was grueling, demanding work which sapped a man's energies and paid miserably.

Right before Christmas, he came down with pneumonia. When he was released from the charity ward, he made up his mind. He'd never eat fish again as long as he lived. He wouldn't even set foot in a restaurant that served fish. But more important, he was through with Brooklyn. It was a dead-end place, and no one knew it better than he. He wanted to be in the real New York. In the picture-postcard New York of skyscrapers and clogged streets and noise and lights and excitement. He didn't even return to the rooming house where he'd been living to pick up his clothes and precious few belongings. If he returned, he'd have to pay the back rent. Besides, a new beginning was better done completely from scratch. He bought the only thing he needed to pursue his dream. A subway token. Then he took the BMT across the East River into Manhattan and never looked back.

Manhattan was a whole different world from Brooklyn. A world with a distinctly different set of rules. Bavier's instincts immediately told him that here opportunities awaited those with foresight, intelligence, and ambition. There was an excitement in the air which you couldn't find in Brooklyn. You could feel it wherever you went, uptown or downtown, East Side or West Side.

642

The first thing Bavier did when he got into Manhattan was to walk all day and all night long. He listened, he watched, he smelled, he learned, and he absorbed. When he couldn't stay awake any longer, he boarded the subway and slept sitting upright, riding around within the bowels of the city. After he woke up, he made it his first order of business to look for a place to live. The Lower East Side was cheap, so he went there first. He found a two-room cold-water tenement apartment on Rivington Street.

There were four apartments to each floor, and they shared a common toilet in the hall. The bathtubs were in the kitchens. The stairwell was dimly lit with naked low-wattage bulbs which threw bizarre shadows onto the walls. There was one overpowering smell here which, like the fish at Sheepshead Bay, Bavier could never seem to get out of his nostrils. It was the smell of boiled cabbage and boiling laundry. Then, too, there were the sounds in the building. Not that he minded them, for they covered up the creaking of the building and gave it its mantle of life and dignity. There were the cries of babies and the sounds of families which proved that, despite all the poverty, the cycle of life went on. The languages he heard around him were a strangely exotic mixture of German, Polish, and Yiddish.

He wasn't at all intimidated by the bleak surroundings or the foreign flavor. He looked upon them for what they were —the first rung up the ladder toward success. He was in *Manhattan*, he kept telling himself. It was here, and only here, that opportunity upon opportunity beckoned. And Rivington Street was a symbol. Not only for him, but for all the thousands of others who had flocked here. Many years later when Bavier was rich and living on Sutton Place, he would look fondly back upon Rivington Street as the place where it had all begun. Even as his millions accumulated, he never once lost sight of those humble beginnings. He took an immeasurable pride in having started at the bottom and having made it to the top.

For quite a few years he played with his wealth as a child tends to play with his favorite toys, making and losing several fortunes in the process. Finally he decided that it was time to stop taking chances and put everything on an even financial keel. He bought the penthouse co-op on Sutton Place and tried to break into high society. Even with his wealth, it wasn't easy. You needed a social background as well as money, or at least good manners and a quick wit. Bavier lacked all the social graces, and he was looked upon as being brash and somewhat vulgar. He'd never had the time to acquire polish. He had been too busy working. Now he tried to make up for it. When he bought the penthouse, he hired the services of an interior decorator. He went to an expensive art gallery on Madison Avenue and let them pick out the paintings to hang on his walls. To his untrained eye they looked crude and baffling, as if a demented child had randomly splashed paint on canvas. But he thought that they gave him an instant veneer. It took him a while to discover that they didn't.

With the same misguided intent, he started haunting the best restaurants and nightclubs, only to discover how much he still had to learn. He had bought an off-the-rack tuxedo, and had gone, proud as a peacock, to El Morocco. Since he hadn't known that it was customary to tip the maître d', he had been seated at the worst table in the house. And to add to the insult, he had actually been mistaken for a headwaiter in his store-bought tuxedo. The next day, his lesson learned, he ordered tailor-made suits and tuxedos.

And then he met Z.Z.

Up until he met her, Bavier had very little contact with women. Not that he disliked them. On the contrary, he worshiped them and put them on a pedestal. Quite simply he'd never had the time for them. As a result, most of his relationships so far had been with prostitutes, for he had deemed sex to be as necessary as bathing or eating or brushing his teeth. For him, prostitutes were a convenience: he didn't have to waste any precious time on a relationship. He got what he wanted, and so did they. Then slowly he began to find that these sexual acts just weren't enough. That something vital was lacking. He thought about it and came to the realization that prostitutes mechanically did what was required of them, but no more. And that he now needed more. He was a rich man and it was time he had a woman he could call his own. No, not just a woman. A wife. But one with an acceptable society background, a credit to his wealth. One who could open all those doors that were still locked to him.

He met Z.Z. at a party given by a business associate. As soon as he saw her, he knew he had to have her. His unfailing instincts told him that she was special. That she was unlike any of the women he had ever met so far. He put her on an even higher pedestal than he had put any other. She was beautiful, with shimmering blond hair, a husky, cultured voice, and a graceful way of moving that brought an excitement to his loins such as he had never felt before. She had an aloof coolness about her, and yet he felt he could detect the smoldering passions which lay beneath the surface of her flawless skin. When she brushed against him, he felt a shiver tingling down his spine. Several days later, he proposed to her. She lowered her green eyes demurely and told him that she was flattered but needed more time to think.

Had Bavier known more about the complicated workings of a scheming woman's mind, he would have realized that it was not he who had proposed to Z.Z., but she who had proposed to him. Without his even knowing it, she had baited the hook, dangled it in front of him, and then made him sweat it out before she reeled him in. Bavier took his having to wait as the sure sign of her being a lady. The truth was, Z.Z., who was in her early twenties, had been waiting to get married until she found a man who was rich enough to supply her with what she needed. Then she played her game. As far as sex and love were concerned, they were luxuries she never considered indulging in. What drove her was wealth, which translated into power. And she knew how to play her game. It was one which Bavier didn't even know existed.

In the beginning, theirs seemed a marriage made in heaven. The moment they left St. Patrick's Cathedral as husband and wife, with Z.Z. resplendent in a white gown and veil and both of them ducking to avoid the showers of rice as they sprinted down the steps to the waiting limousine, Bavier was as light-headed as a sweepstakes winner. For the first time in his life, he had someone to shower his affection upon. He was a dutiful husband and he generously let Z.Z. have anything she wanted. A beautiful woman, he rationalized, was born to be spoiled. Besides, she was opening doors to a society he hadn't even known existed. And he was grateful.

It took him a year to discover that the society he had entered was one he would gladly have done without. He didn't like the cocktail parties where he had to stand around talking about the stock market. He preferred to play it. He couldn't stand the interminable, boring dinners, or the Monday nights at the opera. He couldn't care less about Thoroughbred horses or the Kentucky Derby, the Preakness, or polo matches in Palm Beach. He didn't like talking about sailing. He preferred to sail. Slowly his disdain for Z.Z.'s crowd grew deeper and deeper. He despised the shallowness of these people. The constant snide social chitchat. The petty backstabbing and scheming. The gossip. The spiteful glee whenever misery struck someone they knew. And he discovered, to his dismay, that Z.Z. thrived on all these things. She was the most backstabbing, scheming gossiper of them all, and as venomous as the queen of the cobras. When someone wronged her, she inevitably got her revenge tenfold, even if she had to spend months weaving her web. When it came to that, she had the patience of a spider. Bavier became as disenchanted with her as he had with her whole social scene. If it had been possible, he would have washed his hands of the whole affair, but he was trapped. Slowly at first, and then with gathering momentum, he looked for escape whenever he could. He drifted into affairs with other women. He knew that Z.Z. knew. He also knew that as long as Z.Z. thought he was being discreet enough, she didn't care what he did. He could do anything with her blessing as long as it would not compromise her social position or cause her fellow vipers to turn their tongues on her. She even helped push him into his affairs. She found them to be agreeably convenient. As her maids freed her time around the house, so Bavier's mistresses relieved her from certain domestic duties she found distasteful. Slowly Bavier came to the conclusion that his wife hated sex. Not only with him, but with anyone. He got no comfort from the fact that she didn't sleep around. The truth was, he would have preferred that to a libido which had given up the ghost. At first her lack of desire confounded him. In time, he discovered the answer. When he did, he didn't know whether to laugh or cry. Z.Z. was terrified that having sex would leave her looking dissipated and give her hollows around the eyes.

When Bavier took his various mistresses out on the town, they always went to out-of-the-way places. For Z.Z.'s sake, he kept them out of her way.

As far as Z.Z. was concerned, her husband would always come crawling back to her, no matter how far he strayed. And whenever she realized that the gap between herself and her husband had grown a little too wide for comfort, she would play her old game, the one she had snared him with. She would fling out the bait, reel him back in, and devote herself exclusively to him. She would even give herself up to him in bed and pretend to enjoy it. If she thought these little bouts were strengthening their relationship, she was sorely mistaken. On the contrary, these moments of contrition were so predictable that Bavier could even forecast their longevity to the day. They never lasted longer than a week. After that, Z.Z. would be climbing the walls and things would invariably return to the way they had been.

Had Z.Z. taken the time to analyze their relationship more carefully, she would have been aware of how truly precarious it had become. But she honestly had no idea how weary her husband had actually grown of her. She would never have believed that he needed someone more stimulating than herself.

In Hélène he found everything that was missing in Z.Z., and much more. Hélène possessed the exact qualities for which he had been unconsciously searching in a woman. She was entirely feminine, but in matters of business she was practical and thought like a man. Whereas his occasional crude manners and salty figures of speech embarrassed Z.Z., Hélène just naturally accepted them. She saw Bavier for what he was. A giant among men, but a kind giant. In many ways, he reminded her of Edmond. She felt she could rely on him in any circumstance. And be totally protected. But even more important, she truly loved Siegfried Bavier. In business, he was feared, and his lack of compassion toward anyone's interests except his own was legend. Hélène knew that that side of him existed, but she never saw it. Her Siegfried was kind and gentle, lusty, earthy, and spirited.

After the tugboats nudged the SS *United States* against the West Side pier, Hélène and Bavier parted company, but not for long. They ended up seeing each other nearly every day, even if they could snatch only a few precious minutes at a time out of their busy schedules. Neither of them minded this inconvenience. They respected each other's priorities and needs. Just having met each other seemed to have spurred them both on to new ambitions. Bavier was putting together a diversified investment package while Hélène rented two floors high up in the RCA Building in Rockefeller Center. She was setting up the American edition of *Les Modes*. Not only that, but she had come to a major decision which was to change her life. She loved New York. She loved its vitality, its larger-than-life glamour. She loved the frenzied creativity. But above all, she loved Bavier, and he loved her. Under the circumstances, it only made sense to stay here and move her headquarters over from Paris. The European editions would be put under a new umbrella: Hélène Junot International, Inc.

HJII was born.

For the first time in ages, Bavier felt like his old self. The weariness that had come over him after being saddled with Z.Z. had suddenly dropped away. Just knowing that Hélène was around seemed to be enough. It caused him to thrive as never before. For some strange reason, he and Hélène gave each other even more drive than either of them had ever had on their own. He sent his mistresses packing and worked himself to a frenzy.

Two months later, he met with Z.Z. and her lawyers to arrange for a quick divorce. Z.Z. took the news quietly, without undue concern. She didn't even try to put up a fight. She was certain that Bavier and Hélène were doomed. She began getting concerned only after he and Hélène got married in a quiet civil ceremony. Still, her concern was limited. Sigi would come crawling back. She was sure of it. All she had to do was reel him back in.

Edmond and Petite Hélène flew in from Paris for the marriage ceremony. Afterward Hélène and Bavier moved into the twelve-room co-op apartment they'd bought. It was on Fifth Avenue at Sixty-sixth Street and overlooked Central Park. Bavier never told her what getting his freedom from Z.Z. had cost him. Seven million dollars, the house in the Hamptons, the Sutton Place penthouse, the four-million-dollar art collection, and the priceless antiques. He thought the exchange well worth it. After all, he had a knack for making money. He'd make up for the losses in no time.

Nor did he tell Hélène that Z.Z. was pregnant. That news had caught him totally unawares, but he didn't let it influence his decision. Nor had he wanted it to influence Hélène's. Besides, the baby would pose no problem because Z.Z. had sworn she would get an abortion. Under the circumstances, it was the best solution.

What Bavier never knew was that Z.Z. decided against having the abortion. She was going to have the baby and try to use it for leverage to win him back. Not for himself, but so that no one else would have him.

And Z.Z. had made up her mind about one more thing. Already she was patiently beginning to spin her web.

Given time, she would destroy Hélène Junot.

11

Bavier and Hélène honeymooned in Acapulco for a week. The days flew by so fast that it seemed as if they had just arrived when they had to pack their bags and leave again. Like it or not, they had to get back to New York. Both of them had pressing business awaiting. But even after they returned, Bavier made certain that the honeymoon did not come to an end. He constantly showered Hélène with gifts. The first week after their return he gave her a small but exquisite Utrillo painting depicting a Parisian street scene. The next week came the square-cut eighteen-carat emerald from Harry Winston, which she refused to take off her finger even when she went to sleep. And finally, in the third week there was the pièce de résistance. The gleaming white 135-foot Feadship motor yacht which they christened the *Petite H*. It had cost six million dollars and carried a permanent crew of ten. It boasted three salons, a small discotheque, two speedboats, a master suite on deck, and four guest staterooms below. Bavier had had the yacht brought up from the broker's in Fort Lauderdale to the Seventy-ninth Street marina. After he and Hélène cruised around Manhattan on it in the moonlight, he instructed the captain to sail it on to Spain without them. They decided to keep it moored in Barcelona, planning to use it for vacations.

Unfortunately, there were to be no vacations. Fate played a cruel trick, and within weeks of their marriage, Siegfried Bavier dropped dead on the floor of the New York Stock Exchange. The doctor said it was caused by an aneurysm in the brain. Hélène was too numb to understand any of it, and she took little comfort in the fact that it could never have been detected in a checkup. Once again, it seemed that her happiness had reached its peak only to be flung back down into the ashes.

Bavier's death made headlines in *The Wall Street Journal*

and in the business section of the New York *Times*. The funeral was held at Campbell's on Madison Avenue. The chapel was packed with businessmen who had come to pay their last respects. When Bavier died, so had one of the last great gamblers on Wall Street. Hélène wished she knew who some of these people were, but most of them were strangers. She sat through the eulogy with a stony expression. The tears would come later. She didn't want to have to share them with strangers. Least of all with Z. Z. Bavier, who sat in the row behind her. It was Z.Z., she thought bitterly, who seemed to know everyone present. And who was receiving the condolences meant for the wife.

In his best boardroom voice, the president of a Fortune 500 corporation droned on and on about Bavier's merits and achievements. Hélène listened raptly, but not a single word penetrated her shroud of pain. All she could think about was the morning Bavier left to go to work for the last time. She had never seem him healthier or happier.

When the service concluded, she walked slowly out of the chapel, every step a special effort. She probably would never have made it past the third aisle if it hadn't been for Edmond and Petite Hélène. Holding her arms tightly, they somehow managed to propel her forward. Then suddenly her step faltered as she found herself unexpectedly face to face with Nigel Somerset. He had stepped quickly out from one of the aisles and was standing in front of her. She stopped walking and returned his stare. Her knees went weak and she could feel them shaking. Somehow she managed to keep her face composed. She didn't want to see Nigel. Not at a time like this. Or at any other, for that matter. What had once been between them was over, and she had no desire to start any relationship anew. But she couldn't turn her back on him, either. He had flown all the way from England for the funeral, and propriety, if nothing else, demanded she exchange a few words.

She turned to Edmond and Petite Hélène. "I'll see you outside," she said awkwardly.

"Will you be all right?" Edmond asked.

She nodded wordlessly and watched them leave. Then she turned back to Nigel. She was unaware of the businessmen filing out into the sunshine. All she could do was stare into Nigel's gold-flecked eyes. She felt the way she had at Auteuil when she had unexpectedly run into him. As had happened then, words seemed to fail her now.

"I'm terribly sorry about your husband," Nigel said.

"Thank you, Nigel," she said in a stiff, husky voice. "I'm so glad you came."

But she wished he hadn't. Just seeing him only seemed to reopen all the old wounds. Was it possible that they had never healed completely?

She looked down, and her face contorted in a pained expression, but when she looked back up at him, it was once again serene. Only she knew what an emotional toll that stoic mask cost her.

"I too am sorry, Nigel," she said politely. "I read about your mother's death last month. I'm afraid I didn't send any flowers . . ."

He looked at her gently. "I can't say that I blame you. On her deathbed she told me how she chased you from Fallsworth. You must believe me . . . I never knew."

"I believe you."

"I know you'll find little comfort in it, but in the end Mother realized she had done the wrong thing by forcing me to marry Pamela. She admitted it. She didn't often admit to her mistakes."

Hélène nodded numbly. Pamela. She remembered the pictures she had seen of Lady Pamela Grey, the woman who, instead of her, had become the sixteenth Duchess of Farquharshire. So she had been right. Nigel's mother had arranged it all. But that came as no surprise. In her heart, she had known it all along. Now the Duchess was dead, but the deed lived on after her.

"I should never have married Pamela," Nigel was saying softly. "I never loved her. Nor she me. Her parents forced her into it. And now . . ." His voice trailed off.

Hélène looked at him pityingly.

Nigel turned away. "Neither of us loves the other," he murmured. "The marriage is a sham." He took a deep breath and she could feel the pain that emanated from within him. "Unfortunately, a divorce is out of the question." He smiled grimly. "Social situation and all, you know."

Hélène reached out and touched the side of his face with her fingertips. "I'm sorry Nigel. It must be very hard on you."

He sighed and placed his hand atop hers, pressing it firmly

to his cheek. "Darling, I know this isn't the time or the place." He quickly looked around, lowered his voice to a discreet whisper, and stared into her eyes. "But I'd like to see you—"

Hélène took a step back. She had to look away so she wouldn't be drawn to his eyes. "I . . . I don't know, Nigel," she stammered, unsure of herself. "I'm sorry. It's just too soon. I need time to think about it . . ." Her voice cracked. And without another word, she turned on her heel and fled Nigel and the chapel and the stifling smell of chrysanthemums.

Two days later, unknown to Hélène, Jacques sold his HJII shares to Z. Z. Bavier and Marcello d'Itri.

12

The saying is true: time heals all wounds. And in time, although it seemed to her a very long time, Hélène's life returned to normal. Unquestionably she felt the unfairness of fate, the unfairness which gave her so much but relentlessly took from her its purest joys. However, she knew that with the help of Edmond and Petite Hélène, her family, she would be able to continue on, nourishing her dream. And now her dream had brought her to Venice,

It was after eleven o'clock at night by the time the last workman picked up his toolbox and left. Hélène saw him to the door and watched him getting into the waiting motorboat. As it surged away down the moonlit Grand Canal, she pushed on the massive carved double doors of the palazzo. Slowly they clanged shut with an echo of finality. Then everything was quiet save for the water lapping against the doorstep outside.

For a long moment she closed her eyes and leaned wearily back against one of the doors. She was dressed in a man's plaid shirt which she hadn't bothered to tuck into her faded

Levi's, her hair was pulled back from her face by a white silk bandanna, and on her feet were white tennis shoes.

With the back of her wrist she wiped the perspiration off her forehead. She heaved a sigh of relief. Little by little, she could feel her body starting to relax as her adrenaline slowed down. At last, everything was finished. And not a moment too soon, either. The party was tomorrow.

Had she anticipated at the outset what she was up against, she would gladly have left everything to the Czarina. But for once she'd insisted on organizing a party by herself. She had thought the occasion too important to trust to anyone. Even Luba. She laughed softly to herself. To date, except for holding intimate dinner parties, the biggest problem had always been what to wear to someone else's party, and then standing for hours in the stuffy ateliers while the couturiers and fitters tugged here, tucked there, pinned, stitched, hemmed, and re-hemmed in order to get her gown just right. While she had been a model, she hadn't minded all that standing around: it had been part of the job. Now she found it tedious and nerve-racking. But that was nothing compared to the two months of planning and hard work she'd just been through.

Once again she shook her head in disbelief. The biggest, most ambitious party she'd ever planned, and she'd expected to do it all herself! What a fool she had been. But who would have thought so much work was involved? Even trying to locate the help—florists, waiters, butlers, caterers, cleanup crews, orchestra, rock band, kitchen help . . . the list seemed endless—had been a mind-boggling job. Hiring those who seemed the most capable and then trying to explain to them just what was needed had been a nightmare. If one of her experienced friends hadn't come to the rescue, she would have had no choice but to cancel the affair. Well, she'd learned one lesson from this that she would never forget. In the future, she would spare herself these headaches and hire a professional coordinator. Even her fluent Italian, which she had been relying on so heavily, hadn't done her a bit of good. Venice was different from Milan, she'd discovered almost too late. Things were slower here. Less cosmopolitan, less efficient. Knowing the language just wasn't enough. You had to know the mentality of the locals you dealt with as well.

The problems had begun with the location, hunting for the appropriate—and available—palace in which to hold the party. Party, hell, she corrected herself. The ball. The Golden Ball.

From the beginning, she had envisioned it being held in Venice. As far as she was concerned, no place else could come close. Not for the splendor she had in mind.

Fine.

And at first it had all seemed so effortless. Even Peggy Guggenheim, when she'd heard that Hélène was in town searching for a palace, had generously stepped forward and offered her the loan of her own massive Palazzo Venier dei Leoni. This extraordinary palace was on the prestigious Grand Canal. An additional wing had been built on one side of the garden to house Peggy's world-famous collection of modern art. The Palazzo Venier dei Leoni was indeed one of the cultural highlights of Venice, but Hélène had politely refused the kind offer. Somehow, just the idea of a modern-art collection reposing under the same roof where the Golden Ball was being held took away from the magic of the ancient Venice that she was trying to recapture. Not only that, but she didn't want to be responsible for a magnificent home filled with millions of dollars' worth of museum-quality treasures while three thousand guests milled around in it. Besides, the type of place she wanted for the ball was one of those huge crumbling old palazzos whose rooms looked like gilded bird cages. Inside and out, except for the plumbing, it had to be unchanged since the time of Canaletto. She had discovered, to her delight, that many of those were available. So far, so good. An old, dilapidated palazzo should pose no problems. They were white elephants as far as everyone was concerned; many of them were up for sale. But for rent?

"Yes, for rent also," the real-estate brokers had assured her smoothly.

Then, when they had heard her out: "But surely not for such a short time, signorina!" they wailed, throwing up their hands in despair. "And certainly not for one party! Please, be *reasonable*!"

Finally she found an agent who was willing to accede to her terms. He showed her one palazzo after another. After inspecting nine of them, she found one she was crazy about.

It was enormous, situated halfway between the Rialto Bridge and the mouth of the Grand Canal. It had everything she had hoped for, and more. There were several tall, skinny pillars at the entrance where gondolas and speedboats could tie up by the marble threshold. Once inside, there was a baronial hallway with a sweeping staircase and decaying but splendid sixteenth-century murals attributed to Tintoretto. And when the agent had pushed open a pair of heroically scaled doors, Hélène caught her breath.

In front of her stretched the biggest ballroom she'd ever imagined. She entered slowly, hardly daring to trust her eyes. That one damp room alone was two stories high and took up almost the entire first floor. Between the marble pilasters, the walls were painted with peeling Byzantine-style murals. She leaned her head way back and stared up at the groin-vaulted ceiling. It was a heaven of rich, patinaed blue liberally sprinkled with gold-leaf stars. Her heart began to pound with the heady thrill of the discovery. This was *it!* This huge, forgotten room was the perfect setting for her Golden Ball. She could already visualize it. With the chandeliers lit, the gleaming gold stars would pick up the glow and actually look as if they were winking in the night above. With an orchestra in one corner and a discotheque set up in one of the other rooms, with buffet tables laden with feasts, with real gold dust captured in carved ice sculptures, with hundreds of magnums of Dom Perignon flowing freely, with three thousand guests resplendent in gold costumes, with all this, and more, the hollow emptiness of the palazzo would come to life as never before in its five-hundred-year history.

The agent watched Hélène as she walked slowly around the dim room, studying, absorbing, calculating, inspecting, and planning, the little wheels in her mind turning swiftly and clicking with the speed of an automatic shutter. Finally she marched determinedly over to him. Her voice was businesslike and brusque. "Whom do I see about signing a short-term lease?" she asked. "You or the owners?"

A week later, the gold-engraved invitations went out. Around the world their destinations were the international jet-setters, film stars, celebrities, and the socialites who set the trends for the times. The ball was scheduled to be held in six weeks. Hélène figured that would give everyone just enough time to rush to Paris, knocking each other down in their scramble to be the first one at the couturiers'. It was always that way whenever there was a theme party.

Yes, Paris was going to be humming, Hélène thought with satisfaction. There would be a run on gold fabric, on gold lamé, on gold lace, and on gold thread. Tempers were going to fray and Givenchy would rake in a fortune. Ilias Lalaounis, more than anyone, was going to do a brisk business selling jewelry, since they specialized in gold. Because for the Golden Ball, gold costumes were de rigueur. Without one, it wouldn't matter who you were: invitation in hand or not, entrance to the palazzo would be strictly forbidden.

Hélène smiled to herself. Yves St. Laurent had finished Hélène's own gold costume over two months ago. She, the hostess, had the jump on everyone. Including the press coverage of her ball. At this very moment, Luba was carefully leaking news of the ball to selected reporters and paparazzi, but only a handful were actually being invited to cover the occasion from within.

Now came the second step. Hélène realized that it was already high time to start decorating the ballroom, that what she had in mind would take weeks. The palazzo was bare. Furniture would have to be found and brought in. And above all, the ballroom would have to be turned into the most festive, gilded fairyland imaginable. She envisioned everything in gold. Gold festoons, gold buffet tables, gold chairs. What she needed now was someone who could interpret her ideas and make them into a happy reality. The Golden Ball had to be one of those elusive fantasies that never would, never could, ever be repeated. She needed someone who was more than just an interior decorator or a stage designer. She needed, in short, a magician.

She sat down behind the ornate desk in her suite at the Hotel Danieli and scooted her chair forward. From the top drawer she took out a blank sheet of the hotel's stationery and put it down in front of her. Thoughtfully she picked up her pen and started to draw up a list of the best interior decorators she knew of in both Europe and America. Of course, whoever she picked would be exorbitantly expensive for one fleeting night only. But for this occasion, monumental extravagance was called for. Besides, what was more extravagant than the new product she was about to launch? A perfume worth its exact weight in gold. That was why she was throwing this ball in the first place. To draw attention to d'Or. The more lavish the ball, the more talked and written about d'Or would be. Word that a new, instant status symbol was available would swiftly spread down from the socialites and media to the uninvited masses. It was all perfectly timed with the massive, coordinated advertising blitz which was in readiness. The day after the ball, the ads would flood the market.

D'Or.

Hélène knew that whatever she spent now would be well spent. Would help seal d'Or's success. There were some things you couldn't scrimp on.

When she finished making her list of decorators, she went over each name carefully.

Impatiently she drummed her lacquered fingernails on the desk as her eyes scanned the list. Each had his or her own trademark, but none seemed to match d'Or. Could there really be so *many* designers? Would none of them do?

She let out a sigh, placed her elbows on the desk, and wearily rested her chin on her balled-up hands. For a moment she just sat hunched there like that. Then suddenly the idea surged up inside her from out of the blue.

Of course! Why hadn't she thought of it before? Her friend Yvette, with whom she'd worked the hat-check at the Folies de Babylon so many years ago, had become an enormously successful restaurateur and nightclub owner. Hélène had been as surprised by Yvette's success as Yvette had been by Hélène's.

Yes! Yvette was the perfect person to organize the ball! Hands down, she was acknowledged to be the world's most gifted party-giver. She would know exactly who was capable of decorating the ballroom. Who was the best caterer. What needed organizing and what didn't. Just hearing the magic name "Yvette" would be enough to set a fire under the locals. Especially if they thought there was a possibility that an Yvette's club might open in Venice. That would mean long and steady employment at good wages. Hélène wouldn't tell them that, of course. The name alone would be enough to get them jumping to conclusions. What they chose to believe wouldn't hurt her.

There was only one foreseeable problem. Would Yvette be able to spare the time to help her? After all, she was an extremely busy woman with all those worldwide clubs to run. Hélène stared at the telephone. There was only one way to find out. She reached for the telephone and placed a call to Yvette's International in Paris. That particular luxurious club on the rue Princesse had been the first of the clubs and had since become the headquarters of the entire chain.

An hour later, Hélène was chiding herself; she should have known better than to think it would be this simple. Yvette wasn't to be found at the Paris club. Nor in Monte Carlo, London, Rio de Janeiro, New York, Berlin, Sydney, Hong Kong, or Singapore. In fact, nobody had the least idea where she might be reached. At first Hélène was baffled by this discovery, but then she quickly saw the wisdom of it. By keeping everyone uninformed as to her schedule, Yvette could swoop down on any one of her clubs without advance warning, thereby forcing her employees to stay constantly on their toes. All Hélène was able to do was to leave a message for her at each of the clubs.

Finally at eight o'clock Venice time it was Yvette who called Hélène from Singapore, where it was the middle of the night. Yvette did not waste her nights sleeping. It was during the days while her clubs were closed that she slept on airplanes while flying from one of them to the next. She was a true night owl, and wide-awake now.

Her breathless, throaty voice bubbled in Hélène's ear. "Oh chérie, of *course* I'd be only too happy to help you out! Together we will see to it that it's the party of the year. No, not the year. The *decade*. Oh, it'll be *sublime*. I can't wait to get started on it. . . . Don't be foolish, I wouldn't dream of accepting a sou. I have enough money, and whatever are friends for, anyway? We'll get along splendidly, I just know it. We always did." From the depths of her throat came the laughter of the memories they had shared. "For as long as I live, I'll never be able to forget that time you blew the whistle on Jocelyne. You were the only person who ever had the guts to do anything about that bitch! Oh, by the way, did you know she's working the *streets* now as a twenty-franc hooker? I ran into her in the Pigalle last year and I almost didn't recognize her. All ugly and bloated like you wouldn't believe. Real down and out, let me tell you. It's really hilarious, though. She actually propositioned me. Took me for a dyke! Can you believe it? Me? A dyke?" More throaty laughter. "Anyway . . . *What? A Golden* Ball? Ooooh, I can see it already. How delicious! And the waiters and bouncers—at an affair like that you've simply *got* to have a squad of bouncers, believe me. . . . Why? There are bound to be party crashers and paparazzi and horrible drunks, that's why. Well, as I was saying, the waiters and the bouncers can be half *naked* and wear nothing but gold paint and bull's masks.

Isn't that marvelous? Oh, loincloths too, it goes without saying. We wouldn't want to get raided, would we? Listen, I repeat, you're *not* imposing. It's the most exciting thing I've heard about in ages! Why didn't *I* think of a Golden Ball? Never mind. . . . No, I haven't gotten my invitation yet. You sent it where? To Paris? Then *that* explains it. I've been traveling for nearly two solid weeks now and nobody in Paris knows where I am. . . . Oh, don't thank *me*. *You're* the one who saved *my* life. I can't wait to hop on the next flight out of here. It's so steamy, and the mosquitoes are deadly. I think they diet while I'm gone and lie in wait to feast on me when I return. . . . I'll call you the moment I get to Venice, I promise! A bientôt!"

Now the palazzo was silent as Hélène pushed open the massive carved doors to the ballroom. Suddenly the glare of all that gold hit her in the eyes. Instinctively she threw up a hand to shield herself against it. Except for the candles, which would be lit tomorrow evening, all the lights were on.

As in a daze, she walked slowly around the room. It was unbelievable—Yvette had truly outdone herself. The ancient ballroom was everything she herself had envisioned, and more. Much more.

With military precision, carved gilt ballroom chairs lined the walls. They were upholstered in a dark blue muslin which, like the ceiling above, was hand-painted with gold stars. The Byzantine murals on the walls were completely hidden by gold-veined mirrors that reflected—and refracted —everything over and over to minuscule infinity. The cold, dark marble floor was covered with a thick sea of tiny wafer-thin gold-foil stars that scattered and danced and swirled around your feet as you walked through them.

Hélène could feel a powerful surge of satisfaction, of having set a goal and then having surpassed it beyond even her own wildest imaginings. It would indeed be the party of the decade, she thought. And it was tax-deductible, for it was heralding the new d'Itri perfume. The perfume which she and Luba had helped the chemists in Grasse to create, and which would be sold only through the d'Itri boutiques and a select number of the world's most exclusive shops starting the day after tomorrow. Already, each of these shops had a special booth set up in the cosmetics departments. Each booth was hooked up to a central computer. Day by day and hour by hour, d'Or's price per ounce, per precious fraction of a fluid ounce, would fluctuate with the price of gold on the international market.

Her eyes rested now on the tall Lucite pedestal which stood in the very center of the room. On top of it was the enormous thirty-gallon crystal bottle of d'Or. Tomorrow, at the height of the ball, Marcello d'Itri would unveil it to a fanfare accompaniment. Each guest would receive one of the half-ounce sizes as a gift. Precious contents aside, even the bottles themselves were valuable and bound to become collectors' items. They were made of hand-cut Lalique crystal. The caps were miniature bars of bullion imprinted with the d'Or logo and the exact fraction of a gram of the real gold used in the plating.

Hélène sank down onto one of the ballroom chairs. Was it possible that all the work was finally finished? That everything for the twenty-eight hundred guests who had accepted was in readiness? Yes, it was possible, she told herself firmly. All the fatigue she now felt told her so. But worn out though she was, she'd take a Dalmane before she went to bed. Tonight, a sleeping pill wouldn't hurt. She needed to get a good night's rest. She'd have to be up early and look her absolute best. This was one occasion when having hollow circles around the eyes just wouldn't do.

She sighed. Morning would begin a gruelingly long day and an endless night. It would start at ten A.M. when a seamstress from Yves St. Laurent was arriving by train, just in case her gown needed some last-minute adjustments or she'd happened to put on a few pounds.

Wearily she closed her eyes. The seamstress wasn't all she had to contend with tomorrow. Alexandre himself would be flying in from Paris at one-thirty to do her hair. And at five, Pablo was arriving from Elizabeth Arden's in New York. He was going to paint her eyes to look like an African butterfly in flight, with ostrich-feather antennae as eyebrows and tiny glued-on canary-diamond tears. And she had to have a last-minute talk with Scavullo. She had hired him to take pictures of the ball for *Les Modes*.

Hélène let out a deep breath. She opened her eyes and shook her head as the staggering schedule sank in. There wasn't a moment to waste.

Before the Golden Ball was even in full swing, word had it that Venice would never see another occasion quite like it. It eclipsed even the Black-and-White Ball that had caused such a furor a few years earlier. Throughout the evening Hélène was everywhere, seeing to it that everyone was greeted, that each guest got just the right amount of personal attention, and that the proper introductions were made. She knew that ultimately it was up to her, the hostess, to see that it would indeed turn out to be the party of the season. She noted, with some satisfaction, that it was certainly beginning to look that way.

Never a big partygoer herself, she suddenly found herself enjoying this one immensely. Without a doubt, she was its star. Her shimmering gown was almost translucent except for its molded gold breast plates. The floor-length hand-painted African butterfly sleeves matched her extraordinarily made-up eyes to perfection. Each time she spread her arms, it was as if she were spreading her wings, ready to take flight. It was clear that of all the costumes, it was hers that was the most original, the most photographed, and the most envied. Yet it never failed to amaze her to what extraordinary lengths the celebrities she had invited had gone to when it came to their costumes. Each one had tried to outdo the other. There were gleaming belts of clinking gold coins, several knights in gold-sprayed armor, necklaces of nuggets, gowns of mesh and coins. The Vicomtesse de Sévigné stole the show as far as arriving in style went. Dressed as an Aztec idol, she had come floating lazily down the Grand Canal on a golden barge she had commandeered from somewhere, no one knew quite where. Not to be outdone, the Czarina wore an antique Florentine ball gown that had once belonged to one of the Medicis. It was sewn and embroidered with gold thread and trimmed with layers of soft gold lace. The train was so long and heavy that it required the services of two gold-clad midgets to hold it up all evening. A gold-costumed monkey (rented from some enterprising organ-grinder, Hélène thought) perched on Luba's shoulder, fascinated with the Czarina's latest trademark—gold Yves Tanguy earrings she had taken to wearing constantly.

As Hélène went past the buffet tables lining the hallway, she slowed down and paused for a moment to appreciate the scene. Gold-liveried servants stood behind the tables serving the hungry guests who were lined up, gold plates in hand. She managed to get a glimpse of the food. It looked even more delicious than it smelled. Once again, she mentally gave thanks to Yvette, at the same time marveling at how it had all been achieved in time, and how the platters of food could be so fresh. Even with the heat generated by the lights and the guests, all the food down to the last sprig of parsley looked bright and unwilted.

She made a left turn and glanced toward the front doors and the floodlit waters of the Grand Canal outside. The entrance was well guarded by the four gold-painted bodyguards hired by Yvette. Past them, outside the open doors, she could see more guests arriving. The armada of paparazzi was so thick that it was practically impossible for the guests to pull up in their gondolas and speedboats. Incessant flashbulbs popped blinding white lightning as the guests' boats carefully maneuvered to the floodlit palazzo entrance.

Hélène lifted her wrist and glanced at her gold watch. Nearly eleven o'clock. In half an hour, Nigel was due to arrive. She permitted herself a smile of eager anticipation. Nigel. It was comforting to know that he would soon be here beside her, dancing, laughing, holding her in his arms. Just his presence would be enough to make everything else about the ball pale. When he arrived, she would be waiting for him here, near the entrance. But in the meantime, she would make a few more rounds to make sure that everything was in order.

14

At eleven-twenty Hélène decided to go back out to the entrance hall and wait there for Nigel. It wouldn't be long now, she told herself with growing excitement, and then he'd be standing here beside her. Ten minutes at the most, if he was punctual.

She had nearly reached the ballroom doors when she caught her breath. Nigel was already standing in the doorway. Dressed in a gold satin tunic and matching breeches, he looked like a grown-up Gainsborough that had just stepped out of its massive gold frame. A breeze swept through the hallway behind him and caught his hair, fluttering through it as he looked around at the mass of golden people. His eyes were searching.

For her, she knew. She straightened. She could almost reach out and feel his anticipation, his disappointment that she wasn't there at the door waiting for him. She felt a surge of pride. He looked so dashing, so handsome.

He was about to step forward; then he checked himself. She realized at once why. He was afraid he'd get lost in the crowds. With this many people, chances were they could pass each other a dozen times without realizing it.

Hélène balanced herself on tiptoe, lifted her arm, and waved. After a moment she caught Nigel's eye. He smiled and swiftly strode toward her.

She threaded her way around some waltzing couples and then ran toward Nigel, throwing herself into his arms.

"For a moment I was afraid I wouldn't find you," he said. "You should have exercised the hostess's prerogative and worn red or white so that you'd stand out."

Z. Z. Bavier couldn't remember just how it had happened, but she and Hubert de Léger had become friends. Well, if not exactly friends, then at least fast comrades-in-arms. It didn't really surprise her. After all, they had a mutual bond. Both of them hated Hélène Junot, although neither would divulge his reasons to the other. And both of them shared the same goal: to destroy her. Yet Z.Z. found herself enjoying every moment she spent with Hubert. With her, he was always polite, always the perfect, charming gentleman, the worldly Comte de Léger. His title was ancient, his manners continental. She had never had a chance to see that other, terrible, childish side of him. But Z.Z. sensed a turmoil boiling within him that he kept well to himself. It always seemed to be lurking just beneath the surface, ready to erupt without warning. She knew that it had something to do with Hélène Junot, and it fascinated her. She only wished she knew what it was.

Hubert had never given Z.Z. much serious thought, but he, too, was surprised. He liked being in her company. He appreciated her biting wit, her sharply honed razor tongue, her ever-ready sense of adventure. It was as if the two of them had been made for each other. But they both instinctively knew that they were too much alike ever to sustain any deep relationship. That was their strength. They did not get emotionally involved with each other. Instead, they kept their mutual goal well in sight.

In silence now they floated down the Grand Canal in the gondola. They sat side by side on the red velvet seat, each immersed in his own thoughts, oblivious of the gondolier at the rear, who expertly paddled the thin, sleek craft through the water.

Z.Z. leaned forward and fished the single red tea rose out of the crystal bud vase attached to the gunwales. She sat back and brought the rose up to her face until her nose was buried in the petals. Then languidly she began tearing the petals off one by one and tossing them into the canal. Another hundred yards to go and they would reach the Palazzo Daniela Donatella, she thought with satisfaction. Another hundred yards . . .

Suddenly she felt the sharp sting of a thorn in her flesh. Angrily she tossed the remainder of the rose overboard and licked the blood off her finger. She stared fixedly ahead through her narrowed eyes and focused her thoughts on Hélène. On the woman who had stolen her husband and left her to deal with her son, Wilfred, alone. She wondered how Hélène would react to her and Hubert appearing at the ball, since they hadn't been invited. She smiled, thanking God that her friend Betty Lindenbaum had come down sick and had let herself be talked into giving Z.Z. her invitation. Poor Betty. After tonight, she probably wouldn't receive another invitation from Hélène Junot for as long as she lived.

With rising anticipation, Z.Z. glanced now at the ancient palazzos as they drifted slowly past. Most of them were dark, their windows shuttered. It was close to midnight.

Suddenly she was aware of Hubert's eyes on her and she turned to him. He nudged her and pointed straight ahead. She sat forward and caught her breath. The Palazzo Daniela Donatella was just coming into view beyond the curve, floodlighted like something out of a Hollywood premiere. Z.Z. couldn't believe her eyes. Every window and cornice caught the light; even the outside had been decorated with festive garlands of gold. And the paparazzi—they must number at least a hundred! she thought as she saw the masses of little craft bobbing dangerously in the water in front of the palazzo.

She took a deep breath. "We're almost there," she said, settling back in the seat. Her long tapered fingers impatiently tapped the legs of her gold-lamé tuxedo. She turned to Hubert, her eyes challenging. "How do you think she'll react to your costume?"

He shrugged. "With Hélène, you can never tell."

"I think I can." Z.Z. smiled wickedly. "I can't *wait* to see her face when you take off your coat!" She let out a hoarse laugh of satisfaction as she reached over and traced a gold-lacquered fingertip down the side of his gilded leather coat. "This is one thing the imperturbable Hélène Junot hasn't bargained for!"

At exactly midnight, the lights in the ballroom flickered and then went out. For a moment there was total darkness. As if someone had thrown a master switch, the music, talking, and laughter subsided.

Suddenly there was a dramatic roll of drums and a single spotlight clicked on overhead. Marcello d'Itri, in a woven gold tuxedo, was standing at the foot of the draped pedestal beside Hélène. Slowly the guests drew closer around them.

Hélène looked around at the shadows of the people encircling her and Marcello. She could sense their curiosity. They were waiting expectantly.

She clasped her hands in front of her, cleared her throat,

and smiled. "My dear friends," she announced in a loud voice that rang out clearly and echoed from the vaulted ceiling. "Surely you are all aware that the theme of this ball is 'Gold.' This theme has not been chosen on a whim. There is a purpose behind it. It gives me pleasure to announce that my friend Marcello d'Itri"—she turned and curtsied graciously to him, and he returned it with a solemn bow— "has created a new and lavish addition to his already superb line of clothing and accessories. This new addition to the line is far more ethereal, and appeals far more to the senses than anything his genius has created thus far." She stopped and looked at Marcello. Their eyes met again. She smiled and nodded.

Marcello d'Itri took a step backward and reached for a corner of the gold cloth that draped the pedestal.

"Ladies and gentlemen!" d'Itri announced. "May I present . . . d'Or!"

There was another drumroll and Marcello tugged on the cloth. In fluid slow motion it began to glide to the floor. All eyes were raised to the enormous cut-crystal bottle with the gold-bullion cap. The facets of the crystal caught the spotlight and flashed fire in all directions, the liquid inside it glowing a deep rich gold. There was a roar of applause.

Marcello stepped forward. "Ladies and gentlemen. In a moment, the waiters will circulate to give each of you a half-ounce bottle. Need I say this is not such a small token?" He paused. "For the price of d'Or, ounce by ounce, is the price of gold on the international market!"

He stopped and bowed again. There was more enthusiastic applause and the spotlight went out. Immediately the chandeliers clicked back on and the music and excited talk started up as before. As quickly as the first notes of the fox trot had begun, they now faded, and the conversation died quickly until the ballroom was silent. People began turning around, craning their necks and standing on tiptoe to see what was happening.

Hélène had been heading toward Nigel. Now she looked around with a puzzled expression. Something was wrong. She could feel the tension in the air. But what was it? What could have happened?

Not losing a moment, she fought her way through the crowd, Nigel following behind her.

When she neared the doors, Hélène's steps faltered. She

came to a standstill, her face white with shock, and she began to tremble.

Hubert de Léger and Z.Z. Bavier stood there smiling, facing everyone. Their eyes were challenging.

It was not the fact that they had crashed the ball which caused the anger to constrict Hélène's heart. It was Hubert's costume.

Slung casually over his arm was a gilded leather coat, and set on his head at a jaunty angle was a visored golden cap. An SS cap. *He was in head-to-toe uniform. A golden Nazi uniform that flashed and gleamed obscenely beautiful.*

As if she had been struck, Hélène caught the nearest person's arm and grabbed hold of it as the ballroom suddenly reeled around her. She closed her eyes. Then she felt firm fingers pushing her into yet someone else's arms. She had been clutching Luba.

Hélène opened her eyes and shook her head like a dazed prizefighter. She barely realized that she was now in Nigel's arms.

She was shaking like a leaf. How dare Hubert come in that getup! Didn't he know that nothing repulsed her more? That nothing repulsed any of the people gathered here more? It was clear that he was trying to ruin the ball. Ruin her.

But that wasn't the worst of it. The worst were the memories that suddenly sprang up in front of her. The terrible things she'd suffered as a child at the hands of the Nazis.

Suddenly a set of footsteps rang out clearly. She lifted her head and turned slightly to the right. Luba was marching up to Hubert, the midgets holding up her heavy train hurrying bowleggedly to keep up.

Luba came to a stop in front of Hubert. For a long tense moment she stared daggers through him. Then wordlessly she flung one arm backward and brought it forward so fast that at first no one even realized what was happening. Only when the sound of flesh slapping against flesh rang out clearly was it obvious.

She hit him again with her open hand. This time Hubert anticipated her move and tried to duck. It was a mistake. Luba's hand missed his cheek and hit him squarely on the nose. Blood began to drip from it, and the monkey on Luba's shoulder screeched shrilly, clapping its tiny black hands together in delight.

Quickly recovering, Hélène signaled for two of the gold-painted bodyguards. Silently they approached the unsuspecting Hubert from behind, grabbed hold of him under the armpits, and effortlessly lifted him up and carried him outside.

Hubert's legs futilely kicked the air. He glanced back over his shoulder, the sweat suddenly pouring down his face as he realized what they were going to do. Indignantly he shouted protests. "No! Somebody make them stop it!" he cried. "Put me down!"

At the entrance to the palazzo, the bodyguards paused. They looked out at the canal, then faced each other. Their eyes gleamed inside the narrow slits of their masks. They nodded and counted aloud.

Hubert started to scream as they grabbed his feet and swung him through the air in an arc. Once. Twice. On the count of three they let go and tossed him far out into the cold, black waters of the Grand Canal.

Hubert hit the water like a cannonball. The paparazzi in their boats quickly snapped pictures and then turned away, protecting their cameras from the sudden splash of water. When Hubert surfaced, he screamed in terror, his arms flailing the water. "I can't swim!" he screeched. "Help me! I'm drowning!"

The Grand Canal closed in over him as he submerged again.

"For God's sake!" Z.Z. screamed from the stoop. "Help him, somebody!" She turned to the two bodyguards who had tossed him in. "Help him!" She clenched her fists and beat one of them uselessly on the chest.

Then flashbulbs popped like lightning and the paparazzi went wild as Z.Z. dived in after Hubert.

Their pictures would make all the papers.

It was dawn by the time the last of the guests departed. Wearily Hélène sat down in the chair next to Nigel's and let out a deep breath. Besides them, only Luba was still there. For a long time Hélène surveyed the chaotic mess with a stern eye. There was nothing more dismal than the remains of a party.

She rubbed her eyes with her fingertips. "I'm exhausted!"

The Czarina smiled. She could move about unimpeded now. The midgets and the monkey had long since been sent home; the train had been unhooked from her gown and was folded neatly over the back of a chair. She sat down opposite Hélène. "But was it worth it! You mark my words," she prophesied. "Within a week, not an ounce of d'Or will be left in any of our outlets." Her coal-black eyes glittered. "We'd better step up production right away."

"Tomorrow," Hélène said weakly, waving away the business talk. "All I want to do right now is to go to bed." She stiffened and clenched her fists angrily. "Hubert de Léger! How dared he crash the ball in a costume like that!"

The Czarina sniffed. "The blood of the de Légers has run bad. Too much intermarriage through the centuries, if you ask me. But don't worry." She leaned forward, patted Hélène's hand, and smiled, her pomegranate lips wide and knowing. "He may not realize it yet, but he's done you an enormous favor."

"Favor!" Hélène looked at her wide-eyed.

"The publicity, of course! You can't buy publicity like that."

Hélène shook her head. "Really, Luba," she said reproachfully, "is that all you can think of? Sales?"

Three days later the telephones in the d'Itri offices were ringing off the hook and the telex kept up a constant chatter day and night. The Czarina's prediction had been correct. The newspapers had been full of Hubert's rescue by Z.Z. from the Grand Canal. There was no way d'Or could not be mentioned, since everything had occurred at the Golden Ball.

As a result, d'Or had taken off, selling out instantly. Hélène quickly called up the factory in Grasse to speed up production tenfold. And as soon as the shelves were re-stocked, they emptied again. D'Or was the hottest-selling fragrance ever.

To Hélène, it suddenly seemed as if the world was paved with gold. It was difficult for her to imagine that she had ever been poor. Even the newspapers began referring to her as "Mademoiselle Midas."

She had laughed at the articles, but deep down inside, she was secretly pleased. She had always been well-known, even before she started *Les Modes*. Her fame and social position had been assured when she had become Madame Kowalsky. But now she suddenly found herself as famous as only a handful of women in the world. She couldn't believe it. Never had anything gone so right.

But things weren't quite as good as she thought. She realized that the instant she got the call from New York in the middle of the night. Once again it was Edmond, with bad news.

"Come back immediately!" he told her. "De Léger and the others have stirred up trouble!"

"What kind of trouble?" she asked. She couldn't seriously believe they could do anything that warranted a call at this hour.

But they had. Z.Z. and Hubert were taking her to court. They claimed she had misappropriated HJII funds for personal use. A subpoena would be awaiting her the moment she set foot in the United States.

Worse, in the morning the IRS was going to descend upon HJII.

15

The warrant was served on her the moment she came through customs. Even while she had been on the plane, IRS agents were already at the accounting department of HJII, throwing everything into chaos. Hélène wanted to drop by and see if there was anything she could do, but Edmond advised against it.

"There isn't enough time, Little French Girl. We have to be at the courthouse within the hour."

The case of *Z. Z. Bavier v. Hélène Junot* was due to begin.

Hélène nodded and stared out the window of the sleek limousine. In less than an hour, and for perhaps as long as the next few weeks, she would be faced with nothing but unpleasantness. She had never been taken to court before, and the prospect of being trapped in a courtroom was highly distasteful. Her only consolation was that she was innocent. There had been no misuse of funds.

By the time a week passed, the accountants, investigators, and lawyers realized it too. Everything began to fizzle out.

To their chagrin, the IRS men discovered that not only was everything tip-top in accounting, and all the taxes owed the government paid, but that the taxes had actually been *overpaid*. By nearly seven thousand dollars. HJII's account would be credited.

Not to be outdone by the IRS, Z.Z. and Hubert's accountants and lawyers had gone at it even more doggedly, but they, too, finally left with their tails tucked shamefully between their legs. Sheepishly they had to acknowledge that not a penny was unaccounted for or misused.

To top it off, the judge took Z.Z., Hubert, and their lawyers into her chambers and gave them a stern tongue-lashing on wasting the court's precious time and threatened them with contempt.

All charges were instantly dropped.

Instead of feeling elated, Hélène seethed with anger. The IRS and the accountants crawling all over the place had set work back by weeks. There hadn't been a single department of HJII that hadn't come under scrutiny. When it was over, she and Edmond met together in her lavishly appointed office high in the RCA Building.

"They're going to pay for this," she said, stalking restlessly back and forth. "But how? What can I legally do to get back at Z.Z. and Hubert?" Her face was flushed with anger and her violet eyes burned dangerously. She stopped at one of the windows, stuck her fingers between two slats of the venetian blinds, and looked down at Rockefeller Plaza. It was curiously empty. It was that in-between time when the Promenade Café cleared its outdoor tables away and the ice-skating rink was yet to be set up.

"You're looking for revenge?" Edmond asked cautiously.

She let the blinds snap back into place. Then she turned her back to the window, crossed over to him, and dropped into a chair. "I'm looking for legal options."

He lit a cigarette, sat back thoughtfully, and crossed his legs. "You could always countersue. For defamation or something along those lines."

"No," Hélène said firmly. "The judge was right. Enough of the court's time has already been wasted. I don't believe in making a mockery of justice . . ." Her voice trailed off as a sudden glint came into her eyes.

He caught her expression. "All right," he demanded

shrewdly, "I can feel your gears turning. Care to share your thoughts?"

She smiled. He could read her like a book.

"I think," she said slowly, "that I have come up with a way to get back at them. It won't make much of a difference to Hubert, of course. He's too rich. But Z.Z. . . ." She smiled. "Z.Z.'s life-style demands money. I happen to know that she overinvested in HJII."

"Oh? And pray tell, how did you happen to come across that information?"

She waved her hand deprecatingly. "I have ways. The important thing is, she's counting on her dividends. Do you think it would be legal if we shrank them?"

"Shrank them!"

"Yes."

"How?"

She leaned forward, the words tumbling from her mouth. "By expanding HJII, Edmond! I've wanted to do that for a while now anyway. This is the perfect opportunity. Let's see . . ." She was beginning to get caught up in her self-induced excitement. "We could start a British edition of *Les Modes*. Perhaps even a German one." She jumped to her feet. "And we could buy a piece of property right here in New York and erect our very own building. The Junot Building! God knows, the way we bounce back and forth across the Atlantic, the company could use a corporate jet, too. We could even get a few cars for the major executives, a Rolls for me . . ."

Edmond smiled suddenly, his teeth flashing. "Little French Girl, you're a blooming genius. Not only will you get what you want, but we'll be cutting our taxes way down in the process."

"It's legal, then?" she asked carefully.

"It's legal. Just don't go overboard," he cautioned. "Cutting the others' profits will cut yours in the process. Make sure you leave yourself enough so that you won't be caught short."

"I'll make do," she said with determination.

Once Hélène's mind was made up about something, she didn't waver. She put her plan into action immediately. She started by purchasing the property on Fifth Avenue and Twelfth Street. She liked the location. Lower Fifth Avenue appealed to her. It was quiet and sedate. The Washington

Square arch a few blocks down reminded her of Paris. Also, the property was already commercially zoned. But best of all, she liked it because she rubbed shoulders with that other fashion giant, Fairchild Publications. They were right next door.

Instead of simply razing the building, Hélène's architects suggested they gut it until it was just a shell. It was a sturdy building and would make a desirable framework for hers. Hélène hesitated, but once the firm came up with the plans for the renderings, she immediately saw their point and agreed.

When first the destruction and then the construction began, she watched over the process with an eagle eye. Not the smallest, most inconsequential detail escaped her. Every day she made it a point to drop by and watch the progress. She roamed endlessly through the shell of the empty building, poking into corners and asking countless questions. She even went so far as to don a hard hat and bravely walk the scaffolding that jutted out over the avenue. She supervised and suggested and egged on the workers so that, miraculously, the Junot Building was completed two months ahead of schedule.

As the inside was totally rebuilt, so the outside was slipcovered with a shell of crystalline mirror. It was one of the first truly face-lifted buildings in the city, and she had to admit that the architects had worked wonders. They had even angled the corners until the original shape of the building was no longer in evidence. It caught all the reflections of the traffic and the neighborhood and the pedestrians. It reflected all the life that went on around it and froze it for a fraction of a second. It mirrored everything, but nothing as gloriously as the changing moods of the weather.

The Grumman Gulfstream II luxury jet she had ordered was completed the same week as the building, and it was flown directly to Italy, whose coachwork is the finest in the world. The interior was being lavishly appointed under the supervision of an internationally renowned interior-design team. And at the Rolls-Royce factory in England, her specially designed Silver Cloud was undergoing the long process of receiving layer upon layer of lacquer.

Hélène should have been content. HJII had gotten its own headquarters—a building named after *her*—and its own corporate jet. Now she could wing around the world in total privacy without having to be inconvenienced by airline schedules. But much more important, both England and Germany had their own editions of *Les Modes*.

The empire had expanded some more.

But Hélène was not satisfied. All her successes so far had been a product of HJII's natural momentum. What she hungered for now was a new success. One which did not involve HJII. One which did not involve Z.Z., d'Itri, von Eiderfeld, or Hubert de Léger.

One which was totally separate from all the others.

A new magazine.

Her own.

Her very own.

16

"Why go out on a limb if you don't have to?" Edmond asked after the Sphinx left the office.

He and Hélène were sitting at the floor-to-ceiling windows where Julie had set up a folding table. It was draped with a crisp white cloth. The flaky croissants and brioches on the paper-thin white bone china were untouched. Far below their feet, the morning traffic on Fifth Avenue was picking up.

Hélène sipped her coffee slowly. "I'm restless, Edmond. I feel like everything's at a standstill."

He laughed. "Far from it. You're busier than ever."

Abruptly she set her cup down in her saucer and got to her feet, restlessly prowling back and forth. "Dammit!" She clenched her index finger and sucked on it. Suddenly she whirled around accusingly, her eyes flashing. "I want a success that's mine. That's mine alone!"

He looked surprised. "Little French Girl. You don't think HJII is yours? Or the d'Itri boutiques, for that matter? Your name is practically a household word. On two continents."

"Sure it is. Maybe that's the trouble. Any magazine I add to HJII's roster is almost certain to be a hit. Not because of me. Because of Luba and the whole staff. *Because* of HJII."

"Everybody should be so lucky. You have everything you've ever wanted."

She vented a deep sigh and slipped into her chair. She reached out and covered his hands with hers, her violet eyes shining earnestly across the table. "I want another success, Edmond. Everything's running fairly smoothly, sure. But I want a new magazine! One that's a challenge. One that's all mine!"

He let out a low whistle. "You're asking for a lot. A whole new publishing company—"

"Damn right. With no one sitting on the board but me." She gave a tentative smile and with a mango-lacquered fingernail toyed with the rim of her cup. "You know, it's funny. There was a time when I would have given anything—*anything*—to be where I am today. And now?" She gave a low husky laugh. "Now it seems like . . . like it was *too* easy." She frowned suddenly. "Like I've cut too many corners to get where I am."

He looked at her steadily. "Are you sure that's it? That that's what your restlessness is really all about?"

She eyed him sharply. "What do you mean?"

"Little French Girl," he said with patent patience, "remember, it's me you're talking to. Edmond."

She gave him a little smile.

"You're sure you're not restless because of . . ." He paused, choosing his words carefully. ". . . because of personal reasons?"

She placed her elbows on the table, rested her chin heavily in her cupped hands, and stared down at the Forbes Building. "I take it you're referring to my love life."

"What else is there?"

"What indeed," she murmured.

"Work is no substitute," he warned with reproval in his voice.

"Edmond, Edmond, Edmond," she said flatly, turning to face him. "God knows I'm no virgin. Oh, don't look at me like that! I'm no nymphomaniac, either. But if I go to bed with a man, I have to feel *something* for him. And it just so happens that the only man I love is Nigel." She smiled sadly. "Fate's played a cruel trick on both of us. We can't help it if we've got to meet discreetly and snatch a few precious hours or nights every now and then. But in his position, a divorce is out of the question. There just isn't any other way. Nor is there anyone else for me. Between our meetings, what else can I do but keep busy?"

"All right. Enough said." He cleared his throat, clearly relieved to be able to change the subject. "The meeting you wanted scheduled with Gore is at ten-thirty. You're sure you want to go ahead with it?"

"Absolutely. I intend to borrow ten million dollars."

"Ten million!" He was shocked. "Why, you started HJII with only—"

"Times have changed, Edmond. Money is no longer worth what it used to be. You should know that better than anyone. Plus nowadays there isn't any room for failure or flukes. I intend to do a heavy TV advertising blitz. Things like that. It'll take a lot of money."

"And this magazine?" He looked at her questioningly. "It will be like *Les Modes*?"

She shook her head. "No, no. One that American women will snatch up even faster. Lately I've been giving it quite a lot of thought. I think I want to emphasize today's working woman. She's supposed to be a new breed, you know."

Hélène couldn't help but smile. New breed, indeed! She and Luba had been working all their adult lives.

"And it would be a mass-market magazine," she added quickly. "Available everywhere, from newsstands to supermarket checkout counters. It would be printed on glossier paper than *Good Housekeeping*, *Redbook*, or *Woman's Day*. Not as slick as *Les Modes*. What I'd like to do is combine today's many-faceted woman—at work, at home, at play. Something like a hybrid between American *Vogue*, *Cosmo*, and *Family Circle*. But big. Hundreds of pages covering everything from thirty-minute recipes to household hints to office management. Features on both white- and blue-collar women. And lots of how-tos. How to apply makeup. How to handle a job interview. How to hire and fire employees. How to dress for success. How to make your husband happy. Or your lover. Plus a whole lot more. Like what to do with your kids while you're at work. The pros and cons of day-care centers, the costs of housekeepers, what psychiatrists have to say about the effects of working mothers on their children. Maybe we can even get some big-name experts to do monthly columns."

Edmond looked thoughtful. "You'll have to get a whole new staff together."

676

"I know that."

"And keep everything separate from HJII. That means every last bank account, bill, printer, distributor, office space . . ."

She smiled. "I intended on doing that all along."

He nodded, and despite his calm, she could sense that his interest was aroused. "Figure out a name for it yet?"

She grinned. *"You!"*

"You?"

"That's right. *You,* followed by an exclamation mark. That's the name of the new slick. What do you think?"

He took a cigarette out of his case and tapped it thoughtfully against the brushed gold. "If it succeeds right off the bat like everything else you've done, you'll make tons of money," he said cautiously. "If it doesn't . . ." He let the unfinished sentence hang ominously.

She nodded wordlessly. She knew what he meant. If the new magazine failed, she would be ten million in the hole. No, more than that. There was the interest to consider, too. It was a frightening prospect, to say the least. Especially since, with the HJII expansion, the construction of the building, the purchase of the cars and the plane, the profits had shrunk. Massively. Even for her.

Her violet eyes were steady and unwavering. "I'm willing to take the gamble," she said softly. "I feel lucky."

She wasn't lucky. She'd never had to swallow the bitterness of defeat before, and now its repugnant taste coated her mouth. From the moment *You!* hit the newsstands it was a miserable failure. She'd gone out on a limb, and the limb had given way under her. She had hoped against hope that perhaps by giving it a few months, *You!* would catch on. By the time the third issue was out, the bell was tolling loud and clear. It could be heard all the way from the newsstands to Madison Avenue and down to Wall Street.

She stood despondently at the floor-length windows looking down at the traffic crawling along Fifth. It was a miserable, windy day, and waves of rain lashed against the windows. Her thoughts were heavy and dark. The failure of *You!* could only be blamed on her, and she felt like kicking herself. For once she had broken her cardinal rule. For every other magazine she had ever created there had been a ready market waiting to snatch it up. *Les Modes*'s secret had been to follow

677

in the footsteps of *Vogue* and *L'Officiel* and *Harper's Bazaar*. They had done the testing on the proving ground, and she'd simply marched in behind them and outclassed them all. She realized now that had she done that this last time around, everything would have worked out fine. But America just wasn't ready for a magazine catering to the working woman. *You!* had two strikes against it. It lacked the slickness and gloss people had come to associate with her, and, unfortunately, it was ahead of its time.

She tightened her lips, walked over to her bookcase, and slid out the first edition of *You!* She stared down at it with a grim expression.

YOU! The tilted letters in the left-hand corner took up half the width of the cover, and they were long and white and sleek, followed by a fire-engine-red exclamation mark.

Directly beneath that was the tilted white legend "The Magazine for Today's Woman."

And under that, on the right and parallel to the logo, were the feature titles, each line decreasing in size from top to bottom.

Staring out at Hélène from the glossy cover was *You!*'s prototype of the new American working woman with her two children. Mommy wearing a chic man-tailored suit, navy-blue silk scarf, white, feminine blouse. Perfectly coiffed, expertly made-up, an arm around each child's shoulder. Junior, seven, blond, shaggy-haired, wearing a Yankees T-shirt. Daughter, red-haired, freckled, cute. Everyone laughing happily.

For a moment Hélène's eyelids felt very heavy. The HJII board members were winning. "The Magazine for Today's Woman" had been resoundingly rejected by today's woman. She wondered if they knew that.

The telephone jangled suddenly. She started, then slowly went over to her desk. She punched down on the button of her private extension and picked up the receiver. It was Edmond.

"Gore just called," he said. "ManhattanBank wants to set up a meeting with you."

She drew in a deep breath, puffed out her cheeks, and slowly let the air out. "What about? The loan isn't due for another few months."

"He didn't say. My guess is that maybe they're getting itchy feet. After *You!*'s disaster, they're probably worried about your ability to pay off the loan."

She tightened her lips in annoyance. In this town, the only thing that spread faster than success was failure. She looked down at the magazine in her hand. It seemed to be mocking her. "Can we stall?"

"I highly advise against it. We can't buy more than a few days at the outside, anyway."

Wearily she closed her eyes. "All right, call Gore. Schedule the meeting for tomorrow afternoon. Then get the comptroller in here. I want to be briefed as to where exactly we stand right now."

"Will do. Anything else?"

"Yes," she said slowly. "Go to Citibank and open an identical account for each account we currently have at ManhattanBank. That includes both our personal accounts. But deposit only the minimum amount required for opening them."

He let out a whistle. "You do play dirty, Little French Girl," he said with a note of admiration in his voice.

Slowly she replaced the receiver. She stared down at the copy of *You!* On an impulse, she tossed it into the wastebasket. Then she collected the other issues from the shelf and threw them away, too.

She had enough reminders of *You!*'s failure.

Yes, the vultures were winning.

Suddenly she slammed her hand down on her desk. "I won't have it!" she shouted, and made up her mind. She would fight to the end. And then, even if ManhattanBank foreclosed and sold her collateral shares of HJII—even then, she would continue to fight.

What was it Siegfried had once said? *If you've made it once, and it wasn't a fluke, you can make it again.*

She would do her damnedest to prove him right.

17

James Cortland Gore III was waiting for them in his office. She kept her face impassive. She had learned one thing about bankers. They're bad poker players. When you're at the top of the world, they fall all over themselves trying to please you. When things aren't going too well, they're polite but curt. And when your world is slowly collapsing around you, they can smell it as clearly as a hungry shark can smell blood from a mile away. And the fat banker was smelling blood. She could tell that the instant she walked into his office.

He rose politely from his leather swivel chair, but this time he didn't come around from behind his big desk. "Miss Junot." He nodded curtly in her direction. She nodded in return. Then he faced Edmond. "Mr. Junot."

Edmond nodded. "Mr. Gore."

The men exchanged handshakes. Then they waited politely until Hélène took a seat. Once she was seated, they sat down too.

Gore cleared his throat and came right to the point. "We had a . . . ah . . . board of directors' meeting yesterday morning, and the subject of your ten-million-dollar loan was raised." His beady gray eyes appraised Hélène from beneath his bushy black-and-white eyebrows. "The board is considering calling in your loan."

She felt as though she'd been shot, but she managed to keep her face impassive. "Mr. Gore, I'm sure you're aware that the loan is a nonrenewable note," she said smoothly. "It is due in four months' time. Surely ManhattanBank is not so desperately in need of ready cash that it is calling in its oustanding loans early?"

"Miss Junot." The bald banker folded his hands on his desk and leaned forward. "Please try to understand our position. The directors are only trying to look out for the bank's best interests." He sighed regretfully. "They are troubled because they think you may be in the midst of a severe financial crisis."

She raised her eyebrows. "Indeed," she said coldly. She turned to Edmond. "Would you like to brief Mr. Gore on my current financial situation?"

Edmond started to reach for his briefcase, but Gore gestured for him to put it away. "Miss Junot," he said solemnly, "the reason the directors are worried is that ManhattanBank takes care of all your banking needs. They have a good overview of your daily financial status, and they have come to the conclusion that there is no way you'll be able to repay the loan in four months' time."

Edmond had been quiet up until now. "Mr. Gore . . ." he said softly.

Gore turned to him.

Edmond took out his gold cigarette case, selected a cigarette, and bought time by lighting it slowly. He inhaled deeply and blew out a cloud of smoke. "Your directors are, of course, aware of all of Miss Junot's financial transactions?"

"I believe that's what I just got through saying," Gore said irritably. "We've been handling all of Miss Junot's accounts for several years now."

Edmond watched Gore carefully. "And just because she *has* been banking with you for so long, you believe that you have financial insight into *all* her accounts?"

"Yes."

"No, Mr. Gore," Edmond corrected him quietly. "You are not completely aware of Miss Junot's financial dealings."

Gore stared at him, then at Hélène. "I don't think I quite understand."

Hélène held her breath, but Edmond smiled easily. "You are aware that Miss Junot is a very wealthy woman?"

"Of course."

"And you're also aware that she has businesses overseas?"

"Of course," Gore said more irritably than the last time.

"Do you happen to know just where her businesses abroad are located?"

Gore sighed faintly, resigned to have to play cat and mouse. "England, Germany, Italy, and France," he said wearily.

Edmond smiled. "And what country do Germany, Italy, and France border on?"

"Switzerland." Gore stared at Edmond. Then he turned to Hélène. There was surprise in his voice. And something else, too. Respect. "You have Swiss bank accounts?" he asked softly.

She smiled mysteriously. "Really, Mr. Gore. I'm sure you understand that I must keep that a confidential matter between the Swiss and myself."

"Then you *do* have eleven million dollars?"

"Ten million, seven hundred and ninety-five," Edmond said quickly. "That is what ManhattanBank would be due if the loan is called in at this time."

Gore steepled his fingers and nodded thoughtfully. "Very well. I shall inform my directors that they have nothing to worry about. Of course . . ." He coughed in embarrassment. "Of course, I shall have to verify that your Swiss accounts can indeed cover the loan."

Hélène rose to her feet. "As you wish, Mr. Gore." She had to force herself to stay calm and collected. But her heart was racing. "Need I remind you that ManhattanBank is holding eleven million dollars' worth of HJII stock as collateral?" She smiled at Edmond. "It seems that Mr. Gore and his directors do not trust us. The checkbooks, please."

She saw Gore watching them nervously, but she chose to ignore him. Edmond put his cigarette out, slung his briefcase onto his lap, and snapped it open. He took out thirteen checkbooks and a sheaf of long-term certificates of deposit. He leaned forward and stacked them neatly on a corner of Gore's desk. Then he took out thirteen more checkbooks. These were from Citibank, and he placed them prominently in two different stacks beside the others. Solemnly he handed his gold pen over to Hélène. She took it from him and smiled wordlessly. Quickly she sat back down and pulled her chair closer to the desk. "Mr. Gore," she said in a clear voice, "I would like the following transactions put into effect immediately." She pushed the long-term certificates toward him. "I know that there is a large interest penalty on early withdrawal, but I would like to convert these into cash. Instantly."

Gore leafed through them, and his eyes widened perceptibly. "B-but . . . they're seven hundred thousand dollars' worth!" he stammered.

She smiled sweetly. "Yes, they are." Then she picked up

the top checkbook from the ManhattanBank stack, flipped it open, and started to write out a check. "Pay to the order of Hélène Junot. Six hundred thousand, three hundred and ninety-three dollars and forty-two cents," she read aloud. She picked up a Citibank deposit slip and filled it out for that exact amount. Then with a flourish she ripped out the check. She looked at Gore. "Would you happen to have a paper clip?"

Silently Gore rolled his chair back a ways, opened his top desk drawer, and handed her a clip. "Thank you," she said. She took it and clipped the check and the deposit slip together. She laid them aside. Then she opened the next ManhattanBank checkbook. "Eight hundred thousand and sixty-eight dollars—"

"Miss Junot!" Gore seemed to have found his voice. "May I ask what you are doing?"

She looked across the desk at him but kept the pen poised over the check. "I'm simply transferring all my business to Citibank, Mr. Gore." She saw his face go pale and quickly added, "Don't worry, I shall inform my Zurich bank immediately and have them transfer to you the outstanding loan plus interest."

Edmond sat back and nonchalantly started to light another cigarette. He smiled at Gore. "No offense intended, of course, but I trust that our comptroller and some of our accountants can meet with the ManhattanBank auditors and determine that everything is in order?"

The banker had broken out into a sudden sweat, and he was mopping his forehead with a handkerchief. "P-please don't be so hasty, M-Miss Junot," he stammered.

"Mr. Gore," Hélène said in a level voice, "a bank is only as good as the services it provides its clients. When these services can't meet one's needs, it is time to change banks. Surely you can understand that. I have nearly four million dollars in various accounts here, my brother has two hundred thousand, and nearly thirteen million a month flow through the HJII accounts. Citibank has assured me that they can handle that volume to my satisfaction." She continued making out the check. Then she tore it out of the checkbook, closed it, and filled out another deposit slip. "I'm sorry, but could I trouble you for some more paper clips?"

"Miss Junot, *please*," Gore pleaded in a small voice. "I will ensure you that your loan will not be called in early. I agree that the directors were acting hastily—"

"I'm afraid you don't trust me, Mr. Gore," Hélène said. "Banking must be based on mutual trust."

He nodded effusively. "Of course, of course. Please, won't you reconsider? We're aware that you're a valuable client. Of course we won't need to verify your Swiss accounts . . ."

She exchanged glances with Edmond. He nodded his head imperceptibly. For now, they had won a round. Gore hadn't realized they were bluffing.

Only when they left ManhattanBank did Hélène realize that she was wrong. Gore *had* known they were bluffing. He'd swallowed the story of the nonexistent Swiss accounts too readily. But why he'd chosen to do that didn't matter now. She suspected he had something to hide, something that an audit would have uncovered. Idly she wondered if his fingers had been in the till, but she really couldn't care less. Whatever it was, it was Gore's problem, and his alone. The bank would cover any losses.

But she didn't have much time to wonder about Gore. When she got back to the office, Julie handed her a message. Nigel had called. She placed a call to England immediately; a few minutes later, she had Nigel on the line. "Darling, is something wrong?" she asked.

His voice sounded tortured and far away. "It's Pamela. She's been in a car accident." There was a pause. "Hélène, she's dead."

"Oh, Nigel! I *am* sorry." Hélène stared at the receiver, then said, "Nigel, I'll be there tonight. Wait up for me, darling."

As soon as she hung up, she picked up the phone again and dialed the airport. The HJII jet was ready for takeoff. Her passport was in her desk. She'd worry about clothes once she got to England.

Five minutes later she was in the white Rolls with the HJII plates, heading toward the airport. Less than an hour later she was already well out over the Atlantic, headed for England.

And that was . . . yesterday.

TODAY

Monday, January 15

1

Hélène listened to the faint rise-and-fall breath of Nigel's sleep. She stared at him, her head resting in the palm of her hand, her elbow digging into the crisp softness of the Pratesi sheets. The thick cashmere blanket rose and fell with each breath he took. His head was turned toward her, lying sideways in the softness of the down pillows trimmed with satin ribbons and scallops of lace. She had watched him ever since he had fallen asleep. Now that the sky was beginning to lighten and let a soft, muted winter glow in through the windows, he was more than just a dark shape.

Nigel. She had waited for him for so long. Now the wait seemed worth it; it almost felt as if so many years had never passed. Nigel was hers, and hers alone.

She pulled her free hand out from under the covers and reached out as if to stroke him. She kept her fingers a bare fraction of an inch above him. Affectionately her extended index finger followed the noble shape of his forehead, down along the bridge of his nose, almost but not quite brushing across his lips. She let her hand linger there, loving the soft feel of the warm whispers of his breath.

"Sleep well, my love," she whispered softly, "sleep well."

That she was awake and he was cocooned in the soothing blanket of his sleep didn't seem to matter. She was content just to know that he was there beside her. That he would always be there. She enjoyed just being able to look at him. Even asleep, he seemed powerful. He slept on his side, his body relaxed.

She twisted slowly around in the bed, afraid that any sudden move might awaken him. She smiled to herself in the pale blue light as she reflected on their night of lovemaking. He had been so strong and demanding. His thrusts had been powerful as he stroked deep and hard within her. Moaning, she had felt herself heat up, and clasped him tightly, responding to his every move. She had experienced one exquisite orgasm after another. Then he had fallen asleep with his head buried between her breasts. Now she felt complete. She was going to be the Duchess of Farquaharshire.

She glanced at the alarm clock. It ticked softly on the nightstand in rhythm with his breathing. The faint green numbers glowed softly. It was a little past six.

They had been up almost all night, and still she couldn't go to sleep. In half an hour she would have to get up. But she didn't feel at all tired. She felt . . . yes—*satiated*. Rejuvenated. Awakened.

Gently she played the fingertips of her right hand across the finger on her left. Once again the massive yellow Somerset Sun was heavy on her finger, this time for good. In six hours they would be at City Hall and together climb the wide, sweeping steps to the marriage bureau. Nigel was hers. Hers alone. She felt better now than she had at any other time in her life.

She reached up to the nightstand and felt for the piece of paper that lay in front of the alarm clock. She wanted to touch it, to make certain it was still there. It was. Nigel had given it to her last night in the Café Carlyle. He had flown to New York to beg once again for her hand in marriage and to present her with the Somerset Sun. And this time, she hadn't refused him. Once she'd let him slip the big ring onto her finger, he had reached into his wallet and pushed the certified check drawn on his account at Morgan Guaranty Trust across the tablecloth toward her. She had stared down at it. It was made out to Hélène Junot for eleven million dollars. She didn't have to be told what it was for. To pay the bank loan and save HJII from the vultures.

She had pushed the light blue check back toward him. "No, Nigel," she said firmly. "This has got to stay out of it. You have your businesses and I have mine. They have nothing to do with our love."

He put his hand firmly over hers. The check was in the middle of the table, caught in a tug-of-war under her fingertips. He shook his head. "Our empires have everything to do with our love, darling," he said softly. "Don't you see? We're builders, you and I. We're both power-seekers. You in your way, I in mine. That's what brought us together in the first place. That's what's kept us together all this time. We share more than just love. We share ambitions and dreams.

Besides," he added quickly, "consider it a loan. You may repay it at your convenience."

"Don't be ridiculous," she said.

"I'm not, don't you be." He leaned back in his chair and studied her levelly. There was a proud, determined pout to her lips. He knew that she needed help. He had also known that she would refuse it. But just this once, he couldn't give in. There was too much at stake and she had too much pride. Much too much for her own damn good. He would have to make her see reason.

He chose his words carefully now and spoke hurriedly. "Hélène, if I'm to be your husband, you must trust me enough to let me help you. Don't always try so hard to be so bloody independent. There are times each of us needs a little help."

"This isn't why I agreed to marry you."

"I know that," he said gently. "It's the reason why you kept on saying no."

She nodded. Silently she looked down at the check, then over into his eyes.

"Go on, take it," he said. Then he grinned. "You accepted a three-million-dollar diamond without qualms. What's wrong with a check for eleven million?"

"It's not the same," she said with stubborn dignity. "You know that."

He reached across the table, clasped both his hands around hers, and pressed them. "Darling, I love you," he said softly. "And I know how important HJII is to you. Too important for you to let it go down the drain because of foolish pride." He looked steadily into her eyes. "Take it," he commanded her gently.

And she had taken it, promising to repay him with interest. And he had laughed. "Marriage is a partnership," he said, "or didn't you know that?"

"I know that," she said in a trembling voice.

He smiled. "Just don't ever forget who'll wear the pants in this family. You'll have your business, but I intend to take care of you. I'm very old-fashioned. Is that clear?"

Suddenly her knees felt weak. She was glad that she was sitting down. Her voice dropped to a whisper. "I . . . I'll be sure to remember that."

Robert Rowen got to the Staten Island ferry terminal about fifteen minutes early. He located the men's room but didn't go inside yet. Instead, he decided to kill time by walking around the terminal. He despised public rest rooms.

A foghorn cried out mournfully as a Staten Island ferry pulled up in the foggy semidarkness, its windows ghostly rows of yellow light. A moment later it thumped against the terminal, sending a tremor through it. As he watched, a mass of passengers hurried off. He shivered and dug his hands into his pockets. It was too cold for a trench coat, even with the heavy knit sweater and jacket underneath. Everyone else was well-bundled for winter. And he felt silly having to wear the red carnation in his buttonhole. It drew too much attention to him. This meeting had all the ingredients of a disagreeable thriller.

As eight o'clock came around, he knew it was time he went into the men's room. Once inside, he glanced around suspiciously. It was deserted. There was no one at the urinals, and all the cubicles were empty.

For a few minutes he waited impatiently for the whisperer to make contact. Then he felt foolish just standing there. He went and pretended to use the urinal. He glanced at his watch. Already it was five after eight.

A few more minutes passed. Then he heard the door behind him opening and banging shut. He held his breath as he sneaked a glance backward. A man in a business suit had come in. Rowen turned his face away as the man approached the urinal beside his and set his briefcase down on the floor. *Zip!* The faint but unmistakable sound of a zipper sounded loud and obscene. Then he heard the splash of urine.

He glanced toward the man out of the corners of his eyes. Already the man was preparing to leave. Again Rowen averted his head; the man was turning around. Then he heard his footsteps. A moment later, the door opened and banged shut. He was alone again.

He wondered now if the voice on the phone had just been playing some kind of sick joke on him. Thinking about it now, he saw how foolish he had been to fall for it. A million dollars! No one in his right mind gave away a million dollars. Not for any reason. Least of all not for ten million dollars' worth of shares in a publishing company. That was an extra ten percent on top of the market price. Whoever wanted them would have a chance to bid on them anyway. Yes, it was high time he screwed his head on right and saw reason. He'd simply forget all this nonsense and go to the office early and get caught up on some backlog. What a fool he had been! A million dollars!

As he turned to leave, something caught his eye. The man had forgotten his briefcase. It was still sitting beside the urinal. He'd have to run after him and tell him. No, he'd catch up with him *with* the briefcase. That was better.

Quickly he went to collect it. Suddenly he felt his skin starting to crawl. An engraved brass nameplate was screwed into the top of the case. The name was his.

Robert Rowen.

Slowly he bent down to pick it up. Was it for real? Maybe he was going crazy and imagining it? Once he had the handle in his hand, he knew it was no mirage. And it was heavy. A lot of money was heavy. But then, so was paper. Or lead. Or any of a dozen things.

He took the briefcase with him into one of the booths and locked the door. Then he sat down on the stained toilet seat and placed the briefcase on his lap. He stared at it in silent fascination.

"You're being a sucker," a miserable little voice warned him. "You're falling for the joke."

But he couldn't help himself. He found himself fiddling with the catches. With a loud snap, they sprang open. His heart started to hammer against his ribs. Slowly he lifted the lid.

He sucked in his breath. Neat bundles of twenty-dollar bills were stacked inside, each bundle held together by inch-wide strips of white paper stamped by the bank. Each package was stamped "$10,000." There were fifty such bundles.

He examined a few of the bills and shook his head. He

couldn't believe it! They weren't phoney. It was really money, all right.

It was no joke.

3

"Double-crossing bitches!" Hubert de Léger's face was white with rage, but the purple splotches on his cheeks that came from burst blood vessels stood out clearly. For a moment he glared at the telephone in his hand. Then he raised it up above his head and brought it crashing down. It let out a painfully weak ring as it hit the corner of his ormolu desk and then bounced to the floor, the expectant crash muffled by the lush, sculptured pile of the Edward Fields carpet. He kicked the offending instrument out of his way as he stomped to the door. Flinging it open, he rushed out of the book-lined library. His chest was heaving and his breaths were coming in short gasps. He didn't bother to take the suede-lined elevator; the stairs were quicker. He went running down them two at a time. Once in the foyer, he stopped and looked around wildly. The town house was quiet. There wasn't a sound to be heard.

"Eduard!" he roared.

A moment later his imperturbable butler opened the double doors from within the living room. "Oui, Monsieur le Comte?" he said calmly.

Hubert glared at him darkly. "My car! Have it brought around immediately!"

"Oui, Monsieur le Comte." The butler turned and started to leave.

"And hurry for once, you slothful, ass-dragging . . ." Fuming, Hubert broke off as he struggled in vain to find the expressive noun he was looking for. More frustrated than ever, he made a contemptuous gesture. His voice was now a high-pitched screech. "Move it!"

"Of course, Monsieur le Comte," the butler said with toneless dignity. His face remained an impassive mask. He was long since used to Hubert's tirades and suffered them in silence. But this was the worst one yet. Vaguely he wondered what had happened to trigger it, but then he swallowed his curiosity. It was none of a good butler's business. He withdrew with implacable calm and left Hubert to pace the foyer impatiently.

When the Mercedes finally rolled up in front of the brownstone, Hubert immediately rushed outside, not even bothering to throw on a coat. He didn't wait for the chauffeur to help him. He jumped right in and slammed the door shut. "The Pierre!" he screamed.

With a burst of speed, the Mercedes surged smoothly off across East Sixty-eighth Street.

A drink. Feeling somewhat better already, now that he had come to some sort of decisive and positive step, he leaned forward, yanked the door of the bar cabinet open, and reached inside. He grabbed a bottle of Armagnac by the neck and fished it out from its shelf. For a moment he turned the bottle in his hands, feeling the smoothness of the glass. He licked his lips. They felt suddenly dry and cracked. He hadn't realized how thirsty he was.

Quickly, without wasting another second, he wrestled with the cork. Then he heard the satisfyingly familiar *plop* and the faint hiss of escaped air. He smiled and lifted the bottle to his lips, drawing on it hungrily, his lips sucking noisily like a starving baby at its mother's breast.

He took a deep breath as the heat of the alcohol burned down his throat and then rushed soothingly throughout his body, bringing a pleasing numbness to his limbs. He sank back in the seat, his hand clutching the bottle by the neck as if someone might snatch it away from him. Clumsily he rested his left elbow on the padded armrest and stared blankly out the side window, his hand at his mouth. Without realizing it, he began gnawing on his fingernails.

She had done it! he thought miserably. Somehow, against all odds and right under his very nose, she had managed to marry herself off quietly—to one of the frigging *richest* men in the world, no less—*and* repay the bank loan! How? How how how how *how* was that at all possible? How, without his knowing it? Had it all been settled when she'd stopped in England in the Lear jet on her way to New York a week ago? When he'd found out where she'd interrupted the flight, he

693

hadn't attached any significance to it. He had been sure, so *damned* sure, that he and the others held all the cards. But now? Now it was clear that she'd kept something hidden up her sleeve. But why hadn't his detectives been on their toes? That's what he was paying them so handsomely for. And above all, *how had Nigel Somerset managed to leave England and sneak into New York without his even knowing it?* Somerset was supposed to be watched night and day.

Hubert's coal-black eyes flashed. All along, his detectives had assured him that Nigel Somerset was still at Fallsworth. Well, he wasn't. That much even *he* knew. And what a fool he'd made of himself! Just six and a half hours earlier, he'd made the five-hundred-thousand-dollar drop to Rowen. A half-million dollars! And for nothing!

He started to shake anew with fury, just thinking of the telephone calls. Until he'd been on the phone, he hadn't even had an inkling of what was up. Nobody had bothered to inform him about anything. And that Rowen! He took a savage swig of Armagnac. Driblets of the liquid ran down his chin from the corners of his mouth. He wiped them away with the back of his hand. That Rowen was a son of a bitch!

He could feel a fiery hatred burning within him. Rowen was enough to make him sick. But he'd get him! He'd *ruin* him! Somehow, somewhere, he'd see to it that his banking career came to an end.

Up until he'd talked to Rowen this afternoon, it had seemed that everything was well under control. He had just called him to have him verify that the briefcase indeed contained a half-million. Not that he'd suspected anything had gone wrong. After all, he himself had watched Rowen from a distance as he'd come out of the men's room carrying the briefcase. He didn't really know what it was that made him call. Instinct, perhaps. Just to make sure. To add a bit more pressure.

"Robert Rowen speaking," the man's deep, familiar voice had said over the wire after the secretary had made the connection.

"Is everything in order?" Hubert had used his whisper, the same whisper he'd used first on Gore, and now on Rowen. "Did you count the money?"

Rowen's voice was very clear and casual. "I beg your pardon?"

694

A sudden foreboding constricted Hubert's heart. "The money!" he hissed sharply. "Did you count it?"

"Who is this? What money are you talking about?" Rowen's voice was properly indignant.

Hubert stared at the receiver. It suddenly dawned on him that something had gone wrong. It wasn't as if Rowen didn't recognize his voice. It was something else.

"You know very well what money!" Hubert hissed harshly. "The money in the briefcase you picked up in the men's room!"

"I'm sorry, sir," Rowen had replied politely. "I believe you must have the wrong extension."

"Listen, you creep!" Hubert spit out venomously. "I warned you about what would happen if you tried to double-cross us!"

"I beg your pardon?" Rowen's voice was noncommittal.

"I'll ruin you!" Hubert was screaming now; the last vestiges of the whisper were gone.

"I'm sorry, sir," Rowen said calmly. "It is obvious that you have the wrong extension. I see absolutely no reason for continuing this conversation. Good day."

Hubert stared incredulously at his telephone receiver. Rowen had hung up on him. Hung up! His mind was flying. *What could have gone wrong?*

He could feel the sweat breaking out on his forehead as his fingers quickly dialed Hélène's office. While he waited, he jumped to his feet and stared out the window behind him. The curtains were drawn aside and there was a good view of his back garden. The trees and shrubbery were bare and skeletal, the ground around the flagstones frozen. He listened as the phone at the other end began to ring. It was picked up halfway through the third ring.

"Good afternoon, Miss Junot's office." The Sphinx's unmistakable voice was brisk and businesslike.

"This is the Comte de Léger. Is she in?"

"I'm sorry, sir. Miss Junot won't be back until two weeks from this coming Friday."

"Two weeks . . . *What!* B-but I don't understand," Hubert stuttered. He turned away from the window and sank back down into his chair. He reached for a handkerchief and mopped his forehead furiously. "There must be some mistake. There was a meeting scheduled for late this afternoon!"

"I was told to cancel it, sir. I just tried calling you, but your line was busy."

For a moment Hubert was silent as he tried to compose himself. Then he found his voice. "Where is she?" he asked softly.

He thought he could detect a gleeful laugh in her voice. "Actually, Miss Junot is no longer Miss Junot, sir. At twelve o'clock noon she officially became the Duchess of Farquharshire."

Hubert could feel the blood draining from his head. It wasn't possible! He closed his eyes. His library was suddenly reeling around him like the world from a merry-go-round. "And the bank loan?" he whispered.

"Which bank loan are you referring to, sir?"

"The one for ten million dollars!" he snapped irritably.

"I'm sorry, sir, but I don't know anything about that."

"Bitch!" Hubert slammed down the receiver. Didn't anybody know *anything*? He stared at the telephone. He'd make one last call. Much as he despised Edmond Junot, he, at least, might be able to shed some light on this mystery.

"Legal department," a woman's voice said hollowly.

"This is the Comte de Léger. Is Mr. Junot in?"

"Please hold, sir. I'll check and see." There was a click and he was put on hold. After a while there was another click.

"Edmond Junot speaking." Even the telephone lines found it difficult to make the resonance of his voice sound hollow.

A grimace distorted Hubert's lips. He didn't like Edmond Junot one bit. Never had, in fact. Although he wouldn't admit it even to himself, something about the man threatened him.

"This is Hubert de Léger," Hubert said, automatically slipping into French.

Edmond chose to speak English. "Actually, I'm in the middle of an important meeting . . ."

"Then I won't keep you long," Hubert assured him quickly. "I was just wondering about the status of the HJII shares. Has the ManhattanBank loan been repaid?"

"That is my sister's business, I believe," Edmond said stiffly.

"I know it is," Hubert said smoothly. "However, as you well know, the status of that loan affects all of Junot's shareholders, myself included. Believe me, I regret very much having to intrude on your time."

696

Edmond was silent for a moment. "Perhaps you are right," he said finally in an even voice. "The status of that loan does affect you and the others." He paused. "It was repaid at ten-thirty this morning."

Hubert's voice was a whisper. "You're . . . you're not joking?"

"Believe me, Mr. de Léger, I don't joke about such matters. At the request of my sister, I went down to Manhattan-Bank to take care of the matter personally."

"Th-thank you."

With trembling fingers Hubert replaced the receiver. He was shaking with fury. *Mr.* de Léger! That peasant knew very well that he was *Monsieur le Comte!*

He got to his feet and looked down at his desk. The telephone seemed to be mocking him, laughing at him with its shrill rings. He hadn't even realized that it had begun to ring. All he knew was that the jeering sounds reverberated crazily in his head. And they had stopped only after he'd smashed the damned instrument and it lay broken at his feet.

Just as the Mercedes limousine pulled up in front of the Pierre, the bottle of Armagnac was empty. Hubert shook it, glared at it, and then tossed it down beside him on the seat. He didn't wait for the chauffeur to come around and hold open his door for him or for the liveried doorman to rush over. He jerked open the door himself and leaped out, leaving it wide open in his hurry. He rushed into the lobby. Not bothering to announce himself at the desk, he marched straight up to the bank of elevators. A minute later he got off on Karl von Eiderfeld's floor.

Impatiently he banged on the door of the apartment. A maid in uniform opened it. He pushed past her into the dim foyer.

"I beg your pardon, sir," she said politely. "Is there someone you wish to see?"

Hubert looked wildly around the foyer. "Where is he?"

"He?"

"Von Eiderfeld!" Hubert said irritably.

"In the living room, sir."

"Get out!"

"Sir?" The woman looked at him as if she hadn't heard right.

697

Hubert drew himself up to his full height. "Are you going to get out or do I have to throw you out?"

Wide-eyed, the maid fled into the corridor. She glanced over her shoulder and then swiftly shut the door behind her.

Upon hearing the commotion, von Eiderfeld had come into the foyer. "My dear Comte, you look beside yourself," he said smoothly.

"She's done it!" Hubert screamed.

Von Eiderfeld drew back and stared at him. "Who has done what?"

"The bitch, who else?" Hubert made a wild gesture as he whirled around and stalked into the living room. He blinked in the darkness, trying to get his bearings. Then he headed straight over to the armoire, flung the doors open, grabbed the first bottle in sight, unscrewed the cap, and took a massive swig. He let out a heavy sigh and banged the bottle back down on the shelf.

Von Eiderfeld was watching him quietly from across the room. He had never seen anyone in such a dangerous rage. Hubert needed calming down; that he could see. But how to do it? Perhaps by just remaining silent. That was what the General Staff used to do when the Führer flew into his rages. Eventually they worked their way out of the system. For the time being, the best thing to do was to humor Hubert.

His whole body shaking, Hubert dropped into a fragile French chair and buried his face in his hands. After a moment, a bit of his composure returned. He looked up at von Eiderfeld with a drawn expression. "You owe me a quarter of a million," he said quietly.

This came as some surprise, to be sure. Slowly von Eiderfeld walked over to the fireplace. There was no fire in the hearth, but the logs were already neatly stacked on the grate. He stared up at the big dark canvas above the mantel, his back to Hubert. He was thinking rapidly. The quarter-million could mean only one thing: half the five hundred thousand Hubert had insisted on bribing Rowen with. He would go just so far in humoring Hubert. There had to be a cutoff point. "Why don't you tell me exactly what has happened?" he said calmly.

Hubert glared at him. "All right, I'll tell you. She's done it. She's gone off, married the Duke, and paid off the loan."

Von Eiderfeld looked thoughtful and rubbed his chin with his fist. "It doesn't really surprise me," he said. There was a note of respect in his voice. "She's a remarkable woman, you know. Survival is at her very core."

"What kind of shit are you mumbling now?" Hubert sprang to his feet. He raced from one window to the next, yanking aside the drawn curtains. The morning sun was gone; the sky was a uniform gray, several shades lighter than the graffiti-covered boulders sticking up out of Central Park. Either tonight or sometime tomorrow it would start to snow.

Von Eiderfeld shielded his sensitive eyes with one hand. "Why don't you compose yourself?" he said quietly, turning his back to the windows.

Hubert's chest heaved and fell. "Compose myself!" he said. "I want a check for a quarter of a million. *Now*!"

"You believe that I should pay for your mistakes?" von Eiderfeld asked softly without turning around. "For your miscalculations? I warned you to wait until five o'clock this afternoon."

"We had a deal to split the bribe fifty-fifty, remember?"

"We had a deal to wait until after the close of the business day," von Eiderfeld corrected him.

"So you want to renege! I should have known better than to trust you! You're just like everyone else! Well, you're through!" Hubert snarled suddenly. "I know all about you! I read those files she had on you!"

Von Eiderfeld turned to look at him. His voice quivered slightly. "So? They are now just a pile of ashes."

Hubert laughed bitterly. "I'll see to it that there's a full-scale investigation anyway. I remember what was in those files. I even copied some of it down. You know what I'll do with that? I'll call the Israeli authorities. You're through, you pink-eyed albino freak! I'll see that you're put on trial and executed!"

"Sit down and compose yourself!" von Eiderfeld commanded.

Hubert lunged at him, grabbed his lapels, and shook him. "Nobody stabs *me* in the back, do you hear? I'll fix you! It'll be like they did with Eichmann! They'll put you in a glass booth like a pheasant under glass!" Hubert began to laugh crazily. Savagely he pushed von Eiderfeld backward and let go of the lapels. Von Eiderfeld stumbled and fell into a chair. He said nothing, just stared. Hubert wasn't rational. He should have stayed as far away from him as possible.

Karl von Eiderfeld didn't doubt for an instant that

699

Hubert's threat was serious. An irrational mind like his was capable of destroying anything and anyone. Still, there was one tiny consolation. Hubert was wrong about the end being at hand for him. One phase of his life, perhaps. But not the end. Call it . . . a new beginning.

After Hubert stomped out and slammed the door, von Eiderfeld got up from the chair with a peculiar sort of dignity. He knew exactly what he had to do. He brushed his sleeves as he crossed over to the windows. One by one, he drew the curtains shut again. Then he stopped at the telephone table. He bent over, unlocked a shallow drawer, and pulled it open. He took out two leather folders. In one was his passport, in the other a wallet. This passport and wallet were always within reach in the event of just such an emergency. The passport was his ticket to a new life. The wallet would help him get there. It was thick with cash and traveler's checks.

Quickly he pocketed both. Then he dialed a telephone number that he had committed to memory long ago. It was to a helicopter service operating out of the heliport beside the Fifty-ninth Street Bridge. He told them to have a helicopter waiting for him in twenty minutes, rotors turning and ready for takeoff. Then he dialed another memorized number in New Jersey. Hélène had specifically forbidden him ever to use private transportation. Up until this moment, he had followed her instructions to the letter. Yet, unknown even to her, he had a private Lear jet in readiness wherever he went, even though he never used it. It was waiting now at Teterboro Airport. Once he boarded, he would give the pilot piecemeal instructions. First, he would fly to Dallas, refuel, and fly on to Mexico City. From there, it was down to Panama City and then over the Andes, jungles, and pampas to Uruguay. He had fifteen million dollars stashed away there. Two million was deposited in a bank, one million in cash was hidden, and twelve million in gold and flawless diamonds was buried in a spot only he and Helga knew of.

After calling Teterboro, he put down the receiver. He was glad that he had had the foresight to foresee an emergency like this. Now that the moment had come, he didn't have to panic. For years he had generously seen to it that the high officials in the governments of several countries were well taken care of financially. When the governments in power changed or fell, as they tended to do with geometric rapidity in South America, he had immediately made contact with the new leaders. Besides Uruguay, he had two other contingency plans open to him, one in nearby Paraguay, the other in Costa Rica. His only regrets were that he would no longer be sitting at the helm of Von Eiderfeld Industrien G.m.b.H. and that he would never be able to set foot on his beloved German soil again. He hated semitropical and tropical climates. He missed the changes of season, and the sun hurt his eyes and burned his skin. In South America, everything was turned around. Efficiency was lacking, and even the seasons, one almost indistinguishable from the next, came lazily at the wrong times of the year. But at least his home in Punta del Este stood in readiness. It had been designed with shady loggias and thick blinds which cut the glare of the sun to a minimum. And Helga would be content. There was an Olympic-size pool.

Another comfort were his sons, Rolf and Otto. On and off, they could perhaps visit with him. That way, he would at least be able to oversee the business from a distance. Even with him far away in the background, Von Eiderfeld Industrien would be able to expand. When Hubert blew the whistle, a scandal would touch the corporation and his sons, but it wouldn't do any of them much harm. The bulk of the corporation was involved in oil and refining; both were in desperate demand. Germany had no petroleum resources of her own. The German government would gladly see to it that nothing would stop the wheels of Von Eiderfeld Industrien from turning. As far as Rolf and Otto were concerned, both were adopted. For once, he was glad about that. They knew he was not their natural father, and the stigma of his past wouldn't devour them. And he had taught them both well. They knew how to survive. Hubert's threats were harmless. Mere irritants. Besides, it was high time he retired. He was old and tired. It was time he spent his remaining years quietly with Helga.

At three-fifteen Karl von Eiderfeld walked out of the Hotel Pierre without even a briefcase in his hand. The sky was getting darker. Already, lights were on everywhere, yellow and bright. He never once glanced backward. He pulled up his Persian-lamb collar, adjusted his hat, and thrust his hands in his topcoat pockets. He walked slowly toward Madison Avenue. Like any tourist or native New Yorker, he stopped at the expensive stores and gazed in at the enticing windows. There was nothing suspicious about his behavior. He didn't flee, he didn't run, he didn't have luggage. He wasn't even nervous. Unknown to everyone, he had in his breast pocket the only two things he would ever need. His wallet and his passport. Everything else could be left behind.

Slowly he continued walking until he reached the heliport at the East River. Only when he was hovering above the glittering canyons of Manhattan and the Bell Jet Ranger helicopter turned and nosed swiftly through the darkening skies toward New Jersey did he let out a sigh of relief.

He smiled grimly to himself. He and Hélène Junot had far more in common than either of them would have liked to admit.

They were both survivors.

4

The snow was beginning to come down in plump white flakes as Hélène's white Rolls-Royce pulled to a stop on the tarmac beside the waiting HJII jet. The chauffeur helped Hélène out of the car. She was cocooned in the soft lushness of a Max Reby Montana lynx coat. Nigel emerged behind her.

Hélène was radiant with happiness. For once in her life, even winter, which she had always dreaded, could not detract from her joy. She felt far too good. It was hard for her to believe that she and Nigel were finally married and headed for—at last—the honeymoon both had yearned for so long.

Above the Rolls, the oval portholes of the jet shone yellow in the night. Small red and white lights along the wingtips and atop the fuselage blinked on and off with mechanical precision. Everything was in readiness for instant takeoff.

Suddenly panic swept through her. Perhaps this was only a dream. Perhaps . . . She took a deep breath and glanced down at her hand. The twenty-eight-carat Somerset Sun flashed on her finger. It was real. This was no dream. A flood of relief flowed through her. She really was Hélène Somerset, the seventeenth Duchess of Farquharshire.

Nigel touched her lynx-clad elbow. "Your Grace . . ." he said teasingly, as if reading her thoughts, and bowed low.

She giggled happily and threw her arms around his neck. "You'd better watch it, silly man," she warned playfully. "As a duchess I demand respect." Suddenly her face became serious and she stroked his cheek. "Nigel," she whispered, "what in the world am I going to do with you?"

He smiled. "Everything, I hope." Then he pulled her close and looked down at her. Delicate snowflakes were caught in her blue-black hair, and in the floodlights they sparkled like multifaceted jewels. Her cheeks were flushed and her eyes were oddly luminous. He shook his head in disbelief. "My God, but you're beautiful," he said in a whisper.

She took a deep breath and looked up into his eyes. "So are you, my darling," she replied softly. As she spoke, a tremor ran through her.

He could feel it. Slowly he inclined his head closer, and she let out a little cry as she parted her lips to meet his. She tasted deliciously soft and warm. Greedily he found her tongue.

He opened his eyes. "Oh, my darling," he said with a smile. "If you could only know how happy you make me."

She smiled back at him. "Mmmmmm," she murmured. Then she kissed his lips again.

In the distance, a 747 lifted off. For a moment its flashing lights were visible as it climbed into the snowy sky. Then it disappeared. The passing rumble sounded like thunder.

Nigel glanced at the HJII jet beside them. "We'd better go inside," he suggested. "Otherwise our flying coach might turn into a pumpkin."

"Or worse yet, our flying coach's runway may get closed down due to the snow," she warned.

They laughed, untangled their arms, and boarded. She was the first one up the folding steps. Once inside the six-foot-high headroom of the jet, Nigel ducked his head. "One inch," he moaned. "Why do I seem to be the only person I know of who had the miserable luck to be born just one inch too tall to enjoy full headroom on private jets and cabin cruisers?"

"Punishment," she teased. "For a lifetime of making everyone look up at you."

She looked around the cabin. Everything was in position

for takeoff. The burnished burl tables were folded down for safety, the overhead lights gleamed, and the recessed cabin lights above the portholes were reflected in the smoked-Plexiglas-and-mirror bulkheads that divided the cabin. The leather-trimmed, limousine-cloth seats were in their upright positions. Up front, in the cockpit, the complicated instrument panels were lit up like a carnival: red, green, blue. Through the tinted windshield, the night looked eerie. Greenish-yellow.

Hélène frowned. The pilot's seat was empty. "Where is Hendricks?" she asked the copilot.

He turned around, and she frowned. He was a total stranger. Not very tall, with brown hair and generally nondescript features. The remarkable thing about his face was his eyes. Behind the silver-rimmed aviator glasses, they were icy blue. Even his crisply starched pale blue shirt held more warmth.

"Who are you?" Her voice was puzzled.

For an instant the Chameleon's eyes bore right through hers. Then he got up and stepped nimbly sideways between the two seats, turning to face her. Hélène's eyes dropped and then flared in disbelief, and her blood ran cold. She tried to swallow, but her throat was tight and dry.

She was staring into the barrel of a Browning revolver.

"Someone named Z.Z. sends you her regards," the Chameleon said evenly. And pressed the trigger.

5

Nine intermitable hours passed before Dr. Weiner finally pushed through the double doors. He pinched the bridge of his nose with his fingertips. He was bone-weary, as if he'd been fighting a losing battle, which was closer to the truth than he liked to admit. His eyes were encircled with the deep, dark smudges of fatigue.

"Dr. Weiner!" Edmond jumped from the plastic waiting-room chair and rushed forward, Petite Hélène at his heels.

"We're doing all we can, Mr. Junot," Dr. Weiner said simply. "If it's any consolation, this hospital is one of the finest in the country, and three of the most eminent surg—"

Petite Hélène reached forward and dug her fingers into the doctor's arm. Her face was drawn and pale, and her eyes were red and swollen from crying. "How soon until we . . ." She swallowed and looked away. "Until we know one way or another?" she finished softly, turning to face him again.

Dr. Weiner looked deep into her eyes, wishing there was some way to give her more hope. But there was so little hope. He and the battery of surgeons had raced against the clock. Against one of the most devastating and dangerous wounds a human being could suffer. The bullet had been fired at nearly point-blank range and had perforated the stomach before lodging in the liver.

Petite Hélène pressed herself against Edmond, her face buried in his chest. "Is there anything we can do?" she cried softly.

Dr. Weiner clapped a weary hand on her shoulder. "Pray," he suggested gently. "If you believe at all in the power of prayer, now's the time to pray."

Petite Hélène entered the hospital chapel and quietly shut the door behind her. Soundlessly she slipped down the aisle and into the front pew beside Hélène.

Hélène turned to her, a questioning look in her eyes.

"The operation is over," Petite Hélène said quietly. "Now all we can do is wait and pray."

Hélène followed her niece's eyes to the crucifix suspended above the altar. Her lips quivered and her shoulders slumped. She covered her haggard face with her hands. Pray, she thought numbly. For ten hours, she'd been trying hard, but the prayers weren't forthcoming. Each time she bowed her head and closed her eyes, the same nightmare vision sprang before her.

"Someone named Z.Z. sends you her regards."

Hélène stared down at the barrel of the revolver, unable to move as the Chameleon's index finger began to squeeze the trigger.

Then suddenly Nigel knocked her sideways with all the

force he could muster. She screamed as her body slammed into the hard plastic cabin wall behind the Plexiglas bulkhead. She caught a blur of movement as Nigel charged forward, his forearm deflecting the Chameleon's aim.

The sound of the shot was like thunder. The bullet slammed into the bulkhead in front of her, the Plexiglas quivering under the impact, the mirror strips adorning it cracking into intricate glass cobwebs.

She felt the blood surging to her temples as Nigel wrestled the Chameleon. Both men's faces were red, and their veins stood out on their foreheads as if sculptured in bold relief. In seemingly slow motion they struggled for control of the gun, their arms quivering as they exerted as much pressure against each other as they could possibly summon. Then, in horror, she watched the Chameleon's gun arm slowly coming down . . . down . . . down. Down into Nigel's body.

Ca-rack!

She let out a piercing shriek and covered her ears with her hands as Nigel staggered forward, staring at the Chameleon in surprise. Then, with a superhuman effort, he somehow managed to turn the gun against the Chameleon. A last blast shook the cabin, and the Chameleon froze. This time it was his turn to look surprised. Then he slid slowly down to the carpet. Nigel bent forward and grasped the bulkhead, gasping for air.

"Nigel?" Hélène's voice was a strangled cry. "Nigel?"

On hands and knees she crawled out from behind the bulkhead and got shakily to her feet. He started to turn. Then his legs gave out from under him, and she caught him as he sagged backward. Slowly she lowered him.

"Nigel . . ." She shook him desperately. "*Nigel!*" Then she let out a cry and shrank back. His abdomen was soaked in blood.

"Oh, God, Nigel, *no!*" she screamed in panic, the tears streaming down her cheeks. "Not *now*! Don't die now!"

And then she cradled his head in her arms, staring as if mesmerized as his blood pumped out from his body, and all her hopes and dreams along with it.

She heard a chilling, high-pitched scream. At first she thought it was Nigel. It was several moments before she realized where it had actually come from—the depths of her own throat.

* * *

706

"Tante Hélène! Tante Hélène!" She felt Petite Hélène's arms around her, compassionately rocking her back into the present.

Both of them were crying, and they cried and cried for a long time.

Nigel lay motionless in the narrow bed, a network of clear plastic tubes coursing into his body. The television monitors on the table beside the bed registered low, painful bleeps and traced listless graphs. Hélène turned and looked at the doctor without speaking. She tried to smile bravely, and touched his arm.

He nodded reassuringly and left her alone in the room.

For a long moment she just stood there looking at Nigel in silence. Then she turned away to stare at the monitors. She saw the unsteady green lines becoming weak mounds before becoming lazy lines again. Then slowly she tore her eyes away from the screen and approached the bed. She sank to her knees and pressed her cheek against Nigel's hand. It felt cool and lifeless. Only the occasional bleeping of the monitors assured her that he was still showing signs of life. She remembered what Petite Hélène had told her—how many hours ago, now?—"Now all we can do is to wait and pray."

Did she know any prayers? she wondered. And could she pray? No, she *couldn't* pray—couldn't since that winter afternoon so long ago when Maman had been carted off by the Nazis; couldn't since Catherine and little Marie's torture and disappearance; couldn't since the day Jeanne had been snatched so brutally from life. She hadn't been able to worship God after he had abandoned all things dear to her. So how could she pray for his help now? It would be . . . two faced. Hypocritical. A desperate, last-ditch attempt just in case all else failed.

She looked up at Nigel, lying there so pale and motionless. He had put his life on the line to save her. She owed him a prayer. A thousand prayers.

She took a deep breath. For a moment she hesitated. Then she kissed his hand. "I'll start praying for you, my darling," she whispered. "I'll pray for both of us!"

Once again she stared back at the monitor. It seemed to have been silent for too long. The bleep, when it finally came, filled her with relief.

She tried to swallow, but there was an immense lump

blocking her throat. Her hands were clammy and trembled. Could she really remember the prayers she had not said since childhood? She had promised Nigel that she would pray for him, but could she summon the prayers up from the dead-letter box that was religion in her mind and begin chanting them? For both Nigel's sake and her own? Could she even begin to believe in the *comfort* of prayer, let alone its power?

She closed her eyes, and again the scene of horror sprang up before her. Nigel throwing her out of harm's way, sacrificing himself to save her.

God bless him, she thought, and those three words triggered it. The long-forgotten prayers began to surface from the depths of her soul. Almost without her knowing it, her lips began to move, and in a whisper she surrendered herself to God.

"Our Father, who art in heaven . . ."

Her heart leaped joyously. So she really *did* believe. She squeezed her eyes shut and bowed her head.

"Hallowed be thy name . . ."

She thought she heard a sound, a quickening of the monitors' bleeps, but she couldn't be sure. Vaguely she heard activity, a door opening, soft footsteps, excited low voices, but nothing could penetrate the invisible wall of prayer that she had erected around her.

". . . Thy kingdom come . . ."

The nurse who had come in ran back out; a moment later, Dr. Weiner came rushing in with her, his stiff white smock flapping around his legs. There was a buzz of conversation.

"The monitors are registering an increase in his pulse," the nurse said quietly.

Dr. Weiner bent down and watched one monitor, then another, nodding slowly. "Maybe," he murmured. "Just maybe . . ."

The nurse turned and noticed Hélène for the first time. "How did she get in here?" she whispered harshly. "No one's supposed to be—"

"Hush," the doctor said patiently, feeling his hopes rising as the monitors' pulses quickened and jumped. "I invited her in. Under the circumstances, I didn't think it could hurt."

". . . Thy will be done. On earth as it is in heaven . . ."

Hélène's eyes were still closed. She wasn't even hearing the doctor and the nurse. Nor was she hearing the jumping pulsebeats of the monitors. Instead, she felt a tightening in her throat. She slumped forward and began to tremble. All at once she was realizing what the prayer was doing. It was stripping away all the years of pain. Like a snake shedding its old skin for a new one, she began to feel lighter. Freer. Like a caged bird must feel after its sudden release. Finally she was stepping over the threshold of heaven after spending an eternity in hell. The demons that had haunted her for a lifetime had been cast back into the darkness.

She looked up and opened her eyes. Then she caught her breath. The doctor was standing there, smiling as though he'd witnessed a miracle. The nurse looked confused as the monitors bleeped happily. And slowly, ever so slowly, Nigel turned his head sideways, opened his gold-flecked eyes, and smiled at her.

"Hélène . . ." he whispered.

A sob caught in her throat. For a long moment she was silent. ". . . *And . . . and forgive us our trespasses,*" she said in a fervent whisper, "*as we forgive those who trespass against us.*"

The Love Makers

This book is dedicated
with love to Gladys Allison
who started me off
many years ago*

* And grateful acknowledgement
is due Etta Barritt and Guy Dolen

Judith Gould's work has been translated into twenty-two languages. SINS was made into a major TV mini-series starring Joan Collins and was shown world-wide. Judith Gould lives and writes in New York State's historic Hudson River Valley.

REQUIEM

REQUIEM

QUEBECK, TEXAS:
August 14, 1985

1

The big Lincoln Continental ate up the asphalt miles between Brownsville and Quebeck. Seated beside her husband on the maroon leather seat, Dorothy-Anne Cantwell stared out the windshield with a blank expression on her face. Everywhere she looked she saw the wide open spaces of Texas, expanses of irrigated fields and citrus groves dotted with occasional, monotonous little towns. Not even towns, she thought, just clusters of sad houses, peeling and dirty and baked by decades of harsh sunlight. The sky, heavy and gray, loomed oppressively over the landscape. Traffic was light and they saw only an occasional car or truck. The landscape was monotonous and hypnotic. And it was worlds away from Manhattan.

She glanced sideways at the big urn on the seat beside her. It was not the usual crematorium urn, somber and plain and poured from a mold. This was one of a kind, the sterling silver intricately hammered and fashioned in a Rococo pattern of auricular scrolls and hand-rubbed to a high gloss finish. The sides flared out into twin handles terminating in delicately fluted ivy leaves which were repeated in swirls around the leaf-footed base.

Buccellati had done themselves proud.

Slowly, she reached over to touch the urn. She half expected it to radiate the warmth of her great-grandmother, Elizabeth Anne Hale, but the metal felt smooth and cold. The urn weighed at least seven pounds, but the handful of gray ashes in it was weightless.

Only three days ago, her great-grandmother had been alive. They had talked and she had smiled at Dorothy-Anne, kissed her. Only three days ago.

13

Now she was ashes.

Dorothy-Anne turned away, her eyes blurring with tears. She found the dampness soothing to the grittiness three sleepless, grief filled days had left in her eyes, but she knew she couldn't give in to tears. If she wept now, she wouldn't be able to stop for a very long time. And, first, she had a job to do.

She felt a stirring within her belly, and, wiping her eyes with a knuckle, she carefully shifted the weight of her body, swollen with the baby she carried.

If only Great-Granny had lived long enough to see this child, she thought sadly. The baby was due in just three weeks. Closing her eyes, she felt for the movement within her womb: a sharp kick, then another, followed by an ever-so-slight shifting of the child. Usually, the kicking filled her with a warmth and closeness for the child. But, now, in her exhaustion, her body seemed strangely alien and dis-attached. She felt her baby move, but wondered if it was in someone else's body.

'Honey? You all right?'

Startled, she opened her eyes and turned to her husband, Freddie. He kept glancing between her and the road, a concerned expression creasing his face.

'I'm fine,' she assured him softly. She smiled and reached over, placing a reassuring hand on his arm. He knew she hadn't been able to sleep since her great grand-mother's death, but she didn't want to alarm him by letting him see how drained and weak she felt now. 'Don't worry, honey. I'm okay. Just tired.' And then she let her head fall back gently on the headrest.

A few more weeks, she thought. Just a few more weeks and then I'll give Freddie his child. But that thought awoke a nagging worry which wiggled in the fog of her exhausted mind like a worm. What if it wouldn't come in a few weeks? What if it were sooner? What if the baby came tomorrow or even today?

She shifted again slightly, shaking her head to dispel the moment of panic. She shouldn't let Dr. Danvers worry her like this. He might be a doctor, even one of the best in the field, but he was just being overprotective when he advised her not to make the trip to Texas. She was, after all, still three weeks away from full term. And Dr. Danvers didn't understand the importance of her great-grandmother's last wish.

It had been a small enough thing to ask that Dorothy-Anne scatter her ashes in Quebeck, Elizabeth-Anne's home. Dorothy-Anne understood the request and knew she had to fulfill it as quickly as she could. That's what Elizabeth-Anne had wanted, and what Dorothy-Anne needed to do. She had to know Elizabeth-Anne's soul was finally at rest – the rest she had waited so long for, and so fully earned. Dorothy-Anne knew she was at the end of her rope, that she had pushed herself as far physically and mentally as she dared – but this was something she had to do, now.

Dorothy-Anne closed her eyes, again trying to ease her sense of restlessness and anxiety. But she knew these feelings wouldn't fade. They sprang from a grief so overwhelming, a loss so profoundly deep, it was physically painful. She didn't know if she would ever be able to get over it.

And then she had a thought that brought a tentative smile to her lips. After all, how could she forget a great-grandmother who had given her a thirty million dollar birthday present?

That had been on her ninth birthday, almost ten years before. Dorothy-Anne felt she would be able to turn the clock back to that day if she lived to be a hundred . . .

October 17, 1974. Autumn, and she was looking out her bedroom window in the big house in Tarrytown, her chin resting on her crossed arms. Below, the gardeners were out in full force, raking the fallen, golden leaves. But she wasn't watching them; she was on the lookout for Great-Granny's car. It would come from between the tall, clipped hedges which stood guard at the far end of the curved driveway.

She had been dressed and waiting for over an hour. Nanny, her governess, had allowed her to wear her favorite red dress, with its starched lace collar and glittering, tiny rhinestone buttons. After all, it wasn't every day that a girl celebrated her ninth birthday, or that Great-Granny came expressly to pick her up and drive her down to the city to celebrate it in style.

Dorothy-Anne glanced again at the china shepherdess clock on the windowsill. Her heart skipped a beat. It was twenty-seven past one. Just three more minutes, and Great-Granny's car would appear. Dorothy-Anne knew this for a fact; Elizabeth-Anne Hale was never late.

Dorothy-Anne sat poised to leap up, watching the second hand of the clock make three last graceful sweeping revolutions, and then at precisely one thirty, she jumped forward and pressed her nose flat against the glass, her breath making a little halo of fog. Her eyes lit up.

There it was, the majestic yellow-and-black Rolls-Royce. The shiny hood with the chrome grille and the big bug-eye headlamps was just nosing out from between the hedges.

Jumping to her feet, she ran from the room and raced down the long, carpeted hall. When she reached the head of the stairs, she got up on the sleek bannister with a well-practiced backward hop. She balanced herself carefully and then let go, beginning the long smooth slide down the wide staircase.

As she slid down to the first-floor landing, she saw Nanny looking up at her with stern disapproval. Immediately, Dorothy-Anne clutched the bannister so that, with a squeak of burning friction against her palms, she came to an abrupt halt. Slowly, she slid off the bannister and walked down the rest of the way with ladylike dignity.

She smiled shyly up at Nanny, but the smile wasn't returned. She didn't really mind. Nanny wasn't a bad sort, even if she wasn't much given to smiling. That didn't matter because Dorothy-Anne was fascinated by Nanny's looks. She was over fifty, with gray eyes and hair, and in profile her body looked remarkably like a silhouetted map of Africa. The stateliness of her bust and buttocks beneath the black dress she always wore was especially surprising in contrast to her thin and shapely legs.

Nanny looked down at Dorothy-Anne and without

16

speaking held out the tan cashmere coat and helped her into it. Then Dorothy-Anne stepped back and awaited inspection. She could almost see Nanny tick off the items on her check list with her critical glance: hair combed and neat, dress buttoned, hem straight. Now came the final test.

Nanny stepped closer and leaned down so that her pointed face was not two inches from Dorothy-Anne's.

'Breathe,' she ordered.

Dutifully, Dorothy-Anne opened her mouth and sighed right into Nanny's face.

Nanny's eyes flickered. She straightened, reached into her dress pocket, and produced a rock-hard white candy. Dorothy-Anne accepted it, unwrapped it from the clear cellophane and handed the wrapper back to Nanny. She then popped the mint into her mouth and with a practiced flick of her tongue, pushed it into the hollow of a cheek. The menthol taste was sharp and mediciney, but she refrained from making a face.

Nanny leaned down again and began to button Dorothy-Anne's coat from the bottom up. 'Now don't you forget your manners,' she warned sternly. 'When you get into the car, say: "Good afternoon, Great-Grandmother. It was very lovely of you to invite me." '

Dorothy-Anne nodded solemnly.

'If you receive a gift, open it *slowly*.' Nanny gave her a meaningful look. 'Don't tear the wrappings to shreds. And don't forget to say: "Thank you, Great-Grandmother. I'll treasure it always." '

Dorothy-Anne nodded again. The mint was making her salivate, but she refrained from swallowing. That way, the awful menthol taste didn't spread.

She then followed Nanny to the main entrance and stepped aside as the huge mahogany double doors were pulled open by the butler. When she stepped outside, the fresh air felt cool and good against her face. A brisk wind was blowing down the Hudson Valley, scudding the white clouds overhead and doubling the work of the gardeners who were still busy raking leaves.

As soon as she heard the door shut behind her, she leaned over the balustrade, turned her face sideways and spat the mint behind the clipped yews, where it joined a pile of others. Then she wiped her lips with the back of a hand and, letting out a whoop of joy, raced down the steps to the waiting car.

Forty minutes later, the big car rolled to a stop under the yellow canopy of the Hale Palace Hotel on Fifth Avenue. Both of the doormen came rushing down the red-carpeted steps, practically falling over each other to open the passenger door. Dorothy-Anne slipped carefully out on the street side, pushed the door shut with both hands and came around the car. Wide-eyed, she stared at the doormen. They were identical twins, dressed in pale blue uniforms with glittering rows of brass buttons and braided gold epaulets on their shoulders.

Max, the chauffeur, went wordlessly around to the trunk and lifted out Elizabeth-Anne's collapsible wheelchair. Max was the biggest man Dorothy-Anne had even seen. He was Japanese, carried his huge shoulders and enormous paunch with pride, and had once been a sumo wrestler. Dorothy-Anne thought Max was a funny name for a sumo wrestler, but Great-Granny had explained that her first chauffeur had been named Max, and thereafter, she had called all the others Max, too.

During the drive down from Tarrytown, Great-Granny's nurse, Miss Bunt, had sat up front beside Max. Now she silently took the chair from him and wheeled it into position on the sidewalk. She held it firmly by the handles as Max ducked into the Rolls.

'Ready, Miss Hale?' he asked.

Great-Granny looked at him dourly, but she didn't move. 'As ready as I'll ever be,' she said in her clear, clipped voice.

Carefully, he scooped her out of the car and deposited her ever so gently into the wheelchair. Next came the lap blanket, which he tucked around her lap and legs.

Dorothy-Anne watched the ritual closely, fascinated as always by anything Elizabeth-Anne did. She idolized her great-grandmother, realizing even at her young age that the elder Hale was a very special type of woman.

Although Elizabeth-Anne's last stroke had left her

paralyzed from the waist down, no one had ever heard her complain; nor did she give the impression that she was helpless. When she had walked, she had done so with erect dignity and, now that she was confined to a wheelchair, she still maintained a regal bearing. Tall and gaunt, she wore her silver hair in a thick, full permanent. Clipped to her ear lobes were large jade cabochons surrounded by a fine lace-work of white gold filigree.

The bright afternoon light showed each of her seventy-one years etched clearly on her face, her skin cracked finely like the surface of an ancient painting seen through a magnifying glass. Yet the light showed more than her age. It also revealed her unique and indomitable strength. That was what was most striking about her, her unmistakable air of inner purpose. She was a woman at home in plush and polished surroundings, but also one of the world's shrewdest and wealthiest entrepreneurs, the founder of a multinational empire which included 432 luxury hotels worldwide.

'Thank you, Max,' Elizabeth-Anne said crisply once she was settled comfortably in her wheelchair. She focused her clear blue eyes on Dorothy-Anne, and raised her eyebrows questioningly. 'Shall we proceed?'

Dorothy-Anne nodded.

Elizabeth-Anne Hale lifted a hand in an imperious but graceful gesture. 'Miss Bunt?'

The nurse stepped aside as the twin doormen took over. They pushed the wheelchair smoothly up the ramp, while Dorothy-Anne and Miss Bunt followed alongside, on the red-carpeted stairs. The chair rounded the top of the ramp and Miss Bunt took over again, pushing Great-Granny toward the gleaming brass and etched-glass doors of the Hale Palace that the doormen already held open. Dorothy-Anne noticed that the doors were flanked by perfect, ball-shaped topiary trees in brass tubs. She fell back as something about the tubs caught her eye. They gleamed like gold and . . . for the first time she noticed the engraved intertwined script H's.

Hale Hotels.

Like the cherry topping a sundae, this last touch made her feel especially important. Great-Granny was a Hale. And so, she thought with a surge of pride, was she.

Elizabeth-Anne had commandeered the Tropical Court so the two of them could have lunch alone. The enormous courtyard was glassed-in eighteen floors above, and Dorothy-Anne thought it was the most exciting place in the world. With the splashing fountains, thickets of exotic foliage and towering palms, the restaurant allowed one to easily imagine it was in the tropics. Especially with the riotously feathered parrots and pale cockatoos with clipped wings that screamed from their perches.

The lunch was accompanied by a string quartet, and served by a moustached maitre d' and two unctuous waiters. The meal itself was simple but delicious: jumbo shrimp cocktails, a salad of red lea and avocado, whole lobsters and sauteed green spinach. Elizabeth-Anne chatted warmly with Dorothy-Anne as the girl happily cleared her plates, even down to the spinach.

When the meal was over, three waiters and the maitre d' brought in an exquisitely frosted birthday cake. Nine tiny candles were arranged in a circle and glowed with little halos. As it was ceremoniously set down in front of Dorothy-Anne, the quartet broke into a rendition of 'Happy Birthday'. Great-Granny joined the singing, her voice surprisingly clear and melodious.

The cake was served with dollops of French vanilla ice cream and a bottle of chilled Dom Perignon. Great-Granny allowed Dorothy-Anne to drink half a glass of it, undiluted. When the desert plates were cleared away, the quartet withdrew and they were alone. The splashing of the fountains and the screams of the birds now sounded very loud. Great-Granny looked across the courtyard, and Dorothy-Anne followed her gaze. Two men carrying attache cases were walking toward their table.

'Gentlemen,' Elizabeth-Anne said, gesturing proudly, 'this is my greatgrand daughter, Miss Dorothy-Anne Hale.'

The men looked down at her and extended their hands. Dorothy-Anne remained seated and shook hands politely.

Both men seemed to have very dry, brittle skin. They were in their sixties and had gray hair and wore pin-striped suits.

'Mr. Bernstein, Mr. Morris,' Elizabeth-Anne said. 'Please, sit down.'

As the men obeyed, putting their attaché cases down beside their chairs, Elizabeth-Anne rested her elbows on the table and folded her hands. She looked at Dorothy-Anne and came right to the point. 'Mr. Bernstein and Mr. Morris are attorneys,' she explained.

Dorothy-Anne looked solemn and Elizabeth-Anne laughed with amusement. 'Don't look at them like that, my dear,' she said briskly. 'They are not here to arrest you.' She smiled and took a sip of her coffee. Then she looked pointedly at Dorothy-Anne over the rim of her cup. 'They are merely delivering your birthday present.'

'Honey?'

The voice seemed to be floating in space amidst swirling memories and flashes of technicolor pictures.

'Honey . . . '

It was a warm voice, a voice Dorothy-Anne knew well and loved. She opened her eyes and snapped back to the present. She shook her head to clear it.

'Are you awake, honey? It sounded like you were talking in your sleep.'

'No . . . no, I was just daydreaming. I'm okay now.' She smiled at him reassuringly, but in truth she wasn't sure if she *was* alright. She had just been in Manhattan, over a decade in the past; the memory had seemed so real, she wasn't sure if she was dreaming now, instead. But, no, the irrigated orchards were still moving past outside the car windows. And the ache in her heart was still there.

'We're about there, honey.'

She looked over at Freddie and tried to smile, then turned back to gaze out the windshield. She wondered how long she had been daydreaming. She didn't feel rested, but knew it must have been quite a while, as night had almost fallen and Freddie had already turned off the main highway, the one no one used anymore.

The sky had darkened some more and on the horizon,

21

Dorothy-Anne saw thunderheads, low and boiling, a menacingly dark charcoal gray. But overhead, they were a yellowish muddy brown, as if the sun were trying to leak through.

'Storm's brewing,' Freddie said. 'It looks pretty bad.' He lit his cigarette with the dashboard lighter and then inhaled so that the tip glowed orange in the darkening light.

Suddenly Dorothy-Anne's attention was drawn to the old billboard up ahead. It was ancient and peeling, a Pop Art relic from long before Pop Art came into being. It was big and rectangular, with a faded coronet jutting out over the top. The little orbs atop the coronet had long since broken away, and the flakes of gold paint had gone the way of the wind and the rain. Now the crown's edge looked like jagged teeth trying to take a bite out of the sky.

She stared at the billboard as it rushed toward her, and she mouthed the faded letters which clung tenaciously to it.

HALE TOURIST COURT

That was what it read, and it had been standing there long before Hale hotels had sprouted like mushrooms after a worldwide rainfall. Long before some clever, Madison Avenue design team had come up with the elegantly intertwined *HH* logo. Because long before everything else, there had been the Tourist Court.

It was just up ahead, on the side of the road, and it wasn't worth a second glance. There were a hundred thousand motels like it across the country on roads like this one, old roads obsolete now that newer highways had been built. The Tourist Court was just another row of dilapidated little cabins separated by carports, their only unique feature their roofs of corrugated iron, high, steep and sloping. They were mansard roofs, once painted bright orange and shining with newness, now weathered dull and rusting.

But still, this particular motel was special in a way no other could ever be. It was the *Hale* Tourist Court, and it was here that Elizabeth-Anne's worldwide empire had begun.

Was it possible? Dorothy-Anne asked herself, gazing at

22

the Tourist Court as Freddie slowed, pulled over and stopped the car. The idea of it spun dizzily in her foggy, exhausted mind. Could one ignoble motel have been the springboard for an empire of international luxury hotels? Could a lone woman truly have had such vision and incredible drive as to build one of the world's largest independently controlled fortunes from these buildings?

As if the answer lay in the Buccellati urn, Dorothy-Anne weakly pulled it onto her lap, holding it close against the baby within her. Now the silver no longer seemed cold or lifeless. She could almost feel a warmth seeping through it.

Freddie helped her out of the car, but she insisted on carrying the urn herself as they walked off through the growing darkness into the roadside orchard across the highway from the Tourist Court. She was moving as if in a daze, feeling more light-headed than ever. Once she stumbled, and Freddie took the urn from her. She felt a strange, cool sweat on her forehead, and so she let him hold it.

Her vision blurred with tears as Freddie unscrewed the cover of the urn. Wordlessly, he handed the urn to her.

She did not speak. Around them, the wind had risen, and the storm clouds roiled low and angry.

Slowly, she tilted the urn. The wind caught the spill of ashes, trapped them in sudden whirls of eddies, and then swiftly dispersed them in a long grey streamer. It was then that the first fat, heavy raindrops came splattering down, forcing the ashes groundward.

Now Dorothy-Anne understood why Elizabeth-Anne had requested that her remains be scattered here.

Because all things must end as they begin.

And then she doubled over as the skies broke open and the first stabbing pain seized her in its grip.

2

In the kitchen of the manager's cabin of the Hale Tourist Court, Mrs. Ramirez heard the rumble of thunder. Lifting

23

her heavy bulk off the kitchen chair, she made her way over to the window, parted the curtains and peered out.

The sky had become almost blue-black as night began to fall, and the flashes of lightning were coming closer. Soon, the downpour would begin, flattening the crops and flooding the irrigation canals. Storms such as this were extremely rare, but she had lived here all her life and could predict the weather by the pain in her swollen ankles - which were much more accurate than those modern weather charlatans on TV. The afternoon had been the kind of damp, peculiarly stifling white-hot day that heralded a terrible storm. The Mexican laborers who had been tending the neat rows of citrus groves had left early, hurrying home before the sky burst open. She wondered whether her husband and son would stay in Mexican Town at her brother's and wait for the storm to pass.

She continued to peer out the window, then suddenly frowned. Through the gloom she could make out a big car parked on the shoulder just down the road. Then she saw the man and the woman. They were slowly coming out of the groves, the woman walking heavily with her legs spread wide. The man was supporting her and the woman was bent over, as if in pain.

Just then, there was a tremendous crack of lightning and the overhead light in the cabin went out. Mrs. Ramirez muttered a curse. As if the storm were not enough, now there had to be a power failure, too.

She waited for a moment for her eyes to adjust to the darkness, then scraped back her chair and went over to the stove where the iron pot of bubbling beans and fatback were cooking for dinner. She found the candle and box of matches, scratched a match against the wall, and lit the candle. As the room slowly brightened, she heard overhead the sudden heavy drumming of raindrops on the iron roof. By reflex, she glanced up. From the sound of them, they were big raindrops, heavy and powerful, the kind that stung your face if you were caught outside.

Just then, she heard the hammering at the door. Frowning, she went over and pulled it open. In the flickering candlelight she could see the tall, handsome man supporting—really half-carrying—a woman and lugging a heavy-looking silver urn in his other arm. Their faces were glistening wet, and they were both soaked through to the skin. Behind them, the rain was coming down in silver sheets.

'Quickly,' Mrs. Ramirez urged. 'Come in before everything is soaked.' Her voice was thick with a Mexican accent.

Once they were inside, Mrs. Ramirez securely shut the door, then held the candle up. There was no time to waste on unnecessary words. She looked at Freddie Cantwell. 'Her time has come?'

'I don't know . . . I think so,' Freddie said, the fear clear in his voice. 'We were in the orchard and she cried out and collapsed. She's barely conscious now.'

'Follow me,' Felicia Ramirez said, taking Dorothy-Anne's other arm and helping Freddie guide her through the small manager's cabin to the back bedroom. She set the candle down on the scarred dresser and Freddie gently laid his wife on the bed. He placed the urn on the dresser, then leaned over Dorothy-Anne and smoothed the hair from her forehead. Her skin felt hot to the touch. 'She's feverish,' he said, turning tense eyes on Mrs. Ramirez.

'How close together come her contractions?' the heavy woman asked.

'I don't know . . . ' Freddie answered hesitantly. 'There was just that one, and she passed out.'

'We will wait for the next, then begin to time them.'

Freddie nodded then picked up the candle and asked, 'Do you have a telephone?'

'In the other room. Leave the candle here. I go get more. It is not good to leave a woman whose time is at hand in the darkness.' Her voice grew quiet. 'If the child enters a world of darkness, it will be forever blinded.'

Startled by the woman's superstition, Freddie put the candle down and started to follow her out, but Dorothy-Anne caught his arm. He turned around and looked down at her. Her eyes were wide and glazed; and her voice was weak. 'Freddie?' He smiled down at her, but her fingers dug into his arm with surprising strength. 'Don't leave me alone, Freddie,' she whispered. 'Please.'

'I'm going to stay right here, honey,' he promised. 'But first I've got to phone for a doctor.'

She nodded weakly.

He pressed her hand. 'Try to relax and get some rest. You'll need your strength.'

She nodded again, and shut her eyes. 'I'll try,' she said softly, giving into the exhaustion that swept over her. She listened as his footsteps receded. Then everything seemed suddenly quiet.

The Tropical Court of the Hale Palace had been anything but quiet. Even as Mr. Bernstein took the documents out of his briefcase, the parrots and the cockatoos continued their screeching. Dorothy-Anne remembered Mr. Bernstein flipping through the stapled papers one last time and then passing them over to Mr. Morris who also looked them over. Finally both men were satisfied that everything was indeed in order.

Mr. Bernstein turned to Elizabeth-Anne. He cupped his hand and coughed delicately. 'You are certain, then, that you wish to proceed with this transaction?'

'Mr. Bernstein,' she replied dryly, 'as you can see, I am over eighteen. Since I can drink and I can vote, I can certainly do with my money and holdings as I please.'

'Of course, of course,' he said soothingly. He looked over at Dorothy-Anne. 'Miss Hale?'

With a start, Dorothy-Anne realized he was addressing her. 'Yes, sir?'

'Your great-grandmother has decided to give you an . . . err . . . well, a rather generous birthday present.'

Mr. Morris nodded solemnly. 'Yes, a very generous gift, indeed.'

'In fact,' Mr. Bernstein continued, 'it is so valuable that although you shall own it the moment these papers are signed, you will not be able to take possession of it until your eighteenth birthday. Do you understand what I am trying to say?'

Dorothy-Anne nodded. 'You mean it's being held in trust for me.'

Mr. Bernstein seemed a bit surprised, but quickly

recovered his composure. Elizabeth-Anne settled back in her wheelchair and smiled proudly, but her voice was clipped.

'Mr. Bernstein,' she said briskly. 'Let's forego the formalities of a lecture, shall we? I may not be of sound body, but I *am* of sound mind. And my mind is made up. Now, shall we sign the papers?'

'There, there is the telephone.' Felicia Ramirez turned from the candles she was lighting and pointed a thick finger to the kitchen wall.

Freddie nodded, reached for the receiver and lifted it to his ear. There was no dial tone. Quickly, he jiggled the cradle up and down with his forefinger. He turned to Felicia. 'It's dead.'

She waved out the match she was holding, at the same time moving toward him. 'Here. Let me.' Snatching the receiver from his hand, she listened, also rattling the cradle up and down. After a moment she slowly hung up. 'It is the storm,' she said. 'The lines must be down.'

'What do we do?'

'Your car?' she suggested. 'You drive into town?'

'It's stuck,' he said grimly. 'I was so upset when Dorothy-Anne collapsed in the orchard that I rushed her back to the car and tried to start too quickly. The wheels dug into the sand, and the harder I tried to get out the deeper they went. It's hopeless now.' He ran his fingers through his hair miserably, then asked, 'Don't you have a car?'

'My husband has it,' she answered quietly. 'He has not returned. In a storm such as this, he is sure to stay in town. It is five miles away and it will soon be night. The trip is impossible in this weather.'

Freddie's head sagged. 'What do we do?' he whispered. 'We never thought there would be a storm like this . . . or that Dorothy-Anne would have the baby now . . . '

Felicia Ramirez drew herself up with calm dignity. She placed a gentle hand on his arm. 'I am a woman,' she said. 'I have six children and I have helped deliver others. I know what to do. Go, stay with your wife. Comfort her and

27

help her rest. I make hot water and get clean towels. It will be a long night.'

When Felicia returned to the bedroom, Dorothy-Anne was awake and tossing restlessly. She tried to sit up, but after a moment let her head drop back down on the pillow. Then, suddenly, she grimaced and arched her back as another contraction seized her. Startled, she opened her eyes widely and gasped from the pain. Freddie grasped her hand in concern, but Mrs. Ramirez seemed reassured.

'Good,' she said, checking her watch. 'A long time has passed since the last. There will be time to rest before the real labor begins.'

Dorothy-Anne collapsed back on the bed as the pain passed. Felicia pulled away the sheet that covered her. Gently, she began to probe with her hands. She frowned to herself and, then, for the first time, began to worry. She was used to her own and her cousin's wide generous hips, built to give birth. But this woman's hips were narrow and bony. The opening would be small and tight.

She gestured for Freddie to draw closer and lowered her voice so that the young woman would not hear what she had to say.

'The passage is narrow,' she murmured with concern. 'She is very small.'

Small. The whispered word drifted to Dorothy-Anne through a mist and set the swirling memories in motion. Yes, she was small. She had signed the lawyer's papers with her small, schoolgirl script then waited as they were witnessed. Then the pin-striped attorneys had congratulated her on the gift she had just received, and left. Miss Bunt had wheeled Great-Granny outside to the sidewalk, and then Great-Granny motioned for the nurse to leave them. The Fifth Avenue traffic moved downtown at a brisk pace. For a minute, they did not speak.

'Dorothy-Anne,' Great-Granny said finally.

Dorothy-Anne moved closer.

'Look up, Dorothy-Anne.' Great-Granny's voice rose to an excited whisper. 'Look up at the Hale Palace.'

Obediently, Dorothy-Anne leaned her head way back

and stared up at the hotel. The thousands upon thousands of tons of pale limestone seemed miraculously weightless. Like a wedding cake it rose in majestic splendor, tier after tier of terraces and balconies, until the twin towers broke off and rose even higher to scrape the fast-moving clouds scuttling across the bright blue sky. After a moment, she lowered her head and turned to her great-grandmother. She looked at her questioningly.

Elizabeth-Anne Hale reached out, took Dorothy-Anne's hand and squeezed it.

'It's *yours*,' Elizabeth-Anne whispered, her aquamarine eyes shining brightly. 'The Hale Palace is now yours, and yours alone. Happy Birthday, Dorothy-Anne!'

Dorothy-Anne awoke to the sound of rain lashing the roof. Freddie was leaning over her, anxiety and fear in his face.

She turned to him weakly, her face pale and pinched. 'Is the storm letting up?' she whispered.

Mrs. Ramirez seemed startled to hear her voice, but shook her head.

'My baby,' Dorothy-Anne said in a tiny voice. She placed a hand on the mound of sheet at her waist. 'My baby will be all right.'

'Your baby will be fine,' Mrs. Ramirez assured her gently. She joined Freddie and leaned over Dorothy-Anne, stroking aside a stray lock of the young woman's moist hair. 'A woman is born to give birth, no?'

Dorothy-Anne nodded her head hesitantly. While Freddie helped her lie back down, Mrs. Ramirez said, 'Now that you are awake, I examine you internally. I was about to wake you anyway.' Mrs. Ramirez turned to Freddie. 'I will need a pan of hot water.'

Freddie nodded and moved toward the kitchen, grateful to be of help. Mrs. Ramirez sat down on the edge of the bed. She reached out for Dorothy-Anne's hands and held them. The young woman's fingers felt cold and moist. 'Do you feel any pain?'

Dorothy-Anne looked up into the woman's dark, liquid eyes. 'Yes.'

'Where?'

Dorothy-Anne leaned forward and slowly twisted around so that the sheet fell to her waist and exposed her breasts, heavy and milk-filled.

Mrs. Ramirez nodded to herself. There would at least be no problem feeding the child. She glanced questioningly at Dorothy-Anne, who reached gingerly behind her and touched the small of her back. 'The pain is here.'

'Your back?'

Dorothy-Anne nodded.

Mrs. Ramirez flashed her an odd look. Then she rose and pulled the rest of the sheet away from Dorothy-Anne's body. The naked young woman shivered from the sudden chill.

'It will not take long,' Mrs. Ramirez said apologetically. She heard Freddie's footsteps and turned around. He was holding a pan of steaming hot water. She took it from him, set it down on the nightstand and then, tightening her lips, she dunked her hands into it. The water was scalding but she did not utter a sound. She washed her hands carefully and shook them dry.

Wordlessly, Dorothy-Anne lay back, scooted down on the bed and obediently parted her thighs. Mrs. Ramirez knelt before her.

Dorothy-Anne could feel the woman's fingers probing the warmth within her. She tensed, the fingers feeling rough and foreign.

'I am being gentle,' Mrs. Ramirez whispered. 'Please. Relax. I will not hurt you.'

Dorothy-Anne smiled wanly and bit down on her lip.

As she maneuvered her fingers, Felicia Ramirez forced herself to keep from frowning. The cervix was still not wide open, though it had dilated somewhat. They still had hours to wait.

She leaned over Dorothy-Anne and placed her ear next to the magnificently swollen belly. She listened for a while and then nodded to herself with satisfaction. She could hear the fetal heartbeat, strong and separate from the mother's own. That was good.

She started to pull the sheet up around Dorothy-Anne again when she remembered there was one more thing to check. Years ago, when she had given birth to Caesar, her second oldest, the old midwife had tested the position of the child.

Mrs. Ramirez lowered the sheet. With one hand inside the mother, and the other on the swollen belly, she gently felt for the child's position. Suddenly the breath caught in her throat. Could she be doing it wrong? She quickly checked again. No, it was true. The child was not positioned right. For a third time, she repeated the maneuver, just to make sure. There was no mistake.

She withdrew her hand and said, 'I go wash,' nodding for Freddie to follow. Once in the kitchen, she turned to him, her elbows crooked, her hands held up like a surgeon's about to be gloved.

'Well?' Freddie demanded.

'The child lays sideways,' Mrs. Ramirez hissed gravely, her eyes wide with alarm. 'It should come head first, like this – ' She motioned with her hand as her eyes flashed like embers in the candlelight. 'Your wife's baby, it lie like this – ' She slashed her hand sideways across her belly.

Before Freddie could answer, they heard Dorothy-Anne moan weakly from the other room and quickly returned to her side.

'What is it?' Freddie asked.

'I heard you whispering,' Dorothy-Anne said faintly. Her brow was still wet with sweat and her eyes glassy. 'My baby . . . my baby is going to die, isn't it?'

Mrs. Ramirez looked at her sharply and crossed herself. 'Do not speak of such things,' she hissed.

'No. I know it's true. I know it is. I'm being punished and my baby's going to die.'

Surprised by her words, but aware his young wife was almost delirious, Freddie smoothed the damp hair back from Dorothy-Anne's forehead and spoke softly. 'Punished? What for? You've never done anything that deserves punishment, darling.'

'Yes, I have,' Dorothy-Anne moaned. She felt a wave of exhaustion, a need to escape her fear swept over her and her eyes closed. But she fought sleep, determined now to speak, to get the truth out into the open. 'You don't know,

31

Freddie . . . Only Great-Granny understood. She protected me, but now she's gone, and I'll have to pay.'

'Dorothy-Anne, you're talking nonsense – '

'No, Freddie. I have to pay now,' she said, her breathing shallow and labored.

'But, for God's sake, what for?'

'Because . . . because I killed my mother. I killed her, and now Great-Granny's gone . . . And she was the only one . . . ' Her voice trailed off.

'The only one who what?'

'Who understood,' Dorothy-Anne answered, her voice the merest, weary whisper.

GENERATIONS
ONE
Elizabeth-Anne

New York City
August 4, 1928

1

The day Elizabeth-Anne Hale arrived in midtown Manhattan with her four children, the mercury hit ninety-six degrees and New York was a blistering furnace. The asphalt streets were baked to a soft goo and the concrete buildings seemed to writhe as they trapped the stifling air and simmered it between their canyon walls.

'Where to?' the taxi-cab driver they hailed at Penn Station asked as Elizabeth-Anne climbed in to the front seat beside him. He was worriedly watching the children clamber into the back, but when he turned to glance at Elizabeth-Anne he was taken aback.

At thirty-three, she was not a beautiful woman, but in her excitement she was radiant. Her face was handsome and strong with its thin, straight nose and sparkling eyes the shade of the clearest, most perfect aquamarine. Despite their jewel-like radiance, her most striking feature was her waist-long, wheat-gold hair, enviously fine and abundant. She wore it tightly plaited and pinned up so that it wouldn't get in the way of things. Her waist was shown off to advantage by her white blouse and full-length, gray calico skirt. Around her neck hung a simple pendant, a pansy encased in glass, that her husband had given her upon their engagement.

She looked at the driver, her eyes wide and sparkling, set in a well-tanned face. 'Could you recommend a hotel? One that's decent but not too expensive?' she asked.

'Sure. There're hundreds of hotels in this town.' He glanced into the rear view mirror at the three girls and little boy in the backseat. The trunk of the cab was half open and tied down, loaded with luggage. 'The Madison Squire's a good hotel. Not cheap, but not expensive either.'

'The Madison Squire it is, then,' she said, thinking they would stay there even if it were too expensive, at least for one night. The journey had been tiring and they could always change to another hotel in the morning. After that, her first order of business was to find an apartment for herself and the children.

The cabbie swung the taxi out into the traffic. 'Where you from?'

'Texas.' Her voice was crisp and clear.

'I'll never for the life of me understand you country people. Why come to this noisy, dirty city for a vacation when you've got all the fresh air you could possibly want at home?'

'We're not on vacation. We're moving here.'

The cabbie shook his head. 'Me, I can't wait till I retire and get a nice house somewhere in the country. Especially when there's a heat wave.'

'We're used to heat.'

'Yeah, guess it gets hot down there in Texas.'

'That it does.'

'What did you do there? Ranch?'

'Ranch?' She was laughing lightly, chidingly. 'No, Texas isn't all ranching, I'm afraid. There are other things there. Lots of other things.' She smiled almost coyly, then turned to watch the city as it flashed by her window, letting her mind wander.

Elizabeth-Anne had owned and run three businesses in Quebeck, Texas: the Hale Rooming House, the Good Eats Cafe, and the Tourist Court she had built along the new highway. She had sold the rooming house and the cafe, and not for a song, either. She certainly wasn't going to advertise the fact, but in her purse was a cashier's check for nearly thirty thousand dollars. That check would nurture her dreams, it was the gateway to a new life, a new future for both herself and the children. A future that would be helped along by the income she still earned from the Tourist Court. It was in capable, trustworthy hands, and she knew it would continue to show a comfortable profit.

With that financial security, it was easier for Elizabeth-Anne to face the task of raising four children alone.

Elizabeth-Anne twisted around in her seat and smiled back at the children, but they didn't seem to notice. Their eyes were glued to the open windows, staring up at the incredibly tall buildings and the well-dressed crowds teeming on the sidewalks.

Elizabeth-Anne looked from one child to the next, starting with Regina. She eyed her oldest daughter fondly, with deep pride. At sixteen, Regina promised to grow into a handsome woman. She reminded Elizabeth-Anne of herself, with her thick, wheat-gold hair which she wore down in a fine mane that reached to her waist. Regina didn't carry a spare ounce of fat on her small, able-bodied frame, thanks to her endless round of chores back in Quebeck. She was a serious girl, well on her way to womanhood, but the freckles around her nose were those of a child. In her lively, inquisitive eyes, Elizabeth-Anne saw stamina and vigor. When the Mexican midwife had slapped her, she hadn't cried out in pain; she'd wailed indignantly.

Her gaze shifted. Fourteen year old Charlotte-Anne had been, of her three daughters, the most difficult to deliver, which Elizabeth-Anne thought ironic, as she was also the most perfectly formed physically. Charlotte-Anne's hair, too, was a rich, ripe shade of yellow, but incredibly fine and silky. She was tall for her age and very slender, with pale flawless skin, pale pink lips, and the Hale aquamarine eyes. But Charlotte-Anne's eyes were so incredibly pale, they enchanted and made one feel ill-at-ease at the same time. The pale hair, complexion, and eyes gave her a peculiar beauty Elizabeth-Anne recognized as truly remarkable.

Rebecca was the youngest of the girls, eleven, and the most sensitive of the four children. She was not startlingly beautiful like Charlotte-Anne, or blessed with the natural intelligence of Regina, but she well made up for it with a quiet determination all her own. Whereas Regina and Charlotte-Anne were both evenly blended distillations of Elizabeth-Anne and her husband, in Rebecca the mix of traits had not been balanced. She was large and gangly, and her face was her father's, strong-boned and heavy. Her eyes were a deeper blue than Elizabeth-Anne's, her brows golden like her Hale hair. Of her three daughters, Elizabeth-Anne respected Rebecca the most. Not because she was the youngest, but because she lacked beauty, grace, and a superior intelligence, yet worked hard enough to make up for her deficiencies. Too, Rebecca's lack of self-confidence was poorly concealed, a vulnerability that kept her close to Elizabeth-Anne's heart.

And that left little Zaccheus. He had just turned four, and whenever she looked at him, the breath caught in her throat. He was the spitting image of his father, a miniature Zaccheus Hale Senior, with the very same purposeful, intelligent gleam in his Hale-blue eyes, and that wonderfully enigmatic, lopsided smile. Looking at him now her heart again skipped a beat and she reached out and stroked the blond bangs out of his eyes. He ignored her; his blue-blue eyes were wide with wonder as he stared out at the city. Yes, she thought, he was indeed Zaccheus's son – his eyes, his lips, it was all there, an eerie reincarnation, a living reminder for her to keep close and treasure.

Elizabeth-Anne shook her head sadly. It was a fine family she had, albeit a fatherless one. She had been without Zaccheus for four years now, four years since the happy days of their marriage had ended so suddenly. Little Zaccheus had still been enwombed within her when Zaccheus had left. The love with which they had conceived their son, the love that was to have lasted a lifetime, had been shattered as easily as a thin crystal flute dropped onto a stone floor.

Zaccheus had been everything to her. After her parents, local farmers in Quebeck, had died, she had grown up with an aunt, a kind and loving woman who had raised Elizabeth-Anne as well as she could while running her rooming house and cafe. Elizabeth-Anne had inherited those businesses in her late teens when her aunt died, and had continued the life of hard work and loneliness she had grown up with. It had often seemed to Elizabeth-Anne in retrospect that she had never really known happiness until she met Zaccheus. Also the child of farmers, he had come

38

from the midwest to Texas to seek his fortune. They had fallen in love at first sight. Brilliant and quick, he was a witty, easy talker, but also a marvelous listener. And handsome too, so handsome that he still brought an ache to her heart. They had started a family together young, but he had proven to be a decent man, a marvelous father and provider, patient and dependable, the perfect lover and friend.

Then it had all ended. Suddenly and horribly, it had ended with one freak and meaningless accident that had shattered their lives forever.

Zaccheus had been at the construction site of the Tourist Court, the motel he and Elizabeth-Anne were building beside the new highway. It had been Elizabeth-Anne's idea, her dream, and Zaccheus had readily agreed to it – even though the construction would take all the money they had saved – because he recognized the passion and conviction of her vision. But now, several months into the project, the work was going badly, held up again and again by mysteriously lost deliveries of supplies from the Sexton warehouse. Soon they would be out of money, but neither Elizabeth-Anne nor Zaccheus saw a solution in sight. They both knew Sexton was sabotaging the construction intentionally. He was the biggest man in the county, owning most of the land and the businesses on it, and from the start he hadn't looked favorably on competition from the Hales.

Late one night after everyone else had left, Zaccheus had gone out to the site to meet Sexton, to confront him about the lost deliveries, and the two men had argued. But Zaccheus had been nowhere near the other man when he had rushed forward in anger, tripped on the uneven ground and fallen, splitting his head open on exposed piping.

Zaccheus had fled, knowing that no one would believe he had nothing to do with Sexton's death. He and Elizabeth-Anne had too much to gain now that the old man was gone. So he had left Elizabeth-Anne a note, explaining what had happened and apologizing, both for the stupid fate that had forced him to flee the certain death sentence a Sexton-family controlled court would hand him, and for leaving without her. He couldn't, his note explained, ruin her and the children's lives by trying to take them with him. Instead, he had pleaded for her to remain, to raise the children, finish the motel and nurture the dream she had started with him.

Thinking of him even now brought tears to Elizabeth-Anne's eyes, but the tragedy was four long years in the past and felt distant to her on this day of new beginnings. She had lived a long time without a word or trace of him, lived through long years of financial struggle, of personal loneliness, of need for her children. She had managed, even succeeded, but she had realized she found too little joy in her accomplishments in Quebeck. Finally, she had known she too had to leave Texas, to get away from the memories of her lost marriage and to find a place where her dream would know no limit, and could be fully achieved.

Oh Zaccheus, she thought again now, unconsciously fingering the pansy charm at her neck, wherever you are, just remember that I love you. Just remain free and enjoy what you can of your new life. You're still mine, enshrined in my heart, and the children's, forever.

And now, as the cab pulled up to the Madison Squire Hotel at Madison Avenue and Thirty-Seventh Street, the memories and hurt receded. Elizabeth-Anne took a deep breath and squared her shoulders bravely to face the hectic, strange new world, and the new life she hoped to carve for herself and the children.

'Thank you,' Elizabeth-Anne told the cabbie after she paid him. 'The children and I can manage the luggage ourselves.'

The doorman took one look at her plain country clothes and then ignored them, stern disapproval showing in his eyes. Even the porter, who usually sprang into action when guests arrived, hung back.

Elizabeth-Anne and the girls unloaded the trunk and then watched in silence as the cab drove off. As it did so, Elizabeth-Anne felt horribly alone. Her determined conviction that the future loomed brilliant before them dissipated like so much mist in a stern breeze and reality started to sink in. Husbandless and mother of four, she was in a strange city where she knew no one, a city of immense crowds and tall buildings the likes of which she had never seen.

She smiled bravely, so that the fear she felt would not rub off on the children. Leaning her head back, she gazed up at the forbiddingly enormous, elaborate hotel rising fourteen stories above Madison Avenue. There was an intimidating, solid classicism about the building's ornate pilasters and carved pediments that made her feel small and insignificant, but she also thought it beautiful. Only later would she learn that only the front of the Madison Squire was so lavish; the other three sides were grimy, utilitarian brick.

She nodded briskly to the children. 'Let's go inside,' she said before her courage could desert her again. She hefted two of the large battered suitcases and the girls took one apiece, grimacing as they lugged them along after her, little Zaccheus bringing up the rear with the shoebox filled with his favorite toys clutched tightly to his chest.

They drew to a halt in front of the revolving doors, wondering how in the world they were going to squeeze the luggage and themselves into the small triangular glass wedges.

The problem was solved for them. Heaving an audible sigh, the doorman pushed open a disguised glass panel next to the revolving door and held it open for them.

'Thank you,' Elizabeth-Anne said, favoring him with a grateful smile. His face remained studiously vacant.

As she crossed over the threshold into the lobby, Elizabeth-Anne supressed the awe she felt, reminding herself that, as the owner of the Tourist Court back in Quebeck, she too was a host to travelers and had a professional interest in her surroundings. She recognized immediately that while the Madison Squire was hardly welcoming in the homey sense, its lavish lobby certainly had a majestic, formal elegance.

Setting the suitcases down she absently fingered the pansy encased in crystal suspended from her neck. Her sharp eyes roamed the lobby, taking in the gleaming marble walls, the veined, inlaid marble floor, and the

41

opulent brass and crystal chandelier glittering overhead. The Louis XVI settees and chairs dotting the room were large and formal, and Charlotte-Anne and Rebecca set down their cases and plopped themselves onto the brocade upholstery. Zaccheus Jr. let out a 'whoop!' and, making a headlong dash, leapt onto a settee of his own. Regina accompanied Elizabeth-Anne, who strode to the massive carved reception desk and fixed the clerk with a smile. It was a totally disarming smile, but it did nothing to soften the dour, haughty expression on his face.

'We need two rooms, please,' Elizabeth-Anne said. 'One with two beds and one with three.'

The slim, dark-haired man took one look at her neat but simple country clothes, sniffed disdainfully, and announced in a haughty voice, 'It's seven dollars for the two rooms. I'm afraid our only vacancies are on the second floor, no view, only an airshaft. With this heat you'll burn up. May I suggest the Algonquin or the Plaza or any of the many other fine – '

Elizabeth-Anne, who quickly estimated there were some seventy cubicles behind the reception desk, half of which had keys signifying vacancies, continued to smile radiantly. 'Those rooms will suit us just fine, I'm sure.'

'Well, if you insist – '

'I do.'

The clerk began to say something, but the steadiness of Elizabeth-Anne's gaze caused him to think twice, and his jaw snapped shut. He fished out two sets of keys, each attached to a large brass tag with the room number engraved on it, and laid them down on the desk. 'That'll be seven dollars in advance,' he said.

Elizabeth-Anne counted the bills out on the desk. The clerk slid them toward him, at the same time smacking his palm on the bell to summon the bellboy, but the moment it clanged, Elizabeth-Anne laid her fingers on it to silence it. 'Just the keys, please,' she said. 'We can find our own way and carry our luggage ourselves.'

'As you wish,' the clerk said with a sigh of disapproval.

'Thank you, Mr. – '

'Smythe.'

'Thank you, Mr. Smythe.' Elizabeth-Anne picked up her two battered suitcases, and, after the children had done the same, they all proceeded toward the marble staircase with its gleaming, solid brass bannisters.

The clerk cleared his throat noisily. Elizabeth-Anne half turned, a questioning look on her face.

'The elevator is that way,' he said, pointing in the opposite direction. 'Just ring the buzzer.'

Elizabeth-Anne inclined her head and changed course. 'Thank you, Mr. Smythe.'

He didn't reply. He didn't have to. It was written clearly in his mirthless eyes: *Country bumpkins*.

Soon after dark, the children went to sleep, exhausted from their long, exciting day.

Elizabeth-Anne crossed her arms, walked slowly over to the window, and leaned out. The desk clerk had been right, she thought. Despite the open windows, the room was stuffy and hot. But she discovered that if she leaned out and angled herself just right, she could catch a thin sliver of view - a tall, compact slice of Manhattan skyscrapers winking and glittering in the night.

She felt conflicting emotions coursing through her - a million fantastic dreams stirring within her - while at the same time she asked herself what on earth she was doing in the midst of the noisiest, strangest city in the world. It was like coming to a foreign country where she knew no one and where many different languages were spoken. After the down-home friendliness she had always known, why had she come here to subject herself to the hustle and bustle of New York, to the hordes of always rushing, unsmiling people?

An unbidden sigh slowly escaped her lips. She knew why. Because Quebeck could no longer feed her ambitions, could not match the scale of her imagination. She longed to build, to create, and the opportunities were *here*, amid the crowds and the noise, amid the energy that made the air crackle with electricity. Here, through sheer hard work, and given enough luck, she felt she could fulfill her dream. The dream she had nurtured ever since she was a child.

43

She smiled to herself, wondering at her ambitious cheek and gall. Other little girls she knew dreamed of meeting a handsome prince and being carried off to his castle to live happily ever after, but not her. No, her dream was far more practical, but just as romantic in its own way. For she, Elizabeth-Anne Hale, had always imagined herself as the queen of a grand hotel. She had seen one such edifice as a child, and it had been engrained in her mind ever since. She remembered the endless games she had played alone while growing up, imagining herself not in the plain rooming house but in charge of a glittering palace filled with bejeweled guests, *her* guests. She would give them elegant meals, gentle music, sumptuous rooms and they would line up to see her, to come stay with her in the greatest hotel in the world.

As she grew, the vision she had created as a child never changed; it simply grew clearer in her mind. Carriages became automobiles, gaslight became electric, but the quality of luxury, her personal touch, remained. And the older she became, the more she envisioned not a single grand hotel, but two, three, even a hundred – and they would all be hers. *Hers.*

The rooming house, the cafe, and the Tourist Court back in Texas had merely been the beginning. She had known that all along. They had been the first step toward realizing her dream. But in order to achieve it, she had had to leave Texas and come to New York City. Here, dreams which were too big to be contained could be forged into reality, of that she was certain. She would become a somebody. Given time, she would shine brighter than all the glittering night lights of Manhattan, more forcefully than the kaleidoscope of colors on Broadway. Because here the very air smelled of prosperity and success, and everywhere you went, you could hear the cash registers ringing. Having been born in Texas, a native-born and bred American, Elizabeth-Anne would not realize until many years later that she, was in effect, not all that different from the hordes of foreigners who had passed through Ellis Island. She did not hail from Lithuania or Greece, but she *was* an immigrant of sorts.

44

No, right now she knew only one thing: Here she would make it. Here she would triumph.

She could sense it.

But first, she had to find a home. Then, when she and the children were settled in . . . then she would set out to conquer this city.

2

Elizabeth-Anne was not prepared for Ludmila Koshevalaevna Romaschkova, nor was the white Russian emigrant prepared for her. They had nothing in common except the townhouse on Gramercy Park South, and it was that which brought them together.

The elegant, five-story house with its pale granite facade and tall, graceful parlor-floor windows had been left to Ludmila by a foresighted admiral in the Imperial Russian Navy who had fled the Bolsheviks with her (his mistress), four Imperial Easter Eggs by Carl Fabergé, and a numbered bank account in Switzerland filled with millions. It was a cruel twist of fate that brought a fatal cerebral stroke to the admiral, to whom Ludmila had been unofficial consort for seventeen years, on the eve of the wedding that would have finally fulfilled his promise to marry her. Only a lengthy and highly publicized court battle, during which Ludmila found herself face to face with the hatred of her departed lover's other heirs, as well as the entire exiled Russian community, had given her even a small compensation for the years she had devoted to the admiral. She received the title to the lavishly furnished townhouse they had shared together but nothing else. Otherwise penniless, she subsequently converted the upper three floors into autonomous apartments and rented them out to selected tenants.

'Who there?' a raspy, thickly accented voice finally called through the door after Elizabeth-Anne had knocked on it the sixth time.

'I've seen the *Apartment For Rent* sign outside,' Elizabeth-Anne called back, trying to speak above the hysterical yapping of dogs on the other side of the door. 'I would like to see it!'

'*Who?*'

Elizabeth-Anne spoke up louder. 'I want to see the apartment!'

There was a pause. 'Now why you not say that before?' There was a series of clicks as various locks were thrown, and the door opened a crack, held there by a thick safety chain. One huge gray eye, dramatically outlined with black liner, looked her up and down. 'Did *they* send you?' The voice was suspicious.

'They?'

'The Bolsheviks!'

Elizabeth-Anne suppressed a smile. 'No, I'm not a Bolshevik.'

'Good.' The door closed abruptly, the chain rattled and clacked, and Elizabeth-Anne found herself face to face with Ludmila Koshevalaevna Romaschkova.

Elizabeth-Anne stared at the diminutive woman in fascination, feeling an immediate liking for this stranger. Madame Romaschkova might have stood little more than four feet three inches tall in her heels, but she nevertheless projected a commanding presence. She held herself with instinctive dignity, and her carriage bespoke another, finer age. Even her thick accent, though exotic, was well-bred instead of amusing; it conjured up visions of ice palaces, tiaras studded with diamonds, and ermine fringed gowns.

Here is a somebody, a character, someone with a past, Elizabeth-Anne thought. She didn't know how right she was.

Although by the time Elizabeth-Anne met her, the glory of Ludmila's life in Russia was long over, you would never know it to look at her. She had retained her air of grace, beauty and privilege simply by making time stand still, by pretending nothing was different. She was as beautifully turned out as she had been fifteen years earlier. Her figure was still excellent with a tiny, cinched waist and a well-mounted bosom, although her fine, oval face had become increasingly lined, the tell-tale webwork of wrinkles spreading deeply into her once flawless skin. She dressed as she had in Russia, in the lavish fashions of pre-1917 St. Petersburg. Her dresses were perhaps a bit moth-eaten and tattered, but somehow that only emphasized the faded beauty. She draped herself with elaborately embroidered, fringed shawls, dressed in regal, heavy brocade better suited to the cold Russian winters than the milder climate in which she now lived, and, after the admiral died, she never took off the necklace he had sent her the morning after they had met – a malachite Fabergé egg encrusted with gold filigree hanging off a web of gold.

The entire effect was enough to make Elizabeth-Anne gape unabashedly.

'Well?' Ludmila Romaschkova demanded. 'What are you waiting for? Come in, come in.'

Elizabeth-Anne glanced down at her feet, afraid that if she moved she would step on one or more of the four white Maltese spaniels yapping at her heels.

'It is okay,' Madame Romaschkova assured her. 'The children, they know when you walk, they get out of way. Quick, quick.' She took Elizabeth-Anne by the arm, pulled her inside the apartment, slammed the door shut, and began locking the bolts across it.

'Are you afraid of burglars?' Elizabeth-Anne asked.

'Burglars? Burglars! Ha.' Ludmila Romaschkova whirled at her, gray eyes flashing. 'If only they were burglars. No, they are worse. Evil. First I have to fear the Reds, then the Whites. Burglars I could take care of.' She glowered dramatically, and then her face softened. 'Come, have tea with me. First we talk. Then we look at the apartment.'

Madame Romaschkova led the way into the parlor, preceded by the dogs. The dim, stuffy room was at once as entrancing as the woman herself. It looked more like the dusty storage room of a museum than a parlor. The furnishings were so tightly packed they had obviously once graced all five stories of the house. As Elizabeth-Anne's eyes adjusted to the dark she could make out two grand pianos, three daybeds, four consoles, a marble column, a

Napoleonic candelabra, two desks, a baroque chest, a medieval chest, a dark, carved Elizabethan table, and a gold and crystal Empire chandelier. Meissen parrots, lamps with fringed silk shades, chairs with gold hooves or claws for legs, tapestries, silver-framed photographs, icons mounted in silver, and coptic fragments behind glass were crammed together and on top of each other, all in happy, riotous, clashing splendor. It was an auctioneer's paradise, but no matter how strapped she was for cash, Madame Romaschkova's emotions won over her practicality. She would never dream of disposing of a single item.

'*This* is real tea,' Ludmila announced as she poured the strong black brew from the huge silver samovar. Elizabeth-Anne accepted the delicate, engraved crystal cup and its silver holder and was about to drop a cube of sugar into it.

'No.' Ludmila cried. 'You put the sugar in your mouth and sip.'

Elizabeth-Anne did as she was told. The tea was bitter and thick, not at all the way she liked to drink it, but when it met the sugar the taste was honey-sweet.

'This is how tea is to be drunk.' Ludmila sipped at hers and sighed contentedly. She was ensconced on a green velvet, four-sided siege, a round chair with four seats built out from a carved center post. It dated from the era of Napoleon III and looked as though it belonged in the lobby of a Second Empire opera house. Facing her, Elizabeth-Anne was seated on a straight-backed Regence fauteuil upholstered with Aubusson Royale tapestry.

Finally Ludmila leaned forward and placed her cup beside the samovar, which sat on an octagonal folding Bedouin table inlaid with ivory. Then she sat back again and made herself comfortable. 'Now. Tell me everything about yourself,' she demanded.

'Everything? About myself?' Elizabeth-Anne looked taken aback. 'Why, there's actually nothing to tell.'

'There is always something to tell.' Ludmila raised her chin and nodded sagely. 'You are married?'

Elizabeth-Anne set down her cup. 'Yes,' she said carefully, 'but I'm . . . alone.'

'Your husband? He is not here?'

She shook her head.

'Divorced?'

'Not really.'

'*Ha*. Men.' Ludmila shook her head angrily. 'Sometimes I wonder why we women put up with them. But do yourself favor. Next time choose nice Russian. They are the best,' she finished with a decisive nod.

Elizabeth-Anne smiled. 'I'll try and keep that in mind.'

'You do that.' Ludmila flipped open a cigarette box made of paper-thin burled wood, carefully chose a cigarette, stuck it in a long holder carved of horn, and lit it. Immediately a strong, pungent blue cloud of smoke enveloped her. She narrowed her eyes. 'You have children?'

Elizabeth-Anne nodded. 'Four.'

'*Four*?'

'Why, yes. I hope you don't mind – '

'Children,' Ludmila said grimly, 'are noisy, dirty and make much damage. I tell people always, you want apartment, no have children.'

'Well, I really ought to be going, then.' Elizabeth-Anne rose to her feet and smiled apologetically. 'Thank you for the tea. It was delicious.'

'You barely touched!' Ludmila wagged an accusing finger at Elizabeth-Anne's cup. 'Sit down, finish. Is a shame to waste.'

'But I really must go,' Elizabeth-Anne protested. 'I have to find us an apartment, and I mustn't lose any time.'

'Who says you lose time? We go upstairs and I show you the apartment. Is small for five people, but very nice.'

'But . . . I thought you didn't want to rent out to anyone with children.'

Ludmila puffed regally on her cigarette. 'Usually I don't,' she said nonchalantly. 'As soon as someone tells me children is no trouble and argue I say, well, Ludmila, you in trouble. If someone says, well, then I must go and look at someplace else, then I know is okay.' She beamed through the scrim of smoke at Elizabeth-Anne. 'Now finish your tea.'

49

Elizabeth-Anne looked at Regina and smiled hopefully. 'Well, what do you think?'

Regina looked around the bedroom thoughtfully. 'It's nice. I think we'll like it here.'

Elizabeth-Anne looked relieved. 'That's why I wanted you to be the first to see it. To see what you thought.' She paced the small bedroom, picking her way around the furniture. 'It's smaller than what I would have liked us to have, and a lot more expensive, but the neighbourhood is very good, and so are the schools. But the best thing about Gramercy Park is the park. Madame Romaschkova . . . I mean, Ludmila – ' Elizabeth-Anne broke off with a laugh. 'Somehow I still find it difficult to call her Ludmila. She just *looks* like a Madame or a Countess or something.'

Regina laughed too. 'I know what you mean.'

Elizabeth-Anne continued. 'Well, she told me the park is private. That only the tenants who live around it have keys, and she has had duplicates made for us. You children need fresh air and a safe place to play, and for that, this place is ideal.'

Regina nodded. 'But it's one bedroom short, isn't it?'

Elizabeth-Anne shrugged. 'Giving up my own bedroom's a small enough sacrifice for the convenience of having park privileges. I'll be comfortable on the chaise in the parlor.' She paused then and looked around fondly. 'And the furniture Ludmila's lent us is so beautiful. It just isn't worth shipping everything up from Quebeck. It would cost a lot more than the things are worth.'

'What's important is that *you* like it here Momma. That *you're* comfortable.'

'And I know you all will be, too.' Elizabeth-Anne hugged Regina warmly, but upon releasing her, she frowned. 'It's still a big change, and in a way, it frightens me.'

'But you wouldn't have it any other way.'

Elizabeth-Anne shook her head. 'You're right, I wouldn't. Come on, let's go sit in the parlor.' She led the way down the narrow hall and stopped in the doorway, studying the parlor with satisfaction. It was small but had a high ceiling and a marble fireplace. The parlor's single window looked down upon Ludmila's overgrown garden in the back of the house. Standing at that window when it was very quiet, Elizabeth-Anne could imagine she was not in one of the world's largest cities, but in a peaceful country oasis instead.

But there was nothing remotely reminiscent of the country inside the apartment itself. Since she was living in Manhattan, Elizabeth-Anne had decided that her home should reflect the mood of the city: electric and vibrant, fashionably contemporary, yet rooted in the traditions of the past. At the same time, she meant the apartment to be a fortress in which she and the children could feel secure, a place to keep at bay the high-charged, bustling energy which greeted them whenever they stepped out the door. She had painted the parlor a rich shade of blue, though she kept the ceiling above the molding white. By using only a few large, bold pieces of Ludmila's furniture, including two huge, gilt mirrors, and balancing these with the lightness of the beige carpet, she had succeeded in creating the illusion of greater space in a unique way.

One entire wall of the parlor was constructed of built-in bookshelves; the multicolored spines of the books belonging to Ludmila gave off a vibrant, pulsating spectrum of color. More importantly, the books covered a wide range of subjects, from the complete works of Charles Dickens to the controversial new science of psychiatry. Elizabeth-Anne knew it could only help to continue her humble education, and was fascinated by the books she now had a chance to read.

Overall, it was a simple room, easy to keep neat and clean. Thanks to the large, eat-in kitchen where she preferred the family to gather, the parlor would be relatively little used, and highly respectable indeed.

'I don't know how you did it, Momma,' Regina said, 'but it already looks like home.'

It was late afternoon on the last Saturday in September,

one of those rare late summer days when all of New York seemed to be taking advantage of the weather. Central Park was filled with families picnicking, children playing ball, and dour nannies pushing baby strollers and carriages along the paved paths, all overseen by an occasional, blue-uniformed patrolman. Overhead, kites flew in the perfect puffball sky.

If it weren't for the tall, sunbathed towers lining the park, Elizabeth-Anne thought, it would be easy to imagine that I'm not in the city at all, but in some pastoral country-side, like the ones in the romantic paintings we saw last weekend in the museum.

She looked around and watched the children shrieking happily and chasing each other up a grassy slope. She hesitated. They were all having such a good time, she hated to have to break it up. But after a moment, she called for them to come over and gather around her. Reluctantly, they approached the bench where she sat, little Zaccheus clamoring up beside her.

'But it's still early, Mamma,' Charlotte-Anne protested. 'Do we have to go home already?'

'No, not yet,' Elizabeth-Anne assured her, 'but I've got something important to discuss with you. Afterward,' she promised, 'you can go right on playing.'

The girls nodded and sat down beside her.

'I've waited a few days to tell you this,' Elizabeth-Anne said, studying each of their faces. 'I've found a job. I'm starting work on Monday.'

Charlotte-Anne stared at her open-mouthed. When she found her voice, she spoke in a tone of incredulity. 'A job? But I thought we had enough money coming in from the tourist court. And besides, you told us we've got a lot saved up in the bank.'

'And so we do. But we've all got dreams to follow. All of you, and me included. Now don't look at me like that. I'm not *that* old, you know.'

'Dreams?' Regina asked. 'What kind of dreams?'

'Oh, you'll find out soon enough.'

'Where are you going to work?' Rebecca asked.

Elizabeth-Anne turned and pointed to the elegant white

building which seemed to rise up from the midst of the trees behind them like some fairy tale castle. 'At the Plaza Hotel.'

'Doing what?' asked Regina.

Elizabeth-Anne sat back and folded her hands in her lap. 'I'm going to be a chambermaid.'

'A chambermaid!' Charlotte-Anne exclaimed in horror. 'Mamma, that's *dirty* work. Back in Quebeck we have *Mexicans* doing that.'

'This isn't Quebeck, darling, in case you haven't noticed.'

Charlotte-Anne hung her head, obviously abashed.

'Besides,' Elizabeth-Anne said, 'I don't intend to stay a chambermaid for long. It's only for a short while.'

'But . . . *why* do you want to be one at all?' Rebecca asked.

'Because I want to see how a big hotel operates, that's why.'

'Well, couldn't we just give up our apartment and stay in one for a while?' she added.

'No, that wouldn't be the same thing.' Elizabeth-Anne sat forward and her eyes gleamed with anticipation. 'You see, darling, I want to see it from the *inside*, from the employees' perspective. I want to discover just how a big hotel works, and what's involved in running one.'

The children all stared at her, obviously surprised.

'The thing which could conceivably be inconvenient,' Elizabeth-Anne continued, 'is that I've got to start by taking the night shift. It lasts from ten at night until six in the morning. But I don't really think it'll throw our lives into chaos. While you're all at school, I'll be sleeping. While you're sleeping, I'll be working. When I get home I'll make you breakfast and see you off. And I'll be up when you get back.'

'But . . . if you want to work in a hotel so badly,' Charlotte-Anne persisted, 'isn't there any other kind of work you can do?'

'You mean other than being a chambermaid?'

Charlotte-Anne nodded.

'I could wash pots and pans in the kitchen or become a

ladies' washroom attendant, if you prefer.' Elizabeth-Anne looked at her curiously. 'Would you like that better?'

Charlotte-Anne narrowed her eyes. 'That's not very funny.'

'I didn't intend it to be. But I do intend on working in various hotels, in various capacities. For now, I'll start at the bottom.'

Charlotte-Anne turned away. 'Well, I just hope you won't advertise what you're going to do,' she mumbled.

So that was it, Elizabeth-Anne thought. She tightened her lips and stifled a sigh, trying hard not to show her annoyance. Charlotte-Anne obviously didn't want anyone to know that her mother was a maid. In all likelihood, she'd probably been telling all her schoolfriends that her family was independently wealthy.

'There's nothing wrong with being a maid,' Elizabeth-Anne pointed out. 'An honest day's work never hurt anyone. There's no shame in it.'

'Mamma?' Rebecca said timidly.

'Yes, dear?'

'If you like, I'll help out. I'll even go to work with you. I think I'd like that much better than going to school.'

Elizabeth-Anne gave her youngest daughter a quick hug. 'I think,' she said with a laugh, 'that for the time being it's best you go to school.'

Charlotte-Anne stared at them expressionlessly. Then she got up without speaking and walked over to the grassy slope, where she sat down in the shadows. When her sisters and Zaccheus resumed playing, she refused to join in their games.

Her first day of work, and she almost blew it. Circumstances had conspired and almost succeeded in making her late.

Now *that* would have been one hell of a way to start off on the wrong foot she thought. And to think that she had been so careful, budgeting every minute of her time. She had believed everything was under control, but there were a million things that popped up right as she was walking out the door. Zaccheus had been fast asleep, but he'd awakened when Regina and Charlotte-Anne had gotten into a violent argument. There had been that to referee, and then Zaccheus refused to go back to sleep unless she sang him a lullaby. The moment she stepped outside it had started to rain, and she'd had to run back upstairs for her umbrella. To top it all off, the subway was delayed. And then, for no apparent reason, the train came to a stop in the tunnel, and interminable minutes crawled by before it jerked and began to roll on again.

With one minute to spare, she rushed through the employees' entrance of the Savoy Plaza. She made it to the maids' dressing room just as that night's shift of chambermaids, smartly turned out in crisp black and white uniforms, were lining up, military fashion, to be inspected by Mrs. Winter, the housekeeper. Already her brisk, sharp footsteps could be heard echoing down the corridor.

Elizabeth-Anne looked around the large, wardrobe-lined room in panic. She started to speak, but one of the maids shook her head and motioned her to silence. She still had no uniform, but realized if she went off in search of one now she would surely be late, even docked. Worse, she might be fired on the spot.

'Pssst!'

She glanced at the small maid at the far left end of the line. She was a petite black woman with merry dark eyes. She was desperately motioning for Elizabeth-Anne to fall in beside her.

The moment Elizabeth-Anne took her place, Mrs. Winter marched into the room, the glower on her face as intimidating as a drill sergeant's.

Elizabeth-Anne leaned her head forward and gazed to her right. The maids were all standing stiffly, chests thrust out like pigeons, chins in the air, hands at their sides. She couldn't believe it! This looked more like a military parade than starting-time for a group of hotel maids.

Meanwhile, Mrs. Winter continued her inspection. She strutted to the precise center of the line, spun smartly on her heel, and faced the maids in a wide-legged stance. 'Good evening, ladies,' she announced crisply.

'Good evening, Mrs. Winter,' echoed the resounding chorus.

Elizabeth-Anne craned her head forward and stared at Mrs. Winter in fascination. She had never seen another woman quite like her. She was tiny, almost dwarf-like, but had an aggressive bearing. Her black wool dress was cut severely; indeed, there was something severe about every inch of her. Once upon a time her hair had been a rich, glowing shade of honey, but now it was liberally streaked with gray. Her eyes were steely hard and her red lips perpetually pursed.

'It has come to my attention – ' Mrs. Winter began before breaking off in midsentence as her gaze fell upon Elizabeth-Anne. Her forehead creased into an irritated frown. 'And what is *this*?' she asked icily.

Elizabeth-Anne stepped forward. 'I was told to report – '

'*Silence.*' Mrs. Winter's voice was like a shotgun report.

Elizabeth-Anne's blood seemed to boil, sending crimson waves of embarrassment up into her face. For a moment, she couldn't believe that she had heard right. She couldn't remember the last time she had been spoken to in such a sharp manner. The obvious pity of the petite maid beside her only seemed to make things worse. She had the curious feeling that everyone else was holding their breath, relieved that Mrs. Winter had found a victim other than themselves, yet at the same time aware that she might at any moment turn on them. Stunned, Elizabeth-Anne found herself stepping back into line.

'Tuck your head back in and face forwards,' Mrs. Winter snapped. 'You are, I presume, a young lady and not a turtle?'

Elizabeth-Anne's eyes flared angrily. She had bargained for many things but not this. Still, she did as she was told.

Grab hold of your temper! she warned herself. You *need* this job. You need to see how this place operates, and you needn't take this kind of abuse for long. Just a few days, a few weeks at the most. Then you'll be moving on to someplace else.

The sharp clack of Mrs. Winter's deliberate footsteps

rang out in the room, and the diminutive woman was standing directly in front of Elizabeth-Anne.

'Your name.' It was not a question; it was a command shot out from between those deceptively tiny lips.

'Elizabeth-Anne Hale.'

'You may speak up. And, when you speak to me, you may address me as "m'am."'

Elizabeth-Anne swallowed hard. She barely knew this goading woman, but already she despised her. She hated standing there and taking this abuse, but knew for now she had little choice. In the future, she'd just have to avoid this Mrs. Winter as much as possible. Above all, she would not do battle with her. She would be above reproach. 'Yes, m'am,' she said quietly.

'I presume the personnel department had you report to me?'

'Yes, m'am. They did.'

'I'm sure they did,' the small woman said drily. She paused, then looked Elizabeth-Anne straight in the eye. 'We are not off to a very good start, you realize that, Miss Hale?'

Elizabeth-Anne raised her head.

'I'll be watching you closely. I suggest you tread very softly around me if you value your job.'

And with that, Mrs. Winter turned on her heels and marched out.

4

'I'm called Dallas,' the small black maid said with a Texan accent, ' 'cause that's where I'm from.' She lifted a towering stack of freshly laundered white towels out of the linen closet and deposited them in Elizabeth-Anne's arms. 'You carry these, and I'll get another stack.' She scooped up a second pile in her own arms and with a well-practiced backward kick of her foot, snapped the closet door shut.

'You're from Texas?' Elizabeth-Anne asked in surprise as they walked down the plushly carpeted corridor.

'Uh-huh.'

'So am I.'

'Really!' Dallas looked pleased. 'Then we better make sure us Texans sticks together, honey. That Miss Winter, she's just looking for any excuse to fire us all. Thinks it gives her power, she does.'

'In that case,' Elizabeth-Anne stated flatly, 'we'll just have to make sure that she doesn't find any fault, won't we?'

Dallas rolled her eyes. 'You're new, honey. You'll find out soon enough. No matter what you do, she'll manage to find fault. You just wait and see.' She nodded emphatically. 'What I can't understand is what a nice lookin' white woman like you is doin' here. There're better jobs in this here city. Lots of them, if you're white.'

A half smile came to Elizabeth-Anne's lips. 'A job's a job, Dallas. There's really no difference whether you're a maid or a housekeeper like Mrs. Winter. She just gets paid more.'

'Does she! Lord. I'd hate to know what she brought home last Thursday.' Dallas shook her head and clucked her tongue. Then she heard the distant jingle of keys and whispered, 'Ssssh.' A moment later, Elizabeth-Anne saw Mrs. Winter turning a corner and heading toward them down the corridor. Only after they had gone into an empty room to change the towels did they speak again.

'You'll help me, won't you, Dallas?' Elizabeth-Anne asked softly. 'You'll show me the ropes around here?'

'Course I will. Miss Winter said I should, didn't she?' Dallas grinned. 'Course, I would anyways. But first, you remember that when you hear keys jinglin' and janglin', Miss Winter's somewhere close by. And second, you get yourself some decent workin' shoes, honey. In them – ' she nodded at Elizabeth-Anne's shoes, 'your feet'll swell up like melons and be killin' you in no time at all.'

Each night for the next week, Elizabeth-Anne pushed herself to the limit. She couldn't believe how hard the work was. She was constantly on her feet, and there was never any time to take a break. Her lower back ached painfully, and it seemed that all she ever did was stoop and carry, stoop and carry. During the very first day on the job, she earned a healthy respect for Dallas. The petite maid always seemed to be in control, and she never uttered a complaint. Somehow, her good humor was contagious. For that, Elizabeth-Anne was grateful.

The night shift, she was learning quickly, was much more grueling than the day shifts because at night the hotel ran on a skeleton staff. She was especially disappointed because she never seemed to get a chance to talk to any of the maids besides Dallas, to whom Mrs. Winter had assigned her for the entire first week. After that, she would be on her own, and she dreaded it. She was inexperienced. There were a thousand things which could potentially go wrong, and she would have to cope with it all on her own.

To prepare her, Dallas tried to remember the various situations in which she had found herself – frenzied moments, heart-breaking moments, funny moments:

' . . . There I was, and there he was, naked as a jaybird. Dallas got out of there fast as her little feet could carry her, that's what I did.'

' . . . That son-of-a-bitch's wife claimed I stole the ring. Sure enough, next mornin' the clean-up crew found it in that carpetin'. Thick as grass it is in that suite, small wonder she couldn't find it herself. But she should of looked. Lord, I nearly lost my job that time, and never heard as much as a peep of apology from anyone.'

' . . . She was havin' a baby right there on the bed, and the house doctor was tied up with a man havin' a heart attack . . . '

Dallas's stories made Elizabeth-Anne aware of the multitude of situations that could go sour, and she knew Mrs. Winter was just waiting for her to make a blunder. It irked her to think that the housekeeper might end up winning their running feud – and that she might end up fired.

But what distressed her most was realizing that no matter how hard she worked as a maid, it would be a long, long time before she would really learn how the hotel functioned. People like Mrs. Winter – the various concierges, the manager, the banquet manager, the battery of desk clerks – had all been hired for their experience. There was simply no way she could hope to cram it all into several quick crash courses. But at least her experience at the Savoy Plaza had given her a basic idea of how the hotel was run, and an early appreciation of the various workers' expertise.

But she was not about to quit. Not yet, at any rate. She had decided that if she did one thing only, she would show Mrs. Winter that she wasn't about to get the best of Elizabeth-Anne Hale.

When she finally got home in the mornings, just as dawn was backdropping the skyscrapers across Fifth Avenue with pale morning light, she was ready to drop into bed and fall into a deep sleep. But that was not possible. She had to stay up for several more hours, waking the children, cooking breakfast for them, and getting them off to school. Somehow she managed to juggle her time, although even she was never clear on exactly how she did it. She only knew that she had to. Owning and running businesses in a small town, she was discovering, had been far easier than working in a huge hotel, where she was at the mercy of the whims of an enormous staff, and the beck and call of hundreds of guests. She had a fine line to tread. Every maid's territory was worked out with specifically scheduled duties, yet not one of them dared talk back to a demanding guest someone else was supposed to take care of – so there always seemed twice as much to do.

'You're lookin' real tired out,' Dallas told her on her fourth day on the job. 'When you get home this mornin', try to get some sleep.'

Elizabeth-Anne smiled wryly. How could she explain to Dallas just how much there was to do? That she had four children and a household of her own to take care of?

Only much later did she learn that Dallas was far worse off than she. Dallas had no money saved up that she could fall back on. She depended on her meager paycheck, and there was never enough; her husband was in prison and she supported their six children by herself. She had to resort to cleaning apartments during the day in order to make ends meet.

When Elizabeth-Anne discovered this, she shuddered

and felt very ashamed for daring to think that hers was an exceptional case.

Elizabeth-Anne thought it a miracle when she collected her third consecutive weekly paycheck. The two weeks she had been working on her own since her apprenticeship to Dallas had gone smoothly. The fifteen sixth-floor rooms which were her area of responsibility had been inhabited by businessmen, an aged widow, several couples, and one family with twin babies. She had been summoned at all hours of the night when the twins had 'accidents', had had to clean up after the businessmen who one night got drunk and sick, had had to answer the old widow's many summons for this or that whenever the woman couldn't sleep and wanted company, but on the whole things had gone well. Nothing tripped Elizabeth-Anne up, and whenever she ran into Mrs. Winter, the housekeeper was tight-lipped.

She's still waiting to find fault with me, Elizabeth-Anne thought to herself with satisfaction, *and it's killing her that she can't*.

The times she saw Dallas, always during the ten o'clock inspections and then again at six in the morning once the shift was over, the other maid smiled at her knowingly, but never said what was on her mind. *Good for you,* the dark eyes seemed to say. But Elizabeth-Anne also recognized the unspoken warning in her friend's gaze. *Mrs. Winter always gets what she's after.*

It was Thursday night, several hours before she had to report to work. She and the children were eating supper around the big oval table in the kitchen. The girls were well-behaved, as usual, but Charlotte-Anne was being especially solicitous, even to Rebecca and little Zaccheus, whom she always liked to lord it over.

Elizabeth-Anne watched Charlotte-Anne cutting Zaccheus's meat into tiny, bite-sized portions. She had never volunteered for that task before. After she had finished, Charlotte-Anne asked Rebecca sweetly, 'Would you like me to pass you some more gravy?'

Rebecca shook her head. 'No, thank you.'

'Some more potatoes, then?'

Rebecca frowned at her. 'No, thank you,' she replied uneasily, wondering what was up.

Elizabeth-Anne pursed her lips, also wondering what Charlotte-Anne was after.

When they finished eating, Charlotte-Anne was the first to scrape back her chair and begin to clear the table. 'It's my turn to do the dishes,' she announced, taking everyone by surprise.

Elizabeth-Anne gazed at her daughter curiously, but still said nothing. She knew that it wouldn't be long before Charlotte-Anne showed her hand.

Only after the dishes were washed, dried, and put away, and Charlotte-Anne had scrubbed the deep, enamel double sinks sparkling clean did she approach her mother. It was nine o'clock, and Elizabeth-Anne was in the curtained-off dressing alcove, getting ready to go to the Plaza.

Charlotte-Anne cleared her throat. 'Mamma?' she said in an uncharacteristically cajoling little voice.

'Yes, dear?' Elizabeth-Anne answered without turning.

Charlotte-Anne took a deep breath. 'I've made lots of friends at school. And for the past three weeks, I've stayed over at their houses every Saturday night.'

'Yes, you have.' Elizabeth-Anne strode out of the alcove to the parlor, adjusting the cuffs of her blouse. She stood in front of the mirror above the fireplace mantel and inspected herself critically. Behind her she caught sight of Charlotte-Anne's reflection. Here it comes, she thought as she watched her daughter tightening her lips.

'All the girls take turns having the others sleep over,' Charlotte-Anne reminded her. 'It's sort of like a pyjama party, even though no one but Theresa has enough beds for us all. We pile up blankets and pillows and – '

Elizabeth-Anne turned around. 'And now you think it's your turn to reciprocate the invitations?'

Charlotte-Anne nodded.

'Then by all means, we'll have a slumber party here,' Elizabeth-Anne said.

'Soon, Mamma? Please?'

Elizabeth-Anne raised an eyebrow. 'How soon?'

Charlotte-Anne's voice grew very small. 'This Saturday? Is that all right with you?'

'*This* Saturday?' Elizabeth-Anne stared at her. 'But . . . that's the day after tomorrow. That doesn't give us much time.'

'You'll have to be at work anyway, and I'll do everything,' Charlotte-Anne promised quickly.

'But you're all young. The other parents will insist you be chaperoned.'

'I've already talked to Aunt Ludmila, and she's promised to keep an eye on us. She won't mind it at all. She's lonely and likes company, you know.' Charlotte-Anne looked at her mother pleadingly. 'I know it isn't much notice but it won't be a bother. Really, it won't.'

Elizabeth-Anne sighed, but gave her daughter a small smile. 'Very well then. It's fine with me as long as you and your friends don't make too much noise and keep your sisters and brother awake all night.'

Charlotte-Anne's face lit up and she threw her arms around her mother's neck. 'Thanks Mamma! I really appreciate it,' she added with a smacking kiss.

'I'm glad,' Elizabeth-Anne smiled. 'I'll cook you all a nice supper before I leave for work.' She looked thoughtful. 'Maybe even bake a cake . . . '

'I'll do it – '

'You just concentrate on having a good time, dear.'

'Oh, I will! You can count on *that*.'

'By the way, what time do you all usually get together?'

'Six, six-thirty.' Charlotte-Anne shrugged. 'Something like that.'

'Good.' Elizabeth-Anne smiled. 'Then I'll finally be able to meet some of those friends you're always talking about. I'm looking forward to that.'

'And they want to meet you too, Mamma. I've told them all about you.'

Elizabeth-Anne looked surprised. 'You have?'

'Well, sort of.' Charlotte-Anne dropped her eyes and her voice grew meek. 'You won't . . . you won't tell my friends where you're going when you leave for work, will you, Mamma?'

Elizabeth-Anne gazed at her daughter expressionlessly. Charlotte-Anne had never really accepted or understood the reasons her mother was working as a maid. Elizabeth-Anne wondered what it could have been that she had told her friends about her. Well, she would find out soon enough, of that she was certain. Charlotte-Anne was a natural spinner of tales, and Elizabeth-Anne was sure she would have made the Hales sound terribly important. No matter what the occasion, she always felt compelled to impress people and to inflate her family's, and especially her own, importance. Strangely enough, it had been Charlotte-Anne who had at first resisted the move to Gramercy Park because of the size of the apartment. Then, once she'd discovered just how exclusive an enclave it was, she'd changed her tune in an instant. You would have thought, Elizabeth-Anne had told herself with amusement, that it had been her idea to make the move in the first place.

A weary sigh escaped her lips. Sometimes she felt that she did not understand Charlotte-Anne at all. She was a total stranger to her in so many ways. And sometimes she feared that perhaps she never would understand her. Still, she was her daughter, and as such she loved her. And she was sure that in her own peculiar way Charlotte-Anne loved her too.

5

The excited chatter of conversation, followed by bursts of laughter, issued forth from inside the apartment as Elizabeth-Anne snapped the door shut and hurried downstairs. It was already nine-thirty, and she knew she was cutting it close. She should have left at least fifteen minutes earlier, but the girls had held her up. If she was delayed again, whether it was the subway's fault or her own, she would be late for work and have to answer to Mrs. Winter.

Miraculously enough, nothing conspired against her. The instant she stepped on the subway platform the train came blasting in and screeched to a stop. She thanked her lucky stars and arrived at the Savoy Plaza in record time. She even had a few minutes to chat with Dallas as she changed into her uniform.

'Lord,' Dallas exclaimed as Elizabeth-Anne hung her best dress in the wardrobe. 'You're sure all dressed up tonight.' She placed her hands on her hips and eyed Elizabeth-Anne slyly. 'Special occasion, huh?'

Elizabeth-Anne smiled. 'Not really. One of my daughters is giving a little party for some of her friends.'

'Well, you look right nice.'

'Thank you, Dallas.'

Their conversation came to an abrupt end when Mrs. Winter's footsteps came echoing down from the hall. The maids snapped into line, and a frowning Mrs. Winter strode along in front of them as they stood in perfect, ramrod-straight formation for the nightly inspection. To date, things were going so well that Elizabeth-Anne stood as tall, and dared to convey as much self-confidence, as the most seasoned maid.

After Mrs. Winter completed her inspection, she puffed out her chest importantly. 'I have been told to give special attention to the sixth floor this evening,' she announced with gravity. 'That means suite six-fourteen in particular, which is within your territory, Miss Hale.' Her eyes gleamed as she turned her attention on Elizabeth-Anne.

Elizabeth-Anne tried to hide her embarrassment. Along with several Irish women, she was one of the few white maids on the staff, and Mrs. Winter insisted on calling the negroes by their first names and the whites by their formal surnames. It was an unfair practice, but there was nothing anyone could do about it, save suffer in silence.

'It is for that reason that I am changing our regular duty roster.' Mrs. Winter motioned to one of the other maids and snapped, 'Minnie, you take care of Dallas's fifth-floor territory, as well as your own. Dallas, you shall take care of all of Miss Hale's sixth floor rooms. And you, Miss Hale, since you have so far managed to keep your nose above water, and since you look the most . . . ah . . . presentable, will be in charge of suite six-fourteen exclusively. You will, at all times, be at that particular suite's beck and call and do nothing else, no matter what. Do I make myself clear?'

Elizabeth-Anne nodded. 'Yes, Mrs. Winter.'

'The rest of you are dismissed.' Mrs. Winter waited for the maids to file out. Then she turned to Dallas and Elizabeth-Anne once more. 'Tonight, we happen to have a very important guest in suite six-fourteen.' She paused for emphasis. 'Miss Lola Bori.'

Dallas let out an exclamation of surprise, but Mrs. Winter chose to ignore it. Even Elizabeth-Anne's heart hammered with excitement. Lola Bori was a legend, the most celebrated star of the moving pictures, the single most imitated and most closely watched of all the millions of women in the nation.

'It is imperative that everything goes smoothly tonight,' Mrs. Winter warned, 'and that every wish Miss Bori might have, no matter how outlandish or farfetched it may seem to you, is catered for. To the letter. Is that clear?'

Elizabeth-Anne nodded.

'Good.' Mrs. Winter paused. 'It is even more important that everyone – the public, photographers, and members of the press – are kept far from Miss Bori. She has requested extreme privacy, and the hotel management intends to deliver it. We have hired extra security guards in the lobby, but in case anyone should manage to get upstairs, it is your duty, Miss Hale, to guard Miss Bori. Of course, you will also not discuss her with anyone.'

'Yes, m'am.'

'Very well, then.' Mrs. Winter gave a wave of dismissal and they hurried out.

'I can't believe it,' Dallas said in a reverential tone as they took the service elevator upstairs. 'Miss Lola Bori! I've seen her in a dozen pitchers sittin' in the balcony at Loewe's. And to think I might get a chance to see her in person. Lordy.' She shook her head. 'Wait till I tell everyone when I get home. They won't believe me, I'm sure.'

'Just be careful who you tell,' Elizabeth-Anne cautioned her.

'Oh, I'll be careful. Mark my words.' Dallas shook her head again and clucked her tongue. 'I still can't believe it.

Imagine, Miss Lola Bori right here in the hotel. A *real* celebrity if ever there was one.'

In her luxurious, three-roomed suite, Lola Bori was both drunk and depressed. The gin coursed through her, and she saw the plush, pink satin furniture of the sitting room through a slightly swirling fog. She pushed herself up from the couch, but once on her feet, she swayed unsteadily. Compressing her lips, she frowned in concentration. 'Gin. Gotta get some more gin.'

She wove her way toward the door and began to fumble with the lock. 'Damn,' she swore under her breath. Then she pressed her face against the door and began to cry softly. She didn't want any more gin. She wanted company.

After a moment she pushed herself away from the door and slowly weaved back to the couch. Catching a glimpse of a face in a tall, gilt-framed mirror, she stared at the reflection, then slowly approached it.

'That's not me,' she mumbled. She licked her lips. 'Not me at all.' She shook her head defiantly at the caricature reflected in the mirror and it shook its head back at her. Her usually perfect, heart-shaped lips were smeared with lipstick, and her famous pale blue eyes were puffy and swollen. For once, the much-celebrated, angular cheek bones did not look worth celebrating; they were hollow and sunken. Her platinum blonde hair was matted and dishevelled.

She stared at the reflection in shock, not daring to believe it was her own.

Then she let out a wrenching sob, collapsing with her head in her hands. This was *not* Lola Bori, her mind screamed. It *couldn't* be.

She was at the zenith, the pinpoint pinnacle of her career. She had intended to stay there forever, reigning from high atop her lofty, gilded pedestal, far above the rest of mankind. She didn't need anyone and had meant to keep it that way. But she hadn't anticipated one thing: talking pictures.

She sank numbly down into the couch and stared blankly

before her. She was through. Finished. It had happened just that afternoon, not eight hours earlier, when that bastard Josef Von Richter, her studio producer, had sat down with her, right here in this very suite, on this very couch. His devastating words still echoed in her mind.

'You cannot have the part,' he had said gravely in his guttural German accent. 'Not *War and Peace*.'

'Of course you're joking, Josef,' she said light-heartedly. But his next words, and the obvious earnestness of his tone, had shocked her.

'No, my dear,' he said softly. 'Your career is over. That is what I have come to tell you.' He paused and looked at her, then turned away uncomfortably. 'Be glad that it has lasted this long.'

At first, she wanted to try to laugh off his words, but they echoed hauntingly in her mind. She had known this was coming, had feared it. Now she could think of nothing, see nothing but the black cloud of doom that was descending around her, suffocating her. She struggled to speak calmly, and her words came out in a ghostly whisper. 'So that's why you made me take the talkies test.'

'Yes.' He bowed his head in a solemn nod. 'You have the face Lola. But you do not have the voice. It is too high. Once your audience heard you speak you would become a laughingstock.'

She had leapt to her feet. 'I should kill you, you filthy bastard!' she had cried, her voice filled with hate. 'I should kill you!' Then she went limp, collapsing into quiet sobs.

'At the premiere of THE WOMAN BEHIND THE VEIL tomorrow,' he said quietly, 'you and your public will see the last Lola Bori film. I am sorry, Lola. You must believe that.'

She cried for a long time, then wiped her eyes with the back of one hand. 'I thought . . . ' She fought to retain the little composure she had left. 'I thought my stardom would go on forever.' She offered it almost as an apology.

His face was an expressionless mask, but she saw the sadness in his eyes. 'You have lived in the pictures too long, Lola,' he said. 'Nothing is forever. It is that way only in the pictures.'

Nothing is forever.

Now the words bombarded her again and again, echoing from the dark shadows in the corners of the room. She shook her head morosely, her eyes glittering with tears. Everything was over.

Was that possible?

She hadn't felt so lost, so completely vulnerable in years. She was helpless, achingly alone. But who was there to turn to? Who could take her bleeding heart and mend it? Who could tell her what to do, where to turn now that she had lost everything?

And then it came to her like a flash of white light: Larry.

Larry, her former husband, the investment tycoon. He had always been so strong and capable. And, during their marriage, he had loved her, worshipped her so. Once, he had tried to buy up all the reels of a Lola Bori film he had deemed too scandalous. He had wanted her to himself. Throughout their short marriage, he had loved her as no one else ever had. He hadn't wanted the divorce. It had been her idea; she had insisted upon it.

But did he still love her?

She clamped her lips together. If he did, she might have a chance. They hadn't spoken in years, not since she had rather abruptly walked out on him, but she knew he was in New York. And, as far as she knew, he was still single. And even richer than before.

Her heart began to pump the same way it always did just before she went in front of the camera. She laughed softly to herself. Josef was wrong. There *was* one more role she could play. She could catch Larry all over again, marry him, and settle down as one of New York City's premier hostesses.

The excitement flowed through her and, fueled by anticipation and gin, she grabbed the telephone and had the hotel operator place a call to Larry's home phone. It had been her home once, too, and she had never forgotten the private number.

She could scarcely contain her impatience as she listened to the ringing at the other end of the line. She was almost rude to the butler who answered, announcing her name and ordered him to fetch his employer. But as soon as she heard the deep, familiar baritone voice, she broke out in a cold sweat. Larry sounded so formal and on guard.

'Lola? What can I do for you?'

She frowned, concentrating on every syllable so that she could speak without slurring the words. 'I need you, Larry.'

There was a pause. It was such a long moment before he spoke again that she was afraid she had been disconnected.

'There was a time I needed you, too, Lola,' he said without any trace of bitterness. It was a matter-of-fact statement, and somehow that seemed to make it worse.

'I know that, Larry,' she said. 'I was foolish. Please? Let's give it another try? For old times' sake?'

He paused for a long minute, then he said softly, 'I'm sorry, Lola. Some things just can't be done over. I'm not God, and neither are you. We can't bring what's dead back to life. What's happened has – ' He sighed, ' – has simply happened. Our two lives didn't mesh. Now if you'll let me – '

But Lola's gasp cut him off. She seemed to see the room go black before her, and she had to rid herself of the terrible vision. 'Larry!' she blurted out, 'I've *got* to see you. I'm alone now. And I'm desperate. I – I can't take it any more, Larry. If I don't speak to someone, then I'll . . . I'll *kill* myself.'

'Another faked suicide attempt?' His words shocked her, like cold water. She shut her eyes and dropped her voice to a whisper. 'No, Larry. This is for real. Honest.' She began to cry. 'It's over, Larry. Everything is over. I'm finished in the movies.'

'But why?' His tone softened. 'You've always loved acting. That's what you do best. Why give it up?'

'Because . . . because of the talkies. It's my *voice*. They don't like my goddamn *voice*.'

'I'm sorry. I didn't know.'

'Neither did I.' Her eyes had a faraway look in them. 'You see, Larry, it really is all finished. All I have left is you.'

'Where are you?'

'The Savoy Plaza.'

'There are some people here, but I can get away soon. All right?'

She nodded through her tears. 'Thanks, Larry. I'll them them . . . the staff, to let you up. They're . . . screening . . . everybody.'

'Just tell them "Larry," ' he continued. 'No last name. No I.D. We don't need the reporters getting word that we're seeing each other again. Not after what they put us through in the past. We don't need that kind of publicity any more. Ever.'

'No, Larry.' Her voice was obedient and contrite. 'I promise.'

'Fine. It'll be an hour or so.'

Emma Roesch had a hand with no engagement or wedding ring gracing it, a night job as a switchboard operator at the Savoy Plaza Hotel, and a boyfriend who worked as a newspaper photographer and kept promising matrimony once he could afford a wife and family.

'We can't get married just yet, honey,' he told Emma over and over. 'I haven't got enough money saved up. The scandal sheets don't pay that well.'

'But I'll keep working,' she had offered. 'With your job and mine we can make it, Barney. I know we can. Lots of married couples have a lot less, and they make it.'

'But I want a wife *and* a family. I want to give you a beautiful big house and lots of children. Tell you what, Em. Soon as I get a real big scoop that pays off we'll tie the knot. But we'll wait until then. Okay?'

She had nodded doubtfully. 'I'll help in any way I can.'

'Hmmm,' he mused thoughtfully. 'Now that you've brought it up, maybe you *can* be of some help.'

She had jumped at the chance. 'How?'

'Well, you work at the Savoy Plaza, right? And lots of important people stay there. What if you listen in on their phone conversations every now and then? If you hear something really important, you can give me a tip and I'll come running with my camera. If it pays off, we're all set, honey.'

71

At first she had been reluctant. 'It's awfully dangerous, Barney. I – I could get fired . . . '

'Not if you're careful. Look at it this way, it's an investment.'

'An investment?'

'Part of our nest egg.'

So she had done as he had asked, but the conversations she had listened in on had all been dull. She hadn't come up with a single item which could help him out. Until now.

As she unplugged Lola Bori's line after placing the actress's private call she once again thought about what he had said. The conversation she had just overheard had been so engrossing that the newsworthiness of it took a moment to sink in. Then she sat up with a start.

What was more of a scoop than anything connected with Lola Bori?

Slowly she glanced around to make sure she would not be overheard. At night, the hotel switchboard had half the operators on duty that it had during the day, so there was no one nearby.

She reached out with her plug and plunged it into the switchboard. Her head throbbed with heady excitement. It was finally happening! At long last Barney would get his long-awaited scoop, his salary would be raised, and she would be dressed in her bridal gown. She almost jumped when he answered his phone.

'Barney?' She spoke in an uncharacteristically low voice. 'Remember what you told me to watch out for?'

When the bell for six-fourteen rang in the maid's station Elizabeth-Anne hurried down the hall to Lola Bori's suite. She was by no means star-struck; from an early age, she had had to face things in a practical way, and that left little room in her mind for daydreaming about film stars. Still, she *had* seen several Lola Bori movies, so neither was she entirely immune to the glamor of a star. But the moment she saw Lola Bori in the flesh, any illusions she might have had vanished.

This can't be the same woman, Elizabeth-Anne thought with shock. This harridan with her unruly white-blonde hair and puffy eyes; this lurching drunk in the powder-blue satin robe slipping off her shoulders; this cannot be the same, exquisitely glamorous star she had seen on the silver screen.

Lola Bori placed one hand on her hip and eyed Elizabeth-Anne up and down.

'I'm going to have a visitor.' Lola Bori held her head high, stretching her swan-like neck. 'I want you to inform the desk, and show the gentleman in the moment he arrives.'

Elizabeth-Anne inclined her head. 'Yes, m'am.'

'The visitor's name is Larry. He is to be asked for his first name only. No I.D. He'll be by himself. No one else is to be let up.' She swayed unsteadily on her feet, then delicately leaned against the doorjamb. 'Is that clear?'

'Perfectly,' Elizabeth-Anne promised her.

Elizabeth-Anne was waiting by the elevator. The night clerk had called to inform her the man named Larry was on his way up. When the car doors opened, she raised her eyebrows in surprise as a short man holding a package draped with a cloth stepped out of the elevator. He was dressed in somewhat shoddy clothing, hardly the class of visitor Elizabeth-Anne would expect Lola Bori to have. But, then, Lola Bori hadn't been what she expected either.

'I'm Larry,' the man said, stepping out of the elevator.

'This way, please,' she said politely. 'Miss Bori is expecting you.'

Elizabeth-Anne led him down the hall, then knocked on the white door of suite six-fourteen.

'Come in,' the muffled voice called from inside.

Elizabeth-Anne opened the unlocked door. She stepped aside to let the man enter, then quickly shut the door again.

Lola Bori was in front of the mirror, combing her hair with drunken fascination. 'You're early, Larry,' she chided. 'You said it would be an hour. I haven't even had a chance to fix myself up – ' She turned to face him, and the color drained from her face. 'Who are you? What are you doing here?' she gasped.

73

Barney flung aside the cloth which had hidden his camera and the shutter clicked, the flash burst, and sparks rained down upon the carpet, capturing, for all posterity, the tragic devastation of a fallen star.

6

In all the years she had worked at the Savoy Plaza, first as a maid, then an assistant housekeeper, and finally head night housekeeper, no one had ever seen Mrs. Winter in such a state of agitation. Her face was splotched with purple spots of rage as she paced up and down in front of Elizabeth-Anne and John Holmes, the night clerk.

Behind her, in the shadows, stood a tall stranger. His hair was shiny black, except for the temples, where it was lightly streaked with silver. Even elegantly dressed in an evening suit and an open, formal cape, his wide shoulders and slim hips were plainly evident. His face was handsome but craggy, with a strong nose and wide, sensuous lips. His right eye was deep blue, but his left was covered with a black eyepatch. He had lost the eye in a hunting accident, and the patch gave him the air of a dashing but distinguished pirate. He stood unblinkingly surveying Holmes and Elizabeth-Anne. Due to the eyepatch, Elizabeth-Anne couldn't read his expression.

'This,' Mrs. Winter said between tight lips, 'is the gentleman Miss Bori *was* expecting. How you mistook the lout you admitted for this gentleman I will never understand.'

Holmes hung his head, but Elizabeth-Anne kept her chin raised, her eyes steely. Only the faint coloring of pink on her cheeks gave away her emotions, which were misread by Mrs. Winter. Elizabeth-Anne was not filled with shame or fear. Stung by the older woman's words, especially in front of a stranger, she was seething with anger.

'Miss Bori,' Mrs. Winter went on, 'had to be given a sedative by the doctor.' She frowned at the floor, crossed her arms, and tapped them with her fingers. 'I don't know how we are going to explain this.' She paused and glared up at Holmes. 'How could you have been so *stupid*? How could you let a photographer upstairs?' Then she twisted her head in Elizabeth-Anne's direction. 'And you! Actually letting him into Miss Bori's room. This is scandalous. *Scandalous*.' She shook her head in disgust. 'Nothing like this has ever occurred in all my years here.'

'I didn't know he was a photographer,' Holmes said miserably, his face ashen. 'He introduced himself as Larry.'

'Miss Bori herself told me to show a "Larry" to her room as soon as he arrived,' Elizabeth-Anne added quietly. 'How could anyone else have known to use that name?'

Mrs. Winter clenched her hands at her sides, ignoring Elizabeth-Anne's pointed question. 'The point is that neither of you suspected that anything was wrong. I find that extremely hard to believe.'

'There was no reason to suspect the press knew Miss Bori was admitting a guest,' Elizabeth-Anne retorted. 'And, anyway, Miss Bori is known to be . . . well, somewhat eccentric. Why should we have expected an imposter?'

Just then, two uniformed security guards entered and Mrs. Winter turned around to face them.

'We've finished searching the hotel,' one of them said with obvious discomfiture. 'The photographer is nowhere to be found. Someone thinks they saw him slip out by the 59th Street entrance.'

'Thank you,' the housekeeper said icily. 'You were both on duty in the lobby at the time of his arrival and failed to intercept him. Therefore you may come in and join us. What I have to say pertains to you also.'

Hesitantly the guards lined up beside Elizabeth-Anne and Holmes.

Mrs. Winter narrowed her eyes. 'As of this very moment – ' She checked her watch. 'All four of you are dismissed.' She smiled grimly. 'Please do not expect any references.'

'But it's not our fault,' Holmes cried. 'I need this job. I have a wife with a child on the way.'

'Then I should think you would have been more careful.'

'Madame.' The voice was soft, but there was no mistaking the tone of authority in it. It was the first time the handsome stranger had spoken, and as he did so, he stepped forward out of the shadows.

Mrs. Winter gazed at him questioningly.

'This incident was most unfortunate,' he said, 'but considering that someone has dared to assume *my* identity, and further, that Miss Bori and I and not the hotel were the actual victims, I believe I might now have the right to say something?'

'By all means.' Mrs. Winter managed to keep her face expressionless, but she failed to hide the irritation in her voice.

The man went on unperturbed. 'You may have gathered that Miss Bori is not quite herself at the moment. She has suffered a . . . a severely painful personal loss. The fault here lies with me, for instructing that I be announced by my first name only.'

Mrs. Winter bristled. 'You are very kind, sir, but still, you are not to – '

'Blame?' He held up a hand to silence her. 'Madame, it is obvious that these particular four employees are blameless. I would think that someone who might have overheard the telephone conversation between Miss Bori and myself, and alerted the press, is the real culprit in this case.'

Mrs. Winter's white face turned scarlet. For a moment Elizabeth-Anne thought the older woman would actually faint.

'I think,' the stranger continued, 'that everything considered, everyone has suffered enough for one evening. I happen to be a personal friend of the owner of this hotel, and I'm sure that a good word to him about all of you, as well as an assurance that Miss Bori and I would like to let this matter die as quick a death as possible, will settle the matter satisfactorily. It would be far more constructive than any punishment meted out hastily.' He bowed his head in Mrs. Winter's direction.

For once, Mrs. Winter was hesitant. She was torn

between conflicting emotions: fury, that her authority was being questioned; fear, that he was obviously going to go over her head and speak with the hotel's owner; and relief, that he and Lola Bori would not hold her responsible for what had transpired. 'Well . . . if you insist, sir . . . ' she stammered.

He smiled, showing even white teeth. 'I do.'

'Very well, then.' Mrs. Winter clapped her hands together. 'Back to your stations, all of you. But let me warn you – ' She wagged a stern finger at the four employees. 'If something like this should ever happen again, and so little initiative is shown in the future – ' She let the threat dangle heavily in the air. 'Return to your posts.'

The three male employees, relief written all over their faces, hurried out of the room.

'Well?' Mrs Winter eyed Elizabeth-Anne coldly. 'What are you waiting for?'

Elizabeth-Anne faced the housekeeper squarely. Her eyes were cold, but she kept her voice even. 'With all due respect, I think you owe us an apology.'

Mrs. Winter stared at her. 'Indeed.'

'And furthermore, as of this moment I am handing in my resignation. Working conditions under your supervision are intolerable. Were I the owner of this hotel, I would never allow my employees to be treated in such a fashion. Perhaps the others need their jobs badly enough to put up with you, but, I thank God, am not that desperate.'

'You . . . you wicked young woman.' Mrs. Winter's voice grew shrill. 'How dare you turn your back on my benevolence.'

'It is you, Mrs. Winter, who are wicked. And as far as your benevolence is concerned, you certainly weren't left with much choice, were you?' She took a deep breath. 'Good night.'

'Good riddance is what I say,' the housekeeper snapped at her. 'I knew you were trouble, from the first time I set eyes on you. Get your things out of wardrobe immediately and don't ever set foot in this hotel again. Don't even bother changing out of your uniform. Get your things and leave this *instant*.'

'Gladly, m'am.'

Aware of the one-eyed stranger's amused expression, Elizabeth-Anne marched shakily into the adjoining wardrobe room. When she came back out, she wore her coat over her maid's uniform and had her clothes piled in her arms. Both Mrs. Winter and the stranger were gone.

Once she was on 58th Street hurrying east toward the Lexington Avenue subway, a car pulled up and followed alongside her at her walking pace. She gave the stately, yellow-and-black chauffeur-driven Rolls-Royce one glance and ignored it.

'Miss!'

She glanced over at the car with irritation. It was the one-eyed stranger.

'I have nothing to say to you,' she said grimly. 'Haven't you and your precious Miss Bori done enough for one day?' She tossed her head and continued walking.

'Could I give you a lift home?'

'I'll take the subway, thank you.' She began walking faster, casting occasional sideways glares at him.

'You're quite independent, aren't you?' There was a peculiar note of challenge in his voice.

She fixed her eyes straight ahead. 'I like to think so.'

Without warning, she turned right on Madison Avenue, and marched downtown. She knew the Rolls had no choice but to either drive straight ahead or make a left turn and head uptown.

When the red tail lights of the stately car joined the uptown traffic she let out a deep breath, leaned against a building, and buried her chin in the pile of clothes she carried. For a moment her eyes stung with tears of frustration. She was furious at the unfairness of it all, not so much for herself as for the others who needed their jobs desperately. Nor was her anger directed exclusively at Mrs. Winter. The stranger, Larry, his drunken film star friend, and their subterfuge deserved it equally. The hotel staff, she realized suddenly, were the pawns of the guests. If Larry hadn't been enough of a gentleman to speak up for them, they would all have been walking the streets and no one would have cared.

How awful of him, she thought with uncharacteristic bitterness as she continued walking. If it hadn't been for him none of them would have been placed in that awkward situation in the first place. The Larrys and Lolas of this world, she decided, were a breed she could easily live without. And as she descended the steps to the subway platform, she hoped she would be able to wipe the unpleasant incident – and any memory of Lola and Larry – right out of her mind. Just as she was certain at that very moment Larry had already forgotten about her.

She was wrong.

When the yellow-and-black Rolls-Royce pulled up outside the double-width limestone townhouse on the north side of 74th Street, the man in the back seat tapped his fingers on the armrest.

By God, but that woman had spirit, he thought. That and something else . . . something about her shows class. An indefinable air of . . . independence. Arrogance. Self-assurance. Of not really being a maid at all.

Who, then, was she?

He wanted to find out more about her, and made a mental note to have her checked out.

But fate did not allow it. The next morning Lola Bori was found dead in her suite at the Savoy Plaza from an overdose of sleeping pills, and he found himself busy exorcising the ghost of his former wife.

The maid from the Savoy Plaza became only a tanta-lizing memory.

For her part, however, Elizabeth-Anne found she was unable to forget the man she knew only as Larry. Having seen him for mere minutes, she could nonetheless at will conjure up his image perfectly: the solitary midnight blue eye she'd barely glimpsed, the tall, trim physique, the carriage of self-assurance. Unbidden, at any hour of the day or night, she would think of the handsome, one-eyed stranger, and a full vision of him would magically appear in front of her.

Not so with Zaccheus. There were those times, and they were increasingly common these days, when she was hard put to conjure up her husband exactly the way he had looked. After the years they had spent together, she suddenly found it difficult to remember him clearly. Some indefinable quality was always wrong, and yet she could never put her finger on just what was missing.

It made her feel angry. And guilty. Zaccheus hadn't been gone much more than four years. He was still her husband – legally and morally – as well as the father of their children. She had no right to sweep him into the recesses of her memory and let a stranger take that honored place of lust and longing. Yet too many things conspired to make the handsome, one-eyed stranger gain preeminence in her waking dreams.

For one thing there was the eyepatch which he wore with such flaunting self-assurance, such *pride*; it spoke of a defiant, independent spirit she felt was akin to her own.

For another, there was his honesty, even if she didn't care to acknowledge it. He *had* spoken up in defense of the hotel staff in front of Mrs. Winter, and she knew, deep down inside, that that had taken courage.

There had been, too, the way he had spoken to her from the rear window of the Rolls-Royce, with those sensual lips bared into that – was she imagining it now? – damning devil's grin.

But most of all, it was the trio of events which had piled up, one on top of the other during that fateful twenty-four hour span, which had etched him dramatically and indelibly on the fabric of her life. First there had been the incidents with the photographer and Mrs. Winter. That had been followed by a terrible fight with Charlotte-Anne once she had gotten home. And, as if to make certain that that night could never, ever, be forgotten, the next morning the newspapers had been filled with the news of Lola Bori's tragic suicide. And the photograph – that very same, damned photograph which had caused all the trouble to begin with – had accompanied the articles.

Together, the events made for the ingredients of one mighty, unforgettable nightmare. And Larry seemed to be at the center of it all.

She hadn't expected things to turn out the way they had.

She had only taken the job in order to acquaint herself with the hotel business. She had quit it because of Mrs. Winter, because of her frustrations, because, too, she had learned all she could as a maid.

During the subway ride home, all she had been looking forward to was a peaceful, quiet few hours to herself, and then a sleep from which she would awaken refreshed and rejuvenated.

That was hardly what ensued once she reached the apartment a little past midnight. Her footsteps were heavy as she trudged up the stairs with her bundle of clothes. For a moment she paused on the landing to catch her breath, more exhausted than during any of the previous weeks when she had worked the entire night through. The incidents with the photographer and Mrs. Winter had drained her both emotionally and physically.

The lights were on in the apartment and Charlotte-Anne's party sounded like it was still in full swing. She could hear the excited chatter of voices and see the crack of bright light under the front door.

She shifted the clothes in her arms, dug in her purse for her keys, and unlocked the door. At first no one heard her come in. When she walked into the parlor, she saw Ludmila on the chaise, fast asleep. Her head was tilted sideways against one shoulder, her hands folded in her lap and her eyes shut. Her mouth was open, and she was snoring heavily. Charlotte-Anne and her friends sat on a mound of blankets and pillows on the floor, busy giggling over some joke. They listened to Ludmila's snores, whispered something, and burst out into more laughter.

'Dees. Dees ees zee way I snore,' one of the girls mimicked. She twisted her mouth in a parody of Ludmila's and emitted a nasal snort.

The others burst into giggles. The moment they became aware of Elizabeth-Anne, however, the laughter subsided.

'Mamma!' Charlotte-Anne looked up in surprise. Then she jumped to her feet. 'I didn't know you'd be back so soon.'

'Neither did I.' Elizabeth-Anne smiled wearily.

'I thought you were invited to stay overnight.'

81

Charlotte-Anne paused and emphasized: 'in *Southampton*.'

Elizabeth-Anne stared at her daughter. This was the first time Charlotte-Anne had actually dragged her into one of her lies. She wanted to put an end to it right then and there, but she stifled the urge, realizing this was neither the time nor the place to lecture her daughter. She would wait until the next day when the other girls were gone.

Charlotte-Anne turned to her friends. 'Mamma gets constant invitations to spend weekends at someone's country house,' she said. Then she drew closer to her mother and lowered her voice. 'Why did you come back so soon? Is something the matter?'

'Nothing that can't keep until tomorrow.' Elizabeth-Anne glanced down the hall at the closed bedroom door. 'Your sisters and Zaccheus are asleep?'

Charlotte-Anne nodded. It was then that she noticed the bundle in her mother's arms. Her eyes went dark as she recognized the clothes Elizabeth-Anne had worn earlier that evening. Quickly she snatched them out of her grasp, turned around to shield them from her friends, and made a pretense of studying them. 'Why, Mamma,' she said over her shoulder. 'These are the things you left in Southampton last summer. It was so nice of Mrs. Belmont to have kept them, wasn't it?' She forced light laughter. 'But she really should have lent you a suitcase.' With the speed one might dispatch a poisonous snake before it struck, she shoved the clothes behind the curtained dressing alcove. Behind her back, the other girls exchanged curious glances among themselves.

Meanwhile, without thinking, Elizabeth-Anne slowly unbuttoned her coat, exposing the black, long-sleeved maid's uniform with its white collar, cuffs, and starched apron. She sank wearily down into an armchair, her head back and eyes closed. Despite Charlotte-Anne's transparent charade, it felt good to be home. At last she could feel herself calming down.

Suddenly she became aware of the girls' animated whispers.

She opened her eyes. Charlotte-Anne's friends were holding a huddled conversation among themselves, glancing at her out of the corners of their eyes. Charlotte-Anne was standing near the door, trembling and white-faced.

Elizabeth-Anne looked at her daughter, surprised by the deathly expression in her eyes. 'Charlotte-Anne? What is it?' she said cautiously, wondering what on earth had happened to affect her daughter so.

Charlotte-Anne looked away. 'N-Nothing,' she mumbled miserably.

Elizabeth-Anne glanced around the room in confusion. The sudden tension seemed almost palpable. She couldn't understand what was going on, but was shocked to realize Charlotte-Anne had, without a word, been ostracized from her circle of friends. And in her own home, yet.

The obvious ringleader of the girls had an arresting face, with a pointed chin and hazel eyes. She got to her feet, signaling that the pow-wow was over.

'It's late, Mrs. Hale,' she said haltingly, refusing to meet Elizabeth-Anne's eye. 'I know we were planning to stay the night . . . ' She glanced at the other girls for confirmation. They all nodded solemnly. 'We'd . . . we'd really like to leave now, Mrs. Hale.'

Elizabeth-Anne looked startled. She sat forward, her hands grasping the arms of the chair. 'Whatever for?' She gazed from one to the other, but they refused to make eye contact with her. 'I thought you were all having such a good time.'

'We're . . . I mean, *I'm* . . . not feeling very well. We'll get our things together and find a taxi. We can go to my house.'

Elizabeth-Anne glanced quickly at Charlotte-Anne. Her daughter was trembling as though with ague.

As the girls prepared to leave, Ludmila awoke with a start and looked around owlishly. 'What time is it? Is it morning already?' she asked sleepily, rolling her 'r's'.

As soon as the girls left, their footsteps trudging noisily down the stairs, Charlotte-Anne exploded. 'I think I'm going to die,' she wailed. 'Oh God, I'll never be able to face them again. I can't even go back to school.'

Elizabeth-Anne stared at her. 'What *is* it?'

'You mean you don't know?'

'No, I'm afraid I don't,' Elizabeth-Anne said evenly.

Charlotte-Anne turned on her mother, her eyes burning with a fierce hatred. The tears were streaking down her hot cheeks and her heart-shaped lips were contorted in pain. 'Just look at yourself, Mamma,' she hissed. 'You came in here and had to flaunt your uniform, didn't you? Your *maid's* uniform.'

Dazedly, Elizabeth-Anne looked down at herself. She was still clad in her working uniform. After everything that had happened earlier, she'd forgotten all about it. And now Charlotte-Anne was convinced she had exposed it on purpose.

'Don't you see?' Charlotte-Anne cried. 'Now they *know* you're a common maid. That's why the party broke up and they don't want anything more to do with me.' And she looked at her mother with the most intense loathing Elizabeth-Anne had ever seen.

'Darling, I didn't mean to spoil the party. You've got to believe me. I've had a terrible evening and I simply – '

'*You've* had a terrible evening!' The cords in Charlotte-Anne's neck were standing out in bold relief. 'I *hate* you!'

'Don't you think,' Elizabeth-Anne said calmly, 'that if you had told the truth instead of making up all those lies, they wouldn't have minded?'

'Oh, you have an answer for everything, don't you, Mamma? Well, I have an answer for you too.' She stamped her foot. 'I *hate* you, Mamma. I *hate you*!'

Elizabeth-Anne stood white-faced and quiet, unable to believe what she was hearing. Perhaps she *had* been inconsiderate in her exhaustion, but Charlotte-Anne's reaction seemed so out of proportion. 'Darling, please calm down. I'm sure we can talk this over and – '

'I never want to speak to you again,' Charlotte-Anne sobbed. 'Not for as long as I live.' Then she covered her face with her hands, ran to the bathroom, and slammed the door with such force that the walls shook.

Elizabeth-Anne stared after her, her head spinning.

Ludmila waited a moment, then pushed herself to her feet. 'I think,' she announced slowly, her accent still thick with sleep, 'that we go down to my apartment and give her a little time to compose herself.' Her eyes sparkled mischievously. 'It may be Prohibition, but I have saved a few cases of a very fine 1909 Bordeaux. Come.' She patted Elizabeth-Anne's arm. 'I think we could both of us use a drink, no?'

Elizabeth-Anne looked down into her wine and swirled it around again. It glowed a hypnotically rich, ruby red inside the baronially proportioned, cut-crystal goblet.

'Well? You drink wine, not watch it grow old,' Luba growled. 'It does that in bottle.'

Elizabeth-Anne smiled apologetically and took a sip. The wine was smooth and fragrant, curiously heady. She could feel it relaxing her tense muscles.

'That is better.' Ludmila nodded. 'So, now. Let me see. The girls, they quickly desert Charlotte-Anne. And she is angry with you. And you have lost job.' She pursed her lips and shook her head. 'Is not very good day.'

'You can say that again. And now what do I do?' Elizabeth-Anne's voice was weary. Even Ludmila's dogs seemed to sense the women's moroseness and kept quiet. 'The only reason I took that job in the first place was to see how a hotel is run. From the inside.' She screwed up her face painfully. 'Well, that's over now.'

Ludmila stared at her accusingly. 'Why not tell me this before?' she demanded sharply. 'I could have told you. You will never see how hotel works, not as maid. What you need, if you want to start hotel, is money. That is all. You simply buy hotel and hire help. Is that easy.' She lit one of her pungent cigarettes and veiled herself inside a noxious cloud of smoke.

'Money!' Elizabeth-Anne gave a low, deprecating laugh. 'That's the only thing there never is enough of.'

'But you say you have money saved up.' Ludmila squinted at Elizabeth-Anne through the smoke. 'Is much?'

'Much?' Elizabeth-Anne's voice was unchanged. 'It depends on what you mean. It's a lot for some people, little for others. But for a hotel?' She laughed bitterly.

'That does not matter. If you want something bad enough, then you will get it.'

85

'It isn't that easy, and you know it. You're always complaining bitterly that you don't have enough money.'

Ludmila made an irritated gesture with her cigarette. 'Enough! What is enough? Me, I am too old to gamble. If I were younger . . . ' Her gray eyes took on a faraway look and she smiled faintly. 'When I was younger, I gamble all the time. I become a mistress. That was a gamble. I go to court in this country for my lover's money, that was more gamble. But if I had a little money and I was your age . . . '

Elizabeth-Anne stared at her. 'Yes?' she prodded, afraid to show her quickening interest.

'You told me you get money every week from the . . . the . . . '

Elizabeth-Anne nodded. 'Yes, from the tourist court.'

'Good. And it is enough to live on, to pay the bills?'

Elizabeth-Anne nodded again.

'So what you have in the bank is, how you say, mad money?'

'No,' Elizabeth-Anne corrected her. 'It's what we can fall back on in case something should happen.'

'How much do you have in bank? Not that I am curious, you understand. Just to see if it is enough.'

Elizabeth-Anne hesitated. What she had on deposit in her savings account was sacrosanct; it was something you did not advertise, not even to your friends.

'Please, I only want to *help*,' Ludmila pleaded with soft urgency. She leaned forward on the siege, took Elizabeth-Anne's hands in her own, and smiled reassuringly. 'If it is hundred dollars or hundred thousand dollars, the amount does not matter to me. It is only what it can do. Do you understand?'

'Yes, I think so.' She took her hands from Ludmila's and sipped her wine thoughtfully. 'There really isn't any reason why I should keep it a secret from you.' She paused. 'It comes to nearly thirty thousand dollars.'

'Thirty thousand! My God, then why you worry?' Ludmila's aging, faded-rose features beamed with pleasure. 'Is plenty.'

'For a hotel?' Elizabeth-Anne shook her head. 'For that I need hundreds of thousands.'

Ludmila wagged an admonishing finger at her. 'Not,' she said pointedly, 'if you are willing to take little chance.'

'I'm not so sure I like the way you said that,' Elizabeth-Anne said slowly. 'I never like to take chances, not with my money. I'm not a gambler.'

'You said you start this tourist court, no?'

'Elizabeth-Anne nodded.

'And if you start hotel, that is gamble, too, no?' Ludmila eyed her shrewdly.

'Well, I *suppose* you could call it that.'

'Good.' Ludmila sat back with satisfaction and exhaled a plume of smoke. 'First, you must change bank. There is man of East Manhattan Savings Bank who will help us. His name is Vladimir Nikolsky. I know him from long ago, in Russia. He is only White Russian I still see socially. He will know who you can see about good chances instead of bad chances. There are specialists for this. But even before that . . . ' For a long moment she regarded Elizabeth-Anne thoughtfully, one cracked-lacquer fingernail poised on her lips as her expressive gray eyes swept over her friend from head to toe. 'Hmmmm,' she said to herself. 'Yes . . . I suppose . . . '

Elizabeth-Anne returned her stare quizzically. 'Why are you looking at me like that?'

'Because,' Ludmila explained patiently, as if to a child, 'it is most important to create an impression. You must look success before you can be success. So first, we do you over. That is all.'

'Do me over?'

Ludmila gave a quick nod and stubbed her cigarette out in the Imari bowl she used as an ashtray. She narrowed her eyes. 'Yes, we do you over,' she stated in such an emphatic voice that Elizabeth-Anne knew it was senseless to argue. Ludmila's mind had been made up.

Lester Lottoman, the assistant manager of the East Manhattan Savings Bank, pursed his lips thoughtfully as his eyes swept the rows of figures covering the most minute fluctuations in the bank's assets. After a moment he took off his silver-mounted spectacles, rubbed his weary eyes, and pushed the ledger aside. There were times when the endless numbers in need of balancing, checking, and rechecking, repaid him for his vast patience with the heady thrill of accomplishment. That was when he caught an error everyone else had overlooked, because he had the patience of a hunter. But there were other times, such as this, when the numbers all merged into senseless hieroglyphics and bored him to no end.

'Mr. Lottoman.'

The sharp voice startled Lester and he jumped, then looked up at the approaching manager of the East Manhattan Savings Bank, Mr. Nikolsky.

'Mr. Lottoman, this is Mrs. Elizabeth-Anne Hale,' Vladimir Nikolsky said, indicating the woman at his side. 'I trust you will see to it that she receives all the necessary banking attention she needs?'

Lester Lottoman nodded, looked at Elizabeth-Anne, and half rose to his feet. 'Please, have a seat,' he said, gesturing to the chair beside his desk.

Elizabeth-Anne sat with a minimum of fuss.

'I shall be in my office with Madame Romaschkova,' Nikolsky told Elizabeth-Anne with a slight bow. 'When you are finished, please join us.'

'Thank you.'

As Lottoman sat back down, he found himself taking an instant liking to this Elizabeth-Anne Hale. She was dressed elegantly, but looked sensible, and carried herself well. 'And what can I do for you, Mrs. Hale?'

Elizabeth-Anne raised her chin. 'I have close to thirty thousand dollars on deposit in this bank, Mr. Lottoman, as well as a respectable monthly income from a motel I own in Texas.'

He nodded encouragingly.

'What I would like is to go into the hotel business. Here in New York.'

'You would like to *buy* a hotel?'

She nodded. 'And it has come to my attention that there are ways I could increase my funds, perhaps enough in order to buy a hotel.'

'You mean . . . by investing?'

'I do.' Elizabeth-Anne took a deep breath. 'Mr. Nikolsky was kind enough to refer you to me because you are related to a highly respected investment banker.'

'Lawrence Hochstetter of Hochstetter Stremmel. Yes, he is my brother-in-law.'

'Then I should like to meet him. You see, Mr. Lottoman, I'm serious about investing my money. As long as the risk is reasonable.'

He stared at her thoughtfully, seeing an attractive, obviously intelligent woman who clearly meant business. His brother-in-law could only appreciate making her acquaintance, and Mr. Nikolsky would approve of any help Lester could give his friend.

'It just so happens that Mr. Hochstetter is giving a party at his townhouse this very evening, Mrs. Hale. I think we should attend.'

'If you're certain it's not too much trouble,' Elizabeth-Anne said hesitantly. 'I wouldn't want to impose.'

'And you won't, I assure you.' He smiled suddenly. 'I'll pick you up at eight o'clock.'

She gave him her address and then they shook hands. As she left, he regarded her with a strangely wistful expression. There was something about her quiet dignity that appealed to him. Lester Lottoman was, perhaps, one of the first to fall under her spell.

But he wouldn't be the last.

'Regina? Anybody home?'

Elizabeth-Anne listened for a moment, then shrugged as she pulled the key out of the lock. She picked up her shopping bags, carried them into the tiny foyer, and returned to make certain the door locked automatically when she closed it.

She listened to the quiet of the apartment. It had that peculiar, empty-house stillness about it. She suspected that Regina had taken her sisters and brother across the street to the park. She missed the greetings of the children, and their excited accounts of their day. But she was also grateful for the silence.

After she and Ludmila had left the bank, Ludmila had headed home and she had gone to do some shopping. Now she was exhausted. She'd had to buy an evening gown to wear that night, even though she knew she couldn't hope to compete with the other guests at the Hochstetter townhouse.

Elizabeth-Anne dropped her keys into the porcelain bowl on the hallway table, took off her hat, and shrugged herself out of her coat. As she hung it on the coatrack she caught a fleeting glimpse of a stranger in the mirror. At first she was startled; then she realized it was her own reflection. She laughed softly to herself. She still hadn't gotten used to the 'new' her, the woman who had emerged from Ludmila's 'doing over'.

She faced the mirror squarely, studying her reflection. Had she really changed that much, or was it only the new clothes and hair-style, the dim foyer and its tricky shadows?

She leaned closer into the mirror. No, she really *had* changed in the three months since she and the children had moved here. She was now beautifully dressed and groomed, thanks to Ludmila. Her friend had been right, Elizabeth-Anne realized. Good clothes and style made life easier. Whether in a store, restaurant, or bank, her appearance insured that everyone worked hard to please her.

But the change, she realized with a start, went much deeper than just her surface appearance. Her features had gained a maturity they had never had before. She exuded a confidence which, combined with her innate sensuality, had caused her bearing to become almost regal.

For starters, Ludmila had changed Elizabeth-Anne's hair style. She had insisted they splurge on an expensive, fashionable coiffeur once, explaining they could then keep up the style themselves. Not for her the faddish bobbed hair of the twenties, or the utilitarian style she had favored in

Quebeck. She now wore her hair combed down from a central part, though this could not be seen with the velvet, helmet-like cloches she wore out of doors. Her ears were hidden by two short braids on either side of her face which were coiled into small, delicate twin knots, lustrous flaxen jewels the color of Kansas wheat which made earrings obsolete. Her pale eyebrows were no longer light; plucked into fine, pencil-line arches, they were tinted a darker shade so that they were more expressive. Her eyes were deepened with the faintest aquamarine eye shadow possible, and other than a muted shade of lipstick this was the only make-up she wore.

If part of her newly acquired confidence came from enhancing her physical attributes, then the rest was due to her new clothes, in which she found herself far more comfortable than the plainer outfits she had worn in Texas. Not for Manhattan the long, severely cut skirts and the pale blouses she had always worn. New York was, after all, a cosmopolitan city which demanded chic. She could not hope to afford the clothes she would have liked to buy, but she had managed by emphasizing quality and style, choosing the cut and the colors which suited her best. In short, she dressed elegantly but within budget, thanks to Ludmila.

Her friend had taken her to the thrift shops of the Lower East Side, which were rife with second-hand bargains. 'Many poor Jewish immigrants have rich uptown relatives,' Ludmila had told her. 'They help poor relations by giving their old clothes.'

So it was on Orchard Street, among the hubbub and haggling, the pushcart peddlers and sidewalk vendors, that Elizabeth-Anne found Seligman's Second-Hand Store and the outfit she now wore. Perhaps it was second-hand, but the fine quality and aura of sophistication it lent her was first class.

'Only two buttons are missing,' Marty Seligman, the proprietor of the store, had pointed out when Elizabeth-Anne had inspected the blouse with its collarless neckline and puffed, sheer sleeves that gathered snugly at the wrists. It was otherwise in perfect condition, but she'd hesitated.

The buttons were unusual, and she knew she couldn't hope to find replacements.

'For you I throw in these for nothing,' Seligman said shrewdly, showing her and Ludmila a box of tiny seed-pearl buttons.

Ludmila had insisted upon clinching the deal. Elizabeth-Anne discovered, to her great delight, that when she and Ludmila replaced all the buttons with the pearls, the blouse was even more beautiful. The shimmer of pearls against the café au lait net was the perfect foil, and made wearing jewelry unnecessary. Instantly, the blouse became her favorite. Both the front and back panels were embroidered with café au lait soutache braid, and the hip-length hem was finished with a border of tiny, pearl-like fringe of crocheted balls, which, coupled with the pearl buttons, gave her an air of refined gentility.

Any other person might have chosen to wear the blouse with a skirt of matching color, but not Ludmila, and Elizabeth-Anne quickly saw her point. Together they chose an off-white, pleated wool skirt of just over knee length, an original from the House of *Worth* in Paris. Before Elizabeth-Anne it had graced an ample dowager from Carnegie Hill, but some judicious tucks had made it a perfect fit. For a jacket, Ludmila had once more insisted on contrast and chosen a cerise wool so cherry bright that it could have been picked off a tree.

Gone forever were Elizabeth-Anne's sturdy, country boots with their myriad eyelets and long laces. She and the girls wore shoes of soft, supple leather now, with modest heels and straps across the ankles. She was, Elizabeth-Anne decided, as well-dressed as many a society matron, and for a fraction of the cost.

Her inspection of herself over, she picked up the shopping bags and went into the parlor. She set the bags down on the chaise lounge upon which she slept, the foot of which was draped with a beige mohair blanket.

From out in the foyer came the sound of a key turning in the lock.

'Mamma? You home?'

The voice burst forth cheerfully, the way Rebecca always

sounded when she came home. As the youngest of the three girls, she was not yet caught up in the shifting moods of her older sisters, who were beset with the magnified worries of adolescence. In character, Rebecca was also the closest to Elizabeth-Anne. She was the most artless of her children, the least prone to tantrums, the most unlikely to talk back, and, above all, the most sensitive. Sometimes, the nagging thought crept into Elizabeth-Anne's mind that Rebecca was her favorite, and whenever it did she would force herself to squelch it.

I've loved each one of them more than the others at one time or another, she reminded herself firmly. *But in truth I love them all equally.*

But these thoughts lasted only an instant and she quickly turned to greet Rebecca with an enveloping hug, 'How are you, darling?'

Rebecca grinned up at her. 'I'm fine,' she said breathlessly, winded from racing up the stairs. And then the excited sentences tumbled out of her in a rush. 'Regina had us walk all the way to Grand Central Station but Zaccheus got tired and we had to take turns carrying him most of the way and Charlotte-Anne's complaining that she's got blisters on her toes – ' She took a deep gulp of air. 'They're on their way up.' She giggled again. 'Regina and Charlotte-Anne and *Zaccheus* are on their way up,' she corrected herself, 'not the toes. Well, those too.'

Elizabeth-Anne laughed and tousled her daughter's hair. 'It sounds like you've had quite an afternoon.'

'Oh, we did! And we were careful, we really were. Regina saw to that. We didn't talk to any strangers. And we saw the most marvelous clothes in a shop window. A sweater Charlotte-Anne said she'd die for! But it's so expensive.' She sighed dramatically. 'But it would look so good on her, Mamma, really it would,' she finished with a knowing glint in her eye that made Elizabeth-Anne smile inwardly.

'Well, maybe you can point it out to me soon,' Elizabeth-Anne suggested, thinking that if Charlotte-Anne wanted it so badly, perhaps she would buy it for her and hide it away until Christmas. The holiday season was only a little more than a month away.

Elizabeth-Anne turned as she heard the others come trooping in. Regina was carrying Zaccheus, who was fast asleep. 'Hi, Mamma,' she called out softly for fear of waking him.

'Hello, darling.'

Charlotte-Anne walked by glumly, her head held low. 'Hi,' she mumbled under her breath, making a bee-line for the bedroom.

Elizabeth-Anne gazed after her in silence. Days had passed since their argument, but Charlotte-Anne still behaved as though it had occurred only hours ago. She had been morose ever since, never saying more than a few perfunctory words.

Well, a few more days would heal their rift, of that Elizabeth-Anne was certain. But even that thought gave her little comfort. She despised dragged-out fights; they took altogether too much out of you. And she hated Charlotte-Anne's silent treatment even more.

They're only growing pains, she told herself, not for the first time. That's all that's the matter with Charlotte-Anne.

Rebecca spied the shopping bags on the chaise.

'Oh Mamma,' she cried excitedly. 'You've been shopping!'

'Yes, I have to go to a dinner party tonight.'

Rebecca seized the bags and rummaged through them. She let out an awe-struck whistle as she held up the gown Elizabeth-Anne had bought at Seligman's. It was made of beige crepe roma, and had a deep jabot which fell in a V from the shoulders to the hem. The sleeves were long, with flaring cuffs, and at the ankles the double skirt ended in an inverted pleat. The gown was feather light and classical in its very simplicity, and fell in beautiful, luxuriantly loose folds. Best yet, it needed no time-consuming alterations. She would be able to wear it that night. Only a spot near the neckline, which could easily be hidden with a brooch, gave away the fact that it was second-hand.

'It's beautiful,' Rebecca whispered in awe. Then her voice grew pensive. 'What party are you going to, Mamma?'

'It's really for business,' Elizabeth-Anne explained. 'A

gentleman from the bank is going to take me to meet an investment banker. That's why I'm going. I'm not deserting you all to just have fun,' she finished teasingly.

Rebecca let the gown drop on the chaise. 'This gentleman . . . is he handsome?'

Elizabeth-Anne gazed at her with a startled expression. 'Why do you ask that?'

Rebecca shrugged. 'Is he?'

'I don't know. I haven't even thought about it.'

'Mamma?'

'Yes, dear?'

'It's been years since we've seen Daddy.'

'I know that, darling,' Elizabeth-Anne replied softly.

'Are we . . . are we *ever* going to see him again?'

'I hope so,' Elizabeth-Anne replied quietly, feeling tears spring to her eyes.

'I hope so, too.' Rebecca paused. 'You know what's the worst thing of all?' she whispered.

Elizabeth-Anne shook her head.

'I . . . I can't even remember what he looks like.' Rebecca turned her tear-streaked face up at Elizabeth-Anne. 'You remember, don't you, Mamma?'

Elizabeth-Anne forced a smile, but she felt a trembling inside herself. 'Of course I do, darling,' she said. 'Of course I do.'

But as she held her daughter tightly against her and closed her eyes, no matter how hard she tried, Elizabeth-Anne could not conjure up a clear vision of Zaccheus Hale.

As Ludmila walked slow circles around Elizabeth-Anne, her sharp, piercing gray eyes were lost in thought. 'The gown is fine,' she said at long last. 'But be careful with the safety pins or you will stick yourself,' she cautioned with an admonishing wag of her finger.

'I'll be careful,' Elizabeth-Anne promised her, grateful for her friend's advice. Trust Ludmila, she thought, to notice where the soft, smooth fabric bunched just ever so slightly, or where it did not quite fall the way it should. She knew the slight alteration was invisible to a less scrutinous eye.

'The shoes, they are so-so. But they will do,' Ludmila said slowly to herself. 'But the jewelry . . . ' Her face wore an expression of disgust as she flapped one hand back and forth in the air. 'That brooch will not do at all.'

Elizabeth-Anne gazed down with dismay at the brooch she had pinned over the spot near the neckline. She had inherited the cameo from her aunt and always treasured it, but she knew that Ludmila was right. 'It's the only brooch I own,' she said slowly. 'I have to hide this spot somehow.'

'Do not worry. I will lend you one.' Ludmila nodded to herself. 'Now, what coat you wear?'

Elizabeth-Anne motioned over to the chair.

'That?' Ludmila looked horrified. 'No, no, *no*, *no*. Never.'

'But it's all I have for this weather.' Elizabeth-Anne protested. 'I have to wear it.'

'I lend you one.'

'Surely it won't fit.'

'Why? Because of my size?' Ludmila looked hurt. 'The coat I give you, it is made for Russian winters. It is long, on me to the ground. Even the sleeves are too long. It will fit. Now, what time is it?'

Elizabeth-Anne glanced up at the clock ticking on the mantel. 'He'll pick me up in less than fifteen minutes.'

'Fifteen!' Ludmila cried. 'Then we have not a moment to lose. I be right back.'

Elizabeth-Anne shook her head as the diminutive older woman rushed out. She wondered in all earnestness what she would do without her Russian friend.

A few minutes later a breathless Ludmila came charging back up the stairs. She carried two large, burled wood jewelry cases in her arms, and towed an enormous coat of pure white Russian lynx bellies across the floor.

'Ludmila!' Elizabeth-Anne was aghast when she saw the coat. 'I couldn't possibly!'

'You must.'

'Not that coat. It must be worth – '

'Much money, I know.' Impatiently Ludmila shrugged aside Elizabeth-Anne's protest. 'You just keep quiet.'

'But . . . what if I should lose it?'

'Lose it?' Ludmila narrowed her eyes. 'No woman *I* ever know lose her fur. Now – ' She deposited the boxes on the table.

'Now,' Ludmila said, 'we choose the jewels.' She bent over the boxes, lifted the lids and began rummaging through them. Elizabeth-Anne let out an exclamation of surprise. Ludmila was always complaining about not having enough money, and if a tenant couldn't come up with the rent on the precise day it was due she threatened to suffer heart attacks. Yet these boxes held what must surely be a king's ransom! Diamond tiaras, belts of rubies, pearls of all sizes and shapes, rings, earrings, bracelets and brooches – all gifts from the admiral. It was all stuffed so haphazardly into the boxes that the ropes of pearls were knotted, and no single earring was with its match.

'*Yes*,' Ludmila cried suddenly. 'This – this is the piece.' She held up a brooch. 'Is beautiful, no?' she asked, not bothering to mask her own pleasure. 'It was created in St. Petersburg by Edward Vilhelm Schramm, who worked for Fabergé. Is a masterpiece, no?'

Elizabeth-Anne could only nod speechlessly.

'Well? Hold it! Do not be afraid to touch it.' She thrust it into Elizabeth-Anne's hand.

Slowly Elizabeth-Anne lifted the brooch. It measured three inches in length and two inches in width, an enamel elipse set with rubies and diamonds and crisscrossed by a ruby-and-diamond Byzantine-style cross. 'Words cannot describe it,' she said.

'So? Put it on. No, here, let me.' Ludmila unpinned the cameo and attached the Russian brooch precisely so that it hung gracefully where the cameo had been. Then she stood back and clapped her hands together. 'Is marvelous,' she pronounced. 'Now. Into the coat.' She lifted it and waited for Elizabeth-Anne to duck down and slip it on.

Ludmila was right, Elizabeth-Anne noticed. The coat, which was oversized on her diminutive friend, fell neatly just below her knees while the lynx hairs at the edge of the sleeves just brushed the backs of her hands.

'My God.' Ludmila let out a deep breath. 'You are stunning.'

Elizabeth-Anne turned to the mirror and couldn't believe the vision of elegance that greeted her eyes. 'I can't thank you enough,' she told Ludmila warmly. 'You're my . . . my fairy godmother.'

'We all need godmothers sometimes – ' Ludmila glanced behind her at the door as the bells chimed. 'Now off with you before your troika turns back into a pumpkin!'

Elizabeth-Anne bent down and hugged Ludmila warmly. The tiny Russian exile returned the embrace Russian fashion, kissing both cheeks and then depositing one last kiss directly on her lips.

8

Lester Lottoman smiled at Elizabeth-Anne. 'Here we are,' he said as the taxi rolled to a stop, double-parking beside a row of gleaming limousines whose chauffeurs were gathered in little groups on the sidewalk.

Elizabeth-Anne peered out the window at the Hochstetter townhouse and felt any last vestiges of confidence seep out of her. This was no townhouse, at least not in the ordinary sense that described the rowhouses lining Gramercy Park or the streets of the Village. She held the lynx lapels of her coat close to her throat, newly grateful for Ludmila's generosity. This house was one of the last of a dying breed, a stately, miniature palace of the type which once lined Fifth Avenue.

As Lottoman helped Elizabeth-Anne out of the car, she continued to stare at the building in awe. It was surrounded by a high wrought-iron fence and stood three proud stories tall. The first floor was raised, with carved double doors and coach lights. The high, mullioned windows were gracefully arched in the French style and were ablaze with light. Elizabeth-Anne could hear the muted strains of music drifting out to the street and wondered at her nerve, coming here to meet Lawrence Hochstetter. How could she ask such a man to help her invest her money, money which, she realized now, was to him surely no more than loose change.

98

Lester Lottoman laughed nervously. 'Well, we can't just stand out here, or we'll freeze. Let's go in, shall we?'

Shyly he hooked an arm through Elizabeth-Anne's and led her to the gate and up the wide, sweeping steps to the front door. The butler recognized him on sight. 'Good evening, Mr. Lottoman,' he said in a low, British-accented voice, his face carefully devoid of expression.

'Evening, Bevin.'

'The other guests are in the salon, sir. I believe Mr. Hochstetter is expecting you.' He bowed his head in Elizabeth-Anne's direction. 'May I help you with your coat, madam?'

Elizabeth-Anne tightened her grip on the lynx lapels. She didn't want to let Ludmila's prized coat out of her sight but with a laugh reminded herself she could hardly wear it indoors. 'Thank you, yes,' she said, recovering her composure.

Bevin took her coat as she gazed around the foyer, where everything was of the finest marble, from the busts perched in their niches to the sweeping staircase that curved up three stories to a huge glassed-in rotunda.

'This way, Mrs. Hale,' Lottoman said, touching her hand and keeping his fingers poised upon it.

He guided her down the length of the hall, where a liveried footman opened two towering doors. At the sight of the salon, Elizabeth-Anne sucked in her breath. The room was covered in murals, skillful portrayals of Rome before it fell into ruin, with distant temples and statuaries, urns and strutting peacocks, columns, cornices, delicate pink clouds and rosy sunsets. The murals covered every surface – the walls, ceiling, even the doors – and gave the room an open, palatial feeling. But it was not museum-like or sterile; the overstuffed chairs and couches of green and gold kept the room cosy. Behind an enormous concert grand piano sat a black pianist in a tuxedo playing Cole Porter and singing softly, and everywhere she looked there were formal floral arrangements. All this on a sea of beige wall-to-wall wool carpeting which matched her crepe gown.

But even more startling were the guests. She counted to twenty and then stopped, realizing that it was pointless to continue. Never before had she seen so many beautifully turned out couples, elegantly tailored tuxedos and lavishly styled evening gowns. Or so many waiters circulating with silver trays of champagne – and at the height of Prohibition.

This must be, she decided, a make-believe, Hollywood world. She almost pinched herself in order to prove it was all real, that she had not entered some fantastically concocted dream. She felt she had stepped over the threshold into another dimension, into the world behind one of the exclusive doors of the socially prominent, the politically powerful, the beautiful, the wealthy, and the accomplished.

'Lester Lottoman, you *rake*!'

The woman swept toward them, wrapped in a form-fitting silver sheath that was missing only its mermaid tail. She wore a necklace with matching earrings of tourmalines and diamonds, and a predatory shark's smile.

'H-hello, Marisol,' Lottoman stammered in such obvious anguish that Elizabeth-Anne glanced at him sharply out of the corner of her eyes. 'I-I didn't know you would be here.'

'My, my, I *bet* you didn't.' The woman's eyes swept over Elizabeth-Anne. Then she turned back to Lottoman. 'This doesn't look at *all* like Henrietta, I'm afraid,' she said with a pout. 'No, not at *all*.'

'Well, no.' Lottoman's Adam's apple was working nervously. 'Henrietta's at h-her cousin's. M-Mrs. Hale here is interested in investing at Hochstetter-Stremmel, so I-I naturally thought the best way for her to meet – '

'When the cat's away, the mice will play, eh?' Marisol's icy eyes sparkled mischievously. 'How *delicious*. And you of all people, Lester! To think we all thought you were a dreary little milquetoast. Well, trust *me* to keep a secret. My lips are *zipped*. If you're good, that is. You see, I've met this most marvelous young German in Newport, and Heinzy followed me all the way here, would you believe?' She lowered her voice confidentially, at the same time making certain Elizabeth-Anne would not miss a word. 'He's hung like a *horse*, I swear. Anyway, I'm terrified he'll find greener pastures, and since there's nothing like a little

100

competition to spice up one's love life, you simply must meet him and help make him jealous.' She flashed a wide, open-mouthed smile, and took Lottoman by the arm, propelling him forward through a throng of guests. 'He won't be but a minute dear,' she sang sweetly over her shoulder to Elizabeth-Anne.

Lottoman twisted around and gazed helplessly back at Elizabeth-Anne. She smiled and shrugged. For a moment she stood there awkwardly, watching the throng swallow him up. She felt curiously empty handed and lifted a flute of champagne off a waiter's tray, but it didn't dull the sensation.

She could feel several guests flick her curious glances while others studied her with longer, openly appraising looks. She turned away, her face prickling with heat. She felt marooned, alone in this sparkling dream world where she knew no one, where she did not fit.

Slowly she crossed the room and stood near the piano, sipping her champagne. Minute after minute crawled by, and Lottoman still did not return. Occasionally she caught glimpses of him across the room. He was craning his neck constantly, his eyes searching for her, but the woman named Marisol was not ready to relinquish him.

'Damn,' Elizabeth-Anne whispered under her breath, tightening her lips in annoyance. She knew she shouldn't have come, but that hardly helped now. She was here to meet Lawrence Hochstetter, one of the country's foremost financial wizards who was, by varying accounts, either a brilliant business tactician or a pirate. The only person who could introduce her had been snatched away. Her doubts were mushrooming, but just as she was about to leave, a deep, familiar baritone voice beside her said, 'Excuse me, haven't we met somewhere before?'

Startled, she turned to face the speaker and nearly spilled her champagne. *It's him!*, she thought with a sinking feeling. Oh dear God. *Him.*

Standing inches away was the attractive stranger she had met at the Savoy Plaza, Lola Bori's friend, the one who had caused so much trouble. The man, a little voice inside admonished her, who had averted just as much trouble as he might have inadvertently caused to begin with. The man she could not, try as she might, forget.

But she ignored that little voice. She was unable to speak, unable to move. All she could do was stare stupidly at him. The unbidden thought occurred to her that he looked even more attractive now than he had when she first saw him. His blue-black hair was swept over his lean skull, the gray at his temples gleaming like polished sterling. He held himself casually, yet peculiarly erect, like a panther ready to pounce. His craggy features, while attractive, were decidedly predatory, and his sensual lips were cocked in a slight smile. He wore tiny diamond studs in his shirt which twinkled mockingly at her. She noticed that this time his black eyepatch was not cloth, but leather, which somehow only served to enhance his devil-may-care appearance.

And here she was, lost in a crowd of strangers, her escort gone, and the only person she'd ever seen before had met her while she had been a maid. She felt like a cheap imposter. She had no right to be here, and now she would be exposed.

'Seems the last time I saw you, you were dressed somewhat differently,' he said, his one eye bold and deep blue. Or was it filled with contempt? 'Do you usually make a habit of crashing society parties?'

She bristled, feeling for all the world like a porcupine raising its armor. 'If you'll be so good as to excuse me – ' She turned to leave but he caught her arm, his fingers feeling strangely warm through the thin material of her dress.

'Not so fast.'

She stared down at his hand. 'I think you had better let me go,' she whispered.

He laughed, his even white teeth flashing. 'I let you go once, remember? I don't know if I should do that again. I'm not used to having to chase after a maid.'

Her face flushed. How dare he hurl such an insult at her! Rallying her forces of self-control, she glanced around the room in hope of finding Lester Lottoman to rescue her from this forward stranger, but he was nowhere in sight. 'I have no intention of suffering insults from you,' she replied coldly.

'Is that so?' he asked, relinquishing his hold on her.

'It is.' She turned and stared at him, and their eyes met. For a long moment, neither could look away, and Elizabeth-Anne felt a wave of something she thought must be revulsion sweep through her at the same time her knees turned weak.

Why does he have this effect on me? she wondered angrily. Why does he look even more handsome than the last time I saw him? And why can't I stand him?

She tore her eyes away from his and craned her neck again, desperately searching the room for Lester Lottoman, who now seemed to have vanished completely.

'Looking for someone?' the stranger asked. 'Your escort, I presume?'

'You presume correctly,' she snapped in reply. She dared not look at him again. Her feelings concerning him were altogether too strong, too strange and overwhelming. How could a stranger fill her so completely with hate and . . . yearning? She drew in her breath and tightened her lips in irritation. She musn't think of him at all. Yes, she would simply pretend he wasn't there. Then perhaps he would ignore her and go away.

'Perhaps your escort deserted you?'

But that was too much to ignore! 'He did not. I'm certain of it.'

'Then may I get you some champagne while you wait?'

She glanced down at her empty hand. In her confused state, she hadn't even realized that she had set her glass down on the piano and a passing waiter had already scooped it away.

'I . . .' she began hesitantly, then changed her mind and sniffed. 'No, thank you.'

'I can't argue with that,' he said, 'especially not during Prohibition. It's a crime, how liquor flows here, isn't it? However, you still haven't told me what you are doing here, and maybe that's a crime, too.'

She thrust her chin out indignantly. 'I needn't tell you anything. But if you must know, I've come to see someone.'

'Oh? And who might that be?'

She glanced sideways at him and gave a triumphant little smile. 'Mr. Lawrence Hochstetter.'

He raised his eyebrows. 'I see. You seem to move in exalted circles. Do you know Mr. Hochstetter personally?'

She could feel her temper rising to the bait. 'Would I be here if I didn't?'

He glanced around. 'Well, it doesn't look like you really know many people here.'

'Looks,' she retorted tartly, 'can be deceiving.'

'I see.' He suppressed his maddening smile. 'Then perhaps you'll do me the honor of introducing me to some of your friends. I'd be delighted, for instance, if I could make the acquaintance of that lady over there.'

Elizabeth-Anne's guard went up. 'W-which one?'

He pointed. 'The one in the white and green.'

Elizabeth-Anne looked over at the woman, noting she seemed the most elegant of all the guests. She stood tall, her angular cheekbones and regal nose hinting at champion bloodlines. Her moon-licked black hair was swept back into a chignon, and she wore an exquisite, three-tiered bracelet of diamonds on her right wrist. A necklace of two strands of huge, black pearls hung from her swan-like throat and her white chiffon gown was diaphanous, embroidered with delicate, pale green leaves.

'You do know her, don't you? I mean, you just got through telling me – '

'Oh!' Elizabeth-Anne clenched her fists at her sides. She was at once angry and afraid. She had talked herself into an impossible situation with this insufferable stranger, and although she was never prone to lying and had little practice at the art, she now found it the only possible course to take. 'Of course I know her,' she snapped irritably.

He nodded. 'She looks familiar to me, too. I know I've met her before, but I can't seem to recall her name.'

Elizabeth-Anne took a deep breath. In for a penny, in for a pound. 'It's Gloria,' she said quickly.

Before she knew what was happening, he was propelling her toward the woman.

'What are you doing?' she hissed helplessly.

'You and I are going to chat with Gloria.' They reached the group where the woman was holding court. 'Gloria – ' he began with a rakish smile.

The woman turned to him in amazement. 'Lawrence Hochstetter, you mean to tell me that after all these years you still can't remember my name?'

He grinned sheepishly at Elizabeth-Anne, who wanted nothing more than to have the floor open up and swallow her whole.

'I'm sorry, Robyn,' he told the woman. 'It's just a little joke played in very bad taste. Blame it on too much champagne. This young woman here . . . ' He glanced at Elizabeth-Anne. 'Why, she looks pale. Perhaps she's ill. Be a dear, Robyn, and show her to the powder room, will you?'

'You are *awful*,' Elizabeth-Anne whispered to him. 'You set me up deliberately – '

But he ignored her, whispering in Robyn's ear, 'And whatever you do, don't let her out of your sight. I don't want her to leave, not under any circumstances. Oh, and tell Bevin to change the seating arrangements. I want her to sit on my right during dinner.'

Robyn narrowed her eyes.

'Well, make that the left. You, dear Robyn, will sit on my right.'

With a satisfied nod, Robyn hurried after Elizabeth-Anne, who was weaving her way through the salon like a somnambulist with slow, trembling dignity.

After speaking with Bevin, Robyn rushed to the powder room where she found Elizabeth-Anne. She pushed her gently down onto one of the chintz-upholstered settees. 'Just relax for a few minutes. If you need anything, let me know. I'll be right here.'

Elizabeth-Anne nodded, but sat numbly, waiting for her blood pressure to lower. She had never felt so humiliated, so insulted, so *angry* in her entire life.

Closing her eyes, she leaned her head back and took a series of deep, slow breaths. She had to calm herself and try to think. It was a fine fix she had gotten herself into, but there was no problem she couldn't solve, either, if she thought it out rationally. Or was there?

'Are you feeling any better?' Robyn asked.

Elizabeth-Anne glanced at her and nodded.

'Good. Some of your color is returning.' Robyn smiled, produced a shagreen Cartier compact, snapped it open, and leaned into the gilt-framed mirror. She began dusting her cheeks with powder. 'I wouldn't worry about Larry too much,' she advised offhandedly.

'Why do you say that?' Elizabeth-Anne's voice still quivered slightly.

'Because he has the worst mean streak of anyone I know.' Robyn eyed herself critically and then powdered herself some more. 'He loves to play practical jokes on people. I take it you were the victim this time.'

Elizabeth-Anne smiled wryly. 'I left myself open for it.'

'Hmph. That's beside the point, if you ask me. But I will say one thing for him.'

'What's that?'

'He treats everyone equally, man, woman, or child. He doesn't make any exceptions for the supposedly "weaker" sex.' Her voice grew wistful. 'Still, sometimes it would be nice if he treated a lady like a lady.' Her powdering finished, Robyn snapped her compact shut. Then she turned around to face Elizabeth-Anne and leaned her hips back against the top of the vanity, smiling faintly. 'I still don't know how you did it. Of course, you're very attractive, but, pardon my saying it, beauty is cheap. This city is filled with thousands of women more attractive than either one of us.'

Elizabeth-Anne looked perplexed. 'I don't think I understand what you mean.'

'Come now. You're the first woman in a long, long time that Larry's been smitten with.'

Elizabeth-Anne felt the hot blood rush to her cheeks. She dropped her eyes to study her lap. 'I'm sure you're mistaken,' she murmured softly.

'Me? Mistaken?' Robyn laughed good-naturedly. 'Not on your life. Listen to me,' she said, approaching the settee, the chiffon train of her gown billowing behind her.

She sat down beside Elizabeth-Anne and took her hand. 'There was a time I wanted Larry very badly. But he married someone else.'

'Is he still married?'

Robyn shook her head. 'No. But he chose her over me, and then he and his wife had a rather ugly divorce which was played up in all the papers. Meanwhile, I married my husband, so when Larry was free again, I wasn't. Now we're simply friends, like brother and sister. But we like each other much more now than we ever did before.'

'But . . . why *didn't* he marry you?' Despite herself, Elizabeth-Anne was fascinated. 'Why did he marry that other woman?'

'Because she offered him what I couldn't. I suppose you have the same quality that he thought she had. Only he was wrong about her. He overestimated her by a long shot. You see, Larry loves nothing more than a mystery. He's always intrigued when he discovers someone who he thinks has a lot more than meets the eye. That way he's got something to unravel. But his wife tricked him. She put on a good front in the beginning, but he found out soon enough how shallow she was.'

'And that's why he divorced her? Just because she was no longer a mystery to him?' Elizabeth-Anne was shocked.

'Well, that was part of their problem. The main reason, though, was a film she'd made. He thought it was too lewd, so he tried to buy up every reel in existence. It made her terribly angry. She accused him of sabotaging her career and God only knows what else. As a result, it was *she* who wanted the divorce.'

'So she was an actress.'

'Oh, yes. A fine one, I'll grant her that much. You've probably heard of her. She committed suicide only recently.'

A chill swept through Elizabeth-Anne. She fidgeted with her hands and her voice dropped to a whisper. 'It wasn't . . . ' she groaned despairingly, 'it couldn't have been – '

'– Lola Bori. The one and only.' Robyn shook her head and smiled sadly. Then she clapped her hands together and brightened. 'Well, I think that's enough maudlin gossip for now. It's time we got going. Knowing this house as well as I do, I think dinner's about to be served. Without us, if we don't hurry.'

'You go on ahead,' Elizabeth-Anne said quickly. 'And thank you.'

Robyn looked surprised. 'Whatever for?'

'Telling me what you did.'

'Oh, pooh, that's nothing. If we're to become friends we shouldn't keep *too* many secrets from each other, should we? I mean, a few always add a little spice, but too many . . .' Robyn shook her head and rose from the settee. She held out her hand. 'Let's go eat.'

'I can't,' Elizabeth-Anne begged off. 'I-I have to be going.'

'Nonsense. I won't hear of it. You're staying.'

'Don't you see? I can't face him. Not now.'

'Why? Because you're still embarrassed by his childish prank?'

Elizabeth-Anne was silent. How could she explain that her humiliation paled in comparison to what she'd just learned? The fact that Larry Hochstetter had been Lola Bori's husband - the same Lola Bori for whose suicide she herself couldn't help but feel some responsibility - had changed everything. Now she knew she would never be able to face him again, not for as long as she lived. Small wonder he took such obvious delight in putting her down. How he must hate her!

Robyn misread her reluctance. 'Don't hold his jokes against him,' she advised lightly. 'As I told you, he's the same with everyone. He didn't single you out. Besides, sooner or later he'll come around and apologize, and you won't want to miss that. And I'm not supposed to tell you this,' she continued, 'but the reason Larry sent me in here after you is because he doesn't want you to leave.'

'I can believe that,' Elizabeth-Anne said bitterly. 'This way he can torture me some more. And I must say, I deserve it.'

'On the contrary, you little fool,' Robyn said with a bright laugh. 'He's *smitten* with you. Now out we go.' Robyn pulled Elizabeth-Anne to her feet and smiled. 'A little food never hurt anyone. Nor did a little conversation. You'll learn soon enough. Neither Larry Hochstetter nor Robyn Morgan ever take no for an answer.'

Elizabeth-Anne gazed into Robyn's eyes. 'Please, can't you just leave me be?'

'I'm afraid not.' Robyn propelled her toward the door. 'Oh, and there's one more thing.'

Elizabeth-Anne raised her eyebrows wearily.

'If we're to become friends, which I'm sure we will, you'll have to start trusting me, all right?'

Elizabeth-Anne gave a little nod.

She wouldn't have believed it, but it was the beginning of a friendship that was to last a lifetime.

The rest of the guests were already seated in the dining salon when she and Robyn came in. Elizabeth-Anne glanced around with a none too sanguine confidence. She felt even more embarrassed than she had before. Dinner had obviously been delayed for her and Robyn Morgan.

Robyn turned to her and smiled reassuringly. 'Take heart,' she whispered gleefully. 'We *must* be important. Had it been anyone else, they would have started already. And for God's sake, slow *down*. This is our grand entrance.' She held Elizabeth-Anne back, forcing her to walk more slowly, while turning her regal whippet's face toward the guests with a flashing smile that wasn't in the least apologetic.

As they approached the table, Elizabeth-Anne saw there were only two empty places to the left and right of the host. She wasn't going to be let off that easy, she thought with a sinking feeling. Lawrence Hochstetter had made certain she'd be rubbing elbows with him, a sitting target for the butt of his jokes.

Reaching the head of the table seemed to take forever. The formal dining salon easily sat thirty-four for a formal sit-down dinner. In a pinch, such as tonight, the dining table accommodated fifty diners, rubbing elbows but eating comfortably. As in the salon, the ceiling soared to a height of twenty feet, but here the dado was painted to resemble carved stone. It reached to waist height, and above it the

walls were covered with murals of shepherds and shepherd-
esses, classical gnarled olive trees, and a cloudy pink sky
with plump cherubs cavorting in midair. The rug underfoot was a richly patterned, palace-size Aubusson and
hanging from the ceiling above the sixteenth century table
were four fragile, Venetian glass chandeliers bristling with
lit beeswax tapers. The fifty matched chairs were genuine
Louis XIV. The china was antique, floral Meissen rimmed
in gold, the crystal was Waterford, and the cutlery was
heavy Georgian sterling.

Elizabeth-Anne couldn't help but show her surprise
when she noticed Lester Lottoman seated beside Marisol in
the least important seats near the foot of the table. He was
staring at her in disbelief, but Marisol's face was far more
expressive. The beautiful features registered pure envy.

'Ladies,' Larry Hochstetter said loudly enough for the
entire company to hear, 'I trust we didn't rush you?'

'You needn't worry, Larry dear,' Robyn assured him
lightly. She leaned down, kissed his cheek, and took a seat
on his right. 'I'm dreadfully vain, I know. But then, so is
Elizabeth-Anne.' She glanced around the table. 'At least
our noses don't shine.'

'Indeed they do not,' he replied,'though ours smell food.
Still, I can't imagine you worrying about anything cosmetic, Robyn. The lily needn't always be gilded.'

'As far as I'm concerned it can never take enough
gilding,' she retorted and they all laughed politely.

Elizabeth-Anne found herself relaxing. So there would
be no mention of her earlier, hurried departure from the
salon. Even her and Robyn's late arrival for dinner was
excusable.

Larry Hochstetter signaled the majordomo, and then an
army of waiters filed in with overloaded trays of food.
Dinner began in earnest.

What followed was the longest dinner Elizabeth-Anne
had ever sat through. It was also the most elegant, and the
most fascinating. Larry Hochstetter was in top form, a
solicitous host and a marvelous raconteur, full of charm
and humor. Robyn was the perfect foil for his wit, and the
two of them got along famously.

But on and off, Elizabeth-Anne found herself feeling sorry for hew new friend. Robyn was obviously in love with Larry, but just as clearly he did not love her, at least not in the intimate sense. Still, they seemed the best of friends, and both of them made an effort to draw Elizabeth-Anne into their conversation. Soon she was glad that she had stayed. She was quickly changing her opinion of her handsome host.

'Larry imported his chefs from Paris,' Robyn confided as the first course arrive, a cold lobster mousseline, served in small porcelain cups decorated with truffles. 'No one in this country can hold a candle to them. Just wait until dessert.'

'Why dessert?'

Robyn smiled secretively. 'You'll see soon enough.'

Elizabeth-Anne found the food not only superb in taste, but beautifully served and garnished. The main course consisted of roast rib of veal. On each tray was a string-bound rib roast for six sitting in a lake of its own juices, each rib end sprouting white paper ruffles. To either side of the roast was a border of scalloped mashed potatoes, executed with a pastry bag and then browned in the oven. These borders kept the veal juices from soaking into the vegetables all around; the inside of each scallop held tiny peas, asparagus tips, and carrots.

But Robyn had been right; the dessert proved to be the pièce de résistance.

'Larry sent his dessert chef to Murano to learn the art of glass blowing,' she said from across the table as the perfect spun-sugar apples, filled with apricot mousse, were set in front of each guest. Elizabeth-Anne stared at hers in amazement. The life-size apple had been blown so artfully it looked as though it were made not of sugar, but of delicate glass, and the apricot mousse inside it glowed richly. She hesitated to eat it, it looked so beautiful. But as soon as she had taken her first bite her taste buds burst to vibrant, glorious life.

The two of them were seated in front of the fire in the upstairs study. The guests had long since departed, and the servants were cleaning up downstairs. Robyn had been the last one to leave. Now Elizabeth-Anne and Larry Hochstetter were alone.

'I must say you've chosen the most convoluted method of meeting me,' he said. 'Why didn't you just make an appointment and come by the office?'

'Because I wasn't sure about the minimum amount of investment capital your company would require. And besides . . . ' Elizabeth-Anne permitted herself a smile. 'I'm not interested in your office handling my affairs.' Her aquamarine eyes went steely. 'I want you to do it personally.'

He took a sip of his cognac. 'You've thought it all out carefully, haven't you?'

'Not really. I'm still very new at this. I just try to be cautious, that's all.'

'And if I decide not to handle your affairs personally? Then what?'

She smoothed her gown over her knees. 'I don't know,' she said after a moment. She looked over at him. 'There are others, I'm sure.'

'There are.' He nodded. 'Investment bankers are a dime a dozen in this town. But they're not Hochstetter-Stremmel.'

She inclined her head. 'And I know that for a company like Hochstetter-Stremmel, thirty thousand dollars isn't a lot of money.' Elizabeth-Anne paused. 'But to me it is.'

He grinned. 'Don't let anyone try to tell you otherwise. It's a lot of money any way you look at it.'

She glanced at him in surprise. He wasn't as conceited about business as he could be in his personal life. 'Spoken like a true banker.'

'Which I'm not,' he pointed out. 'I simply invest money for people. Based on educated guesses, economic forecasts, past performances of companies and gut instinct.'

'Do you think . . . ' she began slowly. Then she laughed chidingly at herself. 'I know it's an unfair question, but do you think I would be able to multiply my money enough eventually to buy a hotel?'

'Given the right investments and a good economic

112

climate, I don't see why you couldn't. Once you've gotten a hundred thousand dollars together, we can start playing little games that can help speed up the process.'

'Games?' she paused and frowned. 'What kind of games?'

'Taking bigger risks. Buying on margin. Buying a hotel by getting a mortgage. That sort of thing. But what we have to do first is invest your money simply and cautiously. Money makes money. The first hundred thousand is always the hardest. The same goes for your first million.'

'And it's relatively . . . safe?'

'Safe enough. But everything in life is risky. There is no such thing as a hundred percent sure-fire bet. I'd be lying if I didn't tell you that.'

'And if you were in my shoes? What would *you* do?'

He grinned. 'Exactly what you're doing. That is, if I had the good sense to seek out someone like myself.'

'Fair enough.' She nodded. 'I'll bring a cashier's check for thirty thousand to your office tomorrow.'

'I'll go one better than that,' he said, raising his glass. 'I'll have my car pick you up and we'll have lunch. You can hand over the check and we'll celebrate.'

She smiled. 'You do have your own way of doing things, Mr. Hochstetter.'

'Larry,' he said with soft intensity. 'If we're to enjoy a profitable business relationship, then you must call me Larry.'

'Larry, then.' She got to her feet. 'Until tomorrow,' she said, holding out her hand in a businesslike manner.

He shook it. 'Until tomorrow. Bevin will see to it that Max drives you home.' It was a long moment before he let go of her hand.

She went downstairs, humming to herself.

He went into the master bedroom suite, whistling softly.

Neither of them could know that in only three hundred and sixty two days, on October 29, 1929, the worst stock market crash in history would bring the world to its knees.

Elizabeth-Anne's gaze wandered past Larry Hochstetter to the windows and out on to the conical roofs and needle-spired tops of the buildings beyond.

Until she and Larry had begun having their bi-weekly luncheons here in the private dining room of Hochstetter-Stremmel, thirty-eight floors atop 70 Pine Street in the heart of the financial district, she had often enough glanced wonderingly at the banking temples of Lower Manhattan. She had tried on countless occasions to imagine what it would be like to look out at the world from so high a vantage point, but imagination had failed her. Now she experienced the soaring elevation first-hand, and often, but it still had lost none of its magic. She felt she could reach out and touch the tops of the surrounding buildings with her fingertips, and she had learned to appreciate just why the crowns of these stone monoliths were so ornate. Not for the people on the ground, who couldn't see them anway; no, they were meant to be appreciated from atop similar buildings. This lofty world was truly more than physically distant from the street far below and ordinary men. From up here, ships entering or leaving the harbor were tiny and insignificant, people were ants, and their problems were nonexistent. Only her own business interests were of importance.

For over ten months, these luncheon meetings had been a tradition. They had only missed two or three in all that time.

She drew her gaze back to Larry and smiled across the table at him. If anyone had told her the night of the dinner at the Hochstetter mansion that her interests would mushroom the way they had in such a short period of time, she would have laughed aloud. But it was no laughing matter.

Larry pushed away his dessert plate and slid the report across the white tablecloth. With her hand she pulled it closer and turned it around to face her. It consisted of four pages. The first was the title page, and it was neatly typed and centered:

She smiled to herself in anticipation as she turned to the first page. Then the smile froze on her face. For an instant, she wasn't sure if she were seeing a typographical error. She glanced sharply across the table at Larry.

His expression was inscrutable.

She consulted the page again. The same figure seemed to jump off it. In less than a year her thirty thousand dollar investment had been parlayed into . . . was it possible? She didn't dare think so.

She gazed down at the figure numbly.

'One hundred and sixty-seven thousand, three hundred and forty-three dollars and ninety-two cents,' she murmured slowly.

No, she decided, there had to be a mistake.

She flipped the pages and ran her index finger along the rows of numbers breaking down the individual investments, dividends and, in one case, a stock which had split. There was also a new mining company stock. Horseshoe Investments of North Dakota, which had struck a minor vein of ore a week previously.

Finally she let out a deep breath and closed the report. For a moment she couldn't trust herself to speak.

'I'm impressed,' she said in a soft voice. 'It's almost . . . *frightening.*'

'If it seems to have grown a little faster than we anticipated,' Larry explained, 'it's only because you gave me carte blanche to do as I saw fit. Once in a while a little bird whispers a hot tip in my ear. Not that it happens often, mind you, but if it sounds good, and not too good to be true, then I follow my intuition. Still, it was ultimately your decision to stay out of everything and let me handle it the way I saw fit that made it possible.'

She chuckled. 'Well, I'm certainly glad I did.'

'So am I.'

'Larry . . . ' she began tentatively. She glanced up and waited as Berty, the Hochstetter-Stremmel cook-butler, cleared away their plates. He was a pale, ghost of a man, but he cooked like an angel. 'It was delicious,' she told him with a smile.

He bowed his head gravely. 'Thank you, madam. Coffee?'

'Please.'

He poured it from a silver pot on the sideboard and brought the cups over to the table. The coffee was black and steaming, served in translucent English bone china.

Once Berty was gone, Elizabeth-Anne toyed with her cup. Her face was expressionless. 'I feel a little guilty, Larry.'

'Guilty?' he grinned suddenly. 'Why on earth should you feel guilty? Because you've come by a little honest money?'

'You know better than that.' She frowned again. 'It's you, Larry.'

'Your ever faithful servant, m'am.' He bowed his head gallantly.

She was not amused. 'It isn't fair,' she argued. 'The only reason my money has increased this much is because you've been giving my account your undivided attention. Far more than it warrants.'

'Guilty, m'am.'

She steepled her fingers and rested them thoughtfully against her lips. Over the past ten months, she and Larry had grown very close. From the beginning, there had been that intense physical attraction between them, but she had suppressed it, confused by her memories of Zaccheus. So, in his own fashion, Larry had doted upon her. Oh, the sparks hadn't stopped flying, but they had had to grow beyond that. They had gained a healthy respect for one another until one day they realized the friendship they had built had blossomed into something more: he loved her, and she him.

It had been slow in coming, especially on her part, but once the realization dawned it had hit her squarely, knocking her senseless. He had begun asking her up to the house for dinner, or out to restaurants and the theater. And for the first time since Zaccheus had left, she had invited a man into her own home, wondering how the girls would take to him. They all did, although they were uneasy at first. In fact, it had been Charlotte-Anne whose reaction had surprised her the most. On the one hand, Charlotte-Anne was delighted to make the acquaintance of a true society celebrity, rumored to be one of the five richest men in New York. On the other hand, when Larry left to go back home she had turned to Elizabeth-Anne and snapped, 'He's nice enough, Mamma. I like him. But nobody can take Daddy's place. Not *ever*.'

Elizabeth-Anne had looked at her in surprise. 'Whoever said I wanted him to?'

Charlotte-Anne looked at her curiously. 'It's plain to see, Mamma. Whenever he's around you flush and your whole face lights up. When you know you're going to see him, you sing to yourself all day. It's not that I mind your seeing him. I *like* him. But Daddy's still out there, somewhere, I *know* he is. I don't think you should share yourself with anyone, at least not until we know for sure what's happened to Daddy.'

'Darling, I'm not sharing anything with Larry. Like you said, he's a very nice man, clever and attractive. But you needn't worry.' She smiled faintly. 'I'd never do anything which might compromise the way I feel toward your father.'

'Yes, Mamma.'

The evening after that, Larry took her to the theater, and then he and Elizabeth-Anne ate a late supper at the townhouse. The meal was light, the champagne was heady, and they both wanted to make love. For a long moment Elizabeth-Anne felt horribly torn. Then she'd pushed herself away from him and said huskily, 'No, Larry. It's not right. Not yet, at least. Not while Zaccheus is still alive somewhere.'

He had acquiesced, and she'd left soon after. The tension between them became unbearable. They didn't see each other again until their next bi-weekly lunch. At first they had both felt the strain, but then he'd asked her out again, and things had returned to normal. They never discussed their physical intimacy *again*. They never so much as kissed one another. Yet somehow their love for each other kept growing steadily, fueled, perhaps, by their frustrated physical desires.

She stared across the table at him now. He was gazing back at her in his usual quiet mamner.

For a moment she felt very bad. She loved him, of that she was certain. And he loved her. Since he couldn't show her physically how he felt about her, he showed it to her in the next best way he knew how, obviously going out of his way tending to her investments. And all for what . . . she asked herself. Not even a kiss?

Here she was, an adult in New York City, a woman of substantial means, with the rare opportunity to love a second time, and she was afraid to make love to the man she . . . loved? Desired?

No, she wasn't *afraid*, she corrected herself. Nor was it simply lust. She felt *guilty* about loving another man, that was all. Guilty because somewhere inside her she still loved Zaccheus, still loved all that he represented, even if she could no longer visualize him clearly. And guilty because she loved the children she had had with Zaccheus, the tangible, living product of the love they had shared. Whenever she felt doubts, she had only to look at the children.

But Zaccheus was gone, she reminded herself, and she couldn't let the children rule her life. It wasn't fair. Not to Larry and not to herself.

She took a deep breath and her voice trembled. 'Larry . . . ' she said softly. 'Tonight . . . ' She gazed across the table into that fathomless, single, midnight-blue eye of his, and it was like being sucked into an ever deepening vortex. 'Tonight . . . let's see each other tonight? I've waited so long. I don't know if . . . '

He regarded her sadly. He loved and respected her too much to force himself upon her. 'Are you sure?' he asked softly. 'Absolutely sure?'

She nodded. 'I'm sure.'

There was a sudden knock on the door, then a middle-aged, severely dressed woman stuck her head into the room. 'Mr. Hochstetter,' she said apologetically, 'there's a call from a Mr. Wharton. He says it's extremely urgent. I can transfer the call in here.'

'Please.' He pushed back his chair, smiled at Elizabeth-Anne, and crossed the room. He picked up the extension phone and listened for a while. After speaking briefly, he slowly put the phone down, his lips puckered thoughtfully. Then he hurried back to the table, seized Elizabeth-Anne's financial report, and punched the intercom button.

'Miss Gordon, bring me the file of my own investments. Quick.'

'What's happened?' Elizabeth-Anne asked. 'Is something wrong?'

'Wrong? No, not at all. Someone's feeding us a red herring, and I can smell it. It stinks. That was my contact at Horseshoe Investments. The stock's starting to drop like crazy.'

'But . . . why?' She stared at him. 'I thought they just hit a new vein.'

'Which petered out.' He smiled grimly. 'So they say.'

'So we're going to sell?' she guessed.

'Yes and no. We're going to sell everything *except* Horseshoe, which we're going to buy up.' He compressed his lips and nodded to himself, thinking aloud. 'Something's up. Old Man Carruthers would never leak the word if a vein petered out, not unless he sold his shares quietly first. No, he's buying up even more stock. They must have struck the mother lode. My guess is Carruthers is trying to bring the stock prices down and then buy it all up cheap.'

'And we're buying, too?'

'We're going to try like hell to buy up every share before he gets his greedy little paws on them. We're liquidating everything in order to raise cash.'

'And . . . ' Elizabeth-Anne's voice trembled. 'And if you're wrong?'

'Then, my dear Elizabeth-Anne,' he said lightly, 'we're up what's proverbially known as Shit's Creek.' He grinned then, his face flushed with excitement. She had never seen him like this. Now she understood the panther-like image he brought to mind.

'Now off you go,' he instructed her. 'I'll see you tonight. Meanwhile, I've got a lot of trading to do. For you and for me. By five o'clock, I want us both to own the majority interest in Horseshoe Investments.'

At six o'clock that evening Larry called Elizabeth-Anne at home. She snatched up the phone.

'*Fait accompli*,' he said. 'Congratulations, Mrs. Hale. We are now both for better or for worse, the majority stockholders in Horseshoe Investments.'

'Should I be pleased, or is it too early to tell?' she asked cautiously.

'It's still a little early, but certain rumors I've heard sound good. Carruthers was waiting for the stock to go down to four dollars a share from eight fifty. I beat him to it. I snatched up all the shares for four fifty. I hear he's livid. Especially since he started the run with his own shares, and was waiting for everyone else to dump theirs.'

'So he's out of the picture completely?'

'No, he's got a few shares left. Not many, just enough to become an irritant.'

'So it looks good.' It was a statement, not a question.

'I dare say it looks very good.'

'And if – ' She stopped herself just in time.

She heard his laughter echoing across the wire. 'And if I turn out to be right, how much are you worth? That's what you wanted to know, isn't it?'

'Well, I mean, I couldn't help wondering, but . . . '

'If, and I repeat if, I am right, then you can count your blessings. You'll be worth – '

She held her breath.

Abruptly he changed the subject. 'Get dressed up real nice and pretty. We're going to celebrate tonight.'

She tightened her grip on the telephone. 'Larry! That isn't fair. You started to say it, now out with it.'

'No, it's not fair,' he chuckled.

'That's better. Now tell me.'

'All right. Just remember that it's a gamble. We won't really know for sure for a week or so.'

'I . . . I'll keep that in mind,' she promised in a shaky voice.

'Well, as of an hour ago, you *could* be worth over a million.'

She sucked in her breath and stared at the telephone. 'A . . . million,' she gasped.

'Or more. Or nothing.'

'I think,' she said slowly, dazed by the prospect of losing or winning those kind of stakes, 'I think I feel like I'm going to faint.'

'No you're not, darling. You're going to get all gussied up. Just for me.'

'Yes, Larry.'

As she hung up, she sighed softly to herself, her eyes sparkling. The prospect of being a millionairess no longer seemed important.

He had called her darling.

Pulled by a single white horse, the landau rolled slowly past the dark, whispering trees of Central Park. The hack in his top hat was perched on the raised driver's seat, and Larry and Elizabeth-Anne sat in the back, just forward of the furled black canvas canopy. All around, Manhattan had decked itself out in its most glittering, beguiling jewelry. The city surrounded them, a three-sided jewel box sparkling with a million lights. Overhead, the sky was a sea of dark velvet, the perfect backdrop for the thousands of diamond stars. They seemed so close that Elizabeth-Anne felt she could reach up and pluck a handful.

She snuggled further beneath the coarse lap blanket. 'Would you believe I haven't been in a buggy since I left Texas? There we longed for cars. And here it's the reverse. It's a *treat* to ride in a buggy.' She laughed softly.

He turned to her, his arm draped around her shoulders.

Her face became serious. 'Thank you, Larry,' she said softly.

'Why? What did I do?'

'For understanding how difficult this is for me to . . .

121

well, to do what we're going to do.' She laughed nervously.

He placed a hand on her chin and turned her to face him. 'Say it,' he said softly. 'There's nothing to be ashamed of. Love is beautiful. Put it into words.'

She took a deep breath. 'To make love, then.' She smiled timidly. 'Was that better?'

'Much.' He hugged her close, and she could feel the warm strength of his arm, smell the faint pleasant manliness of him. She leaned her head back on his shoulder as she gazed up in wonder at the night sky. 'What I really meant was, thank you for making it so easy for me. So romantic. First the candlelight dinner. Now the ride.'

He tightened his grip and leaned down to kiss her. For a long moment he looked deeply into her moonlit eyes. The aquamarine pupils were dilated in anticipation, a deeper, richer, more fathomless shade of clear blue than he had ever seen them. 'My God, but you're beautiful,' he marveled in a whisper, his lips brushing against hers, his breath warm and full of longing.

A surge of expectation rippled through her, bolts of electricity dancing from her head to her toes. He lowered his face and covered her mouth with his so that their lips were united, and their tongues tasted of each other's softness and warmth. She shut her eyes and reached up, pulling him down even closer. If anything could last forever, she prayed silently, let this be it.

'I think,' he suggested quietly, whispering against the soft skin of her cheek, 'it's time we headed home.'

She opened her eyes then, and gazed up at him with such trusting tenderness that it was the only answer he needed.

His bedroom was on the second floor of the house, and the drapes were pulled tightly across the windows. The room was a haven, a serene, private world of its own. As was the case downstairs, the walls had been painted by a master artist from Italy, and the muted trompe l'oeil architectural features – paneling, pilasters, and ceiling moldings – seemed real enough to touch. The bed was huge, replete with a rich, green silk canopy and a headboard trimmed in elaborate gold applique which completed the heightened, sensuous feeling of grand luxe.

But Elizabeth-Anne was oblivious to her surroundings as Larry held her close.

'You have beautiful hair, my darling,' he whispered softly, unpinning the braided coils at her ears. The freed hair fell loosely and he stroked it almost reverentially, letting it flow between his fingers like soft molten gold. 'Beautiful,' he murmured over and over.

She shook her head, loosening her hair completely. Then she felt him fingering the miniscule buttons at the back of her dress. 'You have perfect shoulders, too,' he whispered as he pulled the dress down around her breasts and planted a light kiss on each shoulder blade. 'You don't know how I've dreamed of touching you like this.'

Then he kissed her deeply on the lips, and she felt light-headed and lost. He moved behind her, suddenly as naked as she was, his powerful legs pushing against hers, his stiff, erect penis brushing the small of her back. He kissed the nape of her neck reverently, then turned her so he could cup her breasts in his hands, ever so gently kneading them while he kissed her deeply, as if trying to discover the well-spring of her femininity. She moaned, letting her head fall backwards, her hair cascading free all around her, marveling in the exquisite sensations he brought her. 'Love me,' she murmured. 'Love me now, Larry, now.'

He showered little kisses on her ears, mere whispers of breath, then drove her to mad, excruciating ecstasy with the faintest, circular whorls of his tongue. His lips moved downward, brushing against her breasts, flicking against her hard nipples, tempting her, teasing her, giving her but the faintest taste of what was to come. His tongue caressed her navel and then traced its way across the tautly stretched, sleek flesh of her abdomen. When at last he licked, tentatively, at her firm, blonde mound, she moaned aloud and gripped him fiercely by his muscular shoulders as she exploded, lost again and again in waves of shuddering pleasure. She felt so extravagantly exquisite, so sublimely rewarded, so clearly driven out of her mind that she wasn't altogether certain the world wasn't coming to an end.

Without warning he scooped her effortlessly into the air, one hand under her spine, the other supporting her bent knees, and carried her, like a sacrificial offering, to his huge, canopied bed.

And then he lowered her gently into that sea of green and gold, so very gently that at first she wasn't even aware of his putting her down. For a moment he could only stare at her lying there, her golden hair fanning out in all directions.

When he climbed carefully on top of her, she was transfixed by the sight of his well-proportioned body, each contour heightened in definition by the shadows cast by the dim lamps. He knelt silently over her, his head bowed. She felt his moist thumbs stroking her nipples, and she arched her back in an instinctual feline motion, her sinuously curved torso lifting clear off the bed, her long white throat exposed, her lips half open, the rows of teeth perfect and smooth. Flesh touched flesh, and his tongue wrought a trail of sweet anguish from her navel up to the cleft of her bosom, around her ear and neck. He burrowed, moaning, into the smooth pit of her arm, and then moved his lips again to her mound, cleverly playing among the spirals of her hair. She clutched him urgently, but he forced her arms to her sides. 'Later,' he whispered. 'Just lie still now.'

She nodded and swallowed. It was a torturous game. After a few minutes she could no longer stand it, and she grasped him fiercely, her mouth emitting gasps and eloquent little screams of pleasure. He fell forward in a lunge, grabbed her up, and kissed her deeply. She could feel his penis growing ever more erect, and for a moment she panicked, suddenly fearful of completing the act.

He seemed to sense her hesitation and pressed himself to her, entering her in one sure, powerful stroke. She closed her eyes, raising her pelvis instinctively to meet him as the pure, warm thought filled her mind: *Yes, this is right. This is perfect.*

They lay utterly still for a long time, savoring the fullness of the moment they had waited so long for. And then he thrust again slowly, a long, sure caress that he repeated again and again until each stroke seemed to pull out of her a deeper well of ecstasy and he was plunging into her over and over with raw passion. She cried out, gripping him tightly with her thighs and arms, clinging to every surging, bucking movement he made and then suddenly he moaned deeply and was filling her and she felt her own body tremble and explode. He shuddered and collapsed, burying his face in the soft, ambrosial comfort of her breasts. His breath was coming in gasps, each lungful of air he exhaled a cool whisper against her burning flesh. She couldn't speak for a long time, and they lay still, not needing more than each other's bodies.

Finally he asked, 'Can you stay the night?' His voice was muffled.

'I wish I could.' She traced her finger along the ridge of his backbone. 'But I can't. You know that. The girls . . . I *am* supposed to be a role model for them, and a good mother doesn't stay out all night.'

He laughed, then shifted around to face her, his head leaning on his elbow. 'In that case,' he said soberly, 'it's time for round two.'

She gazed at his phallus. Remarkably, it was erect again. She grinned. 'Insatiable bastard.'

When she got home it was already past two o'clock in the morning. She slipped quietly up the stairs and managed to let herself in without making a sound. She locked the front door, then tiptoed into the living room. There, she stopped in her tracks. The girls were seated on the chaise, wide awake but avoiding her gaze. Their faces were red. Clearly they had been crying.

A dark shadow of shame and self-revulsion swept through Elizabeth-Anne. She was overcome with guilt as she stared slowly from one to the other. Then she dropped her gaze. The pain of seeing them so hurt tugged excruciatingly at her heart.

So they have somehow guessed what I've been up to, she thought. They know that I've cheated on my husband, on their father. I should have known better. I should have, but the temptation was too strong. I've failed them as a mother.

God forgive me, she prayed silently.

'Girls . . . ' she whispered hoarsely.

Charlotte-Anne and Regina pushed their sister to her feet. As always, it was Rebecca who was made to speak up for the others.

With trembling hands, Rebecca held out two sheets of paper. It was a letter. 'I-I think you'd better sit down, Mamma,' she said, handing it to her and bursting into tears.

Elizabeth-Anne stared down at the two sheets of paper, at her husband's small, familiar script. She couldn't believe that suddenly, after so long with no word, she now held a letter in her hand. And tonight of all nights . . . But, then, before her guilt could blossom further, she began to read – and the pain of the words seared her very heart and soul.

My dearest wife and beloved children,

I know this letter coming out of the blue will be a shock. After so long without word, it grieves me more than I can say that this is all I have to send you. Because by the time you receive this, it will all, thank God, be over. It's best this way. You must trust me and believe that with all your heart.

I'm writing from Texas, but I have not returned here as a free man. I am writing from my prison cell. The past has finally caught up with me, and I'm through running at long last. Please understand when I say I'm relieved, almost grateful that the running is over. It gave me nothing, because it kept me from you.

I have been sentenced to death. I know those words will be so hard to read, but please understand how grateful I am. I'll be free of the past at long, long last. The warden is a good man and he promised to keep this letter and not mail it until the sentence is carried out. I asked him to hold onto it because I'm afraid that otherwise you would come here, and if there is one last request I have, it is to shelter you from that painful goodbye. That is my last wish, and probably one of the only things I can do anything about anymore. Please forgive me for my long silence. This letter is not intended to distress you. Please, receive it in the spirit in which it is written. I love you, my dear wife. All these years of hiding and running – I've loved you throughout them. That love was what kept me going, and that love is what makes this ignoble end for me somehow noble. You and our children, that is all that matters. That is all that has ever mattered.

Darling, you are young and beautiful, and the young, they say, are resilient. Be so, for my sake. Don't let it all have been in vain. Now that you know my fate – look at it through my eyes if you can. At least now we'll both be free. The past is behind us. I can stop running and hiding, and you can build a new life for yourself. A new and better life. Don't shut yourself away. You have so much love and happiness and laughter to give, and my one hope is that you can rebuild your life with a man more deserving of your love than me. Whatever you do, don't mourn for me. Don't shed tears. I know you've done all that these past few years. If my conscience would permit it, I would not write this letter at all to save you from more grief, but you must know what is happening so that you can at last be free. Free to choose your life and loves. Free to start over. Do that, darling, for me. Otherwise, my death will have been for nothing, and I can't bear to think of it that way.

Remember one thing, and one thing alone. I am not sad. How could a man be sad when he leaves the one thing behind which matters most – a wonderful family? That is my legacy, and that is what gives me peace and the courage to face these last hours.

What more could a man ask for?

*My love always,
your husband and father.
Z.*

Elizabeth-Anne's face was like ash.

Her life, everything she had ever lived for and loved, seemed to melt to ruins before her eyes.

Zaccheus – her husband. Her falsely accused husband, the father of her children. Zaccheus – dead.

Could it be possible? Could a man be executed for a crime he hadn't committed? Was his life really over? The last time she had seen him he had been so alive, so full of vibrant warmth. Was this cold paper really the last she would ever have of him?

The room seemed to reel around her, the children's tear-streaked faces revolving faster and faster, until everything was a featureless blur, until everything was black. Blessedly, she passed out.

It was past midnight, the morning of Friday, October 29, 1929. In just a few hours the stock market would crash and the Great Depression would begin.

All America would grieve, but it was a reality Elizabeth-Anne would be unaware of for a very long time. Because her own grief was too all consuming. Losing money was one thing. Losing a loved one in the flash of a sudden bolt of lightning was another thing entirely.

10

The world had turned mad. Her life had exploded, and everything was suddenly crazily off kilter.

Like a mortally wounded animal, Elizabeth-Anne crawled into her nest and ceased to function. She lay dazed on her chaise lounge, half-dressed, and covered with the cashmere blanket, refusing to get up except to drag herself to the bathroom. It was as though she were sick. And she was. She was sicker than she had ever been in her life, only it was not a malady for which a doctor could prescribe medication. It was an illness of the spirit. Zaccheus had died, and something within her had died along with him. From the moment she had read the letter, the world stopped spinning and ground to a halt. Seconds, minutes, even hours and days were no more.

She withdrew completely, not even able to communicate with the children. They locked themselves in their room, as miserable and mournful as she. But they at least could still shed tears. In her, the pain festered and rankled her soul. The pain manifested itself physically, and was so all-pervasive, that even little Zaccheus, who was too young to comprehend what had happened, realized instinctively that something was terribly wrong, and that Mamma wasn't herself at all. He became just as quiet and withdrawn as Elizabeth-Anne, but with a pitiable difference. He was frightened.

Two days and a night passed. The pain which consumed the girls had not decreased, but at least they managed to function in a zombie-like state which could pass as the first step, however trifling, of the many which they would have to go through in order to fully cope with, and accept, the tragedy that had engulfed them.

Elizabeth-Anne, however, was catatonic, not in the true medical sense of the word, but she was in so deep a state of shock that she no longer cared about anything. She could come to no decisions, nor feel any lessening of the brutal pain which stabbed her so deeply. She was aware of what was going on around her but it was all unfolding as if in a dream. She knew that the children needed her now more than ever in their lives, for the first time she was incapable of coping. Her own pain was too unbearable. All she had been able to do was erect an invisible wall between herself and the world that no one seemed able to penetrate. The past days had eaten up her entire resources of strength. There were simply no more reserves she could fall back upon.

When another three days had passed, the resilience of the young began to manifest itself more visibly. The girls were still broken hearted and given to periodic outbursts of tears, but at least they had begun to function a little less by rote. Regina cooked for them, and all the girls took turns attempting to force food upon their mother. But Elizabeth-Anne would only stare at it blankly. She didn't touch a bite.

The sisters gazed at one another in worry.

Five days, and their mother was wasting away.

Ludmila was alarmed.

She couldn't recall a day going by without her and Elizabeth-Anne paying each other a visit, and now she hadn't seen hide nor hair of the Hales. She knew that they were at home because she had heard them moving about in their apartment. She had been tempted to go upstairs on countless occasions, but something had held her back. Intuitively, she sensed that Elizabeth-Anne and the children wanted to be left alone. Whatever the reason for their sudden need to shut themselves away, she was certain that it was a private matter, but it hurt her feelings that they did not share their heartaches with her. Still, she respected their need for privacy.

But when day after day passed and she still did not hear from Elizabeth-Anne, and the stairs did not tremble with the sound of the girls traipsing out to school in the mornings, her soft, old face went tight with worry. Anxiously she began pacing her cluttered apartment.

This was totally unlike the Hales, she told herself. So out of character. Whatever could have happened?

Then a terrible thought flashed through her mind. Today was Saturday, the second of the month, and Elizabeth-Anne's rent was due. Elizabeth-Anne had never been late in paying it. What if . . . what if she had lost all her money in that horrible stock market crash? Slowly Ludmila sank down onto the siege, lost deep in thought. Hadn't she, Ludmila Romaschkova, been instrumental in suggesting to Elizabeth-Anne that money could be invested? Hadn't she paved the way for her to seek out an investment counselor in the first place? And what if her well-intentioned but ill-timed advice had caused her friend's entire nest egg to be wiped out?

Ludmila's head spun dizzily and she shut her eyes. Who could have foreseen the future? Who could have guessed that such a disaster might descend upon the country and wipe out so many fortunes in one fell swoop? If her worst fears were confirmed and Elizabeth-Anne now found herself penniless, then Ludmila felt she was at least partially to blame. She would have to make it up to her friend somehow.

She nodded to herself. Elizabeth-Anne was proud. Perhaps the reason why she was holed up was because she could not pay the rent on time.

She might even have lost every penny she had.

Or perhaps she was so shattered by the loss that she could not bear to face it – or the woman who had suggested she invest her money.

Or worse, she could be contemplating suicide.

Every day, the papers were full of reports that dozens of

people who had lost their fortunes or life savings had leapt to their deaths, had shot themselves, gassed themselves, slit their wrists.

The thought of it filled Ludmila with icy terror. She sprang to her feet, no longer able to just sit and wait. She knew something was terribly wrong upstairs. Elizabeth-Anne, the girls, and little Zaccheus were more to her than mere tenants; they had all become fast friends. They were *family*.

She was going to go upstairs at once to find out what had happened.

At first she had rapped softly on the door. She heard movement inside the apartment, and one of the girls' muffled voice. Rebecca, she guessed, though it was harder to tell. When no one came to the door, she had knocked harder. And then harder. Finally she pounded on the door with her shoe.

Pausing to take a deep breath, she heard a creaking of the floorboards. She could see a shadow darkening the crack of dim light under the door and sensed rather than saw someone peering out at her through the tiny peephole.

'It's me, Ludmila,' she called in what she hoped sounded like a cheerful voice.

The floorboards creaked some more, and she heard muffled whispers. Finally the door opened as far as the safety chain allowed. Rebecca's huge eyes peered out at her.

'Rebecca, thank God you are all right . . .' Ludmila's voice trailed off and her face creased with a frown. Rebecca usually projected a lively, radiant quality. Now her eyes were dull and lifeless.

' 'Lo, Auntie Luddie,' she murmured quietly.

'Hello, Rebecca,' Ludmila said, cocking a curious eyebrow. 'How nice to see you. May I come in? I want to talk with your mother.'

'She doesn't want to see anyone.' Rebecca started to shut the door.

'Wait.' Swiftly Ludmila wedged her foot between the door and the doorframe. Drawing herself up as imperiously as her four feet, three inches would allow, she used her most commanding tone of voice. 'I demand you open door, immediately.'

Rebecca hesitated. Her sisters might not have listened, but she was just young enough to obey an adult's command. She nodded morosely, waited for Ludmila to remove her foot, and closed the door. Then she unhooked the chain and let Ludmila in. The tiny Russian dashed over the threshold calling, 'Elizabeth-Anne! Elizabeth-Anne!'

As she hurried into the dim gloom of the living room Ludmila felt something give under her feet. There was a splintering crack and she looked down at the floor, then wrinkled her nose in disgust. She had stepped on a dinner plate crusty with leftovers. She frowned to herself and gazed around the usually perfect room in disbelief. The curtains were drawn and the air was stale. Clothes were strewn all over the floor. Dirty dishes and smudged glasses were piled up on the tables. This was very unlike Elizabeth-Anne, to whom cleanliness was next to godliness.

Then she spied her friend lying in death-like silence on the chaise. She drew in her breath sharply. Elizabeth-Anne was staring right at her, but Ludmila realized that the aquamarine eyes were unfocused. They seemed to gaze right through her. With a shock she noticed how haggard Elizabeth-Anne looked.

She approached the chaise and took a seat on its edge. 'Are you sick?' she asked softly. When Elizabeth-Anne did not reply she placed a hand on her forehead. 'No, there is no fever.' Slowly she withdrew her hand and stared down at her friend.

Elizabeth-Anne let her head loll sideways, staring vacantly away from her.

Ludmila leaned closer to her. 'I be right back,' she said softly, patting Elizabeth-Anne's shoulder. 'Do not worry. I call doctor.'

For the first time Elizabeth-Anne seemed to show signs of life. 'No,' she whispered hoarsely. 'Don't call a doctor.'

Ludmila glanced up as Rebecca scuffed slowly toward her. The sight of the child tugged at her heart; she was walking like a defeated old woman. Then she shook

Elizabeth-Anne gently. 'Then what is it?' she cried urgently. 'Is it because of money? Did you lose money?'

Elizabeth-Anne's eyes drooped shut. 'Please,' she begged in a whisper. 'Leave me alone. That's all I ask.'

'*No*. We are friends. Or do you forget?' Ludmila reminded her. 'If something is wrong, then I have right to help.'

'No one can help,' Elizabeth-Anne sighed. 'Not even God. Not anymore.'

Ludmila glanced sharply at Rebecca. The girl nodded her head solemnly.

'In God's name,' she demanded, 'what has happened here?'

Rebecca shrugged wordlessly and drifted away, joining Regina and Charlotte-Anne, who were standing in the bedroom doorway. They all gazed at Ludmila with much the same empty expression that was still on Elizabeth-Anne's face. What on earth and in heaven could have happened to bring on such moroseness, Ludmila wondered.

Suddenly little Zaccheus pushed his sisters aside and came running out of the bedroom. He threw himself at Ludmila and buried his face in her lap. He began sobbing noisily.

Ludmila stroked his head with one hand, and with the other she sought Elizabeth-Anne's hands. Touching them, she sucked in her breath. They were cold as ice, lifeless. She realized she might never discover why Elizabeth-Anne and the children were all so miserably dejected. Well, in the end, it was none of her business. If Elizabeth-Anne ever decided to tell her, then fine. If not, then that was fine, too. Meanwhile, there were more important matters at hand. Somehow she had to pull Elizabeth-Anne and the children out of their despondency. She had to get their minds off what was bothering them so deeply.

Ludmila was no stranger to crises. She had gone through enough of them herself to know just how to deal with them. In this case, action was called for.

She rose abruptly to her feet, marched over to the window, and yanked aside the curtains. Glorious sunlight came streaming in. She pushed the window as far open as it would go. The sudden gust of air felt deliciously refreshing.

Ludmila turned to the girls and clapped her hands. 'Now,' she proclaimed in a voice which discouraged any talking back, 'we will all clean house. It is disgusting mess. You, Regina, get broom. Charlotte-Anne, you get mop. Rebecca, help me tidy.'

The girls stared at one another, and a signal seemed to pass between them. Slowly, albeit reluctantly, they obeyed.

Ludmila hurried downstairs, dug through her dresser for her oldest, most worn Hermès scarf, and tied it around her head. For several hours, she worked alongside the girls, scrubbing, polishing and dusting. It was good therapy; the girls even began talking to each other in low voices. Their conversation was far from cheerful, but it was a beginning.

'I'm hungry,' Zaccheus finally complained.

Ludmila stopped washing a window and frowned. She had been too preoccupied to realize that she was hungry, too. Now that she thought about it, her stomach began rumbling.

'I go cook,' she declared. She put down her rag, went downstairs, and came back with an alarmingly small amount of groceries. While the girls continued to clean, she set to work in the kitchen. Just before she was ready to serve the food, there were a series of urgent knocks on the door.

'Answer it, somebody,' she called over her shoulder. 'I'm in kitchen, cooking.' She dipped a spoon into the hot oatmeal, lifted it to her nose, and sniffed it critically. To her, it smelled wonderful. It wasn't simply run of the mill oatmeal; it was an expensive Irish oatmeal, much coarser than the regular kind, and she considered it a rare treat. She neither noticed the girls' faces nor heard their groans when they had come in to see what she was preparing.

There were more knocks on the door, this time louder, more insistent.

With a dark face, Ludmila marched out into the hall and flung open the door. 'Oh, is you,' she growled.

Larry Hochstetter looked down at her in surprise. He couldn't contain his laughter. Ludmila looked thoroughly ridiculous in her ancient brocade dress, the fringed shawl draped around her shoulders, the malachite Fabergé egg hanging around her neck, and the old scarf knotted around her head. She looked for all the world like a cross between a miniature empress and the most lowly scullery maid.

'Well?' she hissed. 'You think something is funny?'

He tried to wipe the smile off his face. 'No, not at all.' He swallowed with difficulty.

'And don't just stand there like an idiot. Come in.'

'Greetings and salutations, madame,' he said with a flourish of his hat and a wink. 'There's nothing like a warm welcome, especially from a beautiful woman.'

She waved the spoon threateningly. 'You better watch your tongue, young man.' She squinted dangerously up at him. 'It took you long enough to come and visit.'

'I called a hundred times, but no one would answer the telephone. I took it to mean no one was at home.' He frowned, sniffed the air, and wrinkled his nose. 'What on earth is that ghastly smell?'

Ludmila indignantly drew herself up to her full height. 'That smell, *monsieur*,' she said acidly, 'is my cooking. You don't like it, you don't eat it.'

'I stand corrected. It is my mistake. In fact, it must be that smell emanating from downstairs that I thought I smelled here. But *this* smell.' He made a production of sniffing. 'This smell is delicious. Truly.' He grinned at her.

Her face softened. 'What took you so long?' she whispered conspiratorially. 'It has been five hours since I called you.'

'The meeting took forever,' he explained. 'I didn't get out of the bank until fifteen minutes ago.'

'I only hope you can do something. No one will tell me what happened, but they act as if the end of world has come.'

He handed her his coat and hat and took a thick envelope out of his breast pocket. Waving it excitedly, he said, 'This, if anything, will get her up. You'll see.'

Ludmila regarded him dubiously. 'I hope so. She just lies there and says nothing.'

She watched him go into the parlor. The moment he

caught sight of Elizabeth-Anne lying on the chaise, he froze. But Ludmila smiled encouragingly and gestured him to go closer. She noticed that his face had undergone a rapid transformation. Gone was the teasing good humor, replaced by extreme concern.

'Elizabeth-Anne,' he said, his voice thick with concern as he approached the chaise. 'Darling, what *is* it?'

She stared up at him. No, she wasn't staring *at* him, he realized with a pang. She was staring *through* him.

'What's the matter, my love?' he asked softly. He brushed his fingers across her cheek. 'What is it? Are you ill?'

Her lips moved faintly, and he had to lean close to catch the words she mumbled. 'At least you aren't dead, too. At least you're alive,' she whispered through cracked, parched lips. Then she shut her eyes in relief.

He placed an index finger on her lips and felt them. They were dry and split. 'Jesus, you're dehydrated.' He turned around. 'Get me some water, somebody,' he called out. 'And stir plenty of sugar in it.'

'Not thirsty,' Elizabeth-Anne mumbled thickly.

'Yes, you are. You'll drink what I give you.'

'Leave me alone,' she pleaded. 'Nobody wants to leave me alone.'

'First you'll drink, then I'll leave you alone. Is that a deal?'

She nodded wearily. Charlotte-Anne brought over a cup of water. He took it from her, placed a hand behind Elizabeth-Anne's head, and made her sit forward. He put the rim of the cup against her lips. 'Drink.'

Like a child, a very sick child with no fight left, she obeyed. After she'd drained the cup, he gently lowered her head. Then he got up and gestured for the girls to follow him into the kitchen.

'Something's got to have happened,' he whispered angrily, 'I've never seen anyone in such a – ' His eye caught the murky, bubbling oatmeal. 'You're going to eat *this*?' he asked incredibly.

'And what,' demanded Ludmila from the doorway, 'is that supposed to mean?'

'You all stay here. I want to talk to you, but I've a call to make first.' He marched back into the living room and called his townhouse.

Bevin, the imperturbable butler, answered the phone on the second ring. Larry told him to connect him with the kitchen. A moment later, the head chef came on the line.

'Marcel? Mr. Hochstetter here. How fast can you prepare a feast? An hour? No, it's got to be a lot quicker than that. I'll give you twenty minutes. Make sure it's hot and meaty. Plenty of fruit and vegetables. And something sweet. Pack it in picnic hampers. I'll send Max up with the car to fetch it. Have someone drive back down with him.'

Ludmila folded her arms and watched Larry from the kitchen. Her gray eyes held an expression of quiet respect. Ah, she thought dreamily, this was like the old days in Russia. This was like something her Fedor, God rest his soul, would have done.

Larry went downstairs to speak to his chauffeur. When he came back upstairs, he joined Ludmila and the girls in the kitchen. 'Well?' he demanded. 'Anyone care to tell me what happened to throw your mother into such a depression?'

The girls avoided his gaze.

'I'm waiting.'

Rebecca swallowed. 'We-we can't tell you,' she said in a shaky voice. 'It was too awful! Too awful!' Suddenly she burst into tears and ran to Ludmila, who coiled her arms around her.

He sighed. 'As you wish. Just remember, if you want to talk to somebody, I'm available at any time. All right?'

Regina and Charlotte-Anne nodded wordlessly.

He went back into the living room and sat on the edge of the chaise. 'Elizabeth-Anne?'

'You promised you'd leave me alone,' she mumbled.

'I need your signature on something.'

She nodded. 'Okay.'

He slid the papers out of the envelope, unfolded them, and handed her a pen. 'Here.' He pointed. 'You have to sign here.'

She didn't protest or even ask what the document was.

She signed her name sloppily and held out the pen. 'Here. Now please,' she begged. 'You've gotten what you've come for.'

He flipped through the pages. 'You have to initial each page, too.'

She listlessly did as she was told.

'And once more here, where it's been changed.'

He folded the papers and laid them down beside her.

'You haven't even asked about the investments.'

'No.'

'In fact, if memory serves me right, I haven't talked to you at all since before the crash. Don't you want to know where you stand financially?'

She shook her head morosely. She didn't care.

His voice grew excited. 'Elizabeth-Anne, listen to me. Our gamble paid off. The mine's struck a motherlode. Much more than I ever dared hope for! By sheer coincidence, we sold all our portfolios a few days before they were worthless. But the mine's going strong, crash or no. You're probably worth millions. *Millions*.' He frowned at her. 'Did you hear what I said?'

'Millions.' She turned her head sideways on the pillow and stared out into space.

He shook her gently but firmly. 'Did a word of what I just said sink in?'

'Something about millions. You lost millions.'

He rolled his eyes in exasperation and shook her more roughly, as though he were trying to shake some sense into her. 'Would you listen to me, goddamn it? *Neither* of us lost a *dime*. We're worth more than ever.'

She frowned. 'I don't understand.'

'Horseshoe Investments. Does that ring a bell?'

She shrugged. 'So it's gone. It doesn't matter anyway.'

'But it's *not* gone.' He laughed. 'You're a genuine, twenty-four karat millionairess.'

'What good is having money if the banks have shut their doors?'

He laughed again. 'Banks! Who cares about banks? It's *gold* we're talking about. Beautiful, yellow, rich as Croesus gold! At first I was afraid that vein was just a stringer. You know, a few inches thick and not too long? But it isn't. We're yielding forty-eight ounces of pure gold a ton.'

'What?' Her forehead creased with a new expression. Realization was slow in coming, but it was dawning nevertheless.

'Hold out your hands, darling. I've something to give you.'

She did so and he said, 'Look here.' He reached into his pocket, took out a handful of what looked like rough pebbles, and dropped them into her hands like so much loose change. 'There's a lot more where these come from.'

She clenched her fingers and brought her fists up to her face. Slowly, she unclenched them, then sucked in her breath. Glittering in the palms of her hands was gold, rough, beautiful, glittering gold nuggets. She stared at them, mesmerized by the sight of that rich yellow as mankind has been mesmerized by it for thousands of years.

'You mean . . . ' Her voice faltered. It was almost more than she could comprehend. 'We really haven't lost everything?'

'Lost it? Hell, no! We're probably the only two people in the entire country who're way ahead of the game.'

'But . . . how could that be?'

'You trusted me and I gambled. And we won.'

Her face suddenly seemed to lose its drawn slackness, as thoughts spun crazily in her head. Zaccheus was gone forever; he had been cruelly snatched from this earth and there was nothing she or anyone else could do about it.

But Larry was alive. Not only alive, but with her, here and now. And thanks to him, her fortune wasn't lost. If he was right, she was rich. Rich enough to fulfill her dreams. Could that be? Could the fates have decided that tearing Zaccheus away from her and the children was enough cruelty for the moment?

'Now, look at the papers you signed, darling,' Larry said softly, a mysterious smile hovering on his lips. 'Look what you just bought yourself for a thousand dollars down.' His one eye sparkled with excitement.

'But . . . if money is so scarce, why spend it? Shouldn't I hang onto it?'

'No, you shouldn't, because all over this city and clear across the country, property is going begging. It's a buyer's market. People are wiped out financially. They can't meet their mortgage payments. The banks are repossessing left and right, and they're trying to cut their losses. Of course, you'll have to pay off the remaining twenty-three-thousand-dollar mortgage, but you got yourself a bargain, young lady.'

'Twenty-three thousand dollars! But – ' her mouth hung wide.

'You can afford it, believe me. For you it's a drop in the bucket. What we'll do is this. Every two weeks, you'll buy another piece of property.'

She shook her head in disbelief. This couldn't be happening. It was all too much, too fast. She was dreaming. Perhaps Zaccheus's execution had been a nightmare, and her mind was forcing a more pleasant dream to take its place.

'What did I buy for twenty-four thousand dollars?' she asked softly.

'Well, read it.' He thrust the documents she had just signed under her nose, rattling them. '*Read* it, for God's sake.' He dropped them into her lap.

She stared down at the pages. Slowly, she began to read. As recognition dawned, she read faster and faster until she was tearing breathlessly through the pages. Finally she sat back and stared at him with a stunned expression. Her breathing was coming in rapid gasps, and her ribcage was pounding uncontrollably. 'The . . . the *Madison Squire Hotel*?'

He nodded.

'It's mine? It's true?'

'As the children say, "cross my heart, hope to die, stick a – " '

'No, we won't! Enough has been stuck in one of your eyes to last you a lifetime.'

He smiled faintly. 'I'll concede it was a poor choice of a ditty.'

'But . . . Larry.' 'She sat up straight, half in excitement, half in new-found anguish. 'But we *can't*. We can't just walk in and . . . and take advantage of people's misery. It's *stealing*.'

'No, it's not. What you're actually doing is bailing people out of bad trouble. If they can't meet their payments and the banks repossess, they're bankrupt. They lose it all anyway, but legally they still owe the rest of the mortgage. Don't you see? You're *helping* people. And at the same time, you're helping yourself.'

She was unable to speak.

'And this is just the beginning,' he cried exultantly. 'You'll see. You wanted a hotel, right?'

She nodded.

'Well, you've got it. But you're going to get a lot more. This is just the beginning. Apartment houses, hotels . . . you'll buy a string of them. All for pennies on the dollar. Never in my life have I known a riper time to buy property. The economy will change, you'll see. And you'll own a *chain* of hotels stretching clear from coast to coast.'

'It's frightening,' she said in a tiny voice.

'Is it? Or is being poor even more frightening?'

She nodded.

His eye gleamed. 'And with the gold coming in steadily every day – just think of it, darling. You'll clean up. Your dream has come true. Not once, but a thousand times over.'

But she couldn't think of it in those heady terms. Not yet. At the moment, she could think of only one hotel at a time. Even that was difficult.

She stared down at the legal documents. 'It's mine?' she whispered in disbelief. 'The Madison Squire is really mine?'

'All yours. Lock, stock, and barrel. One hundred percent yours.'

'Oh, Larry.' And, finally, she began to cry. She lunged forward and flung her arms around him. 'I-I don't know what to say. Just when my whole world was collapsing all around me – ' She looked up, startled. 'Who could that be?'

'That,' said Ludmila, hurrying across the room, 'is door.' She went to open it. Elizabeth-Anne craned her neck. One of Larry's uniformed servants was standing with a huge wicker hamper shaped like a large suitcase, in each hand. She stared at the servant, then turned speechlessly to Larry.

'That happens to be food,' he said. 'You'll need your strength, darling. You don't look like you've eaten in days.'

Tears were rolling down her cheeks.

The servant looked around, quickly moved some chairs out of the way, and spread a blanket out on the living room floor. When he opened the hampers, Elizabeth-Anne couldn't believe her eyes. They had been custom made and compactly held fine bone china, heavy sterling cutlery, hand-cut stemware, and artfully folded white linen napkins. In amazed silence, Elizabeth-Anne and the girls watched the man deftly arranging the place settings. He opened bottles of champagne, and then out came the food: paper-thin slices of smoked salmon with rows of lemon slices and parsley, ice-cold dishes of Beluga Mollasol caviar, toast and water wafers and pumpernickel, deviled eggs and steak tartare, tiny cornichons, several cold roast chickens, piles of rare pink roast beef, pickled vegetables, velvety peaches and ripe bananas, and wonderfully glazed petit fours and creamy Sacher tortes.

Elizabeth-Anne realized she was ravenous.

'Once we finish our little picnic,' Larry said, 'we'll head uptown to inspect the hotel. Tell you what: As owner's perogative, why don't you and the children move into the royal suite and live there? I was there once for a party for a European duchess, and if memory serves me right, it's an enormous penthouse duplex. It even has a kitchen, although I think you'll be too busy to cook. You'll probably use room service or the dining room mostly. But best of all, it's got a wrap-around terrace planted with trees and shrubs.'

'The royal suite? Us?' She stared at him. 'Could we? I mean . . . *really*?'

He laughed. 'Can't you get it through that thick skull of yours? It's *yours*, darling. You own it.'

'B-but I can't be seen – ' She sputtered as vanity took

142

hold of her. She grabbed handfuls of her hair and pulled her fingers through it. 'I need to wash my hair, bathe and get ready. I can't go anywhere like this. Charlotte-Anne, run a bath for me. Regina, sweet, fetch my beige shoes – '

'Whoa! Not so fast,' Larry laughed. 'There's time for all that. Let's eat something first, shall we?'

She laughed suddenly. 'I think I'm going to cry.'

He stroked the tears from her cheeks with his fingers. 'You are crying, darling.'

'Oh, Larry, I'm so happy. You've saved my life.'

'Well, I wouldn't put it quite like that.'

'I would.' She nodded solemnly. 'You did.'

'Then you owe me one. I want to come along and see the hotel. Is it a deal?'

'See it?' She jumped out of bed. 'You'll see it all right, Larry Hochstetter! You'll see it till you're sick of it, if I've got anything to say about it – '

The excitement was infectious. Suddenly, miraculously, the girls and even little Zaccheus joined in, all of them talking animatedly and laughing and crying. Magically enough, in the midst of their greatest tragedy, they had all come to life.

And so had Hale Hotels.

11

This time when they pulled up outside the Madison Squire, they were received quite differently. The Rolls-Royce worked wonders. The moment the huge car approached, the doorman and porter came running. They fell all over themselves to be helpful, even before the seven passengers had piled out of the car.

'Good afternoon, madame. Good afternoon, sir,' they chorused solemnly.

Larry ignored them, Ludmila sniffed, and Elizabeth-Anne smiled graciously. The children stared up at the huge building with wide, excited eyes.

143

'The luggage, please,' the porter said to Max.

The big chauffeur stood with crossed arms and shook his head wordlessly. The porter retreated hastily, and the doorman made a beeline for the giant brass-and-glass doors. He unlocked a side door and held it wide for them, his eyes focused straight ahead.

Inside the lobby, the same self-important Mr. Smythe stood sentinel behind the reception desk. This time, there was nothing disdainful about his attitude; he clearly did not recognize them.

'Good afternoon, mesdames,' he greeted them. 'Good afternoon, sir.' He favored Ludmila, Elizabeth-Anne, and Larry with a tight, nervous smile, and didn't as much as blink a disapproving eyelash as little Zaccheus let out a whoop and tore across the lobby. He raised his eyebrows inquiringly. 'Do you have reservations?'

Elizabeth-Anne smiled faintly. 'No, Mr. Smythe, we do not.'

For a moment he looked faintly surprised that she knew his name. Then he smiled self-importantly and adjusted his tie with the lacquered fingertips of one hand. 'Of course, reservations are not really necessary,' he conceded.

'I didn't think so,' she said pleasantly. 'You'll have someone show us up to the royal suite?'

She couldn't help but feel a faint triumph at how that *really* threw him. 'Of-of course, madame,' he stammered. 'R-right away.' He clapped the bell on the desk with the flat of his palm and opened up the reservations ledger. He pushed it around to face her. 'If you'll be so kind as to register?'

Larry stepped forward and flipped the ledger shut. 'I don't think this is necessary, do you?' he asked softly.

Mr. Smythe's throat made a warbling sound as he cleared it. 'Well, sir, the hotel regulations require that – '

'Mr. Smythe, is it?' There was no misinterpreting Larry's tone.

'Yes, sir.' Mr. Smythe was bewildered and looking painfully uncomfortable.

'You might not know it yet, my good man, but from this moment on it is Mrs. Hale who makes the rules around here. You see, she intends to take up permanent residence in this hotel.'

'Yes, sir, but – '

'Also, I think you should know that she is now the proud owner of this establishment.'

Mr. Smythe blushed crimson. 'Oh, I-I . . . of course,' he stammered, now at more of a loss than ever. 'In-in that case, I'll show you up to the royal suite personally.' He raised a hand and snapped his fingers once. A gaunt, well-groomed, middle-aged woman hurried out from the office behind the desk. 'Mrs. Carleton,' Mr. Smythe said without turning around to look at her, 'take over for me, please.'

'Yes, Mr. Smythe.'

'I'll be up in the royal suite if you need me.' He came around from behind the desk and turned to Larry and Elizabeth-Anne. 'If you'll be so kind as to follow me, please,' he said with a slight bow. He crossed the marble lobby to the bank of elevators, his leather heels clacking noisily.

Elizabeth-Anne, Ludmila, Larry, and the children followed, but they took their time. Elizabeth-Anne was taking the opportunity to study the splendid lobby. She breathed deeply as she gazed around, unable to believe that this small, glittering, palace-like hotel was now truly hers. It seemed impossible, like something out of a dream.

Mr. Smythe was waiting for them outside the elevator, and the uniformed elevator operator was holding the door open. By the way the man was acting, Smythe had clearly let him know just who Elizabeth-Anne was.

Once they were all inside, the operator shoved the door shut, and pressed down on the brass handle. As they rose smoothly skyward, Mr. Smythe cleared his throat and said apologetically, 'The royal suite takes up the entire top two floors of the hotel. I'm afraid the elevator only goes as far as the first of those floors. There are two staircases, however, connecting both floors of the duplex. One is quite grand, and the other is for the staff and emergency use.'

'That is quite all right, Mr. Smythe,' Elizabeth-Anne assured him.

He nodded then stood silently, his fingers ticking

nervously against the sides of his trousers. Elizabeth-Anne gazed up at the sweeping hand of the floor indicator above the door. As they approached the eighth floor, a bell chimed and a yellow light went on indicating a stop call, but they rode on without stopping.

'Just a moment, please,' Elizabeth-Anne said.

Both the elevator operator and Smythe turned to face her. The elevator bobbed to an abrupt halt between floors.

'Someone is summoning the elevator on the eighth floor, I take it?'

'Yes, Mrs. Hale,' the operator said timidly.

'From now on, unless there is an emergency, I want every elevator to stop whenever and wherever it is summoned. It doesn't matter who is on it. I intend for the guests to be king around here, not me and my family. The guests pay good money to stay here, and we will pamper them and keep them coming back to stay here time and again. Is that clear? No inconvenience for the staff, or my family, is too great when it comes to satisfying my paying guests. They're going to get more services for their dollar here than anywhere else.'

'Yes, ma'am,' the operator said in a tiny voice.

Elizabeth-Anne nodded. 'Fine. Also, I would like to point out that there are smudges on the paneling of this elevator. And the brass needs a good shining.'

'Yes, ma'am.'

'I'm going to inspect every elevator in this building at noon tomorrow. I want them all to gleam like new.'

'Yes, ma'am.'

She smiled. 'Just so we understand each other and don't get off on the wrong foot. Now, let's backtrack down a floor and pick up whoever summoned this thing.'

As she looked away, she caught Larry's approving gaze, and she shrugged. As long as she would have her way – and with Hale Hotels she *would* have her way – one motto would ring out loud and clear: Nothing under the sun would be too much when it came to her guests. She would have them coming back. Again and again.

And that, she knew, was what would make her hotel shine above all others.

By the time they reached the royal suite several minutes later, the word was obviously out. The moment the elevator door slid open, a maid greeted them. She was a short Irish woman in her late thirties, and her black and white uniform was crisply starched. 'Good afternoon, Mrs. Hale,' she said in a thick brogue. 'Welcome to the Madison Squire. My name is Moira, and I'm permanently assigned to this suite. Anything you want, you just call me.'

'Thank you, Moira.' Elizabeth-Anne smiled warmly at her and turned to Smythe. 'I believe that Moira can show us around just fine. I appreciate your taking the time to show us up here.'

Smythe tried his best to hide the fact that he was perturbed. He didn't like to be summarily dismissed. 'As you wish,' he said, bowing stiffly.

'Meanwhile, Mr. Smythe,' Elizabeth-Anne said slowly, 'could you tell me when the day shift lets off?'

'At five o'clock.'

Elizabeth-Anne consulted her watch. 'Very well. That gives us half an hour. Please see to it that everyone from the day shift is assembled in the dining room at that time. I wish to have a talk with the day staff.'

'Yes, Mrs. Hale.'

'And I want you to do the same thing for the night shift. And the morning shift. Assemble them after their shift is over so that I can speak with them.'

'But . . . the shifts are eight hours apart. Wouldn't you care to rest and – '

'Mr. Smythe,' Elizabeth-Anne said patiently, 'rest is for the guests, not the staff. From this moment on, I am not only the owner of the Madison Squire, but a member of the staff as well.'

'Yes, Mrs. Hale.' Rebuked, he backed into the elevator. Only once the door closed, did he allow himself to wipe the beads of perspiration off his glistening forehead.

No one had to tell Elizabeth-Anne what it was like to meet the boss for the first time. She remembered only too well the day she had met Mrs. Winter.

'Nervous?' Larry had asked her as she'd prepared

herself for her first meeting with the staff.

She'd nodded and shut her eyes.

'If you like, I'll be there with you,' he'd offered.

She'd opened her eyes then and smiled painfully. 'Sorry, no,' she'd told him softly. 'This is something I have to do alone, Larry. Otherwise I'll never gain their respect.'

His look told her that he understood perfectly.

She could feel the day shift's tension and anxiety crackling like electricity in the air of the dining room the moment she came in. It was a big room, and everyone was seated around the white-draped tables which had already been laid out for dinner. As soon as she made her appearance, Mr. Smythe approached her, and everyone quickly rose to their feet. Maintenance men, maids, book keepers, telephone operators, kitchen help, reception clerk, porters, bellboys, waiters, chefs and the doorman – the entire life blood of one eight-hour shift at the Madison Squire was assembled before her. And life blood of the hotel they were, she well knew, for without the essential human services the staff provided, the Madison Squire would be but an empty shell.

Slowly she made the rounds of the room, her keen aquamarine eyes appraising everyone as Mr. Smythe introduced her. She shook hands with everyone and tried to remember the faces and names as best she could. There was such a large staff. But in time, she was certain, she would learn to call them all by their names and learn a little about them.

Finally, the personal introductions over, Elizabeth-Anne stood alone in the front of the room. 'Please, be seated.' Her voice sounded suddenly weak, and she cleared her throat.

There were the sounds of chairs scraping and starched uniforms rustling, but otherwise the tense silence could have been cut with a knife.

Elizabeth-Anne took a deep breath. She felt as nervous as everyone else, but she knew that she must not show it. She had to appear in total control. This was her staff, and in order to get them to do her bidding, she must not only gain their respect, but their affection also.

Swiftly she counted heads. There were twenty-seven employees sitting before her, and they were now her responsibility. The weight of it made her feel overwhelmingly alone. She took a deep breath to steady her nerves. Then she clasped her hands in front of her.

'Ladies and gentlemen,' she began softly. 'I know you've all had a rough day, and that you're tired and anxious to get home. So I'll try and make this relatively brief.' She paused and smiled reassuringly. 'You do not know me, and I do not know you. That, at least, puts us on an even footing. However, within a few days we'll all be better acquainted with one another. Some of you have been here for a long time, others not so long. It is especially traumatic for long-term employees to find out that the business they have worked for is undergoing a change in ownership, because that usually means a change in management as well. Usually, but not always.

'I understand the way you feel perfectly. New bosses can be tough, and you'll have to prove yourselves all over again. Some of you will not like me. And I will probably not like some of you either.'

She allowed herself a chuckle. At least the ice was broken, she noticed. The staff looked a little less worried already.

'However,' she continued, 'that is all beside the point. The only persons with whom you must be popular is the guests. I intend to make the Madison Squire the shining star of all the hotels in this city, indeed the *country*, and in order to do that, I need the help of each and every one of you.'

She paused, her eyes sweeping the faces before her. They were all sitting at attention, digesting every word.

'You will find out that I am a fanatic when it comes to cleanliness and services. We're going to glow and sparkle, all of us. And since I live upstairs, I'll have an easy time keeping my eyes on each and every one of you. Which doesn't mean I intend to frighten you. Not at all. It's only to keep you all on your toes.'

She paused again, watching them exchange wary glances.

'Starting tomorrow, I want the person in charge of each section of this hotel to give me a guided tour. That includes bus stations in the dining room, linen closets in the halls, and even the boiler and heating equipment in the basement. This is all necessary, because I wish to know this hotel inside and out, and no one knows it better than all of you. I also wish to get to know each and every one of you personally, because we are a team. I may happen to own this hotel, but I'm as much a member of the staff as any of you.

'Now to some rather unpleasant business. When you arrive for work in the morning, I want every one of you to drop by the personnel office. You are all to hand in letters of resignation.'

A sudden murmur rose from the employees.

Elizabeth-Anne raised a hand to silence them. 'This is not to say that any of you will be let go. You will be instantly rehired, but on new terms. Each of you will again go through a probation period. This will give us a chance to see how well we work together and if we discover we don't get on, you will not be fired summarily. You shall receive severance pay and references. I know this is not easy to live with, but I believe it will give all of you an opportunity to prove your worth.'

She inclined her head.

'By Friday of next week, I also expect the head of each department to prepare a report describing how things can be improved.' She dropped her voice so everyone would have to strain to catch what she was saying. 'You will discover that, although I am demanding, I tend to reward hard work. Those of you who deserve it will get raises. Naturally, I won't be giving any of this away for nothing. It will be up to each and every one of you to prove you deserve it.'

She stopped and smiled brightly. 'Meanwhile, let me reiterate that I welcome the opportunity of working with you. And don't forget, we are all a team. I'm counting on you to make the rest of us look good. I want this hotel to be filled to capacity at all times, and to do that, our reputation must spread. That is all in your hands. And to give you some incentive right away, despite the resignation letters I expect from all of you, I am hereby raising all salaries by ten percent.'

There was utter confusion mixed with the wariness now.

She continued to smile. 'Now, let's hope you all earn it. Good night.' She turned and left the room. In the silence that followed her out, one could have heard a pin drop. Only after she closed the dining room doors did pandemonium break out.

Larry was waiting outside the dining room for her. 'I caught your speech,' he said with a chuckle.

'Eavesdropping, eh?'

'No. I was just on my way out, and I happened to overhear it. You're good. Very good.'

She smiled nervously. Now that the meeting was over, she allowed her misgivings to show.

'In fact,' Larry added admiringly, 'you were brilliant. You not only hung a killing sword over their heads to make sure they work their damnest, but at the same time you gave them across the board raises to let them know just how much they stand to lose.' He grinned hugely. 'It seems I've underestimated you. You're quite a businesswoman. Much more of one than I realized.'

'More than I realized too,' she admitted in a weak voice.

'Well, now that you've proved it, what do you say we ride up to the house? I still have plenty of champagne in the cellar.'

She shook her head. 'Thanks, but no. Not that I couldn't use a drink, but it's been one helluva day.'

'You can say that again.' He leaned forward and kissed her on the lips. 'I'll drop by tomorrow, how's that? Then I'll bring the champagne. A whole case as a housewarming present.'

Her smile was dazzling. 'I'd like that. And Larry?'

He raised his eyebrows.

'Thanks.'

'What for?'

'You know what for, Larry. Everything. Everything.'

*　　*　　*

The star-spangled night was cool and velvety as Elizabeth-Anne stepped out through the French doors and stood on the terrace. All around her, Manhattan glittered and shimmered, a vertical fairyland of crystalline towers and gleaming lights. She had tried to sleep, but it was impossible; too much had happened too suddenly.

She was filled with a soaring sense of anticipation and wondrous excitement. Not all that long ago, she and the children had been in this hotel under very different circumstances. It seemed yesterday she had leaned out of a window in this very building, determined to take the city by storm and forge out a brilliant future for herself and the children. Now it was starting to happen, and this terrace, as well as the entire building, a whole square block on Madison Avenue, was hers, and hers alone.

She breathed deeply of the sweet night air and her own heady success, a gleam of sparkling resolution shining in her eyes. Yes, she had come far in a short period of time. But not far enough, she thought. There was still so much to be done. So much more to be achieved and built and forged out of nothing. By God, she would conquer this city, she would tame this cacophanous, teeming giant and call it her own, and after she was through with that, she would conquer the country, and then the world.

Hale Hotels.

She savored the sound of those two short words on her tongue, tasting them, letting their power and strength course through her. From up here, high atop the city, it was easy to take strength from the present, and see into the future, to feel the pulse of the entire world. It wasn't difficult to imagine an empire of hotels spanning the earth.

For a long time she stood alone on the terrace of the Madison Squire, a solitary woman gazing out at a sleeping world, planning and dreaming, determined to make everything she ever wanted come true.

She did not hear him, but she felt his presence as he came out onto the terrace and stood behind her. She turned slowly to face him. 'I thought you had left,' she said softly, gazing at his moonlit face. 'I thought I wouldn't see you until tomorrow.'

'I did leave,' Larry answered. 'But tomorrow seemed too far away. I had to come back and see you. I knew you'd be standing out here. Surveying your world.'

She laughed. 'Guilty.'

'It's beautiful, isn't it?'

She nodded, the tears shining in her eyes. 'Larry,' she whispered quietly, 'Oh, Larry. You've made me the happiest woman in the world.'

He drew her close to him, wrapping his arms around her. She sighed contently as he held her against the rugged warmth of his body.

'I want you to be happy,' he whispered, nuzzling the nape of her neck with his lips. 'I want you always to be happy. You and I, we're special, Elizabeth-Anne. That's why we're standing here right now, instead of down there. We dare to dream, both of us. We dare to take chances and lock horns with fate to make our dreams our reality.'

'I love you Larry.' Her voice was the barest whisper in the night.

'And I love you.' He kissed her, tasting her vital urgency, feeling her powerfully trembling body. They kissed a long time, the lights twinkling all around them, and then he took her by the hand and led her inside, up the sweeping stairs to the second floor of the duplex, to the huge master bedroom where they celebrated success and dreams, achievements and each other by making fierce, urgent love until the sun rose brightly in the east.

GENERATIONS
TWO

Charlotte-Anne

NEW YORK CITY,
March 20, 1931

1

At precisely seven a.m. on this Friday morning, just like on every other weekday morning of the year, three sharp, business-like raps on the bedroom door awoke Charlotte-Anne.

'Go 'way,' she mumbled, which was exactly what she mumbled every weekday morning. As usual, her words were ignored. The door opened and Dallas, Elizabeth-Anne's friend from the Savoy Plaza, whom she had lured away to be her family housekeeper at far better pay, came bustling in full of good cheer. For once she wasn't loaded down with the huge breakfast tray room service normally sent up. Elizabeth-Anne had left strict instructions that the family would breakfast together that morning.

'Morning,' Dallas sang out cheerfully. She crossed over to the French doors and yanked aside the thick, butter-yellow drapes.

'Go *'way*, Dallas,' Charlotte-Anne moaned irritably. She scowled as she buried her face under the pillow.

'Now, now, Miss Charlotte-Anne, your Mamma said you got to be up at the stroke of seven, and I aim to get you out of bed just when she said. Breakfast's at the table this mornin'. Your Mamma, she wants to discuss something important with you all.'

Dallas grasped a corner of the off-white, satin comforter, and pulled. She and Charlotte-Anne had suffered through this daily ritual hundreds of times, and Charlotte-Anne, knowing full well what was coming, grabbed hold of her end of the comforter. A fierce tug of war followed. Dallas won out; she always did. For one thing, she was wide awake, which Charlotte-Anne wasn't; for another, the

157

satin was slick and liked to slip out from between Charlotte-Anne's fingers.

Once Charlotte-Anne gave way to Dallas's swift, forceful yanks, the comforter slid to the foot of the bed like a rumpled, soft sculpture accordion. Charlotte-Anne shivered, but knew she would get no sympathy from Dallas, who was not one to coddle children and considered Charlotte-Anne, at seventeen, very much an adult in any case.

Elizabeth-Anne Hale had given Dallas carte blanche to run the apartment and the children as she saw fit. Dallas knew their mother trusted her implicitly, and took seriously her responsibility to see that the children became nicely behaved and dutiful adults. Mrs. Hale had become an extremely busy woman, and she didn't always have much time on her hands to see to the children herself. She had had to delegate a lot of authority, and Dallas wasn't about to let her down.

Charlotte-Anne lay there in her ecru lace nightgown, still huddled against the chill with her head buried under the pillow.

'Come on, Sleeping Beauty,' Dallas growled softly, giving the fluffy, down-filled pillow gentle but firm smacks with the palms of her hands. 'It's a lovely day out. Still a little on the dark side, mind you, but it's gonna be beautiful. Can't you just smell it?' She lifted her head, sniffed appreciatively and smiled. 'Spring is finally in the air.'

As Charlotte-Anne continued to refuse to respond, Dallas shook her head, gazing about her and wondering for what must have been the hundredth time why such a beautiful room was wasted on such a lazy girl. Of all the rooms Dallas had seen in all the years she had spent working in luxury hotels, this particular room was her favorite. The entire decor spoke of femininity and grace. The walls were covered in richly carved French Provincial paneling, but all the other furniture – the chairs, the curvaceous headboard, the bombé chests with their pregnant wooden bellies, the lady's dresser with mirror and settee, the sheer gauze curtains and heavier drapes – it was all done in soft, creamy ivory with just a hint of butter yellow for accent. On the dresser, chests, and nightstands stood potted, papery yellow daffodils. There was something intensely lady-like and yet sunny about the room; even on the dreariest of rainy days it seemed to Dallas that the sun was shining here.

It was a room fit for a princess, which was how Dallas looked upon Charlotte-Anne and her sisters. And little Zaccheus was a prince. Crown prince and princesses of an empire which was already comprised of seven hotels, three right here in New York City, along with one each in Baltimore, Philadelphia, Boston, and Washington, D.C. And that wasn't counting the Hale Tourist Court in Texas. Not to mention, Dallas reminded herself, something about shares in a very lucrative gold mine. And from what Dallas's small but alert ears had picked up, Elizabeth-Anne Hale would be off to buy another Tourist Court today, somewhere on Route One.

Elizabeth-Anne's success didn't fill Dallas with envy. It had just the opposite effect: it gave her hope for all woman-kind. Sometimes she still had trouble believing that the woman she had first met as a fellow maid was now the mistress of the growing Hale empire.

I'm glad she has what she does, Dallas thought to herself with a satisfied chuckle. She deserves it, and so do I. I'm paid handsomely now, and the working conditions are sure a lot better than any I've ever known elsewhere. She nodded to herself. No longer was there need for her to work two jobs, and she didn't have to spend a dime on food, either. Leftovers from the hotel kitchen were hers to lug home. Unbelievable as it seemed, she was even starting to tuck a little money away each week for her own children's future.

'C'mon, now, honey child,' Dallas warned Charlotte-Anne, grabbing hold of the creamy ivory pillow and tugging on that too.

'All right, all right,' Charlotte-Anne mumbled grumpily, her voice muffled by the pillow. She flung it aside angrily, then sat up, yawning. She rubbed the sleep out of her eyes with her knuckles. Even dishevelled, her beauty was startling.

Since the Hales had moved to the Madison Squire almost a year and a half before, Charlotte-Anne had matured considerably and now looked much older than her seventeen years. All of her youthfulness had been shed. Her gangliness was gone, and her body was tall and slender. Her handspan waist, coupled with the rich, solid swell of her breasts provided a voluptuous figure that was in tantalizing contrast to her pale complexion, which lent her a flawless, haunting porcelain beauty. Her hair was her mother's, the same rich, ripe shade of ready-to-harvest wheat, but her eyes, with their peculiar, unsettling shade of pale aquamarine were the slightly tilted, slanting eyes of a predatory cat. At the same time, small and defiant as her face was, she could appear deceptively frail and sweet looking, thanks to her tiny, pale pink lips and perfect, pearly small teeth. She gave off an air of flawless and enchanting doll-like beauty, but that was on the surface. Beneath the demureness she affected was a poorly concealed toughness, a stubborn will of iron, and a feisty, tiger's mind of her own. No one knew this better than Dallas, who was the first person to set eyes on her each morning before she could settle into the image of sweetness she tried so hard to project.

'Best you hurry,' Dallas warned her. 'You've got half an hour. Breakfast's at seven-thirty sharp. Your Mamma's expecting you to be on time.'

'I hear you, I hear you,' Charlotte-Anne answered testily.

Dallas eyed her suspiciously and then left, closing the door softly behind her.

Charlotte-Anne waited until the door closed, then stuck out her tongue. Without further ado, she swung her legs out over the bed, her feet doing a tip-toe dance as she felt for her slippers. Finally finding them and wiggling them on, she stood up and stretched lazily. Then she pulled on her rose silk robe, tied the pink sash around her miniscule waist, and walked over to the French windows. She looked out for a long moment. It was indeed a perfect, early spring day. As she watched, the city grew lighter and came into sharp, stony focus.

160

On an impulse, she opened the terrace doors wide and stepped outside. Briskly she massaged her forearms against the sudden chill and did a quick little dance. The terracotta tiles were cold, and the chill soaked right through her thin slippers. But for the moment, any discomfort was quickly forgotten. She leaned forward on the brick parapet wall and stared dreamily out over the city. Thirty-three stories below, the traffic on Madison Avenue was still light, waiting for the morning rush hour.

She shook her head. Considering all the traffic and bustling people, and the low vacancy rate of this hotel, she'd never have known that the country was plunged into the depths of the Depression. From up here, she couldn't see the pitiful look of hopelessness worn by so many walking on the street below her. The suites in the Madison Squire were filled, and so were most of the expensive rooms. It was the inexpensive rooms which went begging. Which only showed, she thought in bewilderment, who was really hurting.

She pushed herself away from the wall and turned to go back inside when something pinkish caught her eye. Could it be?

She stooped down in front of the redwood planter to investigate.

It was! The first of the season's crocuses was braving the weather, its tightly cocooned, wing-like petals peering out from beneath the dark soil. It was an omen, she decided.

Humming softly to herself, she went back inside. Today was special, and so far, everything was working out perfectly, much better than she'd hoped.

She danced through her bedroom, arms extended, and swooped toward the bathroom door.

Yes, everything was going *much* better than she'd anticipated. She could sense that. The fact that her mother was going to be gone all day proved it; the fact that she wouldn't be back until tomorrow reinforced it further.

Her hum turned into a song as she filled the ceramic washbasin with ice cold water. She slipped out of the robe and nightgown, and splashed handfuls of ice cold water into her face. As she dabbed herself dry with a huge, soft

161

white bath towel, she eyed herself critically in the mirror. She was pleased with what she saw.

She ran the big, tortoise shell comb through her hair. Suddenly she froze, the corners of her lips drooping into a distressed frown. Maybe everything wasn't as perfect as she thought. Perhaps her mother *had* gotten wind of her plans. Why else would she have insisted on them all having breakfast together this, of all mornings?

Charlotte-Anne ran down the gracefully curving, carpeted stairs of the duplex, her fingers nervously tying her hair back with the silk, navy blue ribbon. She could hear muted voices in the living room.

Damn, she thought to herself, her lips tightening in frustration. She was late again, and they were probably waiting for her to start eating.

She knew that with each passing day she was taking longer to dress, but it was all because of her despised school uniform. Each morning, she was determined to somehow make it look more stylish and she would experiment in front of the mirror. It wasn't her fault, it was the Brearley School's. The elegant building on East Eighty-Third Street might house one of the finest girls' schools in the country, but she hated going there. Even more she hated dressing sedately in plain white blouses and dark blue skirts like some child. She considered herself much too sophisticated for the schoolgirl look, with the short white gloves and her hair tied back with a ribbon. Worse yet, the school was for girls only. How she yearned to throw off the shackles of that school! She would have liked nothing more than to burn her uniform and have her hair styled nicely for a change.

Well, she would do that soon now, she promised herself. Very, very soon. *If* everything went well. And if it didn't, she would make sure another opportunity presented itself.

She stopped running before she reached the living room doors, and entered the room with a slow, gracious walk.

The rest of the family was already seated around the table at the far end of the room, just as she had feared, waiting for her. Elizabeth-Anne, Regina, Rebecca, Zaccheus, and Larry Hochstetter turned to gaze at her.

Seeing Larry startled her. She hadn't expected him. Family breakfasts were rare enough, due to her mother's grueling schedule, but breakfasts with guests were rarer still. She wondered what had prompted this unusual turn of events.

'Morning,' she said in what she hoped was a light, cheerful voice. Her mother held up her cheek and she kissed it. Charlotte-Anne favored Larry with the best smile she could muster, ignored her sisters and brother, and slipped into her seat.

'Now that we're all here,' Elizabeth-Anne began, without so much as a disapproving glance at her errant daughter, 'we can have our little discussion. As you all know, I've never made a serious decision which might affect you without consulting all of you first.' There was a radiant smile on her fact and her cheeks were tinged with a pinkish color that made her look much younger than her thirty-six years. But, from her fidgeting hands, Charlotte-Anne saw that her mother was unusually nervous.

Charlotte-Anne instantly felt the heavy load slipping off her shoulders. She had been fretting for nothing. This breakfast discussion had nothing to do with what she had feared. Gratefully, she tried to concentrate on what her mother was saying.

'As you all know, it's been nearly a year and a half since your father . . . died.' Elizabeth-Anne had carefully planned her speech, but her voice trembled nevertheless.

The children nodded, their faces suddenly solemn. Elizabeth-Anne glanced quickly at Larry, who sat beside her and held her hand in silent encouragement, his face carefully expressionless.

'There comes a time,' Elizabeth-Anne said slowly, 'when each of us must take a good, hard look at our lives. We must look behind us, to the past, to promises made. We must consider the present, in which we live now. And we must look forward to the future, to what it might hold for us. As you all know, I loved your father very much, as did all of you. And I *still* love him. However, the fact remains that he is gone. We've all mourned him for a long time. We were alone for years before he died. But, now, while we will

163

always hold him dear to our hearts, we must look toward the future. This was his last request.' She paused, letting her words sink in. Then she smiled and looked hopefully around the table. 'I think you all like Larry?'

Her children nodded.

'As you all know, Larry and I are leaving for New Jersey this morning to buy a new property. But we have other, more important plans in addition. As soon as the papers are signed, we're planning to go on to Elkton, Maryland. It isn't much further, and civil marriages are performed there with a minimum of fuss and delay.' She paused and added softly, 'Larry and I decided we'd like to get married.'

The mention of marriage was totally unexpected, a shocking bolt of lightning out of the blue. Regina's hand slipped, and she knocked over her glass of orange juice, which spread across the white linen tablecloth. Charlotte-Anne sat still as a statue, her slice of toast in one hand, her butter knife in the other. Only her pale eyes moved, and they swept around the table at the silent tableau.

Her mother and Larry were facing each other, exchanging encouraging, hopeful smiles.

Regina's mouth was hanging open as she stared in horror at the yellow stain of the juice.

Rebecca still held a cup of hot chocolate poised at her lips.

The silence was broken by eleven-year-old Zaccheus. 'Are you going to be our new Daddy?' he asked Larry in his clear voice.

The spell was broken and everyone began to move at once. Rebecca lowered her cup, while Regina righted the glass and dabbed at the stain with her napkin.

'I like to think so,' Larry told Zaccheus. He glanced around. 'It all depends on you and your sisters.'

'I told Larry long ago,' Elizabeth-Anne said hesitantly, 'that we always discuss an important decision which affects us all. We'd like to hear all your opinions.'

'Yes!' Zaccheus cried excitedly. 'I think yes!'

'Regina?'

Regina stopped dabbing the stain and looked across the table at her mother. Now eighteen, she spent her days, and a good portion of her nights, at Columbia University, where she was immersed in her studies. She hoped eventually to become a pediatrician. Regina realized only too well that with each passing day, her own life was just unfolding, and her mother's, which until now had been an intrinsic part of it, no longer revolved around her. Both mother and daughter needed separate lives, and she understood this. Eventually, all birds flew off to make their own nests, and she was certain she would soon too. She had been hoping for a long time that her mother would have a second, luckier chance at love, and the news of her impending marriage had startled her because it seemed too good to be true. It was everything she had prayed would happen.

Regina nodded solemnly, her brow wrinkling as she sought the correct words. 'You both have my blessings,' she said huskily. Then she jumped up, hugged her mother, and kissed Larry.

The tears sparkled in Elizabeth-Anne's eyes as she said, 'Thank you, dear. Both Larry and I appreciate it.' She switched her gaze. ' 'Becca?'

'I miss Daddy, of course,' fourteen-year-old Rebecca said slowly, biting down on her underlip. 'But I know nothing will ever bring him back.' She stared down into her hot chocolate, as though the answer lay somewhere in her murky cup. 'And you're right, Mamma. Life goes on.' She nodded and looked up, meeting her mother's gaze. 'It's okay by me.'

Elizabeth-Anne let out a breath of relief and smiled warmly at her youngest daughter. Then she leaned further across the table and asked, 'Charlotte-Anne?'

Hearing her name, Charlotte-Anne jerked her chin up. Throughout the conversation, her mind had been swirling with the unexpected news as she quickly tried to evaluate how it might affect her own plans for her brilliantly plotted future. Like Regina, she was just realizing that her own life was beginning; unlike her sister, she saw ahead of her a life which was far removed from what she considered the pedestrian orbit of her mother's world. As long as the marriage didn't interfere with what she wanted, and she knew it wouldn't, then it was fine with her. In fact, upon second thought it was one of the best things that could have happened. Her mother led an extremely busy life, and had little enough time left over for the family as it was. Now with a husband, she'd be more occupied than ever, and that, Charlotte-Anne observed with a twinge of hope, meant that her plans would come to fruition even faster. She'd have to account for even less of her time.

She nodded and gave a brief hint of an assenting smile.

'That's settled, then.' Elizabeth-Anne sat back with obvious relief while Larry quickly got to his feet, leaned down, and kissed her happily.

'Watch it,' she said with a good-humored laugh. 'You'll muss my hair.' Elizabeth-Anne then watched joyfully as Larry rushed from chair to chair, kissing and hugging the entire family.

'Mamma could do a lot worse,' Regina told him. 'A *lot* worse.'

He laughed, pleased. And then everyone began talking at once – everyone except for Charlotte-Anne, and nobody noticed her thoughtful silence. When Larry sat back down, he tapped his coffee cup with a teaspoon.

They all fell silent and looked at him expectantly.

'First of all, on behalf of your mother and myself, thank you. Second, I want you to know that I'm not going to try to take your father's place. No one can do that. You won't have to call me "Dad" or anything like that, unless you want to. "Larry" will do just fine. And third, your mother and I would be honored if you would all come along to Elkton with us and attend our wedding. I should warn you, though, we won't be back for a week. From Elkton, we're going on a working honeymoon of sorts, to see what the staffs of the Calvert Hale in Baltimore, the L'Enfant Hale in Washington, and the Penn Hale in Philadelphia have been up to. If that interferes with your schoolwork or other plans, you could always head straight back here from Elkton. If you even want to come that far, that is. We'll leave it all up to you.'

Zaccheus clapped his hands, and Rebecca cried out, 'Oh, I'd love to come!' She giggled. 'Especially if I get to miss school.'

Regina frowned thoughtfully. 'Speaking of school, I've got an exam today but . . . '

'Then you stay, dear,' Elizabeth-Anne said quickly, reaching across the table and patting her hand. 'Larry and I understand perfectly. I know you've been studying like crazy for this exam. It would kill us if it were all wasted now.' She smiled. 'Charlotte-Anne?'

Charlotte-Anne looked up quickly. Her pale eyes were curiously veiled. 'I-I'd love to come, but I've got . . . I've got exams today, too,' she lied.

Elizabeth-Anne glanced at Larry. 'Perhaps we should wait a while longer,' she suggested. 'Then we can plan the wedding to coincide with everyone's schedules. It doesn't have to be so hurried.'

'Absolutely, definitely, certainly *not*. I won't hear of it,' Charlotte-Anne cried quickly, turning to them with an expression of sheer, utter disappointment. Her pulse was racing. The success – or failure – of her plan depended on her being left to her own devices. The marriage played into her hands, and their being gone an entire week was manna straight from heaven. It *had* to take place.

'You two go ahead and tie the knot,' she said forcefully. 'I won't hear of the marriage being put off on account of any of us. Not, that is, if you want *my* blessings.' She eyed them shrewdly and added, 'If you're willing to wait, then you can't be absolutely sure you really want to marry each other, can you?'

'Oh, but we are,' Elizabeth-Anne assured her.

'Then prove it.'

'Well, if you insist,' Elizabeth-Anne said doubtfully.

'I do. And I'm sure everyone else feels the same way.' Charlotte-Anne looked down at her plate, lowering her eyes lest anyone caught the triumphant gleam in them. She felt a surge of anticipation coursing through her. On her way to school this morning she would stop by the hotel office on the second floor under the pretext of typing up an article for the school newspaper. She'd done that on fifteen or twenty occasions already this past year. Except that there had never actually been any articles. Instead, she had been typing notes on Hale Hotels letterhead. Just like all the

167

others, the note she typed this morning would beg that she be excused from the second half of the school day for a doctor's appointment. Then she would forge her mother's signature. Much practice had made it near perfect.

She smiled, thinking what fools her teachers were. And how they worried about her fragile health! She constantly had to fight to keep from laughing out loud, they were so solicitous of her. The truth was, she hadn't been near a doctor's office in close to a year. She was the very picture of perfect health.

What was it Mickey Hoyt had told her that last afternoon they had spent together?

'No sacrifice is too much.'

That was it. *No sacrifice is too much.*

Not for what she wanted.

2

The perfect morning turned into a rotten afternoon.

By one o'clock, the Manhattan sky was awash with boiling gray clouds. Charlotte-Anne glanced up at the sky and cursed herself for not listening to the weather report, not arranging to be excused from school at noon sharp instead of twelve-thirty, and refusing to take an umbrella. She should have listened to Dallas, who'd warned her that it would rain. But she was sick of having to listen to Dallas. If you weren't careful, she would mother you to death. And if you didn't obey, she'd rat on you in no time.

Well, today she wouldn't. The happy couple were off to get married, far from any worries about what Charlotte-Anne was up to. And who, she asked herself, had the time to worry about something as mundane as the weather when the rest of her life was at stake?

She hurried down the crowded sidewalk, pushing and shoving as the first fat, cold raindrop splattered on her shoulder. Scowling and holding her book over her head with one hand, and hanging tightly onto her bulging briefcase with the other, she began to run, ducking to avoid the masses of umbrellas which, with the first drops of rain, sprouted up everywhere like a forest of giant, black mushrooms. She reached Madison Avenue, had to wait for the light to change, and then hurried across the street, heading east on Forty-Second Street at a run. One more block and she'd be inside Grand Central Station.

The cloudburst soon became a deluge and her tan, camel's hair coat was soaked by the time she got inside the dry, cavernous warmth of the station. Now she was sure she'd catch hell from Dallas later. She stopped to shake off the excess rain and catch her breath. She was drenched through and through, and her teeth were chattering.

Well, right now *that* was the least of her worries. She was here to change in the ladies' room anyway. Whenever she had a rendezvous with Mickey Hoyt, she carried a change of clothes instead of books inside her ample briefcase. After all, she couldn't show up to meet him looking like a frumpy schoolgirl, not after all the stories she'd made up about herself.

She'd told him she was twenty and unhappily married to a very jealous man, which was why she had to meet him so furtively. She'd even bought a cheap wedding band, which she always slipped on her finger before she met him. No detail was too minute, as long as it added credibility to her ruse. She had the strong suspicion that if he should ever find out the truth - that she was actually seventeen and living at home with her family - she'd be in a real pickle. He was too well known in this city, too famous to walk away from it untarnished. His career, which meant everything to him, could only suffer so many scandals. If his reputation were threatened he'd drop her like a hot potato. And if that happened, then all her glorious, glamorous hopes would be dashed.

Well, it wouldn't happen. She simply wouldn't let it.

She rushed into the ladies room, to any observer a frantic schoolgirl, but emerged fifteen minutes later an entirely different person. Walking with stately grace, she was a radiant breathtaking beauty, a stylish, modern young lady from the top of her head to the tips of her shoes.

Striding through the shopping concourse on her way to the baggage lockers, she caught sight of her reflection in a darkened store window. She felt the first real thrill of pleasure since it had started to rain. Soaked or not, she looked terrific.

She had dried her hair as best she could, then pinned it up so she looked even taller and more mature. She topped it with a tiny, forest green flannel hat, rather like a bellboy's, with a long scarf attached that she tied at the back of her head. The matching jersey blouse was the same green, too lightweight for this cold, atrocious weather, but it had been the only thing she could find to match the skirt, which was of a circular cut, of heavy-weight flannel. Her tan colored accessories – a foulard neckerchief, a belt of calfskin, and lisle stockings – contrasted wonderfully with all that green. The gloves she wore were soft, supple suede, just a shade of green lighter than the blouse and the skirt.

The clothes belonged to her mother who, thank God, was nearly the same size she was, and she'd had to sneak them out of the apartment. They didn't quite go with her sedate, schoolgirl's coat, but she had no choice but to wear it. Trying to sneak out one of her mother's bulky coats past Dallas's eagle eyes was more than she could manage. She just thanked her lucky stars that she'd been able to sneak out as many clothes as she had on so many occasions thus far. But she'd been careful. After she wore them, she sent them down to the hotel dry cleaners, and then intercepted them on the way back and hung them up.

When she reached the baggage lockers, she found one which was empty and locked her satchel and sopping wet school uniform inside it. She dropped the key into her miniscule, pale tan calfskin handbag. All physical evidence of the schoolgirl was gone. Even her mannerisms had changed. Her walk was charged with a disturbing sensuousness, at once fresh and arresting, and she gave the impression of being curiously remote, yet fully secure in the effect she projected. Her pale eyes glittered with brilliant lust, her creamy, smooth skin bloomed with an anticipatory flush, and every gesture she made was swift and fluid.

This was the adult in her which struggled constantly to break through the schoolgirl mold, but at home, around family and friends, she kept this grown-up part of herself locked away. She was afraid of ridicule, of being teased and condescended to. But now, she felt deliciously free and unburdened. Men turned to stare appreciatively, and women appraised her with envious glances. She pretended not to notice, to be aloof from it all, but she savored every moment of it.

As soon as she got back outside, she shivered. It was raining even harder than before. If she waited around for it to let up, she would be late, and Mickey wouldn't like that. Like her, he was stealing these precious hours, and every minute counted.

She turned up the collar of her coat. She hated getting drenched again, but she saw little choice. She mustn't do anything to irritate Mickey, especially not after the promise he had made her the last time they had been together.

She began to dash west across Forty-Second Street. The Algonquin wasn't that far, and with any luck, the rain would taper off.

Which, of course, it didn't.

While she rushed through the storm, her mind was not on the rain but on her career and Mickey Hoyt – in that order.

As far as she was concerned, her fate had been sealed the moment the curtain had risen on her first Broadway show nearly a year earlier. Sitting in the audience, thrilling to the excitement of what was unfolding onstage she knew then and there where she wanted to be. Not in the audience, but on the stage. She hungered to become a star, like the ones who were captivating her. She wanted to become a great lady of the American theater, an actress who reveled in applause. But, even more important, *she* would become that rarest of the rare, a truly *great* actress. With her own emotions, she would milk her audience of theirs. She would manipulate them to laughter and tears, to love and hate. It didn't seem all that far-fetched. She had the talent. Everyone said so.

In school the previous year, she had joined the Dramatic

Society and had tried out for a play. The role she had won had been a minor one, but she had applied herself so diligently that she'd managed to stand out and steal the show. She had been so good that this year, there had been no contest. She had been cast in the starring role of a short, brilliant drawing room comedy by James M. Barrie.

She had let her studies slide as she threw herself into her part with such abandon that her teachers felt compelled to send a caustic note to her mother.

'*If Charlotte-Anne would only apply herself as diligently to all her school work as she does to her acting . . .*' the note had begun. She had seethed with fury. Couldn't they see, the fools? Were they blind? It was *acting* she had to learn about, not economics or endocrine glands.

But the night of the play, at the final curtain call, she knew that all the aggravation, and her failing grade in geometry, had been worth it. She was inundated with so much intoxicating applause that she'd had to take deep breaths to keep from getting dizzy.

She had played the role so perfectly that the incredible had happened. As the play progressed, she had actually *become* the character. The rounds of applause she had earned catapulted her to the loftiest heights she had ever known.

Everyone in the school suddenly admired her. She was told time and again that nobody had ever noticed how beautiful she was. Even classmates who had once snubbed her or who had never spoken to her before, and especially boys who had ignored her up until now, finally clustered around her. She was asked out for dates, her advice was sought. She had never been so popular in her life, and she'd never realized just how powerful that would make her feel.

Her fate, which had revealed itself so clearly to her when she'd sat through that first Broadway show, was now truly sealed. She would become an actress. She was determined to see her name in lights.

Even her mother and sisters had congratulated her profusely on her performance, although none of them took her acting ambitions very seriously. 'Someday,' she promised them softly as they drove home after the play, 'I'm going to be an actress.'

'That's lovely, dear,' her mother had said. 'You were really very good. For a while, I actually forgot it was you up there on the stage.'

They were flattering words, the very compliment any actress was dying to hear. Yet she could sense that no one, especially her mother, greeted her announcement with the seriousness it was due. No one seemed to understand that beside acting, everything else paled in significance.

Her name in lights.

She didn't need to study history and mathematics. She needed to study dramatics, *theater*.

She even went so far as to try to discuss this with her mother one night. Elizabeth-Anne had smiled at her. 'But, darling, everyone needs to learn the fundamentals. After you've conquered the basics, of course you can go to college and study theater. No one is trying to stop you.'

'But . . . you've often told me that *you* didn't get much formal schooling,' Charlotte-Anne pointed out, hoping to somehow wheedle out of attending Brearley and being able to take acting lessons from a coach instead. 'It hasn't hurt you any.'

'That's true,' Elizabeth-Anne had replied. 'But believe me, there are many times when I wish I'd have been able to learn a lot more.' She sighed. 'But in Texas, things were different. There, school wasn't nearly as necessary as it is here.'

Charlotte-Anne had nodded silently. Somehow, she just couldn't get her point across. Oh, her mother understood about her wanting to do something . . . But what she couldn't seem to get her to understand was how important it was to stop wasting time on useless learning and to concentrate wholeheartedly on the career she had chosen. She had gone to bed with a leaden heart. She couldn't even close her eyes. She thought all night about acting, and it consumed her.

Then suddenly, in the wee hours of the morning, just before dawn, the idea had occurred to her. Why hadn't she thought of it before? She was right here, in Manhattan, for

God's sake! Why didn't she just go to auditions? Then, if she got a part, nobody would dare stop her. Not if she proved herself.

Of course, she did have school to contend with.

If necessity was the mother of invention, then ambition was the father of deceit. The idea didn't so much germinate, as explode in her mind.

There *was* something she could do about school! She would simply play hookey. There was no reason she shouldn't be able to get away with it. She was an actress, wasn't she? And if she was caught, then too bad. It was worth the risk for the chance to see her name in lights.

And so it began – the conniving, the typing of her 'mother's' notes excusing her from school, the 'suffering' from a multitude of ailments for which she had to 'consult the doctor,' the painstaking practice and forging of her mother's signature, the changing clothes in the ladies room at Grand Central. She called herself Carla Hall, since she hadn't dared to use her real name. The Hales were becoming too well known in the city. And every actress needed a stage name, she rationalized. Carla Hall was an easy name to remember; she was going to make sure no one would ever forget it.

She scoured the papers. Each time she saw an ad for an open audition somewhere, she resurrected one of her ailments and spent the afternoon trying out for whatever show it was. All the auditions seemed to be held in dingy lofts or dirty, rickety rehearsal halls on the West Side.

It had been a rude awakening. She had expected something very different, but there was nothing remotely glamorous about auditioning for a show. Most of the time she didn't even get a chance to see the script before it was handed to her to read aloud. It was simply sink or swim. She was made to feel like an insignificant steer in a huge herd of cattle.

She didn't exactly know how, but she persevered, although there were countless times when she thought she might as well give up and go back to school. The competition was stiffer than she had ever imagined. She had never guessed that there were so many beautiful girls in this city, all far more talented than her. And they all seemed to have one thing in common: they all wanted to become actresses.

It wasn't long before she could recognize her fellow aspiring 'theater trash,' as they called themselves. They all looked hungry, starved for food as much as for success. Without fail, they tended to downplay their beauty, as though trying to prove they were mere putty, malleable for any role. Their clothes were rather seedy and very casual. They didn't seem to care at all how they dressed. All that mattered was the greasepaint they were certain flowed in their veins. At each audition, Charlotte-Anne was only too painfully aware that she was too finely dressed and glowing with good health.

If the auditions were grueling, then the reactions she provoked from the other aspiring actresses were even more torturous. She could feel the waves of open hostility rolling toward her. One girl would poke another in the ribs and gesture at her; yet another would mimick a lady, haughty chin in the air, hands adjusting the flounces of an imaginary gown. She caught whispers of the nickname they had dubbed her with, 'Miss Rich Bitch.'

Their icy expressions were all the same, and she could read them with no difficulty: What's *she* doing here? Who does *she* think she is? Does she really think wearing a hundred dollars on her back will get her a part?

She felt so alone, and there was no one she could turn to for encouragement. Only two things kept her going: hope that an opportunity to showcase her talents would arise, and the belief that she was special. That *she* was one of the chosen few. But whenever she looked at the others, her heart would sink.

If they only knew! she cried to herself. She didn't want to look different. She would have given anything to blend in with the crowd. It was ridiculous, but the crux of the problem was that she didn't have anything suitable to wear. Her school uniform was definitely out of the question. Nor could she wear her own clothes, which made her look too young, too girlish. She had had but one option – trying to look older than her mere seventeen years. As she saw it, she had no choice but to sneak out with her mother's clothes.

The only trouble was, all her mother's outfits were now expensive, extremely well cut, and very ladylike.

It's just another necessary sacrifice, and a damn strange one, she told herself over and over. Let them all laugh behind my back. Let them call me 'Miss Rich Bitch.' I don't care. I'll show them. *I'll* make it.

Audition followed audition, and she always heard the same words repeated over and over. They might as well have been a recording. 'Thank you. If we decide to use you, you'll hear from us. Next!'

For weeks, she didn't dare audition for a musical or any show which required dancing. She knew she could neither carry a tune nor perform the simplest dance step. But finally, out of desperation, she decided to try it. It couldn't hurt, she told herself. What could they do other than turn her down?

The show was a long-running, smash musical revue called *Reach for the Stars*, for which a new cast was being assembled. The rehearsal hall where the auditions took place, like the others, was in the West Forties. If anything, it was an even more dilapidated building than all the others she had been in so far. She was the twenty-eighth girl in a line-up of about fifty, and she recognized a lot of the actresses from previous auditions. It seemed that nobody ever got a part. Yet there was a peculiar air of brave camaraderie about the girls. Most of them knew each other and tried to put one another at ease. But they ignored Charlotte-Anne.

With trepidation, Charlotte-Anne sat quietly on one of the rickety benches, awaiting her turn. With each passing minute she was filled with a mounting sense of dread.

One by one, the other girls before her went into the rehearsal room. She heard them all sing, accompanied by an out of tune piano. They were all so good. Even through the closed door, she could tell that much.

Oh God, she prayed silently. I can't carry a tune or read music. I can't even dance. I'll just make a fool of myself.

Just as she made up her mind to leave she heard a name being called out.

'Carla Hall!'

She froze. They called her again, and somehow she managed to get up, her legs weak, her body shaking. She armed herself in the only way she knew how, by squaring her shoulders and assuming an aloof, steely, lady-like veneer.

The big audition room was bare and dim. An upright piano had been placed in one corner, so that the player faced out. Four men and a woman sat in the shadows at the far end. A young man in baggy trousers thrust a sheet of music at her. She stared at it stupidly and turned to the piano player. He looked grizzly and unkempt, half hidden behind a veil of cigar smoke. Then the out-of-tune piano began to pound. She stared down at the undecipherable notes she held in her hand. She took a deep breath. Perhaps she could fake it. She had heard enough renditions of the same song for the last two hours.

She opened her mouth to sing, but no sound came out. The piano player stopped after playing the first few bars. Horror-stricken, she looked at the four men at the other end of the room, but they didn't seem to be paying any attention to her. Slowly she turned to face the piano player, who was rolling his eyes. He started over.

Again nothing happened.

The young man in baggy trousers marched toward her and snatched the music out of her hand. He flung open the door. 'Next! Ethel Broward!'

In dismay, Charlotte-Anne stared at the four men and the woman. She had been dismissed, this time without even an if = we = want = you = we'll = give = you = a = call.

She hadn't even rated that.

As though in a dream, she saw the next girl come in, a confident, smiling brunette in her mid-twenties. Charlotte-Anne knew she had to leave, but she couldn't move. Her feet seemed to be nailed down to the floor.

'Well?' the young man demanded. 'You waitin' for a miracle?'

That snapped her out of it. She turned around and, clapping a hand over her mouth, ran from the room. Her eyes were burning as she burst out into the waiting room where the others were staring at her. She hurried down the flight of steep stairs. She thought she was going to be sick before she ever got outside.

She leaned against the grimy brick wall, taking deep lungfuls of fresh air. The queasiness slowly left her, but she was sobbing loudly, the tears spilling down her cheeks. She had never felt so humiliated in her entire life.

She heard footsteps behind her and turned away, hiding her face.

'Hey, there's always another time, kid,' a man's tenor voice said gently. 'Not everybody was cut out for song and dance. You just came to the wrong audition is all. Mistakes like that happen all the time.'

She wiped away her tears and sniffled. 'I'm not a kid,' she said quickly. 'I'm twenty years old.'

It was her first lie to him, the first of many. But at the time, it didn't seem to matter.

'So you are.'

She turned around slowly. He seemed to tower above her, handsome, rugged, yet somehow slick and polished. His eyes were agate and hypnotic, and a half smile hovered on his lips. He was one of the four men who had been sitting at the far end of the room, but now he looked curiously familiar. She had the feeling she should know who he was, but she couldn't place him.

He grinned apologetically. 'Sorry. I didn't mean to call you a kid. It's just an expression.'

She smiled and nodded. Then suddenly her heart seemed to shrink. Now she knew why he looked so familiar! She had seen his picture in the newspapers and magazines on countless occasions. She had even caught one of his shows the year before. He was Mickey Hoyt, one of the most brilliant stars of the New York stage.

His eyes shimmered with a marble-like gloss. 'Come on, I'll buy you a cup of coffee.'

For the first time in her life she felt an instinctive physical longing well up inside her. It was as though something deep within her, which had always lain sleeping, was suddenly awakened. She found herself nodding. She was spellbound.

He placed a hand under her elbow and guided her

toward Times Square. 'Been having a tough time of it?' he asked as they walked.

She nodded, trying to keep up with his long strides.

'I know what it's like. I've been there, too.'

'You?'

'Sure. You don't think I was born onstage, do you?'

She shrugged. 'No. It just comes as a surprise, that's all.' She frowned. 'Sometimes it seems like I've cornered the market on rejections.'

'I wouldn't worry too much if I were you. You're beautiful, possibly one of the most beautiful young women I've ever seen, and believe me, I've seen a lot. But you've got them all beat. You project a certain quality, something the other girls don't have. There's something of the reserved New England lady about you.'

'I'm from Texas originally.'

'I know that. Your speech says so. But your attitude is strictly Bostonian.'

Her brow furrowed. 'Maybe I should try to get rid of my accent?'

He shook his head. 'I wouldn't worry about that. What you need are good roles. There're plenty of those which call for your kind of accent.'

'And they're impossible to get.'

'Not really.'

She looked at him with quickening interest. 'Do you know something I don't know?'

'No, but I've got something you don't have – connections. Lots of people in this town owe me favors. This business is strictly "you scratch my back, I'll scratch yours." All I have to do is call in some old debts to see about getting you some decent scripts. Some you can study and try out for without going through those humiliating cattle calls.'

She couldn't believe her ears. 'You could really do that?' Her voice was a whisper.

'Why not?' He grinned easily. 'I'm Mickey Hoyt, aren't I?'

She nodded solemnly.

'It'll take time, though. The most important thing is to

179

find you the right script. But I warn you, it won't be a big part. Just a decent one. The rest is up to you. Think you can handle that?'

'Can I!'

He stopped walking. 'Here we are.'

She stared up at the lovely building. 'This isn't a coffee shop,' she said softly.

'No, it isn't. It's the Algonquin. But room service does send up a decent pot of coffee.'

She looked hesitant.

'And I confess, I did lure you here.' He smiled disarmingly. 'Under the most dishonorable pretext.'

A faint flush crept through her skin and she looked away.

'You don't have to come up. But I'd like it,' he said softly. 'We can always sit downstairs in the lobby and just talk.'

'No, that's okay.' She glanced up at him. His eyes seemed to reach out and become part of her. As he held her gaze, she had the sensation that the earth had stopped moving, that they were the only two people alive.

As though she was under hypnosis, she followed him into the hotel and up to the nineteenth floor. When they reached room nineteen-nineteen, he closed the door and locked it.

He turned around and smiled at her. 'Don't worry, I won't get you pregnant. There are other ways to make love, you know.'

She watched him unzipping his trousers. She stared down at him with fascination. His phallus was already semi-erect, large and reddish purple. So this was 'the plumbing' all the girls in school whispered about. When her brother had been a baby, she had seen his tiny genitals, but this was the first time she had ever seen a grown man's penis. She had had no idea that it could be swollen so large, or look so angry. For a moment, panic seized her.

She felt his hands on her head, pushing her down to her knees. The carpet was thick and soft. She stared up at him. His eyes were glowing intently, like burning embers.

'Come on, baby,' he said, his voice soft and husky. 'Eat me. Eat me good.'

It wasn't making love, she realized; but it didn't matter.

180

She did as he asked, when he let out a growl, she instinctively removed her mouth and turned her face away. Semen spurted thickly through the air. Then he held her, and the only thing she could tell herself was that it was worth it.

No sacrifice was too much.

When she arrived at the Algonquin, she was as wet and lovely as a drenched swan. No one stopped her as she hurried through the lobby. Despite her soggy state, she looked like she belonged. She had the nonchalant bearing of one accustomed to luxury.

She headed straight for the elevators and went directly upstairs. He was always waiting for her, always in the same room, and always on Friday afternoons. Now, after all these weeks, room nineteen-nineteen had become her home away from home.

And perhaps today . . . Dare she hope that today, at long last, he would finally have found the perfect script for her to read?

When she stood in front of the door, she brushed some of the rain off her coat, took off her hat, and shook it dry. She patted her hair and took a deep breath. Then she knocked softly three times.

She could hear footsteps on the other side of the door. In a moment it would open, and he would stand there, tall and handsome, melting her with his dazzling smile and the promise in his eyes.

A key turned in the lock, but when the door swung open Charlotte-Anne let out a strangled cry. It wasn't Mickey Hoyt standing before her; it was Elizabeth-Anne.

'I think,' her mother said in a quivering voice, 'that it's time you and I had a serious talk.'

3

When Charlotte-Anne came out of the examination room, her face was pinched and she avoided looking at her mother. She didn't think she could ever face anyone again, but especially not her mother.

Dr. Rogers, a large, lugubrious man with watery gray eyes, caught Elizabeth-Anne's gaze. He shook his head discreetly and went back into his office.

Elizabeth-Anne allowed herself a deep sigh of relief. Then she sank back in the waiting room chair and closed her eyes.

During the ride home, Charlotte-Anne stared morosely out of the car window. Neither she nor her mother exchanged a word. She realized it wasn't just because her mother was disappointed with her, but because she was embarrassed too.

When they got home, her mother silently followed her into her room and shut the door.

'You're still a virgin,' she said softly, sinking down on the edge of the bed. 'Thank God.' She looked directly at Charlotte-Anne.

Charlotte-Anne's face blazed scarlet. She sat down on the chair of her dressing table and hung her head in shame.

'I won't pretend that this hasn't come as a shock,' her mother said. 'Just before Larry and I were set to leave, the telephone rang. It was one of your teachers. She was very worried about your health and wanted me to reassure her that you were all right.'

Charlotte-Anne groaned inwardly.

'Do you realize,' Elizabeth-Anne asked softly, leaning forward, 'that you've missed twenty-seven afternoons of school this year? *Twenty-seven*?'

Charlotte-Anne closed her eyes. She'd known she'd been 'ill' a lot of days, but even she hadn't realized they added up to that many. 'I . . . I can explain,' she whispered falteringly.

'I wish you would.' Elizabeth-Anne looked at her daughter curiously. 'This day has been no end of unpleasant surprises. After the call from school, Dallas was in here making your bed when your phone rang. Naturally, she answered it.'

Charlotte-Anne felt her stomach turn sour. She should

never have given Mickey Hoyt her number. She'd only done it because he insisted.

'It was someone named Mickey,' her mother continued, 'and he asked for Carla Hall. Of course, Dallas was too surprised to correct him. He left a message for you. He said he couldn't meet you today, but that he'd be at the Algonquin next Friday, as usual.'

'And he just came out and told Dallas that?' Charlotte-Anne asked in bitter disbelief. 'Just to try and end everything between us?'

'I can't speak for him,' her mother said. 'Perhaps he wanted to do that, perhaps he didn't. But for us it was a simple matter of deduction. Larry went to see the desk clerk at the Algonquin who, of course, was very discreet and claimed to know nothing. Under the circumstances, that was to be expected. But when Larry took him aside and told him you were underage, that he was prepared to go to the police and file charges, and that this could possibly result in a case of statutory rape, he recalled everything. It seems,' she added drily, 'that room nineteen-nineteen was becoming quite well known for your Friday afternoons.'

Charlotte-Anne shook her head miserably.

'Of course, Mr. Hoyt should have known better. He's too well known in this town to think he could get away with something like this. However, I'm sure it's not entirely his fault, although I might like to think so.' Her mother looked pained. 'I won't pretend I'm not disappointed in you, Charlotte-Anne. I am. However, we are all human. We all make mistakes. Especially when we're young.'

'I'm not a child anymore,' Charlotte-Anne said softly. 'I'm a woman, Mamma.'

Her mother looked at her and nodded. 'It seems impossible that you've grown up so fast. I still sometimes think of you as a child. Now I realize that was my mistake.'

'It wasn't your fault, Mamma.'

Her mother sighed wearily. 'Perhaps it was, and perhaps it wasn't. I don't think we'll ever know the answer.' She rose to her feet. 'I have some serious soul searching to do. I suggest we wait until tomorrow to decide how to handle this.' She crossed the room to the door.

Charlotte-Anne lifted her head and looked at her. 'You hate me, don't you, Mamma?' she asked thickly.

Her mother turned and looked at her with surprise. For the first time, Charlotte-Anne was truly aware of her mother's strength. 'No, I don't hate you, Charlotte-Anne. There are things you do that I might not like or approve of, but you are my daughter.' Elizabeth-Anne's voice grew gentler. 'I could never hate you, no matter what you did. I love you. Someday, when you have children of your own, you'll understand.'

For a moment Charlotte-Anne looked at her in amazement. Then her vision blurred with tears. 'Mamma?'

'Yes, dear?'

'I love you, too,' Charlotte-Anne whispered.

Elizabeth-Anne smiled. 'I know that.'

'I'm really sorry, Mamma,' she cried despairingly. 'For all of this. All I've been thinking about was my – Oh, damn! I've ruined your plans and Larry's. I've been so selfish.'

A soft expression veiled Elizabeth-Anne's eyes. Her mother was, Charlotte-Anne realized, handling this highly unpleasant matter with the utmost fairness. Somehow, Elizabeth-Anne Hale was managing to keep her own emotions under tight rein.

'The property is still available,' Elizabeth-Anne said, 'and I'll sign the papers for it in a few days. And Larry won't run off, that much I know. Nothing was postponed that couldn't have waited a few days, anyway. The only thing that matters to me is that you don't get hurt.'

Charlotte-Anne gave a little nod. A lump was blocking her throat and she could not trust herself to speak.

Elizabeth-Anne opened the door. 'I'll see you later, dear.'

'Yes, Mamma.' Charlotte-Anne watched her mother leave. Only after the door closed did she fling herself onto the bed and burst into tears.

She was desolate with humiliation and remorse, and terribly angry with Mickey. God, how she *hated* him. He had not only been indiscreet, but his behavior had been downright despicable. She should never have trusted him. She had told him that she was married, and that no one must find out about their Friday afternoons. It didn't matter that she had lied to him. She had had a reason, and a good one. But he had gone out of his way to disgrace himself and her, the bastard!

She could only deduce that he'd deliberately tried to end their relationship, in the ugliest way possible. And that meant one other thing as well, which was what hurt her the most. He had never meant to help further her career. It had all been idle talk. Just a way for him to control her.

She felt dirty, tricked, and used.

'I have come to a decision,' Elizabeth-Anne told her the next day as they sat in the living room. 'Painful though it may be, I think that in the long run, it will work out for the best.'

They were sitting alone, facing one another on the matching apricot couches. Charlotte-Anne had been awake half the night long, and had finally come to terms with the truth about Mickey Hoyt. She had not loved him, she saw that clearly now. She merely had been dazzled by who he was, and what he had promised to do for her. And he had liked her for those needs of his which she could fulfill. It hadn't been easy to look at it in those bare-boned, brutal terms, but it had been a necessary exercise. Coming to grips with what she and Mickey shared – or more importantly, what they hadn't shared – had left her with a new kind of maturity, and for the first time she was seeing her mother not from a youthful vantage, but as a fellow adult.

She felt she was appreciating her mother for the first time. Elizabeth-Anne Hale was an attractive and well-groomed woman, very much the lady, in her exquisitely tailored, Jane Regny suit with its jacket flaring slightly at the hips, and its skirt reaching to midcalf. No one would ever guess that she came from a small town in Texas. Looking back at the past few years, Charlotte-Anne realized that she had never known anyone quite as adaptable as her mother, who could accomplish so much and do it with such style.

Up until now, Charlotte-Anne had been listening attentively and speaking only when called upon to do so. She had decided, for once, that no matter what decree her mother meted out, she would not put up an argument.

'As we both know,' her mother was saying, 'your grades at Brearley this past year have been . . . well, shall we say, unsatisfactory?'

Charlotte-Anne smiled wryly. 'They've been atrocious.'

Elizabeth-Anne laughed. 'Whatever you say, but there's no need for us to hurl insults. I realize now what I, and I suppose every mother in the world, does not want to have to face.' She sighed sadly. 'That a child she loves dearly has grown up right in front of her eyes. You are now an adult, Charlotte-Anne, and I think it's time I treated you as one.

'At any rate, I believe your unsatisfactory grades in school have been due in large part to the energies you have lavished upon your theatrical ambitions instead of your studies. Therefore, I think it would be nice now if you expended at least half as much attention on your studies as you have on the theater. However, you are nearly grown up, and some things cannot be forced. Whether more schooling serves you or not is to be seen. But as a young adult, I think there is no harm if you acquire a little polish. I'm sure even the actress in you will agree with that.'

Charlotte-Anne nodded.

'I want you to know that I don't blame you for what has happened,' Elizabeth-Anne continued. Her voice was soft and wistful. 'I have been lax also. I've been paying altogether too much attention to the business, and neglecting my family in the process. I should have seen what was happening with you, but I never took the time. However, that's all water under the bridge now. We can only look back upon the past to learn from it. Otherwise, the past is useless.'

Elizabeth-Anne paused for a moment. It was important that Charlotte-Anne realized that what was coming was what she believed was best for her and not a punishment. She had thought about it all night long, and this morning, she had made some telephone calls. Still, good intentions all too often pave the road to misery. It seemed so difficult to try and set things right.

'I surmise,' Elizabeth-Anne said gently, 'that you have been hurt by this involvement with Mr. Hoyt?'

Charlotte-Anne looked thoughtful. 'Yesterday, I thought I was, but I'm not so sure about it today. He used me, I see that now. But I tried to use him, too. Only I wasn't as good at it.'

Elizabeth-Anne nodded. 'That's a very mature outlook, and I'm pleased. I know it hurts to have to put things in such brutal terms. Nevertheless, I think it would be a lot easier for you to get him totally out of your system if you were further removed from his orbit. Residual feelings always linger a while, especially with a well-known person. Each time you see his picture in a magazine, or his name on a billboard, you are bound to feel a little pain.'

Charlotte-Anne frowned thoughtfully. 'I don't think that will pose much of a problem now. I can handle it, I think.'

Elizabeth-Anne held up a hand. 'Nevertheless. The school to which I've decided to transfer you is a boarding school.'

'Mamma!' Charlotte-Anne cried, truly surprised.

'Please hear me out, dear. You must understand that this is not a punishment of any sort. It's a fine school where they can teach you a lot. And not just about mathematics and history, though they teach that too. L'Ecole Catroux is basically a finishing school. They turn girls into young ladies and prepare them to face society. Besides, I don't think a little bit of international exposure will hurt you.'

'Interna . . .'

'A young lady needs to travel, Charlotte-Anne, and I hear Switzerland is quite lovely. At the risk of repeating myself, a little grace and polish has never hurt anyone. L'Ecole Catroux is in Geneva, and it comes highly recommended. A lot of American girls go there, as well as English girls and others from all over the world, all from the finest families. You will make new friends and acquaintances that you would otherwise never have an opportunity to meet. Neither will it hurt you to pick up another language.'

Elizabeth-Anne paused, her face set with pain. 'It hurts

me to see you go. You *must* believe that. I still find it difficult to face the fact that you're grown up now. If it were up to me, I'd like nothing more than to keep you with me always, and smother you. But that's selfish, and I refuse to ruin your life. You must learn to be independent. I know that now. That's what made you try so hard to become an actress, and drove you straight into Mr. Hoyt's arms. He was not so much to blame as I.

'It is my sincerest wish that you will remain at Catroux until the end of next year. However, if you wish to come home or quit on your eighteenth birthday, which is only six months from now, I leave the choice entirely up to you. You will be of age and, legally at least, be capable of making your own decisions from then on.

'If, at any time, you still want to avidly pursue an acting career, I will help you in any way I can.'

Charlotte-Anne looked at her mother. 'Switzerland sounds so . . . so far away. I've never been gone from home.'

Elizabeth-Anne leaned forward and reached out, placing her hands over Charlotte-Anne's. Her voice was as gentle as her touch. 'There comes a time, Charlotte-Anne, when each of us must take the first step toward independence. That is what you will do now. Try to look at it this way: as a result, you'll be better prepared to face the world than most.'

'About your offer, to help me pursue acting when I return. It stands even if I come back in six months?'

'Yes.'

'I mean . . . you'll really help me?' Charlotte-Anne stared at her mother.

Elizabeth-Anne faced her squarely. 'I think you know by now that I never make promises I don't keep.'

Charlotte-Anne nodded.

'If you're serious, yes, I'll do what I can. I'll support you financially so you can concentrate fully on acting and *nothing* else. I'll pay for acting classes, or coaches, or whatever it is you need. And you can live away from home if you like. I'll even try – if it's within my power, that is – to open whatever doors I'm able.' She smiled mysteriously. 'I hear that investors in shows can sometimes pull enough strings to get someone a part. God knows, I have enough money. I'm sure some producer wouldn't mind parting me from some of it.'

'Oh, Mamma!' Charlotte-Anne looked ready to burst into tears. She was at once relieved and elated. She had expected her mother to lecture and punish her. Instead, she was being offered everything she wanted. On an impulse, she jumped up from the couch, slid over to her mother's, and squeezed her tightly.

'I hope,' Elizabeth-Anne said, 'that you'll promise to learn as much as you can at Catroux, and give the teachers as few problems as possible. And as for the trip across the Atlantic, you won't be alone. Robyn Morgan is sailing for Europe next week on the *Ile de France*, and I've arranged for you to take the same crossing. She said she'd be delighted to have you accompany her.'

Charlotte-Anne was overjoyed. They'd known Robyn for years now and Charlotte-Anne not only liked her, she admired her. Robyn Morgan wove that indefinable spell around herself which Charlotte-Anne hankered for. And while six months spent at a strange school in a foreign country frightened her, it wasn't really *that* long. She'd waited in vain for at least three months for Mickey Hoyt to pop up with a script.

'And now,' Elizabeth-Anne said, getting to her feet, 'I think it wouldn't hurt if we did some shopping. You'll need some new clothes. We can't have a Hale arriving in Switzerland in rags, can we?' Her eyes twinkled with amusement. 'Or in her mother's clothes?'

Charlotte-Anne looked contrite. 'I'm sorry, Mamma.'

Elizabeth-Anne laughed. 'I will say one thing,' she said, putting an arm around Charlotte-Anne's shoulder. 'You do my clothes justice.'

'Mamma?'

Charlotte-Anne's tone was so serious that Elizabeth-Anne looked at her daughter worriedly. 'Yes, dear?'

'Larry . . . you're going to marry him, aren't you?'

'Of course! We've got it all set up. In fact, he's running around town making the arrangements right now. We'll be married here in a civil ceremony downtown, followed by a very small wedding at The Little Church Around the Corner. Just for family, and a few assorted friends like Robyn and Ludmila.'

'I hate to have to miss it.'

'And I wouldn't have you to, not for the world.' Elizabeth-Anne laughed. 'I told you Robyn was coming, didn't I? Well, she can't be in two places at once. And neither can you. The wedding will be held the afternoon before you sail.'

Charlotte-Anne felt the warmth of the bond between herself and her mother. Suddenly she realized how much they loved each other, although they'd never said it. She took her mother's hand and lifted it to her lips. 'I'm glad, Mamma,' she said. 'I wouldn't want to leave with any hard feelings between us.'

'And I wouldn't want that either.'

'It's funny, you know?' Charlotte-Anne looked at her. 'I never knew we could talk like this.'

'Just remember. Anytime you want to discuss something with me, feel free to do so.'

Charlotte-Anne nodded. 'You know what?' Her eyes began to well with tears. 'I . . . I feel that we're closer than we've ever been before. Like we're not just mother and daughter. I feel like we're . . .'

Elizabeth-Anne smiled into her daughter's eyes. 'Friends?' she asked.

4

Spring burst upon New York in its glorious splendor just in time for the wedding. It was one of those rare, sparkling days, a balmy surprise tucked between two late winter cold spells. It took little imagination to fancy Elizabeth-Anne as a June bride.

The little church on East Twenty-Ninth Street was filled with white lilies, roses, carnations, tulips, and peonies.

Charlotte-Anne gasped as her mother was led to the altar, a tiny white bouquet of lilies of the valley in her hands. Elizabeth-Anne had never looked more lovely. She wore a dove gray lace dress, gray satin picture hat, and gray satin pumps. Around her neck was the three-tiered pearl necklace Larry had given her that morning. And he looked splendid beside her in his custom-tailored dark suit with a white carnation in his lapel, and a dark, velvet patch over his eye. It was hardly the society wedding of the year, although if they had so chosen it could easily have become that. It was simply a lovely wedding for family and a few close friends, which was just the way they had wanted it. Ludmila cried and blew her nose noisily through the ceremony.

Then, a few hours later, it was time for Charlotte-Anne to leave. Larry's stately yellow-and-black Rolls-Royce, which Elizabeth-Anne was to keep in perfect running condition for the rest of her life, and which was still festooned with garlands of white flowers for the wedding procession, was loaded with new Vuitton luggage, a going away gift to Charlotte-Anne from Larry. They drove over to the West Side, where the *Ile de France* was berthed.

Elizabeth-Anne and Larry had secured her a large, first class stateroom next to Robyn's, but they hardly had a chance to glance at it. Shortly after they had boarded, a deep blast of the liner's horns carried mournfully across the water.

'It's time we left,' Larry said. 'All visitors have to get off now.'

Charlotte-Anne nodded. It was with both excitement and a heavy heart that she bid her family farewell. For the first time since she could remember, she felt truly close to them all. Now she realized with a pang just how sorely she would miss them.

'Well, Mrs. Hochstetter,' Charlotte-Anne said to her mother. 'How does it feel to be married?'

'Truthfully, quite the same as before,' her mother said with a smile. 'I've loved Larry for a long time. But the hotels will still be called *Hale* hotels; I'll keep my own "stage" name, so to speak. In public I'll still be Elizabeth-

Anne Hale. But in private life, I'm Mrs. Lawrence Hochstetter.' She smiled at Larry, then looked intently at Charlotte-Anne. Her voice broke. 'I'll miss you, dear.'

'And I'll miss you, Mamma. Too bad I won't be around for the move.'

'Move?' Elizabeth-Anne looked puzzled. 'What move?'

'To the Hochstetter mansion, of course!'

'Oh, dear me, no. It's the other way around. Larry is moving into the penthouse with us. We decided quite some time ago that we'll be comfortable enough there. Besides, I'd feel strange rattling around that mansion. And then, there's the economic side of it. Why pay for a huge staff of servants when we have the entire hotel staff at our disposal. Dallas and a chauffeur is all we need. The hotels will simply absorb Larry's servants. This way they won't be out of work, and at the same time, we cut our costs.'

'Always the businesswoman,' Charlotte-Anne smiled. 'You'll never change, Mamma.'

Elizabeth-Anne pretended to look shocked. 'I surely hope not.' The tears shone in her eyes as she hugged her daughter. They exchanged kisses and she pressed a small box into Charlotte-Anne's hand.

'What's this?' Charlotte-Anne asked curiously.

'That's your father's necklace. The pansy charm. I want you to have it to remember us by.'

A sob escaped Charlotte-Anne's lips and she hugged her mother again.

Larry enveloped her in his arms and she stood on tiptoe to kiss him. 'Thank God stepfathers are never wicked.'

'I'll miss you, big girl. Just make sure you don't stay over there too long.'

'Oh, I wouldn't.'

'Don't be so sure. Europe has its magic. Some people love it and stay forever.'

Then Zaccheus shook her hand and gave her a reluctant peck on the cheek. 'Gee, you sure I can't come along, sis? This boat sure is neat.'

Charlotte-Anne smiled at him. 'I'm sure,' she said, smiling down at him sadly. She turned to Rebecca, and they embraced.

'I know we didn't always see eye to eye,' Charlotte-Anne told her thickly, 'but I'll miss you. I love you, and always will.'

'Me, too.' Rebecca kissed both her cheeks.

Charlotte-Anne nodded and threw her arms around Regina, who burst into tears. 'This is the first time we've ever been apart.'

'Don't worry,' Charlotte-Anne assured her oldest sister. They exchanged quick kisses. 'I'll be back real soon. And I'll be the actress while you'll be the doctor. Bet you'll even deliver my kids, huh?' Her voice grew husky. Her bravado was deserting her. 'We'll see each other in no time.'

Regina nodded and smiled through her tears.

Neither of them could know that Charlotte-Anne would never see Regina alive again. Or Rebecca and Zaccheus, for that matter.

Charlotte-Anne watched as her family got off the ship. She stood outside on the deck, gripping the varnished railing as though trying to draw strength from the wood. She leaned over and looked for them in the crowd at dockside. Finally she spied the familiar faces, and she waved excitedly. There was another deep, mournful blast of the horn.

'Why, you're crying!' a voice said from beside her.

Charlotte-Anne turned and saw Robyn, looking stunning in a small hat with a short veil shading the top half of her face. She was smoking, and her cigarette was stuck in a long, ivory holder.

'*I* only cry at weddings and funerals,' Robyn declared. '*Never* at sailings.' She took a puff on her cigarette and exhaled. 'I did cry a little this afternoon at your mother's wedding, you know. Weddings always have that effect on me.' She paused. 'Larry's found himself a fine lady.'

Charlotte-Anne nodded. 'I know.'

'Well, I suppose I'll go inside and make certain the maid is unpacking my things. If clothes are kept in suitcases for too long, they take forever to hang out. I'll leave my side of the connecting door unlocked in case you need anything. Feel free to visit anytime. After all, we're neighbors now.'

'Thank you, Mrs. Morgan.'

'Mrs. *Morgan*?' Robyn tilted her head back and laughed. 'You dear, sweet child. Don't make me feel so terribly old. You and I have six or seven long days ahead of us, and we'll be running into each other every time either of us turns around. We might as well call each other by our Christian names.' She inhaled on her cigarette, exhaled a plume of smoke, and cocked her head. 'On trains and ships it *is* the thing to do. You must call me Robyn.'

'Robyn,' Charlotte-Anne repeated tentatively.

'That's better.' Robyn flashed her a smile, gave a tiny wave with her fingertips, and went back inside. The horn blasted again, this time with more urgency. Charlotte-Anne waved down to her family as the lines were cast off and the heavy ship began to move away from the pier, nudged by the tug boats which surrounded it like a gaggle of ugly ducklings clustered around a beautiful mother swan. Charlotte-Anne kept waving long after the individual faces receded from sight. Soon the ship was backed out into midstream and the tugs poked at it until the bow faced downriver.

Charlotte-Anne blinked back her salt tears and lifted her head. Dusk was coming rapidly, and the purple sky overhead was streaked with reds and oranges. On the shore, the massive concrete monoliths already glittered with a million lights. Only now did she realize that in the years since she'd come to New York, she had never noticed how truly beautiful and impressive the city was. She had gotten too used to it. When she'd walked on the sidewalks or crossed the streets, she had never taken the time to look *up*. That was how you had to see this city, with your head tilted back. She thought of so many things she'd never done, so many little, seemingly inconsequential things. They all seemed so important right now.

'Damn,' she swore in a tight little voice. 'I don't want to leave. I don't want to go to school in Switzerland. I only want to go home.'

For a long time she stayed out on the deck. Darkness came swiftly as the ship sailed down the island and off through the harbor. Charlotte-Anne walked back along the promenade deck, watching the Statue of Liberty slipping by. Then the ship headed out into the Narrows and the lights of the city receded, growing dimmer and dimmer in the distance. She had the impression that New York was Atlantis sinking slowly into the sea. Then it was swallowed up completely by the blackness of the ocean and the sky.

They were at sea. A brisk, chill wind tugged at her clothes, fluttering and snapping her skirt. The other passengers had long since gone inside. She was alone on the deck.

'Charlotte-Anne! Goodness, what are you still doing out here? I've been searching the entire ship for you. I've even had you paged. Why didn't you answer? For a while I was sure you'd gone overboard.'

Charlotte-Anne turned around. Robyn stood resplendent in a floor-length gown of cascading ruby taffeta, with a matching stole that she clutched around her creamy, bare shoulders. Her ears, neck, and hands sparkled with rubies and diamonds.

'You look beautiful.' Charlotte-Anne's pale eyes swept Robyn from head to toe. 'Is there a party?'

'Party! We've both been invited to sit at the captain's table, and you're not even changed yet.' Robyn shook her head in despair and murmured, 'Is there a party!'

Charlotte-Anne turned away and stared sorrowfully out at the dark expanse of the sea. The long, receding wake glowed with phosphorescence. Somewhere far behind it was home, where she longed to be now. She needed some time to herself, alone, to sort out her feelings and adjust to the temporary shipboard world, and, even more importantly, to prepare herself emotionally for life in a foreign country.

'I really don't think I feel up to it tonight, Robyn,' she begged off.

Robyn's eyes flashed. 'Nonsense. An invitation to sit at the captain's table is practically a royal summons. And besides, you're not going to rob me of the pleasure of arousing everyone's envy as we descend the staircase of the Grande Salle à Manger together. We're clearly the two most beautiful women onboard, and I intend to break some hearts. There's the most marvelous Italian prince in a suite

195

right down the hall from us. He's been invited to the captain's table too. Luigi di Fontanesi.' A little sigh escaped Robyn's lips. 'I met him once or twice. He's so dashing, and *filthy* rich. And a bachelor yet! Women throw themselves at him left and right, but so far he's managed to keep himself from getting involved with any of them. There was even a rumor going around a couple of years back that some girl in Deauville had tried to commit suicide over him.' Robyn looked temporarily deflated. 'Too bad I won't have it said that I rob the cradle. He's just a wee bit too young for me. He's older than you, though, but not that old. Somewhere in his late twenties. Now get inside, or do I have to drag you in and dress you myself? I took the liberty of going through your things, and I picked out what you're going to wear. The maid's already steamed it and laid it out.'

Charlotte-Anne was somewhat overwhelmed by Robyn's barrage of chatter, but she managed to plead, 'Not tonight. Please.'

'Yes, tonight!' Robyn's tone left no room for further argument. 'I promised your mother I'd take care of you. And to Robyn Morgan that means two things. First and foremost, protecting you from all things evil. And Luigi di Fontanesi is *deliciously* evil. And second, exposing you socially. I refuse to take no as an answer.'

'By the time you've finished dressing,' Robyn growled impatiently, lighting a cigarette and pacing the stateroom, 'dinner will long be over.'

Charlotte-Anne glanced at Robyn's moving reflection in the tilted mirror. 'I'm *hurrying*,' she mumbled, her mouth full of bobby pins. She was sitting in her slip in front of the built-in dressing table, deftly pinning up her hair. 'There, finished,' she said finally. She removed the remaining pins from between her lips, pivoted on the stool, and faced Robyn. 'How does it look?'

Robyn stopped pacing and nodded with approval. She had never seen Charlotte-Anne with her hair up, and she approved of how it furthered the impression of slender height. 'Wait a minute. Hold this.' She handed Charlotte-

Anne her cigarette holder, leaned down, and pulled loose a few carefully chosen tendrils of Charlotte-Anne's hair. 'It shouldn't be *too* perfect,' she explained. 'You've got a young innocence about you, and we should emphasize it.' Her fingers worked deftly, arranging several 'vagrant' tendrils of hair to frame Charlotte-Anne's face. 'There. Perfect. Now turn around and look.'

Charlotte-Anne pivoted again and studied herself in the mirror. Robyn was right. The new arrangement heightened her heart-shaped face and emphasized the widow's peak she was hardly aware she had.

'Now, into your dress.'

'Just a moment.' Charlotte-Anne pulled open a drawer and took out the slim box her mother had pressed into her hand just before sailing. She lifted out the pansy charm. For a moment she held it suspended between both hands and looked at it closely. She had never really studied it before, and now she admired its fine filligreed silver and the deep purplish-blue hue of the pansy captured in the crystal, the richness heightened by the flower's center of rich yellow.

She was glad her mother had given it to her. It was something familiar, a link to the past, and she realized at once that it would mean as much to her as it had meant to Elizabeth-Anne.

'Here, let me.' Robyn took the necklace from her and secured it around her neck. Charlotte-Anne touched the charm. It felt cool and smooth, and filled her with confidence.

She rose from the stool, crossed over to the bed and picked up the sleeveless evening gown her mother had chosen for her. Made of layers of pure white, diaphanous chiffon, it was Grecian in its simplicity. She lifted it over her head and let it float down smoothly over her.

'You look,' Robyn said, stepping back in disbelief, 'like nothing I've ever seen before.' She sounded delighted. 'Believe *me*, next to you everyone else will look garishly overdressed.'

'Oh.' Charlotte-Anne's face settled into a frown. 'It isn't enough? Perhaps a bracelet or some make-up or – '

'No, no,' Robyn laughed. 'I meant it as a compliment.'
She removed the cigarette from the holder, stubbed it out
in an ashtray, and dropped the holder into her clutch purse.
She took Charlotte-Anne by the arm and led her to the
door, then opened it and switched off the lights.

'Let's go knock 'em dead.'

5

The Grande Salle à Manger towered three decks high, and
the murmur of conversation and the strains of elegant
music wafted up to the top landing of the grand staircase.
Charlotte-Anne clutched the bannister on the top floor and
gazed down. All her confidence seeped out of her. Even
from this height, the dining room was a sea of elegantly
turned out men and exquisitely gowned women. She
wished she had inherited her mother's easy confidence and
adaptability.

She looked pleadingly at Robyn.

'You look exquisite,' Robyn assured her with a smile.
'Your mother chose well for you. The gown is just right for
your age and figure, and I never knew anyone could
project such clashing worldliness and formal innocence
with pinned up hair. You're simply ravishing. Now down
we go.'

Charlotte-Anne took a deep breath. Below, the first
course was just being served by an army of white-jacketed
waiters. She saw heads leaning back as diners looked up at
her and Robyn. Even from three floors below, she could
feel the eyes appraising them. The grand staircase had been
designed for sweeping entrances, and it terrified her
because she realized that just as it could show off elegance
and grace it would magnify the slightest, humiliating flaw.

She clutched the bannister more tightly, the glances from
below making her knees go weak. Oh, if only they hadn't
arrived late! If only she hadn't spent all that time out on
deck, they would have been just two more in a crowd

descending the staircase. Now, making a grand entrance by themselves, she was certain something terrible was going to happen. She would trip on her hem or stumble on the carpet and go falling down an entire flight of steps.

'Chin *up*,' Robyn sang softly under her breath, her lips composed in a careful smile as she led the way. Charlotte-Anne couldn't help but marvel at the older woman's poise, at the swanlike neck with its regal chin, and the elegant definition of the slanting, patrician cheekbones. Robyn was lithe and polished, and seemingly unaffected. As she stepped forward beginning the long descent, her ruby taffeta gown billowed out from her tiny waist and the snug fit of the low cut bodice.

Here goes, Charlotte-Anne told herself, following Robyn as she admonished herself: Just go steady. Put one satin slipper in front of the other, and repeat that process until you reach the landing. After that, there's only one more deck to go, and then you're on the bottom.

Once more, she glanced down at the sea of upturned faces. This was like . . . she caught her breath. Yes, just like being onstage. Somehow that thought gave her confidence and she squared her shoulders and moved on, more relaxed. She was still unaware of the sensation she was creating. She was so young, and unaffected, so like a young gazelle in her freshness and grace, that she was breathtaking. The white chiffon accentuated her every move, and with each step she took, her confidence grew a little more.

Only when she reached the middle landing, where Robyn turned and waited for her, did she realize the effect she was having on the diners below. Her audience was captivated, she could feel it. It was like the electricity coursing between an actor and his audience. Together, she and Robyn swept down the last flight, two elegant swans, one red and one white, and all eyes in the Grande Salle à Manger were upon them.

She wondered if it was her imagination, or if the orchestra really did switch to an elegant waltz to accentuate their entrance. Her face blushed pinkly, and the rosy glow only served to heighten her beauty. Robyn turned to her, a half-smile on her lips, her eyes sparkling.

The instant they reached the foot of the staircase, the maitre d' appeared as though by magic. 'Madame. Mademoiselle.' He bowed gracefully to each one of them in turn. 'This way, if you please.'

He led the way through the sumptuous mirrored room. They swept through the sea of tables, white draped and gleaming with silver and crystal, past millions of dollars worth of jewelry, on dazzlingly clad women. The *Ile de France* was a flagship of ocean-going luxury, and once again Charlotte-Anne marveled that, despite the misery of the Depression, there was still so much wealth in evidence.

When they reached the table of honor, the captain was already on his feet. He stood with his shoulders squared and his resplendent black uniform seemingly gilded with ormolu. His face was distinguished, his hair silver, and his eyes dark.

'Bonsoir, Madame Morgan.' He bent over Robyn's proffered hand and kissed it with a flourish. 'It is an honor to have you aboard once again.'

'You flatter me, Captain Louvard, that you even remember me.'

'No, it is I who am flattered, to have you sail with us so often, Madame.'

Robyn turned to Charlotte-Anne. 'May I introduce my traveling companion, Miss Charlotte-Anne Hale.'

'A pleasure indeed.' The captain bent over Charlotte-Anne's hand. 'Mademoiselle.'

The captain made the introductions with the gentlemen, all in ties and tails, standing and the ladies remaining seated.

'May I present Mrs. Reichenbach,' Captain Louvard said, beginning on his right.

'Mrs. Morgan and I are old friends,' the buxom woman with thinning red curls and several chins elucidated. 'I'm pleased that we're making the same crossing, my dear. It's nice to run into familiar faces.'

'Especially those who aim to win back their poker losses?' Robyn teased.

Mrs. Reichenbach laughed heartily, her bosom heaving. Then she eyed Charlotte-Anne and sighed softly. 'You look so lovely, my dear. Though it's devastating to be reminded of one's own lost youth.'

Charlotte-Anne smiled gratefully. This was an accolade indeed. Mrs. Reichenbach was well known as one of New York's premier hostesses, and the wife of the country's richest and most powerful newspaper publisher. More powerful, it was rumored, than even William Randolph Hearst.

Captain Louvard gestured across the table. 'His Eminence Giovanni, Cardinal Corsini, special envoy to His Holiness, the Pope.'

His Eminence smiled politely, but with little warmth. His face was that of a medieval prince of the church, thin and hollow. He inclined his head. 'Ladies.'

'His Grace the Duke of Fairfax, and Her Grace, the Duchess of Fairfax.'

The Duke, standing, bowed; seated beside him, his wife nodded and smiled graciously. The Duke was thin and white-haired, the Duchess much younger, and very beautiful with her rosy English complexion.

'His Excellency, Ambassador and Señora Cabral de Perez,' the captain said next, and added gallantly, 'Ambassador and Señora Perez are Argentina's latest diplomatic gift to France.'

The ambassador was an elderly man with the face of the aesthete. Señora Perez was a pale-skinned Buenos Aires beauty with coal black eyes, sensuous lips, and jet black hair pulled back in a chignon. She wore a gown of gold brocade, and around her neck hung the largest emerald Charlotte-Anne had ever seen.

'It seems, captain,' the ambassador said with a smile, 'that your country lost a fine diplomat when you decided to devote your life to the sea.'

The captain smiled and his gaze shifted. 'The Honorable Chief Justice Alexander Goode of the United States Supreme Court, and his wife, Mrs. Goode.'

Charlotte-Anne shifted her gaze. The Justice was a portly, imposing man with a leonine mane of white hair. He looked uncomfortable in formal dress. His wife was tiny and projected good humor. 'How do you do?' they both chorused, then laughed. 'It seems,' Mrs. Goode said, 'that we're always saying the same thing at the same time. Rest assured, it's not rehearsed.'

Charlotte-Anne laughed politely.

Captain Louvard turned to the next guest. 'General Erich von Kersten, from Munich.'

General Kersten was red-faced, meaty, and teutonically correct. He took a few steps back, walked around the table, and clicked his heels together smartly. He bowed low over their hands, and smiled broadly. 'One charming lady is a gift, but two charming ladies are heaven-sent.'

Charlotte-Anne could almost feel the effort it took Robyn to keep from cringing. Even she was glad when the general went back to his seat.

'And last, but certainly not least,' the captain said softly, 'His Highness, Prince Luigi di Fontanesi.'

Charlotte-Anne turned to her immediate left, by reflex now proffering her hand. He was standing directly beside her, and took her hand gently in his. It was then that she met his eyes. Their gaze held, and for an instant she felt paralyzed.

He was by far the most handsome man she had ever encountered. His bold, tawny yellow cat's eyes seemed to burn through her, and his white teeth gleamed predatorily. He seemed to tower over everyone, and even though he was formally dressed she could sense the sheer power of his physique, the wide animal shoulders of the athlete tapering down to a small waist and narrow, tight hips. She could almost taste the unabashedly lusty appetite in his sensuous lips and feel the cynical indolence of his bearing.

He bowed low over her hand and his breath lingered a moment too long. She felt a chill, mixed with a blast of heat coursing through her.

'You are very beautiful,' he said so softly that she strained to hear the words.

Startled by his highly charged, brazenly lengthy touch, her cheeks blazed crimson. She snatched her hand back and dropped her eyes. For some reason she felt curiously violated. She had never known a man who could simply look at her, and with an ever so light touch reach deep down to the depths of her soul. She was glad that everyone else had resumed the meal. It took her several moments to collect her composure. At least, she thought, her reaction to him hadn't been noticed by anyone.

But then Robyn caught her gaze and smiled knowingly.

Charlotte-Anne flushed again. Were her feelings *that* transparent?

'Mademoiselle?'

Charlotte-Anne turned to Captain Louvard and smiled awkwardly as he held her chair for her. She took a seat at his left, and then he helped Robyn into hers at his right. At first she was relieved not to be sitting beside Robyn. She didn't want to have to put up with her knowing looks. What was it she had said up on deck? The prince was 'deliciously evil'. And, Charlotte-Anne amended, danger-ous. Why else would that woman in Deauville have tried to commit suicide over him?

Yet, while she was glad to be spared her friend's scrutiny, she felt uneasy in this crowd of strangers. Everyone was so much older than she was, and so much more accomplished. What could she possibly have in common with ambassadors and cardinals and princes? She found herself yearning to sit unnoticed at one of the other of the hundreds of tables in the room.

She gazed hesitantly around and then suffered her second shock. Only now was she aware of who was sitting on her left – Prince Luigi di Fontanesi.

She slid her napkin off the serving plate and unfolded it slowly in her lap. Then she raised her head, having decided she would avoid looking at him or speaking with him. Everything about him frightened her – his indolent self-assurance, his striking good looks, the physical power radiating from him, his unsettling ability to look deep into her soul.

She was grateful when a waiter placed the first course in front of her. Looking down into her shallow soup plate, she saw four poached quail eggs in mushroom caps floating in a rich golden sauce sprinkled with real caviar. Ordinarily, such a treat would have delighted her, but now all she saw was bountiful satisfaction for an appetite which had deserted her. Still, eating was something to do. She seized upon her spoon, intending to concentrate fully on the food before her. Her efforts were in vain.

From her left, she couldn't help but sense his amused, searing gaze burning through her with such intensity that her hands began to shake. It infuriated her, because she knew good and well that he strove exactly for the effect he was achieving. And she knew he must be silently laughing at her.

She tightened her lips, disgusted with herself for allowing him to cause such a violent reaction to rage within her. But 'allowing' had little to do with it. She felt totally helpless.

She couldn't wait for this dinner to be over with.

She concentrated more closely on her plate, absently pushing the food around with her spoon. Around her, the conversations became more heated, and snatches of phrases seeped into her consciousness, becoming a collage in her distracted mind.

'Are you entering the Monte Carlo Grand Prix this year, Prince Luigi . . . '

'The social reforms begun in Argentina in the last decade . . . '

'Economic chaos . . . '

'Since 1924, Duke Fairfax, when the labor government first . . . '

'Really, Cardinal Corsini, the Treaty of Conciliation between Cardinal Gasparri and Premier Mussolini . . . '

'Isn't Paris in the spring *just* like Buenos Aires in the winter . . . '

'The effects of the Hawley-Smoot Tariff on world trade . . . '

'No, the Weimar Republic and President Hindenburg . . . '

'Prince Luigi, as an aviator . . . '

'But despite the Depression, the Empire State Building *is* nearly completed, isn't it . . . '

'My dear, dear Mrs. Reichenbach, if you only . . . '

'Germany will not permit herself to be shackled . . . '

The various statements rippled and rose in intensity around the table, punctuated by the clinking of crystal and china, and the scraping of silverware. Charlotte-Anne felt out of her league, possibly because she wasn't paying attention. She was too busy concentrating on one thing, and one thing only – trying to avoid Prince Luigi di Fontanesi's attention.

'And what do you think, Mademoiselle Hale?'

Charlotte-Anne started and turned to her right. The voice belonged to the captain. She'd totally missed his question. And somehow, during it all, the plates had been switched. She hadn't even noticed the whole, spiny lobster, red shell stuffed with crabmeat, that was now sitting before her.

'I'm sorry, captain,' she said apologetically. 'I wasn't paying attention to anything but the food. It looks so . . . so *extravagant.*'

'And a smart young lady you are.' General Kersten boomed from across the table. 'In my country, work and politics are for the men, and the kitchen and the bedroom are for women. More women should feel the way you do.'

Charlotte-Anne was too shocked to speak before Mrs. Reichenbach said, 'Indeed. I'll have you know, General, that many women are as accomplished as men, and some even more so. History will bear me out. Every year, more and more women are making gains, both politically and professionally.'

'With all due respect, Mrs. Reichenbach,' the general said, laughing, 'you disagree that giving birth to, and caring for children, are not a woman's commitment?'

'I said nothing of the sort,' Mrs. Reichenbach retorted. 'All I'm saying is that one must have an open mind. One should strive not to nurture preconceived notions about men and women's roles.'

'I think Mrs. Reichenbach has a point,' Robyn put in. She placed her elbows on the table, leaned forward, and gestured to Charlotte-Anne. 'Miss Hale's mother is a businesswoman. She started by building one tourist court in Texas, and she now owns a chain of tourist courts and hotels. She is doing extremely well, and continuing to expand. And, I might add, she has four children she has

205

been raising herself, without the benefit of a husband. As a widow – '

'Ach,' the general said irritably, cutting her off and waving away Elizabeth-Anne's accomplishments with a flick of his hands. 'An individual! Life is not for the individual.'

'And who, pray tell, *is* life for?' Mrs. Reichenbach asked indignantly.

'The masses, of course. One cannot judge all women by one remarkable woman, especially a successful one. Name me other women who can match men point for point.'

'Amelia Earhart.' The soft voice belonged to Luigi di Fontanesi.

Surprised, Charlotte-Anne turned to him without thinking. For once, he was not gazing at her, but had locked eyes with General Kersten.

'Ach, Fräulein Earhart!' The general laughed. 'So the intrepid Fräulein Earhart and two other fliers flew from . . . well, across the Atlantic, at any rate.'

'Newfoundland to Wales, in 1928,' Prince Luigi said quietly.

'See?' the general intoned. He smiled tolerantly at Robyn and Mrs. Reichenbach. 'But did not your Charles Lindbergh fly from New York to Paris in . . . in . . . ' He looked at Luigi.

'1927,' the prince said softly.

'You see! His transatlantic flight took place one entire year earlier than Fräulein Earhart's,' General Kersten said with smug triumph. 'And *he* flew without a crew. Fräulein Earhart would do well to stay at home and have children.'

'General,' Luigi said easily, 'I myself have on two different occasions tried to fly the Atlantic. Once solo, and once with a crew of two, just like Miss Earhart. Twice, I was forced to turn back. If I could not accomplish something that a woman could, does this speak ill of me as a man, or well of her as an aviator?'

'Surely, my dear prince, accidents of fate occur every now and then. I would not let Fräulein Earhart get the better of me simply because she managed a flight when you could not. There are always extenuating circumstances.'

'But you agree, then, that Mr. Lindbergh, and not I, is the better pilot?'

'Well, perhaps,' the general said uncomfortably.

'And if Mr. Lindbergh is the better flier, because he accomplished what I could not, then do you not think that Miss Earhart might be, also? For exactly the same reason?'

'As I said before,' the general answered heatedly, 'accidents of fate occur. I stand by what I have said before. Men are born leaders. The American, Herr Lindbergh, has proven that. But, in the coming years, even the Americans will be outdone. By the *Germans*. My government will see to that. On land, in the air, and on the sea. All you have to do is look at what is happening around the world. India, once the backbone of the British Empire, is boycotting British goods and rejecting the idea of taxes without representation. England is weakening by the day. America has slipped back into the lull of isolationism, licking her wounds. One by one, the major powers are getting weaker. But one day soon, Germany will prove herself more powerful than ever before. We will be a nation to be reckoned with.'

'I see,' Chief Justice Goode said drily. 'Then you are privy to more information than any of us. It was my opinion that Germany is weak. The Weimar Republic has difficulty keeping up with its reparation payments. How do you suggest that Germany will increase in strength when multitudes of her people cannot even buy bread?'

'And whose fault is that?' The general's face grew even more red. 'Germany is being sucked dry by her enemies,' he hissed, leaning across the table with fiery eyes. 'But we Germans will not stand for it much longer. The French,' he said, smiling at Captain Louvard, 'and with all due respect, the British also,' he added, nodding apologetically at the Duke and Duchess, 'everyone in Europe and America has ganged up on the Fatherland. But time will tell.' He clenched his hand into a fist. 'I know one thing. Germany will not always be weak.'

'Perhaps you know that, General,' Ambassador Perez said, 'but I happen to know that the evening is young, the dinner marvelous, the wines excellent, and the ladies exceptionally beautiful. I propose – '

But once started, the general was not about to give up graciously in mid-stream. 'The Fatherland is like the proverbial phoenix,' he cut in forcefully. 'Germany will rise out of the ashes stronger than ever, her peoples united as one. It will not be long now. President Hindenburg's days are numbered. A new man named Adolf Hitler has growing support – '

Mrs. Reichenbach laughed lightly. 'I've heard of your Adolf Hitler, and his Beer Hall Putsch – '

'Herr Hitler was premature, that was the problem. When the phoenix that is Germany finally rises again, things will change.' General Kersten nodded ominously. 'You shall see. And the stranglehold the Jews have on us – '

There was a sudden clatter as Mrs. Reichenbach's fork dropped onto her plate. 'Begging your pardon, General Kersten, I, for one, am Jewish. And let me assure you – '

'As I have said before,' Ambassador Perez broke in, 'the evening is too young and beautiful for us to talk politics.'

'The ambassador is quite right,' Captain Louvard added quickly.

'And you,' a voice said softly from Charlotte-Anne's left, 'have not yet eaten a bite of your two courses. Perhaps that is what makes you the most beautiful woman aboard?'

Charlotte-Anne colored as she met Luigi di Fontanesi's predatory gaze.

'I would be honored,' he said, 'if after dinner, you would accompany me to the ballroom.'

'I'm . . . sorry.' Charlotte-Anne tore her eyes away from his and stared at her lobster. 'But I'm otherwise engaged,' she murmured. 'I have made plans.'

'Then change them.'

'But they're very important.' She was still frightened of him, yet fascinated by the way he had stood up for women and Amelia Earhart. She couldn't shake the feeling that he had sparred with General Kersten only for her benefit. Or was that merely her ego?

Robyn leaned forward and smiled. 'Oh, but my dear,' she said cunningly. 'Of course I won't mind if you change our plans. I wouldn't dream of holding you to them. Besides, there's something else I am simply *dying* to do. Like win back my past poker losses from Mrs. Reichenbach. You and the prince go ahead and dance.'

Charlotte-Anne felt her stomach shriveling into a tight, nervous chestnut. She cursed Robyn's fine-tuned hearing. Did nothing escape her? And what did she think she was trying to do, anyway? Play matchmaker between her and the one person who frightened her more than anyone else she had ever met?

Charlotte-Anne didn't want to dance. Not with anyone, and especially not with the prince. Besides, she didn't know how.

She did not dare look at Luigi. 'I'm afraid my dancing is awful, Your Grace,' she murmured more to her lobster than to him.

He laughed suddenly. 'I can tell that you Americans are truly democratic. However, the Duke and Duchess are "Your Grace." I am simply "Your Highness." '

She blushed again, aware that every eye at the table was on her.

'However,' he continued, 'I would be honored if you exercised your democratic perogative and called me "Luigi." '

She turned slowly to him.

'And as for your dancing, which you are afraid is not very good, believe me when I say that mine is excellent. No one can dance terribly when they dance with me. I know how to lead.'

'In that case,' Robyn said lightly, 'I'm sure that Miss Hale would not only be honored, but she, too, would like to extend to you the courtesy of being called by her first name. Wouldn't you, dear?'

Whether Robyn's statement was a comment or a rebuke, Charlotte-Anne did not know. In either case, it left her with no choice but to go dance with Luigi di Fontanesi. Charlotte-Anne lifted her chin and stared straight into Luigi's dark, smoked-glass eyes. 'In that case,' she said in a trembling voice, 'I suppose I must thank you, and accept.'

Even as she said these reluctant words, her heart gave an

209

excited leap. Which, when she considered it, was not at all unpleasant.

He escorted her by the arm to the Grand Salon, where the etched-glass windows soared to a height of more than seven yards. Already, the ballroom was a sea of floating couples. Above the elegant strains of the waltz in progress she could hear other, more muted sounds: the swishes of silks, the rustles of satins and taffetas, the whisper of velvets. Couples danced across the shiny parquet floor like graceful, miniature music box dancers captured inside the massive jewel box of the ballroom.

He led her to the edge of the dance floor, conscious of her nervousness. She smiled stiffly, but the effort was fading fast, and her heart was sinking rapidly. Luigi had promised to lead her, had assured her that she would dance beautifully. But now, faced with the effortlessly graceful dancers surrounding her, she wasn't quite so sure it would be possible. Every woman present was letting her gentleman guide her, but they were also *dancing*. She felt miserable and foolish. She was certain that she would make a spectacle of herself.

She found herself yearning for L'Ecole Catroux. Why couldn't she have already attended the school and have gained the polish so necessary to a young lady? Why had she been thrust into the midst of all this luxury while she was still so unprepared for it?

She looked at Luigi, and the breath caught in her throat. He was gazing out at the dance floor, his eyes searching for an opening, his face in glorious profile. It was a classic Roman face carved from alabaster, the nose perfect and strong, exactly like Michaelangelo's David, the chin determined, the lips curved and jutting sensuously, the black hair gleaming and combed slickly back. He was a Roman marble come to life, sinuous and powerful, his face and body a reminder of his heritage. He was the perfect image of the languid playboy, but any vapidness about him was dispelled by the high cheekbones and the two strong, almost cruel lines running from his nose down to the corners of his mouth.

He turned to her, his face coming into full view, and again she caught her breath. He bowed, a mere forward motion of his head, and then she felt his hands slip onto the small of her back, sending ripples up and down her spine. He touched her other hand, enfolded her gently, like a most precious flower, and then began to move, sweeping her onto the dance floor. She gazed down at someone else's feet and tried to imitate the steps. She stumbled and he caught her, drawing her closer.

'No, no,' he said, his breath a whisper. He began twirling her slowly, gracefully. 'Do not look down. Do not try to do anything. Only move along with me. Like this. See . . . It is not so difficult. Do not concentrate on it . . . Now you are doing fine.'

She nodded, her mind reeling as she felt the heat of his lithe body, the crackling electricity of his touch. She looked up into his face and let herself go. Before she even realized what was happening, he was sweeping her around the dance floor, his every move perfect, leading her so exquisitely that it appeared that she was as proficient a dancer as he. The strains of the waltz were a soft, muted pulse, seemingly tailored to their every move.

He gazed down at her, his lips curved into a smile. 'You dance beautifully,' he said softly.

'Do I now?' She smiled crookedly and cocked her head. 'I thought you told me it would be because you lead so well.'

'Ah, but I am, am I not?'

'Are you always this sure of yourself?'

'Almost always. I have a way with beautiful women.' His eyes flashed mischievously. 'Or so they tell me.'

'I see. And what if I told you that I have a way with handsome men?'

He grinned at her. 'Then I might believe you. After all, you attracted me, did you not?'

'Did I – '

'What do you think?'

'I think you're very cunning,' she said. 'It was you who watched me throughout dinner, trying to make me uncomfortable – '

'Now *you* are the one who is being cunning.'

She simultaneously blushed and glared at him, but they continued waltzing without missing a step.

'And you look even more beautiful when you are angry,' he smiled. 'When your eyes flash brilliantly.'

She looked away from him. The massive salon moved around them like a merry-go-round, and the other couples swished and laughed softly . . . exchanged secrets. Women gazed at Luigi longingly, and eyed her enviously. She caught sight of Robyn dancing in the arms of Ambassador Perez, smiling that knowing little smile of hers. So Robyn wasn't playing poker with Mrs. Reichenbach, she thought. It had been a trick to get her and Luigi together. But she couldn't think about it for long. The waltz stopped with a flourish, the figures on the dance floor stood frozen for an instant, with only the ladies' gowns still swaying. Then everyone clapped politely.

Another waltz began. Before she knew it, Luigi was spiriting her around even more effortlessly than before.

'Ah, so the fire has finally died in your eyes,' he said at long last. 'Then you are no longer angry with me.'

She was silent.

'Are you going to stay in Europe long?' he asked.

Despite herself, she had to gaze back up at him. There was something magnetic about him which drew her. 'I don't know. Six months at least. Longer perhaps.'

'I wish it were for a very long time.'

She didn't speak.

'Perhaps forever?'

'Don't,' she begged in a whisper. 'Don't talk like that.'

'You are uncomfortable?'

She nodded.

'Then I will change the subject.' He paused. 'This is your first trip to Europe?'

She nodded again.

'You are on what the Americans call "The Grand Tour"?'

'No. I'm going to Switzerland. To finishing school.'

'Then you are very young.'

Startled, she gazed at him. His voice had been one of surprise.

212

He frowned. 'How old are you?'

She sighed. 'Does it matter?'

'Sometimes it does. I do not wish to rob the cradle.'

She laughed, remembering how earlier that evening Robyn had said the very same thing about him.

'Is something funny? He looked hurt.

'No. I'm sorry. It was just your choice of expression.'

'Then my vernacular? It is wrong? If so, you must tell me.'

'No, it's correct.' She struggled to look more serious. 'But I'm not exactly still in the cradle.'

'That much I am very aware of.' His gaze burned deep into her, flooding her body with shocking warmth. He pressed her closer to him, and she felt the tightening of his hands, the heat of his legs through her diaphanous chiffon, and the hard strength of his manhood. 'I think,' he said in a whisper, 'that I am in love with you.'

Now her step faltered, but he caught her, swirled her on.

'Do you say that to all the women you meet?' she asked with a tinge of bitterness.

'No.'

'Then why to me?'

'Because you are young and beautiful. There is a fresh innocence about you which is lacking in most women.'

'Is that what you think?' She looked up at him in a childlike way, her hands light, as thought she were about to extricate herself.

'Aren't you innocent?' he prodded gently. 'Or am I wrong?'

'You . . . frighten me.'

'Why?' he asked. 'Because you have heard something about me? Because I have a . . . a rather tarnished reputation?'

She met his eyes. 'Don't you?'

His face was devoid of expression. 'I am afraid I do.'

She nodded. 'That is part of what frightens me. The rest is . . . well, your title. Your self-assurance. And you are probably the most handsome man – ' Damn! She bit down on her lip. Why had she let something foolish like that slip out? Now she felt like a schoolgirl.

'Physical attractiveness can be a millstone around anyone's neck,' he said. 'You should know that. You yourself are extraordinarily beautiful. Surely you have noticed that beauty hampers?'

She was silent.

'Am I the first man who you were ever attracted to?'

She thought briefly of Mickey Hoyt. She had been attracted to him, yes. But she'd been more attracted by who Mickey was than by anything else. She shook her head. 'No. I've never really been attracted to a man. But I've . . . I've been hurt. And I don't want to be hurt again.'

He stopped dancing abruptly, and they stood in the middle of the floor facing each other. His hands were still holding her. The waltz strains and swirling couples flowed around them. 'And you think,' he asked softly, 'that I have not been hurt also?'

Her voice was husky. 'I . . . I don't know.' Then, before she knew what she was saying, she blurted out, 'At Deauville – the woman who tried to commit suicide over you – '

'That much publicized case.' He laughed shortly. 'She wanted to marry me. What else is new?'

'And you didn't want to marry her?'

His gaze was level. 'No. Not her.'

'But she died, or nearly died. Over you.'

His smile was grim. 'Nearly died? She took pills, yes, but not enough to kill herself. She tried to trap me into marriage. Nothing was too much, as long as she got what she wanted. Which she did not.'

Charlotte-Anne turned away.

'You don't believe me?' he asked gently.

'That a man like you can be trapped?'

'Am I so different from other men?'

'Yes. No.' She was confused. 'I don't know.'

'That woman in Deauville. She was a baroness. I warned her before we ever saw each other seriously that it was to be a brief affair. Somehow she thought that it wouldn't matter. That she would gain a hold over me nevertheless. She tried. It was not until several weeks after we met that I realized she would do anything to marry me. She thought that by making love to me . . . ' His voice trailed off in midsentence.

'That you would marry her?'

He nodded. 'She waited long enough until she could tell me she believed she was pregnant.'

Charlotte-Anne looked startled. 'Was she?'

'I don't know.' He shook his head. 'I suppose now I will never know.'

They began to dance again, this time more solemnly.

'But . . . did you try to find out if she had a child?'

'She never showed pregnancy, if that is what you mean. If she was carrying a child, she could have lost it when she tried suicide, or had an abortion. Or else it was just another ruse.'

Charlotte-Anne stared into his eyes. 'I feel sorry for you,' she said slowly.

He smiled then. 'I have gotten over it. But it is nice to know that somebody believes the truth. Most people don't. I have been made out to be a womanizing ogre. Nobody wants to believe otherwise.'

'I do.'

'Why? Because somebody wanted you also? Or you him?'

'Because *I* wanted him,' she said, sighing. 'Because, like the baroness, I would have done anything. Only . . . ' She tightened her lips.

'Only what?' he prodded gently.

'It wasn't him I wanted. It was what he could *do* for me. Now, looking back on it, I'm very ashamed of myself.'

'You are young and inexperienced. Perhaps you did not know better.'

'But I did. And you?' She raised her chin. 'You are experienced?'

'Yes, I suppose you could call me that. But I was no match for a much older, and even more experienced woman.' He grinned. 'I'm afraid I am very weak when it comes to temptations. It seems I can never say no. Not even to you now.'

'But I'm not trying to tempt you.'

He held her closer. 'I know that. Which makes you all the more tempting.'

Her eyes fell and they danced on in silence. The waltz ended, and another began.

'I'd like to share the night with you,' he whispered.

She pulled herself away. 'I'm sorry.' She shook her head. 'I'm not ready for that. I've got to go. It seems we've danced forever, and I'm tired and out of breath.'

They stopped and he led her off the floor. 'Perhaps you would like some fresh air?' he suggested. 'We could take a walk on deck.'

She shook her head. 'No, I think I need time to myself.'

'Because I frighten you?'

Her features contracted in a little frown, and she shook her head again. She didn't know what was happening to her, only that she ached deeply for him, longed for his touch. How could she explain to him that her own feelings frightened her far more than anything he could do to her?

He held both her hands in his. 'Then I will escort you to your stateroom.'

'No, I'd rather you didn't.'

He looked deeply disappointed. 'If that is what you wish,' he said.

'I do. And thank you.' She gave a little smile. 'It was a most memorable evening.'

'I will see you again?' he asked hopefully. 'Tomorrow?'

'Perhaps tomorrow.' Then she turned and quickly left, leaving him standing alone, his face brooding.

Robyn came up to him from behind. 'And to think that you never once asked me to dance,' she said chidingly.

Scowling, Luigi turned to her. 'I'm sorry. I do not feel like another dance. Perhaps some other time.' Then he turned away again and stared across the massive room.

Robyn said nothing, but her sharp eyes followed his gaze. Charlotte-Anne had just reached the door, a slender figure in white.

It was the first time in years that a woman Luigi had danced with had not ended up in his bed.

'You,' Robyn said pointedly as she took a seat in the narrow, green-leather armchair, 'disappeared awfully fast last night.' She was wearing a pale, Empire-style peignor with a high bodice and a matching gossamer robe, and she held a cup and saucer in her hands.

Charlotte-Anne sat up in bed and shrugged. 'I was tired,' she mumbled evasively.

'Were you now?' Robyn cocked her head and eyed her curiously. 'Or were you running away?'

'Running away? From what?' Charlotte-Anne stood up and stretched.

'Not from what,' Robyn corrected. 'From *whom*.'

Charlotte-Anne flipped a strand of hair out of her eyes. 'What time is it?'

'Nine-thirty. In other words, time to have breakfast and get some fresh air. We can't have you sleeping your life away. You're far too young to do that. And besides . . . ' Robyn took another sip of her black coffee. 'I gather that someone is waiting up for you.'

Charlotte-Anne went into the small bathroom and looked at herself in the mirror above the sink. She was pleased with her reflection. She couldn't ever remember looking as well rested, or having slept so soundly. 'What time's breakfast?' she called over her shoulder.

'Any time you want it,' Robyn called back. 'I took the liberty of ordering it on a tray. If I hadn't, by the time you'd get to the dining room they would be serving lunch. Your breakfast's on the dressing table in my stateroom. Help yourself.'

'I don't mind if I do.' Charlotte-Anne came back out of the bathroom. 'I'm ravenous.'

'It's the sea air.' Robyn smiled. 'I'm the same way.'

Charlotte-Anne went through the connecting door to Robyn's stateroom. After a moment she came back. 'That's *all* there is to eat?' she asked in disbelief.

'A lady,' Robyn said, 'does not need anything more in

the morning than a cup of black coffee and a single croissant. That's all I had, and that's all you'll have.'

'*Robyn*.' Charlotte-Anne scowled at her in disgust. 'I'm used to having eggs and toast and sausages. There's not even any sugar.'

'And you don't need any. You'll get used to black coffee soon enough.'

'But . . . it's so bitter.'

'It's an acquired taste, and I think it's high time you acquired it.'

'And I hardly ate a bite at dinner last night,' Charlotte-Anne protested. 'Besides, I'm not fat. I don't need to go on a diet.'

'No, you don't,' Robyn agreed. 'Not yet, at least, because you are young. But when you're my age, you'll thank me. As to dinner, I know you ate next to nothing. That's not my fault, it's yours, so don't complain. Now have your coffee and croissant, and then get bathed and dressed. I've made a date for shuffleboard at ten. You'll like it. It's a lot of fun.'

'And what if I don't want to play?'

Robyn made a gesture of impatience. 'Don't always be so argumentative. If you don't want to play, you won't have to. It's that simple. But eat your breakfast and get ready, for God's sake. I'll run you a bath.'

'I might be a while,' Charlotte-Anne murmured, a frown drawing her brows together. 'Why don't you go on up ahead? I'll join you later.'

'Oh, no, you don't. I'm staying right here; otherwise you'll never get out of this cabin.'

Charlotte-Anne sighed and went to get the breakfast tray. She carried it into the bathroom with her and ate while soaking in a tub of fragrant bubbles.

She was surprised to discover she was humming softly to herself.

But Robyn, pressing her ear against the bathroom door and listening, wasn't in the least bit surprised. Not by the humming, nor by how much care Charlotte-Anne later took getting dressed.

* * *

The sun shone brightly and the salt air was tangy and fresh. The winds of the North Atlantic were cool, whipping the pennants and fluttering the French tricolor which hung from the stern. Overhead, the wind tugged the dark plumes of smoke out of the massive funnels and pulled them backward toward the horizon. All around, the ocean looked endless and bluish gray, each triangular wave topped with foamy little crests.

Robyn looked very stylish dressed in a pair of loose-fitting, gray twill trousers, a white sweater, and a string of marble-sized pearls. It was considered a rather daring, if casual morning outfit, but as long as she didn't wear it past noon it was acceptable shipboard attire.

Charlotte-Anne, standing off to one side and watching the game of shuffleboard, was dressed in an oyster-coloured cashmere-and-silk sweater, a modest, off-white pleated wool skirt, and oyster leather shoes. She had brushed her hair and tied it back with a silk ribbon, and it make her look much younger and more vulnerable than she had the night before. The moment Luigi caught sight of her from a distance, he hurried toward her. At that moment, he knew she was truly the most beautiful young woman in the world, at least for him. He was used to armies of cool, sophisticated society beauties, but Charlotte-Anne's fresh radiance was something entirely new to him, and made any woman he had ever known pale by comparison.

'Good morning. You are a sight for sore eyes,' he marveled, smiling at her. 'I trust you slept well?'

She smiled at him and nodded. He looked even more handsome in daylight than he had in the Grande Salle à Manger, or on the dance floor. His complexion looked more marble-like, and the dark blue blazer, white slacks, and paisley ascot suited him perfectly.

'Now that you're well rested,' he said, taking her by the arm and leading her away from the shuffleboard game, 'I insist on one thing.'

'Oh?' She turned her back to a lifeboat and raised her eyebrows at him. The wind whipped at her skirt. 'And what is that?'

'That you devote the entire day to me.'

219

'Oh! But I couldn't.' She made a little gesture. 'I mean, I'd bore you in no time at all.' She glanced at a ripe-bodied brunette who paraded past, eyeing him openly.

He looked at the woman, then back at Charlotte-Anne with a grin. 'As you can see, there is no contest. I would much rather be with you.' He took her hands, held them, and gazed deep into her eyes. 'I want *only* to be with you,' he emphasized softly. 'Is that too much to ask?'

She didn't reply.

'Do I have your permission to share your company, or must I get it from someone else?'

Charlotte-Anne laughed, and suddenly all her nervousness seemed to drain away. In the bright daylight, he seemed far less threatening than he had the evening before. 'If that's what you want,' she replied, 'who am I to ruin your day? But you must promise me one thing.'

'And what is that?'

'That you won't let me starve. Robyn thinks that every woman needs to watch her weight, and I'm *famished*.'

'In that case, I will not let you starve. The Café-Grill should already be open. If not, I am certain a steward can bring us something. Myself, I have feasted on shad roe for breakfast, but there is nothing we Italians like as much as a woman with an appetite.'

'Prince Fontanesi, you have yourself a deal.' She stuck out her hand and they shook on it.

The rest of that first day at sea flew past in a magical blur. They swam in the long swimming pool; he tried to teach her to play tennis up on the sun deck; they watched *The Champ* with Wallace Beery in the theater; they shopped in the arcade, where he insisted upon buying her a blown-glass unicorn she admired; and then they dined once again at the captain's table. And somehow, during it all, they found time to talk about themselves. That night, after dinner, they went up on the sun deck and stood under the canopy of stars. It was late, and they were alone. The moon was a crescent riding high in the heavens. The waves slapped softly against the hull many decks below, and from somewhere forward drifted the muted strains of a waltz. Common sense told her that the *Ile de France* was a floating city filled with hundreds of passengers and crew members; yet somehow, she felt as though she and Luigi were two people standing alone atop a bluff which rose up out of the middle of the Atlantic Ocean.

She had never felt so tormented, so torn in two.

As the lightheartedness of the day had worn on and evening had approached, she once again found herself reverting to the opinion she'd formed of Luigi yesterday - that everything about him was quite frightening. Yet at the same time, she envisioned his arms intertwined with her body, imagined running the palms of her hands down his broad naked back, which she knew would be smoothly muscled and warm. She trembled, at once fearing yet hungering for his touch. But most of all, she was tormented by the thought that his touch might never come.

He was so unpredictable, as though he was of some other species. He was unlike any of the American men she had met. None of them had that sensuous, dangerous sense of purpose lurking beneath a thin veneer of alabaster skin. One part of her insisted she resist him when the time came; another whispered that she plunge headlong into any offered passion, no matter how short-lived or ill-timed it was, no matter how much she could get hurt in the process.

She had never before felt so many conflicting emotions, and was desperately confused. She wished she could seek advice from somebody, but realized instinctively even Robyn could not help her; she was on her own. She had to choose to either follow or abandon the dictates of her heart.

It was with a shock that she suddenly realized she barely knew him. It didn't seem to matter.

Already, she was deeply in love with him. But he was Luigi di Fontanesi, one of the most sought after and eligible bachelors in the world, and she knew that could mean only one thing. Her love for him, whether she gave into it or not, was a doomed thing, because surely it was one-sided.

How was she to know that Prince Luigi di Fontanesi, heir to one of the oldest titles in all Italy, the only child of one of his country's richest and most respected families - was thinking exactly the same thoughts about her?

She glanced at him out of the corners of her eyes. He

stood with his back to her, leaning against the railing, with his hands tucked in his pockets as he stared out at the sea. The pale moonlight and muted deck lights cast his shadow along the teak planks underfoot. His face was cast in a frown of indecision, his lips tightly compressed in thought. His eyes seemed faraway, but that was only an illusion. His thoughts were focused on something very nearby. On Charlotte-Anne.

Slowly, he turned to face her. She stood tall and slender, sheathed in wraithlike white. The wind swirled and tugged at her gown. Her pale eyes caught his gaze and glowed iridescently, like a cat's in the night.

He, too, had never been so at odds with himself. And suddenly he knew why: he had never really been in love before.

For once, he was taken completely by surprise. Could it be love? God only knew, he'd had more than his fair share of women, especially considering he was only twenty-nine years old. But always, whether the woman was aristocrat or peasant, blonde, brunette, or redhead, single or married, of creamy ivory skin or rosy English complexion, he found that the moment they first made love the relationship began to die its sometimes slow, sometimes quick, but always inevitable death. Because all those women had one thing in common; they had all believed that his bed was a direct line to his wedding band. They never stopped to consider that he would recognize the true nature of their desire, that their lust was for his principality, and not for him.

But Charlotte-Anne had not thrown herself at him. Indeed, she had at first fought him off. He knew she was special. There was a natural aura, an innocence blended with a regal poise, that made her the perfect candidate for his principessa. She looked born to the part. But far more important, he thought she was the most desirable woman he had ever seen. Until now, love and sex had been separate entities in his mind. Now these two desires – one a physical longing he had never had any problem sating, the other a mystery which had always eluded him – had merged neatly, creating one strong, throbbing emotion which pulsed so powerfully through him, he was confused. He found himself yearning for the simple, familiar relationships of his past, for the advantages of never becoming involved. But there was a disadvantage too, and he only realized now what he had been missing. He had never before felt quite as incredibly alive, or exhilarated, as when Charlotte-Anne was with him.

Here was a woman who seemed to embody everything he had ever sought. For once, he was frankly terrified. He wondered how to proceed. He did not want to do anything which might frighten her off. If love was this rare, and this enchanted, then he wished to nurture it forever.

She would make the perfect Principessa di Fontanesi.

He wanted to marry her.

He stood there for what seemed an eternity. He devoured her with his eyes. His body craved her, but he realized that his heart craved her just as much, if not more. And she just stood silently, gazing back at him, her head held high, her hair gleaming like molten silver in the moonlight.

'Charlotte-Anne?' His voice was soft as he reached out and gently pulled her close. She looked up into the sculpted planes of his face. It was at once so strong and firmly molded, yet so aristocratic and delicate. His black hair gleamed sleekly, and his lashes were dark and thick around his glowing eyes.

Her jawline tightened, and her eyes glittered up at him as his strong arms enveloped her.

'I love you,' he said simply.

She sighed then, and looked away.

'I want to marry you,' he whispered into the shell of her ear.

Her head jerked and she stared at him with a startled expression. 'What did you say?'

'I want to marry you,' he repeated.

Her pulse raced. 'But . . . but you don't know anything about me,' she protested in an unsteady voice.

'I know enough.' His voice was sure as he pressed his lips to hers. It was a velvet kiss, not short, not long, somehow almost chaste. He smiled down at her. 'You have not given me a reply. Or perhaps you have, with your kiss?'

'No . . . I mean . . . I don't know anything about you,' she went on helplessly.

'What is there that you need to know?' He tightened his arms even more firmly around her. 'Only that you love me.'

'Other things,' she said weakly. 'Little things.'

He met her gaze then, and seeing her earnestness, chuckled softly. 'Let me see. I am twenty-nine years of age and I have no brothers and no sisters. My parents live in Italy, and they constantly chastise me because they think I am wasting my life flying airplanes and racing cars. I have spent the last few months traveling across America, and now I am returning to Italy. Premier Mussolini has summoned me, and when Il Duce calls, people respond. Even di Fontanesis. It seems he has plans in mind for me.'

'Plans?'

He nodded. 'He wants me to take a commission in our armed forces, which probably means I will have very little time to fly and race, both of which I love with a passion.' He smiled good-humoredly. 'Is there anything I have left out?'

She looked up at him for a long moment, her face serious. 'You're teasing me,' she said.

'Perhaps. But it is all true.'

She took a deep breath, her body trembling. Her mind was swirling in a vortex. It was all doubtless the truth, but those few, threadbare facts were a fraction of the fabric which composed his whole self. Love required mutual compatability, and that was composed as much of strong bonds as of thousands of idiosyncrasies. What was he like when he was angry? What were his favorite movies? Where had he been to school? What was his favorite color? Was he ambitious?' How could she love someone when all these, and so many other things about him, were a total mystery to her. After all, what *did* she know about Luigi di Fontanesi?

Next to nothing.

Yes, she knew only one thing. And it was the only thing that mattered.

She wanted him.

She yearned to share all his secrets, craved to discover all the little things about him. Wasn't that love – that endless journey of discovering a person over a period of many years.

She sighed, her mind a swirl of confusion. Her deep-rooted physical fear of him, as well as that paradoxical physical yearning which consumed her . . . the way he seemed able to arouse her passion with a single burning glance . . . the electrical charges that tore into her whenever he touched her – was that love? Or was it merely an overpowering chemical reaction rooted in physical attraction?

No, it must be love, she decided. Why else, when he was near, did she have no control over her emotions? Why else did she let him guide her heart. Her very soul?

'You are very silent,' he said. He grinned down at her warmly, and she drew a deep breath of fear mixed with anticipation.

'Luigi – ' she began, but he swooped down and his lips sought hers with a hunger she had never known. For a moment she struggled, gripping his hard, muscled arms with her fingers, and then she went limp and shut her eyes, losing herself in the heat of his kiss. His hands caressed her, his arms trapped her. She felt her breasts pressed flat against his solid chest as he kissed her even more deeply. His thighs rubbed against hers and she felt the warmth radiating from him, felt too the firm, urgent outline of his penis straining against the fabric of his trousers. And then she let herself go completely. Warm currents of lust lapped at her around the edges, receded, and then came curling in on a tidal wave which swept violently over her. She felt she was drowning helplessly, and she couldn't remember a time when she had ever felt anything sweeter.

He raised his head, and her eyes opened slowly. His gaze and hers lingered and merged, and with one hand he let go of her to stroke the creamy skin of her cheeks, the graceful curve of her neck, raking his fingers through her hair, running his hand softly down the youthful hardness of her breasts.

'I think,' he said between urgent little sucks on her lips, 'that it is time to consummate our love.'

225

Her eyes flared and she stiffened, but words deserted her.

'I never take no for an answer,' he whispered, 'not when we both need it so much.' He knew how he felt about her, and knew there was no longer any need to wait.

He gripped her more fiercely and kissed her again. His lips moved slowly, taking soft little nibbles out of hers, and then he kissed her deeply, until she was dizzy and lost in his desire, in her own. As though in a dream, she found herself being led off to the plush luxury of the Trianon Suite.

When they reached his suite, he took her by the hand and led her to the bedroom door. She hesitated for a moment, and he raised her hand to his lips and held it there without speaking; words were not necessary. Then he stepped aside, so that she could enter first. For a long moment she looked into the dark bedroom, where only twin pools of light glowed at each side of the bed. Then she gazed at him. His head was tilted, his eyes glowing softly. She took a deep breath and entered the room.

Champagne was already uncorked on the nightstand, the gold-sheathed neck of the bottle sticking out of the silver ice bucket at a jaunty angle. The music of gentle violins wafted from the speakers built into the paneled headboard. The quilted satin coverlet on the big double bed shone with the rich softness of burnished gold.

Her heart skipped a beat, and anger swelled up within her. So he had expected her to spend the night and make love. Why else was there music and champagne? He had planned this, connived it. He had known she would come.

He saw her sudden stiffness and said, 'I always listen to music and drink champagne at bedtime,' he said. 'Other people prefer a brandy or a cognac. I prefer champagne. I find it helps me to sleep.'

She nodded and bowed her head. The anger seeped back out of her as quickly as it had risen. A clock ticked softly. The air smelled salty, and faintly of cologne.

She sensed that he was right behind her. The moment he closed the bedroom door, she felt his hands at her waist. Almost without applying any pressure, he turned her around to face him. She gazed up into his eyes, and the secret of all the little things she yearned to know about him began to be revealed to her. She noticed the slight indentation in the very middle of his underlip. He gazed at her half-open lips, at the slight, charming overbite, the pearly smooth whiteness of her perfect teeth.

She lifted her arms, gently draping them around his neck. And so the night began. They made love with great care.

He is a sorcerer, she thought, and I am under his spell.

His hands were a silken glide along the smooth velvet of her bare arms. She no longer feared what might happen. This was a rite which women have passed through since time immortal, and her primordial instincts guided her.

She watched in rapt fascination as he removed his clothes, enthralled by his economic movements as he slipped out of his shirt and trousers, and folded everything neatly on a chair. His tightly packed muscles rippled and shifted with his every move. His buttocks were small and firm, his hips almost nonexistent. She hadn't realized how slender and lean his body was, or how long it stretched gracefully from waist to shoulders.

He turned to her again, his face alive with a strange animation, his sex strong and erect.

He led her to the bed, then leaned over and snapped down the burnished gold coverlet. As he straightened, she laid her hands on his shoulders, then parted her lips, and he opened his mouth to receive her kiss. Her body trembled as the last vestiges of her youth fell away, shed by this night. He held her away from him and gently raised her white gown over her head. The silken fabric felt like cool, clinging fingertips lightly massaging her flesh. When she was naked, she stood silently with her hands at her sides, as though waiting for his appraisal. He slid the pins out of her hair, one by one. When she shook her head, the blonde curls bounced lightly down around her face. He seemed pleased, smiling as his fingers flowed through her soft curls and she let her head loll backwards. He pulled her to him then almost roughly, pressing her full breasts against his chest and his rigid penis against her soft belly. She moaned and he lowered her backward onto the bed. She felt the satin coverlet shifting gently under her as his smooth flesh

227

slid atop her own. Moist lips brushed moist lips, and darting tongues playfully sought each other, caught up in a sensuous dance.

He closed his lips on her nipples, and rolled them gently between his teeth. Then he kissed her everywhere, awakening every inch of her body with his tongue, gently teasing her shoulders, elbows, the soft inside of her knees. Her body trembled with pleasure and, no longer able to lie still, she returned his caresses, raking her nails ever so lightly across his buttocks, then taking his small, hard nipples between her own fingers. His lips returned to her breasts and as he bit her gently she felt her nipples swelling and becoming erect. Closing her eyes, she let herself float among the exquisite burst of pain and pleasure, returning each sensation to him as he electrified her.

Slowly he let go of her nipples and kissed her deeply, then turned her on her side, kneading and kissing the smooth velvety skin of her buttocks. He ran his tongue up and down the ridges of her spine so that she cried out and tensed, and then his mouth nuzzled the nape of her neck. She had never felt sensations quite so delicious or so entirely consuming. Every nerve of her body seemed tuned to him as he turned her again and trailed a line of burning kisses down from her neck, between her breasts and over her flat belly. Then slowly, tantalizingly, he bowed his face between her thighs. Without needing to be guided, she rolled her hips up to meet him. His tongue caressed the taut mound, then sought out the very core of her ecstasy, his tongue playing at the velvety flesh until she felt herself mad with desire and arched her entire body in fine agony.

As he rose and prepared to mount her, she swallowed hard and wet her lips. Suddenly she was afraid. She felt his legs rubbing against hers, and then she felt his organ probing between her legs. His penis nestled there, poised, and then as he kissed her deeply she felt a searing pain. She moaned, and he froze, then began to pull out of her.

'No,' she whispered, her eyes glazed over with a loving determination. She shook her head. 'It's alright, Luigi. Don't stop.'

'You are sure?'

She nodded, and then he kissed her again, at the same time slowly but surely thrusting into her. She grabbed a corner of the pillow and bit down as something within her tore and gave. She could feel a dampness seep down her thighs, as he continued to gently slip in and out of her flesh. His pace, at first slow, built steadily until her pain was forgotten and she found herself pressing her hips against him to match his rhythm. He reached under her to clasp her buttocks and press her closer, and then she felt they were truly one, welded together as he reached again and again more deeply into her. Tension filled her body and her breath was coming in short little gasps when she suddenly felt herself leap free of a precipice and fall into a world of thick, exploding pleasure. Wave after wave enveloped her as he buried himself within her and froze, crying out, his whole body taut as the ecstasy throbbed between them.

Then he collapsed on top of her, his breathing raspy, his skin slick with perspiration, their bodies still joined.

When, after a long moment, he lifted himself off her and lay down beside her, she looked away, afraid to meet his eyes.

She felt his firm hand on her chin as he turned her to face him. 'I love you, Charlotte-Anne,' he whispered solemnly, kissing the tip of her nose. 'I must marry you. You must be mine.'

His eyes melted her fears, and her heart began to beat again.

'And you?' he asked softly. 'Do you wish to marry me?'

She smiled tremulously. Her eyes glowed, but her heart was weary. Oh, if it were only so easy! But for another six months, she was still underage. She had promised her mother to attend L'Ecole Catroux, for at least half a year. What if he didn't want to wait that long?

Still, she found herself nodding, and a warm contentment rushed through her. She stared up at the ceiling as he raised the coverlet over them both. The room went dark as he turned out the lights.

His body felt warm against hers. He draped an arm over her, and nuzzled close to her. She felt so safe, so relaxed that sleep wasn't long in coming.

Her last conscious thought was that now she knew, she no longer felt torn.

And suddenly an acting career no longer seemed important at all.

7

The suspense was killing her.

Elizabeth-Anne had never felt so nervous in her entire life. Her ears were ringing with tension, and her mouth was dry. Outwardly, though, she appeared calm, if a little sleepy with indifference. She glanced at Larry, sitting across from her at the white-draped table. He too looked the very essence of languid ease, although she knew that his insides were just as knotted as hers.

She and Larry were closing in for the kill, and neither of them had any way of knowing whether or not the quarry was going to escape.

'It's a game,' Larry had told her forcefully in the yellow-and-black Rolls-Royce on the way to this meeting. 'Just don't forget that. It's just a poker game and, though the stakes are high, forget they're even there. Remember, you win some and you lose some. The only trick is to win more often than you lose.'

But that, she thought now, was easier said than done.

This particular 'poker game' was not taking place in a casino or the smoky back room of a seedy bar. They were seated at a long dining table in the lavish banquet room of the Shelburne Hotel on Fifth Avenue and Sixty-Second Street. Besides the two of them, the other 'players' were four lawyers, two representing Elizabeth-Anne and two representing Milton Shelburne, an accountant for each of them, as well as a representative from each of their respective banks.

Elizabeth-Anne glanced at Milton Shelburne. He was their quarry, and a formidable one. He was tall, with a paunchy stomach that kept him a foot back from the table. His black, olive eyes were shrewd, his thinning dark hair combed back, and his moustache was well-trimmed. He wore a custom-made suit, and heavy gold cufflinks shone from under his pin-striped cuffs. He looked every inch a wealthy and powerful man, and the pungent Havana cigar he was smoking only reinforced that image. Although Elizabeth-Anne realized that he was in all likelihood even more nervous than she or Larry, he did not show it either. In fact, despite the stakes, everyone at the table looked sedate enough for a church social.

Elizabeth-Anne was dying to check the time, but she didn't glance at her wristwatch. She reiterated over and over to herself just how important it was to give the impression that she and Larry believed time was of no consequence. They had to lull Milton Shelburne into a false sense of security, as though there were no pressure to finish the negotiation quickly. If they didn't, Shelburne might get wise and manage to wiggle out of their trap by, somehow, working out a better last-minute deal with one of the other bidders who had since dropped out.

As things stood, it was the most peculiar negotiation Elizabeth-Anne had ever, and would ever, partake in. To begin with, it had come as a totally unexpected, eleventh hour sale, although she was not supposed to know that. She and Larry had been in New Jersey, finally buying the Tourist Court whose purchase she had delayed, along with her wedding, after she'd discovered Charlotte-Anne's affair with Mickey Hoyt. Charlotte-Anne had departed for Europe a week before, and Elizabeth-Anne had finally felt ready again for business. As soon as she had gotten the message that the Shelburne had unexpectedly come on the market, she had insisted they change their plans. Instead of going on to Baltimore, Washington, and Philadelphia to check on Elizabeth-Anne's hotels there, they had hurriedly returned to New York. After an all night session with her lawyers and accountant, a bleary-eyed Elizabeth-Anne had met with her bankers at nine that morning, then gotten busy and called around town.

And had hit pay dirt.

One of her many contacts had the lowdown on Milton Shelburne, and had given it to her. It was supposed to be a well-kept secret, but the word was that Shelburne was in a very bad state. True, it was the word of only one source, but Elizabeth-Anne had trusted her contact implicitly in the past and it had paid off. So now she felt confident that no matter what impression Shelburne projected, there was no way he could hold out. He had until five o'clock of that very afternoon to come up with a buyer, or else all would be lost.

At a few minutes to five, he would take whatever they offered.

Elizabeth-Anne knew that she had to have the Shelburne Hotel. It was the kind of opportunity that arose only once in a lifetime. The Shelburne was located two blocks north of the Hotel Pierre, and it took up an entire city block. The imposing structure had been designed in 1887 by Henry Janeway Hardenbergh, the same man who had given New York the Dakota Apartments and the Plaza Hotel. But nowhere was Mr. Hardenbergh's genius as readily evident as at the Shelburne Hotel. The sprawling lobby could have come straight from a Renaissance palace, with its gracefully arched ceilings and triforium walkways. But it was the huge central courtyard which made the structure so distinctive. Elizabeth-Anne could already picture the fantasy jungle she would create under that soaring ceiling of skylights at the Shelburne, rich with lush palms, splashing fountains, and masses of potted orchids. But the one thing she and most every New Yorker agreed was the building's *tour de force* were its lofty, majestic twin spires that rose high above the street to scrape the clouds.

She knew that if she did not get the Shelburne today, in all probability it would forever elude her.

The time to buy property and buildings had never been better. All over the country, the real estate market was as depressed as it had ever been. Without an end to the Depression in sight, buildings went begging. Even so the Shelburne was one of those unique buildings that, unless you were blessed with exceptional luck, was forever out of reach.

But luck was smiling upon Elizabeth-Anne. She could *feel* it. In order to make buying the Shelburne an affordable reality, all she and Larry had to do was drag out the negotiations until a few minutes before five.

She felt a cramping stab of pain in her intestines. How much longer did she have to wait until five o'clock? She felt she had been sitting at the table forever. At ten o'clock that morning, three other parties had converged upon the Shelburne along with her in order to bid on the hotel. Negotiations had dragged on all morning, and Milton Shelburne had been playing it close to the chest, never budging from his asking price. Elizabeth-Anne, who knew of his financial predicament, couldn't help but admire him for his bravado, but the three other bidders eventually got annoyed. One by one, they had left, two of them withdrawing their initial offers and the third hotelier telling Shelburne that his offer still stood, should he be interested.

Elizabeth-Anne's hopes had soared. What the hotelier hadn't realized was that Shelburne only had until five o'clock to conclude the deal. What remained now was in the hands of fate. If Shelburne reached that hotelier in time, then the Shelburne Hotel would elude her. On the other hand, if he couldn't reach him . . .

She exhaled slowly, silently. It occurred to her that it was poetic justice that both she and Milton Shelburne should wear the exact same armor – seemingly infinite patience and a look of total nonchalant ease.

So far, she, Larry, and their two laywers had not so much as submitted a single monetary bid. They had merely sat back quietly and let the others haggle. She had planned to wait until the very last minute, as if she would then top the highest offer Shelburne had received. She had felt, correctly, that any bargaining on their part would only serve to push the price up. Their silence had not gone unnoticed by the others, and especially not by Milton Shelburne. Their presence only seemed to weaken the others' positions and strengthen Shelburne's, who believed he would be rewarded for holding out. It never occurred to him that Elizabeth-Anne had discovered his Achilles' heel.

In prosperous times Shelburne's fortune had accumulated to a staggering sum, but very little was composed of real money. He had owned large parcels of commercial real estate through Manhattan and Brooklyn, and had watched the Crash, the Depression, and the banks gobble up his properties, one by one. His credit had always been good, and he had originally amassed his wealth by overextending at the banks; he was well-known for buying marginally and for making swift thrust-and-parry deals. By keeping every building and property he owned totally separate from the others, each run by a differently incorporated company, he had set things up so that should the worst ever happen and any number of his companies topple, the rest would remain staunch and strong. But even he had not been able to predict a calamity on the scale of the Depression. His empire did not, perhaps, topple all at once, but it fell ignobly in bits and pieces. The Shelburne Hotel was his last holding, as well as the single most valuable piece of real estate he had owned. As the others had been, it was mortgaged to the hilt. Ever since his empire had begun crumbling he had quietly sought a buyer for the Shelburne, but one thing or another had always come up. Either his asking price had been too high, or his potential buyers bowed out at the last moment. When he had finally found someone serious, a cruel twist of fate had ruined that opportunity as well. The day the papers were to be signed, his buyer had found himself bankrupt overnight. It was one of the harsh realities of the Depression, but the fact that those occurrences were commonplace hadn't made it any easier a pill to swallow. It seemed to him that his financial future was doomed.

Until now.

His decision to auction off the hotel had created sufficient interest for four potential buyers to show up and bid on it. The fact that two of them had backed off and walked out didn't worry him. After all, one offer still stood. And, from what he had heard about Elizabeth-Anne, she was grabbing up property all over the place as if there were no tomorrow. Her presence could only indicate one thing: She was serious. She meant to end up with the Shelburne Hotel.

His fatal mistake was that he didn't know just how serious she was.

He glanced casually to his left trying to read her thoughts. Just as she had all day, she appeared calm, quiet. She sat tall and straight, her dark suit, pale blouse, and rope of pearls conveying an air of sedate financial solidity. Her aquamarine eyes were veiled with a faraway look and the slight, dark circles caused by the past two grueling days were artfully hidden by carefully applied powder. She looked, for all the world, like a spectator watching a stage play with only the mildest amusement.

Aware that Shelburne's gaze had shifted to her, Elizabeth-Anne kept herself composed. When she felt his eyes wandering away from her, she glanced at Larry. Then she frowned at some papers, and shuffled them in front of her. It was a subtle way to check her wristwatch without appearing to do so. She pursed her lips thoughtfully before finally speaking.

'Of course,' Elizabeth-Anne said slowly, 'we would all like to get this matter settled as quickly as possible.' She frowned at the papers in front of her. 'What worries me, and I know it worries Mr. Hochstetter also, is that the patronage of the Shelburne has declined markedly over the past year. And from glancing through the books, the operating expenses are very high. The Shelburne requires an extraordinarily large working capital.'

'The Shelburne is a first class hotel,' Milton Shelburne put in smoothly. 'The staff could always be trimmed.' He inclined his head in Elizabeth-Anne's direction and permitted himself a faint smile. 'From what I have heard about you Mrs. Hale, you're very proficient at trimming costs without visibly sacrificing any services.'

'Be that as it may, the Shelburne is an entirely different ball game from my other hotels.' Elizabeth-Anne rattled the papers in her hand. 'My other hotels are more modest and easily manageable. The Shelburne, as you know, is one of this city's largest hotels with over seven hundred suites and rooms, many of which require extensive remodeling and renovation. The public areas have become rather seedy as well and require a considerable investment.

Frankly, I'm worried that I may have a difficult time operating the hotel as well as paying a heavy price for it.'

'But you haven't even mentioned a price yet,' the senior partner of Shelburne's two lawyers pointed out.

'No, I haven't.' Elizabeth-Anne picked up a pencil and scribbled a few doodles in the margin of one of her papers. Then she pulled back her suit sleeve and looked pointedly at her wristwatch. 'Gentlemen, I'm afraid it is getting late. I suggest we break off for today and continue again in the morning.' She made as though to rise.

'Wait.' The blood drained from Shelburne's face. 'I'm sure we can come to some sort of satisfactory agreement.' Shocked at Elizabeth-Anne's suggestion, he was for the first time feeling the noose of panic tightening around him.

Elizabeth-Anne held her breath and watched Larry closely. The trap was about to be sprung, but Larry's face was completely devoid of expression. Even now that the time to pull off the coup was at hand, no matter how much excitement they felt, they would keep it subdued and continue about business in a totally unemotional and impassive manner. Business, Elizabeth-Anne and Larry both knew, allowed no room for emotions.

'In that case, Mr. Shelburne,' Elizabeth-Anne said quietly, 'let me make you our offer.' She glanced at Shelburne's banker and his lawyers. 'Gentlemen, I am offering to assume the mortgage on the Shelburne as it stands now. I also offer to pay you, Mr. Shelburne, the amount of sixty-five thousand dollars in cash.'

Shelburne looked as though he had been struck. Then he gave a hollow, mirthless little laugh. 'You're joking, of course.'

Elizabeth-Anne shook her head. 'No, Mr. Shelburne. I never joke about business matters. I am dead serious.'

'But . . . but that is preposterous,' Shelburne sputtered.

'Is it?' Elizabeth-Anne folded her hands in front of her and leaned across the table toward Shelburne, her eyes gleaming with a hardness Larry had never before seen, and which he now found extremely interesting. It emphasized to him just how much she really had learned and grown since they had met.

'Mr. Shelburne,' Elizabeth-Anne said patiently, 'the outstanding unpaid mortgage on this hotel is still a quarter of a million dollars. When you purchased it, you paid a hundred and fifty thousand dollars down, and over the past ten years, you have paid off another quarter of a million of the principal. I needn't remind you that money is in short supply at the moment, or that the market for real estate has plunged. And much as I hate to have to bring it up, I have checked around, Mr. Shelburne. You are in no position to bargain, nor to turn down the offered sum. You are, in fact, dirt poor. If you do not accept my offer, which will at least pay you sixty-five thousand dollars, not only will you lose this hotel in . . . ' Elizabeth-Anne pointedly consulted her watch, then looked back up and met Shelburne's eyes, 'in twelve minutes, but you will not even have the satisfaction of having sold it. You will see it repossessed, and who knows? I might even get a better bargain if I wait a few more minutes.' She paused, and her voice grew softer, almost pitying. 'Look at it this way, Mr. Shelburne. You have one of two choices open to you: make sixty-five thousand dollars, or lose everything.'

Shelburne was trapped, and he knew it. 'Who told you about five o'clock?' he whispered hoarsely, his face pale. 'Did you?' His head snapped accusingly toward his banker, a gaunt, brittle man with a high, sloping forehead. At the moment, he projected not so much the image of a banker as that of an undertaker.

'No.' The man answered, shaking his head and clearly miffed by the suggestion. 'The First Mutual Bank of Manhattan, as you well know, is the very soul of discretion.'

'Well, somebody must have leaked the word,' Shelburne snapped. He was suddenly sweating profusely, beads of perspiration popping out all over his forehead. He tugged his handkerchief out of his breast pocket and unceremoniously mopped his face. Then he got unsteadily to his feet and turned to Elizabeth-Anne. 'I'm afraid that I must refuse your offer,' he told her with weak dignity. He smiled stiffly at her, then at his banker. 'I think you are both forgetting that I've had another offer for four times that amount earlier this very afternoon.' He allowed the faintest smile of relief to hover at the corners of his lips. 'And that offer still stands. You all heard it being made.'

'We heard it, yes, and you stand to make four times what I offer *if* you accept before five o'clock,' Elizabeth-Anne reminded him. 'Don't forget, after five the bank will repossess the Shelburne, and it will belong to them. Not to you.'

Milton Shelburne stared at her, realization dawning. 'You tricked me,' he hissed. 'You dragged things out all afternoon just to trap me.'

Elizabeth-Anne looked at him with a stony expression. 'Call it whatever you wish,' she said easily, 'but remember, our offer still stands. Until five o'clock on the dot, that is. You have ten minutes, Mr. Shelburne, in which to conclude your deal with the other party. Whether or not you decide to deal with us is entirely up to you. However, at precisely five o'clock, if you have not accepted our offer, it will be withdrawn.'

Shelburne turned to his lawyers. 'She can do this? And get away with it?'

They nodded wordlessly, avoiding his eyes.

'This . . . this is sheer *lunacy*.' Shelburne's voice rose with indignation.

With deliberate slowness, Elizabeth-Anne pushed back her chair, got to her feet, walked to the foot of the table, and picked up the telephone. Whipping the cord around, she brought the telephone to Milton Shelburne and set it on the table in front of him. 'You are welcome to call the other party and accept their offer immediately.' She looked at Shelburne challengingly. 'However, should that deal fall through for any reason, you are still free to accept our offer, as long as it is before five o'clock. Either way, you can't lose.' She amended that statement gravely: 'Well, at least not everything.'

Shelburne licked his lips and stared down at the telephone.

'Call,' Shelburne's banker urged. 'For God's sake, Mr. Shelburne, place the call.'

With trembling fingers, Shelburne reached for the telephone and dialed.

For a moment, Elizabeth-Anne had to shut her eyes. It was almost more than she could bear. This was not business. This was a jungle with no rules and no laws. She felt heavy with guilt, at the same time she knew her actions were necessary, *fair*. Hadn't it been Shelburne himself who had refused the other offer to begin with because he had been so certain she would top it? His greed and lack of acumen was causing his downfall, not her.

'Get me through to Mr. Spencer.' Shelburne's voice was high-pitched with tension. 'Tell him it's urgent.'

Everyone looked away from him, unable to witness his growing misery.

'What do you mean he hasn't come back this afternoon? He left here hours ago! You've *got* to know where I can reach him . . . ' His voice cracked. ' . . . Well, if he gets in before five o'clock, have him call me.'

Elizabeth-Anne let out a weary sigh. There was no sweetness in this victory. Her intestines were as knotted as they had been all day.

Shelburne let the receiver drop from his hand. It landed on the table with a clatter as he sank back down into his chair.

The minutes seemed to crawl by. No one spoke. Everyone kept glancing at their watches and staring at the telephone.

The telephone did not ring. By 4.59, Mr. Spencer still had not called.

At precisely five o'clock, Milton Shelburne buried his face in his hands. 'All right, Mrs. Hale,' he whispered hoarsely, his voice muffled by his fingers. 'I accept your offer.'

Just before nine o'clock Elizabeth-Anne finally laid down her pen and pushed the last of the papers away from her. 'There,' she said softly.

She didn't show it, but she couldn't remember a time when she'd been as relieved to get something over with. The two days she had now been awake, and the tension of the Shelburne negotiations, topped by Milton Shelburne's heart-wrenching defeat, had taken their toll on her.

Nothing sounded more pleasant than to go home, crawl into bed, and sleep as long as she pleased.

But she wasn't only tired. She felt frightened too. Sixty-five thousand dollars up front, as well as assuming a mortgage of a quarter of a million dollars, may have been a bargain, but the amount of money she had just spent staggered her. She knew too that refurbishing the hotel to its former grandeur – which she felt *must* be done, would require another staggering sum. Nor had any of her other properties been bought outright. All except the tourist court in Quebeck were partially financed. Larry's motto had always been to use OPM – Other People's Money – whenever possible. OPM had its definite advantages, to be sure. It could also, however, lead to disaster. A deeply rooted fear kept gnawing at her: should the rich vein at the gold mine peter out, and Horseshoe Investments collapse, she would find herself in the exact same straits as Milton Shelburne. 'Gentlemen,' she said in a weary but sure voice, 'I think it's time we called it a day, don't you?' She smiled thinly at them.

They nodded. Shelburne himself had left hours before, signing the necessary papers and leaving the rest to his lawyers. Now they, as well as the rest of his and Elizabeth-Anne's negotiating teams, placed their copies of the contracts in their briefcases, snapped them shut, and rose to their feet. Each man perfunctorily shook her hand and murmured congratulations before filing out of the room.

As soon as Elizabeth-Anne and Larry were alone, the big room seemed empty and oppressive. Elizabeth-Anne allowed herself to show just how drained and exhausted she was. She took a deep, noisy breath and sank down into the maroon leather chair she had occupied all day. Her eyes were burning in their sockets and she rubbed them with her knuckles.

'You're tired,' Larry said.

She nodded, tilted her head back, and shut her eyes.

Larry came over and stood behind her chair. He placed his hands on her shoulders. 'Let's go home,' he said. 'You've had a tough day.'

'I'll be all right,' she said. 'Just give me another minute.'

'We're in no hurry.' He began massaging her back, rubbing her knotted muscles with firm circular motions of his fingers. 'You don't look very happy,' he said, 'but that doesn't surprise me. It's like postpartum depression. I can't remember a time when I haven't felt depressed after pulling off a deal like this. Still, I must congratulate you. Together, we've managed one of the biggest business coups of the Depression. You bought this hotel for a fraction of its real market value.'

'I know that. And it bothers me.' She let out a strangled sigh as he continued massaging her back. 'Business is business, and I'll not forget that. It's Darwinism, pure and simple. The survival of the fittest. But I don't have to like it.'

'No, you don't.' He paused, his fingers suddenly still on her back. 'But do you think for an instant,' he asked her, 'that if the shoe were on the other foot Shelburne would have hesitated to take *you* to the cleaners?'

'No, I don't doubt that either.' She reached up, covered his hands with hers, and held them on her shoulders. 'I'm frightened, Larry.'

He chuckled, 'Why?'

'For one, the survival of the fittest. Today I was the fittest.' She twisted around to look up at him. 'But what about tomorrow? Where will I be then?'

He knew she didn't expect an answer. 'And the other reasons?' he asked.

'I suppose it's because the numbers all add up to so much. And because paying off what I owe is all tied in to Horseshoe Investments. Larry, what if the gold mine should dry up? What then?'

'Then we're both sunk,' he said grimly. 'But I don't think that will happen. Not for a long time. Bear in mind that in business you've got to run ahead of the tide, and that's exactly what you're doing. There are times to be conservative, and times to be daring. The trick is to know which way to lean. Today was one of the times to be daring, and it paid off.' He leaned down and kissed the nape of her neck. 'It's healthy never to grow overconfident, but you can only worry so much before you worry yourself sick.'

She nodded. 'I'll try and keep that in mind.' She smiled wanly.

'Anything else bothering you?'

'Many things. For one, I own a good chunk of real estate which is worthless should the bottom of this country's economy drop out any further.'

'The economy will pick back up, trust me.' He paused. 'Do you have any idea just how many depressions and recessions we've gone through in this country?'

She shook her head. 'No.'

'Well, listen to this, and then I'm sure you'll feel better,' he said. 'In 1869 we had what the financial community likes to call "Black Friday." It resulted from investors trying to corner the gold market.'

She gave a low, mirthless laugh. That was hitting just a little too close to home.

'In 1893,' he continued, 'we had another similar financial panic which resulted in a four-year depression. Then the same thing happened all over again in 1907. We've recovered each time, darling. Rest assured, the United States will pick itself up by its bootstraps and pull itself out of this Depression just like it has from all the others, or my name isn't Lawrence Hochstetter.'

'All right, you've convinced me. As long as there's enough money around for our guests to afford to stay at our hotels, I'll try not to worry too much.'

'That's the spirit.'

'Now, what about running all these hotels and tourist courts? Larry, they're scattered all over! I'm running myself ragged trying to keep up, and now we have the Shelburne, too. It's time we set up an umbrella company. As I've found out, I can't keep managing a growing empire this size all by myself. I'm spreading myself much too thin.'

'This umbrella company, whatever you choose to call it – ' Larry interjected.

' – Hale Hotels,' she said promptly.

He laughed. 'We've been married seven days, and you still insist upon using Hale instead of Hochstetter. They warned me about liberated women.'

'It's only because Zaccheus and I had the vision to start

242

the tourist court, which began all this. I owe it to his memory, Larry. And the children are Hales. This will give them something to grow up into. A chance to *be* somebody.'

'I know that,' he said gently, 'and I'm secure enough to accept it.'

Then Elizabeth-Anne's voice grew more businesslike. 'I can head up Hale Hotels. Directly under me, I'll have to have two or three good executives – vice presidents, I suppose – whom I can trust. Each will be responsible for running a certain number of the hotels and tourist courts, and they'll be answerable only to me. The individual managers of the hostelries, in turn, are answerable directly to the executives, unless, of course, I give a specific order and thereby supercede theirs. The rest of the staff of each individual hotel or tourist court is answerable to the managers. But any executive order, and especially an order from me, can supercede the manager's. You get the general idea?'

Larry nodded his assent. Tired though she was, the gears of Elizabeth-Anne's mind were clicking everything into place. 'In other words,' she concluded, 'we set up a chain of command, with me sitting at the top of the pyramid.'

He grinned. 'Just like Cleopatra, my sweet.'

She smiled. 'Now don't sweet talk me!' She poised a finger against her lips. 'I suppose it would be a good idea if we gave each executive a specific territory,' she said. 'He'll handle everything within that particular territory, and nothing else. Say one gets New York. Another has Pennsylvania and New Jersey, the other has Baltimore and Washington. That'll cut down on a lot of running back and forth. Maybe he should even be based in his area instead of here in New York.'

'That's a good idea,' he said admiringly. 'You catch on fast.'

Elizabeth-Anne's face grew pinched. 'But how do I know I can trust anyone else to wield so much power?'

'If you intend to keep expanding, you'll have to delegate authority and hope you can trust the people you hire. In fact, you'll have to even if you don't expand any further and just decide to keep managing the hotels and motels you own now.'

She nodded. 'And I don't think I'll have to worry about finding good executives. Not if I offer a decent salary and a good bonus to whoever drums up the most business. Nobody thrives on keen competition like an executive. And in these times, it's an employer's market. There are thousands of terrific executives out there, some of them out of work, and others looking for better jobs. That's what we'll do,' Elizabeth-Anne said with finality. 'But we have to make sure the executives we hire are *very* good. I only want the cream of the crop.' She paused. 'How long do you think it will be before we can set up the Hale Hotels umbrella corporation?'

'No more than a few days. A week at the most.'

She smiled. She was already beginning to feel a little less nervous, and her doubts were under control. But her physical weariness wasn't. As she and Larry continued to talk, her eyelids started to droop. She almost fell asleep sitting up when a knock came on the closed door. Startled, her eyes flew open. 'Come in,' she called out. She turned to Larry. 'Who can *that* be?'

He stubbed out his cigarette and got to his feet just as the door opened. Two girls, one blonde and one brunette, stood in the doorway. From their dress, Elizabeth-Anne saw they were obviously prostitutes.

She stared at them in disbelief. What had come of this hotel, she wondered, to let girls wander in off the streets? And why hadn't the hotel detectives intercepted them? The next thing you knew, they would be working the lounges or sitting in the lobby drumming up business. This was one thing she would have to put a stop to.

But before she could open her mouth, Larry was striding across the room toward them. She watched in amazement as he took out his wallet and counted out five crisp one-hundred-dollar bills for each of them. They smiled at him, tucked the money into their bosoms, and blew him a kiss before turning and leaving.

'What was all that about?' Elizabeth-Anne asked. Then suddenly it dawned on her. For the first time since they had met, she felt she could murder Larry. 'You didn't,' she hissed at him in a shocked whisper.

He looked at her, his face cool and expressionless. 'I did,' he admitted lighting another cigarette. 'You didn't really expect me to leave anything to chance, did you?'

'Oh, Larry! It makes everything so . . . so cheap.'

'Why? Because when Spencer walked out, the girls had been arranged for? Perhaps it was ruthless, but sometimes the end justifies the means. It was a gamble, but it paid off, didn't it? While Shelburne was trying to get hold of Spencer so desperately, he never even suspected that he was right upstairs.' He grinned.

'I'm so *ashamed*,' Elizabeth-Anne whispered. Despite the warmth of the room she hugged herself with her arms and shivered. 'You lured him into a sexual trap just so Shelburne couldn't find him.' She shook her head miserably. 'And I thought he simply couldn't reach Spencer.'

'Elizabeth-Anne, it worked. You must remember that. Because of this, a lot of people turned out happy. Spencer had a wonderful opportunity to release his tension without his wife ever finding out about it. The girls got paid twice, once by him and once by me. And you got the hotel for a song.'

Elizabeth-Anne shut her eyes. She couldn't believe what she was hearing. Her victory had been sour enough before finding this out. Now it had curdled completely.

Wearily, she pushed herself to her feet. They might as well go home now. Just remaining in the hotel left the taste of bile in her mouth.

It had been a day of surprises. Thank God the surprises were over.

But when they got back to the Madison Squire, the desk clerk handed her a cable. She tore it open, then realized that the surprises had just begun.

She stared down at the message and had to read it and reread it several times before it sank in:

MAMMA PLEASE DO NOT BE ANGRY STOP HAVE MARRIED AND AM VERY HAPPY AND

VERY MUCH IN LOVE STOP I AM NOW THE PRINCIPESSA DI FONTANESI STOP I WILL WRITE IN DETAIL SOON STOP PLEASE DO NOT BLAME ROBYN STOP I LOVE YOU VERY MUCH AND HOPE YOU GIVE US YOUR BLESSINGS STOP MUCH LOVE CHARLOTTE-ANNE AND LUIGI DI FONTANESI

8

Three thousand, five hundred miles across the Atlantic in the dark, mountainous Alps, the train's iron wheels protested with a long, ear-splitting screech as it braked to a halt. The express was one carriage longer than usual; coupled to its rear was the luxurious, royal blue private coach emblazoned with the coat of arms of the di Fontanesis. The carriage's interior was like a compact, luxurious house, with a parlor, bedroom, small kitchenette, bath, and quarters for the private steward.

In the small bedroom paneled in rich, Carpathian burled elm, Charlotte-Anne was awakened more by the sudden stillness than by the drawn-out screech itself. She opened her eyes. She could hear voices barking sharply outside on the platform. She sat up. Then, careful not to awaken Luigi, she got out of bed and slipped into the rose colored robe Luigi had bought her in Paris. She tied the sash around her waist and went over to the window, parted the heavily fringed, thick brocade curtains, and looked out.

She had to shield her eyes. The platform, the cluster of buildings, and the train were bathed by blinding floodlights which gave everything a startling surreal quality.

The train had stopped at the Italian border.

She slid down the window and leaned out. The mountain air felt thin and chilly. Everywhere she looked she could see uniformed officials and border guards wearing glossy high riding boots, peaked, visored caps, and flared breeches. The uniforms looked very official, and somehow very intimidating.

She heard the soft bang of a door. Then she saw Aldo, the white-jacketed private steward of the di Fontanesis' coach, hop down to the platform. He stopped to talk to some officials directly under her window and she repeatedly caught the words 'Prince di Fontanesi, Principessa di Fontanesi' amid his rapid-fire burst of Italian. She saw him offering them his, Luigi's, and her own passports, but the officials shook their heads and didn't even bother to check them. Then one of them happened to look up. The moment he saw her, he touched his visor with his fingertips, murmured *'Scusi,'* and moved on to the next car.

She frowned thoughtfully to herself. When the *Ile de France* had docked in Le Havre, her and Luigi's faces had been carefully scrutinized and compared with their passport photos. And again, when the train crossed the Swiss border, they had been required to go through rigorous border formalities. The ever-efficient Swiss had even given the private carriage a thorough search. What they intended to find, she had no idea. The fact that the coach belonged to the Di Fontanesis, or that Luigi was a prince, hadn't seemed to matter in the least.

But to the Italians it obviously mattered a great deal. They didn't bother to glance at the passports. No officials walked through the coach. It was as though she and Luigi enjoyed diplomatic immunity. It was the first time she was made truly aware of the awesome power the di Fontanesis wielded in their own country. She was not yet used to the courtesies accorded to the nobility and she found it peculiarly unsettling.

She was about to push up the window when a commotion further down the platform caught her attention. A young man had jumped off one of the carriages in the front of the train and had broken into a run. The border guards did not bother to chase him. It was unnecessary as other guards all around the platform easily encircled him. He sensed that he was trapped, stopped running, and raised his arms above his head.

With a shock, Charlotte-Anne watched as one of the guards slipped the revolver out of his gleaming holster. The guard stretched out his arm, aimed, and fired a single shot.

The crack of the gunshot reverberated like thunder. The young man jerked as the bullet slammed into his back, and the force of the shot threw him forward. She winced as he fell heavily to the concrete. He landed on his face and lay without moving.

Two guards ambled over to him. One of them had his hands on his hips, the other was replacing the revolver in his holster. Without warning, they gave the man a sharp kick and flipped him over on his back. The young man slowly raised his head. His face was screwed up in pain. The guard raised his boot, and with all the force he could muster, slammed it down on the prone man's face.

Charlotte-Anne heard the agonized scream. She could almost feel the crunching of her own facial bones and felt the gore rise in her throat.

She ducked her head back inside and slammed the window shut. For a moment she leaned back against it and took a series of deep breaths. After a moment the nausea began to subside.

She heard a movement in the passage outside the bedroom. Crossing over to the door, she opened it and saw Aldo, the steward, returning to his quarters.

Aldo gave a little bow. 'Yes, Principessa?'

She glanced behind her. Incredibly, Luigi had slept through the gunshot and the screams. She closed the door so the sound of their voices wouldn't awaken him. 'Aldo,' she whispered in a trembling voice, 'they just shot a man . . . '

Aldo nodded, his features carefully composed. For a moment, she imagined a flash of hatred in his dark eyes, but when she looked closely, it was gone. Or it had never been there in the first place. 'I saw, Principessa,' Aldo said in his heavily accented English. 'It was probably an *anarchista*.'

'But . . . but there was no need to shoot him. He had surrendered.'

The steward shrugged. 'The leader of every country has many enemies. Il Duce has his fair share also.'

'But . . . couldn't they have just arrested him? Did they have to shoot him in the back?'

Also looked down at the floor. 'This is Italy, Principessa.

The laws are different here from in America.'

'But – '

'Try to forget it, Principessa,' he advised softly. 'Pretend that it never happened.'

She stared at him. 'But it *did*. I can't just stand by – '

'If there is nothing else . . . ' Aldo gave another little bow and went on to his quarters. She watched him leave, then slowly returned to the bedroom. She glanced at Luigi, who was sleeping soundly on his side.

She slipped out of her robe and crawled back into bed. The mattress shifted and Luigi stirred and turned over on his other side, facing her. His eyes opened and he squinted sleepily at her. 'You are awake.'

'Yes.' She nodded. 'We're at the border.' She took a deep breath. 'Luigi – '

He yawned. 'Hmmmm?'

'They just shot a man.'

'Who did?'

'The border guards.'

'Do not worry about it,' he said with a yawn. 'No one would dare to shoot you.'

She looked at him with shock. 'That's not what worries me. They shot him in the *back*. An unarmed man. It was terrible – '

His voice was a soft murmur. 'Do not concern yourself with such things. It was official business. Do not involve yourself.' He coiled an arm around her. 'Tomorrow is a long day. Try to get some sleep. You will need it.'

She stared at him, but his eyes were already closed. Then she heard his soft snores. He was fast asleep again.

Even long after the train had begun to speed into the darkness again, sleep eluded her. Finally she slipped out of bed, put her robe back on, and walked to the plush parlor at the front of the carriage. For a long time she sat on a tufted velvet armchair by the window. The Italian Alps were majestic and deceptively peaceful in the morning light. The sky seemed clear. The landscape was somehow sharper, more dappled with light than any she had ever seen before.

Italy.

She was in Italy now, yet another country where she had never set foot. The country which was her home.

She shuddered as the real significance of her marriage hit her for the first time. She was not just any woman any more. She was a princess, a member of one of the most powerful families in all Italy. She was an important part of a culture which was entirely new to her. This was now her home, a land ruled by fascism. She had read about Mussolini in the papers back in New York, but he hadn't made much of an impression on her. Italy had always seemed so far away. She had never thought Il Duce or fascism would ever really affect her. But now it did, and she realized it was a situation that disturbed her deeply. She had witnessed a man being killed, or at least seriously wounded, treated sadistically. This was a horror of fascism she hadn't known about. Yet for a di Fontanesi, life was coddled. Something as routine as a passport check had been waived.

What was it Aldo had said?

'This is Italy. The laws are different here.'

She wondered if she could adjust to this new climate. What kind of laws condoned outright cruelty and murder? What kind of country would be her new home, anyway? She knew fascism well enough now for it to be repugnant to her. Could she live under its iron fist?

Many dark shadows and doubts flitted batlike through her mind. She was filled with dread. She couldn't help wondering how her mother had taken the news of her marriage. Surely she'd long since received the cable, sent two days earlier, from Le Havre.

She smiled to herself grimly. Knowing her mother, she'd probably be furious, but there was nothing she could do. Charlotte-Anne was, after all, the Principessa di Fontanesi, and her mother would simply have to adjust to that fact. She might have been born a Hale, but she was a Hale no longer.

But much as her mother's reaction concerned her, and the scene at the border horrified her, neither was truly the cause of her anxiety now. Rather, she was thinking of the night before.

Aldo had turned down the lace-edged sheets, which Luigi informed her had been embroidered by the nuns of the order of Our Lady of Peace. After she and Luigi had had a nightcap of champagne, they had made love. She had felt strange, making love on sheets embroidered by nuns who had taken vows of silence.

Then, just before they'd gone to sleep, Luigi had told her the thing that now filled her with such dread. She shuddered again even now, her heart jumping with icy fear.

Luigi had not yet informed his parents of their shipboard wedding.

He was bringing home a bride no one expected.

9

The nearer the winding country road brought them to the ancestral home of the di Fontanesis, the more Charlotte-Anne sensed her husband coming to life. An undercurrent of excitement emanated from him, his eyes shining with an intense pride. It only served to make Charlotte-Anne feel very much the outsider, and to deepen her doubts.

For him, there were memories around every turn. Proudly he pointed out the sights to her. Here he had once been thrown from a horse; there his family's properties started, continuing for twenty kilometers as far as the eye could see blanketing the hills, there were their olive groves; those shorter, well-tended green furrows were vineyards; that entire village had paid annual rent to the di Fontanesis for the past four hundred years. Of course, he explained, the rent was still being collected only because of its long, time-honored tradition. It was the family's varied other business interests - notably banking and industry - upon which its real fortune was based.

In Rome, their private railroad car had been disconnected from the train, and they had spent the night at the di Fontanesi villa bordering the Borghese Gardens. Then they had driven the remaining seventy-five miles southeast to the country estates of the di Fontanesis in the shiny new red Bugatti which had been waiting for Luigi in Rome. After Larry's stately yellow-and-black Rolls-Royce, riding in the smaller, sporty Bugatti convertible was, Charlotte-Anne thought to herself, like taking a ride on a roller coaster. Especially with Luigi at the wheel. He was an expert driver, but a fast one. Along with aviation, racing was his great love, and although she constantly begged him to slow down, he only laughed.

The closer they got to his home, the faster he seemed to go, which increased Charlotte-Anne's discomfort because she was not nearly as eager to reach the palazzo as he was. She was increasingly nervous and worried, convinced that he should have let his parents know about their wedding. She should have insisted upon it. What kind of reception could a mystery bride expect? In her mind she conjured up a vision of his parents, grim and aristocratic: his father, the Prince Antonio, a thin aesthete with a threatening, almost ecclesiastic demeanor; his mother, the Princess Marcella, a Medici descendent with a cunning, cold nature. The di Fontanesis could trace their lineage back to the twelfth century; one of their ancestor's fifteenth-century offspring had even been pope.

Despite her fearful anticipation, she couldn't help admire the beauty of the landscape they passed through. Between the villages, they drove along humpbacked hills, their sunny sides clad with the green vineyards which had been reclaimed from the reluctant, rocky soil and cultivated over many centuries, their shadier sides grayish-green with olive groves. Here and there rose the occasional, piercing spires of the stately cypress trees. Tiny rambling villages precariously crowned the hilltops or nestled deep in the valleys. Everywhere along the twisting road, local farmers tended their fields with the same implements their ancestors had used. As they drove past, the farmers would lay down their tools and stare at the bright, fast car with expressions of wonder.

Each time they entered a village, Luigi slowed down impatiently, though Charlotte-Anne was grateful for it.

Chickens strutted the narrow, dusty streets, pecking the ground for food, until the red car sent them fluttering and squawking. Charlotte-Anne leaned her head back and stared up at the buildings. The stucco was peeling, exposing the thick stone walls beneath. In every village, tall stone church steeples towered over the roof tops, which were speckled with different colored tiles. It was a land where time seemed to have stopped centuries before. The border incident Charlotte-Anne had witnessed began to seem further and further away.

'I didn't think it would be so beautiful here,' she said.

Luigi glanced sideways at her. They had just left a village behind them and were speeding along an open stretch of road. 'What?' he called over the rush of the wind and the roar of the engine.

She cupped her hands and shouted, 'I said it's beautiful!'

He grinned then, and once again she was struck by just how handsome he was, how he could simply look at her and make her melt.

Abruptly he slowed down and pulled the car over. As he engaged the handbrake, she looked at him in surprise. 'Is something wrong?' she asked.

He shook his head. 'We are almost there now. It is only a few minutes further.'

She nodded.

He reached for her hand and held it. 'You are nervous?'

She grimaced, then nodded again.

'There is nothing to worry about,' he assured her. 'My parents do not generally eat young ladies for dinner.' And with that, he threw the car back into gear and they hurtled around one last curve, where he abruptly braked, turned right with a protesting screech of the tires, and swung off the road onto an even narrower drive that was smooth and well paved.

'This is it,' he exclaimed as the car burst past two enormous stone pillars guarding the entry to the property. Charlotte-Anne twisted around in the red leather seat and looked back. Each receding pillar was topped with a gray, crumbling fragment of a marble statue.

The road wound, gently climbing up the hillside through

the olive groves. Both shoulders were planted with cypresses which flashed past the fast moving car.

'Is that the house?' she called, pointing to her left. Across the valley another hill, half a mile away, was crowned with what looked like a rambling, yellow stone fortress complete with crenelated wall and towers.

His eyes flicked sideways at her. 'No, that is the Convent of the Order of Our Lady of Peace, the ones who embroider our linen. Our house, or I should say the house of my parents, is directly above us. When the wind blows from the west, you can hear the church bells from the convent.'

The road rose higher, making its way up the hill in an ever-rising spiral. Charlotte-Anne looked down, and between the cypresses, she could see the green, gently sloping vineyards and olive groves, and villages dotting the valley.

'Look up,' he said, pointing with his hand. He slowed the car down to a snail's crawl and her eyes followed his pointing finger, getting her first glimpse of the ancestral home of the di Fontanesis.

Jutting out above them was a broad, balustraded terrace. The house itself was recessed, half-hidden behind a cluster of cypresses, but even from the little she could see, she realized it was of dishearteningly palatial proportions. Squatting atop the leveled hilltop, it commanded a sweeping, three-hundred-and-sixty degree view of the entire countryside.

The central portion of the house, she learned once they came around the next bend, was four stories tall. Three soaring arches on the ground floor created a recessed loggia, flanked by three tall French doors on either side. Directly above that, on the second floor, three massive, arched windows mirrored the first floor. The third floor was made up entirely of octagonal windows, except in the center, where the second-floor arches ended. The top floor had three smaller windows; from under the center one a flagpole carried the fluttering crest of the di Fontanesis.

Two long wings, each two stories in height, stretched out from each side of this central pavilion, and with the roofline and the staggered effect of the facade the palace gave the impression of being a gently sloping pyramid, white everywhere except for the gabled roofs, which were tiled as were all the houses in the region.

Only when the car curved further around the hill did Charlotte-Anne notice, with awe, that what she had previously glimpsed was only the tip of the iceberg. All four sides of the palace were identical; the palace was perfectly square, with an open, central couryard. The building was enormous, the size of one of her mother's grand hotels. She took a deep breath and tried to stifle her growing trepidation.

'I grew up here,' Luigi said, still driving at a snail's pace. 'Of course, this was not my only home. The Villa della Rose, in which we spent last night in Rome, is where I usually live now, unless I come here to visit my parents. Rome is where you and I shall be living. And then there are the other houses. The neoclassical palace my grandfather built on the shores of Lake Garda, the chalet in the Alps, and the palace in Venice. But this one is my favorite. All the locals call it Palazzo Bizzarria.'

'Palazzo Bizzarria? What does that mean?'

'The literal translation is The Bizarre Palace. Its official name, however, is the Palazzo di Cristallo, the Crystal Palace.'

She took her eyes off the approaching house long enough to turn and glance at him. 'But why? I don't see much glass other than the windows. Why not simply call it the Palazzo di Fontanesi?'

'You shall see soon enough.' He smiled mysteriously. 'There is, in fact, a Palazzo di Fontanesi. The palace in Venice is called that, but in Venice one simply calls a palazzo a Casa. Ca' for short, so it is the Ca' di Fontanesi.'

'I think,' she said, staggered, 'I'm slightly confused.'

'Do not be.' He laughed. 'You will sort it out soon enough.'

'You said that this house is your favorite. Why?'

'Because it *is* the crystal palace. And because of its history. You see, this is our ancestral seat, but there is nothing much left of that. My great-grandfather was a little . . . how do you say it? Touched?' He tapped his forehead.

'Touched.' She nodded. 'Yes.'

'The result of too much intermarriage among the other branches of our family, probably. He was our own Mad Ludwig. He had gotten it into his head to raze the original house, which I understand was splendid by any standards, in order to build this one. He had rather strange tastes, as you will see. He traveled a lot in his youth, and the Turkish palace of Dolmabahce on the Bosphorus affected him deeply. When he returned, he decided he had to have something just like it. Unfortunately, he tried to outdo the Sultan Abdul Mecid. Building this house, in fact, nearly bankrupted the family. Only the rentals coming in from the villagers and farmers saved my family from total financial ruin, and even that was almost not enough. As a result, although the tenants would now like to buy their properties from us instead of renting them, my family will not hear of it.' He shrugged. 'At the moment, we are very rich, but who knows? Maybe some time in the future the rental income will save the Fontanesis once again.'

She stared directly ahead now. They had crested the landscaped hill, and in front of her sprawled the Palazzo di Cristallo. It seemed to stare right back at her, its unblinking, dark, mullioned windows framed by ocher pediments.

The moment they pulled up in front of the arched loggia, the massive front doors opened. Before Luigi could even switch off the engine, an ancient couple came hurrying down the steps, their faces wide with happy smiles. 'Luigi!' they cried in thin, brittle voices.

Luigi hopped out of the car and quickly embraced them. 'Cinzia! Marco!'

He turned toward the car. Charlotte-Anne was getting out, the expression on her face one of palpable relief. Perhaps she had worried too much, she thought. Luigi had been right, after all. These people did not look like they would eat her for dinner.

'Your parents look very happy to see you,' she ventured with a hesitant smile when Luigi turned to her again.

He laughed then. 'My parents? No, no. Cinzia and Marco helped raise me, but they are not my parents. They are servants.'

She blushed crimson, realizing then just how much she had to learn. And until she did, she would be far better off keeping her mouth shut.

'So *this* is why it's called the Crystal Palace,' Charlotte-Anne marveled in a bare whisper as Luigi, who had passed his arm through hers, led her inside. Her faux pas of moments ago forgotten, she thrilled to the splendor which greeted her in the main hall. Luigi's great-grandfather might have been slightly mad, but the effect he had achieved was miraculous.

The grand marble double staircase rising before her was U-shaped and covered in deep Oriental rugs. The ceiling of the rotunda, four floors up, was glass and from it hung a massive cut-crystal chandelier, its countless, many faceted prisms sparkling in the sunlight. But what made the staircase of the Crystal Palace so magically unique was the balustrade, made up of glittering, swirling cut crystal, reinforced on the inside with delicate rods of brass.

'There are thirty-two thousand individual pieces of Baccarat crystal in the various staircases alone,' Luigi said. 'Five hundred candelabrum, and two hundred chandeliers are scattered throughout the palazzo. That one, however – ' he pointed to the chandelier suspended over the landing, ' – is the most magnificent by far. It is said to weigh more than a ton.'

She could only nod, her eyes darting about the cavernous hall. Everywhere, it seemed, marble pedestals held enormous crystal candelabra. The walls were either marble, or beveled mirror set into marble. Rare pieces of Roman antiquity looked out from marble niches. The elaborately carved cornices were gilded.

She disengaged her arm from his and took a few steps forward. Gazing up, she saw that each landing of the staircase was lined with marble columns sprouting gold-leafed, Corinthian capitals. And the balustrades of sparkling crystal rose four flights up. It was an icy splendor barely softened by the rich hued rugs, it hit upon that mad, secret nerve of the fantastic which was hidden deep in every mind.

'Do you like it?' Luigi asked at last.

She turned to him and swallowed. 'I-I could never have imagined anything like it.'

'Neither could I. Only seeing is believing. Now you know why this palazzo has earned both its official, and unofficial, names. It is crystal, and it is bizarre.'

'The most peculiar thing of all,' she said, 'is that it should be *here*, and not in Rome.'

'As I told you, my great-grandfather was quite peculiar. Rest assured, neither my grandfather, nor my father or I, inherited his particular madness.' He smiled. 'Come, let me take you up to our apartment. Marco will carry the luggage upstairs, and you will have a chance to freshen up before you meet my parents.'

10

The day was one she had no wish to repeat, ever.

They had left Rome in the late morning. Already exhausted by their quick stop in that ancient city, filled with the strange sights, sounds and smells of a foreign country, and then the long drive through the countryside, she found the overwhelming palazzo almost more than she could take. Its outlandishness soon became only another, nightmarish reminder of just how far removed she was from her own familiar, comfortable world.

Then she had met Luigi's parents. They at least spoke English, but the meeting was formally polite and very cool. They were everything she had imagined them to be: his father, stern and aristocratic, and his mother, meticulously well-groomed and cold. When they learned of the wedding, they had offered no congratulations. His father had ignored the news completely. His mother had simply raised her patrician eyebrows, and had then digested it in silence.

That evening, they ate in the huge dining room on plates of silver, a tablecloth of lace. Everything else, from the candelabra and serving platters down to the stemware and salt and pepper shakers, was, distressingly, of cut crystal. The conversation had been reserved, and immediately after the meal, the Principessa Marcella Luisella Uberti di Fontanesi had pushed back her throne-like dining chair, risen regally to her feet at the foot of the absurdly long table, and smiled coolly.

'Luigi, I am certain that you and your father have much to discuss,' his mother had said in the hesitant but excellent boarding school English she had learned long ago. 'We ladies shall retire to the music room to get acquainted while you two go on to the smoking room.' She had looked at Charlotte-Anne then, her lips composed in a slight, polite smile, but her eyes were a steely black which held little warmth.

Charlotte-Anne had turned pleadingly to Luigi, but he had only smiled at her and said, 'It is a good idea to get acquainted with your new mother-in-law.'

The Principessa had led the way to a surprisingly small, intimate salon where there was not so much as a stick of crystal in sight, a fact for which Charlotte-Anne was extremely grateful. The room was completely feminine, with fragile French furniture instead of the heavy, ornately carved Italian pieces elsewhere in the house. The decor was all done in pale tones of light blue with delicate gold striping. A huge grand piano angled out of one corner; a gilded harp stood in another.

'You would perhaps like a coffee?' the Principessa asked before they sat down.

'No, thank you,' Charlotte-Anne replied.

'Good. I never drink coffee in the evenings. I find it makes it difficult to sleep. Here in the country, we go to sleep very early.' She paused, then said, 'Please, have a seat.' The tiny woman gestured toward a settee and Charlotte-Anne sat down warily, her back erect. She wasn't aware of it, but it was the exact pose her mother would have adopted under similar circumstances.

The Principessa Marcella di Fontanesi was a fine-boned woman of fifty-seven, as beautiful as her tall, balding husband was handsome. It was easy for Charlotte-Anne to see where Luigi had gotten his looks. The long-waisted, well-built body of the athlete which he carried with such ease came from his father; the strong, sculpted features from his mother. Diminutive though she was, the Principessa did not give off an air of petiteness or helplessness. On the contrary, she seemed bigger than life with her well-groomed head of white hair, her severely tailored black suit, and the single strand of magnificent pear-shaped pearls around her throat. Her eyes were as darkly intense as Luigi's, but larger, more incisive. But Charlotte-Anne soon learned that her stately calm was deceptive: she was a shrewd, tense, and severe woman. From her, Luigi had inherited that not-so-subtle air of a panther ready to pounce.

'You are very beautiful, Miss Hale,' the Principessa began, remaining standing and pointedly looking down on Charlotte-Anne. 'I see why my son was attracted to you.'

Charlotte-Anne looked up at her and met those piercing black eyes without flinching. 'I am no longer a Hale, Principessa,' she said softly. 'I am a di Fontanesi.'

The Principessa looked at her and made an irritated gesture. 'That,' she said directly, 'is a matter of opinion, Miss Hale. It was a shipboard romance, a hasty civil wedding. One becomes a di Fontanesi only by being married in, and having the marriage blessed, by the Holy Mother Church.'

'That's all you think it is?' Charlotte-Anne asked, shocked. 'A lousy shipboard romance?'

'Come, come. Let us not fool ourselves, Miss Hale.'

Charlotte-Anne raised her chin stubbornly. 'Luigi and I love each other,' she said with fierce but quiet pride. 'We will love each other forever.'

A faint smile hovered on the Principessa's lips. '*Really.*' She crossed the room, leaned back against a little writing table, and folded her arms in front of her. The smile never left her lips. 'How much do you want?'

Charlotte-Anne looked startled. 'I beg your pardon?'

'I said,' the Principessa repeated patiently, 'how much money do you want in exchange for calling off this foolish marriage?'

'You're trying to buy me off?' Charlotte-Anne said with disbelief.

'In whatever currency pleases you. For some it is money. For others it is jewelry, or favors. Everyone has a price. Only the currency differs.'

'I don't believe this,' Charlotte-Anne said, springing to her feet and crossing the room. She towered over the shorter woman. 'I don't think you heard right,' she said. 'We are already married.'

The Principessa tilted her head back, her gaze still piercing. 'Are you, now? You're certain of that?'

Charlotte-Anne nodded. 'Of course I'm certain.'

The Principessa shook her head sadly, as though trying to get through to a stubborn, recalcitrant child. 'You forget one thing. You are now in Italy, Miss Hale,' she said in a quiet voice. 'The laws here are different. We are a Catholic country. Your shipboard wedding was a meaningless ritual.'

Charlotte-Anne narrowed her pale eyes. 'Well not for me it wasn't,' she snapped.

'Then you are deceiving yourself. And that is a pity.'

Charlotte-Anne's expression did not change. 'So what are you trying to tell me? That the marriage isn't recognized?'

'Ah. Now you are getting the point.'

'And Luigi . . . he knew it wouldn't be?'

'Surely you cannot think that my son is ignorant of the laws of his country and his church?'

The fight seemed to seep out of Charlotte-Anne. She felt suddenly dizzy. She didn't know if what the Principessa claimed was true, but she was frightened.

'It can't be true,' she told herself silently. 'Oh God, why do I have to face this creature alone? Why can't Luigi be here at my side now of all times?' Her shoulders slumped and her eyes fell wearily.

The Principessa seized upon the moment, misinterpreting Charlotte-Anne's desolate pain for defeat. 'Leave him now, while there is still time,' she whispered hoarsely. She dug her fingers claw-like into Charlotte-Anne's arms and shook her. 'You are merely infatuated with each other.

But love? What can you know of love? You are too young. When you are older, you will thank me for not letting you make this mistake.'

Charlotte-Anne jerked back, loosening the woman's painful grip. Slowly she shook her head, still in a state of shock. She knew now how wrong she had been to underestimate Luigi's parents. She hadn't expected them to welcome her, but even in her wildest nightmares she had not expected a battle such as this.

Defiantly she raised her chin. 'Principessa, I think we are agreed on one thing,' she said in a trembling voice. 'You do not like me, and I do not like you. So be it. However, I love Luigi.' She blinked back the tears which threatened to fill her eyes. 'I love him so much that I will fight to my dying day to keep him, and I believe in my heart that he will do the same for me. The way I see it, you have two choices left open to you. The di Fontanesis have power and influence. You will either accept us, and make certain our marriage is recognized, or you will lose your only son. I don't want your money or your favors. I don't care what your twisted mind may come up with, but I will never be bought off.'

'Call it what you will.' The Principessa's face was rigid with cold self-assurance. 'It is as I have said. Everyone has a price. You need only state yours.'

'Damn you, *I won't be bought off*.' Charlotte-Anne exploded in spite of her choked-back tears. 'Can't you get that through your head?'

'Do not be so emotional.'

Flushed and breathing hard, Charlotte-Anne whirled around and ran toward the door.

'Where are you going?' the Principessa called after her.

Charlotte-Anne spoke without turning around. 'I'm going upstairs to pack.' She paused, her fingers on the door handle. 'And as soon as I'm through, Luigi and I are returning to Rome. I can see we aren't welcome here.'

The Principessa laughed. 'You are bluffing.'

'Am I?' Charlotte-Anne let go of the door handle, clenched her hands at her sides, and retraced her steps towards Luigi's mother. 'Try me,' she challenged.

'Besides, we'll be far better off in Rome than in this . . . this museum of an ice palace. You know, I think in your own way, you're as mad as Luigi's great-grandfather. This place is addling your brain.' She paused and added slowly, 'Believe me, Luigi and I will be happy in Rome.'

'And Luigi's career?' The Principessa had recovered her momentary lapse into mild fear; her voice was once again smooth and well modulated. 'What about that? Il Duce has let it be known that he has great plans for Luigi.'

'What about them? Luigi loves flying and racing; he'd be content to do that for the rest of his life. So Il Duce wants him in the armed forces. So what? He'll either take him or leave him. And, anyway, from what I've seen so far, Luigi'll be a damn sight better off if he doesn't run around with that pack of murdering fascists.'

The Principessa gasped and her face went ashen. 'You fool,' she hissed. 'You would be best off to keep your political views to yourself. It's not safe to speak that way.'

'It isn't, is it?' Charlotte-Anne permitted herself a smile. 'Well, in that case I'd better run through this morgue and shout out my opinions before anyone gets the wrong idea. And then I'd better go from village to village, and city to city.'

'Please,' the Principessa urged quietly. 'Calm down.'

Charlotte-Anne felt like laughing and crying at once. What a farce this was, she thought. She had found the Principessa's two weaknesses: her height, which was why she hadn't taken a seat, and, more important, her immense fear of the fascists. Apparently the powerful di Fontanesis were not that powerful after all.

'You may be infallible around here, Principessa,' Charlotte-Anne said contemptuously, 'but I see I was wrong. You do have more than two choices open to you.'

'And what,' Luigi's mother asked, 'might else there be?'

'Specifically, I will promise to keep my political views to myself. *If* you stay out of our lives and stop trying to meddle.'

'And if I do not?'

'Then I'll shout from the rooftops. I'll make the biggest anti-fascist stink this country has ever seen.'

263

'You would not live for a day!'

'Without Luigi, life is not worth living for me. And believe me, if I go, I'll drag you and your entire family down along with me.'

The dark eyes shone with fear. 'Please, be reasonable,' the Principessa gasped.

'No, *you* be reasonable. I think you'll agree that we'd better start accepting each other's presence. I won't have my husband torn between his wife and his mother. Do I make myself clear?'

The Principessa stared at her with shocked hatred.

'We'll be polite and civil,' Charlotte-Anne continued. 'We don't have to pretend to love each other. We'll do our best to stay out of each other's way. And this, Principessa, had better be our last fight. Oh. For another thing, you might as well get used to calling me Charlotte-Anne instead of Miss Hale. Just as I'll have to get used to calling you "Mamma." '

The Principessa cringed.

'Now, I suggest you go and use all your influence to make certain that this marriage is recognized.'

And with that, Charlotte-Anne stormed out of the music room. She left a quivering Principessa Marcella Luisella Uberti di Fontanesi standing alone staring at the door.

As she hurried down the cold, gleaming marble corridor lined with crystal candelabra, Charlotte-Anne smiled grimly to herself. The Principessa had been both right and wrong, she thought to herself.

Everyone had a price.

Silence, it seemed, was golden. And as such, very expensive.

It had cost the Principessa her son.

The moment Charlotte-Anne left the music room, a secret wall panel concealed by the striped, blue-and-gold wall fabric swung soundlessly open. His Eminence Giovanni, Cardinal Corsini, the same man Charlotte-Anne had met at her first dinner aboard the *Ile*, stepped gracefully into the room, his ankle-length soutane rustling as it swirled around his legs. His thin face with its high, angular cheekbones held an impassive expression. He pushed the panel shut with the palm of his hand.

The Principessa Marcella di Fontanesi turned wearily to him. 'You heard everything?' she asked in Italian.

He nodded and slipped into a chair. 'She has spirit,' he said expressionlessly.

'Spirit!' The Principessa snorted. 'She is asking to be shot. And she will end up getting us *all* shot. These modern American girls – they think they are entitled to everything. It is true what is said about them. They are only interested in one thing – to marry titles.'

His Eminence steepled his bony fingers and held them against his brittle lips. 'This one cannot be bought off,' he murmured. 'I see now that I have misjudged her. I was wrong.'

'Yes, you were wrong.' The Principessa took a seat opposite him, but the fight seemed to go out of her. 'However, I am still grateful that you hurried here and warned us about the marriage before they arrived. To show our gratitude, the church will, of course, receive a sizeable donation, as always.'

'Whatever charity you find it in your heart to give, Principessa,' the cardinal said softly, 'the church is grateful for.' He stared at her with an expression of hurt. 'I did not come because of the donation.'

The Principessa smiled tightly. 'Of course not.' She glanced down at her hands as she wrung them nervously in her lap. 'It seems we have all underestimated the girl,' she mused aloud. She looked back up at him. 'How do you suggest we proceed?'

He half-smiled. 'With utmost delicacy.'

'Of course.' She tightened her lips. 'Much as I hate to admit it, she has threatened our sole vulnerability. And perhaps she really does love Luigi. Only time will tell.'

'Then you wish the marriage to be recognized?'

'Do I have any choice?'

The cardinal shrugged. 'Not much. It depends on how serious she is about carrying out her threat.'

'The results of which, your Eminence,' the Principessa reminded him drily, 'we cannot afford to even consider.'

He nodded gravely. 'These are difficult times,' he sighed.

'But it is true that their marriage, as it stands now, is not recognized?'

'It depends, Principessa. In the courts of America, England, and Germany, it is official. According to Rome, however, it is not. Prince Luigi and his wife are living in sin. Any child they conceive would be conceived in sin. She is not even Catholic. I discovered that on the ship.'

The Principessa nodded and pursed her lips. 'In that case, I suppose we have no choice. We must make certain this marriage gets recognized with all due haste. Of course,' she added delicately, 'we will only be too happy to show just how grateful we are for any red tape you are able to cut.' She eyed him significantly. 'Not for yourself, of course. For the church.'

'Of course,' he replied, his face still impassive. 'I shall put it to the Holy Father at once.'

11

The room smelled faintly moist and musky from recent lovemaking. Their labored, anguished breaths had calmed again to become soft, steady breathing. The bright country moonlight streamed in through the open windows. The faint, distant sound of the church bells rode over on the cool breeze from the convent on the hill across the valley.

Charlotte-Anne stared up at the dark ceiling of heavy damask canopy covering the bed, her mind drifting. In the moonlight, her face was pale silver and deeply shadowed.

She sensed Luigi's eyes studying her. Then she felt his satin skin against hers as he gently prodded her to turn over on her side. He took deep, appreciative sniffs of her salty skin. 'Nobody makes love like you do,' he whispered into her spine as he buried his face against her naked back. He made an animal-like growl, pretended to take a bite out of her flesh, and nuzzled her roughly.

'And nobody makes love like you do either,' she retorted, but it was a weak, half-hearted attempt at good humor. The listless tone of her voice gave her away.

'What is the matter?' He shifted on the bed, switched on the silk-shaded nightstand lamp, and lay sideways, supporting his weight on his cocked elbow. He was watching her intently.

'Oh, nothing really.' She rolled over and lay flat again, her eyes tracing the swirls of damask. She puffed her cheeks full of air and let go of a deep breath, blowing stray tendrils of hair out of her eyes. 'I was just thinking, that's all.'

'About what?'

'You. Me.'

'What about us?' he asked. 'Aren't you happy with me? Don't I satisfy you in bed?'

She couldn't help laughing. 'You're perfect. But you know that.' It amused her that Luigi di Fontanesi, the notorious ladykiller, should need such reassurances.

'Then what is it?' he asked worriedly. 'You look so preoccupied.'

'Do I?'

'Yes, you do.' He leaned over her face. 'When we made love just now, you were so . . . *determined*. It was as though you wanted to use it to forget something.' He paused. 'I only want you to be happy,' he said, kissing her lips. 'I want you always to be happy.'

'I know that.' She smiled faintly up at him.

'And we must never keep secrets from each other. Not ever. Not for as long as we live.'

She nodded, feeling ashamed of herself for keeping something from him so early in their marriage. Their *unrecognized* marriage, she reminded herself with a stab of fear, remembering the Principessa's icy, self-righteous words. There was nothing she wanted to do more than to confide in Luigi and tell him about her confrontation with his mother, but she knew she would never be able to discuss it with him. What had occurred was between the Principessa and herself, and it had to stay that way. She was not about to see her husband torn between his wife and mother.

'Then will you tell me what is disturbing you after such wonderful lovemaking?' He paused. 'Was it my mother?'

She gave a start. It was as though he could read her mind. She let out a low laugh which she hoped sounded convincing. 'Whatever gave you that idea?'

'You were with her this evening. Afterwards, when we made love, you were tense. I have never seen you so tense.'

'I suppose I *was*,' she said slowly, choosing her words with care, 'but that's only to be expected. It isn't every day that a girl meets her in-laws.'

'And that's all that is bothering you?'

'Should there be anything else?'

He shrugged his shoulders. 'Knowing my mother, who knows? Sometimes she intimidates people without even realizing it.'

'Does she now?' Charlotte-Anne regretted the sarcasm the instant the words slipped out.

He nodded. 'Yes, she does.'

She let out a breath of relief. Luigi's English was good, but the sarcasm was completely lost on him.

He was baffled. 'If it is not me, or my mother, then what is it?' he prodded. 'I do not want us to have any problems.'

'I don't either,' she said quickly. She turned on her side to face him, her pale eyes glittering. 'But Luigi . . .'

'Yes?'

'Your mother . . . well she . . . she hinted that we might face some problems.'

'Problems? What kind of problems?' he asked in a puzzled voice. 'Hopefully not any which are insurmountable.'

'Knowing you, no problem is insurmountable.' Nevertheless, she bit down on her lip. 'It's about our marriage.'

'What about it?'

'Your mother is afraid it won't be recognized by the Church.'

'That is a problem.' He nodded gravely. 'However, I've thought about it and I am not so certain it cannot be worked out. If we must, we will simply get married all over again.'

She tightened her lips. 'I want us to be married already,

Luigi,' she said with soft intensity. 'I want our marriage to have been official all along. I know it sounds silly, but I want to know that I am your wife.'

'Then do not worry,' he smiled. 'I am a di Fontenesi, and so are you. And God knows, we give enough to the Church. Have no fear. Our cardinal will work things out.'

'*Your* cardinal?'

'Yours, too, now that you are a di Fontanesi.'

'But . . . I don't understand.'

'You will in time. All the powerful Italian families have a "family" cardinal, so to speak. It is like having a family doctor, or a lawyer. Our cardinal will straighten things out. It may cost us, but then, nothing in life is free.'

'Who is this cardinal?'

'You have already met him. On the *Ile de France*.'

'You mean Cardinal Corsini?'

'The very one. So stop worrying. Knowing my mother and the cardinal, together they will move heaven and earth to set things right. My mother is a very determined woman. She always gets what she wants.'

Charlotte-Anne nodded.

'Now wipe that worried expression off your face. I said it would all be fixed, did I not?'

She smiled. 'Yes, you did.' She bent forward and kissed him deeply. Somehow, just hearing him tell her it was all right made it seem so.

'Now look what you made me do,' he accused as he drew away from her.

'What?' she asked.

He laughed, flipping off the embroidered sheet and looked down. She followed his gaze and shook her head in disbelief.

The Principessa Marcella moved down the marble corridor on slippered feet. As she passed Luigi's apartment, a perverse kind of curiosity came over her. For an instant she wavered between stopping and continuing on her nightly rounds.

Her curiosity won out. She drew close to the door and pressed her ear against it. Her elegant lips curled with disgust as her acute hearing caught the muffled, urgent sounds of lovemaking. She could hear her son's anguished moans and the cries of passion that the *putana* he had brought home emitted as she urged him on.

Now more than ever, the Principessa was thoroughly convinced that the girl was the worst kind of tragedy which could be visited upon the di Fontanesis. Only an *animal* relished such disgusting acts, the Principessa hissed to herself with revulsion. She could not believe that her son could have stooped so low.

For a moment, the Principessa was reminded of her own youth. How different that had been!

She had married Prince Antonio thirty-one years earlier. He had been young and intensely studious, and she had been the most famous beauty in all Umbria, some said in all Italy. And everyone agreed that they made the perfect couple. What they didn't know was that choosing him had been an easy decision for her. She had received countless proposals of marriage, but she had turned them all down in favor of the prince. Not because she had been physically attracted to him. His handsomeness had had nothing to do with it. On the contrary, she had chosen him above the others because he was the least physically demanding of her suitors. She had had the feeling that she could control his passions.

And control them she had. For three decades now, she had been the irreproachable chatelaine of the various pallazi, the model hostess, the legendary beauty, and the perfect wife in every way but one. She knew about her husband's mistress of longstanding, and she was not at all threatened by her. She was, in fact, relieved that he took those disgusting urges elsewhere to relieve himself of them. She despised having to make love. She had consented to it in the beginning only in the practical interest of producing an heir. After she had become pregnant, she had moved to her own room and never allowed her husband to make love to her again.

She could only wish that her son had inherited her own physical frugality, but from the stories which had found their way back to her, she knew he hadn't. How peculiar that Luigi had come to possess the womanizing qualities she herself found so revolting. He had certainly not inherited that from herself or his father. The prince's discreet mistress was his only bed partner. But Luigi was different. He loved women – *all* women – and that was his great weakness. She wished, not for the first time, that Luigi was quieter and more studious. He reminded her too much of everything she found revolting in a man.

The moist, succulent sounds of lovemaking coming from Luigi's apartment unearthed all the long-buried memories of everything she had found so demeaning. She could not understand what on earth could drive a woman – any woman – to accept it. A man's urgency . . . well, that was understandable. Physically, men were animals. But for a woman to enjoy it? No woman who embraced it with such fervor could, in her opinion, be a lady.

She heard the distant, echoing footsteps of one of the servants approaching from around the corner. Quickly she moved on so she wouldn't be caught eavesdropping.

I *wasn't* trying to eavesdrop, she told herself as she continued on her rounds down the seemingly endless corridors. I pass this way every night after checking to make certain that everything in this house is in order, she assured herself.

But what, then, a small voice in the back of her mind asked, *prompted you to stop and place your ear against that door in the first place?*

And she answered herself, with an audible snap of her jaw: *Just to make certain that I wasn't making a terrible mistake. I had to be sure my initial instincts about the American were correct. And they were. She is everything I feared she was. And worse.*

When Marcella reached the apartment she shared with the prince, she went directly to her bedroom. She was about to undress, but she felt so agitated that she wanted to speak to someone. For a long time she stared at the connecting door leading to her husband's bedroom. She had not knocked on his door for years. She hated to do it now, but finally she cocked a knuckle, took a deep breath, and knocked.

'Yes?' His muffled voice sounded surprised.

271

She opened the door. 'Antonio,' she said softly. 'Are you still awake?'

His room was dark. In the wedge of light flooding through from her room, she saw him sit up in bed and squint. Then he reached across the bed to his nightstand and switched on the lamp. It bathed his face in soft yellow light. 'Marcella? Something is worrying you?'

'Worrying?' She laughed as she drew closer to his bed, careful to make sure that she kept at arm's length from him. Her voice held a disapproving tone. 'I am happy that Luigi is back. But as for that American . . . '

He nodded. 'Did Cardinal Corsini leave yet?'

'No, but I had a chance to speak with him. I put him in his usual guest suite in the opposite wing. He will leave in the morning, before they wake up. They will never know he has even been here. I have warned the servants to remain silent.'

He looked at her. 'You have had the opportunity to talk to Luigi's wife. What happened?'

'Wife!' The Principessa snorted. 'She is nothing but a common *putana*. As I passed their bedroom door – '

' – Yes?' A spark glowed in his dark eyes.

She was so involved in her hatred for Charlotte-Anne that she didn't notice her husband's quickening interest. 'You should hear the sounds coming from within the apartment,' she spat disgustedly. 'You can hear it all the way out in the hall. It's revolting, I tell you.'

'Sounds? What kind of sounds?'

'You know . . . ' She made an agitated little gesture.

'Love-making?'

She blushed and turned away. 'That girl is no good. I cannot bear to think of her as a di Fontanesi.'

'She will not leave, then?'

She turned back to face him, her eyes flashing. 'She refuses. She claims to love him. She has gone so far as to tell me, his mother, that he will stand by her no matter what. It must be our money she's after. Either that or . . . or what they do at night.' She wrung her hands in despair. 'She threatened me.'

'How so?'

272

She told him about Charlotte-Anne's threat to publicize her anti-fascist feelings. A tiny smile hovered at the corners of Prince Antonio's lips. No one had displayed the courage to stand up to his wife for many years. The girl had spirit, and silently he applauded her. 'As long as Luigi is happy,' he said carefully, envying his son, 'that is all that matters.'

'Perhaps that is all that matters to *you*. Men always stick together. But do you have any idea what it will cost us to have this marriage recognized? And if we don't, think of the scandal.'

'There need be no scandal, you know that. Another generous contribution – '

'And another, and then another,' she said testily. 'I have never seen anything as ravenous as Rome. The Vatican eats up our money. Do you have any idea how much it has already gotten from us?'

'We can afford it,' he said mildly. 'I don't mind. And besides, you are a good, practicing Catholic.'

She raised her chin and nodded. 'Yes, I am,' she said gravely, his irony lost on her.

'Then it seems we have no choice other than to embrace her into this family.'

'Perhaps we have no choice, but I won't embrace her,' the Principessa growled. 'Not now. Not ever. She is a whore. It grieves me that Luigi should fall for her. He has always had such cheap taste in women.'

'If she makes him happy, so be it.'

'Any woman can make him happy, if that kind of gratification is all he seeks.'

'She seems quite charming to me,' the Prince said. 'A little shy, perhaps, but under the circumstances that is understandable. She is very beautiful.'

'Yes,' the Principessa admitted drily, 'she is beautiful. But many women are beautiful.'

'You are beautiful still,' he said smoothly. 'Even more beautiful than you were in your youth.'

She stared at him. 'That is because I am a lady. I have not allowed physical dissipation to take its toll on me. But she is different. Her beauty will fade quickly.'

273

He felt his own physical needs suddenly rising. Beneath the covers, his phallus throbbed and grew.

'Marcella,' he whispered gently, reaching out for her. '*Cara mia.*'

But she had already turned and was walking briskly through the connecting door to her own bedroom. It closed with a soft but decisive click.

The Prince sighed and dropped his head wearily back down on the pillow. How long it had been now since their love had died! It had stopped when she was pregnant with Luigi. That had been Marcella's excuse then, and a multitude had followed. In time, he had stopped trying altogether. Perhaps she had never loved him. Or perhaps love did not exist.

He closed his eyes, imagining the sounds of his son and daughter-in-law. Almost without realizing it, his hand drifted down to his penis. He had a sudden vision of Luigi and Charlotte-Anne naked together, him riding her mercilessly.

Prince Antonio di Fontanesi had barely touched himself when he felt himself explode.

His last thought before he drifted into sleep was that, whatever the price, having the girl in the family would be well worth it.

They soon discovered that even for the mighty di Fontenesis, it wasn't all that easy to appease the powerful Vatican. The laws of the state were one thing, the laws of the Church something else entirely. Only after six months could they arrange to have Charlotte-Anne and Luigi's marriage officially recognized by Rome.

During that time, Charlotte-Anne was forced to keep a low profile at the Palazzo di Cristallo. Meanwhile, Luigi was in Rome. She was not allowed to accompany him there. According to Cardinal Corsini, this was no time to flaunt an unrecognized marriage before society and the Church. Strict conventions had to be observed. This became even more imperative when Charlotte-Anne discovered she was pregnant.

The truce she had worked out with the Principessa

Marcella was an uneasy one, and both women did their best to stay out of each other's way. Living under the same roof for over six months was difficult for both. When their paths did cross, they were polite, but no love was lost between the two princesses.

Charlotte-Anne hated being away from Luigi, even if it was only a distance of seventy-five miles. It might as well have been seven thousand. His commission as colonel in the Italian Air Force kept him in Rome, and too often he didn't return to the palazzo for weeks at a time. She was dying to move into the Villa della Rose with him, but she could only wait. Whenever he came to visit he would whisper, 'Soon now. Just have patience.'

It took the patience of Job.

It was January before a final agreement could be worked out between the Vatican and the di Fontanesis. In the end, it cost the di Fontanesis five hundred million lire, along with the donation to the Vatican of three coveted works of religious art.

The day the marriage was recognized, the Principessa Marcella came to Charlotte-Anne's apartment. Luigi was in Rome, and Charlotte-Anne faced her mother-in-law alone.

'Congratulations,' the Principessa Marcella said drily. 'You now have the satisfaction of having had one of the most expensive marriages in history. I suggest that, since you have gotten what you wanted, you start packing and leave at once for Rome. Furthermore, I strongly suggest you keep any and all political views to yourself, unless you want to jeopardize your own and your husband's lives. Your car is waiting.'

The Principessa closed the door without so much as saying good-bye.

But still, the Principessa and the Church seemed to have had the last laugh. Their child, 'conceived in sin,' was stillborn. And though Charlotte-Anne became pregnant regularly, she suffered a series of seven miscarriages during the next five years.

In the beginning, their life together was a fairy tale dream come true.

But for her problems with child-bearing, Charlotte-Anne considered the next few years as near perfect as any could possibly be. The moment she finally left the loveless splendor of the Palazzo di Cristallo, she felt liberated as though from a dark, stifling prison into the joyous, brilliant sunshine. *It* might have taken time and cost a fortune, but finally she really *was* the Principessa Charlotte-Anne di Fontanesi and Luigi *was* officially her husband.

Since arriving in Italy, she had exchanged numerous letters with her mother. The first had been full of explanations, the rest to keep up with what was happening and to fill the loneliness she felt at the palazzo. It had come as a pleasant surprise to her that Elizabeth-Anne held no hard feelings because of the hasty shipboard wedding.

As long as you're happy, darling, her mother had written, *that is all that counts. Hopefully, we'll both be able to travel and visit each other often. I love you dearly, and the only thing which saddens me is that Italy is so far, far away . . .*

She had felt immense relief when she had read that first letter, and was filled again with that rich feeling of closeness to her mother. The last thing she had expected was her mother's swift blessing. Eventually, she was certain Elizabeth-Anne would come around, but to have her approval forthwith both amazed and delighted Charlotte-Anne. In this way the thousands of miles that separated them brought her a new outlook on her mother. Her respect for her increased immensely. Elizabeth-Anne Hale was some lady, she realized now. Her only regret was that it had taken her so long to discover it.

Rome quickly became home. Charlotte-Anne fell under the spell of the Eternal City as people had for thousands of years. Her first priority was to transform the formal Villa della Rose from the haughty palace it was into a warm, comfortable home. She banished the massive, carved furniture into storage. In its place, she furnished the rooms with the warm honey tones of finely waxed fruit and nut-wood veneers, and the soft glaze of flowered chintzes. She was tired of palaces. She wanted a home where they could raise a family.

As the work progressed, she and Luigi lived in another wing of the villa, and she made him promise not to go and look at what she was doing until it was finished. Then, she showed him around, her nervousness highly apparent. She was so afraid he would hate what she had done and would want it all put back as it had been.

He gazed around, silently walking from room to room. His frequent nods revealed nothing of his thoughts.

Finally he turned to her and grinned. 'I like it,' he said, hugging her tightly. 'It is comfortable.' Then he kissed her long and hard. 'Above all, it is now our *home*.'

She knew he had paid her the highest compliment she could hope for. The only note which soured it was when his parents came on an unexpected visit.

'It looks rather plebian, don't you think?' the Principessa asked Luigi. 'But then, it's a matter of taste . . .'

Charlotte-Anne fought to keep her fury to herself. She was only too grateful that her in-laws didn't stay long. And that their future visits were exceedingly rare.

It seemed to her, in those early years, that she and Luigi were as one, except when his long hours working as attaché of Italy's fledgling Air Force kept him away. But when he was at home, and his time was his own, they spent every waking and sleeping hour together.

Still, she thought, it's not enough. Even if we could spend twenty-four hours together, every day for the rest of our lives, it wouldn't be enough. It was a romance made in heaven, and she was certain it could never end.

Luigi had planned to take a few weeks off so that they could go on a belated honeymoon, but he never found the time. 'Il Duce insists he needs me, and I am afraid that things are only going to get busier,' he said apologetically.

'I don't care,' Charlotte-Anne declared. 'With you, Rome is honeymoon enough.'

When he had the time he showed her the city inside and

out, until she knew it by heart. She became familiar with the tourist Rome – the lush banks of azaleas rising up the one hundred and thirty-seven stairs of the majestic Spanish Steps, the Colosseum and its multitude of marauding cats, the ecclesiastic splendor of the Vatican, through which Cardinal Corsini personally guided them so that she could view both the public and the private chambers. She and Luigi dined regularly on the Via Veneto, and he took her to the Diocletian Baths and Sant'Angelo Castle, where Hadrian's mausoleum was located. Every way she turned, it seemed, there were visible remnants of a civilization long past.

Under Luigi's patient tutelage she came to love Rome – how different it was from the maddening hustle and bustle and grime of New York! She found herself falling under the spell of the monumental panoramas, the splendid ruins, and the wide sidewalks lined with cafés. She loved the contrast of the very old, the merely old, and the new. But most of all, she loved the clogged sidewalks, the sweet sounds of tenors singing, the screams of the children as they played in the alleys and on the terraces. Rome was magic and enchanting, and if it hadn't been for the ever-present signs of the military – the precisely strutting fascists parading down the boulevards, the forced civility whenever soldiers were within earshot, and the suspicious glances over people's shoulders – her love for the city would have been complete. She had to keep reminding herself that Luigi, too, was now in the military. And he wasn't a monster.

He took her everywhere, and taught her the local customs. Once, when they spent an afternoon walking, they stopped at a sidewalk vendor to buy fruit to eat along the way. Charlotte-Anne had never seen such huge, golden peaches or tomatoes of such a deep, lush red, or bunches of grapes tied together with vine. Everything looked inviting, but she settled upon a bunch of grapes. She asked how much they were in the halting Italian Luigi had taught her.

The vendor, a thin old crone, told her they were sixty lire. Charlotte-Anne was about to start counting out the money when Luigi stopped her. 'No, no!' he cried. 'You must bargain.'

'But . . . why?' she stammered. 'She said they were sixty lire.'

'Watch, and listen carefully.' He took the grapes from her, held them up to inspect them, then frowned. Shaking his head, he put them back down and picked up another bunch. He squeezed a few peaches, a few plums. Then she watched him wave the bunch of grapes she had chosen in the first place in front. She followed the conversation only roughly, recognizing phrases here and there that she had learned. 'Thirty-five lire,' Luigi began.

'Signor!' the vendor protested. ' . . . *Bambinos* . . . they starve . . . fifty.'

He shook his head and scowled. 'Grapes . . . bruised . . . Thirty-five.'

'Forty-five.'

'Forty.'

Despite herself, Charlotte-Anne was intrigued. 'Enough, enough,' the vendor finally mumbled. She shrugged. 'So the *bambinos* starve . . . you drive a hard bargain, signor.' And then the haggling old crone beamed broadly, her gold teeth flashing.

Charlotte-Anne counted out the forty lire and started popping grapes in her mouth as they continued to walk on. 'That poor woman,' she scolded, shaking her head. 'How could you do that to her?'

'She expects it,' Luigi said. 'Anything else would be to rob her of the joy of her trade. Watch.'

They halted and looked back. An old man was buying an even bigger bunch of grapes, fiercely haggling with the vendor. He got them for thirty lire. 'You see?' Luigi said, smiling. 'Things are not always what they seem.'

Charlotte-Anne kept her ears and eyes open, and she learned.

But Luigi didn't just show her the tourist sights for which the city was so famous. He took her to the Rome tourists never saw at all. They dined in a ridiculously cheap restaurant he loved which was frequented only by the working classes and was located underground in the two thousand year old ruins of the catacombs. He was convinced the chicken cacciatore there was the best in all Italy.

'This is the best-kept secret in all Rome,' he told her. 'I make it a point never to tell anyone about it. If society were to discover this place, it would be ruined.'

Her discoveries of Rome did not cease while Luigi was at work at the Ministry of Defense. She delighted in taking walks through the gardens of the Villa Borghese, whose rambling ancient stone wall comprised the wall of their own backyard. These walks, though without him, were put to good use; she had hired a tutor to teach her Italian, and while she and the tutor walked, she learned her new language. She spent hours on this secret project, which she had begun at the Palazzo di Cristallo to while away her empty hours.

Finally, when she felt she was ready, she met Luigi at the door when he came home one evening and spoke to him in fluent, flawless Italian.

'I'm so proud of you,' he whispered back in his native language. And he proved it by showing her off to all his friends.

There were little irritants, too, which she discovered gradually. In the beginning, whenever he came home, he had changed out of his colonel's uniform and brash regalia. But slowly, he started to wear his precisely tailored suits and silk shirts less and less until finally it occurred to her that he had stopped wearing them altogether. It disturbed her, and when she mentioned it to him, he said, 'Il Duce wants all his officers in uniform all the time.'

'But you're at home now. Surely his orders don't reach into our house.'

'So? I'm comfortable.'

She didn't go on to point out that when he wore his uniform out their evenings were different than they had been before. People were always so carefully civil and polite, their stony faces giving nothing away.

It hadn't been like that in the beginning. Due to his title and his military position, Luigi moved in lofty circles, but he had always been equally at home with common people.

280

She had been both surprised and pleased when she found that he treated everyone equally well, with a total disregard for class or wealth. What amazed her was that everyone seemed to genuinely like him. His easy, contagious laughter, familiarity, and sincerity transcended all social barriers. She had to remind herself constantly that to her he was a husband, but to everyone else he was a national hero of sorts: he had won countless car races, and though his aviation records were not comparable to those of Lindbergh or Earhart, he was, after all, Italy's premier flying ace. But whether he was prince, or sportsman, or the common man's friend, everyone liked him. Until he was in uniform.

In those heady, first few years together, several things occurred which marred the otherwise perfect scheme of things and which, looking back upon them much later, Charlotte-Anne realized should have warned her about troubles to come. But those were such happy and carefree times, and troubles seemed so far away. They were together, invincible, and she believed that nothing could ever come between them. The incidents were spread so far apart that they seemed disparate, and she didn't make the connection until it was much too late.

On one sunny spring Sunday, the first thing occurred which caused her to feel anxious, and told her that everything was not quite as perfect as it seemed.

Luigi drove her to the outskirts of town for a picnic, stopping to point out in the distance behind them, a low-cost housing project which he explained Il Duce had recently erected.

She was startled by the sudden change in his voice. As he spoke about the dictator's work, she realized just how much Luigi was coming to admire his leader.

Inwardly, she cringed. He should never have brought her here, at least not on such an otherwise perfect day. The mention of Il Duce seemed a cloud obscuring the lemon sun.

She was silent for so long that he knew something was wrong. 'What is the matter?' he asked her.

'Please, Luigi. Let's go back.'

'But why? You look so upset.'

She shook her head. 'I'm not upset,' she corrected him tightly. 'I'm confused, that's all.'

'Confused?' He looked at her with a perplexed frown. 'What about?'

'Please, let's forget it,' she pleaded.

'*No*,' he said, and she saw the hurt, mingled with anger, which shone in his eyes. 'If it concerns the way we feel about each other, I am entitled to know about it.' He paused. 'Well?'

She waved a hand at the sterile, poured-concrete apartment blocks behind them. 'I'm confused about those.' She gazed at him. 'And about you.'

'I do not understand.'

'You seem to . . . ' She tightened her lips, wishing that she'd never started to explain. 'Your voice . . . well, it just sounded as though you're starting to like Il Duce.' She gazed up at him.

He laughed. 'And that worries you?'

'Yes.'

'Why should it?'

'Because . . . because he is *bad*, Luigi. He frightens people. Even your own mother let me know how terrified she is of him.'

'When was this?'

'That first night at the palazzo.'

'She might have been then, but not anymore, she isn't. The more Il Duce trusts me, the safer she feels.'

She shivered. 'And Il Duce . . . he trusts you?'

'More and more, yes.' He nodded.

'And you?' She looked at him with a curious kind of defiance. 'Do you trust him?'

'I'm beginning to understand him,' he said carefully. 'He wants what is best for Italy. I see that now. At first I did not believe it, but now I do. Certainly, there are things he does which I do not like at all. But he wants a new Italy, Charlotte-Anne. A stronger Italy. An Italy as strong as it was in the times of the Caesars.'

She shivered again. There was a conviction in his voice she had never seen before, and she found it frightening.

'And you, Luigi?' she asked softly. 'What do you want?'

'Me? I want what is best for you. For my family. For all Italy.' He smiled. 'In precisely that order.'

But, somehow, she wasn't sure that was the order of his priorities. He was changing, she realized, changing before her eyes.

He seemed to sense her fears, and took her hand. 'Come, let us not be so serious. It is a weekend afternoon, the sun is shining, and I am off from work. It is time for *amore*, not for worries.'

She looked at him, her eyes sweeping over his hated, elegant uniform. She couldn't help thinking: yes, you are off from work, but why can't I shake the feeling that your work is with you always, that you bring it home in your head? What happened to the dashing Luigi I met? The prince who loved the sport of flying and racing? Now, planes were only weaponry. And cars no longer mattered. There was no more talk of racing.

She pasted a weak smile on her face. 'You're right. It's silly to spoil a lovely afternoon. Let's forget it.'

And soon she had forgotten about it altogether.

13

It was some months before the next incident occurred which aroused her anxiety.

'We're invited to a formal reception at the Ministry of Foreign Affairs the day after tomorrow,' Luigi said casually one evening at dinner.

She had been about to take a bite of veal off her fork; now she put the fork down on her plate. 'The Ministry of Foreign Affairs?'

He nodded.

She let out a low whistle. At this point she was used to their burgeoning social life, and although it had intimidated her at first, she had quickly discovered that she was well-liked and admired. But previously their social life had revolved around internal affairs and the military, along with the old-line nobility. That they should be receiving invitations to a reception at the Ministry of Foreign Affairs was an indication that they were being swept into yet another social sphere.

Usually, Charlotte-Anne did not like the stiffly formal receptions and dinners with the self-important, uniformed officers strutting around on the arms of their gossiping wives, but this time she looked forward to going. She was just recovering from her second miscarriage and, as with the first, she had locked herself away in the villa until she came out of the ensuing depression. While she had been recovering, Luigi had not even mentioned any functions where she was expected to accompany him, and for that she had been extremely grateful. She knew he had waited until now because he sensed that she was finally ready to get out.

'I want you to look beautiful, as always,' he smiled across the table at her. 'Perhaps you should get yourself a new gown.'

'Another one?' She couldn't help laughing. Men were so vain, and Luigi was more vain than most. He loved an opportunity to show her off, and seemed to take a special pride in dressing her.

'I think something sapphire-blue would look nice,' he mused, nodding. 'Yes, very nice indeed.'

'But you know I prefer pale colours,' she protested. 'And, besides, two days is hardly enough time for Signora Bella to sew a gown.' She lifted her goblet and took a sip of white wine.

'I don't think she'll mind,' he said with a vague smile. 'Besides, you've given her enough business that she'd be a fool not to drop whatever she's working on to knock out a gown for you.'

Charlotte-Anne knew better than to argue with him. The next morning, as she walked into Signora Bella's little shop, the gray-haired seamstress smiled broadly and brought out a bolt of sapphire-blue velvet. 'Your husband had this delivered to me yesterday morning,' she said, fingering it between her thumb and forefinger. 'It is lovely, no?'

'Yes, it is certainly a lovely fabric,' Charlotte-Anne had to agree, despite her anger toward Luigi for disregarding her wishes.

'And do not worry, Principessa,' Signora Bella said. 'You will look absolutely marvelous in it.' She made a circle with her thumb and forefinger, and her massive bosom rose and fell as she sighed appreciatively. 'It will be *bellissimo*.'

'But it has to be completed the day after tomorrow,' Charlotte-Anne pointed out.

'So it shall be,' the old dressmaker said, her hands tugging at the ends of the yellow cloth tape measure which always hung from around her neck. 'I have, after all, your measurements on file, so I have gone ahead and cut and pinned portions of the gown together. See?' Signora Bella picked up a partially finished bodice from her paper-clad worktable and held it up. 'Now I must see that it fits you to perfection and compliments you. Then, this afternoon at four, I will need you to come in for another fitting, and once again tomorrow morning, when we will see to it that any last minute adjustments are made. It will be delivered to your villa by three tomorrow afternoon at the very latest.'

Signora Bella was even better than her word. At just past noon the following afternoon, the completed gown arrived. As soon as Charlotte-Anne lifted it out of the box, any irritation she had felt toward Luigi seeped out of her. She should have known. Luigi's taste was flawless. The gown was indeed a masterpiece.

He only wants what is best for both of us, she had to remind herself.

She felt strangely exhilarated when her hair was done and she got dressed. Luigi walked circles around her, his hand on his chin as he nodded and smiled his satisfaction. He looked tremendously pleased with himself. 'I have never seen you look quite so beautiful,' he said. 'You are breathtaking. The gown is very becoming.'

Looking at her reflection in the tall, gilt-edged mirror in the bedroom she knew he was right. The richness of the sapphire-blue velvet seemed to change the color of her eyes.

Instead of their usual pale, unsettling color, they glowed like two rich, round sapphires.

'Now for the crowning touch,' Luigi said softly. 'I have a necklace I would like you to wear tonight.'

He reached into a pocket of his dress uniform tunic and took out a long, slender black velvet case and two smaller, square velvet boxes. 'To show you how much I love you,' he whispered.

She stared at him. Then hesitantly, she took them from him. First she opened the long, slim case. She let out a startled gasp. Cushioned against the black velvet was a necklace of seventy-nine finely matched, pear-shaped diamonds. The pendant center was a five carat, flawless round blue sapphire as deep blue as the moonlit sea.

'Luigi,' she gasped.

Without speaking, he took the necklace from her and fastened it around her neck. It felt cool and deliciously heavy against her skin. She turned to face the mirror. The diamonds glittered, and the sapphire illusion of her eyes appeared heightened.

Slowly, she opened the lids of the two smaller boxes and discovered matching diamond-and-sapphire drop earrings. In the other, she found a ten-carat sapphire ring surrounded by marquise-cut diamonds.

She felt ashamed of herself for feeling irritated by the way he had dictated her choice of clothes and jewels. Of course he had to pick the sapphire gown – so it would match the jewels. How ungrateful she was!

'Luigi, they're . . . they're too much,' she stammered. 'Far too extravagant.'

'When will you ever learn, *cara*,' he chuckled. 'Nothing is too extravagant when it concerns you.'

'But . . . it's not even my birthday,' she sputtered.

'Does it have to be?' he asked as he clipped the earrings onto her lobes. 'When I saw these, I knew they were meant for you.' He paused and looked suddenly pained. 'I know, these can never make up for the loss you have suffered, but take them as a token of your husband's deep love.'

'But what for?'

'For taking in stride the hardships and loss you have had

to endure,' he whispered, turning away. 'I know how much you wanted to have our baby, and how much the miscarriage affected you.'

Her eyes filled with tears. 'Now look what you're making me do!' she said in a choked voice as she dabbed her eyes with a lace-edged handkerchief. 'You're making me ruin my make-up.'

The Ministry of Foreign Affairs was not far away, but they rode there in the chauffeur driven Daimler, circling the Piazza del Popolo with its obelisk in the center, and down the Via del Corso, to the Piazza Colonna. During the short ride there was a nervous energy about Luigi which she found rather peculiar. He was always the very picture of calm, and she wondered what now caused his agitation. She wondered if there were something special about this evening he hadn't told her about. But she knew it was useless to pry. She would have to wait and see.

The reception began very pleasantly. She had expected to meet only strangers, but there were quite a few guests she knew and hadn't seen since before her miscarriage, and they greeted her warmly. She was introduced to the Minister of Defense, a tall, sleek, bald-headed man in a well-cut tuxedo who bowed over her hand, kissed it, and introduced her to his plump, shark-toothed wife. And there were a multitude of people she had never seen before, but who seemed to know who she was.

She made several new friends that evening. Being an American who, it was rumored, came from a very wealthy family and had married into one of Italy's most powerful clans seemed to fill everyone with curiosity, admiration, and respect.

She found herself the center of attention.

And then came the first unpleasant surprise of the evening. Just after the dancing began in the great marble hall, the Minister of Defense asked her for the first waltz. Then she danced with Luigi, and when he was taken aside for a discussion with the Minister and some generals, Charlotte-Anne went over to the white-clothed buffet tables. They were laden with silver trays of imported caviar and salmon, paper-thin slices of prociutto, and artful little canapés. Domestic wines and foreign champagne flowed freely.

'*Cara*,' Luigi said suddenly from behind her. 'I believe you two have already met?'

She turned around slowly and drew a deep, startled breath as she found herself face-to-face with General Kersten. She remembered the German all too well from the crossing on the *Ile de France*, and he looked exactly as he had then, red-faced and meaty, with pin-prick blue eyes. She was as instinctively revolted by him now as she had been then, and she remembered how he had cruelly goaded Mrs. Reichenbach and talked so horribly about the Jews. She struggled not to show her distaste. He was not in civilian clothes as he had been on the *Ile de France*. His gray uniform, with its red, white, and black swastika armband, flared riding breeches, and high gleaming boots, was curiously intimidating. It was only then that she realized how many other guests were wearing similar uniforms. The reception was top-heavy with Germans.

As when they had first met, General Kersten clicked his heels together noisily and kissed her hand. 'You look even more charming now than the last time we met,' he said loudly. 'I congratulate you on your marriage.' He turned to Luigi, smiled, and faced Charlotte-Anne again. 'It was a most auspicious crossing, *nicht wahr*?'

'Yes, it was,' Charlotte-Anne agreed politely, warning herself that she had to be very careful not to let her personal feelings show. This party was too important to Luigi's future.

'And to think,' General Kersten continued, 'that I have been transferred to Rome. Such a lovely city! We must see a lot of each other. Perhaps you will be so kind as to show me around every now and then?'

'Yes,' she murmured, 'of course,' silently vowing that rather than run into him everywhere she would lock herself up at the villa like a hermit.

'It seems that General Kersten and I,' Luigi informed her, 'shall be working closely together.'

'Oh?' She looked startled. 'But – but I thought you were the Italian Air Force attaché, Luigi.'

'So he is,' General Kersten boomed. 'But things in Germany are now different. Herr Hitler has become chancellor, and his first order of business is to strengthen ties with our Italian brothers. He is an ardent admirer of your Premier Mussolini, you know. The Führer wants for Germany as Herr Mussolini wants for Italy – a thousand-year Reich. And to do that, Germany *must* be strengthened. It seems your premier has kindly loaned your husband to Germany for a while.'

'I-I don't understand.' Charlotte-Anne looked at Luigi.

'I only heard about it myself a few minutes ago,' Luigi told her. 'It seems I'm going to be made General.'

'Oh, Luigi,' she whispered, forcing a smile she did not feel. 'How wonderful!'

She gazed quietly around the room at the men in formal wear and dress uniforms, the ladies in their finest gowns and jewels. It was so deceptively peaceful and lovely, and yet she could sense a frightening, invisible undercurrent. It was as though something obscene had entered the marble hall. The talk of thousand-year empires frightened her; she didn't know why.

'Ah, I see that you have already met General Kersten,' the Minister of Defense said as he approached with his wife. He smiled at Charlotte-Anne, then looked at Luigi. 'I take it you do not mind if I borrow the lovely Principessa for a few minutes?'

'Not at all,' Luigi replied. 'And I shall borrow your beautiful wife in the meantime.'

The Minister's wife took his arm, her smile displaying her unfortunately long teeth to disadvantage.

Charlotte-Anne bowed her head and slipped her arm through the Minister's, grateful for the opportunity to get away from General Kersten.

'Are you enjoying our little reception?' the Minister asked as he led her across the hall.

'It is lovely.' She favored him with a smile.

'And you, Principessa, are the single loveliest woman here. I look forward to your adorning more of our functions.'

'As you wish.' She blushed and inclined her head,

289

expecting him to lead her in a dance. Instead, he took her past the dance floor and out to an anteroom. She looked at him with surprise as he closed the padded door. The music sounded muted and far away.

'I hope you will forgive me for being so mysterious, Principessa,' he said as he turned to her, 'but I wanted to speak to you in private.'

She felt a sudden alarm. 'Is something wrong?'

'No, no, not at all,' he assured her. 'Certainly not. I just wanted to speak to you about your husband's future. And your own.'

'I don't think I understand.'

'You will, in time. Forgive me if I do not elaborate, but there are forces developing in many countries which will soon change the world as we know it; what these are is unimportant at the moment. What *is* important is that it will be for the better.' He paused and smiled. 'Your husband is an important man, Principessa. Il Duce is relying upon him more and more. He has great expectations for him.'

She nodded. She had heard all this before, and she was wondering where it would eventually lead.

'A lovely wife is, of course, a tremendous asset to a man's career, and in that the Prince is very lucky.'

'You flatter me,' she said softly, meeting his eye. 'But one thing I do not understand. Sometimes you call my husband Colonel. Other times, you refer to him as the Prince. Which is he, Signor Minister? A prince or a colonel?'

'Both, of course.' He looked vaguely unsettled; then he said smoothly, 'As I was saying, you are a tremendous asset to your husband. And you will have the opportunity to be an even greater one. The Colo – the Prince – will shortly be made general, and as you know, even among generals there is a . . . well, to put it bluntly, a pecking order.' He smiled wryly. 'Your husband can either become a very powerful general, or merely one in a crowd. Much of that depends upon you. I sincerely believe that it would behove this country if he were to become very powerful. Your husband has many attributes that this country needs now as never before. He is a well respected member of an old and titled family. Il Duce believes that what his government needs to function more smoothly is the support of the aristocracy, who at present do not universally give him the respect he deserves. Times are changing, Principessa. Italy is finally entering the twentieth century as a major power in her own right, and your husband's expertise with automobiles and aviation – well, in the near future, that expertise is going to be very important for Italy. It will make the difference between success and failure.'

'In what way?'

'That, I'm afraid, I'm not at liberty to say. However I, and indeed most of Italy, would appreciate it, immensely, Principessa, if you did everything within your power to help your husband rise swiftly within our government. Who knows? Soon he might become second only in power to Il Duce.'

'And how do you suggest I help do this?' she asked curiously. 'By socializing more? By giving more parties, arranging charity functions – '

He smiled. 'That, too. But I'm thinking mainly about something else.'

'Yes, Signor Minister?'

'You are still an American citizen, Principessa. In order to help your husband fully and for you to become totally accepted in society and by the government, to gain true credibility for both your husband and yourself, you *must* renounce your American citizenship and become an Italian.'

She stared at him, instantly bitter at his proposal.

'You will do it?' he asked hopefully.

She schooled herself to speak calmly. 'I will certainly consider it, Signor Minister.'

'Of course,' he said soothingly, 'but please. Do not think about it for too long. For events that are coming . . . well, I cannot over-emphasize that speed is essential.'

'But acquiring a country's citizenship takes time, does it not?'

'It usually does.' He nodded, then smiled. 'But in your case, Principessa, I'm certain that the time-consuming steps can be dispensed with. It can be done with much speed.'

'I see.' She nodded, frowning thoughtfully. 'As I said, Minister, I will certainly give it careful but quick thought.'

'I knew you would.' He paused. 'But please, do not take too long to make up your mind.' Then he bowed, pivoted on his heel, and left the anteroom.

For a long time, she remained alone. She wondered if Luigi knew that this conversation had taken place. Or that it had been planned. Perhaps that had been the cause of his uncharacteristic nervousness.

Her hand went to the necklace round her throat where the diamonds and sapphire felt cold against her skin. What was this necklace, she thought, besides a slave collar? How much choice did she really have about keeping her American citizenship?

She knew only one thing. She loved Luigi with all her heart and soul. She would do anything in her power which might help him, with no questions asked. She had told the Minister that she would give his request thought, but she already knew what her answer would be. She would do as he had asked.

Still, she couldn't help thinking that the sapphires and diamonds had been a bribe.

14

Only some time later did the third occurrence, which was by far the most ominous, take place, and it was then that the previous events took on their true significance. In the meanwhile, Charlotte-Anne went on with her life in the Villa della Rosa with blissful ignorance.

Rome was a social whirlwind. There were no end of private parties and official functions to attend, and everywhere conversations turned to politics. She had little interest in the subject and her ever-increasing popularity was based, in good part, on the light-hearted, charming social bantering she preferred. With her, people felt at ease. They didn't have to watch every word they said, or defend their views. The reasoning behind this was simple: when she was around she put a stop to all political talk, and adroitly turned the conversations to lighter subjects.

Nonetheless, she increasingly sensed a growing turbulence under the placid surface of Roman society stemming from the 'events' the Minister had hinted at, and which were indeed beginning to flourish. There were rumors of unrest, military build-ups, and an air of impending war. Overnight, receptions and dinners became military strategy sessions; wives worked the parties, jockeying for their husbands' promotions; generals sought out industrialists and vice versa; favors were exchanged and deals consummated amid the free-flowing champagne, caviar, and waltzes.

She sensed the carefree days drawing to an end, but she didn't want to believe what was happening. She tried every way she could not to face it, and for a time she was successful. Europe might have been in the midst of a gathering hurricane, but the power centers, the capitals, seemed to be at the eye of the storm, and were deceptively peaceful. However, eventually her unspoken anxieties grew too strong to ignore. She was terrified that if she mentioned them to Luigi, he would agree that her fears were founded. His promotions – now coming in quicker succession – would soon make him chief general of the Air Force. She was increasingly aware of the political turmoil, but tried to tell herself that it was only because of the more powerful social circles they moved in. She wanted desperately to believe that the charged unrest was something she hadn't felt before simply because their sphere of friends and acquaintances hadn't included so many foreigners as it did now. Rome was, after all, filled with them.

Germans were everywhere.

Despite these misgivings, time still seemed to fly past in a blur, and so did the string of miscarriages which truly darkened her life. She was her happiest when Luigi was at her side. Unfortunately, he couldn't be there always. As time went by, she saw less and less of him, and their time together became all the more precious. She wasn't in the least bit interested what the duties which he carried out for Il Duce were; she cared only for the time he was with her. After their fourth year together, when Luigi was sent on more frequent, and lengthier assignments to Germany, she started to become depressed because she felt so alone. Whenever he was not with her, she found herself caught in an emotional limbo.

'I want to go with you,' she told Luigi, not for the first time.

He smiled good-naturedly. 'I must go alone, *cara*,' he replied sadly. 'Armed forces bases are not places for women.'

Her face fell, and he urged her to spend the time he was gone at the Palazzo di Cristallo. His parents, he was sure, would look forward to her visit. She shook her head. 'I like Rome, Luigi,' she said. 'Besides, when you return you come to Rome first. I want to be here, waiting for you.'

He smiled. 'I shall miss you.'

'And I shall miss you, too.' She paused. 'Luigi . . . '

'Yes?'

'Why do you have to go to Germany so often? I didn't think Germany was allowed either an army or an air force after the last war.'

'They are allowed a small one of each, but Adolf Hitler is now in power, and he is trying to end all that. He believes Germany must be strong in order to survive.' His voice grew more fervent, and his eyes took on a glazed glow. 'You wouldn't believe what is happening in Germany, *cara*,' he whispered. 'The flying. Every weekend, thousands and thousands of weekend enthusiasts take to the air in gliders. It's like the national sport! They're training for when Germany will have a real air force again. Il Duce is lending me to the Germans to help teach them, and to point out areas for expansion.'

She turned to the window and looked out at their sunlit backyard and its manicured lawn, its oval swimming pool, and the ancient walls of the Borghese Gardens behind it. 'What is Adolf Hitler like?' she asked.

He hesitated a moment. It was as though he hadn't yet

made up his own mind and had to collect his thoughts. 'He is a very complicated man,' he said slowly. 'But there's something about him . . . a kind of magnetism he radiates, which draws people to him. I've never seen anything like it. He's very much like our own Il Duce, but much stronger. He seems to throw off an aura of power. When he's at a rally, he can literally drive people berserk. When he's not pleased with something, he rants and raves and throws worse tantrums than a spoiled child. Yet in private, he can be exceedingly charming and polite. He's a contradiction, but a fascinating one.'

She did not take her eyes off the backyard view. 'Do you like him?' she asked.

'I don't really know. I suppose I've never given it any thought.'

'Doesn't he . . . frighten you?'

He frowned, then laughed. 'Yes, you know, I suppose he does.'

She turned around then, not wanting to hear any more. She should never have asked. It was all too frightening. She smiled. 'I'd better have Magda press an extra uniform. You won't want to look all rumpled when you arrive in Berlin.'

And as she left the room, she felt an ache in the pit of her belly. It wasn't until half an hour later, after she'd calmed down, that she acknowledged its cause: fear. She could no longer lie to herself; she knew that things were not right. She loved Luigi, but hated fascism in all its ugly forms. She would never forget that incident at the border for as long as she lived. But she had made her bargain with the Principessa Marcella: she would never do anything which might hurt Luigi or the di Fontanesis. She loved Luigi too much. She was his model wife, and because of that, he was one of the most envied men in all Rome. Other wives, it was whispered, were known to conduct discreet affairs when their husbands were out of town for any period of time. But Charlotte-Anne would never dream of such behavior. She lived for one thing only.

Luigi.

Often, she thought of how she failed him constantly, and

she was always trying to find new ways to make it up to him. She knew how badly he wanted a son and it hurt her deeply since, after the stillborn child, she failed to carry another full term.

'Next time, *cara*,' he always told her gently. 'Next time.'

But miscarriage followed miscarriage.

The time Luigi was gone always crawled by. The time he was with her was a blur. Whenever they went to visit his family, or on the rare occasions when the Principessa Marcella and Prince Antonio came to visit Rome, everything was seemingly perfect and polite. On the surface, Charlotte-Anne and the Principessa were friends. Over the years, they had perfected the charade. Only when they were alone, did the fangs come out.

'I hear you had another miscarriage,' the Principessa once told her drily.

Charlotte-Anne stared at her. 'Italy is a small country, I see. Word gets around quickly.'

'For a di Fontanesi, yes,' the Principessa said pointedly, hinting that in her mind Charlotte-Anne would never be a real di Fontanesi. 'We have ears everywhere.'

The next day, Charlotte-Anne changed gynecologists.

And then the winds of political change threw their life into a tailspin.

Luigi was gone for longer and longer periods of time, and she saw precious little of him. Slowly, and with growing fear, Charlotte-Anne watched her husband, who had previously been only a token fascist, being converted by the aphrodisiac of power. There was no longer time for the little pleasures of life. Germany had become Luigi's second home.

'I'm very sorry you feel this way,' he said one day after she fussed because he was going to be gone for sixty days, 'but this is military business.'

'Luigi, for God's sake, I'm your *wife*. I don't get to see you half as much as those Germans do.'

He looked at her with a stony expression. 'Please, *cara*, don't whine. It is unattractive.'

She stared at him. It was the first time he had ever talked

to her in such a condescending tone and she wanted to burst into tears. She managed to remain dry-eyed only by reminding herself that he had many responsibilities weighing on his shoulders. She musn't add to them by making wifely noises.

The only thing which hadn't changed with his increased hunger for power and ambition was his passion. When he was home, his ardor was as great as it had ever been. But there were times she got the feeling that it was not he who lay in their bed. He looked like Luigi, spoke like Luigi. But increasingly, she was under the impression that he was no longer the man she had married.

She wanted the old Luigi back.

The night before he flew to Germany for two months, he took her to bed as usual. He entered her quickly, and rode her hard, bringing her swiftly to orgasm just as he exploded inside her and let out an anguished, drawn-out cry. Then he collapsed wearily beside her.

Like a slap in the face, she realized how much their lovemaking too had changed. Gone from their bedroom was the sensual torture of protracted foreplay. There was a new kind of efficiency even in his sex: he entered her, achieved orgasm, and collapsed. As if there were time for nothing else.

Luigi,' she whispered, opening her eyes.

'Hmmmm?' He was half asleep already.

'Luigi . . . you said you'd be gone for two months?'

'Hmmmmm.'

'Well, it's been ages since I've last seen my family. What do you say I sail for New York and visit with them while you're gone?'

'I don't think so,' he yawned.

She frowned and sat up. 'Why not?'

' 'Cause . . . you can't go.'

She flushed with uneasiness. 'You mean you won't let me?' she asked incredulously.

He yawned again. 'If it were up to me you could go anywhere you pleased.' Then he rolled over and his breathing came at low and regular intervals. He was already fast asleep.

She stared at him for a long while, turned off the lights, and crawled under the covers. She pulled them up to her chin and lay awake for hours. What did he mean, if it were up to him she could go anywhere she pleased?

She found out the next morning, after Luigi had left. She had gone to the passport office, realizing that since she had renounced her American citizenship, she no longer held a valid passport. To date, they'd never had the opportunity to vacation outside Italy, so she'd never bothered getting one.

At the passport office she received the ominous news: she was not allowed to travel outside the country.

She couldn't believe it. There had to be some mistake. Finally she called the Minister of Defense.

'I am sorry, Principessa,' he told her with a soft but final tone of voice. 'Things are happening.'

'Yes, indeed they are,' she snapped. 'I can't even travel! I'm a prisoner here.'

He laughed soothingly. 'No, Principessa. It is just that your husband is handling a very delicate mission, and for that reason the powers that be think it best that you stay in Italy. Please, feel free to travel all you want within this country. There are many beautiful things to see.'

'Thank you,' she said sarcastically, and slammed down the receiver. She closed her eyes and took a series of deep breaths in order to calm her nerves. For a moment, she felt compelled to go to the American embassy, but she realized the futility of that.

She was no longer an American. There was nothing they would be able to do for her.

Whichever way she looked at it, one thing was clear.

She was a prisoner.

The following day, Tuesday, was when the letter arrived. Charlotte-Anne always looked forward to receiving news from home, and went to read it outside under the shade trees beside the pool. As usual, it was written in her mother's slanting, elegant script, but she immediately noticed that the words weren't neatly formed as if at times Elizabeth-Anne's hand had been shaking.

298

This time, it was a letter which brought pain and shock into her life.

July 21, 1936

My darling Charlotte-Anne,

How I miss you, especially now of all times! And oh, how it grieves me to have to write you this. It's been two weeks now since I've written last, longer than any other time between letters, and I know you must have wondered why. Now the bad news must come.

Your sister Rebecca died yesterday. I know you will have to read and reread that terrible sentence again and again before you can believe it. She was hospitalized with pneumonia, but there was nothing they could do to save her. Oh, Charlotte-Anne, what am I going to do? You, your brother, and your two sisters are everything in my life. A woman's children are the legacy of herself and her husband. It makes this loss doubly painful for me. It was as though not only Rebecca, but your father, too, had died all over again. I don't know if I'll ever be able to get over this loss. I know time is supposed to heal all wounds, but I don't know if that's really true. Still today, I sometimes relive old wounds I received in my childhood. Nothing ever heals, not completely at least. The scars always remain.

When the hospital called and we rushed over, I could not believe it. Rebecca looked so at peace, so restful. I was certain it was a trick, or some kind of joke. She looked as if she were sleeping.

Larry is so good to me, especially now. It's strange, you know. He isn't your real father, but he feels like a father toward you all. Rebecca's death seems to have hit him harder than anyone else. Last night, when I thought he was asleep, I woke to find him crying.

It is heartbreaking, but just last week Rebecca was starting to make plans to visit you next summer. It would have been so nice for you and she to have seen each other, but I realize that Italy is far away. Do not try to blame yourself for not having seen her in so long. We are all mere mortals, and we cannot see what the future holds for us. There is a power beyond our comprehension in whose hands our destinies lie.

I know from your painful letters in which you confided to me about your tragic miscarriages, that all is not perfect with you

*either. Life, alas, is never perfect. I know now that if you and
Rebecca had been able to see more of each other, it would have
made no difference over life or death in the end. It just seems such a
terrible shame – and hurts so much – that one so young can so
suddenly be struck down. She was only nineteen! How little we
still all know.*

*Dearest darling, I know how you must feel reading this, but
please take heart. Your sister was a good person. I know that she
is in heaven and someday we will all be reunited. I don't believe
that this is just the hopeful rambling of a woman in much pain.
There is a greater design to the world than we know – there must
be – and in the depths of my heart I know that, no matter how he
tests us, God is good.*

*Perhaps this coming year, if you cannot come to visit us, Larry
and I will at least come to Rome. He has business interests in
Europe which, due to the international situation, he thinks he
might do well to liquidate; perhaps we can combine business with
a short visit with you. I would really love to do that. How I ache
to see you again and put my arms around you, and hug you.*

*Take care, my darling, for Larry says all is not well in the
world right now, and I have learned to trust his judgment. If there
is anything we can do to help you, please let me know.*

Your loving Mamma

Charlotte-Anne let the letter drop to her lap. She covered
her face with her hands and wept. It was doubly cruel that
Luigi was not at her side to comfort her. She wanted him to
hold her, to murmur soothing words, to share some of this
burden with her. But he wouldn't be back from Germany
for two months. Only now did it occur to her that out of the
hundreds of people she knew in Rome, there was not one
close friend she could call upon in a time of need.

She had to suffer the burden of Rebecca's loss by herself.

And as she did so, she realized it was more important
than ever to get her passport and receive permission to visit
with her family.

But even when Luigi returned, that dream proved
impossible to attain.

'I'm sorry, *cara*,' he told her, his voice gentle and
sympathetic, 'but they are afraid.'

'Afraid? They?' She stared at him, 'Who are *they*, and why are *they* afraid?'

'Because of my job. It's highly sensitive, you know that, and with things going the way they are in the world, they are afraid that if I told you anything, perhaps even talked in my sleep, and you let any information slip out, however innocently, great harm could come to this country.'

His words infuriated her, but she knew that there was nothing that could be done.

If a di Fontanesi couldn't pull those kinds of strings, then who could?

15

Elizabeth-Anne and Larry arrived in Rome during the first week of April, 1937. Charlotte-Anne was doubly delighted. Not only was she going to see them again at long last, but Luigi had juggled his schedule and managed to take an entire week off in honor of the occasion. That, she well knew, was no small matter, and she was touched by his thoughtfulness. She felt as though it was a combined family reunion and second honeymoon.

Luigi came along with her to meet the train at the Terminal Railroad Station. The moment it chugged in, Charlotte-Anne caught sight of Larry and her mother leaning out of the window of a first class carriage, and tears of happiness rolled down her cheeks. She'd missed them both more than she'd realized. Her mother looked so different, she noticed with surprise. She seemed older, but somehow less distant. Charlotte-Anne had to remind herself that she hadn't seen her mother in six years; Elizabeth-Anne was just forty-three and she was now twenty-three.

'Mamma,' she sobbed as soon as the train jerked to a halt and Elizabeth-Anne came hurrying down the steps. They fell into each other's arms and held their embrace for a long time.

Elizabeth-Anne was crying, too. 'Look what a sight we make,' she said, laughing through her tears as she dabbed first her daughter's eyes and then her own with a white-lace handkerchief. 'Oh, darling, let me look at you!' She held her daughter at arm's length and shook her head. 'I still can't believe that it's really you. It's been so long.' She pressed her cheek against Charlotte-Anne's.

'I know.' Charlotte-Anne smiled and pulled away from her. 'And Mamma, this is Luigi.'

He stood tall and dashing in his uniform, then bowed somewhat formally. Elizabeth-Anne broke the ice by kissing and hugging him warmly. Then, as Larry shook his hand and hugged Charlotte-Anne, a porter picked up their luggage and followed them out to the waiting Daimler. The two women walked arm in arm. The men led the way, taking the opportunity to get acquainted.

'I know you invited us to stay at the villa,' Elizabeth-Anne said, 'and we really do appreciate it. I hope you won't be offended that we made reservations at the Excelsior.'

'The Excelsior?' Elizabeth-Anne looked at her with dismay. 'But why stay at a hotel? We have plenty of empty guestrooms at the villa.'

'Thank you, darling, but no,' Elizabeth-Anne smiled. They had reached the car and waited for the chauffeur to fold down the jump seats. Then Elizabeth-Anne ducked inside and waited for Charlotte-Anne to follow. 'It's nothing personal, I assure you. I really do prefer to stay at the hotel.'

'Don't forget,' Larry grinned as he and Luigi took a seat on the leather-upholstered jump seats facing them, 'hotels are in your mother's blood.'

Elizabeth-Anne leaned forward and slapped his thigh good-naturedly. 'There he goes again! He loves to make it sound as though the hotels are all I care about.' Then her tone grew more serious. 'But really, I've been waiting a long time for just this opportunity, and I intend to take full advantage of it. It isn't every year that I get the chance to come overseas to spy on the grand hotels of Europe. I've made up my mind to stay at every one I can, in order to see

302

what needs improving with our own. I can only do that by experiencing first hand what the competition is offering.'

'In that case,' Charlotte-Anne said, 'I can't very well argue with you, Mamma, can I?'

'No,' Elizabeth-Anne said with a laugh, 'I'm afraid you can't.'

After Elizabeth-Anne and Larry got settled into their suite at the Excelsior, Charlotte-Anne sent the car around to bring them to the villa for dinner. She had done herself proud, bringing out the 1878 Ginori china with its cobalt-blue and gilt ribbon edges, the Baccarat crystal, the di Fontanesi heirloom silver, and the heavy linen embroidered by the Sisters in the Convent of Our Lady of Peace. The candles cast a soft, flattering light, and everyone had dressed for dinner. She had instructed the cook to prepare a true Southern Italian feast, made up of the authentic peasant dishes that were her favorites. And what food it was ! The generous platter of antipasto, and the chilled sliced eel on beds of shaved ice were followed by Pasta alla Siciliana – spaghetti baked with tomato sauce, eggplant, zucchini, and olives. Then came the Saltimbocca Romana, 'sandwiches' consisting of outer layers of veal and prociutto, and filled with melted mozarella cheese. The red wine came from the di Fontanesis' own vineyards, and the fresh baked bread came straight from the oven, garlicky and steaming hot. For dessert there was a choice of tortoni, spumoni or ripe fresh fruit, as well as cups of thick, rich black espresso.

'If I eat another bite,' Larry announced as he wiped his lips and then placed his crumpled napkin on his plate, 'I think I'll burst.'

Charlotte-Anne smiled. As she looked around the table, she was filled with joy. Except for Regina and Zaccheus, everyone she loved was seated in her home for dinner. It seemed too good to be true.

'So you are not returning to the United States together?' Luigi asked politely as they headed back into the salon.

'No.' Elizabeth-Anne shook her head. 'Larry has some

303

business to attend to in Germany, but I'm not going along. He doesn't want me to.'

'It's clear Germany is a powder keg right now,' Larry said worriedly. 'The situation is much too volatile. I don't think anyone should go there unless it's necessary.'

Charlotte-Anne glanced at Luigi to try to read his expression, but his face was studiously blank. He crossed over to the fruitwood sideboard, and while a servant came in with a tray of liquors in tiny glasses, he picked up his humidor, opened it, and brought it over to Larry. Larry selected a cigar, sniffed it appreciatively, and rattled it next to his ear before lighting it. Luigi merely selected one at random and lit it. The two men sat down together on facing easy chairs to discuss politics while Charlotte-Anne and Elizabeth-Anne sat on a couch and caught up on the latest news of family and friends.

'Zaccheus has grown so tall for a thirteen-year-old,' Elizabeth-Anne said proudly. 'And he's become so handsome. I've brought you a picture of him, but I left it at the hotel. I'll give it to you tomorrow. You'd never recognize your brother. He's the spitting image of his father.'

'Has he decided what he is going to do yet?'

'Well, I eventually want him to go to college and join the hotel chain, but he's dead set against it.' Elizabeth-Anne shook her head in disbelief. 'He wants to go to Annapolis.'

'The Navy?'

Elizabeth-Anne nodded. 'He won't let us talk him out of it.'

'You're afraid of all the troubles brewing, too, aren't you Mamma?'

Elizabeth-Anne's face wore a sprained expression. 'Yes,' she said quietly, 'I am. I'm especially afraid for Zaccheus. If another war does come, and Larry thinks it's inevitable . . . ' She shrugged eloquently. 'Well, I'm a mother. No mother wants to see her son go off and lay his life on the line, no matter what the reason.'

'I understand how you feel,' Charlotte-Anne said. 'I feel the same way about Luigi. His being in the military . . . ' she paused, reluctant to worry her mother with the truth.

'Anyway! Enough of this maudlin talk.' She sat up. 'How's Regina?'

'She sends you her love. Her graduation from medical school was wonderful; we combined it with a celebration of her twenty-fifth birthday. I wish you had been there. She's on her way to being a fine pediatrician, you know. But I must admit I'm not looking forward to her marriage. Her fiancé's orthopedic practice is in San Francisco, so she'll join him there.' She looked pained. 'It's so hard for a mother to watch her children scatter all over the place. Rebecca is dead, Zaccheus wants to join the military. Now Regina's going to be across the country and you're here across the ocean . . . None of my children want anything to do with Hale Hotels.' She shook her head. 'And yet I know if you try to keep your loved ones on too tight a rein, and don't let them do what they want, you chase them away all the faster.'

'You didn't chase me away, Mamma,' Charlotte-Anne said softly. 'I fell in love.'

'I know you did.' Elizabeth-Anne smiled and squeezed Charlotte-Anne's hand. Her voice dropped to a whisper. 'And I can see why. Luigi is awfully handsome.'

They both stole a sideways glance at him and smiled, but their good spirits soon faded as they listened to the men's conversation.

'You keep referring vaguely to Germany's problems. So what,' Luigi was saying between puffs of blue smoke from his cigar, 'kind of problems do you think Germany has?'

Larry smiled crookedly, without humor. His one eye watched Luigi intently. 'Hitler.'

'But do you not think the Germans want Hitler?'

Larry sat back, making himself more comfortable. 'The way I see it, they haven't much choice. Not anymore, at least.' He blew out another thick stream of blue smoke. For a moment he studied his cigar in silence. 'Hitler is now fully entrenched in power. It's too late to do anything about that now. He'll never step down voluntarily. And so far, Germany's economy has been so bad that the people are under the mistaken impression that he's their only

305

salvation. Besides, he's claiming to bring dignity back to Germany by repudiating the Versailles treaty and the reparations agreements, and by remilitarizing the Rhineland. The Germans look upon him as their savior. And why not? They're desperate. And in their desperation, they are unable to see things clearly. They do not see that in the long run, all he can really bring them is despair.'

'I have been to Germany quite often,' Luigi said casually. 'Il Duce and the Führer are strengthening ties.'

'And both Germany and Italy are supporting Franco, I know, but I think the only result of the Spanish Civil War will be a compounding of an already tragic situation. Hundreds of thousands, even millions, are going to die.'

'In Spain?' Luigi asked curiously.

Larry shook his head slowly, his expression grim. 'I think you know better than that.'

Luigi shrugged noncommittally and smoked on in silence.

'In Spain,' Larry said. 'And in all of Europe. There will be much bloodshed, I'm afraid. Bloodshed like there has never been before.'

'But why do you think it will involve all of Europe?'

'I've listened to Hitler's speeches.' Larry's voice was quiet but ominous. 'Of course, there are those who wave it off as the ranting and raving of a lunatic. And there are others who simply scoff or laugh at him.' He sat forward, his body tensed. 'Personally, I don't subscribe to either opinion. Or perhaps I would, to both, if the situation weren't so deadly serious. Hitler's out to do what he preaches, you mark my word. And he is a very persuasive personality.'

'Then perhaps people shouldn't listen to him so closely,' Luigi suggested. 'Perhaps he is simply telling them what they want to hear.'

'Is that what you think?' Larry asked, staring at him steadily.

Luigi did not reply. For a moment, they all sat quietly in the growing, uncomfortable silence.

Charlotte-Anne, ever the perfect hostess, knew from experience just when it was time to change the subject. She sat up straight and clapped her hands together. 'I have an idea,' she said brightly, intending not only to break the silence, but to keep her mother in Rome longer. 'What if Mamma stays here while Larry goes to Germany? Then you can both meet here for another week-long stay before returning to the States?'

Elizabeth-Anne shook her head. 'Thank you, dear, but no. We've worked out our schedule and it leaves little leeway for extending our trip. We can't stay here that long. We've both got to be getting back as soon as possible. And it's as I said before, I'm keen on seeing what the grand hotels of Europe have to offer. From here I'm going on to Venice to stay at both the Danieli and the Gritti Palace, to Paris for a look at the Georges Cinq, the Ritz, the Crillon, and the Plaza Athénée, and London for the Ritz and Claridge's. Then I'm sailing home from England, and Larry's going from Germany. I think it's high time New York had a world class hotel of its own, don't you?'

'There are some fine hotels in New York,' Luigi commented diplomatically.

Elizabeth-Anne surveyed him with raised eyebrows. 'Some fine ones, yes,' she corrected him, never one to mince words. 'But a truly legendary hotel? No, we don't have one of those. And I intend to give the city one. When we bought the Shelburne Hotel. I had plans for it, and now I intend to see them to fruition. I'm going to renovate the entire building, top to bottom, down to every last room. It will be the ''flagship'' of the entire chain, and I'm even renaming it. It will be the Hale Palace.'

'Mamma,' Charlotte-Anne laughed, 'you'll never change, will you? Always building, building, building.'

Elizabeth-Anne smiled faintly. 'What else is there to do in the world? One can either build things, destroy them, or rest on one's laurels and watch the time go by. Myself, I've never been one who was able to sit still.'

The seven days flew by so quickly that it seemed to Charlotte-Anne that Larry and her mother had barely arrived before it was time for them to pack their bags and leave again. Larry was taking the train to Germany;

Elizabeth-Anne was traveling with him as far as Venice.

'I wish you could have stayed a lot longer,' Charlotte-Anne told them regretfully as they all rode to the Terminal Station together in the Daimler. The late afternoon shadows were a deep tide of purple creeping slowly across the sidewalks.

'In other circumstances, we would have,' Larry assured her, 'but with thirty-seven hotels and tourist courts to look after, your mother has become an extremely busy woman. And for my part, I want to get all our business finished here as quickly as possible, and then reinvest the money in the States. The world is in turmoil right now. It's a time bomb. It won't be long before someone lights the fuse.'

Charlotte-Anne shivered. 'Don't frighten me, Larry,' she said in a low voice.

He looked pained and patted her hand. 'I find it frightening, too, but I'm realistic. That's the way things are. Fooling ourselves does no one any good. Besides, there are always two sides to a coin. In times of war and turmoil, nations' economies change. Some for the better, and some for the worse. It's high time to put some of our money into munitions and aircraft plants in the States. Those are the investments of the future.'

'Aren't you forgetting something?' Elizabeth-Anne asked with a sidelong glance at him.

'Of course not.' He laughed, breaking the tension. 'And the hotels,' he said pointedly with mock seriousness, 'keep growing.'

On the station platform, Larry took Charlotte-Anne aside and held her close. 'Listen, if there's anything you want, anything at all, you'll let us know?'

She nodded. For the first time she saw him not only as her mother's second husband, but as a father to her too. She stood on tiptoe and kissed his cheek. 'Yes, Daddy,' she said softly, for the first time not using his Christian name.

He looked deeply touched and hugged her tightly. 'You're sure you don't want to come back to the States and sit things out for a while? At least until the troubles here are over? You've always got a place at home with us.'

She thought fleetingly how tempting that offer was, but it was no use. And she couldn't admit to Larry and her mother that she wasn't allowed to leave Italy.

'I'm sure,' she said, switching on her brightest smile. Then she added softly, 'My home is here, beside Luigi. He's my husband, and I love him. But thanks anyway.'

She was quiet with sadness now that they were about to leave. It was as though she had a premonition that her life was changing. If Larry was right, the neat order of things was about to be upset. She would no longer be able to govern her thoughts and actions. With marriage, she had crossed over a threshold over which she could not return.

'We worry about you,' Elizabeth-Anne told her as she took her daughter in her arms.

Charlotte-Anne pressed her head against her mother's breast. 'Whatever for?' she murmured. 'I'm like you, Mamma. Indomitable. And besides, I'm being well taken care of.' She pulled away gently, sought Luigi's hand, and gave it a firm squeeze. Then the conductor's shrill whistle resounded down the platform, they all quickly exchanged a few last kisses, and Larry helped Elizabeth-Anne up into the first class carriage.

Charlotte-Anne and Luigi watched the train as it pulled out slowly. She followed her mother's waving hand, and she waved back with a white handkerchief. Soon the hand and the train disappeared from sight.

'They are very nice people,' Luigi observed as they walked back outside to the car. 'They love you very much.'

Charlotte-Anne nodded. 'And they both liked you, even if Larry didn't agree with all your opinions.'

'He is a very bright man. Perhaps he did not agree, but he understood.'

'He thinks it will all end in tragedy.' She stopped walking and stared at Luigi in silence for a moment, gazing into those darkly hypnotic eyes of his. 'Do you think that too, Luigi? You never talk about it.'

He shrugged. 'I can do many things, *cara*, but I cannot read the future.'

She laughed then and hooked her arm through his. The visit had done them both a world of good. She hadn't felt so light-hearted and alive in a very long time. And it had been ages since she had seen Luigi for so long without interruption.

'What I still can't get over,' she marveled, shaking her head in amazement, 'is the fact that it's possible to fly from Germany to New York in a little over fifty-one hours. Larry can get there in two days from Frankfurt, while Mamma's crossing will take six or seven days. It's as if the world is shrinking right in front of our very eyes.'

'That is nothing, compared to the future,' Luigi speculated. 'Someday, it will be a matter of mere hours.'

'Is that the aviator in you speaking?' she teased him.

'It is.'

'Well, we'll just have to wait and see. Myself, I can't comprehend that. But someday, I *would* like to fly across the Atlantic like Larry's going to do. I think it's exciting.'

'And someday you shall.'

'Maybe you'll be my pilot.'

He made a face. 'Not until passenger airplanes can make that trip. I'm an airplane pilot, *cara*. I don't consider those Zeppelins to be flying machines. All they are is giant balloons.'

'But fast ones.'

'You think they are fast? Not compared to airplanes they're not. They are slow and clumsy.'

And, it was proved on May 6, 1937, they were unsafe as well.

Exactly one year after a regular passenger service was inaugurated between New York and Frankfurt, the *Hindenburg*, while mooring in Lakehurst, New Jersey, exploded and burned. Of the ninety-seven people onboard the giant dirigible, there were thirty-six who lost their lives.

Larry Hochstetter was among them.

16

Much later, when she looked back on it, Charlotte-Anne realized that in a way Larry had been lucky. She knew it was often said that death was worse for those left behind, the loved ones who had to face the world, suddenly alone. When she thought of her mother's grief, expressed in Elizabeth-Anne's long and eloquent letters, Charlotte-Anne didn't doubt the truth of that saying. Through the letters, she felt Elizabeth-Anne's pain and disbelief at again having to endure the loss of her husband, just as Charlotte-Anne herself felt the unspeakable devastation of losing a second father. But her mother didn't lose herself in misery long; she steeled herself to her new, lonelier world and threw herself into her work, finding her own kind of comfort and sustenance in running the Hale empire.

But it wasn't only the struggle for recovery that Larry was spared. Difficult as their personal tragedy was, Charlotte-Anne found herself more frightened and over-whelmed by the political drama that was unfolding. For Larry had been right. The bloodshed he had predicted indeed came, enveloping Europe. Hitler was hungry for power and, together with Mussolini, began to swallow up entire lands and peoples. Europe simmered until it finally reached the boiling point.

By 1937, Italy had conquered Ethiopia.

In 1938, Italy followed the example of its ally Germany and adopted anti-Semitic laws.

In January of 1939, Il Duce announced the annexation of Albania, a conscious imitation of the 'victories' of ancient Rome.

On March 31, 1938, after four years of the right wing dictators Schuschnigg and Dollfus in Austria, Hitler marched in from Bavaria and the resulting *Anschluss* made Austria an integral part of Germany.

In 1939, Hitler signed a non-aggression pact with the Soviet Union.

It was quickly broken.

By that time Charlotte-Anne had ceased going to social functions unless Luigi was in town. She could no longer bear to hear the self-congratulatory tone of people's voices, or the excited discussions of the new, rising Roman Empire. No one seemed to take into account that the victories had been so easy because many of the conquered had hardly reached the beginnings of the mechanized age. Too often, the victory was nothing more than the slaughter of innocent, virtually stone age tribes by tanks and machine guns.

And then, between the first and the twenty-seventh of September, 1939, the powder keg exploded. Both Nazi Germany and the Soviet Union invaded Poland, dividing a country which had tried to fight twentieth century battles with the weapons of the nineteenth.

But Hitler's scheming came to its ridiculous but tragic head after he met the ineffectual British Prime Minister, Neville Chamberlain, in Munich. Chamberlain, as well as his counterpart in France, anxious to spare their countries from the voracious appetite of the Axis powers, gave the Führer the sanction to dismember Czechoslovakia. France and England promised not to interfere.

As she nervously paced the deceptively peaceful gardens of the Villa della Rosa, Charlotte-Anne could only wonder, *Where will all this lead us next?*

She never answered herself, for the reply was too frightening. She worked hard to keep the world at bay; to her, the walls surrounding the Villa della Rosa made it an oasis from reality.

In the fall of 1940, when Luigi came home from a tour of duty after carrying out yet another of his mysterious assignments for Il Duce, he and Charlotte-Anne had made love in the afternoon. While they lay in silence with the curtains drawn over the late sun, waiting for their breathing to return to normal, Charlotte-Anne put her fears into words. 'Luigi,' she whispered, 'what is happening to the world? What is it going to do to us?'

'Don't worry, *cara*,' he said casually, nuzzling her naked back with his lips. 'It's all for the best.'

She sat up and pressed the rumpled sheet against her breasts. 'But only yesterday I saw people beaten up in the streets and then herded into trucks. I asked someone what was happening, and he said it was because they were Jews.'

'I suggest you don't concern yourself with the Jews,' he said darkly.

'How can I not?' she said fiercely. 'Hitler's gobbling up

312

Europe like some famished emperor, and he's throwing Il Duce the crumbs. What will happen if this continues? Hitler and Mussolini want to conquer the world! Luigi, what if the United States enters into this?'

'The concerns of Europe are not the concerns of America. The United States has had its fill of war from the last one. You will see. America will wisely stay out of this.'

Famous last words, she thought, when on December 7, 1941, the Japanese attacked Pearl Harbor.

It was not long before Japan's allies, Germany and Italy, declared war on the United States.

The United States, in turn, declared war on Germany on December 8, 1941.

And on Italy three days later.

Charlotte-Anne di Fontanesi, born in the United States and an American in her heart, suddenly found herself an enemy of all she held dear other than her husband.

On opposite sides of the Atlantic, Elizabeth-Anne and Charlotte-Anne greeted the declarations of war with equal fear and dismay. Diplomatic relations between Italy and the United States were cut, and mail exchange was no longer possible through normal postal channels. Only through the efforts of Cardinal Corsini, who acted as middleman, did Charlotte-Anne and her mother stay in touch. Vatican intermediaries smuggled their letters, which necessitated going through a lengthy chain of archdioceses. The Vatican was officially neutral, but Pope Pius XII was considered by Hitler to be a pest. Rumor was that the Führer was considering moving the pope and his entire baliwick to Germany or, God forbid, to Liechtenstein, where the Vatican could be monitored much more closely and be far less influential.

So exchanging letters took time, generally eight to ten weeks, but sometimes as much as five months. Each time a letter got through, Charlotte-Anne seized upon it, pressed it to her heart, and then read it over and over. The news from New York was good, and bad, and bittersweet.

. . . *Things are very hectic without Larry, and how I miss him!*

Sometimes I wonder how I manage to get everything done without him. He was such a terrific administrator, I only realize that now. He's made certain that the empire practically runs itself . . .

I just added three new tourist courts to the chain. Of course, it being wartime, a lot of the executives are gone fighting, and it's making for a lot of extra work for me. With the men gone, I've had to hire a lot of women, and they're working out just fine . . .

Zaccheus has been shipped to active duty in the Pacific. He was so excited to finally be part of what he calls the "fighting navy," but he's only 18! I worry about him constantly . . .

I hope everything in Rome is fine. The reports we get here are all so vague. I really don't know what to think, but I know now, with Luigi on the other side, and you there too, how people must have felt during our Civil War, with brother fighting brother . . .

I'm so devastated. I don't know if I can bear this new tragedy. Zaccheus has been sent home, and he's in the hospital. I don't know what to think or do, other than pray. He's had to have both his legs amputated, and sometimes I fear he's even lost the will to live . . .

I'm so happy about Zaccheus's nurse, Janet. She's kind and plain, but a sensible woman, and she's nursing him so well. For the first time, Zaccheus seems to be gaining some of his old fight back . . .

You wouldn't believe it, darling! I cried and cried all through the ceremony. Janet will make him such a wonderful and understanding wife. Only a year after his horrible injury and now they love each other so dearly, and it's heartwarming to know that she can take good care of him . . .

Janet is pregnant! I'm so overjoyed. At least something good has come out of this damn war!

For a while, it was impossible for Charlotte-Anne to guess which side would win. Germany had the support of Italy and Japan, but the Allies consisted of the United States, France, England, and the Soviet Union. Battle after battle seemed to be the turning point, leaving one side or the other in the stronger position.

Since the United States had gotten involved, Charlotte-Anne no longer tried to hide but followed the war avidly.

She started going out again, if only to catch up on the latest news.

Charlotte-Anne's circle of acquaintances knew more than most, as they were the power brokers of Rome. Not everyone was as discreet as Luigi, and gossip flowed freely. If the generals and their wives weren't lying, she quickly discovered, then what she read in the newspapers and heard on the radio wasn't the entire truth, not by a long shot. Listening to the official Italian reports, one would have thought that the Allies were taking a devastating beating. At first this was true, but as time went by, Charlotte-Anne learned from her select circle of friends that the Allies were beginning to win. Charlotte-Anne didn't dare let on how desperately happy this news made her.

And when, on September 9, 1943, the Allies invaded Italy, she sat in the garden of the Villa della Rosa and broke open a bottle of champagne and celebrated quietly by herself.

She had celebrated prematurely; she found that out all too soon.

On September 10, Luigi returned to Rome. He had one night to spend with her before being transferred down to the boot of Italy with an Infantry division in order to try and stop the Allies in their tracks. For once, he allowed his worries to show. The fact that Il Duce had put his premier flying ace in charge of mere foot-soldiers spoke for itself. Luigi couldn't hide his awareness of the fact that it would only be a matter of time before Italy was conquered.

Charlotte-Anne was more terrified than she had ever been. It was common knowledge that in any war, infantrymen suffered the heaviest casualties. Now she feared for his life so deeply that she berated herself for cheering the Allies on. But she had little time to torment herself. She had to put on her best face for Luigi; after he was gone, she could torture herself with worries all she pleased.

The precious hours flew by. When the staff car arrived to fetch him, she saw him out to the front gate. The night was still and, with one hand, she clutched her nightgown around her shoulders. A sliver of moon floated like a white gondola in the sky. He kissed her deeply and urgently, and then he extracted the promise from her.

'Please, *cara*. There is something you must do for me.' His voice was thick. 'I don't have the time, or I would do it myself. Go to the Palazzo di Cristallo and persuade my parents to come to Rome and stay here until it is all over. They'll be safer here. I'm afraid there's going to be a lot of fighting and bloodshed to the south.'

She had no wish to ever see them or the palazzo again, but she knew she could not refuse him this one wish. He loved his parents, and she loved him. She had never let him know how much she and his mother hated each other and never would, especially not now, when he was being shipped to the front. He would have enough things on his mind without her adding to his misery – important things, such as staying alive.

So she promised.

Umbria lulled one into a sense of false security. On the surface, wherever she looked, Charlotte-Anne saw a world at peace. The vineyards were well tended, the grapes lushly hanging on the vines.

No matter how much she argued, the Principessa Marcella would not allow Charlotte-Anne to persuade her and the Prince to travel to Rome. 'I wouldn't dream of leaving here,' she snapped at her daughter-in-law. 'A di Fontanesi never turns tail and runs.'

'But it's going to be dangerous,' Charlotte-Anne protested. 'And, anyway, it wasn't my idea. It was Luigi's.'

The Principessa's dark eyes were hooded. 'There is danger everywhere. Even in Rome.'

'But Luigi thinks that Umbria will become a battle-field.'

'Then let it be so. I, for one, refuse to be driven from my home.'

'But don't you care about your well-being?' Charlotte-Anne argued incredulously. 'Or about living? Must you be so stubborn and selfish?'

'Stop being so melodramatic,' the Principessa said

irritably. 'If *you* want to leave and return to Rome, then you're welcome to do so.'

And Charlotte-Anne thought: *I would, if only I could. But I promised Luigi that I would see to it that his parents are safe and taken care of. How can I do that if I return to Rome?*

So she stayed on for several more days, and before she knew it, the days became weeks. Then she began to feel unwell. At first, when she missed her period, she didn't pay much attention to it. It had happened often enough before. Then each morning, and anytime she smelled food, she began to feel nauseated.

Suddenly she was afraid for more than herself and Luigi's parents.

Even before she went to see the doctor, she knew she was pregnant once again.

As the date of her delivery drew nearer, so did the war, but Charlotte-Anne stayed on at the Palazzo di Cristallo. A promise was a promise, and Luigi, misguided though he might have been politically, was her husband. She could not let him down. If his parents refused to leave, then she had no choice but to stay with them.

Umbria became a cauldron of speculation. Rumors about the Americans abounded. People said that they were advancing, others that they had been driven back into the sea. Still others whispered that they were committing atrocities.

Charlotte-Anne didn't listen to any of it. She knew the Americans weren't monsters. But she was fearful for her unborn child. Ever since her first stillborn child, she had never carried a child fullterm. Day after day, she prayed that she would be able to this time. Now that the world had gone mad, and there was so much death, she wanted more than ever to bring a little joy, a new life into the world.

Each day which passed without the feared miscarriage seemed a miracle.

Months passed, and her body grew swollen. She found it increasingly difficult to walk around. When eight months had passed, she wept silently for joy.

In her ninth month, the Allies had beaten the retreating

Germans and Italians to within ten miles south of the palazzo.

Once again, Charlotte-Anne pleaded with Marcella, who steadfastly reiterated, 'This is my home. I will not leave.'

Now when the wind blew from the south, it brought along with it the reverberation of artillery barrages. The night sky began to look like it did back home on the Fourth of July. Then they became aware of the retreating wounded Germans and Italians.

And finally, the Allies were but two miles away.

It was then that Charlotte-Anne formulated the plan. She knew little of military strategy, but she knew two things: the hill upon which the Palazzo di Cristallo had been built, and the hill on which the convent was located, were two of the highest points in the entire region. The Germans and the Allies would each surely try to gain control of them, for whoever was king of these hills could control the surrounding countryside with ease.

She smuggled off one last letter to her mother, informing her that she was now in her eighth and a half month of pregnancy, and then she saw to it that a storm cellar was dug in the middle of the vineyards, much like the ones they used to have in Texas in case of tornadoes.

If worst came to worst, and she and the di Fontanesis found themselves in the middle of a battlefield, they would be able to hide out there in relative safety.

The shelter was barely completed before she was grateful for her foresight.

17

She wasn't sure how long it had been since they fled the palazzo. It seemed days at least since they had hidden out in the vineyard.

There was hardly room for the three of them, and they could barely stretch out all at once. All they had with them was some candles for light, which they used frugally. Above them, the hastily contrived trapdoor was a piece of thick wood, camouflaged by a huge grapevine which they had pulled over it. The little food they had managed to take with them had run out quickly and now they were hungry, thirsty and tired. Their nerves were on edge. Charlotte-Anne feared that at any moment they would reach the breaking point, lose control, and turn on each other.

The dark pit of the shelter stank from the bucket they used in the corner and from their own sweat. The battle above seemed to last forever. All they ever heard was the constant roar and echo of artillery barrages, the muffled rat-a-tat-tat chatter of machine guns, the whines of stray bullets. Too often, shells landed nearby, causing tremors in the pit, and stones and earth would come loose and slide down the wall.

Charlotte-Anne was certain they were going to be buried alive.

'Our home!' the Princess Marcella di Fontanesi wept over and over. 'All our treasures. Everything we own is going to be destroyed! Generations of – '

'Hush,' Prince Antonio di Fontanesi, the father of Charlotte-Anne's husband, hissed at his wife. 'At least we are alive.'

'Not for long,' his wife whined. 'You wait and see. We'll all be dead. When Luigi comes back, it'll be to bury us. If he ever finds us down here, that is. We would have been safer staying in the palazzo!'

Charlotte-Anne felt the first pain at the height of the bombing. Several times, she started to tell them, but each time she waited for it to subside. Finally, there was no way she could deny it.

'I'm going to have the baby,' she said.

'What? Now?' The Principessa Marcella's voice was a hiss in the darkness. 'Here? We have no food to eat, and we've run out of water to drink . . .'

Charlotte-Anne struggled to spread out more comfortably. 'I can't do anything about it,' she said apologetically. 'I know the timing's bad. Please, you must help me.'

'You are Luigi's wife. Of course we'll help you,' Prince Antonio said. 'Won't we, Marcella?'

'If only the battle would let up,' the Principessa wailed. The carefully modulated, cultured tones of her voice had deserted her, and she sounded like any frightened, whining fishwife. 'How can we help? We can barely see what we're doing? There is only one candle left. And this place is so *filthy*.'

Charlotte-Anne reached out and touched her mother-in-law's arm. 'But it's safe, at least for the time being.'

Another mortar round landed close by, and the ground shook crazily. Simultaneously, a million hailstones rained down on the trapdoor.

Principessa Marcella let out a shriek. 'It's the end!' she screamed. 'The end!'

'Quiet,' her husband hissed. 'We must remain calm.'

'Calm!' his wife cried. 'How do you propose I stay calm?'

'We *must*. We have a baby to deliver.'

The Principessa began to laugh hysterically. 'If it weren't for *her*, and her precious *baby*, we wouldn't be in this fix. I'm leaving! I'm getting out of this trap. You two can stay here till kingdom comes, for all I care.' Her voice took on a mocking tone. 'Ironic, isn't it? *Her* countrymen have invaded Italy. It's because of them that – '

The sound of the Prince's hand was like a gunshot against his wife's cheek. She let out a shriek and quieted down. Then she began to whimper softly.

About six hours later, as the battle reached its zenith, the angry cries of the baby filled the pit.

'It's a girl,' the Prince said with soft pride. 'The house of the di Fontanesis has another princess.'

Principessa Marcella laughed. Her voice was shrill. 'Another princess! That's just what we need, you old fool, isn't it? Luigi's away in battle, killed for all we know. Who's to carry on our name? It's a *son* our house needs, not another daughter.'

Despite her exhaustion, Charlotte-Anne heard the Principessa's hysteria and was afraid that the Prince would once again strike his wife. Instead his voice trembled with dignified control. 'Be quiet, Marcella. Can't you, for once, count your blessings?'

Charlotte-Anne's eyes filled with tears. She had forced herself to hold on, to endure the ordeal for the child's sake. But now the darkness, the filth, the Principessa's hysteria and cruelty, her own unutterable exhaustion, it all became more than she could bear. The Prince held the child and she let herself slip into dark unconsciousness.

She had no idea how long she slept, but the baby's cries awoke her.

'I have to feed her,' Charlotte-Anne murmured.

Carefully, the Prince handed her the child.

'Hello, little daughter,' Charlotte-Anne whispered, her voice full of love.

'What are we going to name her?' the Prince asked.

'I don't know,' Charlotte-Anne answered. 'We'll wait for Luigi.' She was too exhausted to say more, so instead she uncovered her breasts and turned to the child. She laid her near her left breast, where the baby instantly found the nipple and began sucking purposefully. Then fear gripped Charlotte-Anne's heart. The baby suckled, but she wasn't getting any milk. Quickly, she moved the child to her other breast, but it, too, was dry.

A cold terror filled her. It was no use, she thought. She had no milk to give the child.

She stroked her baby gently. The infant sucked madly, then began to cry again. Charlotte-Anne's voice was a frightened whisper. '*I don't have any milk.*'

Principessa Marcella let out a groan of exasperation. 'See? What did I tell you? These modern American girls cannot do even that. I told you, didn't I? Why couldn't Luigi marry some nice Italian – '

'*Shut up, Marcella,*' the Prince roared. 'For once, will you just shut up!'

A wild kind of triumph crackled in the Principessa's voice, even above the miserable cries of the child. 'But how's the baby going to eat? Eh? You tell me! I suppose we just walk into the kitchen and heat it some milk – '

'Please!' Charlotte-Anne begged, her voice surprisingly strong. 'Stop it. You're only frightening the baby.'

Outside, the artillery barrage was coming closer, but there was a sudden silence in the pit. Even the baby was quiet, apparently exhausted. But it wasn't long before she began to wail again with hunger.

'Hush, hush, little baby, don't you cry,' Charlotte-Anne sang in English, feeling not only fear, but shame for failing in her most basic duty as a mother. The singing did little to quiet the child, and finally Charlotte-Anne wept in misery.

Eventually, the infant fell into a fitful sleep, as did Charlotte-Anne, but it didn't last long. The baby soon woke again from the pain of her hunger. The crying went on for hours, and there was nothing any of them could do.

Charlotte-Anne knew her baby would die.

Finally, she could stand it no more. She kissed the baby's soft cheek and whispered, 'I'm going to fetch you some food, Miss No-Name.'

'You cannot leave,' the Prince gasped, unbelievingly. 'Not while the battle is raging all around us. Besides, you are too weak.'

'Then who will get milk for the baby?' Charlotte-Anne asked quietly, painfully pushing herself up.

The Prince was silent. For once, even the Principessa did not speak.

'Momma will be back soon,' Charlotte-Anne told the baby. She kissed her and then reluctantly handed her over to the Prince. 'Take good care of her.'

'I will,' the Prince said solemnly.

Carefully, Charlotte-Anne rose, lifted the trapdoor lid, and peered out. It was night, but flashes of hellish artillery lit the sky, and the sounds of shelling were like thunder. She took a deep breath.

'We'll pray for you,' the Prince said in a shaky voice.

Charlotte-Anne looked down at her in-laws. In the flashes of shell-bursts and flares, their eyes gleamed up at her, wide and frightened. Then, without hesitating further, she slowly climbed out of the shelter, struggling for the strength to mount each step of the ladder. At the top, she let the trapdoor slam shut and collapsed. Her nose was filled with the stink of cordite and fire; she was surrounded by the stifling air of hell.

Slowly, torturously, she began to crawl on her belly.

Each movement was agonizing, but she imagined she thought she still heard her baby's cries and crawled on.

Before she managed to get fifty yards, she heard the chatter of a nearby machine gun. Two bullets slammed into her arm and her side. She rolled over on her back and looked up at the fireworks sky, feeling nothing so much as surprise. She tried to get up, but she could not move. She was confused, because rather than feeling pain, she couldn't feel her body at all.

Before she slipped into unconsciousness, she began to pray. Not for herself, but for her newborn child, who she feared would starve before the next day was through.

18

The three old crones dressed in tattered black moved slowly through the carnage. Black oily plumes of smoke billowed from various spots around the field. The whole scene seemed like a dreamscape. The intense blue of the cloudless sky, the spires of the tall cypresses, the heat from the fires all around which made everything shimmer, the destroyed weapons, the men lying silent or moaning, the blood-splattered corpses of those who had died or those who would shortly die – it was all unreal and thus, somehow, more bearable.

'It is over,' the first of the hunched-over old women whispered in a dry, brittle voice. 'All that is left now are the dead.'

'And the dying,' amended the second woman, clutching her ragged shawl with arthritic claws. Her sharp, pinpoint eyes moved down to the body lying face-down at her feet. It was one of the Italian men. She could tell from the uniform.

With her foot she nudged the stiff body so that it rolled over. The bloody face looked up at her with unseeing eyes.

'Do you recognize him?' hissed the third woman.

She shook her head and gazed all around her. The smell of death was strong in her ancient nostrils. She made a quick sign of the cross. She was an old woman, and death was no stranger to her. She herself had cheated death on at least three occasions. Hadn't she watched the other villagers starve to death? Hadn't she seen relatives and friends lined up against the village wall, shot to death by the firing squads? Hadn't she received letter after letter informing her that her grandchildren and her children were dead? All that was left now were the very old and the very young. And not even many of those.

She heard one of the other old women let out a sharp cry of delight as she spotted the glint of gold on the finger of a blood-encrusted hand. She shook her head, her lips working slackly on toothless gums. Nothing was new, not life, not death. There was simply more death now. But hadn't she predicted this? Hadn't she alone dared hiss aloud her hatred for the fascist pigs?

She continued to work her gums as she skirted the deep bomb craters and picked her way through the destroyed, dismembered bodies. Then she saw it. 'Quick, quick,' she called out, motioning for the others to come.

They hurried over and looked down. 'It is the Principessa,' the first woman hissed. 'In death all are equal!'

'No, she is not dead,' whispered the second. 'See? She still breathes.' She made a swift sign of the cross.

'Principessa indeed,' hissed the third. 'It is the Americana. She married him for the title only. I spit upon her!' She sprayed spittle onto the inert body. 'Even death is too good for her.'

'Do not speak so of the dying,' said the first, placing a dry, wrinkled hand on her arm. 'Come. We must see if there are any men we know lying here.'

'I spit upon you,' the third one hissed again.

'Wait,' the first said sharply. 'Listen!'

They all cocked their ears as they caught the muffled, high-pitched cry.

'It is a child,' said the first.

'No, it is just a soldier crying out,' said the second. 'In death even the men sound like the children.'

'Or it is the wind,' added the third.

The black apparitions slid slowly out of her line of vision as

Charlotte-Anne came to once again. Without moving her head she glanced around, her gaze confused. The white clouds were receding. In their place, she could see a vast blueness all around her. She was under water, staring up at the surface. The black apparitions had been people gazing down into the pool in which she lay quietly, like a fish afraid to move and draw attention to itself. She thought she recognized the strange smell which had eluded her earlier and which now seemed more pronounced than ever. She had smelled it once before, many years ago, when she'd been rushed to the emergency room with an appendicitis attack. There had been a highway accident somewhere that night, and she had smelled that same metallic, overpowering scent then.

It was the smell of death.

Death? She stared up at the blue sky. No, she couldn't be dead, she thought fuzzily. Not in this curved, beautiful, watery universe, where her entire being felt so pleasantly numb and good.

Slowly, ever so slowly she turned her head sideways and caught sight of a shattered arm. She frowned to herself. For a moment she couldn't comprehend the sight. Then she felt a dreamy fear growing within her, and it all came back to her in a flash.

The shell-shocking bombs, the whines of the bullets.

The earthquakes that shook the ground beneath her.

The strangely painless numbing of her body as fiery pain after fiery pain had flashed through it.

The quivers as things lodged within her.

The quick, powerful roar as her life blood rushed to meet the wounds, seeking escape from her body.

The geysers of blood, thick and red, solid streams at the bottoms flowing outward like ruby showers of rich, warm raindrops.

Her mind reeled now with the memory, and fear possessed her. Her heart pumped more madly, though she fought weakly to slow it down. She tried to calm her breathing, take more shallow breaths. After a moment her pulse slowed as she felt herself slipping away once again into unconsciousness.

She was dying. The revelation was sudden. Oh, but how beautiful it was, now that she thought about it . . . The strength seeping out of her, the whirling sensation, like being spun into an ever-quickening vortex. The dimming of everything around her and then the sudden, blinding white light, brighter than a thousand suns. How easy it had been to give herself up to that beguiling, dazzling light!

She felt a rivulet of something wet crawling down one cheek, toward her lips. She parted her lips and then tasted the salty tear. She was still alive.

Images swirled lazily in her mind, magically becoming fragments of her life . . .

She was a child, tightening her lips purposefully as she carefully and ever so slowly walked beside her mother, who carried her father's ashes . . .

She was a child, running breathlessly up the stairs, clutching her report card proudly . . .

She was half-girl, half-woman, laughing hysterically, the tears running down her cheeks as her best friend, Gina, mimicked the flirtatious walk of a society lady . . .

She was a sober young woman standing on the deck of the *Ile de France*, on her way to boarding school in Italy, the stone canyons of Manhattan slipping slowly past along the shore . . .

New York . . . home . . .

Slowly she closed her eyes, the lids flickering. She was so tired. She didn't want to be under water any more. She didn't want to be here, wherever she was. All she wanted was to go back, to long ago. To another world, another time.

The Principessa di Fontanesi, the richest woman in all Italy, born Charlotte-Anne Hale in a small town in Texas and raised in New York, wanted to go back home, where everything had been sane, and warm, and safe, and sound.

Her mind swirled as it reached back to the beginnings of her memory, and her life was a dream rushing upon her, flashing from long ago to the present, a whirlwind of memories, what seemed like a millennium crammed into a few short minutes.

And lost among the moans and cries of the hundreds of

mortally wounded lying all around her, there came yet another sound, higher pitched, and more angry, but no less afraid.

It was the cry of her child.

Her baby, who she had left buried in the shelter underground while she had crawled through the raging battle in order to bring it food and water, so that it might live . . .

19

'*Help me. Somebody please help me.*'

Her cries echoed like thunder in a canyon, bouncing back and forth with decreasing audibility. A radiating heat seemed to burst outward, then contract, then flare again somewhere deep in her right side.

'*Help me, please . . .* '

The two stretcher bearers, their white armbands with the red crosses on them splattered with blood, stopped and looked down at her.

'It is a woman!' exclaimed one of them in surprise. He dropped his end of the stretcher and got down on one knee beside her, placing a hand on her forehead. He looked up at his partner. 'She is cold as ice.'

'Is she badly hurt?'

He examined her side. The moment he saw the pool of gelatinous blood in which she lay, he shrugged impassively. 'Everyone is badly hurt.'

'There are so many wounded. Do we take her to the hospital now? Or does she wait for her turn? We were told to – '

The man leaning over her tightened his lips. 'At sea, it is always the women and children first. I think in battle also. We take her now to the Sisters of Mercy.'

Gently, they took hold of her and rolled her onto the stretcher. She moaned with the pain, but they seemed oblivious to it. When they lifted the stretcher, each step they took seemed to jolt her insides, causing the pain to flash ever more violently. She screamed and screamed in agony, but she was the only one who seemed to hear it.

After they had gone a few yards, the man leading the way stopped and looked back over his shoulder. 'She is so quiet. Is she still alive?'

The other man looked down at her. He nodded. 'She is still alive. But she is in great pain. She does not have long, I think.'

'Sometimes it is better this way,' his partner replied philosophically as he continued walking. 'At least in death she will sleep in peace. She will not feel her misery.'

She stared up at the bouncing, roiling plumes of black smoke. '*You're wrong,*' she shouted soundlessly. '*Everyone is wrong. Dying is cold and wet and painful. No matter what anyone tells you, it's goddamn hell.*'

Everything everybody had ever told her was a bold-faced lie.

She knew that now.

She had not been quite four years old then, and she had been sitting on her father's lap, listening carefully to the fairy tale. The moment he closed the book, she stirred restlessly and looked up at him. 'That's all there is?' she asked in disappointment.

Her father smiled and put the book aside. 'I'm afraid it is.'

'But what happens after it says "and they lived happily ever after"?'

'It means just what it says. They were happy for the rest of their lives.'

Charlotte-Anne nodded slowly. 'But when she bit into the apple she died, didn't she?'

'Yes . . .' her father said carefully.

'And then, when the prince kissed her, she woke up again?'

He nodded.

'What would have happened if he hadn't kissed her?'

'I suppose she would have gone on sleeping forever and ever.' Her father smiled reassuringly. 'But don't worry about that. The prince came and woke her up, just like it said he did.'

'Daddy?'

'Yes, dear?'

'I'm not going to eat any more apples.'

328

He laughed. 'Oh, I wouldn't go so far as that, if I were you. It was only a fairy story. Things like that don't happen in real life. I'm not so sure people even know how to poison apples.'

'Oh.' Charlotte-Anne paused. 'But people die, don't they?'

'Yes.' Her father's voice was soft. 'We will all die one day. But you needn't worry about that, either. It's a long, long way off. Why, you were just born.'

'But when we die, does a prince come around and kiss us awake? When Billy's mother died, no prince came, and she's still gone.'

'What happens, Charlotte-Anne, is that when we've outlived our time, we die.'

'Does it hurt?'

'I don't think so.'

'And what happens after that?'

'Then a prince comes and wakes us. Only he isn't really a prince. He's God. He wakes up our souls, and if we've lived good lives, then we go to heaven and join Him and live happily ever after.'

'What do we do once we get there?'

'Oh, I don't know. Whatever makes us happy, I suppose.'

'Like baking cookies?' Charlotte-Anne asked eagerly.

'Like baking cookies.' He laughed again and kissed her affectionately.

'But . . . God does wake us up? We don't keep on sleeping and sleeping? He doesn't forget about us?'

'No. He never forgets,' her father said warmly, enfolding the tiny, inquisitive body in his arms. 'God comes and wakes us all up. He's our real prince.'

20

The Convent of Our Lady of Peace was built high on a terraced hilltop overlooking the countryside. Only a fluke of military strategy and its proximity to an even higher, more strategically important hill – where the Palladian palazzo of the di Fontanesis, which was now a smoldering ruin sat – had spared the convent from destruction. The battle had raged for eight days, and now the sweeping view of the countryside through the arched loggias was a vision of hell.

The ancient foundations of the convent dated back to the

twelfth century, and it was surrounded by thick stone walls which shut out the world. Inside, the enormous groin-vaulted main hall was filled with cots pushed closely against each other and spilling out into the hall and dormitory. The ancient ceilings and loggias echoed with the screams of the wounded, the murmured litanies of prayer, and a thousand tumultous, foreign sounds. The stench of urine and feces mingled with the copper smell of blood. It was late afternoon, and the steady stream of wounded being carried in had still not slacked off, bringing even more noise and chaos into the usually hushed halls.

Sister Maria Theresa sat on the edge of a cot, sponging the caked blood off the chest of the young soldier. She had not set eyes upon a man for years, and never in her life had she seen one naked until now. She kept her eyes studiously averted, working by feel and the tell-tale moans of the soldier, rather than by sight. Behind her, stretcher bearers were bringing in yet more wounded.

'I don't know where we're going to put them all,' a female voice whispered from Sister Maria Theresa's right. 'They're carrying in more. There must be hundreds.'

Sister Maria Theresa turned and locked eyes with Sister Magdalena. Despite the din, Sister Maria Theresa too spoke in a whisper. For seventeen years, she had scrupulously kept her vow of silence, and now that it had been temporarily lifted, the sound of her own voice was hoarse and foreign to her ears. 'We ran out of food and medicine hours ago,' she hissed. 'Most of the water is contaminated. What are we going to do?'

'We shall pray, Sisters,' a steady voice intoned from behind them.

Both nuns looked up to see the Mother Superior, standing staunchly erect, her inner strength glowing despite her weariness of body and soul.

'A cigarette,' croaked the injured soldier whose chest Sister Maria Theresa had been sponging. 'A cigarette? Please?'

Sister Maria Theresa looked around helplessly.

Wordlessly, the Mother Superior looked down at the soldier. Her eyes hid the compassion within her. She knew he was only a child, seventeen, perhaps. And he was another who would not last the night.

The Mother Superior reached into the blood-caked folds of her once-white gown, now a stiff russet, and sought one of the packets of American cigarettes one of the liberators had given to her. She handed it to Sister Maria Theresa, who took it reluctantly.

'Light one for him,' the Mother Superior said gently.

'Yes, Reverend Mother,' Sister Maria Theresa answered. She tightened her lips and fished a cigarette out of the pack, then took the matches the Reverend Mother handed her. Then she sat still in confusion.

'Well, Sister? Put one in your mouth, inhale as you light it, and then let him have little puffs.'

'Yes, Reverend Mother.' With shaking fingers, Sister Maria Theresa did as she was told. As she lit the cigarette, she broke out in a spasm of coughing. Then she held the cigarette to the soldier's lips. He took grateful puffs.

Sister Maria Theresa handed the pack back to the Mother Superior.

The Reverend Mother shook her head. 'No, you keep it. When you run out, see me. I have more. Give one to any of the wounded who request it. If they do not have lung wounds.' The Mother Superior handed another packet and a box of matches to Sister Magdalena.

The Mother Superior stood there for a moment, watching the two nuns and the soldier. She knew that this was a time of trial, a moment when her faith was being tested as never before. She, too, was confused and horrified by the sights which assailed her, but she knew that she could not succumb to weakness. But there was so little she could understand, so little real comfort she could give. She had devoted her entire life to God and, through Him, to man. Ever since she could remember, she had been filled with a deep faith. When she had looked about her in calm times, she had seen God everywhere. In His birds, His heavens, on the very earth she humbly trod. As a young novitiate, she was certain that God had things well in hand and was winning. But now she was old, her face parched and creased, her sagging jowls squeezed tight by the wimple which framed her face, the white gown and veil covering her soaked with blood. And now it occurred to her, although she tried to suppress the blasphemous thought, that God was no longer in control, and evil ruled the world.

She turned away wearily as two stretcher bearers approached her. 'Where can we put her?' one of them asked.

The Mother Superior sucked in her breath at the sight of the pale woman, badly wounded and only half-conscious, who lay on the stretcher. She immediately recognized Charlotte-Anne as the Principessa di Fontanesi, daughter-in-law to the family that had always been so generous to the convent. She lifted the sheet which draped the Principessa's body and winced at the sight of the shattered arm. Then she noticed the wound in the Principessa's side. The kidneys, she thought with despair. Involuntarily she let the sheet drop.

Turning back to Sister Maria Theresa, she said, 'Go, show them to the dormitory. Have them put her in my room. In my bed. Do not leave her side, Sister.' The Reverend Mother turned. 'Sister Magdalena, find one of the doctors and send him upstairs to see to the Principessa. And hurry.'

She struggled to open her eyes. Lifting her head slightly from the pillow, she peered faintly through the gauze of her eyelashes. How heavy her lids were. Whiteness was all she saw, and the dim white blur of a figure moving with the disembodied slowness of an apparition. Out of the whiteness came the dull rumble of murmured voices, distant and muted, like the sea on a lonely shore.

Then sleep rose once more, darkening the whiteness. Her bee's-winged eyes folded to black and the sounds faded from her mind.

It was a world of white satin and soft acoustics, and she was a princess lying in a huge soft bed. Cut crystal sparkled and flashed fire and ice. Through a white-draped doorway floated her satin prince, coming to wake her with his kiss. She was dead, sleeping her fairy tale death of a hundred years, and he was finally coming closer and closer, growing in size as he approached. His face drew near. Asleep, dead, dead, asleep, she seemed to sense the lips which would awaken her, and she responded, her mouth seeming to float up through satin air. She smelled his sweet breath, could visualize those narrow pale lips, his white satin doublet with the puffy sleeves, his legs encased in the soft satin riding breeches of the fascists, and tucked into white boots. His skin was smooth and she could see his shiny teeth inside his hollow mouth. She could feel her own lips as they rose and pursed, but before his lips could touch hers, he began to recede as mysteriously as he had appeared, and she felt his life-giving power draining away. He became even smaller and more distant, and then began to whirl faster and faster as he was sucked into the vortex of a swirling satin dream.

Her eyes opened with less effort when she awoke again. Her leaden lids were lighter now, and the thin gauze of her eyelashes, which had veiled her vision, was drawn away. The whiteness had softened to yellow. She looked upwards, blankly beginning to register the flatness of the white ceiling above her.

Lying there she let her eyes wander. Her mind struggled to order what she saw – the flatness of white walls, a white ceiling and, suspended above her, an electric light, yellow and bright. The light bulb seemed to grow as she stared up at it, filling her vision. She was in a box with nothing in it but a great light bulb above her. It seemed to radiate an awesome heat.

A box? She blinked dreamily at the great yellow glow of the light. No, surely it couldn't be a box. Perhaps it was a square universe, and she was floating in it. Weightless and powerless, she might drift forever, basking in the warmth of this electric sun. She sighed soundlessly and the light grew tinier and tinier until it disappeared altogether.

She climbed slowly through the clouds, the wisps parting in front of her. The climb was an effort. She was not as strong as she used to be. But then the last of the fog's clinging fingers parted, and she was in a room.

333

The space was tiny, spare, and white. It was more like a cell than a room. The stone floor was bare, the narrow iron cot was covered with a thin, lumpy mattress, and a single wooden chair was pushed against one wall. Above the bed hung an old polychrome crucifix. There were no curtains at the tiny window. Consciousness came fleetingly and went, came again. Her eyes focused and she noticed a white apparition seated on the chair.

The apparition seemed to sense she was awake. It rose and drifted to her side. Charlotte-Anne stared up at it. It seemed to hover over her, huge and white. It was a beautiful angel.

Then her mind cleared. It was not an angel after all. It was a nun dressed all in white: only the pink hands and face, and the black rosary dangling from her middle disturbed the white of her veil, wimple, bid and gown. That, and the splatters of dried blood.

'You are safe, Principessa,' the nun said gently, but to Charlotte-Anne the voice sounded distant and hollow, somehow distorted. 'No one will hurt you now. The doctor has been to see you. We are doing everything we can.'

Something struck Charlotte-Anne as very funny, and she wanted to laugh, but no sound would come forth. Her eyes looked at the nun with an expression of amusement. Why on earth did she need a doctor? She couldn't remember ever having felt better in her life. She was floating on a cotton candy cloud. Everything was soft and painless. She couldn't feel a thing.

'We ran out of medicine, but the Americans brought some more,' the nun explained. 'We have given you morphine.'

Charlotte-Anne didn't seem to hear her. She knew that there was something important she had to say, but her mind was dulled by the sweet, fuzzy cloud of well-being. Every time the thought drifted close it seemed to dance away playfully, just out of reach.

'You are going to be fine.' The nun smiled reassuringly and steepled her fingers. 'We have been praying for you, Principessa. All our prayers are with you.'

Charlotte-Anne tried to speak. Her mouth formed the

words, but no sound would come. 'Do not pray for me,' she tried to say as the thought which had been skipping in and out of reach suddenly came close and revealed itself. A tear slipped out of the corner of one eye. 'I . . . don't . . . need . . . your . . . prayers . . . Sister. But . . . I know . . . someone . . . who . . . does.'

21

She drifted headlong out of the numb zone.

Despite the constant pain, the crashes of thunder, and the roar of lashing rain, she had managed to slip in and out of sleep. She had no idea how long she had been asleep. Long enough, she realized, to allow the clear sky she had remembered to cloud with a violent storm. The moment she gazed through the haze of her eyelashes, she moved her head slightly to one side. The nun seemed to be right over her, her white-framed, scrubbed-pink face glowing in the warm, yellow light. Charlotte-Anne smiled weakly up at her.

When the nun realized she was awake, she wiped the worried look off her face and tried to smile reassuringly. Charlotte-Anne's eyes moved past her. The doctor, who she was vaguely aware had examined her earlier, had his back turned to her. A priest was peering out the tiny window, trying to see through the rain-streaked darkness.

Charlotte-Anne struggled to lift her head. Her face was starkly pale.

'She is dying,' she heard the doctor say.

The priest turned away from the window, his soutane swirling around his legs. He shook his head sadly.

'My . . . baby,' Charlotte-Anne tried to say. She stared up at the nun. 'My . . . baby. Was it . . . found?'

The nun smiled gently down at her. She leaned over Charlotte-Anne and stroked aside a stray lock of her moist hair. 'Do not try to speak,' she murmured.

Charlotte-Anne gazed at her and let out a thin, reedy moan. The nun tucked the sheet around her neck.

'She is dying,' the doctor said again. 'There is nothing more than I can do. It is now in the hands of God.'

The priest turned back to the window, his hands clasped behind him.

She is dying.

The soft inflections of that sentence kept floating lightly in Charlotte-Anne's ears. She closed her eyes to try and shut out that voice, but it kept repeating itself, like a recording, the three words playing over and over in her mind.

She is dying.

She is dying.

Sister Maria Theresa prayed quietly, her lips emitting an occasional sibilant whisper.

She was still seated beside Charlotte-Anne's bed in the Mother Superior's cell. Two and a half days had passed since the Principessa had been brought in, and still her condition was unchanged. It seemed a miracle that she was alive at all.

Sister Maria Theresa attributed it to the power of the prayers she offered up to God. She prayed for the Principessa, for all the wounded and dead, for all of poor, ravished Italy. After not being able to sleep at all through the days and nights of bombing, and now with caring for the wounded, she was surprised to find that she was still wide awake. Her body felt heavy and burdened, but she was mentally alert. That too was a miracle. It was as though God had blessed them all with incredible strength to see this tragedy through. Even while she prayed her eyelids never drooped and her eyes never left her patient's quiet, prostrate form.

The Mother Superior floated soundlessly into the little cell. She placed a hand on Sister Maria Theresa's shoulder. 'How is she, Sister?' she asked softly.

The nun looked up and saw that the Reverend Mother's usually serene face looked haggard and sad.

'She is unchanged, Reverend Mother,' the nun whispered.

'I suppose that is more than we could hope for. She is in

the hands of almighty God. Whatever He decides, it is His will.' The Mother Superior nodded and then managed a faint smile. 'Would you like to take a few hours and rest, Sister. I can have one of the other sisters replace you. It is going to be a long night and an even longer day tomorrow.'

'No thank you, Reverend Mother. I'm still fine. Perhaps later, when I need it.'

'Bless you, Sister. I am proud of you. You are very brave.'

Sister Maria Theresa said nothing.

The Mother Superior cocked her head to one side. 'What on earth is that noise?'

Both nuns listened for a moment. The faraway chant seemed to be made up of a multitude of voices. Sister Maria Theresa rose from her chair. 'It seems to be coming from outside,' she said.

Both nuns drew over to the tiny window and looked out into the night. They saw a bonfire burning in the middle of the village, the pink glow of which flickered on their faces.

'There are torches everywhere,' Sister Maria Theresa interjected. 'And those chants . . . It is as though a celebration is going on.' She stared at the Reverend Mother.

'Either that, or yet another tragedy,' the Mother Superior mused gravely. 'Somehow those chants do not seem happy sounds. I hate to think what could be going on now.'

A flurry of sounds echoed from the stone-paved corridor outside and caught her attention. A muted roar drifted up from the valley below and filtered into the little room and through her consciousness. Charlotte-Anne was too weak to speak or to move, but upon waking her hearing was again exceptionally acute. Every nuance, every rustle, even the faintest faraway whisper made a loud impression through the thick scrim of her mind.

'The Mother Superior said so,' a hesitant, meek woman's voice said. 'There are many more wounded coming in, and there is no more room downstairs. We must put them in our quarters.'

'In here, Sisters?' It was a much louder, deeper voice. Without thinking about it, Charlotte-Anne realized it belonged to a stretcher bearer.

'No, no, not in there. That is the Mother Superior's room. The Principessa must be alone.'

'Even in defeat, the fascist princess is living like a queen,' one of the men grumbled.

The nun ignored the comment. 'Here, put him into this room. Line up the cots close together.'

There was a loud commotion as hob-nailed boots clicked down the corridor.

'What is going on?' one of the men asked.

Charlotte-Anne recognized what she thought was a familiar voice. She did not know where she had heard it before, but it seemed it had been sometime since her foggy consciousness had swallowed her up.

'There is madness in the village!' someone shouted breathlessly. 'If it isn't stopped soon, there is going to be an ugly riot!'

'But why? I thought the Allies had moved in. They are supposed to be keeping the peace.'

From somewhere far away came the cracks of gunfire. 'See? Listen! Even the Americans cannot stop it! The people are angry!'

'I don't understand. I thought it was all over. That the battle had moved to Cassino.'

'So did I.' The man gave an ugly laugh. 'But that's not a battle you're hearing. That is a mob. It seems that Prince Luigi di Fontanesi, Mussolini's right-hand man, has returned to the village. They discovered him trying to make his way back home on foot, disguised as a peasant of all things. They've killed him and hung him upside down from a scaffold in the piazza and . . . and . . . I'm afraid it's not for your ears, Sister.'

A nun's scurrying footsteps and swishing robes echoed faintly and then died away.

'Well, what?' another of the stretcher bearers hissed excitedly.

'They cut off his cock and balls, that's what,' the man whispered, 'and shoved them into his mouth!'

Sister Maria Theresa, sitting motionless in her chair, overheard the terrible conversation. Her hand flew up to her forehead and she quickly made a sign of the cross. 'Oh my God,' she whispered, aghast that such terrible things should be discussed in a holy place. Turning quickly to look at Charlotte-Anne, she prayed that the Principessa was still asleep.

Charlotte-Anne stared up at the ceiling, her paler-than-pale eyes unblinking. Only much later, when the Principessa still had not moved, did Sister Maria Theresa realize that she was dead. Muttering a Hail Mary, she smoothed Charlotte-Anne's eyes shut and pulled the sheet up over her.

'Thank you, oh Lord,' the nun prayed as she fell to her knees on the cold stone floor and bowed her head. 'Thank you for sparing the Principessa such terrible news. It is far better that she died, rather than hear such an awful thing.'

But Sister Maria Theresa was wrong. Only Charlotte-Anne's love for her husband had driven her to cling shakily to life. The instant the brutal words had registered, the fight had gone out of her. At the awful realization of her beloved's fate, she had allowed herself to drift up, up into that welcoming, peaceful nothingness which was death.

22

The shadows beneath the hill crowned with the convent became long and purple. All around, the incredible destruction seemed out of place against the familiar magnificence of the pink streaks of sunset.

Never in their wildest nightmares had they imagined such devastation.

The Principessa's face was tear-streaked and dirty. From more than a week in the storm cellar, and then wandering through the ruins, her clothes had become torn and mud-smeared. She looked more like a haggard peasant than the proud, well-groomed matriarch of the di Fontanesis.

Prince Antonio stumbled after his wife. He had taken off

his jacket and wrapped it around the newborn infant in order to keep the little girl warm. He carried her gently, full of fear because the baby had become so listless and quiet. She had not cried for hours and she lay so still that he was afraid she was already dead.

From somewhere in the north came the distant booms of shelling. The Allied army had moved on to conquer another hill at Cassino. More deaths, more destruction, would follow. The Prince shook his head mournfully. Would the nightmare never end?

The Principessa sank down on a heap of stones which had once been part of the western wing of the Palazzo di Cristallo. She covered her face with her hands and began to weep noisily. All that remained of the proud palazzo were jagged fingers of wall reaching up into the sky, and mountainous piles of shattered crystal which reflected the setting sun like a king's ransom in diamonds.

'Gone,' Marcella whispered in a strangled cry through her tears. 'All *gone.*'

'Come, come *cara mia*,' the prince said gently. 'It is time we moved on.'

She turned her face up to him. 'Why? *Why* did this have to happen?'

'Because the world has turned insane,' he replied with a peculiar, quiet dignity. 'Because too many people, our own son included, came to look upon Il Duce as some kind of god, because he promised a return to the times of the Roman Empire. Too few people realized Il Duce was nothing but a power-hungry, mad buffoon.' He too started to shed tears, but unlike his wife, his crying was soundless. 'We had to learn the hard way that long ago, the twilight of the Caesars marked their end for good. Ghosts cannot be resurrected. It was the scheme of a madman.' He paused and wiped his eyes. 'Come, while I am talking foolishness it is getting dark. Soon we will not see where we are going. We must find food for the child and a place to spend the night.'

'I don't want that child,' Marcella whispered numbly. 'The whore from America has brought ill luck upon our family. Her offspring is the spawn of evil things.'

'Hush! Do not talk such nonsense.'

Her eyes blazed. 'Nonsense, you say? Doesn't it strike you as peculiar that she should have had the foresight to dig that hole in the vineyards?'

The prince did not reply.

'It was she, Antonio. I tell you, she had her hand in this.' She began to wail louder. 'She was a spy of some sort. How else could she have been prepared for what has come?'

He took his wife by the hand, pulled her to her feet, and they began to stumble downhill, careful to skirt the treacherous, yawning bomb craters which had opened up the earth. Everywhere, the landscape was pockmarked with them.

The sunset became twilight, and then night fell quickly. It was a dark, cloudy night, with only occasional, ghostly patches of moonlight to aid them. It seemed an eternity before they reached the base of the hill. Above them towered the silent ruins where once their proud palazzo had stood sentinel.

'Listen,' Prince Antonio said sharply. 'I think I hear something.'

'What could you possibly hear other than the sound of that bombing?'

'No, I do hear something approaching.' He listened again, and then his voice grew excited. 'It is a horse, I think.'

'So?' she hissed. 'What good do you think a horse will do us?'

'Perhaps none.' He shrugged. 'Then again, perhaps everything. But whatever you do, Marcella, this is not the time to play the lady. Say nothing of what you are. We are simply ordinary people who have lost everything and have nowhere to go.'

'Why should I want to do that?' she snapped. 'I am the Principessa Marcella di Fontanesi!'

'Because,' he explained patiently, 'Luigi is too well known, and too hated for working with Il Duce. Believe me, it is much safer for us this way. Otherwise, God only knows what fate might befall us. There are those who would find great joy in tearing us from limb to limb.'

And that, he noticed, took the wind out of his wife's sails.

Suddenly he felt the bundle in his arms shifting slightly, and once again he offered up a silent prayer of thanks because the child was, incredibly, still alive.

As the horse-drawn wagon neared them, Antonio Di Fontanesi hurried forward to meet it. In the dim glow of moonlight breaking through the clouds he could see the crude, creaking wagon was packed full of people. As he walked past the horse, it radiated such intense heat that he knew at once it was on the point of collapse.

'Please, help us,' the prince begged as the wagon drew to a halt. 'My wife is ill, and we have a newborn child with us. Have pity, please. We must get it something to eat, or else it will surely die.'

The man sitting on the driver's seat looked down. 'We can't take you, you gotta walk. The horse is already half dead.'

Wait,' an authoritative voice said from the back of the wagon. There was a scuffling sound, that of people moving, and a man jumped down to the road. He moved quickly forward. 'Let the woman ride in my place. I can walk.' As the man drew nearer, Antonio di Fontanesi could make out the dark soutane and the white clerical collar of a priest.

'Thank you, Father, thank you,' Antonio murmured gratefully.

Antonio walked Marcella to the back of the wagon, and with his free hand helped her climb up into it. People shifted to make room for her. Many appraising eyes glittered in the moonlight. Antonio lifted up the child to Marcella, but she recoiled and refused to take her. 'You want her,' she snapped, 'you carry her.'

He nodded miserably. He was too hungry and tired to argue with her.

The wagon began to roll on, and Antonio di Fontanesi and the priest walked alongside it.

'Where are you headed?' Antonio called up to the driver.

'To the convent,' the driver replied. 'We hear the Sisters have turned it into a hospital. Many of us are hungry, sick, or wounded. They say there's food and medicine there. And Father Odoni says they are probably short-handed. He's going to offer his help.'

Antonio di Fontanesi fell silent and hung his head. Despite the overwhelming tragedy and devastation which had befallen everyone, little signs of humanity and caring were cropping up as people tried to cope with their own pain and help others. Sometimes it seemed as though it took a tragedy to bring out the best and the worst in people.

He was ashamed to realize that for both Marcella and himself, it had brought out the worst.

Only by a mere fluke of fate did the di Fontanesis' path cross with the Viganòs'. In peaceful times, when the lines of society were strictly drawn, the closest they might have gotten to each other was by passing on the road, one family trudging along on foot while the other roared past in the luxurious confines of an expensive, chauffeur-driven automobile. They had nothing in common, other than that in years past, Paolo Viganò had at times toiled, along with hundreds of others, in the fertile vineyards of the di Fontanesis.

Until the bombing had started, Paolo Viganò had always considered himself a lucky man. He was hardly rich, being a mere grapepicker, but he had always *felt* wealthy. True, at times the meager contents of the kitchen cupboard had to be stretched, but he had never known a day of sickness in his entire life, nor had he known real hunger. In his simple mind he equated hunger with laziness, so he had made certain that he always worked hard. Everyone said that no one knew the grapes like Paolo Viganò, and when he heard the compliments his chest would swell with pride. He had even been spared the tragedy of leaving his family to fight in the war because of his clubfoot, which was not bad enough to hurt his work but did keep him from being a useful soldier.

His wife, Adriana, was a simple, large sun-browned woman with gentle eyes and a quietly pleasant smile. In her youth she had been a great beauty, one of the rare and treasured blonde-haired, blue-eyed Italians. But she had never wanted more than her Paolo. The love they shared had only grown with each passing year of their marriage. She helped out at harvest-time, picking grapes in order to supplement their income. Other times she kept the house and tended the kitchen garden and the goats and chickens she raised.

Their six-year-old son, Dario, was turning into a lovely, intelligent child. He was possessed of a quick mind and studious manner, and he filled Paolo with pride. When one day Dario startled his parents with an announcement that he was determined to become a priest when he grew up, both Paolo and Adriana had been filled with warm pleasure, though they regretted the possibility of having no grandchildren. Then six years after Dario was born, Adriana found herself pregnant again. With that joyful news, Paolo's joy was complete. He had felt rich indeed.

Now, waiting by the roadside, he felt neither rich nor blessed. His wife, whom he had half-carried for miles, was resting beside him against a tree, watched over by Dario. Paolo was as devastated as the shelled, war-ravaged land around him. Two nights earlier, at the height of the bombing, his wife's time had come. One moment she was in the kitchen baking bread; the next, she could no longer stand on her feet. There was no doctor or midwife to be found, and Adriana was sick, burning up with a fever. The child she gave birth to died within the hour. His wife had been too delirious even to comprehend the tragedy which had occurred. Paolo, sure that she was going to die, felt frightened and helpless. He could not conceive of a life without his beloved Adriana.

When Paolo heard the horse-drawn wagon approaching in the distance, he held his breath. Was it possible that his luck had not deserted him after all? With growing anxiety he waited for the vehicle to round the curve, then cried out to them.

'Please,' he desperately urged the driver. 'My wife is terribly sick. I'm afraid she is going to die. Could you find it in your heart to give her a ride?'

'Can't she walk?' the driver asked gruffly.

'No, she is much too feeble. I've already had to half

carry her for kilometers. She is so sick she can hardly move.'

'Then you are in luck,' the driver told him. He motioned up to the hill and the convent etched blackly against the weak moonlight. 'We are on our way to the Sisters. We hear their convent has become a hospital.'

Paolo felt a surge of hope. 'Then you'll take my wife?' he begged.

The driver hesitated. 'As long as someone else who is now riding will walk.'

For a fleeting instant, Antonio di Fontanesi was tempted to order Marcella down from the wagon, but another woman volunteered. Antonio decided he was just as happy not to have his wife walking beside him.

As soon as room was made in the wagon for Adriana Viganò, Father Odoni helped Paolo lift the stout woman up onto the back.

Only once his beloved Adriana was in the wagon and the party was headed up the hill toward the convent did Paolo once again dare consider how lucky he was. Perhaps, just perhaps, things might turn out all right after all. His sick wife was on her way to the convent. His son had survived the war. His humble home was still standing. And under his coat he had the two loaves of bread Adriana had been baking when her time had come. They had clothes on their backs, there was help at the convent, and he had had the foresight to bring along some food. What else could a man possibly want?

Antonio, Father Odoni, Paolo, young Dario, and the woman who had volunteered to walk went on foot beside the slow-moving wagon. For a long time no one spoke. Everyone was weary, and the steady uphill climb was tiring. It was Paolo Viganò who finally broke the silence. He had caught Antonio lowering his ear to the bundle in his arm.

He tapped Antonio on the arm. 'What are you carrying all wrapped up like that?'

Without losing a step, Antonio parted a portion of his coat. The baby looked pale and lifeless in the moonlight. 'She is my son's,' Antonio explained sadly. 'Something has

345

happened to her mother. Perhaps she is wounded, perhaps she is dead. Perhaps we will never know. The mother's breasts were barren. She left our shelter during the bombing to find the child some food, but she has not returned. Now I am afraid the poor thing is going to starve.'

Paolo shook his head miserably. 'My wife, too, just gave birth,' he said, commiserating. 'It too was a daughter, but she died right away.' His voice grew choked. 'Now I am afraid that my wife will die also. The only comfort is that she is too delirious to know that the daughter she has carried is dead.'

'I don't know what I'm going to do,' Antonio whispered. 'If the Sisters have no milk . . . '

Suddenly Paolo reached out for the bundle in Antonio's arms. 'Let me have the child,' he said excitedly. 'Surely my wife, ill though she is, has plenty of milk in her breasts.'

Antonio stared at him, then quickly he handed the child over.

'Stop for a moment,' Paolo called to the driver as he hurried to the back of the wagon, climbed over the tailgate and bent down over his wife. She was lying on her back, perspiring heavily. When he touched her forehead it felt cold as ice. He opened the blouse and exposed a huge, swollen breast.

Antonio had followed him and now watched as some instinct brought the child to life. Greedily she found the nipple and began to suck the milk from Adriana Viganò's copious breasts.

'Just look,' Paolo murmured, the tears sparkling in his eyes. He was at once saddened and filled with joy. He wept for his own dead child, and then he dried his tears and smiled proudly that his ailing wife should, without even being aware of it, save the life of another.

God truly worked in mysterious ways, Paolo thought. He had not turned a blind eye on them after all.

In the midst of tragedy, He was out working His miracles.

From across the room, Antonio watched as Paolo Viganò

leaned low over the cot and kissed his wife. The cot was in the makeshift ward which was actually the chapel of the convent. The pews had been carried outside and cots were lined up everywhere. A young nun was burping the baby, patting her on the back. Then she handed the infant back to Paolo. He turned and waved at Antonio, then, with Dario, circled around the sea of cots to where Antonio and Marcella waited against the far wall to one side of the altar.

'Adriana stands a good chance,' Paolo burst out as soon as he neared Antonio. 'It may be some time until she recovers completely, but the Sisters and the doctor are convinced everything will turn out fine. They said she was brought here just in time.'

Antonio smiled and clapped a hand on Paolo's shoulder. 'I am very glad to hear it.'

'I am so relieved.' Paolo said, tears in his eyes. Then, almost reluctantly, he handed Antonio the baby. 'She *must* have been hungry. She has eaten once again.' He shook his head in disbelief. 'I don't think I ever saw such a hungry child. She may be tiny, even for a newborn, but she is so beautiful.' His face grew mournful and his voice fell to a whisper. 'Do you know, for a moment my wife was aware of the child? It was as though the touch of the mouth against her gave her new strength. For an instant, she looked at me with total consciousness and smiled and said, ''My beautiful, beautiful baby.'' ' Paolo bit down on his lip as the tears spilled from the corners of his eyes. He shook his head miserably. 'I did not find it in my heart to tell her the truth. Not yet, while she is so ill.'

Antonio nodded. 'I understand.'

Paolo wiped his eyes with his fingertips, put an arm around his son's shoulders, and drew Dario close. 'I'm sorry,' he said to no one in particular. 'I do not usually cry.'

Antonio smiled, drily. 'I do not either, but lately I find I've been crying a lot.'

Paolo looked at him. 'Did you find out about the availability of milk yet?'

'No,' Antonio answered, shaking his head. 'But we were

told to wait and speak to the Reverend Mother about it. We will see what she can do.'

'Should you find it necessary,' Paolo said politely, 'my wife is producing plenty of milk. It has to be drawn from her breasts anyway.'

'Thank you, my friend,' the Prince said.

'By the way, my name is Paolo. Paolo Viganò.'

'I am very grateful for what you have done, *Signor*. My name is Antonio. And this is my wife, Marcella.'

'Signora. Signor.' Paolo bowed politely, but Marcella merely gave him a frosty smile and turned away.

'There is the Reverend Mother now,' Antonio said. He watched as the Mother Superior swept through the chapel doors in her blood-stained white robe, every few steps stopping to give words of comfort to some patient.

As she came closer, she happened to look across the row of cots and met Antonio's eye. For a moment, her gaze roved on elsewhere; she didn't seem to register him or the Principessa in their dirty, changed appearance. Then recognition clicked in her mind and her eyes swept back toward him. She hurried over, still inquiring of various patients, but doing so more quickly.

When she reached them, she gave them a strained smile. 'Prince di Fontanesi. Principessa.' She inclined her head.

Paolo gasped. 'You are . . . the Prince? And the Principessa?' He stared at them; then his eyes fell and he quickly bowed his head. '*Scusi, scusi,*' he murmured.

'For what?' Antonio asked.

'For being familiar.'

Antonio touched him under the chin and raised his head so he could look him in the eye. 'I am not sorry. I am grateful for all you have done to help.'

The Reverend Mother cleared her throat and folded her hands. 'I'm afraid I have become the bearer of much sad news of late, and now I must bring yet more bad tidings.'

'Charlotte-Anne is dead, then?' Antonio asked.

She nodded. 'I'm sorry, and you have my deepest sympathies. The stretcher bearers found her and brought her in, but it was too late. She had suffered too many internal injuries. There was nothing more that we could do, other than make her as comfortable as possible. She was, and is, in the hands of God.' The Mother Superior touched Antonio's arm gently, in a gesture of comfort, and only then noticed the child. Her eyes flared in surprise, and for the first time in days she allowed herself to smile. She bent down to inspect the infant. 'A newborn!' She looked back up at him.

'Yes, and now she has no mother,' Antonio said bitterly. 'Nor is there any milk to be found.'

The Mother Superior tightened her lips. 'I'm afraid there's none here.'

'And we ourselves don't even have any food to eat,' Marcella growled. She looked at the Mother Superior hopefully. 'We have not eaten for days.'

'I'm sorry, Principessa.' The Mother Superior's tone was dry. 'If we only had some we could spare I would give you all I could. But the wounded and sick do not have enough. We are waiting for the rations of the Americans.'

Marcella grumbled and turned away.

'I have some food, Principessa,' Paolo offered, proudly opening his coat. 'Two loaves of bread. See – ' He handed one of the crispy, golden loaves to the Mother Superior. 'It is the least I can do, Reverend Mother.'

'Bless you,' the Mother Superior said.

He broke an end off the second loaf and held it out to Marcella, who seized upon it greedily. She took a large bite and began to chew as though someone might snatch it away from her at any moment.

'Thank you,' Antonio told Paolo quietly. 'You have my lifelong gratitude, first for your wife feeding the baby, and now for feeding us.' His eyes fell. What had happened to turn his wife into such an animal so quickly? Or had she only needed the opportunity to show her real self. He had never been as ashamed of anyone as he was now of his wife. In mere days, Marcella had taken on all the worst characteristics she had once ascribed to the peasants. And it was the peasants who were now behaving with dignity.

'But the child,' Antonio murmured worriedly. 'What are we going to do about the child, now that there is no milk and her mother is dead?'

'And her father also,' the Mother Superior said softly. 'Perhaps you have not heard?'

Antonio stared at her, his face suddenly drained of all color. 'How did he die? Was it here?'

She shook her head. From what she had heard about Luigi di Fontanesi's death, that was information which could surely wait. They would find out about it soon enough.

As the silence continued, the fight seemed to go out of Antonio. As if he guessed the horrible truth of his son's fate, the Prince seemed to shrivel and age right before their very eyes.

Marcella finished her hunk of bread and a calculating glint came into her eyes. In her near madness, she didn't even seem to register the news of Luigi's death. She stared at the rest of Paolo's loaf. 'Why don't you take the child?' she suggested in a sharp whisper. 'It no longer has a father or a mother.'

Paolo stared at her. 'I beg your pardon, Principessa?'

'I said – she's yours. For the rest of that loaf of bread, you can have the baby.'

'Marcella!' Antonio was shocked. She was haggling like some fishwife bargaining at the market – and using the child as currency. Too much had happened, he supposed. The walk through the ruins of the Palazzo di Cristallo had confirmed the worst of everything to her; it had broken her.

Marcella snatched the child out of his arms and held her up to Paolo. 'Look how beautiful she is,' she hissed. 'An angel. Your wife need never know that she is not of her own flesh and blood. Yours was a day old. This one is not much older. You can have her, substitute her. And see this necklace her mother put around her neck?'

Paolo could only stare down at the pansy charm, numb with surprise.

'The necklace is yours, too. I don't want it. You can have her and the necklace! All we want for her is the rest of that loaf of bread.' Her eyes gleamed crazily.

Antonio turned to face the wall, the tears streaming down his cheeks. The Mother Superior had to turn away also. She could not bear to see the ugly impression on the Principessa's face.

'Don't you see that it's all for the best this way?' Marcella hissed at her husband. 'At least this way the child can eat. And she'll have a mother and a father. And we can have some bread to eat, too.'

'You . . . you would do this?' Paolo asked softly.

'Yes, yes,' the Principessa snapped. 'Here!' She thrust the baby into his arms and snatched away the rest of the loaf of bread. 'I hated the baby's mother. She was nothing but a fascist *putana*. I knew my son was doomed the moment I first saw her. It was all because of her that he died. Who wants the child of the slut who killed her husband.'

Paolo stared down at the baby. Her tiny, wrinkled pink face was one of wide-eyed innocence. The fluffy, down-like hairs on her head were golden, and the eyes were wide and aquamarine. She was indeed an angel. And his wife would never doubt the child was not her own; their coloring was so similar. Paolo looked over at Marcella, who was already walking away, biting off another hunk of the bread. She had not even offered a piece to her husband, who followed after her with a slow step and stooped shoulders. The Mother Superior bowed her head and prayed silently. Under ordinary circumstances, she would have tried to intervene, but the situation was hardly ordinary. It would have been useless to challenge the aristocratic authority of the di Fontanesis. Everywhere, there was death and destruction. Better the child lived in a family of simple people with loving hearts, than try to keep her in the presence of the shrew who was willing to sell her for a loaf of bread.

The Mother Superior watched as Paolo put one arm around his six-year-old son's shoulder, dropped to his knees to show him his new baby sister, and extracted from him a vow never to tell his mother what he had just witnessed.

Then Paolo looked up. 'Reverend Mother, this child does not have a name.'

She nodded. 'I suppose it doesn't, or else they would have told us.'

'What was the mother's name?'

'Charlotte-Anne.'

He frowned thoughtfully. 'Anna. Yes, we shall call her after her mother. We shall call her Anna.'

The Mother Superior smiled her approval.

Yes, it was much better this way.

Somehow, God in his Wisdom had seen to it that the child would at least be loved.

23

The suitcases lay on the bed, their lids yawning open.

Elizabeth-Anne watched in silence as Janet folded and packed their clothes. She glanced over at Zaccheus. Her son had pulled his wheelchair up in front of the window, and he was staring out at the hills of Umbria as though some elusive, last-minute answer lay hidden in that view. She knew what he was thinking. She was thinking the same thing.

They had come to Italy to find Anna, but had finally had to admit failure. There were so many pieces to the puzzle, and she was afraid that no matter how hard she searched or how deeply she dug, she would never find them all.

She crossed the room and stood behind Zaccheus, wearily placing a hand on his shoulder. For a moment he turned and glanced up at her. Her features were composed; she felt there was no need to show the terrible pain she felt as she stared out at the now-familiar hills.

When she had first arrived, she had imagined she felt closer to Charlotte-Anne here, where she had lived, but she knew now that that had merely been an illusion. These hills could not make up for her loss. Charlotte-Anne was buried in Italy but her spirit was no longer here. Elizabeth-Anne had to accept that fact and come to terms with the tragedy, just as nature did. In places, the bombed vineyards had already been replanted with surviving vines. There was a lesson to be learned from that.

Life went on, she thought dully. Despite the most tragic devastation ever visited upon the world, life went on.

She steepled her hands and held her forefingers poised against her lips. She knew that her family had not been singled out to suffer. Millions of other lives had been destroyed in the past few tragic years. But the toll the war had extracted from her and her loved ones was high: a son who was crippled; a daughter dead at only thirty, whose very name inspired such loathing that the Italian peasants would spit and curse upon hearing it; a missing grandchild; a son-in-law who had been fallen upon by his people, stabbed to death with pitchforks, and then ignobly hanged upside down in the village piazza and mutilated, because he was the symbol of a government which abused its power and oppressed its citizens. They had taken their anger out upon Luigi di Fontanesi because he was a remaining tangible manifestation of a country gone mad.

What had happened to the human race, to turn people into such rabid animals?

She had asked herself that question a thousand times, but there was no answer. There were so many questions, and no answers to any of them.

Slowly, she turned around. She decided she might as well help Janet pack. Just moving around in a zombie-like state did not do anyone a bit of good, least of all herself. They had come here and done all they could, which had amounted to nothing. Now the sooner they were packed, the sooner they could leave. She knew now the best thing they could do was go home and come to grips with their losses. It was time to face the truth. Her granddaughter had disappeared. Like an unwanted puppy or kitten, she had been given to passing strangers by her other grandparents. No matter how far and wide she continued to search for her, Elizabeth-Anne realized that the search would be fruitless. She would never find Anna. The parents she had been given to had no doubt heard about her search, as Elizabeth-Anne had had it so widely publicized, and they had disappeared into the night. The worst part of it was, in all her fifty years she had never learned to accept defeat.

She clenched her hands and let out a silent moan of anger and impotence. The many voices and images of the last few weeks seemed to swirl in her mind.

The Mother Superior, her face sad, her voice torn and tortured: 'Signora, the child is happy. You must believe me. It will only hurt her to be torn from the only family she knows and loves. Please, Signora. Have a heart. If you insist, yes, I will tell you. But please, Signora. It will be a grave mistake.'

Her own voice, hollow and faraway: 'I have to know. I must. She is my daughter's child.'

The Mother Superior: 'Very well, then, Anna. Anna Viganò. Father Odoni himself baptized her.'

And the Viganòs's neighbor and landlord: 'They left in the middle of the night, like thieves running from the law. Who knows where they went? They left owing me two months' rent. Good riddance I say.'

Elizabeth-Anne's heart and soul burned with the pain. She had been so close to finding Anna. Now she was once again gone, lost forever. Who knew where the Viganòs had fled to in order to keep the child?

Memories, so many, many memories assaulted her. There was so much that she blamed herself for. So much could have been different if only . . .

If only I hadn't sent Charlotte-Anne to Europe, she might still be alive.

If only I'd spent less time with the hotels and more time being a mother.

If only I'd kept a tighter rein on her.

There were so many 'ifs.'

And so many startling truths which only now came into focus. Charlotte-Anne had been headstrong and rebellious, so very determined to get her way. And that, Elizabeth-Anne knew, was one characteristic which had been inherited from herself. She and Charlotte-Anne had much more in common than either of them had ever wanted to admit. But unlike herself, Charlotte-Anne threw caution to the winds. She never gave any thought to the potential consequences of her actions.

Oh, if only I'd prodded her in the right direction. That was all Charlotte-Anne had needed. Why hadn't I noticed that? Why had I been so blind?

But it was too late to dissect the past, to dream of doing

things differently. Charlotte-Anne had been tragically killed. She was gone forever, and what Elizabeth-Anne had to do was keep alive the good memories.

Eventually, she knew she would come to terms with Charlotte-Anne's death. But she also knew she would never understand what the di Fontanesis had done. Nor would she find it in her heart to forgive them.

How could they have given the child away? And for food? Did they think they were the only ones on the point of starvation? Only the arrival of the Allies, and their generous dispensing of rations, had kept all of Italy from starvation. But it was love which, despite the scarcity of sustenance and the preponderance of disease, had sustained families and held them together. Perhaps . . . she dared think . . . perhaps Anna was best off without such loveless people as the Principessa Marcella and her husband.

Still, she would never be able to come to terms with the fact that Anna was missing. Death was final. Sooner or later, everyone had to die. A grave, at least, was tangible. But a disappearance? No, that was one thing which was truly unacceptable. Not knowing what had happened to Anna would forever gnaw at her. But, for now, she had to accept defeat, accept the fact that, no matter how much effort and money she continued to expend, the child would never be found. She could only pray that, whoever had gotten her would lavish all the love in the world upon her.

Yes, it was indeed time they all went back home and picked up the shattered pieces of their lives. Janet and Zaccheus's son, Henry, was in the States with the governess, waiting for their return. It was time to concentrate on the here and now, on the living. It was time to take stock and count their blessings.

Wordlessly, Elizabeth-Anne moved over beside Janet and picked up a blouse. She folded it carefully, the tears sparkling in her eyes.

The war was over, but the suffering would continue for a long time. And eventually, it would become diluted, more bearable, leaving only memories and sharp little jabs of pain in its wake.

Life had to go on. But that didn't mean that the good memories had to be stifled. She had to open her mind to them, welcome them to fill her, and permit herself to have a good cry.

Despite the tragedies which had occurred, the love for her dead daughter and missing granddaughter did not have to die. In her, the love could thrive as potently as if she were still with them.

And that, she thought, was the key to survival.

But still, she knew there would be those countless days when the nagging thought would creep into her consciousness and wedge there, refusing to budge:

What on earth had happened to her Anna?

GENERATIONS THREE

Anna

Rome, Italy
May 22, 1964

1

It was forty minutes past ten by the time the all-too-familiar bus crossed the Cestio Bridge to the far bank of the Tiber. The Roman sky was a sea of calm blue, with a regatta of fleeting, gold-tipped clouds sailing across it. But Anna Viganò felt anything but calm.

Of all days to be late! she moaned to herself. Of all days for her brand new Vespa one cylinder scooter to break down! She had saved so long, hoarding money she could ill-afford to put aside, hoping the scooter would be a way to avoid the infuriating, snail paced morning rush hour traffic. And for a while it had. But then, today, the most important day of her life, it had suddenly and mysteriously died. She had tried to get the scooter fixed, but after waiting for the mechanic for an hour, he had pronounced the problem hopeless.

And now she might miss the opportunity she had waited so long for. Her chance to be the one hand-picked employee of the Hale Roma who would be sent to the company's Management Training School in New York, and thereby become an Assistant Manager. It was the opportunity of a lifetime.

Glancing out the window, she saw the bus was finally nearing her destination and pulled the cable to request a stop. As she went to the front of the bus, she snapped at a man who got in her way. How unlike her! She must get control of her nerves. Usually, she was the very picture of politeness. Her job required it. It was up to her to smooth over rough edges, to wipe away any irritants in the hotel guests' lives. And she was certainly used to the hustle and bustle of Roman crowds. Having lived here for all but three years of her life, she had had plenty of time to develop patience.

Apologizing to the man with a pleasant smile, Anna got off the bus and hurried down the sidewalk. Time was of the essence. The manager would have a fit if he saw her come in at this hour. Even if someone had tried to cover for her, he had surely found out that she hadn't been in yet by now.

She cringed, just thinking of him. He was a pompous martinet who moved with the speed of lightning and the stealth of a spider. He seemed to be everywhere at once. Nobody had the keen ears and reptilian eyes of Romeo Corvi. Although he was leaving his late forties behind, he certainly didn't show it. All sleekly groomed, with a slightly disdainful, but not so slightly unctuous air, he acted as though he should be behind the counter of Van Cleef or Cartier. She shuddered, thinking of his thick black hair combed straight back and his irritating habit of cocking one dark eyebrow to immense heights while he surveyed one with a look of total disdain. After all she'd been through that morning, having a confrontation with Corvi was something she did not relish.

With that thought, she hurried toward the huge, square-block building with its pedimented windows set behind classical, collonaded balconies. On the sloping roof facing her were large gold letters facing outward, announcing her destination:

HALE ROMA

Even before she reached the hotel she saw the long line of taxis queued up, waiting for the day's before-noon check outs. As she went by, she pointedly kept her gaze fixed on the pavement directly in front of her, to avoid the cabbies' glances. Nevertheless, she heard an appreciative wolf whistle, which only made her speed up, her heels clickety-clacking a swift staccato rhythm on the pavement.

She fairly flew past the main entrance with its wide, red-carpeted steps and gleaming glass and brass doors, her destination the employees' entrance around the corner in the cobble-stoned side alley.

As she neared it, she had no choice but to slow down

because of the uneven cobblestones. Her mind only half on the treacherous alley, she lectured herself silently.

Whatever happened today, no matter *what*, she mustn't put her job in jeopardy.

If Romeo Corvi raised a stink about her coming in so late, then she must take his tongue-lashing in silence, be very humble, and above all, *not talk back*.

She mustn't do what she had been tempted to do on a thousand other occasions and what every employee in his secret fantasies dreamed of doing, too: she could not put her hands around that haughty thin neck of his and squeeze the last bit of breath out of him.

Today, of all days, she had to tread carefully. Not only because of the chance of being picked to attend the Management Training School; even without that, this job was too important to her. Getting it in the first place had been a miracle. It had taken considerable connections. When the Hale Roma had opened a year and a half previously, jobs there had been at a premium. The salaries were high in comparison with those of the other hotels, and advancement opportunities were said to be excellent, because everyone had to start from the ground up. Thousands had applied for the jobs, and thousands had been turned away. Only two hundred lucky Romans found employment, and she had been one of them.

Her influential Cousin Fabio, who had his fingers in many pies, had been responsible for getting her the initial job interview. But all even he had been able to do was open the door. The rest had been up to her. She'd landed the job, and then sailed on with flying colors. In the year and a half she'd been at the hotel, she'd proved her worth time and again, swiftly getting promoted from monotonous hours spent typing in one of the tiny cubicles on the second floor to helping all around: manning the reception desk when things got particularly hectic, filling in for the public relations manager when she had come down with appendicitis, soothing an hysterical guest and aiding to track down a lost earring, guiding women to boutiques where silk scarves were to be had at bargain prices or cobblers' custom-made shoes in three days, finding a suitable baby-sitter for a couple who wanted to leave their child behind while enjoying a night on the town, and searching the city for the one *Drogheria* which could fill a guest's rare and necessary medical prescription. And throughout it all, she was always friendly, polite, eager, and patient. She bedazzled all with her ever-present smile, was dependable and went out of her way to be helpful. She made herself indispensable by creating a job for herself where none had existed before; she was an unofficial jack of all trades, summoned whenever there was a need, and she was well-liked and respected by everyone, staff and guests alike.

Everyone except Romeo Corvi.

Just thinking of him was enough to bring her blood to a boil. He looked for fault with everything she did, and she had finally discovered why. She was too naive to have realized it herself, but after someone else had mentioned it, she realized the problem. She was altogether too efficient, and in too many areas. He was afraid that she was ultimately more qualified for his job than he was.

But just as she knew she wasn't out to steal his job, she also recognized there was no way to convince him of that. Confronting him on the issue would only confirm his worst paranoia. It was a no-win situation.

Office politics. *How she hated them.*

Two weeks ago, her troubles with Romeo Corvi had come to an explosive head. The New York headquarters of Hale Hotels had just sent word that the Roma Hale was to submit a list of their ten brightest employees. Each was to be interviewed by an executive officer from New York for a future opening as assistant manager, either in Rome or at the Milano Hale, now under construction. Besides earning regular pay, the chosen candidate would receive an all expenses paid trip to New York in order to take part in the Hale Hotels Management Training Course.

Anna knew that it was the opportunity of a lifetime. Money had always been a problem, and she was determined to overcome it by working her way up through the complicated hierarchy of a major business. She was sure sheer hard work and dedication would take her where she wanted to go. From the beginning, she had faced her qualifications with brutal candor. She had taken stock of her advantages and disadvantages, and knew she had more things going against her than for her. Her education was adequate, but she had only attended public schools. She was young, a woman, and, worst of all, far too attractive for her own good.

At almost twenty, her beauty was pronounced and startling. She stood nearly six feet tall in her stockinged feet. Her wheat gold hair was straight, cut to shoulder length in an attractive but no-nonsense style that bounced with her free stride. Her skin was smooth, pale butterscotch in color, and her eyes were arrestingly blue, too deep for aquamarine, and too light for sea blue. She had a small waist, generous hips, and long, powerful legs. She exuded the very picture of health. She strode swiftly, with an economy of movement, as though there was a purpose to her every step. She was a woman in the midst of a man's world, and she was determined to prove her worth. The chance to attend the Management Training Course was manna from heaven.

She'd expected her name to head the list of candidates. In all fairness, it should have. Everyone agreed that she knew the overall workings of the Roma Hale better even than the current assistant manager.

That she had managed to look over the list of candidates had been a total fluke. As luck would have it, Corvi's personal secretary, Gabriella Di Donato, had been out sick. The girl who filled in for her was new, and didn't know how to operate the telex machine. She'd asked Anna for help.

'Don't worry about it,' Anna had offered. 'I'll send it.'

She sat down in front of the machine with the typewritten message. The moment she saw that it was the list of candidates, her heart seemed to stop dead.

Her name was not even on it.

Romeo Corvi had seen to that.

She'd been on the verge of tears when the idea occurred to her. Since *she* was sending the telex, she would simply include herself on the list. The only problem was, New

363

York had specifically asked for a list of ten names. Not eleven. And there were already ten names listed.

She sat for a moment, deep in thought, having pangs of conscience about who to scratch. Then she noticed the seventh name, and she breathed a lot easier. Maurizio Corvi was Romeo's younger brother who, thanks to family nepotism, had been given his job over many more qualified applicants only weeks earlier.

It was no contest. She struck Maurizio from the list and put herself on it instead. After she sent the telex, she filed the copy and waited for Corvi's explosion. Sooner or later it was bound to come as it was only a matter of time before he would find out what she had done. Her only satisfaction was that it was a *fait accompli*. He would be able to do nothing to change things. Except fire her. If he threatened that, she'd have to be slippery as an eel and wiggle out of it somehow.

Last week, a telex reply had chattered in over the wires from the New York headquarters. It gave the arrival date of the Hale Hotels representative, as well as a list confirming the names of the candidates who should be ready to be interviewed. Romeo Corvi had been apoplectic with rage. Only his brittle, self-important dignity had kept him from calling her a thousand choice epithets. He had gone so far as to threaten to fire her, but she had wisely pointed out to him that that would look awfully peculiar. After all, one didn't fire an employee who, only a week earlier, had been in such good standing as to deserve a place on the list. He'd gone purple with fury, trembling visibly while he fought to keep his anger in check. Then, after a stern warning, he had stormed off, his chest puffed out, his head held high and tilted back.

She shuddered every time she thought about how close she had come to getting fired. If she had been, there would have been nothing anyone, not even Cousin Fabio, could have done to help. Not that she would want any more of Fabio Pegrone's help. Not ever again.

Her hatred for Cousin Fabio was second only to her detestation of Romeo Corvi. Ever since she could remember, all she had ever heard was, 'We have our

364

Cousin Fabio to thank for this,' 'We have our Cousin Fabio to thank for that.' Sometimes, Anna thought she would scream if she heard another word about having to be grateful to Cousin Fabio. Gratitude and niceness, in his case, meant letting him walk all over you.

Fabio Pegrone was a distant cousin on Anna's father's side, and the two men had never been close. Her father came from the poor branch of the Viganò family, while Fabio hailed from the rich Pegrone branch. When Anna had turned three, and the Viganòs had come to Rome from Umbria, her father had sought out Cousin Fabio for help. He'd been given a job in Fabio's construction firm doing mean, manual, back-breaking labor. Her father had never been heard to utter a single complaint, not even on the day he dropped dead of a heart attack.

Nor had her mother ever complained. Not once in all these difficult years.

Ever since arriving in Rome, they had lived in one of Cousin Fabio's tenement blocks. For that, her mother always said, they'd had to be extremely grateful. Inexpensive housing was difficult to find, and if Cousin Fabio hadn't let them have the apartment, they would have had to live on the streets.

Only when Anna was old enough to understand the difference between the tenements which Cousin Fabio owned, and the lavish penthouse duplex in the exclusive Parioli District where he and his family lived did the injustice of it all make an ugly, lasting impression. She felt ever more rankled by the lavishness of Fabio Pegrone's lifestyle, which he maintained by squeezing every last lire out of his tenants. In winter, the apartments had little or no heat. Boilers broke down constantly and were not repaired for months. Toilets got clogged and stayed that way for weeks. Rats roamed the dark hallways biting babies and spreading disease, while cockroaches skittered around the floors and inside the walls. Anna grew to hate the ever-present smells of cooking intermingling with the stench of garbage, the lack of fresh air and light, the squalling of babies, and the huge families crammed into one or two miniscule rooms. When she was seven, and first learned to read, one of the first things she deciphered was the graffiti scratched deep into the walls and doors of Fabio Pegrone's tenements: Pegrone the pig.

She was ashamed to be related to him. And even more ashamed to let anyone know where she lived.

What pained her the most was that, when her father died just after she had turned eight years old, her mother had had to take in the Pegrones' laundry in order to make ends meet. The little Adriana Viganò earned seemed to jump right back into Cousin Fabio's pockets. It was a vicious cycle, and there was no avenue of escape. Dario was too young to get anything but erratic, low paying jobs so it was the laundry that kept the family going. Over and over, her mother reiterated that they had to be grateful to Cousin Fabio for letting her do it. Otherwise, they would starve.

Money – or rather the lack of it – was the specter which haunted them ceaselessly. How often had she wondered, if she had a lire for every single rat, mouse or cockroach she saw, how rich they would be? But that was an idle dream conjured up by anger and helplessness, emotions fed by the continuing injustices she saw as she grew up. The rent for the tenement was often raised without warning from month to month. Behind their mother's back, Anna and Dario often went to see Cousin Fabio about it, but all the pleading in the world never did them a bit of good. He sent them to his manager, who insisted they were entitled to no favors just because they were distant relatives of Signor Pegrone.

Somehow, miraculously, they survived. When Dario was old enough he left home to study to become a priest. It was their mother's fondest dream that he do so, and she refused to even consider that he work to support them instead. At least it was easier with him gone, as there was one less mouth to feed. But Adriana's health was fast eroding, and she found it more and more difficult to do laundry. Anna's job at the Roma Hale literally saved them. It paid far from a splendid wage, but finally set things on an even keel. She continued to live at home in order to help stretch the income: every week, she handed her paychecks over to her mother. She knew it was up to her to give her mother the financial support which had been lacking in the household for so long.

And so it was that her ambition was fueled. Not by greed, but by the lack of basic necessities which they had suffered for so long.

If I'm the one who is chosen to go to New York to take the Management Training Course, and if I become assistant manager at a princely salary, then we can finally get out from under Cousin Fabio's thumb once and for all. Then I can finally chase away the bleak ghosts of hunger and wretched despair.

Oh, but everything depended upon so many *ifs*. And there was still never enough money to go around, she thought despairingly.

Sometimes, she was under the impression that no matter how hard she worked, it was still futile, as if there were a bottomless drain in the house down which every last, precious lire swirled. Not that her mother wasn't careful. Far from it. Adriana Viganò scrimped and saved every last lire till it bled. She mended old clothes and, when they started to fall apart, mended them all over again. She haggled for groceries and bought days-old loaves of bread. But the years of poverty had taken their toll, and now Adriana had fallen ill. Doctors were expensive; specialists even more so. And then, a year ago, just before Anna had started work at the Roma Hale, she herself had had to be hospitalized. All because of Amedeo Battistello.

And the way she had fallen for him.

2

Amedeo.

It had been a year and a half since she had met him. God, how she had come to hate him! But she hadn't hated him in the beginning. He had dazzled her, and she had fallen head over heels in love with him.

She had been sixteen years old at the time and just finishing her last year of school. It was one of those chance meetings which could never have been arranged. Every afternoon, when school was over, she would take the bus to the Parioli District and pick up a bag of the Pegrones' laundry. Every morning, on her way to school, she would drop off the finished laundry which had been washed, dried, and carefully pressed, then packaged in brown wrapping paper and tied with twine. 'As professional looking as any expensive laundry's,' Adriana would say proudly.

Anna had to get up very early to get the deliveries done on time, because the tenenemt was located far from the exclusive district which was a favorite with industrialists, film stars, diplomats, and the likes of Cousin Fabio. One morning, after she had dropped off the laundry, she rushed out of Cousin Fabio's building, afraid she was running late, and collided with a tall, handsome stranger.

'You're in a terrible hurry,' he said, grabbing her by the arms to keep her from falling.

'I-I'm sorry, Signor,' she said hastily, lowering her eyes.

'It is I who should be sorry.' He smiled then. 'Or perhaps not. It isn't every day that a man encounters such a beautiful young lady.'

She stared at him for a second or two, caught off guard by his flashing eyes and the touch of his hands. He was young, tall and broad, and his dark, well-cut suit and white silk shirt were custom tailored. The striped, black and tawny-yellow tie matched his dark hair and predatory cat's eyes. His nose was prominent, and his lips were soft and sensuous. His gaze and touch set off warning bells in her head, and she quickly pulled away from him and began hurrying down the sidewalk. She heard quick footsteps behind her, and then he was at her side again, easily falling in step with her long-legged stride. He smiled at her. 'I have a car. Can I give you a lift?'

She shook her head and kept her eyes riveted on the sidewalk in front of her.

'We should be friends,' he said equably. 'I mean, we are, after all, practically acquainted, aren't we? Bumping into each other like that?'

She stopped walking and turned to face him. He was

grinning, his teeth perfect and white against his swarthy tan. Off to one side of his upper lip he had a tiny, freckle-like mole, odd and dashing. His skin was stretched tautly across his high, almost Slavic cheekbones, and his eyes seemed to reach out into hers, and she felt her mind go blank, then spin with wild thoughts.

He seemed cultured and cultivated but exuded an air of peril and adventure. Although he looked to be in his early thirties, he had an irresistible, easy, boyish charm about him.

'I have to go,' she said with sudden vehemence, jerking herself back from that mesmeric countenance. 'I'm late.'

'Wait.' He caught her arm. 'I don't even know your name.'

She took a deep breath. She could feel the pulse in her temples, the slight clamminess of her hands. He was so close that his face was mere inches from her own. She could smell the sweet perfume of expensive soap, and the even more expensive, crisply masculine fragrance of eau de cologne, but she never felt his fingers on the thin, tan sweater she wore draped over her shoulders as he tugged loose one of the brass buttons. While he held her gaze he slipped it into his pocket.

'Really, I must go,' she said finally, almost sadly. As she walked away, her low heels clacked an ever-quickening beat until she was half running. When she rounded the corner she stole a glance over her shoulder. He wasn't trying to follow. She slowed down and let out a breath of relief.

And felt curiously disappointed.

That afternoon, when school let out, she returned to Cousin Fabio's building to pick up the day's bag of dirty laundry. She kept her eyes peeled for the stranger, but he was nowhere to be seen. Again, she felt let down somehow.

That night, lying in the narrow bed in her tiny, humid room, she stared up at the ceiling for what seemed like an eternity. She had trouble going to sleep, but she had no trouble imagining those hypnotic eyes burning into hers, the tiny mole near the corner of his mouth, and those white-white teeth gleaming in the dark. She found herself fantasizing about him until she finally fell into a deep, dreamless sleep.

By morning, she had all but forgotten him. But after she dropped off the Pegrones' laundry and left Cousin Fabio's building to head to school, there he was, leaning nonchalantly against the downstairs door, a crooked grin on his face. He held up a hand, and a brass button caught the sunlight and glinted brightly.

'Oh, you found it!' she cried with delight. 'I was wondering where I'd lost it.' As she reached out for it, he playfully held it beyond her reach.

'You can have it on one condition.'

She looked at him wordlessly.

'You'll come and have an espresso with me.'

And so it began.

Amedeo Battistello. How easy it had been to fall for him! He was so unlike any of the young men in her mean, tenement-strewn neighborhood. He was sophisticated, wore well-tailored clothes, and always seemed to have a crocodile wallet full of money. He drove an expensive little Alfa Romeo convertible while the boys in her neighborhood just dreamed of owning cars. They struggled to hold on to low paying menial jobs while he worked for his uncle, a producer at Cine Città, Italy's answer to Hollywood. The boys in her neighborhood had their fun, but were expected to find a nice girl, get married and have children. Building a family was one of the few things Amedeo never seemed keen to discuss. The one thing he did have in common with the young men around whom she had grown up was that peculiar, hungry look in his eyes.

She found herself rearranging her schedule in order to meet him. She started leaving her books at home, and hiding the Pegrones' laundry in her school satchel. She never told Amedeo who she was and he took it for granted that she lived in Cousin Fabio's building. She lied about her age and claimed to have a job. She liked the fantasy of being someone other than poor Anna Viganò, the daughter of a widowed laundress. It was, after all, a harmless deception. Nobody could get hurt by it. Could they?

At first Amedeo took her to sidewalk cafés for espresso

and cake, or a cool glass of wine, usually on the Via Sistina, which passed by the top of the Spanish Steps. They sat in the piazzas, walked along the Tiber, or tore recklessly around Rome with the convertible top down. He took her far from the cloying smells of greasy cooking and the infestations of rats. He was glamor and wealth personified, and seemed part of another, more beguiling world. She believed implicitly that he was the most exciting man alive.

Then he told her that he wanted to take her home. But because he lived in the building next to hers, he instead took her to the Hotel Hassler, atop the Spanish Steps. It was there that she lost her virginity.

When he'd signed them in at the reception desk of the Hassler for the first time, the desk clerk had looked at the scrawled registry, smiled politely, and called her 'Signora Battistello.' She'd blushed proudly, pleased as a genuine newlywed that someone would even consider that she, Anna Viganò, could belong to someone as extraordinarily handsome and rich as Amedeo Battistello. How many times during the past few weeks had she tested the name Battistello silently on her tongue, savoring the mere sound of it?

But then, everything about Amedeo was wonderful. He brought out a radiant glow in her which seemed to change her entirely. She had always looked mature for her age, but now she seemed positively sophisticated. At first, she had been afraid to make love, but with Amedeo it was anything but the lascivious, purposeful copulation about which coarse jokes were constantly bandied about in the tenements. How often, on hot, humid summer nights, with her window open, had she unavoidably heard the grunts and groans coming from the other windows facing the courtyard? But it was never like that with Amedeo. His love making was a graceful, tender ballet full of passion and promises.

That first time, he had led her upstairs slowly, then whispered her name and taken her in his arms. The door was locked and the shutters closed, so that the late afternoon sunlight streamed through the slats into the semidarkness. She had watched his every move, her heart hammering with excitement while a terrible fear gnawed into the flesh inside her belly. This was her first time, and she knew it was wrong to be with a man like this before she was married.

But the man was Amedeo. How could it be wrong? Theirs was a love so powerful that *nothing* else mattered.

As his strong arms held her, any hesitation she had left evaporated, seemed to drain visibly out of her. Her lips trembled, dry with a mixture of anticipation and dread. She'd heard the stories of how much it hurt the first time, but Amedeo was so kind and gentle and loving, she couldn't believe the stories were true.

He bowed his head to the side of her neck, his lips forming a gentle little kiss, a whisper of desire. His hands caressed her arms and breasts, then coursed down her sides to her thighs. Through her thin cotton dress she could feel his touch tingling across her flesh. She swallowed, shut her eyes, her lips parting. She was unable to resist the surge of passion she felt when she savored the fact that he, Amedeo Battistello, was doing these things to her, bringing such a prickling, intense heat to her body and an ache to her soul.

Slowly, almost reverentially, he unfastened the buttons at the back of her dress, and then he parted the fabric and pushed it down off her shoulders. It glided, whispering softly, down to her ankles. She stood in silence, her cheap, coarse slip out of place in the soft luxury of the room.

'*Anna. Anna.*' His lips were at her neck again, his tongue flicking moist, warm little circles against her skin. She felt his fingers stroking her shoulders, brushing at the nape of her neck, coiling her long blonde hair around them.

'*Anna.*' His voice was a bare ghost of breath as he pressed himself, still fully clothed, against her half-clothed body. She could feel the quickening of his heartbeats merging with her own. She inhaled the intoxicating aroma of his eau de cologne mingling with the even stronger, more tangible masculine smell of him.

'*Anna.*'

She trembled as he held her face in his hands, kissed her deeply, then paused, to slip out of an item of clothing before kissing her again and helping her shed another piece of her clothing. Finally they stood facing each other naked.

She averted her gaze in embarrassment, but he took her face back in both hands and whispered, 'It is beautiful. Don't be ashamed.'

She still could not face him.

'*Look at me*,' he commanded sharply.

She forced herself to do so, tears sparkling in her eyes.

'Look,' he whispered more gently as he took two steps backwards, as straight-backed and proud as a dancer.

As though hypnotized, her eyes swept from his face downward. He was well-muscled, but thin and wiry, and it surprised her. When he was clothed, he seemed broad because of his wide shoulders. He was tanned all over, except for a thin, white bathing suit line; by contrast, her own body was sadly pale. His chest was curly with wiry coils of black hair, making it seem even darker, and the pelt reached down his belly and gathered force at the thicket in his groin. His penis was large and superb, hard and dark red.

'*Anna.*' His voice was a whisper that roared in her ears. She lifted her gaze and stared straight into his eyes. He stepped forward and pulled her into his arms, pressing her fully against his nakedness. His body felt so warm and hard, so unyielding and different from her own. And oh, how the touch of his flesh seemed to sear into hers.

She felt his hot tongue exploring her mouth, filling her with warmth and wild abandon as his penis pressed hotly against her belly. Her nipples grew erect, aching for his hands and his lips, longing for him to take her.

He placed one hand under each of her buttocks, lifted her and carried her effortlessly over to the bed. He laid her down gently, as though afraid she might break, and crawled atop her. His thumbs and forefingers kneaded her nipples while his lips and tongue caressed every inch of her body, bringing the surface of her skin to tingling, vibrating life.

She arched her body and sighed a breathy kind of moan as he began to enter her. Instinctively, she clamped her muscles together against the unfamiliar intrusion, but then she began to experiment, to open herself up for him, to welcome him into her most private and precious place. Her eyes stared up at him, wide and luminous.

He pressed his erection more deeply against her, sending little shock waves down her spine, until he met the obstruction of her hymen. He stopped and looked at her in surprise. 'You're . . . a virgin?' he asked.

'Go ahead,' she whispered, smiling faintly. 'I want it. I want you.' She reached up with her fingers to stroke his cheek.

He prodded at her twice, but her hymen was unyielding. She tensed in anticipation and with a hard, brutal thrust, he tore into her. Pain exploded in front of her eyes, a searing fireball red in the center and flaring outward into yellow ragged circles. But the starburst gradually faded, and Amedeo transformed it to white hot desire.

She found herself instinctively raising her hips and working her torso in a purposeful rhythm to meet his own. Her pelvis rose and swayed against him, bringing delicious waves of burning pleasure. She drew her legs up, bending her knees and opening herself wide.

He thrust deeply into her then, drawing out each stroke at an ever quickening pace so that she sucked in her breath, swallowing the exclamations of surprise as wave after heated wave engulfed her. This was an explosion, a coming *alive* she had never even dreamed of before. She was enveloped in wanting and lust, in hotness and pulsing. For this, she knew, she had been born, just as in every massive thrust there was a little death.

Suddenly, he gave a sharp cry. His body arched, and she felt him lunging yet deeper into her as he clutched her and filled her with a throbbing explosion. His head swooped back, his eyes pressed shut, and he jerked uncontrollably.

Both their bodies were coated with a veneer of sweat. He sprawled panting atop her, his breath labored and his penis small. She felt as though her mysterious insides had survived a most delicious assault. The room was dimmer. The glowing horizontal zebra stripes cast by the shutters had disappeared as outside a cloud scudded in front of the setting sun. Even now that it was over, their thumping heartbeats seemed synchronized.

From somewhere below on the Spanish Steps drifted the faint, muted sound of lovers laughing.

That first time was like no other. It was a time when the joy of discovery and exploration was as intense as the burning of their passions and desires. It was the moment she had stepped over the threshold into womanhood.

Everything had been so beautiful, so filled with pleasure, so softly clean as they lay on the freshly laundered sheets in the late afternoon sun. She had never even given a thought to pregnancy, then or in the months that followed. She didn't want to spoil what they shared by even thinking about it. Naturally, she had heard whispers about prophylactics. Even if the Church forbade their use, they were available. She had never seen one and the only time she had mentioned it, Amedeo had scowled and said he didn't like using them. And besides, who could give a thought to consequences in the midst of such delicious, overwhelming ecstasy?

After that first time, they had met regularly twice a week, always at the Hassler Hotel, and it was on one of those eight heady occasions that their baby was conceived.

She told him about it on a bleak day of thin light and steady rainfall. She had battled with her emotions for weeks, unable to come to terms with her pregnancy or even to tell him about it. Every time she had tried, she had lost her courage and instead tried to forget in yet another afternoon of passion.

She was afraid. It was as though by telling him she would be confirming her condition to herself. She knew that the longer she waited, the more irreversible the situation became. But what would it matter? It was irreversible as it was.

Already her mother had noticed that she was putting on weight. Amedeo had, too. Twice, he'd jokingly called it her 'baby fat.'

Poor Amedeo, she thought. And poor mother. If they only knew the truth. She realized that sooner or later she would have to tell them both, and the very idea of it filled her with terror. She would have preferred to hole up somewhere and die.

On the fateful afternoon when she'd finally broken the news to him, they had made love as usual. Afterwards, when they lay in silence in the dim room, she had stared up at the ceiling with blind eyes. 'Amedeo,' she had finally said in a soft, frightened whisper.

'Yes?'

She took a deep breath and closed her eyes. 'I'm pregnant.'

The announcement had all the impact of an explosion. He sat up as though he'd gotten a sizzling jolt of electricity. '*What*?' He stared at her.

She nodded and bit down on her lip. 'Don't be angry,' she pleaded huskily, turning to him. 'Please. I'm scared.' She reached out to hold his hand, but he was poking around on the nightstand for a cigarette. She watched tensely as he fumbled with a match and lit the cigarette with trembling fingers. He let the smoke out of his mouth and inhaled it into his nose. 'How long?' he asked at last.

'I think . . . three months.'

He groaned and let himself fall back down on the bed with such force that the box spring shook under the impact. He lay there and smoked on in silence. Finally he stubbed out the cigarette and sighed deeply. 'Of course, you'll have to get rid of it.'

She froze then, and her whisper sounded strangled. 'I-I don't understand.'

His laugh was unexpected and bitter. 'You don't understand?' He turned to her, his eyes cold. 'Do I have to spell it out for you? An *abortion*.' His eyes turned into hers. 'Now do you understand?'

She struggled to sit up. With one hand she clutched the rumpled sheet against her naked breasts. She began crying softly. 'But . . . it's illegal.'

'That doesn't mean it can't be done,' he said matter-of-factly. 'I know plenty of girls who've gotten abortions.'

'Plenty of . . . girls.' Her voice trailed off. She wondered how many others there had been before her. She had never

376

given that any thought. She was amazed at her own naiveté. Of course she wasn't the first.

Nor would she be the last.

'Sure.' He shrugged casually. 'They say it doesn't hurt half as much as having a tooth pulled. It's nothing, really.'

'Nothing?' She stared at him. 'It's killing. It's wrong.'

'Having an illegitimate kid isn't wrong?'

'But it doesn't have to be illegitimate,' she said. 'We could get married.'

'*Married*?' he asked in amused disbelief. 'You and me? You're joking.'

She shook her head wordlessly and turned away.

'Oh, no. I'm not about to marry anybody. I like things just the way they are. And don't try to argue. I'm not going to change my mind.'

Her voice was tiny. 'I thought you loved me.'

He was silent.

'But you told me you did.'

'People always say things they don't mean in bed,' he said irritably. 'I like you. In fact, I like you a lot. You're a lot of fun.'

'Fun?' She stared at him. 'That's all I am to you? Fun?'

He scowled suddenly. 'That's the trouble with women. Sooner or later all of you start nagging.' He sat up, swung his legs out over the bed, and reached for his jacket. He dug into the pocket for his wallet, then handed her a sheaf of lire notes. 'The last time, it cost me twenty thousand. Here it is. This should take care of it.'

She made no move to take it, and he threw the money at her. It fluttered all around her like confetti. 'Arrange to get rid of it,' he said grimly. 'I don't want to hear another word about it.'

'But . . . where do I go?'

'How should I know? I'm not a woman. Ask around.'

'Amedeo,' she whispered. 'I want to have your baby.'

'Well, I don't want you to,' he snapped. He started getting dressed.

'Amedeo. Please. Don't be angry.'

He ignored her. 'Why didn't you tell me before? Why did you have to wait three months?'

'Because,' she replied truthfully, 'I was afraid that when I told you, you wouldn't want me anymore.'

His face was cold and expressionless as he buckled his belt.

'Amedeo – ' She tried to catch his arm, but he was already on his way to the door.

When he reached it, he turned around. '*Get rid of it*,' he repeated bitterly. 'None of you ever learn, do you? You all think that by becoming pregnant, I'll marry you.' Then he left, slamming the door behind him. Even across the room, she could feel the powerful gust of wind it created.

She sat hunched over, her body and soul aching. She knew she would never see him again. Strangely enough, she no longer felt frightened. It was as though a load had been taken off her shoulders.

She stared down at the lire notes. In a sudden rage she began throwing them off the bed. She didn't want his money. She didn't want anything of his any more.

After a while, she dried her eyes and got dressed. She looked in the mirror, hardly recognizing the pale, tear-streaked countenance which stared disconsolately back at her. Slowly she tied her scarf around her head.

Once she got outside, she didn't bother waiting for the rain to subside. As though sleepwalking, she trudged over to the front of Trinità dei Monti, the church with its twin bell spires which stood at the top of the Spanish Steps. They were deserted. The rain had chased the hordes of tourists indoors.

She smoothed her belly with her palms, then again wiped the tears from her eyes as she descended the steps. She was moving quickly, starting to feel she wanted to flee, get as far away from Amedeo and all that had happened as quickly as she could. Almost blinded by her tears and the heavy rain, she half ran down the steps, then suddenly felt her heel slip on the rain-slicked surface.

She screamed as she fell heavily, then somersaulted down the first flight. The sharp concrete tore at her skin, battered her bones and scored her face with its sharp edges. When she finally tumbled onto the landing, she lay deathly still. Then she was seized with a bolt of white-hot pain in her uterus, and with a scream she curled up and clutched her belly.

In the hospital, the doctor told her she was lucky to be alive, but had unfortunately lost the baby. In addition, he explained it would now be dangerous for her to ever carry another child. Too much within her uterus had been damaged by the fall. She would probably not survive another pregnancy.

She had closed her eyes, covered her face with her hands, and wept.

She had given Amedeo everything, and he no longer wanted her. She had offered up all of her love with her virginity. Because of him, she would never be able to have a baby. If she did, she would die.

She shut her eyes and sobbed. Even when Adriana came to comfort her, soothing her and telling her that there was no shame, none at all, Anna barely listened. The hatred for him burned terribly within her.

Amedeo.

How she despised him.

3

During the morning shift, Mirella Brino was in charge of the reception desk.

The moment she saw Anna hurrying purposefully through the cool, cavernous marble lobby with its wall-to-wall cabbage rose carpeting, she left her post and cut her off halfway. 'Careful,' Mirella murmured under her breath as she glanced around. 'Corvi's on the warpath. We tried to cover for you, but . . . ' She shrugged her shoulders expressively without finishing the sentence.

Anna smiled. 'Thanks anyway,' she said, giving Mirella's arm a squeeze.

Mirella nodded. 'By the way, the Hale representative is here for the Management Training Course interviews. They're being held upstairs in the Amalfi Suite.'

'What time's mine?'

Mirella tightened her lips across her teeth. 'It was the first one scheduled for this morning. When Corvi found out you hadn't come in on time, he juggled the schedule just to make sure you'd miss yours. The bastard.'

Anna's heart sank as though weighted suddenly with lead. 'Well I might as well go upstairs and see what I can do. Maybe I can get interviewed later.'

'Maybe.'

There was something in Mirella's tone that set off the warning bells in Anna's mind. 'Why "maybe"?'

Mirella shook her head woefully. 'How come it's always up to me to tell you these things?'

'Mirella, what *is* it?'

'Corvi took the opportunity of substituting his brother in your place.'

'Maurizio?' Anna stared at her. 'You've got to be kidding!'

'I only wish I were.'

'Well, it's worth a try, anyway.' Anna squared her shoulders.

'By the way, guess who they sent over to do the interviews?' Mirella's eyes gleamed with secret knowledge.

'Who?'

'Henry Hale. The second in command of the company, would you believe?' Her face held a dreamy expression. 'He's so handsome. And so young! They say he's a genius,' she sighed. 'I think he's just my type. And he isn't wearing a wedding band. I made sure to check.'

Despite herself, Anna had to laugh. 'You're incorrigible, Mirella! Anything in pants is your type, or haven't you noticed?'

'When you get to be thirty and you're still single, you take what comes,' Mirella said morosely. 'Anyway, watch out. He's a cold fish. When I met Signor Hale I smiled, fluttered my lashes, and laid on the charm nice and thick. But to no avail.' She sighed again. 'He's made of stone, apparently. Or maybe I'm slipping.'

Anna clapped her friend affectionately on the arm. 'Don't worry, Mirella. It won't be long before some man discovers your charms, and you'll sweep him off his feet. If it's not because of your looks, it'll be because of your cooking.'

'Sure,' Mirella said with a weary smile.

Anna took a deep breath. She glanced over her shoulder at the brass-doored elevators. 'Well, I've wasted enough time. I'd better get on upstairs. Wish me luck?'

Mirella held up both hands and crossed her fingers. Anna returned the signal. Usually it inspired confidence, but today was one day when she was afraid her luck her run out.

'*Maurizio*,' she swore angrily under her breath. 'If he gets sent to New York I'll break his legs first. I deserve to go, and so does nearly everyone else. But Romeo Corvi's snide little brother? He can't do anything right, but it never seems to matter.'

And with that bitter thought, she strode rapidly past the yawning elevator doors and stabbed the button marked 'ten.'

On the tenth floor, Henry Hale tried to concentrate on the matters at hand, but his mind was wandering. Luxurious though it was, the Amalfi Suite was merely an extension of his New York office. He looked puffy and tired under his clean shave, but he managed to smile reassuringly at the sixth interviewee for the Management Training Course who was being shown out. Then he told Romeo Corvi to hold off for fifteen minutes before showing in the next one.

When he was alone at long last, he got up from the gold-brocade couch and poured himself a much needed, golden jigger of Johnny Walker red. He carried the cut-crystal glass out onto the terrace and surveyed the terra cotta roof-tops of the Eternal City.

He gripped the glass tightly and made a throaty sound of exasperation. He felt both worn down and aggravated. He was long since used to the psychic and physical strains of overloaded work schedules and bone-wearying globe-hopping, so that wasn't the cause of his boiling anger. As a Hale, he knew it was expected of him. Sadly, he thought of his parents, who had died in a car accident two years before. He missed them still. He had been raised by a doting mother, and much as he loved Janet Hale, he looked to his father and grandmother as his role models.

He had seen little enough of his father; while growing up Zaccheus Hale, Jr. was an enigma who seemed to be constantly swallowed up by his work, a remarkable achievement considering he was paraplegic. His father had thrown himself whole-heartedly into his short but brilliant career, perhaps to compensate for his physical disability. Maybe because he had known from the start the lifespan of paraplegics was not long. Little had he expected the sudden death that did take him.

His grandmother's obsessive dedication to the business was legendary, and looking to her and his father, Henry had set stern goals for himself as a child.

He had begun working when he was twelve, hanging around the hotel kitchens during summer vacations and doing odd jobs after school in order to acquaint himself with his legacy. For other children, their hometowns were their world; for him it was the major cities of four entire continents. He loved nothing more than to accompany his grandmother on trips around the world, looking after the sprawling, ever-growing empire. As the only Hale heir (his aunt Regina had never had children), Henry realized at an early age that he was being groomed for a lifetime of work and dedication, and it had always seemed perfectly natural. By the time he turned sixteen, he was already spending seven days a week hard at work, for either school or the business. By then it had already been many years since he had enjoyed a real vacation. He graduated from Harvard and Harvard Business School in record time, so that at twenty he was ready to step into a senior executive position.

Even now, wearing the coveted crown of being perhaps the youngest-ever vice president of a major international corporation, sixteen hour workdays were the rule rather than the exception. If anyone were to suggest he slow down, would he laugh? No, he considered, he wouldn't laugh. He would simply not understand why he should, because he took his career seriously and thought nothing of juggling a hundred duties at a time.

As the most eligible of American bachelors, he was particularly frustrating to women. He never seemed to find the time to devote to them.

The only thing he asked from others was the same, steadfast dedication with which he threw himself into even the most minor chore. Unfortunately, he was quickly discovering that in Rome that was asking for the inconceivable.

The orange rooftops shimmered in the heat, a gently undulating sea reaching all around to the base of the Seven Hills of Rome. Though a city of stunning beauty and splendid history, Rome was not, he was realizing, a city where things got done. At times, he was amazed Rome was still standing and populated. Romans were a breed unto themselves, as different from the Northern Milanese or the Southern Sicilians as Scandinavians were from Arabs. They were immensely proud of being Romans, and did things in their own sweet time, in their own peculiar ways. There was no changing them.

He sighed wearily and pressed his lips together. Today, he decided, was just not his day. But then, yesterday hadn't been much better.

For starters, there had been the flight from New York, which at best was an uneventful and tiring proposition. However, yesterday's Boeing 707 had developed engine trouble halfway across the Atlantic and had had to hobble crippled into the Azores for an emergency landing. The landing, though hairy, had gone off without a hitch, and the relieved passengers had broken out into enthusiastic applause for their pilot. Nonetheless, it had been an emotionally grueling experience. And, as a result of the unexpected, hours-long Azores layover, by the time he reached London his connecting flight to Rome had long since taken to the skies, and he'd had to kill four hours before the next flight. That didn't leave quite enough time to head into London from Heathrow, and yet it was too long to wait to sit patiently around the airport doing nothing. Time was money, and four wasted hours added up to a lot of it.

When he finally arrived in Rome, the limousine which was supposed to have met him at Leonardo da Vinci Airport was not there. When he reached the Roma Hale, Romeo Corvi greeted him effusively, practically prostrating himself as he apologized over and over for the inexcusable limousine mix-up. He had personally shown Henry up to the Portofino Suite.

On the surface, everything in the suite looked fine. Corvi had arranged for a hospitality package, containing a bottle of champagne and a huge formal floral bouquet, as well as a fully stocked bar. Henry, however, had thrown Corvi by refusing to stay in the Portofino Suite and insisting upon the less grand Amalfi Suite instead. Elizabeth-Anne had a firm rule that when she or anyone else in the family stayed at a Hale hotel, rooms and suites were to be switched two or three times a day without advance warning. It was irksome to the staff, but a wise practice, as Henry was now finding. So far, in Rome, altogether too much had gone wrong.

When he'd taken a shower, the drain was sluggish and the tub had filled with water.

When he'd switched on one of the nightstand lights, he'd found the bulb was burned out.

He'd tried to call New York, but the switchboard operator, not yet alerted to who was in the Amalfi Suite, had been slow in placing his call.

He sent his suit down to be pressed, and it had been returned to the wrong room and then gotten lost.

All those problems in a suite for which people paid the equivalent of $100 per day.

Then, to top everything off, after he'd called Corvi on the carpet and told him he wanted these problems alleviated – *pronto* – it had still taken far too long to fix things. When he'd had to complain about the problems a second time, that slimy little bastard had had the gall to tell him that 'in Rome things are different.'

Henry's eyes had narrowed into dangerous slits, and Corvi had finally snapped to it. By 4.30 most of the problems had been smoothed over, but the misplaced suit still hadn't been found. Henry began having doubts he would ever see it again. Instead of waiting, he had changed to another suit and then went to the car dealer's to pick up a new Masseratti he had ordered, and which he planned to ship on to New York after he left Rome.

When he'd gotten back to the hotel for the interviews, that oily, unctuous, self-centered Corvi – who, as every hour passed he could bear less and less – had been constantly trying to suck up to him. For all of Corvi's efforts, even the interviews, so far, had gone far from smoothly. For some reason, the schedule had been rearranged at the last minute, causing no end of confusion. But worst of all, of the six people he'd interviewed already, there hadn't been one he'd not have doubts about recommending for the course.

He shook his head and tossed down the last of his drink. He'd need the fortification. He still had four more employees to interview, and he wasn't at all sure he even wanted to go through with it. Romeo Corvi seemed to employ only morons like himself. Everything considered, Henry thought it incredible that the hotel ran as smoothly as it did. It certainly couldn't be due to Corvi or the employees he'd met so far. He'd have to ask around and find out who kept things running from behind the scenes. Whoever it was would have to be complimented . . . even moved into Corvi's position.

One way or another, Romeo Corvi had to go, and the sooner that was done the better off the hotel, and the entire Hale organization, would be. Nor would he alone get his walking papers. Maurizio Corvi would, too. His had been the single most unbelievably embarrassing interview of all. The identical last names of the two had not been lost on Henry.

A major shake-up was due at the Roma Hale but Henry knew he would have to wait a few days. Elizabeth-Anne had a firm rule that no one was ever to be fired unless there was a replacement waiting in the wings. Once one was lined up, then management could proceed with the professional insensitivity of a surgeon.

All in all, Henry thought, shaking his head as he went back inside the suite, the Roma Hale reminded him just a little too much of the Hale Hotels in Mexico and Hong

Kong. There, too, things had been run in a maddeningly sloven fashion. That is, until Henry had arrived on the scene to put a screeching halt to all that. For the time being, the Azcapotzalco, Cozumel, and Victoria Hales were running at peak efficiency. For a man his age, he had already become a master at shaking things up. But, then, trouble shooting was his job, his talent, just as helping to run the most luxurious hotel chain in the world was in his blood.

Henry was about to call for the next interview when his attention was diverted by a loud voice right outside the suite. 'What the hell – ' he muttered aloud as he crossed over to the double doors and threw them open.

As the elevator had risen higher and higher, so had Anna's adrenalin. By the time she got off on the tenth floor, she had reached a state of rage.

Corvi, that deceitful, disagreeable, disdainful little *shit*. He didn't miss a single opportunity to trip her up. She had *had* it with him. If he thought she would take this latest scheme lying down, he had a surprise coming, the sorry bastard.

She clenched her hands together and took a deep breath, fighting for control. When she got off the elevator she stopped to check her appearance in the ornate mirror hanging above a gilt console in the corridor. She wore little make-up, and the pulsating anger made her face look curiously hard. It was hardly the way she wanted to face anybody for an interview, but it would have to do. Anger alone would give her the nerve to barge in to see Henry Hale.

She marched down the creamy carpet to the white-lacquered door of the Amalfi Suite, then hesitated only a fraction of a second. Tightening her jaw, she raised her clenched hand to knock and then heard a lisping voice that froze her arm in midair.

'*What do you think you're doing, Signorina Viganò?*'

Anna turned and found Romeo Corvi rushing toward her. She faced him squarely, by instinct spreading her feet in a fighter's stance.

'Steady,' she warned herself silently as her heart knocked like a trip-hammer against her ribcage. 'Don't lose your cool. He's going to bait you, and you mustn't rise up to it like a starved fish.'

She spoke aloud then, trying to make her voice sound casual. 'I was about to see about my interview.'

'Your *interview*?' He smiled an ugly smirk which made his lips and thin nostrils look curiously shark-like. 'I'm afraid you're *not* scheduled, Signorina Viganò.'

She felt the hairs at the nape of her neck beginning to rise. 'I'm going in there,' she announced quietly but firmly, 'and you cannot stop me.'

'I wouldn't try it if I were you,' he hissed. The smirk was frozen on his lips.

'And why not?'

'Because the moment you step through that door, you will be fired.'

She stared into his face, trying to read the seriousness of his threat. Instead, she saw something that surprised her: fear. He was afraid of Henry Hale. The realization struck her with the force of the courage she needed.

'We'll soon see about that,' she said coldly. She grabbed the polished brass door handle, but quick as a cobra his hand struck out and seized hers. She glared into his face, his eau de cologne cloyingly sweet and overpowering at such close range. 'I'll trouble you to let me go,' she said, her voice hard.

'You are fired, Signorina Viganò,' he hissed. 'As of this very moment. Go collect your things and leave at once.'

Whether determination or sheer fury caused her to act, she would never know. She feigned to loosen her grip, and he let go of her hand. The moment he lifted his fingers, she moved to open the door again, but he grabbed her by the arms and pushed her roughly away.

'Let me . . . *go*,' she cried, fighting to reach the door handle again as he held her back. 'Let me go, you . . . you *worm*!'

And at that precise instant the door to the suite was flung open from the inside. Both Corvi and Anna froze in the middle of their struggle, twisted their heads around, and stared at the tall, handsome blond man silhouetted in the doorway.

Anna's eyes flashed. For a split second she couldn't take it in that it was actually *him*, that this was how she was to meet her interviewer. Then she slumped, and all the fight seeped out of her.

Henry Hale stared at both of them for a long, silent moment. He couldn't believe the display before him, and was at first disgusted by another one of Corvi's tricks. Then he noticed the girl.

What jumped out at him first were her startlingly corn-flower blue eyes. He had never seen eyes like that – so radiant, so alluring. But then he realized he had never seen anyone quite like her before at all. She was not just the only woman he had ever really noticed; he was certain she was the most beautiful woman on earth.

All this flashed through Henry's mind in an instant, while Anna and Corvi remained frozen in their ridiculous tableau. Then Corvi seemed to suddenly realize he was still pinning down Anna's arms. He let go of her, his face glowing red with embarrassment. He yanked out his white handkerchief and dabbed at his forehead as Anna began brushing her arms with her fingers, as though trying to rid herself of the remnants of Corvi's crawling touch.

'So would someone like to tell me just what the hell is going on here?' Henry asked.

Corvi spoke first. 'This woman insisted on going in to see you unannounced,' he said disdainfully in his thickly accented English.

'Indeed?' Henry's eyebrows arched. 'And why should she want to do that?'

'Because,' Corvi said, raising his chin, 'she is a born trouble maker.' He punctuated the word 'troublemaker' with a quick, birdlike nod, his eyes glaring at Anna.

'Is this true, Signorina?' Henry asked, gazing at her.

Her eyes flashed for a moment, and her fingertips froze in the midst of brushing her arms. 'That's a matter of opinion,' she answered with all the dignity she could muster.

Henry raised his eyebrows in surprise. Her English was exceptionally good, with little trace of an accent.

'She was fired,' Corvi snapped, taking advantage of the moment. 'She was fired, but refused to leave. The *gall*.' He drew himself up, tucked his handkerchief back into his pocket, and adjusted his silk tie. Anna remained silent.

'And why,' Henry asked her, 'were you fired?'

'Because she refuses to obey specific – ' Corvi began heatedly.

Henry's quiet but sharp voice cut Corvi off in mid-sentence. 'I asked the Signorina.'

Corvi shut his mouth, but stood simmering.

'I was fired,' Anna explained, as calmly as she could, 'because Signor Corvi took it upon himself to rearrange the interview schedule for the Management Training Course, and I wouldn't stand for it. I was unavoidably late and he took the opportunity to stick his brother in my place.'

'Maurizio Corvi,' Henry said thoughtfully, rubbing his chin with his thumb and forefinger. His expression was grave, but his eyes were now dancing with amusement. Everything was beginning to fall into place.

'Yes, Maurizio Corvi.' Anna rolled the name on her tongue with distinct distaste.

'Might I add,' Corvi said in a brittle voice, 'that Maurizio was initially scheduled? That when the telex went out with the list of applicants, Signorina Viganò herself struck his name off the list and put her own in its place.'

Henry looked at her questioningly.

'I did,' she conceded. 'But Maurizio didn't deserve to be on it. If anybody did, it was me.'

'Be that as it may.' Henry turned to Corvi. 'Signor Corvi, as the manager of this hotel you, better than anyone, should know that employees do not fight in the public areas. There are plenty of employees' areas where you can do just that. Our guests do not pay premium rates in order to watch squabbles. We are a hotel, not a colosseum.'

Corvi swallowed, his throat suddenly dry.

'And you, Signorina,' Henry continued in an equally cold voice, 'as an employee, you should not only be aware of the same thing, but should at least obey the orders of your manager.'

Her eyes fell. She felt tears of anger stinging in them, and was ashamed to show it. She was boiling inside, but she knew that this was no time to erupt. She must stand rebuked. The only outward signs of her anger were her tightly compressed lips and the swift heaves of her breasts.

'I think,' Henry suggested, 'that we would all benefit if we simply forgot this unfortunate incident. You, Signor Corvi, may go back to whatever you were doing.'

'But . . . but what about her?' Corvi spluttered.

'The Signorina may come inside my suite. That is contingent, of course, upon her temper.' He turned to face Anne, his eyes shining.

Anne nodded with relief and slipped past him into the suite. Henry followed her, shut the door, leaned casually back against it, and burst out laughing.

She bristled and stared at him in fury. Alone with him now, she couldn't help but notice how handsome he was with his wheat-gold hair, strong profile and cleft chin. He was a big man, tanned and expensively dressed and when he met her eyes with his own surprisingly blue ones, Anna's breath caught. She guessed him to be about her age, but he obviously came from the other side of the tracks – the *right* side. That, on top of the attraction she would have preferred not to feel – that she had believed she would never feel for a man again – and his blithe laughter at her predicament, all combined to make her strike out in anger. 'I suppose you think this is all very funny?' she asked as coldly as she could.

'The fight, you mean?' he asked, still laughing.

She nodded stiffly.

But he hadn't stopped smiling. 'No, it's not funny. But you are.'

'Me!'

'You.' With a huge effort he pulled himself together and reassumed his grave, businesslike manner. 'I don't believe I've ever met anyone quite as forward or determined as you seem to be.'

'I did what I had to do,' she replied.

'Of course you did,' he said. 'You rose to the occasion quite courageously.'

Somehow, this didn't make her feel any better.

He cocked his elbow and slid back his cuff to look at his watch. 'It's nearly lunch time.' He adjusted his cuff. 'You couldn't, by any chance, recommend a good restaurant for a business meeting?'

She seemed to shrivel visibly. Apparently, he didn't have time for her after all and had only called her into the suite to further humiliate her.

'And the interview?' she asked morosely.

He came toward her and placed his hands on her arms. 'It is you I want to have lunch with,' he said softly.

'You mean . . . I still stand a chance to go to New York?'

'Yes, you do.'

She smiled then, her entire face lighting up. She almost couldn't believe it; despite Romeo Corvi, the opportunity toward which she had for so long worked was still within reach. She let out a deep breath of relief.

But Anna would never make it to the Management Training Course; Mirella Brino was the one who finally went. For after lunch, Henry took the rest of the day off, and spent it with Anna. Something magical clicked between them, and neither had to delve into their hearts to understand their feelings. Their reaction to one another was immediate and instinctual.

That weekend, they drove to Naples, took the hydrofoil over to Ischia, and spent the weekend together, lying in the sun during the day, and making love at night.

Henry Hale, who had never done an impulsive thing in his life, and Anna Viganò, who after her luckless relationship with Amedeo had sworn she would never fall for another man, quietly got married before the weekend was up.

For the first time in his life, Henry had done the unthinkable. Those who knew him well were astonished. Henry had never taken a single day off from work, let alone two entire weeks.

'We're going on a honeymoon before heading to New York,' he announced to a surprised Anna as they lay together in bed the morning after the wedding.

'But . . . your work,' she protested.

'It'll keep for two weeks. Believe me, Grandmother will see to it that nothing suffers.'

'What about your family? They don't even know we're married.'

'They'll find out soon enough,' he assured her. 'Right now, I want you all to myself.' He gripped her in a gentle bear hug and held her close.

'Where do you want us to go?' she asked.

He kissed the tip of her nose. It had happened so fast, he was still amazed at the happiness he had found with Anna. To love someone so much that he wanted to spend every waking and sleeping hour with her was a joy which he had never anticipated. 'We'll go wherever you desire,' he promised softly, 'as long as it's far from any Hale hotel. And we'll be alone, just you and me. Name the place, Mrs. Hale.'

She tilted her head back and laughed. 'I don't have the faintest idea of where to go!'

He smiled at the mixed expression of bewilderment and delight on her face. 'Never mind. I have an idea. We'll play an old American game. It's called Pin the Tail on the Donkey.'

'Pin the . . . what?'

'You'll see.' He released her, patted her once on the bottom, and then telephoned down to the reception desk. He instructed the clerk to send up a map of the world. 'And also have the gift shop pick out a scarf,' he added. 'Preferably one of dark silk. Oh, and a brooch as well. Charge them to my suite.' When the clerk said she wasn't sure if they had a map, he simply replied, 'Then I'm sure you'll be able to improvise something.'

Anna was speechless. If fairies and sugar plums were the stuff of childhood dreams, then this was the adult version of the same. The magic that great amounts of money could perform was still unimaginable to her. Being able to pack up and travel at a moment's notice to any far corner of the earth without even having to consider the cost was something entirely foreign to her.

The travel desk wasn't able to produce a map of the

world, but the receptionist had sent up a packet of the next best thing, brochures and pamphlets for tours and cruises the world over. Henry nodded to himself. They would do. They all had maps of one specific area or another, which he quickly tore out. Then he pushed aside a couch, lifted a picture down off the wall, and began taping the maps to the walls in a reasonable facsimile of the globe. He stepped back to inspect his handiwork, and they both burst out laughing. It was a mismatched world consisting of a magnified Mediterranean, a giant Mexico, a small Scandinavia, a tiny East Africa, and only small bits of the Far East.

Henry lifted the scarf out of the shallow gift box and fashioned it into a blindfold, which he then solemnly tied around Anna's eyes.

'Really, Henry,' she protested mildly, her hands instinctively touching the blindfold.

'Ssssh,' he said, kissing her lips. 'Indulge me . . . Now here, hold this brooch and stick the needle end of it into the wall. Wherever you stick it is where we'll go. Watch it! You don't want to stab yourself. Now, hold it out . . . this way.' He placed his hands on her shoulders and led her toward the map. She moved with cautious steps, uncomfortable with the blindfold. Then he turned her around and around, so that she completely lost her bearings.

'Now pick a spot. Remember, whichever place you pick is where we're going on our honeymoon.'

'Henry . . . ' She turned in the direction of his voice.

'I'm deadly serious. Do as I say.'

She nodded obediently and stepped forward, feeling her way with an outstretched hand. She held the brooch out, moved it hesitantly up and down, left and right, and then without further ado stabbed it into the wall.

He slid the blindfold off her and she stared at the wall. 'C-Cozumel?' She turned to him, her blue eyes wide.

'Cozumel it is,' she smiled.

'But . . . we don't have any clothes for Mexico,' she sputtered.

'We'll buy whatever we need on the way, and whatever else we don't have, I'm sure we can buy there.'

'Henry . . . ' She was starting to cry.

'Aren't you happy?' he asked worriedly, pulling her toward him.

She sniffed and nodded. 'Being sad isn't the only reason to cry,' she sobbed into his chest.

The two weeks they spent alone together were amongst the happiest they could recall.

They didn't stay at any of the big beach-front tourist hotels. Henry called up a friend, a film producer by the name of Schulkin, to see about renting his house. Two years previously, Elizabeth-Anne had invested in one of Schulkin's pictures. Henry had been in on it, and when the picture turned out to be a good investment, they had all become friends. Now, not only did Bernie Schulkin agree to the rental, he also swore on his mother's grave to keep Henry's whereabouts a secret.

'I get it, you son of a bitch,' Bernie laughed over the phone. 'Making it into a love nest, eh? How many girls you taking?'

'Goodbye, Bernie.'

Bernie sighed wistfully. 'Sure would love to come along.'

'At least two of us here would hate it,' Henry quipped, and halfway around the world, Bernie gazed at his white telephone receiver in puzzled astonishment.

He had never before known Henry Hale to crack a joke.

'If any place is heaven, this is it,' Anna breathed the moment the canopied jeep pulled up in front of the villa.

Far from the big hotels along the beach, the ocean front estate was made up of multi-level terraces leading down to the sea. The house was sumptuous, but not ostentatiously furnished. Made of rough stone, the villa boasted a proliferation of arches, no two of which were the same, giving the house a unique charm as well as plentiful access to cooling ocean breezes. There were twenty rooms in all, and two swimming pools, one saltwater and one fresh. Both pools were made up of craggy rock formations, which had been carefully blasted hollow in order to leave boulders jutting up out of the water. The grounds were tended by a gardener whose job it was to maintain the jungle-like patches of palms, eucalyptus, sea grapes, bougainvillea, and passion flowers without making them appear at all manicured. Two other full-time servants staffed the house, while the gardener doubled as the driver and so picked Henry and Anna up at the airport.

The estate was a paradise of utter privacy. Each day, Henry and Anna swam, went boating, ate on the loggia, and made love. After a week, they both had even, fruitwood tans.

Lulled by the fragrant flowers and tropical breezes, neither Henry nor Anna noticed as their two weeks rushed past in a blur. But as the time approached for them to fly to New York, Anna became increasingly filled with misgivings.

On their last afternoon, they were lying on the chaises under the sun when she said, 'Henry, what if your family does not like me?'

He gazed at her pinched expression and smiled. 'They will.'

'But they don't even know we're married yet. We told no one.'

'It isn't such a big family. Two minutes, and they'll all know.'

She nodded, but her lips were twisted in a frown. 'But still . . . your grandmother . . . ' She slipped off her chaise and knelt at the side of his.

'My grandmother.' He was silent for a moment, thinking of Elizabeth-Anne. 'I wouldn't worry about her if I were you. She'll like you just fine.' He took her face in his hands. 'Don't be such a worry wart. Nobody's going to bite you. Now finish your pina colada, and then we'll take a swim and cool off.'

'In the fresh-water pool. Salt burns my eyes.'

'It burns mine, too,' he agreed with a laugh.

They both turned and glanced at the villa at the same time. Somewhere inside it, the telephone had started ringing. It stopped on the third ring.

'At least it's not for us,' Henry said, shaking his head. 'I still can't believe how wonderful it is not to be tied to a phone. Still, every time I hear one ring, I feel the compunction to answer it. I'm like Pavlov's dog, I suppose. Conditioned.'

'Excuse me, Señor.'

They turned around, finding the maid had carried out a long-corded telephone.

'What is it?' Henry asked, feeling almost shocked.

'Is for you, Señor.' She held out the telephone.

'Knowing Bernie, he wants me to do him another favor,' Henry told Anna with a smile, despite his own bewilderment. 'Trust good old Bernie.'

The maid shook her head. 'No, Señor. Is not Señor Schulkin.'

'But no one knows we're here.' Now he was truly alarmed.

'Someone does,' the maid said gently. 'Is Señora Hale.'

Anna turned sharply to Henry, who rose to take the phone. For a long moment he stared at the receiver. Then he lifted it to his ear. 'Grandmother?'

'Henry, dear!' Elizabeth-Anne's voice floated crisply across the wires, only slightly marred by the static. 'How's the sun?' She sounded bright-eyed and chipper enough to bring Henry to his senses.

'How did you know where to find me?' he asked sternly.

Elizabeth-Anne laughed. 'You left a trail a mile wide. Don't forget, the Roma Hale made the reservations for Ischia, and the hotel there made the reservations for your flight to Cozumel.'

'That backstabbing Schulkin,' Henry growled under his breath.

'Bernie? Why, it wasn't him at all. In fact, it took my secretary four hours to track you down to the house, but track you down she did.'

'What did you do? Offer her a bounty?'

She laughed. 'Perhaps I *should* do that in the future. Anyway, I'm glad you finally took a vacation.'

'Don't I deserve it?'

'Of course you do,' she said soothingly. 'However, you could have let me know where you were.' There was no reproach in her voice; it was merely a statement of fact.

'Yes, perhaps I should have.'

'Are you enjoying yourself?'

He looked over at Anna and met her gaze. He couldn't help but smile. 'That I am,' he said into the phone, wondering what Elizabeth-Anne would say if she knew just how happy he truly was.

'Good. Enjoy your last day, then.'

'How did you know about – oh, I get it. The reservations for the return trip.'

'The reservations,' she agreed. She paused. 'I'll see you tomorrow. Do drop by the Madison Squire after you get in. I'll be home all evening.'

'Will do.'

'And Henry?'

'Yes, grandmother?'

'Be sure to give my best to your bride.'

Before he could say anything, the connection was broken. Thoughtfully he replaced the receiver.

'What is it?' Anna asked.

He looked at her with a dumbfounded expression. 'She already knows. It's incredible. I don't know how she does it, but she already the hell knows.' He smiled wryly and shook his head. 'She said to tell you hello.'

4

It was close to ten o'clock at night when they arrived at the Madison Squire. Henry didn't announce himself at the front desk; there was no need. Most of the Squire's employees had bounced him on their knees as a child and they greeted him with genuine warmth.

Entering the lobby, he was filled with a sense of warm nostalgia. Nothing about the Squire had changed; it never did. Half the staff had spent the better part of their lives with the hotel. Paula Kelley, the head switchboard operator, had been on the staff forty-nine years, and hers was not an unusual case. Many worked well past retirement age. The Squire was their life and joy, and they intended to keep working until the day they died. There was a pride, an esprit de corps, a feeling of being part of the family at the Squire that was sadly lacking in most hotels.

In the same way, Elizabeth-Anne had never allowed the hotel to become ostentatious. She emphasized warm personal service, and rather dowdy luxury, which was kept just this side of frayed so the atmosphere remained nice and cozy. As a result, the Madison Squire had developed a loyal following. More repeat guests stayed here than at any of the Hale hotels, and the Squire employees prided themselves upon remembering a client's name after his very first visit.

'Everyone seems to know you,' Anna observed as they got off the elevator on the penthouse floor.

He nodded, a wistful expression on his face. 'I practically grew up in this hotel.'

'I like it. It's so . . . so *warm.*'

'Personally, I think it could use a little sprucing up. It's beginning to show just a little more seediness than it should.'

'But that would spoil it,' Anna cried.

'My sentiments exactly,' a crisp voice seconded from the end of the hall.

They turned and found Elizabeth-Anne, bathed in the glow of the wall sconces, looking very stately and beautifully groomed, as always every inch the lady.

For a long, drawn-out moment time seemed to freeze as the two women's gazes locked. They sized each other up frankly in a split second, the way only two women meeting for the first time, and sharing the love of the same man, can do.

But for Elizabeth-Anne, this meeting was far more than it seemed. Outwardly, she appeared to be a composed, handsomely elegant sixty-six year old, with her warm smile and perfectly tailored, oyster wool Chanel suit. But her mind was a blur with conflicting emotions and anxious thoughts.

Looking at the lanky, poised young woman with blue-blue eyes who stood before her, Elizabeth-Anne felt like a teenager on her first date. She searched Anna'a face for the tiniest hints of recognition, and as she peered closely into those clear blue eyes so much like Henry's own, she shivered.

Could it be? she asked herself.

Tears sprang to Elizabeth-Anne's eyes. At first she hadn't wanted to believe it. The startling news of Henry's marriage had shocked her deeply, tearing open the old wounds that had never properly healed. It had started when she had tried to call Henry in Rome, and she had been informed that he and the Signorina Viganò had left for Ischia.

Viganò.

The name had frozen her tongue, had sent memories of defeat and a thousand dead hopes spinning wildly through her mind. When she had finally managed to find her voice, she had haltingly asked for Signorina Viganò's first name.

Anna.

It could not be! she had told herself over and over. It was some sort of cruel trick. It had to be! Anna had been given away, and disappeared. This sudden resurrection was nothing short of miraculous – and Elizabeth-Anne didn't believe in miracles. No, it must be money this bogus Anna was after. She must be a sly, insidious fortune hunter who had somehow found out about Anna and decided to impersonate her. That wouldn't be very difficult to do. After all, no one had ever seen Anna.

Oh, but how devious she must be to manage to worm her way into Henry's affections so swiftly! Henry, who had never looked at a woman twice. Henry, who had never heard the story of Anna, who never even knew such a cousin existed. She, Janet, and Zaccheus had all found the subject of Charlotte-Anne's lost child too painful to discuss, ever; it was taboo.

After Elizabeth-Anne had made the initial discovery about this Anna, she had expected Henry to call at any moment with the news that he had found his cousin. After all, the woman posing as Anna would expose herself to him, wouldn't she? Since it was part of the Hale fortune she was obviously after, that would be the next obvious step in her plan. And Henry, not knowing anything about her, would in confusion call his grandmother.

But the woman obviously wasn't ready to lay her cards on the table, at least not yet. Henry's silence only increased Elizabeth-Anne's inner turmoil. Finally, she had been unable to wait any longer, and had placed some calls.

It was then that she found out about the marriage.

The news left her dumbfounded. Henry married. Without even calling to tell her? But this was no time for hurt. She had to come to grips with this bogus Anna Viganò, *now*.

What bothered Elizabeth-Anne was that the marriage didn't make sense. Unless, of course, the fortune huntress had found it an unexpected but easier route to the family coffers. Yes, that could be it. Or . . .

Elizabeth-Anne had groaned aloud, not at all wanting to face the other possibility. It was because of the marriage that the new nagging doubt began to form in her mind.

If it was really Anna, then she might not even know it herself.

Could she, after all, really be Anna Viganò? Miracles did happen occasionally, didn't they?

Suddenly nothing made sense anymore. Elizabeth-Anne knew only one thing. She had to find out who Anna Viganò really was.

So she had had her checked out through a private investigator while the honeymooning couple had been soaking up the sun in Cozumel.

'I want to know her past,' Elizabeth-Anne instructed the detective. 'Specifically, who she is. I don't want her personal life dissected. I don't want to have any of the so-called "goods" on her. I only want to know where she was born, and who her family is. Whether or not she was adopted. Nothing else. Is that clear?'

The investigator had been quick and thorough. The news he had returned with had been enough to strengthen Elizabeth-Anne's feeble hopes.

Anna Viganò, she was told, was a nineteen-year-old resident of Rome, who had moved to that city from

Umbria when she was three. Her father, a laborer, was now deceased; her brother, Dario, was a priest; and her mother had just moved out of the family's ghetto apartment to one in a considerably more fashionable neighborhood. Her new, more comfortable lifestyle was apparently financed by her daughter, who had recently married quite well. The mother, it seemed, knew her daughter to be nothing but her own flesh and blood, though she admitted to having been ill at the time of her birth, so that her memory of the event is not clear.

It was enough to make the impossible suddenly seem very possible. But Elizabeth-Anne knew the true and final test remained. She had to see this Anna Viganò herself, for only by meeting her face to face could she decide whether there was anything in the girl's visage of her beloved Charlotte-Anne.

And now, her heart pounding wildly, she saw before her in the young girl's gaze eyes that were heart-wrenchingly familiar. If they weren't Charlotte-Anne's, then they were very, very close. And the regal di Fontanesi nose . . . yes, she saw the girl's father there, too. But what was most important to Elizabeth-Anne was that seeing the girl now, she *knew*. This was Anna.

Her Anna.

These thoughts flashed through her mind in the first seconds of their meeting. Both she and Anna had been momentarily paralyzed as they stood facing one another in the warmly lit hallway. Then, at the same moment, Elizabeth-Anne and Anna found their feet. They hurried into each other's arms and embraced. And it was then that Elizabeth-Anne knew it. Hanging from a delicate silver chain around Anna's neck was the pansy charm that had once been Elizabeth-Anne's own.

'Welcome, Anna,' Elizabeth-Anne said softly, the tears slipping down her cheeks. She reached up with her fingertips and gently touched Anna's face. 'Welcome. Welcome . . . to your home.'

'Thank you,' Anna whispered. Tears filled her own eyes as she was overcome with the strange feeling that, in this strong woman's embrace, she truly was at home.

Elizabeth-Anne then turned to Henry. He was smiling broadly with the light in his eye that told her he was happier than she had ever before seen him. And it was at that moment that she realized the horrible dilemma that faced her. *Henry had married his cousin.* He and Anna didn't know – and when they found out it could destroy their love. And that, Elizabeth-Anne now saw, would destroy Henry.

For now, Elizabeth-Anne forced the radiant smile to remain on her face and turned to embrace her grandson. She would savor this moment, and face its repercussions later.

Henry was overwhelmed; he had never seen his grandmother like this. He held her tightly and kissed her cheek, all the while thinking that although he had hoped that she would like and accept Anna, he had never expected the intense, warm reception she had just given his new bride.

5

Elizabeth-Anne sat stiffly on the apricot couch, wrestling with her conscience. She had been perfectly still for hours, ever since Henry and Anna had left. The silk-shaded lamps cast warm, yellow pools of light in the otherwise dark livingroom of the Madison Square duplex. Elizabeth-Anne's eyes were locked on the sterling framed photograph she held in her hand.

The most recent snapshot of Henry, it captured his face in three-quartered profile. His handsome features were unsmiling, almost stern. She stared at it, remembering the joy she had seen in his eyes earlier that evening, and felt as if her soul were torn in two.

How could she *not* tell Henry and Anna that they were cousins? Marrying a first cousin was illegal in many states of the Union. Was it illegal in New York? It would be easy enough to find out, but Elizabeth-Anne wasn't sure she wanted to know.

What, then, about the morality of the marriage? As a

Catholic, Anna would see her marriage as incest, the most heinous of mortal sins. How could she live – much less love – with such knowledge?

The power to tell her and Henry the truth lay solely in Elizabeth-Anne's hands. And her mind was tormented by the question of what to do. Should she accept Anna as a daughter-in-law or as a grand-daughter? Her longing to embrace Charlotte-Anne's child, to find again a little of all that she had lost, was almost overpowering. To do so would be the fulfillment of a hundred buried dreams . . . but they were her dreams, old dreams. What would such an act of selfishness do to Henry and Anna's hopes for the future?

What, then, was her responsibility as matriarch of the family. Could she make a moral and legal choice for Henry and Anna? Telling them the truth would be the 'right' thing to do, but it would end their marriage.

And all the happiness they had found together. Henry had always been so serious, so soberly determined to play his part in the Hale empire, to prove himself one of the youngest and most brilliant businessmen in the world. Now, suddenly, he seemed to have learned life was for other things as well, for joy and spontaneity, for knowing and loving a woman.

Elizabeth-Anne had lost Zaccheus's love so long ago . . . then lived through that impossible pain again when Larry died. Hadn't the Hales had their share of suffering?

Could she really in the name of truth, take this delicate, exquisite flower that was Henry and Anna's love and poison it, crush it with the knowledge of their incest? Could she be so cruel? So heartless? So *righteous*?

Suddenly, she knew that they must never, *never* know. It was a secret which must be kept from them at all costs, one which she would take to her grave. They loved each other too much. She could see that just by the way they looked at one another, by the warmth bridging their gaze.

Her frustration and indecisiveness melted away.

Leave well enough alone, she told herself. *Leave them be.*

Besides, she thought with a sudden light-hearted smile, how many grandmothers were there who could love their grandson's wife as deeply as she could?

No, they must never find out. And it was up to her to make sure they didn't.

She sat there for a while longer, then she went upstairs to bed, little suspecting she had just planted the seed that would destroy so much happiness for her great grandchild, yet unborn.

6

When Henry, Anna and Elizabeth-Anne stepped out of the cool, dark house, they were blinded by the glaring sunshine. Squinting, they made their way down the front steps and skirted the antique yellow-and-black Rolls-Royce which was being buffed by the chauffeur. As they headed across the manicured lawn, Anna fell behind, letting Elizabeth-Anne and Henry talk. They were walking slowly, their heads bent forward, and Henry had his arm around his grandmother's waist.

Anna dug her hands into the pockets of her plaid wool skirt, stopped walking, and breathed deeply. How different from the city it was here, how much cleaner and fresher! She could hardly believe this magnificent estate was merely forty-five minutes from midtown Manhattan. Here, only the trills of the birds and rustle of leaves broke the silence. The air smelled richly of freshly mowed grass.

Turning, she admired the house again. An elegant Colonial, it stood three stories tall on the crest of a high hill above the blue waters of the Hudson.

She heard the fading murmur of Elizabeth-Anne and Henry's voices, and hurried down the gently sloping hill after them. When she rejoined them, they were still deep in conversation.

'I know it's *big*,' Elizabeth-Anne said, 'but you need a large house. After all, Henry, you and Anna have your social positions to think of.'

'But, grandmother, this is the last thing on earth we expected for a wedding present.'

404

'I should hope so. I'm not in the habit of giving away houses. Anyway, I know the present was a long time in coming. It took me quite a while to find it. Estates like this one don't come on the market every day.'

'It must have cost a fortune.'

Elizabeth-Anne turned to him and laughed. 'It didn't cost you a penny, so you can stop worrying about it. And you know I can well afford it. It's a drop in the bucket for me, if that much. All you need are a few people to help . . ' She waved her hand casually around the grounds.

'A few! We'll need an *army* of servants just to keep this place up. Several gardeners – '

'So you hire an army,' Elizabeth-Anne said flatly, refusing to let him persuade her. Then she laughed and tugged at his sleeve with mock resignation. 'Don't be so impossibly conservative all the time, Henry. For God's sake, if we were financially strapped I could understand your hesitancy. But we're not.'

'If we're careful,' he said stiffly, 'we need never be.'

'You sound just like a banker,' she said irritably. 'Still, you must agree that there *are* some investments it doesn't hurt to spend money on. Real estate is one of them.' She paused, looked over her shoulder to see if Anna was within earshot, then dropped her voice to a whisper. 'And clothes are another. Anna could use a new wardrobe, you know.'

'Why? She's happy with what she has. When she needs something she goes out and buys it.'

'When she needs something,' Elizabeth-Anne corrected him, 'she waits and goes to Gimbel's or Alexander's when there's a sale. Really, Henry, don't you think you could take her to Sak's or Bergdorf's? I mean, she doesn't need Paris couture. She's very attractive and she can get away with wearing anything. But something nice, eh?'

'She has this thing,' he said slowly. 'She's been poor all her life, and now she's afraid to waste money.'

'No, she's afraid to spend it. There's a difference.' Elizabeth-Anne couldn't help the faintly ironic smile which hovered on her lips. When she had first learned about Anna, she had been afraid she was a gold digger after the Hale fortune. Now, looking back, she saw how wrong she had been. If Henry was ultra conservative, then Anna was downright frugal. Idly, she wondered if she saved plastic bags and glass jars and reused them. 'Haven't you told her we're rich?' she asked Henry.

'She knows that.'

'But have you told her just how rich?'

'I have.'

'And?'

'She doesn't believe it. She says there can't be that much money in the world.'

'Sometimes,' Elizabeth-Anne said, thinking aloud, 'even I still can't believe it. Two hundred and fifty million dollars!' She shook her head and laughed again. 'Anyway, let's all go back to the house. You're stuck with it. You can't go and exchange it like a table setting from Tiffany's, you know. It's been paid for, and it would be very bad manners to refuse it. It was a present, and it's up to you to accept it graciously.'

'You are a dear, grandmother. But an impossible one.'

'You and Anna are my grandchildren. Let me indulge you every once in a while,' she growled.

'Then we thank you.'

'You already did, over and over.' She stopped walking and looked around. 'Just think of the advantages of this place. Even commuting to the city is easy. If you like, you can avoid the traffic altogether.'

'How?' he asked, mystified.

'By buying a boat. The real estate agent told me that the last owner commuted to the city in his speedboat. I guess he got the idea from the millionaires who lived up here before the Depression.'

He smiled. 'We'll see.'

'Have we lost Anna?' Elizabeth-Anne asked, twisting her head around. 'Oh, you're right behind us.' She held out her free arm so that Anna could hook hers through it, and together the three of them began walking the perimeter of the property. 'I can't wait till you see the orchard. It's too far to walk today. Altogether, this place is made up of forty-three acres. But they're necessary, and so are the extra bedrooms in the house. A growing family needs space. You *are* planning to give me plenty of great-grand-children, aren't you?'

Elizabeth-Anne smiled disarmingly at Anna, whose face went pale.

'Is something wrong?' Elizabeth-Anne asked with concern.

Anna smiled, but not before Elizabeth-Anne caught the most implacable, inconsolable look of sadness deep in Anna's blue-blue eyes.

'No, no,' Anna assured her hastily. 'I was just thinking about something, that's all.'

Anna sat on the bench in Central Park, stonily watching the parade of Fifth Avenue nannies pushing expensive, imported baby carriages. It was late morning of a perfect, blustery day, and the sun was out in full force. So were her depressed spirits. She couldn't remember ever having felt so miserable.

Until now she had never really taken a moment to stop and think, to sort out her own life and Henry's. Now, the prospect overwhelmed her.

Henry. How she loved him! If she had ever been certain of anything in her life, it was that. From the very first, they had been so sure of each other. Neither had felt the need to hesitate or analyze their feelings. How precious little she had known about him then. And how little she still knew. Which was part of the excitement of their love, the joy of discovering each other day by day.

But all that was over.

Oh God, she thought, her eyes glazing over as she felt the familiar, dull ache in the pit of her belly. She had had that ache on and off for days, and knew it would soon culminate in nausea. That was where her pain and misery lived, deep inside her stomach. Whenever she felt depressed, the physical manifestation would show itself there.

Why, oh why, she asked, hugging herself, why hadn't she told him about Amedeo?

But, in truth, she knew she had taken advantage of the fact that she had never been pressed to tell him. From that

407

first time, Henry had known she wasn't a virgin. It hadn't seemed to make any difference to him.

But she knew she owed him an explanation. Because Henry had a right to know that when she had fallen down the Spanish Steps and lost Amedeo's child, she had lost *their* children, too.

Why hadn't she come out and told Henry about that before she married him?

But she had been too happy then. After they had met and made love, she had been selfish and self-centered. She had wanted him all to herself, and the thought of children had been as far from her mind. Only now did she realize the magnitude of her mistake. Henry was a *Hale*, the heir to an empire and, as such, he of course needed an heir of his own. A man in Henry's position wasn't free to just fall in love.

She pressed her fingertips to her forehead. Her mind felt numb with her guilt and regret. She slowly got to her feet and walked from the bench. She passed a nanny and pink-faced baby playing a game of peek-a-boo. The woman hid her face with both hands and cried, 'Where is Rhea?' before parting her fingers and cooing, '*There* she is.'

Even as she continued to walk on, Anna could hear the woman and child's laughter. Their happiness seemed to mock her, and she shut her eyes with a heavy sigh. Ever since that day in Tarrytown, when Elizabeth-Anne had given them the house, Anna felt she saw children, especially infants, everywhere, reminding her of what her own damaged body could not produce.

She sighed deeply once again, then shook herself. Checking her watch, she saw she only had fifteen minutes to meet Henry at 21 and would have to hurry to get there on time. Squaring her shoulders, she briskly made her way out of the park. No matter what, she promised herself, she mustn't let Henry know how worried she was, or why. It was a problem she had created, and she must find the way out of it. She couldn't burden him with her troubles, not until she decided what to do. She loved him too much for that. He was everything to her. She loved him enough to . . .

She stopped cold, her heart pounding excitedly. Was it

true? The realization, the solution to all her problems, had come so suddenly it almost overwhelmed her. She took a deep breath to calm herself and reconsider. But there was nothing to think about; this decision was as immediate, as instinctual as her love for him had been. Because it was born of her love for him.

She loved Henry enough to try to give him a child.

She felt suddenly omnipotent with the joy of that knowledge. The weight of her depression slipped away – she felt all powerful, free and so *lucky* to have found such love.

But, even in her joy, she knew Henry must never know the extent of the gift she would give him. He must never know the risk she would knowingly take, never know that by giving life to their child she was very likely sacrificing her own. Only she could decide to take the chance; he would never allow her to if he knew. But giving life to their love was the only thing that had meaning for her now. Her decision was clear. So she would keep it from him at all costs.

She immediately realized how difficult that would be. There were so many things to consider. Both the family doctor and her gynecologist were the finest in the city, but they were also Elizabeth-Anne's personal physicians. And Anna knew Elizabeth-Anne was on friendly terms with both of them.

Well, she would simply have to find new doctors. That shouldn't prove too difficult. New York City was, after all, not Italy. It was the heart of the most advanced country in the world, a wonderland of physicians and specialists and hospitals. People came here from all corners of the world with their assorted disorders and diseases. Surely it was possible that with such expert medical care she would not only succeed – but survive. It was a dream worth pursuing, an irresistible possibility. Yes, with the power of a love such as hers, anything was possible.

She reached Fifth Avenue and began to rush down the sidewalk in her excitement. Her eyes shone, and every breath she took seemed effervescent. She felt delirious with joy. She practically danced down Fifth Avenue, smiling at everyone she passed – especially the children, the infants!

Yes, now that she had decided she felt herself tingling with the love coursing through her, she felt irresistibly and completely *alive.*

7

Henry and Elizabeth-Anne were in Greece negotiating construction contracts for the Ierápetra Village resort when the call came through. Sotirios Kyrkos, Hale Hotel's Greek resident executive officer, answered the phone in the Pericles Suite of the Athens Hale.

'It is for you, Mr. Hale,' he told Henry, covering the mouthpiece with his hand. 'It is the New York office.'

'I'll take it, thank you.' Henry got up from the white cotton couch and crossed the polished marble floor to the telephone table. Elizabeth-Anne remained seated, studying the art boards spread out in front of her. They portrayed the Ierápetra Village, her idea for an exclusive Aegean resort modeled after an idyllic fishing village, right down to the waterfront *tavernas* and windmills. The instant she caught the sudden change in Henry's tone of voice, she looked up and listened intently.

When Henry finally replaced the receiver, he stared across the room at her, his face white. 'That was Dr. Dadourian,' he said thickly. 'Anna's been hospitalized.'

'What?' Elizabeth-Anne jumped to her feet and crossed over to him. 'Did he say what was wrong?'

He shook his head. 'Only that she stands to lose the baby.'

'Oh, Henry!'

He turned away, stepping out onto the sun-drenched terrace. He stared blankly out across the city toward the distant Acropolis, his hands thrust deeply into his trouser pockets. Elizabeth-Anne followed him outside and squinted in the glare of the Greek sun. She placed a hand on his arm.

'She also stands to lose her own life,' he said tightly.

Elizabeth-Anne felt the words plunge into her like a knife. *No, it couldn't be.*

But when Henry turned to her and she saw the cold fear in his eyes, she knew it was. Then it was as if the naked desperation she saw in his face galvanized her. Now was not the time to indulge her own fear, she told herself. No matter how worried she felt, she had to be strong. Henry needed her.

'You stay put, dear,' she said firmly. Then she hurried back inside, to confer with Sotirios Kyrkos. 'Mr. Kyrkos, could you please make travel arrangements for us? We must leave for New York immediately.'

Kyrkos didn't know what news the Hales had gotten, but their distress was obvious. 'I am so sorry, Mrs. Hale, but there is no afternoon or evening flight. I'm afraid you will have to wait until tomorrow morning.'

'Tomorrow morning is too late.' She paused briefly to consider the alternatives. 'Our only choice is to charter a jet. Could you arrange it for us? I'll take anything as long as it has transatlantic range. Nor do I care what it costs.'

'Yes, Mrs. Hale.'

'And please ask for a car to take us to the airport right away. We'll wait there until a plane is ready.'

'Yes, Mrs. Hale.' He gave a polite bow and left the room.

Elizabeth-Anne went back outside. Her face felt tight. 'We won't bother with packing,' she told Henry. 'Either the staff can pack up our things and send them, or we'll get them when we return. All we'll need is our passports. We're leaving right now.'

He turned to her slowly, his eyes filled with tears.

'I love her,' he said in a choked voice. 'God, how I love her. If anything happens to her - ' His voice broke off in a sob.

Elizabeth-Anne took Henry in her arms and held him. She shut her eyes against her own tears, unable to look him in the face and see her own sinking heart mirrored there. 'I know that, Henry,' she said softly. 'I love her, too.'

More than you'll ever know.

At half past two in the morning, they rushed into the Columbia Presbyterian. Dr. Dadourian was pacing the lobby, waiting for them. When he saw Elizabeth-Anne and Henry burst in, he hurried forward to meet them.

'How is she, doctor?' Elizabeth-Anne demanded at once, not breaking stride as all three headed toward the bank of elevators.

'Not good, I'm afraid.' He punched the button for the elevator and they began an impatient wait for it to arrive. 'For the past eight hours she's been in the operating room.'

'And the problem?' Elizabeth-Anne looked into his eyes.

The doctor sighed painfully. 'She should never have had the baby,' he said. 'She must have known from the start. I've examined her, and the problem was caused by a trauma years ago.'

Henry stared at him. 'But . . . she never said anything – '

Dr. Dadourian shook his head sadly. 'Nor did I even realize she was pregnant, not until she called today to tell me that something was terribly wrong. I hadn't seen her for over ten months. She called to tell me she had been seeing another doctor, that she was pregnant. But the other man was out of town, and she was terribly frightened.'

'She never told me,' Henry repeated dully.

'Will she pull through?' Elizabeth-Anne asked.

'I honestly don't know.'

'And the baby?'

'Who cares about the baby?' Henry suddenly asked in a sharp, hissing voice.

Elizabeth-Anne and Dr. Dadourian exchanged glances, but before they could speak the elevator finally arrived.

They rode up in silence. On the fourth floor, Dr. Dadourian led them to the nurses' station. The beige colored corridors were empty and silent, the air heavy with the sharp medicinal odor indigenous to hospitals the world over. Elizabeth-Anne found the atmosphere unspeakably oppressive, but she saw Henry was in too deep a state of shock even to notice.

Dr. Dadourian confered with the nurse, who told them Anna was now out of surgery, but they would have to wait for the attending surgeon, Dr. Loomis, to learn more. The nurse escorted them to a glass-enclosed waiting room filled with molded plastic chairs.

'Come,' Dr. Dadourian said, bringing Elizabeth-Anne and Henry seats. 'There's nothing we can do but wait.'

Exactly twelve minutes later, Dr. Loomis joined them. He was a tall, distinguished man with silver sideburns and the hands of an artist. His face was drawn, and the green eyes behind the thick glasses were red-rimmed. He had shed his blood-soaked surgery greens; long ago he had learned that the sight of them did little to reassure his patients' loved ones.

'How is she, doctor?' Henry asked, jumping to his feet.

Dr. Loomis sighed wearily. 'The good news first. We've managed to save the child. Congratulations.' He smiled weakly. 'You have a beautiful daughter. She's in the incubator. As you know, she was premature. We had to deliver her by Caesarian section. She'll have to stay in there for a few days. You're welcome to see her whenever you like.'

'Damn it, man,' Henry growled, grabbing Loomis's sleeve. 'My wife! How's my *wife*?'

The doctor's eyes dropped. 'Not good at all, I'm afraid. We're doing everything for her that we can.'

Henry shut his eyes. His face drained of color. He stood motionless but for a slight swaying. It was as if he had become unmoored and stood rocking in a wind. When he opened his eyes again, the effort for control he was making was obvious. 'I . . . I would like to see her.' His voice came out low, like a growl.

'Of course,' Dr. Loomis answered. 'This way, please.' He led the way back to the elevators and on the ride upstairs explained Anna's condition. 'Apparently, Mrs. Hale should never have tried to have the child. It seems that long ago her uterus suffered rather severe damage. It's a miracle that she wasn't forced to check in long ago. Or perhaps she did have to, but was afraid for her child. We would have had to abort the pregnancy and maybe she knew that.'

'Will she pull through?' Elizabeth-Anne asked quietly.

The doctor was silent a moment, then said, 'Of course, there is always the possibility of recovery. The human body

413

is most remarkable. One never knows its capabilities completely. They change from person to person.'

Elizabeth-Anne met his eyes. 'But you think she won't. Survive.'

The doctor met her gaze fully. 'In this case, I would say the chances are slim,' he said gently. 'Very slim indeed. I'm sorry.'

Elizabeth-Anne took a deep breath and nodded once, tightly holding onto Henry's arm. Even as all the life seemed to drain out of her, she realized she was supporting him.

Outside the recovery room, Dr. Loomis stopped once again. 'I know this is very difficult for you,' he said softly, 'but please try to be brief. And if she doesn't recognize you, or she's still under . . . Well, bear in mind that she's heavily sedated. And very low.' He opened the door for them. The two doctors waited outside while Henry and Elizabeth-Anne went in.

The nurse on duty avoided their gaze. Elizabeth-Anne held tightly to Henry as they approached the bed. There he fell to his knees, seeking Anna's hand and holding it in his. It felt icy to the touch.

He stared at her in disbelief. He'd last seen her only a few short days before. She had been so healthy, so alive and glowing with the happiness of carrying their child. Now she looked pale and gaunt; for a moment he was afraid she was already dead. But watching closely, he saw the faint movement of her breast as she took in weak breaths. No, not yet. She wasn't gone yet.

He felt dull and empty. How could this still, helpless thing be Anna. Anna, who had always been so exuberant, so bursting with energy. Now, lying in the recovery room with tubes taped to her arms and another coursing out of her nostril, she looked shrunken.

'Anna,' he whispered. 'Can you hear me, my love?'

He watched her unmoving face desperately, silently, until Elizabeth-Anne came up behind him and put her hand on his shoulder. He turned and looked up at her. He saw what was in Elizabeth-Anne's eyes, but he couldn't face it and almost frantically turned back to stare into

Anna's still face. But it was there, too. This wasn't Anna, his wife. It couldn't be. It was only a shadow of her.

'Anna.' He reached out with one hand, trembling as he touched her soft face with his fingertips. The tears were stinging in his eyes. 'Anna,' he whispered again.

He did not know how long he knelt at her bedside. Only after the nurse came over and gently pried his hands loose did he realize Anna had slipped away from him.

She was gone. She had never regained consciousness. He hadn't even been able to say goodbye.

Henry collapsed, his sobs shaking his strong body. Elizabeth-Anne took him in her arms and rocked him gently. She too was weeping. 'I know, Henry,' she whispered, her voice unsteady with pain, her aquamarine eyes glittering. 'I know. Don't hurt, baby. Please don't hurt.'

Elizabeth-Anne walked stiffly into the seedy, dark bar on the lower level of Penn Station. She made her way through the bar to the tiny booth in the back. Henry was hunched over, both his hands clutching his glass. After the funeral, three days before, he had stalked off, white-faced and grim. It had taken her as many days to find him. She had finally done so only by luck. One of the Hale Hotels executives, who commuted daily between New York and Port Washington, had spied him in that same bar twice in the same day. It was he who had told Elizabeth-Anne where Henry was.

'Henry,' she said softly. 'Come home, Henry.'

He looked up at her, his eyes glassy. When he spoke his voice was slurred, but he managed his simple sentence. 'Leave me alone.'

'Henry.' She took the seat opposite him and reached for his hands. He yanked them back, spilling some of his drink in the process. She fought her revulsion as she smelled the rancid odor of bourbon emanating from him.

'You can't go on like this, Henry. Come home.'

'Home?' He gave an ugly laugh and stared at her. 'What home? Yours or mine?'

'It doesn't matter. They're both your homes.'

He just shook his head and took another pull at his drink.

'Please, don't make this so difficult,' she pleaded. 'It's hard enough as it is.'

'She's everywhere.' His voice dropped to a hoarse whisper. 'She's everywhere. I can smell her perfume. I see her clothes. The pictures she bought. She's everywhere.'

'She's in our hearts. She'll always be there. Come home with me. To the Madison Squire.'

'No.'

She leaned across the table. 'Look, Henry. We're all entitled to mourn, you especially. But drowning your sorrows in drink isn't the way to do it.'

'No?' He scowled at her glassily. 'Then what is?'

'You can have a good cry,' she suggested.

'I've cried.' He took another drink.

'Henry, please listen to me,' she urged desperately. 'Anna is *dead*! Nothing will bring her back. You can't just drown yourself in alcohol. *Please*.'

'Why not, grandmother? It's my life.' He drained his glass, then set it down with a bang.

'Because of the child, Henry,' she said gently. 'Your child and Anna's. That's why you've got to pull yourself together.'

'I told you before. Don't want that kid.'

'Henry, she's your daughter,' Elizabeth-Anne said in despair.

'So?' He met Elizabeth-Anne's gaze with hard, glittering eyes.

Elizabeth-Anne sighed. 'Come on Henry. I've got the car waiting upstairs. Let's go.' She pushed her chair back, paused, and added softly, 'Today's the day your daughter is being released from the hospital. Let's go fetch her, Henry. Let's bring her home. Together, you and I.'

'Nope.'

She sighed wearily. 'But don't you see? She's Anna's too! I thought you loved Anna.'

'Yes, I loved her,' he said, suddenly ferocious. 'I loved her more than my own life. And that baby *killed* her.'

'The child did *not* kill her.' Elizabeth-Anne hissed harshly. 'Anna knew the consequences, but she wanted a child. She wanted *your* child. She wanted it so badly that she was willing to risk her life to give you one.' She paused. 'Do you want to throw away everything?'

He narrowed his eyes. 'You want the baby? You're welcome to her. I never want to see her.' He signaled the waiter for another drink, then turned back to Elizabeth-Anne. 'Now, leave me alone.'

Elizabeth-Anne rose to her feet and went out, passing the waiter who was carrying an oily glass of bourbon over to the booth.

On the escalator on her way to the street level, she wondered why everyone was staring at her. She didn't even realize it until she got into the Rolls.

She was weeping.

8

The white-uniformed nurse smiled as she handed the squalling bundle to Elizabeth-Anne. The baby was clothed in a christening frock of off-white cotton sprinkled with eyelets and trimmed lavishly with Belgian lace. Elizabeth-Anne had bought it especially for her, and was now touched at how it emphasized the child's angelic sweetness.

Elizabeth-Anne cradled her great-granddaughter in her arms, careful to support the tiny, down-covered head with one hand. The child seemed to sense safety and warmth and love, and instantly stopped crying. It was as though they were communicating in a secret language. The miniscule doll's mouth broke out into gurgling, toothless laughter.

'I think you two will get along just fine,' the nurse said, laughing and patting Elizabeth-Anne's arm.

Elizabeth-Anne nodded and smiled. She rocked the baby soothingly back and forth in her arms as she studied the tiny face closely. The baby looked so familiar, an eerie image of all four of her children a few days after their birth. But this child seemed even more precious, if that was at all possible.

A hint of tears glistened in Elizabeth-Anne's eyes. The child was so tiny, so blonde, so blue-eyed. The familiar features were all there. She was a true Hale.

Just holding the infant pushed Elizabeth-Anne's depression to the back of her mind. Only once she got downstairs, and sank into the supple leather backseat of the yellow and black Rolls-Royce, did she again feel weighted down with despair.

This child. Anna's child.

She was holding more than just her first great-grand-daughter. She held in her arms a most precious, living part of Charlotte-Anne, the daughter she'd lost, as well as the child's mother, Anna, her own granddaughter. The agony she had felt over Charlotte-Anne's death and Anna's loss, old pains that had never healed and new ones that had not had time to, now, finally, felt salved. Even Anna's untimely, tragic death, painful though it was, seemed somehow more bearable. She could start to come to terms with it. Because of the child.

She stared thoughtfully out of the side window as her car headed downtown along Riverside Drive. Between the rich foliage of the trees and shrubbery, she caught occasional flashes of the wide, silver Hudson.

By all rights I should be taking her in the opposite direction, she was thinking, up the Henry Hudson Parkway to Tarrytown, to her own home. But instead, she's coming downtown, home with me. Not that I won't want her. How I do! But she should be with her father now, not me, no matter how temporary it might be.

Elizabeth-Anne sighed and shook her head morosely. Strangely enough, she felt saddened and hurt rather than depressed and angry. A father didn't just declare that he never wanted to set eyes on his daughter, and then run off, no matter what the reason. Surely once Henry got over his mourning, he would come to his senses and accept his loss and understand his gain. His daughter was, after all, his own flesh and blood. Wounds took time to heal, but eventually they did.

No one knows that better than I.

But if he didn't, what then?

Her aquamarine eyes narrowed and she thrust out her chin. In that case, she would take care of this radiant child for as long as she had to. She would hire a nanny and juggle her own busy schedule. Somehow, she would find the time to lavish love upon this darling baby until Henry pulled himself together and fought his way out of his depression.

Yes, in the meantime, she would take the baby under her wing. Eventually Henry would accept her. He had to, Elizabeth-Anne told herself grimly. The poor child had lost her mother; she needed her father twice as much.

Who knew what the future might bring? she reflected morosely. To date, she'd put all her hopes into Henry, counting upon him to become her successor and head Hale Hotels after her. But she'd never known until now that he was this flawed . . . this *weak*. That's what his reaction to Anna's death showed her. Not just grief, but weakness in blaming the infant. It wasn't the baby's fault that her mother had died in childbirth. Couldn't he understand that? *Couldn't he comprehend that Anna was still alive – in his daughter?*

Elizabeth-Anne cooed softly and rocked the baby in her lap. 'Don't worry, little darling,' she whispered down at her. 'I'll love you and look after you, even if no one else will. Everything that's mine will eventually be yours.' She leaned down and rubbed the baby's nose with her own. 'You are, after all, a *Hale*.'

The child stared up at her through solemn, wide blue eyes. A look of intelligent understanding seemed to glow in the tiny face – or was it only her imagination?

'And of course, we'll have to come up with a name for you,' Elizabeth-Anne continued. 'I suppose that's up to me now, too, since your Daddy won't have any part of it. Let me see . . . ' She sighed thoughtfully. 'Adele . . . no, somehow you just don't *look* like an Adele . . . Alice? Barbara? No, no. Carla? Dorothy? Yes! *Dorothy*. We'll name you Dorothy-Anne Hale. Somehow it just sounds *right*.'

The child broke out into happy, spontaneous laughter, her fingers reaching up as though trying to grasp the name out of the air.

It was as that very moment that the special bond they would share for the rest of their lives was cemented. And both of them seemed to sense it.

The years would only strengthen it.

'Your Daddy will have a change of heart, Dorothy-Anne,' Elizabeth-Anne promised. 'You mark my words. This won't last long. He's just hurt, but he'll get over it.'

But she was wrong.

Henry would never get over the loathing he felt toward his daughter. Not even when she moved in with him in the big house in Tarrytown. To him, she would be a constant reminder of everything he hated. Of pain and loss. Of death.

For him, Dorothy-Anne would always be his beloved Anna's murderer.

GENERATIONS
FOUR
Dorothy-Anne

Quebeck, Texas:
August 14, 1985

1

The wind howled outside in the rain-lashed orchards and the dim light of the single candle left the room steeped in deep shadow. Freddie leaned over Dorothy-Anne as she lay on the bed, struggling for breath and sobbing deeply, her body drenched in sweat, her cheeks wet with tears.

Freddie had been as stunned by her declaration as he was now anxious to comfort her. 'Dorothy-Anne, my darling, how could you say such a thing? Your mother died in childbirth. You're not to blame for her death.'

'No, Freddie, I am,' she answered, struggling to get the words out. 'They told me . . . I heard them say it.'

'What do you mean?'

'Oh, Freddie – ' Suddenly her face contorted with pain and she squeezed his hand tightly as a fresh contraction seized her. Her body tensed, her back arched and for a long minute they did not speak. When it finally passed, she felt her muscles relaxing like melting butter. Freddie saw that she would not be able to fight sleep, and, as the contractions would soon be coming closer and closer together, she would need her strength. But her obvious panic had alarmed him and he had to ask 'Dorothy-Anne, what do you mean, "*they* told" you?'

She shook her head weakly, her eyes already closed. 'My father . . . my father said it . . . he said he hated me . . . On my tenth birthday . . . ' But she couldn't go on. She was swimming in a black, warm pool, far from the Hale Tourist Court. She was receding in time, everything spinning faster and faster until she reached Tarrytown and she was ten years old. Then the spinning abruptly stopped and it was the day of her birthday and she was back in the big house overlooking the river.

423

She was standing alone in the sitting room. The clock on the mantel ticked noisily. She half-turned toward it and saw it was nearly one o'clock in the afternoon.

She tightened her lips and turned back to stare out through the high French window. The river below was wide, unusually blue-gray and placid. Overhead, the sun shone brightly in a powder-blue sky. Across the river, the hills were blanketed in oranges and yellows. Indian summer, and Mother Nature had decked herself out in all the finery she could summon. But Dorothy-Anne was not enthralled. She felt more miserable than she had ever felt in her life.

She turned away from the view and plopped down onto the couch in front of the fireplace. She avoided looking around. She didn't like the sitting room. Like much of the rest of the house, it was filled with large, stately furniture. She felt inconsequential and uncomfortable, out of place in the only place she could call home.

She sat unmoving for several minutes until her governess came into the room.

'Your father couldn't take the day off,' Nanny said gently as she marched into the room with her stately walk. She held an enormous, beautifully wrapped present out in front of her. She smiled at Dorothy-Anne. 'But he's left you something very nice.'

Dorothy-Anne didn't look up. The empty despair that had been feeding on her for the past two days sat in her stomach like lead. For once, she wasn't even looking forward to seeing her great-grandmother. She didn't want to see anyone or anything. All she wanted was for the pain and loneliness to stop. She wanted her head to be empty, she wanted to wake up and be someone else. She wished . . . she wished she were dead.

'Daddy doesn't like me,' she said. 'He never has.'

Nanny made a sympathetic clucking sound with her tongue. 'Now, now, child. Don't be silly. Your Daddy loves you.'

'He doesn't. He's never around, especially not on my birthdays.' Dorothy-Anne continued to sit with a stillness unnatural for a child her age. 'Why does Great-Granny always celebrate my birthday with me instead of my Daddy?'

'I told you, child, he's a very busy man.'

Dorothy-Anne turned to look Nanny in the eye. 'Great-Granny's even busier than Daddy,' she said flatly. 'She owns Hale Hotels and runs them. Daddy only works for her.'

'Your father is president of Hale Hotels,' Nanny said severely.

Dorothy-Anne still held the older woman's gaze. 'And Great-Granny's chairman of the board.'

Nanny wasn't a governess for nothing. She knew when she'd lost an argument. Sighing, she set the wrapped box down on a rose silk-covered footstool. 'Aren't you going to open your father's present?'

Dorothy-Anne stared at it. 'No,' she said with a sudden flash of insight. 'Daddy didn't buy it for me. He had somebody else pick it out. I overheard him talking on the telephone to his secretary. He told her to call F.A.O. Schwarz.' She paused and closed her eyes. 'And he's not at work either. He's in La Jolla. With a woman.'

'Now how would you know that?' Nanny sat down in exasperation and folded her plump white hands in her lap. She looked at Dorothy-Anne. 'You've been overhearing a lot of things lately, it seems.'

Dorothy-Anne sat in silence, hunched over.

'Ladies,' Nanny said succinctly, 'do not listen at doors or keyholes.'

Dorothy-Anne didn't look up. She knew from experience what expression Nanny would be wearing. Her pointed features would be severe, her eyes pinched with disappointment.

'I wasn't listening through keyholes,' Dorothy-Anne said with sudden savageness. Then she fell silent again.

Nanny did not speak. She knew that the girl's outburst was merely to mask her pain.

Dorothy-Anne bit down on her lip. She could feel the tears threatening to fill her eyes, but she would not let them come. She got up slowly. 'I have to go to the bathroom.'

'Well, you better hurry up, then,' Nanny said. 'Your Great-Granny will be here any minute, now.'

'Yes, Nanny.'

Dorothy-Anne left the room. She did not use the bathroom off the downstairs hall. Instead, she took the staircase up to the second floor, where she glanced around quickly to make sure that none of the servants were about. She slipped into her father's suite and closed the door behind her.

His bathroom was huge and smelled faintly of disinfectant. She got up on tiptoe. She found what she wanted in his medicine cabinet.

And slashed her wrists.

All because the telephone had rung yesterday.

She had been coming down the sweeping stairs when the hallway telephone had begun to ring. She hurried downstairs to answer it. It was the servants' day off, and her father was busy upstairs in his study. After picking up the ivory receiver, she was about to speak when she heard a second, almost instantaneous click.

'Henry Hale speaking.'

She recognized her father's voice and was about to hang up when she heard a cultured, purring woman's voice answer. Something made her stay on the line and listen in. Perhaps it was because the caller was a woman.

'No 2, is that you, darling?'

'I'm not No 2, Chessy,' he growled. 'You know very well I'm Henry.'

'My, my.' The throaty voice held a hint of mocking laughter. 'Aren't we touchy this morning.'

'Look, Chessy – ' he began irritably.

The playful voice changed instantly. 'I'm sorry, darling,' she said quickly. 'You know how I love to tease you.'

'Sometimes your jokes aren't very funny.'

'Ah, but you don't mind my teasing you nights, do you, darling?' She laughed softly. 'But listen, darling, the reason I called was because you mentioned you might be coming out here to La Jolla, and since CeCe's birthday is tomorrow . . . '

Dorothy-Anne brightened. CeCe's birthday. Who was CeCe? Was that a nickname for her that she didn't know about? After all, *her* birthday was tomorrow –

'Oh, shit,' Henry broke in harshly.

Dorothy-Anne held her breath and tried to keep her heart from pounding. Had she made a noise? Had her father discovered she was listening?

'What is it, darling?' the woman asked. 'Is something wrong?'

'No, it's nothing. I just remembered my daughter's birthday is tomorrow, too.'

'Oh, Henry. I am sorry. I didn't mean to take you away from your little girl. You've got to be there.'

'No, Chessy, it's alright. I'll be happy to join you in La Jolla. There's no need for me to be here. In fact, I'd rather not.'

'Henry, how can you say that? She's your own daughter – '

'I prefer not to think of her that way.'

'Henry,' the woman said, shocked by his words, 'you sound as if you hate the poor thing.' She laughed tentatively, uncomfortable with the turn the conversation had taken.

Henry paused for a minute, then spoke in a strangely expressionless voice. 'I do. I can't stand to be around her. You see, tomorrow is also the anniversary of my wife's death. I do hate that child. Especially on the anniversary of the day she killed my wife.'

She first became aware of invisible angels humming softly all around her. The cool currents stirred up by their wings caressed her face. She heard faint, ethereal whispers. She listened closely, but they made no sense. A peculiarly buoyant, floating sensation held her in its spell. It was not at all unpleasant. Rather like floating lazily in a swimming pool. The water felt soft and warm, and smelled vaguely of chlorine. Through half-closed eyes she tried to look around her. Big, soft white shapes moved gracefully in ever-so-slow swirls. Wherever she was, she had never been to this place before. She couldn't understand what was happening. Nor did she really care. The buoyant feeling felt so good. So good . . .

She closed her eyes and let everything recede as she gave herself up to that pleasant nothingness.

Next, she noticed that her sense of smell was heightened. A sharp, mediciney odor seemed to emanate from within her. It seemed to come and go in waves, teasing her nostrils.

She lifted her head a few inches. Her eyelids felt heavy, but she managed to see out through the haze of her lashes. The world was drifting by as if she were watching it through a white scrim. Shadowy white apparitions moved in a dreamlike, slow-motion ballet. Everything was white, a hundred different shades of white. All but the thin, ruby-red line which rose from her arm to be swallowed up by all that white. Murmured voices seemed to chant incantations in a monotone.

The whiteness and the red line went slowly dark, receding once more into sleep.

The clouds and white scrim had turned warm and yellow when she awakened again. It was easier to open her eyes now; the lids didn't feel nearly as heavy as they had before. She stared up into space. She could make out a flatness above her.

Without moving her head, she glanced around. Her eyes were deep green, confused. The clouds were receding. In their place, she could see more flat surfaces all around her. She was in a two-toned box. The top half of the walls were white, the bottom half, bilious green. The warm yellow she had seen was emanating from an electric light. She thought she recognized the strange smell which had eluded her. She had smelled it once before. Three years ago when she'd had her appendix taken out. She was in a hospital.

A hospital? She stared up at the flatness. No, it couldn't be a hospital, she thought dreamily. The semi-gloss ceiling was a monotone landscape, topsy-turvy and seen from a hundred miles out in space. A crack of river, held up by gravity, flowed between a valley of mountains. She felt a peculiar longing. She didn't want to be in outer space. She wanted to be home.

She turned her head sideways and caught sight of a small pale hand, bandaged at the wrist. Her eyes widened. For a moment she didn't understand. Then she could feel a tightening in her chest as it all came back to her.

The metallic-gray razor blade, paper-thin and yielding easily from the pressure of her fingers. So thin she almost bent it.

The strangely painless parting of her soft flesh as the blade sliced into it.

The pop as the artery was severed.

The mighty, pulsating roar as her blood rushed to meet the wound, seeking escape from her body.

The geyser of blood, a thick, powerful stream at the bottom spraying outward like a ruby fountain, the droplets falling all around like warm rain.

Her stomach churned with the memory, and a flash of heat engulfed her. The moment she tasted the bile starting up, she lunged forward and held a hand to her mouth. She swallowed, breathed deeply, desperately.

Bit by bit her head cleared. She remembered every painful detail. Now she knew why she didn't have a mother like other children. Because she had killed her. She didn't ask herself how or why. She never even remembered seeing her mother. But Daddy had said she killed her, so it must be so. And he hated her so much for doing it that she had tried to kill herself.

And failed.

The breath hissed out of her as she sank back down. The mattress was hard, the sheets starched and scratchy. They weren't her own sheets.

She *was* in a hospital.

She closed her eyes, feeling helpless, ashamed. She couldn't bear to face anyone. Not after what she had done.

Death. Oh, how peaceful it had seemed . . . The falling sensation, like being sucked into a slow, powerful maelstrom. The darkness that first engulfed her becoming blinding light, brighter than a thousand suns. How easy to give herself up to that beguiling, dazzling light!

She felt a moistness sliding down her cheeks, toward her

lips. She tasted it with her tongue. The tears were salty. Suddenly she was glad she was alive.

She heard a door opening. A mannish-looking nurse in uniform came toward her, stopped, turned on her heel, and went right back out. The door sighed closed, opened again. She heard the faint squeak of pneumatic tires. She struggled up. The nurse was holding the door wide and Nanny was wheeling Great-Granny into the room.

Except for the wheelchair, Great-Granny hadn't changed a bit since Dorothy-Anne's earlier memory of her, though Dorothy-Anne knew she was now over 80. The erect, regal posture, the sterling silver hair perfectly coiffed, even the wrinkles at the corners of her eyes didn't seem to have changed at all. The only thing that was different was how Great-Granny got around. She hadn't let that slow her down any, either.

Dorothy-Anne was relieved she wouldn't have to face anyone but her great-grandmother. If anyone would understand, she would.

Elizabeth-Anne was the only person in Dorothy-Anne's life who had ever truly shown how much she loved her. She was the only one who understood her, who was there when she needed someone. Yes, she was glad she was alive, if only for Great-Granny's sake. They had had a special rapport all Dorothy-Anne's life, as if they had recognized even when she was an infant how alike they were.

These thoughts flashed through Dorothy-Anne's mind in the moment that passed before Elizabeth-Anne raised her right hand and said, 'This is far enough. Please leave us now.'

Nanny nodded. She cast a worried glance at Dorothy-Anne but left the room, shutting the door behind her. Elizabeth-Anne placed her hands on the wheels of the chair and negotiated her way to the bedside.

Elizabeth-Anne smiled at her great-granddaughter. 'Good evening, Dorothy-Anne.' She reached out and took the girl's bandaged hand in her own. 'How are you feeling?'

Dorothy-Anne looked at her sheepishly. 'You're not

angry with me, are you, Great-Granny?' she asked in a tiny voice.

'No, I'm not angry,' she answered. 'But I am disappointed. If something was troubling you, you should have come to me.'

Dorothy-Anne bit down on her lip, preparing herself to be chastised. But she had forgotten one thing: Elizabeth-Anne Hale was some lady. She knew her priorities. Smiling conspiratorially, she reached under her cashmere lap blanket and produced a stack of comic books. 'I know for a fact that Nanny doesn't allow you to read these, but just this once, I thought we could break the rules. What Nanny doesn't know won't hurt her, eh?'

Dorothy-Anne was awed. 'How did you ever manage to sneak them in past her?'

'I sent Nanny on an errand while Miss Bunt wheeled me into the bookshop.' Elizabeth-Anne shook her head in marvel. 'I picked them out myself. My, my, you can't even find a simple Superman comic anymore. Just those ghastly creatures like Hydraman and Granite Woman. Brrr!' She made a production of shuddering. 'Hide them under your blanket. Nanny will be in a little later.' She paused as Dorothy-Anne slid them under the covers. 'Do you hurt?'

Dorothy-Anne shook her head. 'No. But I feel kind of . . . weird.'

'I shouldn't imagine. Probably the result of blood loss. I talked to Dr. Sidney. He assured me you'll be out of here in no time. Thank goodness Nanny and I found you in time. Otherwise you might have died.' Elizabeth-Anne paused, bowed her head, inspected her hands. 'I've always been of the opinion that there can't be effects without causes. Some people may say certain acts are never justified, but I'm not one of them. People usually do things for a good reason.' She lifted her head and gazed at Dorothy-Anne. 'Do you want to talk about it?'

Dorothy-Anne shook her head. 'You . . . you wouldn't understand.' A look of hurt came into Elizabeth-Anne's eyes. Dorothy-Anne felt instantly contrite. 'I didn't mean it that way, Great-Granny,' she said. 'I know you would understand. It's just that . . . ' She took a deep breath, frowned, then shook her head again. 'It's just that *I* can't talk about it. At least not yet.'

Elizabeth-Anne cocked her head to one side. 'I've lived a good many years, you know, and one of the few things that I have learned was never to coop up any hurt inside you.' She paused. 'You just concentrate on getting better. Just remember, I'm not advising you to do it, but if you feel you don't want to talk about it – ever – well, I'll understand that, too.' She smiled gently.

Dorothy-Anne returned the smile, her eyes moist. 'Thank you,' she whispered.

Elizabeth-Anne rearranged her lap blanket. 'Well, I'd better be going before the nurse charges in here and throws me out. Five minutes, I was told, and no longer – '

As if on cue, the door opened and the mannish nurse poked her head in. 'Five minutes are up, Mrs. Hale,' she said.

'I'm going, I'm going.' Elizabeth-Anne shook her head. 'To several thousand people I may be the boss, but when it comes to doctors and nurses, *I'm* the one who gets pushed around.' She laughed, maneuvering her chair back to the door. 'You just make sure they take good care of you,' she warned. 'After all, you're a Hale. I didn't set up an endowment for a new wing here for nothing.'

'Great-Granny?'

Elizabeth-Anne stopped wheeling the chair. 'Yes, dear?'

'Why are men the way they are?'

Elizabeth-Anne started; then a veil seemed to drop down over her eyes. She moved the chair around so that she faced the bed. 'I honestly don't know, dear,' she said. 'That's one question I haven't been able to answer.'

'And Great-Grandfather? What was he like?'

'Zaccheus?' Elizabeth-Anne steepled her fingers and raised them to her lips. Her eyes held a faraway look. 'He was sweet. And I loved him.'

'Was he like Daddy?'

Elizabeth-Anne's eyes flashed. So that was it. Henry had driven his daughter to this, caused a mere child to reach for solace in death. As stunned as she was, she wasn't surprised. She had always admonished him to do more for his daughter. Yet what was more impossible to fake than a love that was not there?

'Your Daddy doesn't mean to be cruel,' Elizabeth-Anne said. 'It's just that he's still hurting from something that was no one's fault. He's angry that he couldn't control things.'

Dorothy-Anne paused for a long minute, then asked, 'Are all men like that?'

'No, my love, not all men. Someday, you'll see. Just be patient and someday you'll see.'

The day Dorothy-Anne was released from the hospital, her great-grandmother had to leave for Tokyo to inaugurate the newly completed Hale Imperial Palace. The most ambitious hotel in the Hale chain, the Imperial Palace rested amidst an ancient rock garden of lakes and cherry trees. It boasted every modern luxury, but also respected traditional Japanese design. Elizabeth-Anne had been applauded for insisting that the authentic design also spoil as little of its ancient setting as possible. 'Art,' Elizabeth-Anne had told reporters at a much-publicized press conference before the hotel was built, 'must be respected and preserved, no matter the price.'

The price had been a million dollars more than anticipated.

'There's been so much fanfare that I've got to be there.' Elizabeth-Anne explained when she stopped by the hospital to visit Dorothy-Anne before leaving. 'The press will be there, and so will the American ambassador, as well as an emissary from the emperor. I've spoken to Dr. Sidney. You're to go home this afternoon. Nanny will have my car at her disposal and she'll come to pick you up. Also, I've spoken to your father. He should be home this evening.'

Dorothy-Anne nodded. She had been in the hospital for two days, and that had given her plenty of time to think. She had been hoping that when her father got back and was told what she had done, things would change. At least she knew why he hated her. That was a start. She promised herself that she would try her best to make things up to him. Perhaps, in time, if she tried hard enough, he would find it in his heart to forgive her for killing her mother. They would get along better together. He might even learn to love her. He'd celebrate her birthdays with her. Take her out to dinners. Even to his office, where he would proudly introduce her to his associates.

Now that the time to face him was nearly at hand, Dorothy-Anne wished that she didn't have to see him. She had counted on Great-Granny being there, giving her support. Without her, the dreams of reconciliation vanished. Much as she needed to, she knew she would never be able to explain to her father why she had tried to kill herself. Worse, she felt like a stupid, weak bungler for having tried it. She knew how her father despised weak people.

She felt miserable during the drive home. Once she got there, she stayed in her room until her father arrived and Nanny came upstairs to get her.

She was surprised when she entered the big sitting room. Four people were there: her father, a beautiful woman she had never seen before, and two girls about her age. The woman was tall and blonde, a combination of femininity and virility, elegant but athletic. She studied Dorothy-Anne with wide blue eyes set in a tanned face. The two girls were mirror images of her, smaller, but just as self-assured.

Her father cleared his throat. 'Dorothy-Anne?'

She stepped timidly forward, hugely conscious of her bandaged wrists. She hid her hands behind her back. 'Yes, Daddy?'

'This is Chessy,' he said, gesturing at the beautiful woman. 'And these are her daughters CeCe and Diane.' He indicated the two girls.

Dorothy-Anne stared first at the woman, then at the girls. She didn't understand why they were there. She looked stupidly at her father.

'Chessy and I stopped in Las Vegas this morning and got married,' Henry Hale said. 'Aren't you going to kiss your new mother?'

Dorothy-Anne stood stock-still. For a moment she couldn't believe her ears. It was too much to bear. 'You're not my mother!' she shouted angrily. 'You'll *never* be my mother!' Then she burst into tears, ran upstairs to her room, and locked the door.

Chessy got to her feet to follow her, but Henry Hale waved her back. 'Leave her be,' he said sternly.

Chessy looked at him dubiously, but sat back down.

'He didn't even ask why I did it or how I was,' Dorothy-Anne sobbed, clutching the pillow to her. 'He couldn't have cared less if I had died or not . . .'

She wept all night long, long after no more tears would come. She was still sobbing when morning came. Her face was red and tired, her eyes swollen, and the nubby pink bedspread was rumpled and damp. But the cry had done her good. It had anesthetized the hurt.

Sitting up slowly, she wiped her fingers across her eyes. During the endless night, the answer had come to her. She was too sensitive and vulnerable. Hurting herself did no one any good, herself least of all. Instead, she would arm herself with her own defenses. She would be stoic. Poised. She would never again show emotion, never let on how hurt she was.

She would be just like great-grandmother Elizabeth-Anne.

2

Freddie took a last drag on his cigarette. The ash glowed red in the dim room, then he stubbed the butt out in a saucer. Reaching for the cup of coffee Mrs. Ramirez had brought him, he looked up at her. 'Thanks,' he said gratefully, taking the cup with both hands.

'*De nada.*' Felicia Ramirez nodded toward the bed. 'Your wife. How is she?'

'Resting.' He blew on the hot coffee, then sipped it carefully. It was thick and bitter, but it would help keep him alert. Help him do what he now realized he had to do.

Mrs. Ramirez drank from her own cup, then said quietly, 'I try the telephone while I make the coffee.'

He looked at her with raised eyebrows.

'It still does not work,' she said.

Freddie glanced at his wristwatch. The dial glowed pale green, showing past ten o'clock. He had thought it was much later; the minutes seemed to have crept by like hours. He looked up at Mrs. Ramirez. 'Do you think I should go outside and see if a car passes?'

Mrs. Ramirez shook her head. 'No one but the locals use this road anymore. They know better than to travel in this storm. The bridge down the road sometimes washes away.'

Freddie looked over at Dorothy-Anne, who slept quietly. 'She'll need a doctor.'

Mrs. Ramirez laid a hand on his arm. 'We must wait until the storm is past.'

He shook his head. 'It may be too late, then.'

Felicia Ramirez stared at him, her face pulsating in the flickering candlelight. She knew it was true. The contractions were coming more frequently and still the young woman burned with fever. 'What do you suggest?'

Freddie tightened his lips. 'I'll walk into town. You give me the directions and I'll come back with the doctor.'

'The best way is through the orchards.' Her eyes clouded over. 'You may get lost. It is a long way.'

He met her eyes. 'I'll have to take that chance,' he said softly. 'I have no choice.'

Minutes later, Dorothy-Anne struggled to rouse herself. When she opened her eyes everything was at first a blur. Then her vision cleared, and she saw Freddie at the foot of the bed, shrugging himself into his jacket. Mrs. Ramirez handed him a black rain slicker, saying softly, 'Here, you will need this.' Freddie took the slicker, his expression grim.

'Freddie?'

He looked up sharply, then forced a smile. 'Hi, honey,' he said cheerfully. 'Feeling any better?'

'Yes, a lot.' Dorothy-Anne hesitated. 'Where are you going?'

'To get us some doughnuts.' He came toward her, sat on the edge of the bed, and took her hands in his.

'No, I mean really,' she said, smiling weakly.

436

'I'm going to see about a doctor.'

'But – '

'Ssh. It's just a short walk across the orchard into town.' He glanced over his shoulder. 'Mrs. Ramirez told me the way.'

Dorothy-Anne's voice was thick with fright. 'But I don't want you to leave me.'

'Don't you want to have a healthy baby for us?'

She nodded solemnly.

'Then you'll have to trust me. You do trust me, don't you honey?' With one hand he smoothed her glossy forehead.

'Yes,' she whispered, 'I trust you.'

A particularly sharp gust of wind tore at the tin mansard roof above them; the roof buckled inward and then snapped back, like tin shaken for theatrical thunder.

'I love you,' she whispered urgently.

'And I love you, too.'

'You'll be careful?'

Taking her hand in his, he pressed it firmly against his cheek. 'Of course I'll be careful.'

'I wouldn't . . . '

'You wouldn't what?'

'I wouldn't want . . . in the wind, anything could happen.'

'Don't you worry your pretty head about me.' He leaned forward and kissed her, then got to his feet.

She looked up at him. He seemed so tall, so strong and in command. She was awash with gratitude, with love for him and the child of his she carried. 'I love you,' she whispered again. 'I've loved you ever since the first time I saw you.'

He smiled at the memory and whispered, 'And I've loved you, Dorothy-Anne.'

They stared at each other in silence, the memory a visible bond between them.

October 17, 1983 was a windswept autumn afternoon in Chicago. The giant skyscrapers stood out in sharp relief against the sparsely clouded sky. One could smell the tang of the lake, a mere three blocks away. The beaches along

Lake Michigan were chewed by the breakers, and the sun peeked out from behind the clouds as Dorothy-Anne got out of the rental car.

She tilted her head back, squinted up at the large grimy building, and shook her head in despair. It did little to inspire her. Still, her great-grandmother had sent her to scout out the work of Freddie Cantwell, so scout it out she would. Although she couldn't for the life of her see why she was doing it.

Slamming the car door shut, she picked her way gingerly across the debris to get to the planks coursing up into the high dark doorway of the building. The stairs had been removed. The sidewalk was torn up, and the sand was thick and deep. She would have to cross ten feet of it in order to get to the planks.

As soon as her feet sank into the soft sand, she was irritated. She had spent a hundred and fifty dollars on the Maud Frizon shoes, and now they would be ruined. She hadn't anticipated such a mess; it was the last time she would ever wear good clothes to a construction site she wasn't familiar with. But she hadn't had a choice. She had flown in, rented the car, and she'd have to fly back to New York again this very evening. There wasn't time to go to a hotel and change.

Suddenly her left ankle twisted sideways and she let out a short cry at the sharp pain. Bending down, she massaged her ankle gingerly.

A burly black construction worker in a silver hardhat and sleeveless T-shirt hurried over to her. 'You okay, Miss?' he asked.

She tilted her head to look up at him. 'No, I'm not all right,' she wanted to snap, but she nodded, bit down on the pain, and refused to show either it or her irritation. 'Yes, thank you. I'm fine.'

'You sure don't look it. I mean, you look right sharp in that outfit but it's all wrong for this place.' He tilted back his hardhat and scratched the front of his gray, woolly scalp. His face held a puzzled expression. 'What you doin' here, anyway?' He eyed her keenly. 'Are you from the bank?'

She straightened and shook her head, her wheat-gold bangs and page-boy cut swaying gently. 'I'm afraid I'm not.'

'Good.' He grinned with relief. Then, as she took a few tentative steps, he automatically reached out to help her.

'Thank you.' She smiled at him faintly. 'Do you work for Freddie Cantwell?'

He grinned widely. 'Sure do. Wouldn't want to work for anyone else, either.'

'Oh? And why's that?'

''Cause he's a genius. He can take an old building like this one, gut it, and make it better than anything ever been built. Better looking too. He can cut corners and costs, but he knows where to cut them.' He grinned even more broadly. 'But most of all because he hires folk like me.' He saw her puzzled expression. 'You see,' he explained, 'I ain't got much of a chance to work. Neither have many of the others. We've all had trouble in the past, jail, drugs and stuff. Mister Cantwell's the only person who gives us a chance.'

'I see.'

'You want to see him?'

'That's what I came for.'

'He's up there.' The black man took off his hardhat, leaned his head way back, and squinted as he pointed toward the roof of the building. A crane was lifting a pallet of bricks skyward, and then swung its cargo gracefully out of view.

'Fine. Just lead the way.'

'That's the way up.' He gestured at the crane. 'But we gotta wait till the pallet puts down empty.'

'You mean . . .' Her voice faltered. 'That's the *only* way up?'

' 'Fraid so. We ain't got no money for nothing else.' He smiled apologetically. 'But I'll go up with you. I won't let you fall, don't worry.'

Sooner than she would have liked, Dorothy-Anne found herself clinging onto the big black man's arm as the two of them rose gracefully into the sky, perched on the pallet. She groaned in dismay as she glanced down between the wide gaps in the pallet wood and saw the ground sink swiftly away. She glanced sideways at her companion, who casually held onto the cable.

'Old Sepp, he's the operator,' the big man said admiringly. 'Handles this baby smooth as silk.'

Dorothy-Anne nodded and forced her eyes to look up. She hated heights, but she didn't say a word. A minute later, the pallet swung gently toward the roof and set down without a quiver.

'See? What'd I tell you? Smooth as silk.'

She smiled gratefully. 'You'll help me? On the way down?'

'Sure will. You just signal for me. My name's Luther. And over there, that's Mr. Cantwell.' Luther pointed to the far end of the roof.

Dorothy-Anne's gaze followed his pointing finger. A man was kneeling on the roof with his back to them. Spread out before him were sets of blueprints weighed down with a brick at each corner.

'Hello? Mr. Cantwell?' Dorothy-Anne called out.

The man didn't appear to hear her. She narrowed her eyes, squared her shoulders, and made her way toward him.

'Mr. Cantwell,' she said sharply, when her shadow covered the blueprints. 'I'm Dorothy-Anne Hale, of Hale Ho – '

He turned around then, and suddenly, for no explicable reason at all, she lost her voice.

Perhaps it was his smile, or maybe the magnetic, bottomless depths of his eyes, or even the easy charm which emanated from him . . . Dorothy-Anne had the sensation of suddenly tumbling into a vacuum, of somersaulting through airless space, of being drawn, in slow motion, into those hypnotic eyes.

In that instant, her mind seemed to snap, clicking a sharply focused photograph of such impossible intensity, such surreal clarity, that she knew it would be frozen in her mind forever. She had captured his face, been drawn into the inescapable image of his pale gray eyes with amber flecks and fine, thread-thin streaks of emerald. She would

440

never forget his soiled, sleeveless T-shirt which showed off his thick, muscular shoulders tapering down to a slim, tight waist. His stormy good looks were dark, and his face tanned and rugged, but with laugh lines sculpted deep around his eyes. Even close-cropped, his hair was blue-black, his chin strong and cleft, his mouth sensuous and sensual.

One instant he had been a stranger, and the next she could think of nothing but his touch, his hands holding her against his powerful chest.

One instant she was a young lady, a mere eighteen year old just out of school and the next she was a woman, a full grown woman with a desire that shook her to her very core.

In that instant, all the frustration she had felt over soiling her shoes and hurting her ankle evaporated. Instead, she saw him, and knew with an uncanny certainty that he was just as keenly aware of her. For a long moment he locked eyes with her.

She felt the blush creeping up into her face. 'I have come all the way from New York to see you, Mr. Cantwell,' she said, her voice curiously unsteady.

'Have you now?' His eyes appeared to be laughing at her.

'I have,' she said a little too sharply. She swallowed, trying to regain her calm. 'I am here as a representative of Hale Hotels. We're interested in your work. You not only have a reputation for coming in under budget, but for renovating and designing buildings which . . . ' Her voice trailed off under his unblinking gaze. She felt acutely uncomfortable.

'Yes?' he asked quietly.

Suddenly she was burning with anger. She was not used to being treated like this, to being thrown off kilter so completely by a perfect stranger. He was obviously not only aware of her discomfiture, but seemed to relish watching her flounder. She knew then that he wasn't about to come to the aid of her faltering conversation.

'I have come,' she said between clenched teeth, 'to see some of your work first hand.'

'But most of all,' he added shrewdly, 'to see if I can be bought by the Philistines?' He winked at her.

She ignored the wink and the jibe. 'Well? Are you going to show me around?'

He placed his hands on his lean hips and grinned disarmingly. 'No,' he said matter-of-factly.

Her eyes widened. 'And may I ask why not?'

'Because,' he said without taking his eyes off her, 'it's way past lunch-time, for one thing.'

'Then I'll take you to lunch.'

'Sorry.' He shook his head. 'I can't take the time. I've still got too much to finish today.'

She growled in exasperation. 'Mr. Cantwell,' she said curtly, 'I've flown here all the way from New York just to see you.'

'Something which neither I, nor anyone else here, asked you to do,' he reminded her.

She inclined her head. 'Granted.' Then she raised her face, her stubborn chin jutting outward. 'Under the circumstances I should think you would be only too happy to see me and show me around.'

'Oh? And why should that be?'

'I happen to know for a fact that you're financially strapped. You've put everything you have into this project, and it's still far from completion. It'll be a miracle if you ever finish it.'

'Ah. So you've been checking up on me. How deeply did you happen to delve into my resources, Miss – '

'Hale. Dorothy-Anne Hale.' She shrugged. 'We checked you out perfunctorily. Nothing more than the surface. But we know you need money, and lots of it.'

'And you can provide it, I take it? As long as I join your organization?'

'Perhaps.'

'I don't want it.'

'I haven't offered it yet.'

'But you will, won't you?' He gazed at her intently. 'Why else would you have flown all the way out there?' He paused. 'The answer is no.'

'You mean you won't show me around?'

'I mean, I don't want your money. I happen to like my independence. I don't want to work for anyone besides myself. It's nothing personal, you understand.'

She smiled grimly. 'Oh? Then what is it?'

He smiled disarmingly. 'I just don't happen to think it's healthy for a husband and wife to work together.'

She looked startled. There was a quiet intensity to his voice which turned her knees to jelly. Then she recovered her composure. 'Mr. Cantwell,' she said quietly, stressing every syllable, 'I do not appreciate jokes. I take my business very seriously. And my time happens to be precious.'

'And so is mine.' He reached out and took her hand. He smiled hugely then, and his unexpected touch sent a tremor through her.

'Let's . . . ' She took a deep breath. 'Let's be serious, Mr. Cantwell.'

'Freddie,' he corrected her calmly. 'You should call me Freddie. After all, this isn't the Victorian age when husbands and wives called themselves by their formal surnames.'

'Stop joking,' she said in a whisper.

'I'm dead serious.'

'But . . . you don't even know me,' she sputtered. Suddenly she couldn't face him, and looked down at his hand. He was still holding hers.

'I know enough,' he said confidently.

There was a long silence then. In the background, the sounds of construction equipment sounded distant and unreal. From somewhere below, she could hear a workman's harsh, clipped voice yelling, and then she heard the clearing of her own throat. She was aware of Freddie's gaze softening, the gray-and-black limpid pools of his eyes surveying her tenderly, his teeth even and white and flashing as he smiled good-naturedly, his natural, instinctive charm in brilliant evidence as he said, 'Naturally, I don't expect your reply right now. You've got to think it over first. And for that I've got all the time in the world.'

'You're persistent, aren't you?' she said with grudging

admiration. She smiled, her coolness thawing.

'That I am. And like I told you, we've got time. Lots of it. Because before I get married, I intend to finish this project. Without any help.'

'And why's that?' she found herself asking. 'It might be a year. Even two.'

'I wouldn't want you to get the wrong idea,' he smiled. He let go of her hand.

'What do you mean?'

'I wouldn't want you to think I'm after your money. It's like I said. I'm independent. Now, since that's settled, can I buy the lady a cup of coffee?' he asked.

And like a fool, Dorothy-Anne blushed a bright crimson and she found herself sputtering, 'Yes, thank you . . . I mean . . . if you really want to – '

'I do,' he said gently, hooking his arm through hers and leading her toward the pallet. His words echoed in her mind . . . She couldn't believe this man meant to offer those words to her as a promise . . .

Do you, Frederick Cantwell, take this woman to be your lawfully wedded wife, to honor and cherish her, through sickness and through health, until the day that you die?'

'I do.'

I do. Tiny, simple words. Huge, grave words of responsibility. But they were only a short year later. Meanwhile, Dorothy-Anne and Freddie lived together on weekends. During the workdays of those many, many weeks, he was in Chicago, and she traveled constantly on business. Until the building he was working on was finished, without any help from her, he refused to tie the knot.

For the time being, there was her flight back to New York, a smooth flight through soaring emotions she would never forget. The day seemed to billow and sail along with her spirit and her thoughts were filled with the image of Freddie Cantwell's eyes. Only when she arrived back in New York, and met Elizabeth-Anne at the airport, did she remember what day it was. And, even then, Elizabeth-Anne had had to tell her.

The night in New York was clear and star-studded. Traffic on the Long Island expressway was light, and moving along at a swift clip. Elizabeth-Anne unsnapped her large Bottega Veneta handbag, and rummaged through it. She took out a thick, vellum envelope. 'Dear?' She held it out to Dorothy-Anne.

'Yes, Great-Granny?'

'Please. Accept this graciously.'

Dorothy-Anne took the envelope and switched on the reading lamp on her side of the Rolls. She looked down at the envelope, frowning in puzzlement as she stroked a stray lock of hair out of her eyes. The left-hand corner of the envelope was embossed with a blue return address:

Shatzkin, Morris, Bernstein and Bidgood, P.C.
666 Fifth Avenue
New York, N.Y. 10036

Slowly, she tore the envelope open. She unfolded a sheaf of legal papers, held them up to the light, and then turned to Elizabeth-Anne. 'But . . . but it's a deed,' she murmured in surprise.

'Don't you think I know that?' Elizabeth-Anne said with mock crossness.

'But – '

Elizabeth-Anne held up a hand, gloved palm facing outward, as if to ward off an attack. 'No "buts," dear. We've waited a long time for this day.'

'What do you mean?'

'Don't tell me you've forgotten!' Elizabeth-Anne eyed her great-granddaughter shrewdly. 'Dorothy-Anne, darling, it's your eighteenth birthday. Don't you remember? Today, the Hale Palace Hotel, which has been held in trust for you since your ninth birthday, is officially *yours.*'

'Oh, Great-Granny, I *had* forgotten. But . . . I thought that maybe – '

'Maybe what?'

'Well . . .'

'When I give someone something, I give it to them for keeps.' Elizabeth-Anne smiled faintly.

Dorothy-Anne threw her arms around her great-grand-mother just as, in the distance, far beyond the Silver Lady hood ornament, they could already see the distant, winking

445

skyline of Manhattan pushing up over the industrial buildings and factories of Long Island City.

A flash of lightning lit the little room like a strobe and the scene became a frozen tableau. The past merged with the present, and Dorothy-Anne returned to the Hale Tourist Court outside Quebeck, Texas. She looked up at Freddie. Her eyes were solemn and her face was pale.

'More pains?' he asked.

She shook her head and breathed deeply. 'Freddie? I don't want you to go out into that storm.'

'It'll be all right, hon.'

'You'll be careful?'

He grinned and held up a hand, palm out. 'Scout's honor.'

'You were never a scout,' she said weakly. He smiled, but she was still worried. 'Freddie?'

'Hmmmm?'

'I'm afraid.'

'Don't be.' He smiled down at her. 'All I'm going to do is to get a doctor. Remember what you used to tell me? As a child, whenever you heard a siren wailing, and you were frightened, what did your great-grandmother tell you?'

'That it doesn't mean that something bad has happened,' she whispered. 'It means that help is on the way.'

'That's right. Just keep that in mind.' He paused and flashed her his most enigmatic smile. 'Who loves ya, baby?'

This was an old game between them. She smiled faintly. 'Kojak,' she whispered.

He kissed her forehead. 'Atta girl.'

And he was gone.

Dorothy-Anne had drifted into a restless sleep, and woke easily when she heard Mrs. Ramirez come back into the room. She struggled to sit up. 'How long has he been gone now?' she asked anxiously.

Mrs. Ramirez checked her watch. 'It hasn't been that long,' she lied softly. She turned away and busied herself blowing out one of the candles that had nearly burned itself out. She stuck a new taper into the candlestick, then lit it before setting it back down on the dresser.

Dorothy-Anne stared up at the ceiling and listened to the drumming of the rain. It seemed to be coming down even harder now. 'The storm's not letting up,' she said tremulously.

'No, not yet,' Mrs. Ramirez said. 'But soon.'

'It seems to be getting worse.'

Mrs. Ramirez cocked her head and listened. She nodded. 'Sometimes it is at its worst right before it ends,' she said reassuringly. She reached behind Dorothy-Anne and fluffed the pillow. 'You just rest. And stay covered.' Mrs. Ramirez leaned over her and patted her hand. 'You will need all your strength.' Then she smiled and lowered herself onto the chair she had pulled up alongside the bed. 'Do not worry,' she said gently. 'I will not leave you alone.'

Dorothy-Anne nodded gratefully. Then she sighed and let her head drop back down on the pillow. She shut her eyes and listened to the violent drumming of the rain. It was coming down heavily, as it had been on the day of her fifth birthday.

It had been raining cats and dogs then, too.

That had been in 1970. Outside the thunderstorm had raged and flashed. Inside the sitting room of the big house in Tarrytown, it was warm and cozy. A fire crackled in both of the two big fireplaces.

Dorothy-Anne had been seated on the tiny, Louis XVI children's chair, working the giant jigsaw puzzle Nanny had given her for her birthday. She kept frowning at the picture of the giant Mickey Mouse on the cover of the box, wondering how on earth to recreate it. Opposite her Nanny was seated very erect on the gold brocade sofa, watching her intently, but gave Dorothy-Anne no clue as to where the puzzle piece she held in her hand fit in. Dorothy-Anne knew better than to ask for help. Nanny was a great believer in letting one figure out problems by oneself.

Nanny seemed to sense rather than hear the bald, black butler come silently into the room. She turned around. 'The car has arrived,' he announced.

Nanny nodded. 'Thank you, Franklin.' She rose to her feet and smoothed her dress. 'It's time we left, Dorothy-Anne.'

Dorothy-Anne looked up at her, the puzzle piece still in her hand. She looked sorely disappointed. She didn't want to leave. 'I'm not done yet,' she said unhappily. 'Can't we wait?'

'I'm afraid not,' Nanny answered firmly.

Dorothy-Anne sighed and pushed herself to her feet. Nanny came toward her, knelt down on one knee, and adjusted the collar of Dorothy-Anne's party dress.

'I want you to look very nice,' Nanny told her. 'Your great-grandmother is a great believer in neatness. And so,' she added pointedly, 'am I.'

'Why isn't Great-Granny coming here?' Dorothy-Anne asked.

'She would have, I'm sure, but she called to say she's very busy today,' Nanny explained. She straightened and took Dorothy-Anne by the hand. 'Come child. It's time we left.' With her free hand Nanny scooped up Dorothy-Anne's shiny, red plastic raincoat.

Dorothy-Anne eyed the raincoat with disgust. She didn't like it. It made her feel hot and sticky. 'I don't want to go to the city!' she announced suddenly, withdrawing her hand from Nanny's. 'It's too noisy and there are so many people.' She shivered and rubbed her arms. 'It frightens me.'

'You have nothing to worry about,' Nanny assured her, giving her an affectionate squeeze.

Dorothy-Anne stared up at her.

'Besides, your Nanny will be there, won't she?' Nanny asked. 'And so will your great-grandmother. You want to see her, don't you?'

Dorothy-Anne nodded solemnly.

'I happen to know for a fact that your great-grand-mother is going to take you to a very special place.'

Dorothy-Anne's eyes glimmered with anticipation. 'She is?'

Nanny nodded. 'She is. But I can't tell you any more. It's supposed to be a surprise.'

Dorothy-Anne's face broke into a grin. She tugged at Nanny's hand. 'Well?' she demanded. 'Let's *go*.'

The rain didn't let up even after they reached the city. During the drive down, Nanny had explained that the average thunderstorm only lasted about twenty minutes, so there must be several thunderstorms piled up and passing over New York one after another. Dorothy-Anne listened in fascination, watching the rain bead up on the windows of her father's sleek black limousine. She snuggled further into the corner of the gray velour seat. With one hand, she wiped the foggy side-window clear. It felt cold and wet to the touch. The world outside was blurry and gray. Timidly, she glanced sideways at Nanny.

Nanny held out her arms. Quickly, Dorothy-Anne scrambled over to her. She let herself be enveloped in Nanny's protective warmth.

'We're almost there,' Nanny said as the car turned on to 72nd Street, then entered Central Park. Ten minutes later, they pulled up alongside the tall steel-and-glass office building on Park Avenue and Fifty-First Street. 'Here we are,' Nanny said. She handed Dorothy-Anne the raincoat. 'Put it on or you'll get soaked.'

Dorothy-Anne made a face.

'You'll have to wear it,' Nanny said firmly. 'Otherwise we'll drive right back to Tarrytown.'

Scowling, Dorothy-Anne shrugged into the coat. The chauffeur opened the passenger door and held an umbrella over them as they hurried through the driving rain to the big revolving glass doors.

Once inside, Dorothy-Anne looked around the cavernous marble lobby with awe. The ceiling was so high and there seemed to be marble everywhere. 'Is this one of Great-Granny's hotels?' she asked as Nanny held tightly to her hand. They were walking through the crowded lobby toward the elevators.

Nanny shook her head. 'No, this is not a hotel. It's an office building. Many people work here, including your great-grandmother. You see, her hotel business is so big that she has to have separate offices just to run everything. She owns hotels all over the world.'

Dorothy-Anne nodded sagely as she digested this. 'And this whole building belongs to her?' she asked as they waited in front of an elevator door.

Nanny chuckled. 'Lord, no, child. But as far as I know, she rents two entire floors, which is a lot of office space, believe me.'

Dorothy-Anne looked up at her. 'Does Daddy work here too?'

A mask seemed to slide down over Nanny's face. 'I'm not really sure,' she said quickly. 'You'll have to ask your great-grandmother.'

Dorothy-Anne's face fell. 'Nobody ever tells me anything about him,' she said quietly. 'Every time I ask, I get told to ask someone else.'

Nanny looked at her with a sad sympathy Dorothy-Anne was too young to recognize. 'That's because it's good manners to mind your own business,' she said lamely.

'But what Daddy does *is* my business, isn't it?' she asked with the damning, incisive insight of the very young.

Nanny was saved from answering by the arrival of the elevator. After they stepped inside, Dorothy-Anne watched as Nanny pressed a button marked '32.' The moment Nanny's finger touched it, the number lit up. Dorothy-Anne's eyes grew big. Tentatively, Dorothy-Anne reached up and fingered one of the numbers. She squealed with delight as it lit up. She pressed another, then another.

Nanny slapped her hand lightly. 'Stop that,' she scolded. She looked apologetically at the other passengers, but no one returned her smile.

Stung by Nanny's slap, Dorothy-Anne tightened her lips. For a moment, she thought she would cry, and she tried very hard not to. And then the doors were sliding open and Dorothy-Anne found herself face-to-face with an entirely new world.

'Is this where Great-Granny works?' she asked as they got off.

Nanny nodded solemnly. 'It is.'

Dorothy-Anne took a deep breath as she felt a strange pride at the thought that all this belonged to her family. The reception area was lavishly furnished in a style that spoke of opulence, grand comfort, and a solid financial footing.

The walls were paneled in mahogany and the carpeting was a delicate, oh-so-pale pink. The sprawling sofas and chairs were masterpieces of the art deco artist Andre Groult, and worth a small fortune. The huge marble fireplace was artificial, but looked as if it belonged.

The only hint that this was not the lobby of a luxury hotel but instead the headquarters of a vast business empire, was a discreetly engraved gold plate facing the visitor from atop the receptionist's Persian desk. The plaque read merely, *Hale Hotels, Inc.*

The receptionist was young and blonde. She seemed startled to see a child, but she recovered her composure with a cool smile. 'May I help you?' she asked Nanny.

'We'd like to see Mrs. Hale,' Nanny answered.

'Do you have an appointment?'

Nanny sniffed. 'We do.'

'And whom may I say is here to see her?'

Nanny smiled down at Dorothy-Anne and gave her hand a squeeze. 'Miss Dorothy-Anne Hale,' she announced.

The name worked magic. The receptionist's professional smile thawed. 'If you'll have a seat for just a moment, someone will be right out,' she said with new warmth. She picked up an ivory telephone as Nanny led Dorothy-Anne over to a sofa. Before they had even settled down, the tall French doors leading down a long, pink-carpeted corridor opened, and an impeccably dressed woman with raven hair strode toward them.

'Miss Hale?' she asked, leaning down and smiling at Dorothy-Anne. 'I am Mrs. Goldstine, Mrs. Hale's secretary.'

'How do you do?' Dorothy-Anne asked solemnly as they shook hands, but inwardly she winced. Mrs. Goldstine's hand was cold and dry.

'I'm fine, thank you.' Mrs. Goldstine smiled, turned to Nanny, and shook her hand also. 'Please,' she said, gesturing elegantly. 'If you'll follow me?' She led the way through the tall doors, walking briskly so that Nanny as well as Dorothy-Anne had to hurry to keep up with her.

The hallway seemed impossibly long. They passed countless closed doors, then turned the corner and faced a wall of glass that looked onto a huge, windowless room, crowded with rows of desks.

'That's the typing pool,' Mrs. Goldstine explained.

'That's where I want to work when I grow up,' Dorothy-Anne announced. 'Because of the pool.' She craned her neck. 'But where *is* it?'

'It's only an expression. It's called a pool because it's where a lot of people work together in one spot.'

'Well, maybe I *don't* want to work there after all,' Dorothy-Anne mused thoughtfully.

'I think,' Mrs. Goldstine said, 'that when the time comes, your great-grandmother has bigger plans in store for you than the typing pool.'

A little further on, they passed another, almost identically glassed-in room.

'Another pool?' Dorothy-Anne asked brightly.

'That is the accounting department,' Mrs. Goldstine explained. 'The people you see in there take care of all the money your great-grandmother's hotels bring in from all around the world.'

Dorothy-Anne nodded. 'But don't you ever get lost here?' she asked as they continued walking.

Mrs. Goldstine laughed. 'I *was* a little confused in the beginning,' she confessed, 'but you get used to it very quickly.' They turned another corner. 'Here we are.'

The first office was Mrs. Goldstine's. It had a big Renaissance desk and the chairs were upholstered in genuine brocade. The office beyond was Elizabeth-Anne Hale's. They faced two huge, tall French doors with bevelled glass windows and opaque blue curtains. Mrs. Goldstine knocked, then swung one of the doors open. Dorothy-Anne stood in the doorway, Nanny's hands on her shoulders and gazed across the room at her great-grandmother.

Elizabeth-Anne Hale was standing beside a sofa, speaking on the telephone. The moment she glanced toward the door, she quickly said something and hung up.

Ever since she could remember, Dorothy-Anne had been immensely impressed by her great-grandmother. Elizabeth-Anne always looked so imposing and in command, with never a spun-silver hair out of place. She stood tall and slender, and looked much younger than her seventy-two years in her classically styled peached-colored woollen suit. A single strand of matchless South Seas pearls encircled her neck.

'Great-Granny!' Dorothy Anne cried, ~~and she dash~~ed headlong toward Elizabeth-Anne's outstretched arms.

'Mrs. Goldstine,' Elizabeth-Anne called over Dorothy-Anne's head as she embraced her, 'please hold all calls.'

Mrs. Goldstine nodded and smiled.

'I'll wait outside,' Nanny said discreetly, and then the French door closed soundlessly and Elizabeth-Anne and her great-granddaughter were alone in the room. For a moment they held their tight embrace. Then Elizabeth-Anne held Dorothy-Anne at arm's length and gazed deeply into her eyes.

'Is this office all yours, Great-Granny?' Dorothy-Anne asked in wonder.

'It is,' Elizabeth-Anne replied. 'Do you like it?'

Dorothy-Anne twisted around. The room was huge, with floor to ceiling windows looking out over Central Park, the huge apartment buildings lining the West Side, the wide silver breadth of the Hudson, and all the way into New Jersey. The rainswept view was gray, but no mere gloomy weather could dampen the plush comfort, and the office was at once warm and cozy. The furnishings were similar to those of the reception room, but dominated by rich peacock blues and warm wood. Elizabeth-Anne's desk was a large, ornately carved Italian piece facing two plush armchairs. Dorothy-Anne thought it beautiful, but felt comfortably at home at the same time.

Elizabeth-Anne's aquamarine eyes glanced toward the rain-streaked windows. 'It's still coming down,' she said, 'but that's all right. The car is waiting for us, so we won't get wet.'

'At least the thunder's stopped,' Dorothy-Anne said softly. 'It frightened me.'

'I can understand that. I was the same way when I was your age.'

'You were?'

'Of course I was.' Elizabeth-Anne strode toward the telephone and placed a call. She did not refer to the caller by name, nor did she have to identify herself. Her crisp, clear voice was unmistakable. 'I'm ready to go to lunch now,' she said. 'We'll meet here in my office.' She hung up the telephone and winked conspiratorially at Dorothy-Anne.

'Who was that?'

Elizabeth-Anne smiled secretly. 'You'll find out soon enough.'

'Nanny said we're going somewhere special.'

'And indeed, we are.' Elizabeth-Anne came forward, patted Dorothy-Anne's shoulder, and turned as she heard the door opening.

Dorothy-Anne turned around too. Her eyes bulged in disbelief. Seeing her father in the flesh was more than a minor miracle. Although she lived under the same roof as he, their paths rarely crossed. She was too young to realize that this was purposeful, that unlike her, most children saw their fathers daily, and that hers tried his best to avoid her. Dorothy-Anne could hardly know that, after hiring Nanny, her father had told the governess that her job was not so much to provide child care as to act as a guard. He had explained to her that he wanted to see as little of his daughter as humanly possible. Nanny had disapproved of this thoroughly, but upon seeing Dorothy-Anne's sweet elfin face, she had been unable to refuse the post. The child had clearly needed someone.

Luckily, although Dorothy-Anne mourned the fact that her father was elusive, she did not think his behavior at all strange, because it was all she had ever known. She loved him unquestioningly and with all her young heart. To her, he was the most handsome man in the world, and now, looking across the room at him, she was filled with love for him.

'Daddy!' she squealed, racing across the deep blue carpet toward him. She flung her arms around his thighs and hung on for dear life.

Henry drew a deep breath and seemed to recoil. He clenched his hands at his sides and his face went dark as he glowered across the office at Elizabeth-Anne. '*This* is the luncheon appointment?' he asked in quiet disbelief.

Elizabeth-Anne raised her chin. 'It is, Henry,' she answered. 'Need I remind you that it's her birthday today?' Her clear eyes glared at him challengingly.

But he matched her gaze without wavering. 'How can I ever forget?' he asked. 'It's the fifth anniversary of her mother's – '

'*Henry.*' Elizabeth-Anne's warning tone cut him off. She came over and, taking Dorothy-Anne in her arms, carried her away from her father. 'Be a good girl and wait outside with Nanny and Mrs. Goldstine, dear,' she said in a strained voice as she took Dorothy-Anne to the door. 'Your father and I have something important to discuss in private. It won't take but a minute, I promise.' Elizabeth-Anne attempted a smile, and hoped Dorothy-Anne didn't notice how false it was.

Dorothy-Anne's face fell. She didn't understand exactly what was going on, but she could tell Elizabeth-Anne was tense, and that was something she had never seen before.

Dorothy-Anne's small shoulders slumped as she stepped out of the room and the doors closed behind her. The moment they clicked shut, she heard voices raised in anger from behind her. Helplessly, she gazed over at Nanny, who was seated on one of the gold brocade chairs facing Mrs. Goldstine's desk. Behind it, Mrs. Goldstine busied herself by beating furiously on her sleek red typewriter, obviously attempting, though unsuccessfully, to muffle the tirade seeping through from behind Elizabeth-Anne's office.

'Goddamnit, Grandmother,' Henry Hale said bitingly, 'can't you the hell ever stay out of anything? Do you always have to meddle in *all* my affairs?'

'You're my grandson,' Elizabeth-Anne replied with a calm tone. 'Dorothy-Anne is my great-granddaughter. She's also a minor, and as such, needs someone to protect her interests. I don't think I should have to remind you that she's your daughter, Henry. Your much neglected daughter.'

'You think I don't know that?' Henry Hale, usually the cool, composed executive found himself losing control. His face was red and his neck cords stood out in bold relief.

'You *dare* stand there and tell me who is or isn't related to me?' he shouted. 'You *dare* tell me how I should treat that child? I suppose the next thing you'll try to tell me is how I should forgive her and forget it all, isn't it? After all the pain and heartache she's caused?'

Elizabeth-Anne was angry, but she did not allow herself the luxury of succumbing to her emotions. 'Henry,' she said, 'what happened was a tragedy, but it was not Dorothy-Anne's fault and you know it. If anyone was to blame it was Anna. The doctor warned her, but she ignored him. Nor did she even tell us the danger she was in.'

Henry made a sharp, dismissing gesture and turned away from Elizabeth-Anne. 'I don't believe you could say such a thing,' he said with angry disgust.

'What do you mean?'

'How could you speak of Anna like that . . . blame *her*! You act as if she's nothing, as if all you cared about were that child!'

'She's all that matters now, Henry,' Elizabeth-Anne answered sadly. 'She's your daughter and my great-grand-daughter. She's our living legacy. Everything else was yesterday. Dorothy-Anne is *today*. She's all we have. Don't waste it, Henry, don't live in the past. What's gone is gone. You've got to leave it behind you.'

'Sure.' He laughed bitterly. 'And kiss her at bedtime. Tell her stories. Tuck her in.'

'Yes, Henry. That's exactly what I mean.'

'*Never*,' he answered, his voice cold as ice. 'And this – this is one thing I can do something about.'

The odd words, and the ugly vehemence behind them, caused the terrible truth to sink in. Elizabeth-Anne shook her head and compressed her lips. She was aghast with the realization that Henry would never change. He couldn't. He didn't just ignore his daughter, he wasn't just indifferent to her; he detested her. Somehow, in the grief twisted state he had been in just after Anna's death, he had turned Dorothy-Anne into some kind of villain in his mind. And now he clung to that belief as the bedrock of his sanity. It was his lifeline, as if he couldn't face the world, couldn't live with his loss, unless he blamed it on someone, on the inhuman devil that he believed his child to be.

And now Elizabeth-Anne understood why. To Henry, Dorothy-Anne was not just a symbol of death, but a living proof of his own mortality. He had believed himself invincible, a match and master for any challenge. But the one battle that had really mattered was the one he had lost, the one that cut him down to mortal size. Death had won out, and he blamed the child.

'Henry,' Elizabeth-Anne begged softly, 'can't you find it in your heart to forget the past?'

'Forget?' he answered in disbelief. '*Forget*.' He turned on her again, his eyes blazing with a light that frightened her, that took the heart out of her struggle. 'Just remember one thing, Grandmother,' he spat out. 'You may pull the strings around here, but I won't let you do it in my home. Your power stops right here, at Hale Hotels. My life is my own.' He turned and strode toward the door, and with his hand on the doorknob spoke again in a chilling voice. 'And as far as *that child* goes, you can have her. I would prefer it if I never saw her again.'

With that he was gone, striding through the outside office without a backward glance.

Elizabeth-Anne dropped her head to her hands. She looked terribly old, as if all the years she had lived had suddenly caught up with her.

Dorothy-Anne twisted her head around and gazed after her father's departing figure in confusion. She glanced over at Nanny, but her face was stoically expressionless. Mrs. Goldstine kept right on typing, as if trying to pretend nothing unusual had happened.

Finally, Nanny pushed herself to her feet. 'Come dear,' she said gently reaching for Dorothy-Anne's hand. 'Let's go see your great-grandmother again.'

Together they headed back into Elizabeth-Anne's

office. But once they saw Elizabeth-Anne, Nanny frowned and let go of Dorothy-Anne's hand. Elizabeth-Anne was swaying unsteadily on her feet and Nanny rushed forward to catch her as she collapsed in slow-motion. Nanny stretched the old lady out flat on the floor and loosened the constricting collar of her blouse.

'Mrs. Goldstine!' she cried over her shoulder. 'Quickly, call for an ambulance!'

In the outer office, the machine-gun typing stopped abruptly as Mrs. Goldstine jumped up from her chair. She peered around the corner of the doorway, her hand poised on her breast, and then lost no time in snatching up her telephone.

Dorothy-Anne stood quietly, a jumble of fleeting images flashing through her mind. She did not know what was happening, only that Great-Granny and Daddy had had an awful fight.

And now Great-Granny was lying motionless on the deep blue carpet.

Dorothy-Anne was filled with a black, chilling fright, and began to cry soundlessly.

3

While they waited for the ambulance to arrive, Mrs. Goldstine got busy on the telephone. Elizabeth-Anne hadn't hired Natalie Goldstine, trained her over the years, and raised her income to the princely amount of fifty-five thousand dollars a year, for nothing. Elizabeth-Anne considered it a small price to pay for the services Natalie Goldstine was capable of providing. And, right now, she was proving her worth.

First, she called Elizabeth-Anne's physician of many year, Dr. Vartan Dadourian. Then she called up Henry's office, and finding him out demanded that he be sought.

'But when he walked out, he looked so . . . so angry,' Ruby Schaber stammered uncertainly. 'I don't know if I should bother him – '

Among her other talents, Natalie Goldstine was a woman who knew how to collect gossip and when to use it. 'Miss Schaber, if you value your job, you'll do everything within your power to locate Mr. Hale as quickly as possible. And that includes calling the numbers in his little black book, which you have so indiscreetly let everyone know you have access to.'

With that, Mrs. Goldstine hung up, but even Miss Schaber's fear-inspired efforts failed to turn Henry up by the time the ambulance arrived.

Mrs. Goldstine, Nanny, and Dorothy-Anne followed the stretcher bearers down to the lobby. They knew Elizabeth-Anne was gravely ill, but decided not to call her sole surviving daughter Regina, who had lived alone in California ever since her husband's death, until they reached the hospital and conferred with the doctor.

'I'll ride with Mrs. Hale,' Mrs. Goldstine told Nanny as they reached the ambulance. 'You two follow in Mrs. Hale's car and we'll meet at the hospital.'

Nanny looked hesitant, loathe to let Elizabeth-Anne out of sight. If she should die, perhaps she would come to first and want to see Dorothy-Anne.

Mrs. Goldstine seemed to read her thoughts. She laid a hand on Nanny's arm. 'I don't think the child needs to be exposed to the horrors of an ambulance ride just yet, do you?'

Nanny shook her head and Mrs. Goldstine climbed up into the back of the ambulance. The paramedics ducked inside, slammed the door, and the ambulance nosed into the thick traffic, siren wailing.

Nanny led Dorothy-Anne by the hand to Elizabeth-Anne's familiar yellow-and-black Rolls-Royce, which was double-parked a few yards away. Nanny's sharp eyes did not miss the fact that Henry Hale's limousine, which they had taken into the city, was gone. He had obviously used it for his escape.

They caught up with Mrs. Goldstine in the Hale Wing of Columbia Presbyterian. 'Any word on her condition?' Nanny asked as she and Dorothy-Anne joined Mrs. Goldstine in the waiting room.

Mrs. Goldstine shook her head. 'None yet. It's too early to tell, I'm afraid. Dr. Dadourian is in the emergency room. We'll just have to wait and see.'

They sat down and began their impatient vigil. The busy sounds of the hospital's emergency waiting room – the hurried coming and goings of doctors and nurses, the cries of patients and worries of their loved ones – all seemed to be taking place at a great distance. Dorothy-Anne was lost in another world of fear and confusion.

Nanny's face was pinched and set in an expression of tight anxiety. Mrs. Goldstine kept fidgeting, constantly consulting her tiny gold wristwatch, and jumping up to use the pay telephone.

'Did they get through to him?' Nanny asked the first time Mrs. Goldstine returned from calling Miss Schaber.

Elizabeth-Anne's secretary had shaken her head morosely. 'Nobody knows where to reach him,' she said, 'and the mobile phone in the limousine isn't being answered. This just isn't *like* him.'

Thereafter, each time Mrs. Goldstine returned from using the telephone, she merely shook her head in a negative response to the hopeful question in Nanny's eyes.

'I'll get us something to drink,' Mrs. Goldstine said finally, needing desperately to keep busy. She brought back three styrofoam beakers from the vending machine, but she and Nanny didn't take more than one sip from their coffee before putting their cups down. Dorothy-Anne finished off her hot chocolate. It was not at all rich and creamy like the cocoa the cook made at home, but the sitting and waiting in the big airless room for so long had made her thirsty.

After what seemed an eternity, Dr. Dadourian pushed open the swinging doors of the waiting room to see them. He was a large, burly man with bushy salt and pepper hair. As soon as they caught sight of him, Nanny and Mrs. Goldstine sprang to their feet but Dorothy-Anne, whose experience with Dr. Dadourian had been limited to countless childhood innoculations, tried to make herself look as inconspicuous as possible. She sat swallowed up in the big, green vinyl chair, her feet sticking straight out in the air in front of her.

'Mrs. Hale has suffered a severe stroke,' Dr. Dadourian said heavily in his thick, guttural accent.

'Can we see her?' Nanny asked eagerly.

'Not just yet, I'm afraid.'

'When *can* we see her?'

Dr. Dadourian sighed. 'Perhaps tomorrow, but I'm not certain you'll want to.'

Nanny looked at him in alarm. 'Why not, pray tell?'

Dr. Dadourian looked at Nanny and Mrs. Goldstine, then Dorothy-Anne. His eyes fell. 'Mrs. Hale won't respond to you,' he said quietly. 'She's in a coma.'

Dorothy-Anne didn't hear what he said, but she saw both Nanny and Mrs. Goldstine's faces turn white. After a moment, Nanny came over to her. 'Let's go home,' she said quietly.

And that was what Dorothy-Anne remembered of her fifth birthday.

4

The storm had worsened considerably. Flashes of lightning were followed by deafening peals of thunder as the wind-slashed rain hammered fiercely against the corrugated roof and the windows. Shrieking drafts of wind found their way inside the house, mocking the delusion of human shelter and threatening to throw the sheltered world into darkness. Dorothy-Anne felt it all swim before her eyes like a live creature.

Elemental chaos.

Angry gods.

Fear.

And pain.

Pain which was more than she could endure.

She was lying perfectly still now, her face shockingly white. She had no strength left to move. This contraction seemed the worst yet, seemed to take over her entire body with all-encompassing pain. Chills slashed up and down her spine while deep inside her, something which struggled to get out, whose time had come, was wedged unnaturally.

Was trapped.

Mrs. Ramirez sat in frightened silence. For a long time now she had been thinking, studying her memory, looking for some half-remembered answer. Long forgotten tidbits were recalled from the dark depths of her mind. A story told once surfaced slowly and rippled the pond of her memory.

But then it was gone, and her mind again was blank. I must remember! she told herself again.

She crossed herself, then glanced at the young mother-to-be. Dorothy-Anne Hale's eyes seemed lost in foggy thought, so far, far away.

Felicia Ramirez wondered where the young woman was, and what she was seeing.

Faraway.

Another time.

Another place.

The private recovery room of the Hale wing of Columbia Presbyterian Hospital.

It was a week after Elizabeth-Anne had come out of the coma. She had been unconscious for four months and three days. Upon awakening, the first visitor she had summoned was her grandson, Henry. She had warned him to be prepared. She expected a detailed report of business matters.

He was surprised when he walked into her room. She was confined to the bed, her legs rendered useless by the stroke, and he knew the prognosis was that she would never walk again. Fortunately, the doctors had said, she had suffered no other serious, long-term damage from the stroke. They promised she would eventually fully regain her strength and be able to carry on with her business.

Elizabeth-Anne, typically, wasn't about to sit around and wait for this to happen. She had never been sick in her life and was determined not to bow to illness now. If her strength was to be regained, she would see that it was in the shortest possible time.

Although the hospital continued to enforce a recuperative schedule, Elizabeth-Anne persuaded Dr. Dadourian
that she was at least well enough to visit with her grandson.
And for that, she would have to look her best.

After applying light make-up earlier that morning, she
had made a fuss until her hairstylist from Kenneth's was
allowed to come to her room. During the coma, her hair
had grown considerably and turned completely white. Now
she had it tinted its usual shade of sterling silver and set in a
permanent.

By the time Henry walked in, Elizabeth-Anne had never
looked better. She was sitting up straight in bed, wearing
not a hospital gown, but a beautifully embroidered bed
jacket. She was surrounded by piles of business-related
reading material – back issues of *Forbes*, *Fortune*, and
Business Week, as well as the *Wall Street Journal* and the
business sections of the *New York Times*. On the nightstand beside her, a pot of water was kept heated on a hot
plate, and a silver tea service, along with a can of herbal
tea, was within easy reach. The room was a mass of
flowers, with the more formal arrangements, sent by
friends and acquaintances, hidden behind forests of pink
peonies. She hated formal arrangements, and she had done
her best to hide them from sight.

Henry bent down to kiss her cheek. 'You look,' he said
pointedly, shaking his head in disbelief, 'like you're
vacationing on the Côte d'Azur.'

She smiled at him. 'Thank you, Henry dear. But a
forced vacation, I'm afraid, is really no vacation at all.'

'How are you feeling?'

'I'll feel a lot better,' she answered, 'once I know what's
been happening at Hale Hotels over the past four months.
Pull up a chair. I suggest you begin at once.'

They were at it for two hours. After the nurse insisted
Henry leave, Elizabeth-Anne sent for Dorothy-Anne and
Mrs. Goldstine. She napped before they arrived, but they
were allowed to visit for only fifteen minutes. Elizabeth-
Anne had little intention of respecting this directive, and
finally, Dr. Dadourian had to come personally to escort
Mrs. Goldstine and Dorothy-Anne out. He wasn't

surprised or annoyed by the chore; Vartan Dadourian had been a personal friend of Elizabeth-Anne's for years and knew her stubbornness. He wasn't even taken aback when Elizabeth-Anne pleaded to have Dorothy-Anne stay a minute more.

'For God's sake, Vartan, I just want to look at my great-granddaughter. After all, I haven't seen her for four months. You're not going to begrudge an old woman that, are you?'

He studied her chart. 'And since when do you consider yourself an "old" woman?'

She raised her chin stubbornly. 'When it suits me.'

He glanced sideways at her. 'I thought as much.'

Dorothy-Anne was allowed to stay, and what she witnessed was an extraordinary battle of wills. Because in one thing Dr. Dadourian was determined to have his way, and he was insisting that Elizabeth-Anne plan an extended stay at one of the European spas. She was equally dead set against such a plan.

'Vartan, I'm *not* sick. Perhaps a bit disoriented and weak, but that's not surprising, considering I feel like Rip Van Winkle must have after he woke up. I need a little time to catch up on things and gather my wits. But that's all.' Her years of stubborn pride would not allow her to admit she needed coddled care, and her bright eyes flashed like cold steel. 'I'll be damned if I'll allow myself to be hospitalized around sick people.'

'Those spas aren't exactly hospitals,' Dadourian corrected her.

'Well, as far as I'm concerned, they are.' Her eyes were steady. 'And don't tell me they're fashionable resorts. You know how I *hate* resorts of any kind. I *despise* programmed days and nights. I refuse to sit around water fountains in parks or take part in group therapy. And I *don't* need to take any curative waters, thank you very much. The water which pours out of my faucet at home suits me just fine.'

He sighed. 'You do try my patience sometimes, you know.'

'Vartan, if you didn't have me to spar with, you'd be bored to death.'

464

'You really do need rest and professional care,' he insisted gently. 'You need time to readjust, I repeat, *readjust* to life as it is experienced awake, as well as to adjust to the fact that you're paralyzed from the waist down. You need a period of *transition*.' He permitted himself a rare smile. 'Don't forget, you're not a spring chicken anymore.'

'No one knows that better than I.' Her lips smiled at him, but her eyes looked at him hard and long. He was a fine doctor, the finest there was. As well as the most expensive. But, most importantly, he was a decent man who had been a friend to her for years. Perhaps if he thought she needed therapy and rest, it was for the best. But not at one of those dreary dress-up spas where patients strolled around in minks. She didn't want it, and she wouldn't have it.

Suddenly, she remembered what Henry had first said to her and she had an idea. 'Vartan . . . ' she said thoughtfully, 'you know, maybe you *are* right after all. Perhaps a *vacation* – ' she stressed the word, ' – would do me some good. God knows, I haven't had one in decades.' Her lips tightened. 'But I don't want anything remotely smacking of hospitals and clinics and sanitoriums.'

He nodded slowly, suspiciously.

'And I won't go alone,' Elizabeth-Anne added. 'I'd be bored to tears and get far too restless.' Her eyes twinkled mischievously as she glanced across the room at Dorothy-Anne. 'I don't really want to go at all. I want you to know that for the record. But I'm not adverse to it under one condition.'

Dadourian sighed wearily. 'And what is that, pray tell?'

She smiled at her great-granddaughter. 'That Dorothy-Anne accompanies me.'

Dadourian turned around and stared at the child. Under the circumstances Elizabeth-Anne's five-year-old great-grandchild could only be a liability. What his old friend and patient needed was rest and therapy. However, the child did have a governess. Perhaps having company would even do her some good. That too could be therapy of sorts. Especially since the old woman and the young child were such fast friends. He turned back to Elizabeth-Anne. 'I suppose you'll take her whether I like it or not,' he said at last.

'I knew I could count on you, Vartan.'

Elizabeth-Anne settled upon the south of France. A real estate broker was called, and he combed the Maritime Alps until he found a suitable villa to lease. A local doctor was contacted who would drop by daily and keep his eye on her. Meanwhile, Henry had come up with a pride of private nurses who would accompany Elizabeth-Anne. There were three of them. The first a Miss Hepple, Elizabeth-Anne hated on sight. She was short and stout, a no-nonsense, middle-aged woman who was gruff and tight-lipped. Miss Hepple and Henry got along all too well for Elizabeth-Anne's liking. She could sniff out a spy when she saw one. She suspected that the woman had been instructed to report the slightest infraction of Dr. Dadourian's orders to Henry. She knew she would have to be careful. She wasn't planning on just lying around on chaises and sunning herself. She and Natalie Goldstine were going to be doing a lot of business over the telephone, contrary to doctor's orders. But she liked the other two nurses, Miss Bunt and Miss Kinney, and she sensed at once that they weren't very fond of the dour, overbearing Miss Hepple either.

The trip was planned swiftly. The Hale jet would fly Elizabeth-Anne, Dorothy-Anne, her nanny, and the three nurses to Paris, and then on to Nice. From there, hired cars would drive them to St. Paul de Vence.

The morning of the departure, Vartan Dadourian paid Elizabeth-Anne a last visit. 'You won't have to worry about a thing,' he assured her. 'Miss Hepple, Miss Kinney, and Miss Bunt are fine nurses. I've also arranged for a Fräulein Ilse Lang to meet you in St. Paul de Vence. She comes highly recommended. She's reputed to be the finest physical therapist in Europe.'

'And I suppose you'll tell me next that if anyone can help me walk again, it's she?'

He made a gesture of irritation. 'No, I won't. You know better than that. I've never kept anything from you in the past, and I'm not about to start doing that now. It's possible, of course, but none of us think you'll walk again. There has been too much damage.'

Elizabeth-Anne nodded. 'Thank you, Vartan. It's cruel of you, but I need to know the truth, not a bunch of lies.'

He eyed her sorrowfully. 'If I could – '

'I know you would.' She held his hand and smiled. 'And I'm grateful, really I am. Perhaps the vacation will even do me some good.' She bit down on her lip. 'If only Miss Hepple weren't coming,' she murmured.

'You don't like her?'

She met his eye. 'Not a bit. My grandson Henry chose her for me because she's his spy. I can tell. She'll report back to him on everything I do.'

'I could help recommend another nurse.'

She shook her head. 'Don't bother. Knowing Henry, he'd make sure she was another Miss Hepple. At least I know who I need to watch out for.'

Dadourian squinted his eyes dangerously. 'This doesn't mean you've lied to me, does it?'

'Lied to you?'

'Just remember what I told you. You're to do absolutely no work. At least not yet.' He paused. '*Absolutely* none.'

Elizabeth-Anne was not one to lie, even for convenience. She simply nodded vaguely, which she felt he could interpret any way he chose. She had extracted a solemn vow from Mrs. Goldstine to phone her regularly to keep her posted on any and all important business developments. She had a feeling that the transatlantic telephone wires would be buzzing. She knew all too well that if she, the center of power at Hale Hotels, was out of touch for too long, Henry could simply take over without anyone's knowing it. He could fire the staff which was loyal to her and replace them with his own people. Elizabeth-Anne alone could prevent this from happening. She knew once she lost control, she would have difficulty regaining it.

Henry was her grandson, and she loved him dearly, despite his faults. But he was hungry for power. Far too hungry, and with her gone, his appetite could be sated far too easily.

467

Somehow she would have to manage to keep him at bay.
The alternative was too frightening.

5

The villa was named Le Fleur de Matin, the Flower of the
Morning, and it was a picture postcard come to life.
Nestled on a wooded hillside high above Cannes, the
original portion of the house dated back to the thirteenth
century. Fortified, renovated and expanded many times
since, the villa was now an odd conglomeration of rambling
buildings. It ranged from one to four stories in height,
while a certain homogeity, and a guarantee of privacy, was
provided by high walls surrounding the entire six acre
property.

Upon arriving, Elizabeth-Anne stared up at the house as
the driver lifted her out of the car and gently set her down
into her wheelchair. She let out a sigh of relief, seeing at a
glance that she would be more than comfortable here. This
was a dream house, a fanciful collection of dark stained
wood and sturdy stone surroundings on a colonnaded, grown
vaulted terrace on three sides. Through the huge arches of
this terrace, one could see for miles, and directly below it
lay the villa's courtyard and garden, a sumptuous collection of cleverly clipped plane trees and lush vines.

While the drivers, supervised by Miss Kenney and Miss
Hepple, unloaded the mountains of luggage from the three
cars, the real estate agent showed Elizabeth-Anne and
Dorothy-Anne around. Even before they were shown the
inside of the house, both great-grandmother and great-
granddaughter were enchanted. This was their paradise,
their own secret garden.

The inside of the house posed few problems for
Elizabeth-Anne's wheelchair, as she could live entirely on
the ground floor. This arrangement was essential to her
fierce pride in self-sufficiency and need for relative freedom
of movement. All in all, the villa offered beauty, and
comfort and privacy.

But even paradise has its drawbacks.

Despite days filled with Ilse Lang's therapy exercises, Dorothy-Anne's company, and hours spent on the phone with Natalie Goldstine (who called under the code name 'Alicia' to throw off the prying Miss Hepple), Elizabeth-Anne found herself growing increasingly restless. She was sick and tired of constantly sitting, sitting, sitting. She came to despise her wheelchair. It was at once her mode of transportation as well as the symbol of her affliction.

But worst of all, she despised doing nothing. The therapy, the games, the telephone calls . . . it was all make-work. That was the worst part. She had spent a lifetime building and creating, managing and expanding. She ached for the thrill of accomplishment, the tension of even an average business day. There were only so many games one could play before one tired of them.

She felt as if she had been put out to pasture.

She would sit in the fragrant, shady courtyard and a single thought would enter her mind and fester there.

If only there was something to do.

It started out as a game.

It turned into Les Petits Palais, an entirely new string of ultra luxurious, small hotels operating under the Hale Hotels banner.

One early afternoon, after finishing lunch in the courtyard, Elizabeth-Anne and her great-granddaughter were in the midst of one of their usual, now lackadaisical, games. Dorothy-Anne would toss a huge, inflated beachball at her great-grandmother, who would catch it, toss it back to her, and then move her wheelchair around a tree to another position. Dorothy-Anne soon tired of it, for which Elizabeth-Anne was extremely grateful. It was a game which was boring beyond endurance and taxed her energies severely.

'Now we'll play hotel,' Dorothy-Anne announced out of the blue.

Elizabeth-Anne felt tired. She eyed her great-grand-daughter sadly, then closed her eyes for a moment. 'If only we could, darling,' she said. 'But this isn't a hotel.'

'Yes it is!' Dorothy-Anne nodded emphatically, secure in her childhood knowledge. A house was more than just four walls. It could be a cottage, or a castle, or even a hotel. 'We'll *pretend* it's a hotel. Anything's what you pretend it is.' She began to skip toward the house. She turned around and motioned excitedly for her great-grandmother to follow.

Shaking her head, Elizabeth-Anne pushed on the wheels of her chair. 'Where are we going?'

'Out front to the parking lot. We'll pretend we just got here, and we've got to unload our suitcases. That's the first thing that happens at a hotel, right?'

'It certainly is, young lady.' Elizabeth-Anne regarded Dorothy-Anne with warm affection, delighted by her eager imagination. But Elizabeth-Anne wanted to play this new game even less than she'd wanted to play ball. It would only emphasize how far she was from her empire, from the heart of the passion which made her tick. But she was determined not to disappoint her favorite little girl; and besides, without Dorothy-Anne's company and vivacity, life would be completely unbearable.

So Elizabeth-Anne followed Dorothy-Anne up to the house along the gently sloping ramp which had been constructed over the raised threshold, and then through the cool, dim downstairs halls and out to the large raked-gravel parking lot outside the walls. She looked at her great-granddaughter curiously. 'Well? What do you suggest we do now?'

Dorothy-Anne's eyes sparkled. 'I'm riding in a car. See?' She raced to the end of the long drive, dwarfed by the two facing, sentinel rows of cypruses lining the smooth expanse of gravel, oblivious to Elizabeth-Anne's cries of caution. Then she spun around and came rushing back the way she had gone, but her demeanor had changed. She was pretending to drive a car, her hands clasped around an invisible steering wheel. She pulled up beside Elizabeth-Anne with a pretended screech that drove Elizabeth-Anne to clap her hands over her ears.

Dorothy-Anne snuck a tiny, sideways flick of an eye at Elizabeth-Anne. 'Now I'm getting out, getting my luggage,' she explained.

She mimed it to perfection, a wealthy dowager stepping out of the car, nonchalantly slamming the door and unlocking the trunk. She lifted out two enormously heavy, invisible suitcases and lugged them up to the front door.

'Wait,' Elizabeth-Anne called quickly. Despite herself, she was getting caught up in the game. 'A porter has to come running and get the suitcases for you. A lady never needs to carry her own luggage. Not at a fine hotel!'

'Oh yes! Here he comes now.' Dorothy-Anne quickly set down her imaginary luggage and placed her hands on her hips. 'You're late, young man!' she chided threateningly, parodying someone she'd once heard. 'This is no way to earn a tip.' She glanced at Elizabeth-Anne. 'What do I do now?'

'You tell him you have a reservation.'

Dorothy-Anne held her head high with regal hauteur. 'I have a reservation,' she announced importantly.

The game continued for an hour. Dorothy-Anne 'checked in' at the 'front desk,' a refectory table in the hall behind which Elizabeth-Anne quickly wheeled herself, pretending to be the concierge. Dorothy-Anne was then led by an invisible bellboy to the nonexistent elevator. She rode upstairs to her room (which was really still on the ground floor), and then she had lunch in the courtyard.

And as Elizabeth-Anne watched the fantastic game, something slowly began to stir in the back of her mind.

A small lobby with a desk, precisely where the refectory table was located.

The image flashed through her thoughts, and she closed her eyes.

All around her, the building seemed to come to life. She could almost hear the sounds of clattering dishes in the courtyard, the murmurs of earnest conversation, the lighthearted tinkle of silvery laughter. She could almost feel people gazing down from the colonnaded terrace above her.

The quiet, whispering feet of bellboys.
The ringing of the concierge's bell.
The scraping of suitcases on the tiled floor.

Startled, she opened her eyes and gazed around. Lithe,

dancing fingertips prickled up and down her spine. A powerful surge of excitement billowed through her, and her eyes glittered with feverish excitement.

'Great-Granny!' Dorothy-Anne called urgently. 'What is it? Is something wrong? You didn't bring me my drink!'

But Elizabeth-Anne didn't hear her. She was lost deep in thought. She was in another world. The very world Dorothy-Anne had described to her earlier.

Anything's what you wanted it to be.

Yes! It could be!

Slowly she spun her wheelchair around and gazed up at the immense, rambling house. The more she thought about it, the more she realized that it *could* be more than a villa. It really could! It could be –

A hotel.

A small, intimate luxury hotel in the heart of Provence. From what the help had told her, there were countless bedrooms upstairs.

The farmhouse next door was deserted; a gallery could connect the two buildings.

The courtyard would be the dining area.

She glanced up at the colonnaded loggia. The loggia would be yet another dining room.

An elevator would have to be installed.

A staff found.

More bathrooms put in.

But the kitchen was big enough. She had seen it.

The thoughts raced through her mind, one upon another.

Suddenly she reached out and pulled Dorothy-Anne close. 'Darling!' Her whisper was solemn and intense, but her face was radiant. 'How would you like to turn this house into a hotel. A *real* hotel?'

Dorothy-Anne stared at her. 'Oh, Great-Granny,' she breathed finally. '*Yes*.'

'But it's got to be a secret,' Elizabeth-Anne warned. 'No one must know.'

'Oh, I can keep a secret. I promise.'

Elizabeth-Anne raised her chin with satisfaction. She had found something to do.

Now came the logistics.

Buying the property, as well as the one next door. *If* they were for sale.

Finagling finances; her banks were located three thousand miles away. Large sums of money would have to be transferred to a local bank. She couldn't use Hale Hotels money; Henry would get wind of it immediately. But she had millions of her own tucked away.

Hiring a contractor. And a hand-picked staff.

And while all that was going on, she had to be certain Miss Hepple was far removed from it all. For now, she would change her to the night shift. And, something else hadn't escaped her sharp eyes. She had noticed the dour woman staring at the young, live-in gardener. She hated to do it. She was a business woman, not a pimp. However, no one knew better than she that special circumstances required special solutions.

A thousand francs changed hands. The gardener began to speak to Miss Hepple, who was icy and insulting. And intrigued.

The real estate agent who had leased Elizabeth-Anne the house was sent to Paris, where he successfully negotiated for its sale.

Two million dollars were wired from New York to the local bank.

The deserted farmhouse next door was soon hers too.

Another thousand francs were paid to the gardener. Miss Hepple was thawing, and soon he was taking her on long drives around the countryside. His instructions were specific: to keep the nurse away for as long a period of time each day as was humanly possible. Miss Hepple quickly became an authority on the local landscape and customs.

Soon the time was ripe. Elizabeth-Anne gave the gardener twenty thousand francs, and the promise that his job would not be jeopardized. He then lured Miss Hepple into an upstairs bedroom, where he and the unsuspecting nurse were 'accidentally' discovered making love. The gardener was 'fired' on the spot, and Miss Hepple was sent home in disgrace. Elizabeth-Anne called Henry and assured him that two nurses and one therapist were quite adequate. Besides, she insinuated, after the incident with Miss Hepple, she could no longer trust his judgment when it came to hiring nurses. The young gardener was immediately rehired.

Money spoke. And spoke.

As the renovations on the villa progressed and Elizabeth-Anne immersed herself in other arrangements, she came to glorious life. She had never felt better or looked better. She supervised every step of the villa's conversion. It was a game – a game that cost millions – but even Ilse Lang agreed that it was the best therapy Elizabeth-Anne could have had.

She was building another hotel, but one so vastly different in concept from the others, that it was a true challenge. And she was doing it all behind Henry's and Vartan Dadourian's back. She relished simply pulling it off and proving to herself, once and for all, that a wheelchair-ridden old woman need not stop living or working. But best of all, the conversion of Le Fleur de Matin from villa to hotel became a labor of love for everyone involved, and that was the key to its subsequent success.

Never had Elizabeth-Anne known so many people working hand in hand. The construction workers became her fast friends; two of them in particular, Bertrand Delcroix and Francois Bricteux, became not only her protectors, but co-conspirators. Early in the morning on certain days, they would lift her, wheelchair and all, into the back of their open lorry, tie the chair securely down, and then hoist Doroty-Anne up beside her great-grand-mother. Then the truck would rumble off, with Elizabeth-Anne in her throne in the back, holding a parasol, while Dorothy-Anne gazed out over the tailgate. It was a sight which made her famous to all Provence.

But these extraordinary outings did not merely serve as entertainment for an eccentric old woman. Elizabeth-Anne was on a mission. Bertrand and Francois drove her all over Provence and the neighboring provinces of Dauphine and Languedoc, scouring the countryside for anything which would embellish their jewel-like little hotel.

Their frequent searches for art and antiques paid off

handsomely. Invariably, they returned to Le Fleur de Matin at night loaded down with precious finds. For instance, at a fifteenth century château which was being demolished, they haggled for an ancient, fifteen-foot high, baronial fireplace mantel. They scoured far and wide for more fireplaces; every room was to have one. They bought antique Provençal beds and chairs, and then they discovered the richest, most unexpected find of all – a huge, marble, pre-Christian era sarcophagus which was to become the famed bar in the courtyard. After they transported it back, it was discovered that it was too huge to fit through the gates. Undaunted, Elizabeth-Anne ordered a section of the wall ripped out, and the sarcophagus was moved in.

The villa was connected to the neighboring farmhouse by a two-story, arched gallery and the buildings became one. The new structure was even more rambling, and thus charming, than the last. The colonnaded loggia over-looking the courtyard became the protected dining terrace Elizabeth-Anne had envisioned, and she spent hours there, thanks to the elevator she had installed which gave her freedom of movement throughout the four floors.

Elizabeth-Anne decided that the staff of this tiny hotel must be exceptionally gracious, and she hand-picked every-one from the concierge to the chef, who she lured from a three-star restaurant in Dauphine. Small wonder, then, that Le Fleur de Matin became an exclusive club of sorts. Everyone said that staying there was like staying with friends. Which was, Elizabeth-Anne congratulated herself, exactly what she had set out to do in the first place.

However, even she had not dared to predict the hotel's phenomenal success. It had been a therapeutic labor of love, and because of that, she'd have been content to underwrite a losing proposition. Instead, she found herself most pleasantly surprised. Although, with its mere twenty-five guest rooms, it was the smallest of all the Hale Hotels, Le Fleur de Matin quickly became the most famous in the entire chain, and one of the most celebrated inns in the world. Within its very first season its standing as the favorite haunt of internationally known artists, writers, and film stars was firmly established. It was at once forbiddingly expensive, terribly exclusive, and overwhelmingly casual – but on the intimate, lovely, and friendly scale that few first class hotels ever achieved.

As the years passed, Elizabeth-Anne was to create other *Les Petits Palais*, the small palaces, as she called them. They were all conceived along the same lines of exclusivity and beauty as Le Fleur de Matin, and were all just as hugely successful. The second was a Tuscan villa with muraled rooms and formal gardens that overlooked Florence. Next, Elizabeth-Anne found a turreted, white, fairy-tale château on the Loire which overlooked the farmlands and river from within its one-hundred-acre wooded park. Then a fifteen-story, stucco villa rising from the beach up an entire hillside in Puerto Vallerta, each floor boasting its own tiled swimming pool overlooking the Pacific Ocean. And the list went on from there, each more fantastically beautiful and warmly charming than the last.

These were Elizabeth-Anne's pride and true passion; with *Les Petits Palais* her role of the innkeeper as hostess was brought one step closer to her lifelong idea. She became the chatelaine of far-flung palaces and villas, as well as friend and confidante to the world's most celebrated guests. Even heads of state were drawn to these private hotels, many to write their memoirs, some just to relax in the rarefied, enchanted atmosphere. Selectivity was the key to the success of Les Petits Palais, for they were the very essence of the lifestyles of the rich and famous. They quickly became one of the worst-kept secrets in the world.

6

Although no one knew it, as 1985 began, the last days of Elizabeth-Anne Hale's life were drawing to a close. There were some things Elizabeth-Anne told everyone, some things she confided only to her nearest and dearest, and a few things she kept to herself and never told a soul. The cancer was one of the things she kept to herself. She didn't see any reason to upset her family and friends by telling them about it. Everyone would know soon enough, anyway.

Above all, Elizabeth-Anne didn't want Dorothy-Anne to know. She and Freddie were too happy. Bad news traveled fast. Too fast, she thought as the big yellow-and-black Rolls-Royce sailed sagaciously through the thick New Jersey rain.

Elizabeth-Anne rested her chin on her hand as she stared out the rain-streaked window. The tires hissed on the wet pavement, and the windshield wipers thumped steadily, tossing aside the heavy, thick sheets of rain.

Suddenly, Elizabeth-Anne pressed the button which lowered the glass partition between her and the driver. With the sterling head of her Baccarat crystal cane, she rapped on the slowly descending glass. 'Faster, Max,' she said urgently.

Max hesitated, his eyes glancing at Elizabeth-Anne in the rearview mirror. She seemed so strong, so sure of herself. But her usual, imperturbable calm had for once deserted her. 'We're already going the speed limit, Mrs. Hale, ma'am,' he said politely. 'The road's slick. Everybody else has slowed down.'

'My vision is still excellent, thank you,' Elizabeth-Anne replied crisply. 'Perhaps those people are not pressed for time.' She paused deliberately. 'I *am*. And you might bear in mind, Max, that I am *not* everybody else.'

He took a deep breath and tightened his grip on the steering wheel. This was the first time she had ever chewed him out, or told him how to drive. He let out the deep breath slowly. 'Yes, ma'am, Mrs. Hale.'

'Well? Then step on the gas!'

Elizabeth-Anne sat painfully forward and craned her neck so that she could see the speedometer inching upwards until it reached seventy-five miles per hour. The car was a tank, nearly three-and-a-half tons of fine-tuned machinery, and once momentum was achieved, it surged majestically forward through the rain.

A satisfied expression came into Elizabeth-Anne's blue

eyes. She sat back in her seat and pressed the button; the glass partition rose soundlessly.

She pushed up the cuff of her white silk blouse to glance at her wristwatch, then sighed. Rush or no, the watched pot never boils. She decided to try to get some work done, hoping that, once immersed, she would lose all track of time.

Still, she couldn't help wishing that she weren't so vain. Flying to Baltimore would have been much easier, but Max would have had to carry her from the car onboard the plane, and upon arriving a virtual stranger would have had to carry her off. She couldn't bear the thought of it. Then, too, Max was the only person she trusted to keep mum about her whereabouts. Anyone else was bound to talk. It was still too early to let anyone know why she was visiting the Johns Hopkins University Hospital.

As long as the car ride didn't take much more than four hours, she preferred driving to taking a jet anyway. A lengthy car ride was difficult enough. She always had to plan in advance, cutting down on her fluid intake twelve hours before each ride so that rest stops were not necessary. Something as simple as going to the bathroom was no longer simple. Oh, how she hated this infirmity! Her fierce independence was rankled no end by her powerless, atrophied legs. She despised having to use the wheelchair. She'd been in it for years, and she still hadn't been able to get used to it. She was only grateful that at least she had enough money to be able to employ people to compensate for her legs.

She sighed angrily. All her life long she had despised people who felt sorry for themselves. The last thing she needed now was to join their ranks.

Without further hesitation, she reached for the Vuitton attache case on the seat beside her. The sturdy, miniature suitcase had served her well for decades; just the sight of it reassured her now.

She placed the case on her lap, flipped it open, and reached for her small, Ben Franklin-style reading glasses. Perching them on her nose, she snapped on her reading lamp and took out a three-inch thick report bound in clear plastic. She gazed down at it. Printed at the top right-hand side of the page was a letterhead:

Hale Real Estate Acquisitions Board
Empire State Building
350 Fifth Avenue
New York, New York 10001

The logo at the top left-hand corner of the page was the emblem of Hale Hotels, Inc., a blanket corporation and the parent company of the sprawling empire Elizabeth-Anne had built. The symbols of her home state, Texas, were artfully intertwined: a stylized pecan tree, a mockingbird, and a bluebonnet inside a Lone Star outlined in blue. On either side of the Lone Star were two smaller red stars, four altogether, symbolizing not only the state where her empire had had its roots, but that rarest of the rare in the hotel business: a conglomeration of five-star hotels worldwide.

The title of the report was neatly centered on the thick cream stationery:

COMPILED FEASIBILITY STUDY
Potential Conversion
of Central Park South Site
into
Mayfair Hale Hotel

And under the title were typed the legends:

Property Still Open For Negotiation
Other Known Bidders: None
Suspected Secret Bidders: None

Hotel Possibilities Previously Explored By . Best Western
. Helmsley
. Sheraton

Elizabeth-Anne's face creased into a frown. She would have to check into just why the other three hotel corporations had turned down the site. But she was gratified to see the red ink stamped onto the title page and onto each of the subsequent 526 pages within. The single word warned: CONFIDENTIAL. Smaller red letters, also stamped, further warned:

ORIGINAL ONLY COPY IN EXISTENCE
UNDER NO CIRCUMSTANCES
MAKE COPIES OF ORIGINAL

The melodrama was, in fact, necessary. Elizabeth-Anne had long ago learned that corporate espionage was rife even in the hotel business. Furthermore, when it was learned that Hale Hotels had its eye, however lazily, on a certain piece of property, she could count on the real estate price invariably, greedily, skyrocketing. To counter this, once the Hale Acquisitions Board had recommended a certain property be bought and she had endorsed it, the sale was slyly negotiated through a third, secretive party.

She opened the report and began to read.

The feasibility of the new hotel, indeed all the possible pros and cons which could be imagined, had been discussed in scrupulous detail. The report started by cold-bloodedly reducing the property and its existing, sweetly gaudy Belle Epoque-style building to their value in dollars and cents, then projected the future worth of the property alone under various depressed and inflated financial climates. It had also predicted the cost of converting the building into a hotel, as opposed to the staggering fortune necessary to raze the structure and start from scratch. It then went on to project the number of rooms versus the years the hotel would have to operate at various vacancy percentages in the red, before it could be turned around to operate in the black.

The legal department had studied that essentially New York phenomenon: the effects a potentially outraged citizen's group would have upon the razing, or even conversion, of the existing building, if it decided to fight to protect the structure by seeking landmark status for it.

An independent marketing survey rated existing New York hotels and had sent out 15,000 questionnaires to regular Hale Hotels business customers, whose addresses were on file in the central Hale data bank. The return-postage-paid questionnaire sought answers as to what, in particular, enticed travelers to any one hotel.

The creative department had mapped out the potential hotel's particular style: from ballroom, to theme restaurants, all the way down to the last napkin ring.

The hotel managers of the existing Hale Hotels reported on what essential services all world-wide hotels offered, what significant services were offered exclusively by Hale Hotels, what was lacking in any one hotel, and what, in particular, would make the projected new Hale Hotel far more desirable than any other hotel in the city and, indeed, the world.

The in-depth coverage of all possibilities was mind-boggling.

Elizabeth-Anne felt overwhelmed by it. Nothing had been like this in the beginning. No longer was the slightest, most seemingly inconsequential item left to acumen, instinct, chance, and a galloping, maverick, gambling spirit. It made her feel somehow useless, as if she were a lone dinosaur plodding through the modern world. And she wasn't at all certain that she liked the way the business world had changed. In the age of computers and surveys, she had no choice but bow to the report writers. But that didn't mean she had to like it. Everything was so . . . so cut and dried. The chances for errors were greatly reduced. But, somehow, that had taken all the *life* out of it.

She felt a tinge of regret, and a stirring of gratitude . . . gratitude that she had been born when she had, at a time when a person could still have vision and spunk and fulfill their dreams on ne'er but faith and hard work.

She closed the report, marking her place with her thumb. Taking off her glasses, she pinched the bridge of her nose, then stared out the rain-streaked window. The visibility was even worse than before, and the tattoo of rain on the roof was a muffled, but constant drumbeat.

With an abrupt gesture, she slammed the report back into her attache case. She had been a fool to even open it! She was in no mood to deal with work now. She couldn't simply distract herself from the mental anguish that plagued her. There was no turning away from the inevitability of the truth. Perhaps when the trip was over, when her mind was once again fresh and at rest, reassured about her own future, she could pick up the report again. But not until then.

Not until the tumor inside her, of which no one but she and the doctors were aware, was cut out, exorcised from her body.

The doctors had assured her that her chances were good, despite her age.

Why, then, did she feel so darkly convinced that she was dying? That this was the beginning of the end?

7

These memories. There were so many of them.

Time seemed to have become frozen, and the minutes stopped ticking.

She felt something soft and deliciously cool against her forehead. She opened her eyes and smiled wanly up at Mrs. Ramirez. 'I'm scared,' she whispered.

'Do not be.' Mrs. Ramirez smiled with gentle reassurance. 'It will be fine. Everything will turn out fine. See?' She stopped wiping Dorothy-Anne's head, reached into the front of her blouse, and held out a tiny glittering medallion hanging from a thread-thin gold chain. 'It is the medal of the Blessed Virgin. I wear it all the time. José, a nephew of mine, he and his wife went to Fatima. They brought it back.' She paused. 'It has been blessed.' On an impulse, Mrs. Ramirez put down the cloth, reached behind her neck, and unclasped the necklace. Then she hung it around Dorothy-Anne's neck. 'You wear for now. The Blessed Mother, she look after me. Now she look after you, too.'

'Thank you,' Dorothy-Anne whispered.

She watched Mrs. Ramirez rinsing out the cloth in a bowl. Then the big woman crossed the room, then stopped in the shadows near the doorway. 'I see about the telephone. Maybe is already fixed.'

Dorothy-Anne heard Mrs. Ramirez's voice, but the face did not seem to belong to her. Suddenly the face she saw was a handsome one with a stubborn chin and the angular cheekbones, a head of silver hair, and arresting aquamarine eyes with their wise, all-knowing expression.

Dorothy-Anne sighed softly and shut her eyes. 'Great-Granny,' she whispered, although she knew it could not be. Not here. Not today. Not ever again.

*   *   *

It had been the last time she had seen her great-grandmother alive.

Three short days ago a lifetime that had spanned the better part of the century had ended.

It had been the night of Elizabeth-Anne's greatest triumph, the crowning touch to an empire which had been forged out of nothing.

The crowning gem: The Hale Castle.

It was Elizabeth-Anne's shining achievement, a lasting monument to herself and her family, to her dream.

Only now that she looked back on it did Dorothy-Anne realize that the day the Hale Castle had been conceived had been the beginning of the end. She should have realized it at the start – that the grandest of all the grand hotels would be Great-Granny's last achievement. But how could she have known? Great-Granny had always been building and expanding. It had been in her life's blood. Only after it was all over, and Elizabeth-Anne was dead, had she realized the truth.

Elizabeth-Anne Hale had been secretly battling the cancer for years, but had never let anyone know. She had sent her loved ones away on business trips or vacations, or had disappeared herself, supposedly to relax, but in truth to enter the hospital for surgery or treatments. She had done it all quietly behind everyone's back. And while the cancer was eating deeper and deeper, and her time was running out, she had gone on to build her greatest achievement of them all, and had fought to live until the day it was completed.

It only proved to Dorothy-Anne how little she knew of the remarkable woman to whom she had been so close all her life.

All those years together – and yet in the end Elizabeth-Anne hadn't confided her deepest secret.

Oh, how could I have been so blind?

For three long and sleepless days and nights now, she had been torturing herself with that same question.

Even on that last night, I didn't realize she was at the point of death.

But how could she have known? Even on that last night

483

of Elizabeth-Anne Hale's life, during the inauguration of the newest star in the hotel chain, the old lady had gathered the last remaining vestiges of her strength and had given the illusion that all was well with the world and with herself.

The inauguration had been more than just that. It had been Great-Granny's farewell party to all she held near and dear.

And no one had known it until after it was over.

The grand ballroom of the Hale Castle had been filled to capacity. Two thousand guests had been invited, and over eighteen hundred had shown up. At Elizabeth-Anne's request, Dorothy-Anne stood on the right side of the wheelchair on the dais, Freddie on the left. They each held one of Elizabeth-Anne's hands. Behind the chair, Miss Bunt stood silent with grim decorum, an expressionless sphinx whose eyes alone gave away her impatience with Elizabeth-Anne's insistence on attending what she considered a senseless event. In a group off to one side were Henry and Chessy, although Regina had not traveled all the way from California for the event.

The pride glowed in Dorothy-Anne's face. She didn't think she had ever seen her great-grandmother looking quite as beautiful as she did on this particular evening. There was something regal about the way she sat poised in her wheelchair, as thought it were a throne. And why shouldn't she be such a commanding presence? Dorothy-Anne asked herself. Elizabeth-Anne was, after all, the supreme ruler of an empire that dotted the globe, and she looked every inch the royal sovereign.

At ninety, her eyes were lively and sparkling, and her aquamarine silk gown lent her a delicate, luminous beauty. Her face wore an expression of ceremonial amusement as though she were being entertained by an army of court jesters. Occasionally, she would tilt her head sideways and look up at Dorothy-Anne through her hooded eyes, a sly twinkle saying, 'See? See what we've done together, you and I? All is revel and merriment. They kow-tow to me, and tell me what they think I want to hear, but deep inside they all hate me. And you know why? They're wondering how we've done it, that's why? But we'll never tell them the secret. Vision and hard work, daring to dream, and putting every last bit of energy behind it - that's all it took, and the fools don't even know it! They all think it was some kind of luck or magic, or, worst yet, a talent of mine! Oh, if they only knew the truth, how disappointed they'd all be.'

Dorothy-Anne saw all this in her great-grandmother's gaze and, squeezing her hand, she nodded happily as tears shone in her eyes. Beneath the voluminous folds of her maternity gown, her child was approaching the time for delivery. A new child was soon to be born, the first of Great-Granny's great-great-grandchildren. 'I hope it's a girl,' Elizabeth-Anne had confided in her only a few days earlier. 'In this family it's the *women* who make the difference. Oh, don't get me wrong. The men have done their share. But the women - they're the strength, the backbone! Oh yes, I *do* hope it's a girl! What more could a silly old woman want?'

A great-great-granddaughter.

And the Hale Castle, conceived and built against all odds, completed at long last.

Yes, what else indeed?

No wonder she looks so happy, Dorothy-Anne thought. *This is her moment to bask in the sun. And she deserves it, by God. She deserves every last accolade, every bit of comfort, every outpouring of love and respect. Ninety, going on ninety-one this week, and she's still not resting on her laurels.*

Instead, she had built the Hale Castle. All told, the cost had come to more than a quarter of a billion dollars after the price of the property, design, construction, and decor had been tallied. It was said to be the single most expensive structure in the entire world.

It towered seventy-two stories above Fifth Avenue in midtown. Just to accumulate the entire square block property had taken several years of patient, secret bidding. Dozens of real-estate agents, none of whom were aware of the identity of his client, had bought up the individually owned parcels of land, one by one. Then the existing buildings had been razed, the rubble trucked off, and the foundations dug. Elizabeth-Anne had hired one of the nation's pre-eminent architects to design the Hale Castle. Not for her one of those carbon copy, steel and glass boxes. She wanted something that would add an extra cachet – her own – to the New York skyline.

Dorothy-Anne had sat through many of the countless meetings between client and architect, and she had followed every phrase of the progress closely.

'You have carte blanche,' Elizabeth-Anne was fond of telling the architect, half in jest, half in seriousness, 'as long as I end up with what *I* want.'

The architect had laughed, but Elizabeth-Anne's vision had been specific and he found himself inspired by it. She wanted a modern building of medieval style. The plaza would be graced by a modern version of a medieval draw-bridge and a moat with a narrow reflecting pool. She wanted the public rooms to be imposing, 'baronial' in scope. And the top was to be crowned with turrets and towers, like something out of a childhood fairy tale.

The architect had managed to achieve all this brilliantly. From the moment that the plans were first made public, the building became the focus of a raging architectural debate heard round the world. Some critics praised the daring design concepts combining the fifteenth and twenty-first centuries; other denounced it as an abomination.

Elizabeth-Anne knew she had made her statement.

She was delighted. The furor only fueled everyone's excitement, and it was the sort of publicity that no amount of money could ever have bought.

And, once the luxury palace had been completed – ready for occupancy by the hotel, as well as condominium buyers and office space renters – Elizabeth-Anne had further amazed her staff. 'Charge through the nose,' she had instructed. 'Make it as expensive and exclusive as it can possibly be.'

And as she knew it would, the Hale Palace had snared the rich, the famous, and the powerful. One Arab business-man bought three entire floors of condominiums, and combined them to become what was probably the largest and most expensive triplex – including indoor swimming pool – in all of New York, possibly the world. Even before the building had opened, all but two of the ninety condominiums had been sold.

Now, watching Elizabeth-Anne closely, Dorothy-Anne reveled in the excitement of the glittering event before them. Their guests had come from near and far. The mayor, governor and vice president were rubbing shoulders with supreme court justices, society dowagers, businessmen, tycoons, members of the press, novelists, and film stars. All the movers and shakers had come out in full force to celebrate the grand opening.

It had all the makings of a Hollywood premier, down to the red carpet on the sidewalk and the searchlights crisscrossing the sky.

By ten o'clock, the reception line had long since fizzled out, a fact for which Elizabeth-Anne was extremely grateful. The palms of her hands were sweaty. She was feeling tired, and wished the party were already over, but she had the determination of a last wish, a last goal to achieve to carry her through. Once she had done what she had come to do, then she would have her rest. A long and final rest.

She glanced over at the orchestra and caught the conductor's eye. At a signal from her, he added a few, flourishing finale notes to the dance music and then moved straight into a pulsating rendition of 'If You Wish Upon A Star.'

'This is it.' Elizabeth-Anne turned to Dorothy-Anne. 'Wish me luck.'

Dorothy-Anne smiled, leaned down, and kissed her great-grandmother on the cheek. 'Good luck, Great-Granny. Though I'm sure you won't need it. You never do.'

'Flattery,' the old lady said crisply, 'will get you everywhere.' She twisted her head around to look up at Miss Bunt. She gave a regal nod, and the ever-faithful nurse wheeled the chair forward, to the edge of the dais. As soon as the music came to a crescendo, the lights dimmed, and a single white spot bathed Elizabeth-Anne in its startling, silvery glow.

The ballroom became very quiet. People pushed their

way forward and faced the dais. A gray-haired man in a tuxedo was setting up a microphone in front of Elizabeth-Anne.

Elizabeth-Anne smiled her thanks at him. Then she cleared her throat and spoke in her precise, ringing voice. 'Ladies and gentlemen, I thank you all for coming and making the inauguration of this building such a success. And I thank you even more for taking a few minutes out to listen to the ramblings of an old woman.' After some polite laughter, she went on.

'As you all probably know, many said it couldn't be done. Not a building like this.' She waved one hand in a dramatic gesture. 'Not one combining stores, offices, rental apartments, condominiums, and a hotel. In fact – ' She broke off and allowed herself a nervous little laugh. 'For a while there, I wasn't quite so sure it could be done, either.' She pretended to let out a deep breath of relief, and the crowd again laughed good-naturedly.

'Nevertheless.' She clapped her hands together. 'What is done is done, and I'm glad it's finished. The New York skyline has changed a little bit once again, and that is what gives this marvelous city its magical excitement and its character. I love the constant state of flux, of things always changing. I'm proud to have been part of it for so long.

'I love this city. I came here in 1928, and I've been here ever since. I've been proud to call myself a New Yorker. This city has been good to many of us, and to no one so much as myself.'

She paused again as a murmur of approval rippled through the crowd.

'However, to show you just how much times change, and without taking too long, I would like to read you an advertisement which Hale Hotels ran recently in the *New York Times*.'

She turned around and held out her hand. Miss Bunt produced a pair of reading glasses and a newspaper clipping. Carefully, Elizabeth-Anne put on the glasses.

'I should warn you that I wasn't even aware that this advertisement had gone in. Of course, why should I be? Hale Hotels has become so big that I really can't know

488

what's going on in every department. Anyway, I saw this advertisement and I read it. Now I would like to share it with you.

' "Technical Support Analyst. Hale Hotels Corporation has an immediate opening for a Data Processing professional to handle new software releases, evaluate software packages, troubleshoot program inefficiencies, system tune the IBM 38 and provide procedures and standards for a group of programmer analysts. The ideal candidate will have a college degree, at least three years of RPG III experience, and in-depth knowledge of the IBM 38." ' She took off her glasses and folded her hands in her lap, then stared out at the sea of upturned faces. 'What the *hell*,' she asked with a wry smile 'are "troubleshooting program inefficiencies," "system tune" and "RPG three?" '

There was a roar of laughter, and thunderous applause.

She nodded. 'My sentiments exactly. It just goes to show how much times change. Why, for heaven's sake, I started Hale Hotels without even graduating from high school! However, I'm too old and cantankerous, and much too set in my ways to start changing now. So, in light of this, and in light of the fact that I'll be turning ninety-one this week – '

A burst of thunderous applause cut her off. She had to wait for it to subside before continuing. She inclined her head. 'Thank you, thank you,' she said crisply. 'However, longevity itself does not deserve applause. Nor does success which is directly due to longevity. As *Forbes Magazine* quoted me as saying in a recent interview, anyone can get where I've gotten. You've only got to live long enough.'

There was more applause and laughter.

'Now, down to serious business. Since I've finally grown up and decided to join the ranks of senior citizens, I might as well start collecting my social security. Therefore, I would now like to appoint my successor. Lord knows, everyone has waited long enough for this moment. Well, it is finally that time. *At long last.* I think I could use a little peace and quiet. After all, I'm no longer as young as I used to be.'

There was more hearty applause; the orchestra broke into a few stanzas of 'Auld Lang Syne.'

Elizabeth-Anne held up her hands to silence the guests. 'It is possible,' she said with typical candor, 'that when you first see who I've chosen to succeed me, you'll say to yourself, "Well, the old girl's finally flipped her lid."' She smiled patiently, shook her head, and wagged an admonishing finger. 'Believe me, I haven't. I built this corporation when I was a single mother raising four children, and though I'm not the spring chicken I once was, I *am* of sound mind and body. Furthermore, as the advertisement I have read to you indicates, it is indeed time for young blood to take over.' She paused and took a deep breath. 'Ladies and gentlemen, I am proud to introduce my successor, the new, and probably the youngest-ever chairman of the board of a corporation of this size, Dorothy-Anne Hale Cantwell.' And with that, Elizabeth-Anne took her great-granddaughter's hand in hers and lifted it high.

Dorothy-Anne stared down at her great-grandmother, open-mouthed. Tears were welling up in her eyes. 'Me?' she asked in disbelief.

'Yes, you,' Elizabeth-Anne answered. 'You will succeed me as head of the Hale empire I have built.'

There was thunderous applause as Elizabeth-Anne was wheeled back a few feet on the dais, holding Dorothy-Anne's hand in her own.

'Like me, when I first started out, you are soon a mother,' Elizabeth-Anne told her great-granddaughter. 'But that is beside the point. Women are just as capable of running a business as men, and mothers as capable as single women. It's up to you to prove that and clear out the myths.' She smiled. 'Believe me, darling, nobody is as well suited, or as talented, to run Hale Hotels as you. Nor do I trust anyone else as implicitly. You've been living hotels ever since you were a baby. Do you remember?'

Dorothy-Anne looked as though she was going to burst out crying. 'Do I remember?' she whispered. 'How could I ever forget?'

She laughed then, feeling the tension break, and wiped her eyes. Leaning down as far as her swollen belly allowed, she embraced Elizabeth-Anne. Then Freddie kissed both their cheeks in turn. The other members of the family stepped forward to offer their congratulations to Dorothy-Anne. Only Henry did so perfunctorily, a cold, fathomless look in his eyes. For an instant, Dorothy-Anne felt a pang of regret. She knew that her father had always thought he would be the one to step into Elizabeth-Anne's place when she retired. At forty-one, this could only be a bitter disappointment to him. But she knew there was nothing she could do. They had never mended the open wound between them. Dorothy-Anne couldn't reach out to him now.

Elizabeth-Anne took a deep breath, the tears shining in her still bright eyes. 'And now,' she said softly to Dorothy-Anne, 'you'll have to excuse me. I'm a little tired. It's way past my bedtime, and tonight I can rest easy. Hale Hotels is in good hands. The papers have already been drawn up, and I've done what I came to do. Now I plan to go home, relax, and enjoy myself. Right now, with a good night's sleep, and tomorrow, with breakfast in bed. Maybe I'll even get a chance to watch some television.' She raised her voice. 'The rest of you stay and enjoy the party. But you'd better listen to my great-granddaughter when she breaks it up! She's a tough cookie. Like me.' And with that she leaned back wearily, her face clenched as if she were in pain.

'Great-Granny,' Dorothy-Anne asked worriedly. 'Are you all right?'

Elizabeth-Anne opened one eye and glared at her with an expression of amusement. 'Of course I'm all right!' she snapped in pretended irritation. 'Why shouldn't I be? Doesn't a retiree get any peace?' Then she turned around and raised one hand, the fingers making a fluid forward gesture. 'Home, Miss Bunt!'

Sniffling noisily, Miss Bunt wheeled Elizabeth-Anne down the ramp. The crowd fell back to make a path, and throughout the ballroom, the music and applause were deafening.

The queen had abdicated. A new queen had been crowned.

*　　*　　*

When they returned to the Madison Squire, Elizabeth-Anne told Miss Bunt, 'I think I'd like to sit outside on the terrace by myself for a while, if you don't mind – ' Her voice was soft, but she was cut off by a wave of pain that arched her back like a cat's and contorted her face. Miss Bunt recognized the symptoms; over the past few months she had grown familiar with them.

'Has your pain killer worn off?' Miss Bunt asked thickly. 'Shall I get you another pill?'

But the attack had passed, and Elizabeth-Anne now only breathed somewhat heavily in its aftermath. Her spirit was still strong. 'Now why should I want that?' she asked irritably.

The nurse knew there was no point in arguing with Elizabeth-Anne, even about this, and dropped her gaze.

'Good.' Elizabeth-Anne sat back, her lips a grim line. She had never discussed her cancer with the nurse, but knew the medication, the furtive visits to the hospital, and the recent bouts of surgery all spoke for themselves. After all, Miss Bunt was a trained nurse. Elizabeth-Anne was grateful for her silence and discretion, her respect for her employer's obvious desire not to let her condition become known. It was a relief not to have to explain – even to Miss Bunt – how completely the cancer had spread. The surgery had never cut it all out. It had been impossible to do that, and now it was everywhere, gripping her vital organs in a tight, unyielding vice.

'The terrace, Miss Bunt,' Elizabeth-Anne said softly.

Miss Bunt nodded and took Elizabeth-Anne out through the French doors. She set the hand-brake, then gently tucked a plaid lap blanket around her.

Elizabeth-Anne chuckled, then snapped with good humor, 'No leave me alone, for God's sake. I'm not a child.'

Miss Bunt hesitated. 'Do you . . . would you like me to stay out here with you?'

'No, I'd really rather be alone.' Elizabeth-Anne reached for her nurse's hand and held it, smiling faintly. 'Faithful Miss Bunt,' she said softly. 'What would I have done without you?'

The nurse shook her head. She appeared to be on the verge of tears.

'No, don't cry,' Elizabeth-Anne whispered sternly. 'Tears are for those with regrets. I have none. None at all. I've lived my life to the fullest.' She paused. 'I've left you well provided for. You can finally retire. You've been good to me, and I thank you.'

Miss Bunt nodded silently, beyond words, and turned to leave.

'I have one last favor to ask you.'

'Yes?' Miss Bunt's voice was shaky.

'Do not come out here to check on me. Leave me here until morning. Don't call anyone. Is that a promise?'

Miss Bunt couldn't turn to face Elizabeth-Anne and only whispered, 'Yes.'

'There's no use ruining everyone's party. They'll find out soon enough. Let them enjoy themselves tonight.' Her voice rose. 'Now leave me be.'

Miss Bunt hurried inside, not quite shutting the tall French windows.

Elizabeth-Anne sat motionless in the wheelchair, her clear, aquamarine eyes scanning the city which for almost sixty years she had called home. The clear August night was humid, but the breeze which rippled past was delightfully cool against her face. All around her, the monoliths of Manhattan glittered with jewel-like sparkles. Peering above them, she could see out to the floodlit towers of the Hale Castle.

She took a deep, satisfied breath. The roses in the redwood planters perfumed the air, and the breeze rustled through the birch trees. It was a velvety night, a perfect night, and far below on Madison Avenue, through the iron railing of the terrace wall, the dark asphalt was ruby with the tail lights of traffic.

How good it felt to be alive! How fabulous this city was, this pulsating behemoth which had the power to create or destroy with equal swiftness, the power that had granted her the greatest opportunity under the sun.

Hearing the drone of an overhead jet, she watched its flashing lights float past overhead.

493

She smiled to herself. How this terrace had changed in the decades since she had first moved to the Madison Squire penthouse, before there had even been jet planes. How the trees had grown, the trunks thickening with every passing year, and how the wisteria, and ivy which she had planted so long, long ago now crept up the brick walls, cloaking them completely with heavy green. She had watched the seasons change from here, many, many times. How often she had smiled at the gray, thin winter sun, the spectacular spring sunsets over New Jersey to the west, the bright lemon mornings of summer. And how often the terrace plants had shed their leaves, only to renew themselves the following spring.

She had traveled so far and wide in her long life, seeing to her far-flung empire, but had always been overjoyed to return here, to her beloved sanctuary. How long now had she lived and fought, built and traveled, watched her children being born and die? And how short the span of years had seemed at times. How much pain, and joy, and bittersweetness she had encountered. How good it was to be alive! And oh, how good, too, it would finally be to rest. To shut her eyes a final time.

It was time to stop fighting, and bow to the inevitable. She had lived long and full and well. Her empire was in order, and so were her personal effects. Her last will and testament had long since been prepared, signed, and witnessed. It was safely locked away in her lawyer's vault. How lucky she had been to have had the time – and forewarning – to put everything in order. To provide for her descendants. To install Dorothy-Anne at the head of the empire.

And what an empire it was. The hotels and motels, the investments and the treasures. And most of all, Dorothy-Anne, pregnant with child.

The greatest gift of all.

She sighed happily, wondering why now, of all times, as she felt her strength sapping slowly from her, she should feel such contentedness. She would never for the life of her understand why people were afraid to live, and afraid to die. Life and death had to be experienced to the fullest.

494

She leaned her head back and stared up into the star filled sky, imagining that each winking light in the firmament was a living soul. Up there were her parents, her aunt, Zaccheus and Janet, Rebecca and Charlotte-Anne, her beloved Larry, her much-mourned Zaccheus, and Anna, the unexpected treasure. They all seemed to beckon to her, calling her silently to join them.

She closed her eyes, savoring the imagined music of their voices as she felt the strength slowly ebbing from her body. She knew the pain was rising, but somehow didn't feel it. Instead, she leaned her head back and the faint, enigmatic smile was frozen on her lips as she lost consciousness. In the morning, she would not wake. It would be frozen there forever.

8

Lightning flashed, followed by the peal of thunder and then the eerie silence, filled only with the machine-gun staccato of the rain. The rich smell of burning wax from the candles filled the room.

The contractions were close together now, racking her body with bursts of pain, squeezing her into white-hot flashes, billowing outward, radiating to her extremities. Through her closed eyes, she saw fire-like patterns, showers of sparks.

Pain.

And regrets. So many regrets. They circled in a frenzy through her mind. Regrets for a thousand things she could have done for Great-Granny and didn't. Things she had always wanted to tell her and hadn't. Regrets for not staying home and waiting until the baby was born before coming here. But how could she have known? How could she have held back with Great-Granny waiting, with the vision of her anxious, tired eyes before Dorothy-Anne's own fogged, exhausted mind.

Regrets. For foolishness and selfishness. But how could she know?

She hadn't this morning, when they had boarded the Hale Hotels Boeing 727-100. Twenty-thousand feet over the Gulf of Mexico, the jet engines had changed pitch as it had swung around in a miles-wide semi-circle and slipped into its landing pattern. Even then, there had been time to change her mind, but she had never even considered it.

The plane's interior had been constructed to look like a living room with oversized, plush beige couches and bolted-down easy chairs. She and Freddie had sat side by side in intense silence. He was holding her hand, but he did not speak. He knew that physically she was beside him, but mentally she was not. Her mind was wandering elsewhere, besieged by the tidegate of memories which had been opened when Great-Granny Hale had died.

He squeezed her hand to reassure her that she was not alone. She turned to him, nodding gratefully, her lips smiling a sad, tired smile; then her eyes filled with tears. They took on that distant look as wave after wave of rememberance washed over her. There were so many of them. And they were all good.

She closed her eyes as she heard distinct voices, both recent and from the past . . .

Great-Granny, on her ninth birthday: '*The Hale Palace is yours, and yours alone . . .* '

Mr. Morris, the ancient, gray-haired senior partner of the law firm, reading from Elizabeth-Anne Hale's Last Will and Testament: '*The remaining bulk of my estate, which includes all property, both real and personal, the entire chain of hotels and motels I bequeath to my beloved great-granddaughter Dorothy-Anne . . .* '

Freddie, gazing at her with shining eyes during the cremation: '*She'll never be dead, Dorothy-Anne, not really. Not as long as we keep her memory alive. Not as long as a single Hale Hotel remains standing . . .* '

Dr. Danvers, every inch the well-meaning pediatrician: '*Dorothy-Anne, I have known you since you yourself were a child, and you've always listened to my advice. Please do so now. Wait to travel. Your time is too near . . .* '

And Great-Granny's last wish, spoken through the brittle, impersonal voice of Mr. Norris: '*I wish to be returned*

496

to Texas, my ashes scattered where those of my first husband,
Zaccheus Hale, were scattered so long, long ago . . . '

Her eyes were sparkling with tears.

Elizabeth-Anne Hale was returning home at last.

9

The rain slashed at Freddie's face, stinging his skin with
the force of needle-nosed bullets. He staggered ahead, his
torso hunched forward as he kept his face down. A flash of
lightning crackled, illuminating the blackness all around
with a silver strobe of pulsating light.

He took the opportunity to look around and get his
bearings. He was in the midst of the orchard. Straight rows
of citrus trees extended into the distance all around, each
row looking just like the last. The leaves were being torn off
the trees and the fruit rained down from the flailing, wind-
whipped branches. Every direction he turned, he saw
identical rows of trees.

He could only hope to God he didn't lose his sense of
direction.

He stumbled on, keeping his face down. The wind
shrieked with the high-pitched, agonizing screams of death.
The wet ground sucked at his feet. Every step was an effort.
In his mind, he repeated his words of determination like a
litany: He couldn't fail. He couldn't lose his way. He had
to get to town and find a doctor.

Thoughts of death bombarded his mind from all sides.
Dorothy-Anne's pain-tensed face . . . the baby within
her . . .

Death was primordial. It was everywhere. It had always
been, and always would be.

It was up to him to keep the grim scythe-bearer at bay.

He fought on, his eyes closed against the wind until his
feet caught on something. His arms shot out, he flailed the
air as he fought to retain his balance. One foot met
nothing; for a moment he seemed suspended in midair.

Then he crashed down into the water, chilled even though it was lukewarm.

He had fallen into an irrigation canal.

The water closed in over his head, and his feet touched the sludgy bottom. Sputtering, he surfaced, shook his head, and waded to the bank. He clutched at the mud and pulled himself out. Slowly he got to his feet. He stared all around, waiting for a flash of lightning to show him the way.

But when it came, he only stood in confusion, trying to remember which way he had come. Where was he headed? He couldn't even tell if he had crossed the canal, or had returned to the side he had fallen from. The rows of trees were so damned identical, everything the same in every direction, each tree seeming a carbon copy of another, and another, and another.

He had no idea of which way to turn.

He hesitated only a moment. There was no time to lose. If he was wandering off in the wrong direction, the sooner he found out about it, the better.

It was all up to him now. His wife needed a doctor. The unborn baby needed a doctor.

It was up to him. He alone could keep death from his family's door.

The wind shrieked its carnival barker's message.

Hurry! Hurry! Hurry!

Silently Mrs. Ramirez cursed the largeness of her hands. They were working hands, thick-fingered and thick-wristed. What she needed was tiny, delicate hands with narrow, tapered fingers and very thin, elegant wrists.

'I am no midwife,' she muttered, disgusted with herself.

Dorothy-Anne sucked in her breath, biting down against the pain for as long as she could. The scream, when it came, seemed to shatter the night. Her back arched as she tried to pull away from Mrs. Ramirez's probing touch. The fingers felt rough and foreign, alien protrusions inside the soft safety of her womb.

'Please, please,' Mrs. Ramirez gasped. Her dark skin gleamed with beads of sweat. She was unused to this position, half kneeling and half lying between the young woman's splayed legs in order to see inside her. She was much too old for these kinds of acrobatics. 'Your pains. They come every thirty seconds now. We *must* move the baby! You understand?' Her eyes glittered.

'But Freddie. He's going to bring help.'

'There is no time. By then it may be too late. Think of the baby! Please you must listen to me!'

Dorothy-Anne looked at her with fear widened eyes.

'I am not going to hurt you. You must believe that.'

Dorothy-Anne nodded as best she could.

'Is tiring, I know. But you must be brave. You must breathe deep, and push.' Mrs. Ramirez's huge breasts rose and fell as she demonstrated. 'You can do?' She narrowed her eyes.

Dorothy-Anne squeezed her eyes shut, imitating the short barks of rhythmic breathing.

'There. Is fine. Now let me try again,' Mrs. Ramirez said soothingly. As gently as she could, she once again began to poke the fingers of one hand up inside the moist warmth of Dorothy-Anne's vagina. With her other hand, she felt along the outside of the abdomen.

Defeated, Mrs. Ramirez withdrew her hand.

'Is it all right now?' Dorothy-Anne asked hopefully.

Mrs. Ramirez stared at her, then shook her head. 'No,' she said softly. 'It is impossible.' She got up and moved over to the enamel basin on the nightstand and began wearily washing her hands. Suddenly, she froze and let out a sharp cry. 'Oh, now I remember!' She smiled broadly, then even laughed out loud.

'What is it?' Dorothy-Anne whispered.

Mrs. Ramirez's voice rose with excitement. 'There is a way! Now I remember.' Suddenly, the story she had been searching for came back to her, the one that had teased her memory all night. Jorge, her second oldest nephew, had also been in a difficult position. The doctor had insisted that her sister Mariana have a Caesarian section, but the local Mexican midwife had managed to shift the baby around without. All night she had tried to remember *how.* And now she had! It was so simple.

'Let's do it,' Dorothy-Anne gasped, struggling to sit up.

'Do not move.' Mrs. Ramirez paced the room, rubbing her hands. 'There is only one problem.' She bit down on her lower lip. 'I will need help.'

'Help?'

'I need someone else. Someone to help me with you . . . ' She lowered her voice, repeatedly shaking her head. 'Now why I not remember this before I let that poor man go off in to the orchard. *Stupido!*'

Freddie squinted through the silver sheets of rain and let out a strangled cry.

The pale lights in the windows had drawn him to this house, had given him a surge of renewed hope. He had run toward the lights, and in his haste collided with the metal hulk in front of him.

A car.

He stared at it, stunned. The big Lincoln Continental was all too familiar.

He shut his eyes, dropping to his knees beside it. He let out a keening moan of self-disgust. How stupid could he be? He had gone off and gotten lost and ended up right where he had started.

As if to reinforce this tragedy, a flash of lightning lit up the tourist court. The sloping, galvanized roofs and the sagging porches throbbed silver white, and then were once again lost in blackness.

Sighing, he staggered to his feet and leaned against the hood. His mind was in turmoil. He could either continue, trying once again to cross the orchard, or else he could waste precious moments by going inside and seeing Dorothy-Anne.

She was so close. Just across the road.

He hesitated only a moment more. Then he ran across the asphalt toward the tourist court.

The moment Felicia Ramirez heard heavy footsteps pounding on the porch boards her heart gave a hopeful leap. So the Blessed Mother had heard her prayers, and had answered them. Just when she needed somebody, somebody had come.

She crossed herself thankfully and rushed toward the door. But when she flung it open and saw Freddie, her face fell. 'No doctor?' she asked.

'No. I got lost.' He took a deep breath and leaned wearily back against the wall.

She shook her head. 'Is all right. I need you. I remember something.'

He gripped her arm before she could rush off. 'How is she?' he asked, the fear obvious in his eyes.

'The same.' Mrs. Ramirez sighed softly. Then she smiled. 'But I think maybe we can do something. Come. We have no time to lose – ' She gestured impatiently.

He saw the hope shining in her dark eyes, and hurried after her.

'Freddie,' Dorothy-Anne moaned in an exhausted whisper as soon as he came in to the back room. She lay pale and drenched, barely able to move. 'You're back. I'm glad.'

'Hi honey.' He held her hand tightly in his, trying to give her a reassuring smile.

'I need your help to change her position,' Mrs. Ramirez said without further ado. 'We *must* get her on her knees.'

'I'm so tired,' Dorothy-Anne protested weakly.

'Later you can rest,' Mrs. Ramirez said harshly. 'Right now we have work to do.' She nodded once at Freddie. 'You stand on that side of the bed. I remain on this side.'

She flipped off the sheet, and Dorothy-Anne shivered in the sudden chill. Except for her magnificently swollen belly, she looked gaunt, bony, and haggard. Her teeth chattered. 'I'm cold,' she whispered.

Mrs. Ramirez ignored her. 'Now, when I say so, we move her over to her left side. Then we make her kneel.' She raised her eyebrows questioningly. Her expression made it clear that any argument was useless. 'You ready?'

Freddie nodded hesitantly.

'Good. Now we both hold her, and rock her gently.'

Slowly, they both pushed on Dorothy-Anne, rolling her over on her side. She let out a muffled scream. Freddie cringed and went pale.

'Now we get her on her knees.' Mrs. Ramirez leaned

close into Dorothy-Anne's ear. 'We need your help also. *Help us.* Support yourself on your elbows.'

Dorothy-Anne clenched her jaw as Freddie and Mrs. Ramirez helped her get into position. It wasn't an easy maneuver, not in her state of exhaustion, and with the clumsy, swollen belly getting in the way. When she finally stood on her knees, Dorothy-Anne let her head sag down between her arms, her triangular shoulder blades jutting from her naked back like two shark's fins, her limp hair hanging down over her face.

'Good. Very good.' Mrs. Ramirez, ignoring Dorothy-Anne's apparent collapse, sounded pleased. She knelt beside Dorothy-Anne, pressing the outside of the abdomen ever so lightly with the palms of her hands. The skin was stretched tautly against the pear-shaped belly. 'Is better?' she asked.

'I – I think so,' Dorothy-Anne whispered in surprise. 'It – it doesn't seem to hurt nearly so much now.'

Mrs. Ramirez nodded with satisfaction. 'Is because of the pressure. The little one no longer pushes on the wrong spot.' She gestured to Freddie. 'Now, move her back and forth. Gently. Like so. Like she is on a boat.' She made a cradle of her arms and demonstrated a steady rocking motion with her hands. 'Meanwhile, I feel for the baby. Now do it!'

Freddie began rocking Dorothy-Anne, holding onto her very gently, yet firmly so she would not collapse on her side.

Suddenly Dorothy-Anne sucked in her breath.

'What is it?' Freddie cried with concern. 'Did I hurt you?'

'No. it's the baby.' Dorothy-Anne looked sideways through her curtain of limp hair, her voice taking on a tone of wonder. 'It's – it's *moving.* I can feel it *move.*' Her back arched and tensed, and she lifted her head slowly, staring in wide-eyed amazement first at Freddie, and then at Mrs. Ramirez.

But Mrs. Ramirez was not looking at her. She had eyes only for the sagging belly. Even from the outside, she could see that the bulging outline which was the child was perceptively shifting from one side to another.

502

Mrs. Ramirez held her breath. 'A little bit more,' she whispered under her breath, wiping the tickling sweat off her moustached upper lip. 'A little bit more.'

The bulge stopped shifting. Then, after a moment, it continued to move.

Mrs. Ramirez let out a short sigh of relief. 'Stay like that,' she commanded as she changed her position on the bed so that she could insert her fingers into Dorothy-Anne's vagina. For a moment she felt around, she squeezed her eyes shut and heaved a massive sigh.

'What *is* it?' Freddie whispered.

Mrs. Ramirez slowly withdrew her hand. Suddenly she burst into laughter. 'The head! I feel the head! It is now down at the opening where it should be. *Dios mia*! We have done it. *We have done it.*' Tears of relief flowed from her dark eyes. 'Now quickly. We must turn her over – '

'You mean . . . it's all right now?' Freddie asked in disbelief.

'Is fine, is fine.' Mrs. Ramirez's head bobbed happily up and down. '*Quickly*, get her on her back – ' Then in a softer voice she added, 'It will still hurt, but it will be a normal hurt . . . But now we can deliver. Do you hear?' Her eyes gleamed triumphantly. 'We can *deliver* the little one. We have done it!'

GENESIS

Quebeck, Texas
August 15, 1985

Dorothy-Anne had never known anything so glorious, so filled with amazement and wonder, as the moment she heard the first cry of her newborn baby.

'Look, a beautiful girl!' Felicia Ramirez cried happily. 'You have a perfect little daughter.'

Tears filled Dorothy-Anne's eyes, but they were tears of pure joy. The awful pain of the long night of labor was over, gone with the storm that had crashed and howled as ferociously as she herself had cried out. But that was all a memory now. The morning sun broke through the small bedroom window and lit the room with a warm glow like the happiness in her heart.

Freddie sat beside her, tears coursing down his own cheeks as he cradled their child in his arms. Dorothy-Anne savored the sight of them, then let her eyes wander to the Buccellati urn still standing atop the dresser. It gleamed brightly in the morning sunlight.

She took a deep breath. She felt immensely drained, but she was exhilarated, too. She could hear the sounds of the birds and crickets returning, and Mrs. Ramirez making little cooing noises over the infant. And she could smell the moist, damp freshness mingling with the scents of citrus. A choked feeling came up in her throat, and she could feel a tear of sadness roll slowly down her cheek. She stared at the urn. It seemed to fade as the first ray of sunlight hit it directly, throwing off a blinding glare.

Great-Granny's voice was a dry whisper. 'Look up, Dorothy-Anne!'

She leaned her head way back, her eyes following Great-Granny's finger as it pointed up, up, to the Hale Palace. The thousands upon thousands of tons of pale limestone looked buttery soft and weightless, and the sunlight bathed the windows and turned them into silvery mirrors. The

507

ornate twin towers scraped the fast-moving clouds that scudded across the Wedgwood-blue of the sky.

How could one adequately express thanks for such a gift, for the flagship of an empire that took a lifetime to build. How can one repay such a legacy as Elizabeth-Anne had left her?

Suddenly, she knew. The night had passed, and a new day had begun. Today was August the fifteenth.

Elizabeth-Anne Hale's birthday. She would have been ninety-one.

Dorothy-Anne turned around and reached out with her hands. Freddie gently laid the child in the crook of her arm.

Dorothy-Anne looked down at her tiny daughter and smiled. She was so lively, and looked so tiny and fragile. An almost angry scowl was on her face, as if she were protesting the indignity of her birth. Her tiny hands were smaller than a doll's and she kept clenching and unclenching them, grasping at air. Like a true Hale, the child's few, silky strands of hair were gold, and her large, inquisitive eyes were aquamarine.

Dorothy-Anne held her daughter close. She glanced up at Freddie. 'Elizabeth-Anne?' she asked softly.

He nodded. 'Elizabeth-Anne it is,' he agreed, 'though I warn you, it won't be easy for her to follow in her namesake's footsteps.'

'Not easy, no,' Dorothy-Anne said pensively. Then she smiled. 'But she'll do it.'

And Dorothy-Anne's lips moved slowly, soundlessly. So soundlessly that even Freddie couldn't hear.

'Happy Birthday, Great-Granny.'